MW00627089

Toly's Ghost

Toly's Ghost

by "BS" Levy

the fourth novel in *THE LAST OPEN ROAD* series

Cover, Graphics and Art Direction by Art Eastman

Editing by John F. Gardner and Bill Siegfriedt

Incredible Backup Support from Carol Levy and Karen Miller

Additional editing, research & assistance thanks to:
Henry Adamson, Mike Argetsinger, Dick Carlson, Tim Considine, John Fitch, Bill Gehring,
Bill Hallandal, Harry Heuer, Phil Hill, Bruce Kessler, Denise McCluggage, Jim Sitz, Sam Smith,
Bob Storck, Tom White, Janos Wimpffen, Woody Woodhouse, Brock Yates, Bob Ziner
and assorted semi-comatose members of Age & Treachery Racing

Think Fast Ink L.L.C.
Oak Park, Illinois
www.lastopenroad.com

2006

PUBLISHED BY:
THINK FAST INK
1010 LAKE STREET
OAK PARK, ILLINOIS, 60301
WWW.LASTOPENROAD.COM
E-MAIL: THINKFAST@MINDSPRING.COM

WRITTEN AND MANUFACTURED IN THE UNITED STATES OF AMERICA

FIRST EDITION
JUNE 2006

OTHER TITLES BY "BS" LEVY

THE LAST OPEN ROAD 1994
MONTEZUMA'S FERRARI 1999
A POTSIDE COMPANION 2001
THE FABULOUS TRASHWAGON 2002

LIBRARY OF CONGRESS CATALOGING IN PUBLICATION DATA
LEVY, BURT S., 1945-
TOLY'S GHOST
1. AUTOMOBILE RACING IN THE 1950s 2. AUTOMOBILE MECHANICS
LIBRARY OF CONGRESS CATALOG CARD NUMBER:
2006900529

ISBN: 0-9642107-6-2

DEDICATED TO

PHIL HILL

A RACER, A HERO, A GENTLEMAN AND A TRUE AMERICAN CHAMPION

AUTHOR'S NOTE: *In the process of writing this book, there were many, many times when I found myself mired in a dilemma regarding the progress of my fictional plot and the actions of my fictional characters versus the true facts of racing history and the lives and accomplishments of many of the real-life motorsports heroes I grew up cheering for from the sidelines and following breathlessly in the magazines I read from cover-to-cover every month as soon as they arrived. I hope those still living and the ghosts and loved ones of those who have passed on—along with you, dear readers—will understand and forgive what I have attempted to do and appreciate the spirit in which it was done.*

Chapter 1: A Change of Scenery

Cal Carrington's driving career really started taking off after that photo-finish win in California wine impresario Ernesto Julio's Ferrari at Road America in September of 1955. That was the weekend I finally conned my friend, best customer, part-time father confessor, occasional bigmouth blowhole and all-purpose business partner Big Ed Baumstein into letting Cal drive the Trashwagon. But then Ernesto's famous European hero driver Jean Behra got socked in someplace in France (some said under a skirt, but I don't know that for certain) and so he offered Cal the drive at the very last minute. At the big racers' party at Siebkens the night before the race, in fact. I was pretty well crushed when Cal told me about it, but in the end I could see it was the right thing for him to do. It was exactly the kind of break he needed. Besides, a hungry, driven, self-centered and ambitious guy like Cal was going to take the drive whether it was the right thing to do or not. It's just the way things had to be.

Everybody agreed that Cal put on one hell of a show the next day—especially considering he'd never so much as sat in Ernesto Julio's Ferrari before—and the race went back and forth for 200 miles between Cal and his old nemesis Creighton Pendleton the Third in one of Briggs Cunningham's D-Type Jaguars. It came down to the very last corner of the very last lap, and Cal set him up perfectly and swept past to take the win—by no more than the thickness of that Ferrari's bright yellow paintjob!—against what most folks figured should have been a faster car. Ernesto Julio was impressed enough to ask Cal if he'd like to do a little more racing for him out on the west coast, and my buddy Cal was ready to leave for California before they even made it to the victory celebration. But then, victory celebrations were never exactly a big deal for a guy like Cal. And neither were pewter mugs, marble-based trophies, mahogany wall plaques or even engraved sterling silver loving cups. Nope, that stuff just never meant very much to Cal Carrington. In fact, nothing much mattered to Cal once the engines shut down except when they'd be firing up again. That's what it was really all about as far as he was concerned. Oh, sure, he liked to win and prove he was better than the next guy. Who didn't? And he was cocky enough to think he was about the best damn racing driver who ever pulled on a crash helmet and a pair of split-window goggles. Or at least he'd never seen anybody better. But for Cal, the magic was in the actual *doing* of it: to be out there devouring asphalt and leaving the real world in your slipstream while you chased the future like you could reach out and grab it with both hands. That's the way it is with *real* racers. They just can't help themselves. Cal wanted his chance behind the wheel of the leanest, fastest, meanest damn racecars on the planet—cars that made you ache to look at them and bubbled the wax in your ears whenever they fired up. Wanted to feel them come alive in his hands like some wild, beautiful, mysterious and dangerous creature he had to tame and make love to at the same time. Moreover he wanted to run those cars—flat-out and wheel-to-wheel—on all the great racetracks against all the other guys who figured they were the best damn drivers in the universe. See if he had what it took to put them in his mirrors and keep them there.

The look in his eye told you he was pretty damn confident that he could.

He told me all about it that soft autumn night we spent out on the front stoop of one of the rough little cabins at the Seneca Lodge: "This is the only thing I've ever really wanted to do, Buddy," he said while we stared up at a low, fat sliver of a harvest moon. But his eyes were focused light years beyond it. "This is the only thing I've ever been really good at in my whole life," he added dreamily. "I mean *really* good at. I can *feel* it." He flashed me one of those helplessly dazzling and dangerous smiles of his. "Everything starts when I fire up an engine and pull out on a racetrack. Goes from black-and-white TV to Cinemascope and Technicolor. You know what I mean?"

"I guess I do," I shrugged. And maybe I did. Although to tell the truth I was a little bit jealous about it. Okay, maybe even more than a little bit. Even though he was my very best friend and I was proud as hell of what he could do with a racecar. But it ate at me why some guys get to be the Ace Hero/Leading Man/Racing Drivers of life while the rest of us wind up doing all the grunt work and mopping up behind them. So I asked him: "What about the rest of the time?"

"The rest of the time?" He mulled it over, looking way past the moon again. "I haven't really thought too much about it. It's just time in between, isn't it?"

"But you can't spend your whole blessed life in a racing car," I argued, sounding an awful lot like my old man giving me one of his post-Yankees-game, post-six-pack-of-beer backyard lectures.

Cal shot me another unassailable smile. "I can sure as hell try!" he grinned. And if anybody could get away with an attitude like that, Cal would be your man.

So it didn't come as any huge shock when Cal threw his helmet and his battered-but-expensive leather overnight bag into the back of Ernesto Julio's tow rig around dusk Sunday evening at Road America and rode straight back from Elkhart Lake, Wisconsin, to southern California with the guys hauling Ernesto's yellow Ferrari Monza. Just like that. "What about the rest of your stuff?" I asked him while Ernesto's guys loaded up the Ferrari.

"What stuff?"

"You know: clothes, bedding, bank book, bible…."

"Look, I'll call you." He climbed up into the cab of the truck and smiled down at me. "You'll help me work it out, won't you, Buddy?" he said like there wasn't even a question about it. And then he waved and he was gone. Just like that. The jerk didn't even bother to say goodbye….

Anyhow, that's how my pal Cal Carrington wound up in southern California. He said it was one hell of a cross-country road trip—even in a damn car hauler—while his car owner Ernesto Julio hopped in his twin-engined Aero Commander at the Milwaukee airport and flew back to San Francisco, 400-odd miles to the north, where his brand-new Bentley Continental was waiting for him at the airport. Turns out old Ernesto was living two very different lives out in California. Up around San Francisco, he was a solid citizen known for the rolling, highly productive sprawl of vineyard acreage his family owned in Sonoma County. Acreage that pumped out thousands upon thousands of gallons of cheap, familiar reds and whites that sold in staggering (often literally!) quantities across bars and checkout counters all over the whole blessed country. Not to mention the popular, modestly priced pink and white champagnes sold under the *Bon Temps* and *Fairpeiper* labels that had become the Great American Standard for prom-night first feels and New Year's Day hangovers from coast to coast. Ernesto called them *"the Chevrolet of sparkling wines"* after he'd had a scotch or a brandy or two, and took pains to explain their success. *"It's the sugar content and the fizz that makes 'em go down so easy. High school girls think they're drinking soda pop! But they'll whack you good if you're not careful. And they can be BRUTAL in the morning. Hell, I get a subscription to the Fruit of the Month Club every year from the guys who make Alka Seltzer and a couple nice boxes of cigars from the folks at Bayer Aspirin."*

My motoring scribe buddy Hank Lyons told me all about how Ernesto's grandfather started up in the winery business straight off the boat from Italy. Or at least after a long, painful wagon ride across the entire expanse of the new American frontier in a wagon with springs like iron ingots and no seat cushions of any kind. Two generations later, his son retold that story over and over to little Ernesto while he was growing up and learning the family business. *"My fadder, he's a-no siddown again in his a-whole life after dat a-ride. Not-a even inna da outhouse! He's a-sacrifice plenty to make dis-a place for us, an' I'm a-no gonna sit-a by while a little stroontz like-a you fucks it up, unnerstan?"* And then he'd give little Ernesto a good hard crack across the face. Unless he was being really good and paying close attention, in which case he'd give him a not quite so hefty crack across the backside.

This was known as "education" in many traditional Italian families.

But Ernesto's father was a sharp, shrewd, hard-working type with calloused hands and a flinty look in his eye who always took care of his family and the wine business his own father started. And also of the sneaky and even scary-looking East Coast and Midwestern business acquaintances who wore big fedora hats, pricey Italian suits and heavy overcoats—sometimes even in the summer—that occasionally clanked when they walked. Those were the guys who bought, transported and distributed a lot of Ernesto's father's wine, and made absolutely sure that it was kept behind the counter of little neighborhood Italian restaurants all across the country. And particularly in New York, New Jersey, Philadelphia and Chicago. And a lot of those little streetcorner places (along with other, somewhat harder-to-find places owned by the above-mentioned gentlemen with the clanking overcoats) continued to serve a little of that wine even during prohibition. Or maybe even more than a little. Ernesto's father managed to quietly keep producing thanks to a loophole in the law that you could drive a damn truck through (or a whole convoy of trucks, and tankers at that!) which said you could still make wine for religious services even during prohibition. So Ernesto Julio's father made sure to produce enough fermented grape products to keep every blessed church congregation in the country well supplied, from the high Episcopalians through the Roman Catholics, Greek Orthodox, Russian Orthodox, Lutherans, Presbyterians, Christian Science and Jehovah's Witnesses clear down to the Methodists, Quakers, Calvinists and Baptists who supposedly didn't drink the stuff anyway. But he made plenty for them, too. And maybe even a little extra for all the Jewish temples, Eastern shrines and down-home, backwoods snake-handlers who might require a wee snort or two to juice up their prayer services. I'm not saying that wine actually *got* to all those churches, shrines and synagogues, mind you. I'm just saying Ernesto's father made sure there was plenty to go around.

Ernesto really started taking his place in the business during those difficult prohibition years, and it was obvious right away that he was the kind of natural-born salesman and entrepreneur who could charm the birds out of the trees when he needed to and cut somebody off at the knees when he needed that, too. Ernesto had a rare and decisive flair for wheeling and dealing, and while his father made wine for the guys with big fedoras and clanking overcoats, Ernesto concentrated on "filling out the line" with imported hard liquor he smuggled up from Mexico, down from Canada or slipped in through the docks at San Francisco. And while most of the other vineyard owners wrung their hands and wailed *"woe is me"* during prohibition, Ernesto saw an open wound of financial opportunity. With his father's help (and even more from his clanking overcoat buddies in the "distribution" business), Ernesto started buying up distressed vineyards all over Sonoma County. By the time prohibition ended in 1933, Ernesto and his family owned an incredible expanse of acreage—a sixth of the whole county, some said—and they were geared up and ready to produce and ship the instant the 18th Amendment was repealed.

In 1927, Ernesto Julio married the daughter of one of the other vineyard owners he was trying to buy out—a nice, solid, old-school Italian girl with plenty of respect and traditional breeding—and they moved into a luxurious, Spanish-style manor house he'd built for them where his grandfather's shack once stood next to the very first rows of grape vines on that very first piece of vineyard property. They lived quietly, privately and respectably (except for Ernesto's taste for fast, flashy sports-cars) and had four children together, two boys and two girls. All around the San Francisco area, Ernesto Julio was known as an upright citizen, devoted husband and doting father. Which he was. Or at least when he was home, anyway. But Ernesto had to travel a lot to look after the wine business—especially after his father passed away a few months after the Japs bombed Pearl Harbor—and that's where the other side of his face started to show.

Because, in the respected old Italian tradition, Ernesto Julio had built an entire, semi-secret side life for himself down in southern California, and the wine business in Sonoma County became only one part of a large and growing list of Ernesto Julio deals, holdings, interests and enterprises. It all started with a piece of a well-known luxury hotel in San Francisco, which was famous for elegant society weddings and legendary, no-limit poker games that went on occasionally in the penthouse. But

Ernesto rarely attended such things personally. At least not in San Francisco. He didn't much fit in with or care for San Francisco society. Not even the SCMA sportycar clubbies, who were mostly toney, old-money types like the ones we'd become familiar with back east.

Besides, it was too close to home.

Four hundred miles down the California coast in Los Angeles was where Ernesto Julio started keeping the *other* half of his life. That's where he had the luxury apartment he moved Cal into up in the Hollywood hills plus a not-so-silent partnership in a highline foreign car dealership in Santa Monica called *Moto Italia* that sold Fiats, Alfa Romeos and Lancias and repaired and/or race-prepped just about anything with four wheels and two seats. The shop in Santa Monica also served as Ernesto Julio's racing headquarters and, more importantly, as a plausible tax-dodge cover for his incurable sportycar habit.

Ernesto also dabbled a bit here and there in the movie business in Hollywood, which was always on the lookout for rich wheeler/dealer types with unusually deep pockets to back movie projects in return for little side benefits like dates with eager, aspiring young actresses fresh in from Omaha or Texas or Brooklyn or Poughkeepsie and hungry for a taste of the limelight. Not to mention regular invites to the infamous, weekend-long house parties at sprawling Beverly Hills mansions, Malibu beach houses or posh hideaways up in the Hollywood hills where famous names and instantly-recognized faces mingled with producers, directors, casting agents, deal makers, power brokers and hot-and-cold-running starlets. Parties where anything not only *could* happen, but was more or less expected to….

When Cal Carrington first arrived in L.A., Ernesto Julio kind of temporarily set him up in the fancy apartment he had up in the hills overlooking Los Angeles. He could stay there as long as he wanted (or at least as long as he stayed in Ernesto Julio's good graces, which seemed deceptively easy at the time) as long as he understood that he might have to vacate the place at a moment's notice so Ernesto could send the smiling old Mexican woman who took care of the cleaning and housekeeping over to tidy things up for whatever sort of evening or weekend activities Ernesto had in mind. That didn't happen very often, but when it did, Cal was pretty much on his own until the all-clear sounded, usually around 11am or so on the following Monday morning.

Even so, it was one hell of a nice place to stay (rent free, no less!) and there was even a part-time job in it for Cal—if he wanted it, anyway—at Ernesto's Italian car dealership down near the ocean in Santa Monica. Cal's duties there amounted to mostly shuttling cars around from one place to another (and that could just as easily mean across town to a trim shop in Culver City or hustling some hot new sportscar clear across the country from New York to Los Angeles), hanging around with the race mechanics and chatting up the customers. Which didn't figure to be too difficult given Cal's natural-born line of bullshit. But Cal never really worked out as a car salesman because he didn't have the necessary tolerance for kissing ass and suffering fools gladly, both of which are prime considerations in the retail automobile business—no matter if you're selling Fiats, Frazer Nashes, Model T Fords or the latest Ferraris. And Cal simply *hated* hanging around the showroom waiting for some rich drool to walk in through the front door and want something. Plus Cal didn't really have to work. He was past 21 by then—just—and getting a little money he never much talked about every month from some kind of trust fund. Or maybe that should be "lack of trust" fund. He'd joke about it, though. "I'm a Remittance Man," he told me later at Sebring through that sly cobra smile of his.

I had to admit I didn't know what one was.

"Oh, they're very big in wealthy families. Especially on the east coast. And it's practically an institution over in England."

I gave him a blank look.

"A Remittance Man is a disagreeable or disreputable sort of chap who gets a check from his family every month—sometimes a very sizeable check—in return for simply staying the hell out of the family's hair, out of the family's business, as far away as possible. And, most especially, out of the newspapers." He shot me a wink. "Especially the tabloids."

As a result, Cal was very punctual about rolling through the front door of the dealership by 11:30 or 11:45 every single weekday morning. Or at least on the mornings he showed up, anyway. But working at the dealership was hardly what Ernesto Julio had in mind when he brought Cal out to L.A., and whatever else you could say about my buddy Cal Carrington, he was devastatingly quick in a racing car. As he started proving to Ernesto Julio and everybody else as soon as he got to California. Cal's first race came barely two weeks after he arrived on the west coast, an SCMA club event out at the Salinas airport, which was about 100 miles southeast of San Francisco and a solid 300-plus north of LA.

Ernesto told Cal he wanted him to drive up in the brand-new, gleaming silver Mercedes-Benz 300SL Gullwing he'd just gotten in a five-car swap with another dealer in Los Angeles. 300SLs were still a really hot item in the fall of 1955, and were the "production" version of the war-machine Mercedes race cars we'd seen out-run, out-plan and outlast the Ferraris down at *La Carerra* in November of 1952. Mercedes went on to pretty much dominate the international motorsports scene throughout the middle '50s—or at least wherever they chose to run, anyway, and they picked their spots with cunning precision—but the terrible wreck Hank and I witnessed at Le Mans in June of '55 really soured the taste of all that success. That was when Pierre Levegh's magnesium-bodied 300SLR launched into the air off the back of an unsuspecting Austin-Healey, hit a concrete support stanchion at 150-plus and went into the crowd along the pit straight like an exploding meteor, killing Levegh and 80-some innocent spectators. By that time there were already rumors floating around that Mercedes-Benz was going to withdraw from racing at the end of the '55 season anyway. I mean, what did they have left to prove? They'd generally mopped the floor with Ferrari, Aston Martin, Jaguar, Porsche and Maserati to win the World Manufacturers' Championship for sports cars in 1955, and the old Argentine master Juan Manuel Fangio had come through to win back-to-back World Grand Prix Driving Championships for them in Mercedes' Formula One cars in '54 and '55 to add to the one he'd already won for himself at Alfa Romeo in 1951. You have to understand that Mercedes didn't always have the fastest or most powerful cars—for sure they didn't down at *La Carerra*—but they had the whole blessed rest of the package you needed to win: design, engineering, relentless development, top-notch materials, quality manufacturing, incredible organization, thoughtful strategy, unbelievable team discipline…oh, and driving talent. Mercedes was always on the lookout for the very best drivers they could find. So they not only hired Juan Manuel Fangio (who most people agreed was the best damn racing driver on the planet at the time) but also blew off one of their own, solid German guys to add Stirling Moss to the team for the '55 season once it became clear that he was The Next Big Thing. Having a keen eye for driving talent (not to mention the money to sign it up!) is a real key ingredient for any successful racing team. And Mercedes was always a lot different from Ferrari when it came to hiring drivers. Old man Ferrari always figured he had the best, fastest and strongest cars—and he was right more often than not—and so he figured it was a damn privilege to get to drive one of his cars. So a lot of his drivers wound up paying him to drive instead of the other way 'round. Or at least they did in the beginning, anyway. North American Ferrari importer and part-time talent spotter Carlo Sebastian put it all in perspective for me one day at his shop in Manhattan: *"I don't care how good they are, if they have money, they pay…."*

To tell the truth, old man Ferrari was as terminally addicted to motorsports as any star-struck racing driver. Hell, he started out as a driver. And then became a team manager for Alfa Romeo during their glory years between the wars before striking out on his own. So he *needed* to win once he had his own company and was building cars under his own name. Needed it like a bride needs a groom or a junkie needs a fix. It was as simple as that. No question Enzo Ferrari's ego was one of the eight great wonders of the industrial age, and it had to be fluffed and preened and petted and cared for with kid gloves the same as any other glorious Italian *prima donna.* Mercedes was different in that the purpose of their racing was always to prove (and improve the image of!) their bread-and-butter road cars, while a lot of folks—Hank included—thought Ferrari only built road cars to generate enough money to feed his racing habit. But I guess that's the difference between Germans and Italians in a nutshell, isn't it? Heart versus head. Mad Passion versus Master Plan. All I know is that no Mercedes ever gave me a hot flash like a blood-red Ferrari and no Ferrari ever awed me with its cool mechanical excellence like a Mercedes SLR.

But that's why there's chocolate and vanilla, right?

Anyhow, Mercedes' new 300SL production version of the 300SLR was still rare, expensive and hard to come by in late 1955. Particularly the all-alloy "competition" versions with the knock-off disc wheels. Carson and Big Ed and me saw one on the stand at the New York International Auto Show in April of 1953, and no question it impressed the living crap out of us. It was the first production car ever with fuel injection, and they had to use those strange, up-and-out "gullwing" doors on account of Mercedes' three-dimensional tubular space frame chassis was easily a foot deep and so the rocker panels had to come halfway up the sides of the car. There was just no other way to do it. But you could see it was really well built and beautifully finished in that cold, meticulous, machined-from-solid-metal German way. Even if 300SL Gullwings were hard as heck to get in and out of. Women in skirts wouldn't even attempt it. Or at least not in broad daylight, anyway. And word got around pretty quick that 300SLs could be a real steam bath inside on a hot summer day. Which is why you occasionally saw them parading around a July or August racing paddock with the gullwing doors wide open over the roof in the "ready for takeoff" position. But even so, they were the cars to have if you really wanted the latest hot new thing, and so naturally Ernesto Julio just had to have one. And he found a way to do it, too.

But the car wound up at his shop down in Santa Monica after that five-car dealer trade, and Ernesto wanted it up in Sonoma County where he could play with it for a while. And having my pal Cal drive it up to the races in Salinas seemed like a good way to do it and get the car broken in at the same time. Like a lot of guys (Big Ed included), Ernesto always believed that you made a car quicker by breaking it in hard and fast—no matter what the manuals, salesmen or service managers told you—and what better way than by having a hotshoe like Cal smoke it up the coast road from L.A. to Monterey followed by a short blast east on Highway 68 to Salinas? It was hardly the fastest route, but it was the right one to take if you really wanted to wring out a new sportscar.

Or that's what Hank Lyons told me, anyway. And he ought to know, since he wound up going along for the ride. Turns out Hank lived somewhere south of L.A. with his mother and stepfather when he wasn't out hop-scotching around the country—or even across the ocean—from one racetrack to another as a motoring scribe. He'd dropped by the dealership in Santa Monica to take a closer look at Ernesto Julio's new toy as soon as he heard it was there. The sales manager at the official, franchised-from-God Mercedes dealership in L.A. kind of frowned on certified non-prospects like Hank crawling all over his cars. And test drives were out of the question. But Ernesto liked Hank and enjoyed the stuff he wrote—especially when he wrote about Ernesto and his cars—and so he pretty much gave Hank carte blanche to nose around his Italian sportycar store in Santa Monica as much as he wanted.

That's where Hank ran into Cal, and naturally the two of them got to talking about the race coming up in Salinas and next thing you know it was just past dawn on Friday morning, September 30th, 1955, with Cal's battered leather overnight bag and Hank's canvas duffel full of socks, underwear and fresh steno notepads crammed behind the seats of Ernesto Julio's new 300SL as they took off up the coast route towards Salinas. "That was one *hell* of a drive!" Hank told me later. "I was scared shitless all the way from San Simeon to Carmel. Honest to God I was." He shook his head and sighed. "But I was lovin' it, too," he admitted. "You ever been on that road?"

I told him I hadn't.

"Well, that first section heading north out of L.A. takes forever, but after Morro Bay it's 100-plus miles of climbing, diving switchbacks—coiling and uncoiling all the time—with ragged rock faces on one side and sheer dropoffs all the way down to the ocean on the other. I swear, you never saw an ocean that big or blue or endless. The scenery is just flat unbelievable. It's the most beautiful and breathtaking stretch of sportscar road you ever saw in your life." He thought it over for a second and added: "Scariest, too…."

"Cal was driving?"

Hank nodded.

"In a brand-new 300SL?"

Hank nodded again, his eyes bulging a little from the memory.

"That must've been one heck of a ride."

Hank offered up a weak grin. "I think I maybe made the whole hundred miles on one breath. Or at least that's what it felt like, anyway." He shook his head again. "Boy, can that guy ever *drive!"*

"You're telling me."

"Once he gets a feel for a car and gets his rhythm with it, it's like watching a damn symphony conductor."

"I know exactly what you mean."

"And that 300SL isn't exactly the easiest thing to sling around. It's big and kind of heavy, and the rear end can get mighty squirrelly if you're not careful with it."

"It's the low-pivot swing axle," I explained, kind of showing off what I knew.

"Well, whatever it is, it can scare the living crap out of you. Especially if you're riding in the suicide seat."

"You have any religious experiences?"

Hank thought it over. "Let's call them 'stirring encounters with the laws of physics' and let it go at that. I'm generally not the religious type."

"Rides like that will *give* you religion."

"I suppose. Or at least they'll teach you how to pray…."

"Amen to that," I agreed.

"But I gotta admit, Cal had that car figured out pretty damn quick. At least after he got us into one hell of a tank-slapper and almost put us over a cliff."

"I don't think that would've made Ernesto Julio very happy—drop-kicking his brand-new 300SL into the ocean!"

"No doubt about it. But Cal wasn't worried. He said we never would've survived the crash anyway."

"That's my Cal…."

Chapter 2: The Hollywood Connection

Naturally Cal was really revved up about driving Ernesto Julio's Ferrari in that race at the Salinas airport the first weekend of October. He'd only arrived in California a few weeks before—direct from Road America, in fact—and the season was generally over and done with back in the East and Midwest. But not out in California, where they race pretty much all year 'round. And even though it was just a garden-variety SCMA club event, that race weekend at Salinas turned out to be famous for a lot of reasons. And none of them very good. Oh, it started out well enough. Cal and Hank arrived late Friday afternoon in brilliant, warm, sunshiny California weather and Cal was thrilled with the whole new flock of keen, eager racers and rows of bright, shiny sportscars that he'd never seen before. The layout at Salinas was different from the wide-open, broad-shouldered airport tracks Cal had driven on before on account of it used a lot of the perimeter and access roads around the runways instead of just the runways themselves. Which made for a fairly interesting 2.8-mile circuit with two long straightaways and eleven turns, even if it was flat as an ironing board and didn't have any of the character or scenery or elevation changes—or greenery or element of risk, for that matter—of the true road courses Cal cut his teeth on back east. And the whole California scene was different, too. To begin with, the cars were generally neater and cleaner and prettied up much nicer than what we were used to back east. Flash and style always counted for a lot out in California. Why, the bodywork and paint on a lot of the cars—even some of the homebuilts and "backyard specials"—was done to near-show-car standards. Hank said that was on account of the hotrod and custom car influence out in California, and no question it was a far, far cry from what Cal had gotten used to with me and Big Ed and the Trashwagon.

Fact is, a lot of guys were building their own cars out on the west coast (or having them built for them, anyway) and what grabbed Cal's eye right away were a pair of tough-looking Kurtis 500 sportscars out of Frank Kurtis' well-known Kurtis-Kraft shop in Glendale, just outside of Los Angeles. Kurtis had been building highly successful Indianapolis racers, sprinters and midgets for years—his low-slung "roadsters" with the engines offset so the driveshaft ran alongside the driver were pretty much dominating the Indianapolis 500—and underneath the cycle fenders and sheet metal, his "sportscars" were nothing but Kurtis Indy roadsters widened enough to fit a passenger seat and covered up with some two-seater aluminum bodywork. Frank Kurtis had been building topnotch oval-track racecars for quite a while, and he was also responsible for the somewhat odd-looking and oversized four-seater "sports car" with the Buck Rogers body styling that Earl "Madman" Muntz bought the rights to and turned into the Muntz Jet—like the one Big Ed owned for a while. Meanwhile somebody gave Frank Kurtis an Allard to try (according to chatter in the Salinas paddock, he spun it around backwards in short order!) and it dawned on him almost immediately that he might be able to do a bit better. Not to mention picking up a little extra folding money selling cars to the bucks-up sportycar trade by turning his successful, strong and well-proven Indy roadster design into a two-seater sportscar. They were genuinely brutal-looking machines—all broad shoulders and a big, toothy, bar-bouncer snarl on the front end—and built solid as a set of railroad tracks. At first Frank Kurtis offered them up in kit form as the 500KK, but he didn't get many takers. So he started selling complete cars—called the 500S—and you could order them with any big, honking engine you wanted slipped between the frame rails. One of the cars at Salinas had a hot-rodded Caddy V-8 and the other one had a big old chuffing monster of a Buick engine under its quivering hood louvers, and Cal said they both came out of the corners like they were shot out of a damn cannon. In the right hands, a Kurtis 500 could take on the latest and fastest Ferraris and Jaguars and stand a pretty fair chance of beating them. Or at least they could on a nice, wide, flat airport circuit with tight corners leading onto long straightaways like Salinas, where brute acceleration really counted for more than aerodynamically slippery top speed or outright handling finesse. Oh, maybe their Indy-style solid axle front and rear suspensions didn't much like the road crowns, iffy pavement, elevation changes and sudden switchbacks of a *real* road course, but they were sure hell for fast on the airport tracks.

There were some nifty smallbore machines, too. Like expatriate Brit Ken Miles' slick, tiny and indecently quick little MG special that everybody called "The Flying Shingle" for obvious reasons. He beat all the Porsches with it more often than not. To the point that California Porsche distributor John von Neumann eventually asked Ken to race Porsches for him—as much to get him out of that damn MG special as anything else! And he kept right on winning, because Ken Miles was one hell of a sharp, talented and mechanically savvy racing driver. He was a tough, skinny, wiry sort of guy with a sly grin, a side-of-the-mouth British accent and a face like the business end of a tomahawk, and Hank said that gorgeous little "Flying Shingle" MG special was so tiny and petite that the shadow of Ken's nose extended halfway down the hood whenever he drove it.

Then there was Pete Lovely's ingenious (if somewhat strange-looking) miniscule Porsche-powered Cooper chassis that he and everybody else called "the Pooper" with tongues so far in cheek that they almost came out their ears. But it went fast as stink. Hell, nobody was building cars like that back east. And they *flew!* But what really impressed Cal was the lack of all that blue-blooded, Old Money stuffiness he'd grown accustomed to at places like Bridgehampton and Mount Equinox back east. Everybody seemed so tanned and relaxed and happy on the west coast racing scene. But Hank said that could be a little deceptive. Everything was on the surface out in California. Everything was appearances. And *looking* like you were on top of the world (and just naturally enjoying the living hell out of it!) was maybe even more important than actually *being* there. But a lot of that was on account of the strong connection between the L.A. racing scene and the movie business in Hollywood, where the line between fantasy and reality was blurry at best. Not to mention that when Big Money arrived in the movie business—if it arrived at all—it came in a sudden, gushing avalanche of exceedingly large-denomination bills that just begged to be spent on something extravagant, excessive, exotic, flamboyant and, if possible, just a wee bit naughty and dangerous.

Sportycar racing was a perfect fit….

Turns out there was always a lot of crossover between the movie business and the California racing scene. Like Hank told me Clark Gable—yes, *that* Clark Gable—had served as Honorary Race Chairman at the races out at Hansen Dam in the middle of June. Can you imagine? But I guess that was to be expected. After all, racing and the movie business were both about money and flash and style and risk and unreasonably high expectations, and the only real difference was that you could pretty much tell where the hell you were and how things were going and whether you were winning or losing in racing, while that kind of certainty was always up for grabs (or at the very least open to interpretation) where the movie business was concerned. So the Hollywood types not only liked racing because of the color and speed and danger and atmosphere and excitement, but also because it was a lot more finite and made a lot more sense than making movies. Like Hank always said, starring roles and Oscar picks were essentially whim-and-fashion gut shots—style points, you know?—but in racing all you needed was a stopwatch to know who really had the goods.

Of course Cal didn't know many of the west coast racers. And they didn't know him, either. Except that he'd shown up in Ernesto Julio's brand-new (but now rather dusty) 300SL and that he'd been entered to drive Ernesto's latest Ferrari in the big-bore "modified" feature on Sunday. And that was more than enough to make him the subject of a lot of whispering, finger-pointing and shrugging of shoulders. Hank introduced him around as best he could, and Cal was typically, cockily confident that they'd all sure as hell know who he was by the end of the weekend. That in spite of the fact that our old *La Carerra* friend and hero Phil Hill—who was pretty much regarded as *the* top California road racer at the time—was entered to drive John von Neumann's Ferrari Monza in the very same race. Phil was also supposed to run von Neumann's quick little Porsche 550 Spyder in the smallbore race, and you'd have to say he was penciled in as the favorite in both groups.

John von Neumann had become quite a key fixture in southern California sportycar circles by then. He was originally from Vienna—just like that Max Hoffmann guy who imported Porsches and just about anything else he could get his hands on back in New York—where von Neumann's father was some kind of bigshot society doctor with an impressive international reputation and some very famous names on his patient list. But he decided he had to get his family the hell out of Europe before the war came, and so they pulled up stakes (and bank accounts) and moved to New York City. Not long after that his father died and John eventually wound up messing around with cars out in California. It'd be easy to simply pass him off as a silver-spoon type who'd always had money in his pocket, but John von Neumann was also a shrewd thinker, hard worker, tireless organizer and had learned a lot of tough lessons about trust and self-reliance. Anyhow, he'd always been nuts about fast, interesting cars, and he and a couple of his car-crazy California buddies (along with their wives and/or girlfriends) started doing these loosely organized, highly illegal point-to-point highway speed runs to test and show off their latest toys. Most often at night, when the canyon, desert and shoreline roads were empty and the cops were generally parked on a stool in a diner somewhere or home having dinner. Those runs would inevitably wind up at some restaurant with good food and a well-stocked bar where everybody could brag and lie and swap excuses, and out of those nighttime speed runs grew an organization called the California Sports Car Club—or Cal Club, as it became known—which turned into kind of a more relaxed, less stuffy, *ain't-that-neat/run-what'cha-brung* southern California alternative to the local SCMA regions. And particularly the San Francisco region, which tended to be more like the blue-blooded, blue-nosed, let-me-see-your-family-pedigree stuffed shirts who had far too much influence on the sportycar scene back east. Cal Club welcomed hot rodders, customizers, Bonneville speed-record freaks and roundy-round types as well as European sportycar enthusiasts—hey, if it made noise and went fast, it had their attention—and quickly turned into a thorn in the side of the local SCMA regions. Especially after Cal Club started putting on their own races. Even though the two clubs were sanctioning and promoting the same kind of races—and often for the same exact cars and participants!—there was an ongoing political border war between the two. Which is another way of saying that the Charlie Priddle types in both clubs were at each other's throats often as not. As for the real racers, they couldn't have cared less! It just meant more events and more race weekends and more places to run!

Besides being seriously infected with the sports car disease, John von Neumann was also a pretty clever and far-sighted businessman, and he got into the sportycar business in a very big way out in Los Angeles. It all started with a place called Competition Motors in North Hollywood, where he started selling MGs and Hillmans and such to the local enthusiast crowd. And also to the fashion-conscious Los Angeles Boulevard Cruiser types who didn't know a double-clutch from a double scotch-on-the-rocks, but thought those precious little European sportscars were terribly *chic* anyway. Like Hank always said, there was never a better market for anything bold, loud, flashy and different than California. And that went double for anything that could attract attention in Los Angeles!

Later on von Neumann added Porsche—buying them one at a time from Max Hoffman in New York and driving them across the whole blessed country to North Hollywood—and those cars really caught on in California and made John von Neumann one whale of a lot of money. Then he worked himself a deal to become the Volkswagen distributor for the entire state just when Volkswagen was starting to catch on. Like I said, smart. But it was more than dumb luck and being in the right place at the right time. According to Hank, von Neumann always ran a tight ship and did things the right way, and moreover made damn sure that the sports cars he sold were out there being raced where the buying public could see them. And winning, too....

But even though he was selling and racing Porsches, von Neumann's real love was always Ferraris. He generally had a couple of old Enzo's latest and fastest street and racing models in his stable along with the MGs and Porsches and such. Like a lot of guys who get bitten by the bug, at first he just drove them himself (and so did his wife Eleanor and her daughter Josie in the Ladies' Races) but John von Neumann was realistic enough to see that there were faster guys out there. And some of them—like Ken Miles—were even working for him as mechanics. I'm proud to say that a large percentage of great racing drivers—and virtually *all* great racing drivers born without that lucky silver spoon in their chops—started out as grease-monkey wrench-spinners. Taking cars apart and putting them back together and dealing with whatever broke gives you a pretty keen feel for how cars work and what they'll put up with.

Anyhow, pretty soon von Neumann was offering drives to some of the most promising young west coast hotshoes—like Phil Hill and Ken Miles and Richie Ginther—in order to give his cars the best chance of winning. Which also helped their careers along no small amount. But John von Neumann was hardly the only rich sportycar enthusiast/car-owner/race entrant type out in California. Ernesto Julio and John Edgar and Tony Parravano always had hot cars—lots of them!—and Tony in particular was a hands-on kind of guy out of the concrete and construction businesses who loved exotic hardware and enjoyed the heck out of spinning wrenches and twisting screwdrivers on his Ferraris and Maseratis himself. Hank said he could be a hell of a nice guy (so long as his cars were running at the front of the pack, anyway) although it was quietly whispered that nosing around in Tony's business affairs wasn't the healthiest sort of thing you could do. But he and von Neumann and John Edgar and Ernesto Julio all loved the fast cars and the excitement and drama and color and sportsmanship and camaraderie of the race weekends. Not to mention the thrill, power and control of being a hotshot racing team impresario. There was huge satisfaction in seeing their cars come home first—especially if they were beating the other bigtime west coast racing team impresarios in the process! Why, it was almost as good as being in the driver's seat! In fact, sometimes (with the aid of a few stiff drinks) they couldn't tell the two apart. Plus there were always lots of parties and pretty girls and wild, famous or unusual characters on the scene, and that made race weekends a hell of a lot more entertaining and interesting than everyday life. In fact, the social scene was the main attraction for an awful lot of the west coast racers and hangers-on. There were beer busts and barbeques in the paddock, motel pool parties where everybody eventually wound up in the drink—whether they were wearing bathing suits on or not!—and boozy, sunburned commando-raid invasions of entire small-town cocktail lounges, corner bars, supper clubs and sit-down restaurants. Racing in California always came with a whoop-it-up party atmosphere that moved through the paddock like a 90-proof tide as soon as the last engine fell silent and continued till damn near dawn for some of the heartier participants.

The cars those bigshot car owners bought to race against each other were always the very latest and fastest—Jaguars and Ferraris and Maseratis and such—and they'd hire the best of the available hotshoes to drive them. Like tough ex-oval track racer Jim McAfee and lightning-fast failed Texas chicken rancher Carroll Shelby and that rich Masten Gregory kid (who by then was known as "The Kansas City Flash" and getting some of his rides without even having to pay for them) and quick local boys Phil Hill and Richie Ginther and Bob Drake and Billy Krause and even Indy 500 stars like Troy Ruttman, whose names were already household words. Although some of the roundy-round drivers seemed a little out of their element at first in the sportycar world. It wasn't that they didn't know how to drive—hell, they were *great* racing drivers!—but, like Sammy Speed once told me, ovals and road courses are as different as country music and a string symphony, and it takes time to get used to either one if you're coming at it from the opposite direction.

Meanwhile those rich car owners planned and schemed and watched and evaluated and maneuvered against each other from trackside, trying to find that elusive extra edge. Hank said the competition between those guys was every bit as fierce as what their drivers were trying to do to each other out on the racetrack—maybe even moreso—and there was always a secret, behind-the-scenes side battle going as to who could get the inside line on the latest, hottest new car or who could spot fresh driving talent and bring it to the finish line first. Which is precisely how Phil Hill wound up entered in John von Neumann's Ferrari and Porsche 550 out at Salinas. But as soon as Phil arrived he had to turn around and head back home after word came through that his brother-in-law Dan Parkinson—who was also a well-known, well-liked and highly successful and respected California racer and car builder—had inexplicably committed suicide. It was one of those strange, hard-to-fathom deals that make everybody look in a mirror and wonder. Especially out in a perfect, Garden-of-Eden spot like southern California. Why would anybody who seemed to enjoy life so much ever want to do such a thing? Especially a racer, since racers can get a lot of stuff out of their systems that ordinary people have to keep bottled up inside where it gnaws at them. But you never know how it is for other people, do you? They usually only show you the shiny side.

But with Phil Hill on his way back to L.A., Cal figured to have an even better shot at winning his race at Salinas. And don't think for a moment he didn't appreciate the implications. That's something you have to understand about genuine race-car drivers: the really good ones are predatory, cold-blooded realists. And opportunists to a fault. But they have to be. Any advantage, any break, any turn of fate that can help you out is a plus. No matter how dark or ugly or unfortunate it may be for somebody else. Even if it's your friend. Sure, you may feel lousy about it. But you *take* it, just the same. And that's something that sets the *real* racers apart from all the duffers, journeymen, playboys and wannabes who fill up the majority of the starting spots on race weekends. It's tight, serious stuff up there at the sharp end of the grid. And the better you are and the higher you go, the tighter and more serious it becomes.

But Cal Carrington didn't really know all that stuff yet. All he knew was that he was happy as hell to be out there getting ready for his very first race in California, and that one of the guys he was worried about—I mean *really* worried about!—he didn't have to worry about anymore. You'd think racing drivers would spend a lot of time mulling over mixed feelings and feeling conflicted about that sort of thing. But believe me, they don't. Personally, I think the best of them are immune….

Ernesto Julio wasn't scheduled to show up until later that evening and his Ferrari was still on its way up from Santa Monica (but most definitely *not* by way of the coast road!) and so there wasn't much for Cal and Hank to do but hang around the paddock, chat up the locals and check out the cars. Dusty as it was, Ernesto's 300SL was attracting quite a bit of attention—300SLs were still new and rare and unquestionably a little bit sinister—and Hank felt compelled to take a clean T-shirt out of his duffel and wipe the car down. Cal couldn't have cared less. In fact, he took his shirt off, stretched himself out on the hood with his aviator sunglasses on and went to work on his tan. At least he put his shirt down first (although Hank said it was more to keep the road dust off of him than to keep the finish from getting scratched).

At any rate, it wasn't long at all before another 300SL cruised into the paddock—a dark blue one with the rare knockoff disc wheels—and pulled to a halt right next to them. The big gullwing doors swung open and out stepped two young kids who looked like they were barely out of high school. The driver was a handsome, smooth-cheeked teenager with Ray-Ban sunglasses and a perfectly sculptured sweep of California blonde hair across his forehead. He glanced at Cal laid out on the hood of Ernesto Julio's 300SL and then ran his eyes up and down the car. "How long you had yours?" he asked.

"About eight hours," Cal told him without looking up. "But it's not really mine. I'm just breaking it in for a friend."

"You breaking in the hood or the whole car?" the other kid asked. He wasn't as trim or blond or handsome as the one who was driving, but he had a wiseass smile and a shitload of mischief dancing in his eyes. Cal aimed those aviator sunglasses at him but didn't say a word.

"You drove it up from L.A.?" the first kid asked.

Cal nodded.

"You take the coast road or 99 and 101?"

"We took the coast road," Hank broke in. "He scared the living shit out of me."

A tight-lipped grin slowly spread across the blonde kid's face. "I wanted to take the coast road, too. But we were running late and I figured we didn't have the time. Besides, I wanted to see what she'd do on a long, flat stretch."

The second kid rolled his eyes.

"Whad'ja find out?"

"It won't do 150. The salesman told me it would, but it wouldn't."

"Maybe after it's broken in?" Hank offered.

"Maybe. But I could only get around 140 and change out of it. At least on the speedo, anyway."

"That's still pretty respectable," Hank allowed.

"Yeah, but it's still not 150." The blonde kid's lip curled under. "If the salesman tells you it'll do 150, it oughta *do* 150."

He obviously had a lot to learn about car salesmen.

The kid looked the two cars over again. "So, you gonna race that one?"

"I don't think so," Cal told him. "We just brought it up for a friend, like I said. Ernesto Julio. You know who he is?"

The kid shrugged. "I think I've heard of him."

"Cal here's gonna race his Ferrari this weekend," Hank explained grandly.

The blonde kid looked thoroughly unimpressed. "Well, I'm racing this one," he said, nodding towards his 300SL, "and my friend Bruce here is gonna get some laps in, too. We were kind of hoping to have somebody to race against." There was a mild hint of a challenge in his voice, and Cal and Hank instantly shot glances at each other. It had occurred to both of them that the kid didn't really look old enough to be racing. Hell, he didn't look old enough to be shaving. The SCMA rules said you had to be at least 21 to get a racing license.

"You been in many races?" Hank asked him.

"This'll be my second. I raced at Santa Barbara over Labor Day weekend."

"First time?"

The kid nodded.

"You do any good?"

The kid looked down at the gill slits on the flanks of his 300SL. "It was my first try," he said without looking up. "I'll get better."

"You'd better," the other kid wisecracked. The first kid shot him a glare you could see right through the Ray-Bans.

"Y'know," Cal told them in a friendly, Dutch Uncle kind of way (but putting the old psych job in at the same time), "300SLs aren't exactly the easiest cars in the world to drive. Especially for a beginner. Oh, they may be the best damn sports car in the world out on the open highway—smooth and solid as a ball bearing—and you can cruise all day long at seven- or eight-tenths, no sweat. But try pushing one to nine- or ten-tenths and they can get a little hairy. It's that low-pivot swing axle. The handling's kinda freakish out there at the limit. And they're sorta heavy, too…."

"Mine's got the all-alloy bodywork," the kid broke in. "I had a regular one, but the salesman said I really needed one of the lightweight ones if I was gonna race it. Bruce and I had to go all the way up to this warehouse in San Francisco to find it."

The other kid nodded. "The guy told us to look through all the cars until we found a silver one with the knockoff disc wheels."

"But this car's blue," Hank observed.

The two of them looked back and forth at each other. "He had it repainted," the wiseass one explained.

"I was maybe trying to fool some people into thinking it was the same car," the blonde kid said sheepishly.

"Right," the other one laughed. "You didn't want your mother to know you bought *two* 300SLs."

"She doesn't care," the blonde kid said like he almost wished she did. He looked the car over with a hint of uncertainty in his eyes. "It's supposed to be the only lightweight on the coast. Or at least that's what the salesman told us, anyway."

"And we already know what a piece-of-shit liar he is, don't we?" Cal laughed.

The kid frowned, but then a big, genuine smile blossomed across his face. "Yeah, I guess we do," he agreed, and stuck out his hand. "Reventlow," he said. "Lance Reventlow. And this is my buddy Bruce Kessler. We went to school together in Arizona."

Handshakes all around.

"Lance, huh?" Cal repeated with an unmistakable edge of sarcasm. "That's a pretty lah-de-dah name, isn't it?"

The kid stiffened. "It's a family name. Anything wrong with that?" You could see he had a pretty short fuse. And obviously one heck of a bank account, too. Getting those alloy body panels and knockoff wheels on a 300SL cost damn near as much as an entire new MG.

"So it wouldn't hit 150, eh?" Cal mused, trying to change the subject.

"Nah. But I didn't keep my foot in it too long. Wanted to save it for the racetrack, you know?"

Cal and Hank nodded in unison.

The other kid shook his head. "But you should've seen this guy in a silver Porsche come past us! It was one of those new 550 Spyder jobs. Wow! We must've been doing every bit of 100, and he went sailing by like we were nailed to the damn road."

"Did the car have a number on it?" Hank asked.

Lance Reventlow nodded. "130. It had '130' painted on the rear deck. And that's damn near what he was doing."

Hank grinned. "And underneath it said *'little bastard,'* didn't it?"

"Yeah, it did, come to think of it."

Hank's grin grew even wider. "That was James Dean."

"The James Dean?" Cal asked.

Hank nodded. "The same."

A year earlier, nobody in Hollywood or anywhere else had ever heard of James Dean. According to Hank, who saw it all happen firsthand, he was just another faceless young actor from nowheresville peering in through the dirty plate-glass window of fame. But then—as happens so regularly in Hollywood—some producer or director or studio executive saw him, liked what he saw, and put a sizzling match to the waiting skyrocket of his career. After that, it was about all he could do to hang on for the ride. A smoldering, intense, good-looking kid out of Indiana by way of southern California and the Actor's Studio in New York, James Dean had been in a few plays and television show episodes out east but still had to work as a busboy in the theater district just to make ends meet. And then he did a screen test for Elia Kazan's production of *East of Eden* and the skyrocket took off. I saw that movie with Julie, and he was perfect and devastating in the part of Rink. Hank told me it helped a lot that Raymond Massey (who played his father in the movie) flat couldn't stand James Dean. Didn't like his style or his manners or particularly his acting methods. Like that riveting scene where Dean breaks down and slobbers all over his father's shirt genuinely disgusted Raymond Massey, and the way he drew back from Dean was the real thing. But it was dynamite on film—oh, was it dynamite!—and that's really all they care about in Hollywood.

East of Eden had just come out a few short months before the Salinas race, but Dean had already starred in two more pictures that had yet to be released, *Rebel Without a Cause* and *Giant,* and, just like that oil well in *Giant,* the money pipeline was gushing. Dean was a lifelong car and motorcycle nut, and now—finally—he had the wherewithal to indulge himself. He bought sports cars and motorcycles in an absolute frenzy, but had no real time to enjoy them thanks to the location work and shooting schedules. Not to mention that the studios frowned on contracted actors taking unnecessary risks. Especially while a picture was in production. It was bad enough when some key actor or actress got sick or dropped dead or went on an extended drunk or overdosed on pills or got themselves thrown into jail or locked up in a loony bin. Those things were going to happen from time to time. Particularly out in Hollywood, where grueling work schedules were inevitably intermixed with too much free time and entirely too many ways to get yourself in trouble.

Anyhow, James Dean bought himself a Porsche Speedster from John von Neumann's Competition Motors in North Hollywood, and managed to run a couple races with it during the spring of '55 after the *Rebel Without a Cause* shoot was over and before he started work on *Giant.* And the bug bit him hard. It was obvious from the start that he was going to be one of the fast guys. James Dean was quick and brave and always drove like there was something chasing him. And maybe there was. In less than a year he'd had it up to here with all the Hollywood posturing and bullshit, and he found a perfect release from all of it in the freedom, speed, solitude and blessed self-reliance of sportscar racing. Hank thought maybe he'd worked so hard for so long without getting anywhere that when success finally came—suddenly, easily and effortlessly—it maybe didn't live up to the expectation. Didn't *mean* anything, you know? Maybe that's why he had the words *"Dean's Dilemma"* painted on the tank of the Triumph motorcycle he used for blasting through the Hollywood canyons on vacant weekday afternoons. But no question he took his acting seriously, and stopped playing with his cars and motorcycles completely when he went to Texas to shoot *Giant.*

There'd be plenty of time for that afterwards….

Even so, Dean was stockpiling all kinds of hot sportscars and motorcycles to use later when he finally got the chance. He'd shown he was quick and sharp and had plenty of nerve in his Porsche Speedster (even if some felt he was a tad over-his-head reckless) and he quickly ordered himself a brand new Porsche 550 Spyder to race after the filming of *Giant* was over. That would be his first "real" racecar, and a very big step up in speed and handling performance from the Speedster. Some of his Hollywood friends warned that it might be too quick or too nervous for him at that stage of the game, while other Hollywood types who didn't care much for motorsports—like Alec Guiness and sometime girlfriend Ursula Andress—thought he ought to give up racing entirely. But James Dean wasn't having any of it. Hell, he'd tasted the magic, and he knew that he had to have more.

Besides Porsches, Dean was fascinated with the low, lightweight and futuristic (if a wee bit flimsy?) Lotus cars Colin Chapman was building over in England. Naturally the British motoring magazines swooned all over them, and they were quickly gaining a reputation as "the cars to beat" in smallbore English club racing. So Dean ordered himself one of those, too. Only without an engine. He and his wrench-spinning buddies had plans to shove in an Offenhauser four-banger—the kind they used in oval track midgets—which churned out about one-and-a-half times the power of the Coventry Climax and hopped-up MG engines Chapman usually put in his cars. If it worked, it was going to be fast as a damn bullet!

But James Dean never so much as saw that car. Let alone sat in it. And everybody was stunned into silence the next morning as news filtered through the paddock that James Dean had been killed in a highway accident on his way to the race. Not long after he swept past Lance Reventlow and Bruce Kessler in the 300SL, doing something like two miles a minute and straining for more. Turns out Dean had originally planned to break in his new racecar and get to know it by bombing around the canyon roads he knew so well north of Hollywood, then have it towed up to Salinas. That made a lot of sense, since the 550 was really a purpose-built racing car and pretty damn Spartan for road travel what with no top, side windows or insulation. So a long haul run up from Hollywood to Salinas would surely be drafty, noisy, gritty, hot and uncomfortable. But the car only arrived a week before the race, and then Dean got a little parking-lot ding the very first time he took it out. So he wheeled it straight over to his friend George Barris' body shop to get it fixed before he allowed his new racecar to show its face in public. I mean, he was sure to catch a lot of flack and snide remarks if he showed up with a dent in his brand-new racecar. And he knew George Barris would take care of it in a hurry and so that no one could tell. George did a lot of bump and customizing work for the Hollywood car crowd, and the wild cars he built were always staring back at you from the covers of the hotrod and custom car magazines you saw on the newsstands. Hank dropped by George's shop pretty regularly just to see what he was up to, and that's where he saw James Dean's little 550 Spyder getting masked for painting. As long as it was in George's body shop anyway, Dean wanted his racing number painted on the nose and sides and the nickname *"little bastard"* lettered across the back in lower-case script.

In the end they flat ran out of time for James Dean to break the car in or get any meaningful seat time on the canyon roads. So, at the very last minute, Dean decided to just drive the damn thing up to Salinas. Competition Motors' ace Porsche wrench Rolf Wuertherich tagged along in the passenger seat—on loan from the dealership to keep an eye on the mechanical stuff—and they headed north out of L.A. on Route 99 early Friday afternoon with a couple more race buddies in tow (including a magazine photographer who was planning to do a photo spread on Dean at the races), just one of so many migrating L.A. racers making that long, *banzai* run up the spine of California towards Salinas that weekend.

Only James Dean never made it.

It was a little before dusk and they were barreling east on Route 446 between 99 and 101, roaring through the flat bottom of the hot, barren, antelope-brown valley between Lost Hills and Paso Robles, heading into the afternoon sun. And Dean was *flying.* Not that he probably felt it by then, since they'd been traveling fast for hours and you get used to the speed after awhile. Especially when the landscape is so empty and wide open that you can see clear to the ridge of the next range of foothills 15 miles away. They'd been going the kind of fast where if you slow down to 50 or 60, it feels like you can almost open the door, get out and walk....

But coming along in the opposite direction (and also at a pretty fair clip, although nothing like the speed Dean's 550 was doing) was an unfortunate, wrong-place-at-the-wrong-time college student named Donald Turnupseed in a Ford Custom Tudor sedan, getting ready to take a gentle angle-sweep left onto Route 41 just a little past the dusty little town of Cholame. Although it's been written and talked about ever since, nobody really knows if the guy in the Ford didn't see the tiny silver Porsche hurtling towards him out of the shimmering blacktop mirage or lost the low, gleaming little bullet in one of the almost imperceptible roadway undulations or simply (and understandably) misjudged its closing speed as he cranked the wheel of the Ford over to make a fast left off the main highway. People who looked the spot over—and there were plenty of them in the days, weeks, months and years that followed—figured that Dean reacted like any good race driver, not slamming on the brakes and locking up the tires so he couldn't steer but rather taking aim and trying to shoot the quickly narrowing gap between the Ford and the righthand side of the road. But the Ford was moving at a pretty healthy clip, and the hole closed before Dean ever got there. The impact was enough to push the Ford's front wheel all the way back to the firewall, and the flyweight little 550 took it right square in the driver's side.

And that was pretty much the end of it.

Chapter 3: Cal in California

Cal wound up winning his class and finishing a close, right-on-his-decklid second overall up at Salinas after one hell of a battle with Bill Murphy's lumbering Kurtis 500S with that big, rumbleguts Buick V-8 under the hood. Cal was actually in front going into the last lap, but the brakes were grabbing real bad by that point thanks to a chunk of lining coming loose in one of the drums (crappy relining job was my guess) and so he couldn't go real deep into the corners. Cal tried pulling to the inside to block in order to keep the Kurtis behind him—I mean, hell, it was the last blessed lap!—but of course that killed his exit speed out of the corner and that big old Kurtis just torqued right by him on the straightaway. There was nothing he could do. But it was still one hell of a drive in a crippled car, and as a reward Ernesto let Cal run his new 300SL in the 1500cc-3000cc "Production Car" race just to give that Lance Reventlow kid something to think about. And Cal won that, too. It wasn't even close. But the kid came in second in the 3-liter class—a distant second, to be sure—and he seemed pretty pleased to have won his first tin cup. He even came up afterwards to congratulate Cal and thank him. It may seem odd that anyone would thank somebody for beating them, but you see that kind of thing all the time at racetracks—like a dog rolling over on its back to show its jugular to what it realizes is a bigger, meaner, and altogether tougher type of dog—and Hank said it sounded pretty genuine. The kid went on to allow as how he was planning to take their advice and maybe try something a little lighter and handier than the Mercedes next time.

Still, a terrible shadow hung over that whole weekend at Salinas, what with Phil Hill's family tragedy and James Dean's terrible accident on his way up from Hollywood that left him laid out on a slab and that poor Porsche mechanic in the passenger seat—who was somehow catapulted out before impact—in pretty bad shape at the hospital. And things got even worse when word came around that there'd been yet another bad wreck on the way to the races. This time coming down from San Francisco, where Masten Gregory's brother Ridelle, who was also quite an active racer at the time, had been badly injured when he got run off the road by a couple hotrod kids drag-racing on the highway. Although people who knew Ridelle thought it was entirely possible that it might have been a three-way race to begin with. But whatever it was, it split his head damn near wide open, and it was touch-and-go for quite a while as to whether he'd pull through. All of which made it a mean, sad weekend, and afterwards nobody much cared who won or what the hell happened out on the racetrack. It just didn't seem that important.

But life goes on, you know? Especially out in Hollywood, where there's always another race weekend or another fabulous party or another hot new star or exciting new film project on the horizon. Coming Attractions are always a big thing out in Hollywood. They just keep coming and coming—and always bigger and better than ever, of course!—and Hank says it maybe keeps everybody so damn focused on the future that they don't pay much attention to what they're doing at the time. Just like the distant, shimmering-wet mirage James Dean's Porsche may well have hurtled out of on Route 446, they see the future out there—dancing like quicksilver, you know?—but they can never actually reach it. "Yeah, this is the promised land, all right," Hank laughed. "*Everything* gets promised. Even if not too awful much gets delivered...."

Even so, there was a lot to like about living in Hollywood, and Cal fell hook, line and sinker for all of it. And Hank saw it all firsthand, since he wound up more or less bunking in with Cal at Ernesto Julio's fancy apartment up in the Hollywood hills. It happened almost by accident. After the Salinas race, Ernesto took his handsome new 300SL gullwing up to Sonoma County to play with for a while and Cal and Hank brought the graceful and beautiful Lancia Aurelia B24 convertible "demo" he had been driving (that would be the one with the odometer cable disconnected!) back down to the dealership in Santa Monica. The Lancia was a gorgeous car with soft, smooth, feminine lines flowing back from a handsome medieval shield of a grille, and their factory racecars (which were about as much like standard-issue street Lancias as D-Types were to XK120s!) had very briefly been the cars to beat in international sportscar racing. With the famous Vittorio Jano designing the cars and a driving team led by the incomparable Argentine champion Juan Manuel Fangio, Lancia D24s finished an amazing 1-2-3 at *La Carrera* in November of 1953, were running 1-2-3 at Sebring the following March but dropped out with mechanical problems and scored another outright win with reigning World Grand Prix Champion Alberto Ascari at the wheel in the grueling *Mille Miglia* in May. And their short, snarling grand prix car built for 1954's new, 2.5-liter Formula One looked ready to win races, too. But then it all fell apart. The racing was expensive and not enough road cars were being sold to pay for it, and so the company was woefully short of money. On top of that the awesome Mercedes steamroller and new, faster cars from Ferrari and Maserati all appeared on the scene in 1954. Mercedes even managed to hire Fangio away from Lancia, offering him an irresistible opportunity with a fantastic car and a superbly organized and disciplined team (plus a *very* large bag of *deutschmarks,* of course). The final blow was when their remaining ace, the great and movie-star popular (at least in Italy) Italian champion Alberto Ascari, got himself killed in a stupid testing accident while trying out his friend Eugenio Castellotti's new Ferrari sportscar on a quiet Thursday afternoon at Monza. Lancia pretty much threw in the towel as far as racing was concerned after that.

Even so, Lancia's road-going sportscars and *Grand Turismo* coupes were still neat, rare, elegantly engineered, and had wonderful looks and handling. Hank said the Lancia made for quite a contrast to the bank-vault-solid 300SL he and Cal drove up to Salinas on Friday. It didn't feel nearly as powerful, strong or sturdy, but it was a lot more forgiving and far more graceful and lighter on its feet than the big Mercedes. Besides, it was a convertible, and that always counted for a lot when it came to tooling down the coast road in California. Especially at night under a fat, silvery moon….

As you can imagine, Cal's eyelids were drooping dangerously by the time they hit the heavy early-Monday-morning traffic a little more than 50 miles north of town. "So where y'gotta go once we get there?" he yawned at Hank.

Hank looked over at him. "My mom and stepdad live way south. Past Orange County. It's over an hour each way. Maybe two during rush hour." And then he added sheepishly: "I could maybe catch a cab or a bus or something…."

"In Los Angeles? On a Monday morning?" Cal scoffed. "Look, why don't you just bunk in with me at Ernesto's apartment? Hell, it's got three bedrooms. Well, two bedrooms and a den, anyway. Plus a living room and a dining room and a kitchen and a Mexican lady who comes over and makes the beds and cleans the place up three times a week. And a balcony that looks out over the whole damn city, too." He was tired. Rambling. "Anyhow, there's plenty of room. Y'even get your own bathroom."

"Sounds better than sleeping on my mom's front porch."

"You sleep on a porch?"

"Lotta times I do. It's cooler out there." Hank checked through the clothes in his duffel bag as he added: "Besides, my mom and my stepdad don't always get on real well. It's quieter out there, if you know what I mean…."

Cal nodded without saying anything.

"…But, hey, it's a place to lay my head and get my clothes washed for free whenever I'm in town. And I'm not in town all that much anymore. Fact is, I'm hoping to get assigned over to Europe next summer. Or maybe the summer after."

"Sounds like a pretty soft deal."

"I don't know how soft it'll be. I think I may be eating a lot of my dinners out of a sardine tin and sleeping in old Fiats or on railroad station benches. But I'm pretty sure it's what I want to do."

"Hey, if it's what you *want* to do, it's what you've *got* to do," Cal said like he knew what he was talking about. "That's the way I've got it figured."

"Me, too."

And that's how my scribe buddy Hank Lyons wound up more or less moving in with Cal at Ernesto Julio's fancy apartment up in the Hollywood hills. And got to witness it all firsthand while Cal fell deeply, desperately in love with California.

Meanwhile it was the ugly, gray, glum and overcast beginning of winter back here in Passaic, and Cal would call me from time to time to see how things were going and razz me mercilessly about how great things were out in California. "It's beautiful out here, Buddy," he'd coo into the phone while I looked out at the cold, slick streets and the carpet of wet leaves in our yard and the raindrops that would soon be sleet and then snow drooling their way down the windowpane. "Why, I was just down by the pool working on my tan."

"Screw you, Cal."

"There's plenty of that out here, too, Buddy. More beautiful girls than you've ever seen in your life. And you'd be amazed how many of them are available. There's a couple of them down at the pool right now…"

"I'm married, Cal. I've got a wife and kids here."

"Hey, as long as you're happy."

Then he'd go back to pulling my chain about the climate. It always seemed to start with the damn climate. Shirtsleeve and swim suit weather damn near every day of the year. And that's only if you felt like wearing a shirt. Or a swimsuit, for that matter. "You wouldn't believe it, Buddy. I can go down to the beach in Santa Monica and have my breakfast under a palm tree looking out at the ocean if I want to before I go to work."

"You get up early enough for that?"

"Well, actually it's more like lunch."

Sure, I'd argue back and forth with him—like New York and Jersey people always do—about how much we loved our seasons back east, and how I just couldn't imagine life without winter blossoming into spring and spring easing into summer and summer fading into fall and fall icing up into winter every year. Even if it did bring more sweltering heat, freezing cold, pouring rain, gloom, sleet, slush and snow than anybody in their right mind would really care for. Cal'd listen politely at the other end and then reply: "Yeah, it's pretty hard to take out here in Los Angeles. One God Damn perfect day after another…."

But there was a price to pay. With no season change, winter break or garage hibernation to split the years up for you, it's maybe harder to tell that you've grown a year older. Hank always said that was a bonus, because it allowed Californians to kid themselves into thinking they weren't getting any older because of the way all the years start melting together. "We've got the fountain of youth out here," Hank would brag. But then he'd add kind of sheepishly: "Unfortunately, you only see old people drinking out of it."

Sure, I'd grill Cal about all the weirdos, nutcases and fruitcakes everybody said were all over the place out in California. But he had a pretty simple answer: "They came here for the weather, just like everybody else."

Then there was the damn landscape. I hadn't seen it yet, but Cal told me you could drive less than the time it takes to get from Passaic to Watkins Glen and be in your choice of palm trees, pine trees or sagebrush and cactus. Or ocean beaches, rocky foothills, snow-capped mountains, Death Valley badlands, dense forests, flat farmland, parched deserts and damn near anything you could think of in between. Although he had to admit not very much of it was green like we know green back east. Not green like the Berkshire Mountains in Connecticut or the Adirondacks in upper New York State or the beautiful Kettle Moraine district around Elkhart Lake, Wisconsin. No, most of California looked more like antelope hide. Or maybe dry toast. But I suppose you get used to that. Especially when the sun shines all year long and the racing season runs from one year right into the next without a break. Hell, back east we'd pretty much packed up our stuff for the winter by the time that sad race in Salinas took place the first weekend of October. But the west coast bunch still had a full schedule of races that ran all the way through until spring. Like I said, it made you just a wee bit jealous. Particularly if you were looking out the window at a cold, gray New Jersey sky and a yard full of wet leaves your wife pretty much expected you to rake sometime before the first snowstorm hit.

And meanwhile your buddy/hero Cal Carrington is out there in California wearing tee shirts and aviator sunglasses and chatting up girls at the pool and working on his blessed tan and waiting for the next damn race weekend to roll around. And that won't be much of a wait since there's a Cal Club weekend coming up at Torrey Pines down near San Diego on October 22-23. "You really ought to come out here, Buddy," Cal grinned into the phone. "We've got sunshine, fun and racing all year long. Believe me, this place is the Shangri-La for sports cars."

"I got a life and a family and a business to take care of back here in Jersey," I told him, sounding just a little miffed. "I can't just take off and re-plant myself someplace else."

"Oh, you'd *love* it out here," he said like he was daring me. "If you can't come to stay, why don't you just come out for a visit? Just a race weekend or two…."

Sure, I knew he mostly just wanted to show off the fancy place he was staying and the super neat cars he was driving and the girls in their two-piece bathing suits down at the pool and all the other well-known earthly delights of California. But I also got the notion that Cal might be just a wee bit homesick. Otherwise why would he keep calling me and bugging me to come out there? No doubt being out on your own can be a wonderful sort of thing, but it can also be a dream with a hole in the bottom.

Cal called me again after the Torrey Pines races, which were held at the old, abandoned Camp Callan Army base near La Jolla, just north of San Diego. In spite of the scenic-sounding name, Torrey Pines was just some flat, dusty scrubland between the Pacific Coast Highway and a set of steep, sheer cliffs that dropped about five stories down to the ocean. The few stunted pine trees that actually grew at Torrey Pines were mostly about waist-to-armpit high, and what with the hard, gritty wind that came blowing in off the ocean, it wasn't exactly the handsomest or most hospitable sort of place to host an automobile race. But it was there, it was empty and it was available, and with all the hordes of speed-crazy sportycar junkies frothing at the bit out in southern California, both the SCMA and Cal Club held races there starting as far back as December of 1951. Hank said there were rumors flying that the October '55 race would be the last one ever at Torrey Pines on account of they were turning the property into a golf course. Although another reason might have been that the July race there turned into a real disaster. The SCMA put it on in conjunction with the San Diego Junior Chamber of Commerce and, as you can imagine with two volunteer groups attempting to joint-organize the thing and a double-serving of self-important Charlie Priddle armband types running around in circles trying to flex their authority, not too much actually got done. Or done right, anyway. Maybe it was just bad luck and maybe it was poor planning, but there were two fatalities plus a serious injury, and that's just not the kind of thing you want happening in the public eye. Especially after that celebrated mess Hank and me had witnessed at Le Mans earlier in the year.

The trouble started as early as Friday night, when some know-nothing idiot with maybe a few too many belts under his belt decided to sneak out onto the "closed" racetrack for a couple hot laps. He crashed out there in the darkness and managed to kill himself. Then, come Sunday, one of the female drivers in the "ladies race" flipped her car at turn one and she died in the wreck, too. I don't know exactly why, but a woman getting killed always seems to get the press and the public do-gooder types a lot more worked up than if it happens to a person of the male persuasion. Does that seem fair to you? But that's the way it is, and everybody and their brother knows it. Plus in between they had a serious brushfire in the infield—Hank said southern California is nothing more than one big tinderbox during the height of summer—and another spectator with maybe an oversupply of alcohol for fuel wandered over the edge of the cliff and fell all the way down to the beach below. It probably should have killed him, but drunks have that uncanny ability to go all rag-doll in desperate situations rather than stiffening up like any normal human being, and that probably saved his stupid life. In any case, they had to dispatch a Navy rescue helicopter to lift him up off the beach in a canvas sling.

Naturally there was a lot of arguing and posturing and finger-pointing afterwards about who was responsible for what—not that it would help either of the dead people or the taxpayers who ultimately paid for the helicopter and its crew—and the general consensus was that the golf course project was being prodded along pretty smartly after that. So between that and the grim, lingering hangover from the Salinas race a couple weeks earlier, it was a rather subdued crowd of racers that filled up the paddock at Torrey Pines that fourth weekend of October. And the weather mirrored how they felt, what with a grim, ugly fog bank parked on the edge of the ocean and a cold, damp breeze that Hank said cut right through you blowing in hard off the water all weekend.

Cal Club's schedule featured a just-for-fun six-hour enduro on Saturday along with two one-hour feature races for under-1500cc and over-1500cc "modified" cars, two 30-minute races for under-1500cc and over-1500cc "production" cars plus a 20-minute "ladies' race" and a 20-minute "Formula III/Formula libre" race for open-wheel single-seaters on Sunday. The amazing thing was the number of entries Cal mentioned, what with over 165 cars set for Sunday's races and more than *70* entered in Saturday's enduro. That's one hell of a lot of cars for any racetrack, let alone a tight, flat, narrow strip of blacktop like Torrey Pines.

That Lance Reventlow kid was there again with his fancy lightweight 300SL—this time co-driving with his wiseass, bucks-up Arizona prep school buddy Bruce Kessler—but they hit trouble in the enduro with lousy pit stops and a flat tire and finished well back. Kessler drove it again the next day (Cal thought maybe the club might have been making a few small inquiries about Lance's real age, but I guess Bruce Kessler didn't look much older!) and he won going away. Cal allowed as how this Kessler kid looked to be a pretty damn decent driver, and that was high praise indeed from an ace like Cal. There was another all-alloy 300SL on hand for the enduro piloted by a guy named Paul O'Shea, and both Cal and Hank said that car was really fast. Plus he was co-driving the enduro with none other than Phil Hill, and so it was no big surprise when they came home a solid second overall in the six-hour behind a "real racecar" C-Type Jaguar that had an unusually uneventful, trouble-free run. Which is exactly what you want in an endurance race.

Ernesto Julio didn't want Cal or anybody else running his Ferrari in the enduro, figuring it would be stupid to take that many hours out of the car for a "who cares" kind of race—especially since it was being scored on handicap (like that incomprehensible "Index of Performance" thing at Sebring and Le Mans) so one of the little tiddlers with a tiny engine and great gas mileage was almost sure to win. But that left Cal making the rounds of the paddock Friday night and early Saturday morning, trying to line himself up a ride. He thought he had a deal to drive one of those little French DB "Douche Bag" things (which would have been just the ticket for a race scored on handicap) but I guess the ride had already been kind of half-promised to some fuzz-faced "car writer" named Henry N. Manney. Can you imagine trusting your racecar to some hotshot scribe who thinks he can drive just because he knows how to pound words about it out of a typewriter?

How stupid can some people be?

In the end Ernesto managed to find Cal a co-drive in one of those hot new Porsche 550 Spyders like the one James Dean got himself killed in just a few weeks before. It belonged to some Hollywood director type who wore huge, rose-tinted sunglasses, pointy Italian leather shoes, riding pants, a cocked French beret on his head and a polka-dot silk ascot underneath a pale salmon colored silk shirt. Cal wondered if there was maybe some kind of costume party going on out in California that he didn't know about. "Oh, he was a nice enough guy," Cal allowed, "but we had to keep him kind of tied down so he didn't float right up out of his shoes."

"How was he as a driver?"

"About how he looked. Maybe a little worse."

"And how'dja like the Porsche?"

"Aw, geez," he almost gushed, "once you get used to the handling, you can run rings around cars with twice, even three times the power."

"So you liked it?"

"I *loved* it!" Cal enthused. "It's just such a light, tight, solid little package. Nimble as the dickens. Fast as stink, too. Or at least so long as you keep your momentum up. And it's easy on tires, easy on gas, and it feels like it'll just run and run all day long. It's *strong!* Built German, you know what I mean?"

"You're talking to a guy who sells Volkswagens for a living."

"Then you know what I'm talking about. But you know what the best part is?"

"Tell me."

"It's having the damn engine behind you and no radiator or anything up front. We had a pretty cold weekend at Torrey Pines and so I actually got a little chilly in the car, but usually you're just *dying* in there from all the heat and fumes off the engine pouring over you!"

"So you had a good race?"

"I suppose I did…but as a team we didn't do too great."

"What happened?"

"Aw, I think we could've maybe won the damn thing outright if he'd let me drive the whole way by myself. Or at least come in second."

"Only second? That doesn't sound like you."

"Oh, one of those popcorn-popper DoucheBag things like they run for Index at Le Mans won on handicap. Went the whole damn distance on one tank of gas. Never stopped for anything, can you believe it?"

"It must've had one hell of a gas tank."

"Yeah. And the driver must've had himself one hell of a bladder, too!"

I hadn't thought about that, but suddenly realized what a major concern it might be. "What about your race?" I asked.

"Let's just say the guy who owns the car was already more than two laps behind when he handed it over to me. I fought and clawed my way back onto the lead lap—went just as fast as the fastest 550s there, maybe even a little faster—but then he insisted on getting back in and lost us another two laps again before the finish."

"So the guy couldn't drive?"

"I'm not sure if it was couldn't, wouldn't or didn't, but he really might want to consider another hobby."

"O.S.B., huh?"

"O.S.B.?"

"Yeah: *Other Sports Beckon.*"

Cal laughed out loud at that one.

"Hey," I reminded him, "neat cars have no control over who owns 'em."

"Amen to that, brother," Cal agreed. "Amen to that."

I shifted around in my chair. "Y'know, lots of people figure that Porsche 550 is the best smallbore racecar in the whole blessed world."

"It probably is, but it wasn't this weekend."

"Oh?"

"Nah. This Ken Miles guy—he's that skinny little hawknose Brit with the nifty MG special…."

"You've told me about him."

"Well, he beat all the Porsche 550s with that thing in the smallbore feature on Sunday. The OSCAs, too. It was pretty damn amazing." The idea that you could beat the best purpose-built, overhead-camshaft, alloy-engined racecars Germany and Italy had to offer with some kind of homebuilt special powered by a hot-rodded MG engine sounded pretty damn preposterous. But apparently this Ken Miles character was hardly your average, garden-variety backyard mechanic. Or driver, come to that!

Poor Cal's race in Ernesto Julio's Ferrari ended before it even started on Sunday when a fuel line coupling came apart on the pace lap (which indicated to me that some wrench-wielding idiot disassembled it for cleaning or something and just plain forgot to tighten it back up properly) and naturally it was some oddball, orphan fitting with a hollow bolt and a necked shank so if you didn't have the exact right part there was no way in hell to jimmy it back together. As best as Cal and Ernesto's mechanics could figure, that special bolt was out there somewhere on the race course (or, worse yet, off in the sand, scrub brush and weeds) and so there was nothing to do but pull up a patch of sand and a cup of hot coffee with a shot or two of brandy in it—Cal said it was way too cold for a beer—and watch the blessed race.

"It was a pretty good race," Cal allowed. "That Bill Murphy guy won in the Kurtis-Buick I raced against in Salinas, but he got pushed plenty hard by something called the Troutman and Barnes Special."

"I've heard of that one, too." And of course I had. After all, *Car & Track*—not to mention all the other well known or here-today/gone-tomorrow sportycar magazines in this country—were almost all published in southern California. So it only made sense that they paid a lot of attention to what was going on in their own back yard. Seems this Dick Troutman and Tom Barnes were top-notch metal fabricators out of the aircraft industry who also moonlighted pretty regularly in Frank Kurtis' Kurtis-Kraft shop in Glendale, building Indy cars, midgets, sprinters and such. Anyhow, they got this notion to do a sports car together, and built it around a hotrodder's favorite Flathead Ford V-8 that everybody said would never last as a road racing engine or make near enough power to run with the bigger, overhead-valve V-8s from Caddy, Chrysler, Buick and the rest. Let alone the fancy DOHC engines from overseas. But the car they put together was light and straightforward and simple as a stone axe, only they used the same sort of materials, detailing, craftsmanship and build quality as a top-flight Indy car. And could it ever *go!* Especially when they put this guy named Chuck Daigh behind the wheel. I'd met him at Elkhart Lake and then again out at Bonneville, only I never knew how to spell his name right on account of the "gh" was as silent as the "p" in "phish." He was an ace wrench and fabricator by trade (not to mention one hell of a seat-of-the-pants engineer) and I guess what he really wanted out of life was to race in the Indianapolis 500. But until that kind of opportunity came along, he figured he could keep his racing addiction in check by helping build Indycars and driving this sportycar special for Troutman and Barnes. He won a bunch of races with it, too. Flathead Ford and all! Although he came up a wee bit short at Torrey Pines and had to settle for second. But you could tell from Cal's voice that he was pretty damn impressed with both the driver and the car. And so was that Lance Reventlow kid with the alloy-bodied 300SL Mercedes....

"Oh, by the way," Cal added before hanging up, "there's a car out here that's almost as ugly as your Trashwagon."

"It can't be," I argued. I mean, if there was one thing my Trashwagon had in spades, it was *ugly.* In fact, I'd gotten kind of sensitive about it.

"I ain't lyin'," Cal assured me. "It's called the Morgensen Special, and it's got a whole bucketload of ugly going for it. I'll send you a picture." And damn if he didn't. And double-damn if Cal wasn't right. And here I'd always thought *I* could lay claim to being the Worst Damn No-Talent Panel-Beater on the Face of the Earth....

Torrey Pines was hardly the last race of the year out in California. A week later there was road racing at the Sacramento Fairgrounds, then at the Glendale Airport in the middle of November, Palm Springs the first weekend in December and even a long jaunt down to wild-man promoter Red Crise's new Nassau Speed Weeks in the Bahamas in the middle of December for those who had the free time and money for it. And a lot of those California racers did. Then it was back to Torrey Pines again for the second (and this time *really* final) "last race weekend ever at Torrey Pines" in the middle of January. Followed by Palm Springs way out in the desert in February and, well, then the season kicked into high gear with races damn near every two weeks again for the balance of the year. They had a hell of a selection of tracks, too. Even if a lot of them were pretty makeshift. There was sportycar racing around Hansen Dam near Los Angeles, at a new, purpose-built racetrack called Willow Springs out in the barren high desert country near Palmdale, airport races at Santa Barbara, not to mention events at Stockton, Bakersfield, Santa Maria, Seattle, San Diego and Pomona. Why, they'd even had racing right through the middle of Golden Gate Park in San Francisco!

But the real jewel in the crown of California road racing had to be Pebble Beach out on the Monterey Peninsula. Some sharp property developers connected with the Del Monte canned fruits and vegetables money were busy creating a very exclusive resort and don't-you-wonder-what-these-folks-do-for-a-living residential area in the dramatic, handsomely forested hills along the Pacific coastline there, and they saw the kind of people—and bank accounts!—road racing attracted to places like Bridgehampton and Palm Beach. So they rightly reasoned that a set of road races might be just the ticket when it came to pumping up the local real estate business. In fact, that's precisely how Ernesto Julio wound up with a large chunk of severely sloped, ocean-view real estate on the scenic, snaking switchbacks of 17-Mile Drive. Along with an overpriced architect on retainer, a contractor who drove a new Packard, an even more overpriced Interior Desecrator waiting in the wings and a Founding Membership in a fancy-schmancy golf club that was just going up on the ocean front. Even though Ernesto Julio didn't know how to play golf at all.

"Oh, you'll absolutely *love* it," the real estate people told him.

"I will?"

"Absolutely."

"It looks too hard. And a little unnatural. The way you gotta stand like you got a rod up your ass and swing those clubs and all."

"But that's the beauty of it. You'll see."

"I dunno," Ernesto Julio told them. "I got a lotta friends who play golf, and the thing I notice is that the better they are at it, the more miserable it makes them."

Chapter 4: A Little Home Cooking

To tell the truth, I was a little jealous about all the sportycar stuff going on and all the racing Cal was doing and all the damn fun he seemed to be having out in California while I was stuck working my butt off from dawn-thirty every morning until half-past-dinnertime every night taking care of our budding Volkswagen dealership and sportycar shop in Passaic. Maybe even more than a little jealous. Sure, all the hard work was starting to pay off for Big Ed and me, but it didn't seem fair for me to be Vice President in Charge of a Bewildering Assortment of Aggravations and Blindside Daily Disasters hitched to that grindstone of that car store while Cal played Wealthy Playboy Race Car Driver under the endless summer sunshine of southern California. On the other hand, it's kind of nice to have wild, freewheeling, devil-may-care friend/heroes to follow and root for—even if they do happen to be self-centered jerks who never once pause to think about other people or what the right thing to do might be—because it lets you live a little bit of that wild, freewheeling life yourself right through them. You know what I mean? So I kept close tabs on Cal and his life out in California, and it gave us lots to talk about around the shop besides sports and news headlines and who appeared last night on *The Ed Sullivan Show* or how much the latest grinning egghead had won on *The $64,000 Question.* It gave me stuff to daydream about, too. Even working stiff grownups need stuff to daydream about.

To hear him tell it, Cal was having the time of his life out in Hollywood, slipping back and forth between the overlapping social whirls of the local movie business & sportycar set. When you think about it, Cal was always more or less sneaking around in the shadows of his parents lives back home at Castle Carrington (or out at their summer beach house in the Hamptons or down at their winter place in Palm Beach, Florida) even though he hardly ever ran into them face-to-face and did pretty much whatever the hell he wanted most of the time. But out in LA, he could do it all without sneaking or getting yelled at or grounded or threatened for the umpty-umpth time with the loss of his inheritance. Not that old Cal Carrington ever stayed grounded for very long. Or at least not after Sylvester showed him how to go behind the dashboard of damn near any car and jimmy the wires to fire it up. It was pretty easy if you knew what to look for. Plus now he had that trust fund money he never talked much about coming in every month—and even a small paycheck twice a month from Ernesto Julio's *Moto Italia* sportycar store in Santa Monica. And that beat hell out of embezzling from his college fund or rifling through his mother's purse or his father's dress pants while they slept one off.

When you get right down to it, Cal was really on his own—and I mean *really* on his own—for the very first time in his life. And he was making the most of it. Or that's the way he made it sound, anyway. There were races or parties every weekend (or races *and* parties every weekend) along with a lot of generally available girls who didn't have to be home at any special time on account of home was actually someplace back in Portsmouth or Pittsburgh or Pocatello or Poughkeepsie or Plano, Texas. I guess most of them came out to Hollywood to have the kind of life they read about in the movie magazines and saw at the Saturday matinees, and there was apparently a near-endless supply of them. Just like there's always a near-endless supply of wannabe racing drivers. There's even a pretty healthy crop of both that have the talent and chops for it. And even more with all the hunger, drive and ambition you could possibly need. But the number who actually make it to the top amount to a scant handful. One out of ten thousand, maybe. Or maybe even fewer than that. That's just the way it is. But that doesn't keep them from coming. And trying. And hoping....

So there were always plenty of girls around, and you had an inkling that Cal Carrington did well with the ladies. It was something you just *knew*. Like you knew that the sun rose in the east or a Lucas voltage regulator would eventually need replacing. And sooner more likely than later. Not that you ever saw him squiring girls around much when he lived back home at Castle Carrington. But of course I only saw Cal around Old Man Finzo's Sinclair or my Aunt Rosamarina's garage or away on race weekends where he was always hustling like hell just to get there and get something to drive. Cal generally kept the rest of his life—his life away from cars and racing—pretty much private. He never brought girls to the track like a lot of guys did. But maybe he figured they'd just get in the way. I mean, you can only keep so may balls in the air at a time, and I've observed from my own personal experience that women require a serious investment in time, courtesy and attention if you want to keep them happy. Or even if you just want to keep them from yelling, crying, stomping off in a huff or throwing stuff at you, come to that. Or that's the way it's always worked in my life, anyway. Not that I'm any kind of expert, since I think I only had maybe two dates before I met Julie and those probably don't even count since they both ended with handshakes. Still, I'd heard stories about girls Cal picked up here and there (even once or twice when we were away on race weekends) and no question Cal was smooth and cool and utterly confident when it came to women. And it wasn't just because he was handsome and graceful and came from a lot of money, but also because he was one of those exciting, irresistible, silver-spoon desperados who didn't give two shits about anybody or anything but themselves. Don't ask me why, but most girls can't keep their hands off guys like that. And not just the fast girls, sluts and tramps, either. It's like even nice girls can't wait to stick their fingers in the fire. And, no, I can't figure it out, either.

Fact is, my friend Cal Carrington had been kind of a lone wolf ever since I'd known him, and the only time I ever saw any female of the species really register with him—and I mean deep down where you could really see and feel it—was when he ran into that quietly determined, sleek and beautiful little Angelina Scalabrini at the New Years Eve party we went to in Greenwich Village the winter before Julie and me got married. Boy, you could feel the heat between those two just standing there in the darkened hallway. It wasn't the sort of thing you could miss. I remember he took her home to her folks' place in Brooklyn (and left us pretty much stranded at the party in the process, but by then we'd learned to expect that kind of thing from Cal) and I know for a fact he went out with her once or twice after that. Or at least he did until she and her mother pretty much vanished off the face of the earth. Or at least out of the greater metropolitan New York area, anyway. I remember Cal went over to the little Italian restaurant her father ran in Brooklyn to find out what happened to her, but her old man was pretty tight lipped about it. Angry, too. To tell the truth, I don't think he liked Cal very much. And he sure as hell didn't trust him.

But for whatever reason that Angelina Scalabrini made quite an impression on Cal. And it wasn't just on account of those catlike green eyes and shimmering black hair and skin you dreamed of using for a pillow. Or that racehorse of a figure with a waist you could pretty much clasp your hands around plus curves above and below that made your eyes bug out. To be honest, I thought she was the single most beautiful female creature I'd ever seen. Marilyn Monroe, Cyd Charisse and Sally Enderle included. But there was something more. You could see it in the clear, keen focus of her eyes and the proud, almost arrogant grace of her posture and the soft but utterly determined set of her jaw. This was a girl who expected to go somewhere and get something out of life. And God only help you if you didn't take her seriously or tried to stand in her way. I knew that kind of look and attitude because I could see the same exact things in Cal every time he sat down to drive.

Cal called me again—collect, natch—the Sunday night after the SCMA races at the Glendale Airport in November. He'd driven Ernesto Julio's Ferrari again and he was feeling pretty cocky and expansive because he'd won his race and had perhaps been persuaded into a few celebratory beers afterwards in the paddock. Not that such a thing ever required much persuading after a race win. Cal was never what you could call a regular, every day, rummy-style drinker—he kept an eye on it, but not so's you'd notice—but he could cut loose pretty good on special occasions. And winning a race was always a special occasion. The champagne, beer and booze flow freely after the checker comes down, and folks always keep handing you mugs and tumblers and paper cups of the stuff whenever you're the lucky chump carrying that flag under your other arm. So it never dawned on Cal that it was actually early Monday morning back in Jersey when he decided to ring me up. Naturally it woke Julie and the kids—both of whom started bawling immediately—and of course Julie's mother came flying down the stairs like a load of coal down a coal chute, demanding to know who'd died.

"Nobody died." I explained sheepishly. "It's just my friend Cal calling from California."

"Izzie inna hospital?" Julie's mother wanted to know.

"I don't think so."

"Izzie inna jail?"

I shook my head.

Julie's mother's eyes went down to mean little slits. *"Then he's-a no good a-sonofabitch,"* She shook her fist at the phone. *"You tella the inconsiderate rat a-bastard f'me: he's-a no good a-sonofabitch."*

"MOM!" Julie screamed, her eyes just as narrow and dangerous as her mother's, *"Please don't talk like that in front of the kids!"*

Little Vincent stopped bawling, looked back and forth between Julie and her mother, and a look of grand, celestial serenity blossomed on his face. I hadn't seen a look like that since he used to drop a particularly satisfying load in his pants before he was potty trained. *"He's-a no good a-sonofabitch!"* Vincent agreed through a winning, radiant smile.

Of course that set Julie and her mom off again, and that startled little Vincent and got him bawling again, and then the baby joined in on general principles and it took the better part of twenty minutes to get Julie and her mom calmed down and the kids fixed up with their necessary trips to the bathroom and glasses of water that would just make them want to go pee again and get everybody packed off to bed so I could get back to the phone in the kitchen. Cal was still on it, of course. Waiting. And why not? After all, he was calling collect.

"Married life sure sounds like a lot of fun," Cal laughed as soon as I got back on the line. He was always a master at sticking the old knife in and twisting it.

"Hmph," I snorted back at him, "You'll never know." And then I started in like my old man: "You'll never grow up enough or care about any other human being enough to get married. You haven't got it in you."

"You're breaking my heart, Buddy," he sniffled into the phone. And then he blew his nose into the receiver. "Why, you'd be amazed how mature and grown up I've become out here in California."

"Yeah, you're *real* grown up," I growled. To tell the truth, I was plenty mad at Cal for waking us up. But it was kinda funny, too. Cal had a way of making most any serious adult topic seem stupid and absurd and even hilarious. It was just a knack he had.

I looked at the clock over the stove. It was coming up on one-thirty in the morning. "Do you know what time it is?"

I could see Cal looking at his watch on the other end. "Jeez, it's 10:30. Sorry I called so late."

What could you say to that? "So," I asked him, "you workin' every day?"

"I'm working on my tan every day," he snickered into the phone. "You really ought to come out here, Buddy. The sun shines all the time and the cars are amazing and there's races every other weekend right through the winter and the girls are plentiful, easy and beautiful."

"You make me sick."

"Hey, is it my fault how well things turned out for me?"

"You need to get a job and a family and some kind of medical condition that makes your skin rot and your teeth fall out of your head. Get a little misery in your life. See how the rest of the world lives."

"I can see the view from here," he assured me. I could see that sly cobra smile of his on the other end of the line. "But I gotta look *waaaay* down to see it."

"Anybody ever tell you what a prince of a guy you are?"

"The guy in the mirror tells me that every morning."

"I just bet he does."

"Hey," Cal shrugged, "he can't help himself."

And that was true enough.

"Listen," Cal started in again, finally getting to the reason he called, "we're racing out in Sacramento in a couple weeks, and that's damn near halfway back to Jersey. Why don'cha get up off your ass and come out for it?"

"Are you out of your mind?"

"Hard to say. Hard to say. Upstate vote isn't in yet. But you oughta come out here. See for yourself what it's like."

"Oh, sure thing. I'll just fire up our VW demo, point it west on Pine Street and put a brick on the accelerator. That should do the trick. And maybe I'll put a *'gone fishin'* sign on the shop door for a week or ten days while I'm away. I'm sure all our fine service customers will understand. So will Julie. In fact, I just can't wait to tell her. Why, she hasn't hit me with anything in at least a week...."

"She'll understand," he said expansively.

"Sure she will."

"And you won't be gone for eight or ten days."

"Have you ever tried driving through the mountains in a Volkswagen Beetle?"

"No, listen. I've got it all set up for you. See, they just got one of those pretty new Alfa Romeo *Giulietta Sprint* coupes coming in for us at the New York docks, and normally one of our guys—me, most likely—would have to fly out and drive it back. But I told them how you were already out there, and it'd be just as easy for you to pick it up for us, grab some stuff for me from over at my folks' place, drive it out here, meet us at the races at Sacramento and then we'd fly you back home on Monday. It's the same difference to the guys at the dealership either way."

I knew I was in serious trouble when Cal's plan started sounding reasonable to me. But I also knew it was precisely the kind of thinking upon which marriage counselors and divorce lawyers base their livelihoods. "Look," I told him, "I just can't do it. I got a wife and kids and a mother-in-law who can't stand me to take care of. I got a car shop and a Volkswagen dealership to look after. I can't just be dropping everything and taking off whenever some grand new road adventure falls in my lap. I just can't *do* that anymore, see?"

"Buddy, Buddy, Buddy," I heard Cal *tsk-tsk*-ing on the other end, "you're turning into a genuine old fart. You know that?"

I did know that. And it made me sigh. "Look, we can't all be knights of the realm like you, going on great quests and slaying evil dragons and rescuing maidens in distress. The world just doesn't work that way for the rest of us. We've got shit to do. We've got *responsibilities.*"

"Use that ugly word again and I'll come over there and wash your worthless mouth out with soap."

"All the way to New Jersey?"

"All the way to New Jersey. Just see if I don't."

I had to laugh. But it was kind of a sad laugh.

"Look," I told him, "let me know if you do come out this way. Maybe we can have lunch or something."

"Lunch?" he snorted. "You sure you can spare the time?"

Cal did come out a couple weeks later to pick up that new Alfa Romeo, and I had to admit it was great to see him. Even if it did make me sick that he looked so tan and relaxed and like he was getting entirely too much sun, fun, female companionship and beach, surf and pool time, while us poor working stiffs back in Jersey were generally about the color of library paste at that time of year. Except for the circles under our eyes, of course. And I had to admit that *Giulietta Sprint* coupe was one sharp, smart, sweet and sexy little machine. It had a real face on it, you know? And a personality that went right along with it. Turns out Alfa had sponsored a contest to pick a name for their new little sportscar, and some typically moonstruck Italian came up with *Giulietta* (that's *"Joo-lee-et-ta")* after the romantic teenage heroine in that famous—but kind of mushy, sad and tragic—Shakespeare play. Even though she kills herself in the end.

Anyhow, Cal tooled up in front of the our shop out of nowhere late on a Tuesday afternoon—unannounced, of course—so I could disconnect the speedometer cable for his drive back west. Naturally we took it for a spin, and what a marvelous, happy, warm-blooded little machine it was! And what a great sound it made, too. More of a fuzzy, feline sort of purr and growl than anything you heard out of a rorty British four-cylinder. And it drove and handled the same way—smooth, soft and supple, just like a big, slinky house cat—with light, tight steering, good pedal feel through the brakes and the most amazing shifter I'd ever stirred. The lever was long, but it went right into the top of the gearbox and so it had this terrifically smooth, solid action. Almost like a joint on a human body, you know? And when we put it up on the grease rack to check things out underneath, I was really impressed by the *Giulietta Sprint's* unibody-style chassis, where the body and the frame were really all one structure. More like an ant or a crawfish rather than something with a skeleton inside and skin on the outside. It was made out of all these almost organic-looking structures of stamped, welded-up sheet steel, which gave it a much deeper, stronger and yet lighter third dimension than an ordinary, old-fashioned set of frame rails with a separate body bolted on top. Makes for a really nice balance between rigidity and light weight if you do it right. At least if you get good steel, anyway—but that's another story.

I was also impressed with the stuff underneath the fenderwells: elegantly made, strong and yet lightweight front control arms, coil spring rear suspension with this nifty triangular piece on top of the axle to control side-to-side movement and torque windup, plus big brakes with gorgeous finned aluminum drums. Just like a blessed racecar! Not to mention all the handsome ribbed aluminum castings for the engine block, transmission case and even the damn center section of the rear end! Unlike your average mainline British sportscar builders, the gents at Alfa Romeo didn't care too much for cast iron. "Wow! This thing is like a junior edition of a Ferrari underneath!" I said to no one in particular.

"That's exactly what the guys at the shop in Santa Monica call them," Cal grinned. "The poor man's Ferrari."

But of course that made perfect sense, since old man Ferrari worked for Alfa Romeo and ran their racing team for years before he ever split off and started building cars on his own. Alfas had an engineering and race-winning pedigree that went all the way back before the First World War, and they were pretty much the cars to beat in European endurance and grand prix racing all through the twenties and thirties. Or at least until Herr Hitler started pumping a bunch of money into the Mercedes-Benz and Auto Union teams just before World War Two to put the fear of God (or at least of The Fatherland) into the rest of Europe.

After the second war, the first two grand prix World Driving Championships ever (Giusieppe Farina in 1950 and Juan Manuel Fangio's first title in 1951) were won in Alfa Romeos. And that was using cars they'd basically designed and built back in the thirties. In fact, the Alfa team steamrollered everybody so badly that the FIA guys in Paris changed the rules to a new, smaller formula for 1953 just so's there'd be a little competition. Besides, running a racing team was an expensive proposition, and even though Alfa was pretty much mopping the floor with the opposition, they really needed to start paying more attention to their everyday, go-to-market models if they wanted to grow and prosper—or even survive—in the postwar economy.

See, road-going Alfas had historically been exclusive and expensive and upscale, but that new *Giulietta* series was aimed a little more towards your John Q. Public/Fred Average kind of sportycar nut. All I knew is that I loved everything about it: loved the way it looked, loved the way it was built, and more than anything loved the way it drove. What an eager, happy, *willing* little car! Oh, sure, the engine was only 1290ccs (or a whopping 79 Cubes American!) but it was all alloy—even the damn engine block!—with hemispherical combustion chambers and double overhead camshafts, just like an all-out racecar. You didn't get stuff like that from MG or Triumph or Austin Healey or even Porsche! And boy, could that thing ever pull for just 1290ccs! Like old skinflint Henry Ford himself once said: *"I always tip my hat when an Alfa Romeo passes by...."*

Anyhow, my buddy Cal hung around the shop and we shot the shit for the rest of the afternoon between the usual, umpty-kazillion interruptions that go along with running a damn garage business. It just never ends, you know? Afterwards we went on another little drive over to Castle Carrington to pick up some more of Cal's clothes and toiletries and stuff, although naturally I called home first to clear it with the boss. After giving me the usual full order of shit plus a heaping side helping of disgust and indignation, Julie grudgingly asked if Cal would like to join us for dinner once we were done at Castle Carrington. "That's really nice of you," I cooed into the phone.

"Hmph!" Julie snorted, and hung up. Then again, you take your chances when you place an unexpected, plan-changing call to the woman who's been stuck at home with your two kids and her mother all day. Especially when those kids have the energy levels of whirling dervishes and the attention span of fleas and the mother…well, the less said about Julie's mother the better. Suffice to say that if she isn't already irritating the shit out of you, she's busy looking for a way to do it.

So we tooled over to Cal's folks' stately and isolated old mansion out in the bucks-up section of the Jersey countryside, and he said it'd only take a few minutes to gather up his stuff since it was wintertime and that meant his folks were off getting stiff before dinner someplace down in the Caribbean. It kind of bothered me a little the way Cal talked about his folks. I mean, my old man was a certified, class-A jerk—no question about it—but we almost always had dinner together as a family while I was growing up. Even if it was just so's he could go around the table picking on us and telling us how badly we were behaving and what terrible choices we were making and how we were totally, irreparably screwing up our lives. Meanwhile my mom smiled like the world was nothing but one big ice cream sundae, served us up her wonderful meat, fish, poultry, vegetables, pasta and gravy and did her best to run sort of minor league interference.

But at least we were together, you know?

It didn't sound like Cal ever had much of that, and that he and his folks and his sister had become like people staying in different rooms on different floors of some grand but creepy-quiet old hotel. At least when they were all at one house at the same time, anyway, which I guess didn't happen very often. Sure, I knew Cal came from a lot of old, back-to-the-Mayflower money, but I still wasn't quite prepared for the sheer size, heft and stature of Castle Carrington. Jeez, it looked more like a damn bank building or oversized mausoleum or something rather than a house where people actually lived. There were fluted stone columns on either side of a massive, double-hung front door you could damn near walk an elephant through if you had both sides open. Cal grabbed a heavy brass knocker the general shape (and size!) of a ram's head and banged it once for me. It echoed like the sound of a dump truck full of percussion instruments crashing into the bottom of the Carlsbad Caverns.

"I usually sneak in through the kitchen door around back," he explained sheepishly, "but you might as well get the full treatment."

A few moments later there was a muted shuffling inside and one side of the huge door groaned open like a railroad turntable. Behind the door was a timid, tired-looking little elf of a man in a black suit and bow tie but wearing house slippers. I noticed the bow tie was one of those clip-on jobs and only connected to one side of his collar. He had sad, watery eyes, a few wisps of white hair swept west-to-east across the top of his head and the same pale, waxy complexion as the guests of honor at wakes and funerals. Behind him I could make out a huge, marble-tiled foyer done in alternating gold and cream slabs, a massive spiral staircase with cream-colored carpeting and a matching gold banister and an enormous, dimly glittering crystal chandelier. "Good evening, young Mr. Carrington," the old guy in the jacket said without smiling. "I'm afraid I wasn't expecting you. There's nothing prepared."

"That's all right, Henry. We won't be staying long. I just have to pick up a few things."

"Would you like some supper?"

"No, that won't be necessary." Cal turned to me. "Henry, this is my friend Mr. Palumbo."

Henry slid his eyes over in my direction. He had this way of looking up at you without raising his eyelids hardly at all. "It's a distinct pleasure, sir. May I take your coat or get you anything?"

"Nah. I'm fine. It's really more of a jacket anyway."

"So it is," Henry agreed. I noticed he was kind of eyeballing me, and that's when I realized I was still in my shop clothes with about a half-pound of muffler dust and at least a pint of 30-weight smeared and streaked about my person.

"Yeah, we're fine, Henry," Cal assured him. "Just go back to whatever it was you were doing."

"Thank you, sir," Henry nodded, looking more than vaguely relieved. He turned and started shuffling back across that gleaming marble floor in those goofy little house slippers, but then he stopped and turned around again. "Your sister Penelope is in the back parlor if you'd care to see her."

Cal's eyes darted towards the back of the house. "Is she alone?"

"She's with a gentleman friend. Watching television, I think. There was a benefit luncheon today. They've been here ever since…." Henry paused with his mouth hanging half open like he was going to add a few more details, but then he seemed to think better of it, gave a little two-inch bow, rotated 180 degrees and shuffled off into that dark, silent cavern of a house.

"You never met my sister, did you?"

I shook my head.

A wry, unpleasant look floated across Cal's face. "C'mon," he said through an ugly smile. "Let me show you how the other half lives."

Cal led me back through darkened, high-ceilinged rooms the size of high school gymnasiums, past a set of leaded French doors leading out to a lawn that seemed to stretch halfway to Albany, and finally to the back parlor, which was an overstuffed kind of room full of studded leather, polished wood, thick tapestries, two entire walls full of books that all looked like dictionaries and encyclopedias and a bar that could have passed for the United Nations General Assembly of distilled alcohol products. Cal's sister and her "gentleman friend" were sprawled out on this big, puffy, oxblood leather couch across from an absolutely enormous Zenith color television set that kept flipping back and forth between a somewhat purplish Red

Skelton with fake buck teeth and his hat brim turned up, a prize fight sponsored by Gillette Blue Blades and Groucho Marx cracking wise and insulting the contestants in *"You Bet Your Life."* I'd never really seen a color set before, and certainly not one with a cosmic ray gun-style Flash-Matic remote control that could flip from one channel to another from anywhere in the room. Quick as you could pull the trigger! I wondered how the hell they did that without wires, you know? But you couldn't really follow any of the programs because Cal's sister Penelope was clicking back and forth from one channel to the next about every twenty-third heartbeat. Even though her eyes looked to be focused a good six hundred yards past the screen. Penelope was a thin, pasty, washed out-looking young socialite with hollow cheeks and a thoroughly blank expression under a perfect-earlier-in-the-day Park Avenue coiffure of disorganized, bottle blond hair. To my eyes, she had what appeared to be a lot of late nights that turned into early mornings and hard, expensive miles on her. Penelope was kind of half-sitting, half-reclining with her chin resting deep into her chest and her legs splayed out both ways in front of her. The Flash-Matic remote was more or less growing out of her left hand and there was an empty bottle of Pernod and an ashtray full of crushed-out Terrytons on the floor next to her. Her "gentleman friend" was laid out like a felled corpse with his head resting serenely face down in her lap. You could hear him snoring, and he'd left a nice little pool of drool on her cocktail dress.

"This is my sister Penelope," Cal said expansively. "Say 'hello,' Penny."

Penny looked up at me with weary, insolent eyes. *"'Lo,"* she gurgled.

"And who is your friend?" Cal asked.

She looked down in her lap as if seeing him for the first time. Bewilderment slowly turned to recognition. *"This's Fred,"* she said with commendable certainty.

"How nice for Fred."

"He'sh fun when he'sh awake," she assured us.

"I'm sure he is."

"Y'wanna drink?"

"Probably not a good idea. I'm supposed to be driving to California tonight."

She didn't look impressed. *"Thass a long way. You might want a drink firs'."*

"Maybe I'll just take one of the bottles along for the road instead."

"Don't take the Pernod," she warned. *"Fred an' I are drinking Pernod."*

"And it looks absolutely stunning on you!" he grinned disgustedly. Then he went over to the bar and surveyed the bottles. There must've been a hundred of them at least. "You want anything to take home?" Cal asked. "They'll never miss it."

"I don't usually keep a lot of hard liquor over at the house," I told him. "My dad and my brother-in-law get into it, and they're bad enough with just the beer."

"Here, take this anyway. It'll dress the place up a little." He handed me a musty, gilt-encrusted bottle of fine Napoleon Brandy, then grabbed another for himself. "Never know when something like this might come in handy."

"Yeah, right. Just like that bottle of your old man's Pinch almost made us burn my Aunt Rosamarina's garage down. On the Fourth of July. Remember?"

A big smile spread across Cal's face. *"Remember?"* he scoffed. "Why, it was one of the highlights of my youth!"

"Oh, yeah. Like you're so grown up all of a sudden."

"I'm a young man on the rise, Buddy. A young man on the rise. No question about it." By way of celebration, he poured us each a wee snort of Napoleon brandy. Or maybe it was more than a wee snort, but you couldn't hardly tell because he used a pair of those big, goldfish-fishbowl-on-a-pedestal Society Grade brandy snifters. You know, the ones where a hefty double shot barely coats the bottom of the glass. He even warmed the outsides of the snifters by holding them under running hot water in the sink before he poured. Personally, I could never understand why you needed so damn much wide-open space over your drink. And I told Cal as much.

He looked down his nose at me. "Appearances," he explained condescendingly. "Putting your booze in a bigger glass makes it look like you're not drinking quite so much. That counts for a lot up here with the croquet-and-ivy set. We absolutely insist on using proper glassware. It's so much more refined than guzzling straight out of the bottle."

"I see."

"Of course you do." He poured a little more into our snifters and clinked them together. "Here's to the future."

"Here's to the future," I agreed.

"May you get what you want."

"May you want what you get."

Two or three deceivingly empty-looking brandies later we loaded a suitcase and a laundry bag full of Cal's clothes and shoes and stuff into what the dealership sales brochures optimistically referred to as the "back seat" of the *Giulietta Sprint,* and I could feel the brandy working around inside me as we took off across the cold, dark, damp and undulating countryside between Castle Carrington and Passaic. I remember it felt particularly warm and cozy inside the Alfa—partly because of the brandy and partly because I was used to traveling in drafty British roadsters and VW Beetles—and the ride was just what I needed to shake off the hollow, empty, upper-crust chill of Cal's folks' house. I couldn't imagine what it might have been like growing up in such a place. But that was something a blue-collar grunt like me could never really understand. Some writer once said that the rich are very different from you and me, and the best I could do was press my nose against the frosted glass and try to see in.

Fact is, I was a little embarrassed that Julie and the kids and me were still living in the old duplex on Fourteenth Street with her mom just a thin layer of lath and plaster away in the apartment upstairs. Not to mention worried that Julie might be a wee bit peeved seeing as how it was already well past 8:30 and no question if I could feel the brandy, she'd notice it, too. Sure enough, she'd set a nice table for us with the linen tablecloth and the good dishes and everything and whipped up a pretty nice meal out of whatever we had on hand in the fridge. But then of course the kids got hungry waiting for us and had to eat something and now they were both tired and cranky and Julie's mom was tired and cranky on general principles and so Julie's smile looked exceedingly strained and artificial when she met us at the doorway. She sized me up through both barrels while Cal gave her a brandy-laced, aunt-and-uncle peck on the cheek.

"What took you so long?" she asked airily while fixing me with her best *you-just-wait-until-later* glare.

"We were needlessly detained," Cal said like it meant something.

"The dinner smells great!" I gushed.

She glared at me some more. "So do you."

"We brought *this* for you," I continued, handing over the fancy, gilt-encrusted bottle of Napoleon brandy.

"I'm surprised there's any left."

To tell the truth dinner was a little edgy, what with little Vincent so tired he was damn near face down in his mashed potatoes and lima beans and little Roberta on the sniffly, sobby end of a full-tilt wailing binge and Julie's mom staring at us like we were a couple escaped axe murderers on account of she was missing *The $64,000 Question* and Julie looking at me every now and then like I'd brought a contagious case of Bubonic Plague into our house. Cal tried making a little polite conversation, but to tell the truth all he had to talk about was the racing and the weather and the parties out in California, and none of that really struck a chord with the kids or Julie or most especially Julie's mom. So we mostly ate in one of those uncomfortable silences where the simple noise a fork makes scraping across a plate sounds like a bulldozer tearing into pre-stressed concrete.

After dinner Julie put the kids to bed and then she and her mom did the dishes while Cal and I stayed at the table, talked cars and racing and shared another couple snorts of brandy. Only this time out of juice glasses. I mean, what else was there to do? "I'm sorry about the dinner," I whispered once I heard the dish water rushing in the sink in the other room.

"There's nothing to be sorry about," Cal whispered back.

"I'm afraid it wasn't a very good time," I said even softer.

"Good times aren't everything, Buddy. I've got more good times than I know what to do with these days."

"You poor thing."

"Besides," he continued, leaning in even closer and whispering even softer, "you're lucky to have what you have here."

"I am?"

Cal's eyes made a quick sweep around the room. "Sure you are. This is a homey kind of place. It really is."

"You sure you don't mean 'homely?'"

"Not at all." He leaned back and took another sip of brandy. "Everything's in its place here. Everything fits."

"Fits what?"

"Just fits. You don't see that very often."

I thought of all the countless dining room tables in all the countless other houses and apartments and duplexes on all the countless other little tree-lined residential side streets in Passaic and New Jersey and all across America and all around the world, for that matter. "You're nuts." I told him. "You see it all the time."

He shrugged. "Maybe *you* do."

I couldn't believe it, you know? Here was my dashing, daring, Hero Driver friend Cal Carrington envying *me.* Buddy Palumbo. The guy who had to get up at five ayem the next morning to go to work with a throbbing brandy hangover and who still most likely had a hushed-but-heated tongue lashing coming up on the old Household Things To Do list yet that evening. And that was the sort of thing you just had to stay awake for, even when you're the kind of tired that suddenly, silently oozes up around you like quicksand and threatens to suck your eyelids clear down your face.

But I guess it gets a little cold and lonely out there in the perpetual free fall of racing, and a reasonable excess of brandy plus a trip home to the museum-grade emptiness of Castle Carrington was just the sort of thing to bring it out. Cal Carrington wasn't the type of guy to let his guard down or let you see inside him very often—and never when he was on his game—but you could see his eyes were down to narrow slits and the brandy had worked him over more than a little. Truth is, Cal seldom drank all that much, and almost never to where you could actually see it. "Look, Cal," I told him as I rose unsteadily to my feet. "I goddagodabednow." No question that fancy brandy had likewise snuck up on me like sledgehammer wrapped in velvet. I looked around the room. "Lissen," I told him, "you can catch a few winks on the couch if you wanna." I mean, it didn't make sense to send him back to Castle Carrington or off on his way to California if he felt anything like I did.

"Won't the wife mind?"

I glanced over at the doorway to the kitchen. The water was still running in the sink. "Hey, I'm already in the shit. I don't think it'll make much difference either way. Besides," I clinked our juice glasses together one last time, "wives won't unload on their husbands in front of company. It just isn't done."

"Even among the lower classes?"

"Even among the lower classes," I assured him.

And that was pretty much true. Although it didn't do much except postpone the inevitable. And sure enough I got a full dose-and-a-half the next night about *how could I leave my rich bum friend passed out on the couch when I left for work* so that he was there and saw Julie's mother in her nightgown and slippers when she came down to fix her coffee and oatmeal the next morning.

"He had to drive all the way to California," I argued lamely. "I figured he needed a little rest."

"You mean he needed to sleep it off!"

"Okay, have it your way. He needed to sleep it off."

"He saw my mother in her nightgown!" Julie screamed at me.

"The poor bastard," I muttered under my breath.

"WHAT DID YOU SAY??!!"

"I said *'it doesn't matter.'*"

"Doesn't matter? Doesn't matter? I'll show you doesn't matter, Palumbo!"

And so it went. On and on and round and round like some mean, mangy old cur chasing his own tail. But that's the way flare-ups between husbands and wives go, isn't it? They rarely get anything settled or resolved. Nope, they just keep roaring around in circles until they run out of steam. In one way, I could easily see what Julie was so blessed steamed about. I'd compromised the sanctity, privacy and peaceful coexistence of our home by bringing my racing buddy Cal over late and ever-so-slightly drunk for a dinner Julie tried very hard (and at the last moment!) to make nice and presentable for us. And then, after I'd spoiled the dinner, I'd let Cal flop like a damn hobo on our living room couch. So he was there to see the Queen of the Harpies in her nightgown and slippers when she came down to make her coffee and oatmeal the next morning. I mean, why couldn't she have her damn coffee and oatmeal upstairs in her own damn apartment instead of coming down to our place as soon as she heard my VW demo burbling out of the driveway? And moreover what the hell difference did it make if I shared a couple snorts with a great pal of mine that I hadn't seen in ages and then furthermore let him catch a few winks on our living room couch because he was bone tired from traveling (okay, and the brandy a little bit, too) and didn't have anyplace else to go except back to Castle Carrington or all the way out to California? Not to mention that Julie's mom broke the sanctity, privacy and peaceful coexistence of our home on pretty much a regular and on-going basis, and I never said one blessed word about it. Or at least not when she was in the room to hear it, anyway.

But those are things you learn in marriage about husbands and wives and old, single buddies and omnipresent mothers-in-law and most especially the naked, inescapable truth that logic, reasoning and well-thought-out conclusions are no match whatsoever for a wife's feelings and emotions. And the sooner you realize that, the sooner you will have some basic understanding as to how and why you keep getting in Dutch all the time….

Chapter 5: Long Distance

Cal phoned me again a few weeks later on a Wednesday afternoon, and I knew right away something was up because they'd had a race out in the desert at Palm Springs that weekend. If he'd done well, he surely would've called as soon as he got up Monday morning. If not smack-dab in the middle of the night before. "So how was the drive back to California?" I asked him.

"Long and boring, mostly. The section through the mountains was pretty neat, but there's sure one hell of a lot of corn, cows and flatland between Pittsburgh and The Rockies."

"Amen to that," I agreed. "How was the car?"

"I fell in love with it," he said matter-of-factly. "It's just such a sweet, soft, eager little ride."

"You make it sound like sex."

"So? What's wrong with that?"

"Not a thing. Is it fast?"

"Well, there's fast and there's fast. It's not fast and powerful like a Jaguar or a Ferrari or anything. But it *feels* fast. And it *sounds* fast. And you can maintain some pretty damn amazing average speeds once you get it rolling. It just hums right along at 80 or so."

I nodded like he could see me. "So how about the racing last weekend? How'd that go?"

"Oh, not too bad," he said airily.

"Not too bad?" That's not the way Cal Carrington usually talked about the races. But then, he usually won. Or at the very least ran at the front. And all of a sudden I realized there was more than just news and chitchat behind this phone call. He wouldn't say it, of course, but I could tell something was eating at him. "So what happened?" I grilled him. "C'mon. Tell poppa."

He made a gagging sound on the other end. But then he spilled it. "Oh, we had a little problem with the engine. Valve spring or plug wire or something."

"Boy, you're one hell of a mechanic. Didn't I teach you *anything?* There's one hell of a big difference between a busted valve spring and a broken plug wire."

"Hey, not to me. We lost a cylinder and that was that. What difference does it make if it was a valve spring or a plug wire?"

"It makes a big difference to the poor slob who's gotta fix it."

Then it got quiet at the other end. Quiet like the echo in a seashell. So I knew something was really wrong. "So c'mon," I prodded. "What happened?"

"Oh, I dunno," Cal said sullenly, "Masten Gregory was there in Tony Parravano's new Maserati 300S. He won the damn thing." I heard him swallow at the other end. "Truth is, I'm not sure I could've run with him even if the car'd stayed together."

"Really?" That sure didn't sound like the Cal Carrington I knew.

"Yeah, he was really flying at Palm Springs. And—hey, I gotta say it—I think that Maserati maybe handles a lot better than the Ferrari."

So *that* was it! All of a sudden it was starting to dawn on Cal that Ernesto Julio was hardly the only wealthy car owner/race entrant type out in California, and that Cal was only one of a whole fistful of fast, hungry young drivers trying to land the good ride and put a match to the skyrocket of their careers. And those rich car owners only put them behind the wheel because the thing they most wanted in life—more than the fame, glory, women, health, money, power and maybe even breathing—was to beat all the other rich car owners to the checkered flag. Because winning was all of those things all wrapped into one. And first place was the only position they cared about. Sure, most of the west coast racers were just like most of the east coast racers: a ragtag bunch of rookies, duffers, hacks, journeymen, idiots and wannabes who would never amount to anything when it came to going really fast or knitting whole races together. But there was also that special, serious, upper-echelon pool of talent that back east included guys like Cal and Tommy Edwards and John Fitch and Phil Walters and Dick Irish and Bob Fergus and that new hotshoe phenom Walt Hansgen and even that stuck-up jerkoff Creighton Pendleton the Third. And you could split those guys up and rank them even further if you had a mind to. Which took place at every bar within driving, swerving, walking, staggering or down-on-all-fours-crawling distance from a racetrack a kazillion times over on your average race weekend. Well, they had the same thing going out on the west coast—in spades!—plus a lot more sought-after seats to fill in all the latest hot cars entered by rich car owners like Ernesto Julio and John Edgar and Tony Parravano and John and Eleanor von Neumann. Hungry young drivers like Phil Hill, Carroll Shelby, Masten Gregory, Jim McAfee, Ken Miles, Bob Drake and Ritchie Ginther knew all about those cars—hell, most of them worked in the business!—and always knew who owned what and who had what coming in fresh from Europe on the next boat, train, plane or transcontinental car hauler. The hotshoes circled around those rides like bees around honey. And they were all pretty damn good, too. Every blessed one of them. These weren't the kind of mid-pack-to-backmarker chumps you could just dazzle with your speed or mesmerize with your brilliant moves. Because they had 'em, too!

Cal was discovering that there's a compression of talent up near the top of any sport or profession, and the higher you climb, the tighter and tougher things become. Fact is, you really needed to be in the right car—or at the very least an *equal* car—to have a decent shot at getting the job done. Not that Cal was ever a pot-collector like Charlie Priddle. He never gave a rat's ass about hardware for his mantelpiece or all the cheering and the hoopla that came after the checkered flag. Or not much, anyway. All Cal ever wanted was to get back in and *drive.* Get back out there on the racetrack where life came alive for him and things made sense. More than anything on earth, he wanted to be out there in the best damn car he could weasel his ass into, running like hell against the best damn drivers in the biggest damn races on the planet. Just to see what he could do once he got them in his crosshairs, you know? And also just to keep the magic flowing....

But in order to get there, you had to have good rides, and in order to get and keep those rides, you had to produce results. And since all the car-owner types were always vying for the latest and fastest new racecars (and often bidding against each other to see who got them!), you needed to be in the right car at the right time. And then drive a pretty smart, sweet, shrewd-as-the-dickens race to be in front at the checker when it counted.

"It's like I told you." Cal explained sullenly. "I'm learning a lot of things out here. Getting ahead. Self-reliance. Making sure my laundry gets done."

"So how does it feel?"

"The truth? Pretty shitty some of the time."

"Welcome to the real world."

"It stinks."

"Still think you're the fastest thing on four wheels?"

The swagger came right back. "No doubt about it," Cal assured me through what I knew had to be that sly, familiar cobra smile. "Only now they gotta be the *right* set of wheels…."

Cal, Ernesto and everybody else were really impressed with the run Masten Gregory put in behind the wheel of Tony Parravano's new Maserati 300S at Palm Springs. Not to mention the way Ken Miles dusted off all the Porsche 550s in the smallbore modified races driving Tony's *other* new Maserati, a 1500cc 150S that looked like nothing more than a shrunk-down version of the 300S Gregory drove the same weekend. But then, Ken Miles was more than a little bit special as a driver, and he won the under-1500cc race with that Maserati just like he'd won them before in his slick little MG special and just like he would continue to win them after John von Neumann made him one hell of a deal to please start chauffeuring Porsches around instead of beating the crap out of them all the time with some other kind of car. Ken Miles was that good.

Even so, it was obvious Maseratis were really starting to come into their own again towards the end of the 1955 racing season. Oh, they'd had a hell of a history, what with the four Maserati brothers building great single-seaters and sportscars in Bologna all the way back to the 1920s, and there were truckloads of fancy silver chalices and engraved loving cups gathering dust back at the factory race shops. Beyond the racing cars, Maserati built wonderful machine tools and manufactured spark plugs and such, but they struggled a lot financially because they were always more interested in making great things than making great money. Fact is, they probably would've gone under for good if the wealthy Orsi family from Modena—who had their fingers in a lot of industrial pies—hadn't come along with a fat bankroll and pretty much taken things over and moved the whole shooting match up to Modena in the late-1930s. They continued to build great racing cars—Wilbur Shaw won the Indianapolis 500 back-to-back with one of their 8CLT grand prix models in 1939 and 1940—but the Maserati brothers didn't much like working for the Orsi family in Modena, so they hightailed it back to Bologna to build cars on their own again as soon as their contract ran out in 1947. But the Orsis still owned the Maserati name and most of the hands, heads, hard work and hardware that went with it, and the company really started turning around again when young Omer Orsi decided to take it on as his own, personal pet project in 1952. His designers, engineers and craftsmen built some marvelous cars, and I always thought their castings, fabrication and machine work were maybe even better than Ferrari. Plus they were always absolutely gorgeous—racecars and road cars alike—and that always has a lot to do with how hard a car tugs at your heartstrings….

Ernesto Julio must've felt pretty much the same, since a month or so later he decided he just *had* to have this flashy new two-tone, Frua-bodied Maserati A6G/2000 convertible that he'd seen in a magazine. That pissed North American Ferrari importer Carlo Sebastain off no small amount, seeing as how he was trying to sell Ernesto one of Ferrari's powerful new 375 America coupes at the same time. But there was more to it than that. Seems old Ernesto was still a little steamed over the way he got passed over when the very latest editions of Ferrari's monstrous 4.9 racecars had been doled out to privateer customers earlier in the year. Why, everybody and his brother had heard about Ferrari's fabulous Four-point-Nines, and all the rich amateurs and "privateer entrant" types wanted one! My motoring scribe pal Hank Lyons was happy to fill me in on the details. The "375 Plus" was the first 4.9 back in 1954, and Ferrari teamed burly Argentine ace Froilan "Wild Bull of the Pampas" Gonzales up with the slight, elegant little Frenchman Maurice Trintignant to score a cliff-hanger win over Jaguar's brand-new (and, to be honest, more technically advanced) D-Type at the rain-soaked 24 Hours of Le Mans that year. Sure, the D-Type had a light, aircraft-style monocoque chassis, slick, aircraft-inspired aerodynamics and Dunlop's revolutionary new disc brakes, but you can't use brakes very hard on wet pavement and so a large chunk of their advantage was lost. Not to mention that the big old 4.9 could really accelerate down that long straightaway towards Mulsanne even though the Jag had a slipperier shape and maybe better all-out top speed. And then open-road ace Umberto Maglioli—the guy we saw do so well in that little supercharged Lancia coupe when we were down there in November of '52—used a 375 Plus to win *La Carrera* outright at the end of the 1954 season. Again in a race where sheer grunt and ruggedness were worth more than grace or finesse. The factory built a couple more and they were eventually all sold off to privateers (including a very special "special order" one with a very sexy Scaglietti body for Tony Parravano out in California) while old man Ferrari—possibly inspired by what Jaguar and Mercedes were up to—started fooling around with straight fours and straight sixes in place of his famous V-12s. Only those didn't work out so well against the Jags and Mercedes during the '55 World Manufacturers' Championship season, so he decided to try the big V-12 idea again at the beginning of 1956 in a model called the 410 Sport. It had the biggest, most powerful motor Ferrari had ever shoved under the hood of one of his racing cars, and two were entered in the very first race of the 1956 season, the thousand-kilometer grind down in Buenos Aires, Argentina. And no question they were the fastest cars in the field in the hands of Fangio/Castellotti and Musso/Collins. Only maybe they were a bit *too* powerful, since both cars broke their transmissions and retired. Which should give you a clue as to how much gear-cracking, bearing-rattling, tire-shredding horsepower they put out. To pour salt in the wounds, in spite of an overwhelming majority of Ferraris entered with some really top-notch drivers behind the wheel, rising star Stirling Moss and Argentine newcomer Carlos Menditeguy teamed up to win the damn race in a 3-liter Maserati.

You can bet old man Ferrari was not amused, and the factory team never ran the big 4.9s again. But rich "enthusiasts" and "privateer entrants" all over the world lined up to get one anyway as soon as they became available. I mean, who could resist the most powerful Ferrari sports/racing car ever built? So one went to this deep-pockets Ferrari buyer in Sweden and John Edgar got one out in California and the factory even built three extra "410 Speciale" versions out of various bits and pieces they had laying around. One went to some French guy and the other two were earmarked once again for Tony Parravano on account of he was such a swell customer and threw cash around in such an entertaining manner whenever he went over to Italy to visit the factory. In fact, there were even a few dark rumors floating around that Tony lent old man Ferrari a few large wads of cash when things were tight for him financially, and in return he got special cars at half price directly from the factory. Which can't have made old Carlo Sebastian very happy back in New York….

Ernesto Julio really *wanted* a 4.9. In fact, he was kind of obsessed by the idea. Even though Carlo Sebastian assured him that Ferrari's soon-to-be-available-to-private-owners "big sixes" were going to be even better and that Ernesto's name would be right at the top of the list. As you can imagine, that got old Ernesto well and truly pissed off. But he wasn't the type of guy to scream and yell or piss and moan about it. That never got you anywhere. Besides, he needed to stay on good terms with Carlo for whenever the next round of hot new Ferraris came rolling out of the race shops, seeing as how Ferrari was forever replacing old-model racecars with new-model racecars (or maybe that should be "new"-model racecars with "even newer yet"-model racecars) in order to keep ahead of the competition. Not to mention keeping the old cash register ringing with customer orders for whatever the latest, hottest new Ferrari racecars might be. After all, who wanted last year's car?

The amazing thing was how Ferrari's guys could design and build whole new engines and drivelines for those cars—straight fours, straight sixes and their trademark V-12s, single overhead cam and double overhead cam, single spark plug or dual spark plug, transmission behind the engine or transmission in unit with the back axle or whatever the hell else you might think of—as quickly as most other manufacturers could change their blessed paint schemes. So Ernesto knew it was important to stay on Carlo Sebastian's sunny side. But it also made sense to fire a shot across his bows and let the sonofabitch know there was other stuff out there by buying himself a Maserati.

Naturally Carlo thought that was a pretty terrible idea. Especially since the glass window in his office door faced out onto the shop floor, and sitting right there staring at him the whole time he spoke to Ernesto long-distance was the exact, gunmetal-silver 375 America coupe he wanted to sell him. And underneath all the style and elegance and class and flourish and pedigree, Carlo Sebastian was still basically a damn car salesman at heart. So he was gently trying to pull the old switcheroo and move Ernesto's heart, ass and wallet into what he had available. *"A Maserati? You're not gonna like a-that car,"* he warned Ernesto Julio in Italian.

"Why not?"

"It's a-gotta no guts. No power. It's only a six."

"I thought you were just telling me how alla Ferrari's hot new racing cars were sixes last year...."

"That's a-different. That's a-for the rules. For the highway you wanna the Vee Twelve. You open the hood at a gas station and everybody's a-cream in their pants. Nothing makes a-the power like-a the Vee Twelve. Nothing makes a-the sound like-a the Vee Twelve. Nothing makes-a the SPEED like-a the Vee Twelve."

"But I wannit for-a the street, Carlo. Notta the racing. Just for cruising, capiche? I gotta enough speeding tickets already."

"But it's a-not a FERRARI. It's notta the real thing."

"Ey, Maserati's been around for awhile."

"Sure they've been around. Around and around. They'll go broke and a-then where will-a you be?"

"Stuck. But I've been a-stuck before."

"Listen. Ernesto. Listen to what I'm a-telling you. The old man built the 375 just a-for you. Just a-for America. It's gotta power like you wouldn't a-believe. 300 horsepower! When you plant a-you foot, it'll give-a you a damn erection right a-through the steering wheel. Two feet long! And it's a FERRARI! The prancing horse! Thatta MEANS a-something...."

"Yeah, I know. I know. But it's a-damn coupe. I already hadda one of your coupes. It was a-HOT inside. I needa convertible out here in a-California. That's a-what the ladies like...."

There was a long pause at the other end. And then: *"Don't I do a-favors for you on the racecars?"*

"Sure you do," Ernesto answered warily.

"When I've gotta the latest thing, don' I make a-sure you getta the first shot at it?"

"Sure you do. Just like I gotta the first shot at the four-point-a-nine. I gotta the first shot right after von Neumann gotta the first shot an' John Edgar gotta the first shot an' Tony Parravano gotta the first shot an'...."

"That's notta nice thing a-to say."

"Look. Carlo. My friend. I'll be buying a-lotsa more cars from you. Lots anna lotsa more cars. I LOVE a-my Ferraris. But I wannna this toy to play around with in a-Hollywood for a-while. A convertible. With a-two-tone paint. That's just a-the way it is, my friend. That's just a-the way it is...."

And, sure enough, that's the way it was.

I got another surprise call from Cal on Valentines Day—collect, natch!—and the way I know for sure it was Valentines Day is on account of it came through just as I was putting my nicest, freshly-creased-at-the-cleaners tan pants and new herring-bone tweed jacket from Schmedley's Men's Store over on Fifteenth Street to take Julie out for dinner and a show. To tell the truth, Julie and me didn't get to sneak out like that very often—it's tough when you've got little kids at home and a mother-in-law lurking upstairs who thinks it's her God-given right to be in on everything—but Valentines Day was a big enough deal to qualify as an exception. Even if it did fall on a damn Tuesday that year. There were also a bunch of fresh roses in the vase on our kitchen table, and that was not a normal sort of occurrence around our house except on very special occasions or after I'd unwittingly done something thoroughly and totally unforgivable. You'd be amazed how easy it is for your average blockhead husband to do something thoroughly and totally unforgivable and not even notice it at the time.

As you can imagine, I was eager to get all the latest west coast racing poop from Cal, but also aware that it would likely cost me some time in the doghouse and another bunch of roses if I made us late, so we had to rush through dinner or miss the start of the movie. "So what's the latest from the land of eternal sunshine?" I asked while I tried my best to shine my cordovan brown oxfords while keeping the phone wedged between my ear and my shoulder at the same time.

"Nothing but beautiful days, fast cars and gorgeous women," Cal said like he was ordering toast.

"Yeah. We get a lot of that here, too."

"I know you do. New Jersey's a real damn garden spot. Especially in February."

"Don't rub it in."

"BUDDY, WHO'S ON THE PHONE?" Julie yelled from the bathroom. She had her hair dryer going full blast.

"IT'S NOBODY," I yelled back. *"JUST CAL."*

"WELL, DON'T BE LONG. WE DON'T WANT TO BE LATE."

"I KNOW WE DON'T WANT TO BE LATE."

"IF WE'RE LATE, WE'LL MISS THE START OF THE SHOW."

"WE WON'T BE LATE."

"AND WE DON'T WANT TO HAVE TO RUSH THROUGH DINNER."

"WE WON'T BE LATE."

"AND IF WE GET THERE LATE, WE'LL HAVE TO STAY AND WATCH THE BEGINNING AGAIN AFTER THE END. I HATE TO WATCH THE BEGINNING AGAIN AFTER THE END. ESPECIALLY IF IT'S A MYSTERY."

"I DON'T THINK AROUND THE WORLD IN 80 DAYS IS A MYSTERY."

"I STILL DON'T WANT TO KNOW HOW IT ENDS BEFORE I SEE HOW IT STARTS. IT SPOILS EVERYTHING."

"WE WON'T BE LATE, OKAY??!!"

I listened for the next volley, but when it didn't come right away I knew the All Clear had sounded and we were done. At least for now. You get a feel for the rhythm of these things once you stay married for a few years.

"Wedded bliss," Cal snickered sarcastically.

"You just don't know what you're listening to," I told him. "When married people yell at each other or sound impatient or exasperated or angry or annoyed with each other, it's just their way of communicating, see?"

"Oh, I understand completely. Why, my parents used to communicate all the way to black eyes and split lips sometimes."

He'd never really mentioned that before. "They really used to fight?" I asked.

"Nah, not really. Just once or twice. And it was never much of a fight. My dad was bigger, but my mom was a lot quicker and meaner. Like a weasel. She had more staying power, too. Eventually they settled on separate bedrooms and separate vacations."

"Why didn't they just get divorced? Like Big Ed does?"

"Oh, in their circles it just isn't done."

"Isn't done?"

"It's unseemly."

"BUD-DEEE!" Julie yelled over the hair dryer, *"WE'RE GOING TO BE LAAAY-ATE!"*

"WE WON'T BE LAAAAY-ATE!" I echoed back at her like the blessed Grand Canyon. *"I PROOOMMMM-ISSSE."* And that's about when I looked down and noticed I had cordovan brown shoe-polish about halfway up my forearm. "Look, I gotta get hustling, Cal...."

"Wouldn't want to make the little woman late for the show, would you?"

"No, I wouldn't. I don't need the aggravation. Besides, she's got it coming. She does a lotta nice stuff for me. Like that dinner she made for you."

"One of the landmark meals of my entire life. No question about it. And coffee in the morning with her mother was another experience to cherish."

"You're just jealous."

"That must be it."

Cal had a way of pissing me off and making me want to laugh at the same time. "So did you call for any specific reason or are you just trying to run my phone bill up?"

"Nothing special. Just wanted to see if you'd like to go to Sebring?" he said like it was no big deal.

"Sebring?"

"Yeah, Sebring. You remember. That racetrack down in Florida."

"I know where Sebring is."

"Middle of March."

"I know when it is, too."

"Factory teams from Ferrari, Jaguar, Maserati, Porsche, Aston Martin...."

"Yeah, I've been reading Hank's columns."

"All the top factory drivers."

"I've heard."

"Fangio, Hawthorn, Moss, Behra, Castellotti...."

"I know."

"...plus a friend of yours...."

"Oh? Who?"

"Me."

"You?"

"Yup. Ernesto arranged for Carlo Sebastian to get a ride for me in *a genuine, factory team Ferrari!"*

"You're *joking!"*

"A man of my station does not joke, my good man. It's unseemly."

I had to laugh. "So when did this all come together?"

"At the last minute, of course. Just before the entry deadline. I guess Carlo kind of owed Ernesto a favor or something. But then some things had to line up. And some money probably had to change hands, too."

"I bet." If Carlo Sebastian was involved, that went without saying.

"BUDD-EEE. I'M ALMOST RED-EEEE!"

"Jesus, Cal. I gotta get cracking here."

"Well, here's the deal," he added at machine-gun speed: "If you can help get the car down there, I think I can get you team credentials and have you help out in the pits during the race."

"Help out the Ferrari factory team?" I half-gasped.

"Technically we're a Ferrari North America entry, but that pretty much amounts to the same thing."

"Really?"

"Uh-huh."

"And I think I can get you a free ride home, too. In a private plane."

"Wow."

"In time to have you back at work bright and cheery on Monday morning."

"Right. I'll really be bright and cheery after working the pits on a 12-hour race weekend at Sebring."

"Hey, the race is on Saturday. You'll survive. It'll be just like the old days."

"That's what I'm afraid of." I heard Julie on the stairs. "Listen, I gotta run."

"Let me know, okay?"

"You know I will." I went to hang up, but then one more thing occurred to me. "Who's your co-driver going to be?"

"Toly Wolfgang," Cal said proudly. And then he hung up.

Of course I'd heard about Toly Wolfgang. He was famous. Or maybe infamous was more like it. He was a rich, devilishly handsome international playboy type with about six different shades of blue blood, exceptionally deep pockets and an incredibly shady past—or a shady family history, anyway—who started racing Ferraris only after he got bored with skiing and polo and amateur boxing and Olympic bobsledding and skin diving for sunken treasure in shark-infested waters. Or at least that's what the gossip columns and movie magazines said. And he got his name mentioned in those magazines a lot seeing as how it always seemed to be linked to some famous, glamorous actresses, high-fashion models or hot young starlets. At least when it wasn't being linked to runaway society girls or rich, wayward heiresses, that is. Not that I pay any attention to that kind of stuff. But sometimes I catch it by accident looking over Julie's shoulder in bed or notice it glaring up at me from the waiting-room coffee table at the little beauty shop on Madison Street where Julie gets her hair done.

"You ever hear of Toly Wolfgang?" I asked Julie as she swept into the kitchen. She looked really pretty all dressed up to go out like that.

"Who hasn't?" she answered absently while fussing with one of those three-buck, costume jewelry "diamond ear studs" I'd bought her for Christmas the December after we got engaged. They were nothing but cut glass junk in tinny, nickel-plate mountings, but they were the first real present I ever bought her, so she insisted on hanging on to them as kind of a good-luck charm. And also to oh-so-graciously remind me of what a cheap, thoughtless, inconsiderate sonofabitch I could be. Still, I thought they looked great on her.

"Well," I told her, "Cal's gonna be co-driving with him at Sebring."

"How nice for both of them," she said without meaning a word of it. And that's about when she noticed the cordovan brown shoe polish all over my hands and my beautifully shined oxfords sitting smack-dab in the middle of the kitchen counter where she prepares our family meals. At which point the temperature dropped about 20 or 30 degrees as a deep, dark cloud passed through the room....

Anyhow, we went out to dinner and the show (and yes, we made *Around the World in 80 Days* on time...barely), and I must admit it was pretty good. Even if I personally wanted to see *Invasion of the Body Snatchers* over at the Tivoli instead. But it got us into a pair of pretty good moods and afterwards I took her out for ice cream and coffee and it was nice to be out with just her and away from the kids and her mom and everything. It reminded me all over again that the two of us got along pretty nicely when we weren't busy yelling and screaming at the kids or each other. And naturally I didn't say anything about Cal's invitation to go to Sebring. I mean, why ruin a nice evening?

But I mentioned the possible Sebring trip to Big Ed the next day at the dealership, and to be honest I felt kind of apologetic about it. I mean, it didn't seem right to just take off and leave, you know? Big Ed looked kind of pleased and clapped his arm around my shoulder. "Buddy, my boy," he grinned around his cigar, "you are getting absolutely revoltingly responsible these days." He stared down at the top of my head. "You got any gray hairs up there?"

"Jeez, Ed, I'm only 23."

He shook his head. "Not inside you're not!"

And I knew he was right. I'd done an awful lot of growing up since the day he tooled his new XK120 up to the gas pumps at Old Man Finzio's gas station for the very first time. Maybe even too much. “So you think I should go?” I asked him.

“It’s up to you, Buddy. You’re a big boy now.”

“But you think it’d be okay?”

“Like I said, that’s a decision only you can make.”

“But I’m asking you, Ed. What do *you* think? Do you think it’d be okay?”

“Hell, *yes!”* Big Ed nodded, even taking out his cigar for emphasis. “Me and JR and Steve can watch the place for a few days. It’ll still be here when you get back.”

“You think?”

Big Ed nodded again. “You been working hard, Buddy. You’re entitled to a little blow-off time every now and then.”

“I am?”

“Sure you are. Guys need that.”

“Boy, I sure hope Julie sees it that way.”

“Y’gotta *sell* her on it, see?”

“That may not be so easy,” I told him. “After all, I just do the grunt work around here. *You’re* the master salesman….”

And indeed he was. Which is why he called Julie without even telling me and somehow managed to sell/con/persuade her into letting me go. Believe it or not, when I got home that night, there was a brand-new pair of white Bermuda shorts and a matching white baseball cap laid out on the bed. “What are those for?” I asked.

“For your trip to Florida,” Julie smiled.

“Really??!!”

“Yeah. Why not? You’ve been a pretty good boy.”

“I have?”

“Sort of.” And then she gave me a kiss that made my toes curl under. She could still do that when she put her mind to it.

“Jesus, how the hell’d you DO that?” I asked Big Ed the next day.

“Salesmanship,” he shrugged. “You want something from somebody, you got to show them what’s in it for them. Show them what the *benefit* is gonna be.”

“I don’t get it. What’s the benefit for Julie if she lets me go to Sebring?”

“Well, first of all, you’re taking her to see that new *My Fair Lady* show that’s opening up on Broadway.”

“I am?”

“Sure you are.”

“I thought nobody could get tickets.”

“Nobody can.”

“But *you* can.”

Big Ed just smiled. “Hey, and don’t ask what it’s gonna cost.”

“Why not?”

“Believe me, you don’t wanna know.”

As it turned out, he was absolutely right about that. Still, one night on a suit-and-tie date over to Broadway sounded like an awful cheap exchange for a six-day racing escapade to Sebring while leaving Julie all alone at home with her mom and the kids. And I told Big Ed as much.

"Well, that's not all of it, Buddy."

"It's not?"

"Nah. She gets something else, too."

"What's that?"

A brilliant twinkle lit up in Big Ed's eye. "You'll feel guilty as hell."

And I did, too.

Chapter 6: Another Memorable Road Trip

Our original Sebring plan was for me to leave late Monday with one of the Muscatelli brothers and Carlo Sebastian's Puerto Rican car hauler/clean-up guy, help out with the long tow down to Sebring and then help out a little more getting the cars unloaded and all the tents and benches and tool boxes and wheels and tires and spares and miscellaneous racing gear set up before Cal and the rest of the drivers showed up for practice on Thursday. But then of course the car Cal and Toly Wolfgang were supposed to drive was late leaving the factory on account of it was a privateer entry and one of last year's somewhat unloved 121LM six-cylinder cars, and naturally the new, big-banger 860 Monza four-cylinder cars for the official, *Scuderia Ferrari* factory team drivers like Fangio and Castellotti came first. And so the 121LM was late getting out the door, and then there was one of your typical, brushfire Italian dock strikes because the second cousin of the guy who ran the crane had insulted the husband of the sister of the guy who delivered fish to the grocery store owned by the uncle of the punk kid who had the dock supervisor's job just because his father happened to own the damn freight company. The upshot of which was that "our" freshly rebuilt and repainted Ferrari sat on the docks next to a half-loaded boat in the Genoa harbor for at least a week before apologies were made and accepted and the ship finally set sail for New York.

The rest of the cars and tools and equipment really couldn't wait, so a last-minute decision was made that Cal would fly out to Idlewild on Tuesday, where I'd pick him up at the airport (in the new Ferrari racecar, of course!) and we'd pretty much take off immediately and drive it straight through down to Sebring so as to hopefully be there in time for opening practice on Thursday. It was the kind of thing I'd done so many times in the past without even thinking twice about it (or even once, come to that) but all of a sudden the notion of driving a freshly-rebuilt-by-the-factory Ferrari 121LM racing car with no mufflers and no top and no windshield wipers (or windshield at all on the passenger side!) and no heater and no insulation and not much in the way of seat upholstery straight-through from New York City to Sebring, Florida, sounded just a wee bit nutty. But maybe I was just getting old, you know?

Besides, whatever else might happen, it was sure to be an adventure....

Julie packed a big suitcase for me with enough stuff for a week in the Catskills, but I was smart enough to just keep my mouth shut and thank her and give her and the kids (and even her mom) a nice kiss goodbye before heading over to Carlo Sebastian's place in one of our VeeDub demos. But I stopped at our shop first to pick up a roll-up tool kit and some wire and tape and mashed my toothbrush and about three pounds max of the clothes Julie'd packed for me into a small canvas bag. Along with some cold- and wet-weather gear, just in case. Then I hid that big suitcase with all the rest of the clothes and toiletries and bottles of suntan lotion inside in the trunk of a dusty Jag sedan we had parked outside with the motor and transmission out. So Julie wouldn't see it if she happened to drop by. I knew she meant well, but there was only gonna be so much room in that Ferrari.

Carlo Sebastian seemed genuinely glad to see me now that we were both more or less in the same business (albeit at decidedly opposite ends of the old dollars-and-cents spectrum), and so he took me on another little whirlwind tour of his race shop. The place was pretty much empty because most of the cars and such were already on their way to Sebring, but sitting in the back corner was the one I'd come for. It was one of the brutish but handsome, 4.4-liter six-cylinder models the factory team ran with commendable speed but not all that much success the previous year, and I thought it was absolutely gorgeous! That bright red bodywork flowed and bulged like the front of a young girl's sweater, and you couldn't miss the snazzy little shark fin on the back of the driver's headrest fairing (which was on the right-hand side, seeing as how most tracks run clockwise and so you want the driver's weight and sight lines on the inside on the majority of corners). I never quite understood what those fins were supposed to do—maybe help keep the thing pointed straight at 170 or so down that long, long straightaway at Le Mans?—but a lot of the Jaguar D-Types had 'em and they'd won a lot of races and, hey, they looked neat, so why not? There were two powerful auxiliary driving lights set into the grille like extra eyeballs for night racing and a neat, wraparound plexiglass racing screen on the driver's side. Although I'd have to say I was a little concerned about the aerodynamic aluminum tonneau cover they'd put over the passenger seat. I mean, no way was I going to ride all the way to Florida crammed down into a dark little tin corner full of gear oil vapor and exhaust fumes! And I could see right away there was no way in hell we could take it off and carry it with us. In the end I wound up leaving the tonneau cover behind—even though it kind of spoiled the looks of the car—for one of Carlo's rich driver types to bring down with him on a private plane on Friday. Creighton Pendleton the Third, in fact. Can you believe it?

Naturally the first thing I wanted was to look under the hood, and Carlo was only too pleased to accommodate me. He rotated those special, Ferrari-style metal spring clips at the corners and the two of us gingerly lifted the hood off and set it against the wall. I must admit it seemed strange to see that big straight six nestled between the fenders instead of the usual and expected V-12, but it still looked every cubic centimeter a Ferrari engine what with serious, dull gray bare aluminum castings everywhere you looked and that familiar Ferrari lettering spelled out on the cam covers. Ferrari had been fooling around quite a bit with big fours and sixes—particularly after Jaguar did so well with their big six in the C- and D-Types. Ferrari started with the little 2.0-liter Formula Two four-banger Alberto Ascari used to win back-to-back World Driving Championships in 1952-'53 after the FIA more or less shut down Formula One for lack of interest. Alfa's old supercharged, pre-war Alfettas were pretty much unbeatable at the time (even though Ferrari finally managed it with a 4.5-liter V-12 that got better fuel mileage at Silverstone in 1951) but Alfa wanted out at the top rather than just waiting around for somebody to knock them off, and there just weren't any other manufacturers willing to go to the trouble and expense of building the kind of complicated, expensive cars the existing Formula

One rules allowed. Especially in a struggling postwar economy where what most manufacturers really needed was to build and sell the shit out of everyday road cars just to stay in business. So the World Driving Championship kind of switched over to the simpler, less complicated and expensive *voiturette* Formula Two rules for a couple years in '52 and '53 while everybody found their feet again, and no question those little Ferrari four-bangers were the cream of the crop. Sure, all-out top-end horsepower was less than it might have been for one of Ferrari's whirring, whirling V-12s, but the four-bangers were so much lighter, simpler and cheaper to build, and also produced a lot more in the way of low- and mid-range grunt. And let's face it: horsepower sells cars, but more often than not it's torque that wins races!

Based on the success of the little F2 cars, Ferrari started fooling around with bigger and bigger fours and then even started tacking on a couple extra cylinders to turn them into even bigger straight sixes—hey, there wasn't any displacement limit for sportscars at the time, so why not? Ferrari could just keep hogging them out and hogging them out some more whenever he fancied a little more power. In the end he wound up punching them out all the way to 3.7 liters and then 4.4 liters for the 118LM and 121LM models the factory team ran several times in the races that made up the 1955 World Manufacturers' Championship for sports cars. But they got their heads pretty much handed to them by the torquey, tough, disc-braked and aerodynamically slippery Jaguar D-Types at Le Mans and by the technically advanced and superbly organized Mercedes-Benz team just about everywhere else. Including the 1000-mile *Mille Miglia* that ran right up and down the spine and clear through the emotional heart and gut of Italy, where Stirling Moss' factory 300SLR (with brave, gutsy, onetime-motorcycle-sidecar-monkey-turned-motorsports-journalist Denis Jenkinson doing the navigating in the "I just crapped my pants again" seat) scored a record-shattering win over all the homegrown Italian cars and drivers. And that really must have stung. So Ferrari put new bodies on the fast-but-never-quite-successful six-cylinder cars and sold them off to "wealthy sportsmen" while the factory concentrated on their new, big-inch four-bangers and began working feverishly away on a new V-12 racing model.

But four-cylinder, straight-six or V-12, Ferraris all have that special, singular look and style to them, and so naturally I couldn't wait to drive the 121LM. Only first Carlo had me sign a bunch of papers and took pains to explain that Cal and me would be very much responsible for the car while it was in transit and also very much on our own if anything bad, worse or disastrous happened on our way to Sebring. But I was hardly a raw sort of hand at this stuff. "So what you're saying is: *if we have a wreck, we better die in it,* right?"

"You grasp the situation perfectly," Carlo allowed through a thin-lipped smile.

I also mentioned how nice of him it was to give Cal a shot in the car, and that I was sure Cal would do a good job with it. Carlo just grinned a little wider and told me: "Arrangements have been made." I took this to mean that a significant wad of cash had changed hands under the table someplace. Because that's the way such things were done. Not that any of the participants would ever talk much about it. After all, none of the supposedly up-and-coming hotshoe drivers wanted anybody to know they were paying for rides (or that some angel, sponsor, rich-heiress bed partner or bigshot sugar daddy was doing it for them) on account of they wanted to maintain the illusion that it was all down to skill, talent and deserved opportunity. But of course that's just not the way it works in real life, since it costs a ton of money to build the cars and a ton more to keep them in parts and tires and brake linings and gasoline and entry fees and a ton more after that—maybe even *two* tons—to put a decent crew together to prepare, transport, field and maintain them. A crew, mind you, with their own collection of mouths to feed and weary bones to rest at the end of each day and families to fret over and bank balances to keep afloat. And all that dough's gotta come from somewhere, right? Lord knows there's never been near enough to cover it out of prize money. Even if you won every blessed race. Which of course you can't. As Carlo himself put it: "No matter how much talent a driver has, if he's got money, he pays."

"What if he doesn't have money?" I asked.

"Then he either finds somebody who *can* pay or I find a driver with deeper pockets and maybe a little less talent." He leaned in close and flashed me that klieg-light smile of his. "Grand adventures cost a lot of money, my friend. Glory costs a lot of money. Fun costs a lot of money. Even risk costs a lot of money. That's just the way it is in life."

"But what if some guy is really, *really* good?"

Carlo rolled his palms up in the classic New York street gesture. "There are never more than a handful like that," he said almost sadly. "Not even a handful, really. Just one or two in a generation. Men like Tazio Nuvolari and Guy Moll and Alberto Ascari and of course Fangio. And maybe this new one from England, Stirling Moss. Those men are *different.* You can see it in their eyes."

"You can?"

Carlo nodded. But then he added quickly: "Ah, but those are the exceptions. The rare ones. Hardly enough to even talk about. The rest all have to pay."

But of course all this cash-passing had to be done privately and discreetly and kept very hush-hush. It wouldn't do to spoil the illusion for your best customers. Especially when that illusion amounted to a very large chunk of what they were buying in the first place….

I have to admit my hand was shaking just a little when I twisted the key, listened to the chattering electric fuel pumps filling up the float bowls in the three Weber carburetors—*clickclickclickclickclickclick*—and fired that big Ferrari six up for the very first time. What a sound! Especially there in the shop, where it came echoing back at me from all four walls! Carlo smiled, raised the overhead door, gave me a hesitant thumbs-up and turned me loose on the streets of Manhattan. You should have heard that nasty, unmuffled, impatient six-cylinder growl reverberating off the stone and concrete and rattling windowpanes all the way to the George Washington Bridge! "Be easy with the clutch and rear end," Carlo yelled after me. "They're not really made for city traffic…."

As you can imagine, that snarling, bright red 121LM snapped necks and sucked the eyeballs right out of people's heads all the way to the airport.

Cal looked a little tired but in reasonably high spirits when I picked him up at Idlewild. But that was understandable after a discombobulated, near-endless three-hop plane trip that started in Los Angeles the previous afternoon. "I hate flying west to east across country," he sighed. "It's like you're swimming against the current of time."

"I know what you mean," I told him, although I wasn't really sure that I did.

It took us the better part of a half-hour just figuring out how to fit my stuff and Cal's stuff plus his racing helmet and goggles and two full-size human beings into that Ferrari for our trip down to Sebring. A racing helmet just doesn't conveniently tuck away into a nook or cranny like socks or underwear. But with no windscreen in front of the passenger seat, we decided that whoever was riding over there (and that would be me most of the time, no matter how tired Cal looked) would wear Cal's helmet and goggles. I must admit I felt a little silly putting on a helmet and goggles right there in front of the terminal at Idlewild. Like I'd been caught out on the street dressed up to go to a costume party, you know? But it all seemed all right once we climbed into the car and Cal fired up the engine. *"Sounds pretty sweet!"* he hollered over the exhaust racket.

"Sure does!" I yelled back. And then I added: *"Carlo said to take it a little easy on the clutch and rear end."*

"Right!" he said, giving me a thumbs-up and a big, cheery smile. Then he slipped on a pair of his trademark aviator sunglasses (which looked to be the same exact ones he gleeped off the counter next to the cash register when we stopped for breakfast at that little roadside diner on our way to the Giant's Despair Hillclimb in his raggedy old TC back during the summer of 1952), mashed the gas to the floor, sidestepped the clutch and slewed us away from the curb on two smoke-billowing streaks of burned rubber.

"I SAID BE CAREFUL WITH THE FUCKING REAR END!" I hollered even louder over the shrieking tires, bellowing exhaust and the usual Ferrari symphony of valvetrain whirrs and gearbox whines.

"It's got pretty good power," Cal allowed as he threaded our way crazily through airport traffic, nicking kneecaps and grazing luggage carts and taxicab door handles on both sides. I hadn't ridden with Cal in months—and never at all in anything that fast!—so I pretty much covered my eyes and braced for impact. No question it was going to take a little time to get re-acclimated to Cal's driving style. No question at all....

The 1956 edition of the Rand-McNally Road Atlas said it was roughly a 1200-mile shot from downtown Manhattan to Sebring, Florida, and with a lot of President Dwight D. Eisenhower's wonderful new Interstate Highway System still very much in the planning, excavating and endless, irritating detour stages, the most obvious route was to head straight down US 1 from one end to the other. But US 1 went through a bunch of big cities like Baltimore, Washington D.C. and Richmond, Virginia, and I'd gotten tips from some of the other racers as to how we could skirt around some of that mess on secondary highways and side roads. Plus there was enough truck traffic on US1 to make things really difficult during daytime driving. I mean, what was the point of taking it all the way up to, say, 130 or so just so's you could lean on the brakes to keep from winding up with a truckload of livestock, eggs, wearing apparel, washing machines, snap peas, cedar beams, fresh milk, new cars or a few thousand gallons of carbon tetrachloride in our laps? Plus you had to keep an eye out for cops, since a blood-red Ferrari racing car is pretty much guaranteed to attract their attention.

But you could pin your ears back and *fly* late at night! And that's exactly what Cal was doing, so we made really good time from about 10pm onward. And I was right there beside him—map, route notes, clipboard and flashlight in hand—freezing cold from fingertips to hair follicles and roasting alive from toes to tender bits, hollering for all I was worth over the whipping wind and gear whine and exhaust howl that there was a town coming up or that we had to take an angle right on a side road by the Standard Station or that I had to stop to clean the crap out of my pants after a particularly lurid passing maneuver. Like I said, the Ferrari was right-hand-drive, and that meant *I* was the one stuck with scout duty regarding oncoming traffic any time we got caught behind a big old truck or travel trailer. And once Cal got a head of steam up, it didn't take more than a wheeze, a nod or a lifted finger to make him think he had room to pull out and pass. Which, in some cases, put me directly in the rapidly closing headlight beams of a gargantuan over-the-road semi or some gently meandering pickup on its way home from the local honky-tonk after closing time.

To be honest, it felt a little strange to be heading into the deep south after all the stuff I'd been reading in the paper and hearing on the radio and seeing on the television news every day about bus line boycotts and school integration and those Reverends Martin Luther King Junior and Ralph Abernathy who seemed to be stirring things up and getting themselves in trouble with the law all the time. Like what happened at the University of Alabama just the month before, where this young colored girl named Autherine Lucy got the federal government in Washington to pretty much admit her to college there. And it seemed reasonable to me, you know? But of course up north we have segregation by geography and neighborhoods rather than race, creed or color (although it amounts to essentially the same thing), and no question our system works a lot better….

Anyhow, letting this colored girl into school there didn't sit especially well with the school administration or their admissions department or the bulk of the students (or, more precisely, their parents) or the elected and appointed government officials of the sovereign state of Alabama or the yahoos down at the local pool hall, all of whom were pretty much used to taking care of things themselves without any unwanted advice from the damn federal government in Washington, D.C. Hell, the University of Alabama (along with most of the rest of the government institutions and services in the state) had been pretty much White Only as far back as anyone could remember. Or at least as far back as Lee's humiliating surrender to Grant and his Yankees at Appomattox, anyway.

If you followed it on the news, there were demonstrations and riots and police dogs and fire hoses being sprayed into the crowd over these Negroes wanting to ride at the front of the buses and eat lunch wherever the hell they wanted and have their kids go to school with the white kids down in Montgomery and Little Rock and wherever else in the deep south. Which naturally amounted to a pretty hefty break from the way they were used to doing things down in those parts, and no question it was stirring up a lot of trouble. But what *really* got the local gentry pissed off were all those outside liberal buttinskys coming down from up north trying to make them look like a bunch of cotton-picking rubes. I really didn't know what to make of it, so I asked Sylvester what he thought about it. But it seemed to get him more irritated and annoyed than anything else.

"Ah look like some kinda damn po-litical spokesman t'you?" he'd snarl as he squinted into the wisp of smoke streaming up off the end of his latest Lucky Strike and scraped at the remaining gasket material on a front timing cover.

"Uh, no, Sylvester. I just thought..."

"Y'see me carryin' any fuckin' signs or marchin' in any fuckin' streets?"

"No, but...."

"Lookee here. You payin' me t'fix these damn cars or 'splain the whole fuckin' world t'you?"

"I'm sorry. It's just I don't really get what's going on...."

"YOU don't get it?? Whut makes y'think I do? Huh? I'm jus' a poor ole black man tryin' t'make a livin' in a fuckin' white man's world. Thass all."

And sure enough that was the end of it. Period. Even though I got this sense that Sylvester felt like he'd missed out on something and now the chance was gone and he was mad at himself and everybody else on account of it. But it wasn't the kind of thing you could talk about or work out with him. And that's something you just have to learn about both friends and people you work with: respect for privacy comes first. Even if you're dying to know more or think you have a better idea.

But we were taking about the University of Alabama, weren't we? After the near-riots over her coming to school there, the university kind of suspended this young colored girl to try and calm things down. So this federal court in Washington up and ordered them to let her back in again. And sent a bunch of National Guard troops to make sure everybody went along with the program. Which, as you can imagine, didn't sit too awfully well with the local white folks. They didn't much appreciate some liberal do-gooders up in Washington telling them how to run things in their own hometowns, you know? And I guess I could kind of understand that, too. To tell the truth, it was hard for an ordinary Jersey guy like me to know what to make of it all. Especially cruising through the beautiful mountains, hills and greenery of the south, where everything looked so ordinary and peaceful and harmonious—like nothing special was going on at all! But I guess that's the eternal difference between the way the world looks in person and the way it looks staring at you from the screaming headlines on the front page of your morning newspaper or blasted out at you both barrels through the television screen on the six o'clock news. Hard to believe it's the same place a lot of the time....

Still, it was great being out on another wild, freewheeling road adventure with my racecar driving friend/hero Cal Carrington—just like the old days, you know?—what with the howl of that Ferrari shattering the atmosphere around us while fields and towns and hills and forests and all sorts of handsome countryside went wheeling by in a magnificent blur. Sure, the wind was whipping my face, neck and shoulders, I had a terrible kink in my back and no doubt I was collecting what would surely turn out to be an impressive assortment of first- and second-degree burns all up and down my left leg where the outside exhaust pipes ran just the thickness of one very thin sheet of aluminum away. Yep, I'd forgotten all the pain, discomfort, short, sharp adrenaline bursts of sheer, clutching fear and the droning, endless boredom of the open road that dragged endlessly on in between. Which is another way of saying I was loving every awful, agonizing, hair-raising minute. You have to understand that heroic quests and adventures don't come along very often in life, and you learn to appreciate them—in spite of the ordeal and occasional terrors involved—because you know the stories and memories will last you a lifetime. Plus you can look at every guy-with-a-wife-and-kids in a Ford or Chevy station wagon and every streetcorner soda jerk, insurance salesman or gas pump jockey you pass along the highway and see from their eyes—damn near stuck out on stalks, most often—that they're envying the hell out of you. A guy can smooth over an awful lot of agony with that kind of feeling.

Of course the great lie is that you get to share a lot of deep thoughts, secrets and understandings on a trip like that. And I guess you can when you're traveling in a normal sort of vehicle or hauling the racecar behind on a trailer. But there was no way in hell you could do much more than shout route instructions or tell the other guy you had to take a pee break—and you had to yell your head off to do that!—traveling at a thrumming two-miles-a-minute-plus in a Ferrari 121LM racecar. But it had its compensations. Like when we pulled into a drive-in just a little north of downtown Jacksonville a few hours after dark on Wednesday evening. The carhop came out on roller skates—a tall, striking girl with a slender waist, too much rouge and lipstick and tightly curled blonde hair that wasn't exactly hers. You could say she was something of a looker in a trashy kind of way. In fact, you could say it a couple of times. And you could see she was pretty damn impressed with the Ferrari. And Cal, too, come to think of it. In fact, their eyes locked solid from the instant she came over. I could feel the heat, even from over on the passenger side.

"You don't look like y'all are from around here," she observed through a lipstick-rimmed smile.

"We're from the North Pole," Cal grinned right back at her. "We work for Santa Claus."

"Oh, really? Do y'all make the toys?"

"Oh, no," Cal deadpanned, "we *are* the toys."

It went on from there.

Anyhow, we eventually ordered burgers and fries and a couple cokes, and then we had to figure out what to do when she came back with the tray since there were no side windows or anything to hang it on. "Why don't you just stand there and hold them for us for awhile?" Cal asked through a smile that was also kind of a sneer.

"Oh, I'll get in Dutch for sure," she said like it sounded exciting. "We're not supposed to get too friendly with y'all customers."

She sure sounded friendly. Real friendly, in fact.

"But this is different," Cal argued. "It's an emergency, see?" He looked around at where the windows would have been if the Ferrari had any. "You don't look very busy, and we obviously need somebody blonde and good-looking to hold our tray."

"I don't think I better," she said with a twinkle in her eyes.

"Aw, *puhl-eeeze?* We've been driving straight through…"

"From the North Pole?"

"That's right. From the North Pole, and…"

"Where are y'all *really* from?"

Cal gave her the beagle-puppy eyes. "You don't believe we're from the North Pole?"

She shook her head. "I may be from a small town, but I know a whopper when I hear one."

Cal looked at me. "Looks like our cover is blown, Boris."

"Boris?" I said.

"Boris?" she echoed.

"Yeah," Cal started in again, "this is Boris and I'm Igor, and we're escaped Russian spies."

"Boris and Igor? You sound like y'all escaped from a monster movie at the drive-in." She held the tray out like she might just accidentally dump all the burgers, fries and cokes directly into Cal's lap. "C'mon now, where are y'all from? Boris over there sounds like he comes from someplace around New York."

"That's pretty good," I admitted. "I'm from right across the bridge in Jersey."

But she never even took her eyes off Cal. "And what about you? Are you from around New York, too?"

"Used t'be," Cal admitted. "Only now I live in California," he took one of the cheeseburgers off the tray she was still holding and took a hefty bite out of it. "Hollywood, actually," he added while still chewing. You could see her eyes widen up a notch or two.

"You in the movies?" she gushed.

"Kinda," Cal shrugged. "Everybody is out there."

"But are you *IN* the movies?"

Cal shrugged again. "Now and then. But what I do mostly is drive racecars."

Her eyes bulged even more as they swept over the Ferrari. "Boy, I've never, *ever* seen a car like this before."

"It's a Ferrari," Cal grinned around his cheeseburger. "Comes from Italy."

"From Italy, huh? How much does it cost?"

"Oh, we normally don't discuss that with the general population."

"The general population, huh? How would y'all like this here Coca-Cola dumped right over your head?"

"Okay. Sorry." Cal looked across the street. There was a handsome two-story frame house on the corner with a wraparound porch and flowers in the window boxes. "Y'see that house over there?"

She nodded. "That's where the Warner family lives. Nice folks, too. Their little boy Bill delivers our newspapers." She shot Cal an insider smile. "You should see him go on that coaster wagon of his. Everybody says he's gonna be a race driver one day."

"Hey, all it takes is money, time and talent."

"But what about their house? What does it have to do with anything?"

"Well, you asked how much this car costs, right?"

She bobbed her head.

Cal pointed across the street. "About as much as that house."

That startled her. "No kidding?"

Cal nodded.

She looked at me, and I nodded too.

She stared at the Ferrari again. "Tell me, is it *fast?"*

"Fast enough." He patted the Ferrari on the dashboard and then sneaked his eyes up to hers again. "How about you?"

"How about *me?"* she asked in that innocent little pipsqueak voice girls use to show you they know exactly what you're talking about.

"Yeah. Are *you* fast?"

She managed a blush. But she may have been holding her breath. "I think we were talking about your *car,"* she reminded Cal in that same teasing, singsong voice. "Is your *car* fast?"

"You wanna go for a ride and see for yourself?" Cal asked as he poked through his French fries.

"Oh, I'd get fired for sure."

"How about after work? What time do you get off?"

"In an hour or so. I'm just on for the dinner rush tonight."

I felt the old antennae go up and gave Cal a nudge. After all, we were supposed to be making tracks for Sebring in a huge sort of hurry. Cal glared at me and then looked back at her with a big, sugary smile. "You have any movie theatres in this town?"

She looked insulted. "Of course we do. It's not like we're hicks down here or anything."

"Oh, really?" Cal said through a down-the-nose New York look that made her blush all over again. Only this time for real. "Tell me, what are these parts famous for?"

Her brow knitted up. "We've got the ocean and the beaches," she sneered right back at him. "An' we had the state championship little league team two years ago."

"My, my."

"And the Okefenokee Swamp is just up the road a ways. You probably went right through it."

"Hm. So that's what that smell was."

"Hey, don't knock the Okefenokee," she said, waving a finger at him. "That's where Pogo Possum comes from."

"Who?"

"Pogo," I blurted out. "Pogo the Possum. That's *right!* I read him to my kids in the Sunday funny papers all the time. We love that strip."

They both looked at me like I'd busted in through a locked door. So I shut up.

"So tell me more about the movie theatres," Cal started in again.

"What's to tell? We've got two in town. The State and The Garden. The Garden is just down the street there."

"Hm. What's playing?"

"Invasion of the Body Snatchers. But I've already seen it…."

Cal turned to me. "How about you?"

"How about *me?"*

"Yeah. How about you?"

"How about me *what?"*

"Have you seen *Invasion of the Body Snatchers?"*

I had to admit I hadn't.

And that's how I wound up watching *Invasion of the Body Snatchers* all by my lonesome (and on my own 50 cents, natch) in some little crossroads burg on the outskirts of Jacksonville, Florida, while Cal "went for a test drive" with the carhop girl from the drive-in. He'd never done that kind of thing before—at least not while I was with him—and I was kind of put out about it. Although he did ask if I wanted him to "see if she has a friend?" when she went back inside with our tray.

"Jesus, Cal, I'm *married.* I've got kids, even."

"I know that."

"But do you know what it *means?"*

"Look, I wasn't trying to insult you, it's just…"

"Forget it. Just forget it. Take me to the damn show. But doesn't it bother you that we're supposed to be down at Sebring first thing tomorrow morning? And we've still got registration and tech inspection and all the damn paperwork to go through?"

"That's *exactly* what I'm thinking about."

"It is?"

"Yeah, it is. I've decided that I want us to be a little late."

"Why on earth would you want that?"

He tapped a forefinger against his temple. "This guy I'm driving with—that Toly Wolfgang—he's supposed to be one of the big new international hotshots, isn't he?"

"Yeah. I suppose. He's won a couple races—none of the big ones yet, of course—and he certainly does seem to get his name in the papers."

"But he's never been to Sebring, right?"

"How would I know?"

"Well, *I* know. And he hasn't."

"So?"

"So maybe I'm trying to put him off his game a little."

"Your own *teammate?"* I have to admit the idea pretty much offended me. But Cal just grinned.

"Hey, he's the only driver I really have to worry about. He's the only one I really have to beat...."

And of course right there was the reason why team owners have to be extra careful when lining up driver pairings for long-distance races. The last thing you want or need is two guys trying to prove something or make a name for themselves in your car. Because then they just naturally have to try to go faster than each other. It goes without saying. And there is absolutely *nothing* that's harder on equipment.

"Look," Cal continued. *"I* want to go somewhere in racing and *he* wants to go somewhere in racing, and now here we are, up against the best in the world at one of the biggest races either of us has ever run and driving one of the best cars either of us has ever sat in. Don't think people won't be watching."

"So you're going to purposely show up late just to screw him up?"

"Just a little," Cal allowed through his sneakiest, snakiest cobra grin. "Get him to worrying about where the hell we are and what the hell happened to the car. Keep him from getting his first practice session in. That's all I'm trying to do."

"That stinks, Cal."

Cal's eyes narrowed and stared straight into mine. "Hey, this is for blood, Buddy. For blood. I don't want to be running fucking club races all my life. Not even in Ferraris. Besides, it's not like I planned it out."

"It sure sounds like you did."

"Nah, I just thought about it a little. Kind of ran it through my mind. But then," he nodded towards the bottle-blonde carhop, who was just then leaning over the counter and giving us an excellent view of her backside, "it's like fate lent a hand here."

Cal had sure changed since he'd been living out in California. Or maybe we'd both changed. Or maybe I never really saw that side of him before. But that's the way it is with heroes. If you like and envy somebody and respect what they can do and you can't, you maybe tend to gloss over their human failings and frailties. Because they're your heroes, you tend to simply *assume* that they have such things as ethics and values and virtue and character. After all, that's what heroes are supposed to have, right? Check out any damn comic book, dime novel or Hollywood movie and you'll see exactly what I mean. Only that's not the way it works out in real life. Not hardly.

In any case, I finally got to see *Invasion of the Body Snatchers*—the last 30 minutes and then a cartoon, a travelogue about Yosemite and then, finally, the first hour—and no question it was pretty good. Even though Julie was right on the money about not wanting to see the ending of a show first. But I didn't enjoy it much. I missed having Julie there with me. I hadn't gone to a movie by myself since I don't know when—high school, I guess—and I must admit it felt pretty strange. Lonely, you know? Especially during the creepy parts where Julie would always nuzzle into me back when we were at the drive-in in Big Ed's black Caddy sedan or even Old Man Finzio's towtruck with the damn shift lever sticking up in the middle. And for sure I'd nuzzle right back into her a little, too. After all, that's what nuzzling's for. I looked around the theatre and there were only a handful of people there—hey, it was a weeknight—but even so it was mostly couples. All except me….

After I'd seen the whole show I went out into the lobby and called home from the pay phone, and of course Julie wanted to know if everything was okay.

"Sure it is," I told her.

"I don't know," she said. "You sound funny."

"I just saw *Invasion of the Body Snatchers* is all. It was kinda creepy."

"I thought you were in such a big hurry to get down to Sebring."

"So did I."

The line went quiet while she chewed that over for a moment. But I could tell her mom was right there, glaring at her like a vulture on a fence post, and so it wasn't really the right time to talk about anything. "You want to talk to the kids?" she finally asked.

"You know I do."

So I asked little Vincenzo how he was doing and he told me about a drawing of a bird or an airplane—he didn't seem sure exactly which—he made for the refrigerator door and then his little sister got on and gargled and gurgled into the phone for me, and I swear I felt so damn homesick I could've cried. Especially after I hung up. I was just standing there facing the wall with the sound of the movie coming through all muffled from inside and nobody else in the lobby but me and the high school kid who took tickets running a carpet sweeper in front of the popcorn stand. I wandered outside to see if Cal was there yet, but of course he wasn't so I went back in to see the ending again. And then I had to pretty much leave because it was the last show and they were closing up. There wasn't much to do except just stand there out on the darkened street of this strange little crossroads town somewhere north of Jacksonville feeling lonely and tired and grimy and gritty and lousy about things in general.

Cal and the Ferrari finally came growling up the street about a half-hour after they turned off the lights on the theatre marquee, and I noticed he was wearing a different shirt underneath his windbreaker. "You have a good time?" he asked me.

"Sure," I said sarcastically. "How 'bout you?"

"Not bad," he said without any particular emotion. Then he handed me the helmet and set of goggles again. They smelled of perfume and lipstick and powdered rouge. I really didn't want to put them on. "You'd better," he told me like he knew exactly what I was thinking. And then he revved her up and eased out the clutch and in no time at all we were wrapped in the onrushing wind and noise and darkness again, devouring distance in one long, unending swallow as we rocketed south across the flat Florida landscape towards Sebring. To tell the truth, I was mad as hell at Cal. I could feel it alternately boiling and simmering inside me. Even though I couldn't exactly understand why. Heck, why should it matter to me that he'd met some hick-town blonde carhop that he'd never, ever see again and knocked her over like a damn tenpin in a bowling alley? Why the hell should I care? And no question the cute, trashy little carhop at the burger stand somewhere in the boonies of northern Florida was putting a notch in her belt every bit as much as Cal was. I mean, handsome Ferrari drivers from Hollywood didn't cruise into town very often in those parts. But it bothered the heck out of me anyway. Of course the easy answer is that maybe I was jealous. But I *wasn't* jealous. I know what jealous feels like, and this wasn't it. It was more like disgusted, you know?

And I couldn't figure that one out, either….

Chapter 7: Fast Times in Florida

Cal and me were pretty tired as you might expect, and the weariness hit us hard as we droned on through the cool, heavy, lonely Florida night, heading south on US 1 past St. Augustine and on towards Daytona Beach sometime well after midnight. We were doing an easy two miles a minute-plus on the straight, empty stretches, following the vibrating yellow blur of the Ferrari's headlight beams like the elongated light of some huge, flickering candle stretched out into the blackness. Cal would slow to 90 or so through crossroad intersections (like that was gonna help if some sneak-around husband, old lady heading home from an all-night prayer meeting or stumble-drunk pickup driver trying to find a bar with a later closing time pulled out in front of us!) and blasting past little whistle-stop towns that didn't amount to much more than a street lamp, a closed gas station and citrus stand. But by that point it felt like you could just about get out and walk at that speed. We were so damn exhausted I was starting to see things out in the darkness—shadowy creatures and sets of glowing eyes and of course those spark-showering meteorite space ships from *Invasion of the Body Snatchers* streaking across the sky. Only they always seemed to be behind me or off to one side when I was looking the other way. You know how that goes. So I was thankful when Cal slowed suddenly and pulled off the highway as we approached a darkened little cracker box of a mom-and-pop motel near Ormond Beach. He switched off the ignition while we were still rolling to keep the noise down, and the silent emptiness of the night was only broken by the soft, sweet crunch of gravel under the tires as we coasted gently to a stop in front of the office. My face was still tingling from the wind and the throb of the exhaust was still echoing in my ears like surf rolling in. Or maybe that actually was surf rolling in, since we couldn't have been very far from the ocean at all. Except for that, the night around us was quiet as the inside of a velvet glove. It had to be about 3:30 in the morning.

"Whaddaya say we grab forty winks?" Cal whispered. Quiet like that makes you feel like you need to whisper.

"Makes no difference to me," I whispered back.

A light went on inside the office (which was also the kitchen) and through the window we saw the skinny old guy who ran the place shuffle to the door in slippers, pajama bottoms and a raggedy terrycloth robe that dragged on the floor behind him. *"Hep'you?"* he asked, his eyes still pretty much closed. He had brown, leathery skin under silky white hair and he'd obviously left his teeth in their water glass back beside his bed.

"We were thinking about a room," Cal explained.

"Well," he yawned. *"Y'be sure and lemme know when yer ready t'stop thinkin' an' actually do somethin' about it, okay?"* But then he saw the Ferrari parked behind us and it perked him right up. In fact, his eyelids came up like a set of double-hung curtains at a stage show. "Boy, that's one helluva car y'got there," he observed.

"Yeah, it is," I agreed wearily. We were both dead on our feet.

But it didn't stop the guy with no teeth in his face. "Geez, I never seen a car like that one before."

"I expect not."

"Oh, but I seen *lotsa* fast cars in my time," he assured us, his head nodding up and down like a fishing bobber.

"I'm sure you have."

"Why, this right here in Ormond Beach is the damn birthplace of speed, son! Bet'cha didn't know that."

I admitted I didn't.

"Why *sure* it is! Yessiree." He cocked his thumb proudly over his shoulder. "They useta do speed record runs right back there behind me."

"In your kitchen?" Cal said like he was serious.

"NO!" the guy almost yelled. *"Out on the beach back there, sonny."* He eyeballed Cal for a second. "You're a real wisenheimer, aren'cha?"

"I do my best."

The old guy eyeballed him some more. Then he looked at me. And then he started in again. "Most folks don't remember it anymore, but they had big speed-record runs out on the beach back there years before they had races an' such down the road at Daytona."

"Do tell…."

"Yessir. Seen it myself when I was just turned 17. Nineteen-oh-three, it was. Saw Ransom E. Olds hisself squared off against Alexander Winton, tryin' t'prove whose car was fastest. Went over a mile a minute, they did. Both of 'em! Why, it was the damnedest thing anybody around here ever saw!"

"I'm sure it was."

"Back before the war I seen Malcolm Campbell—that's *SIR* Malcolm Campbell, y'know—break the World Land Speed Record back there a whole buncha times. Four or five at least. Saw him go three-hunnert-an'-one miles per hour! Honest t'God I did. Right back there on the beach!"

"That's absolutely fascinating," Cal said without meaning a word of it. "But we're pretty tired here and I think we're ready for that room about now."

But it was like the old guy didn't even hear him. He was rolling now: "So how fast that car of yours go, sonny? Pedal to the metal. C'mon, wottle she do?"

Cal glanced at me and then back at the old guy. "Hard t'say," he mused, rubbing his chin and kind of mimicking the way the guy talked. "Don't think we've had it much over 300 yet, have we, Buddy?"

"Can't say as we have," I nodded in about the same voice. I mean, 130 or 150 or even 175 or 180 miles per hour wasn't going to impress this guy.

"That's pretty fast," the old guy agreed grudgingly.

"Sure is," Cal continued without missing a beat. "You have to be careful not to smile at that speed or the rush of air'll blow the teeth right down your own throat."

The old guy's eyes got bigger. "No kidding?"

Cal nodded solemnly.

"Yeah," I chimed in. "And we have to wear goggles so the wind doesn't push our eyeballs clear out of our ears."

He looked uncertainly back and forth between Cal and me. "Do tell…."

Anyhow, we got a room at the little motel and slept like a pair of corpses until about seven the next morning, and then the old guy's wife fixed us up with tall glasses of freshly-squeezed orange juice, hot coffee and a couple slices of French toast each before we took off again for Sebring. Wouldn't take any money for the breakfast, either. But I left them a nice 50-cent tip on the bed stand. I figured it was the least I could do.

It turned out to be your typically hot, bright and sunshiny Florida day, but we couldn't make very good time on account of all the trucks, tourist traffic and meandering retirees. Not to mention those infamous little speed-trap Florida towns where a large part of the local economy gets raked right in off the highway. So it was well after noon when we finally turned left off Highway 27, followed the southern shoreline of Lake Jackson for less than a mile and then took a right at the stately old Kenilworth Hotel where a lot of the racers always stayed and headed out through the dusty orange groves towards Sebring's so-called racetrack. In real life, it had been a big World War II military airport purposely hidden way off in the boonies of central Florida, and served as kind of a holding station, training base and jumping-off point for freshly-built bombers and freshly-trained crews on their way to the European and Pacific fronts. But it kind of went to seed after the war was over and, thanks mostly to promoter Alec Ulmann and some fairly desperate local chamber-of-commerce types, those empty runways and access roads got themselves pressed into service as a makeshift racetrack once a year starting way back in 1950. The idea that it had become the biggest, most important and by far most international sportscar race in North America seemed a little goofy—I mean, it was just a broken-down, rusting, half abandoned old World War II bomber base out in the middle of nowhere, you know?—but that's exactly what happened.

And there it was, baking in the sun as usual: a vast, flat, wide-open weed patch and insect sanctuary crisscrossed with cracked, ageing concrete runways and a spider web of matching access roads. There were rusty tin hangers and the crumbling foundations of long-gone barracks and out-buildings here and there, plus rows of decaying, mothballed bombers left over from The Big One parked off in the distance on the far side of the runways. I don't think the government really knew what to do with them, so there they sat—getting cannibalized for spare parts every now and then, but otherwise just laying out there in the baking Florida sun like retirees in deck chairs. As you can imagine, there was no way a gritty, empty, tumbled-down airport like Sebring had the style, class or stature of a place like Le Mans. But by 1956, it sure as hell had most of the same top hotshoe drivers and famous factory teams. In fact, it was the biggest damn sportscar race ever in North America and a full-fledged, fully-supported round of the FIA's World Manufacturers' Championship.

Along with Sebring's impressive entry list and increased status came a lot more "local volunteer" types and SCMA armband people to run things and handle the headaches (or create them, as the case might be), and as a result it took us over an hour and a half to get through registration. Seems Carlo Sebastian's crew had picked up our gate passes for us when they checked in (figuring we'd meet up with them at the hotel that morning before heading out to the track) and so now we needed to get *into* the track in order to get them. But of course we couldn't get in to get them because we didn't have our passes in the first place. And naturally the scrawny, bucktoothed, fruit-fly-inspector-turned-SS Commandant-for-the-weekend in front of us was simply loving an opportunity to flex his authority. "Can't go in without a pass," he said for maybe the fifteenth or twentieth time.

"But we need to get *inside* to get our passes, see?" I explained again, speaking very slowly and distinctly so as not to reveal how genuinely pissed off I was becoming. Especially since I could hear the engines firing up for afternoon practice. "You see that car over there?" I asked, pointing towards our dusty Ferrari 121LM. "Does that look like a racecar to you?"

"Yes, it does," the guy nodded like it made no difference at all.

"And don't you think it really wants to be *inside* the track right now, getting ready for afternoon practice?"

"I expect it does," he smiled up at us. "And it can go right in anytime somebody with a proper track credential comes out to get it."

It would have gone on and on and round and round like that for hours—with the jerkoff in front of us enjoying every minute, of course!—but somebody must've gotten word to Carlo Sebastian's guys that we were stranded at registration, and damn if Toly Wolfgang himself didn't come charging full-tilt out of the paddock on a little red Vespa motorscooter with a prancing horse decal on the front splash apron and a skinny wisp of two-stroke vapor pinging out the exhaust. He was small, neat, quick, dark and intense, and he did not look happy. Of course I recognized him instantly from the pictures in the newspapers and gossip magazines. Especially the eyes. They were so dark they were almost black, and set deep beneath heavy, black eyebrows. I came to learn those eyes could be solid as armor plate, dance like rippling water, turn women to mush, flash over with ice or burn a hole clear through you at a moment's notice. He was smaller than I imagined from the photographs, but taut, tough, aristocratic and wiry, with just the tiniest hint of silver-gray frosting at his temples and at the edges of his mustache. Looking at him, you could easily believe the stories that Toly Wolfgang had been an amateur tennis and boxing champion, a fencer, front-man driver for an Olympic bobsled team, polo ace and accomplished steeplechase rider before he turned to automobile racing. I thought he looked a lot more Greek or Italian than German—a little bit like Gilbert Roland, the movie actor—but that made sense because he was sort of a blue-blooded mongrel, what with a bunch of aristocratic Spanish and Italian ancestry mixed in there with the Russian and German and Austrian and Lord only knows what else. Rumor had it the blood of five or six different royal houses (plus a few willing chambermaids) coursed through his veins, and you could see it in the way he looked and dressed and carried himself. His white linen pants were perfectly creased, his shoes were neatly polished and he wore a black knit shirt with two thin red bands around the left bicep and some kind of important regal crest embroidered over the heart.

As soon as he got the motorscooter flipped up on its centerstand, Toly Wolfgang took a slender silver cigarette case out of his pocket and lit up a *Gauloises* with a matching silver lighter. He took a slow, deep drag as his eyes swept around the registration area, sizing it up, and let the smoke curl up over his lip and twist back into his nostrils in a classic French inhale. He saw Cal and me at the table with the Fruit Fly Commandant and he headed over, glaring at Cal the whole way. "It was nice of you to drop by," he told Cal with a hard, sarcastic edge in his voice.

"We had a few unavoidable delays," Cal explained without really saying anything. I nodded, not knowing what else to do.

"Hmpf," Toly snorted. He took one look at the scrawny guy with the buck teeth in front of us, took another deep, thoughtful drag on his cigarette, and decided without a word that it was useless to fool with him. So his eyes searched the back of the tent until they came to rest on an important-looking gent in a jacket and tie with a medal of some kind pinned to his lapel. In a flash Toly was past the jerk we'd been arguing with and making a beeline for the guy with the coat and tie. The guy in the jacket and tie saw him coming and instantly gave him one of those little head-bob bows of recognition and respect. They shook hands and talked back and forth in rapid-fire French for a few moments—lots of shrugging, mugging and hand gestures—and then the guy with the jacket and tie simply walked over, reached down to the table where the guy with the buck teeth was sitting, selected two passes from the top of the stack in front of him and slipped them into Toly's pocket. Just like that, can you believe it?

That's the way they do business downtown!

Even so, it took us another 30 minutes or so to get inside and get our stuff unpacked and get the car through tech inspection (which was officially closed by then, but Toly got that fixed pretty quick, too) and by then afternoon practice was almost over. Toly jumped into the car—he'd never so much as sat in it before—fired it up while hurriedly strapping on a scruffy black helmet with that same fancy crest on the front and went charging out onto the racetrack. But he only got a couple laps in before the car started coughing and sputtering on account of everybody was in such a big damn hurry to get him going that nobody bothered to check the fuel level. Hey, that's what always seems to happen when you're in a frantic rush at the racetrack. Something simple gets forgotten or overlooked. Every damn time.

The first sign of it was when the car started starving out in right-hand corners, but within a half-lap it was sputtering even on the straight sections and the damn thing finally cut completely halfway down that long back straightaway behind the paddock. There was nothing Toly could do at that point but just coast the rest of the way in—cars thundering past on both sides!—and creep his way into the pits at barely a walking pace. Did he ever look steamed! And then they couldn't find the damn gas can or funnel since nobody much thinks about refueling during afternoon practice. By then the checker had waved to end the session, but he charged back out to sneak in one more tour anyway. There was an armband type with a whistle, a big straw hat and an even bigger beer gut at the end of the pit lane waving for him to stop, but Toly just gunned it and the guy had to jump out of the way at the last instant in order to avoid becoming a hood ornament. As Toly and the Ferrari disappeared around the first turn and wailed off into the distance, the pit steward with the big beer gut picked himself and his straw hat up off the concrete and went into one of those red-faced, arm-waving dervish dances that can only mean one thing when done by a volunteer race official: somebody was gonna catch hell!

But I don't think Toly Wolfgang much cared. It had already occurred to him that it took more than two sputtering, confusing laps to find your way around a track as big, odd, discombobulated and outright strange as Sebring. But he wisely sneaked into the paddock by going the wrong way through the ambulance station at the exit of Sunset Bend and thus avoided an ugly confrontation with the guy he'd almost run over. Who had meanwhile stormed over to Carlo Sebastian's pit box, where he was waving his arms and shaking his fist in the air while he screamed and hollered at us about *"WHOEVER THE HELL WAS DRIVING THAT DAMN FERRARI??!!"* But of course we all played dumb (and like we didn't speak anything but Italian) and slowly but surely the guy's anger melted into a kind of furious but helpless frustration—face beet-red, chest puffing, fists clenching and unclenching—and he finally skulked away, muttering under his breath. And who should be standing there watching the whole blessed performance and trying his best not to laugh right out loud but my old motoring-scribe buddy, Hank Lyons. Geez, it was great to see him!

"I see you conveniently forgot how to speak English," he grinned.

"It was just a momentary lapse."

"You know your Italian stinks."

"It's New Jersey Italian. It only works in restaurants."

"Italian restaurants, or all kinds of restaurants?"

"Everywhere *but* Italian restaurants! Hell, I can make myself misunderstood in five or six different languages…."

We shared a nice laugh.

"It's really good to see you."

"It's really good to see you, too."

"What have you been up to?"

"Oh, the usual motoring-journalist shit. Living like a fat prince on the race weekends and damn near starving to death in between. How about you?"

I shrugged. "You know how it is. Wife. Two kids. Way too much family. Growing VW business. I just show up where I'm supposed to be and do what people expect. I don't even have a life anymore."

"That's too bad."

"Nah, it's okay."

"No, it isn't."

"You sound like Cal."

"Say, how is he?"

"Fine. I rode down with him from New York in the 121LM."

"I heard. How was it?"

I thought it over for a second, picking my words carefully. "Well, let's just say it was as close to heaven as I ever hope to get."

"In more ways than one!" Hank agreed. And he's the guy who would know, since we'd both taken long, fast, thrilling and sometimes terrifying over-the-road sportycar drives with Cal Carrington. It made us kind of a blood brotherhood, you know?

There wasn't much of anything to do until night practice, so we wandered back over by Carlo Sebastian's bivouac to see how things were going for the old home team. Toly Wolfgang still sitting in the car, silently smoking another *Gauloises* while he stared off into space and thought things over. Night practice was coming up right after dinner, and he could see already that Sebring was hardly the kind of circuit you wanted to be figuring out in the dark. Which is probably exactly what my buddy Cal Carrington had in mind, come to think of it.

We didn't have any work to do on the 121LM except wipe it down and check the fluid levels, so Cal and Hank and me decided to take a little tour of the paddock to check out the amazing collection of cars and teams gearing up for this year's race. You really had to be impressed by the turnout of big names, major teams and important cars at Sebring that year, and it occurred to all three of us how much everything had changed since the race we'd seen there just three years before, when it was pretty much just the Cunningham and Aston Martin teams plus a bunch of SCMA club amateurs and rich European privateers. Why, now it was damn near as big a deal as Le Mans, what with front-line, manufacturer (or at least manufacturer-backed) teams from Ferrari, Maserati, Jaguar, Porsche, Aston Martin, Lotus, Cooper and Deutsch-Bonnet among the "thinly disguised all-out racing cars" and genuine, go-to-market "production car" teams that had to somewhat unfairly run even-up against them from S. H. Arnolt and Donald Healey plus a factory-backed team of three new MGAs making their debut in international competition (even though the EX182 prototypes—which were nut-for-nut and bolt-for-bolt identical—ran at Le Mans and in the Tourist Trophy the year before). The MGA was designed to replace the somewhat antique- and upright-looking T-series MGs (although I always thought the TF with its slant-back radiator grille and faired-into-the-fender headlights was rakish as hell) and take on the Healey Hundred and Triumph TR3 in the pitched battle for Yankee sportycar dollars. Like the Healey and Triumph, it used an out-of-the-parts-bin sedan, truck or tractor engine with a cast iron block and head, pushrod-operated valves and not much except a pair of sidedraft S.U. carburetors and a rorty exhaust note to get the technical types excited. But that's what allowed MG (and Healey, and Triumph) to bring the cars in at such a bargain basement price—I mean, not every lunchbucket Joe could afford a Jag or a 300SL—and no question those MGAs were gonna sell like hotcakes here in America. And you had to like the way it was built. Although it had the smallest engine of the three at just 1492cc, it was smooth and pretty to look at and maybe a little more elegantly designed. I was particularly impressed with the curved, soft-looking support members that went from the firewall to the frame rails under the hood. Sure, it takes a mechanic's eye to pick out stuff like that, but you come to appreciate that little details nicely executed are what give a sportscar its feel and character. Even so, those MGAs didn't have a prayer against the "real race car" Porsche 550s and OSCA MT4s running against them in the "1500 Sports" class, but that was hardly the point. Like the Arnolt-Bristols, they just wanted to soldier on, maintain a decent, dignified and disciplined pace and hopefully get all three cars to the finish line without any major dramas or disasters. If you could accomplish that, it went without saying that you'd be well up the order in the final results. After that, it was up to the silver tongues and perfumed pens in the advertising department to get more mileage out of whatever you'd managed to accomplish. And they knew how to do it, too....

But the cars that were causing the biggest commotion at Sebring that year—by far!—were the trio of new 1956 Chevrolet Corvettes in spanking Polo White paint with wide, dark blue racing stripes down the center. Including one with an oversized, 307-cubic-inch monster of a Pontiac engine that was the only entry in the so-called "Sports 8000" class. You have to understand that, at least up to that point, Corvettes had been considered pretty much a joke by the "International Motoring Press" and most of your rank-and-file tweed cap/stringback driving gloves/down-the-snoot European sportycar types. Even the ones born and raised right here in the old U.S. of A. And, to be honest, the chuffly, low-revving old "stovebolt six" in the original Corvettes—like the one Big Ed Baumstein bought—were not exactly what you could call inspiring. Even with three sidedraft Carter carburetors tacked on the side to dress it up a little and the fanciful "Blue Flame Six" moniker (which apparently came from some overpaid advertising guy's wet dream) painted on the valve cover. Worse yet, that anemic, two-speed Powerglide automatic was the only transmission available, and that didn't cut much ice with the double-clutch downshift, heel-and-toe crowd. But the boardroom guys at Chevrolet weren't exactly all asleep at the switch, and they could see what was going on with the sportycar boom here in these United States. So Chevy started getting cautiously serious about this performance business. Which is why they added their promising, neatly packaged and amazingly lightweight new 265 cubic-inch V-8 (all but a half-dozen were ordered with it) and a proper stick shift to the option list for 1955, then heaped more frosting on the cake with a handsomely brutal new shape and face, optional dual four-barrel carburetors and a high-lift camshaft for the '56 model year. And Chevy also decided—very quietly—to try their hand at racing them. But out the back door, of course.

Just in case things didn't go too well....

The new Corvette team was headed up by experienced, sharp and wrench-savvy ex-Cunningham and Mercedes team driver (not to mention our own personal *La Carrera* and Le Mans pal and hero) John Fitch, and he made an excellent front man, field engineer and project manager for the deal. Even though everybody and his brother knew it was a genuine, toe-in-the-water factory effort with funding coming straight from General Motors in Detroit. Even if all the entry forms and paperwork said the cars were entered by some will-o'-the-wisp outfit called "Raceway Enterprises," which apparently operated out of some men's room, grease pit or broom closet at Dick Doane's Chevrolet dealership in Dundee, Illinois. Hank explained as how the "Raceway Enterprises" dodge was just to protect Chevrolet's image in case the cars were slow, broke down, or things got ugly (like they had for Mercedes at Le Mans the year before). Not to mention putting a set of shallow pockets in the line of fire between any potentially aggrieved party or parties and General Motors' well-known and even more well-protected bank accounts.

To tell the truth, most of the European racers figured the Corvettes didn't have a chance of even finishing the damn race at Sebring, much less winning anything. After all, they were pretty much ordinary 1952 Chevy sedan chassis underneath those snappy-but-oversized two-seater bodies, and the smart money in the press-room and all up and down pit lane considered them just big, lumbering boulevard cruisers with dumb (if new) pushrod, cast-iron V-8s and no real performance potential, panache or motorsports pedigree to speak of. And sure enough, they looked awfully big, crude and clumsy parked next to the Ferrari 860 Monzas and Jaguar D-Types running in the same blessed class. Not to mention the 300S Maseratis and DB3S Aston Martins running in the next class down. You have to remember that the FIA rulebook had gotten a wee bit fuzzy regarding the difference between a true, go-to-market sports car and an all-out racing car with a spare seat that never got used except to carry some bosomy pit dolly with a checkered flag in her hand around on victory laps. Or some idiot New Jersey Volkswagen mechanic with a burnt left leg, a crick in his back and flies in his teeth all the way down to Florida.

Anyhow, the way the rules read, if you made 25 copies of damn near anything (or, in the case of Ferrari, if you convinced some willingly snookered Italian FIA liaison that your were *intending* to build 25 copies) then it qualified as a "sports car" as far as the FIA gents in Paris were concerned. And that was a loophole you could drive a blessed truck through. And most particularly an over-the-road car transporter loaded with thinly disguised racing machines! At least if you had a mind to, anyway. And you can bet people like Ferrari, Maserati, Jaguar, Porsche and Aston Martin certainly had a mind to.

Even so, I had an inkling that those Corvettes might wind up surprising a few people. I thought a lot of John Fitch, and that new Chevy V-8 figured to be a pretty sweet race motor once the hot-rodders got hold of it—even if it didn't have overhead cams or alloy cylinder heads or Weber carburetors or any of that other fancy-schmancy European stuff. Why, chief engineer Zora Arkus-Duntov himself (who knew a thing or two about sports cars and had co-driven with Sydney Allard at Le Mans) took one of those new Corvettes to a stamped, sealed and certified two-way, flying mile run of 150.15 miles-per-hour just up the road at Daytona Beach a few months before. And 150 mph is 150 mph, whether you do it by firing an arrow at a bullseye or pushing an anvil off a cliff. Plus they had Fitch and Walt Hansgen in the big-inch, Pontiac-engined car, and I'd put those two up against anybody when it came to talent, skill and savvy behind the wheel. Besides, the Pontiac-engined Corvette was the only car entered in the monster 8.0-liter class, so all they had to do was finish to take home a first-place trophy. And that can be a very comforting thought when you're mapping out your race strategy. Still, like everybody said, the Corvettes were big and heavy and mostly ordinary Chevy sedan bits underneath the fiberglass, and, except for the one with the oversized engine, they had to run even-up against the Jaguar D-Types and Ferrari 860 Monzas and 121LMs in the "Sports 5000" class. Squared off against that kind of opposition, the Corvettes didn't figure to make much of an impression.

Which is why you didn't see any regular, street-issue Jag XK120s or XK140s racing at Sebring in 1956. They didn't have a chance! But you sure saw a whole slew of D-Types running! Nine of them, in fact. Including one privateer entry co-driven by 1955 Indianapolis 500 winner/oval-track star Bob Sweikert. Although the best of them surely figured to be the factory-backed, three-car team in all-American white-with-blue-stripes racing colors entered under the "Jaguar USA" banner. Everybody in Florida knew that "Jaguar USA" was really nothing more than Briggs Cunningham's old squad with Alf Momo as official team manager/prep genius, only now they had a couple of the very latest-spec new D-Types plus some factory team drivers with unmistakable British accents on loan from the factory in Coventry, England.

I thought it was kind of sad that Briggs Cunningham had given up on building and campaigning his own cars. But I guess that was thanks to old Uncle Sam and his IRS tax guys, who could get pretty persnickety regarding the distinction between a hobby and a business if you weren't making any money at it. Hank and me both thought it stunk, since Briggs and his own personal guts, drive and bank account had been fielding the only genuine, feared and respected all-American racing effort in international competition for years. And they'd done pretty damn well at it, what with that outright win we saw the C4R score here at Sebring in 1953 plus a couple competitive and hard-fought third-place finishes at Le Mans and even leading all the Europeans on their home ground at the 12 Hours of Reims until some air got under the car at 150-plus and sent it airborne. And then tumbling. It sure would have been nice if they'd won that race. But Briggs wasn't selling too many of the handsome-but-somewhat-massive (and expensive!) Vignale-bodied Cunningham C-3 *grand turismo* coupes he'd been showing around on the auto show circuit—mostly as a tax dodge, I think, just so's he could write the racing off—and his new C6R competition model just wasn't getting the job done at all. First they tried it with an Indy-style Offenhauser four-banger, but the Offy didn't take the conversion from the alcohol fuel they run at Indianapolis to high-test gasoline very graciously. It just never made the power they expected. And it shook like crazy in the process. All engines have what engineers call "periods of harmonic imbalance" where all that heavy stuff spinning around inside gets a little wobbly and off kilter through certain RPM ranges, but it always seems worst on big four-cylinder engines and it was particularly bad on the Offy. The problem never showed up much at Indianapolis on account of oval-track cars run in a pretty narrow RPM band rather than up and down the scales like a road-racing engine, but the bottom line was that it just didn't work out. So Cunningham's guys tried stuffing a Jaguar engine in the C6R. But by then the IRS jerks were yapping at the door and the sad fact was that Cunningham's C6R/Jaguar just wasn't as good or fast as the Jaguar factory's own D-Types. It was simple as that. So it made more dollars and sense for Briggs to phase out of his own cars and switch to becoming Jaguar's North American importer and official stateside racing team.

It was a shame, but what could you do?

As always, the Cunningham team was super well-organized and the Momo-prepared cars were absolutely immaculate. And all up and down pit lane people were talking about the special, fuel-injected "Jaguar USA" D-Type with first-team factory hotshoe Mike Hawthorn as lead driver. Hawthorn was white-blond and terribly fair-skinned, and as stiff-upper-lip British as afternoon tea. He had a big schoolboy smile and always looked dapper as all getout, what with his straight-stemmed pipes, white shirts, straight or bow ties and tweed jackets—he even wore those blessed white shirts and ties when he drove the damn racecars!—and favored this dashing, wraparound pleastic face shield over the split-window, fighter pilot-style goggles favored by most of the other drivers. But Hawthorn had already gained himself a gunslinger's reputation as a ruthlessly fast, decisive, take-no-prisoners kind of guy behind the wheel. Plus that latest D-Type was rumored to have more than 300 horsepower under its shapely, flip-up front bonnet (which, by the way, they kept closed as much as possible in order to keep prying eyes from the Ferrari, Maserati and Aston Martin camps from taking a closer look at the fuel injection!). Not that you could see all that much. I managed to sneak a peek myself when they were checking fluid levels, and it was just six plain, slightly tapered induction horns sticking out from the side of the cylinder head and not much else. Or at least that's all I could see before the nose came quickly down again! Hank said all the scribes in the pressroom—and particularly that self-proclaimed British know-it-all, Eric Gibbon—figured Hawthorn in the fuel-injected D-Type as the fastest car in the field by a fairly substantial margin. And sure enough the Ferrari timers caught him at a very quick but highly unofficial 3:28 during afternoon practice, which was easily the best time of the day and a whopping *10 seconds a lap* faster than the top qualifying time for the previous year's race. And 10 seconds amounts to a whole lot of distance in a car that can nudge 180mph on the long, straight stretches. But endurance racing is always about more than raw power and sheer, blinding speed, and there were also class wins to think about as well as the overall victory. The

Cunningham—pardon me, "Jaguar USA"—D-Types were over the 3.0-liter limit, so they had to run in the "Sports 5000" class with the big factory and privateer Ferraris and the two Chevy-powered Corvettes, but there were also two good teams in the "Sports 3000" 3.0-liter class—Aston Martin and Maserati—who were likewise in with a shot come the end of 12 long hours.

Of course Cal had already raced against Masten Gregory in Tony Parravano's Maserati 300S in December out at Palm Springs, but I'd never seen one "in the flesh" before, and I thought they were absolutely, positively gorgeous. The 300S was lower, smoother and slinkier than the big Ferraris (and a lot more graceful, too—at least as far as my eyeballs were concerned), plus the machine work and castings underneath that beautifully formed aluminum bodywork amounted to sheer artistry. Even if some of the welding looked like globs of chewing gum! Stirling Moss had already won the first round of the 1956 World Manufacturers' Championship down in Buenos Aires in a 300S (or at least he did after all of old man Ferrari's monstrous four-point-nines broke their transmissions thanks to an oversupply of raw horsepower) and Moss thought the 300S was the best-handling, best-balanced two-seater sports/racer on the planet. And he should know.

But Moss always preferred to drive English cars whenever possible—he had one of those Union Jack patriotic streaks running down his back like a lot of his fellow Brits—and so he'd switched to one of the compact and handsome but somewhat underpowered Aston Martin DB3S models for Sebring. And it was probably a wise move, since the Maserati guys looked more than a bit confused and disorganized in Florida, what with three cars entered but only two actually showing up and one of those pretty much a rent-a-drive deal for two fairly raw hands with fat wallets. Although one of those raw hands was Carlos Menditeguy, a handsome young kazillionaire sportsman and champion polo player from Argentina who got sucked right into the slipstream of countryman Juan Manuel Fangio's incredible success in Europe and his resulting celebrity status at home. I believe Menditeguy wanted some of that for himself. I guess the way he had it figured, he was young, brave, handsome, privileged, rich, strong and fit while the great Juan Manuel Fangio came from nothing and looked more like a paunchy old streetcorner newspaper vendor than a racing champion. Not to mention that Menditeguy had lucked into co-driving with Stirling Moss at that first race of the season down in Buenos Aires, and damn if they hadn't won the thing outright in front of his own hometown crowd! Or at least they did once all of Enzo's thundering four-point-nines shredded their gearboxes, anyway. In any case, winning your first big race in front of your hometown crowd can be a very dangerous thing for a proud, rich and ambitious young driver who doesn't know the ropes yet. Oh, no question this Menditeguy guy was fast as the dickens. Everybody said so—in spite of his lack of experience. But Hank and all the other pressroom wags allowed as how he was brutal on cars and had no patience, pacing or sense of mechanical sympathy. Which is precisely what you *don't* want or need for a 12-hour endurance grind at a rough-and-tumble track like Sebring. Still, Maserati's other team car was in with a real chance, what with tough, hard and determined little Frenchman Jean Behra paired up with perhaps the slyest and most stylish of Italian racing champions, Piero "The Silver Fox" Taruffi. No question both those guys knew how to go fast and win races.

I was thrilled to see my old buddy Tommy Edwards co-driving one of the Aston Martins, even though he reckoned the whole lot of them were down 50 horsepower to the fuel-injected Jaguar and 25 or so to the garden-variety D-Types. But they had a pretty good lineup of driving talent, including our old Texas buddy from Bonneville Carroll Shelby plus Englishmen Roy Salvadori, Peter Collins, part-time dentist (or maybe it was full-time dentist/part-time racing driver?) Tony Brooks and, of course, Stirling Moss. Like I said, most insiders figured Moss as one of those rare, special talents who were good for a few seconds a lap all by themselves. Tommy hinted that team manager John "Death Ray" Wyer was thinking about turning Moss loose as a "rabbit" to try and break up the opposition, but that's pretty hard to do when you're spotting the best of them half-a-hundred ponies. Not to mention that the DB3S was getting a little long in the tooth and looked a wee bit upright and old fashioned compared to the 3.0-liter Maseratis. But if anybody could do it, Moss was your guy. In any case, the Astons looked absolutely fabulous in their gleaming, light metallic green paintjobs, and they had the most marvelous exhaust note you ever heard—like a flock of six French horns blaring out a fanfare in perfect tune and harmony. What a sound! But Tommy couldn't stay and chat with us on account of "Death Ray" Wyer had called one of his famous, top-secret planning and strategy meetings, and you did *not* want to be late—or even crack a smile, for that matter—where one of John Wyer's team meetings was concerned. But we made a date to get together later after night practice to catch up on things. And maybe share a beer or two. It was great to see Tommy all charged up and happy and doing well for himself again. Last time I'd seen him he was going through a bit of a rough patch, and it's always a relief to see somebody you like, admire and care about come out the far side of one of those deals.

Porsche had sent a pair of their newest 550 Spyders from the factory (the lead entry co-driven by upcoming German aces Hans Herrmann and "Taffy" von Trips) and they were backed up by a couple more private entries, including one from John Edgar's stable in California with Jack McAfee and Pete Lovely at the wheel. Hank pointed out that Baron Huschke von Hanstein himself was listed as a reserve driver for one of the factory Porsches and one of the privateer entries as well and, in spite of his lah-de-dah title, von Hanstein was not only a fast, crafty and seasoned racing driver but also head man for the entire Porsche competition department. You have to understand that Porsche did things differently from the other manufacturers. They built their racing models for the express purpose of selling them (and selling them at a profit!) rather than offering reduced-spec "customer cars" or selling last year's factory cars off to privateers once they were through with them. The smart money in the pressroom figured the Porsche 550s as the cars to beat in the under-1500cc class, and likewise the odds-on favorites to win the coveted-if-generally-incomprehensible Index of Performance award.

Even so, the smallbore car that caught everybody's attention was the tiny, almost toylike new Lotus Eleven, which was so low, sleek and slippery it made the newest Jaguar D-Types and Ferrari 860 Monzas look tall and clumsy by comparison. Hell, the new Lotus barely came up to your blessed knee! Better yet, Lotus designer, builder and all-purpose, sleight-of-hand automotive entrepreneur Colin Chapman was on hand in person to co-drive his new creation along with his stateside Lotus sales agent, Len Bastrup. Eric Gibbon made it clear to everyone within earshot that this Colin Chapman gent was one hell of an ace racing driver besides being clever as the devil himself when it came to engineering racecars. There were also a couple of his older Mk. 9 models (those were the ones with the big, soft-looking fins on the back) entered at Sebring in the hands of American privateers, and every one of them was drooling over Chapman's new Eleven. Including Dr. M.J. "Doc" Wyllie and his wife Peggy, who were co-driving their Mk. 9 at Sebring. Both of them did well with their Lotus on the SCMA club circuit, and it was neat the way they traded off on the driving so they each got a chance behind the wheel. You don't see that kind of thing very often between husbands and a wives where racing is concerned. Or anything else, come to think of it! Plus they were really nice people—originally out of South Africa, but now living in Pennsylvania—and very enthusiastic about their beloved Mk. 9 and Lotus cars in general. Fact is, all the Mk. 9 privateers (and a lot of other drivers, come to that!) had a serious case of the old green-eyed envy when it came to Colin Chapman's new Lotus Eleven. Especially after one of the crew guys casually let slip that it weighed less than 900 pounds. And I could believe it, too. I mean, there wasn't much car there, and what there was looked about as simple, light and essential as you could make it. You couldn't miss the way Chapman used lots of short, straight, small-diameter tubes welded together in strong triangular shapes to make the frame, then riveted on sheet aluminum here and there to make it even stronger. That's what made the damn thing so unbelievably light! Although, to be honest, I thought it looked a wee bit fragile and delicate for a race as long and a track as rough and unforgiving as Sebring. But it sure looked hell for fast!

Right across the way was a single, semi-privateer example of Lotus' major opposition over in England—a strange, low, blunt little device from Cooper with the engine parked squarely behind the driver and fully independent rear suspension in the usual Cooper style. I thought it was a really intriguing package, but not exactly what you could call handsome or good-looking. "Let it win a few big races and you'll be amazed how beautiful it'll get!" Hank observed wryly, and I had to go along with him on that. Underneath the sheet metal, the Cooper seemed substantially stronger and sturdier built than the Lotus. But that wasn't saying very much. In any case, you wondered if either one was stout enough to make the distance at Sebring….

Behind all those guys you had the true "production" sportscars that didn't have much of a chance but entered anyway to show the flag, show what they could do and have some fun in the process. Besides, you never knew what could happen in a long, tough, pounding race like Sebring. Fr'instance an ordinary, 4-cylinder Austin-Healey Hundred (or maybe it wasn't so ordinary, since it was one of the "Special Test" factory cars) finished third overall and took first in the "Sports 3000" class at Sebring in 1954. But of course that was before all the big factory teams got involved and moreover the year all the really fast cars broke or hit trouble—including the entire Lancia team—and Stirling Moss and Richard Lloyd won the damn thing outright in a little tiddler of a 1500cc OSCA. Still, a win is a win, and it prints just as indelibly in the record books if you luck into it sideways or fight tooth-and-nail for it from green to checker.

Donald Healey came back with his new 100S competition model in 1955, and the 100S was an amazingly quick car for something that was essentially just an ordinary, blue-collar Healey Hundred underneath the racing numbers. Or at least that's what Donald Healey wanted everybody to think, since he made sure they were almost identical to the rank-and-file Austin-Healeys on display in dealership showrooms. But the 100S was one pretty special Healey Hundred, what with light-weight aluminum bodywork, a better gearbox and four-wheel disc brakes—it was the first true production car to have them—and they'd done what they could with that cast iron lump of a mail truck/milk wagon engine by fitting a higher-compression alloy cylinder head and bigger carburetors and a hotter cam. But even with all the improvements and modifications, the 100S was still simple, basic, rugged and handy as a short-handled sledgehammer. Just like every other Austin-Healey ever made. Plus, like always, old Donald Healey had managed to sign up some genuine ace racing drivers. Including Stirling Moss, can you believe it? Well, Moss did his usual incredible job and co-driver Lance Macklin held up his end as well, and damn if they didn't come home in sixth overall! Unfortunately, a lot of the fast, expensive, exotic "pure" racecars made it to the finish that year, and so their run was only good enough for fifth in class behind two Ferraris and two Maseratis. Still, sixth overall is pretty damn respectable for a cheap-ass British sportscar with a mail-truck engine!

For the '56 race, Donald Healey again sent a couple of his hotted-up 100S models (even though they had to run heads-up against the Aston Martins and Maseratis again in the "Sports 3000" class) and there were a couple of American privateer 100S entries to back them up. One of the factory team drivers was a quick but easy-going young American hotshoe named Elliot Forbes-Robinson and another—who caught absolutely everybody's eye—was this amazing little squint of a Scotsman called Archie Scott-Brown. And when I say amazing, let me point out that Archie Scott-Brown was born without much in the way of a right hand or forearm and with both legs stumpy, short and disfigured. Somehow, he had overcome those handicaps (not to mention the Charlie Priddle types of the European race sanctioning bodies, who didn't want to issue him a license) and not only made himself into a racing driver, but a bullet-fast and wickedly, on-the-edge competitive one as well. At the very highest level. They say a person can move mountains if he puts his mind and spirit behind it, but you tend to pass that kind of talk off as church-sermon bullshit while you're muddling through the drudgery, doldrums and boredom of everyday life. And then you see a guy like this Archie Scott-Brown. See his quick, flashbulb-pop smile and the fiercely determined set of his jaw and the hard-but-happy gleam twinkling in his eye. See the way he can will and force and hustle and toss and caress a race-car around a racetrack. Hell, Hank said some of the English scribes were even mentioning him in the same breath with Stirling Moss! Anyhow, you see somebody like that and you come to appreciate all over again what a special sort of creature human beings can be and that you haven't done nearly enough with your own life….

Just down from the Healeys were S.H. "Wacky" Arnolt's well-turned-out team of white-with-blue-racing-stripes Arnolt-Bristols. Those cars had an uncanny knack for staying out of trouble at Sebring and usually found themselves still motoring happily around (and well up in the standings!) by the end of 12 hours. Just past them was a semi-privateer/semi-works oxcart of a Morgan Plus 4 (I guess the factory in Malvern Link, England, paid the entry fee and helped out with a few parts, but that's about as far as it went) run by a couple of American drivers. And across from the Morgan was Hap Dressel's thoroughly amateur A.C. Ace, which was actually driven to the track from Arlington, Virginia, practiced, raced and then driven back home again after it was all over.

Just like everybody used to do back in the old days….

That pretty much brought us back to Carlo Sebastian's paddock spot, where there were some odd and interesting cars under the awning besides the factory team 857 and 860 Monzas. There was "our" 121LM and the equally "semi-works" 500 Mondial and 500 *Testa Rossa* running in the "Sports 2000" 2.0-liter class, plus a three-year-old Ferrari 250MM that our old buddy Creighton Pendleton the Third had been signed on to co-drive. It belonged to some rich new customer of Carlo's who couldn't drive a lick and even knew it, but really wanted in on all the glamour and fun and excitement and to rub elbows a little with the "real" racers. That's pretty much how someone becomes an "owner/entrant" in the world of sportycar racing. Anyhow, Carlo arranged the whole deal (natch!) and lined up Creighton The Third and none other than Cal and Hank's new California buddy Bruce Kessler to handle the driving chores. And you can bet several fat wads of currency changed hands under the table, and mostly in the general direction of Carlo Sebastian's pocket! Although as anyone who knew him heard often enough, Creighton Pendleton the Third *"never paid for a ride in my life."* Right. I'm sure Bruce Kessler paid, too—he had family money from some big brand-name swimwear fortune—but he turned out to be a hell of a nice guy anyway. Maybe because the family money was still pretty new and hadn't had a chance to grow warts and bony fingers and one of those down-your-nose attitudes like all those snooty Old Money types back east. Plus west coast guys tended to be a little more relaxed and easygoing in general. At least from all outward appearances, anyway. And except for maybe Phil Hill, who always looked serious as a heart attack and tended to be a little tense, nervous and fidgety outside of a racecar. But he could sure as hell drive—fast, smooth, precise and consistent—and he already had his mind made up that he was going to be a professional racing driver over in Europe and that's all there was to it. Phil was never exactly your relaxed, easygoing, *"what-the-hell-let's-give-it-a-whirl"* kind of race driver. He took it seriously and was absolutely dedicated to doing his best every time he climbed behind the wheel. And he knew cars and mechanics inside out—and from the end of a set of wrenches, not from books and hearsay—and that made him even better. Anyhow, he was determined to have a future ahead of him in the professional race driving business, and he was down at Sebring to co-drive Texas oilman George Tilp's new Ferrari 860 Monza with "The Kansas City Flash," Masten Gregory. Masten had already established himself as one of the other hot young American prospects (along with Carroll Shelby) and he could be fast or faster than anybody on his day. But he could also be the least bit unpredictable....

The amazing thing to me was how tall and blubbery that three-year-old 250MM looked compared to the newer cars. Hell, I remembered like yesterday how cars like that knocked me clear out of my sneakers when I saw them for the first time back in the spring of 1952. Why, they were the hottest, sleekest, fastest, sexiest, most dangerous-looking things on wheels! And now—just four years later—that same 250MM looked like something somebody's grandmother might drive. Especially compared to "our" 121LM and the factory team's new 860 Monzas. But at least the 250MM was a V-12, so we'd get to hear that perfectly-meshed Ferrari howl again.

Speaking of engine noises, there were a pair of those little bathtub-fart Deutsch-Bonnet "DoucheBags" things paddocked right across the way from us and painted bright French blue. One was a factory-entered car and the other was a "semi-works" privateer entry fielded by none other than our old Sebring pit neighbor, Seneca Lodge discussion leader and all-purpose, all-American design genius from Milwaukee, Wisconsin, Brooks Stevens. It was really great to see Brooks again, and I was more than a little curious as to why he was running that tiddler French D.B. instead of one of his own Excaliburs.

"Oh," he said kind of sadly, "the Excalibur idea more or less ran out of budget and enthusiasm at about the same time. Kaiser was struggling and they couldn't be bothered, and it was just too much to try and carry on my own. Besides," he added, rolling his palms up, "we never really had a chance against the Ferraris and Jaguars. I thought my guys," he nodded in the direction of his longtime driver Hal Ullrich, who was teamed with Frenchman Gerard Laureau in the D.B., "deserved a real chance."

"A real chance?" I almost laughed, looking at the tiny D.B. But then I felt kind of embarrassed that I'd sounded so rude and dismissive.

"Oh, go ahead and laugh," Brooks said through a warm, friendly smile. "Most people don't get this." And I was surely one of them. To tell the truth, I didn't much fancy the notion of these tiny little corn-popper cars sputtering around the track and getting in the way of the faster cars in the "real" race. But Brooks saw it differently. "This is really the heart of where we'll all need to be headed one day," he nodded in the direction of the tiny blue car squatted on the grass in front of us. "All of us."

I didn't get it. And neither did Hank.

"What do you mean?" Hank asked.

"More out of less," Brooks said gently, patting the sleek little D.B. on its nose. "One day, it's all going to be about getting more out of less."

I still kind of didn't get it, but it made me go a little hollow inside all the same. Just by the way Brooks said it. He sure as hell sounded like he knew what he was talking about....

Anyhow, the two little DoucheBags were essentially running against nobody but themselves in that tiniest-of-tiddlers "Sports 750" class (they were the only two cars entered!), and of course both of them were eyeballing yet another mighty conquest of the who-gives-a-good-God-damn Index of Performance award. For the honor and glory of France, you know? But from the greatest to the smallest and the fastest to the slowest, it was a truly unbelievable collection of cars, teams and drivers that had somehow found their way to the middle of nowhere for the 1956 12 Hours of Sebring. It was hard to fathom what could have caused this huge, colorful, important, fascinating and thoroughly extraordinary International Circus of Speed to migrate across continents and oceans to descend once more—bigger than ever!—on a dilapidated, decrepit, sun-baked and oil-soaked old airport surrounded by silent, dusty orange groves out in the boondocks of central Florida.

And yet, there it was!

Chapter 8: Night Practice

Between the afternoon track session and night practice, the Ferrari factory team and its "favored privateers" had a nicely catered sit-down dinner at a long table under this big white tent with all the sides open and Ferrari flags tied to the support posts. We even managed to sneak our buddy Hank in as a sort of a Visiting Dignitary type (which wasn't all that tough, since everybody seemed to know who he was and moreover liked what he wrote in the magazines, plus there was plenty of extra food and a few empty seats since Carlo Sebastian and Ernesto Julio and some "special guest"—wink, wink—weren't due to show up until sometime Friday afternoon). I must admit the soup, salad, pasta, gravy and garlic bread tasted pretty damn good to me—even if the meat balls weren't near as good as my mom's back home in New Jersey. Way too much breadcrumbs, you know? Makes them mealy. Naturally we had to sit down at the privateer/rent-a-ride end of the table with people like our old buddy Creighton Pendleton (who *"never paid for a drive in my life,"* remember) along with Bruce Kessler and a couple rich "import/export" guys from Venezuela who were running a 500 *Testa Rossa* they'd arranged through Carlo Sebastian in the 2.0-liter class. And next to them sat none other than dark, dashing and thoroughly infamous International Playboy-type Porfirio Rubirosa, who was co-driving a 500 Mondial in the same class (also thanks to Carlo Sebastian, of course!) with a thoroughly out-of-his-depth rookie of an English club racer named Dewey Dellinger, who actually owned the car. Thanks to a sad yet fortuitous yachting accident the previous summer that left both of his dear parents and the family Pomeranian as shark bait somewhere off Barbados, Dewey had come into a rather large instant-pudding, pie-crust and porridge-mix fortune and was "having his first go" at bigtime international racing. "I ran the family Alvis at Snetterton once," he explained through a wide-eyed grin, "but my mother found out and had my father take the keys away." Dewey had only recently ceased wearing a black mourning band around his barely noticeable bicep and no question he really missed that dog....

Hank whispered behind his hand that neither Dewey or this Rubirosa character weren't exactly what you might consider, umm, "stellar talents" behind the wheel, but even so they were in with a decent shot at a class win on account of the rest of the "Sports 2000" class entrants were ordinary, go-to-market sports cars like that oxcart of a Morgan and the Arnolt Bristols and the AC Ace we saw that had actually been driven to the blessed track. None of those cars could hope to match the Ferrari when it came to speed, sophistication, strength, power or handling. In fact, their only real competition was the Lotus Eleven that didn't figure to last the distance and the other 2.0-liter Ferrari in the hands of the rich Venezuelans seated next to them. But those two were already arguing bitterly about something or other in Spanish (complete with lots of arm waving, fist shaking and rude hand gestures that you didn't have to speak Spanish to understand) and looked pretty likely to take it out on the car.

According to Hank, none of the sport insiders took Porfirio Rubirosa very seriously as a racing driver, even though he'd been in good cars at a fair share of major races. Hank said he was no better than your average puddinghead amateur, but he managed to weasel his behind into a lot of interesting rides and his well-publicized amorous adventures with rich, beautiful women had earned him a grudging respect around the paddock. Anybody who ever picked up a newspaper (or, better yet, eye-balled a gossip magazine over their wife's or girlfriend's shoulder) had probably heard about Toly Wolfgang's romantic escapades, but this Porfirio Rubirosa guy put him completely in the shade. Fact is, "Rubi" had pretty much made his living—and a damn good living at that!—warming up the beds of some of the richest, most famous and most glamorous women in the world. Which was quite an accomplishment for a guy whose father was a smalltime, gold-braid-and-feather-plume Strutting Peacock edition of a military general for iron-fisted dictator Rafael Trujillo down in the Dominican Republic (which is pretty tiny even as Caribbean banana republics go, since it only takes up half an island). But Trujillo sent his dad over to Paris to keep an eye on the diplomatic consulate there, and that's mostly where Rubi grew up. So he had quite the suave, continental manner about him. Rubi started out his romantic adventures by marrying no less than the daughter of Rafael Trujillo (who pretty much ran the Dominican Republic lock, stock and barrel—or at least everything on his side of the island, anyway—and incidentally bought himself that bright yellow Pegaso that cost twice as much as any Ferrari right off the stand at the New York International Auto Show!). Apparently being married to the daughter of a powerful Caribbean head of state must've gotten a little stale and confining for a guy with Rubi's appetites and ambitions, so he split from her and took up with an absolutely beautiful French film actress named Danielle Darrieux, who divorced her own husband in order to marry him. Apparently she'd been seeing him right along anyway. But I guess there wasn't enough money or action for Rubi being married to a famous, drop-dead gorgeous French film star, so he left her and traded his way up to American tobacco heiress Doris Duke (you know, as in several popular cigarette brands and the money behind Duke University?), who everybody said was the second-richest available female in all of North America. But Rubi wasn't the kind of guy to settle for second best—not him!—so, for an encore, he blew her off and married the *first*-richest available female in all of North America, Barbara Hutton. You know, the "poor little rich girl" whose grandfather started Woolworth's Five-and-Dime and whose father built up the huge and respected E. F. Hutton investment firm in New York. And who, by the way, had a pretty impressive reputation as a rogue, playboy, scoundrel and womanizer in his own right. To the point where his wife—Barbara Hutton's mother—committed suicide because of it. Or at least that's what the gossip columnists said.

In any case, little Barbara had herself a pretty traumatic and unsettled childhood, followed by an even more troubled, convoluted and confusing adult life, what with four previous marriages before Rubi (including no less than two Russian princes, a Danish count and famous Hollywood leading man Cary Grant) and all sorts of scandalous gossip and ugly rumors about drugs, drunkenness and debauchery and really strange things going on behind closed doors. Not that I ever pay any attention to that stuff. Anyhow, Barbara Hutton's marriage to Rubi lasted all of 53 days and supposedly netted him a cool three-and-a-half million dollars ca$h American in the settlement. And all the while he was playing around plenty on the side, including a well-publicized, long-running affair with Zsa Zsa Gabor, the sexy Hungarian film actress who told the world that: *"a night with Rubi is the greatest present a woman could ever give herself."* Cal whispered in from the other side that the waiters in posh, exclusive, place-to-be-seen restaurants from New York to Hollywood referred to those oversized cylindrical pepper grinders they use to put fresh pepper on your salad as "Rubirosas." If you catch my meaning. And no question you've arrived at some kind of unique celebrity status when waiters at both ends of the country (not to mention damn near everybody in the paddock at Sebring) seems to understand that you're hung like a horse and moreover know how to use the old equipment.

But we had to be a little careful about what we said or even how we smirked or rolled our eyeballs on account of Barbara Hutton was also the mother of Bruce Kessler's great buddy Lance Reventlow, the rich, handsome, and seriously underage-looking 300SL driver Cal and Hank met out in California. She had Lance with her second husband, a blue-blooded Danish Count with a name like a run-on sentence (try "Cort Heinrich Eberhard Erdmann Georg von Haugwitz-Hardenberg-Reventlow") that she married in 1935 and divorced three years later. The story went she almost died having Lance and the doctors told her she couldn't have any more kids after that, which made her even more distraught and unhappy. Although it set Lance up as pretty much sole heir to one of the biggest piles of money the world had ever seen from the day he struggled out of her belly. Not that such a thing makes up for absentee parenting, a merry-go-round of stepdads and growing up with nannys or shuttled off to boarding schools with a bunch of other displaced silver-spoon-types. But you can buy a lot of candy, toys and distractions with the kind of money Lance Reventlow had. Life has its compensations, you know?

Anyhow, the point was that Lance was Bruce's friend (and even Cal's and Hank's a little since they'd met out in Salinas) and old hung-like-a-horse Rubi was more or less one of Lance's growing list of ex-stepfathers. Even if Rubi never paid much attention to Lance and never took his role as stepfather anywhere near as serious as his regular line of work being a high society escort, stud and stallion. In fact, according to Hank, the only stepfather who really tried to be a dad and pal to Lance was Cary Grant, the movie actor. But that's another story, isn't it? In any case, handsome, hung and internationally notorious as he was, Porfirio Rubirosa wasn't all that much of a racecar driver. Even if he did look the part. He was cut from a lot softer stuff than the "real" Ferrari team drivers who actually got paid money rather than paying money (although never all that much, since old man Ferrari was famous for throwing quarters around like they were manhole covers) to sit behind the wheel and could honestly say they raced for a living. But that was part of the magic for the rich Ferrari sportsmen, entrants, privateers and rent-a-ride guys: they got to sit at the same table, break bread, sip wine, pass the salt or butter and be "part of the gang" with the genuine pros.

Hell, that's a lot of what they were paying for, you know?

I could understand it, too. Fact is, it was quite a pleasant shock to find myself sitting down to dinner with rising American stars like Phil Hill and Masten Gregory plus the famous Ferrari factory drivers I'd only seen before in magazines. Especially Juan Manuel Fangio, who was quiet, polite and soft-spoken and actually kind of dumpy-looking—not at all the way you'd expect a hero driver to look—and had maybe the saddest eyes I'd ever seen in my life. But there were reasons for that, and no question he'd proven time and again that he legitimately deserved the title of best damn racing driver on the planet. He was Italian by ancestry, but his parents relocated to Argentina where he dropped out of school at age 12 and went to work in a car shop. He had the bug all right. Hank said Fangio drove his first race at the age of 18, and soon started making a name for himself racing stripped-down, hopped-up Fords and Chevrolets on these incredible, long-distance, open-road races that ran on mostly dirt and gravel roads all up and down the spine of the Andes Mountains. One of them went all the way from Buenos Aires, Argentina, to Lima, Peru—over 3,000 miles!—and took over two weeks to complete. Fangio won that race, and no question it took a lot of guts, stamina, skill and mechanical savvy to get the job done. Not to mention a huge supply of determination. He didn't come from a lot of money and so he always had to work on the cars himself, and I think that's what set him apart from the upper crust "aristocrat" drivers who never got a hot spark off a grinding wheel in their eye or skinned their knuckles raw on a radiator core. It gave Fangio a sympathy and understanding of the machines that most drivers simply don't have. Plus he understood the stakes better than they did, too. He'd had a terrible rollover wreck in the early days back in Argentina where he got badly busted up and his best friend, partner and riding mechanic got killed in the seat right next to him. Most likely because of some mistake or miscalculation Fangio himself had made. That's one hell of a heavy load to carry around with you.

Juan Peron was the all-powerful dictator of Argentina and really loved his motor racing, and he decided to send Fangio over to Europe to show all the European stiffs what an Argentine driver could do. Fangio was 36 at the time and a lot of people figured he was already over the hill, but in his first season in Europe in 1949, he won seven out of ten races in a privateer Maserati—on tracks he'd never seen before!—and got himself hired on by the Alfa Romeo team for the 1950 season. Alfa was pretty much the only manufacturer involved in grand prix racing at the time—their cars were just dusted-off and refurbished pre-war models, but there wasn't really anybody around to challenge them—and Fangio won his first World Driving Championship with Alfa in 1951. But Alfa decided to retire from Grand Prix racing after the season (everybody was sick and tired of the way the Alfas were steamrollering the opposition anyway), and so the FIA in Paris switched the World Championship to 2.0-liter "Formula Two" cars for the '52 and '53 seasons in search of a little more competition. Only old man Ferrari and his designer Lampredi built themselves a really tight, tough and torquey little jewel of a four-cylinder F2 car, and it went on to steamroller the opposition every bit as badly as the Alfas had in '51. Maybe even worse. The story went that old Enzo wanted Fangio to drive for him, but Fangio was a little wary of old man Ferrari and signed with Maserati instead. It wasn't what you could call a great career decision, since Italian ace Alberto Ascari's Ferrari went on to win every blessed race in the '52 championship season while Fangio spent most of the season flat on his back in a hospital bed with a broken neck he managed to collect for himself at Monza. Ascari won the title again in '53—in surely the best car—but Fangio finished second in the championship and scored a surprise upset win at Monza right in front of the home Italian crowd at the very last race of the season. It was the only thing that kept the Ferraris from another clean sweep, and you can bet that didn't sit real well with old man Ferrari....

Meanwhile Mercedes-Benz had gotten itself back into racing in a big way with the 300SL sports cars we saw win *La Carrera* back in November '52, and they hired Fangio on as their team leader for the 1954 season. He won back-to-back World Driving Championships for them in '54 and '55 in the Mercedes grand prix cars, not to mention helping Mercedes sew up the 1955 World Manufactures' Championship in their 300SLR sportscars! But he also saw his Argentine friend and protégé Onofre Marimon killed during practice for the German Grand Prix in a ride Fangio himself helped arrange.

That was maybe yet another reason for those sad, sad eyes.

Even so, Fangio had lost none of his skill, determination or desire, so he finally bit the bullet and switched to Ferrari after Mercedes' wholesale withdrawal from racing at the end of 1955 following that terrible, black day we witnessed at Le Mans. Besides, what did they have left to prove? They'd pretty much mopped the floor with Ferrari, Jaguar, Maserati and whoever the hell else bothered to show up in both sportscars and Formula One. According to Hank, Fangio was still plenty wary about the way old man Ferrari did business and how he put pressure on his drivers, played one against the other and always had a bunch of hungry young lions waiting in the wings. But no question Ferrari was the best game in town for the '56 season, and that's where a top driver has to go if he wants to stay a top driver. No matter who he is. Besides, Fangio was that rare type who never said much or complained about things but just got on with the job. You could see how everybody around the table respected him. It was even in the eyes of the other drivers. Mixed with a little envy, of course. None of them could quite figure out what made that old man so damn good. Hell, nobody could.

Next to Fangio was his co-driver for the weekend, Eugenio Castellotti, who was a cool, proud, dapper and aristocratic young country gentleman from the village of Lodi, near Milan. Like a lot of Ferrari's drivers, he'd originally bought his way into the sport in 1950, but did well enough that he wound up driving for the Lancia factory team a few years later. And then Ferrari after Lancia pretty much folded up its tent and turned its grand prix cars over to Ferrari in the middle of the '55 season. And that's a pretty interesting story all by itself. Lancia had hired on a real genius of an ex-Alfa Romeo designer and engineer named Vittorio Jano, and he was the guy behind a whole series of wonderful machines from Lancia. Including the amazing little supercharged Aurelia coupe that Maglioli took to fourth overall at *La Carrera* the year we were down there and the neat and handsome D23 and D24 sports/racers that finished first, second and third overall at *La Carrera* in November of 1953 and looked set to win again at Sebring the following spring until the leading D24 broke its engine with just 45 minutes to go. As you can see, for a very brief period, Lancias were the cars to beat in major league international competition. And it didn't hurt that they had Juan Manuel Fangio on the payroll, either. Plus this Vittorio Jano had whipped up a very compact, ingenious and promising new V-8 Formula One car to run on the grand prix circuit for the '54 season….

And then it all went to shit.

The big problem behind the scenes was that Lancia simply wasn't selling enough road cars to pay for all the racing glory. And then the Mercedes blitzkrieg came along with magnificent and intelligent cars, crushing organization and reliability and a big enough bag of gold to hire the very best drivers available. Including one Juan Manuel Fangio. Lancia countered by signing on two-time World Champ Alberto Ascari (who'd apparently had about enough of driving Formula One cars for old Enzo Ferrari) as team leader. But then he got himself killed in a stupid, spur-of-the-moment testing accident in his friend Castellotti's new Ferrari sportscar at Monza. You have to understand that Ascari was a huge national hero in Italy after his back-to-back World Championships, and it was a crushing blow to Lancia. Ironically, it came just a week after Ascari made front-page headlines all over Europe for surviving the most fantastic swan dive of a crash anybody had ever seen into the yacht harbor at Monte Carlo! He'd just taken the lead in the Monaco Grand Prix following the thoroughly uncharacteristic mechanical retirements of both Fangio's and Moss' Mercedes, but then he either ran out of brakes, lost his concentration or hit an unseen patch of oil on the approach to Monte Carlo's infamous harbor-front chicane and lost control. The car squirmed this way and that, shot across the road, smashed clear through the barriers and went catapulting into the Mediterranean, where it sank instantly in a hissing puff of steam. Everything went silent for long, agonizing seconds as the water rippled back over the invisible hole where Ascari's car had vanished. But then, just when all seemed lost, Ascari's light blue helmet suddenly popped through the surface like a blessed fishing bobber! He looked around, gasping and sputtering, and then swam himself over to one of the rescue boats they have waiting at Monte Carlo for just such an eventuality. No one could believe he'd made it!

A week later he was dead. Killed trying out his friend and teammate Castellotti's new Ferrari sportscar just to see what it felt like during an impromptu visit to a test session at Monza. It happened on a totally empty track during lunch break on a quiet Thursday afternoon. Some said a dog might have run onto the track. Or possibly some course worker was out inspecting things, not expecting racecars to be thundering around the track at lunchtime. Or maybe it was a mechanical failure. Or perhaps even a mistake? But no matter what, Ascari was gone. Between his death and the terrible disaster at Le Mans less than a month later, Lancia decided it was time to pack it in. Not to mention that the company was going through some really tough times financially and this was a convenient way to bail out of the headaches and crushing expense of running a racing team. Especially when Jano's new V-8 Formula One car was getting soundly thrashed by Fangio and the Mercedes-Benz squad at almost every grand prix.

Anyhow, with Ascari gone, Eugenio Castellotti automatically picked up the mantle as most promising of the current crop of hotshot Italian drivers (with his fiercely determined young teammate Luigi Musso visibly waiting in the wings, of course), and Hank said the reason Ferrari put Fangio and Castellotti in the same car at Sebring was to keep Eugenio from tearing up a car trying to beat the old maestro. Castellotti struck me as very proud, intense and maybe a little aloof, and you could see the way everybody respected and deferred to Fangio grated on him a little.

Across from those two was the occasionally very fast but always very happy second-generation (both his father *and* his mother raced!) "American" driver Harry Schell. But even though he carried an American passport, Harry grew up in France, spoke mostly French and ran a famous racing bar in Paris when he wasn't off on a driving adventure someplace. What a character! He was famous for charming women and playing practical jokes, and he made for quite a contrast with his serious-looking young Italian co-driver, Luigi Musso. To me, Musso looked kind of haunted. But then, he had a lot of pressure on him as a likely candidate for the title of Next Great Italian Racing Champion. Ever since Ascari managed to get himself killed at Monza, every fan and motoring scribe in Italy had their eyes peeled for the next hot new talent. Castellotti of course thought he was the one, but Fangio had managed to put him in his place several times already when they were teammates at Lancia, and so a lot of Italians were on the lookout for somebody else to take up the challenge. The Italians were really passionate about their motor racing, and desperately wanted an Italian to be World Champion again. Especially if that meant beating all the stiff-upper-lip Brits and storm-trooper Krauts and cheese-eater Frenchmen—and, of course, fast Argentinians—in the process. For better or for worse, a lot of them figured young Luigi Musso was going to be their guy. He thought so, too. Even if he didn't look 100% convinced of it....

Naturally all of us were down in the cheap seats (or maybe they were really the expensive seats, come to think of it) at the far end of the table, and I wound up sitting right smack-dab between Hank and Toly Wolfgang. It was amazing to see how Toly came to life at dinner, bantering with everybody at the table—even Cal, Hank and me—in a switchback, free-flowing combobulation of Italian and French and Spanish and both popular brands of English. He could go back and forth between them like it was nothing! And those were only about half of the languages he read, wrote and spoke fluently. Plus he'd ask you things and then actually listen like he really gave a shit while you answered him back, his head cocked thoughtfully to one side while the cigarette smoke curled up over his lip and disappeared up into his nostrils, then gently exhaled out through his mouth again. He could be really funny, too: ribbing Rubirosa in Spanish about going into town for bigger underwear that wouldn't "restrict the circulation," teasing Schell in French about slowing himself down by wasting too much energy on women and eating too much pasta and digging the needle in at Musso in Italian for taking everything way too seriously. He called Ferrari team manager Mino Amarotti "Il Duce" and nicknamed Cal "Hollywood," which stuck immediately. *"My teammate Hollywood came here hoping to drive like Fangio and fuck like Rubirosa,"* he told the whole table in Italian, *"but unfortunately he's gotten it backwards and so he fucks like Fangio and drives like Rubi!"*

That got a pretty good laugh out of everyone. Especially the Ferrari mechanics.

It was common knowledge Toly wanted "in" on the factory team, and so no question he was doing a little politicking for himself. But it came across as pretty genuine. Toly Wolfgang had a boatload of natural charm and personal magnetism—he never came across like one of those blowhard clowns who needs to be the center of attention all the time—and it started to make sense once you learned a little something about his background. No question he was a captivating and unique sort of creature….

To begin with, Toly Wolfgang's full name was long enough to damn near qualify as a sentence all by itself, and his family's history, ancestry, exploits and scandals were pretty much legendary—especially in Europe. He could speak and moreover think quickly in five or six different languages, moved easily through the world of wealth and privilege and seemed to know everyone worth knowing from barons to bartenders and team managers to maitre d's. He supposedly had the blue blood of five or six different royal families pumping through his veins, and everybody knew that his father was one of the cleverest, most successful, most elusive and and most despised arms traffickers and black-market profiteers of World War II. There were even rumors that he'd been a Nazi spy. The French brought him to trial after the war, and he was quickly convicted and sentenced to life in prison. But he still had enough clout, cash and connections to get his sentence relocated to some ancient old castle out in the Ardennes forest. He ultimately died there—by all accounts a suicide. Hank seemed to think Toly was there when it happened, but he wasn't entirely sure. "That jerkoff Eric Gibbon will know the story," Hank told me in a whisper.

As if on cue, who should come wandering out of the gathering dusk looking for a free meal and a few juicy driver quotes but renowned (just ask him!) British motoring scribe Eric Gibbon. He was a pasty-faced little weasel with a scraggly, reddish-brown beard, wire-rimmed glasses, a houndstooth deerstalker hat that he considered very much his trademark and a proud little potbelly budding out from under his tweed jacket. That bulging gut was a testament to Eric's speed and resourcefulness when it came to glomming free food and drinks for himself damn near everywhere he went. Of course, press freebies and hospitality were always part of the motoring journalist game *("eat like a prince and live like a pauper,"* was the way Hank put it), but this Eric Gibbon guy had turned mooching and freeloading into an art form. He had the brass and lack of breeding to simply invite himself in almost anywhere, and most of the racers—especially the Brits and the Cunningham guys—were too polite and/or worried about what he might say in print to tell him to buzz off. I knew Hank didn't care for him very much on account of the little sideline business he had selling lurid crash photos to the tabloids, and it didn't take long to see he was one of those irritating, permanently dissatisfied know-it-all types who sneers and snipes and sniffs down his nose at you when he talks.

"And how are the fine gentlemen from Maranello this fine evening?" he said grandly. No one on the factory team end of the table even looked up. So he tried our end, his eyes going around from face to face as he rattled off: "And how are the fine gentlemen from Maranello by way of New York, Paris, the Dominican Republic, Connecticut, Venezuela," he looked at Cal and Hank, "and California."

"We're doing just fine," Hank answered out of professional courtesy. "And you forgot New Jersey." He gave me a little nudge under the table.

"Oh, that's right. Passaic, isn't it?"

You had to be impressed by what the guy knew and remembered, anyway.

One of the Venezuelans had excused himself to call home or take a dump or something, and without even asking Eric Gibbon loaded up a plate and sat down in the empty chair. He just pushed the plate that was already there out of the way and dug in. One by one, the mechanics and team drivers at the other end backed their chairs away from the table and headed off to prepare the cars and themselves for night practice.

"And how about you?" Eric asked, cocking his eyes towards Toly Wolfgang. "Where are you hanging your hat and slippers these days?" There was a combative, accusing tone to his questions that was easy not to like. In fact, it made you want to punch him in the nose just a little.

"Oh, wherever there's a race," Toly answered, lighting up another *Gauloises.*

"Do you still live on Lake Lucerne?"

"That's where all the fan mail goes."

"Is there much of it?"

"Enough. It's only a small chalet."

You could see Eric Gibbon was stuck for a comeback, so he simply shrugged and dug into his plate again. "How do you fancy Ferrari's chances?" he asked Hank through a mouth full of spaghetti and meatballs. It was hardly the kind of thing most journalists would ask another writer right there in Ferrari's tent. Especially while eating their food.

"I dunno," Hank shrugged. "The big fours should be pretty reliable, I think. And they've got Fangio."

"You think Fangio in the 860 Monza is any match for Hawthorn in the fuel-injected D-Type?" he asked, his eyebrows arching upwards.

"Hard to say," Hank answered, picking his words carefully. "Depends a lot on who wants to push the hardest. Who decides to draw a line in the sand. That's most likely Hawthorn, isn't it?"

"I'll give you that."

"But this is just practice. The race is something else again."

"I'll give you that as well." Eric pushed another shovelful of pasta in his face and chewed on it like he was evaluating the fate of nations. I'd only just met this Eric Gibbon character, and I already figured him for one of the most arrogant and irritating assholes in the entire state of Florida that particular evening. And yet you had to be impressed with what he knew and how he'd come to know it. He'd ask anybody about anything at any time or place, and then press hard for an answer even if it made them uncomfortable. I guess the same things that made him such a world-class jerk of a human being also made him a pretty damn good journalist and race reporter.

And there you had it in a nutshell.

Toly was first out in "our" Ferrari for night practice, and you had to like the way he worked at it and chipped away at the track carefully and sensibly, going slowly at first and coming in twice to have the lights re-aimed while he went back behind the pits and lit up another *Gauloises*. Toly always insisted on having a pack of his favorite cigarettes and a windproof Zippo lighter wrapped in plastic and taped or tied down somewhere in the cars he drove. Just in case he crashed or they broke down and left him stranded out on the circuit. Anyhow, after the mechanics finished up aiming the lights, he went back out and whittled away and then whittled away a little more until he worked himself into the top 10 on the time sheets with a thoroughly respectable 3:33. I could see by the hard line of Cal's jaw that it was starting to gnaw at him just a little. So when Toly came in and handed the car over, our boy "Hollywood" jumped in, stormed out of the pits on two smoking hot streaks of rubber, took one quick warm-up lap to refresh his memory and then shot straight up towards the top of the timing sheets with a real flyer, backed it up with an even faster lap at just under 3:31 and pulled in, cutting the engine for a plug check at the end of the backstraight and coasting the rest of the way. "You can go out again if you want to," he told Toly nonchalantly as he climbed out of the racecar, "but I think that's about enough for me."

"No, that's okay," Toly answered back without skipping a beat. "Let's save it for the race, eh?" He was standing right in front of Cal by that point, staring him squarely in the eyes. "You do understand what that means, don't you?"

Boy, you could feel the frost from 20 feet away! To tell the truth, I don't think either one of them was particularly happy with the way that brutish 121LM handled, but Cal wasn't about to say anything if Toly seemed content with the car—hey, you don't want to come off as a whiner, and especially not with all the Ferrari factory guys within earshot—and Toly sure wasn't about to piss and moan about it while Cal was still faster in the car. That always sounds lame as hell. I started to wonder if those two weren't getting off on the wrong foot, you know?

Chapter 9: Toly

It was getting pretty cold and blustery like it does sometimes at Sebring by the end of night practice—you wouldn't believe how the wind can whip up!—so we packed things away as quickly as we could and headed back to the Kenilworth for a wash-up and drinks. Hank had been planning to camp out at the track *("nobody gets into motorsports journalism for the money,"* he grinned, *"because there isn't any"),* but we allowed as how he could bunk in on a cot or a piece of the floor in our room if he wanted, so he came along, too. Tommy and the Aston team were also staying at the Kenilworth, and the piano bar was so packed with racers, crew people and hangers-on that it overflowed into the lobby and out onto the front steps and into the parking lot in back. I don't think the place had ever seen a crowd like that on a Thursday night. Not ever. And it was kind of neat that you could hear snippets of Italian and French and German and Spanish and British-style English through the hubbub and laughter and the clink of emptying glassware….

And then this wonderful music started.

At first it was your standard piano-bar stuff—you know, Cole Porter, Gershwin, show tunes, that kind of thing—but then it eased into something softer and melting and classical. I thought I recognized the melody, and Hank explained as how it was *Claire de Lune* by Claude Debussy. But of course you couldn't prove it by me. All I knew was that whoever was playing that piano was *really* good. So I snuck into the lounge for a peek and damn if it wasn't Toly Wolfgang crouched over the keyboard, eyes half-closed, cigarette dangling from his lips, shoulders hunched forward and brow deeply furrowed as his fingers gently and gracefully swept over the keys….

As you can imagine, people were crowding in three- and four-deep around that piano, including one very striking young lady—or maybe she wasn't so young or wasn't exactly a lady, but it was dark in there and who was I to know anyway?—wearing a stack of gold bangle bracelets around her forearm and wrist and long, blonde hair that she was forever sweeping away from her eyes. They were big, deep eyes with near-liquid pupils under heavy, exaggerated eyelashes, and the bangles on her wrists jangled a little whenever she brushed at her hair. Just to let you know she was there, you know? And of course that registered like a snare drum roll with every male of the species on the premises. Even the nodding-off drunks. Fact is, she was surrounded by a whole blessed flock of them—including Ferrari team drivers Eugenio Castellotti and Harry Schell plus a couple more from the Jaguar and Aston Martin teams—all eager to chat her up or light her next cigarette or buy her another drink. I'm not sure exactly where women like that come from on race weekends, but there always seem to be a few around. Some are just brash, independent types out looking for a little impromptu romance and adventure. Others are highly dependent types looking in entirely the wrong places for something new to depend on. Many more are simply camp followers, stopover airline stewardesses and bit players on the racing scene plus occasional local talent all polished and prettied up for a grab at the brass ring. Or gold ring, as the case may be. And then you've got the bored-looking gals whose assigned Male Companions For The

Weekend have either pissed them off or are stuck under a car back at the racetrack, off someplace with the boys, or already sleeping it off back in the hotel room. And those especially are often looking to get even, if you know what I mean. But whoever they are and wherever they come from, they're either temporarily unattached, permanently unattached, looking to get attached, or soon-to-be unattached, and that makes the whole blessed lot of them fair game. Hell, even fully attached women can become fair game on a race weekend! But those women are always in relatively short supply compared to the male of the species, so there's always a lot of deceptively friendly-looking competition going on about exactly who is going to wind up going where and doing what with exactly whom. If you catch my drift. And you could tell that this particular example at the piano bar in the Kenilworth Hotel was really enjoying all the attention swarming around her. Just by the way she was pretending to ignore it entirely. That's always a sure giveaway. So while all the guys buzzed around her like bees around a hive, she generally kept those big eyes of hers three-quarters shut, sipped her drink, took long, slow drags off the cigarette at least half a dozen guys had tried to light for her and made sure to faintly jangle her bracelets every now and then as she swayed gently to and fro with the music.

Toly's eyes were shut, too, as he slipped through the last few lilting phrases of *Claire de Lune* and eased his way into Beethoven's *Moonlight Sonata.* But then he glanced up, saw me standing there, flashed me a big, gleaming smile and jumped right into a rolling, rollicking, barrelhouse boogie-woogie. Without skipping a blessed beat, can you believe it? Jeez, could that guy ever *play!*

I listened and watched there for a while—Toly could go back and forth between musical styles as easily as he could go back and forth between languages and facial expressions!—and you should have seen the look on his face when he went back into a little more of that classical stuff we'd heard from up on the stairway. His eyes went all hard and serious and the corners of his mouth turned down into a fierce, commanding scowl as his fingers flew and pounded over the keyboard. Boy, did he ever look serious! And yet that music could lift you right up inside—almost like you were floating—if you just closed your eyes and let it.

Anyhow, by that time the hot-looking blonde at the bar was listening and responding a lot more to Toly's piano than all the over-stimulated racers gathered around her trying to get her attention. But it was really loud and close and stuffy in there, what with people jammed in elbow-to-elbow, a million cigarettes going and not much in the way of ventilation. Not to mention that I kinda felt like a fifth wheel, since you got the idea that Toly really wanted to focus all his undeniable charm and magnetism on the blonde. Undiluted, you know? So I got a round of drinks, headed back into the lobby and found a nice, cozy spot to rest my behind next to Cal and Hank and Tommy Edwards on the stairway landing overlooking the lobby below.

"That's Toly Wolfgang playing the piano in there," I told them.

Cal stared at me. "You're joking."

"No, really. Honest it is."

"I can vouch for it," Tommy agreed, swirling the ice cubes in his gin-and-tonic. I noticed he hadn't even taken a sip of it. "I've heard him play before. He's bloody well marvelous."

"Boy, I'll say."

And then we just kind of sat there, listening to Toly's piano melodies filtering in through the laughter, arguments, and jumble of racing conversations in four our five different languages going on in the lobby below us. Then who should come wobbling up the stairs but professionally irritating British motoring scribe Eric Gibbon. He looked pretty pie-eyed to me (it's usually a dead giveaway when someone's hanging onto the railing with both hands!) but he recognized us immediately. "Good Lord, it appears I've stumbled on a clot of native Americans," he said like he'd discovered some particularly fascinating bug under a rock.

"Easy about whom you're calling an American," Tommy reminded him.

Eric looked at him dismissively. "Oh, you hardly count as an Englishman anymore. Didn't you marry an American and come live over here?"

"Only until the divorce came and the money ran out," Tommy said through a smile that was part grimace. "And I only mention it so you won't bother to."

Eric gave him a nasty little nod of approval.

"So what's up?" Hank asked without any measurable enthusiasm.

"Just the usual crap," Eric snorted. "Boring, boring, boring."

"Endurance racing usually is."

"It is here, that's for sure. At Le Mans you can at least get civilized food. Have a few crepes and a glass of champagne. Go watch the girlie show at the carnival. Ride the Ferris wheel. This place is the bloody armpit of creation."

"You can get fresh orange juice every morning."

Eric didn't look too impressed. He had himself an attitude, no two ways about it.

The piano music wafting in from the bar eased from old standards into beautifully grand and exquisitely flowing classical again. I kind of knew the tune, but couldn't really recognize it. But you could close your eyes and see some grand palace ballroom with marble flooring and crystal chandeliers and all these courtly lords and ladies in silk and ruffles and powdered wigs dancing divinely with each other. "That's Chopin," Hank muttered to nobody in particular. "It's the *Grande Valse.*"

"Oh? And exactly where did you study music?" Eric asked down his nose.

"My mother was—is—a piano teacher," Hank explained. " Or at least she used to be. Just for kids in the neighborhood, you know? To make a little extra money."

"Extra money is *always* appreciated," Eric nodded like an actor taking a bow.

There was no applause.

"Say," I finally asked him, "whaddaya know about Toly Wolfgang?"

"What do I know about Toly Wolfgang?" he repeated dramatically, his eyebrows arching. "Why, simply everything. Everybody knows everything about Toly Wolfgang!" He said it like you had to be from under a rock someplace not to know the story already. "Bloody black-hearted celebrity is what he is." He raised

an unsteady finger in the air. "A knight errant. A dark, moody star in the firmament of royal society." Eric Gibbon wavered for a moment and then sagged down onto the steps next to us, then added: "A brilliant bloody n'eer-do-well prodigy of an international scoundrel."

"Really?" I asked, my ears pricking up. "Tell me about him."

"There's a lot to tell," he almost mumbled. "I'll need another drink."

"Here, take this one," Tommy said, handing him an almost-full glass. "I'm out first tomorrow anyway."

Eric eyeballed the drink in his hand, then looked back at Tommy. "You used to drink eight or ten like these," he said scornfully.

"And I used to pay the price as well."

"An Englishman should drink," he scolded Tommy. "It's unseemly not to."

"Then be my guest."

Eric sniffed Tommy's glass. "Gin and tonic?"

"It's a gentleman's drink."

"I'll have it anyway." He drained about two-thirds of it in one swallow.

"But what about Toly Wolfgang?" I prodded.

"Ah, yes. Toly Wolfgang. Fascinating topic, really." He pounded the last third of the gin-and-tonic. "But where should one begin?"

"Why not start at the beginning?" Hank offered.

"Ah, yes. The beginning. Comes from a family pedigree you simply would not believe. His granddad was one of the Romanovs—God strike me if I tell a lie!—but had the luck, charm and discretion to become a diplomat. Damn good one, too, since he knew where all the bodies were buried and what skeletons were rattling around in the closets of all the finest palaces in Europe. Saved his life, it did, since he was off at some royal court or other when the rest of the men in his family got their balls shot off by the bloody Bolsheviks. The women, too."

"The women got their balls shot off?" Hank deadpanned.

Eric glared at him. "Do you want me to tell the story or not?"

"Sure we do!" I urged, trying to make it sound like I was speaking for everybody. "Please. Go on."

He gave a little sniff of acknowledgement, sucked the last of the moisture out of the bottom of his glass and picked up where he left off: "They say he was patient and calculating as a spider, this Romanov, and quite the ladies' man. The Czar had sent him all over the royal courts of Europe, cavorting with countesses and chambermaids, prancing about with princes and kowtowing as necessary to emperors, cardinals, kings and queens. Had the breeding, blood and manners for it, and that rare taste for intrigue, too. His sister-in-law—the Czarina—well, if you know your history, you know she was the granddaughter of Queen Victoria herself. And the grandmother on his father's side was a full-blooded Prussian princess. Older sister was married off to some stiff Bavarian ramrod, and their dear little offspring turned out to be none other than loony old King Ludwig of Bavaria. You've heard of him even here in the states, I should think…."

"I should think," Hank nodded, even though I didn't have a clue.

"Right." Eric tried to take another drink, but realized his glass was empty. He looked into the bottom, scowled and then shook it at us like one of those Salvation Army guys ringing a bell on a Manhattan streetcorner at Christmastime.

"I'll get you another one," Tommy offered.

"Thanks ever so much. And be a good lad and make it a double, would you?"

Tommy heaved up off the step and headed down into the lobby below. At the piano bar, you could hear Toly was off on another, serious classical piece.

"That's Rachmaninoff," Hank said to nobody in particular. "It's from the second piano concerto…"

"Now where was I?" Eric interrupted, ignoring him completely.

"Mad King Ludwig of Bavaria," I reminded him while shooting an apologetic glance over Hank's way.

"Ah, yes. Mad King Ludwig, poor fellow. Queer as they make them, of course. Mad as a hatter, too. Built some wonderful castles. Have you ever seen Neuschwanstein or Linderhoff? Magic stuff, really. Had an underground grotto built with an underground lake inside, where blindfolded musicians played in the caverns while he and his playmates lazed around in a boat shaped like a swan. Amazing. One of his places had the first electric lights in all of Europe. Built a huge opera theater for his, umm, 'friend' Richard Wagner just so he could stage those monstrous operas of his." Eric eyeballed us over the rims of his glasses. "They were quite close, you know."

I gave Eric a blank look, but Hank and Tommy seemed to know what he was talking about.

"Of course," Eric continued like he was getting bored with it, "poor old loony King Ludwig damn near bankrupted the Bavarian treasury with those colossal castles and building projects of his. Eventually drowned in Lake Starnberg a week or so after they declared him insane. Everyone knew it was murder. But they had to get rid of him. No choice, really." He looked up at Hank and me. "Never would have had any of those fascist Wagner operas if it weren't for old Mad King Ludwig." A thin smile spread across his face. "But I forgive him for it…."

"We were talking about Toly Wolfgang," Hank reminded him. "About his family."

"Oh, yes," Eric agreed, his eyes rolling up into his forehead. Then he leaned in close like drunks do and proceeded to talk loud enough that you could hear him in Daytona Beach. "On his mother's side, this Romanov fellow—Pyotr Romanov, to be exact—was a sort of one-man Council of Nations: part French, part German, part Austrian and part Spanish along with that thick slug of pure Russian blood. If you paid attention in your history class—and you probably didn't—you know the royalty back then used to marry one another quite a bit. Mostly to cement political alliances and keep from being invaded, if you want the truth of it. But of course it played bloody hell with the gene pool."

"Well, you really don't want to mix with the riffraff," Hank joked.

"We English think not," Eric agreed. "In any case, this Pyotr Romanov saw the ugly black clouds on the horizon long before the rest of the bunch, and so he was conveniently out of town someplace on a diplomatic mission when the Russian Revolution started boiling over. And he's no fool! Been quietly smuggling gold and jewels and God-only-knows-what-else out of the mother country for years and socking it away where only he knows where it is!"

"Clever guy," Hank nodded appreciatively.

"So he's rich?" I asked.

"Well, there's rich and then there's rich," Eric allowed. "He's not rich by Czar and Czarina standards—solid gold bathroom handles, emerald-encrusted bedpans, that sort of thing—but he's got himself a nice enough little nest egg. Cash in the bank plus a few random houses, chalets, castles and seaside villas scattered here and there in Switzerland and Austria and along the Riviera and Cote d'Azur. Nothing ostentatious, of course. Just charming little places with hardly anything in the way of staff. And all of it paid for by the blood, sweat and tears of the proletariat. Isn't it marvelous?"

Tommy arrived with another glass of fuel to keep him going. Eric took a slow, deep pull off of it and slumped back against the wall. He looked like he might fade off to sleep right there in front of us. "So what happened to him?" I finally prodded.

"Happened to whom?"

"That Pyotr Romanov. After he escaped from Russia."

"Oh, yes. Of course." Turned out all Eric really needed was another drink and a hint that his audience was hungry for more. In an instant he was hard at it again: "Well, he's sharp as a tack, this Romanov, and it turns out he has quite the head for commerce. Of course, he's used to power and privilege on the grand scale, and that makes it easier. I mean, it's not something you can learn in public school, is it? Especially in England."

"So what happens?"

"Well, by then all the other Romanovs have been taken out behind the barn and shot by the Bolsheviks. They're a classless bunch, the communists, aren't they?"

"So they tell the world."

"So indeed."

"But what about this Pyotr Romanov?" Hank reminded him again.

"Well, he's a man without a country now, isn't he? Money in hand and plenty of connections, but very much on his own." Eric leaned in close again. "But he's bloody well up to it. Sets himself up in Switzerland where the bankers always knew how to keep secrets and goes into business for himself. He can still travel almost anywhere he wants as long as he stays among the bluebloods and aristocracy, and he's got the money and connections to find things out and make things happen if he has a mind to."

"So he was a spy?"

"Let's just say he was a true, free-market capitalist. And as such he was never particularly picky about what he was buying or selling. Only about price, profit and prompt delivery." He looked accusingly at Hank, Cal and me: "It's the American way, you know."

"It's not like we invented it," Hank protested.

"You didn't invent the motorcar, either," Eric sniffed. "But 150 million Americans will tell you otherwise."

"Could we get back to Pyotr Romanov?"

"Oh, yes. Romanov." He rubbed his chin. "Well, during the first war he dabbles a bit in arms here and state secrets there, and I understand he even helped broker the peace once they'd used up enough bullets and bodies. All very much behind the scenes, of course. But the facts are there if you care to dig for them."

"But where does Toly Wolfgang come in?"

"Shortly. You'll see." He took a quick sip off his drink. "Not long after the first war, this Romanov meets a beautiful young Italian girl from a very fine, rich and well-connected family. Roots go all the way back to the Medicis. And—if you believe the historical gossip—the court of Ferrara. That's where old Lucretia Borgia did her dirty work. You *have* heard of Lucretia Borgia?"

We all nodded. Even me.

"Oh, what a bloody little dickens *she* was! The entire family, in fact. Did you know that she was the illegitimate daughter of Pope Alexander the Sixth?"

"I had no idea."

"Oh, you should read up on it. Scandalous business! Married twice by the time she was 18! Second husband was murdered by her own brother. And then she had an affair with some ambitious Vatican lawyer. Can't recall his name. Pity. In any case, he met a most sudden and unfortunate end. Fell on a sharp knife six or seven times and then stumbled into the Tiber River with his hands and feet bound together. They called it a 'terrible accident,' can you imagine? Everyone knew her family did it, of course. But what could you do? And afterwards Lucretia got something of an unsavory reputation for poisoning anyone who got in her way. I believe foxglove was her favorite."

"Fascinating. But what does it have to do with Toly Wolfgang?"

"Just trying to flesh out the background for you," Eric protested, looking profoundly hurt the way only drunks and small children can. "The point is that this lovely Italian girl had a little of the old Medici and Borgia blood in her as well."

"Quite a pedigree."

"Quite indeed. In any case, they fell in love, this Pyotr Romanov and the Italian girl. You know, stars and comets and sweet violin music…the complete business. Not to mention that her family was filthy rich and very well connected in Italy. Or at least they were before Mussolini and his goons took over. But that was later. In the meantime, they were married, the rich, beautiful Italian girl and this Romanov, and they had a child together shortly afterwards. Perhaps even *too* shortly afterward. But then, who am I to judge?"

"Who, indeed?" Tommy echoed, sounding thoroughly bored. But maybe he'd heard the story before. But I sure hadn't. In fact, I was fascinated. You just don't get family histories that go back to the Middle Ages like that here in the states. Not even out towards the end of Long Island.

"So when was the baby born?" I prodded.

"The story's a bit cloudy there—for sure Toly won't tell you!—but I'd make it right at the end of the first war, give or take a year. And, as everybody including you now knows, that child was Toly Wolfgang."

"Wow."

"But what about the spying and the arms business?" Hank asked.

"That came later. In the meantime, the loving couple and little Anatoly were splitting their time between Switzerland, the Riviera and Ferrara, and this Romanov character still had his hand in deep pockets and sticky pies all over the continent. So he was pretty well placed when he saw the next one coming."

"The next one?"

Eric looked at me like I was something on the bottom of his shoe. "World War II, you nitwit. He saw it coming as soon as Mussolini and his fatheads took over Italy. And he'd seen enough of the world to know what it meant. War meant only one thing…."

"Which is?"

"Why, opportunity, of course!"

"But what about the name? Where did 'Wolfgang' come from?"

Eric sighed and looked exasperated. "With the whole rest of his family not only deposed but forcibly deceased, he didn't particularly want to advertise that he was a Romanov. Besides, nobody trusted the Russians. Not even their allies. And people in his line of work have to use a variety of names and identities in any case. At least if they want to stay on the bright side of the grass. When he dealt with the Germans, he was Ernst Wolfgang. Back in Russia he was Anatoly Karchenkov. And Phillip Leeds now and then in London. He was Peter Gulick in the Balkans and someone else again in Paris or Prague or Rome or Austria or wherever the bloody hell else. Having a royal name just didn't mean what it used to by then. Cash was king! A new world order was coming, and it wasn't the blood flowing through your veins that counted any more. No, it was more the blood you could make flow out of the veins of others…."

"So Toly's father became an arms dealer during the war?"

"Arms. Fuel. Guns. Butter. A state secret or two. It didn't matter much to him, so long as the money was good and he thought he could get away with it. He'd moved Toly and his mother to a lovely little chalet on Lake Lucerne. Toly still has it, I believe. And there they stayed until after the last shot was fired. And meanwhile this Pyotr Romanov was doing one hell of a business, selling everything from licorice and lambswool to bayonets, bombs and bullets to anyone who was buying. But mostly to the Germans."

"Why the Germans?"

"They were convenient and their word was good and their gold was as shiny as anybody's. This Romanov never took checks, drafts or paper money from anyone. Didn't believe in it. And I also think he had a bit of resentment built up for the Jews after the way the Bolsheviks slaughtered his family. Blood runs deep."

"Why the Jews?"

"Oh, a lot of the revolutionary instigators in Russia were Jews. Trotsky was a Jew. Marx was a Jew. A lot of them were Jews. Oh, they all gave it up, of course—you know, 'religion is the opiate of the people' and all that—but people like Pyotr Romanov tended to trust family and blood more than the text of manifestos. Plus he didn't much care for Stalin. Not many did. I don't guess he figured on you bloody Americans joining in with the Russians. I mean, the truth is you had a lot more in common with the Germans."

That made all three of us squirm a little.

"So what happened?" I asked to get him kick-started again.

"Oh, the usual when you back the wrong side in a war: stunning success followed by devastating failure. Mind you, he wasn't just dealing with the Germans. He made deals and swapped information with the French and the English and the Russians and the Italians and anybody else who needed something he could supply. And he could supply damn near anything for the right sort of price. I believe he even made deals with the Americans. Sold them the plans to certain buildings and some of Hitler's defenses while they were pushing their way across Europe towards Berlin. Maybe he thought that might save him afterwards, since the handwriting was on the wall even before Normandy. But he was still working the other side, too. People say he sold the Germans a truckload of American radio show recordings to train their infiltrators before the Battle of the Bulge. Had to be American English, don't you see? Proper British English never would have done. There's even a story that the bullets fired at the Russian soldiers as they advanced into Berlin came from him. And that the lead was actually smelted by some foundry or other near Pittsburgh, here in the States!"

"That's hard to believe."

"War stories usually are. Otherwise they wouldn't be war stories, would they?" Eric looked drunkenly up at me. "You of course know the difference between a fairy tale and one of your Yank Marine war stories, don't you?"

I had to admit I didn't.

"Well, it's quite simple. One starts out with *'once upon a time'* and the other begins with something like…" he gave me his best dunderhead Yank leer, "…*'this is no bullshit, see?!!'*"

Tommy chortled a little and I think I actually got a little angry. For my lifer Marine buddy Butch, you know. And all my highschool buddies who got their asses shot off over in Korea, too. But what I really wanted was for him to get back to his story. "So what happened after that?"

"After what?"

"After the Russians took Berlin. What happened to the Romanov?"

"You mean Wolfgang's father? Oh," Eric shrugged, "what you might expect. He was arrested—by the French, of course—and tried for war crimes. No bloody chance, really. The Frogs made a huge bloody fuss about it. Wanted him hanged, naturally. They're a vengeful and vindictive lot, aren't they? Never did learn how to lose a war, no matter how much bloody practice they had at it. But Eisenhower and a few influential Americans apparently stepped in. Seems some of them thought he was one hell of a capitalist, and they arranged a top-secret deal to save him. I believe he'd made a bloody fortune for some of them. Wouldn't surprise me at all if a very large bag of gold was exchanged while no one was looking."

"So he got off?"

"Of course not. That would have been unthinkable. Especially for the French. But he did manage to get life in prison, and you'd have to consider that a victory of sorts."

"Life in prison? That's a pretty ugly sentence."

"It still beats the low end of a rope or playing tin-duck target to a firing squad."

We all had to pretty much agree with that.

"And it wasn't bad duty as life sentences go," Eric continued. "I don't know how it was arranged, but he wound up in this old medieval castle in the Ardennes. All by himself, can you believe it? Must have had a staff of a dozen or more just to look after the place and see to his needs. Some said it was as much to protect him as to punish him. He'd earned himself a lot of high-placed hate and important enemies during the war years."

"But what about Toly?"

"Ah, that's the irony. He and his mother lived peacefully there on Lake Lucerne throughout the entire war. Went through his late teens and early 20s safely tucked away in Switzerland while all of Europe was blowing itself sky high around them. While Toly Wolfgang rode horses, studied with tutors and played soccer! Learned his piano from some live-in Jewish refugee who'd been no less than a concert maestro in Prague. So while a whole generation of young men his age were being shot, maimed, blown up, burned and buried, he was off riding his horses or sitting at his piano overlooking Lake Lucerne, practicing his bloody Beethoven, Bach and Brahms."

"You can see why some people might not like him."

"Not his fault, really," Eric shrugged. "Most would've said the hell with it and done the same if they'd only had a chance. He was just one of the lucky ones, that's all."

"And after the war?"

"Strange, really. Pyotr Romanov tried to stay in touch with his family during the hostilities, but of course it was difficult. Meanwhile Toly's mother was becoming increasingly strange and unstable. Rumor has it there was a live-in nurse who eventually had to give her drugs to keep her quiet. And of course Toly's father could only show his face once in a very great while. He'd arrive unannounced most often, be there for a few hours or a day or possibly even overnight, and then he'd be gone again. Back to the business of war and those dark, smoky, silky-quiet little rooms where the material of war is bought, sold and traded. I suppose he did his best by them, but his wife was further and further gone every time he visited. Eventually she went over the edge completely and killed herself."

"A suicide?"

Eric nodded.

"How?"

"Ugly business. It happened after the armistice and after the trial. The day after they sentenced Ernst Wolfgang to life in prison—or Pyotr Romanov, take your pick—the wife just rowed herself out to the middle of Lake Lucerne in a little green rowboat and jumped right in." Eric gently lowered his eyelids. "She couldn't swim a stroke."

"That's awful."

"I suppose. But living didn't look too terribly attractive to her, either."

"But what about Toly?"

"What could he do but look out for himself? And it wasn't so difficult. After all, there was plenty of money. But he'd never been anywhere or done anything that counted. He'd read a lot of books, was good at chess and riding and played that wonderful piano, but he was chafing at the bit for something to do with himself. Something important. At first it was sports—polo, boxing, steeplechase, fencing, bobsledding—and he was very fit and extremely good at all of them. But none of them kept his interest for very long. Except the boxing. I've heard he won a few small amateur titles, but as soon as he moved up in class he got pounded pretty decisively, and that soured him on it. To be honest, no one with his breeding and intellect belonged in a ring with some brawling Neanderthal off the streets. Besides, he was too old for it by then. Professional boxers are generally washed up by their late 20s, not just starting out. And then there was the traveling. He fell in love with it—the adventure, the distances, the strange characters and wild nightlife he found in cities like London and Paris and Rome and Monte Carlo. He was more than ready to break out."

"What happened to the father?"

"Oh, that's a famous story. Like his mother, a suicide. Right in that castle prison of his in the Ardennes. Made all the front pages and news broadcasts at the time."

"Were Toly and his father close?"

Eric half-shrugged. "The story goes that they were close in a cool, detached sort of way. After the war and the trial and everything, Toly made a point of visiting him regularly in prison after it was all settled. Twice a month or more. But by then the mother was long gone and he rarely went back to Lake Lucerne in between."

"Why not?"

"Why go back to an empty house full of haunting memories? Besides, he was happy—or busy, at least—sampling the darker pleasures of Paris and Prague and Rome and Monte Carlo between the trips to see his father in prison. The war hadn't been over very long, but those were still fine places to go. At least if you had money. Anyplace is a good place to go if you have money."

"I suppose," Cal agreed like he didn't already know it.

"So how'd he get started in racing?"

"Funny story, that. By chance he was in Monte Carlo when the first postwar Grand Prix was held. 1948 it was. He'll tell you he didn't even know there was a race in town except that it was hard to get his usual hotel room at the Beau Rivage overlooking the harbor. He was there with some heaving young starlet or dancer or something, and the sound of the cars practicing woke them up in the morning. He went out on the balcony and watched Farina and Chiron and Villoresi and the rest skittering around Sainte Devote and blasting up the hill towards Casino Square and that was it. He was hooked. It was just a couple of months after his father's suicide."

"You never told us how that happened," Hank reminded him.

"Oh, he found out he had cancer, poor devil. Served him right, I suppose. But he wasn't the type to just waste away there in prison. What purpose would that serve? No hope. No life. No future. No chance to do much of anything except spare himself the agony. And why not? Especially when there's a quick and easy way out. One and done, you know."

"One and done," Tommy repeated under his breath.

"Tough business, though," Eric continued. "Everyone says Toly was the one who brought him the bloody capsule."

"The capsule?"

"The poison capsule his father got from the S.S. Standard issue, really. All their agents carried one sewn into the lapels of their jackets. Cyanide, I think."

"That's pretty grim."

"You don't know the half of it. Toly brought him the capsule—or so the story goes—and first his father explained to him about all the sundry numbered bank accounts and hidden keys and lock box locations he had to know. I'm sure he made Toly write them all down. Then he went on about how Toly had to wait until the poison had worked and he'd stopped twitching, then wait for at least a minute more, and then kick him hard in the head to make sure he was fully dead before calling the guards."

"That's horrible."

"I suppose," he sighed, his eyes slowly closing. "But at least it was the bloody end of it." A moment later Eric was snoring, and it took all four of us to get him off the stairway landing and trundled off to bed. I was pretty much ready for bed, too, but I couldn't help sneaking down to the lounge for one more peek into the piano bar and maybe a nightcap to take back to the room. The crowd had thinned out quite a bit, and that striking blonde with the gold bangles on her arm was now sitting on the piano bench next to Toly. Her head was resting on his shoulder with her hair running down his chest, and they were swaying dreamily side-to-side as Toly worked through his entire repertoire of soft, moody old torch songs….

Chapter 10: Over Before it Started

The next day I went out to the esses with Hank to watch practice, and it was really interesting to see the different styles of the drivers. Hawthorn drove neatly but furiously, hammering the fuel-injected "Cunningham" Jag around the track like he really meant business, while Moss in the Aston was far more relaxed and serene and you got the feeling the whole Aston team was holding back a little and saving the cars for the race. Which is a pretty wise thing to do at a race like Sebring. Maserati had no such discipline, and so Behra was running hard as the dickens. But Hank said the word on Behra was that he only had one speed anyway, and that was pretty much flat-out all the time. The little Porsche 550s were visibly slower than the big-engined cars at the end of the long straights but obviously very light and handy and carrying a lot more momentum through the corners. Although that grating, agonized howl off their cooling fans made you wonder how they could possibly last the distance. Past performances made you pretty damn sure they would, though. And having a quick, nimble, reliable little car that was easy on tires and got great fuel mileage (so it could maybe get away with two or three fewer pit stops!) could be worth a lot of laps by the end of 12 hours. Which is exactly what the Porsche guys were counting on. That made for quite a contrast with the three lumbering Corvettes, which kind of wallowed their way through the corners and gut-rumbled like lazy thunder down the long Sebring straightaways. But that kind of stuff can be deceiving. A big, slow-turning American V-8 makes an awful lot of torque, and no question the Corvettes were showing plenty of acceleration off the turns and some really decent top speed by the end of the long straights. Even if their brakes were a little suspect and they weren't particularly elegant in the handling department.

The car that really impressed the heck out of both of us was that slippery little sliver of a Lotus Eleven, which skated around the damn corners like a water bug on wheels and didn't even come up to the door handles on the Corvettes! Plus that Colin Chapman guy who designed and built Lotus cars could *really* drive. He was neat, precise, used every bit of available road (even kicking up a whiff of dust here and there at the apexes and exits) and threaded his way through the bigger, clumsier cars like a terrier in a herd of buffaloes. I still didn't think anything that tiny, low, light and fragile-looking could possibly make the full race distance, but then it all became academic when Chapman's co-driver Len Bastrup went flying (or got nudged?) off the track and crashed into the hay bale barrier in front of one of the worker stations. I'm not sure how bad the damage was, but a fuel line or fitting must've torn loose and so the car erupted into flames before it even stopped moving. Fortunately the driver was able to scramble out with just minor singes, but there was only one fire bottle at the worker station and that just wasn't enough to cope with a damn-near-full tank of gasoline. Especially when you could still hear the electric fuel pump clicking merrily away through the flash and crackle of the fire! Oh, the corner worker did his best, bravely standing there against the heat and aiming his extinguisher nozzle squarely into the fire. But it was like trying to bring down a tank with a pea shooter, and once the fire bottle ran out, about all he could do was scamper back 50 or 60 paces and watch the damn thing burn. By the time the emergency truck arrived with more extinguishers and buckets of sand, that beautiful little Lotus wasn't much more than a smoky, smelly trash fire. Too bad, since a lot of us really wanted to see it race!

As for "our" Ferraris, Harry Schell looked like he was having fun while his co-driver Musso was crouched forward in the cockpit like something was chasing him. And maybe it was. Cal looked relaxed but serious for a change while Toly steered and shifted with a fierce, almost cruel determination. Exactly the way he looked when he played Chopin's *Grande Valse* at the piano bar the night before. He had a hard, mean edge to his style and a dark scowl showing underneath his goggles, and you could see the tendons on his neck and forearms standing out like cords. Castellotti was also fast, terrifically brave and determined but not exactly precise, his face frowning and severe with the obvious effort of trying to match his team-mate Fangio. The raw Argentine Menditeguy in the 300S Maserati was brutally fast and untidy, taking the corners in a furious collection of slides and saves. "He looks a little wild to me," I mentioned to Hank.

"He's trying too hard. Never does the same thing twice."

"He sure is fearless."

Hank looked at me. "In this line of work, all 'fearless' gets you is white sheets and black shrouds."

I looked at him. "You are a writer, aren't you?"

"Can't help it," Hank shrugged, the color rising on his cheeks.

We waited another three-and-a-half minutes and watched Menditeguy slash past us again, steering furiously as the Maserati slewed sideways across the concrete and kicked up a plume of dust at the exit of the corner. "Think he'll smooth out and get better?" I asked.

"If he lives. But he's thrown himself into the deep end of the pool and just flailing like mad to keep his head above water. Maybe he'll do himself a favor and lose interest."

"Doesn't look like it to me," I observed. "He seems pretty committed."

"That he does," Hank agreed. "That he does."

By contrast, Fangio looked entirely too smooth, serene and graceful to be as quick as he was. And I'll never forget the expression on his face. Almost like he was falling asleep! Even as he slung the tail gently out through the right-hander and then changed direction in one fast, flowing motion for the left-hander that followed. And he only did a few laps before packing it in, saving the car for the race. No wonder they called him *"The Maestro."* He was really something special!

The timing sheets they put up after practice pretty much agreed with what Hank and I had observed firsthand out on the fences. Hawthorn had topped the list for most of the session in the low 3:28s, but then Fangio slipped in an amazing 3:27.2 when nobody was looking. Just to put the needle into Hawthorn a little as much as anything else. Hey, if you think some other driver has the fastest car, sometimes it makes sense to really hang it out for a lap and set a scorcher just to get him wondering. Maybe make him push a little harder than he should next time. After all, endurance races aren't usually about Who Goes Fastest but rather Who Survives and Who Screws Up. So a wise driver or team manager will try anything he can to eat away at the opposition's confidence. Racing is a mental game as much as a physical and mechanical one, and the very best drivers make sure to play all the shots and angles.

Speaking of which, Cal and Toly had gotten into a thoroughly unhealthy little Contest of Speed in the 121LM during Friday's morning and afternoon practice sessions. Cal won the coin flip and drew First Man Out, but it was decided that he'd only run a few laps and then come in and hand over to Toly on account of Toly didn't really know the track as well. Plus it would give them a chance to practice driver changes, which can be a hell of a lot clumsier and trickier than you might think. Especially when the race is on and the clock is ticking. Naturally Cal headed over to the false grid early so he was first in line to go out, and he just flat *took off* as soon as they let the cars out on course. Which, to be honest, isn't the smartest sort of thing you can do in a cold car on a cold track early in the morning. Particularly when you've got a 12-hour grind coming up the next day in the same exact automobile. Still, it looked pretty damn impressive when he came wailing out of Sunset Bend all by his lonesome and roared past the pits with nothing but empty space in his mirrors. Cal was already angling across the track to line up for Turn One by the time the next few cars—Behra in the Maserati, Castellotti in the factory Ferrari and Hawthorn's co-driver in the fuel-injected D-Type—came funneling onto the pit straight.

"He's really cooking," I grinned at Hank.

"He'd better be careful or he's gonna burn it up before the weekend's even started," Hank observed, shaking his head.

But Cal was hardly finished. He put in what the Brits call "a real blinder" the next time around—opening up an even bigger gap to the other cars!—and then pulled in at the end of his third lap to hand the 121LM over to Toly. On my stopwatch, he'd done a high 3:28 on that last flying lap (although I've been accused more than once of being a little trigger happy when I've got a watch on Cal), but no question he was solidly under 3:30. Toly didn't so much as raise an eyebrow. But he didn't exactly smile a whole lot, either, as he climbed into the car, fired it up and went storming out of the pits to respond. He did a couple familiarization laps—you could hear he was short-shifting down the straightaway in front of us, and that's probably exactly what he wanted us to hear—but then he cut loose with a 3:35, a 3:34, a 3:33, a 3:31:5, a 3:31 flat, another 3:33 going through lapped traffic and a thoroughly respectable 3:30 and small change. Alfredo Muscatelli showed Toly his 3:30 on the pit board and waved him in. He came trundling in the very next lap, the faintest hint of a grim scowl creased across his face. "How's it running?" Cal asked Toly in a studiously casual voice.

"Feels okay," Toly allowed like that was really what they were talking about. "The rear is a little squirrelly and the top end power's nothing special compared to Hawthorn's Jag. And the steering gets a little light at the end of the back straight."

"But nothing you can't handle, right?"

Toly glared at him. "No," he said evenly, "nothing I can't handle."

"Good," Cal smiled back like butter wouldn't melt in his mouth. "What are you showing on the tach there?"

"6100. But I'm taking it pretty easy…"

Sure he was.

"…and there's a little vibration in the back end. Did you notice it?"

"Can't say as I did. Maybe I'd better check it out."

"Suit yourself."

So Cal went back out to "check the vibration" and (purely accidentally, of course!) knocked another full second off before he came in. He was right up near the top of the time sheets with that one.

"Yep, I can feel it, too," he allowed as heat waves shimmered off the hood and wisps of smoke rose from the brakes.

"Any idea what it is?"

"Hard to say."

"Let me try again. Maybe I can tell what it is."

"Suit yourself…"

By this time you could see the sparks flying back and forth between their eyes and even a dumbass Volkswagen mechanic from New Jersey could see this was doing that 121LM no good at all. But that's what happens when you've got two fast, tough, ambitious, determined and competitive drivers locking horns like a couple charging bull mooses during mating season and no car owner or team manager around to throw a bucket of cold water on them. Our 121LM wasn't really a factory entry and Carlo Sebastian and Ernesto Julio weren't due to show up until later that afternoon, so it was pretty much just me and Hank and the Muscatelli brothers trying to keep a lid on things. And failing pretty miserably at it, if you want the truth of things. By the time afternoon practice mercifully came to an end, Cal had just cracked into the high 3:27s and Toly was maybe a second-and-a-half behind, give or take a couple tenths. Which was pretty damn respectable on a track he'd never so much as seen before. Oh, and you could hear the gear whine from the 121LM's transaxle over the bellow of the exhaust by the end of the session, too….

After practice Cal and Toly and the rest of the drivers headed over to check out the "official" time sheets and attend a drivers' meeting, while Alfredo Muscatelli and one of the Ferrari factory guys who only knew four phrases in English *("Where find piss hole?" "Where find poop hole?" "Where find American beer?"* and *"Where find American girls?"* although not necessarily in that order) pulled the rear wheels and took a peek at the 121LM's transaxle. I kind of stood around offering lame advice and commiseration, but anybody could see there was way too much slop in the rear end gears. Not to mention no parts on hand to fix it. After all, the factory had switched over to its big four-banger 857 and 860 Monzas for the '56 season and so the 121LMs had been sold off to private owners as "obsolete." Pardon me, make that "ex-works." And you can imagine how happy that made Ernesto Julio and Carlo Sebastain when they arrived in Ernesto's twin-engined

Aero Commander shortly after practice ended. I have to admit it was pretty impressive watching that plane circle and land on the runway behind the racecourse and knowing it was our personal team owners inside. Even more impressive was the small, sleek, stunning looking young vixen in a short, clingy black dress who got out of the plane right behind them. I couldn't make her out too well at that distance—even through Hank's binoculars—except for her shiny, shimmering sweep of black hair and huge, dark, heart-shaped sunglasses that covered most of her face. But you could feel her drawing stares like a magnet as a shuttle Jeep picked them up and whisked them over to our spot in the paddock. An audible hush followed them, broken only by the thud of dropped tools, the crack of craning necks and the squeegee-like sound of eyeballs bulging out of their sockets. As the Jeep drew closer, I had this strange feeling that I recognized her from somewhere. Only I couldn't quite place it. Naturally she vanished into the motorhome to "freshen up" as soon as she arrived, while Carlo and Ernesto came over by the racecar and shook hands grandly all around. And then Ernesto asked how things were going.

"Is beautiful," Alfredo Muscatelli assured him in Italian while giving Carlo Sebastian a quiet little high sign to let him know that everything had actually gone to shit. *"We only looking now at a tiny little problem with the gears."*

"But you can fix it, right?" Ernesto beamed back through a huge, confident smile.

"Of course we fix it," Alfredo assured him. *"If only we have the parts."*

A dark cloud passed over Ernesto Julio's face. He cocked his head towards Carlo Sebastian. "They'll be able to fix it, right?" he asked in English.

"I just got here," Carlo protested, rolling his palms up. "Let me at least find out what's up, okay?" He took Alfredo Muscatelli aside and they started whispering desperately back-and-forth in machine-gun Italian.

Ernesto eyes shifted over to me. "You'll tell me what's going on, won't you?"

I didn't say anything.

"Look. Buddy. I flew all the way across the whole fucking country to see this fucking race. Brought somebody real special along to show her, too. She's never been to a damn car race before."

"She's a *very* pretty girl," I said, trying to change the subject.

"Of course she's pretty," he laughed. "I throw all the ugly ones back."

"I'm sure you do."

Then we just kind of stood there, watching Carlo and Alfredo huddled together with their backs towards us over by the racecar. There was obviously a lot being said. Only it was all in whispers....

Ernesto looked at me, his eyes like aircraft landing lights. "So tell me," he asked in that friendly, just-between-you-and-me voice all great dealmakers have in their arsenal, "what's up with the car? I've got a deposit down on that damn thing already."

I squirmed uneasily. "Well, it's, uh, real *fast...."*

"I *know* it's fast. Why the hell would I buy a slow racecar? But what *else* is going on with it?"

Well, there was no point screwing around. I mean, he was gonna find out sooner or later anyway. So I let him have it straight up: "It looks like we've got a pretty serious problem with the rear end gears."

"But they can fix it, right?"

"Sure they can fix it," I assured him. And then I added: "If they've got the parts."

"Whaddaya mean, *IF* they have the parts?"

"Look, it really isn't my place to be telling you this…."

He took my shoulders in both hands and stared so deep into my eyes I could feel it down to the end of my toenails. "Look. Buddy. We go back a long way. Back to Elkhart Lake, remember? I *like* you, okay? So don't start bullshitting me now…."

I let out a long, sorry sigh. "It's like this," I told him. "I'm not so sure they have the parts. See, the 121LM was last year's car, not this year's car, and I don't think the stuff off this year's cars quite fits."

Speaking of fits, old Ernesto Julio looked like he was about ready to throw one. But at least he was kind enough to rotate 180 degrees and stalk over by the car so he could throw it in the general direction of Carlo Sebastian and Alfredo Muscatelli. For which I was exceedingly thankful. Although I did want to watch. There are few sights in this world more entertaining than watching a small, animated group of Italians having a serious difference of opinion. So long as there are no firearms, straight razors or blunt instruments in the vicinity, anyway.

While I was watching the show, the door to the motorhome swung open with a squeak and that beautiful, taut, slinky looking girl in the clingy black dress was hovering in the doorway above me. Boy, did she ever have a shape! Not big like my Julie, but sculptured like a damn statue. I had to kind of force my eyes the rest of the way up to her face. She'd pulled off her sunglasses, and as soon as I saw her without them I recognized her instantly. Damn if it wasn't Angelina Scalabrini! You know, that beautiful young Italian girl Cal met and took an immediate shine to at that New Year's Eve party in Greenwich Village. The one we all went to at the apartment building where my sister Mary Frances lived with that jerkoff Ollie Cromwell and all their beatnik Bohemian friends the winter before Julie and me were married. I knew Cal went out with her a few times after that, but then she and her mother pretty much vanished. He'd talked about her now and then—including during our long trip out to Bonneville together—and it occurred to me that she was the only female human be ing I'd ever heard him mention more than once. And naturally I wondered just what the hell was she doing here at Sebring? And, more importantly, what the hell was she was doing here at Sebring with Ernesto Julio….

"Y-you're Angelina Scalabrini, aren't you?" I stammered in her direction.

She looked down at me like she was puzzled for an instant, and then a big, friendly smile blossomed across her face. Jesus, she was radiant. "You're Buddy Palumbo, aren't you?" she beamed. "I remember you!"

"From the New Year's Eve party, right?"

"That's it!" she beamed some more. She had the kind of smile that made you want to reach for a bottle of suntan lotion.

"Boy oh boy," I said, shaking my head, "Angelina Scalabrini. We thought you dropped off the edge of the world."

"My mom and I moved out to California. It's almost the same thing."

"So I hear."

"You do?"

"From Cal. He's out there, too." An uncertain look flashed across her face and quickly vanished. "You remember Cal, don't you?"

"Of course I do," she said in a low, careful voice while looking past my shoulder to where Ernesto, Carlo and Alfredo were still arguing mightily next to the 121LM. Then her eyes came back to me. "But it's not Angelina Scalabrini anymore."

I looked at her kind of sideways. "You didn't get married or anything?"

"My God, *no!"* she laughed. "Nothing like that. I just changed my name for work." She gave me a helpless little shrug. "I'm kind of a movie actress now."

"A movie actress?"

She nodded sheepishly. "It's Gina LaScala now," she explained with an odd mixture of pride and embarrassment. She shook out her hair and gave me her most dramatic head-shot profile in the doorway. "Do I look the part?"

"Remember, you're talking to a grease monkey from New Jersey here."

"You buy movie tickets like anyone else," she laughed. Now the Ernesto Julio connection was starting to make a little sense to me. But for some reason it made me feel a little uncomfortable, too. Squirmy, you know?

"So," I asked her, "what movies have you been in?"

"Oh, you haven't seen them."

"Don't be so sure. I take my wife to the movies all the time," I lied. "I'm even taking her to see *My Fair Lady* on Broadway after I get back."

"I'm impressed."

"You should be. The tickets cost a damn arm and a leg. *If* you can get them."

"But you've got connections, right?" she teased.

"Well," I said, blushing a little, "let's just say I know some people who've got connections. Actually, it's more like I know one person who's got connections. My partner, Big Ed Baumstein. But he's got a *lot* of connections."

"That's okay," she said airily. "So long as you've got connections with people who've got connections. That's how things work."

"I've noticed."

"And how about your wife? Tell me about her."

"You remember Julie. She was at the New Year's Eve party, too. We were even already engaged then."

Angelina thought for less than a heartbeat. "Sure I remember her! She's the one with the…" she looked at me uncertainly and then held her cupped hands out well in front of her own quite shapely chest.

"Yep, that's my Julie."

"So, when did you two get married?"

"June of '53."

"You have any kids?"

"Two already."

"You've been busy," she allowed, her eyebrows arching.

"You know how it is," I blushed. "We're good Italian Catholics."

"I can see."

"And it's nice, you know," I said without even thinking about it. "Being married and having kids and all."

"It's nice to hear someone admit it for a change. A lot of men won't."

"Aw, some guys are just like that," I said, thinking about Cal and that smalltown carhop at the drive-in north of Jacksonville and the striking blonde with the bangle bracelets Toly picked up in the piano bar at the Kenilworth. "It's just the way they are—always looking for something new and different."

"And over in a hurry," she added.

"Yeah…" I agreed, kind of blushing again, "…and over in a hurry."

She looked at me. "But not you?"

"Nah, I guess not," I admitted, feeling a little embarrassed about it. "Guess I just don't have the imagination or ambition for it."

She reached out and put her hand on my shoulder. It sent a slow, soft shudder right through me. "Maybe you're just not a rat-bastard sonofabitch like the rest of them. Believe me, it's nothing to be ashamed of." She leaned in and almost whispered: "Your wife's a lucky woman."

"Aw," I blushed again, looking at my shoes, "I always figured *I* was the lucky one." And I suppose I meant it, too. You ever want to know what's really in your heart, just listen to yourself now and then when you talk to other people.

"So tell me," I asked again, trying to change the subject to something more comfortable and less personal, "what movies have you been in?"

"Oh, you haven't seen them."

"How do you know? We go out to the movies a lot. Or whenever we can get her mom or my folks to babysit, anyway. So how do you know we've never seen them?"

"Because they aren't out yet. I just got my first real break a little over a year ago."

"Your break?"

"Well, it wasn't much of a break. It was one of those cheap, outer space monster movies you see at the drive-ins."

"I absolutely *love* those movies!" I told her with genuine enthusiasm. "Which one was it?"

I could see she didn't want to say.

"C'mon," I prodded her. "If it was me, I'd tell you."

"Not if the movie was this bad," she laughed. "The sets were made out of cardboard boxes, and the monster was some big ex-wrestler named Monsoon Cody wearing a gorilla suit, big lobster-claw rubber hands and a space helmet."

"I think I saw that one! What was the name of it? C'mon. I'd tell you…"

"Flying Saucers from Planet X," she finally admitted. "And I hope you didn't see it. It was a real stinker."

"Well, if I saw it, I probably didn't really see it."

She looked at me quizzically.

"Wh-what I mean is," I tried to explain as color and heat crept up my neck, "is that if we saw it, we saw it at the drive-in…" My face must've been about the color of a ripe radish by then. "…So we really didn't see much of it, you know?"

She put her hand lightly on my shoulder. "I understand completely," she nodded, her eyes twinkling. "And believe me, I'm grateful for it, too."

"So tell me," I said, trying to change the direction of the conversation again, "was it a speaking part?"

"Not really," she laughed, "but I did get to scream a lot." She had one hell of a nice laugh.

"And that's what launched your career?"

"No, spilling a plate of Hungarian Goulash in Brad Lackey's lap is what really got my career started. The screaming at the thing in the gorilla suit was just so my mother and I could eat."

"I see," I said, not seeing at all.

"Oh, it's a long story," she sighed, rolling her eyes. "A long, long, *long* story. But the point is that I finally got a bit part in this big historic epic about Napoleon and the Battle of Waterloo." She nodded over in Ernesto Julio's general direction. "He helped me out with that. Ernesto's helped me out a lot."

"That's what helping's for."

She didn't say anything.

"So did you have any lines in that one?"

"Just one line, really. I was this innkeeper's daughter and all I ever got to say was *'more stew, sir?'* to Trevor Howard. Hell of a line, huh? But some big studio people noticed me and then all of a sudden there was an agent and a contract and what I think will turn out to be a really great major supporting role in this big pirate extravaganza that'll be out later this summer." She struck that dramatic, head-shot pose again. "Do I look like a brazen, sultry gypsy dancer to you?"

"No doubt about it. Especially the 'sultry' part."

She rolled her lip into a pout. "Oh, and I worked so hard on being brazen."

"I'm sure you were stupendously brazen."

"It's kind of you to say," she allowed with a little curtsey. But then she sighed and blew out an empty puff of air. "Of course you never really know what it's going to look like up on the screen until the editing's done. I might wind up on the cutting room floor."

"Jeez, that'd be a shame."

She looked off into the distance. "You bet it would."

It went quiet then, and we could hear Ernesto, Carlo and Alfredo still arguing over by the Ferrari with its rear end up on jackstands.

"You know Cal's here," I said evenly.

She slid her eyes over to Ernesto Julio and gave me a barely visible nod.

By this time the "discussion" between Ernesto Julio, Carlo Sebastian and Alfredo Muscatelli had gotten pretty heated—including a few hand gestures that are really hard and maybe even dangerous to use in close quarters—and I figured it was as good a time as any to step into the team motorhome and "freshen up" a little myself. I mean, the last thing I wanted was to get sucked into their argument, and I really didn't know what more I could say to the stunningly sleek, beautiful and amazingly friendly Angelina Scalabrini. Or Gina LaScala. Or whoever the heck she was.

And naturally that's precisely when Cal and Toly popped into view, heading towards us through the clutter of racecars, rental cars, transporters, vans, parts trucks, tents, awnings and team encampments clogging the paddock. For just an instant I thought Gina looked a little panicky, but then she drew a quick breath, squared her shoulders, waved at Cal and flashed him a huge, radiant smile. It hit him like a searchlight beacon—froze him in his tracks, really—but only for a heartbeat. Then he smiled back as easy and unruffled as you please and ambled over towards us with Toly in tow, his eyes locked solid with hers the whole way.

"Well, this is certainly a surprise," he grinned, continuing forward until they were almost touching. She was still standing on the steps of the motorhome, so he was looking up at her. And you couldn't miss the way she eased herself back a little into the doorway.

"It *is* a surprise, isn't it?" she agreed, even if she didn't look like it was a surprise at all.

"So what brings you here?"

"An airplane."

"Oh? Where'd you fly in?"

"Right here."

"Right here at the track?" Cal asked uncertainly.

She nodded, looking a little embarrassed.

"Which airplane?" he started in again like they were just making small talk.

"That one," she answered, pointing out towards Ernesto's twin-engined Aero Commander parked off in the distance on the runway.

"Oh? Who owns it?"

She glanced over to the three men still huddled fiercely around the Ferrari. "It's Ernesto Julio's," she told him matter-of-factly. "He said he wanted me to see one of his cars race." Then she added: "He also told me Sebring was the best race in America."

"I think the people at Indianapolis might have something to say about that," Cal laughed, still locked into her eyes. "Did he tell you I was one of his drivers?"

"I'm sure he must have mentioned it," she said airily. To tell the truth, she was looking a little uncomfortable.

Toly looked around from face to face, sensing the tension. *"And he never mentioned ME to such a lovely creature?"* he demanded suddenly, striking a ridiculously dramatic pose. All eyes swept to him as he waved his fists in the air. "I am *outraged!"* he continued in mock fury, pounding at the air. "Simply *outraged!"* Then he started muttering aloud in a rapid-fire smorgasbord of French, English, German, Spanish, Russian and Italian. It was pretty hilarious, and everybody got a solid laugh off of it.

"Sorry," Cal said sheepishly. "Toly Wolfgang, this is Angelina Scalabrini."

"No, it isn't," I corrected him.

"It isn't?"

"Not any more."

He looked at her uncertainly. "You didn't get married, did you?"

"That's exactly what Buddy asked!"

"That's right!" I agreed.

Cal looked at her more seriously. "But you didn't, did you? Get married, I mean."

"Oh, it's nothing like that. It's just, well…" you could see a little color blossoming up on her cheeks again.

"She has a stage name now," I explained.

"A stage name?"

"Yeah. She's a real, live movie actress. A star. Or at the very least a starlet. Can you believe it?"

She gave Cal an embarrassed little nod. "It's true, Cal," she admitted. "I'm Gina LaScala now."

"Gina LaScala, Gina LaScala…" Cal muttered softly, trying out the sound and taste of it. "…Gina LaScala…."

"Well, whoever you are," Toly interrupted, clicking his heels together and bowing smartly from the waist, "you are a vision of beauty, grace and loveliness." He stared at her for a moment like he was looking for something, then eased his eyes over to Cal. "You have history with this fellow, don't you?" he observed.

"Am I that transparent?" she laughed. "I must not be much of an actress."

"And I wouldn't really call it a history," Cal added.

Toly looked back and forth between them again. "Hmm," he mused softly. "Perhaps we should call it 'unfinished business,' then." He stared straight at me. "And such things certainly don't require the presence of outsiders, do they?"

"No, really," Angelina—or make that Gina—protested. "Please stay."

"We can all go out to dinner or something," Cal offered without much in the way of enthusiasm.

"I hardly think so," Toly insisted. "I have a big race tomorrow and a lovely companion of my own waiting for me tonight." I figured he must be taking about the girl with the blonde hair and jangling bracelets from the piano bar. He looked back at Gina. "But rest assured you haven't seen the last of me. I can promise you that." He held her eyes while giving Cal a playful but stiff elbow shot to the ribs. "And when you grow weary of this dull and tiresome fellow, I'll be waiting to whisk you off on a *real* adventure." And with that he gave another tiny hint of a bow, turned on his heels and headed off alone into the gathering twilight.

That left the three of us kind of standing there, while off under the awning Ernesto, Carlo and Alfredo were now talking quietly with Giuseppe Muscatelli next to the parts truck. And about then is when I noticed that both Cal and Gina were more or less glaring at me. "Look," I said, trying to oh-so-delicately excuse myself the way Toly Wolfgang had done, "I, er, uh, umm…I gotta go use the can."

"You want to go in here?" Gina asked, stepping out of the doorway.

"Nah, that's okay," I told her graciously. "I'll use the public one. It'll be better for everybody that way." And with that I gave them my own little version of a Toly Wolfgang bow and disappeared behind the motorhome. But that's where I stopped dead in my tracks. I could still hear them whispering and then the creak and bang of the screen door as they went inside. And that's when I did the thoroughly unthinkable and just kind of stood there under the side window, peeking in under the curtain to see and hear what was going on. Sure, I know you're not supposed to eavesdrop—especially not on your friends!—but, hey, everybody does it. Besides, I really didn't have to go to the can anyway….

They were standing close together inside the motorhome—not that there's much room inside those things anyway—and at first they just kind of looked at each other without saying anything for the longest time. But you couldn't miss how they were leaning towards each other and then leaning towards each other some more until they just sort of oozed together. Like until they were so wrapped up into each other that you couldn't tell where one of them stopped and the other started up again. They stayed like that a long, long time, and just looking at them made your pulse race and mouth go dry. I don't think I even breathed….

"So it's not Angelina Scalabrini any more?" Cal finally whispered.

"No, I'm pretty much Gina LaScala now," she whispered back. Then she eased away from him, shook out her hair and gave him that same head-shot profile like she'd given me in the doorway. "So do I look the part?" she asked boldly.

"I always thought you did," Cal grinned. Then he put his arms around her and drew her close again. "It's really good to see you again," he whispered into her hair.

"It's really good to see you, too."

"I wondered what happened to you."

"I was hoping you did."

"You just *vanished.*"

"It's a long, long story," she said softly, even sadly. "Do us both a favor. Don't make me tell it now."

They were quiet then. So quiet I was afraid they'd hear my heart pounding just outside the window.

"You can at least tell me what you're doing with Ernesto Julio," Cal finally asked.

"The same thing you are."

Now Cal was the one who pulled away. "What the hell do you mean by *that?*"

She glared at him. "You know exactly what I mean by that. He's a powerful man and he knows a lot of people and he gets things done." Here eyes were focused on him like death rays. "Face it: he's got something you want and he's got something I want."

"Yeah," Cal protested, "but I draw the line at driving his cars."

"Oh, you'd do the same if you could." You could tell she was angry as hell. And not just at Cal, either. "Besides," she added evenly, "nothing's happened yet."

"Whaddaya mean, 'nothing's happened yet?'"

They were eyeball-to-eyeball now. "You know exactly what I mean," she told him. And then she let out a long, slow sigh. "Look, he helped me get a couple parts, okay? Important parts. The kind of parts that can jump-start a whole career." She looked down at the floor. "This weekend's supposed to be the big payoff."

And that's when all three of us heard the rusty-spring creak of the outer screen door as Ernesto and Carlo swung it open and climbed up into the motorhome. You could tell Ernesto sensed something the moment he came in and he eyeballed the two of them suspiciously. Then his eyes darted down and locked hard into mine where I was standing outside, staring up like a Peeping Tom through the bottom crack of the curtain. At first I froze solid, but then made a big, dumb show of pretending to zip up my pants.

"So who wants to go to dinner?" Ernesto asked, still staring down at me. I didn't much like the look on his face.

Sometimes you get a feeling when things are starting to go wrong, and this was surely one of those times. So I begged off on dinner and hung around at the track instead with the Muscatelli brothers, trying to see what—if anything—we could do with the 121LM's rear end gears. Meanwhile Cal, Gina, Carlo and Ernesto went out for what I can only assume was a pretty edgy dinner with some of the rest of the Ferrari privateers. Although apparently things loosened up a bit after everybody'd had a few glasses of Ernesto Julio's special private stock before dinner plus a few more with dinner plus several of those fancy brandy shooters in the way-too-big glasses after dessert. In any case, old Ernesto was in pretty rare form by the time they ran into Toly Wolfgang in the piano bar later on. Although I believe Toly'd already been to bed at least once by that time in the evening. I guess old Ernesto had himself quite a bit to drink, and the way I heard it, Gina was the one who kept pouring it for him. And then pouring it for him some more, if you know what I mean. She pretended like she was doing the same for herself, but short-pouring or pawning her drinks off on somebody else or maybe even ditching some of it under the table.

Meanwhile we were out in the cold and dark at the track—just like the old days, you know?—only this time I was with the Muscatelli brothers and staring at a bunch of beautifully cast and machined Ferrari parts I didn't really know how to fix instead of the busted Jaguar and MG stuff I was more used to. No matter what, you really had to be impressed with the way old man Ferrari made things. The frame tubes were oval instead of round to make them stronger, and the transaxle casings were gorgeous aluminum alloy castings with nice, sturdy webs and ribs inside and out to keep everything strong and stout as well as light. It was just the opposite of that desperately flyweight Lotus Eleven that'd crashed and burned to a crisp earlier in the day. When you think about it, racecar builders are continually evaluating simplicity versus complexity and making endless, difficult compromises between light weight, strength, power and reliability. When you looked into the guts of a Ferrari and saw the way it was built, you understood why they almost always finished races. And won them in the process, often as not. Ferraris were war machines, plain and simple, and in spite of their thoroughbred reputations and exotic specifications, they were tough as nails under the skin.

If there was a fly in the ointment, it was the way Ferrari jumped from one idea to another to another and kept dreaming up new models. Like going from the little V-12s to the big V-12s to the straight sixes like our 121LM to the middle and big-sized four-bangers like the 857S and 860 Monza factory cars. Like I said, Ferrari could whip up a whole new engine as easily as most manufacturers change a headlight bezel or door hinge. And old man Ferrari was nobody's fool. He knew that's what kept all the rich privateer owners like Ernesto Julio and John Edgar and John von Neumann and Tony Parravano coming back—checkbooks in hand—to buy the latest hot new model. Although they were never real happy discovering that the one they'd bought just a year (or even a few months!) before was now considered obsolete by the factory. Especially when that also sometimes meant that parts could be hard to come by….

And that's exactly the bind we were in that night out in the cool March darkness of the Sebring paddock. We had the rear end torn all apart and laid out on shop rags on a makeshift tool bench, eyeballing the pieces this way and that under the cold, white glare and dark-side-of-the-moon shadows of a couple of clamp lights. None of us much liked the wobble and lash in the ring-and-pinion before we stripped it down, or the heat-blued, off-center shiny patches on the gear teeth once we'd taken it apart. But we didn't have any of the replacement parts we needed to fix it (or the special, unit-room tools you need to really put a ring-and-pinion together properly with the right amount of bearing crush, end float, gear mesh and preload), so about all we could do was stare at it and worry over it and stare at it some more. It looked like one of those deals where something starts out just a tiny wee hair off-kilter when whoever-it-was originally bolted it together, and then, as time and miles and the huge torque of that big, 4.4-liter Ferrari six—multiplied through the gears, don't forget—come at it from one side while the grip of the tires and the pounding of the road come at it from the other side, and meanwhile everything is spinning and whirling and rotating and gyrating until the bearings are damn near rattling in their cages….

Fact is, it's a wonder any racecar can survive even a single lap, let alone a 12-hour, motorized gauntlet run like Sebring.

Anyhow, we were there until well past midnight, doing what we could for that sick transaxle while the paddock emptied out until it was just us and the darkness and the distant, barely audible whoops and hollers of the revelers in the infield having a time that damn few of them would remember come the following morning. We wound up making some half-assed shims out of thin sheet steel to try and get the ring-and-pinion gears meshed a little better. Or at least that was the theory, anyway. Then we checked the pre-load with the well-known torque wrench of the wrist, cleaned the outside casing up all nice and shiny just to make it feel better inside (don't laugh, sometimes it works!), stuck it back under the car, re-attached the axle shafts, filled it with gearlube, buttoned everything up, put the wheels back on, took the car off the jackstands, patted it on the fender, stretched the cotton car cover over it, sighed, crossed our fingers, said a little prayer to the vast, deep, twinkling night-time sky, put away the tools, tidied up the workbench, grabbed a gritty fistful of hand cleaner and a shop rag to wipe it off, looked at each other like surgeons who'd just lost a patient, shrugged, switched off the clamp lights and piled into Carlo Sebastian's panel van for the grim, silent drive back to the hotel. I mean, there was nothing else we could do….

Come morning Sebring had erupted into a combination of Times Square on New Year's Eve and the Rose Bowl Parade all rolled into one. It was a frothing sea of shorts, tee shirts, smiles, banners, sunburns, clicking cameras, engines warming up, high school bands and hangovers—overflowing with noise and color!—as what seemed like a kazillion people flooded through the paddock before the race, all jabbering and waving and pointing their cameras every which way and jamming programs and autograph books under the drivers' noses. The drivers didn't seem to mind much. Hell, they needed something—anything!—to keep them occupied and take some of the weight out of the waiting. Carlo Sebastian was there wearing a huge smile under the handsome new Panama hat he'd bought with a Ferrari prancing horse logo embroidered in the hatband. A seriously gaunt and hungover Ernesto Julio was there with Gina on his arm in yet another stunning outfit—this time a kind of ivory-cream silk job with matching shoes and sun visor—and the stares of damn near every guy in the paddock were following her around like a school of mullet. Even so, Ernesto's eyes were nothing more than pained little slits and he looked like he would've much rather stayed in bed. I noticed Gina and Cal kept stealing little glances at each other every now and then. But only when the other one wasn't looking, you know? Everybody's been through those kind of deals, where you're staring so hard you're almost burning a hole through somebody and yet if they glance back at you, you're suddenly looking the other way. And maybe whistling.

Meanwhile guys like me kept busy moving all the parts and tires and tools and gear and fuel cans and jacks and chalk boards and umbrellas and folding chairs and an ice chest filled with water and pop for the drivers and a million other things into our pit stall. You feel like you're in some big monster rush and that you'll never get everything done in time, but by a half-hour before the start you're usually standing around with your face hanging out, wondering what the heck to do with yourself. So you go check the air pressure in all the spare tires again for the umpty-umpth time and take yet another pee (that would make four "last pees before the start" so far this morning, but that's what a lot of coffee and way too much adrenaline will do for you) and then you help the Muscatelli brothers push "our" somewhat suspect 121LM and the little 500 Mondial Porfiro "Rubi" Rubirosa was sharing with Dewey Dellinger and the 500 *Testa Rossa* the two Venezuelans were driving and the big old bucket of a 250MM that Creighton Pendleton was co-driving with our new California buddy Bruce Kessler to the front straight to line them up for the Le Mans-style start. I have to admit it made me swell up a little to see that big white Corvette with the blue racing stripes and that oversized Pontiac engine under the hood right up at the front of the line. Even though I knew it was because the cars were gridded according to engine size rather than qualifying times. Which meant "our" 121LM was also way up towards the front thanks to its monster of a 4.4-liter engine. Ahead of all the D-Types and the factory-entry Ferraris, even.

Cal and Toly flipped a coin to see who got to start and Cal won the flip, but Carlo Sebastian pulled rank and decided to put Toly in first because he supposedly had more experience. Even if Cal had gone a hair quicker in practice and certainly knew the track better. But it was all pretty academic anyway since the car wouldn't fire up when Toly scampered across the track and leaped into it at the drop of the green. He had to sit there, grinding helplessly away on the starter while the rest of the field stampeded past and thundered off into Turn One. You could smell something sort of burning, too. We finally had to push the damn thing over into our pit stall before he ran the battery down to nothing, and of course it took what seemed like an eternity to finally locate the blessed problem and fix it. Seems we'd accidentally pushed against or put too much pressure on the tiny little eye connector where the power wire attaches to the to the electric fuel pump when we were messing around underneath the car the night before, and though it had enough contact to work fine when we fired it up and warmed the engine that morning, it was one of those "hanging by a thread" deals that finally decided to snap in two—right on cue, natch!—somewhere between our warm-up spot in the paddock and our place in line at the front of the grid. Can you believe it? And then of course the bare end shorted against the frame and pretty much melted the wire (Ah-ha! The burning smell!) so we had to run a new wire and put new connectors on the ends and stick in a new fuse and….

And to tell the truth, it didn't make shit for difference anyway. We finally got everything back together, had Toly climb back in, told him to fire it up (while the field was thundering past for about the third or fourth time) and sent him down to the end of pit lane so the marshal could wave him out into a hole in traffic. And damn if it wasn't the same big, fat guy he'd almost run over when he went blasting out of the pits after practice was officially over on Thursday afternoon! So the guy kept him waiting until the whole damn field had gone by. Even the little blue DoucheBag tiddlers at the far back end of the pack! By that time Toly was steaming (and so was the car!) and so he wound it up to about five grand, dumped the clutch, and with a loud squawk from the tires and a hard grinding/shredding noise underneath, stripped the ring-and-pinion gears right there on the spot. Hell, we didn't even make to down to Turn One.

Not even once….

Chapter 11: Twelve Long Hours

Well, I guess you could say it was funny what happened to Cal and Toly and their big six-banger Ferrari at Sebring that year. And I guess it was. Or at least it was after we stood around our pit stall for a while looking stupid and dumb and embarrassed and then spent the better part of 20 minutes dragging all of our gear and stuff back to Carlo Sebastian's spot in the paddock and loading it onto the truck. Not that there was all that much of it, since Carlo's other entries were still running strong. As they should, with less than 20 blessed minutes of the race run! You go into an endurance race all geared up in your head and heart to go the full 12 (or even 24!) hours, and the letdown when it fizzles out like a damn dud firecracker right there at the beginning just drains all the juice right out of you. And we were hardly the only ones. One of the all-American Corvettes spit its driveshaft out the bottom after just three laps (to the sound of much snickering from the British and European scribes in the pressroom, you can be sure), one of the "we're only really racing against ourselves" French DoucheBags in the dwarf 750 Sport class broke its gearbox five laps later and one of the angry Venezuelans in Carlo Sebastian's 500 *Testa Rossa* managed to crash out of the race all by his lonesome on the very same lap. Fortunately without injury, and leaving the way wide open for "Rubi" and Dewey Dellinger to pick up an easy class win if they could just keep the blessed car on the black part and not break it in half. But that's the way it goes in endurance racing: one team's hard-luck story is another team's gift-wrapped Christmas present. And, as Hank reminded us much later after an awful lot of drinks, at least we didn't have to put in all those grim hours of sweat, blood, effort, tension and anguish only to have the whole thing go tits-up at the 11th hour like some poor guys. Plus we had the oh-so-dubious distinction of being the very first car out of the running (although even that was close, since the Corvette lost its driveshaft on lap five), so no question we won some sort of prize at Sebring that year.

There really wasn't much to do after the stuff was packed away but come back to the pits and watch the race for a while. But the pits are a really a lousy vantage point because all you can see is the cars hammering down Sebring's wide, bumpy and ugly front pit straight and listen to the bellow of the exhaust noise echoing off the concrete and the splattering patter of the tires pounding over the tar strips. By nightfall, it'd get to where you could close your eyes and match the engine noise with the speed of the tar strip patter and know exactly which car it was.

Like a lot of the more ambitious teams, the Muscatelli brothers had hammered together a kind of makeshift, elevated viewing/timing-and-scoring stand out of wood planks and 2x4s (with a big, red Ferrari flag and a bright Cinzano café umbrella over it, of course) and you could climb up there and at least see a little bit of the back straight and across part of the infield to where the cars barreled down and got hard on the brakes for the infamous Sebring hairpin. But it was way off in the distance and you really couldn't get a feel for the speed of the cars or see the drivers working the wheel like you could out on the corners. Plus it was pretty damn crowded up there, what with Sid Muscatelli overseeing the stopwatches and lap charts plus Carlo Sebastian and co-drivers Bruce Kessler and Dewey Dellinger all watching nervously over Sid Muscatelli's shoulder while counting the laps and heartbeats until pit stops and driver changes. Ernesto was up there, too, all scrunched in behind them with a pained, squinty look on his face that was obviously a leftover from the night before. But at least he had the lovely Gina LaScala standing right next to him. Even if she was stealing little sideways glances at Cal and Toly down in the pit box below, who both looked about as grim and lifeless as the heads on Mount Rushmore. I went over and suggested as how the three of us could maybe link up with Hank Lyons over by the pressroom and head out to the corners and watch the race develop. Hell, there wasn't much else to do. It always takes time for the irony and humor of a disaster like theirs to bubble up to the surface. Say one round of pit stops and a couple rounds of drinks....

"C'mon," I urged them. "You planning on just standing here in the damn pits for 12 hours?"

Cal looked at me and then up towards Gina on the timing stand above us, shielding his eyes with his hand. "You want to come with us?" he hollered at her over the thunder of the cars (although he tried to make it sound like he was asking everybody above him right up to God and his angels).

Gina glanced at the sour, unhappy expression on Ernesto Julio's face and leaned in to say something in his ear. When she was done, he drew back slightly and stared at her, then down at Cal, Toly and me and then said something to her that we couldn't hear.

She looked back down at us. "I don't think I can," she yelled at Cal as one of the rumbleguts Corvettes and one of the zinging Porshces hurtled by and echoed their way off towards Corner One. "I think we're going to leave soon." She gave a small, helpless shrug, and for just an instant there were no cars passing and it seemed very, very quiet.

"That's too bad," Cal said softly. But you could tell she heard him.

So did Ernesto Julio. He scowled at Gina and then she gave Cal a big, empty mask of a smile. "Who knows," she said airily, "maybe we'll see each other again?"

"You never know," Cal answered back like he was talking to somebody's aunt.

"C'mon," I kind of whispered to him as Hawthorn's leading Jaguar screamed past at full throttle. "Let's go watch the race, okay?"

"Yes, let's go have a few too many drinks and watch the race with Buddy," Toly agreed, tugging on Cal's elbow from the other side. And so that's what we did. Even if getting Cal out of there was kind of like leading a dazed fighter away from the ring. To tell the truth, I'd never seen him like that.

But it didn't last long. In fact, the glint and flash were back in his eye by the time we grabbed a cold six-pack of beer and a mostly-empty bottle of Ernesto Julio's special, high-test brandy from the motorhome, snagged Hank out of the pressroom and headed out to the hairpin to watch the action. Hell, the race was less than an hour old.

Hank refused a cold beer because he was working and figured he really needed to stay awake and keep his head clear for the next 12 hours. "Although," he added with a sly grin, "I've heard Walter Scott from the Milwaukee Journal can do an entire race weekend report from Elkhart Lake without ever leaving his favorite stool at a little bar in downtown Plymouth, about nine miles from the racetrack."

"Oh, really? How does he do it?"

"Uses beer and an occasional rum-and-coke to keep him going, watches baseball on the television all day long and then just listens to the crowd at the bar when they start filtering in from the racetrack. He writes pretty good stuff, actually. Never gets the names right, of course, but pretty good stuff. Even pie-eyed. He's famous for it."

These are the fascinating little insider tidbits you'd never know about without a pal like my friend Hank Lyons. Speaking of which, Hank filled us in about how the race was progressing while we headed over towards the hairpin. To the cheers of the crowd, Fitch's Pontiac-engined Corvette actually led the charge away from the Le Mans start from its position at the front of the line, but the glory only lasted a hundred yards or so before Mike Hawthorn in Cunningham's—er, make that "Jaguar USA's"—fuel-injected D-Type elbowed its way underneath into Turn One and proceeded to simply motor away from everybody. Hawthorn had a 300-yard lead by the end of the very first lap! And he continued to pad that lead—lap after lap—as the field quickly strung out behind him. He was into lapped traffic by the fourth time around!

Meanwhile Stirling Moss made his usual, lightning dash across the pavement, leaped into his waiting Aston DB3S, fired it up and tore away in a haze of rubber dust before most of the rest were even in their cars. Sure, there was a lot of grousing up and down pit lane that he'd jumped the start pretty blatantly, sprinting across the track when the countdown wasn't much past "two." Or maybe even "three." But of course the other drivers had no choice but to follow suit and sprint towards their cars as well once Moss made a break for it, so what could anybody do? In any case, he was driving the wheels off that pretty green Aston, running laps in the 3:31 range (which was a good five seconds a lap faster than any of the other teams thought a DB3S could go!) and damn if he wasn't solidly into second place and holding it confidently once the field sorted itself out. That was pretty damn impressive, and you could see he was carrying a lot more momentum than anybody but the factory Porsche 550s through that fast Turn One sweeper. That guy could *drive!* Plus no question "Death Ray" Wyer's Aston team had kept a few pounds of sand in the bag during practice and qualifying....

But of course the other driver everybody had to keep an eye on was Fangio, who was not only fast and smooth but had that rare, long-vision ability to see all the way to the end of the race from the moment the green flag dropped. Even in a complex, extended grind like Sebring. A lot of drivers—even fast, accomplished drivers—can never see much further ahead than the next blessed corner. Fangio had this uncanny inner sense of what sort of pace might be needed to win a race and the discipline to run that pace regardless of what everybody else was doing. And so he'd calmly, cleanly and methodically eased his Ferrari up through the field to assume third place—right in the wheeltracks of Moss in the Aston Martin—and seemed more than happy to just sit there, a half-minute or so behind Hawthorn in the leading Jaguar. You got the sense he was just marking time and watching Moss drive, even though Fangio's Ferrari was surely faster than Moss' Aston Martin and he could have blown by any time he wanted. The two of them had been teammates at Mercedes-Benz the year before—with Fangio as very much the respected Old Master and Moss as the hot young Whiz Kid—and you could see there was a special understanding between them. I guess it's pretty hard to define what makes one driver better than another or to separate Good from Great from genuine Genius, but you sure as hell know it when you see it. And no question those two had it. I suppose Hawthorn had it too, but it somehow felt a little more desperate and a little less serene as you watched him wailing away in that Jaguar.

The guy who was really catching everybody's eye was that rich and furiously determined Argentine polo-champ Carlos Menditeguy in the 300S Maserati. No question he was trying to impress everybody—and succeeding!—but he was driving like it was a damn five-lap sprint rather than a 12-hour enduro and thrashing the living crap out of that poor car of his. He was twisting it right to the limit in every gear, slamming it from one gear to the next and hammering on the brakes until the tires chirped and shuddered every time. And you should have seen him wrestling that thing through the corners, dropping wheels and kicking up dirt and barging his way impatiently through lapped traffic! But it was working for him. He'd carved and bluffed and charged his way through the faster privateers and even started reeling in some of the factory guys. Particularly the backup team cars like Hamilton in the second "Jaguar USA" D-Type and Musso in the second Ferrari 860 and our pal Tommy Edwards in the second Aston Martin. Some of them probably wanted to race with him—particularly Ferrari's haunted and hot-blooded young Italian, Luigi Musso—but they were under strict orders to maintain pace and take it easy on the equipment in case the first-team cars hit trouble.

Besides, who wanted to mess with this guy?

And sure enough Menditeguy went that little bit too fast going through the chicane and had himself a real whopper of an accident. He skated off through the dirt and a wheel caught a rut or something and before you could even gasp that gorgeous Maserati went somersaulting end-for-end! Poor Menditeguy got tossed out like a blessed rag doll and then the car pretty much rolled right over him! Like a lot of the drivers, Menditeguy believed in the European notion that you were better off not wearing seatbelts and getting thrown out in an accident rather than being strapped to a ton of scrap metal that was most likely going to burst into flames and burn you to death on the off chance that you managed to survive the wreck. In any case, he was tremendously lucky getting carted off to the hospital with serious injuries when it very easily could have gone the other way. Especially the way he was asking for it. But that's something you can't really teach hungry young rookies out to prove something.

They have to learn it for themselves….

We went back to the pits to watch the first round of driver changes, and I had a feeling that Cal was maybe going to try to talk to Gina again if he could just find a way to get her separated from Ernesto Julio. Toly'd had himself a couple healthy snorts of brandy by then, and grandly allowed as how he'd be willing to run a little interference for Cal. You know, set up a diversion by chatting up Ernesto so's Gina could maybe sneak away for a couple minutes. He and Cal had both been getting pretty chummy with Ernesto's bottle of top-shelf brandy. Truth is, I don't think Cal had the slightest idea what he was going to say to Gina even if he got the chance. But by that time Ernesto was looking exceptionally sunburned, bored, angry, hurting and disgusted (not surprising after the disaster with the 121LM and the obvious over-supply of his own fine distilled grape products the night before) and Gina was coming to understand what a gritty, loud, hot, boring and endless sort of slog 12 hours of endurance racing at Sebring can become when you don't have somebody to root for anymore. So the two of them hopped another shuttle jeep back out to where Ernesto's Aero Commander was parked on the far side of the racetrack, and we got back to Carlo Sebastian's pit just in time to see that plane taxi down to the far end of the runway, turn around, gun the engines and soar off into the wild blue yonder with the race barely two hours old. Cal had a hollow, empty expression on his face as he watched that Aero Commander climb through a long, lazy arc with the sun glinting off its wings and head west, getting smaller and smaller until it was just a tiny pinpoint in the sky. And then it was gone….

So we watched the cars pound around some more—Hawthorn still in a commanding lead and, as Tommy often put it, *"going like the bloody clappers"*—and I remember wondering out loud if that was really such a great idea in such a long race. By contrast, I noticed the Phil Hill/Masten Gregory privateer 860 Monza was running at what I considered a beautifully measured pace, and I said as much. And naturally right on cue they started having engine problems and were out of it less than a third of the way home after a series of steamy pit stops. But that's the way it goes in endurance racing: the righteous and innocent get their just (or unjust) desserts right along with the guilty.

Eventually Toly suggested that we should all go back to the motorhome for another six-pack of beer and another bottle of Ernesto's brandy if we could find one. Personally, I thought that was about the last thing those two needed since they were both looking rather pixilated already. But what else was there to do? I begged off on joining them—why step willingly into a train wreck?—and so they headed off in the general direction of Carlo Sebastian's motor home while Hank and me went down by Turn One again to watch the drivers coping with a blind, daunting sweeper that tightened up in a kind of sucker move two-thirds of the way through. It was one of those corners with a hundred ways in and only one way out, and you could always tell when the second drivers were in the cars by the way they went through there. Hawthorn's co-driver wasn't nearly as fierce or forceful (or maybe he was trying to nurse it a little since Sebring is notoriously hard on brakes, and the faster your car will go in a straight line the more brakes you use up trying to get rid of the damn speed) while Behra was putting in one hell of a gutsy run in the remaining 300S Maserati. He was sure one fast, fearless guy in a racing car. Had a great feel for it, too. But, like Hank said, he was generally one of those flip-switch charger types with only one speed—*Flat Out!*—and you had to wonder if the car could take all that punishment. And sure enough he started coming in for unscheduled pit stops almost as soon as he got his Maserati up among the leaders. Too bad, really, since the 300S was such a damn beautiful—and beautifully balanced!—car. Behra was really driving the wheels off of it, too.

Meanwhile Moss had handed the quickest-by-far Aston Martin over to fellow Englishman Peter Collins, and he looked really good in it as well. But then it blew up in a big way (with a bang and a clatter and a near-opaque, bluish-white smokescreen trailing behind) and they were out of it. Before a quarter of the race had been run! Not that everybody and his brother didn't see it coming. Still, Moss had managed to light a big enough fire under both the Maseratis that Menditeguy's had already crashed out and the remaining Taruffi/Behra 300S was making frequent stops at the pits for electrical gremlins, and it was hard not to laugh watching the Maserati mechanics swarming over it in a frenzy of flailing arms, flying tools and shouted prayers, curses and saintly implorations in their best, back-alley Modenese dialect. They eventually got it fixed, but by then the two remaining Astons were left with pretty much clear sailing in the 3.0-liter class and a likely peek at a top overall finish. Maybe even a win if the big Jags and Ferraris faltered. So there was method behind Moss' and Collins' flat-out madness after all, and it made you appreciate what went on behind team manager John Wyer's justly famous and damn-near-impossible-to-read "Death Ray" eyes! Why, he'd even come up with little grab-on tabs on the brake pads so they could be changed quickly on pit stops if that became necessary. Not even Jaguar had thought of that! Although he couldn't do much about the gearbox on the Shelby/Salvadori DB3S, which had started to lose third gear. He instructed Roy and Carroll to not even try using third so as not to risk breaking teeth off the gears and trashing the gearbox entirely, and, although they were still way up there in the standings, it dropped them well off the pace.

As you can imagine, none of this was lost on our old buddy Tommy Edwards when we stopped by to visit him in the Aston pits. He was getting ready to take over and by then their car was solidly in the middle of the top 10 overall, running like a freight train and holding down a quite comfortable first place in the 3.0-liter class. You couldn't miss the thin, cautious smile on Tommy's face as he strapped on his helmet. "Misfortune can be a very beautiful thing when it's happening to everybody else," Hank grinned.

"Hey, you can't win unless some other poor bloke loses," Tommy shrugged as he fumbled with the buckle. "That's just the way it works. And Lord knows I've been on the losing end often enough to bloody well know about it." Tommy tugged again on his helmet strap and fidgeted with his goggles, and I caught myself really hoping and praying that things would work out for him here at Sebring. He needed a break. You could feel it. We stayed for the refueling and driver change—no new tires this time, as the old ones still looked pretty good—and I crossed my fingers as Tommy pulled away under the yellow-orange glow of the late afternoon Florida sun.

After that we wandered around pit lane some more, watching the pit stops and driver changes and some cars being frantically worked on by their crews while others looked all but abandoned in a fatal scent of steam or a gently creeping pool of oil under the engine compartment or rear end. It feels like you've been there forever by that point in an endurance race—you can't feel your way back to the beginning or, even harder, see forward to the end. Just like the teams, all you can do is keep on slogging. And it's right there in the dull, tense, endlessly droning heart of the contest that things quietly, almost invisibly change. The wild, colorful, screaming-flight-of-butterflies sprint you witnessed at the start somehow oozes out of its cocoon as a creeping, slimy caterpillar, evolving before your eyes into a dreary and deadening marathon of sturdiness, stamina, carefully measured pace, raw instinct, crafty intuition, blind-side heartbreak, unexpected opportunity, spur-of-the-moment improvisation and pure, gut-it-out survival.

Castellotti had taken over from Fangio in the factory 860 Monza, and although he was the odd second or two slower than the old master, he was going a lot quicker than Hawthorn's co-driver in the fuel-injected D-Type. But the Jaguar was starting to have brake problems, and that's never a good sign with the race barely half over. Plus there was the usual flap in the pressroom and confusion up in timing and scoring about who was actually where and whether the Fangio/Castellotti Ferrari was just taking the lead or putting a full lap on the "leading" D-Type when Fangio finally swept past for good late in the afternoon. Hank and me decided to head across the paddock to watch the cars braking at the end of the backstraight for Sunset Bend (and to see how it got its well-deserved name!), and along the way we happened by Carlo Sebastian's bivouac to see how Toly and Cal were doing. They were sitting nose-to-nose at the little folding card table with a half-empty bottle between them, deeply engrossed in some desperately serious discussion. "How're you guys doing?" I asked.

"We're discussing love," Toly explained without taking his eyes off Cal's. "He thinks he knows what it is, but of course he doesn't."

"Sure I do," Cal protested with an expansive, almost angry hand gesture that damn near swept him right off his folding chair.

Toly looked up at Hank and me through fierce, bloodshot eyes. "You see what I mean?"

Hank tugged silently at my sleeve, and I had to agree. This was no place for anyone even remotely sober.

"Look, we'll see you guys later, okay?"

But they were already back at it—nose-to-nose—burrowing deep into whatever high, mighty, vital, crucial, soon-to-be-resolved-for-all-eternity or just-as-quickly-to-be-forgotten-for-all-time topic had their attention.

"He doesn't usually drink like that, does he?" Hank whispered as we moved off towards the backstraight. "I never saw him drink like that out in California."

I shook my head. "Not that I've seen. Except maybe once or twice."

"Well," he shrugged, "let's hope it's a one-off. He looks pretty bad."

"That he does," I had to agree. "That he does."

So we watched at the braking zone for Sunset Bend as the sun drooped lower and lower until it was blazing straight in from the horizon and directly into the drivers' eyes. Some of them tilted their heads down to block the glare with the bill of their helmets while others held a free hand up to shield their eyes. Which made you wonder how they managed to both steer and double-clutch downshift with the other, you know? Anyhow, you couldn't miss how the brake lights on the Hawthorn D-Type were flashing several times down the backstraight before they came on in earnest for the turn. "He's having to pump the hell out of the brakes," I observed.

"That's never a good thing. And I think the other team car has already been in once or twice for brakes as well."

"I thought the Jaguars were supposed to have such fantastic brakes?"

"Great at Le Mans and great at Sebring are two different things," Hank explained. "You speed up and slow down a lot more times per lap here at Sebring. And there's no eight-kilometer straightaway with the wind rushing over them at 180 or so to help them cool off. It's hotter here, too."

Dusk came quickly as the sun eased down into the orange groves west of us, and we headed back to the pressroom so Hank could pick up a mimeographed copy the latest official standings. Along the way we ran into Cal and Toly again walking—or should I say meandering, sashaying and stumbling?—through the paddock. They'd obviously been at it pretty hard and were now well into that slow, mellow, sloppy and sentimental stage like a couple of drunken college chums. It felt strange to see Cal all lit up like that—come to think of it, I'd rarely seen him looking particularly plastered before—but I guess he'd taken a couple pretty hard shots what with the split-decision result against Toly in practice, the big race they never got to run because the damn car broke, seeing Angelina again after three whole years and then finding out she was some kind of ascending Hollywood starlet and moreover palling around with his own personal car owner/race entrant/pit-and-paddock sugar daddy Ernesto Julio. And then, to cap it all off, watching the two of them winging off towards California in Ernesto's Aero Commander without ever really getting to talk to her. To tell the truth, he was looking awfully dispirited, disheveled and unsteady, and that wasn't like the Cal Carrington I knew at all.

Not that Toly Wolfgang looked much better.

"So, how's it going?" I asked them.

"The good news is, we're out of it," Cal confided with inebriated certainty. He held up a bottle of Ernesto Julio's cheap champagne. "I toast the end of our misery," he proclaimed to the entire paddock, then took a hefty swig. Obviously they'd run clear through the cold beer and expensive brandy.

"Good fortune ended it early for us," Toly agreed through a crooked, wavering smile. He leaned in close, eyes twinkling. "It made us men of leisure," he whispered, then took a long swig himself and passed the bottle around. Hank said he didn't want any on account of he was still working, but Toly wouldn't hear of it. *"What?"* he demanded, sounding thoroughly outraged. *"Are you a woman? A silly little girl?"*

"It's not that..." Hank started to explain, but Toly stopped him. In fact, he put his hand right over Hank's mouth!

"Ssshhh!" Toly commanded like drunks do. "You must show the proper respect for our delirious misfortune."

"Delirious, indeed," Cal nodded, his eyelids half closed.

Toly clapped his arm around Cal's shoulder, leaned in close again and stage whispered: "And you *must* toast my good friend's broken heart."

"That's right," Cal agreed, leaning into Toly's shoulder. "You absolutely *must* toast my broken heart."

Toly unclamped Cal's shoulders and he almost toppled over. But Toly didn't even seem to notice. He pulled his face in even closer to Hank's and mine. His breath was easily 100 proof all by itself. "It's not *really* serious," Toly confided like somehow Cal couldn't hear us. "My friend here doesn't really have a broken heart."

"I *don't?"* Cal asked, propping himself against a convenient fence post.

"Of course you don't," Toly informed him sternly. "How can you break something you don't have?"

"I have a heart," Cal protested, his head and shoulders wavering. I could tell they were getting into that combative stage again. Drunks generally flip-flop back and forth like that all the time.

"Okay. So you have a heart," Toly conceded almost angrily. "But you've never used it. How can you break something you never use?"

"Oh?" Cal sneered back at him. "So in just one weekend you think you know me so well?"

"Yes I do," Toly answered flatly. "I know what is in your heart."

"The heart I don't have, right?"

"The heart you don't use."

"Whaddaya mean, *'don't use?'"*

"Don't use because you can't open it up for anyone. Can't let anyone inside." Toly turned to Hank and me. "There's no room," he explained, rolling his palms up like it was obvious.

"I see," Cal muttered as he struggled to get his feet under him again. "And exactly how do you know all this?"

"Because your heart is just like mine. It's shut and it's black and it's cold and solid as a tombstone. It can't allow love inside because there's no way in. And no room for anyone else even if they could get in."

Cal thought it over for a moment. And then he raised a finger like drunks do when they're about to make a telling, pivotal point. "If that's true," he intoned solemnly, "how could some heartless bastard like you or I possibly know it?"

There was a moment of weighty, drunken silence. And then Toly started in again. Only quietly this time. Even sadly. With his eyes cast down towards the ground. "I only know what love looks like from the outside," he admitted in a soft, hoarse whisper. "The same as you." But then, barely a moment later, his head popped back up with bloodshot eyes blazing and a cruel, eager slash of a smile creased across his face. *"Come!"* he insisted. *"Let's drink to it!"*

"Drink to what?" Cal asked, losing the thread like drunks do.

"To the love we'll never know!" Toly explained grandly, taking a big swig off the bottle and passing it over to Hank and me. Hank looked a little sheepish as he pretended to take a healthy swallow. Then I took a gulp—a real one—and nearly spit it right back on account of it was all warm and sticky and as full of sugary fizz as the soda pop some smirking cub scout has shaken up to squirt at his buddies. It was hardly what you could call refreshing. "That's awful," I half-gagged, and passed the bottle back to Cal.

But Cal was still deep into the weight, heft and consequences of what Toly had been saying. "To the love we'll never know," he agreed, raising the bottle for all to see. Then he gurgled down the last of it and looked at the empty bottle like he couldn't figure out what the hell it was doing in his hand. He even turned it upside down to see if there might be anything left. "I believe we've used this one to death," he observed.

"That's all right. I know where there's more," Toly assured him.

"Indeed you do. Lead on." Cal tried to focus his eyes back on Hank and me. "Would you care to join us? It's very educational."

"I don't think I'd better," Hank told him. "I've got to cover the race."

"It's your loss." Cal shrugged. "How about you, Buddy?"

"I don't know. It looks to me like you two have one hell of a head start. I think I'll stick with Hank and see how the race comes out."

"Someone will win and everybody else will lose," Toly explained distastefully. "That's what always happens."

"Yeah, but somebody's got to set it all down," Hank reminded him. "Somebody's got to stay up till three fucking ayem getting all the facts and stories straight and writing it up for the damn newspapers and magazines." He looked right at Cal and Toly. "After all, somebody's got to shower the winners with glory."

"Ah, yes," Toly nodded thoughtfully. "And bury the dead. Someone's always got to bury the dead."

We watched as the two of them made a kind of sloppily synchronized U-turn and stumbled their way arm-in-arm back towards the motorhome. "Boy, I wouldn't want to be either one of those guys in the morning," Hank observed.

"Me, either."

No question they were as drunk as any two spectators in the Sebring infield that year. And that's saying something, believe me!

It was full night by then, and you could hear the cars howling and growling and barking their way around the circuit like packs of wild mechanical dogs and see the sweeping glare of their headlight beams clawing into the darkness. We watched at Turn One again and then dropped by the Aston pit to see how our friend Tommy was doing, and sadly arrived just in time to see him pull in with a dull, heavy clatter coming from somewhere deep down in the engine and wisps of oil smoke laced with that telltale foundry smell seeping out from under the hood. With less than a blessed hour to go! What a *shame!* And I wondered as I watched him climb slowly, almost painfully out of the car—soaked with sweat and covered all over in grease, grit, tire rubber and grime—if he was any better off than Cal and Toly, who'd never even made it to Turn One. I really wanted to go up and say something to him, but of course there wasn't much of anything you could say.

Besides, there are times a person just needs to be alone....

Hank stopped by the pressroom once more as the official clock ticked off the last quarter of an hour. By then the Hawthorn Jag had retired with no brakes left at all and so it was the Fangio/Castellotti 860 Monza just cruising along in first overall and first in the "Sports 5000" class, and the other team Ferrari of Musso and Schell sitting solidly in second, two laps behind. They were followed by a gap of another four laps to one of the slower but more prudently driven privateer D-Types in third overall—the one co-driven by owner Jack Ensley and Indy 500 winner/oval track star Bob Swiekert, of all things. Proving once again that, no matter what those European scribes or tweedy tea-bagger types thought, our American roundy-round guys really knew how to drive a damn racecar, no matter which way the blessed track went.

The last remaining Aston DB3S in the hands of Roy Salvadori and our old Texas chicken-farmer pal Carroll Shelby finished another lap back in fourth—wonky gearbox and all—and still managed first place in the "Sports 3000" 3.0-liter class, just a lap ahead of the consistently faster but troublesome Behra/Taruffi Maserati 300S. So there would indeed be some celebrating over in the Aston Martin camp that night, even if Tommy and his co-driver were feeling pretty damn miserable.

Two of those pesky little Porsche 550s managed an amazing sixth and seventh overall and first and second in the "Sports 1500" class (led by the factory car, natch) and I was proud as hell to see the Fitch/Hansgen Corvette—the one with the oversized Pontiac engine, remember?—not only make the finish in its first-ever attempt at Sebring, but come home ninth overall and first in class as well! Then again, it was the only car entered in the "Sports 8000" class, and so all it had to do was make the finish in order to win. Still, reaching the checker at Sebring is no easy task, and I thought they did one hell of a fine job. Some of the European press guys snickered behind their hands about how Chevrolet's hulking, 5.2-liter "Yank Tank" got beaten by a couple 1500cc Porsches, but so did most everybody else.

And damn if "Rubi" Rubirosa and that wide-eyed English rookie Dewey Dellinger didn't soldier on to take 10th overall and a barely contested first place in the 2.0-liter "Sports 2000" class! Naturally they were over the moon about it (even if they had by far the fastest car in the class and drove, as Hank so gently put it, "without any visible genius, verve or distinction") because the trophy's just as shiny and the little line of agate type in the record book reads just the same whether you slay a mighty dragon or swat a dozen shit flies to get there.

Speaking of which, that little popcorn-popper French DoucheBag was absolutely running away with the complex Index of Performance computations until it ran out of gas on the circuit with less than two hours to go. Pushing the car was illegal (at least if you got caught, anyway), and so the driver had to run huffing-and-puffing all the way back to the pits, grab a half-gallon of gas, run all the way back to the car, pour it in and sputter off again into the night. That killed any chances for the "more out of less" Index of Performance award and dropped them down to 16th overall out of the 23 cars that eventually managed to scream, struggle, strain or stagger across the line under their own power come the end of 12 hours. But that was still good enough for a glorious and valiant win in the thoroughly uncontested "Sports 750" class (the Brooks Stevens-entered DoucheBag had blown its clutch before the race was three hours old), even if they did finish a paltry 39 laps and 200 miles behind the overall winners. But their accomplishment was easily overshadowed by Leech Cracraft and Red Byron, whose stubby little rear-engined Cooper survived all sorts of meltdowns, misfortunes and mechanical disasters to waddle home 21st overall, a solid 40 miles behind that tiddliest of tiddlers D.B. Panhard that ran out of gas on the circuit. And yet that was still good enough for a lucky "win" in the "Sports 1100" class seeing as how all the other cars either dropped out or, in the case of the privateer Lotus Mk. 9 co-driven by Colin Chapman after his shatteringly fast new Eleven crashed and burned in practice, got themselves disqualified by the officials. Seems the starter motor in the Mk. 9 had burned out, and the rules were very clear that you had to re-start your car "on the key" and without any "outside assistance" like a set of jumper cables or pushing. Well aware of this (and also realizing that a push start would be extremely easy to spot), Chapman came up with the clever—if somewhat sneaky—notion of jacking the back end up like they were looking at something underneath and then, with the transmission in a low gear, clutch out and ignition switch on, giving one of the rear wheels a quiet little tug to spin the engine so's it'd fire up again.

Only trouble is, they got caught….

All three of the new MGAs finished (in 19th, 20th and 22nd positions overall and fourth, fifth and sixth in class behind the "real racecar" Porsche 550s) and it was kind of neat to see them cruise under the checker together in tight formation, just like a blessed fighter squadron. If you knew anything about how long, hard and tough a race like Sebring is, it made you feel something inside. In fact, you felt that way about everybody and anybody who made the distance. Or even made a good try at it.

Chapter 12: Glamour, Gold and Grindstones

Sunday morning I wound up flying back to New York with Carlo Sebastian and Bruce Kessler in none other than Creighton Pendleton the Third's own personal Beechcraft Bonanza. Which, along the way, Creighton took pains to explain were nicknamed "Doctor Killers" at small regional airports all over the country on account of a lot of rich amateur pilots bought them for personal use and that unusual, V-shaped tail was rumored to make them a wee bit tricky to fly. And land. But I think he was just telling me that to wind me up a little, since he knew I'd never been up in a private plane before. Not to mention that he was still simmering over the way my pal Cal set him up like a pin in a bowling alley and then and beat him fair and square to the finish line at Road America the previous fall. Not that he'd ever say anything about it (except that it had been "a really great race" and "a memorable finish," of course) but you could tell it was eating his liver plenty every time he saw anything that reminded him in the slightest of Cal Carrington. Like me, for example.

Anyhow, I was jammed into what is laughingly referred to as the "back seat" of that Beechcraft Bonanza next to our new California buddy Bruce Kessler, who was on his way to Carlo's Ferrari garage in Manhattan to pick up a car for his friend Lance Reventlow and drive it back out to LA for him. Turns out it was the same blessed gunmetal-gray 340 America coupe Carlo had been trying to pawn off on Ernesto Julio. Anyhow, all I can say is thank God I wasn't back there with somebody the size of Big Ed Baumstein, because I would've spent the whole trip squashed up against that curved plexiglass side window like something out of a Tom and Jerry cartoon. There wasn't an awful lot of room back there. Plus you really felt trapped—like in the back seat of a VW Beetle, you know?—only even worse, seeing as how there was only one flimsy little door and that was way up front on the co-pilot side more or less kittycorner from me where there was no way in hell to get at it or be anything except Last Man Out in an emergency. Not that leaping through that particular door would improve things appreciably, even in the event of a crash dive….

Like I said, this was my first-ever trip in a small private plane, and I must admit I spent most of it feeling every bump, shudder, noise, waver, wind gust and hiccup in the atmosphere like a bolt of lightning shooting up my ass and wondering exactly what size and shape hole a fully loaded Beechcraft Bonanza could make in a cornfield. You couldn't carry on much of a conversation thanks to the engine and propeller noise—or at least not without hollering—and the ride was, as Creighton himself put it, "a little choppy" thanks to a bunch of air pockets and updrafts and such that seemed to hit us every now and then like anti-aircraft fire. Although I got the feeling he was doing some of it on purpose. Especially when the plane would suddenly and unexpectedly drop eight or ten stories in a heartbeat. Usually accompanied by the sudden, soft, smacking sound of my butt cheeks slamming together. And it got even worse when Creighton shot an insider wink I didn't see at Carlo and Bruce and flipped a switch under the dash so the motor sputtered and coughed a couple times and then cut out completely. Let me be clear about this: there is no more chilling sound in the world than the whistle and rush plain old air makes going around the fuselage and wing profiles of an airplane when there's no engine noise to drown it out. It'll open up a hole in your gut the size of Yankee Stadium. I guarantee it! And naturally Creighton played around with all the switches and knobs on the control panel in front of him, pretending like he was trying to get it restarted and looking extremely concerned while the Beechcraft eased gently over into a moderate-but-accelerating nosedive that about put my feet right through the floor skin! The wind was rushing faster and harder now—you should've heard it!—and Creighton was still fussing and fooling around with all the knobs and switches and pretending like we were really in trouble. I even had this crazy notion that maybe I ought to climb right over him and grab the controls myself—not that I had the slightest idea how to fly a damn airplane!—but I figured I couldn't do much worse at it than he was....

And of course that's when Creighton and Carlo looked at each other and burst out laughing. *"I really had you going there!"* Creighton cackled as he calmly flipped the switch that sparked the engine back to life.

"YOU GODDAM SONOFABITCH RAT-BASTARD!!!" I yelled over the welcome roar of the motor. But that just made the two of them laugh harder. Bruce was laughing, too, but at least he was trying to hold it in a little. Just to be polite, you know? *"Th-that was a really r-rotten thing to do,"* I spluttered, my fists clenching and unclenching with rage. Not that they could much hear me over the engine noise. In any case, you'd be amazed how quickly you get over being mad at the person holding onto the stick and rudder controls of the small and exceedingly fragile-appearing airplane you happen to be flying in at the time. And I must admit Creighton was a pretty damn good pilot. Just like he was a pretty damn good racing driver. And, as I kept telling myself over and over (and had told myself over and over and yet over again about Cal): the rich couldn't help being rich any more than the poor could help being poor. It was just unfortunate that a lot of them had to be such assholes about it.

We stopped for refueling and coffee someplace in North Carolina and the guy at the counter had some sandwiches brought in for us from a little diner just down the road. While we were waiting, I kind of eavesdropped on a conversation between Carlo and Bruce and Creighton the Third about the race drivers they'd met and run against at Sebring. And when I say I eavesdropped, what I really mean is that I didn't have much to add. At least not in that sort of company. Besides, I didn't think anybody was really interested in my opinion anyway. But it was pretty interesting just the same. As in the Sebring pressroom, consensus around our little table in the airport hangar coffee room was that three-time World Grand Prix champ Fangio was pretty much in a class by himself. But maybe getting a lot of years and miles on him, you know? Meanwhile, young English phenom Stirling Moss was also in that "very special" league and looked to be closing fast. Behind those two you had a fat handful of almost/maybe/sometime guys who could be genuinely brilliant or would be genuinely brilliant or might be genuinely brilliant if the wind blew in the right direction and God smiled down in such a way that the very best of what they could do blossomed into what they could do all the time. Or at least any time they wanted. Hawthorn and Collins and Phil Hill and Tony Brooks were in that bunch, closely followed by Jean Behra (who was unquestionably brave and consistently brilliant in any kind of car, but never seemed to comprehend when and how to slow down) and guys like Castellotti, Schell and Musso on the Ferrari team. They all had their days in the sun and they all won races. But the overriding excellence and ongoing consistency just weren't there. At least not like Moss and Fangio.

All three of them had taken notice of how fast, smooth and steady Carroll Shelby drove, how unbelievably quick, clever and tidy Colin Chapman seemed behind the wheel, what a tremendous job Walt Hansgen did in that hulking brute of a Corvette and were absolutely wowed by the raw speed, grit and determination of little Archie Scott-Brown.

"What about Cal and Toly?" I finally asked. The other three looked at me. "What I mean is, how do you rate those two?"

Creighton thought it over. "It's really too soon to tell, isn't it?" he sniffed. "I mean, Cal's a good club racer—a *really* good club racer, I'll give you that—but we're talking about the Big Leagues here."

"I dunno," Bruce allowed. "He's got a hell of a lot of talent."

That's what I thought, too. But I didn't say anything.

"Creighton's right," Carlo nodded in a fatherly way. "There's an enormous difference between being some star club racer here on this side of the ocean and becoming a genuine professional over in Europe." He looked right at me. "And it has less than you might imagine to do with talent." He took a bite of his sandwich and mulled it over. "Remember that an amateur can go fast when he feels like it. A true professional has to go fast whether he feels like it or not." He paused for a moment to let that sink in. "You know," he continued, looking back and forth from Bruce to Creighton, "sometimes I think the talent is the easiest part. Have either of you ever thought about what it takes to be a professional racing driver?"

"Money!" Bruce answered instantly, and we all laughed.

Carlo held up a quieting hand. "Money is part of it, sure. And so is talent and so is opportunity. But you need something else before any of that."

"But what else is there?" I asked like the class idiot.

Carlo smiled gently. "The desire, my friend. The *need!"* He shook his head almost imperceptibly. "There has to be something inside that you cannot deny. Something so powerful it overshadows everything else. Without that…" he rolled his palms up "…no sane person would ever even consider it."

"You make it sound pretty bleak," Bruce observed.

"It *is* bleak," Carlo nodded. "But at the same time it's marvelous, too."

There was an unmistakable flash of agreement in Bruce and Creighton's eyes.

"But you can't fool yourself," Carlo cautioned. "Men are killed or maimed for life every weekend. Survival is only one of several possibilities." He took a sip of his coffee and continued. "Accidents are a certainty. You have to accept that." He let out a long, deep sigh. "Racing is a cruel, beautiful mistress, my friend. A glorious adventure, to be sure. It's a magnificent, delicious and all-consuming—but sometimes fatal—addiction." He moved his eyes around the table. "But if you have that need, that desire, that fire in the belly…" he shrugged helplessly, "…well, then there can be no other life, can there? And you will sacrifice anything and everything on earth to pursue it."

Nobody said anything. Outside the window, a Piper Cub taxied across the grass.

"Tommy Edwards says driving a racecar is the only place his life makes sense," I tossed in.

"A lot of drivers feel that way," Carlo agreed. "It's not just a marvelous thing to do, it's also an escape from the rest of life. A place to hide from all the doubt and fear and emptiness. A relief from the drudgery of routine. Most of us spend our lives waiting for things that never happen or worrying about things that inevitably do." He took another sip of coffee. "Would you like to know what my friend Enzo Ferrari says about drivers?"

I nodded. And you could see Bruce and Creighton were all ears, too.

"Enzo says there are only two things that can drive a human being to become a professional racing driver…."

"What are they?" I wanted to know.

"Love or ambition."

"Love or ambition?"

Carlo nodded. "Some just love the way it feels to drive fast and race. Love the feel of the car and the road. Love that sweet, secret place where it all melts endlessly together. Love the blended science, grace, skill, tactics, instinct, discipline and emotion of it. They cannot help themselves. They live for the chess-match duels with the fellows up ahead or just behind. They're addicted to the speed and the sounds and the smells. The feel of the G-forces pressing into you. And, at the very core of it, you have that incredible, almost Godlike sense of control. To drive very fast—right at the limit—is to hold the beating heart of the future in your hands…."

Boy, he sure knew how to talk.

Carlo drained the last of his coffee and continued. "And then you have the ones driven by ambition. Driven above all else to be special. To be different. To be in some way better than the rest. To be a man of value and respect and consequence." He pushed the last small wedge of sandwich into his face. "It's not easy finding such things in life…."

I could see that.

"The interesting thing," he added, still chewing, "is that your friend Cal and Toly Wolfgang are very close on the track—perhaps even closer than either of them realizes—but Cal does it because he's addicted and needs it and loves it while Toly does it because he needs to do something important with his life. To achieve something that's recognized and respected without question." He looked at me. "Do you know any of his family history?"

I nodded. "Eric Gibbon filled us all in at the party Thursday night at the Kenilworth."

Carlo rolled his eyes at the mention of Eric Gibbon's name, but then continued. "The point is the two of them are exactly what *Signore* Ferrari was talking about…"

I was beginning to see it.

"…Cal does it because he loves it. Can't get enough of it. He can't help himself…"

I knew that was true.

"…And Toly Wolfgang does it because he has to. He needs to make some sort of mark in life. Achieve some recognizable measure of success. I think perhaps as much for his father as for himself."

"But his father's dead."

Carlo gave a weak shrug. "What does that matter? It's what drives him, I think. What burns and rumbles inside. And he can't help himself either…."

And there you had it. Plain as the empty coffee cup and sandwich wrapper in front of me. Cal and Toly were funneling down two completely different paths towards the same, intertwined future. And I could see already that those paths were destined to cross and re-cross and split apart and intertwine together over and over again as time went by. It was the kind of thing you could just feel as soon as you saw them together.

"Okay," Creighton announced, pushing back from the table, "it's time to wrap this up and get airborne. If you need to visit the little boys' room, either do it now or be prepared to hold it all the way to New York City. I don't want any wet upholstery. And let's not forget about the bill…."

I reached out and picked it up off the table. "This is on me," I said, trying to make it sound like a couple take-out sandwiches, four bags of potato chips and four cups of coffee were a really big deal. But that's what happens when everybody—including yourself—knows you're a wee bit out of your league socially. The gent with the least winds up paying the bill and the rich guys he's buying for are gracious and magnanimous enough to let him do it. Still, it was damn nice of them to let me tag along since no question I really had to be back at our VW shop in Passaic the following morning.

You have visions of what it's going to be like and how genuinely good it's going to feel when you finally open up the door to your own house again after a long trip away. Even if your house is really just the bottom floor of a duplex with a war-painted battleaxe of a mother-in-law just a short flight upstairs (who generally acts like she can't stand the sight of you and who's furthermore reminding you constantly that her daughter could have done better, you don't have any social graces and the place could really use a little fix-up work that you never seem to get around to). But even so, it was nice to be back home where everything—including your Queen of the Harpies mother-in-law—is in the same familiar place and doing precisely what you expect it to do. Even irritating things can be comforting when they're familiar. Especially after an assault campaign of a race weekend that sure felt a lot longer than six days. For starters, Cal and me had traveled damn near straight-through from New York City to the Middle of Nowhere, Florida, in a Ferrari 121LM with no windshield on the passenger side—the wind blasting my head, the chill night air shivering through the rest of me and my left leg damn near on fire from the exhaust heat. Oh, and I got to watch *Invasion of the Body Snatchers* (starting in the middle, no less) all by my lonesome while Cal went through a graduate-level Applied Anatomy course with that smalltown carhop north of Jacksonville. Then we'd done the whole blessed 12 Hours of Sebring—Thursday practice through the checkered flag at 10pm Saturday night—and that was like a four-day commando raid all on its own. Even though our blessed racecar expired before it even made the first turn! And after that (and the party that inevitably followed!) I'd gotten up at the crack of dawn with a head like a baked mud pie and climbed into the shaky, bouncy, narrow and exceedingly scary back seat of Creighton Pendleton the Third's own personal Beechcraft Bonanza and flown all the way back to New York with some folks who made more money sitting down to take a good crap than I earned in two weeks of knuckle-busting. Plus any endurance racing adventure always feels a lot longer than it actually was in minutes, hours and days. But that's a lot of the magic, isn't it? Race weekends—and especially big race weekends like Sebring—always seem so much broader and grander and busier and more important and more colorful and, well, more *alive* than everyday life. But that's also what leaves you feeling like you've been dragged up a dirt road all the way from Passaic to Poughkeepsie tied to the back bumper of one of Butch Bohunk's old Fords after it's all over. And also like you've been away so damn long you can barely remember what your kids' faces look like or how your kitchen smells or the special way it feels to lay down next to your wife in bed at night. Or just the soft, simple pleasure of curling up in your favorite easy chair with a cold beer or a cup of hot Ovaltine to read the Sunday sports section.

Especially if the Yankees lost.

But of course those notions only last about as long as it takes for the key to click in the latch and the door to swing open on the actual reality of your happy home life, what with your sweet, loving wife screaming at the kids like the captain of a destroyer that's taken two hits to the powder magazine and appears ready to go down with all hands. And all simply because dear little Vincenzo has drawn a portrait of his beloved little sister Roberta—in purple India ink!—on your wife's best Easter-, Thanksgiving- and Christmas-only Irish lace tablecloth. And meanwhile little sister Roberta hasn't taken her afternoon nap and so now she's moody and cranky and only really interested in how far she can mash the remains of her strained beets into the face of her favorite Raggedy Ann doll. And naturally Julie's mother is standing there like a poised hatchet, letting her know in marvelous detail what a lousy job she's doing raising her kids and what a world-class crumb-bum she married in the first place.

It's not exactly what you pictured, you know?

But you get used to it. Or at least you do after a few hours' decompression, during which you kiss your loving wife hello while keeping her from actually breaking all of little Vincenzo's fingers, wipe most of the mashed beets off of Raggedy Ann's face and hug little Roberta to keep her from crying (although it doesn't really help, but you try) and then you give your mother-in-law a peck on the forehead that tastes like sour limestone and take little Vincenzo aside for a wee father-son talk that he almost more-or-less pretends to be listening to. Or at least until he suddenly blurts out of nowhere: "Where were you gone to, Daddy?"

"I was off at a big car race in Florida," you answer with a small blush of pride.

"Oh." And this is where he wipes a big glob of snot out of the end of his nose and looks at it like it might stand up and dance. "Grandma said you were off drinking and wasting time when you should have been fixing things up for us here at home. She called you a *stugatz.*" Then he looks up at you with those big, wide little boy eyes, wipes the glob of snot off on your sleeve and asks: "Daddy, what's a *stugatz?*"

But there's really no time to frame a proper answer on account of now you've got to run upstairs like a good little son-in-law to unclog the bathroom sink in Julie's mother's apartment. Which is most likely clogged because she insists on plucking those huge, hairy black Italian eyebrows of hers just so she can draw them on again with a damn grease pencil. No question Julie's mom would have herself a set of real Woolly Caterpillars for eyebrows if she ever let them grow out....

Eventually you get done with that and then comes dinner, but you're not really hungry after that long, bumpy plane ride on top of a fairly wicked hangover and getting a good, close look at the contents of Julie's mom's sink trap to top it all off. So you pitch in and help put the kids to bed by reading them the adventures of *Babar the Elephant* for the umpty-kazillionth time and then sweetly say good-night to your mother-in-law as a way of letting the old battleaxe know it's time for her to get the hell upstairs. But she doesn't take the hint and so she's still there like a vulture on a fence post when you get out of the bathroom 20 minutes later. But eventually she does go upstairs and then, finally, it's bedtime for you and your wonderful, loving wife. And you look at her fondly as she heads into the bathroom, noticing how—to you, anyway—she still looks like a movie star. Okay, so maybe it *is* Anna Magnani from *The Rose Tattoo,* but that's not the point. Before she closes the door, she stares right into your eyes and snarls: "Well, I suppose *you* had a good time this weekend!" Why, by the time you head off to work the following morning, it feels like you've never even been away....

I have to say things around the Sinclair had changed considerably since Old Man Finzio passed away and my mentor, financier, good friend and all-purpose Dutch Uncle Big Ed Baumstein and me went into retail Volkswagen business together. I mean, it's not like we had one of those big, gleaming, blonde-brick-and-plate-glass-window dealerships like the Plymouth, Ford, Chevy, Olds, Packard,

Chrysler, Cadillac, Studebaker, Mercury, Dodge, Hudson, DeSoto and even Nash dealers had for themselves over on the beltway. Those guys had it made. But we had our little three-car showroom (it was probably more like a two-car showroom, but VeeDubs run pretty small) and a small, clean shop out back to take care of them for our customers. On the other side of the lot we were still running *Alfredo's Foreign Car Service* ("Sorry, Alfredo's not in") out of the old Sinclair plus a little used car lot in front where Big Ed always kept a nice selection of polished-up-but-occasionally-suspect used MGs, Triumphs, Jags and Healeys (and even the occasional Allard, Porsche or Lancia) waiting to either fulfill the fondest dreams of some grinning new sportycar addict or go off like a time bomb in some unsuspecting sucker's wallet. Not that we didn't stand behind what we sold. Sometimes as far behind as possible, in fact. But many of those cars weren't exactly rock-solid reliable even brand-new from the factory, and even some of the nicest ones were only there because the previous owner had a serious rethink of his emotional attachment to the vehicle in question when presented with a repair estimate that ran roughly one-quarter to one-third the cost of the entire car.

Or triple his monthly mortgage, take your pick.

Luckily we didn't have to do too much of the dirty work thanks to our old pal Colin St. John and his partner-in-crime Barry Spline over at Westbridge Motor Car Company, Ltd., on the far side of the Hudson (who were still busily offering *"Thoroughbred Motorcars for Discriminating Drivers"* and getting top-dollar or better every time), since they had no problem handing out fanciful, plucked-from-the-stratosphere repair estimates whenever they figured they could get away with it. Which generally included 8am to 6pm Mondays through Fridays plus half-days on Saturday during the warmer months. As you can imagine, that drove a certain percentage of their customers over in our general direction. Just listen:

Customer (steaming and/or sputtering): *"The damn thing grinds something awful every time I try to put it into gear. Whenever I shift it, too. That English sonofabitch over at Westbridge said I need a complete transmission overhaul. And a clutch job, too. Said it'd take two weeks just to get the parts in and cost damn near a third of what I paid for the whole blasted car!"*

"Well," I allowed cautiously, "let's take a look." The guy was obviously well past angry and, if first appearances were anything to go on, not the pleasantest of human beings in the first place. Even under the best of circumstances. So I climbed in and gingerly probed the left-hand pedal, noting the floppy, nobody-at-home feel until it finally hit a weak little hint of spongy resistance way down at the bottom. Hell, all it probably needed was a good bleed or a rebuilt clutch master or slave cylinder. Or maybe a new hydraulic line. Worst case imaginable, it needed a pressure plate and/or a throwout bearing. But you'd generally put both in (plus a new disc while you were at it) if you had to go in there. I mean, there's no reason not to.

Now let me explain that the temptation to take an angry, abusive, impatient, know-nothing rube like that all the way to the cleaners can be very hard to resist. Why, I could tell him we'd take it apart for a looksee, replace the simple hydraulic crap I was pretty sure it needed, bleed it out real good, get the car back to him the next day (or maybe at the end of the week just for appearances sake), hand him a bill for half or a third what Barry Spline was threatening to charge over at Westbridge and laugh all the way to the bank. But I'm just not built that way. Most likely thanks to my mom, who could be scatterbrained as hell about a lot of things, but always thought about other people first and inevitably did the right thing without so much as thinking about it. Even if all it ever seemed to get her was a sweet little twinkle in her eye and a long-running marriage to one of the biggest jerks I ever met in my life. And I'm not saying that just because he's my old man, either. Ask anybody. But if you're raised a certain way you wind up stuck for life with this stupid, gee-whiz little Jiminy Cricket gene jumping around inside your system, raising his eyebrows and shaking his little green bumbershoot at you anytime you even think about pulling a fast one.

Fortunately for both of us, Big Ed had far fewer moral or ethical compunctions about restricting the natural ebb and flow of greed and commerce. Not that he was a cheat or anything. But he flat *loved* to wheel and deal. So although the rude guy with the presumptive "clutch and transmission job" got off with a rebuilt slave cylinder and a bill for less than 30 dollars (and became a loyal customer ever after, even though he had to drive—or, on occasion, have his car towed—all the way from midtown Manhattan to get it serviced), he did wind up selling Big Ed the car six months later after he put a little gouge in the oilpan crashing through one of Manhattan's justly-famous spring potholes and didn't happen to notice the oil pressure gauge reading "No Sale" until after he started hearing industrial-style clattering noises, smelled molten metal and wondered when somebody put a steel foundry in over on Sixth Avenue....

To tell the truth, it was the perfect kind of deal for us on the used sports car side. The legitimate retail repair bill to fix a seized engine was enough to make anybody's eyes bug out (or water, or both), and yet the car was pretty much worthless without some kind of running motor under the hood. Naturally Colin St. John and Barry Spline would have gone for both ears and the tail, lowballing the value or what was otherwise a pretty damn nice automobile (all the way down to tow-it-away junk, in fact) while simultaneously trying to maneuver the mark into a brand new car with a reassuring "full factory warranty" that didn't cover much of anything after the first 90 days. And then of course Barry would find some engine out of a junkyard and plug it in without much more than hosing it off and putting in a little fresh oil. And then they'd have that new Puerto Rican kid put on a wax job you could see your face in and offer it up for sale without any mention of the big question mark under the hood. Like I've said before, Colin St. John and Barry Spline knew all the tricks and angles. And they were making an awful lot of money for themselves over at Westbridge.

But we tried to do things the honest way. So we offered the guy a measurably fairer price for his crippled car (and even more if he wanted to trade it in on something we had in stock, although this particular one-time sportycar addict looked about ready to run, not walk, back to his local Ford dealer) and then actually rebuilt the damn engine so we knew what was living under the hood when we finally put it up for sale. Mind you, we were still making good money on both ends of the deal. Just not near as much as Westbridge. It took a lot more time, money and effort to do things the right way, but that's what we did. Usually….

The thing you had to understand and eventually accept was that there were going to be breakdowns and repairs and angry, disappointed customers to deal with over on the used sports car side. It went with the territory. Fortunately most of it was little stuff. But every once in awhile something very big would go very wrong. And sometimes not long after they'd taken delivery of their gleaming new/used sportscar. That's when you had to make the customer also understand—sometimes rather forcefully—that once they signed the papers and drove it off the lot, they *owned* the blessed car. Warts, leaks, fractures, blow-ups and all. Big Ed had to call in a few of his buddies with the fedoras and clanking overcoats once or twice to explain that to certain very angry customers in a few extreme cases. There's not much you can do with somebody who's convinced he got a raw deal and that you screwed him on purpose. Which is the really sad, unfortunate underside of the whole blessed thing.

Even worse is how the very nicest people seem to have the worst luck with the used cars you sell them. Especially pre-owned British sportscars, which were often a wee bit marginal right off the showroom floor and furthermore have the kind of eager, top-down, wind-in-your-face personality that tempts owners to thrash the living tar out of them. And some of those owners are precious shy on nuts-and-bolts car knowledge or mechanical sympathy. Here's an example: *"It just quit running, see? Just like that. Do you think it could be the battery?"*

"Hmm. What did it do right before it quit running?"

"Well, there was a little steam and this funny smell. But then it stopped."

"The funny smell stopped?"

"No. Just the steam. Come to think of it, the funny smell got worse. Funnier, too."

"Hmm. Did the temperature gauge go up?"

"Why yes it did! But then it went back down again—all the way to the bottom of the dial, in fact—and so I figured it was plenty cool enough to keep driving."

Well, that's what they do once the engine runs fresh out of coolant. And that's also how an unlucky, ill-informed, inattentive or insensitive used sportycar owner can turn a simple thrown fan belt, split radiator hose or weeping water pump into a blown head gasket. Or worse. And it can even happen just a week or two after they've taken delivery, too. Sure, you try to do something to make it right now and then. But, believe me, it hardly ever works out. I don't think anything I've ever done has gotten people as angry or disgusted with me as some of the stupid favors I've tried to do out of pure, dumb guilt. And that's when you find out they maybe weren't the nicest people after all….

It was totally different over on the Volkswagen side. The cars were simple as a window fan and basically all the same—day after day, month after month, year after year—and although we had certain things we knew to look out for, we could pretty much count on no surprises. At least after the first few major screwups, anyway. We knew you had to make sure they had enough oil and it was important to change it regularly, and you had to watch out for leaks at the valve cover gaskets and broken fan belts—when the little red generator light starts glowing on a VW Beetle, it's generally time to park it and call a tow truck. And I mean right now. They needed brakes and shocks and clutch jobs now and then (but it was a simple, four-bolt deal to drop a VW engine to get at it) and I'd always put our newest guys on muffler and heater cable replacements—especially on older cars—because it was a dirty, dusty, rusty sort of job and you could pretty much count on some bolt or nut or flap being frozen up solid. Fan belt and valve adjustments were a trifle critical but not really difficult once you got the hang of it, and most of our guys could rebuild one of those dinky, one-pot Solex carburetors blindfolded.

I guess the only serious, way-out-of-our-depth trouble we ever had was when I had to overhaul my first VW engine. Now the air-cooled VW motor is not like any other automobile engine you've ever seen (except for a Porsche, of course, but they're really the same thing) on account of it's an air-cooled flat four that sits way out at the ass end of the car and is encased in all this tinny, stamped sheet steel shrouding that can slit your knuckles clear down to the bone or slice your thumb right off if you're not careful what you're doing. Butch called them "The Guillotine Cars" because of it, and always kept a large bottle of iodine and a box of assorted-size Band-Aids behind the parts counter. Including the real big ones. And rolls of gauze and adhesive tape, too.

But VWs are pretty damn easy to work on outside of that, and so I didn't feel particularly awed when one got brought in on a hook (only turned around backwards with the ass end in the air) on account of the engine was seized up solid. That could happen if you ran 'em low on oil or lost the fan belt and just kept driving. So we dropped the motor like we had umpty-dozen times before and removed the clutch and flywheel and all the tin shrouding *(careful!)* and took off the fan and generator and carburetor and manifolds so that we were down to a bare-naked Volkswagen engine. And then I personally took off the valve covers and pulled the rocker arm assemblies from both sides and removed the pushrods and undid the head nuts so I could pull off the heads and the barrels—hey, this was *too* easy—and then I undid the case bolts and ran into the first minor brick wall trying to figure out how to get the blessed case halves apart. I mean without knocking a damn hole in either one. But then we found the wee little hidden bolt I'd overlooked and after that it was all gravy again except that the main and rod bearings were pretty much welded to the crankshaft.

So I took the crankshaft over to my machinist friend Roman Szysmanski and he ground it down and trued it up for me and I took a good look at the rods and pistons and such and ordered a set of .020" over bearings (we maybe could have got away with .010", but I always figure you want to get past where the heat got to) and when everything came back from the machine shop, I buttoned it all back together with new piston rings and a brand-new clutch and plugged it back into the car. Although I must say it took a bit of effort to turn the motor over on the stand in order to do the valve adjustment. Like I had to use a breaker bar with a length of pipe slipped over it, you know? But I just figured it was a little tight because I'd done such a keen, precise job of putting it together, you know? Why, I'd mic'd the bearings and journals as careful as you please and even double-checked everything with Plasti-Gage just to make sure I had all the clearances absolutely, positively right.

What more could you do?

Then I filled it up with oil, checked for leaks, eyeballed the fan belt tension one last time, climbed proudly inside and twisted the key.

Gn.

So I rotated the key back and tried again.

Gn.

"Aha, flat battery!" I thought. So I brought the jumper box over and hooked it up.

Gn.

Okay, maybe a duff starter (although, at least according to the customer, it sure seemed to work fine before the engine seized). Hmm.

"Maybe we should try push starting it?" Steve Kibble offered. So he and JR got behind and started pushing while I sat inside, twisted the key on and eased out the clutch. Which is precisely when the rear wheel locked up solid and both of them banged their knees into the decklid.

"Sure seems a little tight," JR observed from the shop floor.

"Maybe we should try pulling it with the tow truck?" Steve offered while massaging both knees.

So we tied a rope to the VW's front bumper and fastened the other end to the back of Old Man Finzio's old tow truck and headed out onto Pine Street. Again I twisted the key, eased out the clutch and watched the rope snap smartly in two right in front of me.

Obviously a defective rope was the way I had it figured.

So we tried a chain. And that worked a whole lot better. JR got the towtruck up to about 30 miles an hour and I popped the clutch and first there was a Godawful screech from the VW's rear tires followed by a heavy, leaden and laboring *thwah-thwah-thwah-thwah-thwah* sort of rotating sound from the engine compartment. But that only lasted a few seconds before the VW's front bumper yanked clear out of its mounts and went clattering off down the street behind the tow truck.

Yep, that was one tightly rebuilt engine, all right!

Turns out you have to check the cases real carefully on seized-up VW engines to make sure they didn't get ever-so-slightly twisted when the bearing surfaces went molten for an instant and then welded themselves solid a half-a-heartbeat later. If the cases were tweaked, you had to have your machinist true 'em flat and then align-bore the crank and cam bearing holes back to the right size and shape again. But of course I didn't know that. And, like every other hard lesson I ever learned in the automobile repair business, it was expensive, confusing, frustrating and time-consuming. Not to mention that it pissed the customer off no end. The real capper on the deal (once I got it all figured out and put back together properly) was how damn *obvious* and *logical* it was to do it the right way in the first place. But that's the way those things always go, isn't it?

Even so, VeeDubs were pretty damn simple once you knew their tricks, and that turned out to be one of those double-edged Sword of Damocles deals my sister Mary Frances' egghead friends over in Greenwich Village always talked about. On the one hand, their basic simplicity and continuity made VWs really easy to repair and service, and I'd have to say the parts were generally well thought out and engineered even if they weren't particularly elegant or inspiring. Not at all like the stuff you saw inside Jaguars or Ferraris. Plus it seemed like we were doing the same drab jobs over and over and over again. Almost like working on a damn assembly line, you know? No surprises, but no real challenges, either. While with the British sportscars over in the old Sinclair shop—and especially the hopped-up, stripped-down, tuned-to-the-teeth ones that got raced now and then—there was a lot more variety and mechanical ingenuity involved. And that could be very satisfying. But so could making money and meeting a payroll every Friday and seeing your wife and kids have the kinds of things you really wanted them to have and being looked at as a respected sort of gent and citizen whenever you waltzed into the bank to make a hefty cash deposit or showed up with the family at church on Sunday mornings. Of course that last item didn't really apply on the weekends you were off fooling around with racecars, on account of you had other, more interesting, alluring and exciting things to do with your Sunday mornings....

Chapter 13: A Fortune in Bugs and Beetles

Like I said, the VW business Big Ed and me started up at the Old Man's Sinclair was really turning into something by the late spring and early summer of 1956. Sure, it was just a sideline, onesy-twosey deal at first. We'd put one out front under the Sinclair sign and, sure as an Italian rocker panel is going to rust, some tax accountant or college professor-type would show up and walk around it a couple times and then he'd show up again a few days later and walk around it some more and peer in through the window and ask a few questions about gas mileage and cruising speed and how the heck any car could run without a radiator. And then maybe he'd show up Saturday morning with Mrs. Tax Accountant or College Professor-type and that's when Big Ed would come bustling out of the office with an ear-to-ear smile plastered across his face and ask them if they wanted to go for a test drive. And that's when he'd come hollering for me or Steve or JR or Doug or somebody to go along with them, because there was no way a guy Big Ed's size could weasel his way into the back seat of a VW Beetle. Or not without a few stout prybars and a tub of gear-lube, anyway. Besides, that burbling little 1200cc Volkswagen four didn't exactly need another 300-plus pounds to lug around. Not hardly.

I remember one time when we'd just started out, this serious-looking gent with an even more serious-looking wife asked Big Ed to go along on a test drive to "explain the features." He was one of those scrawny, frayed-tweed-sport-coat types with nervous, darty gray eyes under wild gray eyebrows and an even wilder mop of disorganized gray hair on top. As for his wife, I bet the closest she ever got to powdered rouge or a tube of lipstick was when she walked past the cosmetics case at a drug store. But they seemed seriously interested and wanted a test drive, and if there's one thing you learn in the retail automobile business, it's that you never know who's a Real Buyer and who's just yanking your chain until you get to the end of the deal. Which means a savvy car salesman treats everybody like a genuine prospect until he learns otherwise. No matter how strange, suspect, stupid, scary, angry, loud, rude, abrasive, foul-smelling, ill-mannered or generally unappealing they might seem. So Big Ed stretched out an even bigger smile, took a deep breath, opened the door, flopped the seatback forward, and did his best to get in. I swear, it was like watching a water buffalo trying to climb into a steamer trunk! But damn if he didn't do it, and damn if they didn't wind up taking the car as well. Although at the end of the test drive he gently insisted that they "go across the street for a cup of coffee" while he "ran the paperwork." Once they were gone, he hollered at the top of his lungs for Sylvester and me to slide the front seat off the end of its tracks so's he could get the hell back out again.

Which is why whenever someone needed a little test-drive schmoozing (or maybe looked a wee bit snaky or Not To Be Trusted—and you develop a sixth sense for that kind of thing in the retail automobile business), Big Ed had me or Steve or J.R. or even Doug go along "to answer any questions." It was absolutely vital to have somebody from the shop along on test drives seeing as how Big Ed kept the gas tanks in our "demo" VWs damn near empty on purpose. He had it figured almost perfect so the blessed things'd start sputtering and coughing and running out of gas somewheres about halfway between the Jersey Turnpike and our showroom on Pine Street. That's when you'd flash 'em your best car-salesman smile and tell 'em to *"just kick that little lever over on the floorboards!"* The one that flops the half-gallon reserve bucket over into the main tank, you know? Why, you should have seen the look on their faces! It was like you'd handed 'em a thousand-dollar bill! But of course that made sense since *everybody's* run out of gas a time or two. Or at least all the men have, anyway. And the women have most probably been sitting right there beside them, gnashing their teeth and muttering under their breath because now they're about to be *very* late for some stupid family thing at Aunt Nellie's house that neither of them really wanted to go to in the first place. But that's not really the point anymore, is it? And you can bet they *both* remember how very noisy and nasty (or, conversely, stone-cold, deathly silent) it got there by the roadside while they waited for the blessed towtruck to arrive….

No question Big Ed Baumstein understood a thing or two about selling automobiles. Understood it intuitively and instinctively, just like Colin St. John. You had to set things up. You had to watch the eyes. You had to know what would make them light up. And you also had to know what would dim them down, too. Which is why he always had one of the shop guys go out and fire up our VW demo and leave it idle for a bit every half hour or so in cold weather. If you've ever owned a VW Beetle, you don't have to ask why.

Thanks to hard work, a little luck, my darling Julie standing beside me like a rock when I needed it (and behind me with pitchfork when I needed that, too) not to mention a series of clever, stunningly simple, full-page black-and-white ads Volkswagen started running in all the big national magazines, things really started taking off for us at our dealership in Passaic. To the point where we had to build a separate VW shop and showroom on the property we bought behind the Sinclair and expanded them again barely two years later. Like I said, Big Ed turned out to be one heck of a crackerjack car salesman—he loved it, and that's always the key to doing well at any job—and I did my best to make sure all the cars he sold were delivered squeaky clean with a full tank of gas and in tip-top running condition. Not that such a thing was particularly hard to do with Volkswagen Beetles, since they were simple as a mud fence and genuinely well screwed together. I also made sure we took proper care of our customers whenever they came in to get their cars serviced. That's really important in the retail automobile business, even though a lot of dealerships don't get it and think the sales manager's closing office is the center of the whole blessed universe. But it was almost *too* easy. Unlike our chaotic, multi-make sportycar misadventures over at Old Man Finzio's Sinclair (where every seventh or eighth job turned into a damn Ph.D. Thesis on *Why the hell did they build it THAT way??!!),* all those happy, burbling little VeeDubs were essentially the same as all the other ones we'd already put out on the road. And, like I said, they were *simple*. Why, you could train a damn chimpanzee to do a clutch or brake job on a VW Beetle. And beat the heck out of the flat rate manual while you were at it.

Sure, we still did a bunch of sportycar stuff back at the old Sinclair, and Big Ed always liked to keep a few used Healeys or Triumphs or MGs or Jaguars (or sometimes even the odd AC, Arnolt Bristol or Morgan) lined up all gleaming and shiny on the used car lot we put in where the gas pumps used to be. He said they were good for business. Made people stop and look. And we made good money turning those cars over, too. Plus it pissed Colin St. John over at Westbridge off no end that we were poaching a few of his sportycar customers, and that made it all the sweeter for Big Ed and me. But the *real* money was coming more and more out of the Volkswagen business. We could move 'em out almost as fast as we could get 'em in, and even though the prices were low and the margins weren't exactly monstrous, we could get damn near advertised list on every deal and Big Ed was a master at loading 'em all up on the back end with sisal floormats and rubber mudguards and fancy fog lights and chrome-plated bumper overriders and upgraded radios and almost-genuine simulated gnu skin protective seat covers. Plus he was shrewd as hell when it came to throwing numbers on trade-ins, and so we most always made money on those, too. Meanwhile, back in my end in the shop, we did our best to do things right the first time and hardly ever had comebacks on service.

It was all gravy, you know?

To tell the truth, I don't think Big Ed really needed to work for a living by then. In spite of four previous wives and four continuing alimonies. He'd always made money in the scrap machinery business, and then he added a pile more off this not-so-silent partnership he did with a thieving band of shyster lawyers and unscrupulous land developers who wanted to turn the ragged shoreline property where one of his scrapyards once stood into a handsome, gracious, well-manicured spread of upscale, high-end luxury homes with gleaming modern bathrooms and spacious, high-ceilinged living rooms, dining rooms and bedrooms where you didn't dare lean too hard against the walls because your elbow might go right through the wallboard. But they all had three-car garages and breathtaking views of the ocean (it could *really* take your breath away on a hot August afternoon if an overnight storm had left an array of overripe cod, shad, haddock and bluefish carcasses rotting on the beach below!) and easily sold out before half the nails had been hammered through the 2x4s. Or 1½x3s, to be more accurate, since the contractors were getting one hell of a deal on off-spec lumber.

Big Ed had also pretty much retired from racing by then, and that likewise sealed up a major rupture in his cash flow. Oh, he still loved fast, flashy cars and bought new ones that caught his eye all the time. He bought himself one of those burly, brutal-looking new Chrysler C-300s in the early fall of 1955 after reading about how Carl Kiekhaefer's team of hemi-powered C-300s had been cleaning up on the AAA and NASCAR stock car circuits all summer with Buck Baker and the Flock Brothers and even our old roundy-round pal Sammy Speed behind the wheel. He got a hell of a deal on it because it was right towards the end of the model year, and even took the blazing Tango Red one right off the dealer's floor because the factory was already in model changeover and he happened to be in a mood to drive a new Chrysler C-300 home that particular day. Big Ed would spend thousands in fistfuls on hot new cars and took some staggering hits on the Instant Depreciation every new buyer enjoys the moment he drives off of the dealer's lot, but on the other hand, he'd fight the dealerships down to the last nickel and penny on the actual, delivered price every time. To tell the truth, I think Big Ed really enjoyed being on the other side of the table for a change, and he absolutely loved getting some wet-behind-the-ears new salesman—there's always a big turnover in car salesmen, in case you hadn't noticed—and put him (and, ultimately, his sales manager) right through the old wringer. Just for fun, you know? Big Ed knew how to dummy up or get angry or look betrayed or play dumb or give it the old poker face as the situation required, and he rarely (except on impulse, like with the Chrysler) waltzed into a dealership to buy a car without knowing pretty damn accurately what the dealer actually paid for it, what kind of readers, spiffs or factory incentives the dealer had coming for unloading the car or meeting monthly quotas, how much stock he had in inventory (which was an exact barometer of how much juice he was paying on the old floor plan at the bank) and how many similar cars were parked on lots and showroom floors within a 500-mile radius. And that was amazingly easy to do. All you had to do was spend a little phone time calling the various dealers (or having your secretary or office girl do it for you if you had one) and innocently ask: *"This is Mrs. Monongahela over in White Plains. I'm shopping for a birthday present for my husband, and our chauffeur said he wants one of those new C-things."*

"A C-300, m'am?"

"Yes. That's the one."

"Well, that's a fine choice, m'am. A fine choice indeed. Pure luxury and smooth as a baby's bottom, but with as much speed and horsepower as you could ever want."

"I'm sure it's very nice."

"Why, you bet it's nice! It's got Chrysler's famous FirePower V-8 with hemispherical combustion chambers and dual four-barrel carburetors! It's rated at THREE HUNDRED horsepower, Ma'am! Why, it's the fastest car in America..."

"I'm sure it is. But what colors do they come in? I don't want it to clash with the flowers around the driveway."

"Our C-300 comes in your choice of shimmering black, Platinum white or Tango Red. That Tango Red will poke your eyes right out."

"But what colors, interiors and equipment do you have in stock? I mean, right now. You see—oh, I'm embarrassed to say this—I sort of procrastinated on this and I really need to pick one of these silly things up this afternoon. His birthday is tomorrow, you see...."

At the other end of the phone line, the salesman is either twitching and frothing at the mouth or doing a Flamenco striptease dance on top of his desk—or both!—and it isn't two shakes before he's got the old stock book out of the sales manager's office and starts reading the inventory cards off to her like a damn bedtime story.

Like I said, it was simple....

And, unless it was one of Big Ed's impulse deals (which, to be honest, happened on a pretty regular basis), he always went shopping for cars on the very last day of the month. That's when a lot of car salesmen (not to mention sales managers and dealership principals) are staring at their balance sheets, sales records and commission figures with gaunt, desperate expressions on their faces and wondering what it feels like to live on beans for a month. Big Ed said the very best day to go shopping for a car was the last business day in February—hey, it's a short month anyway, the new cars aren't so new anymore, and the weather tends to keep folks inside—and so much the better if there's sleet and hail or a full-tilt blizzard going on outside. And you had to make sure and show up about five minutes before closing and then drag it out for hours until it's just you and the salesman and the sales manager in a little corner office off of a darkened showroom with just a pen, a thin stack of papers and two sets of car keys on the desk between you.

"It's better action than playing craps in Havana," Big Ed would chortle, punctuating with a deep drag off of his fat Cuban cigar and blowing out one of his signature, doughnut-shaped smoke rings.

Anyhow, Big Ed drove that C-300 for less than two months before he traded it in on the very first '56 Cadillac Eldorado Biarritz convertible in New Jersey—the one with the 305-horsepower, 365-cubic-inch engine with dual four-barrel carburetors—and added one of those snazzy new two-tone Studebaker Golden Hawks with that barge-hauler of a 352-cubic-inch Packard V-8 to his stable as soon as they hit the blessed showrooms. Although he had to keep them mostly at home or parked across the street behind the sandwich shop so our VW customers wouldn't see them. After all, we had to keep up appearances. And Big Ed still couldn't get enough of the latest new British and European sportscars. That went without saying. He bought himself a sweet, creamy-white XK140 drophead (with an automatic transmission…shhhhh!) to impress the latest and dewiest-by-far prospective Mrs. B, and he really enjoyed finally having a Jaguar he could drive all day long in city traffic (or at least until it overheated, anyway) without squawking the tires or lurching away from traffic lights.

But you never get over being a racer. Especially after you see the effect it has on other people. So big Ed kept his helmet and goggles and driving gloves plus a few random first-place trophies and wall plaques (none of which he actually won, but that was hardly the point) and all sorts of framed photos of himself in the Jag and even the Trashwagon on the walls of his so-called "sales office" just off our showroom floor. To be honest, it was more like a large nook or a small walk-in closet than a real office, but it allowed the illusion of privacy without really offering any and also gave Big Ed an unobstructed view of the showroom floor, the lot in front, and (if he leaned forward and craned his neck a little, anyway) one end of the row of used sportycars parked in front of the old Sinclair.

Anyhow, he had these racing pictures and plaques and trophies and stuff cluttered up all over the place, and if anybody asked him—and sometimes even if they didn't!—Big Ed was ready to explain in a heartbeat (and at length) where they were taken and how extraordinarily well he was running that particular day until whatever it was broke or blew up or caught fire or wound up parked upside-down in a ditch with the rest of the car. Truth is, I think Big Ed liked *talking* about being a racing driver more than actually doing it—you'd be surprised how many so-called "race drivers" are exactly the same way!—and, like the rest of them, he'd discovered that it was a lot more satisfying to be an accomplished, experienced and respected *retired* racing driver than an embarrassingly slow and ham-fisted active one.

A lot of that attitude was thanks to the fitful and horrendously expensive few races he finally got to run in the eternally-being-rebuilt-at-the-factory Ferrari coupe Javier Premal and I took over the edge of that cliff during the 1952 *La Carrera Panimericana* and that Carlo Sebastian finally delivered to him—"good as new," of course—some three-and-a-half years later! Big Ed's experiences with the Ferrari taught him that he could spend heaping bushels of money and go fast enough to scare himself silly and yet still not be fast enough to scare anybody else. Except for maybe a few corner workers.

Now some guys—Skippy Welcher comes instantly to mind—can find themselves in that sort of predicament and it just doesn't seem to faze them. Or, more likely, it doesn't even register on the old humiliation barometer. But Big Ed was sharper and smarter than that. Hey, he'd had his fling with it, and in the process he'd made a miraculous discovery. Just like Butch Bohunk and his beloved brotherhood of Marines, he learned that once you've been called a racing driver—even if a not particularly marvelous or magnificent sort of racing driver—you were *always* going to be a racing driver. At least as far as the guy across the bar, lunch counter or desk from you is concerned. Or maybe even the guy who stares back at you out of your shaving mirror every morning. And he's the one you've really got to impress, isn't he?

Not to mention that the highway accident in the Trashwagon while racing The Skipper's C-Type back to Siebken's bar after he finally beat the crazy little sonofabitch fair and square at Road America really shook Big Ed up inside. Not at the time, of course. But later. Like it always does. In the middle of the night, when all you can hear is the faint ticking of your alarm clock and the crickets chatting each other up outside and maybe even the sad, moaning echo of a freight train somewhere way off in the distance. That's when fear creeps up on little cat's feet and whispers quietly in your ear about what oh-so-easily might have happened….

Who needed it? Hell, Big Ed was selling the heck out of new Volkswagens and used sports cars and enjoying the living shit out of it. He might have been easy pickings on a racetrack, but Big Ed was smooth, sweet and deadly on a used car lot or showroom floor. And there I was, backing him up on the service side, running what was by then a six-bay shop with two lifts and a grease rack, too. And even though it was a lot of work, I was pretty damn happy about where I was and how my life was going. Including Julie and the kids and everything.

Sure, you piss and moan about your family and your pain-in-the-ass relatives all the time. Especially around a car shop, where grousing about your family is as much a part of the daily lunchtime chatter as discussing the Dodgers and the

Yankees, popular music, favored brands of beer, candy bars or cigarettes, undefeated heavyweight champ Rocky Marciano's retirement from the ring (and he was Italian, too, just in case you didn't know it) or the relative merits of the frontal grillework on the April versus the May pinup girls on the latest Rigid Tools calendar. But I had to admit (at least to myself, anyway) that I enjoyed my time with Julie and the kids between the screaming matches and the things I really didn't want to do and places I really didn't want to go and people I really didn't want to see and the endless marathon of Mandatory Family Gatherings I didn't really want to attend that are all part and parcel of The Great Domestication.

Because you get those other moments, too. You know, those soft, quiet, often totally unexpected surges of real warmth and comfort and caring. Like those little flashbulb-pop smiles from the kids that wash over you like rippling waves of parental pride and understanding. Makes you feel like you've really done something good and righteous and upstanding with your life, you know? Gives you the feeling that somehow, some way, and against all odds, you've turned into precisely the sort of decent, solid, upstanding citizen that neither you—or your father—ever thought you could be. And it all comes together in clear, sharp focus the day you finally sign the deal on your very first house. That's a day no young man will ever, ever forget….

To begin with, it happens in a bank, and you've been going to banks in tow behind your mom or dad ever since you were a smelly little toddler with a load in your pants. And you remember all your life what it was like peering up from down there at knee level, looking up at the tall, fluted marble columns and polished oak counters that were so high you could barely reach them—and on tiptoes at that!—and most especially leaning your head all the way back to stare up at those high, cathedral-like ceilings where even the tiniest whisper or heel click seemed to echo like the last note off a church organ. It made you feel as small as looking up into the sky on a clear, moonless summer night.

But of course that's the way the bankers and their architects and decorators have it figured before the first shovel of dirt comes out of the hole. Just like churches, court buildings, headstones, libraries, opera houses and mausoleums, banks need to look solid and solemn and weighty and permanent enough to be around until the far end of eternity. To tell the truth, it's a little intimidating. And that's exactly what those bankers and their architects and interior desecrators have in mind….

Naturally I had to bring the whole family along, Julie and little Vincent and even littler Roberta—he with a finger rammed up his nose like it grew there in the first place and she kind of dragging her heels and whimpering into her Raggedy Ann doll on general two-year-old principles—because somewhere it is carved in stone that the entire family has to witness an event as life-changing, mysterious and monumental as signing your life away to buy your very first house. As the husband, father and designated wedding, funeral & special-occasion-only Apparent Family Leader, you are naturally expected to understand what's going on. But that's impossible since your average mortgage transaction amounts to an avalanche of incomprehensible paperwork that everybody but you seems to understand perfectly. Or at least the guy on the other side of the desk seems to, anyway. And the bank officer does his best to make you feel like a complete idiot by smiling and chattering pleasantly (as he passes over even more serious-looking forms and papers for you to sign) and acting, in general, like both of you do this every day.

Bank Officer: *"And here's the mortgage note. Sign here, here and here on all five copies."*

You: *"Here, here and here?"*

Bank Officer: Nods.

You: *"All five copies?"*

Bank Officer: Nods again.

Sound of gold-and-tortoiseshell Schaefer pen scratching on bond paper.

Bank Officer: *"Here's the certificate of title. Sign here and here."*

You: *"Here and here?"*

Bank Officer: Nods.

Bank Officer: *"And this is the title insurance form. Sign here."*

You: *"All five copies?"*

Bank Officer: Smiles.

Bank Officer: *"And this is the other insurance form covering the house and property against...*(chuckles)*...well, it covers almost everything imaginable. Fire, flood, theft..."*

You: *"Somebody would steal a house?"* This is your idea of a joke.

Bank Officer allows a precise, one-eighth-inch upturn at the corners of his mouth so as not to appear rude. Hell, he could be handing you a damn death warrant for the Lindbergh baby and you'd sign it without even batting an eye.

But then comes that special moment when you've signed the last document and the bank officer looks at you, smiles, extends his hand, and congratulates you on your shrewd, wise, mature, fortunate and exceedingly astute purchase and now owing his bank more money than you've ever seen piled in one place in your life. And damn if you aren't *proud* of it! All of a sudden it's like you actually *belong* in a place like a bank. And you stride out into the sunshine like a blessed emperor surrounded by centurions. Even if one of those centurions still has a finger growing out of his nose and the smallest little centurion smells like she's badly in need of a change. Just like back when you were that same little kid with the load in your pants visiting a bank for the very first time....

Naturally it was Big Ed who debunked the banking business for me when we went in to do a loan to buy the property next door to Finzio's Sinclair and another a few months later to build our first VW showroom and yet a third time to expand the building and do a floor plan for our inventory when the business really started to grow. See, car dealerships don't actually *own* all those gleaming fenders, polished bits of chrome trim and eager pairs of headlamp lenses that hopefully stare out through the showroom window like the eyeballs of adorable beagle puppies.

Nope, most usually the banks own 'em. Lock, stock and barrel. The dealer's bank lays out the money to buy the cars from the manufacturer or regional distributor and then the dealer pays the "juice"—the interest—on that money until the car is sold. At which point the bank gets paid off and releases the title and the dealer keeps whatever's left as his profit. Or, if times are really tough, he simply pockets the money, puts the paperwork in the bottom drawer of his desk (right under a half-empty bottle of Rye is the usual spot), and keeps paying the "juice" to the bank until somebody gets wise and he receives an unexpected and thoroughly unpleasant visit from a group of unsmiling gentlemen in suits carrying badges and search warrants. Soon after which he may find himself relocated to a state-owned recreational housing facility with bars on the windows.

And don't think it doesn't happen!

But the point is that it's important for any car dealership to have a close and cozy relationship with a bank. And the bank gets it back in spades with the wholesale juice on the floor-planned cars and the even juicier (but riskier) retail juice on the loans the dealership's customers take out to buy the blessed cars. I first started to see how this all worked when Big Ed took me in to do that very first deal on that vacant property by the alley behind the Sinclair where the three-flat mysteriously burned down after the owner died and the place more or less deteriorated and it was all tied up with courts and lawyers on account of the heirs and relatives couldn't agree on anything. It dragged on for months and months, and it was beginning to look like nothing would ever get settled when the place suddenly went up one night like a gasoline-soaked bonfire (in fact, *exactly* like a gasoline-soaked bonfire!) and I have to admit that things got a lot easier for everybody after the place burned down. First off some city inspector (who, strangely enough, seemed to know Big Ed by name) came around and said that the remains of the building—it looked like one of those World War II newsreels of the aftermath at Dresden—had to be taken down and carted off and the hole it left behind would have to be filled in so none of the little neighborhood kids could fall in it and maybe break an arm or a leg. Or maybe get left there to simply starve to death in the case of that nasty little Phil McCracken kid from over on Elm Street who stole stuff from all the shop owners and broke windows every Halloween. But the real point was that tearing down and loading up and carting off all that burned lumber and scorched lath and plaster (not to mention filling in the resulting hole) meant that somebody-or-other among the heirs and relatives was going to have to write a check. And if they didn't take it down and cart it off and fill in the hole, there would be a fine as well. And of course that would mean writing another check.

It's amazing how quickly negotiations moved along after that!

But we were talking about the bank, weren't we?

I got to know that bank pretty well. After all, it wasn't just *our* new house, it was The Bank's new house, too. And it seemed like it was getting more and more like The Bank's new house every time Julie wanted to do something to "fix up" or "improve" it. But Big Ed would just laugh. "It ain't what'cha make, Buddy. It's what'cha can *borrow* that counts." And I must admit, it made me feel pretty special the way the guy at the bank knew my name—hell, he called me *"Mister* Palumbo!"—and always smiled and shook my hand and had the papers in order and ready for me to sign. Like it or not, I was turning into some kind of regular citizen.

Who'd have ever guessed?

But the screwy part is that it all seems to happen so damn *fast* once the fireworks of growing up are over and your life starts to settle down. I swear, it's like somebody snuck a few pounds of lead into your socks when you weren't looking. One day you're just some happy, snotnose kid running down the beach with a tin shovel and a sand pail in your hand—not a care in the world!—picking up seashells and picking your nose and poking dead fish with a stick What could be better? Next thing you know you're skipping stones and playing water games with your buddies, splashing around and hurling clumps of muck at each other and one day you even almost drown. Every kid almost drowns at least once in this life. You remember it, too—that cold rush of water flushing up your nostrils and the sudden, panicky realization that you are very likely *NOT* going to make it back to the surface. *"Is this IT?"* you ask, all terrified, angry, depressed and disgusted with yourself at the same time. That's usually your first real glimpse of what sits out there at the end of the road for all of us—princes, pricks, pie men, presidents, preachers, pickle packers and panhandlers alike—and it comes back and kind of haunts you sometimes when you're all alone in the middle of the night.

Even so, life goes on, and what seems no more than a sneeze and a heartbeat later, you're on that same sandy beach at night with a million kazillion stars overhead and this wonderfully special and beautiful girl (or maybe not so special or beautiful, but who the hell are you to know the difference?) beside you on your mom's old army blanket, and that smooth, warm, mysterious place where your bodies come together feels like the center of the whole blessed universe. It's as deep and dark as the sky is high, and it's almost like you're drowning again. Only this time it's soft and sweet and urgent and delicious, and you want it to go on forever….

But of course it doesn't.

Only you don't find that out until later. You never find *anything* out until later. That's the sneaky, fingers-crossed, behind-the-back, nothing-up-my-sleeves way life works. And you might as well get used to it, because next thing you know you're walking down that same exact beach a fat handful of years later. Only this time you're pushing a baby stroller and there's another snotnose little kid—a great kid, mind you, wouldn't trade him for the world—yanking on your sleeve and screaming bloody murder for another ice cream cone on account of the one you already bought him is splattered all over the boardwalk and somebody's monster black Labrador (which really ought to be on a leash—what the hell is the matter with people?) is inhaling it off the wood planking in one lick. And of course the look in that little kid's eyes leaves no doubt that he expects *you* to fix it. Which is one of the great, overriding misconceptions all children seem to be born with: that daddies can fix anything. I suppose the sooner you get that sort of notion out of a kid's head, the better off he or she is going to be. But, in spite of all logic, you find yourself doing exactly the opposite, reinforcing and re-reinforcing bullshit ideas like that the world makes sense and somebody-or-other is in charge and Santa Claus really does live up at the Noth Pole and flies around the world delivering toys out of his blessed sleigh every Christmas and that—most of all and no matter what happens—everything's going to turn out fine. Unlikely, incredible and illogical as it seems, parents generally find themselves doing everything in their power to make kids believe that kind of crap when they're little just so's they can smash it all to smithereens right in front of their faces a few years down the road. Helps them mature, right?

Don't ask me why that's the way things are—it just is.

And meanwhile you're growing up and taking on responsibilities and becoming more and more aware that the whole blessed world is whirling and gyrating around like an out-of-control merry-go-round spiraling off its axis—especially according to the newspaper headlines and those funeral-faced commentators on the six o'clock news—what with the Russians and us poised hair-trigger on the brink of Total Nuclear Annihilation all over the blessed globe and all those Negroes sitting in and causing riots down south and nothing on the damn radio except that new-fangled rock and roll and your sister Mary Frances' egghead friends over in Greenwich Village listening to "folk music" and reading poetry without any punctuation. I mean, I hate like anything to agree with my old man, but what the hell ever happened to Frank Sinatra and Rosemary Clooney, anyway?

But you've got other things on your mind.

You've still got that same, wonderful, special, beautiful girl walking along beside you (only she's put on a little weight…but then, so have you) smiling brilliantly when she isn't flashing you the hairy eyeball for stealing a glance at some pretty girl in a two-piece bathing suit, and all the while she's explaining in excruciating detail why you'd both be so much better off with aluminum siding like her girlfriend Gina Massucci's husband put on *their* house and why can't we have a clothes dryer instead of hanging out laundry like a bunch of damn hillbillies and, oh, we've got to go over to your folks' house for dinner Sunday because they want to see the kids—*VINCENT!! SHUT UP!! CAN'T YOU SEE MOMMY AND DADDY ARE TALKING???!!!*—and did you happen to see that exquisite dark maple dining room set in the front window of Finkelman's over on Pine Street?

It isn't a fart and heartbeat later that you've got that exquisite new dark maple dining room set along with a nice new dining room to put it in over at the nice new house you're not at all sure you can afford in what everybody says is a much nicer part of town. You know, the yellow one with pretty white shutters and one of those dangerous-looking mother-in-law apartments poised like a vulture's perch over the attached garage. And meanwhile it feels like the ground under your feet is turning into quicksand and you're sinking further and further and deeper and deeper with every step—until it's all you can do just to keep putting one blessed foot in front of the other. And the worst part of it is that you're the only one who even seems to notice.

Don't get me wrong. I love my wife and kids. I love our house that I always seem to be working on whenever I'm not down at the VW dealership organizing things and shuffling people and paperwork and watching our parts inventory so it doesn't go waltzing out the back door under one of our fine line mechanics' jackets so he can finish up some side job he's got stashed away in an alley someplace behind his brother-in-law's house. I also love working on the cars myself now and then whenever I get the chance. That's still—by far—the most satisfying part of the whole deal, because there's a beginning, a middle and an end to every job, a nice little buzz of satisfaction and accomplishment when you finish, and most of all it's something you get to do all by your lonesome. Solitude gets to be a pretty damn precious commodity when you've got a business to run every day and a wife and family to take care of every night when you finally get home.

But that's how things change. That's growing up. That's maturing. That's what has you reaching for aspirin and bicarbonate of soda instead of licorice whips and jawbreakers. The expression on the face of the guy in your shaving mirror pretty much sums it up: *The carefree times are over, Bub. Get used to it.* The days drag on and on and yet the years disappear like sulfur sizzling off a match head. Each one faster than the last. And pretty soon it starts to dawn on you that you're not really running your life anymore.

It's running *you!*

The irony of the whole deal is that the little kid you used to be is still bubbling around inside, jumping up-and-down all goggle-eyed and excited about the marvelous, thrilling and amazing things you still so desperately want to do in this life and impatient as hell for the next great adventure. Only you've pretty much stopped paying attention to that kid, on account of you've got an alarm you don't really need anymore that rings at 5 ayem every morning and a cup of coffee to drink while you read the paper and keep up on all the terrible news you're probably better off not knowing (I mean, you can't really *do* anything about it, can you?) and then you kiss the wife and kids, hop into the VW demo in the driveway and burble off to the dealership. When it's your damn business, you sure as hell better be the first one there. Or that's the way I look at it, anyway. And meanwhile the days are full and getting fuller and fuller until they all start running together and you wake up some mornings wondering where the hell all the years went. In fact, you start waking up like that *every* morning.

Not that I'm complaining or anything….

The other sad part was that I rarely got the chance to work on cars myself or sneak away on race weekends anymore, and I missed the hell out of that. But I was busy. At the shop I was spending most of my time explaining things they seldom seemed to understand to our marvelous service customers—some of whom could be just a wee bit unreasonable, can you believe it?—and meanwhile trying to keep the inevitable differences of opinion between our fine group of line mechanics and my old buddy Butch Bohunk behind the parts counter from breaking out into fist-fights. My Aunt Rosamarina had been hauling Butch over to his therapy sessions at the VA Hospital outpatient clinic a couple times every week—she had to just about drag him by the earlobes at first—and now he was getting around pretty damn good on this wheeled walker cart thing he'd built for himself out of a busted-up hand truck and a stolen grocery cart. He'd welded about a third of the wire metal basket on the front to hold the brake shoes and heater cables and clutch pressure plates and such that our mechanics needed for their jobs, plus a neat little clipboard for his paperwork and an empty can of *Motor Magic Instant Liquid Valve Adjuster* fastened on with two big hose clamps to hold his pens, pencils, bent-up pack of Pall Malls and the windproof, brushed stainless steel Zippo lighter with the famous eagle, anchor and globe crest on it that he'd never been without since his days as a hard hat diver in his beloved Marines. When he built it, Butch was careful to keep the thing narrow enough so's it'd squeeze down the tall, tight aisles between the shelves in our parts department, and he put the bigger, hand truck wheels on the front and casters from the grocery cart on the back so's it could turn on a dime and give you nine cents change. He also engineered this drop-down, rubber-tipped parking brake to keep it from rolling, a flip-up, locking pair of hand supports made out of the folding leg assemblies of some rented-but-never-returned party table plus a built-in step rail on the front so he could struggle all the way up to the top shelves all by himself if he really needed to. Butch hated asking anybody for help—or anything else, come to that—and he'd rather crawl on his belly through an oil fire than ask another human being for assistance. And that went at least double- or triple-strength after his accident.

Although he never said much of anything about it, you could tell that Butch was pretty damn proud of that cart. I mean, he figured it out and built it all by himself, you know? Even polished up the chrome plating on the wire basket, spray painted the rest of it a nice, shiny shade of black and put a little *"Semper Fi"* Marine decal on the front. And then one day Sylvester snuck a chrome bulb horn and some rubber handgrips (you know, the kind with the red-white-and-blue plastic streamers coming out of the ends, like you see on kids' tricycles?) on it while Butch was in the can. Butch really cussed the hell out of Sylvester for that one. In fact, he hurled a thoroughly rebuildable Solex carburetor core at him from clear across the shop floor. But he never took them off. In fact, it got to where he'd honk that bulb horn at the rookie mechanics now and then—like Bozo the clown, right?—any time they were being particularly vague or obtuse about what they needed to finish up a job. Oh, he was still a mean, ornery cuss by nature and, walker cart or no, he'd just as soon spit in your eye and take a swing at you if he didn't like your attitude or the tone of your voice. But that was just Butch, and I figured I sort of owed him something for all the stuff he'd taught me over the years. Even if he reciprocated by resenting it like hell and taking it out on our mechanics and parts customers. Particularly whoever the newest and/or stupidest mechanic in the shop might be at any given time.

Honk! Honk!

And then of course I'd have to schedule a little talk with Butch (or at least with his shoulder, since he'd generally turn the other way so it was like addressing a closed door or maybe the back end of an ox) and explain as how this was a business and we all depended on it for our livelihoods and so we were really all in this thing together and needed to find ways to cooperate and get along with each other.

Really we did....

Honk!

As far as race weekends were concerned, I just didn't have the time. There was always stuff to finish up at the shop on Saturday (we were supposedly only open until noon, but I can't tell you how many times I was still there come dinner time) and there was almost always family shit to do with the kids on Sunday. Plus Julie was a real stickler about going to church and getting communion. It was strange, since I didn't ever remember her being particularly concerned about it before we got married. In fact, I don't think it ever came up at all. But all that changes once you've got kids to save from the raging fires of eternal damnation (even if you're not entirely convinced such a thing actually exists) not to mention a "family unit" and "position in the community" to worry over and protect. That "position in the community" thing is precisely what gets a lot of successful, hardworking husbands into church with their wives and families on Sunday mornings when they'd really rather be off to a race someplace or watching a good ball game or even just back home in bed. And it's also how those blessed (or so they seem to think) church fund-raisers come at you from all angles whenever they need a new organ, basketball court, stained glass window, set of hymnals, fresh padding on the flop-out kneeling rails in the pews or a replacement gold spike for Jesus' feet on the big sculptured crucifix out front. The one everybody and his brother knew that smartass little punk Phil McCracken stole on Halloween.

I must admit it chafed at me that I wasn't heading off to the races with Team Passaic every other weekend, but it couldn't be helped. Besides, the safety vultures had shut down the real road races I loved so much at Bridgehampton and Watkins Glen—to be honest, crowd control had never been much of a priority or success at any of those races—and so the SCMA was running most of its events on flat, featureless airport tracks, narrow private driveways for little cars only like Brynfan Tyddyn and odd, claustrophobic, pretty much makeshift circuits like the "extended oval" up at Thompson Speedway. Sure, I knew there was talk about some local farmer building a small but very real road racing circuit up around a place nobody ever heard of called Lime Rock in the far northwestern corner of Connecticut, plus

Cam Argetsinger and a bunch of the other people who'd created and sustained the original, open-road street races at Watkins Glen were deep into negotiations on building a brand-new, purpose-built racetrack on a big stretch of land just up the hill from town. But there was a lot of politics and logistics involved in both of those deals, and neither one of them was ready yet.

Meanwhile my goggle-eyed undertaker of a brother-in-law Carson Flegley—who loved sportscar racing with a passion but couldn't drive a nail through a slab of shit from behind the wheel—had gone out and bought himself a brand-new Austin-Healey 100-M. It was black, of course, but this time over red since most of them were coming in two-tone, and I guess it was a pretty good upgrade from his original Healey Hundred what with a thinner steel head gasket that upped the compression ratio to 8.1-to-1, bigger 1¾" S.U. carburetors and a hotter camshaft with stronger valve springs, a re-curved distributor with more advance, and the better, stronger, four-speed-with-overdrive gearbox and the upgraded rear end that came with all the second-generation "BN2" Healey Hundreds. Plus it had a nifty-looking "cold air box" under the hood to feed cool, fresh air to those bigger S.U. carbs and two lines of snappy looking louvers down the hood to let the hot air out plus a leather bonnet strap to keep that hood down at high speed just in case all the latch and hinge mechanisms failed in unison. Or rusted through a few years down the road. But it sure looked neat, you know? And of course Carson dressed it up with a pair of "Speed-lite 200,000 candlepower" driving lights that he bought mail order for $11.95 each from one of those small ads in the back of *Car & Track* magazine. And then he damn near burned up all the wiring trying to install them himself. Not that it was entirely his fault, seeing as how he really wasn't much of a mechanic (hint: beware of anything that comes with instructions that promise: *"installs in minutes with simple hand tools!")* not to mention that they were really just marked-up war surplus aircraft landing lights, which, if you think about it, are only intended to be on for maybe five or ten minutes every couple hours and are furthermore wired in to an electrical system with enough designed-in capacity to handle them. In an ordinary, road-going sportscar, they pulled so damn many amps that you could almost hear the suction at the generator terminals. At least until the fuse blew, anyway. Which is probably what tempted Carson—out of sheer, rookie mechanic frustration—to try wiring them direct off the battery terminals and bypassing the fuse box entirely. I mean, what good was a blessed fuse if all it did was blow, right? The only good news was that he ran separate wires instead of going through the loom, so all he did was make a bad smell, scorch a few things, burn his fingertips and permanently weld several strands of copper to the backside of his dashboard.

I tried to go a little easy ribbing him about it since he was my pal and brother-in-law and everything, and also because you could see how bad he felt about it. "It's an altitude thing," I explained to him through an absolutely straight face. "You tried to put aircraft landing lights on a sports car without an Altitude Compensator."

"An 'Altitude Compensator?'"

"Sure. It's one of the trade secrets." I held up a 30-amp fuse in a spring-loaded, in-line casing. The kind you can buy right off the stand-up card on the counter of any auto parts store in America. "Only real, professional mechanics know about these babies," I told him. "This is real insider stuff…."

And sure enough it fixed the fuse blowing problem once I got it all safely wired in and put a neat little flip switch for those "200,000 candlepower" driving lights under the dash. Only problem now was that the filaments in the bulbs would burn out pretty quickly if you kept them on too long. But they were never really designed for extended-use operation in the first place, were they? Even so, they were impressive as hell when they were working. Like a damn flashbulb that doesn't shut off, you know? Why, Carson said they'd freeze a deer like a damn stone statue. Right in the middle of the road, most usually. And he was proud as heck of the way all the dash lights dimmed and the idle dropped a few hundred rpm whenever he flipped them on to show them off to friends in the lot behind the VFW hall where our local sportscar club had its monthly meetings.

Our other Team Passaic regular Buster Jones had moved what he thought was up from his XK120 to a much-raced, often pounded-out and repainted and thoroughly clapped-out Jaguar C-Type that wasn't really competitive anymore even in the best of hands. Sure, that car brought in an awful lot of money for Julie and me, seeing as how it was always needing a major this or a rebuilt that or thoroughly overhauled whatsis in order to stay on its wobbly last legs for Buster for one more race weekend. And I can't say as I had a lot of sympathy for him, since I'd advised him against buying the damn thing in the first place. Hell, it'd belonged to Skippy Welcher at one point, and unbelievably went downhill even from there. But that's the way it always happens:

A world-beater car launches through its glory years on the bigtime international scene, and naturally a bunch of rich guys buy copies thinking some of the old Hero Driver magic will rub off on their backsides right through the seat cushions. And sometimes—for a very brief period, while the car still really has the goods on everything else—it may just do the trick. But then newer, faster cars come along from the same or other manufacturers and the rich guys go chase after them like they're nymphomaniac Hollywood starlets and meanwhile the old nail generally gets sold off or traded in and inevitably winds up with some poor drool with a lot less money but maybe even more desperate dreams of glory. Naturally it all comes to a clattering halt when the guy breaks something he can't afford to fix—hell, if he's honest about it, he can't afford to race that car in the first place!—and then it gets sold off "as is" to some wide-eyed, home-garage wrench-spinner who thinks he's lucked into the greatest "fixer-upper" opportunity in recorded human history. Or, worse yet, to some back-alley, acetylene-torch engineer who thinks he's got the inside scoop on how to make it *"better than ever."* That last one is pure poison, believe me. You should never put good money down on some poor car that everybody and his brother have been patching together, messing with, modifying, "updating" and "improving." No matter how good it looks.

And I must admit that particular C-Type looked really *good* thanks to its freshly pounded-out and puttied-up bodywork and a shimmering coat of light silvery-blue paint that wasn't hardly dry yet and still had a few fly legs and moth eyeballs stuck to the finish. Plus you gotta be doubly careful anytime the guy trying to sell you that C-Type (and take your old XK120 with the loud valves, leaking radiator core and wobbly left-front wheel in trade) is none other than our old buddy Colin St. John over at Westbridge Motor Car Company, Ltd., who was still very much in the business of providing *"Thoroughbred Motorcars for Discriminating Drivers"* at every opportunity. Or at least so long as those "discriminating drivers" had the cash for a down payment and the credit leverage to get themselves done at the bank, anyway.

"She's in tip-top shape," Colin assured Buster through an airy cloud of Cavendish. *"Freshly rebuilt by the factory lads back in Coventry. Every single component."* He paused to watch Buster's eyes. That's where you could see it building. The dreams of glory. The flutter of checkered flags. The thrill of victory and warm, wet kisses from bosomy trophy girls. It was Car Lust all over again. Plain and simple. In fact, it was almost laughable how people couldn't help showing it. At least if you knew what to look for. And Colin St. John surely knew what to look for. Like a cobra, he'd silently, stealthily slink and slither around his prey, watching their eyes, listening for the faint, telltale hitch in their breathing, waiting for the precise right moment to strike….

"Tell you what I'm willing to do, Sport..."

It's too bad I wasn't with Buster that day, you know?

Not that it would have made much difference. Once somebody's got that look in their eyes, it's usually too late to save them.

Even so, that car made Julie and me an awful lot of money at our "Alfredo's Sports Car Shop" over at the old Sinclair. But it took a lot of time, too. And that's what was slowly but surely starting to dawn on me about the racing business: no matter how much you charged, it was damn near impossible to cover the time, effort and hassles it took to do the blessed work. Like chasing parts. Sometimes all the way to Coventry, England. Or making umpty-dozen trips to the machine shop so that this little doohicky over here mated up properly and leak-free with that little doohicky over there. And finished in time for you to stay up all night (and maybe the next night?) to get the damn thing installed. Just so's you could load up enough stuff to supply the entire blessed Normandy Invasion at the crack of dawn the next morning and head off to the damn racetrack. Where you then had to unload everything and set things up—the overhead awning and the army surplus field generator and the "portable" air compressor that weighed as much as a damn Healey six complete with manifolds, carburetors, generator and starter motor. Not to mention the lawn chairs and workbench and tool boxes and spare tires and the table for the sandwiches and the ice chests for the beer and cold drinks and...well, there's just no end to it. After which you wind up running your butt ragged all weekend long trying to keep the damn cars running and fixing whatever busted, melted, fractured, broke or caught fire while simultaneously offering advice, excuses, sweet talk, encouragement or commiseration as required to whichever of your supposed "star drivers" seemed to need it. And then, after it's finally all over and all the races have been run and won—by your guys or, more likely, somebody else—and all the problems have been conquered and dragons have been slain (or not) you have to run the whole entire process again backwards: loading and packing and throwing stuff wherever it will fit and then driving back home in Sunday evening, back-to-the-city traffic with a pounding headache, every bone and muscle aching and your eyelids so damn heavy they're ready to ooze right down your cheeks….

Oh, I didn't mind it so much back when I was young and single and on the loose. In fact it was—by an enormous margin—the most thrilling and exciting thing I'd ever done in my life! But back then I didn't know much of anything (which always helps) not to mention I was mostly just running Big Ed 's cars and trying to put a little something together on the side for my rich but perpetually broke hotshoe pal Cal Carrington. Sure, I knew Big Ed couldn't find his ass with both hands when it came to driving racecars, but he kind of knew that, too—even if he never said as much out loud—and all he ever really wanted out of his race weekends was to have one hell of a great time both on and off the track and maybe beat that crazy little asshole Skippy Welcher to the finish line at least once in his life. Both of which were pretty damn admirable aspirations as far as I was concerned.

And then there was Cal. Sure, he didn't give two shits about anybody else—from Jesus Christ Himself right down to that grizzled old colored guy with the shaky hands and the big lump of a tumor on his forehead who shined shoes for a living in Grand Central Station—but you couldn't help liking him anyway. Or at least I couldn't. Cal had that sly, cocky, dangerous cobra smile, a just-between-you-and-me wink, leading-man good looks, a thoroughly disgusting case of natural physical grace, solid brass balls, a wicked sense of humor, and could he ever drive a damn racing car! It was different when you had somebody like Cal Carrington behind the wheel. Somebody who could really get the job done, even when the chips were down. It made you eager to get up in the morning. Even at three ayem. Or stay up all night long twisting wrenches and spinning screwdrivers if you had to.

But things change in life. Time passes. And guys like Cal move on. I suppose that's what they're meant to do. And when they go, a lot of the eagerness and enthusiasm gets sucked right along in their slipstream. Believe me, the last thing you want in the world is to be left running some kind of weekend mechanical nursery school for spoiled problem children from 0-Dark-Thirty every morning to Half-Past-Bedtime every night, trying like hell to keep the toys running and playground equipment in shape and moreover preventing the idiot toddlers who don't know any better (that would be your fine customers) from breaking their cars in half and hurting themselves. And then, come Monday morning after damn near every race weekend, it felt like you'd been run over by an entire column of General Patton's pet Sherman tanks.

And your *real* blessed workweek was just beginning….

Not to mention that racecars had a habit of sitting in the shop for months on end—you didn't dare leave 'em outside—taking up space you so desperately needed for all those meat-and-potatoes brake jobs and valve adjustments and carburetor rebuilds and clutch-and-synchro replacements for all our fine sportycar customers plus taking care of all the new Volkswagens Big Ed was putting out on the street. And meanwhile the racecars just *sat,* dog-in-the-manger style, waiting for a rebuilt this or a remanufactured that or some special-order framistat gasket or kanooten valve seal that even the blessed factory in England seemed to be out of.

Who needed it?

Well, I suppose I did. Needed it pretty badly, if you really want the truth of it. And that's why I did my best to take care of my old Team Passaic regulars and kept looking after their cars for them—even though I was stretched so damn thin I looked just about transparent. But I'd gotten past the stage of letting it run—or maybe that should be ruin?—my life for me. So on race weekends I generally sent JR or Steve (plus maybe Doug or even Tater as a tire, sparkplug and oil-changer and all-purpose gofer) along with whichever of our Team Passaic guys were planning to go racing. And that seemed to work out fairly well. Oh, sure, I'd make a few of the races myself. But I'd generally have to drive up after closing up the shop and the dealership on Saturday afternoon and so I'd only really be there for the races on Sunday. Or in other words too late to do anything except shake my head, offer commiseration and make a list of what parts we'd have to order and what we'd have to do to the cars to make them race-ready again once we got back home. To tell the truth, things had really changed for me since Cal was gone. You'll happily stay up as many nights as it takes and then tow straight-through from here to hell-and-gone when you know the guy with the helmet and goggles is going to run at the front. But it's hard to get yourself all torqued up when your drivers are mostly duffers, fumblers, tryers, klutzes, whiners and wannabes. Nothing against Buster or my brother-in-law Carson, of course, but it just wasn't the same….

Besides, I was too damn busy to even think about it most of the time. But that's what happens when you've got your own business and it starts to take off and all of a sudden everything in your life gets five or six times as big and ten or twenty times more complicated. Every day you find yourself doing less and less of the actual, hands-on *work* and more and more of playing manager, hand-holder, motivator, compromise broker, prick boss and father confessor to whoever seems to need or deserve it at the time. It never ends. And then you drag yourself home to Julie and the kids and the new house and her mother with the bird-of-prey glare and grease pencil eyebrows and the rest of your extended family (who are usually there on the phone even when they aren't there in person) and that never seems to end, either. Mind you, I still loved the quiet, romantic moments Julie and me got to share at least once every six or seven weeks when the sun, moon and stars came into perfect alignment and neither of us were furious at one another and the blessed phone wasn't ringing off the damn hook and none of the kids were sick or crying or couldn't sleep because they were hungry or thirsty or had to pee or were having nightmares about ghosts and goblins and boogeymen and Julie's mom was off playing Bingo at St. Bonaducci's so we knew she wasn't upstairs with her ear glued to the damn carpeting. Truth is, with all of that going on, I was justifiably proud of the fact that neither Julie or me had ever hit one another over the head with a cast iron frypan or plunged a carving knife deep into one another's ribcage in spite of the occasional, near-irresistible urge to do exactly that.

We had our good times, though. Like the Friday night a few weeks after Sebring when I dressed up in a brand-new Brooks Brothers suit that actually fit real nice and a pair of shiny new Florsheim wingtips, had my folks watch the kids and took Julie to see *My Fair Lady* less than a month after it opened on Broadway. Didn't even care that the tickets Big Ed arranged through one of his Manhattan "connections" cost more than an entire VW clutch job. After all, that night on the town and those king's-ransom seats for *My Fair Lady* were all part of the Understood Reciprocity Agreement for Julie letting me sneak off to Sebring with Cal, and you've got to honor those kind of commitments with a minimum of grousing and grumbling as part and parcel of the Greater Overall Implied and Understood Marriage Contract. At least if you want any peace in this life before they close the casket lid and start shoveling dirt over you, anyway….

To tell the truth, I'd never cared all that much about Broadway musicals, but *My Fair Lady* turned out to be pretty damn good entertainment. The music was catchy, the story was interesting, the sets and costumes and staging were really dazzling and I actually found it easy to stay awake through the whole blessed thing. Even during the slow numbers and mushy parts. But a lot of that was on account of the subject matter, since I could really see a lot of similarities between my own experiences among the hoity-toity east coast sportscar crowd and how that Liza Doolittle felt surrounded by all those snooty English aristocrat types. I mean, she was really just a gutsy little guttersnipe of a Covent Garden flower girl underneath all the tacked-on frills and finery. And here I was: a blue-collar grease monkey from Passaic, New Jersey, all dressed up in shiny new Florsheim wingtips and a brand-new Brooks Brothers suit that wasn't shiny anywhere—not even on the knees or butt cheeks!—sitting eighth-row center next to the lovely, beautifully dressed and still very nicely stacked Mrs. Julie Finzio Palumbo at the hottest damn Broadway show in decades! Can you believe it? Hell, people were offering their children up to the white slave trade just to get tickets for that show! And again just like that Miss Eliza Doolittle, I spent the entire second act pondering over what had happened to me and trying to somehow make myself believe I actually belonged there….

After the show, we went over to no less than the Rainbow Room of the Waldorf Astoria Hotel (you know, where that famous Guy Lombardo guy and his equally famous orchestra play lilting dance music and *"Old Lang's Sign"* right at the stroke of midnight every New Year's Eve?) thanks to reservations Big Ed had personally made for us and the way he insisted that we really had to go. It seems Big Ed had a lot of pull at the Waldorf Astoria thanks to a long-running dalliance with a prospective but never quite actual (or ex-) Mrs. Big Ed who worked as a counter girl at a highly upscale tobacconist shop just down the street where Big Ed bought a lot of his fanciest cigars. Which, by the way, seemed to smell more and more like burning cow pies the more he paid for them. But the point is that both he and the exceedingly ample tobacco shop girl liked the way they did things at the Waldorf. Plus it was convenient, and that counted for a lot when a certain bright-eyed, scrumptious and jiggly young lady might or might not be supplementing her regular tobacconist counter income with a little evening, afternoon or even lunchtime moonlighting at a sideline historically performed in darkened alleys or rented hotel rooms. In any case, Big Ed spent a lot of time at the Waldorf and got a reputation as a *very* healthy tipper, and that sort of thing—more than anything else—gets you first-class service on a first name basis anywhere in Manhattan.

The Rainbow Room was just like something out of *My Fair Lady,* what with rich, silvery draperies, thick carpeting, countless svelte, beautiful, elegantly dressed young women sitting at tables with not nearly so svelte or beautiful but also elegantly dressed older men (many of whom were their fathers, uncles or even grandfathers, of course), chattering pleasantly over tablecloths that looked like they were spun out of pure, molten platinum. Our waiter introduced himself as Henri (pronounced *"On-Ree")* in a thick French accent, and he had slicked-back hair, a pencil-thin mustache and both looked and talked like some suave, sophisticated continental movie star. Plus he just seemed to *gliiiide* his way around the dining room—like he was riding on a pair of silent, invisible roller skates. Henri smiled grandly and called us *"Madame and Monsieur Palumbo"* as soon as we sat down. Like he'd been taking the most excellent close personal care of us for years, you know?

Like I said, Big Ed had a lot of suck at the Waldorf Astoria.

To be honest, I don't think Julie and me had ever sat down to dinner in a place like The Rainbow Room before. Why, I damn near swooned when I saw the prices on the menu—all of which were printed in small, exquisite, wedding-invitation style script on equally exquisite spun platinum cardboard that matched the tablecloths and napkins perfectly. Not to mention that those prices were oh-so-graciously rounded up to the nearest whole dollar—*dealing with pocket change is such a bore, don't you think?* Why, it was like eating money! And I'm talking *large* bills here, not your ordinary, wallet-issue Washingtons and Lincolns. But there's no escape once you find yourself sitting down in an elegant place like The Rainbow Room with a suave, sophisticated and debonair waiter like Henri at your elbow and a spun platinum menu where everything is rounded up to the nearest whole dollar staring you right smack in the face. So I closed my eyes, took a deep breath and told Julie to order whatever the heck she wanted.

"But how much is everything?" she asked. I couldn't believe it. Hell, I had a hard time just getting my eyes to move up from the prices to the descriptions of the blessed entrees. And that's about when it dawned on me that, while *Monsieur's* menu had the prices listed there in small, neat and thoroughly terrifying little numbers, *Madame's* menu most certainly did not.

"Would Madame care to start with a shrimp cocktail?" Henri asked with a practiced flourish. "They were flown in fresh from the Caribbean this very afternoon."

"Looks like they flew first class," I muttered, staring at the price on the menu.

Henri chuckled politely. Like he'd never heard anything so clever, witty or charming in months, you know? And suddenly I began to understand why rich people are willing to spend so damn much money for a blessed meal. It's the way they fluff you up and make you feel about yourself. Even if you're a complete jerk or a total heel in everyday life. Not to mention that the portions are monstrous and everything tastes like it was cooked in God's own kitchen. Which incidentally helped explain why so many rich people tend to be fat as hippopotamuses.

Anyhow, I ordered myself a big, thick, juicy slab of prime rib that surely came from a pampered, highly contented sort of cow who slept on a bed of flower petals and never walked any further than the nearest feeding trough throughout its entire life. Meanwhile Julie ordered herself a whole Maine lobster that was so damn big its claws hung clear over the sides of the serving platter. And of course there were appetizers and soups and salads and side dishes and even a little tiny scoop of sherbet (Henri called it *"sore bay")* to *"cleanse Madame and Monsieur's palate"* right in the middle of everything. Needless to say, when our boy Henri brought the dessert cart around—he needed two assistant waiters just to roll the blessed thing—we were both too damn full to force down another bite.

But of course that was before we saw the Yule Log-sized cannoli or the half-pound wedge of creamy-smooth strawberry cheesecake with fat, fresh strawberries and a glistening red syrupy glaze on top or the brick-sized double chocolate brownie crushed damn near flat in the middle thanks to a virtual Mt. Everest of vanilla ice cream or the 10-inch diameter cherry-maple tart topped off with an entire pint of fresh whipped cream and a bright red maraschino cherry or the enormous, golden yellow Napoleon slice with paper-thin layers of pastry, elegant squiggles of chocolate brown and silver-frost icing on top and thick vanilla filling oozing out between the layers. Or howsabout the matching, half-gallon-sized crystal goblets filled to overflowing with your choice of butterscotch pudding, hot fudge sundae, lemon-orange parfait or chocolate mousse.

It was pretty hard to resist.

So we didn't.

But the real surprise arrived when the check came around. Or failed to come around, to be more precise. Henri brought over a gleaming silver platter with two petit, long-stemmed crystal cordial glasses filled with fine, smooth, caramel-colored brandy and a perfectly folded, spun platinum napkin in between. But when I opened up that napkin and looked inside, instead of the expected bill for more than I used to make in a month, there was nothing but a key. A room key, in fact. For room number 1401 at the very same Waldorf Astoria Hotel.

I looked up at Henri like I didn't get it. And I didn't.

"Compliments of Mr. Baumstein," Henri smiled with a suave, sophisticated wink. "Enjoy the rest of your evening here at the Waldorf." And then he glided gently away on those silent, invisible roller skates.

Well, it sure was nice of Big Ed. And what an experience for Julie and me to spend a night at the famous, fancy and elegant Waldorf Astoria in downtown Manhattan, wrapped up in cool satin sheets and backed up by a half-dozen plump, down-filled pillows, watching a genuine 27-inch color console television set with its own Invisible Death Ray remote control plus a 14th-story view of the busy, bustling nighttime streets of New York City right outside our window. But it felt a little strange to be away from home, you know? Away from our own familiar bed and our kids in the next room and even Julie's mom with her damn ear glued to the floor carpeting upstairs. Plus we were both too stuffed to do much more than belch, groan, sip a little bicarbonate of soda and watch TV. We finally managed to drift off after the last show turned into a test pattern, but neither of us slept particularly well. Or at least not until it was already getting light outside. Then we fell into a deep, near-comatose sleep all wrapped up into each other like a couple very friendly dead people. But that only lasted until we heard a soft, gentle knock on the door just a few hours later.

"'alo?" a young woman's voice said through the door in a pleasant French accent. *"Maid service?"*

I should have put up the damn Do Not Disturb sign.

"Not now," I groaned back at the door. *"Later."*

"Oui, Monsieur," she answered, and padded softly away.

I started wondering if the Waldorf Astoria ever hired anybody who spoke regular American English, you know? Naturally both of us were awake after that, but we didn't feel much like getting up. It was nice just lying there between those cool satin sheets together, still a little sleepy-groggy and nuzzling comfortably into each other and...well, it's really none of your business what happened after that, is it?

To tell the truth, it felt wonderful, mysterious, naughty, strange and even a little bit unreal to find ourselves there all by our lonesome in this elegant room at the Waldorf Astoria in downtown Manhattan, wrapped in satin sheets and propped up against plump down pillows, far away from the kids and Julie's mother and the damn phone line that connected us—like the tentacles of a maniac giant squid—to all those other all-too-familiar family voices, all the problems going on at the shop, all the not-hardly-volunteer church and community commitments you wind up getting stuck with when you're not rude or quick-thinking enough to hang up the phone or come up with some plausible excuse. Not to mention all the other gotta-do's, responsibilities and interruptions that crop up every single day in real life and require your immediate attention....

But that's growing up, isn't it? That's becoming an adult. That's getting married and having kids and settling down and finding your place in the world. Not to mention finding your plate so damn full it's hard to sort out what to do next sometimes. Why, if it wasn't having dinner with Julie's mother it was dropping in on my folks for more of the same. Oh, sure, it was nice how the kids smoothed things over with my old man. Grandkids have a way of doing that. But he could still be a real pill when he felt like it (and he felt like it on a pretty regular basis, especially once he got a couple beers in him). And he never said anything about how good Big Ed and me were doing with our VW dealership. He'd rather choke. Especially after Julie and me got that pretty new yellow house with the darling white shutters that was maybe just a teensy bit nicer than his. Okay, maybe more than a teensy bit. It was like I'd stabbed him in the back, you know?

Felt pretty good, if you want the truth of it.

Of course Julie was always pushing me to do nice things for my old man and spend more time with him—like with a little kindness and attention you could somehow keep an asshole from being all dark and smelly on the inside, you know?—and one time she even talked me into taking him to a Yankees game, of all things. My treat. As I remember the only good part was that the Yankees lost. I picked him up in this gorgeous silver Jaguar Mk. VII sedan that we had in for an oil change—we were still getting a lot of MG and Jaguar business over at the old Sinclair shop on the far side of the lot, and this car was damn near brand-new so you could really smell the wood and leather—but he didn't so much as bat an eye. And then he grumbled, bitched and groused all the way to Yankee Stadium about all the endless heartaches and dire responsibilities of his stinking union shop steward job at that chemical plant in Newark where he mostly sat on his ass all day and bossed other people around. And every once in awhile he'd veer off from his work miseries to do a little light-duty pissing and moaning about my sister Mary Frances, who was still very much single and by then teaching kindergarten over at Our Lady of Perpetual Sorrow in Lyndhurst. *"She went on a damn party from the time she was sixteen,"* he growled, *"an' now she's gonna wind up an old maid because of it."* My old man was really top class when it came to dishing out retribution. You could say it was one of his specialties.

Truth is, I knew a hell of a lot more about what had gone on with Mary Frances than he did, and I also knew that she'd never been quite the same since the day I took her over to that doctor's office on Park Avenue in Old Man Finzio's towtruck so's she could have herself an abortion and get rid of that jerkoff Ollie Cromwell's baby. I mean, there's just no way to dress that up in nicer words and make it sound any better. Oh, she had a boyfriend or two after that. One was that quiet but very nice saxophone player named Pauly Martino that she had over to my folks' house for Christmas in '54. But he was on the road a lot, and you really don't want to know about what jazz musicians do on the road. Even the nice, quiet ones. They'd see each other whenever he was in town and I was hoping maybe something good might come of it, but then he got this steady dance orchestra gig at a place called The Fontainebleu down in Miami and I guess he wanted her to join him down there. But it was as if Mary Frances didn't really like herself too much anymore and so she didn't really trust anybody who felt anything nice towards her, either. If that makes any sense.

And then she met another college-professor type who I didn't like at all (even if he did buy a Volkswagen from us) and then he turned out to be ever so slightly already married, and that was about the end of it with men as far as my sister Mary Frances was concerned. You could see it in her eyes. They looked angry, hurt, betrayed, disgusted, depressed and, most of all, just plain worn out. It tore me up to see her like that. But there wasn't much of anything I could do. I had to give her credit, though. She moved herself back in with my folks for a while—and what a living hell *that* must have been!—and worked in the business office of the local community college while she went to night school and got her teaching certificate. It took her less than a year. And then she went to work in that Catholic school kindergarten taking care of other people's kids. I visited her there once or twice—one time to build a little two-foot stage with steps at either end for their gala Christmas Pageant and another to help out when a steam pipe burst—and I'd have to say that even though she looked pretty harried and maybe even a little haggard from chasing after other people's kids all day, you could see how much each and every one of those kids loved and trusted and depended on her. And I guess that somehow made it all worthwhile. But it also made you wonder and suppose how good she would have been with her own kids if she'd ever gotten married and had a family of her own. And you can bet she wondered about that, too. Wondered about it a lot. Even though she never mentioned it. But then, my sister Mary Frances was never a whiner. She had way too much guts and pride for that. Still, you could see she wasn't what you could call happy or fulfilled, and I got to thinking a lot of that was simply because she didn't feel she had it coming any more.

But you can't fix people's lives for them. Not even people you love and care about. All you can do is smile like everything's okay, offer up a few lame words of support or encouragement and then go off by yourself and feel miserable about it. Not that it does any good. Even so, you'd have to say Mary Frances was doing a lot better than she had been, and in spite of that asshole Ollie Cromwell made sure to keep in touch with all those artsy, overeducated, socially aware and politically hyperactive beatnik/Bohemian friends of hers over in Greenwich Village. Who were naturally still painting and sculpting and reading and writing novels—this new one called *On The Road* had a lot of people very worked up—not to mention plays, political manifestos and poetry, going to art gallery openings, coffee houses and solidarity demonstrations and listening to way-out jazz music until three or four in the morning. Even on week nights. Not to mention spending a terrific amount of time and effort planning out a magnificently fair, equal and equitable new social and economic system for themselves and the rest of humanity. Whether the rest of humanity wanted it or not. And of course my old man wasn't happy about that last part at all, since everybody and his brother knew we were up against it hard with the damn Russkies every place you looked. In fact, my old man and his union buddies were absolutely certain that the commies were behind all those riots and sit-ins and civil rights boycotts down south.

Not that any of them could actually prove it one way or another.

But it was something they just knew in their hearts….

Still, that didn't keep Mary Frances from staying in touch with all her fellow-traveler pinko friends in Greenwich Village, and she made a point of going back over there whenever anything vital to the entire social, cultural, artistic, political or economic future of the world was concerned. Like the afternoon she took a bus-and-train ride across the Hudson to join the solemn, funeral-like candlelight vigil outside the shuttered offices of *The Daily Worker* newspaper after the IRS shut them down for supposed tax evasion on March 27th. Wouldn't you know it, she got her damn picture in the paper—first page of the *Daily News* metro section, no less—and my old man was absolutely furious. I wasn't particularly thrilled about it either, seeing as how I thought all that wonderful "social equality" and "redistribution of wealth" bullshit all her left-wing pinko friends talked about depended to a staggering degree on who or whom was doing the redistributing. Of course they were all thoroughly convinced they could pull it off in a fair, equitable and even-handed way, but I have to say (even though it meant agreeing with my old man) that I had serious doubts. Like everybody except the filthy rich themselves, I kind of relished the notion of running a bulldozer through the bank vaults, investment accounts and lock boxes of all the third-, fourth- and fifth-and-further generations of stinking rich ne'er-do-well bozos who had money up the old wazoo but never did an honest day's work in their lives. Like Skippy Welcher, for a prime example. And not enough to break them, right? Just to skim a wee bit of the dusty, unused stuff off the top. Then, in an even-handed and methodical manner reflecting keen organization, benign social justice and perfect economic equality (maybe we could get the post office to handle it?), we'd spread it merrily around so you and me and every other working stiff who busted their ass from dawn to dark every weekday and at least a half-day every Saturday got a nice fat wad of extra folding money in his (or her) pocket.

Sounds like a swell idea, doesn't it?

But when I thought about all the millions and kazillions of poor, unfortunate, down-trodden, disadvantaged, can't-get-a-break-to-save-their-lives/Buddy-can-you-spare-me-a-dime lost souls, sad sacks, sick folks, sob stories and out-and-out screwoffs down below me on the old social/economic pecking order (including a few undeniable lazy freeloaders who, just like the filthy rich, never did an honest day's work in their lives), I wasn't quite so sure. Especially since taking care of them would probably mean dipping a big fat government soup ladle into *my* personal bank account. In the end, I was pretty damn certain it was something one of those benevolent volunteer charities or government social agencies ought to take care of, you know?

And right there you had the difference between socio-political theory and philosophy—which was what my sister Mary Frances' over-educated/way-too-intelligent egghead friends in Greenwich Village talked about all the time—and the actual nuts-and-bolts, nickel-and-dime realities of everyday life. Like fr'instance the enormous hubbub that went up in every jazz cellar and coffee house in The Village a few months later when this famous French writer/philosopher guy named Jean Paul Sartre (who no doubt had exceptionally deep furrows in his brain seeing as how he'd made an entire career out of writing and philosophizing about nothing) very loudly and even more publicly ended his longtime association with the Communist Party. That would be shortly after the benign and compassionate government of the Soviet Union sent in a few hundred tanks and three or four infantry battalions to crush a little brushfire political uprising in Hungary like a bug on a windowsill. Anyhow, this Jean Paul Sartre character quitting the Communist Party was absolutely *huge* news in Greenwich Village. Why, you'd think the whole blessed world had turned inside out! Even if a quick walk through damn near any other neighborhood on either side of the Hudson would convince you that this Jean Paul Sartre character was hardly what you could call a household name.

"He's a French actor, right? Wasn't he in that movie with whazzername? You know, the blond with the big ones?"

"Yeah, that's it! It was about the French Revolution, and he got his head chopped off at the end with one of those, whaddayacallit..."

"...Guillotines?"

"...Yeah, that's it! Said it was the best thing he'd ever done, too. Can you believe it? Or waiddaminnit. Maybe he was the one who got stabbed to death in the bathtub. I can't remember. But I sure remember the blonde. What a pair of tits! She played Marie Antoinette, and that outfit she was wearing made her look like a couple ostritch eggs poking up out of a satin egg crate."

"Nah, that's not it. He was a German spy, I'm pretty sure—or maybe it was an underground freedom fighter?— in one of the world wars. But I can't remember which one. Lost one of his arms. Or maybe it was both legs. But he got a nice medal for it. Or maybe he got shot by a firing squad...."

"Say, isn't he the pastry chef over at the Waldorf?"

Even so, I think going over to The Village and mingling with all her artsy-craftsy/political-activist friends made Mary Frances feel liked she belonged to something bigger and more important than her life as a blessed old-maid kindergarten teacher living in her folks' house over in Jersey. And also that there was perhaps something more between her ears than the stuff she found in the bottom of the small, soiled underpants she had to change every day at work.

Meanwhile my sister Sarah Jean had married Carson Flegley like I'd always hoped she would and the two of them moved into a nice old frame house not too far from his family's funeral parlor in East Orange and started cranking out babies with astonishing regularity. It was amazing to me that quiet, timid, plain-Jane Sarah Jean was the one who wound up with the nice house, a caring, attentive husband and a growing family while Mary Frances—who was the gutsy neighborhood knockout/spitfire when we were all growing up—turned into the old-maid kindergarten teacher. Go figure.

Or figure Butch Bohunk taking up with my old maiden aunt Rosamarina. There was a match *nobody* saw coming. And it was the talk of every back porch in the neighborhood, too, seeing as how Butch could never get a divorce settled with his Mean Marlene—she always wanted a lot more than he had to sign the papers—and so they were living in sin as far as all the ladies hanging laundry on the back-alley porches were concerned. But my Aunt Rosamarina never had much contact with her neighbors anyway, and Butch eventually managed to get her around to his way of thinking, the general gist of which was that they could all pretty much go fuck themselves.

Chapter 14: Gina

Any woman sitting under any hair dryer in damn near any beauty shop in America can tell you that Gina LaScala's real name was Angelina Maria Scalabrini and that she came to Hollywood from the old Italian section of Brooklyn where you could smell garlic simmering in the three-flats and hear scratchy, 78-rpm Enrico Caruso recordings echoing across the back-alley fire escapes where the laundry hangs out to dry on sticky summer afternoons. They also knew that a lot of movie magazine writers, Hollywood gossip columnists and so-called "film critics" thought Gina LaScala might well be the single most beautiful female creature on the planet. Or at least in Hollywood, which amounted to essentially the same thing as far as those guys were concerned. Not that a lot of those movie writers, gossip columnists and film critic types were attracted to women in the same way a red-blooded American truck driver, pipe fitter or New Jersey wrench-spinner might be, but that's another story entirely.

Thanks to their usual keen investigating, back-door snooping and sticking their noses in where they weren't really wanted, those columnists also knew her father (or maybe it was her stepfather, depending on which story you believed and who was doing the talking) ran a little Italian restaurant over in the old neighborhood where he worked his butt off from the crack of dawn to well past bedtime six days a week and pretty much collapsed in a heap on the seventh. Unless he had communion parties or wedding receptions to cater, anyway. Meanwhile her mother mostly stayed home and played sick while she plotted, schemed and squirreled away money for what she'd already decided she was going to do with little Angelina's future.

It was the second marriage for Angelina's father. His real name was Rudolpho, but all the kids in the neighborhood started calling him "Rudi" when he was growing up, and it stayed with him like a cute scar for the rest of his life. He was a first-generation Brooklyn Italian and the eldest of five tough, serious, streetwise kids whose parents came from a long line of spaghetti strainers, sauce stirrers, veal beaters and sausage broilers from over in the old country near Bologna. Rudi's mother and father opened their first storefront sandwich shop/lunch counter/Italian deli soon after arriving in New York by way of Ellis Island, and naturally little Rudi and his brothers and sisters were expected to pitch in and help out from the time they could hold a slotted spoon. All five of them grew older, wiser and wider behind the cook stove, lunch counter and cash register of that little storefront eatery, and thanks to hard work, frugal ways and a solid sense of family, Rudi's father and mother were eventually able to add a small corner grocery two blocks away and a real sit-down restaurant on 7th Street where everybody knew you could get generous portions of spaghetti, ravioli or manicotti that was never overcooked, great *pasta fazool* or a pepper-and-egg sandwich on the lunch special every Friday and nice, fresh clams on your linguini—not the canned stuff—on the dinner special Friday nights. By that time little Rudolpho was pretty much just *"Ey, Rooti!"* to everybody in the neighborhood, and in his early 20s he courted, proposed to and married a thin, quiet and thoroughly old-fashioned first-generation New York Abruzzi girl who worked and fought and scrimped and saved and struggled side-by-side with him in the family businesses. They had three children in four years—two girls and finally a boy—and Rudi's wife was generally back in the restaurant working again, new baby under her arm, within a week or two after getting out of the hospital.

As eldest son, Rudi naturally inherited ownership and control of the restaurant on 7th Street after his father passed away and his mother grew older and feebler and had to pretty much retire. Middle brother Antonio wound up with the original deli/luncheonette a couple blocks away, youngest brother Paulie got the grocery store and the two sisters got whatever came with the husbands they married, which caused the usual and inevitable jealousies, arguments, lingering envies and simmering hatreds common to a lot of old-school Italian families. Even so, the whole bunch got together for huge and outwardly happy late-afternoon family meals on all the major Catholic holidays, the Fourth of July and Thanksgiving.

But Rudi's wife's constitution was never very strong, and it worsened over time with the birth of the three children and the daily hard work at home and at the restaurant. She was ultimately diagnosed with cancer during the depression years when things were tough for everyone, and had to stay home more and more to try and take care of herself as best she could while Rudi went to work at dawn every day except Sunday, cooked the sauces and made the desserts and set up the appetizer trays and oversaw the organizing of the plates and silverware and made sure all the food purveyors were delivering what he'd ordered and weren't screwing him on the freshness, count or quality. Then he did the lunch rush and after that accommodated the few well-dressed afternoon idlers with heavy bulges in their pockets who always sat by the front window with their eyes peeled towards both ends of the street while their bosses—serious-looking neighborhood guys in expensive silk suits who loved Rudi's *Sauce Bolognese*—discussed the weather and the price of good provolone at a table way in back next to the coat rack. They were his best customers, and they liked coming to Rudi's place because it was clean and quiet and had a good view of 7th Street in both directions out front plus a stout steel back door with two hefty forged iron dead bolts to keep it shut. Rudi always made sure none of the help came over to refill their wine glasses, pour them a little more coffee or read them the dessert menu unless they were summoned with a small cock of the head or wave of the hand. The neighborhood bosses liked Rudi because he was respectful, friendly, agreeable and discreet and had a rare knack for staying the hell out of the little squabbles and differences of opinion that turned a lot of their favorite restaurants into shooting galleries.

Later on he'd cook for the dinner crowd and make his regular, glad-handing tours of the tables—*"Ey, Rooti! Ova heah!!"*— and then oversee clean-up and count out the cash register while the handful of drunks who should have gone home long ago lingered over their beer, wine, cocktail tumblers and little aperitif glasses of anisette until he turned off the lights and gently threw them out. Then he'd go home, kiss his wife on the forehead, tell her how much better she was looking and how much stronger she was getting, have one long, tall glass of wine all by himself and fall into a deep, dreamless sleep. Just so he could get up at the crack of dawn the next morning to do it all over again. Rudi Scalabrini was one of those staunch, solid, old school Italians who don't expect much more out of life than hard work and heavy routine, and who know better than to look too far into the future.

And then he met Angelique....

Angelina Scalabrini's mother couldn't have been more different from her father. She was one of those self-consciously glamorous, stage-struck types who spend their whole lives chasing the limelight so desperately that it could never catch them even if it wanted to. But she could turn heads all right—short, dark and busty under a mane of bottle-blond hair—and looked really striking from eight or ten feet away. Particularly when the room was dimly lit and she had all her makeup on. Angelina's mother told people she was an actress and a singer and a dancer, but like a million other hopefuls who started too late or never had the right sort of breaks or connections (or never had enough looks or talent in the first place), she'd been knocking around the dingy fringes of New York show business since she hit the streets of Manhattan as a wild, hungry-eyed teenager during the height of the roaring 20s. She made the chorus lines for a few Broadway shows as a dancer (although never in the front line or never in the middle or on an end if there was only one line) and worked on and off as a cabaret singer at some of the less elegant local speakeasies. But she always had to flesh out her co-called "stage career" earnings with a little free-form hostessing or working as a dice game/hat check girl. Or, when times were tough, maybe even as an "escort." Or at least that's what some people said, anyway. They also said she always did well on tips.

Her real name was Philomena Angellini, but she went by the single stage name "Angelique" on the three- and five- and eight- and finally ten-year-old head shots they used to put up outside the joints where she was singing, and she found herself spending more and more time in front of her mirror every year, applying more and more makeup in a losing attempt to keep looking like those pictures. Unlike her father, Angelina's mother was a night person by both spirit and inclination, so she could only consider work opportunities that allowed her to pretty much ignore mornings entirely.

Rudi first met "Angelique" at a wedding reception he couldn't refuse attending during the sad, waning months of his wife's long, draining and difficult battle with cancer. The party was for the daughter of one of those tough-looking silk-suit guys who held meetings in the back of Rudi's restaurant on alternate Tuesday or Thursday afternoons (it didn't pay to have too predictable a schedule in their line of work), and the truth of it is that Rudi didn't really want to go. Especially since it was being held at a big, fancy hotel on the other side of the East River in

Manhattan—a posh, stiff, glittery sort of place where he didn't feel comfortable at all—but he knew it would be an insult if he didn't attend to pay his respects and slip an envelope stuffed with cash to the new bride and groom.

As it turned out, "Angelique" was singing that night in the dark, smoky little bar just off the hotel lobby and almost directly across from the huge, bustling banquet room where the wedding reception was going full blast and a 28-piece orchestra was playing every happy, bouncy Italian melody known to man. It was actually supposed to be a 30-piece orchestra, but according to the chatter and behind-the-hand whispers around the tables, the second trombone player had gotten food poisoning from some suspect *scungilli* and the guy who usually clanged cymbals, shook bells, rang chimes and beat on wood blocks at the back of the percussion section during novelty numbers was actually upstairs in one of the top-floor luxury suites with the bandleader's wife.

As you can imagine, that wedding reception was a raucous, splashy, noisy sort of party bubbling over with music, shouts, toasts, laughter and a whirling, jostling dance floor, and it was really the last kind of place Rudi wanted to be. His wife was really struggling then, and so he felt guilty, helpless, miserable and even ashamed about being there. Useless, too, since he wasn't accustomed to parties where he wasn't doing the cooking and serving or at the very least overseeing things in the kitchen. Plus he didn't really know a lot of the people there and those he did know inevitably asked him how his wife was doing.

Which is probably why he treated himself to a few too many cocktails before dinner followed by more than enough red wine with the food courses. Most of which he found pretty disappointing, but what could you expect from a hotel kitchen? The shrimp in the shrimp cocktails were pink enough, but they smelled a little and tasted mealy. The *minestrone* was lukewarm and greasy, the lettuce in the salad was limp, the pasta was mushy, the meatballs were small, hard and dry, the red gravy didn't have any zip to it, the chicken was fleshy and undercooked while the fish course had been cooked until it was dry as corrugated cardboard. But maybe that was just to cover the suspicion that it'd been a few too many days out of the water. But Rudi didn't say anything. That would have been inexcusably impolite. Besides, he didn't really feel much like talking to anybody anyway….

So right after the cake and coffee he excused himself and went into the lobby to escape from all the music, noise and laughter. And that's when he wandered into the dark little bar where Angelique was singing to order himself an anisette. She was doing mostly slow, sad Italian love songs with a piano player, a bass player and a drummer who never used anything but brushes on his drumheads all evening for accompaniment. Her songs were full of loss and sadness and heartache and longing, and Rudi thought they were excruciatingly beautiful. Some of them nearly made him cry. Especially after his third and fourth cordial glass of anisette.

Rudi introduced himself between sets and told Angelique how much he loved her voice, style and choice of material while she looked him up and down—the shoes, the cufflinks and even the label in his jacket when he went to the men's room—and decided he might be exactly what she was looking for. Of course he told her about his wife. In fact, it was the first thing he mentioned after he complimented her on her singing and told her how beautiful she looked. Like I said, it was a pretty dark room.

Anyhow, it wasn't all that long afterwards they started seeing each other a little on the sly—it was hard for him to get away at first, but eventually it got easier—and he finally took the risk of hiring her on part-time at the restaurant whenever her singing and acting careers would permit. Which was most of the time, if you want the truth of it. There were naturally a few raised eyebrows and back-porch rumors running around the old neighborhood to the effect that he'd quietly set her up in a studio apartment he was paying for just across the bridge in Manhattan, but no one had any proof or knew for sure. That's one of the great beauties of a cash business.

Only then she got pregnant. Just as Rudi's wife was lingering through her last, tragic few months. It was a terrible, ugly and uncomfortable situation for everyone involved. But, like all terrible, ugly and uncomfortable situations, it eventually passed and the world moved on. Rudi's wife finally expired just as Hitler's armies were marching into the Rhineland in the spring of 1936 as kind of a Coming Attractions preview of World War II, and another six weeks were allowed to discreetly elapse before Rudi and Angelique got married. They did it quietly in city hall, not in church, and naturally that was a scandal all over the neighborhood, too. But people came to the wedding reception at the restaurant anyway since Rudi had an open bar and was doling out food for free. At least Angelique wasn't showing too badly by then.

Rudi's other three kids hated his new wife, of course. But they loved and respected their father even more and continued working hard and helping out at the restaurant early in the morning and again in the afternoons and evenings after school. They even agreed to watch over things with their Uncle Tony while their father and his new bride took an extended-weekend honeymoon to the Poconos and promised no ill will against their new half-sister Angelina when she arrived right on schedule less than seven months after they'd buried their mother. There was even some speculation around the neighborhood that Rudi wasn't the baby's real father, but it wasn't something you could prove one way or the other. But as Angelina grew through childhood and into her early teens, it became obvious to everyone that she was a genuine, knockout beauty. And not at all like her father. Or her mother, come to that. She had raven black hair and smooth, creamy-white skin and luminous green eyes that glistened like oiled emeralds. And where her father was tall, thick and fleshy and her mother was short and busty, Angelina was sleek, slender and petite. At least until she started filling out before she'd barely reached her teens, and quickly turned into the kind of girl who swivels heads, stops traffic and causes young men to trip over fireplugs and walk blindly into lamp posts. Middle-aged and older men, too....

Little Angelina was exactly the kind of daughter her mother always wanted: a true, natural, knockout beauty that she could mold and shape and protect and hover over and possibly even transform into the kind of radiant, respected and revered stage and screen goddess she herself always wanted to be. In fact, it got to where nothing else mattered to Angelique. Nothing at all. And so as soon as little Angelina was old enough there were acting lessons and singing lessons and dance lessons and sessions on poise and diction and of course auditions. There were always lots of auditions. Not to mention "omens" and "signs" to guide her. In spite of her street-wise, cynical, you-only-get-what's-coming-to-you-if-you-grab-and-claw-for-it nature, Angelique had a deep-seated superstitious streak. But that's the way it is with a lot of Italian women, you know? Sicilians in particular. They can be brutally realistic about almost anything you can think of, and yet full up to here with these dark, quirky little fears about curses, spells, omens and evil eyes. But maybe that's just the flipside to all those repetitive, round-robin prayers to the Holy Mother and all the major- and minor-league saints that a lot of those same women mumble over and over and over again until the words don't make sense anymore.

So every now and then between the auditions and the dance, singing and acting lessons, Angelique would take little Angelina to see this scary old two-bit Sicilian fortune teller who called herself Madame Cellini and worked out of a stuffy little second-floor apartment overlooking the wholesale produce market where all the restaurants got their fruits and vegetables every morning. Usually well before dawn. *"It's a-so noisy out there at four-thirty inna morning!"* Madame Cellini would rasp while she stroked the old, battle-scarred tabby purring in her lap, *"but it's a-nice and quiet inna the afternoons and evenings."* Madame Cellini's apartment was cluttered with ancient books and carved crucifixes and glazed ceramic figurines of the holy family and all the popular saints and bible characters and even a few of the old Roman gods from the days before Christianity got popular.

Madame Cellini also had cats. Three of them. A beat-up old tabby, an orange and white male that spat and clawed and a slinky, arrogant Burmese, and all three of them made little Angelina's eyes itch and nose run whenever she was around them. They roamed the place at will, watching from the windowsill or peering down from the top of the bookshelves or staring directly into the eyes of Madame Cellini's customers from the chair back behind her shoulders. Madame Cellini talked to her cats, too, and when she did they perked up their ears and stared back at her like they understood every word. It gave little Angelina the creeps. As it did when Madame Cellini called her forward, cupped her cheeks in those cold, bony hands of hers and peered deep into little Angelina's eyes. It was like staring into the face of a dying animal in a ditch by the side of the road.

Angelina's mother first started visiting Madame Cellini when she was bouncing around the city looking for show work, and she'd become something of a regular long before she ever met Rudi. Madame Cellini had foreseen it all, of course. She foresaw everything. Or at least that's what it seemed like after the fact, anyway. But no question she'd given Angelique hope and comfort during those long, lean years when she was knocking around New York as a part-time lounge singer, hat check girl and "hostess." Then again, Madame Cellini was in the hope and comfort business, wasn't she? *"You'll meet a man,"* she told Angelina's mother solemnly, *"and he won't be the one, but he'll be the way...."*

"Where will I meet him?" Angelique wanted to know.

"It's dark. The vision is dark. But you'll be singing. I can hear it. And he will be sad. So very sad."

All of which sounds like amazingly accurate stuff. Unless you step back and have a think about what generally happens to bottle-blonde nightclub singers/hat check girl/"hostesses" on the make who work dark bars and lounges where guys with troubled lives go to drown their sorrows. All of a sudden it doesn't sound so damn clever, does it? And naturally Madame Cellini agreed—for two bits, anyway—that there was indeed a rich, dazzling, star-struck future ahead for the quiet, self-possessed little daughter with the shimmering black hair, perfect skin and deep, luminous green eyes.

Angelina always hated those afternoon sessions with Madame Cellini in the cluttered, claustrophobic second-floor walkup over the produce market. But she had no choice. After all, her father was almost always off working, her older half-brother and half-sisters treated her with an uncomfortable mixture of contempt, envy and secrecy, and so except for her mother, she was pretty much a stranger in her own house. Besides, her mother's will was too strong to resist. Nobody could stand up to Angelique once she'd set her mind to something. And especially not Rudi. Plus, as her mother reminded Angelina regularly, did she *really* want to spend the rest of her life in a damn apron? Get married to some fat, boorish young man whose family owned a wholesale fruit business just so she could pop out babies for him one after another and watch her youth and beauty and opportunities fade to nothing while he treated her like a piece of furniture? Is that what she really wanted out of life?

Her mother taught Angelina everything about men. They were to be used, but not to be trusted. *"Men are pigs and they run the world,"* she told little Angelina, *"but they're no match for a woman head-on. Make them tell you what they want straight out in plain English. Most of 'em haven't got the stomach for it. And if they do, just play innocent and pretend like you don't understand. The important thing is to keep them confused and off-balance. That's where the power is. That's where the mystery is."*

Angelique was a master at all of it, and had no trouble dominating her marriage to Rudi completely. She had him right in the crosshairs, you know? Like she complained of a bad back after the pregnancy and so she only had to work at the restaurant part-time on afternoons and a few evenings, and then only as a hostess so she could sit on a stool behind the cash register and keep off her feet. And she insisted on a maid twice a week to help with the house. In fact, there was a big argument over it. But she threatened to leave and take Angelina with her, and the fire in her eyes left no doubt that she would do exactly that.

Rudi loved Angelina like all fathers love their daughters, and I guess she was always kind and thoughtful towards him in return. But he never felt truly at ease around her, you know? There was always a sense of distance. And the more gorgeous and glowing and naturally graceful and beautiful she became, the clumsier, more awkward and inept her father felt around her. But that didn't matter. Shuttling Angelina off to her voice lessons and dance lessons in the city or acting lessons in Greenwich Village or auditions almost anywhere or those strange, creepy afternoon sessions with Madame Cellini in the second-floor walkup over the produce market was all Angelique cared about. And she told her husband straight out—many times, in fact—that once Angelina was ready, she was taking her to Hollywood.

The strange part is that he never actually believed her.

I suppose you can justify damn near anything if you want it badly enough, and Angelique had no second thoughts about making plans and salting money away on the sly for their escape to Hollywood. In fact, she'd been packing secretly for over a week when the day finally came. There was no buildup, no argument, no warning of any kind. Just a sudden, unexpected phone call to the restaurant at 10 ayem on an otherwise unremarkable Thursday morning, right about the time Rudi was turning the soup of the day down to simmer for the lunch crowd and finishing up the pastry trays and putting them in the walk-in cooler. That's when Angelique announced that she and Angelina would be leaving for California by train later that day and that was the end of it. It wouldn't have done any good to tell Rudi the night before. There would have been a scene.

No, it was better this way....

Angelina was barely 17 when she and her mother arrived in Hollywood and settled into a small, cheap apartment just a short bus ride from the studios. Like tens of thousands of other Hollywood hopefuls, she made the rounds of every closed door and casting call in town while her mother burned up the phone lines to agents and producers and casting directors, trying to find that elusive, hidden chink in Hollywood's armor. Not to mention a long-distance call every Wednesday afternoon to Madame Cellini back in Brooklyn to find out what the fates had in store. But finding movie work for Angelina was pretty slim pickings, so Angelique had her take a temporary waitressing job at a lunch counter not far from the famous wrought-iron gates of Paramount Studios. Like her half-brothers and sisters, Angelina had helped out around her father's restaurant from the time she could fold a napkin and knew all there was to know about waiting tables, but her mother scolded her not to act too proficient or professional at her new job. *"When somebody important is in the place,"* she said, waving a finger under Angelina's nose, *"make sure you spill something or drop something or scatter some silverware. Make some noise. That's how they notice you."*

And that's precisely how she met Brad Lackey. The very day she got fired, in fact. For spilling an entire platter of the Hungarian Goulash lunch special directly into his lap. Not that she would have lasted very long at the restaurant anyway. It was only her second week on the job, and the other waitresses already had it 8 to 3 that the owner was going to get rid of her. He probably would have fired her already—he'd never seen a waitress who dropped or spilled so many things!—but she was so incredibly sweet and sleek and beautiful and the way she looked at him with those oiled emerald eyes turned the marrow in his bones to warm butterscotch pudding. He suspected she might be doing it all on purpose, of course, but she was a decent enough actress even then to make it all look accidental. Including the platter of goulash that went tumbling into Brad Lackey's lap only minutes after one of the other girls let slip that he was a second- or third-string assistant something-or-other to one of the bigwig studio executives over at Warner Brothers.

Truth is, Brad Lackey was nothing more than a glorified gofer, errand boy and minor-league arranger of things for one of the big studio vice presidents. Like most everybody in Hollywood, Brad was an out-of-towner—a clean-cut young guy from Dubuque who wore Clark Kent glasses over gee-whiz Midwestern eyeballs—and like all the other gee-whiz kids out of Dubuque, he was enamored to death with all the glamour, sheen and sparkle of the movie business. Not to mention thoroughly mesmerized by the famously decadent Hollywood lifestyle he saw slathered all over the tabloids and gossip magazines but never seemed to come face-to-face with in real life. But he was sure it was out there, and he was even surer he wanted in on it—even if only to watch and marvel—and that's why he'd hocked himself up to the earlobes to get the well-abused MG TD he used to run errands for his boss all over Los Angeles. Brad Lackey knew he *needed* a snappy, snazzy little car like that, even if it blew a little oil and ran a little rough and the gearbox ground angrily every time he shifted from first to second. After all, he had a title and position to think about—Assistant to the Producer—and, like everybody else who saw themselves as genuine Hollywood insiders, he was thoroughly swept up in the frantic, dazzling, desperate rush of things that simply *had* to get done. Like tooling up to those gorgeous homes in the Hollywood hills or the ones nestled high into the seaside cliffs overlooking the ocean or the quietly brazen mansions not quite hidden behind the tall hedges, stone fences and ornate iron gates of Bel Air and Beverly Hills. That's where he'd drop off promising scripts for the stars (or more likely their agents) to read. Or he'd find himself stopping by the carpentry shop to see why that damn Viking ship for the Burt Lancaster movie was taking so long and costing so much. Or he'd be off trying to locate the highly respected but highly eccentric Southern novelist the studio had brought in—for a very large wad of cash—and set up in one of the bungalows on the back lot to do a screen adaptation of his latest best-seller, but who'd apparently slipped off on a three-week bender instead. Or he could be picking up the producer's cleaning and stopping by the little tailor shop for the pants he had altered. *"And make sure nobody can see they've been let out, got it? Oh, and pick up some sandwiches from the deli on the way back. Corned beef on rye with mustard and a pickle for me, a tuna on toasted white for Sheila and a bagel with lox, cream cheese, tomato, red onion, lettuce and a few capers if they've got 'em for Solly. Here, take some money. Oh, and whatever you want too, okay? And bring back some sodas while you're at it."*

To Brad, it seemed like everything in the movie business was either a crisis or an emergency or way over budget or disastrously behind schedule. Or some hideous and unmanageable combination of all four. Unless it was a complete catastrophe, of course, which was even worse. According to my motoring scribe buddy Hank Lyons, Hollywood pretty much ran on its own desperate sense of urgency, and he was sure it was part of a neatly orchestrated and masterfully choreographed plan. The guys at the top kept heaping on pressure and stoking the fire under everybody's feet in order to avoid questions, challenges, close scrutiny or possible consequences. And the key to accomplishing that sort of thing was keeping everybody around them nervous, off-balance, looking over their shoulders and in a constant state of panic.

It worked like a charm.

Anyhow, this Brad Lackey guy did well in that kind of environment because he was young, diligent, observant and ambitious without being particularly shrewd, smart, clever or ingenious. The studio bosses were always on the lookout for talent like that because they were afraid of guys with too many brain cells or too much moxie. So being a little on the dull, gee-whiz, plodding side of things helped Brad immensely with his career. Better yet, he knew how to keep his ears open and mouth shut. You could just about make a career out of that sort of thing in Hollywood.

"Oh, I'm SO sorry!" Angelina gasped as the thick, brown goulash gravy overflowed the pile of egg noodles and beef bits in Brad Lackey's lap and dribbled down over his brand-new Florshiems. And there was no way Brad could miss the restaurant's owner making a beeline towards them from behind the counter or the tears welling up in Angelina's eyes. My God, he'd never seen eyes like that before in his life....

Of course she was fired—discreetly, after Brad left—but she'd gotten his work number because she absolutely *insisted* on taking care of the cleaning bill. And less than two weeks later he'd arranged that screaming-her-head-off bit part for her in the cheapie outer space monster movie a friend of his was shooting for the drive-in circuit. It was only a few days' work and hardly major studio stuff, but it gave her a small screen credit and a tenderfoot's feel for what things were like on a movie set. And three weeks after that Brad was pulling up in front of her mother's apartment in his shiny-but-rundown MG to take her to the studio premiere of *"How to Marry a Millionaire"* starring Lauren Bacall, Betty Grable and Marilyn Monroe. And, after the show, up to a party he knew about at a huge house up off Mulholland Drive in the Hollywood Hills.

And that's where she met Ernesto Julio.

I'm pretty certain Angelina had never been invited to a party like that or seen a house like that in her life. Except maybe in the movies. From the front it looked like just a big white stucco ranch with a fountain and a reflecting pool in the middle of an oversized driveway that was chock-full of Cadillacs, Lincolns, Packards, Mercedes and Rolls-Royces. Not to mention every kind of top-down, two-seater sportycar imaginable. Flashy convertibles with hefty price tags were the things to have in Hollywood. "Jesus, that's a damn *Maserati!!"* Brad half-gasped as they passed by Ernesto Julio's striking new two-tone, Frua-bodied A6G/2000 convertible. "I wonder who owns it?"

"What does a car like that cost?" Angelina wanted to know.

"More than I make in a year."

"Oh? And what *do* you make in a year?"

"A damn site less than some star or studio exec paid for that Maserati."

Although the house only looked one story high from the front, it was built on a steep hillside so the back end amounted to three solid floors of uninterrupted plate glass overlooking the sheet-cake sprawl of Los Angeles. Between the front and the back was a lush outdoor courtyard with a swimming pool and shimmering blue lighting, and the people milling around were wearing everything from tuxedos to swimsuits to—if you included the busy couple hidden in the hedges around by the side of the house—nothing at all. A jazz combo was playing in an enormous, cream-colored living room, and Brad went inside to get Angelina a drink while she took up a strategic position next to the sliding glass doors that separated the living room from the pool area. Her mother had taught her it was just the sort of place you needed to be if you wanted to get noticed. And she knew how to play it cool, too. Nothing real obvious, you know? Just be patient, look radiantly beautiful, stunningly sensual, desperately desirable and thoroughly unattainable and wait to see what happens….

It took her less than an hour. By that time she was standing next to Brad Lackey while he was fawning all over Ernesto Julio about his new Maserati, and Ernesto was smiling and laughing and trying to be at least slightly discreet about staring at Angelina like his eyeballs were about to roll right out of his face. But it was hard not to. As far as Angelina was concerned, Ernesto looked reasonably handsome for his age and very nicely groomed, what with his deep tan, a sculptured mane of silvery hair and dark, flashing eyes under a matching set of bushy, silver-white eyebrows. But she also thought he looked a bit old and thick in the middle for the pirate-style silk shirt he was wearing with half the front buttons undone. But this was business, and she knew it. So did Ernesto, who turned out to be a real expert on how such things were properly and gracefully handled. First he invited Brad Lackey for a quick spin up Mulholland Drive in his gorgeous new two-tone Maserati. Even let him take the wheel on the way back. Meanwhile Angelina waited outside at the top of the driveway, watching the people come and go and listening to the music, chatter and laughter filtering out from inside. Every now and then she'd sneak a glance at that couple behind the hedges. They were finished now. Passed out, it looked like. They'd probably still be there in the morning.

There was no mistaking the six-cylinder growl of the Maserati as it came thrashing down the hill in third gear. Brad Lackey was at the wheel now, all glassy-eyed and breathless, and Ernesto did his best to hide a wince as Brad made a spastic attempt at a double-clutch, heel-and-toe downshift and bounced the Maserati heavily up the steep incline of the driveway. He lurched the car to a stop right in front of where Angelina was standing. *"Wow. That's one HELL of a sports car!"* Brad gushed. *"Geez, thanks, Mr. Julio! Thanks a lot!"*

"It was my pleasure," Ernesto Julio assured him, patting his arm. And then he turned to Angelina. "Would *you* like to try it?"

"I'm afraid I'm not much of a driver...." she answered coyly, never letting go of his eyes.

"Oh, there's nothing to it," he insisted. "Come. I'll show you." And so, while Brad Lackey stood there like the damn emperor with no clothes, Ernesto Julio closed the passenger door behind her with a quiet *"thunk,"* clambered in on the driver's side, fired up that strong, sweet-sounding Maserati six and launched the two of them smoothly off into the darkness.

They never came back.

Who knows what happened that night? Or in the nights and weeks that followed? But surely she spent them teasing him and stringing him along rather than just caving in the way he expected. After all, as her mother had so carefully explained, that's how you kept them interested. The end result was a major studio screen test for Angelina over at Warner Brothers and then, after a few weeks of phone calls and meetings with middle-echelon studio people, she landed a walk-on part in a big budget historical epic about Napoleon's defeat at Waterloo. There was also a new name for her. Gina LaScala. The name change was actually Ernesto's idea, but it was her mother—or, more correctly, Madame Cellini—who dreamed up the exact sound, taste and feel of it. Maybe she saw it in her crystal or read it in her damn tea leaves. But everyone agreed it fit Angelina perfectly. New rising starlet Gina LaScala was only in a single scene in that movie, playing a hot, effervescent and enticing young innkeeper's daughter who happened to be serving up dinner to the British generals just as plans were being laid for the upcoming battle. Her only line was to ask Trevor Howard as The Duke of Wellington: *"More stew, sir?"*

But the camera loved her. It caught her sleek, catlike moves and the radiant sheen of her hair and the unmistakable, iridescent heat and want glistening in her eyes. Those eyes said it all. They made you ache and melt and wonder what it might be like to have a creature like that all to yourself. Just for one night. Hell, just for 15 minutes! And that kind of aching and melting and wondering got your palms all sweaty and made your mouth go dry. It was the kind of thing no acting class could teach and no director could beg, coach, coax, threaten or cajole out of any young actress. Nope, it just had to be there. Where the camera could see, record it and reveal it. Just for the movies....

Chapter 15: Pebble Beach to Paramount Ranch

Speaking of unexpected pregnancies, we had kind of a surprise waiting for us when Julie started not feeling real well in the morning about three weeks after we went to see *My Fair Lady* and then spent the night in that fancy hotel suite Big Ed arranged for us at the Waldorf Astoria. Of course we both knew what it was right away, and I guess we were pretty okay about it even if it did hit us from the blind side. I mean, we'd been being kind of, umm, "careful" about things after little Roberta was born. If you catch my drift. Including certain kinds of "careful" that neither the nuns where Julie went to high school, our local priest, his bishop, that bishop's archbishop, the archbishop's cardinal at the archdiocese or even the old Holy Father himself over in Rome would exactly approve of. And I didn't care for it much myself either, come to think of it. But Big Ed's night at the Waldorf came as a complete surprise and I never carried those things around in my wallet like some guys do. I mean, can you imagine the explaining I'd have to do if Julie ever went in there for a couple bucks to get her hair done or pay the kid who mowed our lawn on Saturday mornings and found a couple of those oh-so-suspicious-looking little foil packets in there? That was a question-and-lack-of-answer session I could very well do without. Besides, I always thought sneaking around on your wife was kind of scummy. Even though I knew—and liked—a lot of guys who did it, got away with it, and figured it was more or less their right as married men. But the point is that Julie and me had shown quite a knack for getting her pregnant almost every time we had a legit opportunity, and damn if we hadn't come through again.

And meanwhile neither me or Big Ed could believe what was going on with our Volkswagen business. It's a matter of genuine historical fact that out of the 51,000 imported cars sold in the United States in 1955, a full 34,000 of the little beauties were VeeDubs. Look it up. And Volkswagen's 1956 sales estimates were hovering around the 50,000 mark all by themselves. But just look at the line we had to sell! Besides the famously economical (and gas prices were getting to be quite a hot topic what with the Egyptians trying to grab the Suez Canal just because it happened to run through their own blessed country—can you imagine!), trendy, popular and fabulously well-advertised little VW Beetle, we had that big, roomy, highly utilitarian and so damn pokey it could hardly get out of its own way VW Microbus to sell to all the outdoorsy, lumberjack-shirt types, thick-glasses college professors, poetry-reading urban bohemians and sturdy-looking females of indeterminate gender. Plus VW had just announced their stylish new Karmann-Ghia "sports coupe" (which, like the Microbus, was just the same old VW innards wrapped up in a different package) and we had people lined up to put ca$h deposits down and wait for months to take delivery. Fact is, Big Ed had to hire on another salesman (or, more correctly, a whole succession of salesmen) to help handle the floor traffic. Especially on Saturdays. And let me tell you what an experience it can get to be once you start hiring—and firing—car salesmen. Face it: nobody starts out in life dreaming of being a car salesman. In terms of status with the neighborhood gentry, "car salesman" falls somewhere between sneak thief, disgraced elected official and axe murderer on the old social pecking order. Not to mention that the profession of "car salesman" has always been kind of a Halfway House for wayward personalities. Mostly bright but flighty types who started out selling something else (Vacuum cleaners? Aluminum siding? Bibles? Cemetery plots?) and come to rest for awhile at a desk in a dealership showroom on their way to a career as either insurance salesmen, investment brokers or smalltime con men and bunko artists. It's also the place where a lot of sharp but disillusioned guys who tried and failed at their own businesses (usually, again, attempting to sell something) wind up while they're "trying to get back on their feet" for another run at the old brass ring. Far as I can tell, you could count the number of real, professional, career-oriented car salesmen in the entire state of New Jersey on both hands and still have enough fingers left over to play guitar and pick your nose at the same time.

As a line of work, car sales generally attracts sharp, ambitious but often lazy characters with an overload of gab, grins and personality but who generally confuse quick thinking with being clever. A lot of them believe deep down in their hearts that they're smarter than other people. And lots of times they are. But they also delude themselves into thinking that they're shrewd, tough, wise and street-savvy on top of it. And the irony is that while most all of them are cynical, sly and sarcastic on the outside, they're generally hopeless optimists and incurable romantics on the inside—soft as the damn goo in a candy Easter egg. Plus an awful lot of them are shortcut artists, point shavers and angle shooters by nature, if you know what I mean.

But we had to hire somebody, because Big Ed simply couldn't handle all the folks who seemed to want to buy VWs from us by himself. Or maybe I should say "order VWs from us," since by the middle of 1956 we had a waiting list for damn near everything and most all the cars were going out at full advertised price plus add-ons. No questions asked. To tell the truth, that took a lot of the magic out of it for Big Ed. Success is always a double-edged sword, and the fun of The Deal—the schmoozing and coaxing and arguing and haggling and cajoling that used to go into every single sales transaction—had pretty much evaporated. "All I am now is a damn order taker," Big Ed would complain. "Hell, *anybody* can do that kind of shit."

Only it turned out they couldn't....

First we hired Roland Montour, who had slicked-down hair and a pencil-thin mustache and a smile like polished piano keys. He used to sell aluminum siding, life insurance and cemetery plots—often at the same time to the same prospective customers—but he figured, *"Hey, as long as I'm there...."* He also rightly figured that VWs were hot and it was a swell opportunity to line his pockets. Only it turned out that Roland liked to drink a little at lunchtime, followed the ponies and wasn't above trying to make a few moves on prospective female customers. Which is not always the wisest thing to do when a very naturally beautiful and athletic-looking thirtyish blonde with a rubber-banded ponytail and heavy makeup comes in to look at a VW Microbus. Especially when it turns out she skates jammer for the New York City Bombers on the Roller Derby circuit. Poor old Roland wound up with one boxed ear, two black eyes and a pink slip.

And then Big Ed hired Leonard "Lenny" Springman, a fast-talking, likeable young Jewish kid from the other side of the Hudson with no experience at all but quite an admirable supply of moxie, chutzpah and sheer, mercenary aggression dancing in his eyes. He was sharp as they come and a hell of a quick study, and he did a great job for us with the customers. But as soon as he got his brain wrapped all the way around the automobile business, he quit to take the sales manager's job over at a much bigger and plusher VW store over on Long Island, where they bought VeeDubs because they were "in" rather than practical, easy to park and cheap to run. Lenny left on a Tuesday and by Friday we had a guy named Joe Mock on the floor. But he was gone within a month once Big Ed caught wise that he was writing multiple orders and taking multiple deposits for incoming cars, turning in only one and more or less pocketing the rest. How he ever figured he could get away with it is beyond me—juggling all those cars and stalling all those customers until the supply of shiny new Beetles hopefully caught up with demand—but it turned out he had a slight drawing-to-an-inside-straight problem and figured, like degenerate gamblers always seem to do, that if he could just ride the "float" of that gotta-pay-it-back cash until he hit a lucky streak, everything would work out.

But of course it never does.

So Big Ed hired "Irish Bill" Moran, who wore a plaid jacket and white shoes and used to work at the Cadillac store where Big Ed bought a lot of his Caddies. But old "Irish Bill" got fired for "curbing" cars on the side, which is where you make a private deal out on the sidewalk to either sell the prospective customer some car your "brother-in-law" has that isn't in the dealership's inventory or to buy the prospective customer's trade-in "for your brother-in-law" at a slightly higher price than what the dealership has offered. You may wonder how anyone can make money buying higher and selling lower than the genuine franchised dealer, but it's amazing what you can do with no overhead to worry about. "Irish Bill" knew how to sell cars all right, but he was used to Cadillac dollars and didn't much like the small prices and thin profit margins on VWs. Or the lack of wheeling-and-dealing on the trade-ins, which is where a sharp car salesman could really make himself some serious money. So "Irish Bill" got into a big, beer-breath argument with Big Ed one Friday evening about marking all the VeeDubs up a hundred or so over the prices printed for everybody and his brother to see in all those clever black-and-white ads VW ran in all the big national magazines. But Big Ed wouldn't do it, so "Irish Bill" quit and went back to hustling Cadillacs.

After "Irish Bill" we had Sam Lombardo and "Wally" Walton and this earnest young kid named Aaron Glickstein with an expression so sincere it made you ache inside just to look into his eyes. And he was actually pretty good. But he left after less than a month to go into the casket lining business over in Paterson with his new prospective father-in-law. We wished him good luck, and we meant it. One Saturday in a pinch Big Ed even tried using our mechanic Doug the Hillbilly as a car salesman—I was amazed to learn that he owned a jacket and tie—but he was over by Big Ed every five minutes with something he didn't understand or something the customer wanted to know and it was harder for Big Ed than doing everything himself. So that didn't last, either.

We were learning that it takes a certain, special kind of personality to be a good salesman—and even more especially a good car salesman—but that not too many people look at it as a longtime profession or a serious career. Including a lot of the people who wind up doing it for a living. Personally, I couldn't understand it. I mean, you could make yourself some really decent money—and pretty quickly, too—if you were selling a hot line in a well-run store. And then, if you worked hard and kept track of your customers and took care of them when they came in for service and always asked how their families, friends, neighbors and co-workers were (and also, just in passing, if any of those family members, friends, neighbors or co-workers might be in the market for a fine new—or used—automobile) you could build up a following and have a nice, well-paying little clientele for yourself. But that's just not the way most of those guys think, you know? We were coming to understand that when it comes to car salesmen, the old revolving door just never stops revolving. It's just the nature of things.

But while my life was turning into a sort of plodding, repetitive, pile-one-job-on-top-of-another-job, stick-your-finger-into-the-next-hole-in-the-dike blur, at least my pal Cal was keeping me up to date on his racing adventures by calling in with race and progress reports at sometimes ungodly hours of the morning. *"How can it be THAT late?"* he'd say like the notion of time zones was front-page news to him. *"It's only a little after 11 out here...."* And now and then Hank would give me a ring or, better yet, send me one of the long, beautifully entertaining letters I imagine he wrote in the dark, wee hours of the morning when he couldn't sleep. Most likely out on the back balcony of Ernesto Julio's fancy apartment up in the hills overlooking the silent, glittering sprawl of Los Angeles. You could tell Hank loved to write—*had* to write—and he had a real knack for telling stories and painting pictures with words. And if that seems simple and obvious to you, just try it yourself one day. No question it's a kind of gift, and I remember Hank and me talked about it that very first time we met, back when we were seat-mates together on that plane down to Mexico for *La Carrera Panamericana* in November of 1952. Hank said even then—and he was just starting out as a tenderfoot scribe at that point—that he really didn't understand the creative mechanics of how he wrote things down or where the words and ideas came from. *"When it's going really well,"* he admitted kind of helplessly, *"it's like I'm not even doing it, you know? Like I'm just the tube it flows through."* He looked at me sort of sideways. "Do you have any idea what I mean?"

I didn't. And I told him as much.

"Yeah," he sighed. "I'm not sure I get it, either. But there it is anyway...."

Anyhow, Cal was still running Ferraris for Ernesto Julio and enjoying the near year-'round racing season they had out on the coast and the easy life he and Hank had going for themselves up in Ernesto's fancy apartment in the Hollywood Hills. In return for the free bunk-in space, Hank took Cal on his rounds of all the nondescript local shops and back-street garages where a whole new strain of the

American racing disease was spreading like mold in a bachelor-apartment refrigerator. Hank also brought him around to the all the after-work hangouts and local watering holes where all the racers, hot rodders and Indycar builders went to wind down, swap stories and ideas and draw up plans for hot new machines on the back of cocktail napkins from the second or third round straight through until closing time. Hank got Cal introduced to almost everybody who counted on the bending, welding, shaping, wrench-twisting, speed-tuning and fabricating end of the LA sportycar scene, not to mention side trips to the shops of hot-rodders like Vic Edelbrock and Clay Smith and customizers like George Barris, "Big Daddy" Roth and Dean Jeffries and oval-track builders like Frank Kurtis, Eddie Kuzma and Quinn Epperly. Cal was frankly amazed by all the dazzling wrench work going on in and around the greater Los Angeles area—and going on year 'round, to boot—and he'd built enough of a reputation driving Ernesto's Ferraris that he was accepted almost immediately as an insider. Not that Cal cared too much even then about the nuts and bolts of building racecars and the tricks and subtleties of making them run right. They were just tools to get the job done as far as Cal was concerned. But you had to know who *had* those tools—had to know who to get close to—if you wanted to get anywhere in racing.

It was already starting to dawn on Cal—particularly since he started hanging around so much with Hank, who wanted more than anything to cover the real, blood-serious professional sports car and grand prix races and championships over in Europe—that the California road racing scene, just like back east and everywhere else here in the States, was pretty much screw-off amateur and most likely to stay that way. Sure, there were plenty of good race weekends and lots of great cars and even a scant handful of really top-notch drivers. But if you were ever going to go anywhere and amount to anything—if you were ever going to *be* something more than a lah-de-dah playboy dilettante or some rich guy's hotshoe lap dog—you had to get your butt overseas and race for money and points against the best in the world. That was the only way you'd ever be taken seriously.

Still, it wasn't the kind of thing you could just hop off and do on your own. Oh, Cal had a little money of his own now—a nice, fat check from the old trust fund on the fifth or sixth of every month plus a little money from *Moto Italia* whenever he bothered to show up—but it was hardly "buy a Ferrari, hire a team and go racing" money. Besides, most guys who took that route never got what they paid for anyway. No, to get the right deal in the right car at the right race at the right time took more than just a fat wallet. It took breaks. It took luck. It took connections. And Cal knew that people like Ernesto Julio and Tony Parravano and John von Neumann and Carlo Sebastian back in New York had exactly the kind of connections he needed. As did, in a much different way, a lot of the greasy-fingernail types with the crew cuts, gunfighter eyes and sly, insider smiles he was meeting in all those shops, garages and after-work eateries and night spots around L.A. *"This is just what I have to do right now,"* he told me on the phone one night, *"and, don't get me wrong,*

I'm lovin' every minute. But if I'm ever going any further, I'll need to get my butt over to Europe and race against the big boys. That's where Phil Hill is right this minute, the lucky bastard. I just need the right kind of break...."

"Breaks have always been a pretty big thing out in Hollywood, haven't they?" I half-joked into the receiver.

"Yep," Cal agreed. "The streets out here are lined with people looking for them."

No question Cal had the skill, talent and faith in his own ability it took to go somewhere in racing. Not to mention a hefty bucketload of desire. Hey, what the hell else was he going to do with his life? Plus that special, gleaming brand of confidence you can only get from a privileged upbringing or haywire genetics—Cal had both—and he was quick as the dickens in a damn racecar. I figured a combination like that would be more than enough to land him a top factory ride over in Europe. Only it turned out that talent was—and is—the cheapest commodity on earth where those kind of opportunities are concerned. Especially when, like happens to most every hero driver somewhere along the line, Cal hit a bit of a rough patch....

First off, it seemed like there was a little bit of an edge between Cal and Ernesto Julio ever since their lame showing at Sebring. I was pretty sure it had something to do with Gina, too, but Cal insisted she was off shooting a western someplace and he hadn't seen her at all. Not even once. Still, I figured if I could feel the heat off them when I saw them together, Ernesto Julio could, too. Not to mention that Ernesto's team was having some major problems getting their "new" 121LM Ferrari (the one Carlo Sebastian pawned off on him after the factory guys in Maranello pretty much decided the six-cylinder cars were pretty much pigs) back into racing shape. It took more than two months for Carlo's parts department to come up with replacement pieces for the transaxle that broke at Sebring. And those "pieces" turned out to be a whole new transaxle (that surely cost its weight in gold!) and which moreover didn't exactly "bolt right in with ordinary hand tools" since the factory had moved on to other things and wasn't really fooling with the old six-cylinder stuff any more. You can imagine the expression on Ernesto's face when some squirmy little parts guy at the factory over in Italy told him during a 3-ayem-California-time transatlantic phone hookup—in the usual irritated, take-it-or-leave-it, machine-gun-fast local dialect—that the reason everything was taking so damn long was because the 121LM was considered more or less obsolete as far as the factory was concerned. The receiver probably turned to ice in his hand.

In the meantime, Cal was stuck with the old Monza he'd won with at Road America in September of '55, and it had a lot of hard miles on it and was getting a wee bit tired and long in the tooth. He managed to pick up a couple wins with it in minor club races where none of the big guns showed up (or, if they did show up, came to drive themselves or let one of their Rich Car Buddy friends drive and left their paid pro hotshoes at home). But if Phil Hill or Carroll Shelby showed up in somebody's newer and faster 860 Monza or Masten Gregory was hanging around with Tony Parravano's sleek and supple 300S Maserati, it was pretty tough sledding. As it was in the smallbore races, where Cal was wheeling a handsome little Maserati 150S that Ernesto bought more or less out of spite after he got passed over for one of those sought-after Ferrari Four-point-Nines from Carlo Sebastian. By then all the hotshot car owners were keeping smallbore racecars around to run in the Under-1500cc or Under-2.0-Liter modified heats that generally served as Sunday-morning curtain-raisers or Saturday Features to the big-bore main events on Sunday afternoons, and Ernesto loved the 150S because it was sleek and petite and perfectly proportioned. Not to mention that he simply didn't think anything as stubby and ugly and shaped like a shiny tin turd as a Porsche 550 ought to be out there winning races. And beating up on all the beautiful, thoroughbred Italian OSCAs and Siatas in the process. No question if you put the two cars side-by-side, the 150S Maserati definitely *looked* a lot more like a race winner than the Porsche 550 Spyder. And that went double if you fired 'em up and gave the throttles a good prod. Why, the Maserati growled, gurgled and spat back through its Webers like an angry tiger cub, while the Porsche sounded more like an oversized Hoover upright gone berserk. But out on the circuit, Cal soon learned that the Maserati was generally not quite powerful, lightweight or handy enough to take care of Serious Fast gents like Ken Miles, Richie Ginther and Jack McAfee in the quickest of the 550 Spyders. Even a talent like Cal needed to be in the right car to run at the front in that sort of crowd.

But he had to soldier on.

Cal had a really decent run going for himself right through qualifying at Pebble Beach in April, and put the Monza solidly on the front row next to experienced west coast Allard star Bill Pollack in Tom Carstens' iffy-handling but bullet-fast-out-of-the-corners HWM-Chevrolet. And—ahem—ahead of established hotshoes like Phil Hill, Carroll Shelby and Jack and Ernie McAfee (who, by the way, were not related despite sharing the same last name) in four of the best and fastest Ferraris in America. But the qualifying results said as much about the racetrack as anything else. The road was narrow, bumpy, up- and downhill and lined with trees, the corners were mostly tight, claustrophobic right- or left-handers and there was only one straightaway anywheres near long enough to let the long-legged, Le Mans-geared Ferraris and such into top. And then for only a moment before it was time to haul them down again for the next tight, twisty section. Pollack's HWM-Chev was basically a raw, stout, cycle-fendered contraption originally built by two Brit racers named John Heath and George Abecassis and intended for 2.0-liter competition with a four-banger Alta engine under the hood. Hank said they only ever built four of those original models, but the cars ran pretty well in Europe in 1950 thanks to being reasonably light and straightforward and having a young gent by the name of Stirling Moss as one of the team drivers. But the effort eventually crumbled to pieces (as most all of those "why don't we build ourselves a racecar and take on the world" deals usually do) and team sparkplug John Heath got himself killed in the last, latest, Jaguar-powered HWM sportscar in the windy, rainy, 1000-mile *Mille Miglia* race in Italy just one week after Pebble Beach. But meanwhile one of those original HWMs wound up as the movie prop "homebuilt special" boxoffice magnet Kirk Douglas (as poor, struggling but wonderfully ruthless and dashing Italian racer Gino Borgesa) flailed through the streets of Monaco in the opening scenes of MGM's fabulous Cinemascope epic *The Racers.* Or at least until Bella Darvi's (what the heck ever happened to her?) little dog ran across the track and Kirk—or make that Gino—swerved to miss it and crashed rather spectacularly into somebody's fancy Monte Carlo front porch. I've seen that movie about a kazillion times, by the way….

Anyhow, longtime Washington state Allard racer Tom Carstens got his hands on the HWM after MGM was done with it and—in what was turning out to be a fairly typical west coast procedure—spiffed it up a little cosmetically, put a little oval-track hardware here and there underneath and stuffed a hot-rodded Chevy V-8 between the frame rails. They called it the "HWM-C"—although eventually it kind of earned itself the nickname "The Stovebolt Special"—and while it wasn't exactly what you might call a refined sort of device (in fact, one driver who watched it from behind said it handled like a wet eel on a hot plate!) the damn thing sure could *squirt* when the road straightened out. One of the main reasons was the Indianapolis champ car-style quick-change rear end they put in to keep up with the Chevy's power. It allowed Carstens to gear it pretty easily for any kind of track, and that was exactly what the doctor ordered at a short, tight, narrow layout like Pebble Beach, where the notion of shaving seconds by driving faster and maintaining momentum through the corners could be a daunting proposition indeed! Besides, once that light, tightly-geared Chevy special got in front, just where the heck were you going to pass the blessed thing? I mean, it was usually full-tilt sideways through the corners and off like a short-fused rocket down the next straightaway. Plus Bill Pollack was a tough, experienced, take-no-prisoners kind of driver, and after all those years horsing a damn Allard around, he probably felt like he was driving a damn Porsche!

As expected, Pollack smoked away from everybody at the start, but Cal was right there behind him. At least for the first 50 yards or so. Turns out that drag-strip launch was a bit too much for the Monza's clutch (which already had a lot of miles on it, and maybe there was a leaky oil seal as well?) but, whatever it was, Cal was fighting some *serious* clutch slip before they even got to Corner One. And of course by the end of the lap he was down to about fifth or sixth and dropping fast as Phil Hill and the two unrelated McAfees and Bill Murphy and Lou Brero in Kurtis-Buicks sailed right on by. Hill found a way around Pollack, too, and quickly started pulling away. He was driving the exact same, "ex-works" Ferrari 860 Monza we'd watched Fangio and Castellotti win Sebring with just a month before. Only now it belonged to John von Neumann, and his guys had fixed it up with a "trick" relocated gas tank to "make it handle better." Meanwhile Carroll Shelby was clawing his way up through the field in another Ferrari Monza (the same one Phil Hill used to win the Pebble Beach race the year before) after starting way back thanks to car problems during qualifying. He shot by Cal like a rocket while Cal did his best to baby that slipping clutch, working the pedals as gingerly as a damn brain surgeon to keep the engine from winding clear through the redline every time he shifted or tried to goose it out of a corner. But it just kept getting worse and worse, and finally Cal had no choice but to pull in and park it. Just three laps before Ernie McAfee came barreling downhill towards corner six in his Ferrari, left it maybe a hair too late (or maybe there was something funny with the brakes?), slithered off the road on screaming tires and slammed head-first into a tree. He was killed instantly.

The balance of the race ran out with, as often happens, most people not even aware of what had happened. Carroll Shelby took a tough win over Phil Hill (whose "trick" relocated fuel tank actually made the car handle worse and worse as the fuel load lightened) but by then news of the fatality had filtered through the paddock and everybody felt sick, betrayed, disgusted and disillusioned because of it. A lot of people—including Hank Lyons—thought the new crop of cars were simply too damn fast for a makeshift, narrow, bumpy and claustrophobic natural road circuit like Pebble Beach. And there was a lot of truth in that. His race report (which finally showed up in the July issue of *Car & Track* some three months later) noted that "expensive cars, petty club bickering and the lengthening shadow of professionalism" were screwing things up, making things dangerous and spoiling all the fun. And I suppose they were. At the very end of the story, Hank quoted some MG regular in the paddock who shook his head and said: *"I remember the old days, when we all drove TCs and actually liked each other!"*

Things got worse rather than better when the mechanics at *Moto Italia* finally got Ernesto's big, six-cylinder 121LM back together. That's when Cal started realizing all over again that it wasn't the handiest thing on four wheels. In fact, it seemed a lot worse than he remembered it from Sebring. He said the damn thing wanted to steer at the back end, which is never the most comfortable or confidence inspiring of sensations under any circumstances. On top of that it was rare to find a straightaway long enough to let all those big Italian horse-ponies do their stuff. Naturally there was a lot of not-always-pleasant back-and-forth between Cal and Ernesto's head wrench/shop foreman guy at *Moto Italia,* the general gist of which was that either the car was put back together wrong or Cal couldn't drive a nail through a slab of shit. Now I knew that was a load of beans—and so did Cal and maybe even the shop foreman guy, too—but you have to understand that racing is all about confidence. Soup to nuts. And that certain ace wrench-spinners can be just as proud, hard-headed, touchy and prickly about their abilities and reputations as even the most notorious of your prima donna-type drivers. And once you've got that kind of misunderstanding, behind-the-hand whispering, hurt feelings, bruised egos and mistrust grinding away inside a team, it's almost impossible to put it back right again….

And it got even tougher whenever Tony Parravano unleashed the monstrous, 4.9-liter "410 Speciale" Ferrari the factory in Maranello had built especially for him. And particularly after Tony put that bib-overalls-wearing/failed-Texas-chicken-rancher Carroll Shelby behind the wheel. Carroll went like stink in that thing.

And it was salt in the wounds that Ernesto really wanted a 4.9 from Carlo Sebastian when he got stuck with the 121LM. But, as Carlo gently but firmly explained, only one had been built *"as a special favor for a special customer,"* and there just weren't any more to be had. Even though Tony Parravano managed to somehow come up with another one later on and some French guy with a fat wallet and even fatter connections right through to old man Ferrari in Maranello wound up with one as well. Ernesto was thinking maybe his purchase of that snazzy, two-tone Maserati instead of the gunmetal-silver 375 America coupe Carlo wanted to sell him might have had something to do with it. And he was probably right. And he felt even more betrayed when fellow rich-California-car-owner John Edgar showed up at the Seattle Seafair airport race in August with yet another 4.9. It wasn't a "410 Speciale" like Tony's car, but rather one of the only-two-on-the-face-of-the-earth, ex-works "410 Sport" models that the factory team ran just once (in the 1,000-kilometer '56 season opener in Buenos Aires in January) and then pretty much gave up on after both cars broke their transmissions. But the big brute was a much better proposition for the shorter, easier, less tooth-and-nail American club races. And particularly on the airport tracks like Seafair where the roadway was flat as an ironing board and grunt down the straightaways really told the story. Plus von Neumann made it even faster by putting old Texas bib-coverall ace Carroll Shelby behind the wheel in Seattle. But that made perfect sense since Shelby already had a little experience hustling monster Ferrari V-12s around thanks to Tony Parravano and his "410 Speciale." The long and short of it was that Shelby pretty much mopped the floor with the opposition at Seafair. "It's a hog, but it *goes!"* was the way he put it afterwards in the winner's circle.

Meanwhile my buddy Cal managed to wreck Ernesto's just-finished 121LM trying to keep Shelby in sight. Oh, it wasn't entirely Cal's fault—maybe just half or two-thirds—seeing as how he got cut off by a backmarker while he was chasing full-tilt after the 4.9. Now airport tracks are generally pretty safe and have lots and lots of runoff area and not too much scenery to hit, but that still leaves the "moving chicanes" known as slow drivers. Personally, I never understood how anybody could be satisfied just trundling around at the ass end of the field, but I knew people—like Big Ed, Skippy Welcher and even my pal/brother-in-law Carson Flegley—who seemed to get a huge charge out of it regardless. The bad part is that some of those guys are just hanging on by their fingernails even though they're going at what appears to be a garden slug's pace compared to the Fast Guys at the front of the pack. And that makes them about the most dangerous wild cards in racing when the front-runners come around to lap them.

From what Hank said, Cal came up behind this dawdling "modified" XK140 and went for a hole that maybe wasn't entirely there. It hardly helped that the guy he was overtaking was thoroughly oblivious, and swung his meandering Jag in towards a ridiculously early apex just as Cal was trying to squirt through underneath. Cal swerved to avoid contact, but there just wasn't enough room and he wound up glancing off the back quarter of the Jag, bouncing high off a pile of hay bales at the corner station and careening way up on two wheels—Hank said he nearly went over!—before flopping back down and slewing wildly sideways one way and then the other while Cal wrestled the wheel this way and that to try and save it. And he damn near had it gathered up when he got smacked *hard* broadside—right in the stupid little driver's-side aluminum door!—by the same blessed Jaguar! The driver of which was apparently unaware that a car doesn't steer so good when you've got the wheels locked up and the brake pedal mashed clear through the firewall. The impact carried the two cars a bit further down the racecourse before they came to a slow, grinding halt in a mess of tangled British and Italian sheet metal and a cloud of stinky steam. Both drivers sat there for a moment while the dust settled—taking a brief inventory of various bones, joints and ligaments to see if everything was still in working order—and Cal was pretty sure right away there was something screwy going on with his right wrist and elbow. After that, there was nothing to do but clamber out and walk away. But the guy in the Jag never bothered to switch his ignition off, and the two of them didn't get more than 20 paces before some fuel from a broken line or fitting leaked onto a hot exhaust pipe or something and all of a sudden there was this little sizzle of flame and then a little bigger sizzle of flame and then one of those *"ka-whumpf"* noises you get when a fire finally finds itself a decent fuel supply. Fortunately the bulk of the fire was on the Jaguar's side of the wreck, but the 121LM had been pushing out a little oil and so naturally that went up, and when it reached the carburetors, the gas in the float bowls and fuel lines went up, too. But the fire damage to the 121LM was mostly superficial and stayed pretty much in the engine compartment thanks to the corner workers who bravely hurried out and emptied their fire bottles on it! But that car looked pretty sad indeed by the time Ernesto's crew guys rolled its bent, blackened and extinguisher foam-caked remains into the trailer and took off for that long, silent trip back down the coast to Santa Monica.

Cal got off with what he thought were just a few bruises, a split lip, a badly banged right wrist and forearm and some splinters off the wood-rim steering wheel in his palms, but by later that afternoon his right elbow had swelled up like a league ball and he couldn't even pick up a damn beer bottle. So they trucked him off to the hospital. Of course he didn't want to go, but he was really in no condition to fight back. Cal hated hospitals even worse than me, and I can't say as I blamed him. A lot of folks who might well survive their illnesses, infections and injuries never survive their stays in the hospital. It's like Butch whispered to me when he was wrapped up in gauze and plaster in that hospital ward after the big wreck in his old Ford that put him in a wheelchair: *"You stay in one of these places long enough and they'll find a way to kill you...."*

Turns out Cal had broken the small bone in his forearm just below the elbow and cracked a bone or two in his wrist on top of it—best guess was he instinctively put his arm out to protect himself as that big Jag zeroed in for impact—and the doc at the hospital put him in a cast from just above the elbow clear down to his hand, with just the thumb and fingers sticking out through some holes. He was plenty pissed off about it—especially since they had another race coming up the following weekend at Paramount Ranch—but I told him I thought he was damn lucky. But he didn't sound so sure. *"Lucky would've been catching Shelby and not having the damn accident,"* was the way Cal looked at it. And I could see his point.

It was pretty tough for Cal trying to be a Hero Driver with one arm out of commission. He somewhat stupidly told Ernesto Julio that he was sure he could still drive—most race drivers think they can simply *will* their way through those kinds of things—but that's just not the way things worked out the next weekend at the inaugural Cal Club races at Paramount Ranch. It was smack dab in the middle of a searing hot Southern California August, but because Paramount Ranch was up in the Santa Monica mountains just 20 miles northwest of L.A., it amounted to a damn near irresistible proposition for all the racers, fans and sportycar flakes in the greater Los Angeles area. And most especially Hollywood, where flashy is every bit as good as fast and style has always attracted a lot more attention than substance.

The Paramount Ranch was one of several "movie ranches" that sprang up around the time talkies came in, and it was really just a cheap dodge to avoid paying film crews higher, "out-of-town" union wages for location shooting. Hank explained as how those "out-of-town" dollars applied to anywhere more than 35 miles from the studios, and so those movie ranches were all neatly—if sometimes just barely—inside the limit. And even though it was hot as blazes in the summertime, Paramount Ranch offered all sorts of scenery and background possibilities just a short drive from the sound stages. To be honest, Paramount Ranch was nothing more than 2700 acres of undeveloped and relatively inhospitable rock, dust, scraggly trees, snakes, bugs and scrub land tucked away in the hill country between Malibu and the San Fernando Valley. But it had forests, plains, big boulders, steep slopes, craggy canyons and enough western-style scenery that a sharp director could pass it off as anyplace from Colorado to Mexico to the mountains of Montana. Or China or a south sea island or even Salem, Massachusetts, come to that. The western Main Street set the studio built and tore down and built and tore down and then built up all over again—only each time a little different for every new picture, of course—hosted all sorts of celluloid showdowns, tearful, *"a man's gotta do what a man's gotta do"* goodbyes and wild bank-robbery shootouts everywhere from Dodge City, Kansas, to Tombstone, Arizona. Fact is, entire generations of famous movie cowpokes came and went over the years, including Hopalong Cassidy, Roy Rogers, Randolph Scott, Duke Wayne, Gary Cooper, Alan Ladd, Burt Lancaster, Robert Cummings, Basil Rathbone, Glenn Ford, Charlie Ruggles, everybody's favorite sidekick Walter Brennan and Bob Hope as Painless Potter and Jane Russell as the girl whose face you never saw because you were too busy staring at her chest in *Paleface* and *Son of Paleface.*

But things changed in Hollywood. The big studios started to crumble under their own, massive weight, the star system pretty much went bust after the studios came to realize it was impossible to get wealthy, glamorous, willful, egocentric, creative, addictive and occasionally downright crazy personalities with entirely too much time on their hands to do what you wanted them to do. No matter how damn much you paid them. Not to mention the flickering little gray television screens that were popping up in living rooms, dens and downstairs "recreation rooms" from one end of the country to the other and causing a genuine panic in the movie industry. Which meant there wasn't so much loose change laying around in the nooks and crannies of those big studio budgets. So Paramount sold the ranch to a couple sharp promoters who put up a sort of permanent Old Western Main Street (which was mostly just flat plywood boarding house, saloon, general store and jailhouse facades propped up with 2x4 framing) and rented it out to the TV westerns—along with as much wide-open-spaces background as anyone might need—to shoot their weekly episodes. They also decided to put in a permanent racetrack, seeing as how the sportycar boom was in full swing and there were more damn sportycar nutcases per acre in and around Los Angeles than anywhere else on the planet.

The track had an unusual layout, what with a figure 8-style flyover bridge on the front straightaway where the track went over itself and then curled around in a big right-hand loop and shot under itself again heading back the other way. Kind of like a big, coiled blacksnake, right? It was sinewy, difficult and demanding, and some of the drivers thought right off the bat it looked a wee bit dangerous. But it was scenic as hell in that hot, dusty, dried-out and sun-baked Southern California way, and the turnout of participants, fans, curiosity seekers and hangers-on for that very first race was truly impressive. Cal was there with a cast on his arm and Ernesto's aging but still very bright-yellow Ferrari Monza for the big car feature and the 150S Maserati for the smallbore go. But it was obvious pretty quickly that he flat couldn't drive with that cast on his arm. Sure, like almost all true racing Ferraris the Monza was right-hand-drive, so he could do all of his gear stirring with his good left wing. But it was awkward as hell trying to steer the damn thing—especially while he was shifting—and his cast kept banging into stuff in the cockpit. After just two laps in the very first practice session he pulled in, went behind the trailer and had one of his mechanic buddies cut the damn cast off with a hacksaw. But that didn't work, either. At first his wrist and arm didn't feel too bad. Or at least not until he got back in the car and tried driving again. Cal went straight off the road the first time he tried to steer the car while his left hand was busy shifting. And it hurt like hell, too. He came in with his right arm kind of dangling down beside him and an expression on his face that nobody had ever seen before. *"I can't do it,"* he hissed through clenched teeth. *"I just can't do it!"*

Well, they helped him out of the car and the mechanic who cut his cast off took him back into town to have another one put on, and meanwhile Ernesto's head wrench guy called in on a pay phone—Ernesto was still in L.A. "on business" at the time, whatever that meant—and then went searching around the paddock for another likely hotshoe to drive the yellow Monza. He came across California golden boy Lance Reventlow and our new friend Bruce Kessler, who had bought themselves a pair of tiny, rear-engined Coopers. Lance had a Climax-powered, Manx-tailed sports/racer—I guess he'd taken Hank and Cal's advice about getting something a little handier than that big 300SL to hurl around—while Bruce was wheeling one of those tiny, 500cc Formula III Cooper/Norton single-seaters that looked like a damn cigar tube on wheels. "You really learn a lot about driving in one of these things," Bruce told somebody he caught looking down his nose at the Cooper. "You've really got to use all the road and the very smoothest, gentlest line to maintain your momentum—hell, it's only a damn motorcycle engine—and you can place one of these things within inches compared to a big car. It really teaches you a lot." Everybody with eyes thought Bruce Kessler was a rising star and had a lot of potential (even if he was a little wild now and then), and naturally he jumped at the chance to drive Ernesto Julio's Ferrari. Oh, sure, he felt bad about it. For about ten seconds, anyway. Even came up to Cal and kind of apologized after he got back from the hospital with a new and even bigger cast on his arm later that afternoon. But that's just how quickly things can change and you can find yourself replaced and maybe even out of a drive.....

Like I said, Paramount Ranch was mostly just a low-key club-racer deal, and the "big guns" amounted to a few Wealthy Amateurs in a couple "customer" D-Types and a Ferrari Monza, Bill Murphy's Kurtis-Buick and a gorgeous "copy" of a 300SLR Mercedes that a local body shop owner named Chuck Porter built for himself out of a totaled "street" 300SL that came his way. A guy named Jack Sutton had done such a splendid job on the hand-rolled aluminum bodywork that there were rumors flying all over the place that this body shop owner from L.A. had somehow got his hands on one of the actual factory Mercedes racecars Hank and me saw run at Le Mans. But of course it wasn't. Hell, the real racecars were straight eights and this was a straight six like every other "street" 300SL. But I guess some folks just can't count. Sure was beautiful, though.

At the far opposite end of the beauty scale was that "Morgensen Special" Hank had told me about, which was uglier than an old three-legged dog with a skin disease. Turns out it was originally a crude-looking homebuilt with an old straight-six Plymouth engine running triple carburetors, but it went fairly fast now and then in club races in '54 and '55. Then it got left off "on consignment" at this fairly notorious sportycar shop near Hollywood that did a lot of work for the movie people who liked fast cars. The shop was run by a husband-and-wife team named Max and Ina Balchowsky, and I guess old Max was as crusty, tough and salty as they come. But he was sharp as hell when it came to figuring out automobiles. A real *maestro,* you know? And his wife Ina knew a thing or two about wrenches and welding torches, too. In any case, Max had done a little sportycar racing himself in an old Ford hotrod he built with a big Cadillac V-8 engine between the frame rails, and I guess some of the purist Ferrari, Jaguar, Porsche and Maserati types got their noses ever-so-slightly out of joint about it. Anyhow, instead of selling that ugly old "Morgensen Special," Max started working on it and massaging it and making it faster. Including shoving a big old "nailhead" Buick V-8 under its lumpy hood. Max drove it some himself, but he was never above putting somebody a little quicker in his cars. Especially if that somebody could sign a few checks to help defray the expenses. Which is how a young kid named Eric Hauser (who was apparently a kind of wallet partner in the project) wound up behind the wheel at Paramount Ranch.

Cal meanwhile wound up watching the Saturday afternoon qualifying races with Hank over on the dull side of the fences. Although he was in a lot of pain and feeling pretty low about things in general, he was alert enough to notice some young hotshoe named Bob Bondurant in a Triumph-engined Morgan and another guy named Elliot Forbes-Robinson in an MGA and mark them both as guys to watch. In the big car race, he and Hank were grudgingly impressed by the smooth, smart way Bruce Kessler drove Ernesto's Monza and the way that ugly old Morgensen Special flew around the circuit in a series of strangely graceful slides, surges and lunges. Oh, it was ugly as hell and that big Buick engine sounded lazy and lumbering—like it was just loafing along, you know?—but the car was fast as stink and no question old Max Balchowsky could build a pretty damn clever racecar. He was sharp as anything when it came to how things worked and went together under the sheetmetal.

Cal was back the next morning with his eyes pointed towards two different horizons thanks to some really potent pain pills the doctor gave him. Hey, *nobody* doles out higher-octane drugs than the highly professional medical types around Hollywood. In fact, they're more or less famous for it. And if it wasn't bad enough watching Bruce Kessler run—and run well—in the yellow Ferrari Monza he figured he really ought to be driving, who should show up on Ernesto's arm but the stunningly svelte, sleek and beautiful Angelina Scalabrini? Or Gina LaScala—take your pick.

Truth is, I don't think anybody knows where this stuff comes from. You pass somebody in a crowded hallway and you catch their eyes and hear their voice and then, all by itself, this warm, aching puddle starts spreading inside your gut. Until it's almost like you're drowning in it. And the really crazy part is that you know—you *know!*—that the other person is feeling it, too. All of a sudden you're in the soup together and neither one of you knows what it is or where it came from or, most of all, what the hell you ought to do about it. Especially when you've got your own life and wants and goals and dreams to look after. Hell, Cal wanted to race cars because he loved it and didn't know what else to do with himself and Gina wanted to be a great movie star because, well, she'd been aimed at it like a loaded howitzer ever since she could walk and talk. So she didn't have any idea what else she could possibly do with herself, either. Fact is, you need to be selfish, single-minded, focused, talented, lucky and thoroughly dedicated to pursue any kind of performing life, whether as an actress or a singer or a quarterback or a shortstop or a saxophone player or a sleight-of-hand magician. Or a racing driver, come to that.

Everything depends on sustained desire and relentless effort—you have to have that cold, burning *need* inside—and that just doesn't leave much room, time or inclination left for anything else.

Back in Brooklyn after they first met, I guess Angelina's mother thought there might be some value in the relationship. After all, Cal was rich and good-looking and came from a prominent family, and there might be some mileage to be made in the tabloids out of his racing. But she sensed very quickly that Angelina was feeling things she neither knew or comprehended, and her mother quickly cut the relationship off at the knees. In fact, that may have been what triggered their sudden move to California in the early spring of 1953. And now the two of them were together again—three years later and 3000 miles away—standing just a few feet from each other along the spectator fencing at Paramount Ranch. But with the tanned, silver haired bulk of Ernesto Julio in between and both of them trying hard as they dared not to look at each other….

Chapter 16: Pros, Politics and Pachyderms

Ever since our adventure with the Ferrari team at Sebring I made a point of trying to keep up with the big international racing scene overseas. But it was difficult on account of the newspapers here—even the *New York Times*—hardly mentioned those Formula One or World Manufacturers' Championship races unless somebody got themselves killed. Not even in the tiny agate underneath the batting averages of every damn scrotum scratcher, undershorts adjuster and tobacco-juice spitter in the major leagues. I mean, who cared about that stuff anyway? Besides my old man and his chemical-plant drinking buddies, that is, who could spout that shit like they were preaching chapter and verse from the Holy Bible. Honest they could. And no way could you find any European racing updates on the radio or television news. Unless there was a huge wreck, of course. And the bloodier the better.

Mostly all I had to go on were the race reports in *Car & Track,* which generally lagged three to four months behind what was actually taking place over in Europe. I used to get *Autosport* via air mail from England and always kept a couple copies on the counter over at Old Man Finzio's Sinclair, but the air freight made them pretty pricey and mostly everybody'd just thumb through the latest issue and then leave it for the next guy to thumb through without ever actually buying one. The Old Man eventually put a stop to it, and out of courtesy to his memory I never got around to re-upping my subscriptions once we opened up the new VW dealership. Sure, I'd see a copy every now and then, but I didn't grab one out of the package as soon as they arrived, lock myself in the john and make noises like I had a bad case of stomach flu until I devoured it from cover to cover. To begin with, I was too busy. Plus it more or less ruined the surprise and suspense of those *Car & Track* stories when they finally arrived. And I have to admit I was getting a little weary of how those British writers were just the teeny-tiniest bit biased in favor of anything and everything that came out of England in any way, shape or form. As far as they were concerned, a good British back-alley rumor was better than anything they could possibly dream up in the race shops in Maranello, Modena or Stuttgart. Or anyplace at all in America, come to that. And that can get a wee bit tiresome if you don't happen to be English. Not to mention the way they praised to the heavens and polished up tall marble pedestals for all their own homegrown British drivers! Mind you, they did have a lot to crow about, what with Stirling Moss nipping hard at Fangio's heels and Mike Hawthorn, Peter Collins and Tony Brooks all coming on strong and looking good enough to beat anybody on their day.

In the right car, of course….

And that was the big question mark for 1956. Could anybody beat Ferrari? Mercedes-Benz had pretty much folded up their tent at the end of the '55 season in the aftermath of that terrible wreck we witnessed at Le Mans. I still had nightmares about it now and then. And so did a lot of other people, I expect. But the point is that Mercedes didn't have a lot more to prove. They'd generally steamrollered the opposition while they were out there—in Formula One and sportscars alike—and most people were left with the lingering impression that Mercedes built the fastest, most advanced, best engineered, most thoroughly developed and most reliable automobiles on the entire planet. And that was the whole idea, wasn't it? Of course, it didn't hurt that they had the two best damn road racing drivers in the world—Juan Manuel Fangio and Stirling Moss—on the old company payroll. That was a tough combination to beat no matter what they were driving. Plus those two always played by team manager Alfred Neubauer's rules and somehow resisted the temptation to race the living crap out of each other when they already had the rest of the opposition covered.

Which was just the opposite of what generally went on at Ferrari, where the Old Man made a point of keeping his drivers stirred up, on edge, at each other's throats (or at the very least looking over their shoulders) and worried sick about where they stood with him and the team. Hank said the Old Man probably figured it made them more aggressive and willing to take chances, and that would make them faster. So he likely relished the notion that Luigi Musso made Castellotti nervous. And he'd hired on the fast, fair-haired young Brit Peter Collins just to keep them both on edge. Plus our pal Phil Hill to help out on the World Manufacturers' Championship sportscar team. And that was a pretty huge deal, since he was the first-ever American to drive for Ferrari. But the cherry on top of it all was signing three-time world champ and consensus Best Damn Racer on the Planet Juan Manuel Fangio, who wound up out of a ride after Mercedes pulled the plug and grudgingly agreed to terms with Ferrari after the Old Man offered him an unusually large bag of gold and it furthermore became obvious that Ferrari represented by far his best chance to keep winning races and defend his World Championship. After all, Jaguar was only really interested in Le Mans (and maybe Sebring for the American market) and Le Mans wasn't even a World Championship round in 1956 thanks to some serious differences of opinion concerning displacement limits between the Le Mans organizers and the FIA in Paris. And if you know anything at all about Frenchmen, you know that argument likely ended with the two parties staring off in opposite directions, arms folded angrily across their chests and a set of engraved dueling pistols on the way. Plus Jaguar didn't even have a grand prix car. And neither did Aston Martin or Porsche, for that matter. That pretty much left just the two Italian teams, Ferrari and Maserati, and while Ferrari was full of politics, plots and intrigues, Maserati could be colossally fragmented, overextended, disorganized and hand-to-mouth.

Oh, there were the usual overblown press releases out of England about bold new British grand prix and sportscar challengers—particularly the new BRM and Vanwall grand prix cars, which were always front-page news as far as *Autosport* and the rest of the English magazines were concerned—but the truth of things was that only Maserati stood in the way of complete Ferrari domination. And Maserati were spread so thin they were damn near transparent, what with trying to build "street" sportscars and *grand turismos* like Ferrari along with the World Manufacturers' Championship sports racers and single-seater formula cars that made their name. They were also struggling a bit financially and hoped that adding "street" sportscars would help keep the old cash register ringing. But there were only so many keen eyes, skilled hands and weary feet to go around and, being true racers, the racing team always came first when push came to shove.

For the '56 season Maserati had true "factory team" grand prix cars for Moss, Behra and Gonzalez and a couple somewhat, umm, "subsidized" team cars for rich, fast but occasionally impetuous and unseasoned rising hotshoes like that Carlos Menditeguy from Argentina, plus slightly out-of-date grand prix cars to look after for a whole fistful of wealthy privateers. Maserati were also committed to fielding their latest sportscars at all the big World Manufacturers' Championship endurance races all over the globe, and it gave them added hope when Moss and Menditeguy won the very first championship round of the season in Argentina after both of Ferrari's monster 4.9s broke their transmissions. The Maserati race shops were also up to their armpits in customer cars that needed building and rebuilding, and that was important because it also rang the old cash register.

Like my buddy Cal, I was captivated by the professional road racing scene over in Europe. Why, the idea that you could do that kind of thing for a living, make big money at it, get World Series/Heavyweight Champ famous, and moreover be taken seriously and as a true professional in even the most hoity-toity continental society was a hard thing to grasp over on this side of the Atlantic. Plus you couldn't miss how the cars and drivers represented—hell, came to stand for—the countries they came from. Unlike our Indy 500 and southern stock car racers that were slathered all over with advertising slogans touting everything from prunes to plumbing hardware, the European teams proudly appeared in their home country's racing colors—Italian red, French blue, German silver and of *course* British Racing Green—and you got the feeling that World War II hadn't exactly ended over there with the armistice. Then again, the Europeans had been raiding, looting, sacking, pillaging, raping, invading, conquering and generally kicking the shit out of each other as far back as history could remember, and so there was plenty of stored-up anger, vengeance, envy, prejudice, hate, bile, fear, piss and vinegar to fuel the old competitive fires.

Racing was big business over there, too. Le Mans amounted to no less than its own, teeming little 24-hour metropolis, and the crowd at a lot of those grand prix races put our own World Series to shame. Even when the Yankees and Dodgers were playing. And those folks not only paid admission, but bought sausage sandwiches and beer or wine or soft drinks to wash it down with and all kinds of souvenirs, too. Why, just about all of Italy shut down and turned out on the hillsides—by the tens and hundreds of thousands!—to watch the *Mille Miglia.* And the same was pretty much true for *La Carrera* down in Mexico. So it should come as no surprise that a few people in these United States started wondering why the same thing couldn't happen here in America?

And that notion had a lot of people very worked up indeed.

An enormous controversy was brewing (and even boiling over now and then!) about whether American road racing should remain a simon-pure amateur sport or go full-tilt, blood-and-guts professional like the Europeans. Which is another way of saying whether it should continue on as a sort of private, upper-crust, isolationist weekend country club for privileged (and properly pedigreed!) duffers, dandies, dalliers and dilettantes, or if it should turn into a professional, take-on-all-comers money-and-blood sport like they had over in Europe. Or right here in the states on the oval-track, Indycar, sprint and stock car circuits. If you listened to the tight-ass Charlie Priddle types, that amounted to pure heresy—unthinkable!—and it ultimately escalated into a Grand Canyon-sized split right down the middle of American road racing.

There was no way you couldn't take sides.

Of course if you talked to the racers—and I mean the *real* racers—hell, they just wanted a place to run their damn cars. But, as is typical of the way things work in amateur, volunteer-based organizations of any kind (and especially when dreamed up and lorded over by a bunch of rich folks with way too much money, privilege and free time on their hands), the cream that often rises to the top is actually the sour, curdled-up stuff right off the bottom. But who else wants to mess with it? Which is precisely how a lot of the people who wind up in charge of such things turn out to be picayune, meddlesome jerks, jerkoffs and jackasses who enjoy flexing their imagined muscles and throwing their puffed-up weight around. Mind you, I'm not referring to the volunteer organizers and track workers who actually put on the events (or not many of them, anyway), but rather the powerful, behind-closed-door types with nothing much better to do who absolutely *live* for the politics, power struggles and intrigues that make their lives and opinions seem so damned important.

So on the one side you had the snooty, sniffy, old guard SCMA hard-liners like Charlie Priddle and his armband gang on the east coast, the movers and shakers of the San Francisco region of the SCMA on the west coast and some white-bread, old-money types like new club president Pearson Cameron and right-hand man Fletcher Wingate out of the Midwest. Although I never met him personally, Hank said Pearson Cameron was exactly what you might expect Central Casting to send over if you asked for a filthy-rich, well-born and perfectly raised young stuck-up, bigoted tight ass. Pearson's family ran a huge dairy business somewhere around Chicago and had lots and lots of money and scads of fancy sportscars (most of which were registered as milk trucks as a kind of tax dodge, but that's another story) and he echoed the sentiments of a lot of the old-money SCMA founders when he whispered behind closed doors that they didn't want a lot of foreigners, paid professionals, riffraff and "ethnic undesirables" crashing their party. And by "ethnic undesirables," he mostly meant rich, high-profile Jews like Erwin Goldschmidt or my friend and partner Big Ed Baumstein, on account of they had no "breeding" and were considered by Those In The Know as loud, pushy and way too clever with money. Not to mention that they killed Jesus Christ. Neither was the club particularly interested in anybody with a touch of the old tar brush, if you know what I mean. Unless they happened to be English-educated Indian princes or fabulously rich and powerful South American dictators, that is. To be fair, that's the way Pearson Cameron and the rest of his silver-spoon buddies had been taught and brought up ever since they could dampen a diaper. After all, those exact same rules applied without question (or mention!) to all the upper-crust neighborhoods they lived in, all the churches they attended—at least every Christmas and Easter, anyway—and all the other golf, riding, saddle, polo, tennis, bridge, social, swimming, racquet and all-purpose athletic clubs they belonged to either up by their summer places in the country or down around their brownstone mansions and posh penthouse apartments in the city.

On the other side of the aisle you had a few ambitious, creative, forward-thinking and promotionally-minded young enthusiasts like Cam Argetsinger and Alec Ulmann, who had been to Europe and seen the racing scene over there—most especially Le Mans—and thought that could be the model for what sportycar racing should become here in the states. Of course Cam Argetsinger was the sparkplug behind the original street races at Watkins Glen, and a lot of the Old Money crowd got their noses out of joint when he fought for—and got—a full FIA international sanction for his race in 1950. In fact, the SCMA threatened to pull out completely—and did, at least on paper—but Cam got the FIA's American representative, the Triple-A (who were sanctioning the Indy 500 and most other professional American oval-track racing at the time) to step up to the plate.

The race came off as a huge success, and that got the above-mentioned blue noses even further out of joint from being rubbed in you-know-what. And a lot of it was because Cam Argetsinger accepted the entry of the above-mentioned Erwin Goldschmidt on his FIA-approved Triple-A license, even though there was no way in hell he could ever get into the club. Some people—including Goldschmidt himself—said loudly and repeatedly that it was on account of he was Jewish. But upper-echelon club types were quick to point out that they did have a few—a very few—Jewish members. Like Max Hoffman, for example. But Max imported and sold an awful lot of the fancy sportycars prowling the streets and byways of New York and New England, and so it would have been a pretty dicey proposition to keep him out. And since a lot of the club members were also his biggest and best customers, old Max treated them with the proper respect and deference. But Goldschmidt was something else entirely. He was rich and brash and proud and loud and arrogant (at least according to many of the old guard in the club) and didn't give two shits if your family came over on the damn Mayflower. No question he rubbed a lot of folks the wrong way. There was a famous story about how Fletcher Wingate overheard him complaining—loudly—at the bar one race weekend that he couldn't get into the club because he was Jewish. *"It's not because you're Jewish,"* Fletcher corrected him. *"It's because you're such a shit."*

Anyhow, most of the snoots and snobs in the club hierarchy didn't want to open the floodgates to guys like Erwin Goldschmidt (or Big Ed Baumstein, come to that) and held Cam Argetsinger personally responsible for allowing him to race his Allard at The Glen in 1950. My Allard friend and hero Tommy Edwards allowed as how Goldschmidt was a hell of a decent driver—no matter what you thought of him personally—and he proved it by finishing a strong second in the curtain-raiser Seneca Cup race for unlimited cars that year. That was good enough to qualify him for the feature Watkins Glen Grand Prix later that afternoon, and that had a lot of the old-guard types very nervous indeed....

A bunch of rather tacky behind-the-scenes maneuvering resulted in all non-SCMA drivers (that would be Goldschmidt and his Allard) being moved to the back of the grid and all the proper SCMA drivers (that would be just about everybody else) put ahead of them. Which made it even worse when Goldschmidt had the unmitigated gall and temerity to work his way through the whole blessed field and win the damn race! After starting at the back! Which was like stuffing a little extra you-know-what up each and every nostril on the old SCMA competition board, if you know what I mean.

The Charlie Priddle types responded by essentially taking the Watkins Glen race away from Cam Argetsinger in 1951 and '52. But they did it in their usual, upright, by-the-book, "all those in favor say *'aye'*" fashion with a thoroughly democratic 4-to-3 vote of the 7-man board they'd lobbied, conned, connived, threatened and coerced and loaded as best they could with sympathetic representatives. In case you didn't know, that's how they do things in the land of winks and nods. Or pick your favorite downtown city hall, for that matter.

But Cam Argetsinger and his Watkins Glen Grand Prix Corporation were pretty much back running things for the "interim" races at the second course up on the hill above town after Tommy's terribly unfortunate crash on Franklin Street where that poor little seven-year-old boy got killed during the '52 event. But the SCMA hard liners were still plenty pissed off and denied Cam a sanction for that first race at the new track in 1953. Plus they spread a lot of ugly rumors and leaked a bunch of stories to the motoring press about how the course was terribly dangerous and never going to be finished in time anyway and even, at the very last minute, that the race had been cancelled. And if this sounds like dirty pool to you, let me just remind you that many of these same folks were veterans of (and major contributors to) various and sundry "conservative" political campaigns, and that's precisely the kind of on-the-job training you need when it comes to influencing, persuading and outright poisoning public opinion.

Cam's friend Alec Ulmann was another thorn in the old guard's side thanks to the success his ambitious, professional and thoroughly international 12 Hours of Sebring was enjoying down in Florida. In fact, the SCMA tried to undermine his second "pro" race in 1952 by running their own 12-hour enduro right up the road at Vero Beach just a week beforehand. They furthermore threatened SCMA drivers with excommunication—er, make that "license suspension"—if they dared to run Ulmann's "outlaw" FIA money event at Sebring. But of course racers being racers, the general attitude among the drivers was: *"You mean we get to run TWO 12-hour races in Florida? Geez, I hope the car holds up!"*

So the lines were drawn, and no question the specter of professional, everybody-welcome international money racing worried the heck out of the old-line

SCMA clubby types. They didn't want to get shown up by a bunch of foreigners of indeterminate breeding, and the American oval track, Indianapolis and sprint car bunch seemed awfully tough, hard-boiled and blood-and-guts serious for their tastes. As for the southern stock car types—hell, they looked like a bunch of backwoods peckerwood bumpkins and snake handlers who chewed tobacco, drank moonshine and ran into each other on purpose. Is that what they wanted their nice, refined sport to turn into? Why, having those guys around would ruin *everything!*

Especially if they were fast....

But the racetracks, bless their cash-starved little hearts, were hungry for any kind of show that funneled people through the turnstyles and put, as my good Brit friend Tommy Edwards put it, "bums on seats." Which is precisely how a 250-mile NASCAR stock car race got booked onto those fabulous, sweeping, rolling, uphill and downhill four miles of Road America smack-dab in the middle of August, 1956. To say the sportycar crowd looked down their noses at the stock car types doesn't quite cover it. Why, not even Pinocchio had a long enough nose for that sort of duty. The general consensus among the tweed cap/badge bar/auxiliary driving light/string-back driving glove set was that stock car racing was, as old squinty-eyed/nutty-as-a-fruitcake Skippy Welcher put it: *"Nothing but a parade of clumsy pachyderms!"* He also figured (along with a lot of the sportycar faithful) that the stock car racers themselves belonged somewhere between orangutans and Piltdown Man on the old evolutionary scale.

Of course I knew better. I'd seen them run on the airport course in Linden, New Jersey, and had moreover talked to a few of them and taken a good look underneath some of those cars—particularly those Smokey Yunick Hudsons, or at least until he shooed me off, anyway—and that was enough to make me see past those slow southern drawls and mannerisms to the shrewd, sly, savvy racers underneath. Mind you, none of those boys had much experience with road racing and no question brakes and handling around Road America's tight, 90-degree corners were going to be a serious problem for them. But I had the feeling they'd figure it out once given the opportunity. I was just about alone in that opinion, however, and the writer *Car & Track* sent to cover the race (who happened to be a dyed-in-the-wool Austin Healey nutcase) couldn't have been more dismissive, mean-spirited or condescending.

Or maybe he could, but it would have taken some serious effort.

It hardly helped that it rained all morning at Road America and the track was still soaking wet as the stock cars finally rumbled out of the pits after a long delay and headed off on their pace lap. My old oval-track buddy Sammy Speed was there and told me all about it. He was wheeling one of the new, "factory-assisted" Dodge D-500s, and allowed that a lot of it was because of his previous road racing experience (mostly thanks to me and my friend and partner Big Ed Baumstein, by the way!). Now most sportycar types didn't pay too much attention to big old American sedans, but I kind of liked to keep my eyes open. After all, I was in the new car business—albeit with Volkswagens—and Big Ed always said you had to look further ahead than the tip of your own nose if you wanted to know what was what and who or whom you had to look out for. And of course the stock cars *everybody* had to look out for in 1956 were the Carl Kiekhaefer Chrysler 300s.

Carl Kiekhaefer was a local-boy inventor/entrepreneur/millionaire who just happened to own (among other things) this enormous outboard boat motor manufacturing company in Wisconsin called Mercury Marine. It seems old Carl took a notion to go stock car racing one day, and in February of 1955 he showed up out of the blue down at Daytona with a whole team of immaculately prepared and perfectly painted Chrysler 300s with *"MERCURY MARINE"* lettering down the sides. Nobody had ever seen a stock car team like it before, what with the cars and equipment all carried inside huge enclosed transporters painted just like the cars and top-notch mechanics in spanking white uniforms with *"MERCURY MARINE"* embroidery on the backs and chest pockets and ace drivers like Tim Flock and Buck Baker and our own oval-track buddy Sammy Speed signed on for more money than most teams had in their budget for the entire year. To tell the truth, they made the rest of the stock car guys look like a bunch of rubes and bumpkins. And those cars went fast as stink, too. Especially on the big tracks where those monster, 331-cubic-inch Hemi engines could stretch their legs. In fact, the well-publicized success of the Kiekhaefer Chryslers was one of the main reasons Big Ed bought himself a brand-new 1957 Chrysler 300C convertible just as soon as they came out in the fall of 1956.

Unfortunately Sammy had a little falling out with the team on account of he really enjoyed running Indycars and sprinters and such while they wanted him to stick to their stock cars. And he probably should have, because the work was steady and the money was better than any deal he'd ever had. But Sammy couldn't help himself. He loved his open-wheel racing—especially on dirt!—but unfortunately managed to break his wrist and shoulder while performing a series of endos during a Thursday-night AAA race on the mile dirt oval in DuQuoin, Illinois, the same weekend he was supposed to be wheeling one of the Kiekhaefer Chryslers on Sunday on the big, almost-round dirt oval in Langhorne, Pennsylvania. Needless to say, that didn't sit real well with his crew cheif—or Mr. Kiekhaefer, for that matter—who quickly pointed out that there was a clause in his contract about not racing other people's cars (or at least not without prior approval, anyway), but Sammy allowed as how the damn contract was nearly half-an-inch thick and he fell asleep before he got to that part. The end result was that Sammy was out of commission for the rest of the '55 season and back on his own when racing started up again come the spring of 1956. He had a pretty good ride going at the Indy 500 that May in a year-old Kurtis chassis—at least until a tire blew and, as he put it, "introduced me to the wall"—and he scored two wins and some other high finishes in Les Gonda's new dirt sprinter running on the bullring ovals and state fair circuit. But it was his road racing experience with me and Big Ed more than anything that got him hired on to handle one of the new, factory-supported Dodge D-500s at Road America that August.

The Kiekhaefer Chryslers were there too, of course, and figured to be by far the most powerful cars and surely the fastest in a straight line. Not to mention that it was a sort of "hometown race" for old Carl Kiekhaefer and his guys, and you can bet they wanted to run at the front. But the Chrysler 300s were big, heavy things, and Sammy allowed as how he thought he might be better off with the Dodge. The D-500 was brand-new in 1956, and the stock car version was a fine variation on an old, old theme that hadn't been played near often enough in Detroit: take your lightest-weight, stripped-to-the-bone two-door coupe and stuff your biggest, hottest engine under the hood. Then step back and watch what happens! The D-500 borrowed a page from old Donald Healey's notebook and set all kinds of ripe-for-the-picking acceleration and speed records at Daytona Beach and Bonneville, and all the magazine ads for the D-500 touted it as a genuine stoplight terror. The Madison Avenue ad types really laid it on thick, too, throwing around thoroughly inflammatory phrases like *"This 'baby' takes 'em all!"* and *"One second you're idling at the light, the next you're off like a flash—out ahead of the pack with nothing in front of you but the wide open road"* or *"Dodge now gives you the red-hot performance you could only get in an expensive custom job"* and *"Keep your eye on the D-500...it's a real bomb!"* to stimulate the salivary glands and pump up the red corpuscles of every 9-to-5 clock-puncher in America with a wife, kids, house, mortgage and a starry-eyed kid/wannabe race driver locked up inside.

The D-500 had a 315-cubic-inch "baby" version of the big, 331-cubic-inch Hemi they used in the Chrysler 300s, along with a hot cam, a four-barrel carburetor and little crossed checkered flags above the "Dodge" lettering on the hood. You could get the D-500 package as an option on any Dodge model for an extra couple hundred bucks, and no question the Dodge marketing guys were out to prove they really had something special. Only they had to tread a little gently on the NASCAR stock car racing side, seeing as how it just wouldn't do to beat up on the flagship Chrysler 300s or the company favorite Kiekhaefer team that was spending so much money and getting Chrysler such great publicity. So while Dodge was setting speed records and such as grist for the old advertising mill, in stock car racing they could only feed independent teams a few trick parts and occasional small wads of cash and hope for the best. Even so, my buddy Sammy was pretty happy about having a D-500 for that stock car race at Road America. He had a hunch that the lighter-weight, handier D-500 might be a far better choice than one of those monster Chrysler 300s on a road course. Even though the Fords and Mercurys were lighter still.

And then the damn rain came down. In sheets and buckets at first, then tapering off enough that they could at least think about giving the race a try. Not many of the stock car guys had ever raced in the rain before (or on a road course, for that matter), but they were there to put on a show—even if there wasn't much in the way of an audience on the other side of the fences—and figured their experience on dirt would be a big help. And I guess it was, since that's where a lot of them wound up as soon as the racing started. Or maybe mud was more like it. *"We were slipping and sliding all over the damn place!"* Sammy told me disgustedly when I talked to him. *"We shoulda been wearing clown hats and rubber noses."*

But the rain eased off as the laps went down, and as I saw in person at the Linden airport, the best of those stock car guys really knew how to drive. Most of them were really getting the hang of it by the time the track started to dry. And that's right about when they started running out of brakes. It made perfect sense when you think about it: as the pavement dried, the cars naturally went faster. And, as Sammy put it: *"There's just no way you can slow a 3,000-pound stock car down from 115 or so to 45 or 50 six times a lap for 250 miles. The damn thing just won't DO it!"* Even so, my buddy Sammy had worked his way into the lead by that point—mostly by downshifting and using the drag of the engine to help slow the car down and take some of the strain off the brakes—but eventually the engine cried *"ENOUGH!"* and blew up in a very big way, spreading oil and scattering connecting-rod fragments and bearing bits all over the braking zone on the downhill slope to Corner Five. Then there was nothing to do but climb out and take that long, sad hike back to the pits to tell the crew. "Damn. I was leading, too," he said ruefully afterwards. "But if I'm honest, we never would have made it to the finish anyway. At least there weren't many people around to see it."

And that was true enough, as the combination of the strange, unfamiliar stock car show—*"a parade of clumsy pachyderms,"* remember?—plus truly crappy weather kept the crowd down to almost nothing. In the end, Tim Flock survived better than anyone else and won it in a Mercury at a relatively snail-like 71mph average, and the snotty reporter from *Car & Track* noted down his nose that was a good 10mph off of what Carroll Shelby averaged in a Ferrari earlier in the year. What a surprise! He also added in a particularly terse, almost shorthand version of English:

"Representatives of FIA present, fawned over, etc. Stamp of approval is 'significant and meaningful,' but to anyone in pit area meaning was highly questionable and significance revolting...Refueling something out of a Buster Keaton comedy...shocking to witness these Fearless Fosdicks at work—barefoot males walking over crushed gravel toting 5-gallon cans of gas...Another character seen pouring gas while dragging away on a cigarette...Crowd in attendance something in excess of what it would have been if no one had attended...but advertised '20,000' figure could not have been obtained even counting mosquitoes."

As you can see, he was hardly impressed. And he was hardly alone.

Anyhow, the big conflict about "amateur" versus "pro" events (or any kind of non-SCMA racing!) on road courses came to a serious head at Watkins Glen just a few weeks later. It was the third weekend in September, and for a change I was on hand to witness the whole thing in person. I hadn't really been to a live race since Sebring in March, and to tell the truth with everything that was going on at the shop and the dealership, I couldn't really afford the time to go to this one, either. But we'd all heard about the new, purpose-built racecourse they'd built (or hadn't finished building, depending on who you talked to) up on the hill above town, and that was something both Big Ed and me figured we had to see in person. "Just remember," Big Ed grinned as we gunned his brand-new, gleaming-black '57 Chrysler 300C convertible out from behind the sandwich shop across the street from the dealership late Friday afternoon, "life is short, and there's nothing so damn urgent today that won't be even more urgent come Monday morning…."

Besides all the stuff going on at the shop and dealership, you may well wonder how I managed to talk my darling Julie into letting me off for the weekend. I mean, she was well into her sixth month with the new baby by then and starting to get as big, uncomfortable, angry, disgusted and dangerously moody and unpredictable as only thoroughly pregnant women can become. If you don't have any personal experience with that sort of thing, just take the highlight moments of those scary, sneaking-past-her-on-tiptoes few days every woman goes through every month and stretch them out so they run from, oh, say, the first through the 30th in September, April, June and November, the first through the 31st in January, March, December, October, May, July and August and the first through the 28th (or the 29th during leap year) if it happens to be February. That should give you some idea. But it can work to your advantage sometimes, too. Like when I casually mentioned that me and Big Ed wanted to take off on Friday afternoon and tool on up to Watkins Glen for the weekend.

"For another race, I suppose?" Julie snorted, not even looking up from the wallpaper catalog she was shuffling through. It was thicker than the damn Manhattan phone book, and there were a half dozen more just like it scattered on the floor around her chair. She was busily trying to find the exact, precise, absolutely *perfect* new wallpaper for the new baby's room—that would be the baby that wouldn't even be born for another three months—but the one she wanted in light cotton-candy pink if (it was a girl) only came in daffodil yellow and the blue one (if it was a boy) was just *way* too dark a blue for the soft, gauzy, pastel robin's-egg blue draperies with the little embroidered toy boats and teddy bears on it she planned to use for the windows. "What the hell is the matter with these wallpaper companies, anyway?" she demanded angrily.

"I'm sure I have no idea," I assured her. And I didn't. But I knew better than to point out that what she was doing might be just the slightest wee bit silly, frivolous, premature, compulsive or unimportant. No sirree. I'd already been through two full pregnancies with Julie, and understood that sort of opinion was going to get you nothing but lumps and trouble. I mean, you have to be pretty stupid to purposely yank on a tiger's tail. Especially when that tiger's in a nasty mood and not inside a cage….

Julie shifted around in her chair like she couldn't find a comfortable position, and right then I felt this huge wave of sympathy for what it must be like to carry another living, growing creature around inside of you for nine months and have to do all the moving, lifting, eating, sleeping, dressing, burping, peeing, crapping and general carrying on with life for both of you. But I must admit to feeling an even larger wave of relief that men don't have to deal with any of it except as accessory hand-holders and part-time shock absorbers. I figure that and peeing from a standing position are two of the grandest benefits of being born male.

"About that race weekend at Watkins Glen?" I asked again, eager to take advantage of the fact that she was focusing an awful lot of anger and attention at the corporate hierarchy of the American wallpaper industry. "We'd be leaving late Friday afternoon, and we'll be back on Sunday…."

"Oh, do whatever the hell you want, Palumbo," she snarled without looking up. "It's like being alone even when you're here…" Then she did look up and glared at me, her eyes like smoldering coals. "Why should I care that you want to take off to go screw around and get drunk with your racing buddies and leave me here all alone with the kids and my back pain and my gut out to here and nobody to help or take care of me?"

"You've got your mother upstairs…." I offered.

"I'm not upstairs!" a shrill voice rasped behind me. It's amazing I hadn't sensed the old battleaxe coming down the stairs or felt her eyes boring icy holes in the back of my neck.

While I stood there, I saw tears of anger and frustration welling up in Julie's eyes like they were a pair of clogged gutters. If you and your wife have had a couple kids together, you know exactly what that looks like. Then her lip started to tremble and she blurted out: *"I don't care what you do, do you hear me? I just don't care. Look at how fat I am! JUST LOOK AT ME!!!"*

"I am looking at you," I said as lovingly, caringly and reassuringly as any man ever has. "You're carrying our baby. You look wonderful to me."

"OH, HOW CAN YOU LOOK AT ME??!!" she sobbed like I'd bitten the head off a live kitten. *"OH, GO TO YOUR DAMN RACE!! JUST GO!! I DON'T CARE ANYMORE!! JUST GO!!!"*

I took that to mean "yes." And ran with it. And if you think that's terrible or conniving or angle-shooting or taking advantage of the situation, let me just remind you that the best place to be during any artillery barrage is well out of range….

So Big Ed and me took off that Friday afternoon in his brand-new, shiny-black 1957 Chrysler 300C convertible—top down, natch—and I've got to admit it was a pretty sweet ride. Even if it was damn near a block long and had fins like a blessed fighter jet. It also had that nifty pushbutton automatic transmission, which the ad guys called the *"Touch of Tomorrow"* when it was first introduced in 1956, but which every streetcorner gas station pump jockey came to know as a Torqueflite. They also quickly learned that it represented a whole new dimension in slushbox automatics as far as stoplight drags and informal street racing were concerned. Why, you could rev it up against the brake or hold it in low until the damn valves rattled running side-by-side with a T-Bird at 35 or so, then punch it into second with your foot still flat to the floor and feel it absolutely *lunge* towards the far horizon. Although that could be a little tough on the old engine and driveline, as countless spoiled college and acne-faced high school punks eagerly discovered at their parents' expense.

As you can imagine, it was great to be out on the road with Big Ed again—just like old times, you know?—even though now we were riding in this big, cushy Chrysler instead of that XK120 we both loved so much. But big as it was, that 300C could gather speed like a locomotive going off a cliff once it got rolling, and Big Ed was always happy to show that feature off to anybody in the next lane who so much as flared a nostril in our direction. Including the owner of a shiny new Pontiac Bonneville who apparently *thought* he'd bought the hottest new car on the road. And it was pretty fast. But not fast enough for Big Ed's 300C (which, by the way, had some very special bits and pieces under the hood thanks to one of Carl Kiekhaefer's engine guys). In the end, every wide-open street drag turns into a battle of nerves. I mean, there's no finish line on the open road, and once it becomes obvious that one car or the other has a little distance in hand and isn't about to be caught, it becomes a question of Who Backs Off First. And Big Ed, in spite of never being exactly what you might call a stellar talent as a racing driver, was never the kind of guy to back off first in a street race. Especially if he had a little lead. Why, I bet he'd blast right past a parked squad car—or even the blessed downtown police station itself—doing triple digits in order to win. And the only way you ever *really* win a street race is by submission. If the other guy hasn't cried "uncle," you ain't got it won yet….

I must admit I was getting a little nervous as I glanced over and saw the mean, determined set of Big Ed's jaw—cigar sticking up at a stout 45-degree angle—the speedo needle right under it wavering past 110, and felt through the seat of my pants the way that big, shiny Chrysler was kind of floating, heaving and wallowing over the gentle undulations of the highway like a cattle boat in heavy seas. You could hardly hear the blessed engine roar over the rush of wind blasting around the windshield and whipping against the side mirrors, and it was quite a relief when I looked into that side mirror and saw the Bonneville suddenly get smaller. Yep, he'd given up, all right. And then came the *coup de grace.* His right-side turn signal started blinking like he maybe had something else on his morning agenda that he really had to do. The Pontiac slowed dramatically and swung into the driveway of one of those cheesy roadside yard statue places where you can buy a cast concrete Apollo or a St. Francis of Assisi with birds on his shoulders and squirrels at his feet or a filigreed birdbath or one of those gleaming, mirror-finish bowling balls on a stone pedestal to dress up your garden. Right. Like the guy was really out to buy a damn yard statue that morning.

"The asshole never had a chance," Big Ed grinned around both sides of his cigar, and patted the big Chrysler on the dashboard.

Submission. It always tastes so sweet....

Big Ed eased us back to a 70 or so—it felt like you could about get out and walk—re-lit his cigar and switched on the radio. "See if you can find anything decent," he sighed, still enjoying the afterglow of humiliating the shit out of that new Pontiac. So I fiddled with the dials and of course most of it was news about the upcoming November election where incumbents Ike and Dick Nixon were taking on that egghead Adlai Stevenson with the hole in his shoe and some senator from Tennessee named Estes Kefauver. Nobody gave those two much of a chance. Plus there was plenty of international news about the looming Suez crisis, which was rapidly coming to a head seeing as how new, left-leaning Egyptian President Gamel Abdel Nasser seemed to think that the Egyptians (rather than the French, English and Americans) ought to control the Suez Canal simply because it ran through their particular piece of desert. Can you imagine? Most Americans (and particularly our fine pencil pushers, position framers, paper shufflers and policy makers in Washington) liked it a whole lot better when fat old skirt-chasing King Farouk was in power. Hell, he was happy to have other people run the damn thing (and he'd sell us all the blessed Egyptian oil we wanted, too) so long as he could continue his lavish, kingly lifestyle and spend all his free time—and that's about the only kind of time he had—cavorting around with luscious ladies, bosomy babes and oversize, eight-course lobster dinners at high society watering holes all over Europe.

Like Toly said, there was a guy who understood what it meant to be royalty!

But it kind of ticked folks off (and particularly his army generals) that old King Farouk was never around, preferred Italian chefs, maids and servants in his palaces (even during World War II, when the Italians were more or less invading his neighbors in North Africa) and didn't seem to especially give two healthy shits about what happened to the rest of the Egyptian people. Plus he'd pretty much bungled the 1948 war against the new, U.N.-mandated *("Excuse me, mind if we borrow a little of your land for a displaced people? You Arab folks don't seem to be using it.")* State of Israel and, at least according to Toly, he'd also developed a bit of a nasty reputation as a sneak thief. Mind you, fat old playboy King Farouk could buy any damn thing he wanted—and believe me, he bought *plenty!*—but he was just one of those guys who *enjoyed* stealing. Just for the hell of it, you know? Look it up if you don't believe me.

Now if you or me or the kid next door gets a case of itchy fingers and tries to do something like that at Woolworth's five-and-dime, they take you in the back room and threaten to call your parents (not that I've had any personal experience with such a thing, of course) but if you're the King of All Egypt and just happen to drop Sir Winston Churchill's prized gold pocket watch down your underwear, nobody can say much of anything about it. I mean, *"Ahh, begging your pardon, Mr. King of Egypt, but could you please pull your pants down and drop your drawers—we think you've got something besides the royal family jewels hidden in there!"* is not the sort of thing you're likely to hear echoing down the halls of Buckingham Palace.

So the Egytians finally booted him out and this ex-military guy named Gamel Abdel Nasser came to power, and he was one of the first smaller country leaders to glom onto how much money, political leverage and notoriety you could get by playing The West and The East (meaning us and the Russkies) off against each other. And naturally we (and the French and the British) weren't real happy about it. Or particularly willing to take it lying down, if you know what I mean. So storm clouds (and troop ships) were gathering. And that naturally got all the good newspaper-reading, radio-listening, TV-watching citizens from the Eastern tip of Long Island all the way to the Pacific Ocean good and jittery, seeing as how the general rank-and-file public perception was that, thanks to us and the Russians, the whole blessed world was turning into a nuclear tinderbox and entirely too many people were fooling around with matches.

But what could any ordinary Joe do about it?

So I twisted the dial to try and find something a little more uplifting, but all I came up with were more depressing news reports about angry white mobs yelling and shaking their fists at some uppity Negroes down south who seemed bound and determined to sit wherever the hell they wanted to on the local bus lines. There was a lot of that going on in 1956. So I twirled the knob again, but the rest was mostly preachy church services and that hot new Elvis Presley music that had all the school kids jumping up and down and screaming like mad and swiveling their hips like blessed burlesque-house strippers. And meanwhile their parents wrung their hands in anguish and fully anticipated the coming of the apocalypse. "Elvis the Pelvis" had appeared on nationwide TV for the very first time on Ed Sullivan's "Toast of the Town" show on Sunday evening, September 9th, and his grinding, gyrating, hip-swiveling, borderline-epileptic performance was the hottest topic of every lunch counter, bar room, front stoop, back porch, barber shop and beauty salon conversation from one end of the country to the other. Listening to the radio, it seemed like Elvis had about every other hit record on the Top 40, and like everybody else with operating eardrums, I'd heard *Hound Dog, Don't Be Cruel, Heartbreak Hotel* and *Blue Suede Shoes* more than enough times to last a lifetime. To be honest about it, I didn't understand the fuss. Nor did I understand the outcry and outrage Elvis' music instantly set off in the byline columns and letters-to-the-editor sections of the newspapers. Not to mention among preachers and their God-fearing flocks all across the country. But I guess it's like this one little high school girl said on TV, a huge, happy grin on her face and tears streaming down her cheeks: *"He's just one big HUNK of forbidden fruit!"*

No question Elvis Presley was a genuine pop phenomenon. Hell, he was *THE* pop phenomenon. And all the right-thinking, God-fearing churchgoers who were up in arms and waving placards and signing petitions about it were just adding fuel to the fire. Personally, I thought it made a lot more sense to just switch the damn stuff off when I didn't feel like listening. That struck me as a far simpler—and more effective!—way of dealing with the problem. Besides, it gave me and Big Ed a chance to talk, which was something we rarely found time to do back at the dealership. Sure, we talked all the time at work about things that needed to be done and stuff we had to take care of, but that was just all the usual problems, details, headaches and hassles of being in business together. It was nice to be out on the road where we could see and think and talk a little further ahead than whatever was at the end of our noses. We both felt sad about how the luxury Italian ocean liner *Andrea Doria* went down off Nantucket after getting rammed by a freighter in a dense fog, and what a genuine tragedy it was that a full load of shiny new Alfa Romeo Sprints and Spiders were down below decks. Oh, and it was a shame about the 52 people who were dead or missing, too. Fact is, Big Ed and me found ourselves talking more about the imported car business, politics and what was going on in the world than sportscars and racing like we used to in the old days.

I guess you could call that maturity.

And you can have it!

The hottest local news in the retail imported automobile business was this second-generation car magnate named Harry Metropolis—his dad owned a fistful of GM stores over on the New York side of the Hudson—who was buying up area VW dealerships as fast as he could find them. And some other guy was opening up a new Citroen-Renault-Peugeot-Facel Vega dealership called *Moteurs Francaise* just a mile and a half up the road from us in Passaic. Now Big Ed really wanted us to take on the Citroen line after he saw the first pictures of their new, spaceship-style DS-19 in one of the magazines. And he was even more impressed and enthusiastic after he took a test drive in one. *"Jeez,"* he said, blowing out yet another perfect smoke ring, *"it's like a damn living room on wheels. Rides smoother than my damn Cadillacs."* I figured it was even money that the next prospective Mrs. B. would find herself driving around town in a new Citroen! And I had to agree that the DS-19 was a whole different kind of car from anything anybody on this side of the Atlantic had ever seen before. Then again, I always figured the French designed cars this way: they looked at what the English, Germans and Italians were doing and said, *"Zut alors, we cannot copy what the Rosbifs, Le Boche and the Italians are doing because we hate them all!"* So the French wind up stuck with whatever's left over. And that makes their cars very different indeed. Oh, they all have wonderful, soft, supple suspension systems that soak up bumpy roads like nothing else on earth. And the DS-19's long wheelbase and air-oil suspension made it about the best of the lot. Plus you could use this little lever on the dash to raise it way up high for rough roads or lower it down to where the rocker panels damn near dragged on the pavement for smooth, fast highway cruising. You could even use it for changing tires without a blessed jack! The front seat was as wide, soft and cushy as an overstuffed velour couch, and you absolutely had to love that one-spoke plastic steering wheel, magic wand shift lever and mushroom-button of a brake pedal, all of which looked like they were lifted right out of a flying saucer! And while the DS-19 wasn't exactly fast in a traditional American *plant-your-foot-and-GO!* sense, you could maintain some pretty impressive average speeds from Point A to Point B once you got your momentum up. To tell the truth, I was almost as impressed with the DS-19 as Big Ed was. But I was also scared to death of it. After all, I was the poor slob in charge of fixing whatever we sold when it broke, and I could see right away that the dumb-but-successful simplicity we enjoyed with the VWs would go right down the shitter if we took on Citroen. Just like the single-spoke steering wheel and all that other space age stuff, that DS-19's hydraulic system looked like it came from another planet. Or it did to me, anyway. And I figured it'd baffle our rank-and-file line mechanics even more. Besides, German and French cars just didn't seem like a good fit together in the same showroom. Or even adjacent showrooms, since I didn't figure our VW distributor would be real pleased about adding on Citroen, either.

Me and Big Ed had argued back and forth about it for months, but the news of that new *Moteurs Francaise* dealership pretty much put an end to it. And I, for one, was plenty relieved. But also worried a little about somebody selling that new Renault Dauphine just a mile and a half-away from us. Everybody and his brother saw the Dauphine as real competition for the Volkswagen Beetle. I'd taken a test drive in one and thought it felt light and tinny and that the shifter was rubbery as hell, but had to admit it was cute and had a lot of charm and personality. Especially that two-tone "Town-and-Country" horn! And style, charm and personality have a lot to do with why people buy cars. Especially women. And no question most women would prefer the clever music of that two-tone horn over the well-known fart-and-burble of a VW Beetle's exhaust.

We did talk some about racing, of course. Mostly about our old Team Passaic guys, who had all hit the road the day before to make Friday-morning practice and were surely gathered around the bar at either the Glen Motor Inn, The Seneca Lodge or one of the downtown joints on Franklin Street (and probably well into their third or fourth rounds!) by the time we reached Binghamton. Carson Flegley had headed up in his Healey 100-M with our race wrench J.R. in the passenger seat to watch over things, and Buster Jones was caravanning right behind them with hillbilly Doug riding shotgun, his somewhat beat-to-shit C-Type up on a trailer behind the second-hand Pontiac station wagon we'd pressed into service as a parts chaser and all-purpose tow ox for *Alfredo's Foreign Car Service* at the old Sinclair. To tell the truth, Big Ed and me both missed being in that caravan. Missed the buzz of getting up before dawn and heading out through those magic, early, quiet hours across Manhattan to Bridgehampton or upstate towards The Glen or out to Pennsylvania for Brynfan Tyddyn and Giant's Despair. We missed that Secret Mission sense of purpose, excitement and anticipation. Missed the giddy, high, illuminated feel of being a part of something daring, freewheeling, desperate, dangerous, and just the wee tiniest bit antisocial and naughty.

Like I said, that's maturity.

And also like I said, you can have it.

There were politics swirling in the air long before Big Ed and me arrived in Watkins Glen late Friday night. Dark clouds had been gathering for months between Cam Argetsinger and his pro/international leaning Watkins Glen Grand Prix Corporation and Charlie Priddle, Pearson Cameron, Fletcher Wingate and the rest of the old-guard SCMA bluenoses regarding Who's In Charge and Who Races Where, and everybody and his brother knew there was a serious showdown brewing. As I said, there'd already been a big flap over the original, FIA-sanctioned "international" race at The Glen in 1950 and again for Cam Argetsinger's "interim" races on the makeshift course they'd laid out on the county roads on the hill above town in 1953, '54 and '55. The SCMA tried to sink it the first year by telling everybody the track wasn't finished and even spread rumors—at the very last minute—that the race was cancelled! But it went on anyway and the SCMA grudgingly granted it a sanction after that, but still didn't much care for Cam Argetsinger and Alec Ulmann's plans for professional, European-style road racing here in the states.

Although its actual safety record was reasonably decent, many of the drivers didn't much care for some of the blind corners and lack of runoff area on the "interim" track, and dealing with the local township governments, permits, insurance and legal problems plus the hassles of transforming ordinary county roads into a temporary racetrack and back for one weekend every year tuned into a bit of a recurring nightmare. A couple solutions were offered up, and one was to create a purpose-built racetrack on private land somewhere in the immediate vicinity and continue the Watkins Glen tradition that way. And it was hardly lost on the local bankers, businessmen, innkeepers, beverage vendors, restaurant owners, souvenir sellers and gas station, drug store and hardware store operators what a welcome boost the races brought to the local economy. The Grand Prix Corporation found and bought 550 acres of rolling farmland not far at all from the original road circuit, and once again Cam Argetsinger spearheaded the whole deal. But naturally there were problems and delays getting the new circuit designed, bulldozed, graded and paved—it didn't help that it rained a lot that summer—and the track was still far from completed as the announced and traditional, third-weekend-in-September Watkins Glen Grand Prix date approached.

Worse yet, Cam had managed to piss off a lot of the old-line SCMA types over the years, and now they wanted a hefty fee—as much as the Grand Prix Corporation could expect to rake in from all the entry fees, in fact!—for sanctioning the event. What, exactly, that fee was supposed to cover was open to a lot of interpretation—especially since the Watkins Glen Grand Prix had come off in the past both with and without the club's blessing—but the official line was that it was in exchange for "the amount of assistance to be rendered" in running the event. As you can imagine, angry letters went back and forth between Cam and his Watkins Glen Grand Prix Corporation and the SCMA top brass from March to May, and the final upshot was that Cam and his organization presented the SCMA with the well-known extended middle finger and resolved to go it on their own. That was a real slap in the face to the SCMA, seeing as how the Watkins Glen race was so well known and well established and moreover since so many of their SCMA drivers wanted to compete.

Things were really up for grabs by the time Big Ed and me sidled up to the bar at the Glen Motor Inn for a couple fast, stiff ones before Last Call came around. We heard they'd barely got the track paved in time for practice to start Friday morning, and to say that it was a rush job doesn't begin to cover it. Seems there were steep dropoffs of a foot or more at the edge of the road in a lot of places. And there was soft, bulldozer-turned soil plus all kinds of construction-site crap strewn over the supposed "runoff" areas. But by far the worst of it was the pavement itself. The blacktop simply hadn't been rolled down hard enough or had enough time to cure. So it was mushy underfoot and coming up in bits, chunks, sheets and buckets-full when even the lightest cars went over it. Cars were getting peppered with flying rocks and spattering pea stone—cracking headlight lenses and shattering windshields all over the place—and, even worse, making the surface treacherous and thoroughly unpredictable. There was a real hubbub about it wherever you put your ear in, and opinions ranged from *"It's an outrage"* and *"How the hell can they charge an entry fee to race on shit like that?"* to *"They've busted their asses to get this done"* and *"There'll be people in the stands who came an awfully long way to watch us, and it's up to us not to disappoint them. We've just gotta be careful, that's all...."*

The whole thing came to a head at the Drivers' Meeting Saturday morning. Telegrams flew back and forth into the wee hours between club officials and the SCMA top brass the night before, and the final one—from the president of the club—was read at the drivers' meeting. It said simply: *"In view of reports of serious and hazardous conditions of Watkins Glen course, undersigned urgently recommend all SCMA members to withdraw from the race. Members participating in event do so in recognition of hazard to safety and welfare of the sport."*

On the one hand you could see it as a fair and earnest warning to keep club members from putting themselves and their machines at risk. On the other you could see it as yet one more attempt to hit the Watkins Glen Grand Prix Corporation and its dreams of real, professional and international racing here in America with a broadside shot deep below the waterline. The irony of the whole thing was that Doc Wyllie—who I knew to be a true, tough racer, a genuine enthusiast and a great supporter of the sport in all its guises—had to read the telegram as part of his duties as the ranking SCMA Drivers' Committee official on hand. There were brief presentations of the club's side of things and the Watkins Glen Grand Prix Corporation side of things, and then nobody knew exactly what to do. So Doc Wyllie asked for a simple show of hands. How many felt it was unsafe to race due to the track conditions and wanted to pack up and go home?

You could tell they were racers.

Not a single hand went up.

Chapter 17: Saturday Night in Watkins Glen

So the races at Watkins Glen came off as promised that third weekend in September—in spite of all the politics and controversy—and to tell the truth, it was a pretty dull show what with none of the West Coast big guns there and all the drivers pretty much tip-toeing around on pavement that was falling apart some places, coming up in clumps here and there and generally the consistency of gritty oatmeal mush everyplace else. That made it hard as hell to pass since there was loose stuff, pea gravel, stones and cinders everywhere but right on the racing line, and you surely didn't want to risk going off anywhere because the wheels might dig right into that soft, loamy stuff and turn you right over! So the experienced hands pretty much came to the fore, and George Weaver's Grand Prix Maserati once again ran away—from a pretty weak field, actually—in the "unrestricted" Seneca Cup race. Then a guy named Grands showed up with one of the new Porsche "Carreras" (essentially a standard-issue Porsche 356 but with one of the terribly fast and even more terribly expensive four-cam motors from the all-out 550 Spyder racecars tucked under the decklid) and he easily blew the doors off all the standard, pushrod-valve Porsches that were busy blowing the doors off all the other entrants in the under-1500cc "Schuyler Carrera" production car race.

It had become obvious by that fall of 1956 that no reasonably recognizable MG could run even-up against the Porsches any more, and so they'd declared an all-MG race—the "Collier Brothers Memorial Trophy"—to give all the diehard MG guys a shot at the limelight. A trio of MGAs came in first, second and third (no surprise there) but the battle at the front turned into pretty much a procession after a hard-charging Charlie Wallace charged just a wee bit too hard and had to take an escape road on lap 6. After that it was just watching the cars go by all the way to the finish. Paul O'Shea did a typically great job of staying between the loose stuff in his "factory recognized if not actually supported" 300SL lightweight, and he grabbed the lead at the start and simply drove away from a lumbering, single-file wagon train of Corvettes and Jaguar XK120s and 140s looking for traction on the iffy pavement. Plus one poor, slow, lonely Thunderbird that maybe took a wrong turn off Highway 14 and wound up on the grid by mistake.

Best race of the day by far came next in the under-1500cc Modified "Queen Catherine Cup," where this guy named Conley (who was a pretty decent driver, no question about it!) led all the way in his new Porsche 550 Spyder while Doc "let's see a show of hands" Wyllie filled his mirrors and feinted around for an opening from the green flag clear through to the checker. But the track was getting even worse as the day went on, and what with the power advantage the Porsche had on the straightaways and up those beautiful, long, sweeping esses, Wyllie's Lotus just couldn't get quite close enough to try a dive-bomb out-braking move into the corners. And it would have been a chancy deal anyway, what with the pavement off-line all cinders and marbles and not really the sort of surface your tires could get a grip on. But of course the spectators didn't know that—and it was a pretty good crowd, in spite of everything—and so they thought they were seeing one hell of a great dice. And I guess they were.

By contrast, the Watkins Glen "Grand Prix" feature was generally a snore. The track crews had been coming out between sessions all day long trying to patch up the holes in the pavement with filler and Sakrete—especially after the big production car race with all those mouth-breathing Corvettes and Jaguars—but it was like putting a band-aid on a cancer. Anyhow, this well-known east coast hotshoe named George Constantine showed up in somebody-or-other's D-Type Jag, and he more or less motored off into the distance ahead of a reasonably strong field that included no less than two other D-Types, some fast but past-their-prime Allards and an older model 4.5-liter Ferrari. Then again, old George had a lot of experience, and that's what you need when the surface is iffy and changing every lap. By far the best dice of the contest was between our own Buster Jones and his long-in-the-tooth, ex-Skippy Welcher C-Type and this raw rookie who probably shouldn't have been out there in a four-cylinder Ferrari *Testa Rossa* he'd just bought. At the driver's meeting that morning when they took the vote about whether to race or not, it was also suggested—because of the high speeds and the iffy condition of the racetrack—that rookie drivers ought not to run. And to a man they all decided not to. Except this bozo, who incidentally had the fastest car of all the rookies entered. Typical, you know? It made for a pretty interesting race, though, what with Buster's tired old C-Type having slightly less speed but a smidgen more seasoning and racecraft between the steering wheel and the seat back and the rookie in the Ferrari absolutely *determined* to keep him behind. So determined, in fact, that he determined his way right off the black part, had his tires dig in to that soft, loamy shit on the shoulder and it more or less levered the car right over. Fortunately without hurting him. The yellow flags flew while the wreckers came out and dragged off his bent-up Ferrari, and after that the parade pretty much continued on to the checker. Kind of a yawner, actually. Although you had to give that George Constantine credit for keeping it on the island under really difficult—and constantly changing—track conditions.

To be honest, it wasn't what you could call a particularly auspicious or inspiring debut for the new, permanent racetrack at Watkins Glen. But it was damn near a miracle they pulled it off at all, and all the racers—every last one of them—thought the new track would be genuinely spectacular once they got it sorted out and properly finished. It was fast and swoopy and scenic and challenging and there were a few spots—in the absolute best European road racing tradition—that an ace driver could maybe take flat-out if he had the nerve, but it would sure make his hands tighten up a little on the wheel….

Naturally we'd decided to stay overnight on Saturday so we could sample a little of the post-race party atmosphere sure to be found everywhere from The Seneca Lodge to the Glen Motor Inn and all up and down the main drag on Franklin Street. And that's where we wound up, since Big Ed and me couldn't do any better than a two-by-four room in this cheesy little tourist-court motel just south of town on account of coming up was a last-minute deal and naturally The Seneca and the Glen Motor Inn were all booked up. But it was fun being downtown for a change—even if most of the racers were staying someplace else—because on a race weekend Saturday night, the entire town of Watkins Glen turned into a monster sportycar party from one end of Franklin Street to the other. It was neat just walking down the sidewalk, past where the old street circuit swept hard right at the end of Franklin Street and then made an immediate left as it started that steep climb up Old Corning Hill. That's where our pal Tommy Edwards had that terrible accident that wasn't really his fault but that he got blamed for anyway back in 1952. It all came flooding back to me as we walked past the Knotty Pine Restaurant and the courthouse and Smalley's Garage where they used to do tech inspection back in the old through-the-streets racing days. It was damn near impossible to believe that they'd run Cunninghams and Cad-Allards and Ferraris and Jaguars and Maseratis and Lord only knows what else down this exact stretch of pavement—right through town, flat-out and foot to the floor!—engines bellowing like mad and the crowd screaming and cheering and whooping it up six- and eight-deep on the curbsides from one end of Franklin Street to the other! It was like remembering the circus after you've grown up, you know? Remembering how the clown's nose lit up like a beacon and everything smelled of popcorn and the elephants seemed bigger than mountains!

And now it was all gone. Changed. Forever. It made me smile and ache a little inside all at the same time. But Watkins Glen on a race weekend was still the center and soul of the whole blessed sportycar movement. Only now there were so many new faces and nameplates: clubby little gaggles and gatherings of Triumphs and MGAs and Healey Hundreds and XK140s and Alfa *Giuliettas* and Lancia Aurelias and Porsche coupes and convertibles and sleek but deadly stern and serious Mercedes SLs. Plus Corvettes and Thunderbirds and big American coupes, sedans and ragtops with a dangerous-sounding V-8 throb coming out of their tailpipes.

Yep, it was the same old disease, all right....

Who should we run into wandering out of one of the taverns on Franklin Street but our old scribe buddy, Hank Lyons. Geez, it was great to see him! *"Hey, what the hell are you doing here??!!"* I damn near screamed, giving him one of those handshakes that more or less melts itself into a hug. "I thought you were out in California."

"Actually," Hank said through a disgustingly condescending grin, "I just got back from Italy!"

"Italy?"

"Do I have to say it twice? It's a country over in Europe, see...."

"I know where the hell Italy is. My ancestors came from there."

"I understand the property values have been going up ever since."

"Very funny." I said, laughing. "Same old Hank."

"Same old Buddy," he agreed. "Always good for a straight line."

"Same old shit," Big Ed grumbled. He was never real big on walking. "Whaddaya say we go inside for a drink or go down to the next joint down the road and get a drink there."

"Suits me."

"Lead on."

So we went inside, and while Big Ed muscled his way towards the bar to get us a round of drinks—no question he was the right man for that kind of duty—Hank somewhat breathlessly explained how he happened to be sauntering through upper New York State on his way back from Italy.

"I got a call from *Car & Track* that their regular European guy got hit by a car while he was shooting pictures during that thousand kilometer round of the World Manufacturers' Championship sportscar race in Sweden."

"My God! Did it kill him?"

"Nah. He was pretty lucky. But I guess it broke both his legs, and that makes it pretty tough to get around as a race reporter and photographer."

"I'm sure it does."

"Anyhow, the publisher himself was gonna go over to finish up the season and do the fall auto salons—had his plane tickets and everything—but he had some family stuff come up and decided to give me a shot at it."

"No shit!!"

"No shit," Hank nodded, his smile nearly floating right up off his face. "Flew first class, too. You ever fly first class?"

I shook my head.

He gave me a look like somebody who'd maybe slept with Ingrid Bergman. And Rita Hayworth, too.

"So what was it like? What happened?"

"Well, the World Manufacturers' Championship was already over by then. Sweden was the last race, and even though Maserati trotted out this monster new V-8—four-and-a-half-liters!—I guess it was still pretty raw and didn't handle or stop real great. And the older, six-cylinder cars just didn't have the power to run even up with those new, 12-cylinder Ferraris. Oh, they gave it a good try, but even with Moss driving his ass off the Ferraris had a little bit too much in hand. Phil Hill wound up co-driving the winning car with that little Frenchman, Maurice Trintignant. I'm pretty damn sure that's a first for an American on the Ferrari team. And I heard there was even a funny part when somebody broke an oil line and three drivers went off into a damn wheat field one right after the other."

"What's so funny about that?"

"Oh, the wheat was so damn tall the drivers had to get out and stand on top of their cars to see the way back to the racetrack!"

"But nobody got hurt?"

"That's why it's funny," Hank explained. "It wouldn't be funny if anybody got hurt."

I could see his point.

"Anyhow, all the Maseratis eventually broke down or ran into brake trouble, and in the end it was Ferrari 1-2-3. In fact, your buddy Toly Wolfgang co-drove the second place car with Peter Collins."

"Good for him!"

Hank nodded. "Did a damn good job, too. They were never the fastest, but they held a good, sensible pace and let the rabbits burn themselves up, then stepped in when the quicker cars hit trouble."

"Just like you should in an endurance race."

We clicked imaginary glasses together.

"Anyhow, that pretty much wrapped up the championship for Ferrari."

"It's hard to argue with a 1-2-3 finish."

"Yeah, I guess. But I think Maserati's *right there* for next year with that new 450S V-8. I got to see it in person at the factory in Modena…"

"YOU GOT TO VISIT THE MASERATI RACE SHOP??!!"

Hank shrugged his shoulders and blushed a little. "Yeah. Ferrari, too."

"You son of a bitch."

"Yeah, I guess I am," he admitted. "Eat your heart out."

Big Ed arrived with our drinks and we all took a nice, hefty pull off of them.

"So what else did you do over in Italy?"

"Well, the main thing was the European Grand Prix at Monza."

"You went to Monza?" Big Ed half-choked.

"You don't know the half of it," I told him. But then I focused right back on Hank, fascinated. "So tell me about it!"

"What's to tell?" he shrugged. "It was only the most fabulous experience of my entire life, that's all." Then he pulled in close and started rattling it all off, rapid-fire: "You should *see* that place. It's got these monster bankings—ten times steeper than Indianapolis!—and these wide, fast corners that make your shorts cinch up just to look at them. Plus it's all inside this big, beautiful park with huge grandstands all up and down the pit straight and the fans—my God, you've never seen *anything* like those Italian race fans!—they come out by the tens of thousands and fill that park up until they're hanging off of every tree, fence and billboard on the property. It makes the damn World Series look like sandlot ball."

"Wow."

"And do they ever *love* their motor racing over there! You've never seen anything like it here in the states. And if it's a red car or an Italian driver, they go absolutely apeshit *NUTS* every time the damn thing goes by."

I could see it in my head, just the way Hank was telling it.

"So how was the race?" Big Ed asked.

"What a race!" he almost hollered, throwing his hands in the air. "It had *everything!* Drama. Surprise. Danger. Disappointment. Victory snagged from the jaws of defeat." He took a long, slow sip of his drink, noticing the people around us giving him the eye and moving in a little closer. But Hank just leaned back in his chair and pretended to look bored. I knew he was just jerking us around.

"Look," I told him. "You start telling us about it *right now* or I'm canceling my subscription to the damn magazine."

"The boss wouldn't like that," Hank sighed. And then he pulled in close and started rattling it off again. "You gotta understand that this was the last race of the season, and the championship was dangling in the balance. It was there for the taking between Moss in a Maserati and Fangio in the Ferrari, with Fangio's young English teammate Peter Collins in with an outside shot if the other two ran into trouble and everything broke his way."

Big Ed and me were all ears. So were some of the people around us.

"But of course Castellotti and Musso are also there on the Ferrari team—and in front of their hometown Italian crowd, too—and so is your buddy Toly Wolfgang."

"Toly made it to the Ferrari Grand Prix team?" I half gasped.

"It was kind of a reward for helping wrap up the sportscar championship for them in Sweden. I guess he'd been pestering the team manager in five or six different languages to give him a shot, and so they finally agreed to give him a car for Monza. It was one of last year's old four-cylinder Supersqualos—not one of the hot, hairy V-8s with the side tanks Ferrari inherited from Lancia—and those old four-bangers never did much even when they were brand-new. But Ferrari figured it was always better to have another bullet in the gun going into the final, deciding race of the season. Even an old, slow bullet. But it was a chance at a first Grand Prix drive for Ferrari, and how're you gonna pass that up?"

"You're not," Big Ed agreed, stating the obvious. "Hey, any of you guys want another round?"

"Does a chicken have lips?"

Big Ed heaved up off his stool and waded right into the five-deep crowd around the bar.

"So how did Toly do in his first Grand Prix?" I wanted to know.

Hank shook his head. "He never made the start. Went off the road in a big way at the *Curva Grande*—you remember that *really* fast corner I was talking about?—during practice on Friday…"

"Jesus! Was he okay?"

"He was luckier than shit, if you ask me. Skated right off at maybe 135 or so and the car just went bananas. It rolled and it cartwheeled and it somersaulted and there wasn't a whole lot left by the time it was over. They had to take most of the remains off in buckets and dustbins."

"But what about Toly?"

"Like I said, he was luckier than shit. He got thrown out on the first tumble and landed on some soft stuff and more or less rolled to a stop without killing himself. Oh, he was sore and bruised, but he didn't even break any bones! Can you believe it?"

I shook my head.

"I think he was maybe trying too hard to impress the team. And everybody else, for that matter. Those Supersqualos had a reputation for being twitchy in high-speed corners anyway…."

"But he was okay?"

"Oh, he looked plenty rattled," Hank allowed. "I saw him in the pits afterwards and he was staring off towards both horizons at the same time. His hands were shaking a little and he had that empty look in his eyes. Like you see on corpses, you know?" I watched a shiver go through him. "It was kinda spooky, actually."

"But he's all right?"

Hank nodded. "By race day he was back to his old self again. A little sore, maybe, but absolutely raring to be out there again with the rest of the heroes and madmen." He looked me straight in the eye. "It's an addiction, you know."

"An addiction?"

Hank nodded. "Race drivers can't help themselves. I mean *real* race drivers, not the posers and paraders. They just can't stay away from it. They *need* it...."

I knew exactly what he meant.

"So what happened in the race?" Big Ed asked as he elbowed his way to our table with a fresh round of drinks.

You could feel everybody kind of leaning in around us for a good listen.

"Well, everybody on the Ferrari team was a little nervous about tires before the start because they'd had more than a few sudden blowouts during practice and qualifying. The bankings put a hell of a load on the tires and steering gear. And of course Ferrari was running on Engleberts because the Old Man made a deal with them to supply tires for all his racecars during the '56 season after he couldn't come to terms with his Italian buddies up the road at Pirelli. They were pretty good tires overall—I mean, just look at all the races Ferrari won this year—but they sure weren't very happy on the high-speed bankings at Monza..."

It made you wonder what goes through a driver's mind after he sees a couple of his teammates suffer blowouts on the far side of 150 when he knows he's out there on the same damn tires.

"...Plus it'd rained all morning, and nobody was real keen about racing Formula One cars at Monza in the wet. But the weather cleared up nicely by mid-afternoon when they wheeled the cars out onto the grid. Fangio'd put his Ferrari on pole ahead of his teammates Castellotti and Musso, but of course they were in front of their hometown crowd and took off like a couple short-fused rockets as soon as the green waved. Like it was a damn five-lap sprint race! I guess Castellotti figured he had something to prove. He'd led a five-car Ferrari sweep of the *Mille Miglia* with a fantastic drive through a heavy rainstorm earlier in the year, and that made him a real crowd favorite everywhere in Italy. But of course Musso had it in his head that *he* was destined to be the next great Italian racing champion and so he wasn't about to let Castellotti sneak off into the distance at Monza under any circumstances."

"What about Fangio?"

"He was too smart to get sucked into a dick-waving contest with those guys. Especially in a long race with the World Championship on the line and all the tire problems everybody'd been having in practice. In fact, he let his championship rival Moss blow right past in the Maserati, then settled into the slipstreaming bunch behind, just waiting to see how things developed." Hank's eyes swept around the table. "He didn't have to wait long...."

We were hanging on every word.

"On the sixth lap, both Castellotti and Musso had explosive blowouts within a hundred yards of each other! At over 165 miles-per-hour!"

"Wow! Did they crash?"

"Nah. They managed to gather it up without hitting anything. Those guys are pretty damn good…."

"I bet there were some fresh dimples in the seat upholstery, though!" Big Ed chortled. Although he was never exactly an ace racing driver, Big Ed surely understood that sudden, seize-your-guts sensation when you're tooling along at top speed and the rug gets ripped right out from under your feet. It's a wee bit disconcerting, to say the least….

"So what happened then?"

"Well, Castellotti and Musso came in for a new set of Engleberts and maybe a quick change of underwear, and that leaves this slipstreaming pack of Moss in the latest Maserati—the one with the engine on an angle so the driveshaft runs next to the driver instead of under the family jewels…."

"So they can get the driver's weight lower and reduce the frontal area for better aerodynamics!" I tossed in, kind of showing off what I knew.

"Exactly right," Hank nodded. "Anyhow, Moss is running at the head of a tight pack with Fangio and Collins in their Ferraris and Schell in that new British Vanwall, the whole bunch of them nose-to-tail and side-by-side and swapping positions back and forth every single lap. It was pretty stirring stuff. Especially the lap when the Vanwall came by in the lead. It sure hushed the crowd, but wouldn't you know I'm standing next to that know-it-all asshole Eric Gibbon on the pit wall, and he's damn near wetting his pants because this dark-green car is running in front of all the bright, shiny red ones at Monza."

"He must have been beside himself."

"Oh, you know how the Brits are. Everything on the inside. But he did have the look of a teakettle getting ready to whistle."

I could see it like it was happening that very instant.

"The show was exciting to watch—back and forth all the time—but I had a feeling some of those guys were holding back just a little because of what happened to Musso and Castellotti. And sure enough that's when Peter Collins blew a tire and had to duck into the pits for a fresh one. Meanwhile Fangio's engine started sounding a little rough and then he stopped, too. Only it turns out it was some problem in the steering gear. Just like the tires, the steering mechanisms were taking an awful lot of guff on the bankings. Anyhow, this huge moan went up from the Ferrari faithful in the grandstands—mixed with wild cheering from the Maserati fans, of course—when Fangio climbed out, took a close, personal look at the steering linkage, and walked silently away from his car."

"So he lost the championship?"

"Oh, wait," Hank laughed. "You guys haven't heard the half of it! There's more. *Lots* more!"

Big Ed and me crowded in even closer to get the rest of it.

"Musso is making this huge charge after his pit stop for tires, and he's worked his way all the way up to third place behind Moss and Schell and ahead of Collins in the other Ferrari. And then he stops for fuel and another set of tires and Fangio is standing back there against the pit wall, and everybody with half a brain is expecting Musso to climb out and hand his car over to Fangio so Ferrari can win the damn championship. I mean, Musso's only got a handful of points and so he's way out of it as far as the title is concerned. But he just sits there in the car, staring straight ahead and making like he doesn't see or hear anything. And he's off the clutch pedal and hard into the gas and streaking full-tilt out of the pits as soon as the last knockoff is hammered tight." Hank's eyes swept around the table once again. He'd drawn quite a crowd by then, and they were hanging on every word. "Well, the fans were stunned. Sure, most of them wanted an Italian driver to win. But Fangio was always counted as an Italian—or at least *mostly* Italian—by the Italian fans since his family came from Italy before they moved to Argentina. And an Argentine/Italian wheeling a Ferrari hit a lot closer to home than some hotshot Englishman in a Maserati…."

Hank paused to let it dangle.

"…Anyhow, you could almost *feel* the quiet after Musso left the pits. And then Collins comes in for his stop. Now Collins is still in with an outside shot at the championship. But he takes one look at Fangio standing there in his helmet and climbs right out of his car. Just like that."

"He hands it over to Fangio?" someone behind me asked.

Hank nodded. "Doesn't even think twice about it. Says afterwards in a press interview that he thinks he's only 25 and really too young to be World Champion. That there'll be plenty of time for him to win a World Championship of his own."

Somebody let out a low whistle on the other side of the table.

"So Fangio shot out of the pits and immediately rattled off the four fastest laps of the race—one right after the other. But he was too far back to make much impression on Moss in the lead or Musso in second place. And right about then it looked like everything was all wrapped up: that Moss would win the race, Musso would take second for his best Grand Prix finish ever and Fangio would take home his fourth World Championship—and third in a row!—by finishing a distant third in the Ferrari Collins so unselfishly handed over to him."

"But that's not what happened, is it?" I knew it by the tone of Hank's voice.

Hank allowed himself half a laugh. "No, it isn't. First off—*with just four laps to go!*—Moss coasts in with a dead engine. *Out of the damn lead, remember!* And guess what?"

You could have heard a pin drop.

"HE'S OUT OF GAS!!!"

I felt a breeze from the collective intake of breath behind my shoulders.

"Well, they fuel him up as fast as they can—funnels and gas cans flying in all directions—and by then Musso has sneaked past into the lead. *Luigi Musso!* The desperately tough young Italian who blew a tire on lap six at 165, wouldn't give his car over to Fangio, and drove like the demons of hell were pursuing him over the whole blasted distance is about to win his first Grand Prix. And right there in Italy, right there in front of that huge, ecstatic—hell, *delirious!*—hometown Italian crowd. Why, you could feel the ground shaking like there was a damn earthquake going on when he came across the start-finish line all by himself in the lead!"

"But he doesn't win it either, does he?" I could tell by the look in Hank's eyes.

Again he shook his head. "Musso's got a lead of over 30 seconds on Moss with just three laps to go. And Moss' engine isn't sounding all that great, either. But then Musso's late coming around. And then there he is! Limping slowly out of the last corner with the car all angled funny and kind of crabbing sideways down the road. He pulls into the pits with one front wheel turned out and rubber-smoke boiling off the tire. Turns out his steering linkage is broken—just like what happened to Fangio's car!—and there's nothing they can do to fix it. I was right there, not more than 20 feet away. He had that same faraway, shell-shocked look in his eyes as Toly when they led him away from the car." Hank drained his drink all the way to the bottom and set down his glass. "So that's the way it finished: Musso broken, Moss limping home first for Maserati and Fangio driving his ass off when it counted but falling six seconds short at the checker. But he did win himself and Ferrari another World Championship, and that had to feel pretty good."

"Boy," I said, "that's one hell of a story."

"It sure is," someone behind me agreed. "And you tell it really well."

"Thanks," Hank allowed, kind of blushing. And then he looked me right in the eyes. "And that's the *real* news!"

"What?"

"I think I'm going back over there."

"Over where?"

"To Europe. And South America. And wherever else the damn circus goes."

"You *are?"*

"Yup!" Hank nodded enthusiastically. "I believe you're looking at *Car & Track's* new world-wide, international racing correspondent!"

"You're shitting me!"

Hank just grinned. I'd have to say it was one of the biggest and broadest damn grins I'd ever seen in my life.

Chapter 18: A Blood Red Season—Part One

Our little Rosalina got herself born in the waning, pre-midnight moments of New Year's Eve, 1956—11:57pm, to be exact—and missed out by maybe one hefty squeeze and a handful of heartbeats being the first brand-new, 1957-model baby on the entire blessed Jersey side of the Hudson. An honor that ultimately fell to a tubby little colored kid named Roosevelt Demetrius Jones—no relation of Sylvester's, I don't think—at some hospital over in Bayonne. It got his pudgy little picture in all the newspapers (along with his proud parents, of course) and I have to admit Julie and me thought it was kind of a gyp. Especially since our little Rosalina was so much cuter and cuddlier.

"Couldn't you have held out just a little longer?" I asked Julie the next morning while eyeballing a picture of a smiling Mr. and Mrs. Jones and a very grumpy-looking little Roosevelt Demetrius on the front page of the Metro section.

Julie just glared at me. "*You* try it some time, Palumbo."

We wound up spending a lazy, worn-out and exhausted New Year's Day in the hospital room with little Rosalina, and of course all the relatives had to file in and out to *"oooh"* and *"aaah"* over the new addition and generally make the kind of noises you associate with drool bibs or failed head gaskets. We'd named little Rosalina after my dead grandmother on my father's side (who I always remembered as being a lot of fun, even if I wondered how she could have possibly spit out such a mean-spirited and miserable cuss as my old man), but of course Julie's mom—mummy dust cheek rouge, shiny black spray-painted hairdo, penciled-in eyebrows, sneaky ferret eyes and blowing gold-tipped Vogue cigarette smoke right in the new baby's face right there in the blessed hospital room and all—was absolutely sure we'd named the baby after her. And I wasn't about to argue with her about it. It was a war you couldn't win.

Naturally I excused myself every now and then to go out and read the paper or watch a little crappy daytime TV in the lobby (the Rose Bowl Parade wasn't due to start until later on seeing as how it was way out in California) or maybe go down the street to the diner for a cup of coffee or something and read the paper some more. Yesterday's paper, too. And even Sunday's. I mean, there's only so much of that syrupy sweet "relatives meet the new baby" stuff you can take, even when it's your own blessed kid. Although I've noticed women appear to have a far higher tolerance level than men where that kind of thing is concerned. In fact, they actually seem to enjoy it. But that's okay, since they likewise have a higher tolerance—a *much* higher tolerance!—for all the icky, slimy, gooey, stinky, messy, smelly and thoroughly disgusting substances that seem to come out of babies at regular intervals (from both ends, and sometimes simultaneously) and that's something we males of the species surely appreciate. Generally speaking, I've always thought newborn babies were highly overrated as an entertainment attraction. I mean, they just *lie* there. Or maybe they cry. A hamster on an exercise wheel or a nice tank of tropical fish is more interesting. And certainly a lot less trouble! But of course when it's yours, things are different. Every little eyeball roll, toe curl, hiccup, burp, fart or lip twitch that might somehow, on some distant planet, be interpreted as a smile is enough to get you all revved up inside. Not to mention opening up the hormone floodgates of every female human being on the premises.

Which, like I said, is why you have to escape down the street every now and again to read another paper and drink some more coffee. I like to think that a lesser man would have stopped in at the corner tavern, too. But I've always made a point of not drinking alcoholic spirits before lunchtime—I've noticed it leads to complications—and even though it was New Year's Day, it didn't seem like a good time to break that rule. Especially since Julie, her mother and all the rest of our Hit Parade of friends and relatives would smell it on my breath. Besides, Big Ed was sure to drop by later on, and he was equally sure to have a toasting bottle of some kind underneath his arm.

Maybe even two.

But until then, it was newspapers and coffee. And I must admit most of the news in those papers was pretty damn depressing. And not just because that fat-faced Roosevelt Demetrius Jones kid got his picture in the paper where I figured our little Rosalina's mug ought to be. There was an awful lot of stuff going on in the world—more than you could find time to worry about!—and it could really give you the jitters if you made the mistake of paying too much attention to the damn news. The front page was slathered with all the latest poop on the big, multi-nation catfight over the Suez Canal. Which was really nothing more than a blessed ditch through the Egyptian desert, if you want the truth of it. But it also happened to be the only way all those tankers carrying their thousands and thousands of gallons of Mideastern crude oil could make their way to America without going clear around the southern tip of South Africa. Which everybody knows is a long, expensive and dangerous sort of journey. Particularly if they've read any seafaring books. Which I haven't, by the way, although I once got through six or seven pages of *Moby Dick* so I could write a book report for Mrs. Gundlefinger's English class in high school—thank God for *Classics Illustrated* comic books! And I'd been around old Butch Bohunk a few times when he'd had a couple and started telling some of his famous Marine yarns. They'd invariably include a few of the bold, seafaring stories he'd overheard from some swaggering Navy swabbies at some dingy little waterfront bar just before he and his Marine drinking buddies beat the living crap out of them. Even though they were outnumbered two- or three-to-one, of course!

Anyhow, according to both *The New York Times* and *The New York Daily News,* we were up against it hard with the Rooskies all over the damn globe, and both papers were full of stuff about that scraggly-beard commie Castro down in Cuba (including somewhat optimistic reports from the presidential palace that he'd been killed in an air-raid attack on a rebel stronghold) and how the Reds were using tanks and guns to crush an uprising in Budapest, Hungary. Worse yet, the Soviet Union had beaten the living crap out of the good old US of A at the Melbourne Olympics. And then *Colliers* magazine folded up—I mean, they'd been around for *ever!*—and

Humphrey Bogart died of cancer and it was all pretty depressing stuff. But there was nothing you could do about any of it except shake your head, cluck your tongue and go right back to doing whatever it was you did for a living and hope like hell that nobody with an itchy finger on either side got anywheres near the trigger mechanisms on those monstrous Intercontinental Ballistic Missiles we and the Rooskies had pointed directly at each others' heads. Why, a guy with enough free time on his hands could turn worrying into a full-time profession.

But I kept reading those papers—just about every day, in fact—and shrugged and sighed and shook my head over my morning coffee like every other Average Joe, hoping and even praying now and then that the problems of the world would somehow avoid crashing right through the kitchen or bedroom ceiling roof of the nice little house with the yellow shutters and the vulture-perch mother-in-law apartment over the garage where me and Julie and little Vincent and littler Roberta and littlest of all new baby Rosalina lived.

Oh, and Julie's jerk of a mother, too.

There was another kind of reading I started really looking forward to every month, and that was of course the stories and features my good friend and great buddy Hank Lyons was writing in the pages of *Car & Track* magazine. I was really proud of him, you know? And kind of flattered that he continued to send me these long, wonderful letters from Europe that really amounted to long-playing editions of the stuff he was writing for *Car & Track*. I came to understand that one of the problems of magazine writing is that the *real* purpose of all those stories and columns and features is to keep the ads from crashing right into each other. See, the so-called "editorial content"—that would be the words and pictures—is what gets people to buy the magazine, but the 35 cents they exchange for each copy isn't really enough to pay the help and get the damn thing printed and distributed and pick up the unsold leftovers from the news stand when the next month's issue comes out. No, the *real* money in the magazine business is in the advertising, and so all those scribes and reporters and photographers and byline columnists are strictly limited so far as how much of that precious advertising space they can clutter up with "editorial content." It was hard for a guy like Hank, who dearly loved his subject, knew hell's own amount about it and moreover really knew how to spin a damn yarn, to *"keep the damn Monza story down to 1200 words."* As he said to me more than once: *"Hell, I want to tell a story till I'm done with it."* But he had to live with the realities of the magazine business like everybody else, getting his work in under deadline and cut to fit the space provided for it.

Worked out great for me, though, since I got the Full Story in these long, wonderful, multi-page *Par Avion* letters I'd get hand-written from Hank on this tissue-thin, half-transparent European airmail stationery after every race or major motoring event. But then, like he mentioned several times, he had a lot of time to write. After all, the pay in the International Motorsports Correspondent business wasn't exactly what you could call excessive. Or even barely adequate, come to that. Oh, you got to eat and drink pretty well off all the press freebie deals (although it could be canned beans and tins of sardines in between) and "accommodations" often amounted to the cramped back seat of a thoroughly clapped-out Fiat Topolino with a few of the springs sticking through the upholstery. But it was an adventure, and Hank was getting to do what he loved and he wrote more than once that maybe there was a book or something in it somewhere further down the line.

No question 1957 was an exciting time to be an International Motorsports Correspondent. To begin with, Fangio decided that he'd had it up to here with the politics, intrigues and bullshit at Ferrari and went across town and signed with Maserati. He'd driven for them before in 1953 and liked the team. Not to mention that when he drove for Mercedes in '54 and '55, there was no question he was Number One and everything was planned and organized and everybody was pulling in the same direction with one goal in mind: for him to win races and for Mercedes to win World Championships. Which they did. But at Ferrari, it seemed like some of his toughest, bitterest rivals were right alongside him on his own blessed team. Hank said he even thought—right or wrong—that he wasn't always getting the best cars. Which should naturally be the right and prerogative of any proven, Number-One hotshoe on any serious professional team. Maserati had their own problems, of course—they were struggling financially and spread so damn thin they were almost transparent—but the cars were good and well-built and there was a real "family" atmosphere that must have been quite a relief after the Byzantine politics and Grand Opera dramas at Ferrari. And Maserati was thrilled to have him, too, since their trump ace Stirling Moss had told them he was planning to do what any good, patriotic young Englishman would do and switching to the promising, all-British Vanwall Formula One team as soon as the European grand prix season started. That left Maserati with the tough, thick-necked little Frenchman and onetime prizefighter Jean Behra—who could be blindingly fast but not blindingly consistent—and Franco/American racing bar operator Harry Schell (ditto) alongside the pretty much unproven Carlos Menditeguy and, later on, Giorgio Scarlatti. Losing Moss left a pretty big hole at the top, and Maserati were thrilled to land a talent like four-time World Champ Juan Manuel Fangio!

Ferrari countered with his "young lions," Italians Luigi Musso and Eugenio Castellotti, plus fair-haired Brit Peter Collins, and also re-signed quirky but blindingly quick young Englishman Mike Hawthorn. Hawthorn had driven for old man Ferrari in '54 and '55, but then left to drive for a couple of the supposed World Beater new English Formula One teams—BRM and then Vanwall—during the 1956 season. But the cars hadn't come good yet and then Hawthorn had a hell of a spat over it with bearing magnate Tony Vandervell, the English industrialist who owned and ran the Vanwall team and, like every English enthusiast, desperately wanted to beat the red cars with something painted British Racing Green. Historically old man Ferrari never forgave or forgot defectors, but since Hawthorn had rather famously beat Fangio in a straight fight at the French Grand Prix the first season he drove for Ferrari in 1953—becoming, in the process, the first Englishman to win a modern, world championship Grand Prix—he was pretty much welcomed back to the team. And then you had Phil Hill, who was still doing just sportscars, and our pal Toly Wolfgang, who was definitely the outsider in this bunch since he was both the newcomer and the oldest driver on the team by at least ten years. It didn't exactly bode well for his future and no question he would get the dregs and leftovers as far as the formula one cars were concerned. But old man Ferrari liked the cold, hard look in his eyes and the way he always seemed to bring the cars home in one piece at the end of a long race. After all, those things were expensive. And picking up points was the name of the game—especially on the sportscar side—and to do that, you surely had to finish.

Hank wrote me that he had this feeling—even before the first green flag of the season dropped in Argentina—that he was going to be witnessing the end of a glorious and magnificent but almost stupidly dangerous era. *La Carrera* was already gone, and many people—including some of the drivers—felt that open-road races like the *Mille Miglia* were too risky. For the public as well as themselves. It was impossible to control the crowds of excited spectators lining the roadsides from one end of Italy to the other and, as Fangio put it: *"No one with a conscience can go fast there...."*

Plus the cars would probably have to change. Many races had been cancelled in the wake of the disaster at Le Mans in '55, and the Le Mans organizers reacted by insisting on a strict 3.0-litre limit for the 1956 race to keep the speeds down. As a result, the French classic was reluctantly dropped from the FIA's World Manufacturers' Championship that year—even though it was surely the biggest and brightest jewel in the crown—and only hesitantly returned to the fold for 1957 as everyone was worried about the ever-escalating speed of the cars. No question the FIA in Paris was seriously considering the adoption of the same three-liter limit imposed by the Le Mans organizers in 1956 as a way of reining in the so-called "sportscars" competing in the World Manufacturers' Championship come the 1958 season. That meant 1957 might well be the last hurrah for the big-banger, wide-open, unlimited-displacement sports/racing cars from Ferrari, Maserati, Jaguar, Aston Martin or anybody else. And there were rumblings that a change might also be in the wind for the open-wheel Formula One cars on the grand prix circuit if the drivers didn't stop killing themselves with such sobering regularity.

Last season or not, the two Italian factories really rolled out the big guns in an effort to beat each other to the title. After all, Ferrari and Maserati were really crosstown rivals—with the *Modena Autodromo* test track conveniently located in between—and the only thing sweeter than beating the British and French and Germans and Americans was beating each other. Maserati had their monster 450S V-8 plus their well developed and better balanced (but not nearly so fast) 300S six-cylinder cars running in the 3.0-liter class as a backup, and Ferrari was loaded for bear with an updated version of the 3.5-liter V-12 Castellotti used to win the *Mille Miglia* the year before—now with double overhead cams and more power. And they kept punching it out for more displacement and more power as the season went on.

Nobody else was really in the picture. Jaguar always focused exclusively on Le Mans and, after scoring outright wins in '51 and '53 with their C-Types and '55 and '56 with D-Types, they decided to close down the factory racing team and sell the cars off to privateers like Briggs Cunningham and the crack Ecurie Ecosse team from Scotland, who had so conveniently saved Jaguar's bacon by winning Le Mans for them in 1956 after the new, fuel-injected factory cars ran into problems. Aston Martin was out there, but wouldn't do the full season, and the little giant-killers from Porsche just didn't have the power to run against the big cars for overall victories. Although they were always good for 1500cc class wins and embarrassingly high overall finishes wherever they raced.

So there it was—Ferrari versus Maserati—a blood-red fight to the death in both sportscars and Formula One. And my buddy Hank Lyons was right there in the thick of it from the first green flag in Buenos Aires in January until the very last checker came down in Caracas, Venezuela, on November 3rd. You have to understand that there were two very different championships at stake here. The World Driving Championship was a battle between the drivers, fought out in roughly three-hour grand prix races—one per country—in the full-out, single-seater Formula One cars. The much-coveted championship went to the driver who amassed the most points in his best five finishes out of the seven races. Of course it was terribly important what make of car he was driving—important to the manufacturers, important to the scribes and newscasters, and important to Joe, Giuseppe, Jacques, Juan, Gerald and Jurgen Average out in the street—and no question the Formula One grand prix cars were the purest, most high-strung, hair-trigger and holiest-of-the-holy damn race-cars on earth. But maybe even more important to the likes of Ferrari and Maserati (and Jaguar and Aston Martin and Porsche and even Mercedes-Benz when they were in it) was the World Manufacturers' Championship for "sports cars," which was fought out by teams of drivers in much longer races—from 1000 kilometers clear up to 12 and 24 hours—since it was the *cars* that seemed to win those races even more than the drivers. And likewise the points championship (and all the press hoopla and prestige that went with it) ultimately came to roost with the winning manufacturer. And Hank would be right there feeding me all of it, just the way it happened—race by race, corner by corner, rumor by rumor and blow by blow—along with, in sadly edited versions, all those readers, subscribers and news-stand page-thumbers who followed the drama, ebb and flow of international racing in the pages of *Car & Track* magazine….

Hank wrote that those first races in Argentina were like the opening rounds of a heavyweight championship prizefight. Naturally Fangio was the huge hometown favorite with the Argentine crowd when the first Grand Prix of the season kicked off in the Buenos Aires Autodrome on Saturday, January 13th. And he came through to win in almost effortless style after the Ferraris of Collins, Musso and Hawthorn all dropped out with clutch or transmission troubles. That left just Castellotti, and although he made a game try at it, the Ferraris just simply couldn't match the pace of the Maserati grand prix cars in Argentina. Then a wheel fell off Castellotti's car, and that was the end of it. Toly Wolfgang wound up the highest placed Ferrari, finishing a lonely fifth in one of last year's cars behind no less than four Maseratis.

You can bet old man Ferrari back in Maranello was hardly pleased!

The 1000-kilometer World Manufacturers' Championship sportscar race was held in the same city a week later, and that gave Hank and the rest of the European speed circus an opportunity to enjoy—and endure—the hospitality of the Argentine government and the local high society. Racing had become really big in Argentina thanks to El Presidente Juan Peron, who was a huge fan and also appreciated the old Roman "bread and circuses" approach to popular government. In fact, it was Peron and a few of his rich, powerful buddies who arranged for and funded Juan Manuel Fangio's original foray into European racing in a privateer Maserati in 1949. But Peron's iron-fisted rule and his unpredictable, sometimes fascist, sometimes socialist, sometimes communistic policies angered, offended and confused a lot of people. Including a lot of folks in Argentina's higher social bracket and a whole boatload of nervous foreign governments, with the good old U.S. of A. right at the top of the list! But his power started to fade after his wildly popular mistress-then-wife Evita died of cancer in 1952, and he was ultimately ousted by his own generals and exiled to Spain in 1955. But the new government wanted to continue the races because the public loved them and expected them to take place. Hank said it felt pretty strange—and just a little scary—to see patrols of uniformed policemen, personnel carriers and columns of heavily armed infantry soldiers everywhere you looked. But that's the way things were done in Argentina.

The World Manufacturers' Championship sportscar race was held on a new and somewhat makeshift 6.35-mile "street circuit" using the wide, sweeping boulevards that ran through the city, and included one desperately fast 2.5-mile stretch with a long, gentle, downhill curve at the end that even the bravest drivers considered suicidal. *"It's crucial to a good time to go fast there,"* Toly explained to Hank, *"but it's impossible to judge or feel through the seat of your pants. You're just hanging on and hoping at 170 or so, and it's all concrete around the outside. Even the tiniest mistake, hiccup or hesitation means death."* Crowd control was also a serious problem. *"The people will sit right on the curbs to watch. They think we're a lot better drivers than we really are...."*

In the end a chicane was hastily installed in that sweeping bend and even more uniformed police and gun-toting squads of infantrymen were brought in to keep the massive crowd at least somewhat in check. And it was *hot!* Brutally hot. Searing hot. Equatorial hot. So careful pace and frequent driver changes would be the order of the day for both the Ferrari and Maserati teams. Moss and Fangio were teamed up in the new 450S Maserati, and Moss took off like a shot at the start and simply drove away from the field, while the Hawthorn/Collins Ferrari had starter trouble and was out before it ever crossed the line. Meanwhile one local driver in a privateer Maserati spun into the crowd—injuring five, two of them seriously—and then another over-his-head local hotshoe crashed his Maserati into a tree and got hauled off in an ambulance in critical condition. There's no getting around it: open road racing is dangerous as hell. That's just the way it's built.

Moss had almost two minutes in hand when he handed over to Fangio, and it looked like the big Maserati V-8 was going to cruise to an easy win. But then the clutch linkage broke, and so Fangio had no choice but to try and shift without it. Which naturally took its toll on all the gears and shafts and bearings in that poor transmission, and soon enough Fangio came by the pits pointing backwards towards the transaxle. He limped in a few laps later with terminal grinds, grates and graunches coming from the back end of the car. The 450S was out of it. This left Ferraris in first and second, and they were being driven by a real musical-chairs rotation of factory drivers as one and then the next wilted under the tremendous heat in the cockpits. Maserati team manager Ugolini pulled Menditeguy's 300S in from third place and put Moss behind the wheel to see if he could do anything about the Ferraris. Hank said Stirling came through with an incredibly brilliant drive, setting staggeringly quick laps with unruffled ease and relentlessly reeling in Toly Wolfgang's undeniably more powerful Ferrari V-12. Moss caught him and passed him for second just before the checkered flag, much to the aggravation of the Ferrari team manager.

Hank talked to Toly afterwards, and once again he had that exhausted, shaken, shell-shocked look of a man who's peered over the edge. He was thoroughly spent—drenched in sweat, grease and grime—and shaking visibly as he attempted to light another *Gauloises*. *"There was nothing I could do,"* Toly mumbled out of an eerily blank, confused expression. *"I was driving as hard as I could...."*

Although Ferrari had drawn first blood in the World Manufacturers' Championship in Buenos Aires, they'd been humbled—hell, embarrassed!—in the Grand Prix. Worse yet, Maserati's monster 450 looked to have the legs on Ferrari's new V-12 if it ever found the strength and stamina to go with it. And then things got even worse for Ferrari. Castellotti had pretty much inherited the mantle of team leader after Fangio defected to Maserati, and he was the guy old man Ferrari called to strike back after Jean Behra set a new lap record in Maserati's latest grand prix car at their hometown *Modena Autodromo* test track. From what Hank heard later, Castellotti wasn't particularly thrilled with the idea. He had a lot of personal shit going on with a wife and family on one hand and an all-too-public affair with this famous and beautiful Italian movie star on the other, and I guess he was off with her someplace when Ferrari summoned him to the test track. As you can imagine, he didn't feel much like dropping what he was doing just to set a lap record that didn't count for anything at the

Modena Autodromo and give their crosstown rivals at Maserati a meaningless black eye. But Castellotti ultimately showed up like any good soldier and climbed into the latest version of the modified and updated Ferrari 801 grand prix car, revved it up, set his jaw, stuck it in gear and steamed out of the pits.

He never came back.

Of course nobody but the team and a few hangers-on were there at the time—it was just a pleasant, quiet Thursday morning in spring everywhere else in the world—and the version Hank heard was that maybe the throttle stuck or a dog ran out on the track or maybe Castellotti was just feeling irritated and pissed off and trying too hard too soon. Or maybe he just made a mistake. But the car crashed almost head-on into the base of a concrete grandstand foundation and that was pretty much the end of it.

Naturally there was anguish and mourning all across Italy, and meanwhile Ferrari had the very real problem of what to do about losing the guy everybody figured to be his team leader after Fangio's defection to Maserati. Naturally it moved everybody already in the queue up a notch. The British pair of Peter Collins and Mike Hawthorn—who knew each other from British club racing and thanks to being thrown together at Ferrari were becoming inseparable companions and calling each other "Mon Ami Mate"—were now Ferrari's front-liners along with the somewhat haunted-looking Luigi Musso. And Toly Wolfgang moved up right behind them. Phil Hill was still regarded by the team as their steady, intelligent and mechanically sympathetic sportscar ace for endurance racing (much to Phil's displeasure, since he figured he was quick as anybody and wanted a crack at Formula One) along with the meticulously quick but careful and experienced little Frenchman, Maurice Trintignant. Ferrari also added the dark, dashing, brooding and intense young Spanish nobleman, the Marquis de Portago. Portago was a fabulously colorful character who always filled a lot of column inches in the European papers—especially the tabloids—and was famous for his polo playing and bobsledding adventures along with his well-publicized love affairs with some of the world's most beautiful women. He started out buying his sportscar rides from Ferrari—he could afford it!—but he'd shown a lot of raw speed and even rawer nerve and the Old Man liked that sort of thing. Besides, Ferrari always believed in the strength of numbers—especially in the unpredictable world of long-distance endurance racing—and he usually cleared out the garage when the time came to load up for a World Manufacturers' Championship race. And that made a lot of sense. But that also meant he was regularly on the lookout for more talented risk-takers to sit in the seats and press on the pedals, and so much the better if they were rich and willing to pay for the privilege....

Maserati evened things up at Alec Ulmann's 12-Hour World Manufacturers' Championship race at Sebring, Florida, just nine short days after Castellotti's fatal crash. Fangio and Behra took the lone 450S entered to an overpowering win, Behra loafing along easily in the slipstream of Collins' leading Ferrari for the first hour or so before pulling out, sweeping past and simply motoring off into the distance. It was no contest. According to Hank, that bellowing Maserati V-8 was flirting with 190mph on those long airport runways at Sebring! He said the patter of the tar strips under the tires sounded like a machine gun firing rubber bullets! I could close my eyes and almost hear it.

Moss had elected to use one of the six-cylinder 300S models because he liked the way it drove and knew it might be more reliable. Especially after the 450's mechanical problems put him out in Argentina. He and Schell drove a fine, smooth, well-judged and trouble-free race to finish second, two laps behind the 450 but still two laps ahead of the third-place, Cunningham-entered "Jaguar USA" D-Type. The best-placed Ferrari was an American privateer entry in fourth and the best factory car was six laps further behind in sixth. It was a pretty dismal showing….

And then came the race that everyone would remember—even people who didn't care a thing about racing—the *Mille Miglia* in May. Hank said it was like nothing he'd ever seen in his life. Like the old, discontinued *La Carrera,* but ten times as big and a hundred times dearer to the hearts of the rabid local fans. All of Italy closed up its shops and factories and businesses and the people swarmed to the roadsides by the hundreds of thousands, cramming the choice viewing spots on the hillsides and second- and third-floor balconies to watch their favorites charge past. The race ran down the length and across the breadth of Italy on ordinary, everyday Italian roads, streets and highways—from Brescia in the north clear down to Rome in the south—only to turn around at the Rome checkpoint and head back up towards Brescia again. A thousand miles of narrow, winding, blind, uneven, pot-holed Italian roadway, including harrowing runs through the mist and rain of the infamous Futa and Raticosa mountain passes on the return run back to Brescia. The *Mille Miglia* was more than a race. It was a national celebration of the fiery-hot, bubbling-over Italian passion for speed, skill, spirit and daring….

Hank said the town square at the starting line in Brescia was not to be believed: filled to overflowing with people and noise and music and vendor tents selling everything from bread and fruit and sausage and soup and sweets to tall glasses of wine, pennants and souvenirs. The cars started rolling down the starting ramp well before midnight, surrounded by popping flashbulbs and a wildly cheering crowd that pressed in so close there was barely enough room for the cars to get through. They started the little tiddlers first, one every 30 seconds—mostly tiny Fiat 600s plus occasional Fiat-Abarths, Renault 4CVs and DB-Panhards—then switched to one every minute as midnight and the wee morning hours passed and the Alfas, bigger Fiats and Lancia Appias chirped their tires, shot down the ramp and spurted off into the night. Hank was particularly impressed with—hell, in love with—the little pumpkinseed-shaped Alfa Romeo SVZ in the 1300 Grand Touring class. It had a special, lightweight, hand-hammered alloy body by Zagato with a beautifully rounded front and rump and that unmistakable Alfa grin on its face. And what a marvelous, angry little snarl it made as it raced into the darkness.

It was several more hours—until right around dawn, in fact—before the tiddlers, middleweights and welterweights gave way to the faster, more serious pure racing cars from Ferrari and Maserati that were really in contention for the overall win. The really big guns came right at the end, with not only a thousand miles of difficult, dangerous roadway ahead but also all the smaller, slower cars that started before them to contend with as well. Moss and his riding partner Denis Jenkinson were teamed up in one of the big 450S Maserati V-8s. They'd amazed everyone by winning the *Mille Miglia* outright for Mercedes in '55 thanks to meticulous preparation, tons of practice, scrupulous note-taking and a special aluminum box with a clear plastic window that carried their route notes on one long, continuous roll of paper. Because of its engine size, their Maserati was the final car to growl its way down the starting ramp in Brescia at just past 5:50 in the morning. But their ride lasted less than 10 miles before the brake pedal snapped clear off! And what a rude shock *that* must have been! Fortunately they skated harmlessly into a farmer's field, mowed through some growing spring crops and didn't hit anything solid. But they were out of it. Worse yet for Maserati, Behra had crashed the other 450S during so-called "practice" the day before. And "practice" at the *Mille Miglia* meant going as fast as you dared in a full-tilt racing car while dodging your way through ordinary, everyday Italian road traffic. Which generally included buses, trucks, bicyclists, horse carts, motor scooters, flocks of sheep, stray dogs, wandering chickens, other "practicing" racecars and swarms of sputtering, downshifting, tire-squealing Fiats being driven flat-out and right-to-the-redline by crazed would-be race drivers who knew they lacked only the luck, funding and opportunity to be racing in the *Mille Miglia* themselves! And rather than blowing whistles, giving chase and writing citations, the local police waved and cheered like everybody else! It was outrageous! It was anarchy! It was magnificent! It was pandemonium! It was delicious and dangerous as hell....

Behra's practice crash pretty much wrote off the second 450S (not to mention putting him in the hospital for a few weeks) and with Moss out in the first 10 miles in the other 450S, the way was wide-open for a full-fledged Ferrari sweep. And that's exactly what happened. But not without drama. And tragedy. You have to understand that the most difficult part of the *Mille Miglia*—besides the 1,000-mile challenge of the road itself—is that no driver has any idea where he is relative to the competition from one checkpoint to the next. Because the cars start a minute apart, you know you're ahead of anybody you can see up ahead of you. And if someone's right there in your mirrors, you know he's ahead of you by far on the time sheets. But what about when you can't see anybody ahead or behind? Then all you can do is motor on as fast as you dare, but at the same time trying to not hurt the car or have yourself an accident.

It's pretty nerve-wracking stuff.

With '56 winner Castellotti gone, most of the locals figured fiercely determined Luigi Musso as the man to beat. But Musso was taken seriously ill the week before the race, and so his car was handed over to de Portago. It was the very latest, 4.0-liter

"335 Sport" version of the V-12, and capable of 180-plus on the long, flat, straight stretches through the Po Valley near the end of the return trip to Brescia. But Portago didn't much care for the *Mille Miglia.* He didn't know the roads and thought it was terribly dangerous. He and his American navigator attempted a practice run before the race in order to make notes, but didn't even make it to the end of the first stage before they clouted a bridge abutment. That was the full extent of their pre-race "practice." Even so, Portago wanted to be seen as a fast young driver on the rise and, after paying for most of his early drives, he surely saw this as an opportunity to become a genuine member of the Ferrari factory team.

Of course the home-grown Italian drivers had a big advantage on the *Mille Miglia* because they've been driving those roads all their lives. That's why Ferrari shrewdly added the wise, patient and experienced old "Silver Fox" Piero Taruffi to his team for the *Mille Miglia,* even though Taruffi had just celebrated his 50th birthday. Only a local expert like Taruffi could attempt the race without a navigator alongside in the passenger seat—at a weight penalty of at least 150 pounds—rattling off route instructions and pace notes while hanging on for dear life and trying not to be sick. But a wise old Italian fox like Taruffi had it all in his head.

Even so, the big news at the halfway checkpoint in Rome was that fair-haired Brit Peter Collins' Ferrari was ahead on the time sheets by almost five full minutes. Followed by three more Ferraris in the hands of Taruffi, Toly Wolfgang (who knew many of the roads almost as well as the natives and desperately wanted to re-impress old man Ferrari), and the young Spaniard de Portago, who was soldiering on and doing his best in spite of the obstacles. And while he was stopped at the Rome checkpoint, Portago's current girlfriend—the beautiful American actress Linda Christian—ran out of the crowd and kissed him passionately. Right there in front of everybody. Hank was only a few yards away, and he said it was like a scene right out of a Hollywood movie. The kind of thing that makes you catch your breath and ache a little inside.

By that point there was no doubt the *Mille Miglia* would end in a Ferrari victory. But the question was: which one? Collins was well ahead, but he'd been pushing the car hard and the difficult mountain passes—the roads Taruffi knew so well—were still ahead. There was cold and even light snow to deal with up in the mountains, and then a light rain as the cars made their last fuel stops at the final service checkpoint in Bologna. All of the Ferraris had made it through the most difficult and dangerous section through the mountains, and now all that stood between any of them and the finish line were the fast, straight roads arrowing across the bottom of the Po Valley. But in racing, things are often more difficult and complex than they seem. Although Collins was still leading handily, the transaxle in his car was breaking up and there seemed no way he would make it to the finish. And sure enough, his Ferrari expired long before reaching the finish in Brescia. Taruffi's car was also making ugly noises from the gearbox, although the old fox sensed it early on and was doing his best to go easy and baby the gears. Toly still held third, but he'd whacked a road marker in the mountains and bent a lower control arm. It wasn't terribly out of whack, but enough to screw up the alignment and make the steering iffy, and that slowed him as well. And then there was Portago. He'd been almost embarrassingly slower than his teammates up to this point—fourteen-and-a-half minutes slower than Collins on the five-hour run from Brescia to Rome!—but of course they had practiced and knew the roads and had spent time in the cars before. Now Portago had the only healthy Ferrari left and just the flat-out speed run ahead from Bologna to the finish!

It was almost too tempting....

Of course it made all the papers—even here in the states—how Portago's Ferrari blew a tire like a gunshot at something over 170 approaching the town of Guidizzolo, just 25 miles short of the finish. The car slewed left, ricocheted off some roadside marker stones, scythed wildly to the right, launched through a ditch, guillotined a utility pole, crashed through a crowd of spectators like a hurtling asteroid, went airborne for 150 yards and came down with a final, violent, shuddering splash into a small canal. Behind it lay a path of unbelievable carnage! Portago and his navigator were killed instantly along with five adults and five innocent little children standing on the hillside overlooking the roadway, and at least 20 more spectators were seriously injured. Blood and bodies were scattered everywhere, and the air was filled with desperate cries, anguished shrieks, pitiful moans and the soft, whimpering gurgle of the dying. When rescuers finally arrived on the scene, they saw that Portago's head had been severed off completely by the hood of his own racecar....

Less than a half-hour later and completely oblivious to the horror taking place just a few miles behind, a weary, grimy but elated 50-year-old Piero Taruffi limped his ailing Ferrari 315S across the finish line in Brescia—a huge grin on his face and fist pumping the air in victory!—to take the win that had eluded him for half a lifetime. Collins had broken not far out of Bologna, and the whispered but never confirmed rumor was that Toly backed off so that Taruffi could win the race. Hank asked him about it later, of course. But Toly just shrugged. "With what happened, who cares? It's not the sort of race anybody wants to remember anyway."

"But did you back off?"

Toly lit up another *Gauloises* and looked at him kind of sideways. "The steering was bad. I'd whacked it up in the mountains."

"But could you have gone faster?"

Toly gave him a smile that had nothing to do with anything funny. "You can *always* go faster. That's the dirty little demon inside all of us. That's what drives us crazy. That's what gets us killed...."

Chapter 19: Meanwhile, Back at the Ranch….

As you can imagine, there was a lot of interest in Maserati's honking new 450 over on this side of the Atlantic, and damn if for once Ernesto Julio didn't have the inside track on getting one thanks to buying that two-tone Frua convertible and maybe even paying a little too much for it. I understand he even made a quiet little trip over to the factory in Modena right after Sebring to put a hefty cash deposit down in return for a promise that he'd have the very first one here in the States. But he kept it all on the hush-hush, you know, so the other bigtime car owners wouldn't get wind of it.

Cal had been running Ernesto's old Monza and the occasionally—okay, maybe more than occasionally—troublesome 121LM at places like Pomona, Paramount Ranch, Stockton, Palm Springs and Hour Glass Field and doing reasonably well with them, but things had been a little cool between the two of them ever since Ernesto caught wind that there might be something going on between Cal and his hot Hollywood protégé Gina LaScala at Sebring the previous year. And for a while right after that Sebring race they were really on the outs. But by the summer of 1957 Gina had already hit the screen in that sexy supporting-actress role as a fiery gypsy dancer opposite—and, by all Hollywood celluloid implications, repeatedly underneath—Yul Brynner in *The Pirate King of New Orleans.* She did a dance number in that movie that would make your mouth go dry. Or toes curl. Or zipper tighten. Or all three at once, come to that. Nevermind that a really close, clinical, Hollywood Insider look quickly revealed that most of the heat, steam and magic came courtesy of a slick choreographer and some pasty-faced editor slaving away at a Movieola machine in a cramped, windowless, dungeon-like editing room tucked away in a basement somewhere on the studio lot. Along with a couple spliced-in, no-face-showing moves and maneuvers performed by a double-jointed circus acrobat/professional dancer from Rio de Janeiro named Rita Tamando while Gina was off taking gypsy diction lessons and working on her lines.

But that's the way it's done in the movie business, and *The Pirate King of New Orleans* was a monster box-office smash. And no question Gina LaScala was the thing most moviegoers found permanently seared into their brains afterwards. Especially the men. The camera just flat *loved* Gina LaScala. Hell, it damn near drooled. And naturally that's when the old roller coaster of Fame & Fortune creeped up over the top and the wild ride began. Almost instantly there were interviews and magazine spreads and radio shows and TV appearances and more blessed scripts than she'd ever imagined for Gina herself, her mother and her agent to skim through and discard or consider. She wound up immediately taking another part as a hot, brazen, sultry and seductive courtier/dancer type—only this time in ancient Egypt—in this huge bible epic spectacular being shot mostly in Spain (where you could get away with using non-union extras and crew people). After that came a strikingly similar role as the svelte, sultry and seductive Bad Girl female heavy (who turns good at the end, of course, and sacrifices herself so the stalwart English hero can sail off into the sunset with the well-bred, virtuous blonde with the creamy skin who comes from a nice, upright, upper-crust English family) in a movie about the defeat of the Spanish Armada being shot mainly in the Caribbean. And already the standard-issue, Hollywood Insider columns and in-the-know interviews were coming out about how this sizzling, sparkling, can't-take-your-eyes-off-her sex symbol Gina LaScala wanted: *"Something different. Something challenging. A real acting part to show what I can do and help develop my craft."* Of course, it was actually Brad Lackey and the fine, experienced crew of wannabe writers and failed English professors over at the MGM publicity department who were actually writing (or at least scripting and choreographing) those interviews. But that's what the public wanted and expected to hear (even as they were staring into her eyes and cleavage on the accompanying, dramatically lighted publicity shot) and, by God, that's what they were going to get!

In any case, Gina LaScala (or Angelina Scalabrini, take your pick) wasn't around town much in Hollywood thanks to all that location shooting. And that was probably a good thing as far as Cal's driving career with Ernesto was concerned. Even better was the Cal Club race he wasn't even invited to drive in at the Santa Barbara airport towards the end of May. Ernesto told Cal he'd kind of promised this studio exec friend of his' hotshot private pilot—a smirking, steely-eyed ex-Air Force fighter jock named Pete Stark who moonlighted now and then as a stunt driver in car-chase scenes—a chance behind the wheel. Not to mention that he wanted Cal to shoot up the coast to Sonoma and swap his two-tone Maserati convert for the brand-new Jaguar XKSS he'd just bought. Now the XKSS was really nothing but a full-tilt Jaguar D-Type fitted with an add-on convertible top, a full-width windshield, side-pipe mufflers, a luggage rack on the back deck and a racing engine ever-so-slightly detuned for street use. Jaguar only wound up building 16 of them before this fire at the factory stopped production (although the rumor going around was that Jaguar only built enough to use up the leftover D-Type parts and then used the fire as an excuse for deep-sixing the project, since all of Jaguar's other production lines were back up and running pretty quickly after the fire).

But the XKSS was one hell of a neat car—imagine driving a real, live, Le Mans-winning sports/racer down to the corner drugstore to pick up a pack of cigarettes and a roll of throat lozenges—and according to *Car & Track* it'd do zero-to-sixty in 5.2 seconds and top out at 149mph. Plus it looked sexier than Gina LaScala (or maybe just *as* sexy as Gina LaScala, since she was way up there near the top of the visible-to-the-naked-eye scale) and so naturally a bunch of hot Hollywood types just *had* to have one. Including TV personality Bill Leyden and actor Hugh O'Brien (TV's Wyatt Earp) along with up-and-coming screen phenom Steve McQueen as soon as the money came in from his breakthrough TV series deal as bounty hunter Josh Randall in "Wanted, Dead or Alive."

Not to mention Ernesto Julio, who generally favored Italian cars, but fell hard for the curves, swerves and mellow, blaring exhaust note of the XKSS. Plus the fire at the factory in February (which by all accounts destroyed nine or ten of the original run of 25 and ended XKSS production forever) guaranteed that they were ultra-rare and hard to get, which of course made them all the more deliciously attractive.

And, in typical Hollywood style, the very first thing Ernesto did with his brand-new XKSS was send it over to George Barris' Kalifornia Kustom shop to have it repainted a green so deep and dark it was like looking into a pupil of an eye. And then it went over to the Mexicans at George Barris' favorite upholstery shop to have the interior redone in a rich tan leather, and after that he had another Mexican kid with a buffing wheel, a tooth brush, a large mound of hand rags and about five tubes of Simichrome polish go over and over those dull-finish Dunlop disc wheels until they shined like mellow chrome.

In spite of all the super-fast, super-exotic cars he'd raced and driven, my buddy Cal was pretty damn excited about getting his hands on an XKSS. Only he was also a wee bit suspicious about the timing. Especially when Ernesto showed up late at the dealership in Santa Monica with his gleaming and glistening new XKSS, so Cal had to fight Friday-evening traffic all the way north out of L.A. Cal had a notion something was up, so he drove like hell to get up and back from Sonoma in record time. Even got chased by the cops at one point, but he said all he had to do was bury the gas and flick off the lights once he had a little distance in hand—there was about half a moon out that night, plenty enough to see by—and then zigzag off on some side roads until he figured the coast was clear. No way could any hopped-up, American sedan cop car ever hope to stay with a well-driven XKSS.

There were more delays in Sonoma when it seemed nobody could find the damn keys to the Maserati. But Sylvester'd showed Cal how to hotwire his mom's Packard convertible back when he was still staying at Castle Carrington and his folks hid the keys whenever they went out of town. And a Maserati wasn't all that different from a Packard (or any other car) when it came to jimmying the damn switch. Cal drove all night to get back down to Santa Barbara—said he averaged better than 100 on a couple stretches in the Maserati and well over two miles a minute now and then with the XKSS on the way up—and the smallbore group was just getting ready to pull out for first morning practice when he rolled into the paddock at the Santa Barbara airport. Sure enough, not only was old Ernesto there with hotshot Hollywood pilot/stuntman Pete Stark behind the wheel of his Ferrari, but Ernesto had Gina there, too. She was only in town for a week to dub some dialog that got spoiled when a helicopter full of tabloid photographers flew over the beach where they were shooting in the Caribbean, and as soon as the work was done she'd be going back on location. Gina seemed genuinely surprised to see Cal at Santa Barbara. And pretty damn happy about it, too.

"Ernesto said you were off getting a car or something up by San Francisco."

Cal slipped her a sly grin. "I bet he did." It felt awfully damn nice to see her again. And he told her so.

"Me, too," she sighed, kind of tilting her head in against his shoulder. "Me, too."

Naturally things got a little awkward when Ernesto came over. "Hey, look who showed up!" he said like he was talking to Cal about Gina and Gina about Cal.

"Pretty amazing," Cal agreed with an almost straight face.

"Isn't it?" Gina added, her eyes going wide.

But Cal knew it was better to just shrug it off and not to make a scene. What purpose would that serve? Especially when he knew Ernesto had that new Maserati 450S in the pipeline….

They made a little small talk and then Ernesto said he had this producer he wanted Gina to meet. So Cal excused himself and went meandering off through the paddock with a glum, aimless expression on his face. He ran into Max Balchowsky—wearing his usual, signature-edition one-piece tan coveralls—Max's wife Ina and the blunt, homely and ungainly-looking Buick-powered special they'd put together that was getting itself something of a reputation on the California road racing scene. The damn thing looked like a junkyard on wheels, ran on whitewall recaps and was painted a kind of Old Maid's Bathroom shade of pale yellow—applied with brushes or brooms, from the look of it—but it always seemed to run pretty well. It'd picked up the nickname "Ol' Yaller" after the famous old mongrel in the popular Disney film, and Max road registered it in Idaho just so he could wear that "Famous Potatoes" license plate on the back. Anyhow, Max knew who Cal was and had seen him drive a couple times—occasionally from directly behind—and decided to strike up a friendly conversation.

"You look like shit," Max observed.

"Ahh, I been up all night."

"You do too much partying, son. Shouldn't do that the night before a big race. Or even a small race. Takes the lead out of your pencil."

"It's not like that," Cal assured him wearily. "It's just I had to run up to Sonoma County to pick up a car last night."

"Up to Sonoma and back in one night?" Max let out a low whistle. "That's some pretty fast highway motoring."

"Yeah," Cal laughed. "I think some of the Highway Patrol guys thought so, too."

Max looked him up and down. "So you drivin' Mr. Julio's big, fancy Ferrari again today?"

Cal eyes oozed down to the ground between them. "Nah, he's got somebody else in it this weekend."

"I saw that," Max nodded, squinting at the top of Cal's forehead. "Any particular reason?"

"Oh, he said it was just a favor for a friend," Cal shrugged half-heartedly. "You know how it is with reasons. They're like assholes—everybody has one."

Max looked down at the same patch of ground Cal was staring at. "So you got anything else lined up?"

Cal shook his head, eyes still focused on the dirt.

"Well," Max said, kind of rubbing his chin, "d'ya think you'd like to take a try in my car?"

Cal's eyes swept up from the ground. "Are you *serious?"*

"Nobody has *ever* accused me of being serious," Max growled at him, "but I am kinda thinking about it."

"You *are?"* Cal could feel his pulse picking up.

"Sure," Max nodded like it was no big thing. "You can drive it if you want."

Cal's looked at him kind of sideways. "But weren't *you* going to drive it?"

"Aw, I was. But I saw you moping around here like a damn lost puppy…" Max looked at him with just the tiniest hint of a smirk in his eyes. "I just can't stand to see a grown man cry."

For once in his life, Cal Carrington didn't know quite what to say. "Th-that's awfully damn nice of you," was all he could come up with.

"Oh, don't start carrying on about it," Max warned playfully. "Ina and me don't allow any crybabies on this team. Better climb in and see how you fit."

Cal climbed into Ol' Yaller. In spite of the back-alley bodywork, it was simple, comfortable and well laid out inside. *"Jesus!"* Cal yelped suddenly, *"I don't even have my helmet with me!"*

A dark cloud passed over Max's face. "Now I said you could drive my car, but I'll have to think twice about letting you use my helmet…."

So Cal drove Max Balchowsky's Ol' Yaller that weekend at Santa Barbara, and damn if he didn't win the blessed race with it. Both races, in fact: the prelim qualifying race on Saturday and the big-bore modified feature on Sunday. Beat all the Ferraris, Maseratis and Jaguars with it, even in the rain! He said afterwards that it was a surprisingly good racecar, in spite of what it looked like from the outside. "Oh, I guess it's not much of a looker," he allowed, "but it's got decent brakes and handles really good for something with all that heavy grunt under the hood. And everything *works!* It brakes straight and true and doesn't get all nervous or squirrely in the corners, and it goes like bloody hell down the straightaways. And God only knows where Max gets those recaps he runs on. Why, I think they may be the best damn tires I've ever driven on! Especially in the rain."

Of course nobody ever suspected anything about the tires, seeing as how Max and Ina always towed Ol' Yaller to the racetrack on a set of dingy, mismatched junkyard blackwalls, then hauled out a floor jack and a set of jack stands and made a bit of a show out of taking the whitewall recaps off her Buick wagon and putting them on the racecar. In fact, I think Max was maybe a little miffed that Cal let on that there might be something special about the tires. *"Aw, I get 'em from a guy who does truck retreads,"* Max would grumble in an irritated voice when anybody started asking about them. *"Hell, I'm too poor to afford new tires like those rich guys run on their cars…."*

Right.

To top things off, hot-shot pilot/stuntman Pete Stark managed to spin Ernesto's Ferrari into the haybales trying to keep up with Cal in the rain, which put a couple nice, fresh dents in the Ferrari's expensive-to-pound-out aluminum bodywork.

Even a big wheel like Ernesto Julio had to feel a little embarrassed about what happened at Santa Barbara, and he showed the kind of guy he really was by putting Cal back in his Ferrari the very next weekend at the old abandoned World War II Naval airbase near Cotati, about 45 miles north of San Francisco. But it turned out old Pete had been a little rough on the gearbox and so Cal wound up limping home second with the car stuck in third gear while Carroll Shelby cruised to a well-deserved if somewhat uncontested win in John Edgar's 300S Maserati. "I would've been a lot better off back in Ol' Yaller," Cal laughed into the phone. And he meant it, too.

Word came through towards the end of June that the new 450S would soon be arriving air freight direct from Modena to the Maserati importer in New York, and Ernesto decided to send Cal east along with the tow rig and crew, seeing as how there was a race weekend coming up at the brand new Lime Rock track in the northwest corner of Connecticut July 27-28, and that seemed as good an opportunity as any to give the Maserati a little shakedown run. Big Ed couldn't make it on account of he already had a three-day holiday weekend in Havana lined up with a brand-new potential ex-Mrs. B—this time an attractive part-time dental hygienist from Weehawken who moonlighted now and then twirling her baton (among other things) at the Tip Top Club in Manhattan. "She's really way too young for me," Big Ed confided out of the side of his mouth opposite his cigar, "but I like a lot of other things about her, too...."

Even though Big Ed couldn't make it, my brother-in-law Carson Flegley and me knew we just had to be there—at least for the feature races on Sunday, anyway—since Lime Rock was only a couple hours out of the city and escaping for just a day wouldn't involve the usual home-front haggling in whims, aggravation, chores, favors, foot-rubbing and New Things For The House that "a weekend away with the boys" inevitably involved. Besides, Carson had this brand new Austin-Healey 100-6 that he'd just picked up from Colin St. John over in Manhattan the week before, and it hadn't really been out for its maiden spin on the open road yet. And even as you get older and wiser and busier than hell and overall less impressed with the world (although generally more fearful of it), a back country road adventure with a brand-new sports car never loses the last of its magic.

Everybody and his brother thought Donald Healey's new 100-6 was a sharp looking thing. It had a grille like a bulldog's smile (albeit full of braces) and that same gutty, sleek and jaunty Healey profile we'd admired so much ever since the first Healey Hundreds hit American shores. Carson's 100-6 was a creamy bright red over an even creamier white—most of them were coming in two-tone—and I was kind of surprised at least one of the colors wasn't black. But I guess there weren't any black ones on that very first boatload (or at least that's what Colin St. John told him, anyway), not to mention that flashier paintjobs seem to go right along with receding hairlines, an almost-too-stable home and work situation and a bunch of young kids running around the house.

To be honest, I think I liked Carson's 100-M better than the "new, improved" 100-6 Colin St. John insisted he absolutely *had* to have even before the first load of them arrived from England. Now a lot of mechanics—myself included—thought that hefty old delivery-truck motor in the original Healey Hundred was a bit of a lump, but that was before we got a chain hoist around that barge-anchor six in Healey's new model. Why, it damn near cracked the roof beam we hung the chain fall from the first time we tried to haul one out at the old Sinclair! And the "new, improved" six actually had 21cc *less* displacement than the old Austin four-banger it replaced. Go ahead and look it up if you don't believe me! Sure, the new six revved a little higher and made—in spite of its humble, commercial vehicle origins—maybe the sweetest raspy purr out the tailpipes this side of a Ferrari V-12. Don't ask me how or why. And a fabulous noise is worth a hell of a lot in any sports-car, whether it's accompanied by real performance or not. But the extra weight of that anvil of a straight six up front didn't do a hell of a lot for the new Healey's handling. And it was hotter than blazes over on the driver's side thanks to the twin exhaust pipes running directly beneath the left-side floorboards. I bet they had a pretty good laugh over that at the factory over in England, seeing as how all that roasting heat runs under the *passenger* side over there. But none of that mattered to my longtime friend and not quite so longtime brother-in-law Carson Flegley, since he'd been smitten by an absolutely savage dose of New Car Lust, and there's just nothing you can do about something like that. Or nothing you should do, anyway. Let them enjoy it while they can, right? It never lasts very long anyway….

Besides, that 100-6 was a damn handsome automobile, and Carson and me truly enjoyed our trip up to Connecticut that Sunday morning. It was perfect top-down weather, and we were cruising north on the Taconic Parkway and enjoying the six-cylinder growl out the Healey's exhaust pipes and especially the way it echoed off the walls of the occasional humpbacked stone bridges (along with the reassuring *bang!* of the undercarriage smacking into the pavement if we went over one of those damn bridges a little too fast!). Austin-Healeys have never been exactly generous when it comes to ground clearance, and we had an awful lot of beer and soda and emergency rain gear and all the picnic food the girls packed for us—enough to feed two dozen people, I swear!—loaded into the Healey's not particularly commodious trunk and those so-called "emergency seats" behind the driver and passenger. Now I considered those "emergency seats" a truly intriguing feature of the new 100-6 all by themselves. The nicely contoured bottom cushions appeared to have all the length and breadth and padding you could possibly require for your average American behind. But legroom could be measured with a damn feeler gauge unless you had the front seats so far forward that the driver had to turn his head sideways so his nose didn't get caught in the steering wheel and the passenger beside him was just about resting his chin on the dash cowling. And with the top erected, headroom in those rear seats ran the entire comfort zone gamut from terribly cramped to nonexistent. Obviously those "emergency seats" on Healey's new 100-6 were intended solely for pets, small children, midgets, pygmies and multiple amputees. And no matter what you put back there, the extra weight made the car bottom out even worse over rail-road crossings and unexpected humps in the road.

But none of that really mattered, since it was such a beautiful Sunday morning to be cruising up the Taconic Parkway in a brand-new sportscar, smelling the green of the forests and fields after the grime and grit of the city and looking out over handsome countryside with lots of trees and rolling hills and not much traffic so we could really open that new Healey up and enjoy it. Although we didn't get to the track until well past noon on account of we kept getting lost trying to find it. We knew we were close when we cut across into Connecticut on Route 44 by way of Millerton, New York, but after that it seemed like we went all around where the track actually was at least half a dozen times without ever getting there. Including one errant run up over the border into Massachusetts! But it was damn pretty country, and I really enjoyed the drive. You couldn't escape the feeling that there was a lot of history and old, old money up in those parts, just kind of quietly sitting around protecting and preserving itself. I found out later that there was once a thriving iron smelting industry in those parts thanks to rich iron ore deposits in the surrounding foothills of the Berkshire Mountains—dating back to before the Civil War—and at one time Lime Rock was full of noisy, pounding, smoke-belching forges and foundries and fiery charcoal blast furnaces that never shut down because they had to keep running 24 hours a day! There was housing for the married workers and a hotel with a dance hall for the unmarried workers and a company store and even a blessed casino, and the rich people who owned all those forges and foundries and the stores and businesses that served them lived in elegant Victorian homes well up the hill on the north side of town where the smoke and the soot rarely drifted. But I guess the rich, easy ore deposits eventually played out and the town and industry mutually faded into history around the turn of the century. And now you didn't see much of anything in the way of factories, office buildings or centers of commerce in that particular corner of Connecticut. And yet all those big, elegant houses remained. Many of them set well back from the main roads and hidden from casual view. It occurred to me that there were a lot more handsome, well-kept old farmhouses than farms.

"Gentlemen farmers," Carson explained.

"What's a gentleman farmer?" I wanted to know.

So Carson explained as how a "gentleman farmer" is some rich guy from the city who enjoys everything about the gentle and pastoral farming experience—wearing flannel shirts and bib overalls, talking about the weather and types of seeds, eating big, hearty meals in the kitchen while looking out over the moonlit countryside and maybe even taking a ride now and then on a tractor or hay wagon—but doesn't really have the time or inclination to actually dig holes in the ground, raise crops, feed or milk cows or chase chickens around a damn barnyard. So they get other people to do it for them. Or they buy one of those farm-type houses with no farm attached and do it that way. "It takes a whole lot of money to do that sort of thing," Carson added respectfully. "A lot of these people are very, very wealthy." And I could see that. I mean, having a farm with no actual farmland out back to support it has to be a bit of a drain on the old bank account.

But I liked it up there in Connecticut (even though I kept feeling like somebody was telling me to "sit up straight") and especially how peaceful, green, clean, well-worn and orderly everything seemed to be. I liked even more that we now had a real, live, purpose-built racetrack less about two hours from Times Square. Or Passaic, for that matter. Even though it took us a couple extra hours that first time because, like I said, we kept getting lost and circling around the place. Eventually we got there by coming back from the east, passing The White Hart tavern, the village square and the old stone church in Salisbury and some of those fine Victorian mansions, took a left at a gas station and growled past yet another fine old church (a white one this time, with its spire pointing importantly up into the sky), took a left at a crossroads a little further south right next to what Carson told me was about the most exclusive damn boys' prep school in the country, sailed over hills and past perfectly trimmed fields, wound down into this woodsy valley and finally found the entrance to the racetrack, which was tucked away over a small stone bridge and up a side road with some really grand and genteel old clapboard homes across the way.

Lime Rock was a quaint, quiet and marvelous little racetrack, nestled comfortably into a valley right smack-dab in the middle of the endlessly green, handsome and sometimes wonderfully misty forests of the Berkshire Mountains. A riffling trout stream ran right alongside the pit straightaway and yet another old stone country church (what else?) stood directly across from it on the main highway. The last services were getting out just as we arrived, and you could see from the expressions on the congregants' faces that they weren't real keen about having this new sports-car track right across the way. Not hardly.

Generally speaking, property is scarce, valuable and hemmed in by nature and neighbors up in Connecticut, and the local farmer/gravel pit owner who built Lime Rock had to squeeze it all into a relatively small chunk of real estate. His name was Jim Vail, and the way the story goes is that his father owned a big, successful farm in those parts and Jim added a sand and gravel business right next door. Then one of his buddies bought an MG TC and they'd use it to go tearing around the gravel pit on Sunday afternoons. Driving a car like an TC on gravel is lots of fun, because you can slide it full-lock sideways and shoot up big, impressive roostertails of dust without actually going very fast. Plus it's always nice to be on private land where no local farmer or woman out hanging laundry is going to shake their fist at you, no cop is gonna chase you and no cows or chickens are going to unexpectedly wander into your path.

I guess word kind of spread about what they were doing, and damn if a bunch of the old SCMA types—including Briggs Cunningham himself!—didn't show up one Sunday afternoon and ask about Jim's "racetrack." Well, they'd been maybe drinking a little beer while they were running that old MG around, and so it sounded like a pretty good idea! So over the next few weeks Jim hopped on his bulldozer and started moving dirt around to kind of shove a bend out of the Salmon Kill River so it didn't run right through the middle of the property, made a deal with his dad to use some of the old man's farmland, got an aerial picture of the property and drew a loop or two on it to show where the track might go and started up a hip pocket corporation to look after the whole thing. He even hired on our old buddy John Fitch—who was freshly back from racing for Mercedes in Europe—as kind of a consultant to throw his two cents in here and there.

The lay of the land plus a hurricane and flood pretty much decided which way the track had to go, and the resulting circuit was *very* short—just 1.53 miles!—but with plenty of drama, excitement and elevation changes packed into that distance. Cal allowed as how the first couple corners that ran through the bottom of what used to be the old gravel pit were pretty straightforward, what with flat ground, moderate speeds, just a single left-hander and plenty of runoff room to absorb excesses of impatience, idiocy or adrenaline. But then things got faster and less forgiving with every heartbeat. The road seemed to narrow as the speed picked up, and then you arrived at a deceptively fast uphill right with the trees and brush so close on the exit that you could almost reach out and touch them. Or that's what Cal said it felt like in the car, anyway. And that was followed by a half-breath straightaway and a fast, grit-your-teeth, maybe flat/maybe not righthander that reminded Cal of "The Kink" at Road America. And then there was only time to take another half-breath and hold it for a steep, blind and thoroughly daunting downhill plunge into an even faster right-hand sweeper onto the floor of the old gravel pit again. Cal said it was by far the most important corner on the track because your momentum through there carried all the way down the front straight, and the only reasonable overtaking opportunity on the whole blessed track was through the braking zone into Big Bend. The rest of it was pretty much single-file unless the guy in front of you flat couldn't drive or had his head up his ass. And God only help you if you went off at The Downhill….

But if you could keep you cool and your hands calm on the wheel through that plunging, sweeping right-hander onto the pit straight and moreover had a herd of big, stomping Italian horseponies under your right foot down the straightaway that followed—like Cal did—there was just no way anybody could stay close enough to dive under you at Big Bend and get past. And that's precisely what our buddy Cal did, using the big Maserati's power to take command right from the get-go and keeping the friskier-handling cars bottled up behind him as he slowly, smoothly and methodically built up a small lead. But then they'd hit lapped traffic somewhere on the backside of the track and all of a sudden they'd be all over him again. "This place races more like an oval than a damn road circuit," one of the drivers on the spectator hill explained to us. "It's all about traffic management, not leaving an opening and finding places to get by."

"That's our buddy in the red Maserati," I said proudly as Cal went by in a full-lock slideways drift with a Porsche 550 Spyder nipping at his heels.

"It handles kind of like a steamer trunk on roller skates, doesn't it?" the guy observed.

"Cal said he's driven handier cars."

The guy nodded appreciatively. "He sure knows how to play cork-in-the-bottle though, doesn't he?"

"If that's what it takes, that's what he'll do."

And that's what Cal did, eventually getting a good break in traffic that sprung him free and after that he just eased off into the distance. It was great seeing him win again and even better seeing that sly cobra grin on his face and that cocky, confident old glint in his eyes. A race driver's got to have that stuff going for him if he wants to get anywhere. And you could see Cal had it back again, too. He also allowed as how Lime Rock was a pretty damn difficult, challenging and demanding little racetrack. "If you can go fast here, you can go fast anywhere," was the way he put it when smooth-talking and occasionally accurate track announcer Ed Conway interviewed him on the victory podium. And all the locals took that as one hell of a nice compliment.

While Ernesto's crew guys were busy loading up, Cal and Carson and me walked over and watched some guys fly fishing in the stream next to the main straight—they weren't catching much of anything—then polished off a few beers up on the hillside overlooking the end of Big Bend and the left-hander. It's amazing how perfectly vacant and peaceful a racetrack can become as evening sets in and the last of the engines have switched off. Especially Lime Rock, where all of a sudden you realize you're your up in these beautiful, green Berkshire Mountains and you can hear birds calling and the faint scamper of squirrels in the leaves and the gurgle of rushing water in the trout stream. It's a pretty damn nice place, no lie.

"So," I asked Cal, "how's life been treating you?"

"You saw for yourself. Things are all of a sudden looking pretty good."

"You're getting along with Mr. Julio?"

"He sent me out here to drive his damn car, didn't he?"

"How about Gina? You seeing her at all?"

"That's not something I talk about."

"You mean you're seeing her but not talking about it?"

"I didn't say that."

"Then what did you say?"

"I didn't say anything. It's like I told you, Buddy: it's not something I talk about."

"Sounds pretty serious."

"It's not serious," Cal corrected me with an insider smile. "Just mysterious."

"You know," I cautioned, waving a finger like any guy with kids soon learns to do, "if Mr. Julio ever catches you two, you'll be fresh out of a drive."

"He won't catch us because there's nothing to catch. In fact, it's kinda because of Gina that I'm here right now."

"It is?"

"Sure."

I gave him a blank look.

"See, it's like this," he explained. "I'm pretty sure Gina's coming into L.A. for a few weeks to do some studio work. Sending me out here to race his new car is a pretty convenient way to ease me out of the picture."

"Doesn't that make you mad?"

"Mad? Sad? Glad? It doesn't make any difference, does it? I'm out here winning races, and that's what I figure I need to be doing right now. There'll be time for all that other stuff later on."

"Later on has a way of never coming around," Carson said softly. It was the first thing he'd said all evening. "You work in the funeral parlor business and you pick on that. In fact, you see it every day…."

It was coming on dusk, so we finished the last of our beers and wandered back over by Ernesto's transporter. The guys had it all buttoned up by then and were just waiting on Cal to hit the road. They were planning to have a nice dinner and stay someplace on the New York side overnight, and then take off again in the morning, heading basically south and a little west to this brand-new road circuit everybody was talking about down near the Blue Ridge Mountains in Virginia. It was called VIR (for "Virginia International Raceway"). and Cal and Ernesto's new Maserati were heading there directly from Lime Rock for VIR's first-ever event the following weekend. *"Hell, we're already out this way, might as well give it a try on the way home!"* was the way Cal put it. And of course he asked Carson and me if we wanted to tag along. We were already bundled into Carson's new red-over-white 100-6 with the engine running, and boy, did that ever sound tempting. To just *take off,* you know? Like we used to do all the time in the old days. But there was no way in hell we could do it. Carson and me had things to do and bills to pay and families to take care of and people to see.

"Well, why don'cha just come down for the weekend?" He patted Carson's Healey on the fender. "Stretch this baby's legs a little. I hear there's some fantastic sportscar roads down there. Everybody says that Blue Ridge Parkway is something else."

But there was no way we could do that, either, since it was a full day's driving and then some just to get there and another full day coming back. That new track at VIR wasn't near much of anything.

"Boy, you guys have sure got your feet nailed to the floor these days," Cal snickered, shaking his head.

"We got responsibilities," I explained, trying hard to make it sound like something I was proud of.

He dragged one of his legs like there was a ball and chain on it.

"Look, one day you'll have a family and a real job and you'll see what it's like," I told him.

"No, he won't," Carson said softly. It was just the second thing he'd said all night.

Boy, you should have seen the expression that passed over Cal's face. It was just for a heartbeat or two, but no way could you miss it.

Cal and Ernesto's big Maserati went on a hell of a tear after that race at Lime Rock. And it was an unbelievable time to be racing in North America. The sport was gaining momentum like a runaway avalanche and new tracks and race sites were popping up all over the place. There was a street race at Put-In Bay on South Bass Island in Lake Erie, a six-hour enduro at this extended oval-cum-road-course in Marlboro, Maryland, more races out west at the California Fairgrounds in Pomona, Palm Springs, Stockton, Santa Barbara and Paramount Ranch, the old standards (only now on permanent tracks) at Watkins Glen and Elkhart Lake, airport races at Bremerton, Washington, Montgomery, New York, Cotati, Cumberland, Hour Glass Field and even Harewood Acres up in Canada, and even more new race courses under construction. Particularly—or at least according to the magazines, which were, after all, published in Southern California—the two brand-new, purpose-built California tracks going up at Riverside, just west of L.A., and on the U.S. Army's Fort Ord property near Monterey, just a little ways south of San Francisco. All the California magazine writers said that new Riverside track was going to be the best and fastest road course in the states (what else?) and no question 1957 was a hell of a neat time to be racing sports cars in North America.

Cal called the next Sunday evening—collect, of course—to tell me how fabulous the track and weekend at VIR was and, just incidentally, how he'd absolutely massacred the Cunningham Jaguar team (not to mention everybody else!) in the big-bore feature race on Sunday. "You should *see* this place!" he just about gushed into the phone. "It's damn near three-and-a-half miles around and there's a set of uphill esses that'll absolutely take your breath away. You can take the first two flat in top gear, *maybe* even the third, but it gets pretty damn hairy after that!"

I'd never heard him quite so wound up about a racetrack before.

"And there's this blind, fast, uphill left that leads immediately—and I mean *right now!*—into this downhill set of corners that'll put you right on the edge of your seat. Especially the last one. It's a double-apex right that you take in third gear, and even after you get the hang of it, you can't shake the feeling that you're going to fly right off the damn pavement. You're going downhill, see, and the car's all up on tippytoes and it just looks like you're never gonna make it. But then the road flattens out and the car compresses on its suspension and all of a sudden you're wondering what you were making such a fuss about. You maybe even think about trying it a little faster the next time around."

"Sounds like you really like the place."

"It separates the real racers from the ribbon clerks, that's for sure. Oh, it's new and a little rough around the edges. And no question it could use a lot of stuff. The track's pretty narrow in some spots and there's zero runoff in a few places where you'd really like to have some. And the straightaways are long enough to make it pretty hard on the little cars. I mean, no way can, say, a Porsche 550 stay close enough to a big car to make a bid heading into the next set of twisties. Of course the Maser (he pronounced it 'Mah-zer') just loved that part…."

"The *'Maser?'*"

"Sure. That's what everybody's calling them now."

I felt like I was really missing out on a lot of stuff, you know?

"...Anyhow, they screwed up my qualifying time and that had me third on the grid behind Hansgen and Wallace in the Cunningham D-Types. But that old Maser just torqued right by 'em. Hell, I had damn near ten carlengths by the time we got to Turn One! Oh, Walt tried to make a race of it—you knew he would—but he shrank down to a damn dot in my mirrors as soon as we hit the back straight, and it was all over but the shouting after that. Besides, he had his hands full with Charlie Wallace in the other D-Type. Or at least until old Charlie sneaked past and then promptly spun out right in front of him. But of course I didn't get to see it because I was too far ahead." He let out a condescending sigh. "It was actually pretty boring...."

"So are you," I shot back. I mean, somebody had to pull his reins in a little and, seeing as how it was my nickel, I figured it might as well be me. "Anything else happen?"

"Oh, it was hotter than hell. A hundred degrees, I think. And there was one heck of a downpour at one point. Wind. Rain. Sky turned green. A real monsoon. Turned all the road shoulders into mud like instant pudding. One Ferrari went off and damn near sank out of sight."

"You're exaggerating."

"Only a little. They really have some work to do on that place. What they need is some hot-shot New York developer to come in and widen it and make more runoff area and build some decent johns and do all the little stuff that needs to be done. But it's still one hell of a great racetrack. Everybody thought so."

"Were the races any good?"

"Well, like I said, mine was pretty dull. At least from where I was sitting, anyway."

"Who cares about your damn race?" I sneered into the phone. "I want to know about the *good* races."

"Well, let's see. One guy got disqualified for triggering a five-car pileup in the first race. Pretty dumb move, actually. And another guy protested because he got bumped clear off the track. And a guy in a TR3 flipped and rolled it into a ball."

"TR3s are getting kind of a reputation for that, aren't they? I think they may be a little too narrow in the beam. Was the driver okay?"

"Yeah. Except for a burning sensation in his bank account, anyway."

"You see anybody who impressed you?"

"Nobody impresses me."

"Nobody except you, anyway."

We got a pretty good chuckle off that.

"Well, let's see," Cal finally continued. "There was one heck of a race between that George Constantine in an Aston Martin coupe and some guy named Robinson in an XK140MC. Damn good race. And I saw some really quick guys coming up in a few of the other classes."

"Like who?"

"Oh, I picked out a couple to watch out for."

"But they didn't impress you."

"No, they didn't impress me. But they looked like guys you'd want to keep your eye on just the same. One was Ed Hugus in a little Alfa Romeo. *Real* smooth and quick. And Bob Holbert was fast as stink in his Porsche 550. He pretty much ran away and hid from everybody in the smallbore modified race."

"Just like you, right?"

"Well, not quite so stylish, of course, but a pretty good drive. And Doc Wyllie did the same to the G-Modified cars a little ways behind. Those two were by far the class of the field."

"Anybody else?"

"Yeah. One more. You remember that dentist from Washington, D.C., who used to race the Jaguar and then the Porsche?"

"Dick Thompson?"

"That's the one. Well, he's beating the crap out of people with a Corvette now. There's a lot of whispering that he's maybe getting help directly from Chevrolet, but let me tell you, he's one heck of a race driver. Absolutely blew everybody's doors off in the big-bore production race. It's hard to make one of those rumbleguts Corvettes look graceful, but that's exactly what he does."

If you knew anything at all about sports cars, you had to be impressed by anybody who could do something like that.

Chapter 20: A Blood Red Season—Part Two

Hank wrote me that Portago's horrific crash just 25 miles from the end of the *Mille Miglia* triggered an unbelievable outcry in the European press—especially in Italy and right up to the steps of the Vatican—about motor racing's senseless lust for speed, risk and danger and its terrible price in innocent lives. And it came as no surprise to anyone that our good friend Eric Gibbon supplied the lurid photos of the crash scene that wound up slathered all over the tabloids. He'd been at the finish line in Brescia with all the other journalists, of course, but managed to commandeer a ride with one of the ambulance crews as soon as word of the accident came through. He told them his sister was married to Portago's navigator, and carefully hid his camera underneath his jacket. It was a pretty low thing to do. But even people like me and Hank, who loved it all so much it made us ache inside, had to admit we felt sickened and disgusted and ashamed. We knew as well as anyone that there would never be another *Mille Miglia.* No one's conscience would allow it. And we also worried—privately, among ourselves—about how this unspeakable disaster was going to affect the present and future of motor racing.

I suppose that's a terribly selfish and uncaring thing to admit, but there it is.

But things go on. That's the way it is in life and that's the way it is in racing. And that's the way it was when the grand prix cars were unloaded just a week after the *Mille Miglia* in Monaco and the sports cars once again at the Nurburgring in Germany a week after that. Hank went to those races like everybody else in the circus, but the grim memory of what had happened in Italy hung over everything like a foul-smelling shroud. Still, there were races to watch and cover and news and rumors to keep up with, and it was Hank's job to get it all, get it down and get it right.

Hank said Monaco seemed like such an unreal, almost cruelly fairytale setting just a week after that black day in Italy. But it was easy to get sucked in. The place was all pink palaces and marble promenades and no poor people to worry about or have to ignore. Behind the jewel-like little principality were steep, rocky mountain cliffs that held the rest of the world back and out of sight, and laid out in front was the yacht-filled harbor and the shimmering blue of the Mediterranean beyond. It was something out of a Hollywood movie, all right—right down to Monaco's new queen, ex-Hitchcock favorite movie actress and arguably the most beautiful, elegant and desirable icy-cool blonde on the planet Grace Kelly. Only now she'd given up movie acting to marry Prince Ranier and become the centerpiece of a real, live fantasy world full of aristocratic grace and upper crust style, all of it played to the sound of string orchestras and trumpet fanfares and the inevitable *oohs* and *aahs* that forever followed that clattering little ball around the roulette wheel in the famous Monte Carlo Casino. Hank said he'd never seen anything like it.

Stirling Moss showed up as lead driver for the up-and-coming English Vanwall team at the Grand Prix of Monaco, and Hank was plenty impressed by the smooth, sleek shape of the cars and the harsh bark of their big, four-cylinder engines. He said they were really nothing more than four of the much-raced and well-proven 500cc Norton Manx motorcycle engines put together on a common crankcase, but they made tremendous torque and the cars were very aerodynamic. Word around the paddock was that a moonlighting de Havilland aircraft designer named Frank Costin (who also did the slippery little Lotus Eleven) came up with the shape and that Colin Chapman had been called in to help refine the chassis and suspension. Still, Hank thought the Vanwalls looked a bit long and tall for a tight, twisty street circuit like Monaco. But Moss stuck his smack on the front row of the grid next to Collins' Ferrari and Fangio's pole-winning Maserati, and he took off like a rifle shot at the start, shouldering his way into the lead on the very first corner. Collins followed suit, passing Fangio for second on the very next lap, and some of the wags from the press bunch started wondering out loud if the old man was losing his touch. They got their answer just two laps later, when Moss—trying *hard!*—locked his brakes and went straight-on into the barriers at the chicane. The impact knocked some wooden barricades and hay bales into the roadway, and Collins went *smack!* into the low metal railing on the outside swerving to avoid them. He was damn lucky not to punch clear through and wind up in the drink like Ascari had a few years before! Hank explained that the downhill approach to the chicane is totally blind, with the roadway disappearing hard left around a barrier and then twisting immediately hard right with nothing but that low railing and the shimmering blue of the Mediterranean beyond. And that's precisely where Fangio showed—once again!—his uncanny feel and genius. He couldn't see the Ferrari crumpled against the railing or the barriers and haybales strewn across the road, and the corner station workers were still scrambling for their yellow flags. But Fangio sensed something was up when he saw all the faces in the stands turned the other way—looking at something just out of sight at the exit of the chicane—and he reacted instantly, calmly backing off, gathering the car up and threading his way through. And right about then Brooks and Hawthorn arrived on the scene, and neither grasped the situation beforehand like the old master. Brooks went hard on his brakes as soon as he saw the mess in front of him while Hawthorn swerved to avoid smashing into Brooks and instead crashed into his teammate Collins' stationary car sitting up against the railing! And there they sat, the top two team Ferraris, into the barriers one almost on top of the other like, as Hank put it, *"a pair of mating insects."* Fangio drove off to an easy win after Moss, Collins and Hawthorn so generously eliminated themselves. "It was pretty damn incredible," Hank wrote. "Fangio just seems to see and feel so much more and so much further ahead than anybody else."

Hardly anybody took much notice of the blunt and ugly little torpedo-shaped Cooper with its engine behind the driver and tough, sullen Australian newcomer Jack Brabham behind the wheel. It was just a Formula Two car, really, built by garage owner Charlie Cooper and his son John in their shop in Surbiton, England, and running an over-the-counter, 1.5-liter Coventry Climax Formula Two engine punched out as far as they dared to 1.96 liters. Not near enough to threaten the 2.5-liter Maseratis, Ferraris and Vanwalls up at the sharp end of the grid. Plus putting the engine behind the driver made it pretty strange-looking and ungainly. One of the Italian journalists said it looked like something you'd find under a rock, and not even Eric Gibbon could call it a handsome or noble-looking machine. Even though it was all-British. But it ran pretty well and seemed to handle nicely, and Brabham was one hell of a hard, fast and steady driver. In fact, as other cars broke and faltered, Brabham and the blunt little Cooper raced all the way up to third place! But then it sputtered and died right near the end. Brabham got out and looked at it—he was a hands-on mechanic and builder in the Cooper shops when he wasn't out racing their cars—saw that the fuel pump had failed and decided to push the car the rest of the way to the finish line. It was hard work but he made it, and got credited with sixth place out of the scant seven cars still running at the finish.

No one much seemed to notice....

Fangio had an even more brilliant drive at the German Grand Prix at the famous Nurburgring in August, and it wound up sealing the championship for him. His fifth, and fourth on the trot—and with no less than four different cars and racing teams! But Hank said that drive in Germany seemed to take a lot out of him. You have to understand that the Nurburgring is a very singular sort of racetrack. It was originally built as a huge public-works project in the Eifel Mountains during the tough depression years of 1925-27. Or just about the time Herr Hitler was getting out of jail and the book he wrote there, *Mein Kampf,* was first getting published and distributed in Germany. From the very beginning, the Nurburgring was conceived—in that typically arrogant but scientific and industrious German way—to be the biggest, longest, greatest, grandest, most testing and most daunting purpose-built racing circuit in the entire world. And, again typical of the Germans, it was. There were two separate tracks, really, and the awesome *Nordschleife* (or "North Loop") used for the Grand Prix and the 1000-kilometer championship sportscar races was an incredible 14.2 miles long. It twisted, turned, coiled and uncoiled, climbed, dived, ran up mountainsides and funneled down valleys, with blind crests everywhere and tall hedgerows lining both sides of the road for much of its distance. That made it look like a dark-green bobsled run, and a driver's memory was the only possible tool for knowing what came next. If you tried to drive The 'Ring on guts and instinct, you'd crash. Or be terribly slow. Or both. The Nurburgring had every type of corner, elevation change and road camber imaginable, and every driver who attempted it agreed: this was by far the longest, most difficult and most challenging permanent racing circuit in the world. Period. It was a place where the very best showed time and again what made them the very best.

Our friend Toly Wolfgang had driven his first-ever race at The Nurburgring earlier in the year in the World Manufacturers' Championship sportscar race, and he was fortunate to get teamed with the steady and experienced little Frenchman Maurice Trintignant while he tried to find his way around. He'd done dozens of laps in a rental car the week before, but there was just no way you could file it all away and commit it all to memory in just a few days' time. No, The 'Ring was something else. Each racing lap was nearly ten minutes long, yet without any extended straight stretch where a driver could take a deep breath and readjust his bearings. When he wasn't braking hard or turning into one corner or trying to correct a slide out of another one, he was clutching the wheel to brace himself as the car shot over a humpbacked crest and went airborne for a few heartbeats before banging down *hard* on the opposite side. You had to make sure you had the wheels straight and the car square to the road whenever that happened. Otherwise the landing on the far side could be frighteningly spectacular. To a newcomer like Toly, The 'Ring had all the fear and uncertainty of an open road race like *La Carrera* or the *Mille Miglia.* But to the racers who really knew and understood it—like Fangio—it was a glorious and mighty place to drive. Even Fangio finished second the first two times he raced there. But, as everyone came to expect, he eventually got the hang of it. To the tune of pole position at the start and first overall at the finish in his next three attempts—twice for Mercedes and once for old man Ferrari—in the German Grand Prix. And now he was back again with Maserati.

But Fangio was never smug or complacent and always looked for the most likely way to win. Even though he'd already won in Argentina, Monaco and France and had a commanding lead in the championship standings. After all, Moss was always a genuine threat, and the Vanwalls had finally come through—in front of their home crowd!—to score their first-ever grand prix win with a resounding 1-2 finish in the British Grand Prix at Aintree. With all the English fans going properly and deservedly berserk in the grandstands, of course….

Fangio and Maserati team manager Ugolini realized that tires might wear alarmingly over the 22 laps and 312.4-mile distance of the German Grand Prix at the Nurburgring, and that the heavy fuel load the cars had to carry at the start—well over 50 gallons—would make it even worse. So they came up with a clever strategy. Fangio would start with only half a tank of fuel, try to pull out a lead on the Ferraris, and then stop in the middle of the race for fresh tires and another half-tank of fuel to take him to the finish. It was a brilliant plan, really. And Fangio once again showed his cunning by letting the Ferraris of Collins and Hawthorn run in front of him for the first two laps, babying his tires and biding his time and letting them set the pace while he waited and watched just behind. And then, on lap three and much to the dismay of the Ferrari team, Fangio swept past the two Englishmen and started pulling away with depressing ease. They hadn't caught on yet that he was running light on fuel, and although the two Ferraris tried their best to give chase, they eventually had to give up. There was no catching the fleeing Maserati, and they could go no faster. And meanwhile Fangio eased away to a half-minute lead.

Then, without warning, he dived into the pits. Suddenly the Maserati scheme was obvious to everyone, and Hank said you could've stuck a grapefruit in the wide-open jaw of Ferrari team manager Tavoni. But things didn't all go according to plan. Fangio's car was quickly refueled, but one of the mechanics dropped the knock-off nut for one of the front wheels and it rolled unseen underneath the car. And then it was frenzied pandemonium as he scrambled about looking for it—around him, behind him, under him, everywhere but where it was!—while the other mechanics frantically searched their tool boxes for a spare. Hank said it was real Keystone Kops stuff—unless you were one of those poor Maserati crew guys, anyway—and well over a minute was lost before they finally found the damn knockoff nut and got Fangio going again.

Things looked pretty hopeless at that point. Hawthorn and Collins—who had been swapping positions back and forth every lap like a pair of playful puppies—swept happily past the pits and into the lead, and they had more than a minute in hand when Fangio finally returned to the track. But instead of charging off after them, he once again took it easy in order to break in his tires, burn off some fuel and lull the whole blessed Ferrari team to sleep. He did two gentle laps—bringing the race to two-thirds distance—and then, with just over a hundred miles to go, he put his foot in it. Without warning, Fangio set an astounding new lap record of 9 minutes, 28 seconds and chopped 12 seconds off the Ferraris' lead. Hawthorn and Collins were still playing with each other, lapping in the mid-to-high 9:30s. Worse yet, there was no way the Ferrari team manager could get word to them on their pit boards for another whole lap! Even so, they were still more than three-quarters of a minute ahead….

Fangio set another new lap record the next time around. He was driving at a level few had ever seen before, taking many corners a full gear higher than anyone had ever attempted. It was the performance of a lifetime. By now the Ferrari pits had gotten the message to Hawthorn and Collins and they did their best to speed up. But their tires were badly worn by that time and there was only so much they could do to respond. Meanwhile, Fangio set another lap record. And then another—tearing chunks out of their lead like a shark ripping into raw meat. The public address announcer was screaming himself hoarse into the microphone!

With three laps to go—less than 45 winding, twisting miles—Fangio had the margin down to 15 seconds. He could smell blood. And his next lap was nothing less than a work of art. He turned the daunting, dangerous 14.2 miles of the *Nordschleife* in an almost terrifying 9 minutes and 17 seconds, and his Maserati appeared right behind the two fleeing Ferraris as they streamed past behind the pits. He dove underneath and out-braked Collins—half on the pavement, half on the grass—heading into the North Curve, then did the same to Hawthorn in exactly the same place a lap later. The crowd was going absolutely insane, and the hollering, cheering and noisemakers were deafening when the three cars came around to take the checkered flag not quite nine and a half minutes later. Fangio had backed off just a bit to a 9-minute 23-second lap, but he was an easy three seconds ahead of Hawthorn and another scant few ticks in front of Collins.

It was the stuff of legends. A race that made everyone who saw it feel a strange, cold glow inside. It even affected Hawthorn and Collins, who looked awed and strangely privileged rather than beaten as they congratulated Fangio on the winners' podium. But Hank said that race did something to Fangio. He had the vacant look of a corpse as he spoke with reporters afterwards. *"I've never driven a race like that before in my life..."* he half mumbled—as if he was talking to himself as much as anybody else, *"...and I never want to drive a race like that again."*

He'd hung himself way out over the edge and gotten away with it. That's how Hank put it in his letter. And Fangio surely knew better than anyone how close he'd come….

Things weren't going near so swimmingly for Maserati in the World Manufacturers' Championship. And that's the one they really wanted to win. Hank said they pretty much expected to cruise their way through the rest of the season after that crushing win at Sebring in March. But then came Behra's practice crash and Moss' snapped-off brake pedal hardly out of sight of the starting line along with Taruffi's hollow win for Ferrari and Portago's terrible crash in the *Mille Miglia.* All of a sudden Maserati's monster 450S wasn't looking quite so bulletproof. The factory cars broke again at the Nurburgring in May and Aston Martin—of all teams—scored their first major international win with their handsome new DBR1. It came down to some really great driving from Tony Brooks, quick pit stops and the usual shrewd team strategy from John Wyer and a truly rotten chunk of luck for Maserati. Moss had taken the lead for them in his 450S, but went missing next time around after a wheel parted company from the car. Worse yet, the outpaced and/or outfoxed Ferraris of Collins and Hawthorn came home second and third behind the Aston Martin, picking up valuable points.

Needless to say, the British motoring press—and particularly Eric Gibbon—were over the moon about the stunning and unexpected all-British victory at the Nurburgring. And he became thoroughly insufferable after another fabulous English triumph at Le Mans. Ferrari had tried for more power to even things up with Maserati's 450, but it was maybe a reach too far and in spite of leading early and cracking off a new lap record, both of the latest-spec 335S factory cars were out well before sunset with engine problems. They'd also entered a pair of brand new, 2953cc *Testa Rossa* V-12s as trial-by-fire preparation for the rumored FIA 3.0-liter limit due to take effect come 1958—Ferrari always kept at least one eyeball peeled towards the horizon, that was for sure—and although he begged for one of the big cars, Toly found himself assigned to one of the 3-liter *Testa Rossas.* But his co-driver managed to crash it pretty comprehensively in practice, and so one of the older-spec 315S V-12 models with the slightly smaller, 3.8-liter engine was quickly pressed into service. It was the only factory Ferrari to make it to the finish, struggling home an unimpressive fifth overall after a careful, conservative run and all sorts of problems with fading brakes.

Maserati didn't do much better. Following a few words with team star Stirling Moss in Buenos Aires at the beginning of the season, they'd quietly hired English aerodynamicist Frank Costin—who'd done such a sleek, svelte, wind-cheating job on Colin Chapman's slick little Lotus Elevens and Vanwall's smooth and handsome grand prix cars—to design them a special, aerodynamic coupe body for their 450S especially for Le Mans. Maserati's regular body builder Fantuzzi was already bursting with work building and repairing the conventional open cars, so Costin's drawings were sent over to well-known and respected Italian body builder Zagato—along with the very first (and now somewhat beatup) 450S they ever built and tested—so the famous *carrozzaria* could bring the whole thing to life in hand-hammered aluminum and have it ready in time for Le Mans. But Zagato had never done and all-out, 180+mph sports/racing car before, and neither were they used to building cars they didn't design themselves (and "design" might not be the exact right word, since Hank said Zagato bodies were more or less "sculptured on the hoof" thumb-and-eyeball style rather than built from drawings). Time was also a problem. The project started late and ran even later, and there just weren't enough hours or free hands available to finish it properly. So Maserati's long, low, incredibly sinister-looking new track weapon seemed barely tacked together as it rolled out of the transporter in France. Hank wrote that it was the most evil- and dangerous-looking automobile he'd ever seen in his life. And by "dangerous," I think he meant to its own drivers as much as the opposition. He sent me a picture of it, and I thought it looked like something one of those caped and costumed villains in the Batman comic books might drive. And I was hardly alone. Fangio walked around it a few times, gave it a good looksee inside and out and told the team he'd much rather race the conventional open car, thank you very much. That left the new coupe to Moss and Schell, and they discovered in the very first practice that it was like racing a combination Dutch oven, Swedish sauna and steam bath. Worse yet, the regular open cars appeared to be faster in a straight line thanks to an incorrectly interpreted air intake that suffocated the carburetors at top end! The new coupe was incredibly hot inside, there was no ventilation to speak of and the fumes were almost worse than the heat, and so the crew immediately set about cutting holes and vents and ducts everywhere to try and make it at least partially livable for the drivers, and of course that played hell with the original aerodynamic contours that were supposed to let it glide through the wind like a shark through water. And it was still hotter than blazes inside! Hank said both drivers looked visibly—if somewhat ashamedly—relieved (not to mention slightly poached) when the rear axle broke just over two hours into the contest. They were running second at the time, but no way could the drivers have made it to the end. The other 450S had already dropped out when a U-joint came apart and the flailing halfshaft split the gas tank wide open, and Maserati should have counted themselves lucky that it didn't go up in flames.

This unlikely and thoroughly unexpected turn of events left the door wide open for the Jaguar D-Types the factory sold off to privateer teams at the end of the '56 season because they *"weren't competitive any more."* Incredibly, those privateer D-Types came home first, second, third, fourth and sixth overall at the end of the 24 hours, with just Toly's limping 315S Ferrari in fifth to break up the parade. Even more incredibly, one of Colin Chapman's toy-like, fragile-looking little Lotus Elevens with a tiny 1100cc Coventry Climax engine under the hood finished ninth overall and absolutely ran away with the Index of Performance award.

Naturally the British press went properly spastic with patriotic joy, smugly trumpeting this great, glorious triumph of British grit, skill, drive, talent, gumption and knowhow over all the faster Italian cars that broke down early and never really made a contest out of it. Not to take anything away from those privateer Jaguar teams—they did one hell of a fine job—but they were racing against essentially each other from about the 10th hour on. Of course none of that mattered to Eric Gibbon, who Hank assured me was inflated like a damn circus balloon and even harder than usual to be around.

But the air didn't stay inside that balloon very long, as most of the scribes in the European motoring press flocked to Italy the very next weekend to witness the expected humiliation of the Indianapolis 500 cars and stars on the steeply-banked oval layout at Monza. The original idea was to have this "Race of Two Worlds" featuring the top American racers against the best that Europe—and particularly Italy—had to offer. And on the surface it looked like a pretty fair proposition. Sure, the American cars had bigger engines, but they were old, long-stroke four-bangers developed out of the original Offenhauser design that dated way back to the 1930s. Plus they had solid axles front and back like a damn buckboard and none of the supposed "sophistication" of the European chassis. And no question on a proper road course like The Nurburgring (or even the grand prix layout at Monza) the Ferrari and Maserati and Vanwall Formula One cars would have disappeared off into the distance. Only the steeply banked oval at Monza was more like an American track, and if there was one thing those American cars could do—and do *well!*—it was race around a damn oval. Ferrari had sent cars over to race at Indianapolis a few times, and each time they came back with their tail between their legs. Sure, Wilbur Shaw's American-run Maserati had won the Indy 500 back-to-back in 1939 and 1940, but the American cars had come a long way since then and Maserati hadn't really done any development work on another oval-track car. So, seeing as how the race was right there in the heart of Italy and didn't count for much of anything—it wasn't part of any series or championship—and seeing as how there'd been a rash of tire and steering-gear failures when the grand prix cars ran on the rough, high banks of Monza in the Italian Grand Prix the year before, and furthermore seeing as how our own, personal buddy Sammy Speed came over with a Chrysler V-8-powered Indy chassis in April to do a little testing and set some lap times that squinted eyes and made lips curl from one side of Modena to the other, both Ferrari and Maserati decided to blow the race off rather than risk getting embarrassed by a bunch of American yahoos on their own home turf. I mean, they had *real* races to prepare for, right?

About ten Indycars made the trip over—every one a front-line job—and the fans who did show up were dazzled by the wild paintjobs and polished chrome plating and the matching crew uniforms that looked like nothing anybody in Europe had ever seen before. Although they'd seem pretty familiar to any American who's ever been in a bowling league. Jean Behra quietly appeared with a couple "borrowed" Maseratis for

Friday practice—thoroughly unofficially, of course—but the best he could average in one of their grand prix cars hastily fitted with a larger, 3.5-liter sportscar engine was around 150mph. By comparison, the fastest of the American cars—Tony Bettenhausen in the howling, supercharged Novi V-8—was turning 175. So the Maseratis were loaded back on their trailer and disappeared even more quietly than they had arrived. And on Friday, of course, before the Italian fans arrived.

The Americans would have pretty much wound up playing with themselves in front of a small but highly disappointed audience if it hadn't been for the Scottish Ecurie Ecosse Jaguar team that had just won so convincingly at Le Mans the week before. Mind you, their D-Jaguar sports/racers were all wrong for this kind of contest on this kind of track against these kinds of cars. The only advantages the Jags had were proven ruggedness and their road-racing, four-speed gearboxes. The Indycars only carried two speeds because that was all they needed on an oval—one for *"let's get rolling"* and one for *"let's go race!"* Because of that, the Jags were able to grab second gear and scream right by all the Indycars at the beginning of each heat. But once the Americans got up a head of steam, they streamed right past again and motored away. It was apples and oranges, really, and hardly a fair fight. And you had to really hand it to those Ecurie Ecosse guys—especially just a week after Le Mans—for showing up to represent the European side in the "Race of Two Worlds" at Monza after Ferrari and Maserati decided to take a pass. Although Hank allowed as how a fat wad of starting money was no doubt involved to ensure their "sporting participation," and you know how Scotsmen tend to be about unencumbered cash.

In the end it was a steamroller performance by the American cars and drivers on a track tailor-made for what they knew and did best. And from what Hank said, they put on a pretty good show, too, with Jimmy Bryan—cigar sticking out of his mouth and all—taking a well-judged win after three tough heats and a lot of the early hard-chargers like Eddie Sachs, Pat O'Connor and Sammy Speed fell by the wayside. In fact, the heat and the pounding of the rough Monza bankings put out all but three of the American cars out by the end of the final heat. Which allowed the three outpaced but tough and reliable Ecosse Jaguars to wind up fourth, fifth and sixth overall at the finish. Or, looking at it another way: dead last, next to dead last, and next to next to dead last behind the remaining American cars. Hank said the very best part was the wind it took out of old Eric Gibbon's sails and the fat wad of Union Jack stuffing it knocked out of him.

Things returned more-or-less to normal at the six-hour Swedish round of the World Manufacturers' Championship on August 11th. Ferrari and Maserati were both there in force, since the coveted title was hanging in the balance with Ferrari a scant five points ahead and strong rumors circulating that the final race of the season scheduled for Caracas, Venezuela, the first weekend in November might not take place. The layout of the Caracas "through the city" racetrack had hardly been settled, and there were still plenty of starting-money, transportation, crowd-control and insurance issues fluttering in the breeze. Not to mention that the local political situation looked anything but rock-solid stable. So both Ferrari and Maserati approached the race in Sweden like it might well be the last of the season and the championship decider. Maserati brought two of their honking 450S V-8s plus a six-cylinder 300S as a backup. But they were missing Fangio, who according to Maserati was "taking a holiday on the Adriatic after his heroic, championship-clinching drive at the Nurburgring." And no doubt he deserved the rest, even though it seemed a little strange that he wasn't racing for them in Sweden when they needed a victory so desperately. Like Hank said, maybe that harrowing drive at The 'Ring took a little something out of him. Or maybe the hefty bonus he had coming for winning the World Driving Championship hadn't quite come through, since everybody and his brother knew how strapped for cash things were at Maserati. The time, effort, cars, money, transporters, equipment, spares, machinery and most especially travel and key personnel involved in fielding both a full-fledged Formula One Grand Prix and World Manufacturers' Championship Sportscar team were absolutely staggering. Especially when the sales of Maserati's road cars couldn't come close to covering the costs. And no way were the race purses enough to balance the budget—even if you won every blessed race! The rumors circulating across town at Ferrari hinted that there were several times the Old Man never would have been able to continue without under-the-table fistfuls of cash, some very creative accounting and wink-and-a-handshake loans of hundreds of thousands of dollars from wealthy "enthusiasts" like Tony Parravano.

Yet Maserati still had high hopes for success. Even with Fangio missing, they still had Stirling Moss, and he was reckoned by just about everybody as heir apparent to the title of Best Damn Driver in the World. And even though their hulking 4.5-liter V-8s had failed to finish a single race since their dominating win at Sebring in March, everybody knew the 450S was the fastest damn sports/racing car on the planet. All the Maserati drivers had to do was bring the brutes home….

And that's precisely what seemed to be happening in Sweden. The two 450S Maseratis of Moss and Behra easily cut the best times in practice, and Ferrari responded by telling Hawthorn to go flat-out from the start and not worry about breaking the car, in hopes that the Maseratis would over-extend themselves trying to match the Ferrari "rabbit's" pace. Especially in a long race in terrifically hot weather on a track that was notoriously hard on brakes. And Hawthorn came through, taking the lead and driving the hell out of his car for the first few laps. But eventually the speed of the Maseratis proved just too much, and by the end of the first hour it was Moss and Behra holding first and second and swapping the lead back and forth now and then just to ease the monotony. But Moss' car started suffering transmission troubles, and retired shortly after he handed it over to Harry Schell. So team manager Ugolini gave Moss a half-gallon of water to drink and five minutes' rest and then stuck him in Behra's car, where he continued to extend its lead over the field.

A terrible rain squall passed through about the middle of the race—turning the hot, greasy track into a skating rink!—but it didn't seem to faze Stirling Moss. In fact, he built up his lead until he had a full lap in hand over the second-place Ferrari by the time he pulled into the pits for gas and tires and handed the car back to Jean Behra. But his work was hardly done, as Ugolini decided to stick him almost immediately into the six-cylinder 300S to see if he could steal third—or maybe even second place?—from Ferrari and get even more points. And Moss responded like a true champion in spite of having driven almost the entire race in terrifically hot weather in three different cars! He drove the wheels off that six-cylinder Maserati, taking the corners in glorious drifts and obviously relishing its light weight and balance compared to the chunky V-8. There weren't enough laps or hours left for him to challenge for second, but he did manage third, and that's how it ended, with the Behra/Moss 450S cruising to an easy and impressive win over the last of the remaining Ferraris with Toly Wolfgang and Maurice Trintignant up. Followed by Moss once again in the 3.0-liter Maserati. But that second-place finish for Ferrari meant everything. It left them a scant three points ahead in the World Manufacturers' Championship. And Maserati wanted that championship desperately. They believed it would finally establish their road cars on an equal plane with Ferrari, and booming sales and financial salvation would surely follow. If only that final round in Caracas, Venezuela, in November would come to pass! After all, they had the two best drivers in the world under contract in Fangio and Moss and no question Maserati's 450S sportscars had the legs on the latest Ferraris....

Meanwhile the Grand Prix season had fizzled down to almost nothing. The Belgian and Dutch races were cancelled in the wake of Portago's terrible crash at the *Mille Miglia,* and there were rumblings throughout the Italian government about banning all open-road racing. In protest (and also because Fangio had already clinched the championship?), Ferrari didn't even bother to send his team to the hastily-added Pescara Grand Prix. Luigi Musso apparently begged Ferrari to give him a car for the race, and the Old Man finally relented. But it came as a private entry, and the rumors going around in the paddock were that old man Ferrari wasn't paying any of the bills.

Musso came through to take the lead in front of a highly partisan Italian crowd, but Moss reeled him in and passed him with the green Vanwall. Fangio hung on in third, waiting to see what happened, and meanwhile cars began dropping out and running into trouble behind them at an almost ridiculous rate. Behra's Maserati blew up, and then so did Musso's "privateer" Ferrari. Fangio spun on Musso's dropped oil and bent a wheel, and by the time he got it replaced, Moss and the Vanwall were long gone, notching up Vanwall's second win of the season. Jack Brabham in the unloved and underpowered little rear-engined Cooper finished dead last among the seven cars still running at the end.

The handsome Vanwalls looked strong again in the final race of the season at Monza on September 8th. And of course both Ferrari and Maserati just *had* to show up in front of their local fans, even though the championship was already settled.

Surely two hefty sacks of starting money were involved as well. The organizers were running the "flat" layout without the bankings after the serious tire and steering problems the year before, but it was still a desperately fast circuit and Maserati had even brought a special, V-12-powered experimental version of their 250F for Behra to drive. The underpowered little English Coopers didn't even bother to show up.

But what a horror for the local fans when the slick, sleek British Vanwalls qualified first, second and third with just Fangio's red Maserati on the very outside of the front row to add a little color! And Moss took off like a shot at the green flag. But there was no getting away from the lead pack at Monza, as the high speed straights and fast corners turned it into a slipstreaming battle royal. Five cars were running nose-to-tail down the straightaways like an arrow through the wind, getting the suction off the car (or cars) ahead and then maybe—just maybe!—pulling out and easing by on sheer momentum. Behra put Maserati's new V-12 to good use by passing Moss' Vanwall for the lead, but Moss got him right back a lap later. Fangio slipstreamed his way to the front in the conventional, six-cylinder 250F, but couldn't hold it against the Vanwalls once he had the point and was forced to give way. After that, the stunned Italian fans were forced to watch the three green Vanwalls running away and more or less playing with each other at the front of the field ahead of Fangio and Behra in their Maseratis. The Ferraris were nowhere. And then the retirements began. Brooks and Lewis-Evans in two of the Vanwalls hit trouble, the experimental V-12 in Behra's Maserati went sick and Fangio stopped for new rear tires. That moved the Ferraris up essentially by default, and Moss sickened the crowd even further when he put an entire lap on Fangio's second place Maserati. But then Moss brought the leading Vanwall screaming into the pits with the race all but over, and the highly partisan Italian fans erupted with joy! But not for long. The Vanwall crew poured in a little fuel, put on a fresh set of tires and sent Moss back out again to cruise to the finish, still well clear of Fangio and the rest of the remaining field. And that's the way it ended. In fact, that's the way the whole 1957 Formula One season ended, with already-crowned champion Fangio finishing a distant second for Maserati and Moss and the ever-improving Vanwall taking yet another British win on a gorgeous fall afternoon in front of a sullen and thoroughly miserable Italian crowd.

Chapter 21: The Shadow of a Small Sphere

Meanwhile, back here in the states, we had rock-n'-roll creeping up our radio dials, a Redstone missile on display in Grand Central Station, air raid drills in the schools (like curling up under your desk would protect you from a damn A-Bomb, right?) and Reverend Billy Graham drawing the biggest crowd in Yankee Stadium history—over 100,000 people!—just to hear him preach the gospel. "Tailgunner Joe" McCarthy dropped dead at 48 after newsman Edward R. Murrow took him on face-to-face in front of the TV cameras, Congress reprimanded him and people stopped paying attention to him, Sugar Ray Robinson won his fourth title—he was a hell of boxer, even if he was colored—and, speaking of colored people, the front pages were overflowing every day with news about the Negroes trying to integrate the schools down south. With a little help now and then from the federal government in Washington, which didn't sit real well with the local citizens at all. Or at least the white local citizens, anyway. Arkansas Governor Orville Faubus even called out the State Police and the National Guard to keep nine Negro kids from attending classes at Central High School in Little Rock. After which President Eisenhower called the good governor in for a little Father Duffy chat about the law of the land. But I guess Faubus didn't seem particularly receptive, so Ike sent federal troops in and had them all around that high school on September 25th to make damn sure those nine colored kids got through the front door. There was a big, angry mob of working-class white folks gathered outside (including what appeared to be a large proportion of previous high school dropouts!) shouting and shaking their fists in the air and hollering pleasantries like *"GO HOME, NIGGERS!"* for the New York network TV cameras. One cowardly nose-picker over in Nashville even set a bomb off at a local high school—can you imagine trying to blow up a blessed high school?—to register his deep personal displeasure regarding the subject of integration. What the hell is wrong with some people? In any case, it was pretty hard stuff for anybody up north to fathom, seeing as how we always kept our school systems segregated the tried-and-true, All-American Big City way by making sure that people of different races, creeds, colors and wealth or poverty levels stayed in their own damn crappy neighborhoods with their own damn crappy schools where they belonged.

And just when you thought things couldn't get any scarier or nuttier, some rich "collector" paid $225,000 for a painting of a bunch of apples done by a crazy French artist who spent his whole life screwing and drinking and died flat broke on some tropical island where the women don't wear shirts. Why, that was more greenbacks than all the blessed houses on our block were worth put together! They ran a picture of that painting in the paper, and I swear that guy couldn't even draw as good as my Julie. Can you believe it? And then the New York Giants and the Brooklyn Dodgers both announced they were moving to California. That last one was really hard to take, seeing as how my asshole father was such a diehard Yankees fan and surely my fondest childhood memories were those rare occasions when the Dodgers creamed the shit out of the New York Yankees in a World Series game at Ebbetts Field. Or Yankee Stadium, which was even better.

With all that going on in the world, it was always a relief to return to the smaller, friendlier and ever so much easier-to-comprehend universe of automobiles, mechanics and motor racing, where aspirations and intentions were generally good, people only got hurt by accident and everything seemed to make sense. Or most of it, anyway, seeing as how the biggest automotive news in the known universe that summer and fall of 1957 was Ford's much-ballyhooed introduction of their new Edsel line. Personally, I didn't get introducing "a brand-new line of fresh, exciting 1958 models" before the leaves were even starting to turn the previous fall. And I didn't much get the Edsel, either. Ford trumpeted all over the place that the Edsel was *"The Newest Thing on Wheels"* and that they'd spent three years and over 250 million dollars on "research and development" alone. My personal guess was that most of that money went into print, radio and TV advertising those last three months before the Edsel was launched—why, you couldn't turn around without seeing a headline or hearing a jingle about the incredible new Edsel!—and damn if Ford didn't sell 4,000 thousand of the blessed things the very first day they hit the showrooms on Wednesday, September 4th! Even if anybody with a floor jack and an ounce of mechanical savvy could see that they were just the same old stuff Ford was using on all their other nameplates and model lines underneath the sheetmetal. And speaking of sheetmetal, Ford somehow managed to bang America square on the funny bone with the "bold new look" of the Edsel. I guess it was mostly the grille. And it seemed kind of unfair in a way. I mean, Alfa Romeo had been building cars with that wonderful, V-shaped vertical piece in the center flanked by horizontal bits on either side and everybody *loved* the way Alfas looked. Hell, they were the most charming, enticing and endearing cars on the whole damn planet! In fact, I was bugging Big Ed almost every week about maybe taking on the Alfa franchise. And then poor old Ford tried almost the exact same thing and you had stand-up comics from one end of the country to the other making fun of it. They called it all sorts of things, but *"a Mercury sucking a lemon"* was my personal favorite! To be honest, except for the goofy grille, some fancy trim and Ford's new "Teletouch" push-button automatic, there was nothing much special about the Edsel at all. And it didn't take old Fred Average and John Q. Public very long to figure it out. Hell, Chrysler'd been selling cars with push-button automatics for an entire model year. Even if Ford did give it a bit of a new twist by sticking the Edsel's buttons in the center of the blessed steering wheel. Lord only knows why. So after an astonishingly successful first few weeks, Edsels went colder than an iced mackerel and Edsel sales fell right off the edge of the earth. I thought the real problem was that they made too much of a fuss and stirred people's expectations up to unreasonable levels.

And, in a way, the same exact thing happened to the new Riverside International Raceway track out in California. Before the place even opened its front gates, all the Southern California sportycar magazines were calling the new, $800,000 racetrack project a "little Nurburgring" and touting its 3.3 miles as "the fastest road racing circuit in North America." And maybe it was. But it was also located out on the hot, dry, dusty and windy valley floor between San Bernadino and Sun City, and looked more like a huge, half-finished construction site than "America's Greatest Racetrack" when it opened for business with a Cal Club event on Saturday morning, September 21st. As you can imagine, our Southern California racing buddy and motorsports scribe extraordinaire Hank Lyons wanted desperately to be there. He was pretty much done with the European racing season after Monza, and it looked like his next race date would be the off-again/on-again 1000-kilometer World Manufacturers' Championship finale in Caracas on November 3rd. But of course the magazine had local guys to cover the Riverside deal (not to mention that there were the usual yearly European car shows coming up in Frankfurt, Paris, London and Turin) and none of those car magazines exactly throw transcontinental airline tickets around like confetti when they've got somebody just up the road who can get the job done. I'm not saying those magazines are cheap, but Hank said they've been known to request signed requisitions for pencils, staples and paper clips….

In the end, I understand it was Cal Carrington who sweet-talked old Ernesto Julio into laying out the money for Hank's round-trip plane ticket to California. Told him Hank wanted to do a feature on the *Moto Italia* dealership racing team plus a photo spread/track test of *"the only Maserati 450S in America."* That actually worked, seeing as how most rich car-owner types have big fat egos to go along with their big fat wallets and will generally roll right over if you promise to give their notoriety a nice scratch. Anyhow, it was a heck of a nice deal for Hank, and I knew he really appreciated it since I got the feeling from some of his letters that he was getting a little lonesome now and then over in Europe and maybe even a little homesick for the old U.S. of A. Maybe even more than a little. On the one hand he was getting to pursue his fondest dreams (and how many of us ever get a chance to do that?), but on the other he was a stranger in a strange land—okay, make that a whole bunch of strange lands—and even if it was thrilling and exciting and invigorating and expanding his knowledge and horizons and all like that, it was also pretty damn lonely. "It's fine when I'm working the races and press conferences and stuff," he told me, "and I can't believe how much I get done when I'm holed up all by myself at four in the morning writing about it. But I feel pretty damn lost out there when I've got time on my hands and nothing to do. I mean, there's only so many old art museums, castles, churches and battlefields you can visit before they all start running together and turning into the same thing." I had no idea personally what such a thing might feel like, but I got a pretty good sense of it from Hank's letters. And I guess that's really the mark of a good writer, isn't it?

Speaking of Hank's letters, it was just as I was reading the one about Vanwall's somewhat unpopular all-British win at the Italian Grand Prix that I happened to glance over and see what appeared to be a picture of Gina LaScala and Toly Wolfgang together in the copy of *Hollywood Tattler* magazine Julie was thumbing through in bed next to me. "Isn't that what's-his-name?" Julie asked absently. I looked again, and damn if it wasn't what's-his-name. And standing right next to (and looking *very* chummy with) what's-her-name Gina LaScala herself. Who by then was becoming such a moon rocket/fireworks display of a movie star that she was only "what's-her-name" to a very small segment of the American public indeed. Or at least the movie-going, tabloid- and movie magazine-reading American public, anyway. "I thought she was going with that rich Cal Carrington friend of yours?" Julie asked like she was infinitesimally interested.

"That's what I thought, too. Lemme see that."

She turned the magazine a good quarter-inch in my general direction. Sure enough, there was Angelina Scalabrini—or make that Gina LaScala, if you like—cozying up to Toly Wolfgang while they were both cozying up to a couple glasses of champagne on the terrace of some swanky hotel during what appeared to be a very expensive party.

"Does it say where it was taken?" I asked.

Julie glared at me like wives do. *"Here!"* she said, shoving the magazine at me like the whole blessed world was starving to death and she was handing me the last morsel of food on the planet.

So I thanked her. It was the least I could do. And then tried to ignore the way she just sat there in bed with her arms folded tightly across her chest and waited for me to be finished. I don't know quite how wives do it, but somewhere in my head I could hear a foot impatiently tapping on a hardwood floor or the sound of fingernails drumming on a solid maple desktop the whole time I was reading.

It didn't take very long. There was just the picture and of the two of them smiling and looking exceedingly friendly with each other and a brief caption underneath. In the usual breathless, leering scandal sheet prose it read: *Hotter than hot young Hollywood starlet Gina LaScala passes the time with dashing professional auto racer and notorious society playboy Anatoly Wolfgang at a party for crown prince Theobald. Tattler's on-the-scene spy hints they left arm-in-arm."* And that was it. Except for the *"Eric Gibbon"* photo credit in tiny agate type right under the picture. Naturally I rustled through the rest of the magazine trying to find something a little more substantial and definitive—you know, the old *Who, What, How, Where, When* and occasional *Why* that everyone knows is the heart and soul of professional journalism. But movie magazines seem to have a different angle on things entirely. It's not what you say, but what you imply that's important. And the juicier those implications are, the better for everybody concerned. Including those Hollywood stars and starlets! You have to understand that the movie business runs on fame, and fame needs fuel—publicity—to keep running flat-out and full steam ahead. And scandals, rumors and innuendo are every bit as good as honors, good reviews and awards when it comes to filling column inches. Better, in fact, because they prod peoples' sleaziest envy, curiosity, fancy and fantasy buttons. You just can't do that kind of thing with a solid review or a Best Supporting Actress nomination.

"That's the little slut who stole what's-her-name's husband. And she was still married to whazzisname herself. And look at that outfit she's wearing. Why, she's falling half out of it!"

"It's terrible."

"And she's gonna be in that new picture with Cary Grant and wazzizname. You know, the drunk who beats his wife. They say she's got a shower scene where all she wears is a cloud of steam."

"I can't believe they let them get away with that. It's absolutely revolting."

"You bet it is."

"Are you gonna go see it?"

"As soon as it comes out...."

But even if Hollywood could be a little strange and unfathomable sometimes, our buddy Hank was thrilled about coming home to California. Even if it was for just a long weekend and entailed a real marathon of airline flight hours. He was all juiced up about seeing Cal and the brand-new racetrack at Riverside and eating a few real, American cheeseburgers again. And then hopefully seeing Cal blow everybody's doors off with Ernesto's 450S so he could write one hell of a great story about it (plus the "track test" feature they had planned for the Monday after the race) and help both of their careers along.

Only things didn't work out quite that way at Riverside.

Our hero driver buddy Cal went storming out of the pits as soon as first practice started Saturday morning, easily pulling clear of the pack and eager as hell to give Hank something to write about by setting the first-ever New Bigbore Modified Track Record at Riverside International Raceway. Only he never made it all the way around. As many other drivers were to discover that weekend, Turn Six was a devilishly deceptive sort of corner, and Cal and the big Maserati went plowing right off and slammed *hard* into the earthen embankment on the outside. The impact shook him up a little and jammed his wrist pretty badly, but outside of that he was thankfully okay. But the Maserati was done for the weekend, what with the left front end bashed in and the steering and suspension on that side seriously deranged. "I was just taking it easy," Cal muttered afterwards, "just cruising up this sweet, smooth, fast set of esses and at the end was what looked like just another fast sweep to the right. Only then it tightened up on me. I mean *really* tightened up on me! Then the car kind of unloaded and the pavement sort of fell away over the top of this little rise you almost couldn't even see and then—*WHAM!*—the damn embankment was *right there!* No runoff at all! Just no place to go. I couldn't *believe* it!" And so that was pretty much the end of things as far as Cal and Ernesto Julio's big Maserati were concerned at Riverside.

I talked to Hank about it over the phone that evening, and of course I wanted to know how Cal was doing. "Oh, the confrontation when Ernesto arrived was a little, ahh...let's just call it *'strained.'* But I've got to hand it to Cal. He walked right up to him and said: *'Ernesto, I banged up your car. It's done for the weekend. It was my fault, and there's not much I can say except I'm sorry. I was just trying too hard too soon.'*"

"He said *that* to Ernesto?"

I could feel Hank nod on the other end. "Yep, that's what he said. Kind of shoved old Ernesto back a bit, too. He eyeballed Cal for what must've been the better part of a minute, and you really had no idea what he was going to do or say next. But then he mustered up this tight, thin sort of smile and told Cal he was glad he was okay."

"That's *it?"*

"Well, he did mention that he'd appreciate it if Cal refrained from doing that sort of thing in the future. Particularly on the very first lap of practice on a brand-new racetrack. And that was about the end of it."

"Wow. Was Gina there, too?"

"Nah. She was supposed to come out on Sunday, but Ernesto went back to L.A. instead. He doesn't much like hanging around racetracks when his cars aren't running."

I couldn't say as I blamed him. "How about Cal? Is he okay?"

"Oh, he's pretty sore. It was a heck of a bang. They've got his wrist taped up and he's taking a lot of fluids. Beer and Tequila, mostly. And he seems to be doing pretty well with one of the volunteer nurses…."

I couldn't really say as I blamed him, either. "How about the car?"

"Oh, it's real fixable. But they'll need some parts flown in from Italy and a couple days in the body shop to hammer it straight again and throw some fresh paint on it."

"That's a shame. How about the new racetrack?"

It was quiet at first at the other end. "Well," Hank said, picking his words carefully, "it sure separates the men from the boys. No two ways about that. There's a couple really fast sections, some sneaky undulations that weight and un-weight the car just as it's trying to turn in and some *really* tricky corners. That one at Six where Cal crashed, in particular. It's deceptive as hell heading into it. Really sucks drivers in if they're not careful. And there's no room at all if you screw up. I mean, there's just this big earthen bank around the outside, and it's not far at all off the blacktop. You mess up at Six and you pretty much eat it."

"Like Cal did."

"Yeah. Like Cal did. But he was hardly the only one. I saw quite a few bent, dusty cars getting towed back into the paddock."

I didn't say anything.

"Don't get me wrong," Hank quickly added, "Riverside's one hell of an impressive racetrack. And *fast,* too! But after you've seen the *real* Nurburgring, well…."

He let his voice trail off.

"What kind of cars does it like?" I prodded. I mean, there are horsepower tracks and there are handling tracks, and you're always curious to know which is which.

Hank thought for a moment. "To be honest, I think the back straight is maybe a little too long. It's more than a mile, and wide-open all the way. Sure, it's neat that the D-Types and such are tickling 150 there, but it doesn't give the less powerful cars much of a chance."

"Gotta have the ponies, right?"

"Yep, gotta have the ponies."

"How about the rest of it?"

"There is no rest of it. It's just a big, fast racetrack and a bunch of dirt. And dust. And grit. And wind. And no shade, either…."

"You don't make it sound very appealing."

"Hey, this is Southern California," Hank laughed. "We're *used* to that kind of stuff!"

But I guess Sunday's races turned out pretty good anyway. Hank called to fill me in with the highlights, and the first thing he mentioned was how Jerry Austin's new fuel-injected Corvette clocked over 137mph down that long back straightaway! That's pretty damn impressive for a genuine, off-the-assembly-line Detroit Iron production car on a closed-course racetrack. But some new guy named Dan Gurney in an ordinary, carbureted Corvette pushed him until he made a mistake and spun, and then more or less motored right away from all the Jaguar XK120s and 140s, Mercedes 300SLs and all the other Corvettes in the big-bore production car race. It wasn't even close, and Hank said this Dan Gurney fellow looked like somebody to watch. "He just seems to be having such a damn good time out there, you know? You can see it in the way he drives."

But the biggest news of the weekend was this 15-year-old Mexican kid named Ricardo Rodriguez, who showed up with a Porsche 550 Spyder and simply waltzed away from all the established West Coast hotshoes in the smallbore modified race. Hell, he wasn't even old enough to hold an ordinary driver's license in the state of California! Hank explained as how his dad was real rich and a huge motorsports enthusiast down in Mexico, and he'd been backing young Ricardo in motorcycles for years. The kid was even Mexican National Champion! And his old man was ready, checkbook in hand, when they decided he should switch to cars. Hank allowed as how the most surprising thing was not how *fast* he was, but how smooth, calm and unruffled he seemed behind the wheel. "He doesn't weigh much of anything, either," Hank added, "and that's always a nice thing to have in your corner."

"Amen," I agreed.

With Cal and Ernesto's 450S scratched from the big-bore modified feature, Chuck Daigh in that simple, lightweight, Thunderbird-powered Troutman-Barnes Special squirted away from everybody at the start. But he had his hands full with Pete Woods in a D-Type Jaguar. The Jag appeared to have more top speed and better brakes, and it passed that T-Bird special several times at the end of the long back straightaway. But Daigh kept battling back, squeezing underneath the D-Type in a series of incredibly ballsy moves going up the esses. That guy could really drive, and according to Hank, it was great stuff to watch. But then the Jag pitted with a split oil line and Daigh had a flat tire and short, skinny little Richie Ginther inherited the very first Riverside feature win at the wheel of John Edgar's 4.9 Ferrari. As you can imagine, that—plus aches and bruises everywhere and a truly hellacious hangover—had my buddy Cal Carrington feeling very sorry for himself indeed. He was sure he could've won that race if he hadn't been so damn impatient on the first lap of practice. And there's just no way you can console a driver when he knows he's the one who screwed things up. At times like that, you're better off to just leave them alone….

But Cal was hardly the only driver to fall afoul of Riverside's Turn Six that particular weekend. A bunch of cars crashed there and one guy rolled his Arnolt-Bristol there in the Under-2.0-Liter production car race. And then the two leading MGAs in the all-MG race crashed almost simultaneously at the same exact spot. One guy whacked the embankment really hard but walked away without a scratch. The other guy wasn't so lucky. His MGA flipped, landed upside-down and he died of his injuries on the way to the hospital. So maybe Cal should have counted himself lucky….

Just two weeks later, on Friday, October 4th, the whole blessed world tilted on its axis when the Russians announced that they'd launched *Sputnik* and beat us into space. Why, it was all over the newspapers, television and radio shows—everywhere you looked!—and it was amazing how that little 22-inch, 184-pound Russian satellite cast its shadow across the entire length and breadth of these United States like a damn solar eclipse. From sea to shining sea. People's faith in our own, God-given American strength, goodness, greatness and superiority had been rattled to the core. Especially since our own space rockets were mostly blowing up on the launching pad, toppling headlong out of the sky or turning into an assortment of *very* expensive fireworks displays. Hank allowed as how it was the Germans who first started messing around with rockets and atomic reactions and thinking about space travel and such towards the end of World War II. And even though all those German rocket scientists were also swastika-lapel-button Nazis and built all their scary rocket hardware with concentration-camp slave labor, there was an enormous secret scramble between the Americans and the Russians to see who could get their hands on those guys first as the war ended. Before the other side did, you know? And now all of a sudden it was turning out that *their* kidnapped-and-transplanted German rocket scientists were better than *our* kidnapped-and-transplanted German rocket scientists on account of they'd beat us into space! It was frightening. It was disheartening. It was unbelievable. It was terrifying. Why, it changed the face of the world in a heartbeat. And it made people nervous in other countries, too. Especially since we and the Russkies were stockpiling nuclear weapons and test-firing ICBMs and generally going toe-to-toe and chest-to-chest with each other with our noses damn near touching and lower lips puffed out like two back-alley bullies squaring off for a fight.

It gave everybody plenty to think about, all right….

Chapter 22: A Blood Red Season—Part 3

Much to Maserati's relief and Ferrari's worry, the FIA and the government of Venezuelan military strongman Generalissimo Marcos Perez Jimenez got their differences ironed out and so that last race of the World Manufacturers' Championship season was indeed going to take place in Caracas on November 3rd as originally planned. Both manufacturers wanted that championship desperately and committed everything they had to the effort. Maserati even made a deal with super-wealthy Colorado land developer and longtime enthusiast/privateer entrant Temple Buell to hustle together an experimental, one-of-a-kind, 5.7-liter (!!!) version of their monstrous 450S model in a huge hurry—in the familiar blue-and-white American racing colors he ran on all his cars—if he would just be so kind as to take delivery down in Caracas and enter it (with his own drivers and on his own nickel, of course) as kind of a privateer backup for the official factory team. Which, by all accounts, was running pretty much on fumes as far as financing was concerned by that point in the season. Trying to field both a top-notch Formula One effort and a serious-contender World Manufacturers' Championship sportscar team was an incredibly expensive and time-consuming proposition. The cars themselves were just the tip of the iceberg. It was the hands and the faces and the payroll and the taking the whole shebang to seven different countries on two separate continents that really sucked the old cash bag dry.

Rumor had it there were even a few late inquiries from the Maserati factory about Ernesto Julio maybe bringing *his* 450S down from North America to beef up the ranks. With our buddy Cal Carrington as one of the drivers, no less! Cal was dying to do it, but old Ernesto wouldn't even consider it. Said there was absolutely no way he could find the time to get away. It was harvest and bottling time for the grapes up in Sonoma County, he had two or three movie irons in the fire and on top of that there were entirely too many important races to run right there in California. Including Sacramento, San Diego, Pomona and Palm Springs plus an SCMA National at Riverside and another race at Paramount Ranch. And right in the middle of all of it was the inaugural event at the new Laguna Seca track on the Monterey Peninsula on November 10th. Or, in other words, just one week after that World Manufacturers' Championship round in Caracas. Ernesto had a lot of plans for that particular weekend, seeing as how Laguna Seca was coming to life on a chunk of underused artillery range property at Fort Ord, which happened to be just a long stone's throw from Ernesto's nearly completed new mansion overlooking the Pacific Ocean on 17-Mile Drive, not far from Pebble Beach. As you can imagine, he had one hell of a housewarming party planned—even me and Big Ed were invited—and no way in hell was some scruffy street race in a dirty, poor, backwards, backwoods South American country where they didn't even speak English going to get in the way. Cal and the 450S had been pretty much mopping up the opposition most places (at least when he didn't stuff it into the trackside scenery, anyway), and the idea of a big, blowout housewarming-cum-victory party following yet another steamroller race win was too tempting to resist.

Of course Cal was pretty blue about missing another chance to square off against the top European professionals (and maybe even impress a few of the top European teams?), but then he caught a thoroughly unexpected break. Turns out it was real important to Temple Buell to use strictly American drivers—and you had to love him for that—and after he signed up the fearless and experienced "Kansas City Flash" Masten Gregory as his lead driver, damn if he didn't ring Cal up to see if he wanted to share the ride! And that made perfect sense, seeing as how Cal had lots of experience in a 450S and had furthermore shown he could run pretty much heads-up against the best of the European guys. And with this being a brand-new race on a brand-new circuit, there was none of the usual Home Field Advantage for the European stars. *"I'm going to race down in Venezuela!"* he just about screamed into the phone at a fairly typical 2 o'clock in the morning.

To tell the truth, the idea got me pretty excited, too.

"Make sure you get your shots before you go," I told him. "And for God's sake, don't drink the water or touch anything with open sores."

"I'll keep it in mind."

I started getting long letters from Hank again about two weeks later—one almost every other day—and he'd had plenty of time to write thanks to yet another set of marathon airplane rides back to Europe for the fall car shows and then all the way down to Venezuela for that final World Manufacturers' Championship round in Caracas. Hank wrote that Caracas was a handsome city built into the smoothly convoluted floor of an elevated valley surrounded by tall mountain ranges and a set of steep cliffs marking the rocky, 2500-foot plummet down to the port of La Guaira on the Caribbean, where the ships that brought the cars came in. Thanks to the high altitude and closeness to the equator, Caracas enjoyed a fine, pleasant climate most of the time, and Hank allowed as how it was truly a lovely place if you just ignored all the poor people and the sprawling, tattered slums and the brutal military dictatorship and the way obscene wealth and desperate poverty lived together like lions and lice around a jungle water hole. There was a lot of money in Venezuela thanks to huge oil profits, but Hank said it wasn't spread around very far.

In the style of a lot of nickel-rocket South American dictators, Generalissimo Marcos Perez Jimenez came to power thanks to a military overthrow of the democratic government he himself helped bring to power in yet another military takeover four years earlier in 1948. But he wasn't quite running things yet (even if he was pulling most of the strings) on account of they'd set up this Lieutenant Colonel Carlos Delgado Chalbaud as more or less the front man. But then the Lieutenant Colonel got himself ever so slightly assassinated towards the end of 1950 (you wonder how these things happen, you know?) and so they held a free, honest and open public election to fill the vacancy. Only when it started looking like this outside guy might be getting most of the votes, the government gently but firmly closed the lid on the old ballot box, stuck it in the back of a dark closet someplace and installed the good Generalissimo as head man.

According to Hank, Generalissimo Marcos Perez Jimenez was a great believer in the old Roman "bread and circuses" form of government, even if there wasn't always enough bread to go around in the poorer sections of the country. But the rich made up for it with a fine selection of white breads, wheat breads, short breads and sweetbreads and any kind of French pastry you might imagine. As to circuses, the good Generalissimo was really counting on his newly internationalized Venezuelan Grand Prix to keep the local population happy and entertained and take their minds off their stomachs and bank accounts for a while. I guess he was a sort of pompous, puffed-up little guy (and no question you didn't want to get on his bad side), but Hank allowed as how he seemed pretty decent as far as ruthless South American military dictators go. Our American government sure liked him because he was viciously tough on communism and sold us all the oil we wanted at bargain basement prices, and that won him the U.S. Legion of Merit and landed his pudgy mug and fancy gold braid-, medal- and ribbon-encrusted uniform on the cover of *Time* magazine in February of 1955.

Back home in Venezuela, the good Generalissimo built magnificent government buildings and a few, somewhat less magnificent public housing projects and encouraged luxury hotels with fabulous views and the finest amenities for the rich. He also built perhaps the most modern, impressive and expensive-per-square-foot superhighway in the world. Even if it only went from downtown Caracas out to the airport. It was called the *Autopista,* and it dove under and swooped over massive, soaring concrete bridges and streamed through tunnels of gleaming, polished white marble. Every mile was lined with tall, modern lampposts and dotted here and there with strong, muscular statues, carved stone obelisks and enormous monuments to the strength and solidarity of (what else?) the apparently rock-solid government of Generalissimo Marcos Perez Jimenez! Hank said one of those monuments looked like nothing so much as a six-story marble headstone! Which was kind of appropriate, seeing as how the good Generalissimo—in spite of winning yet another landslide victory in yet another somewhat suspect "honest, free and open" public election just a month later in December—got himself ousted in yet another South American military coup in January of 1958. This time accompanied by a general uprising and more than a little rioting in the streets. That should give you a little feel for the underlying civic tensions back on the race weekend in November and also explain why there were columns, platoons and squadrons of uniformed and heavily armed soldiers in full battle dress everywhere you looked....

The so-called "racetrack" for the World Manufacturers' Championship round was laid out on 6.1 miles of that magnificent *Autopista* into Caracas that the good Generalissimo and his flunkies were so proud of. Unfortunately, the layout included a ridiculously tight and poorly marked succession of hairpin corners with solid fences around the outside at one end and a bunch of linked-up, concrete- and guardrail-lined cloverleaf sweepers at the other end to head the cars back the opposite way. In between were two long, parallel, undulating high-speed stretches where the only thing between the cars thundering flat-out down one side of the highway and the cars storming back the other way was a little set of curbs with a narrow grass strip in between and a succession of those tall, graceful modern light poles. Plus occasional non-paying spectators who decided to wander out to the median—with cars flashing past at over 170-plus in both directions!—so they could sit on the curbs and get a closer look at the action. And who was going to venture out there to shoo them off?

None of the drivers liked the place at all. It was terribly fast, it was poorly marked, it was uncoordinated to drive and it was dangerous as hell. In fact, Toly Wolfgang missed one of the confusing hairpin turnoffs during first practice and went storming off towards downtown Caracas—flat out in top gear!—and never realized his mistake until he came face-to-face with a heavily loaded gasoline truck heading the opposite way. In *his* lane! "It was kind of a surprise," he allowed afterwards, lighting up another *Gauloises.* "They really need to do something about the road markings. And there are an awful lot of things to hit out there."

"Most of which won't move very far if you hit them," Masten Gregory added with a grim smile. That very night, he had the team mechanics weld a roll bar inside the blue-and-white 450's headrest fairing. Just to be on the safe side….

Toly thought the course looked like it had been designed by Salvatore Dali—you know, that surrealist artist guy with the bug eyes and curlicue mustache who paints all those screwy, fantasy landscapes full of oozing clocks and stuff—and a lot of the other drivers were complaining, too. There was even talk of a boycott, and so the organizers figured they better do something about it. The last thing they needed was for the less fortunate or influential (but highly numerous!) members of Caracas' lower classes to come out of their shacks and hovels and gather on top of the walls and overpasses to watch the good Generalissimo's Great Race Car Circus and find nothing but empty pavement to stare at. That wouldn't do at all. So the army went around and piled low walls of sandbags around some of the larger and more obvious solid objects (not that a wall of sandbags was appreciably softer than a block of granite, but at least the monuments, guardrails and statues were better protected) and they also stationed a soldier with a big flag at that confusing split-off where Toly went barreling into town. The poor soldier's job was to just stand there—with the damn cars bearing down on him at top speed!—and use the flag to wave them on in the proper direction. *"That is either the bravest or the dumbest soldier in all of Venezuela!"* Toly observed wryly.

"Make that all of South America," Hank agreed. But it seemed like they had plenty of soldiers to spare in Caracas. They were everywhere you looked, in fact. Supposedly they were there to help with "crowd control," but such a thing could have new and unexpected meanings in a South American military dictatorship. Hank allowed as how everybody was quietly advised to cooperate with the military at all times and not to smart off to any of the soldiers—particularly not the officers and squadron leaders—seeing as how many of them were staunch capitalists and great believers in the practice of free enterprise.

The good Generalissimo wanted his European and American guests to come away highly impressed with Venezuela, and so he had his tourism bureau book all the drivers, teams and wealthy privateers into the luxurious and exclusive Humboldt Hotel and the neighboring Canamaco Resort, which were located way up on a mountaintop overlooking the city and could only be reached by cable car. That made them pretty much invulnerable to any sort of distasteful activities, social disturbances or out-and-out trouble with the slum folks down below. Hank wrote that the Humboldt was a truly amazing place, what with a fabulous view of the city and surrounding mountains, several swimming pools, an indoor skating rink and a circular ballroom with a rotating floor for hosting huge, lavish parties. Hank didn't personally have an invitation to stay there, but Cal was nice enough to offer him the sofa in the two-bedroom suite he was supposed to be sharing with Toly Wolfgang. "You might as well try the bed," Cal grinned. "Toly doesn't always show up at night from what I understand."

"Sometimes I find somewhere soft to lie down," Toly explained at breakfast the next morning while a perfectly manicured waiter poured freshly-squeezed orange juice around the table.

"Where were you last night?" Cal asked.

Toly just shrugged.

"I saw him," Hank said slyly.

Toly's eyelids rolled up an eighth of an inch.

Apparently he'd rolled into the penthouse bar at the Humboldt late the previous evening with a very classy and attractive local *senorita* on his arm. Hank said she was wearing a plunging black cocktail dress, lots of expensive diamond jewelry and had her raven-black hair cut Veronica Lake-style so it looked like she was peering out from behind her own, shimmering black shower curtain. She was very tan and spoke no English whatsoever, and Hank said you could hear the muffled intake of breath and cracking of masculine neck vertebrae from one end of the room to the other as they walked over and sat down at the piano bar. Cal was trying to get some sleep back in the room, but Hank was far too tired to sleep—you know that weary yet wide-awake feeling when you just can't get the last of the electricity out of your system?—and that's why he was up in the penthouse bar, nursing a snifter of brandy that cost more than most of the meals he'd bought as a motoring journalist in Europe. Then again, Hank never visited fancy places when he was working off his own stack of nickels. He said that was pretty much Standard Operating Procedure in the world of motoring journalists. You got to make up for it—and then some—at long-lead manufacturer press launches and racing banquets. But since it was the last race of the whole damn year and seeing as how it was also such a fabulous, luxurious place—surrounded by glass, brass, polished wood, silver plate and velvet up on top of a hotel up on top of a mountain overlooking the whole damn city of Caracas—he decided he'd splurge and buy himself a decent drink. And hope somebody rich who knew him might waltz in and offer to buy him another.

And that's when Toly swept in with the beautiful young woman in the black dress, black hair and diamonds on his arm and sat both of them down at the piano bar. Hank had an impulse to go over there himself—hell, there might even be a few free drinks in it—but he had an even deeper notion to stay where he was, hidden in the shadows, and just watch how things played out. As you can imagine, it wasn't long before Toly worked his way behind the keyboard, and Hank said it was once again dumbfounding the way Toly Wolfgang could play piano. He started out with some soft, silky old standards like *Moonglow, It Had to be You, Harlem Nocturne* and *The Way You Look Tonight*—all done at a slow, almost melancholy pace. Then he eased into a bit of the Rachmaninoff piano concerto he'd played before at Sebring, but so gently and seamlessly you could hardly notice the transition. And then he caught Hank out of the corner of his eye and rolled into a few bars of rollicking, barrelhouse boogie-woogie. That guy could play *anything!* And it appeared to be having the right sort of effect on the beautiful young Latin girl. Especially when he went all smooth and lush again easing into Beethoven's *Moonlight Sonata.*

It wasn't at all the sort of thing you expected from a racing driver.

Cal and Toly hadn't really seen each other since Sebring, and even though all they left Florida with was a few sob stories about the race and a pair of massive hangovers, I guess they were both looking forward to hanging around together again. Even though they were driving for different teams. And even though they'd surely get around to discussing Gina LaScala, seeing as how yet another Eric Gibbon *paparazzi* shot of Gina and Toly Wolfgang together—drinks in hand—on some carved stone balcony someplace overlooking the Mediterranean had made it into all of the European tabloids and most of the American movie magazines.

"What were you guys up to?" Cal asked at breakfast Saturday morning like it didn't mean much to him one way or the other.

"We weren't up to anything special. She was shooting part of a film in Italy and I was at Monza and, well...." He let his voice trail off. Then he looked straight at Cal. "Does it mean anything special to *you?"*

"Why should it?" Cal shrugged.

Toly leaned in close to Cal's ear. "Look, my friend. She is a wonderful, beautiful, sexy and intelligent girl. There are few such creatures in this world." He tapped his finger against his forehead. "Believe me. I know..."

Cal's eyes narrowed.

"...But I am fortunate," Toly continued. "I have been given money, looks, charm and fame. It's all a sham, of course—you and I know that!—but that's how people see me. They can't help it and neither can I."

"So what's your point?" Cal said, his voice sounding a little strained.

Toly swung his arm around Cal's shoulders. "Only this. I have been burdened with a stunning oversupply of wonderful, beautiful, sensual and intelligent girls. Women, too. I do not claim to deserve them—far from it—but those are the facts, my friend..."

Cal just looked at him.

"...One more or less makes no difference to me. And that is the sad part, I suppose."

"The sad part?"

Toly sighed. "The sad part is that none of them make any difference to me. Not any more. Not really. Not down deep where it counts."

"So?"

"So if this one means something to you, I think you should by all means go out and get her."

"What makes you think she means anything to me?"

Toly looked him straight in the eye and smiled. "Let me be your mirror, my friend. Let me reveal to you the things you cannot see by yourself. I personally think you're in love with this girl."

Cal looked down at his plate. "I suppose I like her okay."

"You *like* her okay?" Toly snorted. And then he shook his head. "It's worse than I thought. Far, far worse than I thought."

"What's worse than you thought?"

"You! You're worse than I thought. You don't even know your own feelings. You don't even know what's going on inside you."

"Oh. And I suppose you do?"

"It's clear to anyone with eyes."

Cal looked at him kind of sideways. "You're just trying to put me off my game, aren't you?"

"Of course I am!" Toly grinned, squeezing Cal's shoulder. "I would not be doing my job for *Signore* Ferrari if I didn't!"

Everybody got a good laugh off that one. But as they all got up to leave the table and head off for qualifying, Toly leaned in close to Cal's ear and whispered: *"At the end of the weekend, I'll tell you what happened."* He shot Cal a wink. *"If we survive, of course...."*

The Ferrari team showed up at Caracas with two of their latest, updated, 4023cc 335S models backed up by two of the new, *Testa Rossa* V-12s they were readying for the 1958 season and the FIA's now confirmed new 3.0-liter displacement limit. Maserati countered with the two factory 450S V-8 entries plus an experimental 12-cylinder version of one of their 3.0-liter, 300S cars as a backup for quick, dapper Swede Jo Bonnier and Englishman Tony Brooks, who had been hired on for this final championship round at the urging of fellow Brit Stirling Moss. Fangio was slated to drive with Moss in the lead 450S and his name was listed on all the official entry forms, but he never showed up in Venezuela. And Maserati team manager Ugolini didn't seem particularly surprised by it, either. They also had Temple Buell's blue-and-white "privateer" 450S with Masten Gregory and Cal Carrington up to bolster the Maserati ranks, and it was obvious after practice and qualifying—as it had been all season—that the big, V-8 Maseratis had the legs on the slightly smaller Ferrari V-12s. Especially on this stupidly fast circuit with ridiculously tight corners at one end that made brute acceleration and sheer top speed more important than handling. The factory Maserati V-8s wound up qualifying first and second on the starting grid, a full three seconds per lap clear of Hawthorn in the fastest of the Ferraris.

But winning a 1,000-kilometer endurance race is always about more than speed and power. It's also about rhythm and pace, stamina and strategy, preparation and pit stops and pure, dumb luck. Not to mention weaving your way through clueless backmarkers and cars in other classes fighting it out for their own small bag of gold and slice of glory. And there were a whole lot of them to deal with in Venezuela. Chevrolet sent John Fitch down with a team of three lumbering Corvettes—two new fuel-injected '58 models and one carbureted '57—and there was even supposed to be a fourth car for Indianapolis 500 stars Troy Ruttman and Johnny Parsons. But the cars were heavy, cumbersome and uncompetitive, and maybe that's why the promised Indianapolis drivers never showed. Things got even worse when the entire shipment of tires for the Corvettes and many of the other American entries got tied up in customs and never made the race. It forced the teams to go scrounging around for local rubber, most of which wasn't really suitable for racing. In the end, the only Corvette driver able to hustle around with any real authority was Dr. Dick Thompson. He was several seconds clear of the other two Corvettes and managed a fairly impressive ninth on the grid, but he was more than *half-a-minute* off the pace of the front-running Ferraris and Maseratis in the same exact class.

There were also a gaggle of Porsche 550s racing for the Under-1500cc prize money plus a slightly punched-out, 1600cc "Type 718" factory car entered for Edgar Barth and team manager Huschke von Hanstein aimed at the Under-2000cc win. One of those privateer 550s was an all-girl American team with Denise McCluggage and Ruth Levy behind the wheel. Ruth already had a reputation as a pretty decent racing driver out in California, but everyone said that this Denise McCluggage was really something special. Hank said she drove just like a man (which some women might take offense to, but he obviously meant it as a compliment), and he also said she was one hell of a writer, too. And Hank would know about writers. Now there have always been a fat handful of motoring journalists who think they know how to drive racecars, and there have also been a few, mostly second-tier drivers who fancy they know how to stitch words together into something you might want to read. But the number who can really do both is very small indeed. Or that's what Hank said, anyway. And I guess he paid this Denise McCluggage about the highest compliment possible when he said she was *"a racer who could write"* rather than the other way 'round.

Besides the Corvettes and Porsches there were a small legion of adventuring stateside amateurs like Eds Crawford and Hugus in one of the fastest Porsche 550 Spyders and Hap Dressel in the same exact AC-Bristol he drove to Sebring, raced, and drove back home again earlier in the year. Plus all sorts of local South

American entries with names like Manuel and Julio and Juan and Santiago and Ramon and Francisco in everything from older Ferraris, Maseratis and Aston Martins to a homebuilt hybrid with a Mercedes-Benz engine stuffed into an older Ferrari chassis and not destined to do much for the reputation of either manufacturer. But no question there were a lot of cars out there besides the obvious front-runners, and the speed, handling, talent, skill and desire levels varied astoundingly from one end of the Le Mans-style grid lineup to the other.

Generalissimo Marcos Perez Jimenez himself—all spiffed up in one of his dazzling military outfits with gold-braid dingleberries on the shoulders and about twelve pounds of assorted medals and ribbons plastered across his chest—strutted down the row of gleaming racecars and made a point of greeting and saluting or shaking hands with each and every driver before the start. Then he took up a position across the track (and safely behind a convenient barrier), raised a huge Venezuelan flag above his head, basked for just a moment in the warm glow of focused attention, and then swirled it grandly through the air. Drivers instantly scampered across to their cars, leaped in, twisted the keys and…mostly nothing! Just the grind of starter motors plus the occasional pop or fart backfire of unburned fuel in the exhaust pipes. Hank said it was either the altitude or the low-grade local gasoline or a combination of both, but it was almost comical how just about everybody seemed to just sit there on the grid—stranded!—before the engines finally started firing and the field peeled, pounced and staggered away. John Kilbourn's chuffing white Corvette was the first car across the line, followed by Masten Gregory in the blue-and-white Temple Buell Maserati he was sharing with Cal. Then came the team Ferraris all mixed up with the Porsches and the other Corvettes and a huge gaggle of local amateurs in all different kinds of cars and then—finally—the two factory 450S Maseratis of Moss and Behra, who seemed to be the very last cars to fire up and screech away from what should have been the very front of the line!

The announcer was screaming madly into his microphone that Gregory was leading, and as you can imagine that got our boy Cal very juiced up indeed. But Masten had just about the entire Ferrari factory team (in the persons of *"Mon Ami Mates"* Mike Hawthorn and Peter Collins) breathing down his neck, and he never made it around to complete that very first lap. He got out of shape and lost control in an 80mph curve, hit the sandbags piled up around one of the many immovable pieces of local scenery, careened off to one side and flipped clear over. The car hammered into the concrete with a sickening *CRUNCH,* and everybody knew in an instant that poor Masten was trapped underneath! Worse yet, the impact split the seams of the filled-to-the-brim 60-gallon fuel tank, and so he was being thoroughly drenched in gasoline as well. The only reason he was even awake or alive to feel it was because of that roll-over bar he'd had the mechanics weld into the head rest the night before….

Sometimes emergencies spark superhuman shows of strength and determination, and that had to be the explanation of how skinny little Masten Gregory managed to kick, bash, struggle and ultimately tear the driver's door right off its hinges so he could scramble to safety before the whole blessed thing had a chance to go up in flames. Which it never did, by the way. But it certainly could have. And that was pretty much the end of the 1000-kilometer, six-and-a-half hour Venezuelan Grand Prix as far as Masten Gregory, Cal Carrington, and Temple Buell's blue-and-white 450S were concerned.

Scratch one Maserati.

The two Ferrari 335S factory cars continued on at the front—Hawthorn playing "The Rabbit" and slowly pulling away—but Moss and Behra in the other two 450S Maseratis were working their way up through the field. In fact, Moss passed no less than 22 cars his first lap and another five the next, and it wasn't long before Behra and then Moss caught right up with the leading Ferraris. They swapped positions back and forth for a few laps, but then Moss seemed to tire of the game, swept past in earnest and began drawing away, setting repeated fastest laps in the process with what appeared to be no effort at all. Behra passed and pulled away from the Ferraris as well, and things were looking nervously giddy in the Maserati pits. No question they had the speed. All they needed was to bring the big brutes home....

Moss was maintaining an unassailable pace, and he had more than two minutes in hand over his teammate Behra—still running a solid second!—barely a third of the way into the race. And then...*disaster!* While overtaking Hap Dressel's AC-Bristol on the very fastest part of the course—the Maserati doing 170-plus at the time—the AC swerved in front of the 450S and the two cars got together. Maybe a tire blew, or perhaps Dressel was just trying to move aside and make room. Or maybe he didn't see the Maserati coming at all—for sure there were no warning flags from the marshals' stations—but whatever caused it, Dressel's AC went ricocheting off to one side and crashed into a light stanchion with such force that it broke the AC completely in two. Dressel was incredibly lucky to survive with just a broken hip, several broken ribs and a concussion. Meanwhile Moss' leading Maserati careened off the other way, swung this way and that, jumped a curb and smashed its way down the guardrail. It came to a grinding halt against one of the guardrail supports, its fortunate driver shaken but thankfully unhurt. But the car was finished—scratch one more Maserati—and Moss trudged glumly back to the pits on foot, thinking he was done for the day.

Even so, this left Behra in the second Maserati safely in the lead, and he stayed there with ease until the time came to head in for fuel and tires and hand it over to Harry Schell. Maserati team boss Ugolini had already thought about putting Moss in the car—no question he was the quickest driver on the squad—and that became an imperative when the back end of the Behra/Schell Maserati burst into flames during the pit stop. It was a huge, erupting fireball of a blaze—it burned Behra's forearm badly as he leapt out of the car—but two Venezuelan fire fighters with hand-held extinguishers responded quickly, bravely and decisively and put it out. But valuable time had been lost, and the lone remaining 450S was now behind the leading Ferraris. Still, there was more than half the race yet to run, and Maserati still had both the fastest car in the race with the 450S and the fastest driver as well in Stirling Moss…

Moss jumped in the car and tore out of the pits with his jaw set. But he returned a lap later, almost comically jumping and bouncing up and down in the seat. Turns out the fire brigade thought they had put the blaze out, but the seat cushion was somehow still smoldering! Surely Moss must have considered pulling over and parking it as he worked his way around those agonizing 6.1 miles with his backside on fire. Imagine sitting down on a barbecue grill while you're trying to drive a blessed racecar! But Moss somehow brought it around and dove back into the pits, and everyone could see his pants were burned clear through as he scrambled out of the car. Someone from the team took him off to have his backside looked after, and the rest of them poured water into the interior, made absolutely *sure* the fire was out, and then sent Harry Schell out with one simple instruction: *"Go like hell!"*

At that point Jo Bonnier in the Maserati 300S was running a strong third, well behind the leading Ferraris, and he pointed a finger and moved over to make room as Schell in the hustling 450S approached from behind. There was still a faint glimmer of hope in the Maserati camp at that moment. Sure, two of their big V-8s were out of it and the third had lost time with the fire and the extra pit stop. But it was running fine now, Schell had the bit between his teeth, the Bonnier/Brooks 300S was solidly in third and nearly half the race remained to be run. Plus misfortune might also pay a visit to the Ferrari pits. That was always a possibility in any endurance race.

But just as Bonnier pointed Schell by, the smaller 300S suffered a sudden blowout and swerved right into the 450S! The two cars ricocheted off each other at high speed and caromed towards opposite sides of the track. Bonnier's car wouldn't steer, and when he saw he was skidding directly towards the concrete base of one of the tall, modern light poles, he just bailed out—*jumping over the side at damn near 80 miles-per-hour!*—and rolled and tumbled to a halt while the car leaped over the curb and crashed *HARD* into the light pole. The noise and motion had barely stopped when there was another sound—a low, deep, metallic *crack!*—and the light pole came toppling down across the car with violent finality. It landed like a felled tree across the driver's seat where Bonnier had been sitting just moments before….

Meanwhile Schell's Maserati careened across the road—completely out of control!—smashed through the railing and into a concrete wall and burst into flames. Luckily it wasn't a head-on hit, and Schell managed to gather his wits and scramble out of the inferno with just a gash on his forehead, a broken nose and an unsightly and surely painful collection of burns.

Scratch the last two Maseratis.

In fact, scratch the whole blessed Maserati racing team.

Ferrari went on to win the race and the World Championship with ease, and rubbed salt in Maserati's wounds by having their cars cross the finish line in a three-abreast formation. Just a week later, word came out of Modena that Maserati was finished with racing. Or at least finished as a factory team, anyway. They would still build cars for privateers, of course, but they were out of money, out of energy, out of spirit and out of passion. The disaster in Caracas had torn the heart right out of them. They were gutted.

Chapter 23: A Party Near Pebble Beach

As tough as things had been down in Venezuela and as screwy and incomprehensible as the world was getting overall—the Russians (or should I say the Russians' captured German scientists) put a damn dog into space the same exact day as the Caracas race—things were going great guns for us at the dealership in Passaic. In fact, we were selling so many damn Beetles, Microbuses and as many blessed Karmann-Ghias as we could get our hands on that we had to bang out the back wall and build an addition to hold four more stalls in the service department—two with their own hydraulic lifts!—and of course that meant trying to find two more savvy, competent, reliable and easy-to-get-along-with line mechanics who could think straight, showed up sober and on time every day, moved slightly faster than still water, didn't curb cars or steal stuff out of the parts department to do side jobs behind their brother-in-law's garage and lacked the imagination to learn all about VeeDubs from us and then open their own shabby, back-alley, low-overhead, corner-cutting independent VW shop someplace close by and try to steal our customers. Not that such a thing happened all the time. But it happened often enough that you knew to look out for it. And the part that really stung was that they were often your best and brightest guys. Or your craftiest, shiftiest and sleaziest, which often, sadly, amounts to the same thing. There may be more difficult things in this world than finding and keeping good dealership mechanics—striking a match on a wet cake of soap would be one of them—but it's right up there near the top of the list.

Naturally all the bustle, activity and responsibilities of the VW store was cutting into the time I could spend just half a block away at the old Sinclair, where *Alfredo's Foreign Car Service* ("Sorry, Alfredo's not in") was still doing very nicely and also badly in need of banging out the back wall seeing as how it was busting at the seams with MGs and Triumphs and Jags and Austin-Healeys and even the occasional Porsche or Alfa Romeo. The owners of all those cars—rightly or wrongly, but mostly rightly—were unanimously pissed off about getting their pockets picked, dignity trampled, credulity stretched and intelligence insulted by the service departments of the dealerships where they bought those cars. I've got to say that Steve, J.R. and Sylvester (I'd moved Sylvester over to *Alfredo's* where the work was more varied and challenging, where he wouldn't set a bad example on the days he showed up late, drunk or didn't show up at all and where he and Butch wouldn't come face-to-face (and nearly to blows) three or four times every week. Sylvester really settled in nicely over there at *Alfredo's,* where he was kind of the Wrenchus Emeritus and the guy all the other wrenches in the shop went to if they had a snapped-off stud to get out of its hole or a stripped nut to get off of its bolt or any of the countless other little scratch-your-head/can't-figure-it-out mechanical disasters that happen in every car shop on a fairly regular basis.

But, like I said, I was running out of time to keep an eye on things and the place was really getting too small to handle the work. We tried shifting some of the service cars over to the VW shop when we had space there, but that didn't work very well what with all mechanics being a little territorial about their work spaces and tools, the parts being half a block away and the fact that the zone rep from VW looked as stony as the faces on Mount Rushmore whenever he spied anything non-VW hanging around the service department. "It's a trade-in," Big Ed would tell him.

"I see. And just who, exactly, is trading in a two-year-old Jaguar on a Volkswagen?"

"Uhh, the VW is for his kid, see? And his wife didn't like the stickshift in the Jag," Big Ed ad-libbed.

"You wouldn't happen to have the paperwork handy on that deal…."

Well, of course the zone rep knew what was going on and of course we knew that he knew—he was really an all-right guy, just trying to do his job—and it was becoming more and more obvious to Big Ed and me that we needed more space. Especially since things were going so good and there were so many interesting, intriguing and enticing new foreign cars out there that we were always jawing back and forth about maybe adding another line. In a separate building, of course, since success had made VW a lot more picky and demanding. They'd decided they wanted all of their dealerships to look like VW dealerships (and believe me, they knew what they wanted VW dealerships to look like, and if you didn't fancy white with blue trim, that was just too damn bad) and to only sell and service Volkswagens on top of it. That was a lot different from the early days—what seemed like half a lifetime ago—when we'd get a Beetle or two from Bob Fergus and set them out under the Sinclair sign like a baited hook under a bobber and wait for a nibble.

I don't know what it is about business and entrepreneurship that makes you want to keep going and keep growing and keep expanding into new things even when you're already making plenty of money and moreover up to your eyeballs with stuff to do and so damn busy and spread so damn thin that you haven't got time to wipe your own ass. But that's the way it is—don't ask me why—and Big Ed and me found ourselves talking more and more about adding another line or even opening another store with another brand or two someplace else (or at the other end of the same lot, like we were already doing with *Alfredo's)* although we were both plenty leery about the risks of having only having two sets of eyes, two sets of legs and two mouths to holler, gnash your teeth or swear through while attempting to run multiple car-store businesses scattered all over the landscape. Some guys could do it—like that Harry Metropolis who was out buying VW stores like it was going out of style on both sides of the Hudson—but I'd learned the hard way that making money in the car business depends on a lot of little deals and even littler details piled one atop the other over a long period of time, and you really need to be around to keep an eye on that stuff or it'll crumble to dust while you're looking the other way. Meanwhile, some of your own, valued and trusted employees will be stealing you blind. Count on it. And yet there was so much new stuff out there that me and Big Ed liked, loved and lusted after and moreover thought we could sell. As I mentioned once before, Big Ed was real soft on Citroens. But I thought it was soft in the head rather than soft in the heart on account of I looked at it like any knuckle-busting mechanic and couldn't really warm up to Citroen's beamed-down-from-outer-space hypo-pneumatic suspension (or the whole rest of its damn hydraulic system, come to that) or that strange, one-spoke steering wheel and the fact that the only things Citroens shared with other cars were four rubber tires (five including the spare) and the fact that they ran—or refused to run—on pump gasoline.

But I agreed it made sense to have another sort-of "move-up" line to offer to our customers, and we looked long and hard at the heavily advertised (at least in the nutball sportycar magazines) Auto Union DKW 3=6. But it was really too close to the VW in price and features and besides, while that three-cylinder, 2-stroke engine made for great ad copy *("Only 7 moving parts! No valves! No tappets! No camshaft!")* it sounded like a fart in a damp tin can and trailed a stinky little oil haze behind it wherever it went. Same thing went for Saab's cute but porky little 93. It was designed and built by a respected airplane manufacturing company over in Sweden, and it was simple, cheap to run, amazingly roomy and comfortable inside (even Big Ed could get in and out of one) and surprisingly fun to drive. Plus, although it wasn't what you could ever call a real screamer—it was more of a popcorn popper, actually—the Saab 93 was great in the wintertime thanks to Wrong Wheel Drive and could maintain some pretty amazing long-distance average speeds once it got a head of steam up. But it was so damn practical it was strange, and you could sense as how Saabs were likely going to turn out like VW Microbuses: they'd have a certain small but loyal following of people who read thick books, took naked sauna baths in mixed company and regularly went to "art house" foreign movies with English subtitles. Several of my sister Mary Frances' egghead friends in Greenwich Village and a whole lot of the locals up around Lime Rock in Connecticut thought Saab 93s were really neat.

The Borgward Isabella was an attractive option (at least if you didn't actually look at it!) and they were running full-page ads in *Car & Track* magazine every month, calling it *"a dream come true"* and *"the continent's most glamorous car."* And from what I personally heard and saw it was solid and pretty well built (which you could more or less count on seeing as how it was German) but the overall shape and styling reminded me of that pale, giggly fat girl with the gap teeth and thick glasses who never gets asked to the high school prom. I have to admit I was kind of taken with Volvo's sturdy PV444 sedan, which was hardly stylish (it looked like a dwarfed-down '40 Ford) and had a center of gravity about halfway to the second story of a three-flat. But it was simple and straightforward and built like an armored personnel carrier. A would-be dealer rep on a little fishing expedition brought one by for us to try, and I liked the way it drove like a cross between a sports car, an economy sedan and a cement truck (especially that long, industrial-grade shift lever sprouting out of the floor tunnel!) and how the more you thrashed it, the better that Volvo seemed to like it.

You might think the natural thing would've been for us to pick up MG or Triumph or Austin-Healey or even Jaguar, but what with Colin St. John and another new thief already operating on the New York side and two other British car stores running their roots (or even Rootes) down into the soil on our side of the Hudson, it didn't look like such a promising proposition. Plus Big Ed was quick to point out that *Alfredo's Foreign Car Service* ("Alfredo's not here") would lose its lofty status as the place to take your MG or Triumph or Jaguar or Healey or whatever once you got good and pissed off at the snooty fast-buck artists at the official, franchised British car dealerships if we went into the same exact business. And that was surely something to think about. "Y'gotta remember which side of yer bread the peanut butter goes on," was the way Big Ed put it, and I could see his point.

It was a deliciously seductive notion to take a chance on some exotic and/or oddball, low-volume, orphan-type English make like Morgan, AC, Arnolt-Bristol, Aston Martin, the ridiculously insect-sized Berkeley or Colin Chapman's incredibly small, smooth and sexy new Lotus Elite. Which looked neat as hell but cost as much as a damn Jaguar and didn't really have all that much in the way of Stomp-On-It-And-Squirt stoplight appeal. Besides which it was tiny (Big Ed could never even think of getting into one!) and made entirely out of fiberglass. Even the blessed chassis frame. You had to admit that was clever as hell, but I had serious concerns about what might happen if you ever got into a wreck in one. Like it'd crack open like a dropped egg. But they sure looked *neat!* But Big Ed and me both knew it would be hard to make a steady profit off strange cars from iffy, small-volume and occasionally fly-by-night English constructors, and our experience with the orderly and well-organized bunch from Volkswagen made us way too wary to even think seriously about it. But it sure as hell was tempting.

So was Porsche—and Porsche made for sort of a natural fit with Volkswagen since they were both pretty much the same car, no matter what the Porsche owners thought—but that Harry Metropolis guy who was buying up all the VW dealerships he could lay his hands on was also into Porsche in a big way, and he already had Porsche showrooms and service facilities operating in two different locations on the Jersey side of the Hudson (although it turned out he was kind of a behind-the-scenes partner in both with a couple shrewd and appropriately square-jawed guys with blonde hair, pale skin and ice-blue eyes named Helmut and Gerhardt).

I was soft in both the head *and* the heart for Alfa Romeos, but Big Ed was kind of skittish about doing business with Italians. And I'm sure he had his reasons. Plus, just like Lotus Elites and Porsches, Alfas were a little pricey for what you got in the way of sheer, all-American, stoplight-to-stoplight-down-the-main-drag performance. "Look what a *Giulietta* costs, fr'chrissakes," Big Ed growled, shaking his head. "And it's only a stinking 1300. Hell, you can buy a 2.0-litre Triumph for less and have enough dough left over for a three-day weekend in Havana. With hookers."

It was hard to argue with logic like that.

But no matter whether we picked up any new lines or just stayed in the used sportycar, service and repair business over at *Alfredo's Foreign Car Service,* we were going to need more space. And it was Big Ed who finally fronted up the notion of bulldozing the old Sinclair—hell, we weren't pumping much in the way of gas any more—and putting up a bigger building that went all the way out to the sidewalk with more space and service stalls inside and a bigger and better organized used-car lot on the outside. *"We could tear it down and build new,"* was the way Big Ed put it.

The idea of tearing down the old Sinclair was like a dagger in my heart.

"Couldn't we maybe buy the property next door?"

Big Ed looked me square in the eye like he was disappointed in me. "That's a nice two-flat, not a piece of shit torch job all tied up in probate like the other place we got. The owner and his wife live on the bottom floor. Been there for a hunnert years. Got their kid and his family living upstairs. And they just put on a new roof and new siding on the garage. It'd take one hell of a wad of cash to move them off the property. You'd have to pay what the damn house is worth—and like I said, it's a nice one—just so's you could knock it down."

Big Ed pulled a fresh cigar out of his shirt pocket and gently crinkled away the cellophane wrapper. "On the other hand, you got this other piece of property—this piece of property you already own, by the way—that's got fucking pump islands where your showroom ought to be and an office that takes up too much space but isn't good for shit and a roof that leaks in the wintertime no matter how many times you patch it and..." Big Ed glared at me. But then his eyes softened and his voice lowered to a patient, fatherly whisper. "...Do I have to go on?"

I shook my head while the dagger in my heart did one slow, cold rotation.

Like I said before, Ernesto Julio had kindly invited both Big Ed and me (and our wives and/or girlfriends, as the case might be) out to California for the grand opening of the new Laguna Seca track on the Monterey Peninsula and the huge blowout housewarming party he had planned at his newly completed mansion overlooking the Pacific Ocean on 17-Mile Drive. And it sure was a tempting offer. Especially since he said he'd be happy to pay our airfare—first class, no less!—send his Aero Commander out to pick us up or arrange a ride for us with Creighton Pendleton the Third in his Beechcraft Bonanza. But you started adding up the travel time and then subtracted the fact that somebody's gotta close things up at the dealership and over at *Alfredo's Foreign Car Service* every night and stick the key in the lock to open things up the next morning and that the bigger and more successful you get the less you tend to trust all the fine folks you've hired (some as recently as last week) to do things the way you'd do them if you were only there. Plus flying all the way across country to go on what amounted to a high-class drunk in some gilded palace of a house overlooking the Pacific didn't hold the same kind of magic that it used to. I mean, the hangover's about the same no matter how nice the hooch, glassware or sheets you sleep it off between happen to be. And although flying backwards through the time zones heading west is always fun (it's almost like you land younger than when you left), the return trip makes up for it in spades. You lose a whole day, and I swear it feels more like two or three.

Sure, I wanted to see my buddy Cal again (and I must admit I was curious as hell about Ernesto's palatial new house), but we had so much going on what with the architect and the builder we were working with on the new building we'd more or less decided to build that I didn't feel like I could get away. Besides, that was the weekend they were going to start tearing down the old Sinclair, and I kind of felt like I had to be there. Even if it was just to get all choked-up sentimental about a bunch of dirty old bricks and rotted old framework and maybe generate a hangover or two on my own.

So for a change it was me calling Cal at Ernesto's new house at half-past-two Sunday morning. You could hear there was one hell of a party going on, complete with a jazz combo in the background, lots of chatter and laughter and the occasional shriek-and-splash of some young thing in a party dress getting nudged, shoved, tossed, thrown or nonchalantly blind-sided into the swimming pool. It felt pretty damn lonely being on the other end of the line. Even if I wasn't exactly alone, since I'd been enjoying the company of that long-leftover bottle of Castle Carrington brandy that I'd been either hoarding or ignoring for just such an occasion.

"Cal there?" I asked.

"Cal who?" An unfamiliar female voice giggled.

"Cal Carrington. The race driver."

"We got lotsa race drivers here…" she swiveled her voice away from the receiver: *"...HEY! STOP THAT!"*

There was a muffled commotion on the other end, then the sound of the jazz combo and another scream and splash, and then all of a sudden I was talking to Angelina Scalabrini. Or Gina LaScala, take your pick. You couldn't miss that voice. Not in a million years. It gave you chills. *"Hello?"*

"Gina?"

"Who's this?"

"Buddy. Buddy Pa—"

"Buddy Palumbo! How ARE you?" Gina just about gushed. I must admit she sounded genuinely thrilled to hear from me. And that sent a few chills up my spine, too. If you've ever seen any of her movies, you know why.

"Oh, you know. Same old stuff. Another day, another dollar."

"You make it sound like a life sentence," she laughed into the phone.

"Nah, things are okay. Better than okay, in fact. I'm just feeling a little sorry for myself tonight."

"Any special reason?"

"Oh, I suppose. We're tearing down the old Sinclair to put a new building up, and I guess I'm a little blue about it."

"You should be out here instead, whooping it up with the rest of the sluts and stallions. This is a pretty damn amazing party. And believe me, I know all about amazing parties these days."

"I bet you do."

"Trust me, they're better to read about in the tabloids than attend," she laughed. "Stupid behavior sounds a lot more exciting afterwards than it looks in person."

"That's why we stayed home. Besides," I took another sip of brandy, "I've got my own little party going right here."

"You do?"

"Yep. I've been keeping company with some of Cal's family's antique brandy. I understand it's supposed to be pretty high-line stuff."

"And is it?"

"It works fine. No question about it." Then something else occurred to me. "Say, didn't I see a picture of you and Toly Wolfgang together over in Europe."

She gave a contemptuous little snort into the receiver. "If you didn't, then Brad Lackey and his publicists aren't doing their jobs."

"You mean it was a set-up?"

"Oh, not entirely. I like Toly a lot—he's quite a character, isn't he?—and charming and dashing as they come."

"Kind of a real-life movie hero, huh?"

"You've got the idea. The studio press hounds heard that I knew him through Cal and Ernesto, and they wanted me to set up something so we could spread a few pictures and a little innuendo around."

"Sounds wonderfully deceitful."

"Oh, it wasn't at all. Or nor much, anyway. Toly understood what was going on. He's quite a big name over in Europe—everything he does is all over the newspapers—and I was over there shooting anyway and two of my pictures were just going into European release."

"So it was all cut and dried. What does Toly get out of it?"

"He gets a couple nice evenings out and a little more notoriety."

"And that's it?"

"If there were any more to it, it wouldn't be your or anybody else's business anyway. I'm not the kind to kiss and tell. Besides, this business is full of people who get paid to do that sort of thing."

I let that notion roll around in the brandy for a while. "So," I finally asked, "is our favorite hero driver Cal Carrington there?"

The phone went quiet on the other end. Just the echo of the sax player easing through a slow solo with brushes on a drum set behind it. Then a distant yell and another splash. "Gina? You there? I asked about Cal…"

"I heard you," she answered softly. And then there was another long pause before she started in again. Coolly. Matter-of-factly. "I don't think he knew I was coming, Buddy. Or maybe Ernesto just didn't tell him…."

Something sounded pretty wrong. "So where is he?" I asked.

"Well," she said slowly, drawing the word out like an archer's bow, "I'm pretty sure he's upstairs in one of the bedrooms."

"Sleeping it off already?"

Another pause. "No, I don't think so…."

And that's when it dawned on my what a stupid idiot I was.

"Geez, Gina, I…."

"Oh, don't say anything, okay?" There was a tight little tremble in her voice now. "Cal didn't know I was coming and he was upstairs with whoever she is before I even got here." She licked her lips on the other end. "It's nobody's fault, really. I don't have any special claim on him and he doesn't have any special claim on me. That's just the way things are. We're both too busy with our lives for it to be any other way…."

Her voice trailed off, and I found myself listening to the sax solo again.

"Look, I have to run," Gina added abruptly. "Somebody else wants to use the phone…" there was another strange, halting pause, "…Always good to talk to you again, Buddy."

"Always good to talk to you, too again, Gina."

"You still married with kids?"

I smiled for the first time that whole weekend. "Like you said, Gina: it's a life sentence…."

Well, it wasn't more than an hour later that the phone rang. At 3:30 and change in the morning. Needless to say, my Julie was hardly impressed. And neither was the baby.

"Jesus, Cal, do you know whatthehell time it is?" My eyelids seemed to be stuck together and my mouth tasted like the small of a bad turnip.

"It's just a little past midnight," he protested.

"It's a little past midnight out there. Do you know what time it is *here?"*

"Listen. You should be happy. I'm not calling collect for a change."

"You're actually *paying* for a long-distance phone call?"

"I didn't say that. I just said I'm not calling collect."

"That's damn big of you." I was awake now, but I didn't really know what to say or where to start. "So how'd things go today?"

"Oh, the track is pretty neat. You ought to see this part they call 'The Corkscrew.' It's *nutty!* Like falling off the edge of the damn earth, honest it is! And that second turn will suck your shorts right up into your crack, no lie."

"That's a colorful choice of words."

"Ah, everybody talks like that out here."

"It's very becoming."

"Thanks. I'm trying to sound like a native."

"And the car's running good?"

"Oh, the 450's all assholes and elbows out here. It's like herding a bull through a damn ballet. Shelby's quicker in a 300S, and I don't think I can catch him."

"Jesus."

"But it's not just me. We've got some mystery stumble we're chasing but not catching. Ernesto's head wrench thinks he knows what it is, but he's said he knows what it is three times already but nothing he comes up with seems to work. He's still back at the track fussing with it right now."

"You should be out there with him, you jerk."

"I'd just get in the way. Besides, I had a little business to take care of."

"So I heard."

"You heard?"

I didn't say anything.

"Yep, God in his infinite mercy found me—what does Toly call it?—'somewhere soft to lie down?'"

I heard a girl's voice say *"who is it?"* in the background.

"Anybody I know?"

"No, this one's a free-lancer. Her name is...*what did you say your name was?"*

I heard something muffled on the other end.

"Her name is Joni and she volunteers in timing and scoring and her uncle's next-door neighbor races a Jaguar." Then he added: "She can stand a quarter on end with her tongue."

"I'm sure that's fascinating. You ought to sell tickets."

"Why don't you put your shorts on, go downstairs and get us a couple drinks?" I heard him say with his hand over the receiver. Then he was back on. "She's a pretty nice kid, actually," he told me. "Cute as hell."

He obviously had no idea. "Did you know Gina was there?"

"Where?"

"There. At the damn party. I talked to her downstairs about an hour ago."

The phone went cold in my hand.

"You there?" I finally asked.

Cal made a kind of puzzled grunt into the receiver. "Did she know I was here?"

"She knew exactly where you were. And what you were doing. The only thing she didn't seem to know was with who."

"In polite circles, that's *'with whom.'"* Cal corrected me, but neither of us thought it was very funny. "Look," he argued quickly (but sounding confused at the same time), "we don't have any special sort of arrangement, her and me. She's got her life and I've got mine. That's just the way things are."

"That's what she said."

"She did?"

I nodded like he could see me right through the phone and told him it didn't sound very convincing from her, either. "Look," I said like I actually knew what the hell I was talking about, "it's pretty obvious to everybody that there's something special between you two. Anyone can see it."

"But how can you tell?"

"Easy. You make each other miserable."

It went quiet again on the other end. "Aw," Cal moaned as he aimed the receiver back towards its cradle, "I just wish people would leave us the hell alone…."

Click!

Pavement Poseurs

for people with the dosh to go posh

★★★★★

EXCLUSIVE!!!

first impressions of the

Hedon Ballistica III

Already ordered a Bugatti Veyron?
Pity.

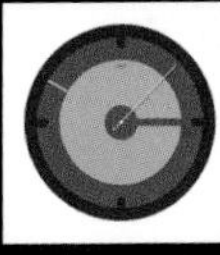

Plus: a host of must-have curbside accessories specially designed to keep your neighbor's glam wheels behind closed doors.

Also: Miami's ***Wolf Den*** wants to *Pimp yur Porsh.*

a **MOI**nternational publication

Advertisers & Sponsors

Phil & Ann **Airey**
Mike & Cheri **Amalfitano**
Bill **Babcock**
Bob & Danny **Baker**
Howard **Baugues**
Mikw & Diane **Besic**
Tom **Black**
Alan **Bolte´**
George **Bruggenthies**
Dave **Burton**
Asa **Candler**
Rick **Carlino**
Lee & Carol **Chapman**
Phil & Judy **Cull**
Keith & Walter **Denahan**
Bill & Shirley **Dentinger**
Michael **DiGiacomo**
Dave & Carolyn **Drake**
Travis **Engen**
Ken **Fengler**
Bob **Fergus**
Linda **Finkleman**
Brock **Flagstad**
Paul **Flowers**
Marc **Giroux**
Bob **Goeldner**
Jamie **Goffaux**
Mike **Gourley**
Tom Sr & Tom Jr **Grunnah**
Pete **Gulick**
Chuck **Gutke**
Les & Laura **Halls**
Neil **Harmon**
Ford **Heacock**
Chris **Heitman**
David **Hinton**
Bill **Hollingsworth**
Ralph **Janelli**
Carl **Jensen**
Mike **Kaske**
Steve **Kibble**
Dan **Kirby**
Tom **Kreger**
Harry **Krix**
Voodoo Bob **Kruger**
Dale **Lagerstad**
Phil **Lamont**
Mike & Sheila **Langenfeld**
John **Langenfeld**
Joni **Lefter**
Jack **Lewis**
Larry **Ligas**
Bruce & Cindy **Lindstrand**
Bill & Renata **Lyman**
Bill & Brian **MacEachern**
Alex **Manzo**
Rita **Manganaro**
Joe **Marchetti**
Rob **McClenagan**
Kevin **McGovern**
Phil **Meany**
Gordon **Medenica**
Ed **Mettelman**
Tim **Michnay**
Richard & Juanita **Miller**
J.R. & Eileen **Mitchell**
Margaret **Mitchell**
John **Mitchell**
Tom & Charlotte **Mittler**
Marc & Marilyn **Nichols**
Connie **Nyholm**
Scott **Paceley**
Bill **Parish**
Tim **Pendergast**
Joe & Carol **Pendergast**
Greg **Petrolati**
Walter & Louiseann **Pietrowicz**
Tim **Pyne**
Paul & Sue **Quackenbush**
Earl **Roberts**
David **Rodgers**
Alex & Liz **Rorke**
Peter **Schultz**
Jeff **Schur**
Michael **Shea**
Harvey **Siegel**
Tom **Simmons**
Mark **Simpson**
Steve & Diane **Simpson**
Glenn **Sipe**
Vic & Barb **Skirmants**
Jeff **Snook**
Hamish **Sommerville**
Hal **Sternberg**
Tim & Margie **Suddard**
Mike **Taradash**
John **Targett**
Daniel **Thompson**
Ed **Tillotson**
Will & David **Tobin**
Geoff **Tolsdorf**
Howard **Turner**
Joe **Tyson**
Tom **Wachal**
Duck & Sue **Waddle**
Bill **Warner**
Roger **Warrick**
Jack **Webster**
John & Lisa **Weinberger**
David **Whiteside**
Jack **Woehrle**
Bob **Williams**
Mike **Williamson**
Bob **Woodman**
Chip **Wright**
Tom & Scottie **Yeager**

EXOTIC MOTORCAR EMPORIUM

MIAMI . FLORIDA

Ferrari 250GT SWB
650ci, 850hp Chevy engine
Porsche Cayenne 4wd • Custom 26″ NBTs
Only one on the planet! Simply astounding!

Bizzarrini GT Strada
Up-graded Chevy engine (555ci, 700hp)
Slammed • 22″ NBT Torsobellas
Graphics by Zoot Ratmann

Lamborghini Miura
Blown Chrysler Hemi (900hp)
230mph • Slammed • 22″ NBTs
Graphics by Zoot Ratmann

Jaguar E-type Roadster
Ferrari V12 • Bennelli 7-spd trans
MegaFlux audio • 20″ NBTs
Ex-Roland Harper-Jones

Lamborghini Countach
Experimental Y16 w/ Settimini FI
GoLux audio system • 22″ NBTs
Electric raspberry & graphite

Aston Martin DB4 GT
Twin-supercharged Chrysler Hemi
225mph • 24″ RoMax wheels
Royal gold & red

Purveyor of Unique Rides for Discerning Individuals since 2001

Se Habla Español

wolf den
miami
Se Habla Español

Siebkens
ELKHART LAKE, WISCONSIN
The Last Open Bar
by Roger Warrick

NBT
Next Big Thing
wheels

the
Monogramos
collection

MR 3300
titanium: pewter & gold luster

Full Machine and Transmission Shop • Restoration/Preparation: Formula Jr./Atlantic
Early Sport Racers to Current Group C Cars • 25 Years Experience with British Cars
Chassis Repair Specialists • Best East Coast State-of-the-Art Fabrication Shop

203.778.8441 • 51 Austin Street, Danbury CT 06810

MR 4100
titanium: pewter & gold luster

The 'Tini Timing Team
Specialists in Vintage Chronography
John, Joni, Margaret and Neil

It *is time* somewhere

MR 2200
titanium: azure & gold luster

all wheels available in 16 - 28 inch diameter

VULGARI
Chromax Jubilee
VULGARI
It's time to make a statement
At fine jewelers worldwide • 95.000 USD

SCARAB
16
7
Meister Bräuser I
Mk1
Mk2

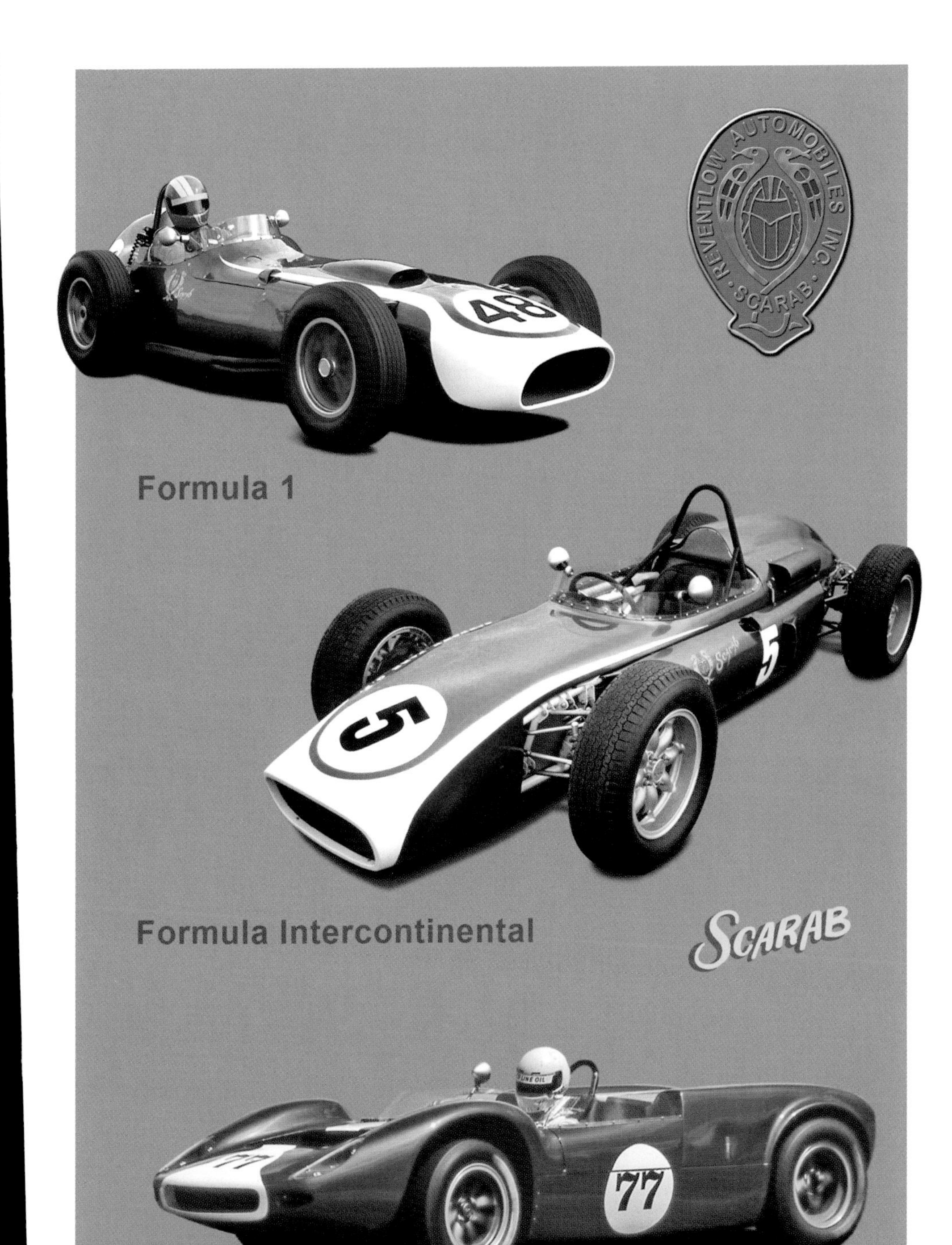

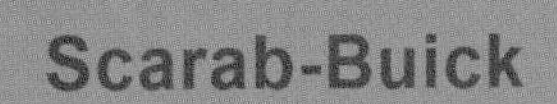

photography by Art Eastman

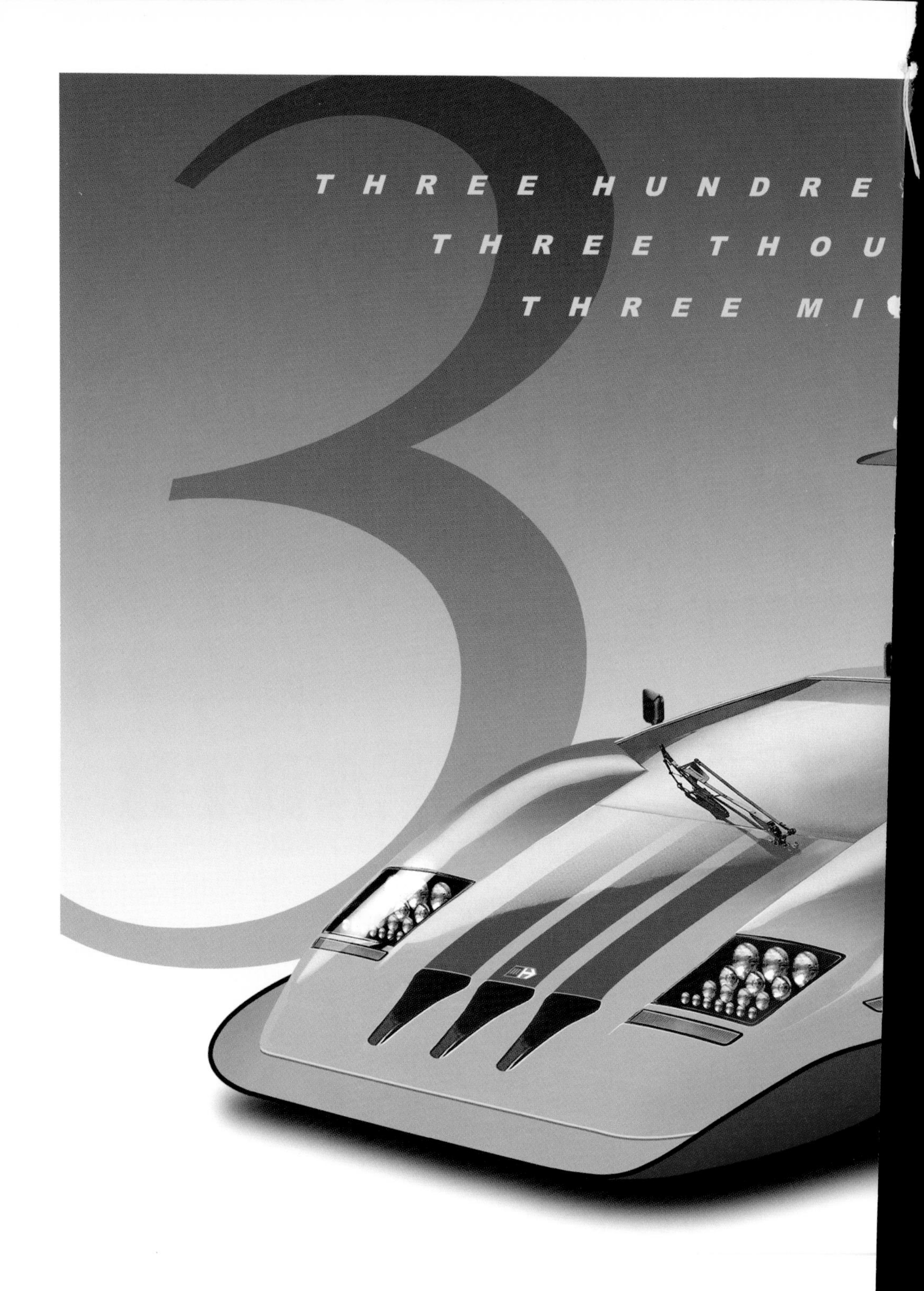

Exclusive U.S. Importer: SAAL's

MILES PER HOUR

SAND HORSEPOWER

LION US DOLLARS

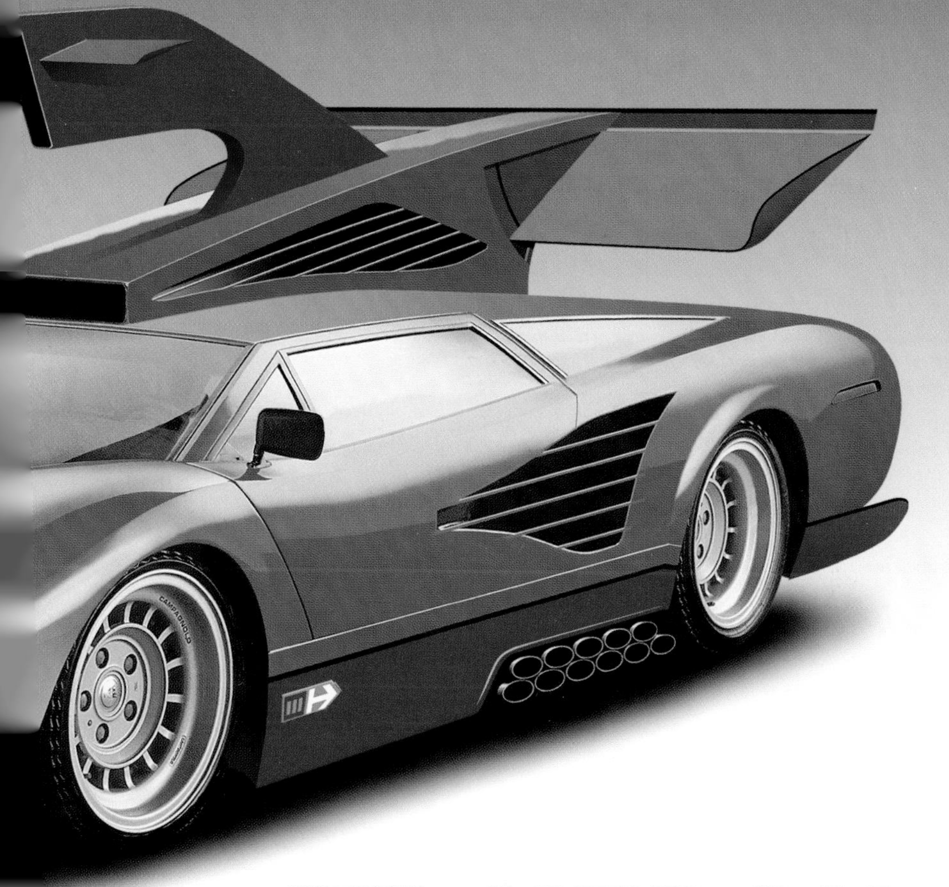

HEDON

BALLISTICA III

Motorcar Emporium • Miami, FL (pictured with optional GoldKast 22-inch wheels)

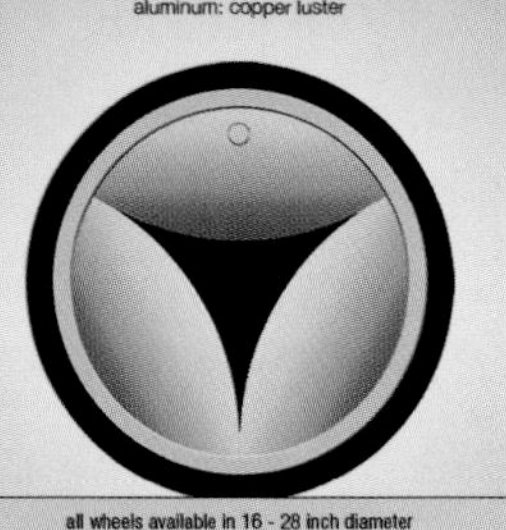

all wheels available in 16 - 28 inch diameter

DO YOU HAVE AN INCORRIGIBLE YOUNG RENEGADE, REBEL OR RUFFIAN AT HOME?

Lee & Carol Chapman's
Weekend Camp
for
Wayward Boys
we put the "man"
in "manic depressive"

TURN HIM INTO THE SORT OF PLEASANT, CHEERFUL, ENTERPRISING AND INDUSTRIOUS YOUNG LAD YOU ALWAYS KNEW HE COULD BE!

"Peter used to beat up all the other little children, but now he only spits and takes their lunch money!" M.G.
"Gordon's turned into a charming, model child thanks to Lee, Carol and his recommended medications." L.M.
"I don't wet the bed any more." T.Y.

LUCKY DUCK
RACING
Local hot-shoe racers
Paul and Sue Quackenbush
show how it's done.
May the force forever
be with you both.
M&M

Heritage
is
Everything
Parish Heacock
Classic Car INSURANCE
Toll Free 800.678.5173
instant quotes online
www.parishheacock.com

CLASSIC
IMPRESSIONS
Automotive Art

"If there is a heaven on earth, it's VIR..." - Paul Newman
VIR America's Motorsport Resort
VIRginia International Raceway 1245 Pine Tree Rd. • Alton, VA 24520 • 434.822.7700 • www.virclub.com

Daniel Thompson

GBC Asset Management, Inc.

ÄúCanada,
Äôs Leading Wealth
Management Team, Äù

website
www.gbc.ca

telephone
514•848•0716
800•667•0716

Featuring Spitfire, GT6, Herald, Vitesse and other Triumph-based Cars

MAGAZINE

Congratulations Burt on the release of Toly's Ghost

www.triumphspitfire.com
800-487-3333
Quarterly Publication
Now in our 5th year
Full color photos
Indepth History
Readers Photo Section
Autojumble & more...
Howard Baugues - Editor

illustration:
Roger Warrick

ALAN BOLTE´

THE VINTAGE VOICE OF SPEED
as heard with HMSA, VARA,
HSR WEST, from CA to W. Va.

ACCURATE, EXCITING, OFTEN FLAT OUT ENTERTAINING P.A. commentary,
The Bolte Group as seen on
Speed TV, TLC, Discovery

www.alanbolte.com

TECH RacinGraphics *Helmet Painting by Al Ribskis*

New Snell '05 Rating... A Fresh Paint Job For You?

Helmet Art by a Fellow Racer • 312.421.3855 • Aribskis@aol.com

SAAL'S

EXOTIC MOTORCAR EMPORIUM

MIAMI . FLORIDA

Tuner cars for the younger enthusiast

Se Habla Español

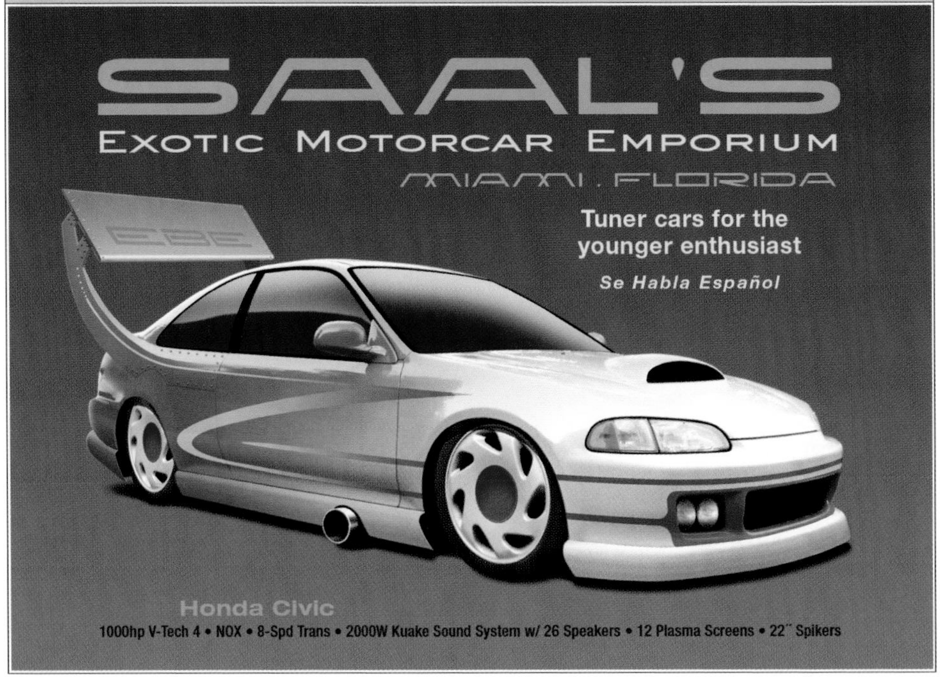

Honda Civic

1000hp V-Tech 4 • NOX • 8-Spd Trans • 2000W Kuake Sound System w/ 26 Speakers • 12 Plasma Screens • 22" Spikers

MASERATI

250F

T61
"Birdcage"

450S

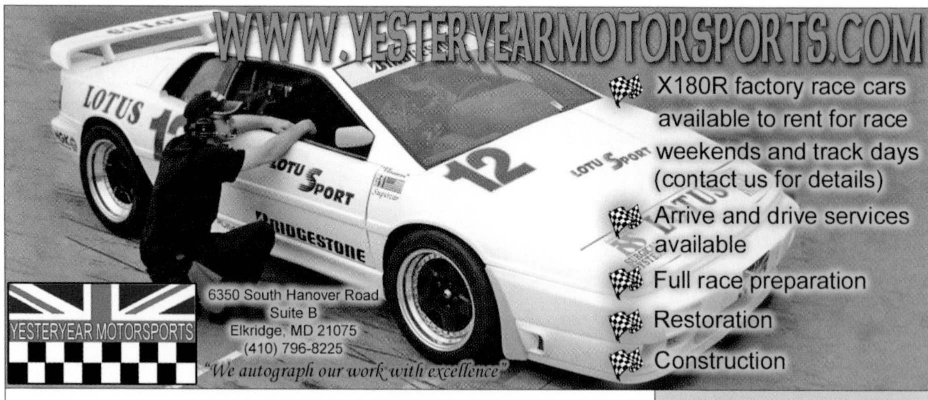
WWW.YESTERYEARMOTORSPORTS.COM
X180R factory race cars available to rent for race weekends and track days (contact us for details)
Arrive and drive services available
Full race preparation
Restoration
Construction
YESTERYEAR MOTORSPORTS
6350 South Hanover Road
Suite B
Elkridge, MD 21075
(410) 796-8225
"We autograph our work with excellence"

Fourth Gear Ltd.
Charlotte, NC
877-221-7837
Custom Embroidery & Screen Printing
www.fourth-gear-ltd.com

Specializing in Exotic, Classic, & Sports Cars of all types.
One of a kind creations or high volume production. For you, your club, our events of all kinds.
When you need something special in wearable graphics think of Fourth Gear first.

The world's best cigars!
SAAL'S
ANNEX
FIREARMS & TOBACCO
MIAMI, FLORIDA

COMMERCIAL TRANSPORTATION SPECIALISTS
Northwest Indiana's
#1 SPRINTER SUPERSTORE!
Dodge BusinessLink
PLUS... Full Line of Hard to Find Chrysler, Dodge, Jeep and SRT Models!
GENERATION GRIEGERS
CHRYSLER DODGE Jeep
~ Ask for Rich Redar ~
U.S. 30 • VALPARAISO, IN • 888-462-4117

Vintage Racing at Its Best!
Whether it's on the old street course at Watkins Glen or the rolling hills of Road America, SVRA is there. The finest and most varied venues in vintage racing is what SVRA is all about. There are classes for all of types of vintage racers from small cc production cars to the most powerful formula cars. Join SVRA in 2006 for the Best in Vintage Racing!
Photos courtesy of R. Harrington Photography
Mike Stott UBS
Sprint Series Sponsor
MOTOR CHECK
Enduro Series Sponsor
stand21
Official Safety Equipment
Panoz Racing School
Official Driver School
Gulick Group
Race Event Sponsor
SVRA Sportscar Vintage Racing Association
Sportscar Vintage Racing Association • 257 DeKalb Industrial Way • Decatur, GA 30030
(404) 298-3323 • FAX (404) 298-3325 • www.svra.com • email: svra@svra.com
©2006 SVRA

FOR SALE: 1957 Triumph TR3 roller (only rolled once, however). Carefully mismatched swaybars (plows like crazy until the rear end snaps impossibly loose). Competition springs & shocks, full belly pan for both car and driver, wets & drys, lots of broken parts (I mean, "spares"), some dubiously legal vintage equipment. Some rust & dents (or is that "some rusted dents?"). Super-trick, highly experimental Mellow Motors-prepared 16:1 short stroke TR4 engine that will rev to 9000rpm (once). Needs housebreaking. $8995 w/out engine, $8500 with.
Call (703) 451-9000 and ask for "Moe" or "Willie"

WANTED: 1951 Sturgeo, KMT Series. Finest Italian/Presbyterian hybrid. Last seen cruising Chicago's North Shore in a 1974 BMW 2002 Tii. Call Alex Rorke (847) 217-5565

FOR SALE: Hedon Balistica III • Every factory option + special order Neutron Pink • Delivery miles only • $4.5m • 305.992.0003

FOR SALE: Laura Bethenia Halls offers one "New Age Torus." Yes folks, this donut-shaped 1,2,3,4 or 5 wheeler (depending on your mood at any specific time) is powered by the revolutionary and totally mystical (we don't even know how it works) "Merlin Epiphany Alternative Fuel" power unit. This machine uses no fuel other than the power of suggestion and the will to move in direct opposition to any and all known planes within the universe. Speed of light plus, is guaranteed and the entire vehicle is also guaranteed against corrosion for, well, the life of the universe as "we" understand it. Of course our disclaimer applies…"your mileage, well as your ability to actually perceive this vehicle, may, in fact will, vary in accordance with your state of mind and yet to be understood, unified theory of the cosmos. Price: Your sanity, your health… or one cold can or bottle of our favorite gutwash. Vehicle might, or might not, be viewed at our pleasure and a suitably dark location.

Will, just as cool as 1965.
Thanks for passing your love of cars on to me. *DJT*

Those who can't do… *TEACH*
Mike "yet another" Langenfeld shows a typical Driving School student how to put a tall, longitudinal crease in the passenger seat upholstery.

WANTED: Second childhood. Must be housebroken, in reasonable condition & good with wife and children. Price negotiable, but occasional race weekend "family vacations" and undying love & thanks will surely be involved.

Rally Engineering thanks all who have made performance rally possible. All are bound in a family thru love of sport. The sport has evolved but the spirit remains the same.
Rally On! Richard and Juanita Miller, Sachse, Texas

WANTED: Sales personnel for Miami's most prestigious exotic car dealer. Criminal record? No problem. Contact Lenny at SAAL's

Now Open
INDOOR EXOTIC CAR GALLERY
Continental AutoSports
Ferrari • Maserati
888.455.0228
420 E. Ogden Avenue • Hinsdale, IL
Factory Authorized Dealer Since 1975
ContinentalAutoSports.com

CONTINENTAL AUDI of NAPERVILLE
1527 Aurora Ave • Naperville, IL 60540
630.388.1000 • ContinentalAudi.com

CONTINENTAL ACURA of NAPERVILLE
RSX
MDX
NSX
TSX
TL
RL
2275 Aurora Ave • Naperville, IL 60540
630.960.2100 • ContinentalAcura.com

Chapter 24: Two Yanks in England

Turns out two of the other visitors at Ernesto Julio's big party near Pebble Beach were that pair of fun loving, stinking rich and ever-so-slightly stuck-up young California racers Hank and Cal met with the lightweight 300SL the weekend James Dean got himself killed on his way to Salinas. Lance Reventlow and Bruce Kessler, remember? Cal wound up sitting around the pool with those two long after most of the party-goers had either left, gone up to one of the many bedrooms upstairs or passed out either face-down in the bushes, sprawled out on one of the lawn chairs or with their heads deep inside the polished porcelain commodes of one of the seven or eight available bathrooms. It's probably not such a great idea to stay up all night the night before a race (unless you're a mechanic slaving away underneath the damn car, anyway!), but I guess Cal was feeling pretty blue and not much like just lying in bed trying to fight his way to sleep. Besides, he'd already been to bed once that night. No, it was better to find somebody to talk cars and racing with and just while away those strange, still, whispery hours before the sky starts getting light. You get to know people at times like that. As if you're all part of some special brotherhood of the wee hours, you know?

Turns out Lance Reventlow and Bruce Kessler first met up at some lah-de-dah private prep school in Arizona for wealthy kids who had asthma, and they became best buddies as soon as they realized they were both absolutely nuts about cars. Lance had a Jaguar sedan to drive around in and Bruce had a hopped-up Oldsmobile, and Lance Reventlow knew more about cars than anyone Bruce had ever met. And they were both stinking rich. Bruce's family ran a highly successful swimsuit company and Lance Reventlow's mother was the original, oft-divorced "poor little rich girl" Barbara Hutton, who was heiress to the whole blessed Woolworth five-and-dime fortune and the subject of more press ink and innuendo than anyone this side of a hot new Hollywood starlet. All of which made Lance—at least according to the newspapers—"the world's richest baby" the very day he was born. His father was this courtly Danish count named Kurt von Haugwitz-Reventlow (who had blonde hair, blue eyes, a ramrod-stiff backbone and all sorts of highly Germanic blue blood pumping through his veins) and he was already her second husband following this apparently charming but boozy Russian prince she married at the age of 20—against her father's wishes—and whose vast family estate back in Russia turned out to be mostly a pig farm. But Barbara Hutton didn't need much of anything in the way of extra assets seeing as how her mother committed suicide when Barbara was only five (think about that for a moment) and left her sole heir to one of the biggest private fortunes in North America. Central and South America, too. Which naturally made her a target for every suave schemer, angle-shooter, international playboy, lounge lizard, greaseball gigolo and con man hanger-on in the hallowed halls of high society. And believe me, there are plenty of those rat-bastards around!

Using her money, Count von Reventlow bought them the biggest, stateliest, most elegant house in all of England (and I'm including the Royal Family here) and that's where world's-richest-baby Lance was born in 1936. Giving birth just about killed his mother, and afterwards the doctors told her she could never have any more kids. That got her very depressed indeed, and thanks to the tabloids—particularly those Fleet Street hatchet rags over in England—she gained a growing reputation for being beautiful, strange, sad, nutty, vulnerable, drink- and drug-prone, unstable, unpredictable and capricious as well as filthy rich. And she gave them plenty to write about by doing stuff like telling them all—very loudly—that she would never marry again the day her divorce from the Russian pig farmer prince was finally finalized and then marrying old Count von Reventlow the very next day….

So Lance had kind of a tough, lonely childhood in spite of all the money and privilege, what with his folks either gone or at each others' throats most of the time and then becoming the central character in a vicious and terrifically well-publicized custody battle when Barbara Hutton and this Danish count finally separated a few years later. She eventually came back to the states, bought yet another palatial home in Beverly Hills and started palling around with famous and almost unspeakably handsome, gracious, suave and debonair Hollywood leading man Cary Grant. Of course he was English and his real name was Archie Leach, and there were rumors floating around that he actually took up with her to do a little investigating on behalf of British Intelligence, seeing as how it was the middle rounds of World War II and Barbara had been awfully chummy with some of the old-line German military aristocracy thanks to her marriage to Lance's father (and that bunch were all wearing swastika lapel pins at the time even if they thought Adolf Hitler was a rabble-rousing, low-life madman). She even had to bribe some higher-ups in the wartime, Nazi-influenced government in Denmark to get her divorce from Count von Reventlow finalized so she could marry Cary Grant in July of 1942. Although the marriage only lasted a few years, he was the closest thing to a real father Lance ever had.

Anyhow, Lance met Bruce at this Arizona prep school for super-rich asthmatics while his mother was off getting married or getting divorced or doing the required lawyering and courting in between, and the two of them really hit it off. Bruce was kind of a cocky, adventurous, wiseass type, and naturally he was the first to want to go racing—even though he was seriously underage—and started out in an XK120 at the age of 16. Lance tagged along and more or less caught the bug from him. They both wound up hanging around L.A. after school was over, and Lance just about lived at Bruce's folks' house in Beverly Hills, which was always a lot warmer and homier inside than his own. Anyhow, they got that 300SL (or, more accurately, two different 300SLs) and started going to the races together, and that's about when Cal and Hank met them for the first time at the race in Salinas. If you remember, Cal talked Ernesto into letting him race the new 300SL he and Hank had driven up from L.A. just to give this young Reventlow kid something to think about, and Cal pretty much cleaned Lance's clock in spite of the fact that Lance had one of the rare, alloy-bodied factory lightweights.

After the race they got to talking, and Cal and Hank both suggested Lance might want to try something a little lighter, handier and easier to manage than a 300SL, and damn if Lance and his buddy Bruce didn't show up with a pair of brand-new, rear-engined Coopers a few races later at Paramount Ranch. They'd bought them off a pretty well-known local guy named Warren Olsen, who'd wrenched on cars for John von Neumann and some of the other West Coast heavy hitters before opening his own prep shop in West Hollywood in 1952. He managed to become the West Coast Cooper distributor by finding homes for a few cars, and happily sold Lance one of the 1100cc bobtail sports/racers with a Coventry Climax engine in back and put Bruce behind the wheel of a brand new Formula III open-wheeler. Warren also prepped the cars and looked after them at the racetrack, and no question he was an ace wrench and also exactly the sort of steadying influence you need to bring a couple rich and privileged but raw, green and wet-behind-the-ears know-nothings along.

To be honest, Cal and Hank never thought all that much of Lance Reventlow as a racing driver. Oh, he did manage to win a handful of races—or at least win his class in a handful of races—in the Cooper Warren Olsen sold him and took care of for him. But they were all minor-league amateur races, and the competition in the 1100cc class was never exactly what you could call stiff. In fact sometimes, it was damn near nonexistent. Nonetheless, he sure looked the part of a hero driver—young, slim, smooth-cheeked and handsome with a perfect, razor-cut sweep of California blonde hair across his forehead—and he always seemed to have lots of beautiful young girls hanging around. Hollywood starlets, mostly. Including a particularly lovely, bright and intelligent number named Jill St. John, who became sort of his main squeeze and proved to be a lot more than just another pretty face. She understood that Lance had a deep, dark hole inside he desperately needed to fill and a serious streak a mile wide. He wanted—hell, he *needed*—to do well at something money *couldn't* buy! Naturally most people couldn't get past the obvious Rich Playboy image, but Lance read and studied and researched and committed to memory everything he could find that had anything whatsoever to do with racing, racecars, driving techniques, chassis design, suspension geometry and engine tuning. Oh, he wasn't much of a natural behind the wheel—not hardly—but he was as focused and determined as anybody you'd ever care to meet. Maybe even moreso, since he had something to prove.

His buddy Bruce Kessler was just the opposite. Bruce was a big, husky kid and sure didn't *look* like a damn racing driver. And he sure as hell didn't know or care much of anything about mechanics. But he was one hell of a natural talent. Oh, he was maybe a little too fearless for his own good (or reckless, take your pick), but Bruce could feel what the damn car was doing and knew instinctively what he needed to do with it. You have to understand that you can't *make* a racecar do things. No, you have to let it tell you what it'll let you get away with through the seat of your pants, and then hope you've got the feel, touch, grace, guts, presence of mind and sympathy to take it there. And Bruce Kessler could do that with maddening ease—right out of the damn box!—while his far more knowledgeable pal Lance had to think about it and work at it and chip away at it like racing was a solid block of granite.

But they both loved it terribly. Like Cal and Tommy Edwards and Phil Walters and John Fitch and Creighton Pendleton the Third and Walt Hansgen and Carroll Shelby and Phil Hill and even Juan Manuel Fangio, Mike Hawthorn and Stirling Moss, they got sucked into it and couldn't get out. Didn't *want* to get out. Sure, it was frivolous and dangerous, but it was just so much *better*—more real and immediate and noble and desperate and hilarious and humiliating and rewarding—than ordinary, everyday life. It was also horrendously expensive. But a guy like Lance Reventlow had the resources to take it as far as he wanted to go. And young Lance decided he wanted to go right to the top. But not as just another promising young hotshoe with a chip on his shoulder and a glint in his eye. No, he had something a bit bigger and more ambitious in mind. See, everybody saw him as this rich, stuck-up, over-privileged, arrogant, ne'er-do-well young know-nothing jerk of a playboy as far back as he could remember, and Lance wanted desperately to turn that around. He wanted to do well at something challenging and difficult and important—something other people would just *have* to respect. It seemed to Cal and Hank that the thing this young Lance Reventlow wanted—more than anything else in the world—was to be taken seriously. And he was willing to do whatever it took to make that happen.

To do that in the world of motor sports, you pretty much had to go race overseas. Everybody agreed that the *real* road racing scene was over in Europe—and particularly in England—and the thing you have to understand is that there was a lot more racing over there than just the big, international Grand Prix races and the World Manufacturers' Championship rounds for sports cars. There were races all over the map every blessed weekend—and especially in England and Italy, where motor sports was nothing less than a national passion—and even big, marquee names like Stirling Moss and Jean Behra and Luigi Musso and Tony Brooks and Mike Hawthorn and Peter Collins and Toly Wolfgang could be found taking on all comers in non-championship Formula One races and second-tier Formula Two races and important national sportscar and *formula libre* races every weekend their schedules permitted. Made for some unbelievably stiff competition and the best place in the world to make a name for yourself if that's what you were really after. If you had the goods, of course. Which is precisely why Lance Reventlow and Bruce Kessler decided to campaign a couple cars over in Europe during the 1957 season, and brought Warren Olsen along with them to look after their cars. They didn't exactly set the world on its ear, but they learned an awful lot. Bruce had a couple good races that raised more than a few eyebrows, while Lance soaked it all up like a blessed sponge....

To tell the truth, I didn't really know all that much about the racing scene over in England. But my great English pal Tommy Edwards brought me up to date the late November morning he came wheeling into our VW dealership—right out of the blue!—in this glistening metallic-burgundy Aston Martin D.B. 2-4 Mk. III coupe. What a car! It reminded you of nothing so much as one of those gleaming old knights-of-the-round-table suits of armor you see propped up in the stairwell corners of art museums. Ferraris and Maseratis had always looked hot and snarly to me, but that Aston Martin was pure British cool. The dashboard in front of the driver was paneled in rich burl walnut like an English men's club, and the seats reeked of soft, hand-sewn glove leather. Nobody in recorded history has ever done that sort of stuff as well as the Brits.

"Tally ho, Sport!" Tommy grinned from behind the wheel.

"Tally ho yourself," I grinned right back at him. "You're a sight for sore eyes."

"And a sorry sight at that," he winked back at me. I hadn't seen Tommy since Sebring, but I knew from the magazines and Hank's letters that he was working and driving now and then for Aston Martin over in England. Turns out he was over here in the states showing this handsome burgundy number around at all the east coast sportycar dealerships before delivering it to Vic Franzese, the longtime racer/innkeeper/enthusiast who owned and ran the Glen Motor Inn just north of Watkins Glen on Route 14.

Tommy's eyes made a quick sweep around the shop. "I see you're doing rather well for yourself."

I felt the color rising on my cheeks. "Aw, we've just been lucky, I guess."

"Nothing of the kind," he corrected me. "Nothing of the kind. I'm something of an expert on the subject of luck, and let me let you in on a little secret: *it doesn't exist!"* He opened the door, clambered out and put his arm around my shoulder. "Except the bad variety, of course," he added in a just-between-you-and-me whisper. "Bad luck is the shit we all step in and the hornets' nests we all stick our noses inside. Can't be helped." He backed away and gave the place another once-over. "But the rest comes down to one's nature and character and sustained effort over time." He looked at me for a second like he was really, really proud of me. "The cream rises to the top, Sport," he assured me. "The cream rises to the top."

Boy, my face felt like it was on fire.

Tommy glanced at a brick-red VW Beetle waiting for an oil change and pulled in close again. *"You know,"* he whispered softly, like somebody might be listening, *"these bloody things are made out of old buzz bomb parts."*

"NO THEY'RE NOT!" Big Ed's voice boomed from behind us. Tommy spun around and found himself face-to-face with the business end of Big Ed's cigar. "Believe me," Big Ed continued with a big, broad smile surrounding his stogie, "these things are made out of solid gold!"

For a minute I thought they were going to grab each other like a couple of silly girls, but then Tommy sort of awkwardly stuck his hand out and Big Ed shook it until it damn near came loose at the shoulder joint. "Damn good to see you, Ed," Tommy told him, "damn good to see you."

"It's good to be seen," Big Ed agreed. And then his eyes wandered over to the burgundy Aston Martin. No question it put That Look in Big Ed's eyes. Aston's D.B. 2-4 struck you like a Jaguar's upper-crust cousin, and you know how Big Ed always felt about Jags. I think he would've written Tommy a check for that car right then and there (even though it was already promised), only we could both see as how Big Ed might have a little trouble fitting inside. The Aston's "2-4" designation referred to the supposed seating capacity, what with the usual, luxurious hero driver/terrified passenger accommodations up front and these fold-down rear seats suitable for legless elves and pixie amputees just behind. But those so-called "rear seats" had beautifully contoured individual rump bolsters, and I couldn't help imagining that, if you took the front seats out entirely, a guy Big Ed's size could actually get one cheek down in each. Of course, there'd be no space left to put the rest of him, but that wasn't really the point.

"So what brings you to America?" I finally asked.

Tommy looked down at the leather key fob in his hand. "I'm embarrassed to say I've been reduced to the capacity of car salesman and delivery boy in the off-season."

"You're over here selling cars?"

"More like selling cars to people who sell cars. I'm delivering this particular one from the factory on behalf of the American distributor, but John Wyer's on his way over—you remember old "Death Ray" from Sebring, don't you?"

"Sure I do."

"Well, I'm picking him up at the airport this evening, and we're going to see what we can do about opening up a few more dealerships here in the states. You can't very well sell cars without dealers."

"You thinking about us?" Big Ed asked. He still had The Look, so he wasn't thinking very clearly.

Tommy's eyes took in the sheep herd of Volkswagens filling the shop from wall to wall. "To be honest, this is more of a social call. Just wanted to see my old master wrench spinner/sometime traveling companion Buddy here. And you, too, of course, Ed. And you, too."

Big Ed looked at the Aston again. "How much does one of these babies sell for?"

"You'd get a bit of pocket change back from seven thousand dollars," Tommy allowed, "but not very much."

I let out a low whistle. It wasn't exactly Ferrari/Maserati/Mercedes 300SL money, but it was well clear of Jaguar's new XK150 or a Corvette. "That's a pretty large wad of cash," I observed.

"It's a lot of car, Buddy. King of the three-liters as far as I'm concerned. And how can you put a price on exclusivity?"

"You're sounding an awful lot like a car salesman these days," I laughed, and Tommy laughed right along with me.

"Be sure you tell that to old Death Ray when you see him. And write a letter to Mr. Brown back in England if you have a moment."

I knew "Mr. Brown" was actually David Brown, the successful English industrialist and gear-maker who bought Aston Martin and brought it back from the brink of bankruptcy. His initials were the "D.B." designation on all the subsequent Aston models, and he'd really turned them into impressive and desirable *Grand Turismos* and put some real sting and purpose into Aston's factory racing efforts. But they were built to a very select taste and bank balance, and none of us could see them selling side-by-side with a bunch of Volkswagens.

"We're thinking of opening up another store," Big Ed said hopefully.

"Oh? Where?"

"We're not sure about that," I admitted.

"What lines are you planning to carry?"

"We're not exactly sure about that, either."

Tommy frowned slightly under his mustache. "Sounds more like a dream or a scheme than an actual plan…."

Big Ed's face brightened. "That's it exactly, Tommy" he grinned. "But trust me, it's gonna happen one of these days. It's gonna happen. And sooner rather than later."

"Well," Tommy said diplomatically, "you be sure and let us know when things firm up a bit. I'd love nothing better than to have the two of you on the team…" his eyes circled around the shop again, "…but it does have to be the right sort of fit. You're not going to move many bloody customers up from a VW Beetle to an Aston Martin Mark Three, now are you?"

It wasn't the sort of question anybody had to answer.

We took an early lunch at the sandwich shop across the street, and Tommy filled us in on what he was doing and what had been going on with the racing scene over in England. "Well, we've got Carroll Shelby and Roy Salvadori, of course, and I'm sort of the steady, fifth-wheel driver for Aston at the big endurance races these days—the bloke who's supposed to bring the bloody second car home no matter what—and I do a lot of test driving on all the new tweaks in between." He looked me in the eyes. "You'd be proud of how bloody technical I've become."

"I was always proud of you."

"Even when I didn't know anything?"

"Especially when you didn't know anything. It gave me something over you."

He put his hand on my arm. "Trust me, Buddy, you've still got something over me. I reckon you always will."

I felt myself blushing again, and naturally that's when the waitress came to take our orders. Which naturally made me blush even redder.

"So," I asked after she left, "you said you do a lot of testing?"

"Well, that's John Wyer's way, isn't it? The bloody Italians—Ferrari especially—why, they're forever coming out with entirely new models, aren't they? Sometimes several completely different cars in a single season. But old Death Ray likes to work and whittle away at something until he thinks he has it at least half-right. And I think our new DBR1 is going to be one hell of a contender over the next several years. We already had our first big international win at the Nurburgring earlier this summer—plus another win in a non-championship round at Spa—and it looks like we'll have bloody Stirling Moss as well now that Maserati's folded up their tent."

That was some hot news indeed!

"Of course, I'll be a bit in the background on the international scene."

"You're the one who has to bring the car home," I parroted back at him, and he gave me a resigned sort of nod.

"But there's a brighter side," he continued. "Someone's got to carry the flag at home when the big guns are off gallivanting around the world doing bloody grand prix races and the like."

"And that's you?"

"Until old 'Death Ray' finds someone he likes better," Tommy said with a mischievous twinkle in his eye.

"And it's been going well?" I asked.

A pale cloud passed over Tommy's face. "Well, you have to understand how things are, Sport. The big endurance races like Sebring and Le Mans are all about bloody strategy and planning and running at a carefully measured pace…"

"Especially for the guy who has to bring the car home, right?"

"Right," Tommy nodded. "Especially for the bloke who has to bring the car home."

"But the English races are different?"

Tommy rolled his eyes. "God, yes. They're flat-out sprints, mostly. No pit stops. No strategy. Just go like hell and hope it all stays together."

"Sounds a lot like the SCMA club races over here."

"And it is. But they're real money races and a lot more bloody hell serious. They draw big crowds in England, and the car manufacturers and the fuel and oil and tire and sparkplug companies are all eager to be involved because of it. You don't have anything like it yet here in the states."

The waitress brought our soup.

"So," I asked, blowing the steam off my spoonful of chicken noodle, "how've you been doing?"

The cloud passed over Tommy's face again. "Pretty well, actually—if it wasn't for this one car and this one bloke who drives it."

"Oh? Who's that?"

"You ever hear of Brian Lister or Archie Scott-Brown?"

Both names rang a little bit of a bell, but I couldn't exactly place them. So Tommy filled me in on the details. And he seemed a little uncomfortable with the whole thing as the story came out. "Well, I suppose it all starts with Brian Lister. Brian's a keen young chap, and his father runs a very successful general engineering firm in Cambridge. Damn good business and a damn fine shop—or at least so I'm told. At any rate, Brian got bitten by the bloody racing bug like the rest of us. Got himself a Morgan first and wound up stripping it down to run hillclimbs and the like. Then he bought himself a Cooper-MG, and that went a bit better. After that he had John Tojeiro build him this absolutely marvelous J.A.P. motorcycle-engined monstrosity he called the 'Asteroid.' Lived up to its bloody name, too." Tommy allowed himself half a smile. "Plummeted to earth almost as many times as it ran."

He carefully eased his eyes over Big Ed's way. "But as things turned out, Brian was never all that fast or successful as a racing driver. Didn't seem to have the natural gift for it, whatever that may be. But he surely loved the cars and very much enjoyed being involved." Tommy drew in a deep breath and then let it out as a long, sad-sounding sigh. "And then Brian Lister met this quirky little Scotsman named Archie Scott-Brown." He looked us both in the eyes. "You have never met anyone in your life like Archie Scott-Brown."

"How so?" I wanted to know.

Tommy searched for words. "Well, to begin with, he was born with no proper right hand and with his legs and feet so badly deformed that the doctors had to break both legs and re-set them when he was a baby. Damn near had to cut his feet clear off and turn them right way 'round to give him any chance of walking as he grew up. Spent a terribly large portion of his childhood in plaster casts and surgical boots."

"That's sad," Big Ed said softly, shaking his head.

"And now he's racing *cars?"* I asked incredulously.

Tommy nodded, his eyes mirroring my amazement. "Old Archie wasn't the sort of bloke to let such inconveniences hold him back. His father built him a little gas-powered buggy when he was small, and Archie spent most of his time seeing how bloody fast he could make it go. Rumor has it he wrapped the bloody thing around the gateposts of their house at least once!"

Big Ed and me looked at each other in disbelief.

"Archie did his national service with the RAF"—Tommy got that same, faraway look in his eye that came over Butch whenever he talked about his beloved Marines—"but of course they never let him fly. His father had been a flier in World War I—a gunner/navigator, not a pilot—and that must have rankled him. But they couldn't keep him out of cars, and so little one-handed, funny-legged Archie Scott-Brown bought himself an MG TD he called "Emma" and decided to give racing a go. Of course there were all sorts of difficulties getting his license approved because of his apparent disabilities, but Archie wasn't having any of it and fought his way through. He started racing in "Emma," and pretty soon she was losing all of her skirts and petticoats as Archie stripped her down and pulled her fenders back to make her lighter and faster."

"Was he any good?"

Tommy's eyes went as wide as I'd ever seen them. "My God, was he *ever!"* he exclaimed breathlessly. "I'd have to rank him as a genuine bloody phenomenon. Like Stirling Moss, almost."

"You're joking. A guy with bad legs and one hand?"

Tommy shook his head. "Would that I were. Because it seems Archie and 'Emma' caught Brian Lister's eye at some club event at Bottisham aerodrome, and Brian offered him the 'Asteroid' to drive. Well, Archie went like bloody hell in it, and on that very day the die was cast: Brian Lister would provide the bloody cars and Archie Scott-Brown would drive the bloody wheels off of them."

The waitress came around with our sandwiches.

"Of course, that was back in 1951," Tommy continued after his first bite of liverwurst, "and nobody knew at the time how things would evolve or what that simple partnership would turn into. Fast as the 'Asteroid' was in its class, it was a freakishly unreliable thing. And now that he had a real ace of a driver behind the wheel, Brian Lister felt compelled to supply him a better piece of kit."

"I've heard of Lister racecars," I offered to keep him going.

Tommy nodded, chewing another bite of his sandwich. "Brian's father Horace Lister wasn't all that sold on motor racing—although I'm sure he was relieved that someone else was doing the actual driving—but Brian was allowed to keep the 'Asteroid' at the family engineering shop and work on it there, and so it wasn't that long a step to start building cars from scratch."

I didn't want to interrupt or correct my friend Tommy, but I knew from my long and sometimes painful experience with the Trashwagon what an enormous step that really is. Although I guess having your own personal welding, metal fabricating and machine shop facilities under the same roof might make things a wee bit easier.

"Brian's first try was an MG-powered thing where the driver's shoulders were barely higher than the top of the tires, and Archie—plus Jack Sears, when there was some additional medical nonsense about Archie's license—went on a real bloody tear with it during the '54 season." A twinkle lit up in his eyes. "You should have seen that thing! It had these supposedly 'aerodynamic' cone-shaped covers over the headlight openings, and everybody thought they looked like a pair of tits."

Big Ed and me looked at each other like school kids about to giggle in class.

"But they knew they weren't going to get very far with an MG engine, so by July they'd finished a Bristol-engined car, and Archie ran right to the bloody front in that one, too. He beat Roy Salvadori in the Gilby Engineering Maserati at Snetterton, and then there was some more silliness about his license and so they put Stirling Moss in the car for Brands Hatch. The best Moss could do was second to Salvadori and the Gilby Maserati—right on his tail, but second place nonetheless—and that should give you some idea of the sort of bloody driver Archie Scott-Brown is."

"That's pretty damn impressive," I agreed.

"To be fair, that was September of '54 and before old Stirling got his factory ride with Mercedes-Benz alongside Fangio, won the bloody *Mille Miglia* and began turning into the current-edition, chiseled-from-marble Stirling Moss who rumor has it doesn't cast a shadow."

There was a hint of bitterness and envy in Tommy's voice that I didn't find very attractive. But that's the way it is in racing. If someone's quicker than you, it grinds at your insides. And if he's quicker than everybody, it grinds at your insides even more.

"So what happened then?" I asked as a way of steering Tommy back on the story.

"Oh, they hit a bit of a rough patch after that. Brian built Archie this Maserati-engined car that they thought would murder everybody in the 2.0-liter class and even give a lot of the big cars fits—and it surely looked it would on bloody paper—but they had nothing but problems with it. A few people even suggested Maserati supplied them a duff engine—and, as disorganized and desperate as Maserati was at the time, such a thing could have happened unintentionally as easily as intentionally." Tommy flashed us a sly, insider smile. "At least when you get something awful from *Signore* Ferrari, you know it was done on purpose and that old man Ferrari knows precisely what he's sent you…."

"I've got a friend out on the coast who could tell you all about that," Big Ed laughed.

"Well, tell him he's got more than a a few cousins in England and Europe, if that's any consolation."

"But what happened to the Lister-Maserati?" I wanted to know.

"Oh, Archie won a few races here and there. But the bloody engine let them down more often than not. They'd pretty much given it up as a bad try and were wondering what to do next when they found themselves caught squarely in the crosshairs of fate and kindly providence."

"What do you mean?"

Tommy tilted his head in my direction. "You know Jaguar retired their factory racing team at the end of the '56 season, don't you?"

"Of course I do. They sold the factory D-Types to people like Briggs Cunningham and that Ecurie Ecosse team from Scotland who won Le Mans this year. After all the faster Italian cars fell out, anyway. And they built a handful of those XKSS sportscars with the leftover parts until that factory fire shut them down."

"Very good," Tommy nodded, looking highly impressed. "And do you know what happened after that?"

I shook my head.

"Well, it went something like this. Jaguar had always been with British Petroleum as a fuel sponsor. Of course they never went so far as to run stickers on the bloody cars like the Americans at Indianapolis, but there were always big ads in the magazines and plenty of signs and banners at every the racetrack so you knew who was winning and what brand of fuel and oil they supposedly ran in their tanks."

I'd seen those ads in *Autosport,* and they were always full-pagers.

"Well, Jaguar's withdrawal left BP dangling in the breeze without any sort of frontline, big-bore sportscar threat in England. Ecurie Ecosse were with Esso and so were we over at Aston Martin. That had the field pretty much covered at the front of the pack."

"So what happened?"

"It seems some gentlemen from BP paid Brian Lister a visit at his place in Cambridge. By then old Horace Lister had seen Archie and the Listers race and win on television and heard all his chums asking him how the company racing team was doing, and so now he was much more pliable when it came to Brian's racecars. In any case, the gents from BP inquired about Brian possibly building something a wee bit bigger to hold an ex-works Jaguar engine. And then get the little Scotsman with the bushy mustache and funny walk who always kept his right hand in his pocket to drive it, of course." Tommy pushed himself back from the table. "And that's precisely what happened. And that's also the little bastard I've been chasing all over England all summer." He shook his head morosely. "And not catching very often, either."

"Wow."

So that's the British home-front racing scene rich young Americans Bruce Kessler and Lance Reventlow found themselves up-to-their-eyeballs in during the heart of the 1957 season. Lance was trying to run a 2.0-liter Maserati sportscar and a Formula II Cooper single-seater, but his entries were often refused because of his age and lack of experience, and it surely didn't help that his looks, name and family notoriety made him a target of behind-the-hand whispers wherever he went. It didn't help even more when Lance managed to flip his Maserati at Snetterton. He was thrown out but the car then landed on top of him, and it was amazing that Lance escaped with just a few cuts and bruises. Plus one hell of a big scare.

Between races, Lance and Bruce visited a lot of the top racecar factories all over Europe—Ferrari, Maserati, Lotus, Cooper, OSCA, and BRM—and Lance also managed to cadge training rides around the Nurburgring with no lesser talents than Stirling Moss, Jean Behra and even Juan Manuel Fangio. That had to be some *very* scary passenger-seat time, no matter how big the reputation of the gent behind the wheel. But no question the national racing meets in England were closer to what the SCMA and Cal Club had going on here in the states and, like Tommy said, the man and car to beat that summer of 1957 was plucky little Scot Archie Scott-Brown and the Lister-Jaguar. "Oh, he's nervous and jumpy as hell when he's waiting for a start," Tommy told us. "You should see him chewing gum while we're waiting on the grid. His jaws are like a set of bloody rocker arms jumping up and down. But when the flag flies, it somehow all melts into this wild, wonderfully smooth flow. There are times running behind him when I find myself damn near mesmerized by what he can do with a bloody racecar...."

But it's always impossible to sort out exactly where the car stops and the driver begins. Or vice-versa, come to that. And that's one of the great beauties and impenetrable mysteries of motor sports all wrapped into one. But whatever was making it happen, the Lister-Jaguar had established itself as the big sportscar to beat in England, and so Lance decided he had to pay a visit to Lister Engineering in Cambridge. It was just a nondescript industrial building surrounded by residential row houses, and Lance and Bruce were given a quick tour by Brian Lister himself. There were two cars being built at the time for private entrants—Brian wouldn't say who, as he figured that sort of information was nobody's business—and Lance spent a lot of time poring over the bare chassis while Brian explained the Lister philosophy.

"I'm not a genius structural engineer like Colin Chapman over at Lotus seems to think he is," Brian said, pointing to the chassis, "so I went with something simple and basic that a person like myself might understand: two bloody great tubes."

Lance stared at the frame from several different angles while Bruce's eyes wandered aimlessly around the shop.

"And I went with parallel, equal-length A-arms up front so you always know precisely where the roll center is—right at ground level—rather than wandering all over the place like it does on some other cars."

He showed Lance the DeDion rear suspension and the way they canted the Jaguar engine over a few degrees for a lower hood line and finally how they'd sculpted the bodywork down tight over the wheels and driveline to minimize the size of the hole it poked in the air. When they were all done with the tour and some meandering talk about prices and delivery dates and even the possibility of putting an American Chevy V-8 in a Lister chassis, Lance thanked Brian politely for his time and ushered Bruce outside. Once they were well clear of earshot, Lance turned to his friend and said: "That thing's a piece of antiquated junk."

"It is?" Bruce asked.

"It is," Lance nodded. "We can build a better car than that."

"Sure we can," Bruce agreed without really thinking about it. He was tired and bored and hungry for something decent to eat.

"You bet we can," Lance assured his friend one more time, his eyes flashing ominously. "You bet we can."

Chapter 25: Hank's Homecoming

By the time our grim, cold and rainy New Jersey winter rolled around, we were getting regular deliveries of our new, 1958-model VW Beetles in at the dealership. And while Ford had just about blown a gasket trumpeting their new Edsel line (which, like I said before, was basically the same old Ford stuff wrapped up in some new—and unintentionally amusing—sheetmetal), the serious-minded Krauts at Volkswagen made do with earth-shaking changes like a bigger, rectangular rear window that made the cramped rear seat feel a little less like a badger's burrow, a slightly larger windshield with re-positioned wiper-arm posts and longer wiper blades for better visibility, a re-arranged dashboard with a bigger glovebox and the optional radio (which Big Ed made sure all of our customers got whether they wanted a radio or not!) now centered smack-dab in the middle, right above the new slide-out, drawer-style metal ashtray that made the most godawful scraping noise you ever heard every time you pulled it out. VW also added a half-pound or so of new sound-deadening material to kill a little bit—a *very* little bit—of the Beetle's natural, inborn exhaust burble, cooling fan howl, gear whine, wind rush, vibrational buzz and echoing, kettledrum thrum. Wow. Not to mention an actual rubber pad instead of a round metal roller on the business end of the gas pedal and a slightly re-designed rear deck lid with an actual flat part for mounting license plates!

It wasn't what you could call soul-stirring stuff, but the folks at VW's ad agency knew exactly how to stick tongue in cheek and a fork in the side of all the big, overblown Detroit manufacturers at the same time, and we were rolling those new VeeDubs out the door damn near as fast as we could get them in. The new building was done over at *Alfredo's Foreign Car Service* ("Sorry, Alfredo's not here") and Big Ed and me had decided to hold off awhile on adding any new lines seeing as how Steve and J.R. had the place filled wall-to-wall with service and repair work and we were making more on a lot of the used MGs, Triumphs, Healeys and such we'd fix up and sell than we did on the new VWs. But fooling around with used British sportscars—and, more particularly, used British sportscar customers—was a lot more involved and time-consuming than keeping Volkswagens running and Volkswagen customers happy. There was a lot more hand-holding (and, okay, excuse-making) involved, and it was occurring to both Big Ed and me that these were more and more two completely separate businesses. We were even fooling around with the idea of moving *Alfredo's* to a new location, setting up a deal where Steve and J.R. and maybe even Sylvester could eventually buy us out and then spiffing up the new building with some carpet and draperies and oak desks and a partition and a potted plant or two and then putting Alfa Romeo and Aston Martin franchises on the showroom floor. And maybe even Lotus and A.C., too! What a dream dealership that would be!

"More like a nightmare," Big Ed said one night after closing when we were talking about it for maybe the umpty-umpth time. It was dark and quiet in the showroom and out in the shop, with just the dim security lights glowing. It made the VWs on the linoleum floor look like they were parked outside under streetlights.

"I thought that's what you wanted to do?" I asked Big Ed.

Big Ed sighed. I kept thinking how tired and worn out he looked.

"Sometimes what we want may not be good for us," he grumbled, looking out through the plate glass window with the big *"THE NEW 1958 VOLKSWAGEN MODELS ARE IN!"* sign on it. This sure didn't sound like Big Ed talking.

"You okay?" I asked him.

"I dunno," he said glumly. "I built up the scrap business and made a lot of money at it and then I got bored and sold it. And now you and me've built this place up and made a lot of money and…" he let his voice trail off.

"And?" I prodded.

Big Ed shrugged. "It's just the opposite of how it is with racecars, you know?"

"What do you mean?"

"The fun part is building the damn thing. Running it is a pain in the ass."

Boy, did I ever know what he was talking about!

But the money was incredible. I never dreamed I'd be taking home the kind of checks and bonuses and profit sharing I was pulling in as Big Ed's partner in Alfredo's and the VW store. The dirty little twist of it is that—no matter how much you make—you and your family will find some way to spend it. Or at least use it up. What with the kids and Julie's mother and all, we somehow decided we were a little cramped for space in that pretty white house with the yellow shutters we'd bought just a few years ago, and so I once again found myself out house hunting in an even nicer and more exclusive part of town. Not more than two tax brackets down the road from where Big Ed lived, in fact. But I discovered pretty quickly that going house hunting with Julie and her mother was both boring and hard on my tongue (on account of how I had to keep biting it all the time) and it was a constant amazement to me how women could go on and on about crown moldings and hardwood floors and the shape and ornamentation of a damn fireplace, staircase or even banister rail. And of course nothing was okay the way it was. That went without saying. Just listen:

"We could knock out the wall there and put in a bay window with a breakfast nook. It'd be darling once the garden came in."

"There's a-too many stairs."

"I love the pool, but we'd need to put a fence around it. I'd be afraid for the children. Or maybe we could fill it in and turn it into a patio."

"I'm a-no wanna live inna damn coach a-house."

"It's too bad the garage has to face the street like that…."

You get the idea.

But even though I hated the idea and effort and expense of moving again, I'd have to say I was pretty happy with my home life. Or as happy as any guy ever is, I guess. Julie had gotten a little dog for the kids—a feisty wire-haired Fox Terrier mix named "Millie"—and it was really nice the way she'd come running up to me and jump up and down and wrap her little paws around my leg like she was hugging me whenever I got home. She was always so terribly glad and excited to see me. Even better was the way she growled and snarled at Julie's mom every now and then—just to keep her on edge, you know?—and how it made the old bat walk around the house with her arms all pinched up against her sides like she was afraid Millie might jump up at any moment and nip one of her fingers off. And if you'd ever seen that little terrier mix jump and snap, you knew she could do it.

Generally dinner would be long over by the time I got home. The kids would be watching TV (or maybe, just maybe, doing homework if there was a test the next day), and the baby would either be bawling her eyes out or fast asleep. Julie'd look up from her magazine or the baby or her ironing and kind of grunt: *"So how was your day, Palumbo?"* and I'd give her a peck and say *"Fine"* and even if I was beat right to the core and still mulling over some shit from the shop or the dealership, it felt pretty damn fulfilling to look around and see what I'd been able to provide for my family. Or at least it did once every couple weeks when I actually took the time to think about it and give a little thanks to Whoever or Whatever unfathomable power had allowed all this to happen.

We'd see my folks for Sunday dinner every weekend—one week at their house, next week at ours—and once a month at least we'd get Carson and Sarah Jean and their swarm of kids in on it as well. To tell the truth, my old man wasn't doing all that good. He had trouble with his eyes and his lungs—I think all that chemical plant crap he'd been breathing for as far back as I could remember was finally catching up with him—and it was a little disheartening to see the biggest sonofabitch I'd ever known turn into just another sad, sick old man. I actually felt sorry for him. And that pissed him off no end, so maybe there's some kind of justice in the universe after all.

Of course my sister Mary Frances was always welcome at those dinners, but often as not she'd have something desperately more important going on across the Hudson in Greenwich Village. According to the people who write in those thin, highbrow magazines with too many words and no pictures, there was a whole new social and literary movement called "the beat generation" going on, and the pulsating heart of it could be found right smack-dab in the bottom of the deepest, darkest, blackest, bitterest, most caffeine-laden cup of espresso in your pick of the streetcorner coffee houses in Greenwich Village. I guess it all started with that Jack Kerouac and his terrifically successful novel, *On the Road.* I never read it myself, of course (like most car people, I just don't read novels), but Mary Frances thought it was terribly important and tried to explain it to me. To be honest, it sounded like it was mostly about wandering around aimlessly and trying to get laid. That seemed to go hand-in-hand with the stuff she kept spouting from that famous French philosopher guy Jean-Paul Sartre—the one with the big, thick glasses and terribly sad eyes—who kept going on and on about nothing and aimlessness and, whenever the mood struck in the midst of all that angst, isolation and desolation, also trying to get laid. Growing out of all that empty murk and mire you had a whole new generation of so-called "beat" poets, who were thankfully not nearly so wordy and generally wrote very thin books with very few pages and a lot of blank paper around the lines and phrases. Mary Frances gave me one about Coney Island written by a gent named Lawrence Ferlinghetti, and I was surprised to find that it wasn't really about Coney Island at all and that I had a hard time making heads or tails of what he was talking about. But I guess he left a lot to the imagination. And it turned out that another popular "beat" poet was none other than that short, pale, pudgy, scraggly-looking Allen Ginsberg guy we ran into at that New Year's Eve party in Greenwich Village the night Cal met Angelina Scalabrini for the very first time. On the one hand, I have to admit to being ever-so-slightly pleased that the "beats" seemed more interested in inward, spiritual things like Zen Buddhism and contemplating their own navels (or any other likely navels that might be hanging around) rather than politics. I'd gotten pretty damn steamed at Mary Frances for getting her picture in the damn paper when the IRS shut the *Daily Worker* down and even moreso when she actually seemed happy about the Russkies beating us into space. But I didn't much care for the concept of poetic aimlessness as a general philosophy of life or the smoking of funny cigarettes as a means to enlightenment. Fact is, I never quite understood if the "beat" in "beat generation" had to do with the jazz music they all listened to (as in "down-beat") or simple exhaustion, seeing as how that's what you can reasonably expect if you stay up smoking reefers and listening to jazz music until all hours of the morning.

Hank called from Idlewild airport early on a cold and blustery Wednesday afternoon—December 4th, as I recall—to tell me he was laid over for a couple hours between flights and that he wondered if we could maybe get together. It was great to hear from him, of course, and I told him to take a cab right over. But he hesitated on the other end and started making lame excuses about how he'd barely get here to Jersey and have to turn right around and head back again, and that's when I realized he was probably too broke to pay for the cab fare. They don't pay race correspondents all that much, and you tend to forget that kind of thing when your bank account has a nice, hefty balance in it all the time. "You stay right there," I told him. "I'll be out front in an hour and we'll go get a nice bowl of pasta for lunch."

"It's almost two in the afternoon," he protested.

"Then we'll have it for early dinner."

Naturally it took me twice as long as I estimated to extract my behind from behind my desk in the service department, and then I had to decide what car to take. Big Ed had his Chrysler 300 parked behind the sandwich shop across the street and I knew I could borrow that, and we had a really nice Jag sedan in stock over at *Alfredo's*. But then I thought about how busted Hank probably was and decided to take one of our run-of-the-mill Beetles. A used one, in fact.

I picked him up at Idlewild and we drove over to a little Italian restaurant I'd heard about not far from the airport. As you can imagine, we were the only people in the place at four in the afternoon. We sat by the front window, and it was the kind of cold, gray, windy day when the chill and damp cuts right through you. "Well," I asked him while we waited for the *minestrone,* "how does it feel to be back in the states?"

"Pretty shitty," Hank grinned. "But that's just because I'm here in shithole New York. I'll be fine once I'm back in California."

"You're a pleasant sort, aren't you?"

"I'm a writer. It's my job to talk ugly. Especially when I'm talking about ugly things."

"You like it better over in Europe?"

Hank's smile faded a little. "Parts of it are wonderful," he said slowly, picking his words, "but there's times already I feel like getting off the damn merry-go-round."

"That happens to everybody," I assured him.

"Yeah, I know it does. Even happens to the drivers. You can see it. The spark just kind of fades out." He looked at me like something was occurring to him for the very first time. "I think it's even happening to Fangio."

"You're joking."

Hank shook his head. "No. You can see it in his eyes. Besides, maybe it's time. He's won five World Championships, and nobody stays on top forever."

"Nobody?"

Hank shook his head.

"Then who's next in line?"

"Oh, it's gotta be Moss. Everybody says so. There's a few other guys who can match him for pure speed on any given day: Hawthorn, Brooks, Behra, maybe even Hill or Gregory..."

"Archie Scott-Brown?"

Hank looked at me quizzically. "How the hell do you know about Archie Scott-Brown?"

"I get around," I told him, twirling my fork around in my spaghetti.

He took a bite of meatball. "Well," he said, chewing and considering, "those guys are all very good. And so is that tough Australian bloke, Jack Brabham. You'll be hearing more about him. Although I can't see those Coopers ever having enough muscle to race heads-up against the Ferraris, Maseratis, Vanwalls and BRMs at the front of the pack."

"I thought Maserati was all washed up?"

Hank raised his shoulders a quarter-inch. "They said they were. But I hear Temple Buell wrote them one hell of a big check and they're building a special small, lightweight version of the 250F for Fangio to drive next season."

"Think it'll happen?"

"Oh, the car'll get built, all right. But you and I both know that's just the tip of the damn iceberg."

"Do I ever," I agreed. The way Hank was digging into his pasta, it looked like he hadn't had a decent meal in weeks. "So you're still happy over there?" I finally asked.

"Hey, I'm doing what I love," he said without much conviction. "How many people have a chance to say that?" He mopped a crusty slice of bread around in the bottom of his plate to sop up the last of his spaghetti sauce. "And how about you?" he asked. "How're things at home?"

So over coffee I told him about the dealership and the shop and the baby and the house hunting and the thinking about adding another line or two, and while I talked I saw his eyes kind of mist over. And that's the real irony of things, isn't it. Whether you're talking drivers or actresses or race correspondents or pop singers or car salesmen or dealership owners or grease monkey wrench-spinners or the guy who picks up trash or the lady who shushes you in the reading room of the local library, nobody is ever satisfied with what they've got. Ordinary people can't help but envy exceptional lives and exceptional people dream of leading ordinary lives.

That's just the way things are.

There was one more race on the endless California racing season schedule—a Cal Club event December 7th and 8th at Paramount Ranch up in the Santa Monica mountains, not far from Hollywood—and Hank arrived back home in Southern California in plenty of time to make it (at least if you consider a shit, a shower, a shave and maybe 40 minutes of shuteye plenty of time, anyway). There wasn't much of a turnout in the big-bore modified class seeing as how all the big, rich guns were off under the palm trees sipping potent rum drinks or tending to their hang-overs at the end of the Bahamas Speed Week in Nassau the same weekend. Hank would've been there, too, except that the editor pulled rank and went down to cover the Nassau races himself. Everybody knew it was one hell of a party and attracted a lot of the top European cars and drivers as well as the cream of the American crop. Which is probably why the editor decided to go down himself. Hey, rank has its privileges. But that was okay with Hank. He was really looking forward to seeing all his old California racing chums again at Paramount Ranch and enjoying a little bright, simple, wholesome, all-American amateur racing fun after all the steely-eyed seriousness and recurring tragedy of the European season. But instead he stumbled once again over the nasty, basic truth that car racing is indeed a danger-ous business, no matter how you try to dress it up in smiles and short pants.

Cal was once again wheeling Ernesto Julio's monster Maserati 450S at Paramount Ranch—there was no way Ernesto could get away for a week to do the Nassau races—and looking to notch up another easy race win against what looked to be pretty thin competition. And it made it even better that Gina was there, too. Even if she was more or less on Ernesto's arm and being introduced around to all these high-powered, behind-the-scenes movie mogul types that Ernesto and Brad Lackey had arranged for her to meet there. Gina had just finished another big, dumb, swords-and-horseback costume swashbuckler—this time about a plot to kid-nap some stumblebum Balkan king from a country about the size of a postage stamp and replace him with a sneaky, double-dealing imposter. Only the good guys (that would be the real king's deputy general, his bumbling French valet and the king's sister, the lovely, radiant Princess Aquianna) secretly kidnap *that* imposter and replace him with the real king's third cousin twice removed, who just happens to be a dashing young English antiquities professor (what else?) not to mention a dead ringer for the king. Right down to a birthmark on his butt cheek (although that turns out to be India ink). And all that happens before you're halfway through the first reel. Anyhow, Gina got the Princess Aquianna part (she naturally falls head over heels in love with the dashing young Englishman, even though anybody who ever read a copy of the *Hollywood Tattler* suspected the actor rather preferred boys), and it was a nice, juicy lead with plenty of screen time that was sure to raise her stock with the movie-going public. I know Julie and me went to see it when it finally came out several months later, and there was more than enough drama and swordplay to keep me awake. Although I always wondered: when the saber- or rapier-brandishing hero takes on eight, nine or twelve of the bad baron's henchmen (and you always know who the henchmen are because they all wear the same dull, drab outfits and none of them can fight worth a damn), what makes them all wait their blessed turn and take the leading man on one-at-a-time rather than just rushing him all at once? But I guess you have to be pretty dumb to take a job as one of the bad guy's henchmen, because you *know* what's going to happen to you in the end….

Anyhow, Gina—with Ernesto's help—was making the rounds of some of the top directors and studio bigwigs trying to find a part that called for a little more brains, depth and character than your average glamourpuss Hollywood heroine. To "complete her as an actress" was the way Brad Lackey put it. But, as far as I could see, it was just another case of not ever being satisfied with what you already have and always looking for something that will make your own mug shine a little brighter in the bathroom mirror every morning. People are just like that. And Cal knew enough to steer clear and give the whole process a wide berth. Plus he was still feeling a little guilty—even though he told himself over and over again that he had nothing to feel guilty about—on account of that missed connection with Gina at Ernesto's palatial house near Pebble Beach when he was up in the bedroom with the girl from Timing and Scoring who could stand a quarter on edge with her tongue.

The weather was sunny and bright that weekend at Paramount Ranch, and surely the sensation of the weekend was young California phenom Dan Gurney in Frank Arciero's 4.9 Ferrari. Hank had already marked him as a guy to watch at Riverside, and Cal was pretty disgusted when most of the stopwatches in the paddock had Gurney a tick faster than Cal after the first practice session on Saturday morning. But that became pretty academic as the day wore on. Ernesto's big 450S started overheating in qualifying, and Cal was sharp enough to smell it before it ever showed on the temp gauge. He eased off and brought it into the pits, and a quick check revealed a murky, frothy, chocolate malt-colored goop drooling off the end of the dipstick.

"Looks like either a cylinder liner or a head gasket," Ernesto's crew chief muttered ominously.

"What does that mean?" Ernesto wanted to know. Gina was standing right next to him, stealing a long look at Cal while Ernesto was busy worrying over the car.

"It probably means we're done. If it's a head gasket, I might be able to fix it. But we don't know if that watered-down oil has done any damage to the bottom end. And if it's a liner, well…."

Ernesto Julio didn't look very pleased.

"I can do a pressure test and maybe get a little better read on it, but my guess is we ought to pack it up before we do any more damage." He looked up at Ernesto from the engine compartment. "Want us to go back and get the Ferrari?"

Ernesto rubbed his chin. "Why don't you check this out a little more first?"

"You're the boss, Mr. Julio."

While the crew chief fiddled away at the big Maserati, Cal, Hank and Gina went over by the fence with Ernesto to watch the cars go by. And they weren't there for more than five minutes before a Corvette driven by a guy named Hugh Woods blew its clutch or flywheel heading into the fast, downhill braking zone into Turn One. Cal said you could hear the *BANG!* and see all the dust and shrapnel scattering out the bottom, and Lord only knows what was happening inside the cockpit once it started coming apart. The clutch and flywheel assembly sits right about even with the driver's lower legs and ankles in a Corvette, and when one of those things breaks apart, it shatters off in all directions like a damn hand grenade. The Corvette went all out of shape, shot straight off the road and hammered head-on into the end of the outside guardrail. It was a massive, ground-shaking impact, and the corner workers were scrambling over to see what they could do before the dust even settled. The session was immediately red-flagged and the rest of the cars brought in, but Hank said you could feel from the sudden, icy quiet and the chill in the air that Something Bad had happened.

Gina had never seen a serious racing accident before. "Is he all right?" she asked again and again. "It doesn't look like he's moving."

Cal didn't say anything.

Although it was only a few moments, it seemed to take forever for the ambulance to arrive and for the workers and the medical team to get the driver out and loaded onto a gurney. The white-clad workers made sure to stand like a rumpled white wall between the medics working frantically on the driver and the crowd of shocked onlookers on the fences. Hank ran down to the corner station to see if he could get any more information while the back door of the ambulance closed with a hollow *"clunk!"* and it pulled away, lights flashing. The driver hit the siren as he swung out of the paddock and onto the main highway, the accelerator pedal buried in the carpet. Cal and Gina looked at each other. Her face was white and her eyes were wide and terrified. Cal didn't even realize she was clutching his arm.

Hank returned from the corner with news only slightly better than the worst imaginable. "He's alive," Hank said encouragingly. But then his tone wavered. "They said he's awful bad, though. Critical condition, I think." He shook his head. There was nothing more to say.

It took quite a while to clean up the mess and gather up all the bent metal and broken shards of fiberglass. But eventually the last of it was swept away with push brooms, and less than an hour after the track went quiet the engines fired up again. Cal, Gina, Hank and Ernesto were still standing along the fence, faces like statues, too numb and shaken to move. The cars pulled out and droned around without grace or meaning—everything seemed disjointed and unreal—and then, without warning, it happened all over again. George Sherrerd's Jaguar got all out of shape right in front of them while braking hard into the downhill sweep at the end of the long front straightaway. The car squirmed this way and that, and then the tires caught traction and spit it into a long, sweeping spin. It would have been relatively harmless if it weren't for that same, insolent piece of guardrail. The Jag hit it full-force broadside—square in the driver's door!—and the car bent damn near double on impact. Hank said you knew before the echo of the thump even faded that the driver was dead....

Cal had one of the *Moto Italia* Alfa Spider demos with him that day—a gray one with dark red upholstery—and Hank had to hitch a ride back to town with Ernesto in the XKSS when both the Alfa and Gina LaScala turned up missing. Ernesto had a strange, vacant look on his face and didn't say much of anything the whole way back into Hollywood. "Where do you want to go?" he finally asked.

Hank was stuck on that one. He didn't want to ask to go back to Ernesto's apartment in case Cal and Gina and the missing Alfa Romeo were there, and he didn't feel right asking for a lift all the way down to his folks' house in Orange County.

"You can stay at my place in the hills if you want to," Ernesto said sullenly, and peeled off 101 on the Mulholland Drive exit.

"You sure it's okay?" Hank asked hesitantly.

Ernesto didn't answer.

But the driveway at the apartment was empty and no one answered the bell. Ernesto let Hank inside and offered him a key.

"Thanks. I already have one."

"Enjoy it while you can," Ernesto told him. "I doubt it'll work after Monday."

Then he turned to go.

"Aren't you going to stay here?" Hank asked.

Ernesto shook his head. "I've lost something," he told Hank in a strangely faraway voice, "and I have to go look for it." Then he climbed into the XKSS, fired it up and growled off into the night.

Hank didn't know exactly what to do with himself. He was terribly tired, but there was no way he could sleep. He glanced in one of the bedrooms, thought better of it, looked in the refrigerator and thought better of that, too, flipped the TV on and then quickly flipped it off again, and finally went out on the balcony to simply sit and look out over the city and wonder just where the hell he was in the universe. And that's where he was, gently dozing, more than four hours later when the little gray Alfa snarled into the driveway and Cal and Gina let themselves in. Hank didn't hear them at first, not the key clicking into the lock or the weary, quietly echoing pair of footsteps across the Italian stone flooring in the entranceway. Cal and Gina went into the open kitchen off the hallway, and that's when Hank eased out of his doze and became aware of them. He was hidden from view behind a curtain in the doorway to the balcony, but he could see them reflected in the glass paneling. And it was so quiet he could hear them, too.

"Do you want anything?" Cal asked.

Gina shrugged without saying anything. The silence was like an earful of cotton. "Nothing sounds good to me," she finally whispered. Her voice was hoarse from crying. "How about you?"

"I dunno," Cal said so softly Hank could hardly hear it. "Maybe a drink?"

"What kind of drink?"

"I dunno. Maybe scotch. Maybe brandy. Maybe nothing." He looked up at the clock over the black marble sink. It was four ayem. "Maybe we should have something. It'll help us sleep."

"Is that what we're going to do?" she asked matter-of-factly.

Cal shrugged again. They were both running on fumes. "Make it a rusty nail, I guess. That's…"

"I know what that is. Scotch and Drambuie. My family ran a restaurant with a bar in it, remember?"

"Not too sweet, okay. The bar's around the corner in…"

"I know where the bar is." She looked at him with no expression at all on her face. "I've been here before."

Gina put ice in two cocktail glasses and disappeared around the corner into the den, and meanwhile Cal leaned forward with both of his elbows on the counter and buried his head in his hands.

Outside on the balcony, Hank didn't know exactly what to do. He felt sneaky and ashamed about spying and eavesdropping on them, but it seemed like it would be even worse to just burst in and announce himself. No question that would destroy the fragile magic of the weary, sad and yet somehow hopeful tension between them.

Gina came back into the kitchen and handed Cal his drink. But when their hands touched, Hank could feel the surge of aligning polarities all the way out on the balcony. They looked into each others' eyes and in half a heartbeat whey were wrapped up together—arms and cheeks and shoulders and backs and eyelashes and lips and hair and even tears—burrowing into each other until in was impossible to tell where one of them ended and the other one began. Hank pulled further back behind the curtain and turned his eyes away, looking out over the gently twinkling silence of L.A. He heard the soft wail of a siren somewhere off in the distance. And behind him, even though he tried his best not to listen, he heard Cal and Gina….

It was 6:30 and a light rain was falling as dawn tried to struggle its way out from behind the mountains. Hank was curled up into a tight, shivering little ball on the patio chair out on Ernesto Julio's balcony. He was cold and damp and his teeth were chattering. He'd dozed a little on and off—not very much—and now the need to get inside and find someplace warm to sleep was becoming overpowering. Besides, he had to pee. So he eased out of the chair—the scrape of the wrought-iron legs on the concrete floor sounded like chalk screeching on a blackboard—and he hesitantly pulled the screen back, took off his shoes and eased himself inside. He was afraid the two of them would still be in the kitchen, sprawled out only God knows how, but he was relieved to find the kitchen and the den and the hallway empty as a hollow grave. The master bedroom door was shut, and he tiptoed past it on his way to the guest bathroom at the end of the hall. He really wanted to take a hot shower and go to sleep, but it seemed unthinkable to make any noise that might wake them up. So he peed carefully around the side of the bowl, didn't flush afterwards and undressed while he gently ran the hot water tap until the thin stream of water was steaming. He soaked the end of a washcloth in the hot water and did his best to silently, carefully sponge himself off. It didn't do much to take off the chill, so he wrapped himself up in one of the fluffy terrycloth guest bathrobes and headed for the far guest bedroom to try and get a little sleep. But before he got there, the door to the master bedroom opened and Cal's head eased out of it. He stared at Hank with half-open eyes. "G'morning," he whispered.

"G'morning yourself," Hank whispered back.

"You been here all night?"

Hank nodded. "I was asleep out on the balcony."

Cal's head swiveled towards the door to the balcony. "It's raining out there."

"I know."

Cal looked back at him. "How'd you get here?"

"Ernesto drove me."

Cal's eyes opened another eighth of an inch. "Oh? What time?"

"I guess I got here about 10:30 or so."

"So you were here when we got here?"

"I suppose I must've been. Like I said, I was asleep out on the balcony."

Cal's eyes slid open a little further. "Where'd Ernesto go?"

"I think he went looking for you."

Cal's eyes found the floor and stared at it. "Look," he finally sighed, "I'm going back to bed." The door closed behind him with a muffled click….

Ernesto's Julio's XKSS growled into the driveway again at a quarter after eight. He got out, walked over to the gray Alfa and stared inside. The red leather interior was still wet from the dew and the light, early rain. But it would dry out. He climbed the stairs to the front door of the apartment and fumbled for his key. But then he thought better of it and rang the bell. It sounded like a set of fine brass chimes. What seemed like at least a full minute later, he rang it again. Then there was some shuffling behind the door and it eased open. Cal was standing there in one of the guest bathrobes, and they stared at each other. "She in there?" Ernesto finally asked.

Cal nodded. "She's in the bathroom, I think."

Ernesto's eyes made a tour around the doorway. Then they looked back at Cal. "Where'd you two disappear to yesterday?"

Cal gave a hint of a shrug. "We just went for a drive. A long drive. First through the mountains and then along the seacoast and even out into the valley." He gave another tiny shrug. "We didn't say much of anything."

Ernesto stared at him some more and then gave a short, sharp sigh. "Well, I guess this is the end of it, then." His eyes locked hard into Cal's. "What you two do is your own damn business. I don't own either one of you. But I don't have to let it happen right under my nose." A tremble of anger was starting to rise in his voice. "And I sure as hell don't need it to happen in front of my friends and my movie people when I'm the one who brought them out specifically to meet Gina!" There was fire in his eyes now.

"I'm sorry," Cal mumbled. And he was. The idea was never to embarrass Ernesto Julio. Even though they both knew it would happen.

The fire melted out of Ernesto's gaze. Now he just looked sad. And every day of his age. "I want you out of here, " he said softly, like he was ordering dry toast.

Cal nodded.

"I don't want to be an asshole about it. You've got until Friday."

Cal nodded again.

"And bring the damn car back to the dealership. I want that done today."

"It's Sunday."

"Just leave it out front. Put the keys in the mail slot." He glared at Cal. "And leave the damn top and windows up, if that's not too much trouble."

Cal looked down at his feet. "What about Gina?" he mumbled softly.

"What about her?" Ernesto answered like they had nothing more to talk about.

Chapter 26: Some Amazing New Bugs

At age 22 and with barely two full seasons of racing under his lap belt, "world's richest baby" Lance Reventlow returned to Los Angeles in the middle of 1957 quietly determined to take on the world. He fully intended to build a car—hell, a whole blessed racing team—that could take on the best that Ferrari, Maserati, Jaguar, Lister, Mercedes-Benz, Aston Martin or any of the other damn European manufacturers might care to toss up against them. The ultimate goal was to win Le Mans with an all-American car, all-American drivers and an all-American team. Essentially the same dream Briggs Cunningham had so desperately pursued—unfortunately without final success—just a few years before. And young Lance was smart and sharp enough not to go off half-cocked. He got himself a lawyer and formed Reventlow Automobiles Incorporated to protect him (and the old family fortune) from any possible lawsuits, cons and legal hassles, and then he officially hired his ace wrench and organizer Warren Olsen as RAI's first employee/head man/team manager and sent him out looking for the brains and talent they needed to get the job done. He didn't have to look very far. Los Angeles was the pounding heart of America's love affair with cars, and its streets and back-alley garages were teeming with hot rodders, Bonneville speed record hunters, oval-track and Indianapolis car builders, stock-car types and sportycar guys. And the planets were aligning nicely for RAI seeing as how a lot of that talent was readily available. Frank Kurtis' cars had dominated the Indy 500 through the middle '50s, but his Kurtis-Kraft shop in Glendale had been bought out by the McCulloch Company (the lawnmower and chainsaw people) so not too many racecars were being built there any more. Warren Olsen easily hired away two ace metalsmiths and fabricators—and racers at heart—Dick Troutman and Tom Barnes. They'd already proven they knew the ropes in road racing by working nights and weekends to build the fast, neat, simple and terribly effective Ford-powered Troutman-Barnes Special, and they eagerly recommended their friend and usual driver, Chuck Daigh, as another likely RAI employee.

You have to understand that Chuck Daigh always considered himself a wrench and builder first and a driver second, and that his real burning desire was to race at the Indy 500. I met him at Elkhart Lake in 1952 back when they ran the races through the streets, and ran into him again when we took the Trashwagon out to Bonneville to run it against Skippy Welcher's C-Type. He never said all that much—why waste words when a glare, grin or glower might do?—but I knew he was shrewd and sharp as they come and knew one hell of a lot about fast automobiles. And Chuck was more than available seeing as how he'd been Ford's and then Chevrolet's point man for their factory racing programs right up until GM president Harlow "Red" Curtice and old Hank Ford got the Automobile Manufacturers' Association in Detroit to drop racing like a hot potato in June of 1957. Some said it was because of that terrible wreck at the *Mille Miglia* the month before and some said it was just good business on account of racing was irresponsible, reckless, dangerous, terrifically expensive and thoroughly unpredictable. But whatever the reason, all the big Detroit manufacturers signed a pact saying that they would no longer be officially involved in racing in any way, shape or form. But the key word there was "officially," seeing as how Ford kept doing its racing business out the back door through shops like Holman and Moody's stock-car garage down in Charlotte, North Carolina. And they were hardly the only ones sneaking around like that.

But Chuck Daigh was more or less out of a job, and made a great pick for RAI seeing as how he knew racecars from both the end of a ratchet wrench *and* behind the wheel. That's not an easy combination to find, and he was a *bona fide* talent both ways. Better yet, he'd been right at the sharp end of race-developing Chevy's new "283" V-8, and even though it didn't have the sheer inner cubes of the bigger Buick, Olds, Chrysler, Lincoln and Pontiac V-8 motors, it was light, compact and intelligently designed and already well on its way to replacing the beloved Ford Flathead as the engine-of-choice for hot rodders all over Southern California. And the rest of the country too, come to that. Daigh pushed for using the Chevy V-8 in the new RAI sports/racer from the very beginning, and Lance was all ears seeing as how he wanted the cars to be truly all-American. Not to mention that Chuck Daigh wasn't the type to go running his mouth off when he didn't know what he was talking about. Not hardly. Lance also told him that there were two rules he had to abide by absolutely if he was going to wrench and drive at RAI: "You can't let me win unless I really *can* win. I mean on my own. And if we're racing over in England, you can never, *ever* be civil to the English press. Especially that snotty little asshole Eric Gibbon."

Chuck allowed as how he didn't think he'd have a problem with either one.

RAI had plenty of engine building talent on tap with a couple sharp local guys named Jim Travers and Frank Coon (who called themselves Traco Engineering) and you have to understand that shop-developing race engines is a whole different proposition from tuning them at the racetrack. Chuck Daigh was the perfect guy to have on your team—and under the hood—once you got out in the field on a race weekend, but coming up with all the internal bits and tricks and moreover putting them together in the right combination needs to be done in the shop ahead of time. And preferably with a big old dyno over in the corner so you can find out if What You Thought is What You Really Know. And it was really Lance, with all of his book car smarts, and Chuck, with all of his practical experience, who kept pushing all the pieces together and keeping their eye on the whole rather than just the details. Like they yanked off the stock Chevy distributor and replaced it with a Scintilla Vertex magneto (which was fairly common hot rod practice) but they mounted that magneto horizontally—right alongside the engine where the generator would normally go—just to get a lower hood line so the car would poke a smaller, slipperier hole in the air. And then they went with short-stack Hilborn fuel injection—like the Indy 500 cars run—for exactly the same reason. Most people figured it would never work. After all, the Indycar engines ran on alcohol and worked in a relatively narrow rpm range, and the Hilborn injection system was an awfully simple approach to mixing fuel up with air into something a racing engine might want to swallow. I heard one mechanic call it "an organized leak," and that was pretty much the size of it. Oh, and remember that generator they had to move out of the way to make room for the magneto? Well, they rather cleverly mounted it way down underneath by the driveshaft, where it was out of the way and the weight of that big old canister was as low to the ground and as far back in the chassis as you could get it.

Speaking of the chassis, RAI got expatriate Brit Ken Miles to drop by and do a little design consulting here and there on the layout, and he was a great choice seeing as how he'd designed and built those two wonderfully handsome and effective MG-powered specials that gave all the west coast Porsches and OSCAs fits with such stunning regularity. Or at least they did until John von Neumann finally got sick of it and hired Ken to drive one of his Porsches instead of beating up on them. Hank Lyons considered Ken Miles a genuine, world-class talent as both a racing driver and a car builder, and clever as all getout when it came to laying out a chassis. Like Hank once said: "All the really great racecars I've seen are made up of thousands of little, perfectly executed details rather than one or two radical ideas. And they always look deceptively simple. In fact, it's that very neatness of design and cleanliness of packaging that sets them apart." I knew exactly what he was talking about, too. I'd learned my lessons the hard way when I was building the Trashwagon: *"If it looks right, it may very well be right. But if it looks wrong, it's pretty damn sure to run wrong, too."*

Of course there were the usual disagreements, arguments, hard looks, hurt feelings, hidden sneers, stalking off and behind-the-hand snickers that you always get when you have too damn many artists, craftsmen, independent thinkers and hip-pocket geniuses working together on one blessed project, but somehow Warren Olsen managed to keep all the egos and attitudes in line so that everybody was pulling in essentially the same direction. And of course it didn't hurt at all that Lance Reventlow was signing everybody's paychecks. I've personally noticed how that has a way of keeping people in line all by itself.

Meanwhile Cal had moved his stuff out of Ernesto Julio's apartment in the Hollywood Hills and stashed it temporarily down in the screened front porch of Hank's folks' house in Orange County while he looked around for a place to stay and tried to figure out just what the hell he was going to do next. The first thing he realized he needed was a car—you just can't get along without one in L.A.—and I guess it was kind of a shock for Cal to go car shopping in person after he'd been enjoying the free use of such an incredible selection of automobiles all his life. Oh, he had money available if he needed it—probably as much as he wanted, in fact—but Cal Carrington hated spending his own money on anything. Not that he was cheap. Why, he could be the most generous guy you could ever meet when he had a little extra cash in his pocket. Even more than a little, come to that. Whatever he had on him, you could rest assured it'd be gone and everyone around would've enjoyed whatever it could buy by the end of the day, evening or weekend. But Cal was a free spirit and freeloader by nature, and he absolutely rebelled at the thought of putting the same old coin in the same old slot and going through life's turnstiles like ordinary people.

"What kind of car should I get, Buddy?" he asked me on the phone.

"I dunno. What kind of cars do you like?"

"Oh, just about anything'll do. A 300SL. A Maserati 3500. Even one of those new Jag 150s would be okay."

"You'd better bring your checkbook."

"Why? How much do those things cost?"

I told him. And then it went quiet on the other end of the line.

"Hmm," Cal finally mused through the receiver, "maybe I ought to get something a little more practical…."

"That's an unusual sort of thought," I told him. And it was for Cal Carrington.

He wound up with a clean-looking but sadly used-and-abused Morris Minor convertible. I told him not to buy it because I knew a little bit about Morris Minors. First off, they were seriously underpowered—hell, you could barely climb a steep driveway in one if you were carrying a few passengers—and I didn't think they were all that well screwed together, either. But this one was cute and bright, shiny blue and I'm sure that car smiled and winked at Cal like used cars are always prone to do when they've really got your number. "If you want something cheap and reliable, you ought to buy yourself a Volkswagen," I told Cal, ever-so-slightly amazed at what a company man I'd become.

"But this is California," Cal protested. "I need a convertible."

"Volkswagen makes convertibles."

"Yeah, but they look like hay wagons in back and something you'd find under a rock in front. They just don't *do* anything for me."

"You like the way a damn Morris Minor looks any better?"

"You should see it," he assured me, his voice going all dreamy. "It's blue." He said it like being blue was some wonderful character attribute all other cars should envy. "And it's cheap, too," he added brightly.

"So are you."

"See?" he agreed with himself. "It's a perfect fit!"

So against my advice Cal bought himself the used Morris Minor that the previous owner had traded in once the clutch started slipping and he found out how much a clutch job would cost. I'm sure they gave him dirt for it, sprayed a little carbon tet into the bell housing to dry the oil from the leaky rear main seal off the clutch disc, had some Mexican kid polish it until you could see your face in the damn wax job and then set it right out front on the lot where it would surely catch the eye of some sucker like Cal Carrington. Probably more than tripled their money on the deal while they were at it, too. It disgusted me more than a little that my friend, part-time hero and longtime motoring pal Cal Carrington bought cars just like old John Q. and Fred Average. Or like their wives, to be more accurate. Color and a cute face first, then price and then, well, color, face and price should about cover it, right?

To be fair, Cal didn't really have any experience buying cars on his own. Hell, he'd gone from his mom's new Packard convert back when he was still living at Castle Carrington right through Ernesto Julio's 300SL Gullwing, Alfa Spiders,

Lancias, Ferraris, Jag XKSS and Maseratis, and I think the only car he ever bought out of his own back pocket the whole time was that ratty '47 TC he was racing the very first time I met him at Bridgehampton in the spring of 1952. And that thing was a piece of shit, too.

In any case, my buddy Cal wound up cruising around L.A. in his new/used and stupendously shiny blue Morris Minor, looking for a place to live and enjoying the dubious freedom of having no idea on earth what he was going to do with himself. He must've cruised past Ernesto's apartment building a dozen times—mostly at night—but the shades were always drawn and the lights were never on and there was never anything parked in the driveway. He also stopped by Gina LaScala's elegant, Spanish-style rental with the white stucco walls and orange tile roof over in Bel Air a couple times, but she was off doing an extended publicity tour for her new movie (the one about the usurped king and the can't-tell-the-players-without-a-scorecard series of imposters) and a maid who didn't speak much English generally answered the door. But finally he wound up face-to-face with Gina's mother on the maid's morning off. Cal said she looked really terrible—pale and pasty-faced with no makeup and rings around her eyes and hair all scraggly and disheveled—wearing a housecoat that looked like a cat slept in it, shaky as hell and walking with a cane. It was just 10 in the morning, but Cal said he could smell liquor on her breath. And he didn't have to get very close to smell it, either. Apparently Gina's skyrocketing success in the movie business hadn't exactly had the expected effect on her mother. "Is Gina home?" Cal asked her.

"Who wants to know?" She asked right back, eyeballing Cal like he was peddling deadly nightshade door-to-door.

"It's me, Cal Carrington."

She squinted her eyes at him like she was trying to get them to focus. Then came an unpleasant flicker of recognition. "Gina's not here," she snapped at him. "So go away. Gina's not here. She's out of town…."

"Where out of town?"

She glared at him. "None of your business. Now go away." And with that the door clunked shut. He rang the bell again—several times, in fact—but there was no answer.

On the way back from Gina's house in Bel Air the clutch in the Morris finally started slipping again, and about 20 blocks of stop-and-go traffic further on it got so bad Cal could hardly drive it. And there was a smell now, too. Cal knew that smell. It was burnt oil. Lots of burnt oil. No question he had to get that car someplace where it could get a little attention. And sooner rather than later. And naturally that's when he heard that old hammering, clattering sound starting up in the bottom end. Cars tend to do that once you've pumped most of the engine oil out into the bell housing. Now Cal understood what that sound meant because he'd heard it once or twice before, and I'm proud to say he had the smarts and mechanical sympathy to switch it off immediately and coast to a halt over by the side of Wilshire Boulevard rather than continuing on until a connecting rod came sailing merrily through the side of the engine block.

At least the sun was shining. But then, it almost always does in L.A. Even on really shitty days.

Well, Cal had the Morris towed over to Warren Olsen's race shop in West Hollywood because it was close by and he didn't know where the hell else to take it, and at first Warren didn't want to raise the overhead door and let him in. "I don't do street cars," he explained from behind the thick, wire-reinforced glass of the little diamond-shaped window in the heavy steel security door at the side of the building.

"Aw, c'mon, Warren. I could really use a hand here," Cal pleaded. Then he flashed Warren that helpless, handsome and infuriatingly lovable rich kid/hero racer smile of his and pretty soon the overhead door rolled open. The two of them pushed the Morris inside.

Warren eyeballed the car. "Okay, what'd you do to it?"

"It's more like *'what did it do to me?'"* Cal explained. And then he told him about the burned oil smell and the slipping clutch. Warren pulled out the dipstick and there was nothing but a blue steel foundry scent on the end.

"It smells like a damn train wreck."

"Sorry," Cal said sheepishly.

Warren Olsen rubbed his chin. "Look, I know a guy named Kent Bain who's got a little foreign car shop over in Pasadena. Does a lot of this English crap. Does a pretty nice job most of the time, too. He could take care of it for you."

"Is he honest?"

Warren shot him a sideways look. "Like I told you, he's in the foreign car repair business."

Now it was Cal rubbing his chin. "What do you think something like this might cost?" he asked, staring at his reflection in the Morris' wax job. "I think the bottom end's starting to rattle."

"You *think* the bottom end's starting to rattle?"

"Okay," Cal sighed glumly. "I know it is."

"Well," Warren mused, "if you caught it in time and the engine still turns free, you might get by for a half a yard or so. But if the crank and rods are messed up or anything really bad is going on inside, it could be more than the whole damn car is worth." He looked over at Cal. "You do want to fix it, don't you?"

Cal thought it over. "No," he said slowly and evenly, "I think I want to sell it."

"Sell it?"

Cal nodded.

"Just as it sits?"

Cal nodded again.

"You won't get anything for it."

"Then that's my problem, isn't it?" Cal shrugged. "Besides, I'm not going to need it any more."

"You're not?"

"Nope," Cal nodded with a keen, solid edge to his voice. "I'm going over to race in Europe."

A little hint of a smile curled up around the edges of Warren's mouth. "And when did you decide that?"

"Just now. Standing right here."

Warren stared at him. "That's a pretty damn big decision."

Cal shot back his patented, rich-kid smile. "Hey, only if you think about it…."

Over by his desk Warren thumbed through the yellow pages, running his eyes up and down the names and numbers in the automotive section. "Here you go. There's this guy named Andy Franko with a foreign car lot and a little shop out back a couple miles from here who's always looking for cheap, fixer-upper stuff like this. He's a little bit of a slippery character, but this is right up his alley. He's just a couple blocks over on Santa Monica Boulevard."

Cal stared at him. *"My God! That's where I bought the damn thing!"*

Warren's mouth spread out into a wide, steady smile. "Ain't life grand?"

While he was in Warren's shop, Cal couldn't help noticing the slick new racecar taking shape in one of the stalls. There was no body on it, just a complete running chassis sitting on a set of Halibrand knockoff mag wheels with a Hilborn-injected Chevy engine nestled inside, but even Cal could see it was beautifully, even artistically built and tremendously well thought out. "Geez, what the heck is *that?"* he wanted to know.

"It's none of your damn business," Warren laughed.

"Hmph. I've been getting that *'it's none of your damn business'* business an awful lot today."

"Maybe it's catching?"

"Could be." Cal allowed as he walked over and took a long, slow look at the new racecar. "Somebody who really knows what they're doing is putting this thing together."

"Remember, you never saw it," Warren warned. And then he couldn't help showing a proud little flicker of a smile. "But that's kind of what we're hoping."

"C'mon," Cal prodded, "you can tell *me*…What the hell is it?"

Warren curled his lip under. "Okay," he finally sighed. "It's Lance Reventlow's new racecar. We had it out at Willow Springs for its first test last Thursday."

"Just like this?" Cal didn't see any bodywork around.

"Yep, just like that," Warren chuckled. "Chuck thought it was a little drafty."

"How'd it go?"

"New lap record, right out of the box."

Cal let out a low whistle.

"And this is just the prototype," Warren continued, a hint of excitement dancing in his usually even-keel delivery. "There's eventually going to be three of them."

"Three of them?"

Warren nodded. "One for Lance and one for Chuck of course, plus one for Bruce Kessler. You know Bruce Kessler, don't you?"

"Sure I do."

It must've been a real treat for Warren to show the car off. Lance was absolutely dedicated to keeping the project secret until it was ready. But showing it off to Cal gave Warren a chance to see it through a fresh set of eyes. Almost like he was seeing it for the first time himself, you know?

"What's he gonna call it?" Cal asked.

"He's calling it a *Scarab."* Warren let the word roll off his tongue.

"What the hell is a Scarab?"

"Well," Warren answered, a twinkle coming up in his eye, "that depends on who you ask. Now some people will tell you that a scarab is the sacred, ancient Egyptian symbol for immortality...."

"I see. And what will other people tell me?"

"Other people will tell you it's a shit beetle."

"A shit beetle?"

"Yeah. One of those fat little desert beetles that roll up balls of camel dung for a living. They had pictures of them in *National Geographic."*

Cal thought it over. "So Lance's new racecar is either named after a symbol of ancient immortality or a stink beetle, right?"

"That's about the size of it," Warren nodded. "And I'll tell you something else."

"What's that?"

"It's gonna *go* like stink, too...."

Our buddy Hank got sent off down to Argentina the third week of January to cover the first Grand Prix of the year and the first World Manufacturers' Championship sportscar round a week later. While he was down there, the biggest news out of South America was that Generalissimo Marcos Perez Jimenez apparently ran fresh out of bread and circuses and got himself ousted from power in Venezuela on January 23rd. There were gunshots and rioting in the streets of Caracas according to the *New York Times,* and I was plenty worried about Hank. Or at least I was until I looked at a map and realized that Caracas, Venezuela was about as far away from Buenos Aires, Argentina as Passaic is from the Paramount Studios in Hollywood. Maybe even further.

Anyhow, it turned out the Argentine Grand Prix was quite a stunner. First off, the paper shufflers and rulesmakers at the FIA in Paris had decided that everybody was going to have to switch from the alcohol-based fuels they had been running in Formula One to 130-octane aviation-grade gasoline (Avgas) for the 1958 season. I guess it was supposed to slow the cars down and allow them to carry less fuel in order to make them a wee bit less incendiary when they smashed into things. But changing over from alcohol-based fuels (like they also ran here in the Indianapolis cars) to even the best gasoline is a lot more complicated than just filling up out of a different jug. Alcohol burns cooler and more efficiently than gasoline and makes a lot more power, but you also need to burn a lot more of it and the mileage isn't nearly as good. So there was a tremendous amount of juggling and fiddling and fine-tuning to be done with carburetion, camshafts, compression ratios, combustion chamber shape, ignition timing and so forth to get everything working at maximum efficiency. Especially for the British grand prix teams like Vanwall and BRM who didn't have sports/racer programs that had been running on Avgas for years. Naturally wily old Enzo Ferrari had the situation sized up early and was testing gasoline-powered Formula One and Formula Two cars with brand new V6 engines by the later stages of the 1957 season. Meanwhile everybody else—again meaning mostly Vanwall and BRM, seeing as how Maserati was pretty much crawling on its hands and knees by then—planned to work on the conversion to Avgas after the '57 season was over. They figured to have everything sorted out and ready in time for the opening Formula One race at Monaco in the middle of May. Only then the Argentine Auto Club asked the FIA if they could please have their grand prix back on the third weekend in January and, much to the horror of all the British teams, the FIA agreed. At damn near the very last minute.

Naturally Vanwall and BRM turned their usual shade of British Sputtering Purple and complained loudly that they didn't have enough time to get their engines converted over to Avgas. Not to mention that it was a long, expensive trek down to Argentina, and old man Ferrari was sending cars and people down there to run *two* races with *two* purses and *two* payouts of starting money, not just one grand prix like Vanwall and BRM. As you can imagine, The British teams wrote letters and drafted documents and even filed official protests against the inclusion of the Argentine race in the Formula One Championship, and the FIA kindly agreed to hear those arguments and rule on them in May at Monaco. Or, in other words, a good four months after the damn Argentine race was over. What probably *really* happened is that the fine gentlemen from the FIA took those letters and documents and protests from the British teams and did what Frenchmen have been doing to Englishmen since the two countries first discovered each other on opposite sides of the English Channel: they folded them into paper airplanes and sailed them out over the *Champs-Elysees* to see which ones would glide the farthest.

Vanwall and BRM responded by pulling their leather caps down, folding their arms resolutely across the buttons of their herringbone tweed jackets and harrumphing that there was no way in hell they were going to go down to race in Argentina. And meanwhile *Signore* Ferrari was surely having himself a happy chortle at everyone's expense but his own. Problem was, not too many spectators figured to show up just to see the Ferrari factory team steamroller a small handful of outdated, privateer Maseratis. So meetings were held and a few sacks of money changed hands and, in the end, Juan Manuel Fangio and Carlos Menditeguy miraculously appeared in what were obviously two of the very latest-spec Maseratis (running as *Scuderia Sud Americana)* plus Jean Behra and Harry Schell in two more reasonably decent "privateer" 250Fs. And another last-minute deal provided one of the biggest surprises in the whole blessed history of motor racing....

Stirling Moss' 1958 Vanwall contract allowed him to drive other cars for other teams when Vanwall themselves weren't racing, and by coincidence rich English gent and top private entrant Rob Walker (of Johnny Walker's Red Label and Black Label whiskey fame) had just gone out and bought himself a nice, ex-works Cooper T43 Formula One car. Or, in other words, one of those "ugly little bugs" that old man Ferrari and the rest of the grand prix establishment looked so far down their noses at it was damn near invisible. As far as old man Ferrari was concerned, John and Charlie Cooper were nothing but hammer-and-anvil *"garagistes,"* not proper racing constructors. Hell, they bought their damn engines off-the-shelf from Coventry Climax. And even bored out as far as it would go, the biggest damn Climax FPF you could build to stick in the back of a Cooper came to barely 2.0 liters. That left it well short of the necessary size and power to challenge the full 2.5-liter motors in the Ferraris, Vanwalls, BRMs and Maseratis. Plus the Cooper's unique rear transaxle was notoriously fragile. But that's because they never had the time, money or expertise to build one up from scratch. So it was based on a Citroen front-wheel-drive unit originally intended for ordinary sedans (although modified with special gears from ESRA) and hardly up to the torque, revs, strain, heat and vibration of Grand Prix racing. But wily old Jack Brabham had casually dropped by the ERSA works in France the previous summer and showed them—hands on—how they needed to beef up the gearbox casing to make them suitable for racing. The first three of those strengthened gearbox casings were picked up and carried back to England as "airline baggage" by John Cooper himself, and he had one hell of a time getting them through customs. As soon as the paperwork was cleared (at about 2:30 in the morning!) he drove straight over to the race shop where the mechanics were waiting to build up a transaxle and install it in a mad hurry, since any cars that planned to compete had to be on their way to South America the next day….

See, the Argentine organizers were tremendously eager to have old Stirling Moss on the grid on account of his drawing card value, and so a very attractive deal was struck at the 11th hour to fly Moss (plus his wife Katie and longtime ace race mechanic, Alf Francis) down to Argentina along with one of Rob Walker's guys and that shiny new Cooper for Moss to drive. It was a slap-dash, last-minute sort of deal, and Alf Francis could only grab a fat fistful of Weber jets, chokes, air correctors and emulsion tubes and hope for the best when it came to "converting" the Climax FPF to Avgas. And what happened next turned the whole blessed racing world on its ear!

Fangio surprised everyone but himself and the highly partisan Argentine crowd when he put his Maserati on pole ahead of all three of the new V6 Ferraris in the hands of Hawthorn, Collins and Musso. Hank thought it was interesting that *Mon Ami Mates* Hawthorn and Collins turned absolutely identical qualifying times in their Ferraris, while poor Luigi Musso was several solid ticks off both of them in the third car. How that must have ground away at him! The best Moss could do with the underpowered Cooper was sixth on the grid (out of only nine cars to actually make the field!), a full two seconds off Fangio's best. Hardly an auspicious start! But what you can do over one qualifying lap with fresh tires and a light fuel load and what you can do over a full, two-hour-plus grand prix distance are sometimes two entirely different things….

The old *maestro* Fangio grabbed the lead as the cars squirmed and spurted away from the start, and poor Peter Collins was out with a broken driveshaft as soon as the flag dropped. Scratch one Ferrari. By the end of the first lap it was a typically charging Hawthorn in front with Behra, a wound-up Luigi Musso and a carefully measured Fangio following in his wheeltracks. And then came Stirling Moss in that ugly little bug of a Cooper, stuck helplessly in second gear and falling back. No matter what Moss tried, he couldn't get it to shift. He was just about to pull into the pits when a stone kicked up by the tires jammed itself in the clutch/gearbox interlock mechanism and—miracle of miracles!—all of a sudden he could shift gears again! It was an incredible stroke of luck!

And it was only the beginning.

By the 10th lap things had sorted themselves out and were running a lot closer to form. Fangio had finessed his way back into the lead and seemed to be pulling out a little distance each lap on Hawthorn and Behra. Much to the delight of the Argentine crowd, of course! Meanwhile Moss had revived, disposed of Musso's more powerful Ferrari after a brief tussle and now, on a clear track, was using the Cooper's superior balance and handling (plus the far smaller hole it poked in the air!) to gain ever-so-slightly on Hawthorn and Behra as their tires wore quickly down on the abrasive Argentine pavement. Hawthorn's Ferrari had to stop for fresh rubber well before half distance, and then so did Musso, Behra and Fangio. That left Moss in the blunt little Cooper in the lead, with over 20 seconds in hand! But there was still plenty of racing to go, and no way could any car be expected to go the full 80-lap race distance on one tank of fuel and one set of tires….

Sure enough, Alf Francis laid out a fuel jug, a set of mounted tires, jacks and lug wrenches in the Walker pits just past half distance—why, the little Cooper didn't even have knock-offs, so they'd have to wrestle with four lugnuts on each wheel!—and as you can imagine, confidence was running high in the Italian pits. Meanwhile Hawthorn had to stop again for another set of tires, Behra lost time with a quick spin and another pit stop and Fangio's Maserati started losing oil pressure and misfiring. That left Musso's Ferrari solidly in second, some 30 seconds behind Moss in the Cooper. But there was no reason for team manager Tavoni to signal him to push it, since the ugly little Cooper would surely have to make a pit stop.

Only it didn't.

With just 15 laps left, it finally began to dawn on the Ferrari bunch that they'd been tricked. By that time Moss' tires were absolutely shot—he could see the white canvas lining showing right through the rubber!—and so he had no choice but to back out of it. Meanwhile the Ferrari pits were urgently waving the "Hurry Up" board at Musso every time he went by. And the Italian responded magnificently, setting his jaw and really putting his foot in it. With fresher tires and a lightened fuel load, the Ferrari was far faster than Moss' limping Cooper, and Musso was driving with fierce, almost desperate determination. He was carving into the Cooper's lead by as much as five and six seconds every lap! And Moss couldn't respond—the cords were showing through on his tires now and he was barely tiptoeing around the corners. In his mirrors, he could only watch and worry as Musso's Ferrari grew from a tiny, distant speck to an ever-larger, ever-closer threat. But the team had judged it perfectly—or maybe they were just dumb-shit lucky—and the race ended with Moss a scant three seconds ahead at the checkered flag! It was a spectacular, stupefying upset, and Hank said you could've stuck a grapefruit in the mouths of all the Ferrari pit guys as Moss crossed the line in first. They were stunned. Gobsmacked. And not a little worried about what old man Ferrari might have to say once they got back to Maranello….

By contrast, the World Manufacturers' Championship sportscar round a week later was a Ferrari rout and pretty much anti-climactic. The only real factory teams were Ferrari and Porsche, and they weren't even running against each other in the same class. Although the engineers at Porsche had bored out one of their engines to a giddy 1581cc so that car could run in the 2.0-liter class. Outside of that, there were just two half-hearted, semi-factory Maserati 300S models entered by enthusiastic Italian Maserati dealer Guglielmo Dei under the *Scuderia Centro Sud* banner, although he had ex-factory aces Moss and Behra in one car and Fangio teamed up with an up-and-coming "paying driver" in the other one. The rest of the field was all local South American privateers plus a few vacationing American amateurs. And then even more air came out of the pre-race balloon when Moss/Behra Maserati broke its crankshaft in practice. Hank said neither Moss nor Behra seemed particularly upset about it, since it was an older-spec, cobbled-up car that had been crashed and repaired, and the handling was nothing like it should have been. Porsche team manager and sometime driving ace Huschke von Hanstein was quick to see the opportunity laid out in front of him, and immediately stepped aside and offered the "big-engined" Porsche Spyder to Moss and Behra. They happily accepted.

And Hank said there was "a wee bit of drama" over at Ferrari seeing as how Mike Hawthorn—who was so fair, blonde and light-skinned that he was damn near albino—picked up a serious case of sunburn between the two Argentine races. So serious he couldn't drive, in fact. And the reason it was so serious he couldn't drive was on account of the worst of it was right where you sit down in a damn racecar. If you catch my drift. Needless to say, there was a lot of winking, snickering and conjecture regarding exactly how an individual might manage to get themselves sunburned in such a spot! In any case, Toly was happy about it because it moved him up to one of the new *Testa Rossas* alongside our old buddy Phil Hill.

The green waved on a hot, mosquito-laden afternoon and local hero Fangio made an uncharacteristically miserable start. So it was the Ferraris of Hill and Musso out front followed by a few privateer Ferraris. And then, on the ninth lap, an inexperienced local driver who had bought his way in—and way over his head!—behind the wheel of an ex-works 300S Maserati lost it in a big way entering the *Autodromo.* The car flipped twice, and he suffered massive head injuries and died on the way to the hospital. But of course nobody at the track knew it at the time, and the rumors and reports echoing around the paddock after the ambulance wailed off were the usual, hopeful: *"they said he's shaken up and maybe broken a few things, but he'll be okay...."*

Right.

Meanwhile Fangio was on a charge trying to make up lost ground. He set a new lap record, but he rather uncharacteristically spun off—not once but twice!—banging things up badly enough underneath that the car had to be retired. Hank saw him in the pits afterwards, and he had this empty, faraway look in his eyes. Not like his old self at all. Like maybe the fire was finally flickering out, you know? Anyhow, that plus the retirement of one of the faster privateer Ferraris put the 1581cc Moss/Behra Porsche all the way up to third overall! Can you believe it? As the pit stops and car problems and driver changes and typical endurance race disasters came and went, the Hill/Wolfgang *Testa Rossa* found itself well in the lead while the little Porsche droned on and on and harried the heck out of Musso and his French teammate Gendebien in the second factory Ferrari. They had a hell of a battle going as the race drew towards its close, and Toly—at the wheel of the leading car—found himself right in the middle of it. Even though he was almost a full lap ahead. And he surely must have impressed all the mechanics and Ferrari team manager Tavoni with way he stuck his car in between Musso's Ferrari and Moss' Porsche and blocked like hell to preserve a 1-2 finish for Ferrari. Moss finally got around him under braking, but by then it was too late and the damage was done. Musso was far enough ahead that Moss couldn't catch him. Toly enjoyed the cheering thanks of the entire Ferrari team as he guzzled champagne in victory circle.

It was his first big international race win.

The next morning Eric Gibbon interviewed him over a breakfast one of the London papers he wrote for actually paid for, and Eric looked his usual, bleary, early-morning self what with reddened eyes under puffy eyelids, a complexion like old newspaper and a stale, lingering stench of alcohol all around him. But Eric was sharp even when he was dull, and he asked Toly a lot of carefully aimed questions about what it felt like to finally be coming into his own at Ferrari and how he had managed to climb the ladder from bought rides to paid drives. Plus who he personally reckoned as the best drivers and Men To Beat out on the circuit. And Toly did his best to answer him honestly. You had Fangio and Moss, of course—you hated to think they were a cut above everyone else, but they kept on proving it, race after race—and then you had a real logjam of speed, skill, talent and desire backed up behind them. Luck had a lot to do with it, too, although a driver hated to admit it. And then, once he'd gotten Toly loosened up and brought his guard down with a lot of racing questions mixed with a little veiled praise and flattery, there was more about Toly's upbringing on Lake Lucerne in Switzerland during the war. About his family. About his mother and his mother's apparent suicide.

And, most especially, about his father....

Chapter 27: A Meeting in Maranello

The old U.S. of A. was pretty damn desperate to hurl something into space that would actually stay there, and they (meaning *our* ex-Nazi German rocket scientists) finally succeeded on February 1st. That was after a series of embarrassing failures with our high-tech, purpose-built Vanguard space rocket that couldn't seem to get more than a few feet in the air (if that!) without blowing itself to smithereens or toppling over in the general direction of the guys who fired it. It was pretty damn embarrassing, if you want the truth of it. Especially since we have a free press over here, so the news cameras were always right there and churning. Over in Russia we heard they just bury the bodies and run a bulldozer over the hole in the ground when one of their rockets got a little out of hand. We'd only hear about it from those guys when everything went right. And then it'd be slathered across the front pages of every damn newspaper in the world. Or at least that's what all my old man's chemical plant buddies said, and I was only too happy to go along with them. Anyhow, this time our American German rocket scientists switched to something a little simpler (a "Jupiter-C" booster based on one of the military ICBMs we'd been shaking at the Russians like an angry forefinger) and it was really just a slightly upscale, 20-story version of the same blessed skyrockets you used to light off in your back yard when you were a kid. And damn if it didn't work like a charm.

Cal Carrington flew back to Jersey just long enough to renew his passport, yank a wad of cash out of the bank and pack himself a duffel bag big enough to hold his helmet, goggles and a few changes of underwear and took off for Havana, Cuba (of all places!) since there was a big, through-the-streets international sportscar race scheduled there for the last weekend in February. It wasn't a championship round or anything, and as a result it was open to all cars regardless of displacement. But the organizers were paying big money (thanks to the Batista government, who were eager to show the world's *touristas* that everything was fine and dandy in Havana and that Castro's rebels were cowering in the jungle and well under control) and promising a hell of a show. My buddy Cal didn't have a ride lined up or anything, but he was hoping to maybe land something at the last minute. Or, at the very least, get something sorted out in advance for Sebring in March.

My pal and partner Big Ed decided to go down for the weekend, too, seeing as how Havana was one of his very favorite places. *"Lemme tell you: it's the best damn party city in the world!"* he'd grin around both sides of his cigar.

"But don't they have trouble with poverty and unrest and unemployment and all those commie Castro rebels you read about in the paper?"

"Didn't they kill Castro in a jungle ambush? I'm sure I read it someplace."

"Well, apparently they didn't kill him dead enough. From what I've heard, he's still out there raising an army and organizing raids and making trouble."

"Ahhh," Big Ed waved his hand disgustedly, "you never see that stuff when you're down there. Oh, sure, maybe out the cab window on your way from the airport. But y'gotta understand that poverty is a way of life down there. Believe me. It's just the way things are." He rolled his palms up—*what can you do?*—but then his eyes went all soft and dreamy. "You should see the inside of those hotels and casinos, Buddy! And the floor shows!" He raised his eyebrows and jiggled them for me. "Don't even get me started about the women...."

Like a lot of rich Americans, Big Ed was very comfortable with his place in the world. And why not? It was a damn comfortable place to be....

The so-called "racetrack" supplied by the Cuban organizers was nothing more than two sides of the big, wide *Malecon* boulevard that ran along the Havana sea wall plus a couple strange, rough, fiddly jinks into town. Almost all the drivers—except for the local amateurs, of course, who were thrilled at a chance to run with the big international stars—worried about the uneven pavement and the long, sweeping corners with high concrete curbs on either side and no haybales, sandbags or anything else to soften the blow or protect spectators. Crowd control simply didn't exist except for the occasional hollered command, snarled threat or brandished rifle on the part of one of the countless Batista military types on the scene. In spite of the sunshine and balmy Caribbean weather, Havana was a pretty scary place for a lot of reasons.

And it got even scarier when a small, well-organized squad of Castro rebels kidnapped Juan Manuel Fangio. He was sitting in the lobby of his luxury hotel, talking to friends, when a serious-looking young man walked over, eased a huge, menacing automatic out from under his coat and suggested in firm but polite Spanish that Fangio should accompany him outside. There was a car waiting at the curb, and Fangio was whisked swiftly and silently away into the back streets of Havana.

Naturally this turn of events created pandemonium—it was an enormous embarrassment for the Batista government—and rumors of bomb threats and more possible kidnappings had all the drivers on edge. But at least it helped Cal get a ride. The Fangio kidnapping left a competitive seat empty, and Maurice Trintignant was quickly moved up to fill it. This left the seat in the older D-Type the little Frenchman was originally supposed to drive empty, and Toly Wolfgang helped arrange things so Cal could get the ride. He was only too eager to take it, in spite of the fact that he'd never driven the car before and hadn't had any practice at all.

A huge, ragged crowd of over 200,000 lined the streets under a baking hot sun and waited for the start while the organizers worked feverishly on possibly sabotaged radio communications and investigated rumored bomb threats. Meanwhile the cars and drivers sweated it out silently on the front straight, feeling naked and uneasy out there in the open under the quiet, pounding sunlight, waiting for the command to start their engines. It finally came, but then the cars sat, engines rumbling, until they started to steam and gurgle and the drivers had no choice but to switch them off again. Then the command to start engines came again. And again the cars sat until temperature gauges pegged and coolant spewed and sputtered out on the pavement. Finally, on the third try—almost two hours late—the green flag finally waved and the field screamed off down the white concrete boulevard with a parted sea of unprotected spectators lined eight- or ten-deep on either side.

Masten Gregory got away like a shot in Temple Buell's blue-and-white Maserati with the huge, 5.7-liter engine under the hood. But by the end of the lap, it was Moss in front (driving Carlo Sebastian's 4.1-liter Ferrari in a kind of one-off deal just for the Cuban race) with Gregory right behind. Toly was up to fourth and trying to figure out a way past Carroll Shelby (good luck!) and Cal was back somewhere in the middle of the pack trying to learn a new car and a new racetrack on the fly. And the circuit was slicker than eel snot thanks to all the leakers, steamers and spewers running around in the Cuban "national" races earlier in the day. The hot sun made it even worse, sizzling the oil, grease and goo up out of the pavement. Even so, Big Ed said it was shaping up to be one hell of a race. He was watching it from a second-floor oceanfront balcony—tall, iced drink in hand and no doubt a young, tawny Cuban girl or two at his side—under a spanking white canvas awning with tassels on the front to shield him from the sun. It was a damn fine place to be. And a damn fine race to watch, too. No question there was a lot of top talent and even more raw horsepower up front, plus a very large bag of gold at the end for the winner….

And then, just seven laps in, the red flags came out. A Cuban driver in a 2.0-liter Ferrari missed a turn (Brake failure? Driver error? Oil on the track? Who knows?) and plowed straight into the crowd, killing six people on the spot and injuring at least 30 more. It was the kind of thing you could have expected, I suppose, but of course no one ever thinks it will happen to them. Not the drivers or the well-meaning race organizers or those tens of thousands of wide-eyed people packed elbow-to-elbow and eight- to ten-deep on the curbsides, leaning forward like flowers toward sunlight in order to get a closer look, hear the noise, smell the hot oil and exhaust fumes and feel the pounding speed of the racecars hurtling by.

While the organizers, track workers, ambulances and emergency crews did their best to get the mess cleaned up, the drivers held an impromptu meeting around the racecars right there on the front straight. A lot of them felt the race should not go on. It was far too dangerous. And too many people had already been hurt and killed. Cal was one of the ones who wanted to keep racing, of course, but Toly took him aside. *"There are times for bravery and times for conscience, my friend,"* he said softly, putting his arm around Cal's shoulder. *"If we continue, whoever wins will have nothing to be proud of. Nothing at all."*

In the end, the drivers more or less agreed not to continue and, since it was already very late, the organizers had no choice but to reluctantly cancel the rest of the show and declare the results official as of the end of the sixth lap. To tell the truth, it was a pretty miserable deal all the way around. About the only bright note was that Fangio was returned—unharmed and in surprisingly good spirits—the following morning. According to the press interviews, he was treated very well by his captors. They moved him from house to house at various intervals for security, but took excellent care of him. He ate well, slept in a fine bed, and there were even whispered rumors around the racing paddocks (which Fangio neither confirmed nor actually denied) that he was not exactly forced to sleep alone. They gave him a big breakfast in the morning before they released him—just down the block from his hotel—and the only apparent ill effect was a slight cramp in his hand from signing so many autographs….

Back in California, Lance Reventlow's Scarab project was nearing completion in Warren Olsen's shop in West Hollywood. They'd made a few adjustments and tested the bare chassis again at Willow Springs, and damn if it didn't set another track record even faster than before. Four seconds faster, in fact! But there was still no body for it, and so Lance and Warren hired an unknown but enthusiastic 18-year-old Art Center College student named Chuck Pelly to draw it up and got one of the best hammer-and-dolly craftsmen on the west coast, Emil Deidt, to pound those drawings into aluminum. The car was still in bare, polished aluminum and the front end was a little disproportioned and ungainly when they took it to a minor club race in Phoenix to shake it down for the first time the first weekend in March. As promised, it went like stink. There were some unexpected problems with Lance's racing license (it had been suspended because he started racing before he was 21 and was never properly reinstated) and so Bruce Kessler wound up behind the wheel. Along with little Richie Ginther, who was invited to take a few exploratory laps to "feel it out" and lopped six full seconds off the previous lap record! But there were teething problems, too. And then Kessler clouted a concrete abutment and rearranged the front end. He did it again while the team was testing at Riverside a few weeks later, and Lance was furious about it. *"DAMMIT, BRUCE!"* he screamed right into Bruce's face, *"WE'RE HERE TO SEE WHAT THE DAMN CAR CAN DO, NOT WHAT YOU CAN DO!"* Lance could be pretty short-fused about things (although he rarely went off without some kind of provocation), and everybody on the team agreed that you definitely did *NOT* want to be in the line of fire when someone set him off.

But the end result was an impromptu, on-the-hoof, cut, bang and weld redesign of the front end, and that plus the addition of a shapely head fairing behind the driver made the RAI Scarab into the most beautiful single racing sportscar anybody had ever seen. Period. And it got even better when Lance and Warren hired famous local hot rod painter and pinstriper extraordinaire Von Dutch to add color to the reshaped body. They wanted to run the traditional American blue-and-white racing colors, but they also wanted to do it California style. So Von Dutch mixed up a batch of subtly iridescent blue metalflake and sprayed it on so it almost glowed from inside like mother-of-pearl. Then he set it off with graceful white scallops that enhanced the Scarab's smooth, graceful-yet-muscular fender lines and detailed it with beautiful white pinstriping. There was even a freehand Egyptian scarab surrounded by rampant, hooded cobras and "Scarab Mk. 1" lettering on each of the aluminum door panels.

The Scarab Mk. 1 was absolutely, positively stunning when it rolled out of the RAI trailer in its final body and paintwork at the 12th annual Palm Springs races April 12-13. But Lance was driving, and he wasn't considered much of an ace by anybody. Or, as one motorsports writer rather unkindly put it (and in large type): *"Lance Reventlow—a young man with cold cash and no talent."* Anyhow, Carroll

Shelby was there in John Edgar's Maserati 450S, and the same writer allowed as how no racecar on earth was fast enough to put Lance Reventlow ahead of Carroll Shelby! Who quickly underlined that opinion by putting the big Maserati solidly on the pole for Saturday's five-lap grid race to determine the starting positions for Sunday's feature. Reventlow qualified the Scarab in third between Dan Gurney in a re-bodied older Ferrari and Max Balchowsky in the pug ugly Old Yaller. But at the start, the Scarab simply screamed past Shelby and took off in the lead. Right up the escape road for Turn One, in fact! By the time Lance got everything sorted out, the leaders were long gone. He clawed his way back to finish a distant third, showing at least a little of the car's potential, but the engine had split a cylinder liner in the process and so the RAI team was through for the weekend.

You have to understand that there were really two road racing scenes going on in these United States: there was California and the West Coast, where Hank grew up and Cal had been racing for the past few years, and then there was the East Coast/Midwest circuit where I'd learned the ropes of the sport. You also have to understand that there was a lot of underlying tension and competitiveness between the two. The West Coast was all chrome and show and flash (at least according to the East Coast guys) while the East Coast was all stuffy and stiff and old-school (at least according to the West Coast guys), and no question more West Coasters were building their own, home-grown style of racecars while most of the East Coast types still looked lovingly and longingly overseas—and particularly to England and Italy—for the latest and best machinery.

No question the top East Coast team was still very much Briggs Cunningham's bunch under the watchful eye of master wrench and car prep *maestro* Alf Momo. Of course they'd stopped running their own cars by then thanks to the old IRS (although never forget: they were the first!) but they'd enjoyed a lot of success running ex-works Jaguar D-Types after that with Walt Hansgen emerging from the pack as their unquestioned lead driver. And he was one hell of a 'shoe, too. Walt could drive the wheels off damn near anything and make any kind of racecar go as fast as it would go. Maybe even faster. And he'd been winning an awful lot of races with Briggs' D-Types all over the East Coast, South and Midwest. They even made the long trek out to Riverside for the big SCMA National meet in December of 1957, where Hansgen's older, smaller-engined D-Type led outright for awhile—in spite of that *loooong* Riverside back straight—and scrapped tooth-and-nail with the 4.5- and 5.7-liter Maseratis of Shelby and Gregory and the 4.9 Ferrari of Dan Gurney before finally having to settle for fourth behind their more powerful cars.

It was obvious to Briggs Cunningham that he needed something newer and faster, and so for the 1958 season, he'd bought himself a pair of brand-new Lister-Jaguars like the one Archie Scott-Brown had been using to tear up the English racing scene all through 1957. And also like the ones Lance had seen at Brian Lister's shop in Cambridge the day he decided he could do better building his own cars out in California. The Cunningham Lister Jags were typically immaculate, and Alf Momo added his usual fine job detailing and preparing the cars so that they were better by far than when they left the factory. Naturally the cars were painted in Cunningham's usual, conservative and traditional American color scheme of stark, refrigerator white with two dark blue racing stripes down the middle. And then, with Hansgen in one car and fast, smart, steady and accomplished Chicago-area racer Ed Crawford in the other, they went out and started winning races all over again.

Thanks in no small part to Toly Wolfgang, Cal had gotten himself a ride in a semi-factory Ferrari 250 GT *Berlinetta* entered by Carlo Sebastian at Sebring (alongside Bruce Kessler, among others), although I'm sure he had to pass a fat fistful of green under the table to get the seat. But he did well with it, running fast and steady and never making a mistake, and in the end they came home in fifth overall and won the GT class for Ferrari, and I'm sure old Enzo had to be pleased about that back in Maranello. Although Cal was disgusted that they were beaten to the checker by a little 1100cc Lotus Eleven that finished just ahead of them (on the same lap, in fact) and took fourth overall. One of the other drivers wasn't nearly as quick as Cal or Bruce, and he compounded things by spinning off twice, lightly crunching the front end and pretty much brutalizing the clutch and brakes. Even so, Cal begged for Carlo Sebastian to put him back in the car for the last stint to try and run down the Lotus and take fourth place, but Carlo wasn't having any of it. *"We're already winning the GT class and that's what we came here to do,"* Carlo shouted over the noise of the passing racecars. *"The brakes are about shot, anyway. All I want is for the driver who's in the car to get the laps he paid for and for the car to make it to the end of the race!"* And that was the end of it. But Hank was right there, and he said he saw a little sliver of a smile creep across Carlo Sebastian's face as Cal stalked away, fuming. He liked guys who wanted to win and were cocky enough to think they had the guts and speed to do it. And old man Ferrari back in Maranello liked them even better.

The Cunningham team was down at Sebring with their new Lister-Jags (including Archie Scott-Brown on loan from the factory as a guest driver!) plus one of the old, long-in-the-tooth, ex-factory D-Types, but they were running sleeved-down, de-stroked Jaguar engines to get them down to the FIA's 3.0-liter limit, and the Jag motors weren't taking to it very kindly at all. In fact, they all retired early on with engine problems. Archie Scott-Brown was the first to go (in rather spectacular fashion!) at the end of lap three, when his engine blew in a big way at the end of the long Sebring pit straight. Toly Wolfgang was just about to pass him in one of the *Testa Rossas,* and both drivers found themselves spinning and skating helplessly with the Lister's oil and water streaming under them. When the cars finally touched, the Ferrari climbed right up over the low, blunt back end of the Lister, and Toly said afterwards it was just plain, dumb luck that it didn't take Archie's head off.

The Lister looked pretty much demolished (although it was mostly just shredded-up aluminum bodywork), but the *Testa Rossa* was all right except for a few harmless scars and gouges in the undercarriage. Toly made a pit stop to replace a bent rim and have things checked over, and he and Musso enjoyed a fairly uneventful run after that. They wound up second in yet another 1-2 Ferrari sweep (their only real challenger was Aston Martin, and both of the Aston DBR1s retired with gearbox trouble) and that was about it as far as Sebring 1958 was concerned.

I remember Elvis "The Pelvis" Presley got himself inducted into the Army the Monday after Sebring—in spite of all his hit records—and I was pretty happy about it since I didn't care all that much for his music. Oh, *"Heartbreak Hotel"* was all right, I guess. But not nearly as good as Perry Como singing *"Catch a Falling Star"* or The Platters doing *"Twilight Time."* But maybe I was just getting old and crotchety, you know? Julie really liked Connie Francis' hit *"Who's Sorry Now"* (in fact, she'd sing it to me sometimes when she thought I deserved it) and we both were kind of soft for Laurie London's rousing *"He's Got the Whole World in His Hands."* And right at the top of the charts and looking likely to stay there was that catchy south-of-the-border instrumental number with just one word for a lyric, *"Tequila."*

Castro was still making all kinds of trouble for the Batista government down in Cuba, the French had their hands full with an uprising in Algiers, that gloating, pig-faced Nikita Khrushchev was made Russian Premier and Elizabeth Taylor's husband, movie mogul Mike Todd, got himself killed in a plane crash. She would have been right there with him, but she had a cold and decided to stay home at the last minute. Oh, and a Vanguard rocket finally worked right after nobody much cared any more and shoved a second US satellite up into space. Big deal.

And on the racing scene, people who were actually there told me you couldn't have scripted it any better as pure fiction when both the Cunningham and RAI teams descended on the fast, swoopy and undulating Virginia International Raceway circuit just north of the Carolina border the first weekend in May. It was the first time the two teams had faced each other, and the Cunningham Listers were back at full strength with their normal, fast and proven 3.8-liter engines after their uncharacteristic meltdown at Sebring with the 3.0-liter units. But what caught everybody's eye was how both teams looked exactly like the places they came from—Wild, Brash & Flashy West Coast vs. Conservative, Button-Downed East Coast Establishment—and it must've been a shock when Reventlow's Scarab absolutely streaked away from the two Cunningham Listers at the drop of the green for Saturday's qualifying race. But VIR was definitely a driver's track—one of the very best, in fact—and while the Scarab looked like surely the fastest car on the track, Lance was still on the steep part of the learning curve as a driver. And there were a lot of people who questioned if he had what it took, no matter how much seat time he accumulated. The two experienced Cunningham drivers slowly, relentlessly hunted him down, and one after the other they slipped by under braking at the end of the pit straight. Lance tried to fight back, but only managed to spin. It was all he could do to claw his way back to fifth at the checker. And there was more of the same in Sunday's feature, what with the two chunky Cunningham Listers taking a dominating 1-2 finish and Reventlow in the Scarab trailing them home in a distant and lonely third place. But the writing was on the wall, and whispers were already circulating that the Scarab was a hell of a damn racecar. All it needed was a driver….

Cal bought himself a last-minute airline ticket after Sebring and flew back to Italy on the same plane as Hank and Toly and most of the rest of the Ferrari team. Except for the rig drivers, of course. On the way, he planned and plotted with Toly and worked on Ferrari team manager Tavoni about getting a drive with Ferrari, and he also made a deal with Hank to share a room at a *pensione* somewhere around Modena if he managed to make any headway with the team. Fortunately for Cal, Carlo Sebastian had already been on the line to Maranello to give old Enzo the low-down on Sebring, and naturally he mentioned the job Cal had done, his obvious will to win and the fact that he was now showing a little patience and maturity in the cars as well as talent and raw speed. Of course Ferrari was full up with drivers at the time, what with *Mon Ami Mates* Hawthorn and Collins plus Italian favorite Luigi Musso on the front line and plenty of other seasoned and experienced 'shoes—led by Toly Wolfgang—waiting in the wings and backing them up for the long endurance races.

But Ferrari always kept an eye out for fresh talent—Hank said to keep the established guys on edge as much as anything else—and so he agreed to meet with Cal just a week or two after they arrived in Italy. Ferrari always insisted on meeting his drivers face-to-face and on his own turf at the Ferrari factory in Maranello. He wanted to listen to what they had to say and watch how they moved and acted and see the look in their eyes. Ferrari was uncanny at reading other men and finessing out the texture and substance of their souls, although Ferrari himself could not be read. He usually wore armor-plate sunglasses and an aloof, unfathomable expression, and even without those sunglasses, he never gave anything away with his eyes. Hank called him a complete politician and a genius at maneuvering and motivating personalities and pitting one against the other to solidify his power and get more than maximum effort out of both.

To tell the truth, I think Cal was plenty nervous about meeting face-to-face with Enzo Ferrari. Even though he'd never admit to such a thing. But I guess he and Hank and Toly all went out for dinner together at a little streetcorner café to talk it over.

"He'll try to steamroller you a little, just to see how you react to being pushed," Toly warned. "But don't fall for it. Trust me, he wants you to drive for him. Otherwise you'd never get the meeting. But he wants you to know you're under his thumb, too."

"He sounds like a real sonofabitch."

"He's not so bad," Toly shrugged, "but he's a genius and a doer and he's crafty and ambitious and conniving."

"Sounds like a sonofabitch to me."

Toly eyeballed him. "You have to understand that great men are not like ordinary men. They are driven by bigger doubts and more dangerous demons. That's what makes them great."

Hank looked at him. "I always thought great men were great because of their ideals and values and character."

"You're such an American!" Toly chuckled disdainfully. "Too many TV heroes and too much Sunday School." He stared back into Cal's eyes. "Do you know what makes great men great?"

Cal wasn't sure.

"They do great things, that's all. They can be terrible people. Sad people. Lonely people. Vicious people. Dangerous people. But look at what they've done—what they've accomplished in life—and that's the real measure of their greatness." He took a sip of Lambrusco. "Ferrari is a great man, make no mistake. But he's blind and a visionary at the same time. And he's tortured inside. He's built his kingdom on the blood and brains of others, and he knows it. But it's *his* drive and *his* ambition and *his* genius for stirring men up and getting more than their best out of them that made it all happen." He looked at Hank and Cal. "You know he lost his son?"

"Dino, right?" Hank confirmed.

Toly nodded. "Not quite two years ago. He was barely through his early 20s and worked with him at the factory when he was able. He'd been sickly for quite a long time. Ferrari visits his grave every day."

After dessert they talked about how Cal should play the meeting with Ferrari. "Do you speak any Italian?" Toly asked.

"Not even enough to order the right pasta."

"That's not good. Can you bring anybody who speaks Italian?"

They both looked at Hank.

"Don't look at me. I damn near flunked Spanish in high school."

"How about you?" Cal asked Toly.

"No, that's no good. It can't be another driver. He'll want to talk about me to you, and he can't do that if I'm there."

"How about Gina?" Cal asked.

"Gina? Is she in Italy?"

"She's in the south of France right now, getting ready to go on location someplace in Spain for a movie about bull fighting."

"Do you think she'd come?"

"If she can, I think she would."

"Oh, she'd be *perfect!"* Toly clapped his hands together. "Mind you, the Old Man doesn't care much for drivers getting involved and married. Too much of a distraction. Takes their eye off the ball and sucks their nerve away. Or at least that's what Ferrari thinks, anyway. He gave Peter Collins a hell of a bad time after he married Louise King."

"Then why would I want to bring her?"

"Because he's also a hypocrite and an old scoundrel at heart," Toly laughed. "He'll take one look at her and he won't look back at you at all. Of course, she won't be allowed in the private meeting in his office. He'll have his own interpreter for that."

"He doesn't speak any English at all?"

Toly smiled. "He doesn't speak it, but that doesn't mean he doesn't understand it. Although nobody knows for sure…."

Gina managed to get away from her script pages for two days in order to make the trip down to Maranello for Cal's meeting with Ferrari, and it went pretty much as Toly said it would. They left their names with the girl at the desk and then waited in the unassuming little reception lobby nestled in a corner of the old brick factory, facing out towards a courtyard. Ferrari came out to meet them—he was a big, imposing, well-dressed man with a mane of silver hair, dark sunglasses over his eyes and a noncommittal frown most of the time—but he smiled when he saw Gina LaScala and smiled even broader when he heard her speak Italian. She was wearing a bright yellow blouse with a red Ferrari scarf around her neck and a Ferrari bracelet on her wrist just to please him. He took them on a quick tour of the factory—the foundry, the machine shop, the assembly room where the bread-and-butter 250 GT coupes and racier *Berlinettas* were coming together and finally the race shops themselves. Tall, wide, almost cathedral-like windows on one side flooded the long, hallway-like shop with light. Mechanics in matching orange coveralls worked at this and that with a quiet sense of measured urgency, and there was always the soft click of ratchet wrenches or the hiss of a gas welder or the hollow echo of a muffled curse rustling in the background. Cal thought it felt like being in church.

The factory team *Testa Rossas* were lined up on one side, being refurbished after Sebring along with a few favored customer cars, and the Dino 246 Formula One single-seaters were lined up just as neatly on the other. The new F1 cars were powered by Ferrari's neat, compact new Avgas-burning V6, and Ferrari was quick to explain that he named them 'Dinos' because his son had a hand in designing them before he passed away. There were abrupt halts and heavy pauses in his voice as he told the story—as if he could barely handle the emotion of recalling it all again—but Gina was professional enough to recognize great acting when she saw it.

After they completed their tour, Gina stayed in the small reception lobby while Ferrari and his interpreter ushered Cal into the old man's private office at the end of the hall. It was simple, stately and gracious all at the same time, and surely the most impressive and imposing thing in the room was Enzo Ferrari himself.

"So you want to drive for me?" Ferrari asked through the interpreter.

Cal nodded.

"Any particular reason?"

This must be the part that was supposed to make him squirm a little. Ferrari sure got right down to it. "Ferrari is the best," Cal answered simply, looking the old man right in the sunglasses. "Every driver wants to drive the best."

Ferrari nodded, and Cal thought he might have even looked slightly pleased. Then he spewed more rapid-fire Italian at the interpreter. "But if every driver wants to drive for Ferrari," the interpreter continued, "why would Ferrari want to hire you?"

"Because I'm the best, too." Cal said without flinching.

"You're better than Hawthorn and Musso and Hill and even your friend Toly Wolfgang?"

"I didn't say that," Cal corrected him evenly. "But how will we know one way or the other unless you give me a chance?"

Ferrari looked at him for what seemed like a terribly long time.

"I have seen and known the best, young man," Ferrari finally frowned through the interpreter. "Nuvolari. Ascari. Guy Moll." Cal noticed he didn't mention Fangio. Or Moss. "They were all very singular men. Difficult to know. Impossible to understand. More than a little crazy, perhaps…." He tilted his head back and peered at Cal out of almost closed eyes. "And if I were to give you an opportunity, which of my current drivers should I move out of the way to make room for you?" Ferrari's eyes eased open a few curious millimeters. "Your friend Toly Wolgang is surely the oldest."

"You shouldn't move any of them," Cal told him. Thanks to Toly, he'd seen this one coming. "Things change in racing," he continued. "Opportunities appear."

They both knew what he was talking about.

"I see. And what kind of cars would you have yourself drive for me?"

"Formula One, eventually," Cal answered smoothly. "But anything you want to get me there."

"Formula One," Ferrari mused, rubbing his chin. "You have a lot of ambition."

"I need it," Cal nodded. "I have a lot of talent."

Even for Cal, that was pushing it.

Ferrari looked at him like he was giving it all the most serious consideration. "I worry that I will have too many American drivers then," he said through the interpreter. "I already have Phil Hill…."

"You sell a lot of cars in America," Cal lobbed right back at him. "More than anywhere else, I'm pretty sure. And America is a very large country."

Old man Ferrari nodded as the interpreter turned it into Italian.

"Better yet," Cal continued nervously, "Phil is from California and I'm from New York City. Or around New York City, anyway. Those have to be the two most important places for Ferrari in America."

Ferrari listened thoughtfully to the interpreter, then leaned back in his chair until the leather squeaked and looked up at the ceiling fixture. "You know," he said softly in Italian, "I rarely go to the races myself anymore…"

"So I've heard."

"Do you know why?"

Cal shook his head.

Ferrari was still looking at the ceiling as if he was thinking of repainting it. "You see, it is too painful for me," he began in a faint, faraway voice. "I cannot bear to hear my cars tortured and abused by their drivers. They are like my children, you see. The only ones I have left…."

The room lapsed into silence. After a long pause, the interpreter stood up and asked if Cal and Gina would care to be *Signore* Ferrari's guests for lunch at the little *Il Cavallino* restaurant across the street from the factory gates. The escarole and bean soup on Tuesdays was particularly excellent. *Signore* Ferrari himself unfortunately couldn't join them because he had a pressing appointment, but he hoped they would understand and accept his hospitality anyway.

The interview was over.

That evening Cal and Hank and Toly and Gina all went out to a fine dinner with several bottles of wine at a little restaurant Toly knew at the end of a narrow, cobblestone street not far from the ancient but clean *pensione* where Hank and Cal were staying. And of course Toly and Hank wanted all the grisly details about what went on with Ferrari. "I don't really know where this leaves me," Cal told them.

"Oh, you'll get a call from Tavoni, don't worry," Toly assured him. "He just wants to let you stew a little. It drives the price down."

"I don't care what he pays me."

"But you have to," Toly insisted. "Otherwise, you won't have his respect."

Gina was looking absolutely radiant and they talked for a while about the new bullfighting picture. "It's based on the Hemingway book," she laughed, "but the script doesn't exactly read like Hemingway."

"Oh?" Hank asked. "What *does* it read like?"

"Balderdash, mostly." She glanced over at Toly. "They don't say or do certain things on the screen in Hollywood. It's considered unseemly."

"So all they can do is hint at it?"

Gina nodded. "And not very well, either. But it's a good part for me. At least I'm finally up into the 20th century!"

Cal and Gina were holding hands under the table.

"We really need a picture of this," Hank said. "It's a pretty special night."

"It surely is," Toly agreed. "Have you got your camera?"

"I *always* have my camera. And my notepad. That's what I do."

Hank stood up somewhat unsteadily and snapped a few pictures of Cal, Gina and Toly. Then he got the waiter to take a few of all four of them.

When Gina excused herself for a minute to go to the Little Girls' Room like little girls of all ages inevitably do, Cal immediately turned to Toly and asked if he could borrow a little money. There was a hint of urgency in his voice.

"What for?" Toly asked.

"Look, you're a friend. You don't need to know what for. All you need to know is that I need it and I'll pay you back."

"No he won't," Hank laughed. "You'll have to chase him for it."

"I thought he was rich."

"Sure he's rich. But he never has any money on him. Not ever."

"I see," Toly nodded, stroking the end of his mustache. He tilted his head towards Hank. "This is how the rich stay rich, you see?"

"Look, I'm not kidding around here," Cal said desperately.

“Well,” Toly sighed, making a big show of fishing around in his pocket, “I’m only doing this because I understand you’re about to get a big contract from Ferrari.” He shot Hank a wink. “Then you’ll be poor like the rest of us.” Toly grimaced, and passed Cal a folded wad of lira under the table.

Cal rummaged quickly through it and laid about a quarter of it back on the table. “This is for my share of the dinner,” he told Toly. They could see Gina on her way back from the Little Girls’ Room. Cal quickly handed the rest over to Hank and whispered that he’d be ever so grateful if Hank could find himself somewhere else to stay that night….

Chapter 28: Summer of the Shit Beetle

My beloved goggle-eyed brother-in-law Carson Flegley had himself one hell of a wreck in his new Austin-Healey 100/6 on about the first really nice spring day we had in New Jersey. It was early April, and it'd been gloomy as hell and raining all week. But then Thursday rolled out sunshine like a blessed red carpet and, what with no funerals scheduled and the temperatures edging into the high 50s, Carson decided it was a perfect day to take his new toy out for a spin. He hadn't driven it much through the winter (and if you've had any serious wintertime experience with low-slung British roadsters with side curtains, you don't have to ask why) and even an unassuming guy like Carson got the old top-down/open-road sportycar itch as soon as the weather broke nice.

Of course Sarah Jean couldn't go because she was busy with the newest baby, and naturally then Carson stopped by the dealership to see if I wanted to tag along. But I had a disappointed and dissatisfied customer (who was right on the brink of becoming an *angry,* disappointed and dissatisfied customer) with a comeback clogging the middle of the service drive plus a few pre-delivery inspections to check out—I always tried to give every one of our new car deliveries a quick, personal once-over, as much to keep everybody on their toes as anything else—plus a mystery engine cutout problem on a dark blue Jag roadster we'd bought cheap over at *Alfredo's Foreign Car Service* and that Big Ed thought he had a live one on. And behind all that was a towering stack of paperwork piling up ever-higher in my office. So there was no way I could go. And I remember the feeling inside—that soft tug of yearning—as I watched Carson and the Healey growl away with the springtime's first real sunshine glinting off the bodywork and flickering off its wire wheels….

But I was lucky I took a pass, seeing as how Carson didn't make it much past the edge of town before he crested a hill on a gentle, blind bend—doing about 70 in a 45 zone while fiddling with a clumsy, lunging upshift from regular third to third overdrive—when he found this bozo in an 18-wheel semi pulling out of a side road directly in front of him. It was one of those classic *No Time To Think* deals, and the only thing that saved Carson was that he was such a terrible instinctive driver. He yanked hard on the wheel to swerve around the back end of the rig (but no way was there enough room to make it, and he surely would've been killed if he hit the semi's rear wheels full on), but he also slammed on the brakes and locked everything up so the front wheels happily wouldn't steer. And then, at the very last instant with the bottom edge of the trailer about to slice his head off, Carson dove down across the passenger seat and waited—eyes slammed shut, clutching the seat cushion!—to be fitted for one of his own blessed caskets as a crushing, grinding, shattering tornado of noise passed over him. Only damn if that Healey didn't go right *under* the blessed semi! Or almost under it, anyway. The semi driver also slammed on the brakes as soon as he saw Carson coming, and the 100/6 just shot underneath like that trailer was a low, rolling tunnel and came squirting out the other side in an elongated crunch of folding metal and a shower of snapped-off side mirrors and shattering windshield glass. And then it meandered off across the road and through the gravel like a headless ox and whanged smack into the support posts for an Edsel billboard with the paper already starting to peel off.

Well, I guess you could say it was kind of a miracle, seeing as how all Carson got out of the wreck was a bump on the head, a split lip, a painful black-and-blue mark about the size of a hardball under his ribs where the shifter got him on the way down and a collar full of broken glass. I shudder to even think what would've happened if somebody else—me, for example—had been riding next to him in the passenger seat….

But the ones you get away with inevitably turn into your favorite bar and cocktail-hour stories, and Carson was pleased to discover he had a new aura and stature with all of our sportycar buddies now that he'd managed to survive A Big One. That still left the little problem of what to do with his smashed Healey. To be honest, the mechanical damage wasn't bad at all. Oh, he put a little tweak in the right-front end and wrecked a wheel and tire when he hit the Edsel billboard, but outside of that he still had title to a fine-running, nearly brand-new Austin-Healey 100/6. Everything else—except the seats and carpeting—was pretty much hopeless. The car looked like somebody ran a damn steamroller down it. Or maybe a Sherman Tank, take your pick. I knew the Greek over at the body shop could do damn near anything with anything (or anything with nothing, come to that), but my guys Steve and J.R. over at *Alfredo's Foreign Car Service* had other ideas….

"You seen that new Devin fiberglass body you can buy for sportscars?" they whispered in Carson's ear. "It looks like a damn Ferrari Monza!"

"Bolts right onto an Austin-Healey chassis."

"With simple hand tools!"

"And it's only 295 bucks!"

"Plus freight, of course…."

Then they handed Carson a folded-over copy of *Car & Track* and showed him The Picture. And that would of course be the picture of the completed, professionally finished, trimmed and painted Devin/TR3 that looked so damn sexy it made your eyes water and mouth go dry. The one that probably cost damn near as much as a Ferrari Monza to get it looking like that. Now I couldn't really blame Steve and J.R. for wanting to take on a project like that. Doing your own car from the pavement up is kind of the accepted Master's Thesis of mechanicing, and it's something every aspiring ace wrench-spinner just has to go through. But, having been through it all myself, I had to explain to them that projects like that are never particularly sound business propositions. "The problem is that no matter how much you charge, it always sounds like too much—to both you *and* your customer—and yet it's never near enough to cover all the effort and time and hassles and things you just never saw the first time you looked at them."

"But it says right here you can do it in your own back yard and that it installs easily with simple hand tools," Steve protested. "Hell, we're professional mechanics and we've got a whole damn shop to work with. It oughta be a snap."

Right.

"And we're thinking of yanking that boat-anchor Healey six and shoving in a Chevy V-8 while we're at it."

"That should be a snap, too," I agreed sarcastically.

But they both had That Look in their eyes and Carson had it even worse, so I knew there was nothing much I could do except tell them that however long they thought it was going to take, it was going to take three times as long, and that the same exact thing went for the money. And I think it all finally started to sink in when the naked, unpainted, unfinished Devin fiberglass body shell arrived from California in kind of a dull, splotchy, translucent baby-shit yellow. Along with instructions about how to cut out the hood and doors (carefully!) with a saber saw. I could see by the somewhat shell-shocked look in their eyes that they were finally beginning to grasp what they'd gotten themselves into. At least I knew where they'd be on evenings and weekends for the next six or seven months….

Cal Carrington drove his very first race as a Ferrari team member at the *Targa Florio* World Manufacturers' Championship round in Sicily, and Hank wrote that he was a little shaken when he arrived in Palermo and discovered that the so-called "racetrack" was really a 45-mile, 700-plus corner tour up into the mountains and back on ordinary Sicilian roads! Complete with humps, dips, pavement patches, ditches, roadside gravel, culverts, bridges, stone walls, fences, kilometer stones and ancient towns with narrow, dusty streets lined with weary old brick and masonry buildings that didn't look like they'd move very far if you hit them. It was a real throwback to the outlawed old days of open-road racing at *La Carrera* and the *Mille Miglia,* but they could still get away with that kind of thing in Sicily simply because it was Sicily and the people were mad as hatters about racing. The local Sicilian government loved the race, too, for all the foreigners and foreigners' money it brought in (as did the mountain bandits and *Mafioso* who really ran things in Sicily), and the deep-seated Sicilian passion for the speed, color, drama, danger and excitement of motor sport easily swamped any twinges of common sense. It was agreed by common public consent that the risks were more than worth the party and spectacle. Especially since most of the risk fell squarely on the competitors' shoulders, and not very many of them were Sicilians. Not to mention that the homegrown Sicilian drivers enjoyed a huge home-court advantage, seeing as how they'd known those roads since the day they left their mothers' breast, and knew each bend, turn, jink, kink, climb, dive and particularly those sphincter-tightening surprise corners that just kept on turning and tightening and turning and tightening long after you expected them to straighten out. The *Targa Florio* was not the sort of circuit you could master with mere talent, skill, force of will, reflexes or instinct. That would only get you wrecked or hurt or killed. And, as Toly advised Cal, the sooner you figured that out, the better off you were going to be.

The factory had given Cal one of the latest 250 GT *Berlinettas* with the idea that he and his co-driver—hot new young Italian comingman Nino Barlini—should easily win the 3.0-liter Grand Touring class with it. Hell, the only other cars entered were an older Ferrari GT plus a couple lardy 300SLs in the hands of some Italian privateers. But it didn't take long for Cal to realize that the real challenge at the *Targa Florio* was the race itself, not the other cars. The full distance was a thousand kilometers—or 626 miles, to be exact—and even the fastest cars could barely average a mile a minute. Meaning the winners would take over ten-and-a-half hours to reach the end! Plus it hardly helped that there was no "official" practice whatsoever. Instead, there were several days of "unofficial" practice where drivers who'd never seen the place before—like Cal—could head out in their racecars (or a factory test mule or, better yet, in rented Fiats!) and try to find their way around. But that kind of "practice" was even more dangerous than the race itself, what with trucks and cows and motorbikes and horse carts and chickens and bicycles and women carrying babies or loaves of bread or bundles of laundry to dodge and watch out for. Along with grinning, toothless, deliriously happy old men standing along the roadsides and cheering as the racers hurled past. Not to mention occasional meandering flocks of sheep and whispered rumors of bandits up in the mountains. The rich car owner with the other, privateer Ferrari GT decided to try it out himself during the unofficial "practice days"—he had two experienced racers signed on to drive it in the actual race—and promptly collided head-on with a delivery truck on the far side of a deceptively gentle rise not far outside of Palermo. He managed to kill himself, and didn't do the Ferrari or the delivery truck much good, either.

Toly was kind enough to go out with Cal to give him a couple tips and show him a few things (or at least he did after a heated argument about who was actually going to drive!,) but it was virtually impossible to commit the whole 45 miles and 700-plus curves to memory in just a few tours. Toly had driven the *Targa* once before in a 1300cc Alfa, so he hardly considered himself an expert. But he did his best to offer Cal some useful advice between bracing his feet against the floorboards and hanging onto the grab handle of the rented Fiat so tightly it damn near came off in his hand. *"However fast you think you can go,"* he warned through clenched teeth as they accelerated down a narrow, uneven, undulating stretch of country road, *"go slower. Otherwise you never make the finish."* The Fiat boomed over a hidden low bridge, went airborne for an instant and banged down loudly on the other side, scraping the hell out of the undercarriage. *"You see what I mean?"*

"It's tricky," Cal agreed as he grabbed for fourth gear, his eyes focused on the road ahead like a pair of death ray beams.

"And remember this," Toly continued as Cal threw the Fiat around an easy, open bend with the tires damn near folding under. *"If you wind up stranded up in the mountains, make sure you have some money in your pockets or a watch on your wrist to give the bandits. As a gift, of course."* Cal quickly heaved the wheel and slung the Fiat the opposite way as the wide-open corner turned into an unexpected switchback. *"And whatever you do,"* Toly added through a tight-lipped grimace, *"DO NOT LEAVE THE CAR!"*

"Why not?"

"Souvenir hunters. They'll pick it down to a bare carcass before you get back. There'll be nothing left to ship back to Maranello...."

In spite of the reconnaissance laps with Toly, Hank said Cal was wearing a pretty grim expression as he waited in the pits for the cars to come around at the end of the first lap. As at *La Carrera* and the *Mille Miglia,* the cars were released at intervals—one every 40 seconds—starting at the ungodly hour of 6:30 in the morning. The littlest tiddlers started first and the big guns came last, and they all began the *Targa Florio* by leaping (or lurching) through a beautiful flowered canopy. Which was hastily removed after the last car left since it wouldn't be long at all before the first cars came around again. At the end of the first lap, the time sheets showed it was Luigi Musso in the lead in one of the factory team *Testa Rossas,* and just 12 seconds behind came Peter Collins in another of the other factory cars. But it was already obvious that at least here at the *Targa*—on this tight, twisty, bumpy, dangerous and diabolically long and difficult circuit—the quickest of the handier little cars were going to be damn near eyeball-to-eyeball with the bigger, more powerful ones. Especially the new factory Porsche RSK with the two stubby tailfins stuck on the back in the hands of Behra and Scarlatti. Along with the pretty little 1500cc OSCAs, particularly the one with seasoned *Targa* veterans Cabianca and Bordoni up. Not to mention the four-cam Porsche Carrera coupe running in the 1600cc Grand Touring category (with team manager Huschke von Hanstein as one of its drivers) which was already looking fast enough to threaten the 250GT *Berlinetta* Cal was co-driving for first GT car home. Handling was far better than horsepower at the *Targa Florio,* and track knowledge meant everything. And track knowledge was hardly the sort of thing you could manufacture on the spot….

Cal's co-driver Barlini pitted at the end of the third lap to hand the car over. There was more than enough fuel left for another lap or two and the tires didn't look too bad, but the front end was bashed in on the passenger side and you could see the wheel rim was wobbling. And young and fit as he appeared before the race, Barlini was absolutely exhausted. Hurling a big, heavy, powerful GT car around the endless twists and turns of the *Targa Florio* and trying to remember what came next was exacting and demanding work. It sucked the spirit right out of you.

The crew changed all four wheels and tires, checked over the front end, gassed the car up and Cal jumped in. He didn't say anything, but Hank was there and said he looked a lot less cocky and self-assured than when he normally climbed behind the wheel of a racecar. But he rose to the occasion and did a hell of a job, keeping it on the old island and turning each lap a solid two or three minutes quicker than his previous one. He finally managed to slip one in even faster than that damn 1600cc Porsche Carrera! But the Ferrari was getting pounded something awful in the process. The steering wheel wasn't pointing straight ahead any more, the shifter was grinding into third and popping out of second and the shocks were fading so the chassis felt more and more like a load of loose plumbing hardware every lap. Cal had lost track of how long or how many laps he'd been out there—it seemed like a long, *long* time!—but he was too busy concentrating on the road ahead to think much about it. All he knew was that he sure felt relieved when they finally flashed him the "IN" sign from the pits, indicating he should stop for fuel, tires and a driver change the next time around. And he had to be happy about the little, handwritten *"Molto Bene"* he saw scrawled at the bottom of the signaling chalkboard.

Only he never made it back around. One of the other cars had dropped a wheel off on one of the endless switchbacks up in the mountains and showered a blind corner with a trail of dirt and gravel. There wasn't much of it, but Cal was the next car on the scene and, pleased with the signal he'd gotten from the Ferrari pits, going maybe that tiny tenth or even hundredth too fast. He saw the scattered patch of dirt and gravel and felt the front end start to plow at almost exactly the same instant. He turned in harder and lifted instinctively to try and get the car to rotate, but the grip simply wasn't there and the Ferrari lumbered helplessly towards the low stone wall on the outside. There was nothing he could do then but jam on the brakes, but it was already too late. The Ferrari banged off the stone wall, ricocheted across the road and thumped down hard into a shallow drainage ditch at the base of a grassy hillside. He could hear and feel the sheet metal crumple and the hard whang of the undercarriage against concrete and saw the windshield shatter out right in front of him. *DAMN!* The engine was screaming wildly even though his foot was off the pedal, and Cal flailed frantically at the dashboard to shut it off.

And then the silence settled in around him....

Cal leaned his head forward against the steering wheel and closed his eyes. Maybe it would've been better if he'd been hurt. Then at least they'd cart him off in a damn ambulance and he wouldn't have to face Tavoni and the mechanics and his co-driver Barlini back in the pits. *"Shit!"* he muttered into the back of his driving glove.

"Pardone?"

Cal looked up to see two young Sicilian men looking in through the opposite window. One of them was wearing what looked like a beret. The other was carrying a rifle. He sat up in the seat.

"Bon Giorno" the young man with the beret said.

Cal licked his lips. "H-hello."

The two men looked at each other, then back at Cal.

"Eh...you OK?" the one with the beret asked.

Cal looked down at himself, did a quick inventory and shrugged. "I guess so."

The man with the beret pointed at his cheek. Cal checked it with his finger. A wet smudge of blood came off on the end of his driving glove. He adjusted the rearview mirror—hell, it wasn't even cracked!—and sure enough, there was a little gash on his right cheekbone. Probably from hitting the damn steering wheel.

The man with the beret leaned his head inside the car. "You..." he fumbled for the English. "You...*come."* He added the universal *Follow Me* gesture with his hand.

Cal licked his lips again. "I'm really not supposed to," he protested. "I'm supposed to stay with the car."

"You...*come,"* the beret repeated with the same hand motion. Then he came around to Cal's side and, with much pulling and yanking thanks to the crushed fender, fought the door open. It made a sound like rusty nails being pulled out of old, dry wood. *"Come,"* he repeated, smiling.

"I'm really not supposed to...."

The beret shook his head and nodded towards the man with the rifle. "He watch. No worry. He watch...."

And so Cal followed the beret up a gentle grass slope while the guy with the gun took a proud, menacing stance next to the crumpled Ferrari. They were somewhere up in the mountains, and Cal was already worrying about all the stories he'd heard about the local bandits. But instead the beret took him to a big stone house the color of an old tombstone. It looked older than any house Cal had ever seen in America, and yet the central courtyard was alive with people and laughter and food and wine. Everyone seemed terrifically happy to see him, and nothing would do but that Cal should sit down and eat and drink with them while the race droned on and on in the background, one car at a time. In less than a half-hour he was *their* brave and heroic American racer, and the way the young girls looked at him almost made him blush.

Cal was feeling pretty good by the time the engine noise stopped and the tow rigs started out from Palermo to gather up the missing cars. Toly had seen the GT Ferrari crumpled in the ditch during his last stint, and he and the rented Fiat—now with a missing hubcap, a bent rim and its exhaust pipe dragging thanks to their "reconnaissance" laps—appeared about a half hour later. He parked it by the wrecked Ferrari and climbed up the grassy slope. Toly looked tired, sweaty, disheveled and grimy in the gathering dusk, but many of the people at the table recognized him instantly. He talked back and forth with a few of them in rapid-fire Italian, then came over and sat down next to Cal.

"You okay?"

Cal shrugged, but the big, wallowing grin on his face gave him away.

"My God, you're drunk!"

"Only a little," Cal corrected him. Then he reached out and patted the empty wine bottle in front of him. "It's pretty good stuff," he beamed. "They make it right here."

Toly looked around the table. "You've done pretty well for someone who doesn't speak any Italian."

Cal shrugged. "I got by."

Toly glanced down the hill to where the Ferrari was stuffed nose-down in the drainage ditch. "What happened?"

Cal rolled his palm up helplessly. "Gravel on the road. Going too fast." He flinched his shoulders. "I made a mistake. That's the long and short of it."

"Jesus, don't tell that to Tavoni!" Toly warned.

"Why not?"

Toly's face opened up in a grand smile. "Because you're a driver, and he expects you to lie...."

The beret handed Toly a glass of wine and a heaping plate of food.

"We should really be getting back," Toly told him in English.

"What the hell for?" Cal asked. "The damn race is over, isn't it?"

"Long gone," Toly agreed.

"So why the hell not?"

"Why the hell not, indeed."

Cal took another long sip of wine. "So," he asked, "how'd you do?"

"Third."

"Who won?"

"Musso." Toly raised his glass. "And good for him, too. He's been going through quite a rough patch, hasn't he? It isn't easy being the Next Great Italian Racing Champion, is it? An awful lot of guys have been crushed by that crown."

"Here's to Luigi!" Cal agreed, and drained the rest of his glass. "So if Musso was first and you were third, who finished second?"

A scowl descended over Toly's face. "That bastard little Porsche with the stupid airplane fins on the back."

"All 1500ccs of it?" Cal mocked.

"At least I didn't wind up in a ditch like some people."

"Well, here's to the little bastard of a Porsche, anyway."

Toly clinked their glasses together. "Fins and all."

"Right. Fins and all."

"Trust me, those little buzz bombs won't be seeing anything but our tailpipes once we get to Le Mans…."

In the end, it was Toly Wolfgang who apparently started the story—right there in the courtyard of that old stone house up in the Sicilian mountains, in fact—that a little dog ran into the road and a little six-year-old boy who loved that dog ran out after it, and that's why Cal had no choice but to swerve and hit the stone wall and then ricochet head-on into the ditch on the opposite side. So he was actually a hero, right? By midnight and six more bottles of wine it was fact in the house in the mountains, and by noon the next day it was a certified local legend. It even got written up in the Palermo newspapers.

Back home in the states, the papers were full of news about how this 23-year-old American kid from Shreveport, Louisiana, named Van Cliburn won this big, famous piano-playing contest over in Moscow—so you thought and maybe even prayed that the Cold War might be warming up a bit—and then a month later Vice President Nixon and his wife Pat got stoned, yelled at and even spat on by mobs of angry-looking folks who really seemed to hate us during their South American "goodwill" tour. Seems a lot of ordinary, rank-and-file South American nobodies and everybodies had their noses out of joint—*"DIE, YANKEE PIG!"*—just because the old U.S. government had been busily backing (and maybe even propping up?) a few gold-braid-encrusted, right-thinking South American military dictatorships that maybe weren't especially concerned about what happened to their poor, ordinary citizens but were eager as hell to Stem The Flow of Communism in South America. Not to mention pocketing a lot of Yankee greenbacks for selling us all the oil and such we wanted at reasonable prices.

Meanwhile, out in sunny Southern California, the summer of the Scarab was just beginning. On Memorial Day weekend, Lance Reventlow finally managed to knit a whole race together—or almost a whole race, anyway—and won the big-bore modified feature outright at the Cal Club races at Santa Barbara. There were several decent Ferraris entered with some damn good 'shoes behind the wheel (although probably the best combination, Dan Gurney in Frank Arciero's older but still fast 4.9, dropped out with a busted diff) but Lance just kept pulling away from the rest of them. He had a 16-second lead built up over Richie Ginther in John von Neumann's new, silver 3.0-liter *Testa Rossa* (John had just picked it up from the factory team earlier in the year after Sebring) but maybe Lance started drinking the champagne a little early, seeing as how he lost his concentration and looped the damn thing two laps from the end. But Santa Barbara was an airport circuit so there wasn't much of anything to hit, and Lance managed to gather everything up, get the car pointed in the right direction and win the race anyway.

Then Lance and the Scarab ran away with the Saturday qualifying race at the Cal Club races at Riverside at the end of June (albeit against pretty spotty opposition) but he broke the rear end in Sunday's feature. Pomona was more of the same, with Lance and the Scarab winning easily both days and setting a new lap record in the process. Again, it was a minor-league, amateur Cal Club event against minor-league, amateur Cal Club opposition, but a win is a win. And all the west coast sportycar magazines were going absolutely ga-ga over the Scarab. But how could you blame them. In a world of imported exotics from Italy and England and a bunch of homegrown, V-8-powered hybrids, mongrels and backyard bombs that generally looked like V-8-powered hybrids, mongrels and backyard bombs, the Scarab stood out as the most stunningly exquisite—and also apparently the fastest—motorized creature in the paddock. The shape, detailing, paintwork, fit, finish, design, engineering and construction of the Scarab set brand-new standards. Or new standards for sports/racing cars, anyway, since the local California Indycar builders (and, more recently, hot rodders) had been building stuff like that as far back as anybody could remember. Sure, it was important that an Indianapolis racecar (or a hot rod, for that matter) was fast and reliable and that everything worked right. But you'd rather paint your face pink than run a new racecar through Gasoline Alley at Indy (or pull your new hotrod up to a stoplight on Sepulveda Boulevard with the engine kind of loping on account of the glass-packs and wild cam) unless it really looked *sharp!* And that meant it had to be painted and polished and anodized and pinstriped and chrome- or nickel-plated plated here and there. Nobody had ever done that kind of thing with a sportycar before, and it sure as hell showed. Made it look so blessed *American,* too. When Lance Reventlow's Scarab slinked and growled and grumbled its way through a racing paddock, it was like Rita Hayworth (or Gina LaScala, for that matter) waltzing through a roomful of knock-kneed high school cheerleaders and bifocaled librarians.

And speaking of beautiful women, the "world's richest baby" was also making news with some of the female types he was dating and bringing to the racetrack, including starlets Natalie Wood and his luscious, intelligent, soon-to-be fiancée Jill St. John. He'd also moved the whole Scarab operation into larger, better-equipped quarters just a few miles away in Culver City, added some new talent to the staff (including Phil Remington, who was like a one-man fabricating shop and could make anything out of anything) and set his boys to work building the second and third Scarabs for Chuck Daigh and Bruce Kessler. They were called Mk. IIs because they had beefed up frame tubes and some other detail differences under the skin. Plus one that anybody could see: the second and third cars were built with right-hand drive. Lance's car had the driver on the left like any normal American passenger wagon, mostly because nobody much thought about it. But it made a lot more sense to have the driver on the right (even though that meant he had to shift with his left hand) on account of most racetracks ran clockwise and that put the driver's weight on the inside and improved his sight lines to the apex on the great majority of the corners. Not to mention that the shift linkage on the Scarab's Corvette gearbox was hung on the left side of the housing, and that put it a painful half-inch into your right thigh if you were sitting on the left.

Lance still harbored dreams of running and winning at Le Mans with his all-American Scarabs, and so he had Jim Travers and Frank Coon over at the Traco engine shop working on a destroked, Avgas-burning, 183 cubic-inch/3.0-liter version of that all-time great Indy 500 engine, the Meyer Drake Offenhauser. It was one of those ideas that looked like it couldn't miss on paper. The Offy was reasonably light, thoroughly developed and tough as a Sherman tank, what with a hellaciously strong bottom end and the block and cylinder heads cast in one piece so there were no head gaskets to blow. And Ferrari had already proven with their big, four-banger 750 and 850 Monzas that you could make some really serious torque with such a motor. And so the third Scarab was set up to run the tall, narrow, handsome Offenhauser four-cylinder from day one.

Only it didn't work out.

In a classic case of book smarts and theoretical thinking crashing head-on into practical reality, that damn Offy just flat refused to cooperate. It didn't much like running on gasoline, had big lumps and flat spots in the power band, didn't churn out nearly enough ponies and, worst of all, shook like it was going to break into pieces. You have to understand that every engine has what engine builders call "periods of harmonic imbalance." And what that means in plain English is that all the stuff spinning and slinging and swinging and pumping and rotating and gyrating and jumping up-and-down inside an automobile engine hits certain speed ranges where everything goes into kind of a Major League Off-Kilter Colossal

Oscillation. Now every engine has these things, but the general rule of thumb is that the more cylinders you have (assuming they're all nicely balanced off against each other as far as reciprocating weight and firing order are concerned) the less of a problem you're going to have with harmonic imbalance. And the less cylinders and inner balance you have—ask any Harley Davidson owner!—the more buzz, fuzz, rock, shake and throb you're going to encounter. Although I've noticed most Harley riders really seem to enjoy that sort of thing….

Anyhow, a big old four-banger like an Offy can be pretty nasty about periods of harmonic imbalance, but it was the kind of thing that never much showed up on the oval tracks on account of it was standard roundy-round operating procedure to fool with the gearing and tire size until you got the engine operating precisely and exclusively in the smooth, fat, sweet and mellow part of its torque band. But road racing was a different proposition entirely, what with the engines running up and down the rev range like a damn piano player doing chromatic scales. And the Offenhauser flat didn't like it. Plus the porting, cam timing, compression ratio and combustion chamber shape of the Offy had likewise evolved on the oval tracks, where it only needed to pull (and pull like hell!) from the when the driver started laying into the throttle in one long, sweeping turn until he charged down the straightaway and backed off for the next. The Offy was probably the best engine ever built for that kind of duty. Especially over 500 miles at Indianapolis. But it sure didn't take to road racing. Not hardly. The RAI and Traco guys tried it with fuel injection first, but it would just stumble and cough and fart and belch flames until it crawled up onto its camshaft and then it would suddenly hook up and go like crazy for a few thousand RPM until you either had to shift or watch it blow up. So then they tried it with Weber carburetors like all the fancy European sportscars used to see if they could maybe spread the power around a little further down the rev range. But the engine shook so bad at certain RPM ranges that it foamed up the fuel in the float bowls like whipped egg whites and threw the mixture all off. They even tried mounting the carburetors on the blessed frame and hooking them to the engine with lengths of rubber hose. Honest they did! But that didn't work, either. In the end, Lance and his guys had to pretty much give up on the idea of racing a team of Scarabs at Le Mans with modified, Avgas-burning Offy four-bangers under the hood.

That setback aside, the Chevy-powered Scarabs were generally starting to blow the rest of the competition into the weeds. Daigh's car was ready by the end of July, and the Scarab team promptly romped to their first 1-2 finish in an SCMA race at Minden, Nevada, near Reno. Only it was hardly without incident. Everybody pretty much knew that Chuck Daigh was a faster, more skillful, more talented and far more savvy and mechanically sympathetic race driver than Lance, and a lot of people wondered what was going to happen when he found himself squared off against a lesser driver in an equal car who just incidentally happened to be the guy who signed his paychecks. The answer wasn't long in coming. Chuck had had fuel injection problems that soaked the plugs and had his car running on essentially six cylinders for the first half of the race in Nevada, and that had Lance pretty much running away with it. But then it finally cleared up and Daigh came charging back. He caught Lance on the last corner of the last lap (can you believe it?) and dove right under him to take the lead! Lance didn't see him coming in his mirrors—he thought he had the race sewed up—and Chuck's move caught old Lance with his pants down. In fact, he spun the car trying to yank it over and shut the door.

To say Lance was a little ticked off is putting it mildly. And probably at himself a lot more than Chuck, if you want the truth of it. He was furious when he climbed out of the car, and stormed away from the racetrack without talking to anyone. The story goes that he smashed his rental car into a tree and wound up picking a fight in a local bar later that evening. Chuck and some of the other RAI guys found him there, still brooding and fuming, and finally Chuck took him outside for a little Father Duffy chat. You have to understand that Lance had a hell of a temper—the kind it's easy to get if you have way too much freedom and money and not near enough parenting and discipline when you're growing up—and it was even money at the bar as to whether Chuck would get fired or they'd wind up trading split lips, loose teeth and black eyes. *"Look,"* Chuck told him, grabbing him by both shoulders, *"you said you never wanted to win unless you could do it on your own. Well, you couldn't."* He pulled in closer and stared right into Lance's eyes. They were damn near vibrating. *"You have to keep an eye on your damn mirrors, Lance! A race isn't won until the checker waves. And you NEVER leave that much room on the inside going into a corner! Especially on the last corner of the last fucking lap! If I didn't do that to you, somebody else will."*

Slowly, the fury melted out of Lance's eyes. His fists unclenched and the spring-tension arch relaxed out of his back. He looked like a hurt and confused 22-year-old kid again. "You're right," he finally muttered. "Let's go have a drink."

Neither one of them ever said another word about it….

After that the Scarabs headed east, looking for another confrontation with the Cunningham team like smart-alecky wild west kids with sixguns on their hips seeking out the established Fastest Gun in Town. They got their wish at an SCMA airport race in Montgomery, New York, just two weeks later. Montgomery sits upstate about halfway between Port Jervis and Poughkeepsie, and naturally nothing would do but for Big Ed and me to take a little trip up there once we heard the Scarabs were coming and squaring off eyeball-to-eyeball against the Cunningham Lister-Jaguars. Besides, Big Ed had just taken delivery of one of Jaguar's brand new XK150S roadsters—creamy white with red leather interior, natch—and a day trip up to Montgomery seemed like a perfect opportunity to break it in. I guess Big Ed was feeling a little pang or two for his old XK120 while he was wheeling that monster Chrysler 300 around, but I figured the bloom would come off the rose pretty quickly seeing as how he hadn't been stuck in rush-hour traffic with a clutch and stickshift for quite a spell. To tell the truth, he probably should've gotten himself a regular-issue XK150 with the optional Borg-Warner automatic, but the "S" was the rare, hot, top-of-the-line model with the straight-port, gold-painted cylinder head, triple two-inch S.U. carburetors, a nine-to-one compression ratio and some 40 more horsepower, and so naturally that was the one Big Ed just had to have. But it didn't come with the automatic. It did, however, have a wraparound windshield and genuine roll-up windows—a real first for a Jaguar roadster—and that was a genuine plus seeing as how side curtains always struck me as a throwback to the old horse-and-buggy days and were a real pain in the ass to haul out of the trunk and plug into their door sockets in a driving rainstorm.

Anyhow, it was a nice day for a drive and we started out plenty early, and I must admit that XK150S could really gobble up the old pavement once we got out of the city. As the highway patrolman who pulled us over was quick to point out while writing Big Ed a speeding ticket with three digits on it. Big Ed tried to talk him out of it, but the State Highway Patrol guys just don't seem to have the same sort of, umm, "flexibility" as most of your local and municipal cops. They take their jobs pretty damn seriously, and if you know what's good for you, you won't flash them a wink or a grin or wrap a tenner or a twenty around your license when you pass it over like you might in certain, shall we say, more sophisticated and cosmopolitan areas. Like Newark, for example. When a crew-cut cop with one of those Smokey the Bear hats on his head calls you "sir" with all sorts of phony respect in his voice (while at the same time his icy eyeballs are saying: *"I've got you, Bub, and your ass is mine!"),* the smartest thing you can do is just say *"Yes, sir"* and *"No, sir"* right back at him without even the tiniest hint of smartass and hope you don't have too many other tickets sitting up in your file drawer in Trenton.

Needless to say, Big Ed was plenty pissed about getting that ticket, and even had me get in and drive afterwards just to make sure he didn't get pulled over again. And I could see why. Boy, was it ever easy to get cheeky with the posted speed limits in that Jag 150S. Why, you could flip it into fourth overdrive and just loaf along at 85 or 90 or so with just 3500 showing on the blessed tach! And Big Ed's Chrysler never hugged the road like that Jaguar. Oh, it was fine on big, wide-open stretches of billiard table-smooth four-lane superhighway, but try running that Chrysler over back roads or gently undulating whoop-de-dos at a high rate of speed and it'd make your stomach queasy and your hands tighten up into a blessed death grip on the wheel. Oh, it was still a pretty neat car, but it was a lot better cruising down Main Street or Madison Avenue than out flogging around the countryside.

Naturally Lance flew in via private plane (what else?) and was at the track and ready to go early Saturday morning. But apparently the Scarab transporter got lost somewheres between Reno and upstate New York, and it didn't pull into the Montgomery airport until almost straight-up midnight. And then the team had to spend the rest of the night thrashing away on the cars to get them ready. So Lance and Chuck didn't have much of anything in the way of pre-race practice. Just the qualifying session Sunday morning. But even so Chuck qualified second between local East Coast hotshoe Fred Windridge in a fast and thoroughly brutish new Chevy-powered Lister and Ed Crawford in the first of the Cunningham Lister-Jags. Walt Hansgen in the other Cunningham Lister was right behind them, along with new-kid-on-the-block Bill Sadler and his exceedingly low-slung and wicked-looking Chevy-powered Sadler Special out of Canada. The Sadler was a lot neater, cleaner, cleverer and more professional-looking than your average backyard home-built but, like everything else on four wheels, not really in the Scarab's class when it came to design and execution.

But Bill Sadler was your typically scrappy Canadian—they figure getting your front teeth knocked out in a hockey game is as much a part of growing up as acne and toilet training—and he rocketed right through the front row to make a grab for the lead as soon as the green dropped. Windridge in the Lister-Chevy was already in trouble with a bum clutch and dropping back, and Daigh more or less "laid a little metal" on Sadler to nudge him gently out of the way at Corner One. Like I said before, he was really a dirt-track oval driver at heart. So Chuck had the lead at the end of lap one, but the two Cunningham Listers were right in his wheeltracks, and they were back around him at the end of lap two. The race quickly boiled down to a straight fight between the RAI Scarabs and the Cunningham team, and there seemed to be an awful lot of bumping, grinding, nerfing, nudging and elbowing going on at the front of the pack. Hardly "gentlemen's racing," I guess, but it sure was one hell of a show! In fact, Ed Crawford had to make a pit stop to get a wrinkled front fender peeled back away from his tire (now how did *that* happen?) and then Chuck Daigh saw his temperature gauge climbing on account of he'd pretty much flattened the Scarab's radiator opening on the back end of the Sadler Special at Turn One. So he had to make a pit stop to have it levered back open. That left Hansgen in the Lister-Jag in front being pursued by Reventlow in the Scarab, while Crawford and Daigh wound up all mixed up with each other again after completing pit stops to pound out the body damage.

In spite of Walt Hansgen's well-known driving skill and the proven speed of the Cunningham Lister-Jags, Reventlow's Scarab was repeatedly able to reel him in and pass him on the straightaways. With ease. Only to have Walt fight back and sneak past again under braking into the twisty sections. It was pretty stirring stuff, no lie! By the middle stages of the race, Lance was having trouble with a slipping clutch and fading brakes, and he finally spun out when he simply couldn't get the car whoa'd down for a corner. He got it going again, but then the brake pedal promptly went all the way to the floor (I told Big Ed I thought he might've got the brakes so hot that the blessed fluid boiled!) and Lance went straight on through the haybales at the chicane.

So Lance was out of it. But Chuck was making one hell of a comeback from his pit stop. He dispensed with Crawford and started reeling Hansgen's Lister in at the rate of two and even three seconds a lap, setting several track records along the way. It's hard to say what would have happened once he caught up, but then Hansgen blew a rear tire just as Daigh closed in for the kill, and he had no choice but to stop and have it changed. Chuck figured he had the race in the bag after that and eased off—hell, he even lit himself a damn cigarette!—but behind him Hansgen was driving like a man possessed after his pit stop. The Lister closed and you could see how hard Walt was trying—jeez, could he ever *drive!*—but the Scarab was still 10 seconds to the good come the checker.

If that win wasn't exactly convincing, the one at Thompson two weeks later certainly was. Cunningham was there with his team of Lister-Jags, and it was kind of a home race for them seeing as how it was up in Connecticut and all. But even so it was the Scarabs running 1-2 by the end of the second lap and easily pulling away from the field. In fact, Chuck and Lance were just flat playing with each other, passing and re-passing for the hell of it. At least it gave the fence-hangers something to cluck over. Chuck's car developed rear axle trouble and had to drop out, but Lance went on to drive an uncharacteristically smooth, smart and unruffled race and managed to lap everybody but Hansgen by the end. Considering what everybody thought of Walt's skill and Lance's natural talent (or lack of it), you had to call it a pretty damn dominating display of the Scarab's superiority.

There was another easy, ho-hum 1-2 act at the new Meadowdale track just west of Chicago (the Cunningham Listers were expected, but didn't show) on the RAI team's way back to Culver City, and then Lance flew ahead to California in order to be there when his buddy Bruce Kessler gave the Offy-powered Scarab its first (and, as it turned out, last) shakedown race at Santa Barbara. You have to understand that this was Bruce's first time back in the cockpit after a really harrowing wreck at Le Mans that killed another driver and put Bruce in a French hospital for a few weeks' stay, and that wasn't the kind of thing you, he, me or anybody else could easily swagger off.

But racers are racers—the great majority just can't help themselves—and so Bruce had the bug back pretty quick after returning to California, and he was eager as hell to climb back in a car, swallow up some pavement and put as many other drivers as he could in his rear-view mirror. I guess you always want to see if you've still got it, you know? Plus the Scarab ride was too good a deal to pass up. Not only was it drop-dead gorgeous, it was also a top candidate for fastest damn sports/racing car on the planet. And if they could just get that blessed Offy to work, they'd be taking it to Le Mans….

The Offy-powered Scarab was every bit as beautiful as the other two (but you could tell it apart by the hood scoop they put in to clear the cam covers on the tall Offy four-banger) but it ran poorly against mediocre opposition at Santa Barbara and vibrated so badly that the shift linkage fell apart. Lance thought the problem might be Bruce's driving as a result of his accident in June at Le Mans and his stay in the hospital, but Bruce was quick to point out that it was bog slow down the straightaways and that when it was off the cam, stepping on the gas was like putting your foot in a bowl of mush. As Bruce somewhat indelicately put it afterwards:

"Lance, this thing is a piece of shit."

Surely the biggest sports car race ever contemplated in California—or anywhere else in the old U.S. of A. this side of Sebring, Florida—was the so-called "Times/Mirror U.S. Grand Prix for Sports Cars" at Riverside in the middle of October. It was sponsored by the Times-Mirror Company, which owned the two biggest newspapers in the L.A. area, and so it came with all the hoo-hah, hoopla and pre-race publicity you could possibly imagine, what with headlines, feature stories, news tidbits and "personality profiles" slathered all over the sports pages for over a week ahead of time. Including quite a few lines and pictures about "world's richest baby" and "Barbara Hutton's son" Lance Reventlow and his homegrown, California-built cars that were named after…what was that again? Something about Egyptian immortality….

The Times/Mirror race also differed from all the usual, rank and file SCMA and Cal Club amateur events in that it was a genuine, $15,000-purse professional road race sanctioned by none other than USAC (the United States Auto Club) who'd been pretty much running the Indy 500 and the rest of American champ car racing ever since the Triple-A pulled out of the race sanctioning business following that terrible wreck at Le Mans in 1955. Now $15,000 was a pretty fat purse in 1958, so the Riverside race attracted a smattering of top Europeans as well as all the best sportycars and drivers on the West Coast. Not to mention a few established Indycar stars and teams plus a stock car guy or two, all eager to pick up a little of that tempting purse money. Carroll Shelby was there with John von Neumann's bored-out Maserati 450S and Masten Gregory was there with John Edgar's 4.9 Ferrari and most of the smart money was on Phil Hill, who'd flown back from Europe to drive von Neumann's new, one-of-a-kind Ferrari 412MI.

The 412MI was a pretty damn special car, seeing as how it was a sportscar re-body of the Frankenstein monster device Ferrari threw together (at the urging of the Automobile Club of Italy) to run against the American Indianapolis cars in the 1958 "Race of Two Worlds" at Monza. I guess Ferrari himself wasn't too keen on the idea—he'd seen the way the purpose-built, Indy-style cars had steamrollered the European opposition on Monza's steeply banked oval the year before—but he had a big, right-sized and thoroughly redundant 4023cc V-12 on hand (the one out of Portago's crashed 335S from that tragic 1957 *Mille Miglia* accident, in fact) and an appropriate size single-seater chassis laying around from one of his 1951 grand prix cars. Not to mention that the prize money at "Monzanapolis" was nothing to sneeze at.

Although the big V-12 had plenty of power to run against the Americans at Monza, the car's relatively short wheelbase and "sophisticated" road racing-style suspension just didn't work all that well on a steeply-banked, high-speed oval. It says a lot about Luigi Musso's guts, pride and fierce determination to do well in front of the hometown Italian crowd that he managed to put the hairy beast on the front row, led the first lap and mixed it up mightily with the best of the American cars. Even though the damn thing was flitting and darting around on the bankings while doing its best to broil him alive. Continual high-speed running and the car's untested aerodynamics were filling the cockpit with engine heat. And exhaust fumes. Musso finally had to pit because of it—pale, woozy and sickened—and the car was handed over to Hawthorn. Musso tried again in the second heat, but again was overcome by the fumes and stopped to hand it over to Phil Hill. Musso was too ill to start the third heat, and so Hawthorn and Hill shared the car. After three grueling heats on a searing hot day and in the hands of no less than three different drivers, the 412MI wound up a distant third to the top two American Indy roadsters. But no question the thing was *fast.* In spite of twitchy handling on the bankings, Musso'd qualified it a thin hair shy of 175 mph! And now, complete with a sleek new sportscar body, a suspension system that was surely better suited to road racing and Phil Hill once again behind the wheel, the 412MI looked every inch the car to beat at Riverside. But not by much, seeing as how the Times/Mirror U.S. Grand Prix for Sports Cars had attracted the biggest, deepest and fastest field of big-inch road racing cars and hotshoe drivers ever assembled in North America.

And the Scarabs were right in the thick of it from the first day of qualifying.

The RAI team had worked day and night to switch the third car over from its terminally unhappy Offy engine to a Traco Chevy like the other two, and also somewhat sneakily added a large additional saddle tank behind the dashboard of Lance and Chuck's cars so they could potentially run the entire, 200-mile race distance without a pit stop for fuel. Nobody else could do that. But they ran out of time to do it to Bruce's car—hell, they were lucky just to get it finished!—and so the general strategy was for Bruce to go like hell and draw the other cars out and then for Chuck and/or Lance to slip quietly and neatly into the lead when everybody else either broke or made their pit stops! It was some pretty clever and far-sighted thinking, and only the RAI crew knew how hard they had been thinking and thrashing for that Riverside race. The cars looked typically perfect, polished, self-possessed and immaculate when they rolled out of the transporter, and the only tipoff as to what had been going on behind the scenes pretty much around the clock for the past four or five days were the bags under everybody's eyes. And the building pile of empty paper coffee cups in the nearby trash barrels.

"We're kind of like a swan," was the way Lance put it to one of the many dimbulb stick-and-ball scribes the *Times* had crawling all over the pits during practice and qualifying. They were there to grab all the latest rumors and hot paddock news for the sports section (even if they didn't get it exactly right) and most of them were your typical baseball/basketball/football types who were new to road racing and had no idea what the hell they were looking at. Or talking about, come to that. And although the attention was always nice, it was a little irritating how those "professional sports writers" acted like they knew you from way back and called you by your first name even if they didn't know how to pronounce it correctly.

"So how's that, Lance? The part about the swan?"

"Oh, all anybody ever sees is how you're just gliding along smoothly and gracefully across the top of the water. But under the surface, you're paddling like crazy!"

"Gee, that's a great quote, Lance. But it's kind of long. The paper likes copy that's hard-hitting and punchy. Have you got anything a little shorter?"

Lance didn't much like newspaper types anyway. And who could blame him? They'd been dogging him and firing flashbulbs at him and sticking microphones in his face and asking him all sorts of questions and then writing whatever the hell they felt like (so long as it would raise a few eyebrows and sell a few more papers) ever since he was out of diapers. Especially those snaky Fleet Street assholes over in England. And he was pretty damn sick and tired of it, too.

But Lance got even more attention after he set third-fastest time earlier in the week on Thursday but then spun off the track during "official" practice and managed to damage the suspension on a hidden drainage ditch while trying to hustle the car back onto the pavement. It was just the sort of unfortunate and ironic story the newspaper guys loved. And especially since it happened to this young punk blonde kid with his own damn cars and racing team, a hoity-toity name and family pedigree and way, *way* too much money, good looks and fame. They had a field day.

Things weren't quite so rosy over at the RAI bivouac in the paddock. The front end on Lance's car was pretty seriously rearranged, and even Warren said there was no way they could get it repaired in time for the race. Let alone qualifying. Now most team owner/drivers would likely have booted Chuck out of his car (the remaining one with the extra gas tank), taken that one for himself, put Chuck in Bruce's car and put Bruce on a lawn chair under an umbrella someplace to keep him out of the sun. But that's just not the way Lance Reventlow thought or did things. Oh, he could be pouty and spoiled now and then (or go off like a damn depth charge if you got his temper up!), but he had a sense of fair play and seemed to understand the Right Thing To Do most of the time. And not too many folks are built like that, no matter what else they may or may not have going for them. In any case, Lance decided that Chuck (who was undeniably the most proven, seasoned and experienced Scarab pilot) would stay in his own car, and that Lance would take the other one, but hand it over to Bruce when he made his pit stop for fuel.

Race day found traffic backed up for miles and a huge crowd of spectators—some said nearly 100,000—filling the grandstands, lining the fences and swarming like ants over Riverside's hot, dry, dusty, barren hillsides. Most had gotten there early for what they'd been assured in the newspapers, television and radio reports—over and over again, in fact—was going to be the biggest damn American V-8 vs. Ferrari V-12, American drivers vs. European drivers, California vs. The Whole Blessed Rest of the World, *us* vs. *them* showdown in motorsports history. And the front row sure lived up to that billing, too, what with the two gleaming blue Scarabs with their beautiful, all-American white scallops and pinstriping sandwiching Phil Hill in John von Neumann's wicked-looking, one-of-a-kind red Ferrari. You couldn't script it any better as fiction….

It was every bit of 100 degrees with the sun glaring down mercilessly when the green flag finally set the field loose a little after 2:00 in the afternoon. The huge, noisy pack roared off and funneled through Turn One, jostling and feinting and fighting for position, and it was all blue right at the front. But not for long, since either Phil tried an iffy move or Lance checked up early (take your pick) but the Ferrari tapped the back end of Lance's Scarab and more or less drop-kicked it off the pavement. Hard to say what really happened (and Phil Hill has *never* had a reputation as a dirty driver!), but the end result was that Lance lost a couple spots and Phil was now hard at it after Chuck in the other blue car. Lance passed Max Balchowsky's rumbleguts Old Yaller to re-take third, and soon after that he had Dan Gurney in Frank Arciero's Ferrari breathing down his neck. And waving like crazy to the corner workers since Lance's car had apparently banged something in the fuel system when it went off course and was now leaving a sloshing trail of gasoline in its wake.

While the Scarab/Ferrari battle continued at the front, the officials black-flagged Lance and he came steaming—and I mean *steaming!*—into the pits. By that time the RAI guys knew what was wrong and they quickly lifted the body and fixed it, and then Lance hollered for Bruce to get in the car. A somewhat bewildered (but oh-so-willing!) Bruce Kessler jumped behind the wheel, fired it up and tore off towards the end of pit lane. Where he was greeted by waving black flags and brought to a halt. The USAC officials apparently weren't about to let him back into the race. And that's about all it took to set Lance off like a damn Hydrogen Bomb. He ran right across the damn track to "talk" to the officials at the starter's stand, and when they couldn't exactly tell him why his repaired car with a fully licensed and registered team driver behind the wheel hadn't been let back out into the race, a certain amount of yelling, screaming, swearing, finger-pointing, fist-shaking, pushing and shoving ensued. A punch was even thrown (although not by Lance, according to eyewitness accounts). And naturally all this happened right in front of the damn press box. At last! Something these stick-and-ball typewriter jockeys actually knew and understood to write about: a *fight!*

But there was another, even better fight going on out on the racetrack, where Daigh in the one remaining Scarab and Phil Hill in the 412 Ferrari were swapping the lead back and forth damn near every lap (and occasionally several times per lap) and the fury of their battle had left the rest of the field far behind. They set the two fastest laps of the race early on and got so close they even touched at one point—the Scarab's wheel knockoff leaving a dimpled, chattering streak down the side of the Ferrari—and Phil was more than a little miffed afterwards about Chuck Daigh's aggressive driving style. But everybody said it was one hell of a show to watch from the stands. The Ferrari had maybe a tiny bit more top speed and almost equal acceleration, but the Scarab was simply the better car overall. Especially considering Chuck was trying to stroke it a little since the heat was getting to the Scarab and his temperature gauge was rising. Even so, he finally managed to get in front and make it stick on Lap 12, and although Phil hung on like grim death for the next dozen rounds or so, but then it was the Ferrari's turn to have trouble with the heat as the fuel started percolating and vaporizing in the big V-12's carburetors. Phil dropped back and then pulled into the pits at half-distance, and after that it was just a matter of stroking the Scarab home.

It was a stunning victory.

Chapter 29: The Fortune Teller from *Tertre Rouge*

Naturally the racing news from Europe took a little longer to filter home, and Hank's letters were getting fewer, shorter and farther in between on account of a lot of the magic, thrill and adventure of his International Motorsports Racing Scribe job had started to wear a little thin. Some of it had even turned into drudgery. But that's what happens with any job if you hang around for more than a week or two. Unless it happens to be an assembly-line job at a factory—or wheeling around drums of foul-smelling shit that'll eat the hair follicles right out of your nostrils at my old man's chemical plant—in which case the magic more or less evaporates by mid-morning coffee break on Day One. The other big change was that now Hank and Cal were more or less sharing the small apartment not far from Maranello when they were in Italy, bunking in with Tommy Edwards more often than not whenever the racing circus took them to England and even spending a few days here and there with Toly at his fancy-schmancy place on Lake Lucerne (the lucky dogs!), so there were far fewer of those long, empty, homesick, sleepless nights for Hank to spend writing me letters. Although I'm sure there were a lot more nasty hangovers involved, too.

In any case, dapper little Frenchman Maurice Trintignant shocked just about everybody—probably including himself—when he pulled Rob Walker's rear-engined Cooper into the winner's circle at the Grand Prix of Monaco in the middle of May. It was the Walker Cooper's second Grand Prix win on the trot, but this time it was more due to smooth driving, stamina and attrition rather than blinding speed or shrewd team strategy. Mind you, the handy, underpowered little Coopers flat *loved* the scenic, narrow, tight, twisty, climbing and diving street circuit that ran up the hill, past the casino and down along the harbor front in Monte Carlo. Trintignant got the ride because Moss was back with the Vanwall team alongside Tony Brooks and Brit comingman Stuart Lewis-Evans, and most of the other top talent was already under contract to Ferrari, Cooper or BRM. Not to mention that Rob Walker rather preferred drivers who could be expected to bring the blessed thing home in one piece. Especially at Monaco, where there were so many curbs, walls and railings just waiting for any mistake. Trintignant had already won the race once for Ferrari back in '55 (after both Mercedes broke and Ascari took his famous swan dive into the harbor) and understood maybe better than anyone what it took to survive a hundred laps around the glittering little principality. It was a track that demanded precision, consistency and concentration rather than balls or bravado, and Maurice Trintignant was always fast and neat there.

The Monaco race not only kicked off the European Grand Prix season, but also marked the debut of Colin Chapman's first Formula One design, the new Lotus 12. It used the same, off-the-shelf Coventry Climax engine as the Coopers (only in the front of the driver, not in back) and looked for all the world like a smaller, tidier, slimmed-down and far lighter Vanwall. And did I mention "flimsier?" Colin Chapman was an absolute mad-scientist maniac when it came to making his cars as light as possible. Maybe even lighter than possible. Eric Gibbon loved to tell people (anyone who would listen, in fact) that he once overheard Chapman say: *"The ideal racecar would be so precisely and exactly engineered that it falls to pieces as soon as it passes under the checkered flag."* And while that may have been a bit of an exaggeration—Eric considered putting words in people's mouths as a justifiable part of any cracking good interview—there's plenty of evidence to suggest that Chapman's designs occasionally fell a wee bit short of making it all the way to that checkered flag before falling apart. He was a genius, all right, but his ideas were right on that keen razor's edge between sheer brilliance and thin air. In fact, the wall thickness of the tubing Chapman specified for the frames on his new Formula One design was so damn thin that the Lotus mechanics started called it "cigarette paper." Although never within earshot when "The Guv'nor" was around.

A lot of people wondered why Chapman hadn't gone with a more radical, rear-engined layout on the new car like Cooper. Especially after the success the Coopers were starting to enjoy against all the established big guns. But Chapman didn't think much of how they did things over at the Cooper Garage. He thought they were unscientific and weak on theory and built cars more by thumb-and-eyeball than pencil, calculations and drafting paper. Not to mention that Cooper had already established themselves as Chapman's toughest rivals in the smaller-displacement sportscar classes that were both companies' bread and butter. Tommy Edwards said that got under Chapman's skin a little. He occasionally called Cooper *"those black-smiths from Surbiton"* and some say he held off on his own rear-engined design because he simply didn't want anybody to think he was copying from them.

The *"Let's win one for jolly old England!"* BRM team was back, and their new car typically bristled with demon ideas, stunning craftsmanship and interesting details, but some of the scribes—even some of the British ones—thought they might be suffering from too much thinking and fiddling rather than too little. In any case, they'd happily hired proven 'shoes Jean Behra and Harry Schell after all the air leaked out of Maserati's factory effort, and that figured to put them in pretty good shape in the driving department. Mind you, there were still a whole bunch of Maseratis around. No less than ten privateer 250Fs were entered at Monaco—in various states of tune and tiredness—but eight of them failed to even qualify. Including one driven by a dark, pretty, upper crust, 32-year-old Italian comtessa named Maria-Teresa de Filippis. Which made her, I think, the first female ever to attempt to qualify for a World Championship Grand Prix. She came from an aristocratic Neapolitan family pedigree that included a fairly large and dazzling supply of lira—pretty young girl or craggy old fart, you always had to have the money to go motor racing—and she absolutely loved the idea, feel, challenge, thrill and adventure of it. Hank said she was kind of a friend/protégé of that tough, pugnacious little French driver, Jean Behra, and she'd already scored an outright win at some Italian hillclimb in a Maserati sports car and came home fifth in a non-championship Formula One race at Syracuse. She was driving for a longtime back-marker/privateer team called *Scuderia Centro Sud,* which was run as kind of a hobby project by bigtime Italian Maserati dealer Guglielmo Dei. *Scuderia Centro Sud* ran a small rental fleet of slightly outdated Maserati 250Fs generally driven by comingmen types trying to show the European factory teams what they could do—including occasional American hopefuls like Masten Gregory, Carroll Shelby (with Temple Buell's money) and even Indy 500 winner Troy Ruttman—along with fat wallet Italian amateurs who wanted to be a little closer to the action than the usual VIP seats. Anyhow, this Maria-Teresa de Filippis apparently made a pretty decent go of it at Monaco. Hank said she'd just gotten down to a nice, even 10 seconds off the eventual pole time—and this in an outdated car with more or less iffy preparation—when it holed a piston and put her out. But good for her, you know? And she did manage to qualify for the Belgium Grand Prix at Spa a month later. Not to mention the Portuguese round and her home Grand Prix in Italy later on in the season. Oh, she never ran anywhere close to the front and only managed to finish one Grand Prix—tenth and dead last among the cars still running at Spa—but you had to give her credit anyway just for taking the shot. It took one hell of a set of balls. Or whatever. Although I hate like hell to admit it, there's no reason on earth why a woman can't drive a damn racecar every bit as fast as a man.

I just hope I never have to sit there and watch it happen, you know?

Anyhow, she was in good company at Monaco, what with 13 other amateurs, no-hopers, poseurs, dilettantes, "social entries," wannabes and shadow professionals also failing to make the cut. Including two outdated but resuscitated racecars from the recently folded Connaught team, which had been bought at a receivership (that's British for "bankruptcy") sale by a singularly sly, shrewd and slippery little English used-car dealer/self-styled racer named Bernie Ecclestone. Although Bernie didn't manage to qualify for the race, he at least made something of a success out of the Monaco weekend by renting the cars out to aspiring Formula One drivers with big dreams and even bigger bank accounts. Including our old California swimsuit fortune pal Bruce Kessler. The cars were pretty much hopeless, and neither of the struggling Connaughts went near fast enough to qualify. But at least the checks cleared….

Saturday's final qualifying session ended with a bit of a surprise in that the whole, three-car front row at Monaco was all varying shades of British Racing Green. Meaning that Eric Gibbon was particularly difficult to take at the elegant participants' reception/cocktail party Prince Ranier and Princess Grace threw the evening before the race. After consuming nearly the entire contents of a crystal punch bowl single-handed, he led the waiters carrying the shrimp appetizers in a rousing chorus of *"Rule Britannia."* Later on he was half-strutting/half-staggering around with one of the orange slices out of the punch bowl over his eye like a monocle and saying things like: *"Orange you glad you came?"* He thought it was terribly funny.

Race day found fast, cool and quiet Brit dentist Tony Brooks on pole in his Vanwall, gutty Jean Behra next to him in the quickest of the BRMs, and then a big surprise in the form of Jack Brabham in the factory Cooper-Climax lining up on the outside. Brabham was running a new, stretched-to-the-limit (and beyond!) 2.2-liter version of the twincam Climax FPF engine, but it was still a solid 300cc and 30-odd horsepower off what the Vanwalls, BRMs and most especially the Ferrari Dino V6s were rumored to have. As you can imagine, we were all thrilled to hear that Toly Wolfgang was starting his first-ever Grand Prix in a rather unusual fourth Ferrari team entry. It was just the old test hack from last season, but Ferrari knew Monaco and figured that adding another car—especially a slower, more conservatively driven car—might help grab some prize money and Constructors' Championship points at the end of 100 laps. The Grand Prix "Constructors' Championship" was a fairly new wrinkle, and although it was never anywhere near as big a deal as the World Chapionship the drivers fought it out for against each other, you can bet old man Ferrari didn't want to see Vanwall, Cooper or BRM trotting off with it, while the Brits—and in particular Vanwall team boss Tony Vandervell—were just as determined that it shouldn't go to "those bloody red cars." In any case, none of the Ferrari Dinos seemed particularly happy through the tight, fiddly corners at Monaco. And neither were their drivers, come to mention it.

Come the race, Behra in the BRM took off like he was fired out of a damn cannon at the drop of the flag, and he had a 100-yard lead by the end of the first lap. But Mike Hawthorn was a hell of a charger—Hank said he never seemed to show his best until the chips were down, but then he could turn into an absolute tiger—and in spite of his lackluster, third-row, sixth-on-the-grid performance in qualifying, Hawthorn's bright red Ferrari came bustling up through the green cars like gangbusters as the laps unfolded. He worked his way past Trintignant and Brabham in the Coopers, Brooks and Moss in the Vanwalls and was harrying Behra for first (wow!) when the BRM ran low on brakes and Behra had no choice but to stop at the pits. So now it was Hawthorn's Ferrari in the lead, but the rest of the cream was also rising to the top and Moss was soon all over him in the Vanwall. Naturally all the Brits in the stands went properly berserk (and Hank said there were a *lot* of Brits at Monaco) when the green Vanwall swept past the red Ferrari with a perfectly judged move under braking. But their joy was short-lived, as Moss was into the pits and out of the race with an ugly valvetrain clatter on the 38th lap. That put Hawthorn back in front, but what with retirements and car problems and pit stops and all, now it was Trintignant in the dark-blue Walker Cooper in second—albeit well back—followed (again, each separated by a wide, empty margin) by Musso, Collins and our boy Toly in the other three team Ferraris. They hadn't been the fastest cars on the circuit—not by a long shot—but the Ferrari V6s were damn near bulletproof. And running first, third, fourth and fifth with the team drivers doing a first-rate job of keeping them out of the walls, pits and trackside scenery. And then, right at half distance, the fuel pump failed in Hawthorn's leading Ferrari—in fact, Hank said it fell right off!—and an even bigger cheer went up from the crowd as Trintignant came skating by in the lead. Apparently there were even more Frenchmen than Brits in the stands at Monaco….

From that point on it turned into kind of a droning procession (although the wild cheers from the Frenchies every time Trintignant went by livened things up a bit) and Hank said the most interesting thing was watching our pal Toly wrestling with a gearchange that was getting balkier by the minute. Sometimes he couldn't get it *into* gear and sometimes—especially on deceleration—the damn thing'd pop *out* of gear. And Hank said the last thing you want on a tight, unforgiving circuit like Monaco is to find yourself steaming into a corner dead-stick with no power on tap to stabilize the rear end. Toly was doing his best to hold it in gear with one hand while steering with the other, but it takes a lot of muscle and effort to herd a big, understeery Ferrari 246 through the streets of Monaco, and the steering wheel was literally gnawing away at his hand.

Then, just nine laps from the end, it all went down the shitter when the gearbox jammed in fourth just as he approached Casino Square. He yanked, tugged, banged and pushed, but it just wouldn't budge. So he flicked his eyes down for half a heartbeat to take a look at it. The next thing he knew, he was in too deep for the upcoming corner. And naturally that's when the damn gear lever decided to pop back into neutral and—*just that quick!*—he was plowing helplessly into the barriers. It wasn't a very hard hit, but it was enough to knock the front wheels cockeyed and put him out of it. Damn. Toly let out a breath it seemed like he'd been holding for the last 30 laps and climbed dejectedly out of the car. Thanks to the gearbox and his repeated orders to *"bring the car home"*—not to mention that it was a tired old hack to begin with—he'd been almost embarrassingly slow compared to his teammates. And now he'd crashed the damn thing! He wondered, as took that long, slow, lonely walk back towards the pits, bathed in the cheers for the calm, smooth and relaxed little Trintignant's brilliant winning drive, how long it would be before Ferrari trusted him again with a Formula One car....

The next Grand Prix was the Dutch round at Zandvoort just one week later, and so Hank and Toly went back to visit Tommy in England in between. There was some question if the Ferrari test hack could (or even should) be repaired for the Dutch race since there was plenty to do on the other team cars. But Toly's instructions were to be there and ready if needed, and so it just didn't make sense to go back to Italy between races. Especially when that meant he'd have to answer the questioning looks of all the workers and shop mechanics at the Ferrari factory. Who needed it?

But things were hardly happier in England. Tommy had just gotten back from a difficult non-championship sportscar race at Spa in Belgium, and he'd already had quite a bit to drink when Hank and Toly caught up with him in the racing pub just a few blocks from his flat. It was a bustling, dark, noisy place that smelled of cigarette smoke, cleanser, old piss and stale beer, and there were pictures, plaques, yellowing sports pages, checkered flags and grotesquely bent steering wheels tacked up everywhere. "Hey, good to see you," Tommy said sullenly as Hank and Toly made their way over to the table.

"Care for a drink?"

Tommy looked at the half-full whiskey in front of him and drained it. "Another just like this, thanks. The bartender knows what I like."

Toly went for a round. "So how was Monaco?" Tommy asked without much enthusiasm.

Hank shrugged. "Beautiful weather. Beautiful people. Exciting start. Boring finish. The usual at Monaco—you've heard it all before."

Tommy's eyes stared down at the table. "And how was Toly's race?"

"Better stick to the beautiful weather and beautiful people when he gets back."

"So it was shit?"

Hank nodded. "Hardly the kind of debut you'd hope for on the Ferrari grand prix team. The car was jumping out of gear for the last 30 laps. He wound up in the fence."

"Was he doing any good up until then?"

"Not really."

Toly arrived with the drinks. He'd brought two for each of them

"Thanks. Cheers," Tommy said, and drained another whiskey. "So I understand your big bloody Formula One debut went straight to shit."

"Straight to shit," Toly agreed through a tight smile. He passed Tommy the second whiskey so they could clink their glasses over it. "Here's to it."

"Right. Here's to shitty races," Tommy agreed, and swallowed half the whiskey out of the second glass.

The table was quiet then. Just the sound of chatter, noise and glassware in the background and two well lubricated idiots at the bar arguing loudly about something Englishman Richard Seaman either did or didn't do when he drove for the Hitler-backed Mercedes-Benz team just before the war. Toly looked across the table at the top of Tommy's head and the way it hung down between his shoulders. "So what's all this about?" Toly finally asked. "You were at Spa, weren't you?"

The top of Tommy's head nodded.

"What happened?"

Tommy's shoulders raised and slowly lowered. "Oh, nothing," he said into the tabletop. "We just lost another bloke, that's all." His face came up slowly. "Just another bloody bloke. Won't make any difference. There's plenty bloody more of us around. Plenty bloody more…."

The story came out slowly, brokenly, in bits and fragments. Tommy's mate Archie Scott-Brown—the tough, fast, plucky little Scotsman with the bandy legs and deformed hand who had fought and scrapped his way into racing and looked likely to fight and scrap his way clear to the top as well—had died just a few hours before from burns he'd received in a horrific, fiery accident at Spa.

"You have to understand the bloody circuit," Tommy tried to explain. "It's just three long, country roads wending through the Belgian countryside. A lot of the bloody war was fought there, you know. In the Ardennes. It's beautiful, really. Or at least it is when you're cruising through in a bloody touring car. But it's nine miles long and blinding fast and terribly narrow, and I don't think a hundred yards of it is actually straight." Tommy took a pull off his Guinness. Toly had switched him to Guinness on the last round and Tommy didn't even seem to notice. "You're averaging—bloody *averaging!*—well over 120, and there's no bloody place to go if you get it wrong." He looked at Hank like he was asking a question: "And the weather just comes and goes sometimes. Just bloody comes and goes...."

That was surely part of it. Archie had been scrapping for the lead with Masten Gregory in the Ecurie Ecosse Lister-Jag, and of course Archie'd been the man to beat for more than a season in Lister's works car. It just wouldn't do to let some privateer team beat them with their own damn weapon, would it? But Ecosse was a keen and experienced bunch, and it seems they'd made some clever modifications—particularly to the bodywork and aerodynamics—that they thought might make their Lister faster than the factory version. And more stable at high speed, which was always a bit of a question mark with the original body shape. Some said it was air packing under the front end, but whatever it was, it made the steering go *very* light at anything much over 120. And the faster you went, the worse it got. Until—at least theoretically—the front wheels lifted clear off the blessed pavement! That wasn't the sort of thing cars generally ran into on the small, flat British airport circuits, but Spa was something else. Plus Masten Gregory could be blindingly, ruthlessly, even frighteningly quick on his day. He seemed to respond to danger like it was rocket fuel, and always did his very best under the most daunting and demanding conditions. And Spa in iffy weather was about as daunting and demanding as it came....

Especially considering what awaited if a driver went off: lumpy fields full of ruts, rocks and tree stumps, stone farmhouses, wooden barns, stands of trees, fences, marker stones, road signs, power poles, ditches and Lord only knows what else lined the roadway close by on either side. And you were going so bloody, incredibly *fast!* In particular, there was one road sign at the end of the fast, high-speed kink named after Richard Seaman that several drivers—including respected Belgian ace Paul Frére—had complained about and insisted be removed. The officials agreed, but it was never actually done.

Naturally it rained on race morning, and the weather was gusty and drying—but still drizzling slightly—as the cars rolled to grid for the 4pm start. Tommy's Aston teammates Shelby and Frére managed to squirt away quickest from the start thanks to tighter gearing, but it was the two Listers back in front by the end of lap one. And quickly pulling away. There were still patches of light rain here and there around the circuit, making each curve and corner different every lap, but Gregory was driving with fierce determination and an almost ethereal touch. Archie hung on and hounded him mercilessly, not about to let him get away. They passed and re-passed many times—much to the delight of the crowd—and it was Archie in front when they came flying into that fast kink at Seaman Bend just after an isolated, heavier rain squall passed through. Some eyewitnesses said Archie just flat lost it on the slick pavement, while others said he saw the wetter pavement, checked up, and poor Gregory—inches behind!—couldn't help tapping him ever-so-slightly from the rear. But whatever it was, it was enough. Archie's car went for a heart-rattling, full-lock slide along the grassy verge, almost seemed to gather itself up, but then clouted the very road sign that had never been removed. It ripped the right-front wheel clear off, and from that moment on, Archie was nothing more than a passenger. The Lister swept through a wire fence, dug its nose in the soft, loamy earth and went somersaulting wildly into the infield, scattering spectators in all directions. It finally hammered down, half-inverted, with Archie hanging limp out of the cockpit. There was a tense moment of agonized silence, and then all 30 gallons of fuel detonated into a raging, boiling fireball.

It took the course marshals several tries before they finally, bravely blasted the flames back with fire extinguishers and got him out. But by that time he'd been terribly burned, and Archie Scott-Brown died in the hospital the next day.

"It's not the bloody cars and it's not our bloody driving," Tommy grumbled as Hank and Toly held him wedged precariously upright between their shoulders and maneuvered him back towards his flat. *"It's the bloody roads. That's what gets us killed. The bloody roads...."*

There was no Formula One Ferrari for Toly at the Dutch or Belgian races—he was just as happy not to drive again at Spa so soon after Archie's death—and both races went to the sleek Vanwalls despite near-equal speed from the Ferrari team. Moss won at Zandvoort and Brooks won (after Moss missed a gear and blew up on the very first lap) at Spa, but Collins fought Brooks for the lead at Spa until his Ferrari overheated and Hawthorn again showed why he was emerging as Ferrari's best hope by finishing fifth at the Dutch race and a hard-nosed second in Belgium, picking up valuable points in both races while the Vanwall drivers were splitting theirs. And poor Luigi Musso had a rear tire blow on his Ferrari at 130-plus at Spa and crashed heavily. He was lucky to escape with bad bangs and bruises but no serious injuries.

In between the two Formula One races came the World Manufacturers' Championship sportscar round at the Nurburgring, where Cal, Toly and Tommy were all back in action again. And there was some joy back for Tommy when Hawthorn's leading *Testa Rossa* shredded a tire and Tommy's Aston Martin teammates, Moss and Brabham, came away with a resounding victory. Moss did the bulk of the driving after Brabham—quick, tough and wily as he was—found it impossible to match his teammate's pace on his very first visit to the *Nordschleife.* And he was hardly alone, even among the top-rank drivers. The Hawthorn/Collins Ferrari hung on for second and Toly co-drove the third-place *Testa Rossa* in surely his best-ever result at the 'Ring. Cal only got a few laps of practice at the wheel of a "semi-works" GT Ferrari, only to have his paying co-driver stuff it into the hedgerows before Cal ever got a chance behind the wheel. It was just as well, since Cal—like Brabham—was finding the 14 blind, twisting, convoluted miles a bit much to absorb in one visit.

For the 24 Hours of Le Mans, Ferrari put Hawthorn and Collins in one *Testa Rossa* and Phil Hill and Olivier Gendebien in another, and decided to give Toly and Cal a chance in the third car since Musso was still recuperating from his harrowing, high-speed crash at Spa. Olivier Gendebien was a wealthy, wry, cool and aristocratic Belgian who'd made quite a name for himself in Ferrari's GT Belinettas, winning the *Tour de France Automobile* outright and taking a solid class win and third overall in one at the tragic 1957 *Mille Miglia.* He was at his best on long, tiring, difficult drives through the worst possible weather and road conditions, and almost always brought the cars home. That made him an ideal running mate for Hill—they were both thoughtful, smooth and steady and always drove with their heads—and it didn't bother either of them that *Mon Ami Mates* Hawthorn and Collins considered themselves the quick boys and team leaders. Of course Cal was thrilled to finally get a shot in one of the front-line cars—it was basic jungle law in racing that you often got your opportunities because someone ahead of you got hurt or killed—and really excited about co-driving with Toly. Even though they were pretty much considered Ferrari's third-stringers, he rather liked their chances. And so did Toly. They were good friends by then and genuinely trusted each other, and both secretly suspected they were dangerously close to equal when it came to sheer speed. More importantly, they'd be trying to show each other what a solid, professional, workmanlike job they could make of it—even while trying to demonstrate to Tavoni that they were definitely (if ever-so-slightly) the quicker of the two. Like Tommy Edwards once said: *"The toughest competition you can ever have is your own teammate. After all, you're both driving the same bloody car on the same bloody day on the same bloody track. There's just no place to hide...."*

But it rained like hell at Le Mans that year, and that changed everything.

Eric Gibbon's story about Toly Wolfgang came out in the London *World Mirror* the week before Le Mans, and it was a festering, dark, innuendo-filled piece that ran in four parts over four successive issues and dug up all the moldy old bones of his father's reputation as an opportunistic war profiteer and his cozy relationship with the Nazis. They ran a doctored picture of his grinning father—Toly recognized it as one from a rare family birthday at home—standing between an imperious and satisfied looking Adolph Hitler and a proud, thuggish, puff-chested Benito Mussolini. The next installment showed a picture of the peaceful, chalet-like house on Lake Lucerne juxtaposed with a grotesque image of dead British soldiers on the beach at Normandy and a background shot of the military cemetery there. The copy delved into his mother's insanity, drug abuse and final suicide along with Toly's rumored part in his father's eventual suicide in prison.

The third installment focused on Toly's aimless, debauched, meandering days after the war—there were plenty of pictures of that on file—when he had money but no country and nothing worthwhile in his heart. And Eric Gibbon's copy said as much. But it also made him sound somehow evil and undeserving. There was a great shot of him on a hotel balcony in Monte Carlo with some French cabaret dancer—*what was her name?*—and they both looked half-naked and stinking drunk because they were.

The last installment—finally—was about his current life and racing career. There were the usual, slippery references to how he'd bought his way in and then bought his way to the top, but also some straightforward praise for his win in Argentina and grudging respect for the fine and feared driver he was apparently becoming (although, by his own admission, not nearly in the same class as home-grown British star Stirling Moss). There was also quite a bit about the possible—*you read it here first, folks!*—convoluted love triangle involving Toly, Cal and Gina LaScala. They ran Hank's picture—how the hell did the slimy little sonofabitch get *that?*—of Cal, Toly and Gina at their dinner at the little restaurant Toly knew not far from the Ferrari factory the day of Cal's first meeting with old man Ferrari. They seemed to be having one hell of a good time. Cal's arm was around Gina and she had hers around him, but the way the flash caught her eyes, she seemed to be leering carnivorously at Toly.

Or that's the way it looked in the paper, anyway.

Gina was in the European news anyway because she'd been shooting a World War II commando raid movie on Corsica with Gregory Peck, Gilbert Roland and Anthony Quinn that spring and early summer, and of course the studio PR flacks made it a point to keep her face in front of the public at every opportunity. But the location work on Corsica finished up the week before Le Mans and so she decided to surprise Cal—and Toly—by dropping in on them unannounced at Le Mans on her way back to Hollywood for the studio wrap-up work. It was no trouble at all arranging credentials—Gina was a big star by then and Brad Lackey took care of everything with a few phone calls—but the weather was turning iffy and the forecast looked even worse when she finally arrived at the circuit with a limousine, a driver and one small overnight bag a little past two in the afternoon on Saturday, June 21st. She had planned to get there much earlier, but traffic had been a mess all the way from Paris. Maybe she should have taken the helicopter? There was one on the set, of course, and she probably could have easily worked it out with the pilot now that shooting was finished. After all, he'd been ogling her from behind his Ray-Bans for weeks. And what an entrance that would have made for the *paparazzi!*

But here she was behind dark-tinted windows in the back seat of a big Mercedes limo instead, stuck in the enormous snarl of Renaults, Citroens, Peugeots, Fiats and Volkswagen Campers trying to find their way into the circuit in time for the race. It was scheduled to start at 4pm, and huge throngs of people had been arriving since well before dawn to stake out their favorite spots and enjoy the carnival midway of rides and sideshow attractions that was already going full tilt overlooking the esses between the Dunlop Bridge and *Tertre Rouge.*

It took almost another full hour for Gina's driver to find his way close to the start/finish straightaway—in spite of the very highest magnitude VIP credentials—only to realize they were on the opposite side from the pits. "Look," she finally told the driver, "let me out here and I'll find my way across."

"Oui, Madamoiselle. But what should I do weez ze car?"

"Just find some way to get it over to the other side, okay? I'll be over somewhere around the Ferrari pits. See if you can find me there."

"Oui, Madamoiselle." The French driver looked pretty happy about getting a free entry into the Ferrari pits at Le Mans! Gina grabbed her credentials and sunglasses and headed for the tunnel under the track, walking right across the place where the terrible, deadly accident had happened in '55. But now it was a rolling sea of moving, jostling people and happy, excited faces. The limo driver called after her: *"Mademoiselle, votre parapluie...your umbrella,"* but she had already disappeared into the crowd.

Gina was used to the way people looked at her now when she was out in public. She'd always been a terrifically pretty girl—more than pretty, in fact—and men in particular would invariably sneak looks, steal glances or even openly leer at her wherever she went. But now they just stared, slack-jawed—men and women alike—stopping and turning and following her with their eyes and pointing or even snapping a quick, fumbling picture as the shock of recognition sank in....

Isn't that so-and-so?

It couldn't be.

I'm sure it is....

It took Gina another half-hour to wade through the crowded tunnel and the bustling, pre-race paddock—naturally posing for a few snapshots and signing a few autographs here and there along the way—before she finally arrived at the Ferrari bivouac behind the pits. They were just getting ready to roll the cars out onto to take their spots across the road for the Le Mans-style start, and she was able to sneak up on Cal from behind because he was deeply engrossed in a conversation with Toly about rev limits, race strategy and the choreography of driver changes during pit stops. And also about driving the Mulsanne Kink at night in the rain, which was looking more and more like a likely possibility. Toly saw her approaching, of course, but she put a finger to her lips and he never so much as fluttered an eyelash before she tapped Cal lightly on the shoulder. There was no immediate response, so she tapped again—harder this time—and he spun around and glared at her.

"Wh-what the hell are you doing here?" he demanded, sounding irritated as hell.

"Well, that's sure a heck of a nice welcome." She looked over at Toly. "What do you think?"

Toly shrugged. "I've heard worse," he allowed sarcastically. "Not very often, mind you. And never in polite company. But I assure you, I've heard worse."

Cal felt the color rising on his cheeks. He leaned over and kissed her awkwardly. "I'm sorry. Really I am. It's just, well..." he fumbled for words, "...it's just I didn't expect you here."

"That was the whole idea." She looked at Toly again. "A surprise isn't a surprise if the other person knows about it, is it?"

Toly raised both eyebrows like a pair of question marks. "Personally, I try to avoid surprises. They can be very hard on the heart."

It was quiet and edgy then, and Cal finally took Gina's hand and led her over by the Ferrari transporter where they could be at least somewhat alone. "Look, I'm really flattered that you came. Honest I am."

"Flattered?"

"Yeah, flattered. You're a big, famous movie star now. Who wouldn't be?"

The ends of Gina's mouth turned down. "That's not the same as *'glad to see you,'* is it?"

Cal licked his lips nervously. "I didn't mean it that way. Of course I'm glad to see you. It's just so…so....so," his eyes drifted off towards the pit straight, "…so *unexpected."*

"It was supposed to be a surprise." She sounded a little hurt.

He took her hands again and looked directly into her eyes. "Look. Gina. This is a very big race for Toly and me. A *very* big race. But it's going to be 24 hours of dull, droning boredom. And according to what we heard from the airport service, it looks like the weather is going to go straight to shit..."

"Oh, *damn!"* she interrupted. "My umbrella!"

But it was like he didn't even hear her: "…I need to focus, Gina. I need to concentrate. I just won't have time to pay any attention to you…."

"I didn't come here because I need someone to pay attention to me, Cal. I get too much attention as it is. I just thought we could spend some time together and I could maybe, you know, help you take your mind off things when you're out of the car."

He thought it over for a moment. "I dunno," he said uncertainly. "And I don't think Tavoni much likes it when the drivers have girls around."

Tina's eyes swept around the nearby paddock. "I see plenty of girls around."

"I didn't say they weren't around, I just said he doesn't much like it. He thinks they're a distraction. So does old man Ferrari. You can tell they don't like it much when Peter Collins brings his wife along."

One of the Ferrari V-12s sputtered to life in the background and revved a few times, getting warmed up for the start. It sounded raw, complex and impatient as the mechanic blipped the throttle, and slowly the hard edge melted out of Gina's eyes and something warm and genuine came behind it. "I won't be a bother, I promise," she said earnestly. "And I'll try my best not to be a distraction, either. Really, I will." Now she was being so damned earnest it was funny. She knew exactly how to do that. "In fact, if you like, I can just curl up under this trailer with a bag over my head, and you can just come by and kick me anytime you feel like talking or need a back rub or anything…."

Cal was grinning sheepishly now. "It *is* good to see you," he admitted fondly. "Damn good."

"You're sure I'm not too much of a distraction?"

"No, you're not too much of a distraction."

"And am I a nuisance?"

"No, you're definitely not a nuisance."

"You're absolutely sure, now? Because I'd hate to think you were just saying that to make me feel better. I mean, the last thing on this earth I'd ever want to be is a distraction or a nuisance...."

"Okay. That's enough."

"...Because that's almost worse than being ignorant or ill-mannered or even smelly or disgusting or if you vote communist or have one of those horrible skin diseases like leprosy. I mean, who would ever want to hang around with anyone that was a distraction or a nuisance. Oh, the unbearable *shame* of it...."

Cal laughed and shook his head. "Screw you, Gina."

"That's more like it," she teased. "Go ahead. Treat me like shit. Abuse me. Call me filthy names. Women are well-known suckers for that kind of thing." She leaned in and kissed him, but pulled back when he went to put his arms around her and draw her into him. "Wouldn't want to do that," she told him airily. "It might be too distracting...."

"Oh, for chrissakes, Gina...."

"Besides, what I really need is to trot off by myself someplace and work on not being such a terrible nuisance and distraction." She flashed him a dumb, silly and radiant movie-magazine smile. "And now I've got to find a ladies' room. I haven't been able to take a pee since we left Paris...."

As she walked away, Cal thought about how she could light him up inside. Make him almost glow. He'd never felt anything quite like it. And, although he didn't even pretend to understand it, he knew he could light her up, too.

The 1958 24 Hours of Le Mans started on a dry track but under threatening skies, and Moss made his usual, slightly preemptive sprint across the track and got away first, tearing off under the Dunlop Bridge in his Aston DBR1 before most of the drivers had even started their cars. The Astons had proved by far the lightest of the big cars when they went through scrutineering—they weighed less than 2000 pounds as compared to slightly over 2200 for the Ferrari *Testa Rossas* and the D-Type Jaguars—and Moss was once again assigned to be John Wyer's "rabbit," running a flat-out sprint pace from the start in order to lure the opposition into pushing too hard and breaking their cars. He made quite a job of it, too, easily pulling away from Hawthorn and the rest of the team Ferraris over the first two hours. But then it all fizzled out when his engine broke a connecting rod and blew it right through the side of the crankcase on the approach to the Mulsanne hairpin. A trail of oil and a billowing cloud of smoke and steam and so much for Mr. Moss. That left the factory Ferrari *Testa Rossas* well ahead of everyone else, but Hawthorn was already in trouble with a slipping clutch and falling gradually backwards, towards his teammates.

Because of his experience, Tavoni had given Toly first stint in the car he was sharing with Cal—probably reasoning that Toly would be less likely to go too fast or push too hard chasing Moss during the early, "sprint-race" stages of what would ultimately turn into a long, slogging, grueling battle of attrition. And things got even dicier just after Moss retired when the black skies opened up in the first massive, teeming downpour, turning the infield to mud, sending spectators scurrying for shelter and swamping some parts of the circuit completely. Visibility went down to almost nothing and drivers hopelessly flipped on their headlamps—as much to be seen as anything else—as the cars sloshed on through the gloom and spray. But the race went on.

The first round of pit stops came shortly after the rain hit, and it was a very taut looking Cal Carrington standing on the pit wall and waiting to take over as Toly slithered the *Testa Rossa* to a halt in front of him. The mechanics swarmed over the car as Toly quickly clambered out. They were running third, a minute and a half behind Hill and Gendebien but only a half-minute behind Hawthorn's fading Ferrari. *"It's like greased eel shit out there,"* Toly yelled in Cal's ear. *"There are puddles all over the place, and you can't see much of anything. Just take it slow the first few laps until you know where they are. Then try to stay out of them. You'll do better tiptoeing around the outside of most of the corners instead of staying on the regular line. That's where it's slickest...."*

Cal nodded.

"And take a spare set of goggles!"

By then Tavoni was motioning him into the car.

Gina was standing behind the pit wall, watching, as Cal fired up the Ferrari and fishtailed away in the rain. She was soaking wet, too, with her eye makeup running down her cheeks and her hair streaming down around both sides of her face like cold, wet seaweed. Toly thought she looked both gorgeous and tragic at the same time, and she had never, ever felt so alone.

Cal tried to do what Toly had told him, tiptoeing gingerly around the outside of the corners and trying to remember where the worst of the puddles were—*Jesus, you can't see shit out here!*—but then one of the English drivers in a privateer D-Type went sailing around the outside like the *Testa Rossa* was dragging an anchor behind it and Cal had no choice but to pick up the pace and try to stay with him. *Fucking English drivers. They don't fucking know any better. That's what it is....*

Just a few laps later, Bruce Kessler had his terribly unlucky accident when a privateer French D-Type swapped ends in front of him on the rain-soaked exit of the fast sweeper under the Dunlop Bridge. Bruce's hurtling Ferrari had no place to go and plowed right into the stationary Jag—killing the Jaguar's driver instantly, although no official word came out about it for many hours—and putting himself in a French hospital for several weeks. Naturally Cal was worried about his friend as soon as he saw the badly mangled D-Type and *Testa Rossa* tangled up together by the side of the road. But he had problems of his own to worry about. He'd never had all that much experience racing in the rain—not nearly as much as the British and European drivers, that was for sure—and trying to do it as darkness settled in on this long, fast racecourse made it even more difficult. Especially when he saw more and more wrecked cars littering the roadside and crushed into the embankments every lap.

By that time the Hawthorn/Collins Ferrari had long since dropped out, and Hank was there in the pits when Phil Hill came in to hand the leading Ferrari over to Olivier Gendebien. He was next to Phil with notepad in hand even before the Ferrari snarled back onto the circuit. *"So what's it like out there, Phil?"* he shouted over the roar of the passing cars and the hard spatter of the rain.

"My God, you just can't BELIEVE what it's like out there! You're aquaplaning all over the place and you can't see a damn thing and the rain seems like it's coming straight at you! And the lights of the cars you're passing blind you right in your own damn mirrors! It's UNBELIEVABLE out there!"

Hank asked Gendebien the exact same question when he came in at the end of his stint two hours later. The rain was still coming down in buckets: *"So, Olivier, what's it like out there?"*

Gendebien looked out from under heavy, almost sleepy eyelids and frowned. *"Eet ees like nuzing,"* he said with a bored, aristocratic shrug. *"Eet ees like going to ze store for a pack of cigarettes...."*

Cal and Toly were also doing pretty well at that point in the race. It was 2:00 in the morning and they were running a distant second to Hill and Gendebien, but under serious pressure from the fastest of the privateer D-Types—those English drivers were just too damn much in the rain!—although Cal had finally gotten accustomed to, if not exactly comfortable with, the cold and the wet and the shitty visibility and the car climbing up on top of the water and skating right across the deeper puddles. The important thing was to *Not Do Anything* and wait for the tires to find traction again on the far side. If you got panicky and tried to steer it and catch the slide, your tires would be pointing the wrong way when they finally got hold of the pavement again. And then you'd *really* be in trouble. But it was a hard thing to do. It took a little faith.

And then, without warning, the headlamps on the Ferrari suddenly dimmed and went out. While hurtling down the eight-kilometer *Les Hunaudieres* straightaway at well over 150mph! Cal blinked, trying hard to see into the sudden, hollow darkness. He could make out a pair of red taillights up ahead—judging by how slowly they were going and how far apart they were, it was one of the little French tiddlers aiming for the *Index of Performance* award—and Cal quickly closed up and fell in step behind them. He had every intention of following them back to the pits. But then the Ferrari's lights suddenly came back on again full blast, startling the driver of the little French car who promptly got it all squirrely under braking for the hairpin, thought he had it gathered up, clipped a perfect apex and performed a grand, lazy *pirouette* right in front of Cal on the way out of the corner. Cal swerved instinctively to avoid a certain collision, but that got him off the pavement and onto the slick, wet grass on the inside, and although the Ferrari actually seemed to accelerate, everything else went into agonizing slow motion as the *Testa Rossa* bounced off the inside barriers with a dull bang, slithered across the track, slid gently up the soaking wet embankment and came to rest with a muffled *WHUMPF!* high-centered on top of the sandbank on the opposite side! *SHIT!*

Well, it took Cal the better part of an hour to dig the car out—in cold, pouring rain, of course—and he knew that if he accepted assistance of any kind, he and Toly would be disqualified on the spot. Not that anybody but corner marshals were even around in a driving rainstorm at something shy of 3:00 in the morning. But he scraped and clawed and used the stupid little folding shovel Ferrari team manager Tavoni had strapped behind the passenger seat of all three cars, and eventually he got it free. Then the damn engine didn't want to start. And when it finally did, it was popping and banging and ran like shit all the way back to the pits. Maybe from all the water, sand and muck it'd ingested down the carburetors?

Toly seemed slightly surprised and even a little discouraged to see the battered Ferrari sputtering into the pits again. Cal climbed out while the mechanics wearily lifted the hood and began looking for the misfire problem. He was covered with mud and sand from head to toe and drenched clear through. *"You look like hell!"* Toly shouted over the popping, backfiring engine and the now-infrequent howl of passing racecars.

"It feels like that's where I've been."

"And now you're going to make me go out and get soaked again, too?"

"It only seems fair," Cal shouted back.

Toly shook his head disgustedly. *"You should have left the damn thing out there...."*

The mechanics put in new plugs and got the engine running again, but Toly only made it halfway around on his next lap before the it started stumbling all over again. Maybe water had gotten in the fuel? But then the lights dimmed and went out and the engine cut completely, and Toly knew it had to be electrical rather than carburetion. But there was no time to worry over it, since he was two-thirds of the way down the undulating *Les Hunaudieres* straightaway between *Tertre Rouge* and *Mulsanne*—dead in the water at 3:30 in the morning in a blinding rainstorm with no taillights to warn any oncoming cars! He barely got it steered over to the side before Gendebien's Ferrari and Jean Behra's Porsche roared by in a hurl of spray like a pair of low-flying fighter jets. Toly sat there, blinking in the darkness, feeling the cold rainwater draining down the back of his neck and the strange, tingling vacuum the fast-disappearing taillights and fading engine noise left in their wake. The pinpoint red lights vanished to the right around the Mulsanne Kink—the Ferrari lifted, but damn if Behra in the Porsche didn't keep it flat!—and Toly could still hear their distant echo as the Ferrari and then the Porsche braked and downshifted for the hairpin at *Mulsanne*. Then there was just the steady patter of rain on thin aluminum all around him. He tried the starter.

Nothing.

He tried again.

Not even a click.

Toly took a quick look under the hood and the decklid to see if it was maybe a bad connection or a loose wire or something simple, but it was dark and cars were hurtling past just a few feet away at over 150 on a soaking wet racetrack. It was cold and the damn rain was still pelting down and they were already well over an hour behind and falling further back with every heartbeat. *"Ahh, the hell with it!"* Toly finally growled, and headed off on the long, wet, lonely walk to the next course marshal's station to try and find a ride back to the pits.

Gina was dozing nervously in the back of the Mercedes limo with the heat going full blast when Cal tapped on the window. She hit the button and lowered it.

"We're out of it," he said simply. His eyes looked like he'd been staring into the sizzling flame of a welding torch for 12 hours.

"What time is it?"

He looked at his wristwatch. "Right at four o'clock."

"Half distance," Toly muttered bitterly from behind his shoulder.

"What are you going to do now?" Gina asked sleepily. She looked genuinely relieved that their race was over.

Cal and Toly looked at each other.

"A hot shower and some warm clothes would be nice."

"Wouldn't they, though?" Gina agreed.

"Pardon, Mademoiselle," the driver's voice came from behind the divider curtain, *"I know an auberge not far from here...."*

So the two of them climbed in the back of the Mercedes with Gina and the driver took them to a sleepy little country inn not far at all from the racetrack. Of course they had to wake the owner and his wife and all the rooms had been spoken for more than a year in advance, but between the chauffeur's charming French and a folded wad of francs and most especially the shock of recognition that lit up in the innkeeper's eyes when he saw Gina and then Toly, they worked a deal to use the owner's own bath—one at a time, of course—but he had nowhere for them to sleep afterwards. There was a barn in back, but the roof leaked and with the pigs and chickens, well....

"I don't think I could sleep anyway."

"Me, either."

"Or me."

So they were back in the Mercedes again just as the sky began turning a sad, cold, pre-sunrise shade of gray. At least the rain had eased off to a chilly, intermittent spatter.

"What should we do?"

"I don't know. You have any ideas?"

"I think I could use some breakfast."

"Breakfast," Gina mused. "And hot coffee. *Lots* of hot coffee." She opened her purse, took out a compact, flipped it open and looked at herself in the mirror. "I look like shit."

"Ah, but Gina LaScala looking like shit still looks better than most women at their absolute best!" Toly assured her graciously.

She leveled her eyes at Cal. "Why don't you ever say things like that?"

"Because I'm not full of shit like he is…."

They had a breakfast of crepes and egg soufflé at a nice little restaurant the driver knew not far from the racetrack—it was just opening up for the race and early church crowd when they got there—and they lingered over cups of hot coffee trying to figure out what to do with the rest of their day.

"We could go back to Paris," Gina offered.

Cal and Toly looked at each other. They both really wanted to be around for the finish, even though they weren't going to be a part of it.

"I've got it!" Toly yelled, slapping his palm on the table. "Let's go to the damn carnival!"

"The carnival?" Cal and Gina were both looking out the window at a singularly gray, damp, gloomy and uninviting morning.

"Sure! Why not? It's not raining too badly right now, and there won't be many people there because it's so early and because of the weather…."

"Including us," Cal answered grimly.

"No, really," Toly insisted. "That's really what we must do."

And, with no better ideas offered up, that's what they did.

Early Sunday morning, the carnival midway overlooking the esses between the Dunlop Bridge and *Tertre Rouge* looked more like a soggy refugee camp than any kind of amusement park. The center aisle was lined with closed wine, beer and food stands, empty shooting galleries, big and little sideshow tents—most with their flaps down—limp banners and sagging awnings. Behind them, a cluster of wet, silent thrill rides towered above the treetops and into the slate gray sky. "They look like they crash landed here, don't they?" Toly observed.

"They're not the only ones," Cal agreed, pointing where one of the little French Panhard coupes sat crushed up against the barriers in the esses, facing the wrong way. Just then the Behra/Herrmann Porsche droned by, all by itself, followed by the usual air-cooled Porsche rasp and two visible tire paths marking the proper line around the wet corner. Toly and Cal knew it was Behra in the car from the little checkerboard band around the base of the driver's helmet. "Those damn things just seem to run on forever, don't they?" Toly groused.

"They're damn good in the rain, that's for sure."

There seemed to be a terribly long silence after the Porsche went by. "I wonder how many cars are left?"

"Not many would be my guess."

More silence, and then a lonely, sputtering Lotus Eleven clawed its way through the esses.

"Sounds like he's in trouble," Cal observed.

"Might be wet electrics," Toly allowed. "The hard part will be making it back to the pits…."

Gina looked at them both. "You two are a real barrel of laughs, aren't you?" She gave Cal a jab in the ribs. "C'mon. It's over, for God's sake. You're out of it. So let's have a little fun and gaiety around here."

"Fun and gaiety it is," Cal muttered glumly.

"Absolutemont!" Toly agreed with ridiculous enthusiasm. He made the three of them link arms—Gina in the middle—and headed them off down the bleak, wet, almost vacant carnival midway whistling *"We're Off to See the Wizard"* to set the mood and pace. It was so perfectly absurd that there was no choice but to join in. *"You know we look ridiculous,"* Cal shouted between choruses.

"That's all right...we are ridiculous!" Toly assured him. And then he brought them up short in front of a small, dark blue tent with silver stars and crescent moons all over it. There was a drawing of a palm, an eye and a tarot card and the name *"Madame Sagesse"* on the rain-warped placard outside. The tent flap was open slightly and they could see a dark, middle-aged woman with gold hoop earrings, heavy makeup and a purple wrap around her head sitting at a small table inside, drinking tea. Several fat ivory candles burned in colored glass dishes in front of her. "Hmm," Toly mused. "This could be the perfect place to start right here!"

"A fortune teller?"

Toly nodded. "What better way to start an awful day than to find out what our futures hold in store?"

"At least we had breakfast first," Cal groused.

"I-I don't know," Gina said hesitantly.

"What's the matter?"

"Oh, I guess it's nothing. But my mother used to take me to this weird gypsy woman in Brooklyn all the time when I was little." A tiny shiver went through her. "If you must know, it gave me the creeps."

"The future gives everyone the creeps," Toly assured her.

"No, I mean this *really* gave me the creeps. My mother believed in all that stuff. She still does…."

"Oh, come on," Toly insisted, and started to lead them into the tent.

"One at a time, s'il vous plait!" the woman inside demanded gently.

"Very well, then," Toly agreed. "I'll go first." He ducked inside and closed the flap behind him.

That left Cal and Gina standing outside in a soft spatter of rain. "You know I saw your mother," Cal said off-handedly.

Gina stared at him. "You *did?"*

"Yeah. It was no big thing. I came over looking for you when you were out of town on some promotional tour."

Gina's eyes narrowed. "I see. And how…how *was* she?"

"What do you mean?"

"You know exactly what I mean."

Cal shrugged. "To be honest, she didn't look too good. And she was pretty short with me." He hesitated for a moment. "I think she might have been drinking or something."

Gina took in a long, deep breath and blew it out. "This is what she always wanted!" Gina spit out angrily. "For me to become some sort of big, successful movie star out in Hollywood. Only she couldn't handle it when it actually happened…."

Cal could see her struggling to say more. "Any particular reason?"

"Oh, God. *Lots* of them. But mostly that the studios cut her out of it."

"Cut her out of it?"

Gina nodded. "When we first got out there, she was running everything—calling people, bugging agents and producers, reading scripts, picking parts, going over dialogue…*everything!"*

"And then?"

Gina gave half a shrug. "Then I started getting more and more offers and she couldn't leave well enough alone. She kept calling people and bugging people and telling people what to do. And demanding things! Jesus, she told one producer she needed full script approval and her own trailer on the set. Finally the studio had no choice but to cut her out of it."

"How'd they do it?"

"The usual way. With lawyers. And a contract, of course. When I took that part in the royal imposter movie, part of the deal was that she couldn't be on the set and wasn't allowed to contact anybody at the studio except Brad Lackey." She let out a sad little laugh. "Poor Brad. She drove him absolutely crazy…."

Cal mulled it over in his head. "And how did you feel about it?"

Gina stared at him. "What are you, a fucking psychoanalyst?"

"No, I just…."

She pressed her fingertips over his mouth to stop him. "It's okay," she told him. "It's nice you care." Gina looked down at the puddle they were standing in. "To be honest, I was pretty relieved when it happened. She'd been all over me all my life—running me, smothering me, making me do things I didn't want to do, see people I didn't want to see, take lessons I didn't want to take…" she hesitated for a moment, thinking about her father back at the little neighborhood restaurant in Brooklyn, "…hurt people I didn't want to hurt…" She looked up at Cal. "She didn't want me getting involved with you, either."

"Is that what we are? *'Involved?'"*

"Call it what you like."

He didn't have a word for it, either. "So what happened then?"

Gina's gaze drifted down to the water again. "Oh, she had some problems with her legs. Or maybe it was her stomach first and then the legs. And then it was her headaches. And then it was arthritis. And then it was something else. Brad found her a couple of those Hollywood doctors and, well, let's just say they wanted to get rid of her and they did."

"Drugs?"

"Drugs. Booze. What's the difference? It's all the same thing…."

Cal put his thumb and forefinger under her chin and lifted it until she was looking directly into his eyes. "I'm really sorry," he told her. "Really I am…."

"What do you have to be sorry for?" she said matter-of-factly. "It's just one of those things, that's all." She straightened her shoulders and brushed the damp hair away from her face. "There are things you can do something about and things you can't do anything about. That's just the way things are, right?"

Cal nodded imperceptibly.

"So there's no point agonizing over something you can't do anything about, is there?"

Cal thought it over. "I guess not."

The conversation stalled like a balloon left hanging in mid-air, but a moment later the flap on the fortuneteller's tent folded open and Toly came out with a bemused but somewhat perplexed look on his face. "You can go in now," he told Cal and Gina. "I gave her a lot of francs, and she said you could go in together."

"You want to do it?" Cal asked.

"Sure," Gina said like it didn't make any difference any more. "Why not?"

So *Madame Sagesse* ushered them in, speaking in a deep, hoarse combination of French and clumsy English. There was only one extra chair, and she sat Gina down across from her and had Cal stand behind. He put his hands on Gina's shoulders and felt her neck backing up gently against his thumbs like a purring cat while the fortuneteller did the Tarot cards for each of them. They both drew "The Lovers" at some point and looked at each other, but didn't really understand the significance. *Madame Sagesse* apologized for her English and how hard it was to make them understand what she was trying to say. Finally, she looked at their palms—Gina's first, then Cal's—and put them side-by-side on the table in front of her, looking back and forth from one to the other. *"Zees 'ands..."* she fished for the words, *"...go well togezzer."*

"I could have told you that," Cal snickered.

Gina gave him a nudge.

The fortuneteller looked into Gina's eyes for a moment, then into Cal's. *"Ees zere ennyzing you wish to know?"* she asked.

Cal and Gina looked at each other. Then back at her.

"I guess not," Cal said sheepishly.

The fortuneteller's face broke out into its own broad, mysterious smile. *"Ees good not to azk too many queztions. Zat way you don't haz to deal wiz ze anzairs...."*

The rain was coming down harder when they came out of the tent, and so the three of them ran back to the big, warm Mercedes and headed towards the paddock again.

"She tell you anything interesting?" Toly asked Cal and Gina in the car.

"Not really," Cal allowed. " She said our hands go well together. And I guess that's true enough. How about you?"

Toly was staring out the rain-spattered side window at the empty grandstands. There were hardly any cars left to watch. 55 cars had started the race, but barely two dozen were still running. And most of them were far, far behind their class leaders and just struggling on to try and make the finish. But even so, those stands would be full of cheering, screaming Frenchmen come four that afternoon—even if the rain was coming down in torrents. Toly closed his eyes and he could almost see them there. Almost hear their shouts. "After she looked at my palm," he said distractedly, "she asked me what I want out of life."

"That's a pretty big question!" Gina laughed. But then she noticed the closed eyes and the strange, faraway expression on his face.

"It isn't really," Toly murmured so softly they could hardly hear him. "Not if you think about it…."

Chapter 30: The Death Ladder

I guess nobody will ever know if it was Eric Gibbon's nasty, four-part story in the London *World Mirror* or that visit with the spooky French fortuneteller on that dreary, dripping Sunday morning at Le Mans (or if it was just something he came up with on his own, you know?), but sometime there in the middle of the 1958 European racing season, Toly Wolfgang decided that he wanted to be World Champion. Wanted it very much, in fact. Maybe because there was such a sense of permanence and finality about being ordained as a true World Champion at anything that mattered. Something like that could never be taken away once it was achieved, and it was big and noble and steady enough to cast its shadow for generations. In both directions, if you catch my drift....

Sure, Toly knew that Moss was quicker (and others might be, too, including maybe even Cal) but he was intelligent enough to know that Moss, thanks in part to his stubborn, Union Jack British patriotism and in part to his rugged sense of independence, didn't always put himself in the best car or best position to win. Toly also recognized that becoming World Champion was only partially about raw speed and skill. It was obvious from the success the Coopers were having (and, to a lesser degree, what the Scarabs had been doing in American racing) that the old, traditional ideas were being challenged by new ways of thinking. The way Hank saw it, the *art* of racing was turning into the *science* of racing, and you had to have the very best of that science behind you and under your butt in order to have any chance at all at a world title. And once that was taken care of, you also had to survive the politics, intrigues, conflicts and personality clashes that are part of any race team—and most particularly Ferrari—and put them to work for you to maximize your chances. That was probably the hardest part of all. But Toly Wolfgang came from a solid family bloodline of proven plotters, ruthless schemers, opportunistic deal-makers and behind-the-scenes connivers, and he had the same, rare combination of raw commitment, shrewd daring, situational flexibility and predatory patience that had served his father so well in his chosen line of work. Or that's how Hank saw it, anyway.

No question Toly took a huge step towards that goal when he signed on with Ferrari. Like a lot of rich hopefuls, he'd bought his way in at first. And when he finally did get a factory contract, it was only for the World Manufacturers' Championship sportscars, and he was very much the spare wheel on the Formula One squad. But Ferrari already had the proven *Mon Ami Mates* Hawthorn and Collins and the brave, proud and determined new Italian hero Luigi Musso signed on ahead of him. Not to mention that old man Ferrari wasn't entirely convinced about Toly's ultimate speed and talent.

But things sometimes have a way of opening up for people with long vision, dedicated goals and the patience of a snake hiding next to a mouse burrow. And the very first breakthrough came just two weeks after Le Mans at the French Grand Prix at Reims. You have to understand that Reims was another of those "knitted together from country roads" European circuits like Spa and Le Mans, and dangerous as hell. It was in the lovely and charming Champagne region of France where all that sparkling, expensive bubbly stuff with the terrible morning-after hangovers comes from. Reims was a beautiful circuit, running through rolling wheat fields and quaint, inviting little farm towns, but some of the corners were almost inexcusably fast, narrow and unforgiving. Particularly the deceptively gentle curve of the *Muizon* corner at the end of the long pit straightaway, which had a curb, a ditch and an embankment running around the outside edge and could, as Hank put it, *"be taken flat-out at 153, but probably not at 154..."* Corners like *Muizon* separated the men from the boys and the fools and madmen from their lives, and Fangio said that taking it flat was worth a full second a lap because it linked two very fast sections together. But you were in the deepest shit imaginable if you ever got it wrong.

Toly managed to more or less buy his way onto the Ferrari Formula One team again at Reims. You would have thought any fourth team entry should have gone to Phil Hill after his great drive for Ferrari at Le Mans, but that's just not always the way things work out in the world of Grand Prix racing. Plus Toly was playing the part of spear-carrier again, back in the old Dino test hack with a tired, older-spec engine under the hood. But the rest of the Ferrari drivers had newly revised engines with as much as 20 more horsepower on tap, and were really looking forward to a high-speed racecourse with two slow hairpins followed by two long, flat-out straightaways where the horsepower of their new-spec engines figured to more than offset the nimble handling of the Coopers and the torque and slippery aerodynamics of the Vanwalls. Fangio was back, too, driving on a circuit where he'd always done well in a very special, *"piccolo"* version of Maserati's 250F that the factory had supposedly built with funding from Denver-area architect, developer, race entrant, motorsports enthusiast and longtime Maserati nutcase Temple Buell. It was smaller and lighter than any previous 250F, but it just didn't have the suds to run with the best of the new Ferraris, BRMs and Vanwalls. Or maybe the old man's heart just wasn't in it any more. Or maybe both....

Hank thought it was pretty neat that there were no less than three Americans entered at Reims—Phil Hill, Carroll Shelby and Troy Ruttman—but they were all in rent-a-ride privateer Maseratis and not really on pace with the newer cars. Carroll and Troy were driving *Scuderia Centro Sud* cars, while Phil Hill was in one of rich and dapper Swiss racer Jo Bonnier's two entries. And Phil did a heck of a job to qualify fastest among the six privateer 250F Maseratis in the field at 2:29. Meanwhile the Ferraris showed off their new power by taking the first two slots on the grid, with Hawthorn on pole at a cracking 2:21:7 (for an *average* of more than 130mph on a 5.18-mile circuit with no less than *two* first-gear hairpins!) and Luigi Musso cinching up his courage to start right alongside in second with a 2:22:4. And it was those two running 1-2 at the front of the pack—and pulling away from the rest—after the usual first-lap shuffle and re-shuffle sorted itself out. And poor Toly got a terrible start, not getting the revs and clutch right and damn near stalling it while the rest of the field rocketed past. Standing starts are a tricky sort of thing (just ask any drag racer!) and require calm, measured precision just when your heart rate is hitting triple digits, adrenaline is spurting out your ears and your nervous system feels like someone's jammed an electric cattle prod up your ass. Not that I know any of that from first-hand experience, of course.

Anyhow, Musso was determined not to let Hawthorn get away—it was still far from settled as to who was really Number One at Ferrari—and every lap approaching that dauntingly fast first corner, he must have been thinking about what Fangio told him when they were teammates at Ferrari in 1956: taking *Muizon* flat was worth a full second a lap! At the beginning of the 10th lap and with Hawthorn inching slowly but steadily away, Luigi Musso finally decided to try it. And you've got to give him his due for the pride, courage and commitment it took to try something that scared the living shit out of him. But he probably should have taken into account that the 246 Dino Ferraris of 1958 arrived at *Muizon* going a fat handful of miles-per-hour faster than the Lancia-Ferrari D-50 V-8s of 1956 ever did….

Musso's car left the road like a runaway rocket sled at something over 150, squirted up the embankment and went somersaulting wildly through the wheat field for more than 200 yards, finally clunking to rest upside-down with the wheels still turning. Musso had been thrown out while the car was tumbling, and was laying like a heap of old laundry at the end of another ugly swath through the wheat—battered, bleeding and already dying. An emergency helicopter was quickly summoned and its chopping rotor sent eerie, rhythmic furrows rippling through the wheat while they gathered what was left of Luigi Musso onto a stretcher and sent him winging off to a nearby hospital to officially die. And meanwhile, the race went on….

Hawthorn was in a class of his own after Musso's terrible wreck, and went on to not only win the race, but also grab that precious extra championship point for fastest lap. Far behind him, Moss in the Vanwall, Schell and Behra in the two BRMs and Fangio in the *"piccolo"* Maserati fought it out for second place. But Schell dropped back with overheating problems and Fangio had to stop at the pits with clutch trouble, and that left Moss and Behra battling back-and-forth for second. Then Behra's BRM lost fuel pressure and stopped out on the circuit, and Moss went on to finish a distant second to Hawthorn. Meanwhile Toly was driving a fine, steady race that eventually netted him third place and his first World Championship points thanks to all the pit stops and mechanical problems. He was pretty thrilled about it—especially finishing just ahead of Fangio in what would turn out to be the old *maestro's* very last Grand Prix—but he knew there was a lot of luck involved and he hadn't really raced wheel-to-wheel with much of anybody for the entire, 250-mile distance. Plus Musso's wreck had cast its pall over the Ferrari team—over the whole Grand Prix circus, in fact—and it was impossible to feel genuinely good about anything….

But Musso's tragic accident moved everybody below him—meaning basically Toly, Phil Hill and Olivier Gendebien—up a rung on the old employment ladder at Ferrari. And so Toly (again thanks to perhaps a little under-the-table greasing of palms) found himself in the third of the three Dino 246 Ferraris entered in the British Grand Prix two weeks later at Silverstone. Unlike most of the continental European racetracks, which were made out of ordinary roads, Silverstone was an airport track laid out on an old World War II bomber base about 100 miles north of London. Although flat as an ironing board, Hank said it was difficult because the track was *too* wide in many places, there wasn't much in the way of visible keys or markers and several really high-speed bends linked up relatively short straight-aways, so maintaining momentum through those corners meant everything when it came to setting a good lap time. Although the average speeds at Silverstone were always quite high, Hank said you'd have to call it as much a "handling" track as a "horsepower" track, and there was always a big home-court advantage for the British drivers who grew up racing at Silverstone and knew every pavement ripple and bit of pea gravel on the premises. Not to mention that the Brits, like the Italians, always managed to come up with a little something extra in front of the hometown (or home country, anyway) crowd. As Stirling Moss proved pretty emphatically when he put his Vanwall on pole at more than 105 mph and Roy Salvadori underscored by placing his underpowered, 2207cc Cooper third on the grid ahead of all the factory Ferraris. And likewise ahead of Cooper's Australian team leader, Jack Brabham. Between them was Harry Schell after another fast qualifying run in the promising (but usually disappointing) BRM P25, and Hawthorn had the quickest of the Ferrari V6s on the outside of the wide, four-car front row. Then came Cliff Allison in by far the new Lotus' best qualifying effort, Collins in the second Ferrari and Stuart Lewis-Evans in the second Vanwall. The usually fast Tony Brooks and Jean Behra were mired back in the third row, and Toly was on the very outside of that row, feeling a little lost in his first-ever race at Silverstone.

You have to understand that Peter Collins had been under some pressure at Ferrari. Rumor had it that old Enzo thought Collins was losing his edge—especially ever since he married that pretty and adventurous American actress, Louise King—and in typical Ferrari fashion, he made sure to let Collins know about it in no uncertain terms. Like by threatening to demote him to a Formula Two car for the French Grand Prix at Reims, for example. And, to be fair, Collins hadn't won a Grand Prix—or even seriously threatened to win one—in over a year. His *Mon Ami Mate* Hawthorn had been showing him up pretty regularly. As had Luigi Musso now and then. But Musso's death meant his place on the team was safe—at least for a while—and he came to Silverstone determined to do himself, and his career, some good.

Before the Grand Prix they had a sportscar race, which Stirling Moss won in fine style at the wheel of the factory Lister-Jaguar, and Hank was pretty excited that our own Jersey boy Walt Hansgen—who'd done such a fine job with the Cunningham Lister-Jags here in the states that summer—was over there to drive the other factory car. The very one, in fact, that poor little Archie Scott-Brown had raced so bravely and successfully and then killed himself in at Spa. It'd been completely rebuilt after the wreck, of course, and naturally Walt really wanted to do well up against an established hero and living legend like Stirling Moss. Walt gave it a hell of a run, too, running second to Moss on a fast and deceptive track that he'd never seen before, but then the clutch packed up and he was out of it. He got his revenge in the big sedan race that ran right before the Grand Prix, though. All the top British "tin-top" drivers were driving Jaguar 3.4 sedans, and they decided to put

Walt in one so he could get a little extra practice time and also as kind of a bonus for making the long trek over to England just to run a preliminary sprint race. He'd wanted to run in the Grand Prix itself, of course, but there just wasn't enough time to make arrangements and no decent car was available anyway. So the sedan race was Walt's last chance to leave some kind of impression on the Brits and Europeans, and damn if he didn't win the blessed thing! Walt Hansgen could drive the wheels off *anything,* and Hank said you simply would not believe the way he slipped, slung, skated full-lock sideways and hurled that big old Jag sedan around the racetrack. Sure wish I'd been there to see it.

When the start for the Grand Prix finally rolled around, Peter Collins absolutely *rocketed* through from the second row to grab the lead, and although Moss in the Vanwall hounded him for the first third of the race (and with Hawthorn's Ferrari right up *his* tailpipe, too!) there was no way in hell Peter Collins was going to be passed or beaten this particular day. Then Moss' car broke a valve spring and the race was essentially settled. Collins cruised to an uplifting (and much needed) win and his teammate Hawthorn finished second, not quite half a minute behind. Salvadori scored a distant but still impressive third for Cooper after a race-long battle with Lewis-Evans in the third team Vanwall, who flashed under the flag literally in the shadow of the nimble little Cooper. Our friend Toly retired with engine problems with just a dozen laps to go after an uninspiring but steady run that had him stuck in a kind of lonely racing no-man's-land, well behind the faster cars but also well ahead of the mid-pack privateers. *"I was playing with myself all day,"* was the way he put it over drinks at the racing pub near Tommy Edwards' flat, and everybody there knew exactly what he was talking about….

All that left the World Driving Championship and the Formula One Constructors' Championship very much up for grabs with just four races left in the season. Moss had two wins and one second place to Hawthorn's one win, two seconds and a third, and Collins had fresh hope with a win and a third place to his credit. Tony Brooks and Maurice Trintignant had a win apiece but nothing to back it up, so it looked like the Championship would likely be decided among those first three. But Moss seemed to either win or break, while Hawthorn always managed to hang around and grab himself some points even when he couldn't win, and that must have been very much on Moss' mind when they headed off for the German Grand Prix at the Nurburgring the first weekend in August.

What with the 14-mile length of the *Nordschleife* circuit, no silver cars in Formula One and close to 200,000 keen German fans expected, it was decided to combine a Formula Two race with the Grand Prix to fatten up the grid a little, add some interest and, not incidentally, put a few home-country Porsches out there for the crowd. The factory car was really just a lightened, 1500cc RSK sportscar with the driver's seat moved to the middle, and although it didn't figure to be as quick as the legit Formula Two Coopers, everybody knew it would be as reliable as a lead sledgehammer and that Porsche's driver, German ace Edgar Barth, knew the Nurburgring like his own blessed driveway. Ferrari also brought a Formula Two car—basically a 1500cc version of the Dino V6 that was used primarily to develop their new Formula One car—and put Phil Hill in it for his very first Ferrari start in a real Grand Prix. Even if he was running in the lightweight class. Phil made a good job of it, though, taking fastest time among the Formula Two cars and winding up 10th on the 22-car grid.

Meanwhile, at the front of the pack, Hawthorn put his Ferrari on pole with the Vanwalls of Moss and Brooks next to him and his *Mon Ami Mate* Peter Collins on the outside, but it was all green at the end of that first long, 14-mile lap around the *Nordschleife.* Moss had pulled out six seconds on Hawthorn and Collins, while Brooks trailed in fourth in the other Vanwall, most likely holding his car in reserve until he saw how things worked out ahead of him. Moss looked every bit the champion as he proceeded to set and then break a series of new lap records over the next few laps while simply motoring away from the Ferraris. But on the fourth lap the Vanwall's magneto packed it in, and Moss was out of it. That left Hawthorn and Collins in front, a good 15 seconds clear of Tony Brooks in the second Vanwall. But Brooks rose to the occasion, running the Ferraris down and passing them both with an amazing move at the North Curve, right in front of the grandstands. The same place, in fact, where Fangio's Maserati passed those two in perhaps the most amazing drive of his career the year before.

So now it was Brooks on the point with Collins chasing for all he was worth and Hawthorn right in his wheeltracks. And then, with just four laps to go and all three of them giving it everything they had—and maybe just that little bit more—Collins' Ferrari slid a bit wide at Pflanzgarten, hooked a wheel in a ditch and went flying off the racetrack. Right in front of his horrified *Mon Ami Mate* Hawthorn. But all Hawthorn saw was the Ferrari going off through the hedges. He was spared seeing the Ferrari tumble through the air and spit Collins out, sending him smashing headfirst into a tree….

Of course the initial reports in the pits were that Collins was fine, but Hawthorn probably knew better and retired with a broken clutch a lap later. Some whispered that he'd given it a "clutch job," over-revving it on purpose with the clutch in until something broke—in this case, the flywheel and clutch—just to get out of the race and find out what happened to his friend, but people who really knew him didn't think he'd ever do such a thing. Especially not while running a secure second with Moss already out of it.

That left Brooks all alone in front to take his second win of the season (and Vanwall's third) while the little bug Coopers of Salvadori and Trintignant finished second and third in a decimated field. Toly came home a struggling fourth, last of the Formula One cars to finish, and then it was some unknown New Zealander named Bruce McLaren (who Hank said didn't even look like he was shaving yet) finishing fifth overall and taking first among the Formula Two cars in a factory

Cooper. The team had also started Jack Brabham in one of their Formula Two-spec cars because they shrewdly figured they had a better shot at the reasonably large (and genuinely attainable) bag of gold for the F2 win plus points towards the *Autocar* Formula Two Championship, which they were leading at the time. Unfortunately Brabham was out on the first lap after a somewhat rough coming-together with one of the privateer Maseratis, and everyone was pretty impressed with the way this McLaren kid from New Zealand stepped in and filled the void.

But the German race left another bad, sour taste in everyone's mouth because of Collins' fatal accident. Formula One was proving to be a dangerous, dangerous game. And especially for the drivers on the Ferrari team. Even so, everybody on the ladder moved up another rung….

The Portuguese Grand Prix rolled around three weeks after Germany, and Hank said you could only imagine what was rolling around behind Mike Hawthorn's eyes. Drivers in general seem to be insulated, isolated, cool, even-keel, lone-wolf types—especially the really good ones—and I think like all other sorts of artists, performers and sports heroes, they don't understand themselves what makes them tick. Then again, who does? Anyhow, here he was, leading the now decimated Ferrari squad and in a pitched battle for the World Driving Championship *and* the Constructors' Title against a fellow Brit driving for a hometown English team who, just incidentally, everybody and his brother reckoned to be the Best Damn Race Driver On The Face Of The Earth now that Fangio had packed his bags and walked away. At, I should mention, age 54, in pretty much one piece and with five—count 'em: *FIVE!*—world driving championships to his credit. Which was a lot more than you could say for a bunch of other title contenders and pretenders without even a single World Championship to their names. Many of which were now etched on slabs of polished marble since they were very decidedly residing on the dark side of the grass.

Like Tommy Edwards said, kind of shaking his head: *"that's not bloody hero worship, it's just plain fact."*

But if there are some things that drive you nuts about the Brits (and top on that list would be how they champion, tout and coddle their own), you have to love their sense of mission, duty, fair play and perseverance—*"getting on with the job and giving it the old school try, don't you know?"*—even when the chips are down and most folks wouldn't even bother rolling out of bed in the morning. England is an old, old country, and it got that way because its people have always thought and felt like that. Then again, that's precisely what makes it feel like such an old, old country….

Anyhow, Hawthorn was dragging around a sack of sorrow and misgivings that would have crushed anybody who paid attention to it, and Moss had the bit between his teeth and a glint in his eye. Oh, everybody knew he was the best (and, typically British, he would never make a big deal of it whether he lost or won—that was for the English press flacks like Eric Gibbon to take care of), but there's a kind of twisting, twirling sense of fate and destiny that goes along with racing, and nobody pretended to know how it would all work out in the end.

Moss and Hawthorn lived up to all expectations by swapping fastest laps all through qualifying and winding up 1-2 on the grid on the old, fast and rough ocean-side street circuit in Oporto (which Hank said smelled of both fish and flowers, since sardine fishing was the major local business) and damn if stiff-upper-lip Stuart Lewis-Evans didn't do his bit for the old Union Jack by putting his Vanwall on the outside of the front row, making Hawthorn's Ferrari the red meat in a British Racing Green sandwich. Toly was in the only other Ferrari because the factory hadn't finished rebuilding another one out of the wrecks, and he was back on the third row behind Brooks' Vanwall and Behra's always fast but usually fragile BRM. And Temple Buell had bought that little *"piccolo"* Maserati 250F from the factory outright (along with renting a few wrench spinners from the old factory racing team) and put Carroll Shelby behind the wheel to see what he could do with it. Shelby put it on the outside of the fourth row, well off the pace of the leaders but also well clear of all the other privateer Maseratis.

Hank wrote that it rained on race morning, but eased off as the start approached, and he saw Hawthorn wandering across the wet pavement towards his racecar with a tweed cap on his head and an overcoat over his white shirt and bowtie, his eyes glazed and unfocused and looking almost like he was sleep-walking. But he came alive once the engines started. Moss grabbed the lead at the start and looked set to pull away, but Hawthorn wrestled it back on lap two, and now it was the red car in front. It went back and forth like that for eight laps before the drum brakes on Hawthorn's Ferrari began to fade trying to keep pace with the disc brakes on Moss' Vanwall (old man Ferrari still wasn't convinced about the superiority of discs—especially since the only ones available came from England), and after that Moss just eased off into the distance. Behra had fought his way up to third after a slow start, and inherited second when Hawthorn made a brief stop to have his overheated brakes adjusted. Toly had to make a pit stop, too, because the hood on his car was flapping loose and coming up threateningly as the air got under it towards the end of the long straightaways. You'd really rather not have it come off like a flying guillotine blade when the next thing it's likely to hit is your head....

Hawthorn came storming out of the pits and really put his foot down in an attempt to catch Behra and regain second place, and reeled off a series of blistering laps. Then Behra's BRM started to misfire—how *that* must have pissed him off!—and he had to grudgingly give way to Hawthorn and then Lewis-Evans, but just managed to hold off Toly for fourth place. And then there was drama right at the end. Moss was leading and had second-place Hawthorn in his sights—almost a full lap down—and his Vanwall teammate Lewis-Evans not far behind him in third, just over a lap down. And that's how things stood when Moss took the checker for his third outright win of the year. But then, *after* the checkered flag and on his very last lap, Hawthorn ran dramatically shy on brakes and went shooting up an escape road! Worse yet, the engine stalled! If the car didn't make it around to the start/finish line under its own power, he'd be classified as a DNF and lose his hard-fought second place. He got out and tried to push-start the car, but the escape road was slightly uphill and there was just no way he could do it. And just about that time, Stirling Moss came around on his cool-off lap and shouted over that it might work better if he turned the car around and tried it going the opposite way on the downhill slope instead. Hawthorn nodded like a light had come on, turned the car around with much grunting, sweating and muttered swearing, gave it a little shove, hopped in, selected second, flipped on the electrics, and popped the clutch. The engine coughed a few times and then sputtered to life, and a relieved-looking Hawthorn floored it, fishtailed back onto the racetrack and completed the lap to claim his second place.

But that was hardly the end of it! Seems the officials were concerned that Hawthorn had broken the rules by going the wrong way on the racetrack when he restarted after his spin—an infraction that could very easily get him disqualified—and they held a little tribunal over it that evening while the cars were being loaded up. And damn if it wasn't Stirling Moss—the guy with by far the most to lose if Hawthorn got the points for second place—who came forward and said that he'd seen the whole thing and that Hawthorn only went the wrong way on the escape road, not on the racecourse itself. And so Hawthorn's second place was reinstated (along with the six points that came with it plus the extra point he got for fastest lap when he was chasing after Behra following his pit stop) and you had to give old Stirling top marks in the Fair Play department. Sure, maybe he felt a little guilty about being the guy who originally suggested that Mike turn his car around, but somehow you couldn't quite imagine somebody like, say, old man Ferrari doing such a thing. In any case, the end result was that the two title contenders were now just five points apart with only Italy and Casablanca to go….

Monza was always a huge race for Ferrari, and never moreso than in 1958. With both titles up for grabs, the hometown team showed up with no less than four cars (for Hawthorn, Toly Wolfgang, Phil Hill and Olivier Gendebien) and had done some serious fiddling with two of them. Hawthorn's car now had Dunlop disc brakes pirated, interestingly enough, off his late friend Peter Collins' street Ferrari GT. Collins had them fitted on his own in an attempt to convince old man Ferrari that they were the way to go. And Toly's car had an experimental engine with 57 more cc, hotter cams, revised cylinder heads, bigger valves, more compression and more horsepower. Toly was pretty happy about drawing the trick engine—Ferrari figured it was too risky to chance something new and untried on Hawthorn's car—since Monza was most definitely a horsepower racetrack. Not to be outdone, Vanwall tried a slippery-looking, bubble-top aerodynamic windscreen on Moss' car, but the gain was negligible and the heat and fumes inside the cockpit were unbearable, so it was given up as a bad try. But the Vanwalls were still sleeker and tidier aerodynamically than the Ferraris, and the front row on race day—much to the dismay of the highly partisan Italian crowd—featured Hawthorn's lone Ferrari surrounded by all three team Vanwalls. With Moss on pole position, of course. The second row was all red with the other three Ferrari entries, but that wasn't much consolation. Toly had purposely taken it easy in qualifying, sticking to a reduced redline to help break in and feel out the new engine, and also not to show his hand too much. After all, if the thing really flew, they might hand it over to Hawthorn….

Hank spent a lot of time hanging around the privateer Maseratis, seeing as how two of them were being driven by Americans Masten Gregory and Carroll Shelby. Of course they were well off the pace of the factory Ferraris, Vanwalls and BRMs, but they were 1-2 among the six privateer Maseratis entered (including Maria-Teresa de Filippis in the very last spot on the grid) and that had to be worth something. And, speaking of Americans, the surprise star of the race was our own Phil Hill in his very first Formula One drive for Ferrari. He was even given the opportunity to "rabbit" for the Ferrari team, and really sunk his teeth into the job at hand, charging through to grab the race lead on the very first lap. And you can bet that put a lump in Hank's throat, seeing an American leading an actual World Championship Grand Prix for the very first time!

But our friend Toly's car was missing at the end of that first lap. And so was Harry Schell's BRM. Seems Schell and Behra's BRMs got their usual blinder of a start, what with Schell squirting up the middle between Toly and his teammate Gendebien while Behra went looking for a hole around the outside. That was all well and good accelerating from a dead stop on the wide front straightaway but, as Toly himself put it afterwards in the hospital in a mocking British accent: *"a certain funneling effect is required going through the two Lesmos...."*

What apparently happened was that the accordion collapsed with nobody willing to give way—typically, no two versions of the accident agreed, and particularly the stories given by the drivers involved—but the end result was that Toly's Ferrari went off and smashed into a tree while Schell's BRM tumbled ass-over-teakettle into the infield. Fotunately Schell got off with bumps and bruises since he landed in a row of bushes that greatly cushioned the impact (but left him with quite a collection of scratches, since they happened to be rose bushes) while Toly came away on a stretcher, lighting up another *Gauloises,* with a hairline fracture in his leg and a dislocated hip. They were both pretty damn lucky, if you want the truth of it.

Meanwhile Phil Hill continued to lead—immediately endearing himself to the Italian fans and amazing just about everybody!—but Hawthorn reeled him in after a couple more laps and eventually went by, and right after that Phil's car threw a tread and had to come in for a fresh tire. All the racing Ferraris were still running on Engleberts thanks to the long-standing contract deal Ferrari had going with the big Belgian tire company, but the general consensus up and down pit lane was that the Dunlops all the British teams were running were better. And faster. And safer....

As was typical at Monza, the battle at the front was among a slipstreaming pack of cars—Moss, Hawthorn, Lewis-Evans and Behra—and while they couldn't shake each other, they'd already pulled well clear of the rest. But Moss' gearbox seized on the 18th lap, and that left a no-doubt delighted Mike Hawthorn at the head of the pack with his only real rival for the championship title already out of the race. He put his foot in it to try and stretch out a lead, but then fate stepped in again as Behra had to call at the BRM pits—this time for brake trouble—and Lewis-Evans' Vanwall started overheating. And then it was Hawthorn's turn to pit for fresh tires (followed by Hill, who also needed new skins) and that, plus heavy attrition, left

Hawthorn barely in the lead over (can you believe it?) Masten Gregory in the privateer Maserati! Hawthorn soon pulled away, but the guy who had been quietly whittling his way towards the front was Tony Brooks in the last remaining Vanwall. Once again, he'd held back in the early stages to see how things panned out, and now he was on a real charge. He passed Gregory for second and began closing in on Hawthorn. And poor Masten Gregory was in trouble. He'd run the entire race nonstop in blistering heat, and the temperature and fumes in the cockpit were starting to get to him. He eventually pitted, crawled out of the car, handed over to Shelby (whose own Maserati was already out of it with engine trouble) and pretty much collapsed in a heap in pit lane.

Meanwhile Brooks was closing on Hawthorn—stalking him—and Hawthorn was doing all he could to fight back. But not so much as to throw it all away. The Ferraris were getting trickier and trickier to drive as their fuel loads got down towards the last few gallons. It changed their balance, their ride height and made them feel stiff and jittery, while Brooks' Vanwall seemed to get smoother and faster as the race wore on. Hawthorn held him off for several laps, but eventually had to give way. After which Brooks simply motored away to take his third win of the season (and Vanwall's fifth!) by 24 seconds. But Hawthorn held on for a solid second-place finish and increased his point advantage over Moss going into the final round in Casablanca the third weekend in October….

It only took grade-school arithmetic to figure it all out. Even though he had three outright wins to Hawthorn's one, Moss had to win *and* take fastest lap in Casablanca to have any chance at all of winning the championship. And even then he also needed Hawthorn to finish no better than third. If Moss won and took fastest lap but Hawthorn still managed to take second place, Hawthorn would win the World Title by a single, slender, solitary championship point. And that's exactly what happened. Only it was much more complicated than that. Much more complicated. And Hank was right there, trying to capture and bring to life—for readers all over America—the most dramatic championship battle ever waged. Not to mention the underlying fight to see who would become—finally!—Great Britain's very first World Driving Champion. And naturally Eric Gibbon and the rest of the frothing-at-the-mouth English press were pouring gallons upon gallons of highly flammable printers' ink over that particular fire.

Hank said Casablanca had a strange, exotic feeling about it—not like the old Bogart movie, but not like East 53rd Street, either—and a large, mixed French and Moroccan crowd showed up to see the show. Including event hosts King Mohammed and his son Moulay Hassan plus a huge party of friends, family, associates, hangers-on and bodyguards, all dressed in colorful Arab robes and headgear. The track was only just built the year before—a fast, smooth, beautifully contoured circuit that ran along the sandy Atlantic beachfront on the outskirts of Casablanca, curled up into the low hills overlooking the sea and then swooped in for another run along the ocean.

Hawthorn and Moss were all over the pre-race headlines and bylines, and they didn't disappoint, gridding the red Ferrari and the green Vanwall first and second—Hawthorn a tenth quicker this time—with the game Lewis-Evans turning in his best-ever qualifying performance ever to put his Vanwall on the outside of the front row. Toly was still on the mend in Switzerland from his encounter with Schell and the tree at Monza, but the rest of the Ferrari team—Hill and Gendebien—were well aware of the job at hand and committed to doing whatever they could to help Hawthorn win the title. As of course were Brooks and Lewis-Evans for Moss over at Vanwall….

Stirling Moss did one of his patented jackrabbit starts and grabbed the lead at the drop of the flag, and Hawthorn waved Phil Hill past to hound and harry Moss while Hawthorn wisely conserved his own car for later in the race. Phil made a hell of a job of it, too, hovering menacingly behind Moss and feinting for an opening at every opportunity to try and snatch the lead. But Ferrari was still fooling around with brake options—Hawthorn had the Dunlop discs he'd used at Monza, Gendebien was on Girling discs and Hill was stuck with an upgraded version of Ferrari's old tried-and-true drums—and sure enough Phil finally overplayed his hand (or, more accurately, his brakes) on the third lap and went scooting up an escape road, putting him out of contact with the race leader. Meanwhile Brooks was doing his best for the Vanwall team by engaging Hawthorn in a hell of a fight for what was now third place. But Brooks' engine couldn't take the strain and blew up on the 29th lap.

Everyone in pit lane expected Hill to slow and let Hawthorn slip through into second before the checker came down, and so now it fell to Lewis-Evans to try and catch and pass Hawthorn to keep him out of second place and save the championship for his teammate Moss. He drove for all he was worth—and he was gaining—but then his engine exploded in catastrophic fashion on the 42nd lap. Oil and parts went everywhere—including under his own tires—and the green car went skating off the pavement with wheels locked solid and oil spewing everywhere and rammed almost gently into a tree. Almost instantly, the oil hit the hot exhaust pipes and caught fire. Lewis-Evans scrambled desperately out of the sudden fireball—his racing coveralls coated with burning oil!—and ran blindly along the trackside, engulfed in flames, while the course marshals chased after him with fire extinguishers. They finally managed to get to him and put it out, but by then he'd been terribly, terribly burned….

So Moss won the race, Hawthorn won the title, Vanwall won the Constructors' Championship and poor Stuart Lewis-Evans flew home heavily sedated on a gurney in the back of the chartered jet carrying the rest of the somber, race- and Constructors' Championship-winning Vanwall team, on his way to a specialist burns unit in East Grinstead where he finally died six days later. By that time, first-ever British World Driving Champ Mike Hawthorn had already announced his retirement from racing.

Chapter 31: Palm Trees and Rum Punch

The 1958 Grand Prix and World Manufacturers' Championship seasons had turned into a hell of an ordeal for everybody involved, and what you really needed after an experience like that was a chance to play in the surf, lounge in the sun, lay on the beach under a palm tree, listen (and maybe even dance?) to some of that infectious island music, drink entirely too much rum and blow off a little steam. And that's precisely what the Bahamas Speed Week in Nassau had on tap from the very first welcome party on Friday evening, November 28th through the very last, bleary-eyed farewell party on Monday, December 8th.

The Nassau races were the brainchild of a P.T. Barnum-style hustler and promoter named Captain (it was never exactly clear what he was a Captain of) Sherman "Red" Crise, and he was a big, loud, strapping kind of guy with huge inner drive, wheeler-dealer instincts and stupendous appetites. He hobnobbed with the rich, well-born, politically connected and powerful all over Florida and the Bahamas, loved fast cars and boats and could be charming, funny, pushy, rude, furious, conniving, clever, obnoxious, engaging or abrasive as the situation required. Some folks considered him a bit of a slippery or even shady operator, but he got things done on a grand scale and promoted some of the most memorable, frivolous, fabulous and amazing race meetings the world had ever seen. Red spent most of his adult life slaloming and slipstreaming his way around between big-money boat deals, car deals, race deals, land deals, tourist excursion deals and Lord-only-knows what other kinds of deals all over Florida and the islands, and everybody agreed it was his personal horsepower, political clout, powers of persuasion and relentless follow-through that got the surf-pounding Nassau-to-Miami powerboat races started in 1956—by far the longest open-water powerboat races ever seen at the time—along with his wild, week-long, one-of-a-kind midwinter sportycar race meet extravaganza/extended cocktail party known as Bahamas Speed Week.

It was a hell of an idea: host a just-for-fun, run-what'cha-brung, not-connected-to-any-damn-rules-or-championship professional race meet on a beautiful tropical island right smack-dab between the end of one racing season and the beginning of the next. Or just about the time the dark, dreary shadow of winter started creeping across the entire blessed Northern hemisphere and the water temperature of the bright turquoise Gulf Stream tide pools around Nassau hovered in the bathwater-warm low 80s. Somehow Red Crise convinced his chums in the local government that the races would be a huge tourist attraction and bring a lot of people to the island. And moreover the *right kind* of people: folks with large, fat wallets in their back pockets (or in the breast pockets of their flowered shirts if they were wearing swimsuits) which they would hopefully empty on posh hotel rooms, party dinners, duty free liquor, perfume and cameras and assorted island trinkets. Or maybe try their luck at one of the thoroughly illegal but open-to-the-public/any-old-cab-driver-can-take-you-there gambling joints. It certainly didn't hurt that Crise was good friends with Sir Sydney Oakes and Lady Greta Oakes (who were divorced by 1958 but still appeared to be great chums—you always wonder how the English do that) and likewise loved fast boats and sports cars. Sir Sydney also by chance and inheritance owned the biggest damn bottling plant in the Bahamas, acres upon acres of prime local real estate and, along with his ex-wife, pretty much ran the wealthy expatriate, displaced aristocrat, fugitive scoundrel and green-eyed tax exile social scene in the Bahamas. Which, by the way, was always on the lookout for something fun and outrageous to do….

More than anything, the Bahamas Speed Week was designed to be a hellaciously good time. Hank told me the first couple race weeks were run on a ragged little course laid out on an abandoned RAF World War II transport base called Windsor Field, but a couple years later—and with full approval of the local brass and bigwigs—Crise moved it to the slightly more hospitable Oakes Field Airport not far at all from Nassau's hotel bars, pools, beaches, restaurants and local night spots. Bahamas Speed Week became famous and then notorious in pretty short order, seeing as how the weather was generally fabulous and the nightly cocktail and dinner parties—including the opulent, black-tie formal affairs hosted by island society types like Sir Sydney and Lady Greta—were so legendary that the pit lane in Nassau quickly earned the nickname "Hangover Alley."

"You oughta come down there at the end of November," Hank told me over the phone during a stopover at Idlewild on his way back to California after that gut-twisting end-of-season finale in Casablanca.

"Oh hell, Hank," I kind of moaned into the receiver. "There's no damn way I can go. I got a business and a wife and a family to look after here in Jersey."

"It's your loss."

I had to admit, it sounded like a pretty good time. Hell, *everybody* was going to be there. But there was no way I could slip something like that past Julie. No way in hell….

"Why don't you take her with?" Big Ed asked me a day or so later when I told him about it.

"Are you *serious?"*

"Sure. Why the hell not? You both been workin' your asses off with the business and the kids and all. You deserve it. You *both* deserve it." He leaned back in his chair, re-lit the end of his cigar and puffed out a perfect halo of a smoke ring for me. "Tell me, when was the last time you took your wife on any kind of vacation?"

I tried to think of something since our honeymoon, but all I came up with was a couple race weekends plus that extended, four-day stay at the shore cottage Julie booked us into down near Atlantic City before little Rosalina was born. The weekend it rained for three-and-a-half days straight and both kids came down with raging stomach disorders thanks to some highly suspect local clam chowder. "You mean without a car race involved?" I asked him.

"I said a *vacation,* dammit."

I thought it over. I thought about velvet-soft tropical nights on the beach with Julie lying next to me in the sand. I thought about waking up in a bright, sunny hotel room with coconut palms right outside our window, fresh-picked fruit and flowers in a bowl on the dresser and no kids bawling or fighting or whimpering in the next room. Or a glaring, pissed-off-on-general-principles mother-in-law up in her vulture-perch apartment over our garage. I thought about the parties at night and seeing all my friends and also—of course—hanging around at the races and feeling that buzz I get in my gut every time somebody fires up an un-muffled Ferrari V-12, Jag straight-six or a rumbleguts American V-8 with lots of compression and one of those hairy cam profiles that make the ground throb under your feet. No question I was giving that week in Nassau some serious thought. Only who was I kidding?

"Look, she's never gonna go for it," I told Big Ed. "She gets one whiff that there's a race involved and the old steel door is gonna slam shut in a hurry."

Big Ed looked at me. "You ever lie to your wife?"

I felt myself kind of backing up in the chair. "Whaddaya mean, do I ever lie to my wife?"

You couldn't miss the little gleam warming up in Big Ed's eyes. "I mean just what I said: *'do you ever lie to your wife?'"* He took another long, slow drag off his stogie and puffed out a series of small, fat, doughnut-sized smoke rings. "It's plain English, Buddy. You been using it all your life…."

"Uh, well…" I kind of stammered, "…no, of course not."

"I see," he continued, eyeballing me right down to the darned ends of my socks. "You ever lie to me?"

I felt heat rising on my face. But then the twinkle in Big Ed's eyes got to me and I started to laugh. "Well," I kind of admitted, "maybe just this once…."

Turns out Big Ed had a typically Big Ed kind of idea—or maybe Dirty Sneaky Lying Scheme would be a better description—seeing as how Volkswagen had this sales contest going and the sales manager of the dealership that sold the most VW Microbuses (which VW of America was ever-so-slightly long in at the time) would win a free trip for two to Hawaii. And we could surely be in the running for that trip if Big Ed managed to close the deal he had cooking with some guy who owned a chain of high-end florist shops to use about a half-dozen Microbuses as delivery trucks for weddings and funerals and such. Of course, the only problem was that the contest wasn't over yet, the trip was supposed to be at the end of January, not the beginning of December, and the specified destination was Hawaii way out in the middle of the Pacific Ocean rather than the Bahamas over on the far opposite side of the North American continent, out in the Gulf Stream not far off the tip of Florida.

"Hey, what the hell's the difference?" Big Ed asked, rolling his palms up. "You seen one ocean, you seen 'em all…."

So I went home that night, grabbed myself a cold beer out of the refrigerator, downed it in about two gulps, and told Julie about the free trip we'd won to the Bahamas the first week in December.

"Oh, there's no way we can go," she shot back immediately. "The kids have school and my mom has her Bingo night and there's the church Christmas raffle I'm helping your mom with. We're in charge of the centerpieces…" she said it like those centerpieces (which, by the way, didn't have to be ready until the 20th of December) were the control rods of a nuclear reactor, "…and how could you even *think* about leaving the kids on their own?"

I moved in a little closer and gave her my very best Basset Hound eyes. "Well, I just thought, y'know, that we've both been working pretty hard and never get away by ourselves anymore and it's just for a blessed week and we've got your mom and my folks and even little Annie Bardelli down the street to help out watching the kids…."

Julie glared at me a little. And I knew exactly what she was glaring at. Little Annie Bardelli had been doing a little freelance babysitting for us every now and then when we took her mom out to a show or went to some kind of church function or other on a Friday or Sunday night. Only all of a sudden little Annie Bardelli wasn't quite so little anymore over the past eight or ten months (if you catch my drift) and Julie had caught me kind of looking at her once or twice—in a purely domestic and totally neighborly kind of way, of course—like I was wondering what she'd look like bending over to pick up little Vincie's plastic toy truck or littler Roberta's Raggedy Andy doll or even littlest Rosalina's pacifier with no clothes on. Wives have a sixth sense about stuff like that, and the very best advice I can give married husbands with little children around the house is to seek out the fattest, ugliest babysitters you can find. It's the smartest thing you can do. And you get a little bonus in that fat, ugly girls usually work hard, love kids and will generally be available on Friday and Saturday nights even well into their senior year of high school….

But we were talking about my so-called Free Trip to the Bahamas, weren't we?

"Whatever you say, dear," I told her in the voice every married woman understands to mean that you're not done pleading and wheedling at all. "It just seems such a shame to pass up a free, thousand-dollar trip up and, well, just *lose* it…."

"A thousand dollars?" she asked, her eyebrows inching up.

I nodded. I thought a thousand dollars sounded like a nice, round number.

"Just *lose* it?"

I nodded again.

"You can't sell it or trade it in or anything?"

I shook my head. "It's non-transferable," I told her sadly, letting my eyes droop so far they damn near melted off my face. "And it's only one tiny little week…."

So that's how Julie and me wound up on the flight down to Miami early Friday, November 28th, to catch the other, much smaller plane over to Nassau for the 1958 edition of Bahamas Speed Week. I mean, for our "Free Island Vacation," right? Oh, I knew I was going to have to come clean about it sometime, but once you back yourself into a lie that big, it gets kind of hard to just casually slip the truth into an offhand conversation. And particularly not when you're out shopping for swimsuits with you wife during a four-hour layover in Miami. As a matter of granite-hard fact, I recommend that husbands avoid going swimsuit shopping with their wives at all costs, because there is nothing that upsets even a thoroughly beautiful woman so much as what she looks like—or at least *thinks* she looks like—in a bathing suit.

"Does this suit make me look fat?" she'll ask as she fidgets in front of the mirror, tugging at this seam or that.

Let me assure you, there is no possible correct answer to that question. And I've tried them all....

Of course the jig was up about 10 seconds after we arrived back at the airport for the little puddle-jumper flight over to Nassau. Hank and Cal were at the gate. And so was Carroll Shelby and Denise McCluggage and Ernesto Julio and Bruce Kessler and Jim Jeffords and George Constantine and a couple guys from Lance Reventlow's Scarab crew and...well, it didn't take a building to fall on her for Julie to figure things out. "Are we going to a fricking *car race?"* she hissed at me between tightly clenched teeth. Her eyes were like a pair of glinting butcher knives pointed in my direction.

Well, there was nothing to do at that point but spill the beans. But quietly, you know. Over by the potted palm next to the men's room where it wouldn't make a scene. I can't remember exactly what I said, but I can assure you it sounded exceedingly lame.

Julie stared at me like I'd set her mother's hair on fire with a blowtorch.

"You *lied* to me!" she snarled.

"If I didn't lie to you, you wouldn't have come," I answered back in a whimpering, bleating sort of whisper. "I wanted us to do this *together,* see?" I said just as earnestly as I could. And then I took a risk and looked her right in the eyes. "We never do anything together anymore. Not just *us.... "* I let my voice trail off and gave her the sad, droopy eyes again. But she wasn't buying it. Or at least not yet, anyway.

I had to suffer a little first.

"You tricked me," she said in one of those dangerously calm, controlled voices that send shivers up your back. "You looked me right in the eye and lied to me."

"It was the only thing I could think of," I pleaded, trying to ride it out. "I mean, we never go off and just *do* anything together anymore." I tried to make it sound real sad and intimate and romantic.

"Right, Palumbo," she snapped right back. "I can't think of anything I'd rather do than go to another fricking car race...."

"But this is so much *more* than just a car race," I assured her. "It's a week-long party on a tropical island. There'll be swimming and snorkeling and walking on the beach and just sitting around the pool ...."

"I don't want anybody to see me in that bathing suit."

"The one you just bought? After trying on every blessed suit in the store?"

"It makes me look fat."

Julie's eyes swept around the boarding area. Everywhere you looked there were clusters of people—almost all racers, crew people and racers wives or girlfriends—and they all seemed to be laughing and smiling and joking and getting ready for one hell of a good time. It was pretty infectious, if you want the truth of it.

"Hmpf," Julie snorted as the fireworks slowly faded out of her eyes. "I just want you to know this, Palumbo. I'm only going along with this because you tricked me. And you'd better pay attention to me while we're there. And you'd better not wander off and leave me alone while you go talk to all your dumb racing friends."

"I wouldn't think of it, Julie," I swore on the graves of my ancestors. "This is going to be *our* time. *Together.* You'll see…."

About then they called for boarding, and you can bet I took her hand and held it as we walked across the flight apron to the plane. Gave her the window seat, too. And then I remember glancing over—as the plane took off with both engines roaring and the earth seemed to tilt on its axis as the somewhat ancient *Air Bahamas* DC-3 climbed into a perfect azure sky over a magnificent turquoise ocean—and seeing the faintest little hint of a smile at the corners of Julie's mouth. Turns out she'd had it about up to here with the kids and her mom and my folks and the damn church raffle, too….

We shared a cab ride to our oceanfront hotel with Hank and Denise McCluggage, and Julie was amazed to discover that Denise was not only a lady racer, but also a lady in a lot of other, very classy respects as well. Not to mention genuinely respected by most of the male racers. Or at least all the fast ones, anyway. Along the way, Hank explained as how the entry was a little down this year and almost none of the big European teams or stars bothered to make the trip on account of Red Crise and the FIA didn't see eye-to-eye about their stupid 3.0-liter limit for sportscar racing. Hey, he wanted the biggest, hairiest damn racecars he could get! Not to mention that a lot of the American SCMA racers who supported the event had cars with way too much engine size to qualify under the new-for-1958 FIA rules. So the FIA was out and the SCMA was in at Nassau for 1958, and the end result was that all the freebie trips and complimentary hotel rooms and $tarting money—not to mention prize money!—the European professionals were accustomed to were replaced by the SCMA's *very* expensive 150-buck entry fee and a big, shiny trophy with no cash money inside for the winner. So even though a few of the big European stars like Stirling Moss and Joakim Bonnier were coming down for a week of fun and sun, they considered themselves professionals and most definitely weren't about to race and risk their necks and reputations merely for the fun of it. That turned the 1958 edition of Bahamas Speed Week into just a big, extended and exotic SCMA amateur race, if you want the truth of it. But that didn't matter much to the participants. After all, the handful of visiting European stars and teams had generally run off with all the big prize money anyway, while the rest of the supporting cast were only too happy to be back down with the sun and sea and palm trees, racing once again in the Bahamas the first week of December.

"Last year was probably the last one for the Grand Prix stars," Hank said ruefully. "And it was neat having them. But Nassau is really about parties and fun racing, and there are always going to be some great stories coming out of it." He looked over at Denise. "Like the fantastic run Denise here had in the Ladies' Race last year…."

Denise kind of squirmed and told him to stop—like he was embarrassing her, you know?—but you could tell she was kind of enjoying it, too.

"You have to understand that just about the whole damn Aston Martin team came down last year," Hank began as the palm trees and native women hawking straw hats, woven baskets and polished abalone shells to the tourists wheeled by. "They liked coming to Nassau because it was good fun and a hell of a nice break at the end of the year. And it was also a heck of a great opportunity to sell off last year's Old Nail to some rich American or Mexican or South American and maybe even take a few orders for this year's car." I could easily understand what Hank was talking about as the cab turned right and continued on along the shoreline. The palm trees were as tall, sleek and graceful and the sun was as bright and the beaches were as white and the water was as blue as anything I'd ever seen on a blessed picture postcard. And the smell! There was salt air wafting in off the ocean and the warm, heavy scent of jungle green and beach sand and huge, ripe tropical flowers sweet with pollen. Nassau was quite a place, even if a lot of it was still raw, scraggly jungle and undeveloped lots full of rocks, weeds, trash and gravel. And you couldn't miss how the native areas we passed (and once we were next to the ocean, we didn't pass many) were all poor, sad-looking shacks and shanties. But the handsome beachfront tourist hotels and the houses and mansions of the wealthy English, European, Canadian, Mexican and American tax exiles who'd come to live with their money in the Bahamas more than made up for it. A lot of those folks believed Red Crise's races would really help bolster the tourist trade. And, even if they didn't, they were guaranteed to be one hell of a good time....

"Anyhow," Hank continued, "Aston had brought down one of their big, new, 3.7-liter versions of the DBR—the one with the Lagonda frame and gearbox behind the engine instead of that damn transaxle they have all the trouble with in back—and Stirling Moss himself was on hand to drive it. Moss absolutely *loved* it down here. When he wasn't swimming, he was sailing, and when he wasn't sailing, he was water-skiing, and when he wasn't water-skiing, he was riding around the island on a motorscooter in his swim trunks. And when he wasn't doing that, well...."

He and Denise exchanged raised eyebrows.

"...Well, Moss looked pretty damn strong in that Aston last year, but he'd also kind of taken a shine to this other lady racer from California, Ruth Levy...."

"Another lady racer?" Julie asked. "Was she any good?"

"Oh, she was good," Hank nodded. "Not as good as Denise here, of course...."

"You watch what you say about Ruth," Denise warned playfully. I guess they'd co-driven together several times, and knew that it's not easy being a woman in a man's game. No matter who you are or how fast you go. Denise looked right at Julie. "Ruth is a *very* good driver," she insisted like somebody's big sister.

"But she's not as good as you," Hank said flatly. "And that's really the point of the story, isn't it?"

"And what story is that?" I prodded, eager to move things along.

Hank and Denise's eyes made an uneasy peace.

"Well, they have a lot of class, heat and novelty races here in Nassau to fill up time between the parties. I mean, the races have to last for a whole week, right? So they have races for islanders only in their own or borrowed—or I guess I should say 'rented'—cars, and traditionally there's always been a Ladies' Race on Saturday."

"A *Ladies'* Race?" Julie asked, sounding genuinely interested.

Hank nodded. "And last year, seeing as how Stirling had taken such a shine to this Ruth Levy, he got the Aston team to lend her his brand-new DBR2 for the ladies' race. Just for jollies, of course."

Oh, of course.

"Meanwhile, our Denise here had a Porsche 550 Spyder on loan from somebody or other, and the two of them got into one heck of a battle for the lead."

"It was a pretty good one," Denise agreed through a big smile.

"Now you have to understand," Hank continued, "that a 1500cc Porsche 550 is just never going to have enough oomph to match a 3.7-liter Aston Martin around a course like the one they have at Oakes Field..." you couldn't miss how Denise was getting a little pink in the cheeks as Hank went on, "...Sure, it's got better brakes and weighs a lot less and handles better, but the Aston's just got too much grunt for it on the long straightaways."

"So what happened?" Julie wanted to know. I was pretty damn happy about the excitement I saw heating up in her eyes.

"Well, they ran it in two heats, and damn if Denise here didn't hunt the Aston down, pass under braking and win the first heat by about a gnat's eyelash after a heck of a tussle." I looked over and saw Denise kind of looking down at the floor mat. "But there was a lot of coaching and pumping-up going on between the heats-—old Stirling was giving Ruth Levy an awful lot of personal advice—and she took off like a shot again at the start of the second heat. As you might expect with a bigger, more powerful car. But Denise closed up through the twisty stuff, squeezed by under braking and got herself back in front, and then the two of them put on one hell of a show. Denise'd really get that little Porsche 550 hooked up and hauling out of the corners, and it'd take Ruth all the way to the end of the straightaway to get back on her tail again. And then Denise'd take her in so damn deep into the corners that there was no way she could get by. It went on like that lap after lap. Once or twice Ruth looked maybe close enough to pull neck-and-neck at the end of the longest straight, but when that happened, Denise here would just duck to the inside so the Aston had no choice but to stay outside and try the long way around. And of course that *never* works...."

"No, it doesn't," Denise chuckled. "Not for Ruth *or* me."

The cab was pulling into the hotel drive. "So it all came down to the last corner on the last lap," Hank continued quickly. "Ruth was stuck behind in second place in what she *knew* should have been the faster car, and she more or less made up her mind that she was *not* about to settle for second...."

I looked over and Julie was on the edge of her seat.

"...So she pulled out at the end of the straight and came storming down the inside without ever touching the brakes." Hank paused for a moment to let the suspense build up.

"Jesus, what happened?" Julie demanded.

Hank looked over at Denise and Denise looked back at him. "Well, she kind of went straight off," Denise admitted sheepishly. "I left her room—I mean, she was coming through no matter what I did, so leaving her room was probably a pretty good idea—and she wound up rolling the car over once or twice."

"It was twice," Hank nodded.

"My *God!* Was she *hurt?"* Julie asked breathlessly.

"Not really," Hank assured her. "Just a few bumps and bruises."

"And her pride," Denise added with just a hint of compassion. "That's always the slowest thing to heal." But you had to love that competitive twinkle in her eye. "I asked her afterwards if she'd run out of brakes, and she told me: *'No, Denise, I ran out of brains....'"*

It was quite a story, and you could see the idea of women racing competitively with each other—or with men, come to that—got Julie pretty juiced up. We climbed out of the cab and tipped the driver and the bellman after they loaded our luggage. "I'll tell you the rest of the story at the welcome party tonight," Hank grinned.

"There's *more?"*

"Oh, yes," Hank nodded. "Oh, yes...."

"There's a *party* tonight?" Julie gasped. "I haven't got a thing to wear...."

"Have you got a swimsuit?" Denise asked.

Julie stared at her. "I'm not going to wear a swimsuit to a welcome party."

"You might as well," Hank laughed. "Odds are you're going to wind up in the pool sooner or later, no matter how you come dressed...."

We ran into Cal and Bruce Kessler and Ernesto Julio and pilot/part-time Hollywood stuntman and even more part-time hired-gun racer Peter Stark in the hotel lobby. Bruce was driving John Edgar's 4.9 Ferrari at the Bahamas Speed Week and Peter Stark was having another go in Ernesto's Maserati 450S, and the three of them were all pretty chummy seeing as how they were all kind of involved in the movie business in one way or another. Turns out Bruce Kessler had a bit of a movie career started up for himself as an assistant director and sometimes even a second unit director (which was really a better deal, since you pretty much got to run your own crew and call your own shots on scenes and footage the *real* director just couldn't get around to) on feature films. Said he really liked it, too.

"Better than racing?" I had to ask.

"Well, it's different," he tried to explain. "The best thing about racing is that it's finite and exciting and immediate and you're holding it right there in your hands while it's happening. And you always know right where you stand, too." He thought it over for a moment. "But I guess that's also the worst thing about it. I mean, when somebody like Moss just drives away from you or when you take your first look at the time sheets after qualifying, there's no place to hide…." he gave me kind of a helpless smile. "…and when a race is over and you switch the car off and climb out and try to walk away, part of you is still *in* the car. Or wants to be, anyway. But not—and here's the screwy part—not because it felt so wonderful and great," Bruce looked me right in the eye, and even though he was smiling and it sounded like off-the-cuff conversation, I could see he'd thought long and hard about this, "but because you're disgusted with yourself and want to go back out and see if you can't do a little bit better. And there's something else, too…."

"The silence," Cal chimed in.

Bruce looked at Cal and smiled. "He knows how it is. Sometimes I think the greatest thing about being out on the track in a racing car is that nothing from the rest of life can get at you. You're just too damn busy and, well, *involved.*"

Cal nodded with his eyes.

"Yep," Bruce continued, "it's a pretty damn special place," his eyes swept around the lobby. "Full of pretty special people, too."

"But you like the movies better?" I had to ask.

"Like I said, it's different. But, yeah, I like it. It's exciting and you have to plan ahead on a grand scale, and yet you need to stay free and flexible and be quick and sharp enough to improvise when you need to and be willing to settle for the best you can get." He curled his lip under, trying to find the right words. "You could say it's the difference between playing music in front of an audience and writing a book or carving a sculpture up in a room someplace where there's no one to see you. When you're performing live—hell, *any* kind of performing live—it's all coming out of you at the moment and you've got to try and keep it all smooth and flowing and fight your way through the missed notes and the rough spots when nothing feels like it's working," Bruce flashed me a near-maniacal grimace. "That's what makes performers so damn crazy when they're not doing whatever it is they do."

"Even racing drivers?" Julie asked.

"*Especially* racing drivers," Bruce chuckled. He glanced over at Peter and Cal, "present company excepted, of course."

Well, nothing would do at that point but for Ernesto Julio to invite us all to have a few rounds of drinks with him in the lobby bar. His treat, of course. You got the sense he felt a little funny about the way things had worked out between Cal and him and wanted to sort of politely put it all in the past—at least for the week in Nassau, anyway—and the easiest way to get that sort of thing accomplished is always in a crowd. And over drinks. So we commandeered a big, glass-topped table out by the French doors that opened out onto a wide flagstone patio overlooking the ocean, and it wasn't long before we had three or four tables filled and pushed together, about our third or fourth round of powerful, fruity rum drinks in front of us and a loud, lushed-up and loquacious Eric Gibbon holding forth on the entire history of the Bahamas….

"Of course it was all pirates and slave traders back in the old colonial days. Blackbeard. Henry Morgan. The whole lot. And forget your romantic schoolboy notions, those Caribbean pirates were nothing but a bunch of cutthroats, thieves and cruel, cold-blooded murderers.You know what they used to do?"

Julie and me shook our heads.

"They used to put out the light in the lighthouse and then tie a lantern onto a donkey's neck and lead it right along there," he pointed out towards the beach.

"What for?"

"Why, to fool ships into thinking it was another bloody boat and that they were still well offshore and in safe water. They'd lure them into the shallows and onto the reefs, run them aground, and then come morning they'd go out and sack and plunder at their leisure. They'd bloody well kill anyone they couldn't get ransom for. A fine bunch! And the slave traders were just as bad. But they didn't have much on some of the people running things here today...."

Julie stared at him. "That's not a very nice thing to say," she told him point-blank. My Julie wasn't about to let a rude remark like that go unchallenged. Especially after a couple deceptively harmless rum drinks with an octane rating well into triple digits.

"Not trying to offend," Eric assured her, stifling a burp. *"I just happen to know the bloody history, that's all. It's quite a story, too. Scandal. Bootlegging. Murder. Espionage. Treason. The stuff of dime novels, really..."*

"I'm working on a novel," Hank muttered into his drink. But of course nobody heard him, because Eric was up and running by then:

"Of course things really took off down here thanks to the American Rebellion..."

"We like to call it a 'revolution,'" Cal corrected him.

"Have it any way you like. But the upshot was that a lot of the well-to-do crown loyalists fled to Canada and the Carribean. The ones who settled here built the town of Nassau into what it is today—the churches, the shops, Parliament Square, Fort Charlotte—and made quite a good business out of smuggling wool for British mills through the Union blockades during your Civil War...."

I had to admit, this was pretty interesting stuff.

"The irony is that smuggling turned into an even bigger business—only going the opposite direction—during your country's silly prohibition. Seaplanes and boats would come over from Miami, load up at the West End with all the whiskey and rum they could carry, and sneak it back to the mainland under cover of night. It was a HUGE bloody business. Made a fortune for a lot of people. Some with highly recognizable names...."

"Like who?"

Eric rolled his thumbs out to either side. *"It's not my place to tattle,"* he teased, *but I understand there are some VERY famous—and notorious!—people and families involved."* Of course, anytime Eric Gibbon refrained from naming names and telling scandalous stories, the bare truth was that he didn't know the details.

"Of course, the real story of modern Nassau and the Bahamas starts with Sir Harold Oakes," Eric continued grandly. *"Not that he had any genuine blue blood you could talk about. Not a bloody drop. American, he was. From some ungodly place up in Maine. Upper middle class at best. Father was a lawyer, I think."* Eric took another hefty sip off his rum punch. *"His parents planned for him to be a doctor and sent him off to medical school, but he heard about some fabulous gold strike up in the Klondike and got this notion to take off and be a bloody prospector. Just like that. Prospected for gold all over the world—Canada, Alaska, South America, California, Australia, you name it—but he wasn't much bloody good at it. All he found in 16 years of living in the wilderness and scrabbling at the ground with a bloody shovel and pickaxe was a bloody iron mine. And he found that with three other blokes."* Eric paused to blow his nose. *"It was a pretty good mine and made him some money, but Harry Oakes was a loner by nature and dead-set on making himself rich with a big gold strike. So he sold out to his partners and went off on his own again. Took him two more long, hard years—damn near froze to death at one point and got mauled by a bear at another—but then he finally found the bloody Big One. Lake Shore Mines up in Canada, just south of Kirkland Lake. Second biggest bloody gold mine in North America. Made him stinking, filthy rich."*

Everybody at the table was listening.

"But stop and think about it. This Oakes chap had been living up in the wilderness all by himself with the bears and the bleeding timber wolves, picking at the earth like it was a scab. And all of a sudden he's the richest man in Canada. Hell, he's one of the richest men on earth!" Eric shook his head like it was a terrible sort of problem to have. *"What to do? What to do?"* he groaned, draining the last of his drink and looking around the table for someone to buy him another.

"I've got that!" a familiar, heavily accented voice shouted from behind me. I wheeled around and there was Toly Wolfgang, propped up on a silver-headed walking cane and holding a half-smoked *Gauloises* clenched between his teeth. I guess he'd kind of sneaked up on us while Eric was talking.

"Hey, good to see you!" I yelped, pumping his hand. Then I looked down at the cane. "How are you doing?"

"Not bad," he shrugged. "I'd like to heal a little quicker. But I'd like to be younger, too, and that's not very likely either, is it?" He looked over at Julie and then accusingly back at me. *"Does your wife know about this?"* Toly demanded.

"This *IS* my wife," I told him. I could see Julie recognized him from the newspapers and tabloids from the Shock Of Recognition in her eyes, and of course Toly knew exactly what to say and how to handle things. He looked back and forth from Julie to me in mock dismay and finally told her: "I know a very good eye doctor in Madrid. You really should have seen him before you did this thing." He signed heavily. "But now I'm afraid it's too late. If you see that doctor now, it will only make matters worse..."

"Julie," I said, "this is Toly Wolfgang."

"Don't listen to a word he says," Cal grinned from the other side of the table. "He's a notorious liar and not to be taken seriously."

"I hope he was serious about my bloody drink!" Eric interrupted.

Toly looked at him. "Heaven forbid I should neglect such an important duty." He looked around the table. "Would anyone else like one?"

Groans and nods all around.

"Very well, I'll bring the whole bar over." Toly started for the bar, and you could see there was a hitch in his walk and he really needed the cane. It had a rubber tip on the end that squeaked on the polished marble floor. *"Do go on,"* Toly called over his shoulder. *"I certainly didn't mean to interrupt a good story..."*

"Where was I?" Eric muttered to no one in particular.

"Harry Oakes had just struck it rich with his gold mine," I reminded him.

"He was trying to figure out what to do with all the money," Cal added.

A light came on in Eric's eyes. "Ah, yes," he mused. And then he was at it full-tilt again: *"So Harry Oakes takes himself a world cruise. Top-class all the way. And wouldn't you know he meets a lovely young morsel of a girl in Australia. Name of Eunice. He's closing in on 50 by then and rough and cranky as an old gate hinge, while she's a ripe young 22."* The waitress arrived with a tray-full of drinks and Eric paused for a swig to let it all sink in, then picked the story up again: *"So they marry and move to Niagara Falls, where he builds her a mansion with 17 bathrooms and air conditioning throughout. AIR CONDITIONING! In nineteen-bloody-twenty-eight! But he's still a crusty old bugger and no pleasure to deal with, but he's become something of a civic fixture thanks to some very generous charitable contributions and the fact that he's paying the Canadian government three bloody million a year in taxes. But that eventually starts to wear thin—seems the richer blokes get, the more desperate they are to hang onto it—so he pulls up stakes and moves his family down to the Bahamas to get away from the taxman."* Eric took another swig. *"Old King George the Sixth is so tickled he makes him a bloody baronet in 1939. So now all of a sudden it's SIR Harry bloody Oakes."* He leaned in over the table. *"You can buy your way into the bloody peerage these days. That's what it's come to."*

"Don't kid yourself," Toly corrected him. "You always could...."

"But what happened to Harry Oakes?" I wanted to know.

"That's SIR Harry Oakes," Eric reminded us, *"and the blighter built most of what you're standing on. To get right to the nub of it, it was his bloody money, drive and ideas that turned this flat, hot, fish-smelling little chunk of rock and jungle into a bloody tropical island paradise. No questions about it, he's the one who made it happen."*

"But what happened?" Cal asked. "I heard he was murdered."

Eric's eyes popped open. *"Oh, it was a delightful scandal. Magnificent, in fact. Stabbed four times in the head. Or maybe hit with a blunt object or maybe even shot—the records from the police investigation are appalling—and then whoever it was laid him out on his bed, poured gasoline all over him and set him on fire!"*

"My God!" Julie gasped. But that just jacked Eric up a notch.

"Whoever it was planned to leave the body and the crime scene all but destroyed. But there was a hell of a rainstorm that night—a real tropical monsoon—and it put the fire out well before the job was done. There was blood everywhere, bloody fingerprints on the walls and feathers scattered all over the place. Some said they were just from his pillow and some said it was some sort of dark island voodoo ritual. The stuff of bloody dime novels, really."

"I'm working on a novel," Hank mumbled again into his drink.

"But who *did* it?" Julie wanted to know. So did I, come to think of it.

"Who knows?" Eric said grandly. *"Happened back in 1943 and no one was ever convicted. But there are plenty of theories. Too many. The big problem with this murder was too bloody many likely suspects...."*

We all waited for him to go on, but of course he held back until someone asked him. In fact, it turned out to be me.

"Well, some say American mobsters were behind it. Lucky Luciano and his bloody larcenous bunch. They wanted to set up legalized casino gambling here like they had in Cuba. But the old bird wouldn't hear of it. Went against his grain. Thought it would ruin the island as a haven for displaced aristocrats and rich society renegades."

"So you think mobsters knocked him off?"

Eric shrugged. *"Who knows? Lots of people think it was one of Harry Oakes' oldest and dearest island friends, Harold Christie. Or make that SIR bloody Harold Christie, and mostly thanks to none other than Harry Oakes."*

"Who was Harold Christie?" Julie wanted to know.

"A bloody Englishman raised right here in the Bahamas. Born dirt poor, but made a fortune buying and selling local real estate. Sold Harry Oakes half the bloody island at one time or another. They became best friends and Christie made himself a fortune and got himself a title out of it."

"But why would he want to kill his best friend?"

Another shrug. *"Some say he was in it with the mob bunch who wanted to do Oakes in because he wouldn't go along with the gambling. Matter of record that Christie spent the night at Harry Oakes' house the night of the murder. In the room right next door, in fact. Oakes' wife and family were away with relatives in Maine, so it was just the cozy two of them. And the servants in the servants' quarters outside, of course."*

"But what did Christie say about the murder?" Julie asked. "Gunshots or a stabbing or a bludgeoning and then a fire in the room right next door...didn't he hear or see *anything?"*

"Told the court he slept right through it," Eric said airily, taking another swig. *"Said he didn't hear or see a thing...."*

"That sounds pretty suspicious."

"Oh, and it runs even deeper. One of the servants said they saw Christie in a car with two men, coming and going from the house in the middle of the bloody night.

And supposedly a strange boat pulled into the harbor that night—in a driving bloody rainstorm—and left again before dawn."

"Supposedly? Didn't anybody see it?"

"Only the harbormaster, and he died in a rather suspicious drowning accident a few weeks before the case came to trial." Eric's eyes swept around the table. *"By the way, he was known to be an EXCELLENT swimmer...."*

"Then this Christie sure sounds like the guy."

Eric shook his head. *"The police didn't think so. They put the whole thing at the feet of Harry Oakes' daughter Nancy's new husband. She was the eldest child and barely bloody 18 at the time. Eloped to New York with a handsome, good-for-nothing French/Mauritanian chap with an embarrassingly shady past named Alfred Fouquereaux de Marigny. Called himself "Freddy," thank goodness. Had a chicken farm here on the island. Bloody good friend of Ernest Hemingway's, too. Or so I'm told. Hell of a notorious womanizer. And most likely a bloody gold-digger with a name like that, don't you think? Local police charged him, but he was acquitted when the case came to trial. The investigation was a hopeless mess."* Eric leaned in and whispered: *"Not really too difficult to fix things here if you've got the money and position...."*

"And that's the end of it?"

"Oh, there's always more here in Nassau," Eric said expansively. *"Seems there was also possibly some Nazi spying and espionage and war profiteering wrapped up in it, too. Not to mention the Royal Family...."*

"Spying and espionage?"

"War profiteering?"

"The Royal family?"

We were all ears.

Eric leaned in again and did the next part in barely a whisper. *"Even in the colonies, you blokes must know about Edward the Eighth abdicating his throne to marry that bloody American divorcee, Wallis Simpson?"*

Julie nodded eagerly.

"Well, as a rule, the royal family doesn't just cast their own adrift—no matter what. So Edward's brother became George the Sixth, and decided to make the happy couple the Duke and Duchess of Windsor as a sort of consolation prize. Three years later, in 1939, he sent them down here and made Edward the crown's first Royal Governor and commander-in-chief of the Bahamas. Which allowed them to gracefully sidestep all that bloody unpleasantness with the Nazis over at home, of course." Eric took another swallow of fuel. *"You have to understand that although he wanted out of the pomp, trappings and circumstance of being king, old Edward was quite comfortable with the bloody resources, pleasures and privileges that went along with it. And his new wife rather fancied them, too. She insisted that the British government re-do the mansion old King George had given them here in Nassau. And she was bloody well upset when they told her they couldn't give her quite everything she asked for because they were a bit caught up in this rather inconvenient war with Germany at the time."*

"The rich are very different from you and I," Hank said like he was repeating something he'd heard somewhere before.

"You bring up an interesting point," Eric nodded. *"You see, there isn't really a lot of regular monthly income in the royalty business. And yet the expenses are truly staggering, what with the parties and gifts and travel and wardrobes and all. No one sends you a bloody monthly check for being a duke or a duchess. Oh, there was something for being governor, I'm sure, but not nearly enough for the kind of parties they liked to throw or the kind of house and staff they needed ot the sort of vacations they liked to take."*

"So what did they do?"

"Well, that's the big bloody question, isn't it? It's a matter of record that they got involved with this somewhat shady Swedish-American millionaire named Axel Wenner-Gren."

"Who's he?" Julie asked.

"That sounds awful German for a Swede," I observed.

"And a lot of other people thought so, too. No question he went to school in Berlin. But he came to America and went to work selling light bulbs for a Swedish-owned company in New York. Did very well for himself, and it wasn't very long before he owned the bloody company. And several other electrical companies besides. Rumor has it he had over 100 million dollars to his name. Bought himself one of the world's biggest yachts second-hand from Howard Hughes...."

Julie was leaning forward in her seat.

"But just like Harry Oakes, he was feeling the old taxman's bite. So he moved his family to a huge bloody mansion right here on the island. Called it Shangri-La, I believe. And naturally he and the Duke and Duchess found themselves wallowing around in the same social circles here in Nassau. It really is a very small little island...."

"So what happened?"

"Well, it seems this Axel Wenner-Gren had some other friends besides those on the bloody island. Including Benito Mussolini and Herrmann Goering and some of his jolly Nazi dancing partners over in Berlin. And that fascist General Maximino Camacho down in Mexico, too..."

"But what has that got to do with Harry Oakes' murder?" Julie demanded.

Eric silenced her with a harsh finger to the lips, and then continued: *"Well, British and American intelligence got a bit suspicious that old friend-of-the-duke-and-duchess Axel was bankrolling deals for bloody arms and oil and rubber and espionage for Nazi Germany..."* he glanced up at Toly, *"...Your father probably knew him."*

"Only on a professional basis," Toly nodded wryly. "They weren't friends."

"But what has that got to do with the murder?" Julie insisted.

"Remember, this was in July of 1943. Right at the bloody peak of the war in Europe, don't you know? British and American intelligence had been monitoring this Axel Wenner-Gren—they were relatively convinced that he was a spy—and

they ultimately froze the assets of a bank he'd started up down in Mexico and started rummaging through the transaction records. And what do you think they found?"

Julie, Cal and me all shook our heads.

"Why, great big bloody deposit accounts for Sir Harold Oakes, Sir Harold Christie and...the Duke and Duchess of Windsor!"

I didn't quite get it, but Hank was quick to pick up on the implications: "Where were the Duke and Duchess getting all the cash? I thought they were having trouble just getting the old Rolls-Royce greased?"

Eric nodded appreciatively in Hank's direction. *"That's it exactly. Just where did all that free money come from? Of course, no formal accusations were ever made and there was never any proof of wrongdoing—heaven forbid a royal involved—but there was surely the hint of foul odor in the air. Plus there were certain, umm, 'irregularities' with the police investigation after Harry Oakes' murder...."*

"What kind of 'irregularities?'"

"Well, it seems that the local Nassau police weren't good enough to do the job. Or at least that was official decision, anyway. And it came right from the top, right from the bloody governor's mansion."

"So who handled the investigation?"

"Two American detectives were brought in from Miami. But they forgot to bring along some of their bloody fingerprint equipment. Isn't that odd? Especially when it seems clear there was a huge, bloody handprint on this folding Chinese screen next to the bed. And there was another interesting coincidence. It turns out that one of the Miami detectives had also served as a personal bodyguard for...the Duke and Duchess of Windsor! Isn't that amazing!"

You had to admit, Eric was pretty damn good with sarcasm.

"Even more amazing was that they did manage to find one absolutely perfect fingerprint. So perfect, in fact, that fingerprint experts testified it appeared as if it'd been taken off a bloody glass, not a silk and wooden Chinese screen."

"So what happened?" we all wanted to know.

"Oh, they put handsome, gold-digging young Freddy on trial for the murder. It was a matter of common knowledge that he didn't like Harry Oakes and Sir Harry Oakes certainly didn't like him—he'd never approved of the marriage from the very beginning, and all of the servants had seen and heard them arguing."

"But he got off?"

"Oh, he was acquitted, all right. Jury voted nine-to-three to let him off the hook. None of them much believed the detectives from Miami. And the local police went in and scrubbed everything down really well before anybody could go back and recheck the crime scene."

"But who told them to do that?" Julie wanted to know.

Eric just grinned. *"Like all the rest of it, my dear, that remains a mystery...."*

Well, it was a hell of a story, and it was already late in the day and we were both about three-quarters buzzed by the time we got up to our hotel room to change for the welcome party. It felt really strange to be two sheets to the wind before it was even dark outside. But it turns out you get used to that sort of thing during Speed Week in Nassau. In fact, I was about ready to call it a day and crawl into bed when that damn music started up right below our hotel room window—that infectious, bouncy, happy Goombay Riddym with the pounding, pattering, syncopated steel band beat and nonsensical, innuendo-laced lyrics that make your toes want to dance right out of your blessed socks. Within 20 minutes I'd showered and shaved and within another 45 or so I'd managed to convince Julie that the white cotton halter top with the white slacks and the black-and-white checkerboard silk scarf in her hair along with the white shoes with the comfortable wedge heels and the little ceramic checkered-flag earrings I'd picked up for her once at Sebring looked just fine. Hell, she'd been in and out of every damn outfit in our luggage by then. But I had to admit: she sure did look terrific!

When we came out of the elevator the music hit us like a wonderful, overwhelming smell. The lobby was already teeming with racers and crews and race officials and wives and girlfriends and hangers-on and hoity-toity island society gents and ladies in dazzling evening gowns and perfectly pressed summer dinner jackets. And Lord-only-knows who else. The party was supposed to be in the main ballroom, but it had already overflowed into the bar and the lobby and spilled out onto the patio and around the pool and even down onto the beach where the band was playing in a little elevated pavilion under a peaked thatch roof. Boy, did that music ever get under your skin! It made your damn hair follicles want to jump up and kick and prance around in unison like the blessed Radio City Music Hall Rockettes....

I got us each a rum punch of some kind and maneuvered us out onto the patio so we could be away from the smoke and chatter and closer to the music. The guy leading the little band was a piano player/singer/songwriter named George Symonette, a tall, slender, snaggle-tooth black guy with amazing rhythm, humor and energy who billed himself as "The Island Troubadour" and seemed to enjoy making his music even more than we enjoyed listening to it.

"Mama don't plant no rice or corn
Very few potatoes
Lima beans and all those things
But Lord, God, tomatoes...."

And it got even better after the evening's second rum drink. A kind of lemony-apricot one this time.

We found Toly out on the patio, and then Hank came over to join us just as the beach torches started to really stand out and sizzle against the darkening, velvet-purple sky. "How you guys doing?" Hank asked over the jangling, rollicking music. To be honest, he was looking a little rocky himself from our afternoon party around the glass-topped table in the bar.

"What's not to like?" I asked, sipping my way about halfway through my second rum drink. "There's certainly no trouble here with the fuel supply."

"Amen," Hank agreed, and the four of us clinked our glasses together.

"You said you were working on a novel?" Julie asked. She sounded genuinely interested and impressed.

"Fooling around is probably more like it."

"What's it about?"

"What I know," Hank shrugged. "Races. Racers. People. Things…."

"You're going to have a tough time trying to sell something like that," Toly said honestly. "Can't say as I've ever heard of any great books about racing. Or not novels, anyway. And I don't think you can count on the racers to read it." He looked at Hank sheepishly. "Those people don't read…."

"I don't care about that," Hank sighed dreamily. "I really just want to see if I can do it, you know?"

"Is it going to have a happy ending or a sad ending?" Julie wanted to know.

"Right now," Hank allowed in a far-away voice, "I'm just hoping it has an ending, period." For punctuation, he sucked the last of his drink up its straw.

It was quiet then. Except for the music and the flame spit off the torches, of course. Toly looked at us and smiled broadly. "Then let's have a party, all right? Did you try any of the food inside?"

"Not yet," I told him. "We just wanted to listen to the music and wind down a little."

"You'd better hurry. The conch fritters are exquisite, but they'll be gone pretty quickly."

"Won't there be more?" Julie asked.

Toly eyeballed her knowingly. "This party is sponsored by the hotel. I'm sure they have to do it in return for booking all the rooms and getting all the racers' business."

"So?"

Toly's lips spread out into an inviting, pit-viper smile. "So expect the free food and liquor to run out very quickly."

Well, you didn't have to tell Julie and me twice. We headed inside and loaded up on chilled shrimp and grouper fingers and conch fritters with cocktail sauce and cold conch salad with lemon and some other stuff we didn't exactly recognize but that went exceedingly well with three or four potent rum drinks. And then who should sidle up next to us but our buddy Cal Carrington again. He was down in Nassau to drive some Texas oil millionaire's ex-works Ferrari. It was one of the 4.2-liter V-12 335 Sport models from 1957 season—like the one Taruffi used to win the Mille Miglia while poor Fon Portago was crashing another just like it into the crowd—and naturally Carlo Sebastian had set the whole thing up. With money coming in from both sides, of course, and most of it winding up in Carlo's own, personal back pocket! He sure knew how to wheel and deal.

"You're a sight for sore eyes," I told Cal. "Haven't seen you since, what was it, 4:30 this afternoon?"

"That was at least six drinks ago. Besides, who wants to talk to you?" He leaned over and gave Julie a nice, playful peck on the eyebrow. "The only reason I hang out with you is because your wife is such a hot number." Julie didn't look entirely pleased with that, so Cal tapped his temple and added: "Smart, too. God only knows what she saw in you…."

"Nice save," I told him, and now Julie was grinning a little bit, too.

Meanwhile, that pulsating, jingle-jangling steel band music was drifting in through the open French doors and kind of swimming and swirling and heating up the atmosphere all around us. Hank walked up again with a mouth full of conch fritters and yet another rum drink in his hand. A pineapply-looking one this time. "They're all really the same, you know?" he explained to no one in particular. "A little fresh fruit juice, a slice of orange or a chunk of pineapple, a maraschino cherry or two, a cute little paper parasol on top and a half-gallon of rum." He took another hefty suck through his straw. "You can pretty much embalm yourself standing up with these things if you're not careful."

"And *you're* being careful?" Julie asked under a set of steeply arched eyebrows.

"I didn't say that," Hank protested. "After all, I'm a motoring journalist." He drew himself up damn near plumb—albeit wavering—and laid on his very best Eric Gibbon impersonation: "As members of the motoring journalist fraternity, it's our solemn duty and obligation to push all the free food we can find into our stomachs and all the free alcohol we can tolerate into our blood streams until the supply bloody well runs out." He leaned in and confided: "It's a matter of fierce professional pride, don't you know…."

To tell the truth, Hank looked a wee bit pie-eyed. Maybe even more than a wee bit.

"Didn't you say there was more to the story you were telling us in the cab?" I asked to kind of help him get re-focused. Like most writers, Hank was fine once he was telling a story.

Hank's eyes hazed over for a second, but then they brightened. He continued the Stirling Moss/Aston Martin story immediately in an incredibly bored, above-it-all and yet down-the-nose Eric Gibbon imitation: "Oh, bloody hell *yes!* The famous Stirling Moss and his bloody well wrecked Aston Martin escapade from last year's race!"

"That's the one."

"Well," Hank continued slyly, "everyone knows that Stirling rather prefers to drive British cars whenever possible."

"Indeed he does!" the real Eric Gibbon agreed loudly from behind us. Hank wheeled around and stared at him with his jaw kind of hanging open. "Oh, but do go *on!"* Eric insisted angrily. "I'm hanging on every *word!"*

Hank's jaw moved a couple times—like he was chewing cud or something—but no actual words came out. He looked pretty damn embarrassed, if you want the truth of it. Pretty damn drunk, too.

"Very well," Eric continued without missing a beat, "let someone who was actually *there* tell the bloody story."

Hank nodded sullenly, looking very ashamed, and Eric quickly squared off to face Julie, Cal and me. He was in that Second Wind phase of drunkenness when it seems absolutely certain that you're the cleverest, most congenial and entertaining conversationalist in all of recorded human history. That stage generally runs until all the air leaks out of the old gas bag and you—or Eric, in this case—find yourself face down in either a puddle of your own piss, a potted palm or a commode. But we hadn't quite gotten there yet. "As my esteemed colleague has already and so accurately pointed out," he began with a flourish, "Stirling has always shown a most becoming and patriotic predilection for English racing cars."

He looked around to make sure he had everybody's attention.

"And it's also a well-known fact that he's never much cared for *Signore* Enzo Ferrari. Or at least not since that bloody rotten business in Bari back in '51."

"What 'unpleasant business in Bari?'" Julie asked.

"Yeah," I chimed in. "What 'bloody rotten business' in Bari?"

Eric looked me like I was a half-pound of spoiled meat. But at least he knew better than to aim that kind of face at Julie. She would've spit right in his eye. Or clawed them both right out. Figuratively, I mean. But maybe literally, too, seeing as she'd had a couple stiff drinks herself and if there's one thing my Julie doesn't like, it's being talked down to. And I know that from ugly personal experience.

Eric eventually sighed, took another pull off one of his drinks (he was carrying two, since the open bar appeared to be in danger of closing soon) and let it rip:

"Well, of course Stirling wanted very much to race for Ferrari—who wouldn't back in '51?—and the gentleman from Maranello with the dark sunglasses had seen what young Stirling could do and claimed to be eager to give him a chance. Remember, this was long before Stirling signed on at Mercedes as Fangio's teammate and so he was still quite an unknown quantity outside of England." Eric drained the last of his first drink. *"You can say a lot of things about old man Ferrari—a few of them even printable—but he's always had a bloody good eye for talent. And a bloody good talent for getting them to drive on the cheap, as well."*

He let it dangle there until we prodded him to go on. *"Well, first Enzo sent a telegram through the BRDC...."*

"What's the BRDC?" Julie asked.

Eric looked at her in silent, awestruck horror while Hank explained as how the BRDC was the British Racing Drivers' Club. Then Julie nodded for Eric to continue, but he wasn't quite done being horrified yet. But finally, when it looked like her attention was maybe shifting to the music outside, he started in again:

"...Ferrari had cabled that he wanted Moss for two races—the non-championship race at Rouen and the British Grand Prix." He leaned in close and whispered: *"Now one can only imagine how badly Stirling wanted to take that ride in the British Grand Prix. It was easily the biggest and most important bloody race in England, and the Ferrari would put him in with a real shot at the winner's laurels...."* Eric started in on his second glass. *"...But Stirling already had a deal with*

HWM for the race at Rouen, and he just isn't the sort to back out of a bloody commitment, no matter what the stakes may be."

"So what happened?"

"Exactly what you might think. He asked Ferrari if he could pass on the non-championship race in France and just do the British Grand Prix." Eric let it dangle there again, and then continued: *"But Signore Ferrari said 'no-no-no-no.' It was both or nothing."*

"Why would he do such a thing?" Julie asked.

Eric performed a perfect crocodile smile for her. *"Why do the innocent suffer? Why do men have black hearts and evil ways? Why do rotten bloody bastards conquer and flourish? It's all the same thing, don't you see. Power is about control and control is about power, and Ferrari understands both. He needs to know that a driver will sacrifice anything—even his character—to drive the red cars."*

"You make him sound like a monster," Julie said.

"An enigmatic god, more likely. Or perhaps just a colossus." Eric rolled his eyes up respectfully. *"Just look at what he's done! One man. Alone. Using, abusing, elevating, crushing, finding, collecting, nurturing and discarding talent, skill and allegiance like some men might fool with a butterfly collection."*

I glanced over and saw the intent, almost paralyzed expression on Cal's face. You could say what you wanted to about that little weasel Eric Gibbon, but he had keen insights and an incredible way with words.

"So what happened in Bari?" I asked again.

"Oh, a meeting was arranged later in the year and Moss and his father went down to see Ferrari in Maranello—Enzo himself had asked for the meeting—and another offer was put on the table. Stirling could drive for Ferrari in the non-championship race at Bari on September 2nd, and then, just maybe, on the Ferrari Grand Prix team in the Italian Grand Prix at Monza two weeks later. If all went well, Stirling would drive for Ferrari in the two South American races in January and then do the full Grand Prix season for them in 1952...."

"Wow," Cal mumbled, almost to himself. "What happened then?"

"Mind you," Eric cautioned magnanimously, *"I only have Stirling's father's side of the story to go on, but it's bloody well apparent that Stirling arrived as promised at the non-championship race at Bari, sat himself down in one of the cars to see how it fit, and was promptly shooed away by one of the Ferrari mechanics."*

"Shooed away?" I asked incredulously.

Eric nodded. *"Seems the car was promised to Piero Taruffi, and no one on the team seemed to know a bloody thing about a car for Stirling Moss...."*

"He came all the way down to Bari and there was no car for him?" Cal frowned.

"Why, that's...*awful!"* Julie agreed.

"You have a fine gift for understatement," Eric acknowledged appreciatively.

It took a moment for it all to sink in. And then I finally asked: "But what does that have to do with Nassau last year?"

Eric's face blossomed out into a self-satisfied smile. *"With the Aston hors d'combat thanks to Mademoiselle Levy, Stirling was very much out of a ride. And that's when one of the rich Americans...."*

"It was Temple Buell," Hank tossed in. Eric glared at him.

"...One of the rich Americans arranged to, shall we say, 'borrow' a car for him to finish out the week. Wound up being a Ferrari—supposedly the exact same one Castellotti used to win the '56 Mille Miglia—and the rest is history."

"What rest?" I asked, not caring that it made me look dumb.

Eric Gibbon leaned his head back so he could look even further down his nose at me. *"Why, he won the bloody Nassau Trophy Race with it, of course. Stirling's first—and possibly last?—major race win in a Ferrari sports car. He rather liked it, too."* Eric drained the last of his second drink. *"Or so I'm told...."*

Later on Julie and me went out on the beach to get away from the smoke and the race stories and the drinking—well, not completely away from the drinking—and we kind of got sucked up into the steel drum Goombay music smiling, snaggle-toothed old George Symonette and his bunch were dishing out from the makeshift bandstand in the little pavilion with the thatched roof. The beachfront in back of the hotel was absolutely alive with that music—jumping, bouncing, swiveling and shaking—and that stuff could really get into your bloodstream. Along with the rum that was already there....

"I kissed her hand
I kissed her lips
Then I lef' her
Behind for you...."

It was loud and wild and special, what with the music jangling in your veins and the torches snapping and crackling against the slick, black sky and a low, slow, steady island surf rolling in behind all of it. Before you know it, Julie and me were kind of dancing with each other. Right there on the sand. Barefoot, even. Now anyone who has ever seen me dance knows I have essentially two moves—sort-of box step and sort-of polka—but that island music seemed to bring its own steps and maneuvers right along with it. You couldn't help yourself. Plus you somehow knew that nobody was looking and nobody really gave two shits anyway. And right there you have the magic of Speed Week in Nassau in a coconut shell.

Saturday brought the first round of practice laps and the first round of ugly morning hangovers out at Oakes Field, and Julie and me slept in a little since we weren't really there with a car or team and didn't have to be at the track at any special time. Which felt pretty damn strange on a race weekend, if you want the truth of it. And then damn if we didn't rent a little powder-blue Italian motor-scooter to ride out to the track. No lie. Julie wasn't real keen on the idea at first, but then Denise McCluggage came tooling up the hotel drive on one—she'd already had her first practice session and was just coming back for a swim and to freshen up—and then Julie wanted to not only rent one, but learn how to drive it herself. And damn if she didn't.

To be honest, the Oakes Field course was not exactly what you could call a stellar sort of racing circuit. It looked like essentially what it was: a pretty basic, flat island airport surrounded by patches of jungle, vacant scrubland where the locals occasionally dumped stuff they didn't want anymore and a few scattered phone poles and power lines for scenery. You couldn't get to a lot of the track as far as spectator vantage points were concerned—or at least not unless you wanted to crawl through bramble bushes or sneak where you weren't really supposed to go across fields of broken rocks full of lizards and insects and Lord only knows what else. By far the best of it was just strolling around through the paddock looking at the cars and meeting all the people. We found Cal and the Ferrari he was going to drive, and right next to them were Ernesto Julio's guys with the big old 4.9 Ferrari he'd brought for our buddy Bruce Kessler to drive. Cal was done with his first practice already—he said the car felt pretty good but the track was all long straights, fiddly little turns and some really abrasive, coral-based aggregate in the paving mix. "Horsepower will get you in the lead here," he told us, "but it's brakes and tires that'll get you to the finish."

The three of us took a little stroll together to see who'd showed up and how badly they were still feeling from the party the night before. We were all taken a little bit aback by the two Rodriguez brothers from Mexico. Older brother Pedro—all of age 18—had a nice, new Ferrari Testa Rossa his daddy had bought for him (the same one Phil Hill and Olivier Gendebien had used to win Le Mans back in June, in fact), while younger brother Ricardo had himself one of the very latest-edition Porsche 550 Spyders. Based on the times from that first practice session, his was the quickest Porsche on the island. Not to mention fastest of all the Under-2.0-Liter cars. No question, the kid could drive. Which was kind of ironic, since he was only 15 and had to be shuttled around the island in cabs and chauffeured limos since he wasn't old enough to legally hold a license. There were a pair of Aston Martins for George Constantine—a GT Mk. III for the production-car race and a DBR2 for the modified race—and Jim Jeffords from Milwaukee, Wisconsin was down with a hideously fast and even more hideously purple 1958 Corvette out of the Nickey Chevrolet shops in Chicago. They called it the "Purple People Eater" after the popular Sheb Wooley Top-40 hit, and no question their chief mechanic, Ronnie Kaplan, knew how to milk an awful lot of speed out of a big, lumbering Corvette. So did Jim Jeffords, come to think of it. Carroll Shelby was signed up in John Edgar's big-engined, 5.6-liter Maserati 450S, and Edgar had yet another 450 Maserati (this one with a Pontiac engine stuffed under the hood) for Indy 500 star Jim Rathman. Way down at the end of the row we found the well-turned-out Scarab team from Culver City, California, with white awnings already up for shade and both of those beautiful, metallic blue-and-white racecars all shined up and gleaming in the sunlight out front. Even Julie could see that they were really something special. "They look like show cars compared to the others," she whispered in my ear.

"They can afford to," I explained.

Then she caught sight of Lance Reventlow and his absolutely drop-dead gorgeous girlfriend, actress Jill St. John. *"My God,"* Julie gasped, *"Isn't that...."*

"HEY, LANCE!" Cal shouted.

Lance looked up from a clipboard, smiled and walked over with his drop-dead gorgeous actress girlfriend in tow. Just like Gina, it was hard not to stare at her until your eyeballs came out on stalks. Handshakes and greetings all around.

"The cars look great," I told Lance. "I saw them run up at Montgomery."

"That wasn't such a great race for us," Lance said apologetically.

"Hell, you won and you beat the Cunningham Listers."

"Yeah, I suppose. But my car ran out of brakes—or maybe I ran it out of brakes!—and Hansgen blew a tire before Chuck could pass him on the racetrack." He looked me in the eye, and I was reminded all over again that this kid was only 22 years old. "We'd like to be a little more convincing than that."

"You sure have been since then," I kind of gushed.

"We've done all right," he allowed, looking a little bit bored with the whole thing. "But what we really want is race over in Europe against the factory teams."

"So I heard."

"But they won't let us do it. At least not with these cars."

"I heard about the troubles you had trying to make the Offy work."

"Yeah," Lance said disgustedly. "That idea just wouldn't come right for us," he stared off into the distance. "I spent a lot of money on it, too...."

"So where do you go from here?" I finally asked.

Lance stared at me. "Can you keep a secret?"

I nodded.

His eyes grew impatient and intense. "I don't want this to get around yet, but we're putting the cars on the block as soon as the races here in Nassau are over."

"You're SELLING the Scarabs?" I gasped incredulously.

"SShh! Not so loud!" he warned.

"But *why??!!* They're the best damn sportscars in the world!"

"I'm glad you think so," Lance nodded. "So do I." He looked up and down the row of cars in the paddock, gathering his thoughts. "I want people to take me seriously. Take American racing talent seriously. And not just a handful of drivers driving for European teams. I'm talking about designers and car builders and engineers and mechanics. We've got a fantastic racing tradition in America, but nobody overseas takes it seriously. Takes *us* seriously." He bared his teeth a little, but definitely not in a smile. "I'd like to see if I can put an end to that...."

"But where will you go? What will you race?"

Lance Reventlow's teeth turned into a sly, mysterious smile. "Use your imagination," he grinned. "Use your imagination...."

Meanwhile Julie had been talking to Jill St. John, and found out that there was a big, black-tie/white-dinner-jacket formal reception at the governor's mansion that night. "Jesus, Buddy," she kind of growled, "you never told me about anything like that."

"Don't worry, it's for participants only," I explained. "We're not invited."

"You can use a couple of our invitations if you want," Lance said off-handedly. "We won't be needing all the ones we have. Besides, you can probably just walk right in. After all, this is Speed Week in Nassau. Nobody's going to stop you."

"But I don't have anything to wear for a formal party," Julie whimpered. "And neither does Buddy." I could tell she really wanted to go.

"You could wear one of my dresses," Jill St. John offered. But of course one look and you could see that was never going to work. Not that I was going to actually say anything like that. I knew better.

Lance looked at us for a moment. "Look," he said, "My mother used to come down here now and then. I'm pretty sure I know a place you can go in town. It's just a little tailor shop, but I think they'll have just what you need."

I felt myself turning a little pale. Sure, Big Ed and me were doing pretty good with the VW business, but I wasn't exactly sure I could go shopping at the same sort of places the sole heir to the whole damn Woolworth five-and-dime fortune could go shopping. Lance must have sensed it and gave me a grin like it was funny. "It'll be okay," he told me. "You'll see."

So Julie and me took the motor-scooter into town, and the quiet, sunlit streets and colorful old buildings really gave you a feel for what this place must have been like way back in colonial days. We found the shop on a side street just off the main square where the slave traders used to auction off their wares, and it was just a tiny, narrow little storefront with a worn wooden counter in front and a beaded curtain behind the counter. But beyond that curtain you could see rack after rack after rack of gowns and dresses and men's seersucker jackets and formalwear and shoes and ties and freshly pressed shirts and a tired old wooden stairway at the back leading up to another floor of exactly the same. A polite, nattily dressed old black guy flashing a helpful grin with two shiny gold teeth in the middle came out of the back and introduced himself. "My name is Simon Longfellow," he said in deliciously friendly King's English. "How may I be of assistance?" I started to explain our situation, but he'd obviously had a lot of experience doing last-minute emergency dress-up jobs for formal parties. To tell the truth, I was kind of nervous about the money—especially since he never mentioned it, just started taking our measurements—but when I asked, he waved his hand and told me that "young master Reventlow's man" had called and so he understood exactly what had to be done. After he measured Julie up, he took her back behind the beaded curtain to this big rack of cocktail dresses and said she could have her pick of *"anything from here to here, my good lady. They should all fit with a minimum of bother."*

An hour later Julie had this fantastic, creamy ivory satin number with a deeply scooped neck picked out (she thought it was a little too daring, but I told her she looked great in it—and she did!) along with shoes, earrings and a beaded handbag to match. And the old black guy had me all fixed up in a white dinner jacket with all the trimmings. Right down to patent leather shoes you could see your face in.

Both outfits needed a few little alterations, of course (personally I thought mine was just fine the way it was, but the shop guy was used to dealing with clients who actually gave a damn about how seams hung, elbows draped and cuffs broke over shoes) and he assured us they'd be at our hotel and ready to go in plenty of time for the party. Naturally I was worried sick about what all of this was going to cost me, but the old black gent just waved it off and told me everything had been taken care of. Just like that. It made me kind of wonder, as we rode that motor-scooter back to our hotel, what it might feel like to have so damn much money that you could do stuff like that and not even think about it. To be honest, I couldn't even imagine it. And neither could Julie. But we got a double-barreled dose of it that evening at the Governor's party….

I don't think either of us had ever seen anyplace like that Governor's Mansion before. Or been around so many spiffed up, elegantly dressed people before, either. The crowd was a real cocktail mix of racers, team owners and the local social register, and it was amazing how you could pick out the blue-bloods, deep-pockets types and society stiffs from the racers even with everybody dressed up in the same blessed uniforms. To be honest, it wasn't near as much fun as the welcome party or the dancing on the beach the night before, but it was interesting to be in a place like that around people like that and see how the other half lives. We ran into Cal and then Bruce Kessler and some of the Scarab bunch—Lance wasn't there, but then he'd probably already had a lifetime supply of those kinds of parties and besides, where the hell would you be if you had Jill St. John for a roommate?

We wound up at a big round table with Cal and Bruce and the rest, plus Hank of course and Eric Gibbon, who naturally wandered over and grabbed himself a seat without asking. He'd obviously gotten pretty chummy with the bartenders already. "Welcome to island society's upper reaches," he announced to the table in general. "Be sure to give your hands a bloody good wash when you get back to your hotel tonight…."

To be honest, the magic of all that pomp and presence and money wore off after about an hour or so. To tell the truth, it was a little stiff as well as stylish. And even the best of manners can get a bit dull after a while. And the lobster was kind of tough. "They give the fresh stuff that's just been cooked to the head table," Eric Gibbon explained. "But that's the way things go when you're a guest of the bloody aristocracy."

"That's not a very nice thing to say," Julie told him for the second time. She didn't think much of Eric or his damn arrogant, know-it-all attitude.

"Sorry," he burbled while sipping the foam fizz off his latest drink. "But you must understand that there are some shifty, slimy characters down here in Nassau."

"I know," she agreed. "I'm sitting right across from one."

Believe it or not, that shut him up.

For a little while, anyway. And then he started in again on something about the 750-kilogram formula from before the war that was even too arcane for me.

"Look," I finally whispered in Julie's ear. "You want to maybe go back to our hotel? This is all very elegant and impressive and all, but I'm tired and I'm bored."

"We've only been here an hour and a half," Julie pouted.

"How much more of this do you want?"

"How much more can you take?"

I looked at her and smiled. "As much as you need, honey. This is your night."

Her eyes swept around the room one more time, drinking in all the dazzling décor and fabulous outfits and inane, elegant chatter. "Okay, Palumbo," she sighed. "Five more minutes ought to do it…."

We took a cab back to the hotel, and the night was warm and soft and smelled of the tropics all around us. But you couldn't see any stars up in the sky. Not even the moon.

If you've never been there, you have to understand that the Bahamas Speed Week was only partially about speed and much more about a week in the Bahamas—or at least that's what all the hotel owners, bartenders, restaurateurs, charter captains and illicit casino operators were angling for, anyway—and they had it all figured out what with the welcome party Friday evening, practice scheduled for Saturday, the black-tie formal at the Governor's Mansion Saturday night, a 100-mile, all-comers, "welcome aboard" fun race set for Sunday afternoon, an outdoor barbeque/pool party/limbo dance & rum guzzling contest at some other island bigwig's house Sunday night, and then a full week's worth of hard partying and high-octane fooling around, a little practicing and tuning, more partying, a bit of swimming, snorkeling, sailing, scuba diving, deep-sea fishing, badminton, horseshoes, shuffleboard, bridge games, sneak-around gambling or just plain screwing around, a few preliminary and novelty races on Friday and Saturday and then the big feature races culminating with the 250-mile Nassau Trophy Race the following Sunday.

You really needed to pace yourself for a schedule like that, but nobody did.

And right at he end was the sad, sullen, last-ditch farewell party at the hotel again on Sunday night. Followed by some very gray, grim and gaunt faces—particularly for people who'd supposedly spent a week in a tropical paradise—climbing onto airplanes out at Oakes Field come Monday morning. Or, if you were lucky, afternoon.

But the weatherman really pulled the rug out from under Speed Week in 1958. After two solid nights of partying, Julie and me woke up early Sunday morning to the sound of rain gushing down like it only can in the tropics. I looked at my watch on the bed stand and it was barely six o'clock. I tried closing my eyes again but the rain sounded like a couple dozen fire hoses aimed at the roof tiles. I got up unsteadily, wandered over to the window and peeled back the curtain. "What's it look like?" Julie asked in a thin, gravelly voice.

"It looks like we're submerged," I told her. And it did. The atmosphere outside was about the same percentage humidity as the inside of a goldfish tank. It looked like algae was floating in it, too. "I don't think they'll be doing any racing today."

Julie groaned and rolled over on her stomach. "Thank heaven for small favors," she mumbled into the pillow.

The rain pounded down even harder.

"Whaddaya wanna do?" I asked the back of Julie's head.

"Do we always have to be *doing* something?" she asked the pillowcase.

I looked around the room. It was warm for temperature, but chilly from the damp, and it all felt strange and foreign to me. "It seems really strange to be away from home, you know?"

The back of Julie's head nodded up and down.

"I wonder what the kids are doing now?"

Her head seemed to sink a little further into the pillow.

"It's Sunday," I said to myself. "Sunday morning. Maybe your mother's taking them to church…."

Julie's face swiveled up towards me. "Are you *trying* to make me sad, Palumbo, or are you just succeeding?"

"I'm sorry, Julie. I didn't mean…."

"Oh, shut up," she said, grabbing my hair and dragging me down next to her. "C'mon," she half-whispered, "let's just make the best of it, okay…."

So we made the best of it. Twice in fact. Not that it's any of your business. And we slept a bunch, too. Not that deep, bottomless-black-pit kind of sleep, but the soft, comfy, dreamy, floating variety where you're all laced up with each other and it's like your mattress is a balsa wood raft drifting way out at sea someplace where no thing and no body can get at you….

"Glad we came?" I asked her.

"Don't push it, Palumbo," she whispered so softly I could hardly hear her.

Chapter 32: Tobacco Politics

It's always nice to get away for a little while to some warm, tropical someplace with just you and your spouse or spousette when it's cold and dreary early wintertime back home and the days are getting so damn short that it's dark before rush hour even starts. But you and your lady (or fella) can only take so much of it before the interruption of your regular daily routines and feeling guilty as hell about ditching out on your responsibilities at home—especially if you have kids and even moreso if you have kids *and* parents circling around your nest—can have you very edgy indeed by the third or fourth day. Not to mention a severe oversupply of focused, inescapable, boiled-down-to-its-mealy-essence intimacy in very close quarters. Which—again by the third or fourth day—is more about nose-picking, belching, hair in the sink, toenail clippings, cold cream, eyebrow plucking, which blessed outfit she should wear down to the damn lobby, where you left your wet bathing suit *("Whadda YOU care, it's not YOUR freakin' carpet!")* and leaving the cap off the blessed shampoo or tube of toothpaste than candlelight dinners, walks on the beach and whispered sweet nothings. If you stick with it long enough, you come to realize that there's a kind of ebb and flow to the way married people get along with each other, and while it's wonderful—hell, it's damn near *miraculous!*—when you go though one of those cozy, cuddly, snuggly and intimate So-Glad-I-Married-You stages, but you always need to bear in mind that it's just another passing phase—like a knock-down/drag-out/if-I-had-a-revolver-I'd-shoot-you-until-all-the-chambers-were-empty argument—and that you'll be back to picking, ignoring, snapping, yelling, screaming and staring daggers at each other soon enough. It's just the way things are. The important thing is to remember that you're in it for the long haul and that men tend to run more on logic, comfort, nuts-and-bolts practicality and line-of-least-resistance laziness and cowardice while women are generally fueled by sympathy, sentiment, style, compassion, whims of the heart (or moment) and the desire to slash at your private parts with a longshoreman's hook about once every 28 days. You just need to remember that you love each other even when you hate each other (and vice versa) and to keep all the firearms, sharp objects and blunt instruments out of reach when you've gotten her really, *really* pissed off. Particularly when she's in season.

Anyhow, Julie and me made it all the way through about Wednesday morning down in Nassau before the dam broke. It started when I saw her picking up the room again so the blessed maid wouldn't think we were a couple of lowlife slobs used to living in a pigsty. Now I thought that was pretty damn stupid and unnecessary. After all, if you don't let maids maid and waiters wait and butlers buttle, they'll all wind up on the welfare roles, right? But there are times (see 28-day cycle mentioned above) when a husband should simply button his lip and go back to trimming his damn toenails. And preferably over a wastebasket or a piece of newspaper or the commode or something, you know? But it was getting to me how disgusted and angry and exasperated and impatient Julie was acting while she tidied up all the horrible, terrible, inexcusable *STUFF* I'd left laying around our room. Like a straw hat, a pair of sunglasses, a matching pair of beach sandals, a couple empty drink glasses, a plastic bottle of Coppertone, my wallet and keys, about two bucks in change, two car magazines, yesterday's Miami newspaper—*Hey, don't throw that out, I haven't read the damn funnies yet!*—my tennis shoes, a pair of socks that maybe could have gone in the dirty clothes bag, the previously mentioned swim trunks (okay, so maybe I *could* have dropped them on the tile floor in the bathroom instead of on the carpet…or maybe even hung them on the balcony railing outside?) plus a couple well-gnawed peach pits neatly wrapped in one of the hand-sized terrycloth guest towels with the hotel monogram on it. Why, you'd have thought I overturned a damn septic tank in her underwear drawer….

But being down there in Nassau was getting to me, too. I wondered about what was going on back at the shop and the VW dealership and how the kids were getting along with Julie's harpy of a mother and my folks and that pretty not-so-little-anymore Annie Bardelli who really needed to stop wearing her skinny older brother's hand-me-down shirts with the top three buttons undone anymore. Not that I was looking or anything. And of course I was also wondering about what I could possibly be doing at night down in Nassau that was making me wake up every morning with a splitting headache and a taste in my mouth like I'd been chewing on a dead camel's balls. The bare fact was that we were both getting pretty damn antsy to get home—tropical island paradise or no. Fortunately things got better again between us before we left. Julie had herself a really desperate and inconsolable, Niagara Falls-style cry, and after that we got cozy again and had a couple really nice, long walks along the beach together—just the two of us, once early in the morning around sunrise and once late at night—and damn if Julie didn't actually learn how to ride one of those rental motor scooters so we spent most of Friday morning put-sputtering all over the whole blessed island on a pair of them. Like I said, there's an ebb and flow to these things and they go in cycles once you both accept the Life Sentence part of marriage and decide to make the best of it. Even so, we were both more than ready to go home long before that rickety, oil-stained old *Air Bahamas* DC3 climbed up into yet another perfectly clear and sunny azure sky and whisked us across a glittering turquoise expanse of ocean toward the mainland.

To be honest about it, the racing we saw in Nassau was okay but not really great. Thursday featured a three-lap race for island residents only in a handful of buzzy little Berkeleys. Now I'd always thought Austin-Healey's new-for-'58 bug-eyed Sprite looked small and basic—and it was—but the little three-cylinder, Excelsior motorcycle-engined, fiberglass-bodied Berkeley made a Sprite look like a damn XK120. They were *tiny!* But, judging by the expressions on the faces of their island resident drivers, they could still go plenty fast enough to thrill—or even frighten—the folks behind the wheel. Hey, a Berkeley or a Sprite may not have the beans to top the magic "ton," but 41 miles-per-hour around a 39mph turn is equally hairy in a Berkeley or a Maserati 450S. Only without the respect and stature….

There were also five-lap heat races for the under- and over-2.0-liter sports/racers, followed by a 25-lap production-car "Nassau Tourist Trophy" feature. In spite of more rain, Jim Jeffords pretty much ran away and hid in that incredibly purple

Corvette from Nickey Chevrolet in Chicago, while George Constantine in an Aston Martin GT coupe finished a distant second (at least he stayed dry!) and a guy named Duncan Furlong brought his AC-Bristol home third. Friday brought more of the same—only finally with some bright, steady sunshine—with a 25-lap "feature" for the sports/racers (won by Lance Reventlow's Scarab over George Constantine's Aston DBR2 sports/racer), but Julie and me were already long gone before it was over. I mean, there's only so much standing around on hot concrete under a broiling tropical sun with engine noise pounding in your ears you can take after a solid week of partying. Besides, she wanted to go ride our motor scooters some more, and you really want to support and encourage that sort of spousal activity, don't you? After all, we still had Saturday's and Sunday's races yet to go at Oakes Field.

Our buddy Bruce Kessler won the all-Ferrari race on Saturday, but not until after a hellacious battle with my boy Cal got settled when rude grinding noises started coming from the back of Cal's 335S and he had to retire. It was just as well, though, since he'd been pushing that old brute pretty hard and it was still on its original-equipment, factory-issue Englebert tires, and the left-rear was right down to the cords from sliding around sideways on that abrasive, crushed-coral-based Oakes Field pavement. Old man Ferrari had already had quite enough of his arrangement with Englebert since by the end of the '58 season he realized—like everybody else—that the British-made Dunlops stuck better and lasted longer. But he was still hammering out his new deal with Dunlop and besides, he still had a pretty heft stack of the old Belgian tires sitting in his warehouse, so that's what all the "ex-works" and "customer cars" were going to be wearing when they rolled out of Maranello over the next few months....

15-year-old Mexican phenom Ricardo Rodriguez showed he was no fluke by easily winning the mostly-Porsche under-2.0-liter race in very smooth style, and our girl Denise won the second heat of the ladies' race—going away—in a borrowed Lotus after retiring with the gear lever stuck in 4th in the first heat. That lady could *drive!* Then there was another big blowout party Saturday night (what else?) and it was kind of amazing how that steel band calypso music could get you jumping inside all over again even after a solid week of hangovers. But of course a fresh supply of rum helped, too....

Sunday brought Speed Week's main event, the 56-lap, 252-mile, welcome-to-all-comers/run-what'cha-brung Nassau Trophy race. And it was kind of fitting that Lance and Chuck Daigh teamed up to give the Scarabs their very last win under the RAI banner. It was a pretty damn dominating performance, too. But of course four days' worth of play racing and partying and beating mercilessly on the cars (and our livers) had thinned the field out considerably. Cal was out before it started with a busted transaxle in the 335S, while Canadian Bill Sadler and his wife didn't even arrive until mid-week after getting stranded with their rig in an ugly snowstorm in upper New York State. Not that they missed much what with the rain and all. But it was good to see them again and the cars looked like they really might be in with a chance at Oakes Field. They'd brought down the "old," red, Chevy-powered Sadler

Special that we'd seen before plus a brand-new one that was even lower and lighter than the original. With the body panels off, those cars made me think about what Colin Chapman might have done if he'd started fooling around with Chevy V-8s back in his early, back-alley-garage-builder days. Sadler didn't have a fraction of a fraction of Reventlow's money or resources, of course, but his cars were straightforward, sanitary, smart, clever and well-built. And they had Girling disc brakes, while the Scarabs still had drums because old Lance didn't want to use "British" brakes on his "all-American" Scarab racecars. Bill Sadler called his new car the "Nisonger/KLG Special" and painted it white-with-blue in honor of some check-writing president of a sparkplug and parts-distributing company, but it suffered the usual new-car teething problems and never seemed to run right for very long for hired-gun driver Bob Said. But the Sadlers were sure neat to look at and could they ever come squirting out of the corners!

Anyhow, There were a bunch of who-cares, five-lap preliminary races on Sunday, and then the cars lined up for the traditional Le Mans-style start for the Nassau Trophy feature. Eighteen-year-old Pedro Rodriguez out-sprinted all the older guys (with all the older-guy hangovers, let's not forget!) and got away first in his Ferrari, but Carroll Shelby in John Edgar's booming 450S had taken over the lead before the end of the first lap, although Chuck Daigh in the Scarab was already third and stalking them both. Meanwhile Lance had to dive into the pits to have the hood on his Scarab fastened down, and for a change he waited patiently and didn't scream or throw a fit while the crew took care of it. But it dropped him down to 10th place. And two laps later Daigh's Scarab was in with a broken half-shaft and had to retire. Not a very auspicious start for the gorgeous metallic-blue-and-white cars from just outside Hollywood….

But I'd been around enough long races to know that it was still early days, and sure enough Lance started working his way back towards the front after his pit stop. Bill Sadler dropped out with mechanical problems and so did Jim Rathman in John Edgar's brutal Maserati/Pontiac, Bruce Kessler had the first of many flat tires caused by the abrasive, coral-based pavement and damn if young Lance wasn't taking a second or two a lap off Carroll Shelby in the 450S. And that right there said about all you, me or anybody else needed to say about the Reventlow Scarabs. There wasn't a person on the whole blessed island who didn't think Carroll Shelby—hangover or not—could drive blessed rings around rich California playboy Lance Reventlow. And yet here he was, losing ground and seconds by the fistful to the young pup. To be fair, Lance was driving really well—and staying within himself for a change—and then Shelby had a flat tire and that pretty much wrapped things up for the Scarab bunch. Lance had a solid lead when he pitted for fuel and tires on lap 29, and he very generously handed the car over to Chuck Daigh so the two of them could share what might very well be their last run—and last win—in the Chevy-powered Scarab sports cars. It was a damn nice gesture, and kind of points up the kind of guy Lance was. Like I've said before, the rich can't help being rich anymore than the poor can help being poor, and when you add on top of that how blessed young Lance was, the staggering, almost crushing weight of his bankroll and the pull-tug-and-ignore way he was raised, you could kind of understand how he could be a hell of a nice pal, a stand-up guy, an arrogant, stuck-up snot, an unbelievably focused and dedicated racer and a screaming, tantrum-throwing punk almost all at the same time.

In any case, he was as good as his word, and the Scarab sports cars officially went on the block right there in victory circle at Nassau—at a fair-and-square $17,500 apiece—and everybody wondered, as Lance and Chuck grinned and joked and posed for the cameras and swilled fizzy champagne out of the huge, shiny trophy Lady Greta Oakes had presented them: what on earth could possibly be next for Reventlow Automobiles Incorporated out in Culver City, California, just a short stone's throw from the Hollywood studios....

Things settled in pretty quickly again back home once the kids got their presents, hugged us both desperately and went back to watch TV, and Julie's mother likewise got hers while complaining bitterly about all the above-and-beyond-the-call-of-duty things she'd had to do and put up with while we were gone. I couldn't believe I'd actually let Julie talk me into buying her a blessed diamond watch, you know? Duty-free or not. What the old bitch really needed was one of those heavy leather hoods like they put over the heads of trained falcons. In a nice, dark color, too. But eventually the old gasbag ran out of wind and vitriol, and she even allowed as how the watch we brought her from Nassau was almost as nice as the one she'd seen down in the jewelry department at Woolworth's five-and-dime.

Back at the dealership we were selling the heck out of the new, 1959-editions of the Volkswagen Beetle. Not that you could exactly tell it from the '58, of course, unless you noticed the chrome horn ring in the steering wheel (before there was just a button) or that they'd finally added an anti-sway bar to the front suspension to try and keep so many unsuspecting Beetle drivers from flying off the road ass-backwards. Particularly in iffy weather. Personally, I always thought the VeeDub's inherent snap oversteer was wildly entertaining (especially on snow or wet pavement) and I didn't think the new one was nearly as much fun. But the Greek over at the body shop had replaced enough rear bumpers, rear decklids and tailpipe tips for us that I figured it was probably a good idea.

My sister Mary Frances dropped by the dealership right after New Years on Saturday morning, January 3rd, and it was nice to see her again and chew the fat a little. Oh, I'd seen her at my folks' house at Christmas, but she was talking kids and cooking with Julie and my mom and Sarah Jean, and I was talking cars with Carson and listening to dirty jokes from my other asshole brother-in-law, so we never really got a chance to chat. You know how it is when you've got somebody in your family that you really like and who maybe lives just 15 minutes away, but you've got a business to run and a family at home to take care of and she's got her teaching job and all kinds of add-on, teacher-type stuff to do getting ready beforehand or cleaning up afterwards plus all those highbrow, lowlife, beatnik pinko friends of hers over in Greenwich Village that she liked to pal around with and stay in touch with and, well, it seemed like we just never got to see each other anymore.

She told me that Pauly Martino musician guy who played big-band saxophone for a living was back in town, and I could tell by what she didn't say as much as what she said that she was pretty excited about it. But worried and careful, too. Didn't want to get her hopes up, you know? You've probably noticed how single women—and particularly single women schoolteachers with a few skeletons in their closet and a little bit of a dark past—tend to get a kind of Old Maid complex and worry a lot about whether they're fit to be out on the open market anymore. Plus, once you get settled into a life—even a boring, lonely, empty sort of life—you kind of hate to risk that well-worn familiarity and regularity on something that may not pan out.

"What have you got to lose?" I asked her.

"I dunno," she shrugged. "Maybe he won't like me anymore."

"He called you, didn't he?"

She gave me a hesitant little nod.

"And he used to write you all the time, didn't he?"

"Postcards," she said, her eyes kind of conflicted and unfocused. "He used to send me postcards from the hotel in Miami. I think they came free in the desk drawer in your room. I must have about a hundred postcards from the Fontainebleu Hotel."

"See," I told her.

"But he never said much of anything. Just the usual crap—*How are you doing? Wish you were here!*—all that lame, trite, ordinary stuff like you'd write to your aunt or grandmother or something…."

"Hey," I reminded her, "he's a *musician,* not a writer. Maybe that's the best he can do?"

"I dunno?" Mary Frances said again, shaking her head. "I just don't know."

"Look," I finally told her, "let's face a few facts. You're not getting any younger. And you liked this guy. You *really* liked this guy. I remember."

"Yeah," she agreed dreamily. "He was nice. I mean *decent* nice, you know? Not just polite nice."

"I thought so, too."

"But then he just, you know, *took off!"* There was some anger creeping into her voice now. "How could he *do* that? How could the sonofabitch *do* that?"

"Didn't he ask you to come with?" I reminded her.

"Sure he did. But what the hell's *that* supposed to mean? That I should drop my job and my work and my livelihood to go traipsing after him like a damn maidservant?"

She was pissed now, but I got pissed right back at her. "Oh, I get it. You don't want to give up *your* life and career to go chase after him, but you want him to give up *his* life and career to stay here with you. Is that the way it works?"

She started to snap back at me with something, but stopped herself. And then she just kind of sank. Almost like a ship going down, even though she was still standing on her feet right in front of me. "Look," I told her in the most caring, understanding and sympathetic voice I think I've ever used outside of a funeral home, "stop making yourself miserable, okay? You like him. He likes you. Give it a damn try. Take a chance again."

She didn't look particularly convinced.

"What happened to the gutsy, ballsy older sister I used to have? The one who gave our father the finger at Thanksgiving dinner, told him where he could stick it and stormed right out of the house? What happened to *that* girl?"

I could see the twinkle coming up in her eyes and the smile wrinkling up at the corners of her mouth as she thought back and remembered. "I guess she sort of died," Mary Frances said wistfully.

"Like hell she did!" I damn near screamed at her. "She just got tired and lazy and chickenshit and forgot what the hell she was made of. It happens to people. I know. I see it all the time." I looked her right in the eyes. "I know you're still in there. The smart-ass little hell-raiser with all the ideals and ideas and causes and crazy notions about fixing this stupid world up and making it a better place."

She looked at me kind of sideways. "You think those ideas are crazy?"

"It doesn't matter what the hell *I* think. I'm just a Goddam car mechanic from Passiac. Who gives two shits about what *I* think?" I grabbed her shoulders in both hands and gave them a hefty shake. "The important thing is what *you* think, Mary Frances. That you *believe* in things! That you're *passionate* about them. That's what makes you special. You care about a world that doesn't give a damn about you. How many people have that much faith? That much gumption? That much tolerance for pain?"

She stared at me for what seemed like a whole minute. "What does any of that have to do with going out with Pauly Martino again?" she wanted to know.

I thought it over. "A person like you *needs* somebody else," I finally told her.

"What for?"

That one had me stumped. But then it dawned on me: *"Because you can't go around being that damn stupid all by yourself anymore!"*

At first she looked angry again. But then her lips spread out in a big, wide smile. "You know," she told me, "you're my favorite brother."

"I'm your only brother," I reminded her.

"You're still my favorite!" She gave me a sweet little kiss on the cheek just to prove it, and I could feel the spot kind of glow a little afterward. It made me all proud and warm and mushy inside.

"So you'll go out with him again?"

"Sure," she said with a little of the old sting and swagger back in her voice. "Why the hell not? What have I got to lose…."

"That's the spirit," I told her. And I meant it.

Right about then who should come tooling up in front of the dealership but my friend and partner Big Ed Baumstein. At the wheel of a shiny new 1959 Cadillac Eldorado Biarritz convertible—dazzling lipstick red with a white top and a matching white leather interior—and, typically Big Ed, he had the top down and the heater going full blast even though it was a chilly January morning. Turns out Big Ed had grown a wee bit tired of fooling around with the stick shift in his Jag 150S—especially in traffic—and I could tell by the creeping height of the clutch pedal engagement that the car wasn't real thrilled about it, either. So it came as no real surprise when Big Ed arrived in that brand-new Cadillac. "Did'ja trade in the Jag?" I asked him.

"Nah, I think I'm gonna keep that one for sunny Sunday afternoons and trips up to the races. This is just gonna be my ordinary, everyday, tool-around-the-city car." Big Ed pushed in the chrome cigarette lighter, waited for it to pop out with a satisfyingly solid, well-oiled *"click,"* and re-lit the business end of his dollar-fifty Cuban stogie. "Besides," he continued, "a Caddy dealer wouldn't give me shit for it." Mary Frances and I ran our eyes up and down that new Caddy. It took a hell of a long time for them to get from one end to the other. The grille in front reminded you of an auditorium-sized Wurlitzer jukebox, and the fins in back looked like they came right off a blessed moon rocket.

Big Ed took a long, slow drag off his cigar and stared at it lovingly while he blew out a series of small, perfectly spaced smoke rings. "I'd better enjoy these damn things while I can," he said sadly.

"Whaddaya mean?" I asked.

"Didn't you see in the papers? That commie asshole Castro with the scraggly beard and the army fatigues took over in Cuba."

"Really?" Mary Frances exclaimed.

Big Ed nodded. "Fuckin' commies 90 miles off the Florida coast." He shook his head. "Can you believe it?"

I shook my head, too.

"That was a great country, Cuba was," Big Ed sighed. "A guy with money in his pocket could buy damn near anything he ever wanted there."

"Maybe that was part of the problem," Mary Frances said with an accusatory little edge to her voice.

Big Ed glared at her. "You don't want to be talking politics with me, sweetheart. I been there, see? *In person.* I know how things are."

"You mean you know how things *were,"* she corrected him.

I figured it was as good a time as any to take Mary Frances out to lunch and get those two out of range of each other. Because that's the thing about politics, isn't it? The more two people get to arguing over it, the more convinced they both become that they're absolutely right and the other person is a misinformed, misguided idiot.

On January 22nd, newly retired, first-ever British World Driving Champion Mike Hawthorn was on his way home—some say from a pub—in a light rain in his hotted-up Jaguar sedan when he spotted whiskey-heir/race-entrant and all-'round enthusiast Rob Walker tooling along the same road in his Mercedes 300SL Gullwing. And of course nothing would do but that Mike should give chase. He caught up and they got into a nice, spirited little race for a ways before they arrived at the Guilford Bypass, and Mike dove the Jag sedan deep down the inside and hurled it into the roundabout in a move I'm sure he thought worthy of a World Champion. Only he lost it a bit on the typically English, rain-slicked pavement and spun the Jag into a tree. It didn't look like much of an accident and when Rob stopped, got out and walked over to make sure everything was okay, he found Mike laid out peacefully in the Jag's back seat like he was dozing off to sleep. Only he wasn't. He was dying. His eyelashes fluttered for a moment, there was the sound of a faint, final wheeze of air coming out of his lungs, and then his eyes gently rolled up and stopped seeing any more. Just that quickly, the brash, brave and dapper young man with the terribly fair complexion, wraparound face shield and white blonde hair, the daring young man who had tempted fate, death and destiny all over the world, lost his best friend, won himself the World Championship and then simply walked away—the lucky young man who had *gotten away with it*—was gone…

It was hard to believe, and even harder to make sense out of.

Then, just a dozen days later on February 3rd, a small private plane shuttling American rock-and-roll stars Buddy Holly, the Big Bopper and Richie Valens to a concert date in Fargo, North Dakota, crashed with no survivors in an early-morning snowstorm near Mason City, Iowa. I'd just heard about Hawthorn's accident from Hank a few days before, and it really hit me when I read that headlines about those three rock-and-roll idols how impermanent things are up in the limelight and how instantly that light can get snuffed out even when you seem to be on top of the world. It was a little scary, actually, and made you look around your kitchen to where your wife was making your morning eggs and coffee and over at the kids watching early-ayem TV when they were supposed to be getting ready for school—I swear, they'd watch anything—and it made you want to quietly rap your knuckles against that light-maple early-American breakfast table just to feel one more time how solid and familiar it felt.

It was a shock to the whole nation when that plane went down, because you always figured that youth and fame came with some kind of temporary immortality. Or at the very least invincibility. You expected heroes like that to live long enough to disappoint you by making the front pages of the supermarket tabloids for divorces, drug addiction, drunk and disorderly (complete with lurid, leering pictures that generally included pasty complexions, black eyes, split lips, shirt tails hanging out, ripped-open buttons revealing several rolls of fat and sometimes even police numbers) before fading ungracefully away. Don't get me wrong, I was never any huge, glued-to-the-radio fan of rock-and-roll. That was for kids, right? Not to mention how the damn Top 40 radio stations played the same blessed songs over and over and over again as long as they were on the charts. Like until you couldn't stand it anymore. Oh, sure, I liked The Platters doing *Smoke Gets in Your Eyes,* Clyde McPhatter's *It's a Lover's Question* and *To Know Him is to Love Him* by the Teddy Bears. Not to mention Jackie Wilson's *Lonely Teardrops,* just about anything Fats Domino ever did and that cool drum instrumental by Cozy Cole called *Topsy, Part Two.* But I'd probably had about enough of *"Hang down your head, Tom Dooley"* by the Kingston Trio after about the five- or six-hundredth time I'd heard it (folk music was getting real big by then, even outside the Greenwich Village coffeehouses my sister Mary Frances went to) and I'd have to say I was sick and tired of David Seville's *The Chipmunk Song* in less than half that time. Although my mom just loved it, you know?

But the point is that Mike Hawthorn managed to kill himself after making maybe the only safe move he ever made in his life. And 12 days later this plane went down and these three other guys died (plus the pilot, of course) just when it seemed like they had the whole damn world by the balls. Money. Fame. Adulation. Doing something you really love and getting paid more than you ever dreamed of to do it. But of course the flip side was that you had to give up a regular, everyday, ordinary life in the process—I mean a life like Julie and me had, you know?—and all that flash and glamour in the spotlight gets traded off against lonely hotel rooms and mornings and afternoons with nothing much to do (which can be even worse than too much to do, believe me) and two-ayem plane rides through a snowstorm that wind up shattered and scattered all over some Iowa farmer's frozen cornfield. Whether you play music or sing with a band or act in the movies or run between the chalk lines in a sports stadium or race a blessed Ferrari on the Grand Prix circuits of the world, you're a performer by trade and you've made your bargain with the devil.

And you have to live with the damn consequences.

Even if you couldn't help yourself.

Speaking of which, my buddy Cal stopped back in town on his way to California to see Gina before the season started in earnest at Sebring in March. There was no January Grand Prix or World Manufacturers' Championship sportscar race in Argentina (or anywhere in South or Central America) that year thanks to the somewhat volatile social, political and economic situation down there, and Gina was back in Hollywood doing some post-shoot dubbing, reviewing of new scripts and flash-us-a-smile/give-us-a-quote promotional work on her newly released World War II commando-raid movie. Cal hoped he could spend some time with her between work and professional engagements, but he didn't call ahead because he wanted to surprise her. And also because that way she couldn't say "no."

Anyhow, Cal came over to our house for dinner while he was in Jersey and Julie and the kids seemed genuinely glad to see him. He seemed even gladder to see them, if you want the truth of it. He'd offered to take us all out for a fancy dinner, of course, but Julie thought he could maybe do with a home-cooked meal and the smell and feel of a place a whole family called home for a change. He seemed to like that, too. Especially since we did it on Thursday night when Julie's mom was always at the church bingo game, and that made it a pretty pleasant deal all the way around.

The bad news was that things weren't working out exactly like he and Toly had hoped over at Ferrari. Following the fatal crashes of Musso in France and Collins in Germany and the retirement (and then fatal crash, although that had no bearing on things one way or the other) of Mike Hawthorn, Toly had pretty much assumed that he and Phil Hill would inherit the positions of Number One and Number Two Ferrari factory drivers, and Cal kind of thought he might finally sneak into the mix sideways as Number Three. Only old Enzo Ferrari had other ideas. I guess he wasn't entirely convinced of Toly's speed or seasoning, Hill's willingness to take risks, desire and long-haul stamina and he really hadn't seen enough of Cal to make up his mind one way or the other. If Cal really was one of those genuinely exceptional drivers, holding him out of Formula One and dangling that carrot in front of him would only make him hungrier, more desperate to do well and more dangerous as a competitor once he finally got his break.

Besides, there was a lot of other top talent out looking for rides….

Tony Vandervell's Vanwall team had won the Formula One Constructors' title in 1958—even though the World Championship eluded them—so in a sense it was Mission Accomplished as far as beating "those bloody red cars" was concerned. Plus he'd spent a fortune-and-a-half in the process, and Vandervell's heart had gone out of it following Stuart Lewis-Evans' game try, horrific crash and ultimately fatal result after Casablanca. So Vanwall was out of it, and that put Stirling Moss and Tony Brooks very much on the open market. Stirling had talked to several teams, and BRM were *very* eager to have him. And their car had shown a lot of promise. Unfortunately, that's *all* it'd shown, and the BRM's reputation as a temperamental nickel rocket with fly-by-night brakes (especially that single, centrally-located rear disc hung off the back of the transaxle) made it a second choice to almost anything. Which is precisely what must have been going through the mind of plucky little Jean Behra, who had driven his heart out for BRM and even led a few races the previous year, but wound up with nine lousy points, a string of DNFs and a collection of badly soiled underwear from all the times the damn brake pedal went straight to the floor.

Ferrari put out feelers to Moss, of course, but he'd seen his fill of the way things were done in Maranello and firmly but politely declined. Aston Martin was building a Grand Prix car, but it wasn't done yet and it looked fairly ordinary and conventional compared to the Coopers. And Cooper were happy with tough, wily, hands-on/greasy-fingernail Aussie "Black Jack" Brabham as lead driver and quick, intelligent young New Zealander Bruce McLaren as his regular sidekick. And no doubt they'd be tougher yet in 1959 what with full, punched-out, 2.5-liter (or 2495cc, anyway) versions of the tried-and-true Coventry Climax FPF behind the driver. Oh, the Climax was still shy on power compared to the Ferraris and BRMs, but the Cooper was light, had great handling, brakes and balance and poked a very small hole in the air. The only other open option was Lotus, but although the cars were gaining speed, they were still a small time team and the cars were still a bit on the fragile and flimsy side of Grand Prix-ready. And there wasn't a lot of money around at Lotus, either, what with energies and resources split between selling Lotus 7 cars and kits to aspiring Boy Racers and Chapman's lovely and ingenious little fiberglass monocoque Elite coupe plus selling customer racecars for the club racing crowd and...well, they were spread pretty damn thin over at Lotus. And Chapman was never known for spending a nickel when a penny or two would do....

In the end, Stirling Moss wound up making a solid handshake agreement with English privateer/Scotch whisky-heir Rob Walker for the 1959 season. They reckoned they'd start off with a Cooper because it seemed to be the best all-around package, but one of the beauties of being an independent team was that they could change cars anytime they wanted to should something better come up. Plus Moss would be the unquestioned Number One with the proven, careful and crafty Maurice Trintignant to back him up, and it also seemed likely that Rob Walker's mechanics—aided by Moss' own longtime ace wrench Alf Frances—might well do a better, cleverer, more flexible and more responsive job of things than the factory teams.

The upshot of this game of musical chairs was the surprise announcement from Ferrari that he'd signed on quiet and unassuming (but blisteringly fast, smooth and steady) ex-Vanwall ace Tony Brooks *and* the occasionally wild but always tough and pugnacious ex-BRM driver Jean Behra to his Formula One team. Ahead of Phil Hill and Toly Wolfgang and squeezing Cal completely out of Ferrari's Formula One plans.

"So what are you going to do?" I asked him over coffee and dessert while the kids watched TV and Julie cleaned up in the kitchen.

"I'm not sure I know," he kind of shrugged. "I've got a contract with Ferrari for the sportscars plus a couple non-championship Formula One and a few Formula Two races. And I've got some fill-in offers to drive here in the states. There's a big United States Auto Club/Cal Club, pro/amateur money race coming up at Pomona on March 8th, and I've got a pretty good shot at a decent ride in that one. Everybody says a lot of the top European guys are coming since they'll be here in the states anyway for Sebring. I'm pretty sure Toly's planning to come out for it, although I'm not so sure there's enough good cars to go around...." his voice trailed off.

"But you really want the Grand Prix circus, don't you?" I could see it in his eyes.

"Well, that's where it is, isn't it? If you want to race the best against the best, it's just got to be Formula One, doesn't it?"

I wasn't entirely convinced. "I dunno," I told him. "It looks just a little bit dangerous to me." Cal's expression turned hard and unfriendly. "I mean," I continued carefully, "it seems like an awful lot of guys get themselves hurt or evn killed over there."

Cal thought it over for maybe a tenth of a second. "It's what I have to do," he said flatly. "Maybe I won't feel that way someday, but right now, that's how I feel." He looked at me helplessly. "Hell, Buddy, it's all I care about anymore."

Now it was my turn to think it over. "You care about Gina, don't you?"

"That's different."

I let my eyebrows sneak up my forehead. "Oh?"

"What I mean is," he said like he was working it out in his own mind at the same time, "I care about Gina when I care about Gina. And I *really* care about her when we're together. But she's busy with her life and I'm busy with my life and that's just the way it's got to be."

"And your racing?"

His eyes turned into death rays. "I care about that *all* the time…."

So Cal went out to California and surprised Gina by being there in her driveway in Bel Air at just shy of two in the morning when Brad Lackey dropped her off following a new release preview showing at the studio and the requisite, glittering, Must Attend party at the producer's house in Beverly Hills afterwards. Cal was leaning against the fender of a gleaming new, gunmetal-silver Maserati 3500 GT that he'd borrowed from his service manager pal over at *Moto Italia,* although odds were good that Ernesto Julio didn't know anything about it. The house was dark and silent, as you might expect at two in the morning, and Gina was a little unnerved by the unfamiliar car and the silhouette of a stranger in her driveway. And startled as hell when she finally got close enough to make out who it was. *"Jesus, Cal, what the hell are you doing here?"* she blurted out in a confusion of surprise, anger, joy and exasperation.

"I was in the neighborhood," he grinned at her. "I thought I'd stop by."

He leaned over and kissed her, and for just an instant it felt like she might melt right into him. But she stopped herself and pulled back. "Do you have any idea what time it is?"

"Los Angeles time or New York time? I'm still kind of running on New York time, so I'd say the sun is about due to come up."

She glared at him. "Didn't it occur to you that you might have called first?"

"That would've spoiled the surprise, wouldn't it?"

A light blinked on in a second story window and Gina's eyes went up to it. A thin, unsteady, wavering shadow was standing behind the curtain.

"Look, I can't invite you inside, Cal. It's not that I don't want to, it's just…."

"Then let's go somewhere, okay?"

Her eyes were still on the shadow in the window. "I can't do that, either. Not now. I've got a call at seven tomorrow morning."

He put his hand under her chin and gently but forcibly brought her face-to-face with him. "Look, I don't care what the problem is inside. We've all got families to deal with and skeletons in our closets. Everybody. It's just the way things are."

"Oh?" she asked, her eyebrows arching. "And when was the last time you saw *your* family?"

"I saw my sister last week," he answered lamely.

"And your folks?"

He couldn't remember. "We're not really that close," he explained. But it sounded thin and lame even to his own ears.

Gina sucked in a breath and slowly exhaled. "Look, this is too complicated for me, okay? Don't get me wrong. I love being with you when we're away someplace together—I mean I really, *really* love it—but things are hectic and busy here and it's just too damn difficult."

"Then let's keep it simple. That's fine with me. We'll just spend a little time together, that's all."

He could tell she was thinking it over, but the frown never left her face. "Look. Cal," she said deliberately. "You don't want to get sucked into my life and work out here any more that you'd want me getting sucked into yours."

"Whaddaya mean?" he argued. *"Sure* I would!"

"Oh? How would you like it if I was there every day at the track, just hanging around like an old stray dog waiting for some attention?"

"I think I'd love it," Cal lied through one of his signature cobra grins.

"Maybe you think you would," Gina continued evenly. "But you wouldn't enjoy it—or love me very much—after awhile. Believe me, you'd get sick of it. Sick of the way I was always just *there* and hanging around and waiting for you and interrupting you and interfering with your work."

Cal didn't say anything.

She drew in a little closer and looked up at him. "Admit it. You know I'm right. For people like us, it's what we *do* that's important, not who we love or how much we think we love them." She laid her head against his shoulder. "It's just the way things are."

Cal thought it over, and he could feel deep down inside that it was true and made sense. "I guess we're both pretty selfish," he whispered into her hair.

Gina curled her lip under. "I don't like to call it that," she said softly, "but I guess that's what it is when you strip all the sugar and bullshit away."

He nuzzled in a little closer. "So will I get to see you while I'm here?"

Another light went on. This time in the stairwell heading down to the main entrance hallway. Gina looked up at him with fresh urgency in her eyes. "Sure, we'll see each other," she said hurriedly. "Tomorrow's a mess but we could do dinner and then maybe go someplace on Friday night. I've got a studio thing, but I could get out of it."

The light went on in the main entrance hallway.

"Look, you've got to leave," she half-pleaded. She pulled away and ran towards the door, fumbling for her keys. "Call Brad Lackey. He'll set it up," she called over her shoulder. But then she stopped under the white stucco archway and looked back at him. "It *is* great to see you," she gushed through a nervous but nonetheless radiant smile.

"It's good to be seen," he called back. But by then the door had opened and she was gone.

Hank was also out in California at the time seeing as how, what with the Argentine races off the schedule, January and February had turned into kind of slow, recuperative months in the pro racer and motoring scribe businesses. Unless you went Down Under to Australia and New Zealand for their summer race season like a lot of the British and European drivers did. Sure, there were always plenty of Cal Club and SCMA amateur races to run out in California—and Cal got a few offers—but he was a pro now and so he occasionally ran into trouble with the Charlie Priddle armband-types who were still very much dedicated to keeping SCMA club racing simon-pure amateur. Plus he had to be a little careful about exactly what kind of shitboxes he sat himself down in, since it wouldn't do at all to get waxed by a bunch of rinky-dink amateurs. Quite a change from the Cal I knew and remembered who'd jump into damn near anything—including my Trashwagon and that brakeless MG TD/Ford V-8 monstrosity he drove one time at Elkhart Lake—without thinking twice. Or even once, come to that.

To kill time until Friday and for lack of anything better to do, Cal borrowed an adorably cute but impossibly cramped little turquoise-over-white Nash Metropolitan from one of his racing buddies at the local BMC dealership (the Maserati had to be back on the *Moto Italia* lot with the keys hidden under the driver's-side floor mat—no questions asked!—before they opened for business the following morning!) so he and Hank could do a little sight-seeing. You have to understand that the Nash Metropolitan was pretty much just a rebodied, single-carburetor MGA under the skin, and so Nash dealers were always shuttling them over to their local BMC dealers for service. "You gotta drop it off back at the Nash dealer by 8 tomorrow morning," his friend told him. "And Jesus, whatever you do, don't wreck it. But outside of that, have fun. Oh, and don't forget to reconnect the speedo cable before you drop it off, okay?"

Cal nodded, did his best to chirp the tires—it was more like a "peep," really—and picked Hank up so they could make the rounds of the local shops and garages around L.A. where all the latest motorized hopes, crazes, projects and pipe dreams were busily taking shape. And that naturally included the clean but nondescript Reventlow Automobiles Incorporated building over in Culver City. It was common knowledge by then that RAI had eyes for Formula One, and that Lance Reventlow fully and even devoutly believed that he could assemble the best American talent available (or at least the best in the greater Los Angeles area, which, as any Southern California sportycar enthusiast would be only too happy to tell you, amounted to the same thing) and take on and eventually beat the best of the British and Italian teams at their own damn game.

It was an unbelievably immense, bold and complicated undertaking, but Hank and Cal found the RAI shop knee-deep in it by the middle of February, 1959. There were fresh, handsome new castings getting unpacked from their shipping crates and machined driveline parts gleaming and glinting on the work benches and a lanky but robust, perfectly welded chrome-moly tube frame taking shape alongside a wooden buck ready and waiting for the hammered alloy bodywork. Every bit of it looked absolutely first-class and toolroom-perfect in every respect. Plus there were drawings on the office walls of what the finished car was going to look like, and was it ever low, sleek and handsome! It had the engine in front, of course, like all the other cars except Cooper (Lance had raced a rear-engined Cooper for awhile, and thought it felt a little twitchier and less stable than the best of the front-engined cars) but the new Scarab F1 car was much lower and sleeker than the Ferraris, Vanwalls or BRMs—at least in the drawings, anyway—thanks to laying the engine over on its side like some of the latest Indy-style cars.

"Yeah, it's a heck of a project," a harried- but determined-looking Lance Reventlow told them when he breezed through the shop to check a few things with Warren Olsen and eyeball the frame and the new rear hub carriers before hustling over to the foundry that was working on the cast-alloy engine block and then squirting up the coast to check on the crankshaft forging, followed by a quick drive inland to talk things over with the engine designer and then down to Halibrand about the wheels and over to Goodyear to talk to them about tires and then…well, let's just say Lance was spread about as thin as cooking oil on a hot plate.

"It's really gonna be something!" he told Hank and Cal while the three of them marveled over the 25 deep, radial fins on the impressively cast and machined aluminum brake drums for the aircraft-style, expander-type front brakes. "Oh, sure, we'll have our setbacks and problems," he said like he really, deep down in his heart, didn't expect to have a single significant one, "but it's going to come together."

"Sure looks impressive," Hank allowed.

"You bet it does," Lance said like somebody'd just poured a little gasoline on his fire. "We should be testing in four to six weeks. I don't think we can realistically make Monaco on May 10th—sure would be nice if we could, though—or the Dutch race at Zandvoort on May 31st. But the next two races aren't until the French Grand Prix on July 5th and the British Grand Prix two weeks after that—I'm pretty sure it's at Aintree this year—and we should be able to make those, no sweat."

"With just the one car?" Hank asked.

"Oh, no," Lance continued enthusiastically. "We'll have at least two cars by then, and we're going to have three on the team when we're done with everything. One for Chuck, one for Bruce and one for me, of course." He looked back and forth between Hank and Cal, the excitement and anticipation absolutely boiling over in his eyes. "I can't believe how quickly everything is coming together! I mean," he swept his arm in a circle and Cal and Hank's eyes followed it around the shop. "Just look at everything we've got done already!"

Although, as any car-project veteran on earth can tell you, it's not the first things that set the pace and finish date, but the very last….

"Looks pretty promising," Hank allowed with a giddy little glow of his own. Of course, all the American sportycar magazines (and all the American sportycar writers, for that matter) were behind the whole deal 110% and itching like crazy for a real American contender—and did they dare dream winner?—on the World Championship Formula One scene. And seeing how much was getting done at RAI and to what incredibly high standards was pretty damn infectious. As was the youthful enthusiasm and nervous confidence Lance radiated like a glowing chunk of uranium ore.

"Let me know if you're ever shy of a driver," Cal said jokingly but not joking at all. "Even if you just need the seat warmed up on a test day." He waited for Lance to look him in the eye, and then added: "I'd be more than happy to fill in."

Lance thanked him—and Hank said it sounded like he really meant it—and then he was off to make his rounds of all the Scarab F1 project suppliers and sub-contractors scattered all over the place around greater Los Angeles and up and down the coast of Southern California.

Chapter 33: A Choice of Futures

Needless to say, the new Scarab Formula One car didn't quite make it to the Monaco Grand Prix on May 10th. Or the Dutch Grand Prix at Zandvoort on May 31st. Or France or England in July or the German or Portuguese races in August or even the Italian Grand Prix at Monza in September. Worse yet, by then it was obvious that the rear-engined Coopers were way too slick, quick and nimble for the front-engined cars. Even the ones with 25 or 30 more horsepower, like the Ferraris claimed to have (although, as I've said before, Italian horses in general tend to run a bit small). Plus there were already ominous pronouncements rumbling out of FIA headquarters in Paris that the Grand Prix cars were too fast and entirely too many drivers were managing to get themselves killed, and so Formula One would be switching from 2.5-liters to 1.5-liters—that's just 91 cubic inches!—for the 1961 season. Needless to say, this didn't sit too well with the British teams (who finally—at long last—seemed to have old man Ferrari squarely in the crosshairs) along with the journalist scribes, race promoters and all-'round motorsports heavyweights who doubted very loudly and publicly that it would happen. After all, who the hell would pay good money to watch the best damn drivers in the world parade around in a bunch of kiddie cars?

And it sounded like even old man Ferrari down in Maranello agreed with them. 1500cc unsupercharged Grand Prix cars? Well shy of 200 horsepower for even the best of them? *Hah! Mere toys!* What sort of dull, lame, uninteresting spectacle would that be? Although meanwhile Ferrari's engine shops were secretly hard at work on a new, 1500cc V-6 "Formula Two" engine with a wide, flat, 120-degree vee to keep the weight nice and low in a rear-engined layout and a projected horsepower output far beyond the best of the 1500cc Climax four-bangers running around in England….

I guess you'd have to say that Lance Reventlow was maybe a little naïve, bold, optimistic and impetuous, thinking that he could take on old man Ferrari and the rest of the Formula One bunch head-to-head in their own back yard with what amounted to a well-financed but not very experienced and basically pretty raw and amateur Southern California racing team. I mean, they didn't know the game and they didn't know the tracks and they surely didn't appreciate how damn serious and even ruthless it was over there. Or what an absolutely mountain-sized chunk they'd bitten off thinking they could build a pure-bred Formula One car up from scratch in a couple months like they had with the Scarab sportscars. But of course the other side of the coin was that Lance Reventlow was young and rich and surely a little bit spoiled—or maybe even more than a little bit—and used to getting what he wanted. Not to mention a little arrogant about what they'd accomplished with the Scarab sportscars (some say he was a little arrogant even before that!), and in particular how they'd gone out and waxed the best in the game—first shot out of the box!—with a beautifully built and finished racecar that they'd brought from scrawls on a cocktail napkin to victory circle in less than six months.

But Grand Prix racing was a far deeper end of the pool. And it was *their* pool, on top of it. Not to mention that Lance had this patriotic, almost religious dedication to the idea that *everything* on his new racecar was going to be cutting-edge clever, built from scratch and, most especially, red-white-and-blue All American from inside out and one end to the other. Which meant—right off the top—that they had to design and build a state-of-the-art 2.5-liter racing engine right out of thin air rather than develop an existing one like they'd done with the Chevy V-8s in the Scarab sportscars. And that's only the difference between warming up a hamburger on the stove and raising a bunch of cattle out on the range somewhere, driving that herd a thousand miles or so cross-country from their grazing pastures in Texas or wherever to the rail head in Kansas City, loading them onto trains, bringing them to the Chicago stockyards, running them through the auctions, sending them through chutes and corrals and then more chutes to the slaughterhouse, banging them on the head (or whatever they do), stringing them up, cutting them open, chopping and hacking and sawing them into handier chunks and pieces, then packing it up and trucking it to all the main street and side-street groceries, meat markets and butcher shops where they'd grind a little up, stick it in a heavy aluminum tray and set it out in the glass-front meat counter with the scale on top where your mom or your wife or whoever could point to it, have the guy weigh it (along with his thumb, if you don't keep an eye on him), pay for it, have him wrap it up in white butcher paper, tie it with string, and send it on home so your mom or your wife or whoever could form it into nice, fat patties and throw it into a skillet with a little butter or bacon grease to keep it from sticking and cook it up for you. And then maybe put a nice slice of Swiss, Cheddar or Provolone on top just when it's almost done.

As you can see, it's a wee bit more complicated proposition….

But you have to remember that Lance Reventlow wasn't even 23 years old when he hatched this idea, and you tend to be a little simplistic, idealistic, optimistic, impatient and short-sighted at that age. I know I was. Why, just look at what happened with the blessed Trashwagon! Not to mention that young Lance had way, *way* too much money and free time on his hands and wanted desperately—more than anything—to be taken seriously by the motorsports community. Not to mention those assholes from the Fleet Street tabloid press over in England. Lance hated them for all the terrible stories they'd printed and all the cruel, snide, vicious, sniping, winking, tongue-clucking, innuendo-laced, horrified-and-yet-chuckling-over-it things they wrote about his mother and father's divorce and the ugly custody battle that followed. And the bastards hadn't laid off any of them ever since. Just to sell a few more fucking newspapers!

No question Lance had enjoyed a little too much easy success with the Scarab sportscars. That can get you to believing in yourself—and your dreams—maybe even a wee bit more than is good for you. But of course you never find that out until later. Hell, you never find *anything* out until later. That's the tricky, nothing-up-my-sleeves/fingers-crossed-behind-my-back way life works, you know? And when you're up there in the public eye, it means everybody and his brother gets a damn ringside seat when any of your pet ideas turn on you and bite you squarely in the ass.

In any case, Lance and his team manager Warren Olsen went on a kind of commando-raid talent hunt to find the designers, engineers, foundry folks and metalsmiths they figured they needed for their Formula One project, and right at the top of the list was 59-year-old engine designer Leo Goossen, who worked for Meyer-Drake in Los Angeles and was already a legend in American racing thanks to his well-known work on the Meyer-Drake Offenhausers and the Novi V-8, which had essentially been the engines-of-choice at the Indianapolis 500 for as far back as anybody could remember. And that Meyer-Drake Offenhauser was one hell of a great motor. Simple. Strong. Torque that wouldn't quit, stone-axe reliable and built like a damn bank vault. To almost no one's surprise, Goossen and Reventlow decided on another big, basic, inline four-banger for Formula One. Same as Vanwall used on their Constructors' Championship-winning cars in 1958 and BRM was still using. Only Goossen and Reventlow decided to lay it over on its side to keep the center of gravity and the hood line low like the latest generation of Indy 500-winning roadsters from Quinn Epperly. Both good ideas. And also, with urging from Lance (who'd maybe read a little too much for his own good and remembered every bit of it) and RAI engine aces Jim Travers and Frank Coon of Traco Engineering, they decided to try a desmodromic valve gear setup like Mercedes used on their incredibly dominant, championship-winning Grand Prix and sportscars of 1954-55.

I don't mean to get too technical here, but you have to understand that the normal way intake and exhaust valves work is that this bump on the camshaft (we mechanical types call it a "lobe") pushes the valve open like when you open your screen door with your shoulder because you've got your hands full of garbage or Christmas presents or something. Then this spring kind of bangs it closed again behind you, right? But valve springs have always been kind of a problem child/necessary evil in high-performance racing engines, seeing as how they're made out of spring steel that has to flex and unflex and flex and unflex a few kazillion bazillion times without cracking or breaking, and moreover do that job over and over and over again at *very* high speed. Like, say, *FIFTY TIMES A SECOND* at 6000 rpm! Not to mention that it's hotter than blazes inside a running race engine. As a result, valve spring breakages, coil bind, valve "float" and all kinds of other spring-related problems are pretty damn common. Especially running at high rpms, and high rpms are vital on account of there's this little explosion in each cylinder every other cycle, and that's what slams the piston down its hole, pushes on the connecting rod and makes the crankshaft turn, and the more of those little explosions you can cram into a minute, the more horsepower you're ultimately going to have spinning off the end of the crankshaft and right on through to the rear wheels.

I hope you've got that all down, because there may be a quiz later on.

Well, what those clever krauts at Mercedes did was rig up an engine with TWO cam lobes for each valve—one to open it and one to close it—and no springs at all. Along with a tremendously clever, monkey-motion system of levers and forked fingers and cam followers and what-have-you to make it all work. Now doing away with the valve springs surely sounds like a grand idea. And deceptively simple, to boot. But believe me, it is not. Imagine that screen door we were talking about is made out of machined tool steel and weighs about 50 pounds and the door frame around it is heavy cast iron set into a two-foot-thick brick wall. And let's say you're banging it open and slamming it shut, oh, say, 50 or even 60 times a second! And imagine that door fits *very* snugly into that frame. Like so tight you couldn't even get in there with your thinnest feeler gauge. And then imagine that, as things get hot, that steel door and that cast-iron frame and the brick wall around it all start to swell a little. Only the tool-steel door swells a little more and a little faster than the cast-iron frame, and the cast-iron frame swells a little more and a little faster than the brick wall around it. And then imagine that everything is done with such force and to such close tolerances that, if everything doesn't line up just exactly dead-nuts perfect every time (and remember, we're talking 50 or 60 times per second here!) the door buckles or bends or breaks clear in half or the cast iron frame cracks or....

Well, you get the idea.

But Mercedes-Benz made it work, right? And beat the living crap out of everybody in the process. Still, it goes to show what a complicated and exacting sort of proposition it was when you realize that nobody—not Ferrari or Vanwall or Jaguar or Porsche or Aston Martin or BRM (and they'd try damn near *anything!)* or anybody else—chose to fool around with desmodromic valve gear even after they saw all the success Mercedes had with it. But young Lance and old Leo Goossen figured they had an inside track. Seems some of the manufacturing brass at Mercedes wanted to take a peek at one of Ford's assembly lines a few years before, and part of the deal was that Mercedes would "lend" Ford one of their championship-winning 300SLR sportscars from 1955—complete with its desmodromic valve gear—to be "put on display" at the Henry Ford Museum at Greenfield Village in Dearborn, Michigan. Which it was, and who knows how many families and school kids on field trips and awestruck, starry-eyed car guys filed by and pointed and shook their heads and clucked their tongues over that sleek and beautiful silver sportscar. But there was a little more to it than that. Seems the engine was also kind of disassembled late at night when nobody was looking. Including—and most especially—that kraut-clever desmodromic valve gear. And it turns out those prying eyes and fingers belonged to two guys from California who were on the old Ford racing payroll at the time: Jim Travers and Frank Coons. So after Ford fell in line with the rest of the chickenshit Detroit manufacturers and got the hell out of racing in 1957 (like a whipped dog slinking away with its tail between its legs, as Hank so colorfully put it), Travers and Coons wound up with all the snapshots and notes and drawings from those late-night, Let's-Take-A-Peek sessions in the Henry Ford Museum at Greenfield Village. Snapshots, notes and drawings that they were only too happy to share with Lance and Leo Goossen for the new Scarab project.

Unfortunately, seeing something and understanding all the subtleties, intricacies and implications of How and Why it works are two decidedly different things, and my own experience has led me to believe that, by the time you finally finish doing something for the very first time, you probably know about two-thirds of what you really should have known before you started. The ironic part is that it seems like the surest method to find the *right* way to do something is by doing it the wrong way first. And the ugly side of that is the bare fact that there is usually only one Right

Way and umpty kazillion, up-a-blind-alley Wrong Ways, and so you can find yourself stumbling around in the dark for a *very* long time without getting anywhere. Except lost. Or maybe up shit creek.

While all of that was going on, RAI's Formula One plans suffered another blow at the big USAC/Cal Club "pro/am" money race at the Los Angeles County Fairgrounds in Pomona on Sunday, March 8th. Heavily promoted by the sponsoring *Los Angeles Examiner* newspaper as a head-to-head-to-head title match between "the best of the European pros" (a lot of them were over here to run Sebring in two weeks anyway), the "top American sportscar aces" and a handful of big-name Indy 500 oval-track stars, the "Examiner Grand Prix at Pomona" drew over 40,000 spectators—at three bucks a head!—to what everyone hoped would be the biggest damn California sportycar shootout since Riverside. But the makeshift track at the Pomona Fairgrounds wasn't exactly an impressive, world-class circuit like Riverside, where big, hairy, powerful racecars could open it up all the way to the throttle stops and top 150 (or even 175!) down that long back straightaway. In fact, the layout at Pomona was terrifically tight, busy and fiddly (11 turns in barely two miles!) and not a little bit dangerous, what with high curbs on both sides through some sections and an ess-bend underpass with a *very* solid-looking concrete bridge abutment right at the edge of the road.

Plus, just like Cal figured, there weren't really enough top cars to go around. Oval-track star Jerry Unser found a ride in an older, Cadillac-powered Kurtis, which was at least a lot like the Kurtis Indianapolis-type racers he was familiar with and trusted. Not to mention that he knew all the little tricks for setting them up. Even if the Kurtis did seem a little bull-in-a-china-shop cumbersome around a circuit like Pomona. But that hot-rodded Caddy V-8 had plenty of power, and that would surely get him up near the front of the pack by the time the pack got to turn one. After that, well, as one Indy star put it out of the side of his mouth opposite the stub end of his cigar: *"Catchin' Jerry is one thing, but gettin' around him is somethin' else agin'."*

The visiting European stars were doing even worse. Dapper little Frenchman Maurice Trintignant wound up in an underpowered Cooper-Climax "bobtail" while his countryman Jean Behra was so disgusted with the smallbore, amateur-level cars he was offered that he didn't even bother to show up. Two-time Le Mans winner Ron Flockhart was stuck with a tired old Jag D-Type and Roy Salvadori could do no better than an 1100cc Lotus Eleven after the Aston Martin he was supposed to drive broke down on Saturday. Cal's hoped-for plum drive in a Maserati 450S likewise evaporated and went instead to some hot new west coast phenom named Billy Krause, and Cal was lucky to wind up with yet another last-minute charity ride in Max Balchowsky's butt-ugly, Buick-powered Old Yaller. Toly was even worse off, stuck in a well-worn, three-year-old Maserati 300S that had a lot of hard miles on it and not nearly enough recent repair or maintenance thanks to a series of slow, uninspired amateur drivers who never really pushed the car hard enough to break a sweat. It started sputtering and misfiring in the very first session and ran that way almost nonstop clear through the weekend. Plus the "visiting team" drivers didn't get much at all in the way of practice laps to learn the track. There was supposed to be open practice on Friday, but a bunch of local residents complained and it was cancelled. And when the cars finally did hit the pavement for a few short practice sessions and qualifying heats on Saturday, a lot of them found their cars clumsy, awkward and cumbersome through Pomona's tight switchbacks and hairpin corners. "I'd give every bit of the prize money ahead of time for one of those Porsche RSKs," Toly muttered disgustedly after retiring with a bad misfire from his heat race on Saturday.

"You think you could win with one of those little things?" Cal scoffed. He'd done pretty damn well with Old Yaller, qualifying it up among the very fastest. But then, he knew the track already. Not to mention that Max Balchowsky's Old Yaller, in spite of its homely, junkyard-dog face and those goofy whitewall tires, was a damn solid racecar. And Max and wife Ina knew how to fiddle around with all the little things, too. Like tire pressures and toe-in and all the other stuff you could adjust and screw around with to get a car running its best on any particular racetrack. In fact, Max even swapped out his beloved whitewall recaps for some secondhand, Scarab-style racing tires at the front in order to loosen the back end up a little around the tighter corners. Lots of cars ran different size tires on the front and back—most of them, in fact—but nobody except Max thought about fudging around with different brands, tread patterns and constructions at opposite ends. Or realized that worn tires—so long as the rubber was still soft and springy—might have better grip than brand-new. But of course Max explained it to anyone who got nosey (like Hank, for instance) in his typically cranky and cantankerous Balchowsky snarl: *"Aw, hell, we had a bad flat spot on one of the fronts thanks to this asshole,"* he jerked a thumb in Cal's direction, *"and the spare in Ina's station wagon is kinda bald and there's a patch in it, so we took these here out of the trash bin behind the Scarab pits."*

In this case, the Scarab Max was talking about was not from RAI's stable, but one of the cars Lance sold off after Nassau. Which was now owned by the Nickey Chevrolet team out of Chicago and painted the same, eyeball-searing bright metallic purple as their infamous "Purple People Eater" Corvette. And, also like the Corvette, it was being driven by Milwaukee, Wisconsin, hotshoe Jim Jeffords. It must have rankled them to watch Max rummaging around in their trash for castoff tires and then seeing the time sheets with Max's mangy Old Yaller way up at the front and their expensive new, best-damn-sportscar-on-the-planet Scarab back in seventh place. But then, Jim Jeffords had never seen the place before, and tight corners and short straightaways were never exactly the Scarab's strong suits.

All the usual west coast Ferraris, Maseratis and thundering, V-8-powered specials were there at Pomona, along with Bill Sadler's pair of Chevy-powered specials out of Canada. Bruce Kessler had been signed on to drive the newest one—the same white-and-blue, "Nisonger KLG"-sponsored car we saw breaking down and boiling over with great regularity down in Nassau—and Mercedes 300SL ace Paul O'Shea was in the older, red one. But Hank said neither one looked like it handled especially great through the corners. In fact, the car that caught everyone's attention was Ken Miles' zippy little Porsche RS, which looked like a hornet buzzing around in a herd of buffaloes out there among the "big" cars.

Poor Toly didn't even qualify for the feature thanks to that persistent misfire, but Cal got the service manager from *Moto Italia* to look at it and he found a serious kink in the little metal elbow bend coming out of the fuel tank. Looked like somebody'd accidentally put a jack under it without looking first. Of course the car's regular wrench had done all the obvious stuff, checking the ignition timing and cleaning out the carburetors and even opening up the fuel pump, but he never bothered to check the line coming out of the tank, and that kink was strangling the fuel feed before it ever got to the pump. Oh, it'd run fine in the pits with no load on it—even if you blipped the throttles and raced it a few times—but once it was out on the track with a load on it, it'd start banging and stuttering and misfiring because there just wasn't enough gas getting through. With the problem fixed, Toly absolutely tore away from the field in Sunday morning's consolation race—he had a five-second lead by the end of the first lap!—but then, with the engine finally singing, the needle on the temp gauge started creeping up while the one on the oil pressure gauge headed in the opposite direction, and he chose to do the right thing and pull in rather than be the Guilty Party in the driver's seat when the damn thing blew up. "I'll leave that for the next guy who drives it," he told Hank through a crooked smile. "Let him get a lapful of oil and take that long walk back to the pits."

Gina showed up around lunchtime with Brad Lackey, who was now driving a shiny new pastel-blue MGA and obviously moving up in the world. She'd been working in one of the studio dubbing rooms since 7:00 that morning, but managed to sneak away when the director got into a huge argument with two of the studio execs about which shot they were going to use and which one would wind up swept out with the trash. The director liked the one with the best acting, dramatic flow and composition, but the two studio guys much preferred the high-angle version where the leading man flubbed one of his lines but you got a really good look down the front of Gina's dress. In any case, she and Brad got to Pomona towards the end of lunch break, just as the first of the cars were being rolled out to the grid, and found Toly, Hank, Cal and Max and Ina Balchowsky gathered around Old Yaller. Brad stared at the car. "Anybody die in that wreck?" he wisecracked.

"You might, if you keep up with that lip," Max snapped at him. It was hard to know when Max was kidding or serious. Especially if you didn't know him. In fact, that's how he picked a lot of his friends. And he could tell right away that he didn't much care for Brad Lackey. Although Gina was sure easy on the eyes.

Toly leaned over and gave Gina a kiss on the cheek. "You missed my race!" he pouted, giving her the old Basset Hound eyes.

Gina looked puzzled. "I thought your race was this afternoon?"

"Not Toly's race," Cal cackled. "He's special. He got to run with the cripples, clowns and old ladies this morning."

Gina looked at him. "Is that true?"

Toly's face contorted in mock anguish. "Sadly, yes," he nodded, stifling a sob.

"Oh? How'd you do?"

His face brightened as he switched into an overdone French accent. "I was—how do you say it in English?—I was *magnificent!"* He struck a dramatic pose and flashed the world a pasted-on, magazine-cover smile.

"That sounds very impressive," Gina laughed. "And how did you finish?"

"I finished without blowing it up!" Toly proclaimed, still preening and posing for some nonexistent photographer. He turned back to Gina and added in a low, confidential voice: "That is what made it so—how do you say it in English again?"

"So magnificent."

"Ah, yes. That's it. That's what made it so…" he struck that leering, ridiculous, leading-man pose again, "…so *magnificent!"*

"Well, look, Mr. Magnificent," Cal chuckled, "why don't you buy Gina and Brad here a couple cokes and hot dogs and take them over by the fences. I've got a race to run in about 15 minutes."

"'bout time you got yer ass in the damn car!" Max Balchowsky growled with just a microscopic hint of a smile at the corners of his mouth.

So Toly and Hank took Gina and Brad Lackey over by the fences in the restricted, Photographers Only area in front of the ess-curve underpass to watch the race. Toly and Hank had credentials that would get them in almost anywhere, they borrowed Cal's pass for Brad Lackey and, well, nobody but nobody stopped Gina LaScala from going anywhere anymore. They just grinned like lucky idiots and made way. To tell the truth, Hank said Gina seemed a little edgy about watching Cal race. But maybe that was to be expected the way things were….

The $15,000-purse *"Examiner Grand Prix at Pomona"* turned out to be a pretty interesting and dramatic race. It started with all the big-inch stuff naturally leaping towards the front, led by new-kid-with-a-big-future Dan Gurney in Frank Arciero's 4.9 Ferrari, Indy 500 star Jerry Unser in that *very* quick and powerful Kurtis/Cadillac, our boy Cal in Ol' Yaller, Carroll Shelby in a 450S Maserati, Chuck Daigh in a one-off drive on a track he knew well in yet another Kurtis (this one with Buick power), and a whole bunch more jostling for position and nipping at their heels. Including Billy Krause in the 450S Maserati Cal was originally supposed to drive, Jim Jeffords in the shiny purple Nickey Chevrolet Scarab out of Chicago, Ken Miles and Sam Weiss in Porsche RS550s (already well up) and Bruce Kessler coming up fast in the white-and-blue Sadler. Jerry Unser's Kurtis-Cadillac faded pretty quickly with electrical problems, and damn if Cal wasn't still hanging onto second place behind Gurney's Ferrari—with Shelby's Maserati 450 right up his butt and Daigh and Kessler not far behind—when Old Yaller's engine blew sky-high right at the start/finish line at the beginning of the 10th lap, scattering parts, smoke and steam everywhere and laying an instant flood of hot oil down on the racetrack. Shelby saw it happening and managed to dodge it and so did Chuck Daigh, but thanks to the low cockpit in the Sadler and having that big, bulky Kurtis right in front of him, our buddy Bruce Kessler couldn't see it coming. Or not until it was too late, anyway. The instant Daigh's Kurtis jinked out of the way—just that quick!—Bruce was on the oil and out of control. He skated off the track with all four wheels helplessly locked solid, hurtled through a roped-off area where a bunch of race officials were standing—scattering them like bowling pins!—went through a string fence and a couple sawhorses and slammed head-on into a row of parked cars. The impact made a huge, ripping/crashing/crumpling noise, followed by half-a-heartbeat's silence and then the soft, confetti tinkle of broken glass coming down like snow….

It was one hell of a wreck, and just plain dumb luck that nobody was killed. Bruce was pretty banged up and bewildered, sitting in the car playing it all back in his head and wondering, as he watched the blood stain spread across his shirt, just what the heck had happened. They red-flagged the race, of course, and wound up taking Bruce and four of the race officials—including Cal Club president Joe Weissman—off to the hospital in ambulances. It took the better part of an hour to clean the mess up, and by that time Cal was up on the fences with Toly, Hank, Gina and Max and Ina Balchowsky, while Brad Lackey was over at a pay phone trying to either arrange or un-arrange something for one of his studio bosses.

"How is he?" Hank asked as soon as Cal arrived.

"Who?"

"Bruce, of course."

Cal shrugged. "I guess he's a little busted up," he allowed, avoiding Gina's eyes, "but I think it's mostly bumps and bruises. Maybe a couple cracked ribs. And a pretty bad gash on his face where it hit the wheel. But he'll be okay."

"That's good. How about the others?"

"Someone said one lady got her legs broken, but I couldn't really get over there. I only know about Bruce from talking to one of the medical guys."

"But you're okay?" Gina asked.

"Oh, sure," Cal assured her. "Not a scratch. Didn't hurt the car any, either." He looked at Hank. "I just feel bad for Bruce, you know? I mean, it wasn't his fault."

"What about *me?"* Max groused loudly. "I told you to *race* the damn car, not blow the damn thing up!" Gina stared at him in disbelief. She didn't realize he was teasing, but the other three picked it up immediately.

"Jeez, Max, if you'd just build the damn things right in the first place…."

"Do you *really* get your engines out of a junkyard?"

"You ought to let Ina build the damn motors. She's a lot more meticulous than you."

"How meticulous can she be?" Max shot right back. "Look at what the heck she married…."

Gina couldn't quite understand how the three of them could be joking and laughing and kidding around after such a serious accident. She didn't realize—at least not yet—how racers use jokes and jibes and patter to take some of the sting out and put some of the swagger and confidence back in. It was also kind of a celebration. After all, each one of them knew it could have been much, *much* worse.

The race restarted about 10 minutes later and quickly turned into a battle of attrition with one after another of the favored cars and drivers stopping out on course or pulling in to retire. In the end it boiled down to pretty much a two-car race, with new-kid-on-the-block Billy Krause running in front in the same exact Maserati 450S Cal thought he'd be driving that weekend. And showing in the bargain that he was a pretty decent pick behind the wheel. But right on Krause's tail and feinting every which way for an opening was—you guessed it—Ken Miles in that scrappy little Porsche RS. As the race wore on and the Maserati's tires wore down and the track got hotter and slicker and hotter and slicker every lap, the advantage seemed to swing further and further in the direction of the light, handy Porsche. But Billy Krause wasn't about to give up without a fight, and according to Hank he was doing one hell of a job of clogging up the track through the corners so there was no room to pass on either side and then using the big Maserati's grunt to gain back a little daylight on the straightaways. It must have been frustrating as hell for Miles, knowing that he had the fastest combination on the track and that the car in front of him was a sitting duck, and yet not being able to find a way by. In fact, he rumpled up the nose on the Porsche pretty badly just trying to get Krause's attention. If you know what I mean. But Billy ignored the taps and nudges and held his ground, while some of the race officials started talking back and forth about whether they should maybe black-flag Ken Miles for "ungentlemanly driving." But, fortunately for the spectators, opinion was pretty much divided as to whether they were watching bad behavior or great, David-and-Goliath-style racing, and the argument went on and on while the show continued. And then, with just one lap to go—two blessed miles!—Krause had a rear tire blow. *POW!* He managed to gather it up without hitting anything, but the best he could do after that was to limp home fourth on a clattering wheel rim while Ken Miles and that little 1500cc Porsche went on to score an upset win in "the biggest-ever Big Sportscar race in California!"

Meanwhile, on the way to the hospital, our buddy Bruce Kessler made a pretty important decision about his future. This was his second horrific accident and second trip to the hospital in less than a year (the other was when he ran into that spun-out French D-Type in the rain at Le Mans, where the Jaguar's driver was killed) and neither of those accidents had been his fault or had anything to do with how he was driving or any mistake he himself might have made. And that was enough for Bruce Kessler. More than enough, in fact. Like he'd told us down in Nassau, he'd started a bit of a Hollywood career for himself as a second unit and/or assistant director, and he really enjoyed the work. But the producers and directors from the studios were afraid to hire him because he might just go out and kill himself (or put himself in the hospital again) in the middle of an unfinished project. And there were plenty enough damn risks in the movie business without going out and looking for more….

So Bruce Kessler was officially out of his supporting-actor role on the Formula One project at RAI. And that was the least of their problems. Besides the desmodromic-valve engine that was still in bits and pieces (some of which had yet to be made, in fact), the new Scarab Grand Prix challenger bristled with all kinds of other innovative, untried and untested ideas. Like fr'instance the brakes. By 1959, even old Enzo Ferrari had caved in and was using British disc brakes on his racing cars. Hey, he was proud, all right—in fact, he was famous for it—but he wasn't stupid. He also understood the notion of "winning at all costs" maybe better than anybody the world of motorsports had ever seen. So Ferrari bit the bullet, swallowed his pride and probably got the World's Best Deal Ever on disc brakes for his racecars by holding out the carrot of using them on all of his production cars, too. That amounted to quite a few sets of brakes, not to mention the advertising and promotional glow of having *your* company's brakes on what everybody pretty much reckoned as the best, fastest, most beautiful, most exotic and far and away most desirable sports cars and *grand Turismos* on the planet.

But Lance didn't want to use any damn British brakes on *his* car. No, sir. He had other ideas. See, Lance and Warren had hired on this 23-year-old aircraft designer named Marshall Whitfield to lay out the chassis, suspension and running gear—he'd already worked with them some on the Scarab sportscars—and he said they ought to take a look at using aircraft-style, expanding pneumatic tube drum brakes on the front of the car and a single, water-cooled disc next to the differential in back. Now the expanding pneumatic tube brake idea looked absolutely brilliant on paper. It was lighter than any cast-iron disc brake setup and, unlike conventional drum brakes, made equal contact with equal pressure all the way around the drums. Why, it was genius! Only problem was that your average airplane only has to stop once, whereas a racecar, well....

And of course the RAI crew couldn't find that out until they tested the car, and they couldn't test the car because parts of the blessed motor were still very much in as-unfinished-yet stages of completion at assorted sub-contractors all over the Los Angeles basin. Meyer-Drake was doing most of the engine work—and they were the best in the business—but they got hit with an unprecedented number of orders for new Meyer-Drake Offys for Indianapolis in May, and no way would any smart engine builder (or any other businessman, come to that) blow off their bread-and-butter customers and the biggest damn race in America just to take care of a one-off, incredibly complicated, possibly fly-by-night or pipe-dream Formula One project for some rich, temperamental, unpredictable and demanding 23-year-old who might just walk away or lose interest if things didn't go his way.

There were also a lot of questions to be answered about the Scarab chassis that was supposed to carry that engine. Lance, Warren and the rest of the Scarab crew had settled on using fully independent, dual A-arm suspension front and rear. Which, at least theoretically, seemed like the best possible design solution. Even though all the Brits and Europeans (except the rear-engined Coopers, which had no choice) preferred to use a DeDion-style rear suspension with a solid tube connecting the rear wheels to ensure that they stayed upright and parallel to each other—and to the fronts—no matter what. Most drivers who'd tried both agreed that the DeDion felt more predictable, consistent and controllable than a fully independent layout, no matter what the mavens, whiz kids and boffins at the drafting tables said or thought about it. But Lance and his guys figured they were wrong.

Like a lot of the Scarab ideas, running a fully independent rear suspension made perfect—even dazzling—sense. Just like laying the engine flat for a lower center of gravity and less frontal area and running the driveshaft alongside the driver to get him nice and low in the cockpit to lower the center of gravity and reduce the frontal area even more. All of which sounded great until you got to the back end and had to figure out what to do with the damn suspension and halfshaft geometry when you had the quick-change diff all the way over on the left side of the car with a ridiculously long halfshaft on the right side and this stubby little short one on the left. And what the hell was the blessed engine doing in front of the driver, anyway, seeing as how....

Hank was right there at ringside when the 1959 Grand Prix season opened at Monaco on May 10th, and it was really no surprise to see Frenchman Jean Behra's powerful Ferrari in the middle of the front row. He could always be counted on for a blistering lap or two and always did well in front of his countrymen, and the majority of shouts and chatter in the grandstands at Monaco were in French. But the bright red Ferrari was sandwiched by a pair of rear-engined Coopers, with Moss in the dark blue Rob Walker car on the pole and Jack Brabham in the Number One factory team entry on the opposite side. The race started with a furious battle between Behra and Moss—another one of those David-and-Goliath deals where Behra used the straightline speed and acceleration of the Ferrari to win the mad dash for corner one, followed by lots of lurid slides and a bit of judicious blocking to keep Moss in his mirrors. But the little blue Cooper was right there, nosing around for an opening at every opportunity, and Hank said it was kind of funny how Moss would shake his fist at Behra—in the middle of a damn four-wheel drift!—to show him what he thought about his tactics. And Behra would just draw his head down a little deeper inside his shirt collar, ignore his mirrors and block some more! But it's almost impossible to keep that sort of thing up forever—especially when your car handles like a pig on roller skates—and Behra finally slipped wide and Moss shot through in an instant. And then just pulled away. Effortlessly, you know?

Three laps later Behra's engine blew up and the Ferrari clattered to a stop on the straight behind the pits. The official word from Ferrari was that a valve spring had broken, but Hank said all the oil pouring out from underneath and all the fine, jagged steel and light-alloy souvenirs the spectators were picking out of the gutters afterward made you wonder if there wasn't perhaps a little more involved....

At that point it looked like Moss was home free in the Walker car with Brabham in the factory Cooper a distant second and only a handful of cars still circulating after the usual Monaco mechanical failures and side trips into the haybales. But one of the "improvements" Alf Frances and the Walker crew made was to take the Citroen-based transaxle out of their Cooper and replace it with a much lighter and more advanced-looking piece they'd commissioned on the sly from Italian driveline expert Valerio Colotti. Which worked wonderfully until it broke on lap 80—just 20 laps from the end—and put Moss out of a commanding lead. Brabham went on to win easily in the factory Cooper after Moss' retirement, and no question the Coopers appeared to be the cars to have on the twisting, climbing, winding, diving, high-crowned and thoroughly claustrophobic street circuit through the little principality.

An interesting side note was that Monaco featured the first-ever major "Formula Junior" race as one of its Saturday curtain-raisers, and Hank said the little open-wheel single-seaters put on a heck of a show. The new class was the brainchild of longtime Italian motorsports nutcase Count Johnny Lurani, who thought it would be great to have an inexpensive Grand Prix "nursery class" based on ordinary, over-the-counter economy-sedan engines and drivelines. It sounded like a pretty good idea, and the cars that showed up for that first major race in Monaco—mostly Italian Stanguellinis powered by 1100cc Fiat engines—looked like lovingly dwarfed-down editions of Ferrari 246 Dinos or Maserati 250Fs. They really looked neat, and Hank said you could just imagine what went through the heads of their drivers as they skittered around the Casino Square and tried to out-brave each other into the hairpin, right in front of cheering grandstands. Hank thought Formula Junior was really going to catch on. Even over here in the states. He worried a little about how they were going to keep a lid on costs, though. You know how racers are whenever there's a checkered flag involved....

Of course Hank's report in *Car and Track* didn't come out until the August issue, and by then it was July back here in Passaic (and, no, I don't understand what magazine cover dates have to do with real time, either) and everybody in the old neighborhood was still jawing over their backyard fences and across porch stoops about how underdog Swede Ingemar "Hammer of Thor" Johansson had knocked out American champ Floyd Patterson to take the heavyweight crown on June 26th. And opinion was pretty mixed (at least in the old neighborhood, anyway) seeing as how Patterson was American and there hadn't been a non-American heavyweight champ for a quarter of a century. On the other hand, Johansson was white, and, well, like I said, opinion was mixed.

The other hot topic of conversation was Vice President Richard Nixon's visit to the American National Exhibition in Moscow escorted by none other than pig-faced Soviet Premier Nikita Khrushchev himself. It seems the two of them got into quite a lively and public little debate (hey, what do you expect when you point a bunch of cameras and microphones at two politicians?) about the relative merits of communism and capitalism. It went back and forth and back and forth, what with Nixon telling Khrushchev how nice it was that capitalism allowed everybody in the US who worked hard and lived right to have TVs and cars and telephones and even electric dishwashers and clothes dryers and maybe even air conditioning, and

Khrushchev volleying right back that Nixon—and Americans in general—"didn't know anything about communism except fear of it." He also explained as how Soviet communism, thanks to its superior planning and organization and management and fairness to everyone, would eventually pass America right on by. *"We will bury you!"* he told Nixon through a confident, gluttonous grin.

Personally, I couldn't see it. Anybody who's ever waited in line at a post office or social security center or even the place where you get your state driver's license can tell you that the government isn't maybe the best outfit you could think of to run damn near anything. Oh, they get the job done, all right. But they do it in their own plodding way and in their own sweet time, and if you're in a hurry or want some damn answers, well, you can just go stand in that line over there. The long one. I guess the point is that you get a certain kind of attitude about things when you know you have to both please your customers *and* make a profit if you want to stay in business under the capitalist system. And when you take those things away, all you have left is a day of shuffling papers and clock watching shoved between a kazillion other days of shuffling papers and clock watching—kind of like my old man's union buddies, you know?—with two weeks off every 50, decent benefits and a nice, cushy pension at the end. I always thought it took a lot of the "got to" out of things, you know?

"Y'know what Churchill said about communism, don'cha?" Big Ed snorted around his cigar.

I shook my head.

"Lemme see if I can remember it right." His eyes rolled halfway up into his head and his voice sounded like it was coming from a half-block away. *"The bad shit in capitalism is the unequal sharing of blessings, while the bad shit in communism is the equal sharing of misery."*

I had the feeling Big Ed didn't have it quite exactly right, but there was no doubt in my mind he had the gist of it.

Speaking of capitalism, things were still going pretty good for us in the VW business. While most of the American car dealers were going through the summer doldrums and wondering how much old inventory they were going to get stuck with and have to deal the shit out of when the new-model changeovers came in September, we were cruising right along regardless of season because VW never changed very much from year to year. And while that might seem like it ought to be a negative, VW's ad guys had turned it into the biggest positive imaginable. They even made fun of Detroit's big yearly model changeovers, and our VW customers just ate it up. So we did pretty good in the summertime. Particularly with the sunroof cars. Although both Big Ed and me were a little curious—not to say exactly nervous—about the new small cars we were hearing rumors about from the big Detroit manufacturers. It hadn't been exactly lost on the fat cats in the fancy, paneled boardrooms at GM and Ford and Chrysler and even Studebaker down in South

Bend that the European makes—and VW in particular—were selling one hell of a lot of cars. It didn't really make sense to them, of course. *Why the hell would anybody want to drive one of those little, bitty, cramped, hard-riding imported things when you could have something big and cushy and substantial and made right here in Detroit instead?* But the one thing no businessman can argue against is numbers, and both the fat cats at the top and their dealers out on Main Street figured they needed something to fight this foreign menace. And sooner rather than later would be just fine.

Studebaker in South Bend was the first one out of the box with their blunt, boxy-looking Lark (although Julie and me both thought it looked more like a pigeon…or maybe a turkey) but Big Ed and me went over to drive one just to see what Studebaker was up to. Professional interest, you know? To tell the truth, it wasn't half bad as something economical to carry four people and their luggage around. But we both thought it was kinda clunky and tinny and looked a little cheap inside. And the six-cylinder model we drove wasn't exactly what you could call "peppy." Wheezy would be more like it. Plus it sort of wallowed around corners with the outside front tire damn near folded under if you tried to push it a little bit hard. "It reminds me of a refrigerator," was the way Big Ed put it, and that pretty much summed it up.

Plus the stateside sportycar press wasn't particularly kind to Studebaker's new breed of American "economy car." Studebaker lent a Lark sedan and station wagon to *Sports Cars Illustrated* for their trip to Sebring that year—and no question the magazine scribes appreciated the way you could fold the Lark sedan's seats down into a bed if you needed to grab a little shuteye or, more likely, sleep one off—but that didn't stop them from giving Studebaker's new Lark a pretty thorough reaming. And I quote: *"We are quite convinced that the six especially is unsuited for heavy cross-country work as its 90-hp leaves it definitely in the poopy category when trying to overtake at 50-plus mph. No doubt about it, we've been spoiled by the horsepower race and we do not like having to plan our passing maneuvers so extensively."*

And these are the same exact writers who went ga-ga over our VWs and Renault's Dauphine (or pick just about any other imported car) when they first became available in this country, calling them "sensible" and "innovative" and "well engineered" in spite of the fact that, just like Studebaker's Lark, you had to make up your mind about passing on two-lane highways at least two weeks in advance. Mind you, I personally liked driving our VeeDubs a hell of a lot better than Studebaker's tubby new Lark. And I thought our cars were better built, too. But I felt kind of sorry for Studebaker on account of the way the sportycar magazines beat them up. Then again, what do you expect from a bunch of journalists? They claim to be "objective," but, based on some of the ones I've met over the years, they can be some of the most prejudiced, opinionated, egotistical and vindictive people on earth. Oh, sure, there are some honest, fair, wonderful ones (like Hank, for example), but a lot of the rest seem driven by this seething, arrogant bitterness towards the life they chose to pursue. Or, like Hank says: *"Hey, those who can't do, teach. And those that can't even teach, well…they write about it!"*

Speaking of the stateside foreign car business, who should pull up in front of our dealership right smack-dab in the middle of July but this jittery, hyperactive little guy wearing a mound of razor-cut hair, white leather shoes, Italian sunglasses and a pastel yellow sportcoat. He was driving a brand-new Caddy Eldorado Biarritz convertible. With dealer plates on it—lipstick red with a white interior, just like Big Ed's—and he waltzed in through the front door like he owned the damn place. He took a quick look around, made a beeline for Big Ed's office and started the conversation off by announcing that he wanted to buy us out. Just like *that!* Buy *our* blessed VW dealership, can you believe it?

Well, of course Big Ed told him it wasn't for sale, and the guy just smiled without taking off his sunglasses and said: "Not at *any* price?" He was one of those impatient, fast-talking hustler types you see a lot of here in Jersey.

Big Ed eyeballed him from head to toe, and then the wheeler/dealer in him took over and he asked without thinking: "What sort of number did you have in mind?"

"What would it take?" the guy shot right back.

Big Ed rubbed his chin. "You're the one who's so interested. Why don't you tell me what you've got in mind?" It was a classic case of what happens whenever two seasoned car-dealership pros start negotiating with each other. Each one knows that the first guy to name a price loses. Every time. It's inevitable. You name a price and the guy either jumps at it (which means you started off way too high) or he unclogs his nose at you and walks away (which means you're probably right in the old ballpark). But this time Big Ed had the high ground. After all, the guy with the big hair and the Italian sunglasses was the one who came sniffing around.

"What would you say if I were to offer you ten million dollars?" The guy finally asked, eyeballing Big Ed closely while he handed him a business card.

Big Ed never flinched. Even though ten million dollars was one *hell* of a lot of money back in 1959.

"I'd say get your checkbook," Big Ed answered evenly. "We'll take it."

The guy laughed. "Of course you would. Who wouldn't?"

Big Ed's eyes narrowed. "So then you weren't *really* offering us ten million dollars, right?"

"Of course I wasn't. Do I look like some kind of prize asshole to you?"

Big Ed looked at him like he hadn't quite made up his mind.

"See, I didn't actually *offer* you ten million dollars," the guy continued without skipping a beat. "I only asked what you would say."

Big Ed's nostrils flared a little and you could see a little color creeping up the back of his neck, but the guy with the shiny new Caddy out front sailed right along. "Let me tell you a little story," he said to Big Ed. "This schoolteacher saves up her money and goes on an ocean cruise, see…."

Big Ed nodded.

"And she's kind of a looker, but always dresses real plain for the kids in the school, see…."

Big Ed nodded again.

"But this time she figures, *hey, what the fuck,* and she buys herself a hot two-piece swimsuit. And it looks real good on her. *Real* good. She's got a nice shape, see…" the guy made motions with his hands like he was holding two basketballs, "…so she puts on the bathing suit and checks herself out in the mirror and she has to admit she's pretty pleased with what she sees. But she's afraid to come out of her stateroom, see? Afraid of what people might think. But eventually she finally says to herself, *hey, what the fuck,* and she goes out on the poop deck. And right there is this guy from Jersey with a big cigar and a big smile and a 10-carat pinky ring—a lot like you, I bet—and he takes one look at her and decides that she is quite a tasty little morsel indeed. But he can also see that she is really quite classy and refined and not exactly the kind of broad you can slip a 50 to and get your horn honked. So he starts chatting her up, and chatting her up some more, and finally gets around to asking if she'll go to bed with him."

Big Ed's eyebrows cinched up a notch.

"Well, she turns red and gets madder'n hell and really tells him off. *'What kind of girl do you think I am?'* she yells in his face. Well, the Jersey guy gets all apologetic and tells her to calm down and that he's very sorry but that she was just so damn striking and hot and beautiful and sexy that he just couldn't help himself. And now of course the schoolteacher broad is a little bit flattered—even though she's still plenty mad—but he keeps working on her and working on her and telling her how hot and beautiful and gorgeous and sophisticated she looks and eventually he gets her calmed down to where she's actually smiling at him. And that's when he asks her, *'You know, you're so beautiful and gorgeous and everything and I'm on this cruise all by myself and nobody here knows either one of us…tell me, would you consider going to bed with me for a million dollars?'"*

Now I'm listening in from over by the parts counter.

"Well, she kind of hems and haws and thinks it over and allows as how a million dollars is an awful lot of money, and finally she figures—*hey, what the fuck*—and she looks down at her feet and blushes a little and tells the Jersey guy that, yes, she would definitely go to bed with him for a million dollars."

I can't wait to see where this is going.

"So then the Jersey guy asks her if she'll hop into the sack with him for a quick 50 bucks. Well, of course she goes ballistic all over again. *'What kind of girl do you think I am?'* she yells at him. Well, the Jersey guy looks right back at her and says *'We've already established what kind of girl you are. Right now we're just haggling over the damn price….'"*

With that the guy grinned, turned on his heels and walked out the door, leaving Big Ed all alone in his office holding a translucent, creamy white vellum business card with just the name *'Harry Metropolis'* and a phone number printed on the front. Nothing else. But the guy said he'd be back. And he was….

Naturally neither Big Ed or me could make sense at first out of what the guy was talking about or what he really wanted, but we came to discover pretty quickly that Harry Metropolis was indeed a genuine player in the retail automobile business in the greater New York/New Jersey metropolitan area. And second-generation, at that. Turns out he already owned three VW stores in Jersey and was out to pick up as many more as he could lay his hands and wallet on. His dad owned four or five Chevy stores and a Buick store and two Caddy stores—all GM—and owning a fat fistful of car dealerships made a lot of sense when you thought about it. First off, if you owned more than one dealership you could achieve certain, ahem, "economies of scale" (as our guy at the bank called them) when it came to ordering everything from spark plugs to window signs to toilet paper for the crappers. It also gave you more leverage with the manufacturers and distributors when it came to getting cars or getting the right cars or better rates from the banks who wanted your floor plan business. Plus if you owned *all* the Chevy or Ford or Caddy or VW or whatever dealerships in one particular area (but continued to operate them under their original dealership names) you didn't have to worry about Joe Blow Motors over in the next 'burb cutting your price in order to make a fast deal.

That made the most sense of all.

VW dealerships were a hot item right then because they were good cars and the company was solid and well organized and the advertising was the cleverest in the whole blessed country. And it didn't hurt one bit that the French and British and Egyptians and Israelis were all still squabbling over the Suez Canal zone and so everybody was in a minor panic about the future price of oil and all the stuff you made out of oil.

Like gasoline, for example.

Not that Big Ed or me had any inclinations toward selling….

Chapter 34: Unlikely Winners

The Scarab Formula One project had been generating a hell of a lot of ink, bar chatter and enthusiasm all over America, but not much at all in the way of actual engine noise. In spite of all the glowing, hopeful prose, cutaway drawings and pictures of handsome engine blocks and shiny, beautifully machined driveline parts and sleek body panels and such in all the nutball American sportycar magazines, the engine was still very much in the Incomplete Pile of Pieces stage of development and the car to hold it wasn't all that much further along since you can't do much in the way of meaningful testing sitting in the driver's seat making engine noises with your mouth. And meanwhile the European racing season went on. And on....

At the Dutch Grand Prix at Zandvoort at the end of May, BRM finally—after 11 years of desperate trying and an awful lot of rude jokes and even ruder noises at their expense (and a lot of those from their own blessed British journalists!)—had the planets and stars come into perfect alignment and won a damn race. From pole position, no less. Bearded Swede Jo Bonnier was at the wheel on what Hank said surely must have been his best-ever day ever as a racing driver (although it no doubt helped that Stirling Moss spent the entire previous week with the team testing at Zandvoort to try and get the BRMs to behave a little better). But Hank said the win wasn't quite so easy as it looked on the result sheets. Ferrari showed up with an experimental "lightweight" car for Jean Behra (actually a smaller Formula Two chassis with a Grand Prix-sized motor shoehorned inside) while "Kansas City Flash" Masten Gregory shocked everyone by rocketing his third-string factory Cooper through to grab second behind Bonnier's BRM at the start and then snuck by to take the lead with what Eric Gibbon called "a fairly mad move" on the second lap! Needless to say, our buddy Hank was going properly nuts on the sidelines seeing an American driver leading a European Grand Prix, and it just served to underscore what he already knew about Masten Gregory: on days when he had that certain cool, calm and yet thoroughly frenzied look in his eyes, the "Kansas City Flash" could be as fast—or faster—than anyone. Although the negative side was that, like Behra, it seemed to come and go when it felt like it and he didn't have the control or command to switch it on at will like a Moss or a Fangio. But he was looking racy as hell at Zandvoort, and Hank and the few American servicemen in the crowd were screaming themselves silly every time he went by.

But Bonnier's BRM was still shadowing him and not looking in any great hurry to force his way by—after all, it was a two-hour race—and then it all went for nothing when Gregory's Cooper started jumping out of gear. And then he lost third gear entirely. He struggled on, but had to let Bonnier by and then his Cooper team leader, Jack Brabham. Brabham patiently nibbled away at Bonnier's lead and finally bluffed his way past on the 30th lap, but neither Bonnier or Brabham seemed willing to push it at that stage of the race. So they were running comfortably in fairly close company while Moss, who had a terrible start and then got bottled up behind Behra's lurid-handling "lightweight" Ferrari for 25 laps before finally sneaking past, closed on the leaders in the dark-Scottish-blue Walker Cooper. Moss caught Bonnier and Brabham from over a minute back—proving once again that he was one of those rare, otherworldly talents who could turn up the wick seemingly without effort—and passed them one after the other to take the lead. Bonnier even waved him past, which Hank said was hardly the sort of sporting, gentlemanly gesture you usually got to see in Formula One. Or not any more, anyway. But you've got to figure that if a guy catches you up from damn near a minute back (and especially when only half the race has been run) it's a pretty sure thing that he's going to get you sooner or later. Unless you put him off in the weeds, that is.

So Moss looked to be on his way to an easy, dominating win when a bearing broke in the Colotti gearbox and put him out with just 12 laps to go. Shades of Monaco! It was too bad for old Stirling, of course, but it allowed Bonnier to take an insanely popular first Grand Prix win for BRM—a win the team had been searching for and dreaming about for almost a dozen years!

Toly wound up a distant sixth, not far behind Behra in the "factory lightweight" Dino 246, and it was a pretty grim and stone-faced Ferrari team heading back to Maranello to pick up the *Testa Rossa* sportscars and head off again for the 1000-kilometer World Manufacturers' Championship race at the Nurburgring the following weekend. To be honest, the sportscar season had started out promisingly enough for Ferrari. Their only real competition at Sebring was a single Aston Martin, three Lister-Jaguars that didn't seem to have the power or stamina to run with the *Testa Rossas* for very long…and the weather. It rained like hell for three solid hours at Sebring—starting around half-distance—and by that time the Aston had long since expired and Moss (who was doing a one-off money drive for Brian Lister and looked to be the only real threat) had run out of gas on course. Then he accepted a ride back to the pits on the back of somebody's motor scooter to get a can of gas, and the officials decided that was "outside assistance" and disqualified the car on the spot. Hill and Gendebien were also out of it by that point with a busted diff in their Ferrari, and Cal and Toly both thought it stunk when Ferrari team manager Tavoni pulled Dan Gurney and Chuck Daigh out of the second-place *Testa Rossa* and stuck Hill and Gendebien in instead. Sure, those two were team regulars and had a lot more experience—especially in the rain—but it really didn't seem very fair to the two Californians. Especially when the car eventually went on to win and it was mostly Hill and Gendebien in the headlines and victory lane photographs and Daigh and Gurney getting mentioned somewhere or other about three or four paragraphs down. Not that I'm blaming Ferrari for that.

Well, maybe just a little….

Toly and Cal wound up a solid second overall after a mostly trouble-free run (they were leading handily at one point, but then wet electrics brought them into the pits twice with a misfire before the mechanics finally fixed it and Hank said the engine sounded pretty flat (for a Ferrari V-12, anyway) for the balance of the race. And then Cal had to take to the grass to avoid Fred Lieb's spinning Turner that was doing its best to avoid a spinning Ferrari GT in the hands of some rich asshole rent-a-driver who got it all wrong during the worst of the rainstorm. It cost Cal the better part of a lap to get the Ferrari restarted and turned back around in the thick muck at trackside.

Still, second place was pretty good behind the other factory *Testa Rossa,* and after Sebring most insiders figured Ferrari wasn't going to have much trouble picking themselves up a fourth World Manufacturers' Championship on the trot.

But all that started to unravel at the Targa Florio in Sicily on May 24th. Neither the Aston or Lister teams bothered to show up, and so Ferrari's only real opposition were the light, whippy little RSKs from Porsche. But the silver cars were at their best on the narrow, bumpy, twisty and tortuous 45-mile laps at the Targa Florio, and there were a lot of long faces in the Ferrari pits when the Porsches went quickest in practice (which was finally held with the roads closed for a change). Ferrari had switched up its driver pairings again since the old man figured it kept everybody on their toes, nose to the grindstone and eyes looking back over their shoulders, and Cal got the call to play rabbit for a change in a special *Testa Rossa* sporting a new, more-powerful engine with six huge double-throat Weber carburetors down the center of the vee. Hank said he did a heck of a job—particularly for a guy who'd only raced at the Targa once before—and let it rip from the moment they turned him loose from the starting line. He'd pulled out an eight-second lead on the time sheets by the end of that first, Banzai Charge lap around Sicily, but he was already in trouble with weakening shocks and sour noises coming out of the back end. In fact, it was all Cal could do to limp around and retire at the end of the second lap with a busted diff. Gendebien's *Testa Rossa* also suffered rear axle problems and retired, while Behra overcooked it a mite while trying a bit too hard and rolled his Ferrari into a farmer's field—the only soft, level stretch of roadside scenery for miles, by the way—and although he somehow managed to get it levered back onto its wheels and back to the pits (surely without any outside assistance from the local Sicilians, of course!) Toly took over and promptly hit a bridge abutment with it. Although he allowed as how it wasn't really steering all that well at the time....

In the end, Porsches finished a stunning 1-2-3-4 overall with a new RSK, an older 550 RS and two Carrera GTs, winning both the "Sports" and the "Grand Touring" categories in the process. It was pretty damn humiliating for Ferrari and a really unbelievable performance from Porsche. Hank said you got the feeling that it wouldn't be their last, either.

If that wasn't bad enough, a week later came the embarrassing, not-even-close Ferrari defeat in the Dutch Grand Prix at Zandvoort, followed a week later by the Nurburgring Thousand Ks on the *Nordschleife.* The irony was that Aston Martin—who, like Jaguar before them, really had their sights fixed solely on Le Mans—wasn't planning to attend, but finally caved in to Stirling Moss' begging and pleading and gave him a DBR1 and a small, skeleton crew to run it at the 'Ring. And Moss returned the favor by putting in one of his most incredible performances. He grabbed the lead early on and simply drove away from the whole Ferrari team, gaining over a minute on them in the first hour. At hour two he handed over to co-driver Jack Fairman, and poor Fairman got cut off by some idiot backmarker and wound up in a ditch. God only knows how he found the strength and leverage to do it, but Fairman single-handedly levered the car out, got it restarted and brought it around to the pits for a quick once-over, tires and gas. At which point Moss jumped back in—now over a minute behind the leading Ferraris—and, just like Fangio in the German Grand Prix on the same exact track two summers before—reeled the leading Ferraris in, passed them both and more or less drove off into the sunset. Hill and Gendebien finished a trying but dispirited second in their *Testa Rossa* and Toly and Cal were another 40 seconds behind in third. And each and every one of the Ferrari drivers was probably wondering just what the hell Stirling Moss was made of and whether he cast a shadow like ordinary men….

Le Mans came and went two weeks later, and it was another debacle for Ferrari's sportscar team with not one of the factory cars still running at the finish and Aston Martin scoring a stunning 1-2 finish with their DBR1s. But Hank said the Aston that really sealed the win never made it to quarter-distance. Crafty old John Wyer sent Stirling Moss out as Aston's rabbit in a special, lightweight car with a hopped-up and freer-running but not nearly so stout four-main-bearing engine under the hood. All the other Astons had the usual seven-main engines, which were hell for strong but didn't make as much power. Moss pushed as hard as he could, and naturally Jean Behra fought hard to match his pace, and meanwhile John Wyer held the other two Astons strictly in check while waiting to see how things would develop. Typically, the Ferrari drivers were running against each other as much as the opposition—particularly through the early stages—and doing their cars no good at all in the process. The engine in Moss' Aston finally broke after 70 laps of merciless thrashing, but by then the damage had been done. One after another, the Ferraris started running into mechanical problems, and the very last of them—the Hill/Gendebien car that had actually been leading by two laps at half-distance!—was pushed to the dead car park with four hours and ten minutes still to go….

Naturally we were all thrilled here in the states that failed Texas chicken-ranch operator Carroll Shelby co-drove the winning Aston Martin with Roy Salvadori, and I was personally just as pleased to see my old British buddy Tommy Edwards coming through to take second as co-driver of the other DBR1. Hank said it was a tremendously disciplined, well-planned and perfectly-executed performance by John Wyer and the Aston team, and actually put them right in the thick of a World Manufacturers' Championship scrap with Ferrari and Porsche with just one race—the Tourist Trophy in September at their home track at Goodwood—to go.

No question the guy who had all the other drivers talking to themselves was Stirling Moss. Except for maybe Brabham, who was tough and shrewd and crafty and rightly rated those things every bit as important as raw skill, and Jean Behra, who was a fighter by nature and believed he could run with anybody in equal cars. But Moss had everybody else pretty much rattled. I mean, you don't get into that game—or not at that level, anyway—without thinking you're awfully damn good. Maybe even "The Best" (whatever that means). So it can be a little disconcerting to have some bozo who puts his pants on one leg at a time just like you do proceed to prove time and time again that he's got a little something extra. And the emphasis here is on "little." But that's all it takes....

Speaking of Moss, whiskey heir Rob Walker had sportingly advised him to look elsewhere for a Formula One ride until they got the teething problems with the Colotti gearbox in the Cooper cleared up, and so Moss appeared in a strangely pea-soup-green privateer BRM fielded by a team called BRP (British Racing Partnership) for the next Grand Prix at Reims in France. Hank said Moss' father and business manager were two of the partners in the deal, and it looked to be a well-timed move seeing as how Reims was a fast, power track where the BRMs and the Ferraris seemed likely to finally have their way with the Coopers.

There was finally some small measure of redemption for Ferrari at Reims in the French Grand Prix, where it was sunny, hotter than blazes and everyone figured the more powerful, front-engined Grand Prix cars would finally have the advantage over the stubby little "bugs" from Cooper. And sure enough Brooks qualified on pole in his Ferrari, Phil Hill was third on the grid in his and Toly took fourth (right next to Moss in that pea-soup-green British Racing Partnership BRM) but damn if Jack Brabham didn't slide his "underpowered" little Cooper into second on the time sheets! The race itself turned into a battle with the track as much as the other cars what with the tar in the pavement melting under that broiling midsummer sun and the surface breaking up badly at the Thillois hairpin. Hank said he'd never seen so many spins, and several tires were cut and radiators punctured by flying rocks and stones. Tony Brooks led from flag-to-flag for Ferrari, Moss lost his clutch at the start but made a hell of a charge anyway, only to spin off at the hairpin and stall it, then collapse in exhaustion trying to get it push-started again in the sweltering heat. In the end Phil Hill took second and Toly finished fourth in their Dinos, while Brabham continued his amazing season by sneaking home third in the Cooper on what Hank, Eric Gibbon and everyone else in the pressroom reckoned to be "a Ferrari circuit."

But the other big news at Reims concerned a Ferrari driver who didn't even finish the blessed race. Jean Behra had got himself hired onto the Ferrari team at the beginning of the season with the understanding—at least in his mind, anyway—that he was going to be Number One driver. But of course that's not how old man Ferrari did things, since he was convinced he got the best out of his drivers—or designers or team managers or anybody else, for that matter—by pitting them against each other and constantly putting the old pressure on and stirring them up. And so there was already a lot of simmering animosity going on before the Ferrari team ever got to Reims. Then Brooks, Hill and Toly all out-qualified Behra (although not by much) and Behra immediately started complaining that his engine wasn't as good as theirs. And there might have been some truth to it, since Reims was a power track and no question he was braver than Dick Tracy and always ran well in front of his home-country crowd. But team manager Tavoni refused to change engines for him (he may not have even had one available) and that brought an even deeper frown and darker expression to the tough little Frenchman's face.

In the race, Behra put on a really heroic charge after a poor start, reeling in the leaders and setting two new lap records in the process before his engine broke a piston and expired in a cloud of smoke and steam on the 31st lap. Behra rolled silently into the pits and was instantly up Tavoni's nose, screaming that his engine was no good and that the blowup proved it. Tavoni—who was busy worrying about the other Ferraris in the race, one of which was actually leading for a change—screamed right back that the engine had broken because Behra had over-revved it. And that's when plucky little ex-prizefighter Jean Behra threw a solid right and pretty much laid Tavoni out in pit lane. As you can imagine, that's also about when Jean Behra's job as "Number One" driver at Ferrari likewise came to an end….

Meanwhile, back in Culver City, the Scarab Grand Prix car finally seemed to be making some visible progress. Oh, the engine was still far from complete, but the team decided to stick the leftover Offy they had laying around from the stillborn Le Mans sportscar project between the frame tubes and at least try and get in some meaningful testing miles. But of course everything on the car had been custom-tailored to the new Reventlow/Goossen engine, and so the Offy wouldn't exactly slip right in. The crew finally managed to beat and bend and pry and grease everything up enough for the engine to go in, and the plain metallic-blue open-wheeler rolled out into the sunshine of a vacant, eerily silent Riverside paddock for the very first time in the middle of July. Everyone was nervous, on edge and boiling with curiosity and expectation when the Offy barked to life and warmed up for a few minutes while Lance and Chuck argued about who was going to take the new car out for its first laps. From what Hank heard, they each wanted the other guy to do it.

Well, it's always hard to get a reading on an untried, untested and somewhat radical car when you take it out for the very first time. Especially when you're using a new kind of front brakes that nobody's ever tried before and running on a brand-new tire from Goodyear, who had never made tires for a Formula One car before. Even so, Lance and Chuck came to almost the same exact conclusions about the new car after only a few laps each: it handled like a piece of shit. The car lumbered through slow corners and was squirrelly as hell through the fast ones, and it was just icing on the cake when one of the Goodyear tire engineers came up with eyes as big as saucers and sputtered: *"Did you know your tires are actually SMOKING through the corners??!!"*

Not to mention that the brake pedal effort was impossibly high thanks to those brilliant-on-paper expanding tube front drums. Which, by the way, started overheating and fading by the end of the second lap. Oh, they kept plugging away at it most of the day, trying to find some kind of handle on the situation, but things didn't look very promising. In the end, Chuck's very best time on a fresh set of tires (and remember, this was with an engine half-a-liter bigger than the still-unfinished Goossen/RAI four-banger) was a scary and thoroughly discouraging 2:09. Chuck had gone five seconds a lap faster in the Chevy-powered Scarab sportscar at the pro race in October. And everybody and his brother knew that a competitive Grand Prix single-seater should be a bunch faster than any damn sportscar….

But the RAI crew didn't exactly have a corner on the frustration market. Fact is, there's always more than enough of that to go around in automobile racing. For example a nationwide transportation strike in Italy kept the whole blessed Ferrari team from attending the British Grand Prix at Aintree two weeks after Reims. Where Brabham (with a little help from a new-spec cylinder head from Coventry Climax) notched up a runaway victory for Cooper over Moss in that pea-soup-green British Racing Partnership BRM.

And then came the German Grand Prix which, thanks to some rather suspicious back-room meetings and political deal-making, had moved from the incomparable, 14-mile Nurburgring *Nordschleife* in the Eifel Mountains to the ugly, unloved and thoroughly old-fashioned Avus track in West Berlin. Originally built by Kaiser Wilhelm way back in 1912 and modified by Herr Hitler to showcase the power and speed of the monstrously fast, Reich-backed Mercedes-Benz and Auto Union grand prix cars of the late 1930s, it was really just two long, parallel straightaways with a big, steeply-banked turn at each end. But unlike other big, banked ovals both here in the states and over in Europe, the bankings at Avus were an incredibly steep 43 degrees and flat, not dished. It's hard to believe even now, but Lang's Mercedes won the 1937 German Grand Prix at an *average* speed of 162mph, and Bernd Rosemeyer's Auto Union set fastest lap at over 170! For a little comparison, Wilbur Shaw won the Indianapolis 500 that year at an average speed of 113.58 mph….

But those Avus bankings were paved with bricks, and although they had no doubt been perfectly and precisely *"ve must hav exzact alignment ov zees bricks"* German Flat when first built, time and weather and being on the losing end of two world wars had left the surface kind of rough, lumpy and uneven. Plus they'd shortened the track a bit and put a stupid, flat, doubled-back-on-itself first-gear hairpin at one end seeing as how the original layout went from what was now West Germany into what was now East Germany, and I'm sure I don't have to point out the kind of complications that created. Fact is, the Cold War and the desire to provide a little entertainment for the locals and focus a little world attention on something positive in West Berlin had a lot to do with moving the '59 German Grand Prix to Avus from the Nurburgring. And I guess those were some pretty good reasons. But the place was rough and dangerous and didn't require much in the way of genuine driver skill—like Hank said, all you could do was floor it and hang on—and none of the drivers or teams were especially happy about running there.

Moss was back in the Walker Cooper (with an upgraded gearbox and one of the new Coventry Climax cylinder heads like Brabham had in the Number One factory Cooper) and so another deal was made to put German ace Hans Herrmann in the pea-green British Racing Partnership BRM to give the locals something to cheer about. The organizers also decided to include a Formula Two class in order to somehow get a few silver Porsches on the grid, and Behra was one of them at the wheel of his own, central-seater Porsche RSK, but he never made the race. Several cars—and especially the low-slung Coopers and Lotuses—were bottoming out on the bankings, and Ferrari brought one car with a special, higher-output experimental engine. They gave it to Toly because it was new and untested, and damn if he didn't put it on pole, more than a second clear of everybody else! Toly told Hank he was pretty pleased with all the attention, but added wryly: *"I hold my foot to the floor so much better than all the others, don't I?"*

The Saturday feature at Avus was a sportscar race for under-1500cc cars (which, as Eric Gibbon put it, translated out of the native German as "Porsche Benefit") and everyone was nervous when the day dawned gloomy, dark and overcast. Then, about an hour before the start, it began to rain. Hank said it made the uneven brick bankings glisten like wet crocodile skin. But a big crowd came in spite of the weather—eager for something to lift their spirits and take their minds off being on the cannon-fodder front lines of the Cold War—and so the race had to go on. Come the second lap, one of the privateer Porsches got too high on the bankings, lost it on the slippery bricks and spun like a top down the following straightaway. It crashed into a cement wall, but the driver miraculously escaped unhurt. One lap later de Beaufort's Porsche also slipped high and shot right over the top of the banking! It bounced and slid down the steep dirt wall that supported the banking—somehow without turning over—and came to rest with a *"clunk"* in the parking lot below. De Beaufort looked around, surely surprised to be there and even more shocked to be in one piece, then fired the car back up, drove it around to the flat part of the circuit and rejoined the race with nothing worse to show for his adventure than a slightly crumpled nose on the front of his racecar. Although they did black-flag him a lap later.

At the front, Behra was chasing hard after the factory-entered Porsches in his own RSK and—once again maybe trying that little bit too hard—skittered up the end of the wet banking at terribly high speed and launched over the top. The car arced through the air, Behra came out like a rag doll and the tough, brave, colorful little Frenchman was killed instantly when his body broke nearly in half against a metal flagpole. Hank actually saw it, and he said it was one of those things you just never get out of your head. One of those horrible, troubling, terrifying images that is always waiting there in the dark on the inside of your eyelids—especially when you're overtired and fighting to get to sleep….

There were meetings that night between the drivers and team managers and even some talk of canceling the race—especially if it rained—but compromises were eventually hammered out that a yellow flag would be shown and no passing would be allowed in case of wet weather, and that the race would be run in two heats to give everyone a chance to look the cars over in between.

It was still wet and rainy come Sunday morning and a heavy gloom hung over the paddock, but thankfully the rain eased off and the track dried out before the race began. Toly used the extra power of the experimental engine in his Ferrari to rocket away first from the standing start, but fried his clutch in the process and soon found it slipping badly on upshifts—particularly into top gear—and by the second lap he had no choice but to pull in and retire. He told Hank behind his hand that he was just as happy to be out of it. *"This is not a good place,"* he whispered so Tavoni wouldn't hear it, *"not a good place at all."* Meanwhile Brabham also dropped out with clutch trouble and Moss pulled in with yet another broken Colotti transaxle after only two laps. That left it almost all-red at the front, what with the other three team Ferraris running in a tight pack and Masten Gregory once again forcing his way up among them by riding tight in the suction of their slipstream down the long, fast straightaways and then gaining back what he lost each time with later braking and better handling through the hairpin. Plus unbelievable bravery on the rough bankings, where his Cooper flitted and darted around alarmingly at tremendously high speed. The four cars were swapping positions constantly and none of them had any chance of breaking away, but the incredible "tow" from the three Ferraris was putting the tach needle on the little Cooper well past the engine's usual redline—in top gear, can you believe it?—and Gregory's motor finally blew in spectacular fashion on the 23rd lap. Eric Gibbon noted rather unkindly that the American driver was the first man to put a rod through the side of a Coventry Climax engine all season, and Hank said it was all he could do to keep from punching the sonofabitch square in the nose.

There were only nine cars still running by the start of the second heat, and that dropped to eight when Hans Herrmann in the pea-soup-green BRM suffered total brake failure heading into the hairpin on the fifth lap. The car blew through the barriers, launched, tumbled and somersaulted in spectacular fashion. Herrmann was spit out onto the hard concrete below but miraculously escaped with just bumps and bruises. Some nearby, right-place-at-the-right-time photographer caught an unbelievable shot of Herrmann sitting there on the pavement with the BRM tumbling near-vertical through the air above him, and of course Eric Gibbon bought it from the guy for quite a sum of money and then re-sold it to all the sensationalist tabloids for quite a bit more. And told everybody he'd taken it, too, of course. Even though he was half-passed-out in the pressroom at the time. He'd also gotten his hands on an absolutely horrific shot of Behra's fatal crash in his Porsche the day before, and that turned out to be quite a little moneymaker for Eric. In fact, it was one of those pictures that almost inevitably got trotted out anytime a mainstream journalist with nothing better to do wrote an outraged, frothing-at-the-mouth "thought piece" about the evils and irresponsibility of automobile racing. But to Eric, it was just more cash in the old till. "Besides," he told Hank coolly, "that sort of thing doesn't hurt racing. It just brings more bloody gapers and voyeurs through the turnstiles. And that's the name of the game, isn't it? Bums on seats…."

Anyhow, at the checker it was Ferraris 1-2-3 with Tony Brooks taking another smooth, calm and well-judged win, and Ferrari fans in Italy finally had something to cheer about. But it didn't last long, as the neat-handling and ever-faster Coopers qualified first, second, third and fourth on the grid for the Portuguese Grand Prix at Monsanto Park in Lisbon three weeks later. Moss was on pole in the dark-blue

Walker car with Brabham and Gregory next in the two factory cars and Trintignant in the second Walker Cooper in fourth. The front-engined cars were nowhere. Moss went on to win easily in terribly hot, humid conditions (the Colotti gearbox finally holding together for him) and Gregory got his best finish ever in second place after team leader Brabham got chopped by a backmarker, crashed through some hay-bales, hit a telephone pole and ricocheted back onto the track, flipping several times in the process. Brabham was thrown out and wound up lying on the track, seemingly unconscious, when teammate Gregory came around again and had to slam on the brakes and swerve mightily to miss him. The sound of screeching tires apparently woke Jack Brabham right up, and he scrambled hastily off the pavement on all fours, much to the relief of the crowd.

It was a hot summer back in New Jersey as well, and working in a shop is always a pain in hot weather. We'd put air conditioning in the showroom, of course, as a way to help lure people in, and it was amazing how many excuses I'd come up with to go in there and check something or other on really hot, humid days. *"Yer gettin' soft,"* Big Ed sneered at me (while sitting in his office which had, by the way, its own, private air conditioning unit besides the system for the showroom).

"Maybe I am," I admitted.

"I remember when you useta work all day at the Sinclair and then work all night over by your aunt's garage—no matter how hot it was!—just to go to the damn races."

I remembered that, too. But it seemed like an awfully long time ago. And, when I thought back, it didn't seem like it got anywhere near as hot back then.

"You remember that race at Floyd Bennett Field over in Brooklyn?" Big Ed asked. "Now *that* was hot."

"Yeah, it sure was," I had to agree. I remembered the steamy Friday night me and Julie went over to Coney Island after practice and took maybe the best Ferris wheel ride anybody ever had in their lives. And I also remembered that stifling hot trip back across the George Washington Bridge in Old Man Finzio's towtruck with Big Ed's dead Jaguar hanging on the back—Julie sitting beside me with her blouse open about four buttons on account of the heat and me stealing glances at it and watching the sweet little beads of sweat running down there until they disappeared behind the cotton—and of course that's precisely when Big Ed's banged-up Jag came off the tow hook and went careening through traffic, bouncing off the steel girders and concrete bridge supports before finally taking out that pharmacist from Hackensack's '51 Buick Roadmaster. Not to mention the DeSoto and Studebaker right behind him, which also got kind of involved.

"You really should've checked those safety chains," Big Ed chortled, as if he was reading my mind.

"How'd you know that's what I was thinking about?"

"It was all over your face."

"It's funny now," I shrugged. "But, boy, it sure wasn't funny at the time."

"That's 'cause you were worried about the inconvenience, pain and consequences, see," Big Ed explained. "You let the consequences evaporate away off damn near any disaster and you got funny. That's the way comedy works. Everybody knows that."

I hadn't really thought about it.

"Believe me," Big Ed continued, warming up to the subject, "all great comedy grows out of tragedy. Only you just need to survive whatever it is and let a little time pass before you get it."

As usual with Big Ed, there was a lot of truth in that.

"So," he said, unwrapping a fresh cigar, "what are we gonna do about this Harry Metropolis guy and his offer?"

"Did he call you again?"

Big Ed nodded. "A couple times."

"I dunno," I said, kind of uneasily. "Whadda *you* wanna do?"

Big Ed shrugged right back at me. "Offers like his don't come around every day," he allowed carefully.

"How much are we talking here?" I wanted to know.

"Well, that depends. I mean, we got the business, and we also got the VW franchise—that's worth plenty all on its own—and then we got the property. And we got the sportscar shop, too. So there's a lot of different ways it could go."

"But you've thought about it."

"Who wouldn't?"

I guess I'd thought about it, too. But I have to admit, it made me nervous. I mean, if you found yourself standing on top of the New Jersey Palisades and you suddenly realized you'd sprouted yourself a fine, feathery set of wings, would you have the guts to jump off? "So what have you got in mind?" I finally asked.

"Well, let's just say if we cashed all of our chips in, we're not just talking about Fuck You money here."

"We're not?"

"Nah," Big Ed said solemnly, shaking his head. "We're talking Fuck *Everybody* money!" Big Ed lit his cigar and took a long, thoughtful drag.

I couldn't understand how such amazing good fortune could make me feel all edgy and squirmy inside. "So you're thinking seriously about it?" I asked him.

"Let's just say I'm thinking about it," Big Ed mused between smoke rings. He gave me a shifty pair of eyeballs. "You should be, too."

"Maybe I should," I nodded without a hell of a lot of conviction.

"That brass ring only comes around once, y'know."

"Yeah," I agreed. "But if you grab at it and catch it, doesn't it yank you right off the damn Merry-Go-Round?"

As you can see, Big Ed and me had a lot to think over. And we figured a little road trip out of the city together would be a great way to do it. Away from the shop and the dealership and all the things you have to worry about and take care of and all the people you either have to look right in the eye or avoid looking right in the eye every single day. So we decided to leave the shop and the VW store in Steve and J.R. and Sylvester and Butch's hands and take ourselves a little Saturday trip up to Lime Rock to watch the USAC "Formula Libre" pro race there on August 29th. And we took the lipstick-red Caddy Eldorado Biarritz, too, on account of the air conditioning.

Maybe I *was* getting old….

You have to understand that the United States Auto Club had been dipping its toe in the sportycar waters a lot that summer, and they liked the no-holds-barred "Formula Libre" rules (which, if you want the truth of it, amounted to no rules at all!) because it pumped up the size of the grids and gave the writers and commentators something to yak about. Not to mention allowing some of the established oval-track teams and stars to take a crack at the sportycar crowd. And the purse money that went along with it, of course.

Still, everybody wandering through the paddock and sitting on picnic blankets on the hillside overlooking the Lime Rock esses thought the presence of a handful of undersized, oval-track midget racers on a sportycar course looked pretty damn ridiculous. Or at least it did until you took a look at the qualifying times, anyway. Rodger Ward (who had won the Indy 500 that year) was there with a really well-turned-out Meyer-Drake Offenhauser midget, and so were Tony Bettenhausen, Russ Klar, Bert Brooks, Duane Carter and our old oval-track buddy Sammy Speed. I didn't recognize him right at first because he was walking with a stick. And not very well, either. His left leg was all jerks and angles, and you could see he was leaning a lot of his weight into his cane. He gave me a wide, tight smile as soon as he saw me. "Hey," I said, sticking out my hand, "good t'see you! How y'doin'?"

He gave me a bony shake and nodded towards his cane. "You're lookin' at it." I felt it was maybe a little rude or impolite to ask, but I couldn't help myself.

"What happened?"

"Langhorne," he said, like that one word explained everything. And it kind of did.

"Bad?" I asked.

"Bad enough." He forced me another smile. "But I'll be all right. It's the left, and so that's good. And I'm drivin' again already," he looked down at his cane. "The sawbones says I'll be done with the prop rod here in a couple more months." Sammy aimed his eyes up into the sky and scanned it from east to west. "He says I'll be able to tell whenever rain's coming, too."

"Those weatherman guys on TV and radio can't do that."

"Yeah," Sammy laughed. "And they're getting' paid!"

I looked over at the midget he was driving. It was deep metallic red—almost a maroon—with engine-turned gold-leaf numbers and lettering and white pinstripe trim. It looked pretty damn sharp. But I didn't recognize any of the crew guys.

"They're local guys out of Pennsylvania," Sammy explained. To roundy-round guys on the tour, "local" meant anywhere within four or five states. Especially since Ike's new Interstate highway system went up. I couldn't help noticing that I didn't see Spud around anywhere.

"You see Spud anymore?" I had to ask.

A worn-down look passed through his eyes. "Not for a while," he admitted. "You know how that goes."

"Sure," I lied.

"I wanted him to come with me on that Kiekhaefer Chrysler deal," he continued, almost to himself. "But you know Spud. Didn't like workin' for anybody or havin' somebody else callin' the shots on the car. And they had a full crew anyway." Sammy licked his lips. "He didn't last but a week."

"So you don't ever see him anymore?"

"Oh, now and then. Now and then. I saw him at Indy this year. He was with Les Gonda's crew. But only for Memorial Day." He gave a little snort of a laugh. "Can't get away anymore. He's got himself a straight job...."

"Spud??!!"

Sammy nodded. "He's the maintenance man—pardon me, maintenance *engineer*—at some aircraft hose and fittings plant down in Texas."

I couldn't believe it.

"It's close to home," he explained. "And I guess there's something not so good going on with his wife's spine," Sammy gave me a helpless little shrug. "You know how it goes."

"Sure," I nodded.

"He says he likes it."

"I'm sure he does."

Sammy looked down at the ground. "You start runnin' out of gas if you do this shit long enough."

I had to agree.

Sammy sighed as his eyes made a slow, careful sweep of the green Berkshire hills around us. "But I sure as hell could use him on a day like today."

"Things not going real good?"

"Oh, they're going okay," he allowed, being careful to turn his back towards the guys with the dark-red midget so's they couldn't hear him. "But we're pumpin' a little oil and I'm not sure this bunch knows what it is or how to fix it. And I think we're maybe a tooth or two off on the gearing, too." He pulled in a little closer and continued in barely a whisper. "Spud was the best ever on these kinds a'deals. He had that little extra sense about what we needed and what we hadda do. It was like he just *knew,* y'know?" Sammy shook his head. "I don't know what the heck that is, but if you could bottle it up and sell it, you'd make yourself a million dollars."

I pulled in a little closer and nodded towards the dark-red midget. "But is the *car* any good?"

"Sure," Sammy allowed. "Hell, they're *all* good. You just gotta catch 'em when they've got good people around 'em, that's all." He shot me a wink that almost clattered. "That's the tricky part, see?"

The three guys around the car headed off for cokes and burgers, so we wandered over for a little closer look. There wasn't a whole lot to an oval-track midget, but what there was looked simple and really solid. And sure a whole world different from any sportscar or formula car I ever saw. You sat bolt upright in a midget with your eyeballs about belt-high and the big, four-spoke steering wheel canted forward at the top like a bus and right in your chest so's you could get some shoulder muscle into the steering. Your elbows pretty much flapped in the breeze on either side, you had one leg folded up on each side of the bell housing and the damn driveshaft ran through a tube right under the crack in your ass. "Say, what happens if the driveshaft breaks?" I had to ask.

"As a rule, they don't."

"But what if one did?"

"Well, if it didn't beat you to death on the spot, you'd still be looking for a new line of work. Singing soprano in a boys' choir, most likely...."

George Constantine's Aston Martin started up right across the way from us. I'd never thought of an Aston Martin as big before, but it looked damn near twice the size of Sammy's midget. "You really think one of these things can run with the sportscars?" I had to ask.

"Hey, a race car is a race car," Sammy grinned. "And this place is a lot different from Sebring or Road America. It *races* like an oval, see? There's really no place for the big guns to use their top end." He patted the little midget on its rollbar. "I think we're definitely gonna surprise us a few tweed caps here today. Yes, sir," he nodded, "just see if we don't."

Well, I knew better than to doubt Sammy's words. But it still seemed so damn *unlikely.* And Big Ed felt the same way. I mean, here on the road-racer side you had George Constantine—who'd just about *owned* Lime Rock that summer in Elisha Walker's Aston Martin DBR2—plus John Fitch in a brand-new Cooper Monaco and Lance Reventlow getting some "practicing for Europe" laps in behind the wheel of his Formula Two Cooper and Pedro Rodriguez in a Maserati 300S and Denise McCluggage in a Porsche RS and my personal pick, Chuck Daigh, driving a white-with-blue-trim Maserati 250F Grand Prix car for a brand new team called Camoradi USA. "Camoradi" was short for "CAsner MOtor RAcing DIvision" (although it was never exactly clear what it was a division of or if it was long or short division) seeing as how the team was run by this hotshot driver/promoter/the-hand-is-quicker-than-the-eye type named Lloyd "Lucky" Casner. Like Lance Reventlow, Lucky Casner had dreams of fielding—and winning with!—an all-American team in Europe. But while young Lance could do it by simply following his whims and signing the checks, Lucky Casner had to do it with quick thinking, fast talking, all kinds of promises to all kinds of people and not a little smoke and mirrors. But you had to hand it to him. Not only did he get his hands on the 250F and whatever money he needed to run it, but he already had another deal cooking to become Maserati's more-or-less factory team in the World Manufacturers' Championship for the following year. And that was pretty impressive stuff.

But even though the Camoradi paintwork was fresh and neat at Lime Rock, the 250F Maserati underneath it was old and tired indeed, and Chuck Daigh struggled a bit to get it up to third qualifying spot on a track it wasn't particularly suited for.

And that he'd never seen before in his life, come to that. I thought he did one heck of a job, but Chuck didn't look particularly pleased. Then again, he never did. George Constantine's Aston Martin qualified second, just ahead of him, and you could hear the jaws dropping open all over the paddock as word quickly spread that Rodger Ward had put the #24 Offy midget on the pole for the first heat, almost a full second clear of Constantine!

Like a lot of folks, Big Ed and me went back for another look at that car (only now you could hardly see it for the crowd gathered around), and I kind of forced myself to see it with fresh eyes and try to understand what made it work so damn well here at Lime Rock. I mean, it was an 11-year-old oval-track racer with just a 1700cc engine, solid axles front and back and little bitty wheels and tires with even smaller brakes inside. But it didn't weigh much—maybe two-thirds of what Constantine's Aston weighed, if that—and it ran on alcohol fuel, which is always good for a few extra ponies. Plus Ward's crew had fitted it with special cams for Lime Rock and jacked around with the torsion bars to make it handle a little better on a road course. Whatever they did really worked, because Ward was past Daigh in the Maserati and all over Constantine in the Aston Martin (and nosing around for a way by!) for the entire first heat. And what a sound and smell it made! That little Meyer-Drake Offy just *screamed* down the whole length of the front straight—all in one gear!—and then it backfired like cannon shots and blew bluish-yellow flames out the tip of the exhaust when he backed off for Big Bend. And then, after it was gone, you'd get that alcohol and bean oil smell up your nostrils that made all the hairs inside kind of swoon.

You couldn't miss that none of the other midgets were running anywhere near as well as Rodger Ward's #24, and Sammy's in particular was sounding a little fluffy and leaving a bluish-white trail of oilsmoke all the way down the pit straight. "We got a busted ring, I think," Sammy explained forlornly between heats. "I'll try it in the next one, but if the engine doesn't clean itself up, we're gonna park it." He rolled his hands up. "There's no point blowin' it up…."

Meanwhile the crew was flailing away feverishly on Rodger Ward's car, trying to get the rear axle ratio changed in time for the second heat. And that was all he needed. Ward squirted into the lead at Turn One and looked about ready to run away with it. But Constantine kept the pressure on and Ward had a little bobble in the esses and went clear onto the grass—right in front of us!—but damn if he didn't keep his foot planted (hell, he'd done about half his racing on dirt!) and got back on right behind the big Aston. They stayed that way until about half-distance—no question the Aston could go deeper into the prime overtaking spot at the end of the front straightaway thanks to those big disc brakes—but finally Ward found a way past in the esses and it was all over. He pulled out a little distance and then just kind of sat there, a comfy three seconds ahead, until the checker fluttered down.

As you can imagine, the final, 60-lap feature heat had everybody's attention. By this point, Chuck Daigh had figured out the 250F and the track a little better, and both he and Constantine got ahead of Ward's midget in the early going. Then Daigh swept past Constantine to take the lead, while Ward just kind of sat there in third, biding his time, saving his brakes and tires and waiting to see how things developed. Smart guy. Constantine fought back with the Aston and re-passed Daigh's Maserati, but then the rear wheel started wobbling and Constantine had to come into the pits and retire with stub axle failure. Too bad, really, since he'd run one heck of a race.

That left Chuck Daigh in the "Camoradi USA" Maserati in the lead. But not by much. He and Ward had lapped damn near everybody by that point. I was also keeping an eye on our Bahamas friend Denise McCluggage, who was running well up in seventh place in her little Porsche and doing a really nice job against a field full of men. But then a flying stone hit Denise right in the goggles—shattering the left-hand lens completely!—and that dropped her back a few spots on account of she couldn't see. I thought she was one heck of a tough, smart and ballsy driver, no lie.

With 10 laps to go, Rodger Ward's midget made its move, and there just wasn't much of anything Chuck and that big, bulky Maserati could do to stave him off. And once the midget got in front, it was all over but the shouting. In fact, the only interesting battle left on the track was a ding-dong dice between local ace and Lime Rock track director John Fitch's new Cooper Monaco and 18-year-old Pedro Rodriguez' Maserati 300S. Fitch caught Rodriguez and it went back and forth a few times before Fitch sneaked by under braking into Big Bend with just a couple laps to go. But young Pedro came right back in the esses, absolutely *hurling* his Maserati underneath Fitch's Cooper and giving John Fitch a pretty clear-cut choice between taking to the grass and two smashed racecars. Always the gentleman (and particularly when left no choice about it!), John picked the grass, and wound up fourth behind Ward, Daigh and Rodriguez at the checkered flag.

Like a lot of sportycar people who were at Lime Rock that Saturday, Big Ed and me were pretty damn stunned. All the way back to Passaic, in fact. "I don't believe what I just saw," he kept muttering every now and then.

"Hey, a race car is a race car is a race car," I mumbled right back, kind of parroting what Sammy Speed had told me.

Come to think about it, we didn't talk about Harry Metropolis or his interest in our VW dealership the whole blessed trip....

Chapter 35: 'Tis the Season

Everybody associated with Lance Reventlow's Formula One project was on hand with sweaty palms, chewed fingernails and expectantly-raised eyebrows for the first bench test of the new, desmodromic-valve Reventlow/Goossen four-banger in the dyno room of Traco Engineering. Even though testing with the Offy-engined car at Riverside had gone from disappointing to discouraging to depressing without any of the usual flashes of New Car Elation along the way. Oh, sure, progress was being made. Lance had finally caved in and agreed to switch to British Girling disc brakes after it became pretty obvious—in spite of everything the team tried—that those expanding-hose, aircraft-style drum front brakes and the water-cooled, single-disc rear weren't working worth a shit. Pedal effort was high, feel was iffy and, more than anything, they didn't stop the damn car. Or at least not once they got a little heat in them. Or a lot of heat, which was more often the case. And the switch to Girling discs created a whole new slew of problems seeing as how the left-side halfshaft was already so short and ran at such steep angles at the end of its motion that there was no way you could sneak a normal inboard or outboard disc brake in on that side without a major overhaul of the whole damn transaxle and rear suspension. Which maybe wasn't such a bad idea anyway, since the Offy-powered test car still handled like a roller skate with a hinge in the middle….

So the crew bit the bullet, scrapped the radical brakes, filed it under "Jesus, we'll never try *this* shit again," ordered a few sets of Girlings from England and set about figuring just how the hell they were going to fit them on the damn car. In the end, Chuck Daigh took out a hacksaw and a grinding wheel and literally cut the whole blessed back end of the frame off—just chopped it right off!—while the pencil pushers at the drafting table and the casting and machining sub-contractors worried over how they were going to move the transmission guts up from the rear axle to behind the engine in order to free up a little space back there. This also gave everybody a chance to do a little rethink on the rear suspension layout and geometry, which certainly couldn't hurt.

And meanwhile the clock was ticking….

You have to understand something else here. Although it's easy to get a feel (like all the nutball sportycar magazines surely did) for the grand purpose, hopeful promise and crusading, All-American Mission of the Scarab Formula One project, you also have to realize it represented the base, beans-on-the-table/milk-in-the-fridge/gas-in-the-gas-tank livelihoods of a whole *bunch* of people. People who very likely couldn't find other jobs that paid nearly as well or gave them the opportunity to work on anything they loved nearly so much. And right at the bottom, feeding and watering the Scarab project with his mommy's seemingly endless supply of money was this handsome, unpredictable, moody, impatient, arrogant—and surely a bit discouraged by now—check-after-check-writing 23-year-old given to elaborate practical jokes and occasional, red-faced temper tantrums. So you can bet all the guys drawing and cashing those RAI checks every week were hoping desperately that something good might start happening before the kid got disgusted or lost interest or just said *"screw it, this'll never work"* and walked away.

So you can imagine the nail-biting electricity hanging in the air of the dyno room at Traco Engineering that day. Everyone had to admit the new engine surely looked the part. It was handsome as all getout to anybody who appreciated fine machinery, laying over flat on its side with four Hilborn injector trumpets pointed up towards the sky and a set of aircraft-style exhaust gas temperature analyzer wires running out of the exhaust header tubes where they came out of the cylinder head. There were bottles of Ernesto Julio's none-too-fabulous *Fairpeiper* champagne on ice in the cooler as they turned the engine slowly over by hand with the plugs out and a big wrench on the front crankshaft nut to bleed the fuel and oil lines and make sure everything moved and meshed properly. Nervous glances all around. So far so good. Then they screwed the plugs in, hooked up the plug wires and starter leads and hit the button…*contact!*

Nothing.

More nervous glances.

Jim Travers and Frank Coons looked all the connections over, scratched their heads a bit and decided things were maybe a little stiff yet or perhaps they'd gone a little weak on the starter motor capacity. So they jump-wired a second battery on, sending 24 volts juicing through the starter motor, and now the engine started to spin. *CONTACT!*

The engine whirred, spat, sputtered, snapped back once or twice and roared to life! And it was a hard, mean and thoroughly marvelous blare of a sound! Almost loud enough to drown out the sighs of relief and the *"POP!"* of corks ricocheting off those cold, frosty bottles of *Fairpeiper* champagne.

And that's about when one of those desmodromic exhaust valves slammed hard into its seat, shattered into pieces thanks to negative clearance once everything got a little heat in it and all the bits tinkled out into the exhaust manifold tubing. Jim Travers' hand went to the control panel like a striking rattlesnake and switched off before any more damage was done, and after that the room fell suddenly, terribly silent. So silent that the fizz off the champagne bottles sounded like surf rolling in….

While the Scarab Grand Prix project foundered through its problems, setbacks, gee-whizzes and disappointments in Culver City, Hank said there was just as much avoiding of eyes and walking on tiptoes going on over at the Ferrari race shops in Maranello. After thoroughly dominating the 1958 World Manufacturers' Championship and having the late Mike Hawthorn win the Grand Prix World Driving Championship for Ferrari on top of it, the bottom had inexplicably fallen out just 12 months later. The sportscar team had suffered humiliating defeats to Aston Martin at Le Mans and the Nurburgring and an even more embarrassing humbling by the little 1500cc Porsches right off the toe of the Italian boot at the *Targa Florio* in Sicily. But their 1-2 finish at Sebring early in the year and second and third behind Moss' Aston at the 'Ring actually left them somewhat unbeliev-ably still leading the World Manufacturers' Championship chase with 18 points going into the final, six-hour round at Goodwood on September 5th. But Aston Martin was only two points behind with 16, and they'd always done well at the Goodwood Tourist Trophy. Hell, Astons had finished 1-2-3 there the year before (although Ferrari didn't bother to show because the championship was already won and there was no reason to risk finishing second to anyone). Not to mention that the offered bag of starting money perhaps looked a wee bit light to old man Ferrari's eyes.

And Porsche could be a real threat at Goodwood, too, even with their little 1500cc engines. Goodwood was a short circuit—just 2.4 miles around—built out of a World War II airbase on the estate of the Duke of Richmond in Sussex. But it was totally different from the point-and-squirt long straights, tight corners and loads of runoff room Cal was used to from the airport tracks here in the states. "Goodwood is like one continuous slide," he told me later through an appreciative smile. "And you're going really *fast,* too..." He shook his head and curled his lip under. "It'll get your attention, all right."

So a car needed handling and balance maybe even more than sheer horsepower at Goodwood, and that put the Porsches in with a definite shot. After all, they were just one point behind Aston in the championship chase with 15. Plus they got great fuel mileage—they'd probably only need two pit stops to Ferrari and Aston Martin's three—and they figured to be quite a bit easier on tires than the big cars. But the surface was abrasive as hell at Goodwood, and so even the Porsches would have to change tires at least once. And while the Ferraris and Aston Martins had knockoff wire wheels, the Porsches would have to struggle with their bolt-ons. And five bolts per wheel, at that....

Even though Ferrari was reigning champion, most of the smart money and pre-race chatter favored Aston Martin. After all, this was pretty much their home track, they'd won the year before, they were acknowledged to have better handling than the Ferraris and more raw speed than the Porsches and, maybe even more than anything, they had Stirling Moss as their lead driver. By the end of 1959, Moss was reckoned by just about everyone as the best damn racing driver in the world—and by no small margin, either—and he had tons of laps around Goodwood. So he knew every inch, edge, divot, dip, dimple and pavement ripple damn near blindfolded. Not to mention that Aston had crafty old John Wyer as team manager, and damn if he didn't pull another, absolutely stunning Secret Weapon out of his bag of tricks towards the end of final practice.

Like everyone else, Wyer knew that Goodwood's abrasive surface was going to eat up tires—and especially the soft compound tires that made the cars go the quickest—and so lightning fast pit stops and tire changes would be absolutely critical. So he borrowed a longtime Indy 500 practice and quietly fitted the three Aston team cars with air jacks hidden underneath the bodywork. But he didn't show his hand until right near the end of final practice, when it was too late for Ferrari or Porsche to do anything about it. Our buddy Tommy Edwards could hardly even retell the story afterwards because he was laughing so damn hard: *"There were only about 15 minutes left to go,"* he told Hank, tears brimming up in his eyes, *"and I'm out on the circuit just pounding around doing a mileage check and bedding in some brake pads and tires. And John shows me the "IN" sign and so I come in and slide to a stop with all four locked up solid like we're practicing a super-quick pit stop—which we are—and of course John's got all the tires and hammers laid out and the brake pad trays, too, in case we need those. But no bloody jacks, right? To tell the truth, I don't think Mister Tavoni over in the Ferrari pits even noticed. Or not at first, anyway. But he sure as hell took notice when one of our blokes ran out and attached an air hose to this fitting we had hidden away in the cockpit. All of a sudden the car bloody jumps off the ground—WHOOSH!—and the guys bang on the wheel nuts and stick on the fresh set of tires and then the bloke pulls the hose off and—WHOOSH!—the car flops back down again and I've already got the rear wheels spinning so we go rocketing out of the pits on two bloody black streaks of rubber—right under Tavoni's nose, in fact!—in less than half a minute!"* He shook his head and dabbed at his eyes. *"Oh, Christ, if you could've only seen the look on his face!"* Tommy choked. *"It turned white as library paste! But his ears were the same bloody color as his cars...."*

Hank allowed as how the psychological edge was maybe as important as the actual time Aston saved with the air jacks, and that the calm, careful choreography, drill-team precision and meticulous, No Wasted Motion efficiency of the Aston crew had as much—or more—to do with their lightning pit stops than the trick air jacks. But whatever it was, it worked, and Hank said you could tell the whole Ferrari team was looking at themselves as underdogs before the race even started. And that wasn't exactly a pleasant or familiar sort of feeling for the previous year's World Manufacturers' Championship sportscar team from Maranello.

But there was plenty of drama yet in store. Moss was naturally first to scamper across the track, vault into his car and fishtail away on the Le Mans-style start. Hank said he practiced that regularly, but there was the usual grumbling and snorting in the press enclosure—especially from the Italian scribes!—that Moss might have once again left the blocks a wee bit early. Like while the starter was still just *thinking* about dropping the blessed flag, you know? But of course once he bolted so did everybody else—albeit a step or two behind—and in any case you're not going to win a six-hour race in the first few hundred yards. Although, as Tommy Edwards was always quick to point out, there's usually quite a traffic jam with a lot of barging, banging, pushing, shoving, wheel-spinning slides, closing of holes and madcap jostling for position going in the middle of the pack during your average Le Mans start, and by far the best and safest place to be in that sort of situation is well in front of it.

Moss' Aston Martin had a clear lead by the end of the first lap with his teammate Shelby, Graham Hill in the surprisingly quick Lotus 15 and, as Hank put it, "the whole blessed Ferrari team" chasing after him. But losing ground every lap as Moss put on one of his usual, professional, icy-calm displays of superior driving. It was something to watch all right, and surely took a bit of the starch out of the guys chasing after him. Moss continued to build his lead every lap and, to put it bluntly, nobody could touch him.

Not quite an hour and a half later Moss brought the leading Aston DBR1 in for fuel, tires and a driver change (to fellow Brit and experienced Goodwood ace Roy Salvadori) and he'd built enough of a lead that they were still in first when Salvadori steamed out of the pits with four fresh Dunlops and a full tank of gas just 28 seconds later. Most of the other cars had yet to make their pit stops! It looked like pretty much a laugher at that point, but there was drama going on behind seeing as how if Aston won and Ferrari finished second, they'd wind up exactly tied on total points and have to more or less share the manufacturers' championship. And nobody but nobody likes a tie....

As you can imagine, damn near the entire motorsports press corps was gathered around the Aston pits at the three-hour mark when Salvadori streaked in for fuel, tires and to hand the leading car back over to Moss again. But I guess the fuel nozzle somehow missed the hole because the car was still moving and gas gushed out everywhere just as Salvadori switched off—sending a small charge of raw fuel cycling through the engine and into the hot exhaust pipe. It ignited with a *BANG!* in what should have been just a loud but harmless backfire. Only it wasn't. In half an instant, the car—and Roy Salvadori—were engulfed in flames! Salvadori bailed out over the side and rolled furiously on the pavement to put his coveralls out while fire marshals and the Aston team mustered to help him and fight the blaze. Hank said it was one hell of a fire, and got even worse when the wooden supports for the overhead refueling rig burnt through and a 55-gallon drum of racing fuel came crashing down onto the pit apron and burst open like an incendiary bomb, sending a raging, black-orange fireball spewing outward and upward in all directions! Hank said it was only pure, dumb luck and a favoring wind that kept the entire Goodwood pits—which were made entirely of wood and loaded from one end to the other with high-pressure refueling rigs!—from erupting like a bombed oil refinery!

People were scrambling in all directions—particularly the motorsports scribes and race-day hangers-on, according to Hank—but the fire marshals and the Aston Martin crewmen fought back quickly and bravely with hand-held extinguishers and a fire hose, surrounding the fire, cutting it off and, finally, smothering it out under a wet, frothy blanket of extinguisher foam and water. But the lead Aston was far too badly burned to continue and the Aston Martin pits were nothing but a charred, drenched, foam-covered mess. Things sure didn't look too good for the home team. Or at least not until you looked up towards the end of the three devastated Aston pit stalls, where John Wyer and his timekeepers were still very much focused on the race and keeping track of their remaining cars. Then Aston Martin privateer Graham Whitehead from the next pit over sportingly called his own car in and retired it so the Aston factory team could have the use of his pit stall, and as soon as everything was scrambled into place, John Wyer brought Tommy Edwards in for fuel and fresh tires and to hand his car over to Moss....

Hank thought the entire thing was a pretty damn impressive display of British spirit, poise, sportsmanship and coolness under pressure, and he said you had to take your hat off to the whole bunch of them.

By the time Moss got back out in the car Tommy had been co-driving with Jack Fairman, it was down in third place behind Bonnier's Porsche and the Ferrari Toly and Cal were sharing. The team-leading Hill/Gendebien Ferrari had retired early on with a broken valve spring—or that was the official story, anyway, even though there was a suspiciously thick pool of oil down on the floorboards—and Hank thought the Ferrari pits might have been showing Toly slower times than he was actually doing in order to spur him on a bit. They'd done that sort of thing before.

A few laps later there was another chunk of drama when "Kansas City Flash" Masten Gregory—who was sharing Ecurie Ecosse's promising but problematic new Tojeiro-Jaguar with some hot young Scottish newcomer named Jimmy Clark—ran completely out of brakes heading into Woodcote corner. Typical of Gregory (and no one else, that's for sure!) he sized up the situation, decided that a head-on, probably fatal crash into an earthen embankment was inevitable, *stood up in the blessed seat and bailed out of the car just a fraction of a second before impact! WOW!* Hank said he went sailing clear over the top of the embankment and rolled and tumbled down the opposite side, banging and bruising himself up pretty badly. But that was about the extent of his injuries, and it sure as hell beat the alternative. You had to wonder what went on inside Masten Gregory's head that made him able to act so immediately, so bravely and so decisively in such a dire situation. Tommy Edwards allowed as how he thought a big part of it was that you could look into one of Masten's ears and see a little light coming through from the other side.

Meanwhile, up at the front, Stirling Moss only needed a little over half an hour to regain the lead. He was just *so* fast and smooth. And after that, he simply drove on away from everybody else and went on to win with ease. By over a lap, in fact. But there was plenty of excitement going on behind him. After the last round of pit stops, Bonnier's Porsche was running in second and Cal's Ferrari was sitting third, just shy of 50 seconds behind with about an hour and a quarter still to go. It was all on the table at that point. If Cal could catch and pass the Porsche and claim second for Ferrari, they'd at least have a share of the World Championship. If he couldn't, then Aston would win it outright. It was that simple.

Well, Hank said that Cal put on one hell of a drive. He was new to Goodwood, but he'd had plenty of seat time by that point in the weekend and he knew the feel of the car and pretty much what he could get away with. And I'd always thought Cal was at his very best trying to come from behind when the odds were stacked against him. He pushed hard, and then he pushed even harder, throwing the Ferrari through the corners in slashing, slithering broadslides and running it 300 or even 400 rpm past the redline in every gear. He even set an outright lap record—even faster than Stirling Moss!—but he did it by running at a pace no car could ever hope to take over a full race distance.

Everyone's eyes were on their stopwatches, watching the gap to that second-place Porsche shrinking by two, three and even four seconds a lap! Tavoni was standing at the edge of the track, waving the *"GO!"* sign over his head on the pit board and screaming himself hoarse every time Cal stormed by. But Bonnier was responding, turning up the wick in the Porsche as far as he dared and setting a new under-2.0-liter lap record in the process, only two-and-a-half seconds off what Cal was doing in the Ferrari! Hank said it was so damn intense you could hardly stand it. Then, just to bleed off some of the frantic, manic helplessness of standing in the pits watching, Tavoni scribbled *"SLOW DOWN!"* on his pit board and flashed it at Bonnier's Porsche. Porsche team manager Von Hanstein saw it and retaliated by holding a *"SLOW DOWN!"* pit board out for Cal! Everyone in the Ferrari and Porsche pits got a pretty good laugh off of it, but all the while they were glued to their watches, scribbling down time differentials and counting the laps left on their fingers. It was going to be unbelievably, unbearably close....

But no cigar. Moss flashed across the line at 6 hours and 46.8 seconds to muffled cheers while everybody's eyes focused and all necks craned towards the last corner, Paddock Bend, waiting to see which car would come through first. And there it was—*silver!*—with the red car charging hard and all up on smoking tippy-toes under braking behind it, just half-a-carlength astern. But it wasn't enough. Cal wasn't going to get him. He'd run out of time.

Oh, if there'd only been another lap!

Just one more.

If only....

Still, it was a hell of a drive, and even in defeat Hank said you could tell that Tavoni—and all the rest of the Ferrari team, for that matter—were proud of Cal and impressed with what he'd done. Although pretty reserved about it since there was no victory celebration to go along with it. And no question old man Ferrari back in Maranello wasn't going to be particularly happy with the way things turned out.

In fact, that went without saying.

Things got even worse for the red cars a week later at Monza for the Italian Grand Prix. Not only was the race right in Ferrari's back yard and in front of all the crazily pro-Ferrari Italian fans and motorsports scribes, but it was also on the long, high-speed Monza racetrack where the Ferraris' power hopefully figured to overcome the little Coopers' handling and balance. But, in spite of a lot of behind-the-scenes lobbying from Ferrari, the organizers refused to use the circuit layout that included the high-speed "Monzanapolis" bankings at one end. Hank said the drivers all hated those high banks at Monza—they were rough and bumpy and dangerous and beat bloody hell out of the cars—but Ferrari figured to have the only car tough enough to take the fierce pounding, and old man Ferrari was never one to look away from a competitive edge, no matter how uncomfortable it made his drivers.

But horsepower advantage or not, qualifying ended with Moss on pole in that infuriatingly quick Walker Cooper. They were fresh from Moss' strong win in Portugal and chasing hard after Jack Brabham in the points race with just two rounds to go, while Brooks was still in with a shot for Ferrari, but really needed to do well here at Monza. So the team brought an extra car for Cal as kind of an unspoken reward for his fine—if unsuccessful—drive at Goodwood the previous weekend. It was Cal's first-ever Grand Prix and he was plenty juiced up about it, even if it didn't necessarily mean he'd made his way onto the Ferrari Formula One team as a regular. Tavoni and old man Ferrari figured quantity might prove equally as important as quality over a full race distance at Monza since cars were going to break—there was no question about that—and having more bullets in the old gun couldn't help but improve the odds.

Hank said you also got the notion that Toly was feeling a little pressure following Cal's furious and mistake-free drive at Goodwood, and he responded by blistering around Monza ahead of all the other Ferraris in qualifying. Fast enough to take second on the grid to Moss, in fact. But he was barely clear of Brabham in the factory Cooper, and Brooks, Hill and our boy Cal in the other three Ferraris weren't far behind. And there was another factor on everybody's mind after qualifying…*tires!* The combination of long, fast corners, soft rubber, high G-loadings and an abrasive surface was producing a lot of tire wear. Especially on the Ferraris. The Coopers seemed much better in that respect, and it surely caught eveyone's eye that BRM showed up with an experimental, rear-engined Grand Prix car of their own stuffed in the back of the transporter. It only ran in practice, but the new car certainly grabbed the attention of the gents at Ferrari, Lotus and Aston Martin, who were all still fooling around with their front-engined racecars.

Moss led away from the start while Brooks fried the clutch in his Ferrari coming off the line and was out on the spot. So much for Tony Brooks. But for a change Stirling didn't disappear off into the distance. Not at Monza, where horsepower and high-speed slipstreaming counted for so much. In fact, the Ferraris of Hill, Cal, and Toly all passed Moss like a rocketing red freight train before the first lap was over, and after that Moss seemed content to just sit there among or behind them, biding his time and letting them set the pace until, around half-distance, one by one the Ferraris started peeling off into the pits for fresh tires.

Moss just kept going.

Tavoni and the rest of the Ferrari team hoped that the Coopers would also need to pit for tires, but they seemed to stick better *and* get better tire wear than the Ferraris (even though they were both now on the same exact tires, although part of that was surely down to the lighter weight, better balance and handling advantages of the rear-engined Cooper chassis). So Moss cruised to an easy win, Phil Hill wound up a strong second, Brabham took third and Toly fourth, while Cal broke something in the back end doing a drag race-style launch after his pit stop in a reckless attempt to get out ahead of his Ferrari teammates. Tavoni didn't look very pleased about that, and Cal worried that his scowl might extend all the way back to old man Ferrari's private office in Maranello.

In any case, it was another bitter disappointment for Ferrari—and in front of the hometown fans, even worse!—and now the World Championship was down to a straight fight between points leader Brabham and the fast-closing Stirling Moss with Brooks hanging onto a slim outside chance going into the final Grand Prix of the season at Sebring in December....

To be honest, the handwriting about rear-engined racecars was already pretty much on the wall when the much-revised Scarab Formula One car tested at Riverside in October and November with its handsome Goossen/Reventlow four-banger finally in place. They'd fooled around with the clearances on the desmodromic valve gear to keep the exhaust valves from shattering against their seats once things got a little hot and the metal expanded, and now the engine was running with respectable reliability if not tremendous horsepower. In fact, it sounded a little flat, and Chuck Daigh wondered silently if the exhaust valves were truly closing all the way or if the engine guys had left in a teeny, tiny, fraction-of-a-fraction-of-a-thousandth clearance to keep the exhaust valves from breaking against their seats. If they did, it would bleed off tiny percentage points of the engine's compression and combustion efficiency and suffocate its power (which was still well short of the horsepower numbers quoted for the Coventry Climax engines in the Coopers and Lotuses—never mind the BRMs and Ferraris). But at least it ran.

The chassis was also improved, what with Girling disc brakes all around, revised suspension geometry, relocated springs and pivot points, anti-roll bars front and rear and the transmission next to the driver instead of way in back with the differential. And they were logging a *lot* of test miles, and that alone was pretty encouraging. So were the lap times, although there was really nothing meaningful to compare them to at Riverside. By mid-November, the Scarab Formula One car was lapping Riverside faster than the outright lap record (which Chuck had set with the Chevy-powered Scarab sportscar the previous fall). But at tracks where both types of cars ran in Europe, the Grand Prix cars were always much faster than the sportscars anyway, so it was hard to really know where they stood. And, although they wouldn't come right out and say it in so many words, neither Lance Reventlow or Chuck Daigh were particularly happy with the way the new Scarab open-wheeler handled—no matter what they did to it. The car went through corners all torqued into a twist like a dirt-track sprinter with the inside front wheel hiked up off the pavement and pawing the air. And it seemed to slide awfully easy rather than stick. Or that's what Cal said, anyway. He was out in California trying to see Gina—she was in the middle of shooting this black-and-white Billy Wilder comedy with Jack Lemmon and Fred MacMurray, and so she was busy most of the time—and Lance invited Cal out to Riverside one day when he didn't have anything better to do just to see what he thought of the car. And Cal was eager to do it, too, seeing as how Ferrari had kept him hanging on the fence about a Formula One drive for the upcoming season. "Back in the spring, I would've cut my arm off for a drive in the Scarab Grand Prix car," he told me over the phone that evening. Or should I say at 1:30 the next morning New Jersey time. "I was even starting to think I might have a chance at the third car after Bruce had his accident at Pomona and hung up his helmet."

"But it's no good?" I asked him.

I could feel him hunting around for words. I mean, no American race fan—driver or otherwise—wanted to write off the Scarab Grand Prix project. Especially before they'd even turned a wheel in anger. We all wanted to *believe,* you know? But the best Cal could say was that it was predictable rather than genuinely nasty and that the engine didn't feel anywhere near as powerful as the one in the Ferrari Grand Prix car he got to drive at Monza.

But of course you never really know where you are, what you've got or what you're up against until you run head-to-head against the competition, and all the American scribes and sportycar fans were hoping that would finally happen at Sebring for the first-ever United States Grand Prix on December 12th. But the Sebring organizers wouldn't offer the Scarabs any starting money like they did for the established European teams—I guess they figured young Lance already had plenty of that and would surely show up anyway for his first-ever home Grand Prix—but they didn't reckon on his stubbornness and unwillingness to be handed the short end of the stick and just take it. So, even though they were pretty much ready, the Formula One Scarabs didn't show up at Sebring, either.

What *did* show was another little Meyer-Drake Offy-powered midget from the Leader Card team out of Milwaukee with Indy 500 *(and* Lime Rock Formula Libre!) winner Rodger Ward behind the wheel. I guess they thought they could maybe repeat the unexpected success Rodger had with that other midget up in Connecticut a few months before. But Sebring wasn't Lime Rock—not hardly!—and the Formula One bunch were just a wee bit tougher company than the hodgepodge of machinery and drivers Rodger had beaten up at Lime Rock. Not to mention that the crew spent most of practice and qualifying trying to get the little 1.7-liter Meyer-Drake to run on Avgas rather than its usual diet of alcohol fuel, and the engine wasn't liking it much at all. In fact, it was all Rodger and the midget could do—in spite of the big, proud #1 painted on its nose—to scrape into the very last qualifying spot in the field, well over half a minute slower than Stirling Moss' pole-winning time in the Walker Cooper.

Horses for courses, you know?

There was a "compact sedan" race and a Formula Junior race as curtain-raisers for the Grand Prix, and Walt Hansgen won both of them for the Cunningham team. He drove a handsome little Fiat-powered Stanguellini in the Junior race and took an Alf Momo-prepared 3.4 Jaguar sedan to a dominating win in the "compact sedan" race, besting a *very* healthy sounding, V-8-powered Studebaker Lark (driven to second place by stock car ace Curtis Turner) plus a motley assortment of VWs, Renault Dauphines, two Volvos, a Valiant, a Saab and one of Chevy's new, rear-engined Corvairs. Which Hank said looked slow and pretty tail-happy on top of it.

Although he wrote an absolutely glowing report about the race for *Car and Track* magazine, Hank allowed privately that the first-ever United States Grand Prix played in front of a fairly unimpressive and underwhelmed crowd at Sebring—especially compared to European races like Monza and the Nurburgring—and that the race itself was more dull and quirky than anything else. Moss and Brooks both needed to win to have any shot at all at the championship, and even then Brabham could ice the title chase by finishing no worse than fourth.

As all the guys in the press corps and most of the crowd expected (except for a few displaced roundy-round diehards who were still cheering wildly for Rodger Ward), Moss did what he had to do, qualifying on pole in the #7 Rob Walker Cooper and taking off from the start like a scalded cat. But it only lasted five laps before he suffered yet another depressing failure of the Walker car's Colotti transaxle. He had no choice but to park it in the esses with the transmission locked in gear and no drive to the rear wheels. For an unbelievable fifth year in a row, the consensus-pick Best Damn Driver In The World watched his championship chances evaporate into thin air at the very end of the season. You could only imagine what must have been going on in his head as he took that long, slow, lonely walk back to the pits.

Tony Brooks wasn't doing much better. His Ferrari got balked at the first corner and Toly, running right behind and absolutely determined to stay up with the leaders, couldn't avoid banging into his teammate's car. It was a pretty hard shot, and Brooks wisely stopped in the pits at the end of the first lap to replace a bent rear wheel rim and have the car checked over. It cost him nearly two minutes.

So now, with barely a handful of laps run, Jack Brabham was looking like a ho-hum shoo-in for the title. Especially since now he was leading the race with his young Kiwi teammate Bruce McLaren following right in his wheeltracks and Toly holding a distant third and losing ground, even though he was trying as hard as he could to atone for running into Brooks. But already his temperature gauge was starting to climb thanks to a hairline split in a radiator seam from the accident, and he was out of it a few laps later with steam pouring out from underneath the hood.

Following all that, the race quickly degenerated into one of those "battle of attrition" parades with one car after another dropping out due to this or that while the two Coopers droned around at the head of the field like there was a damn tow rope between them. Little Maurice Trintignant was really on his game that day and worked his way up into third place in the second Scottish-blue Walker Cooper—even closing on the Cooper factory cars!—while Brooks did an absolutely heroic job of driving back up through the dwindling field following his early pit stop. In fact, those four were the only cars on the lead lap (out of just seven still running!) as the race droned on towards its finish. And, as Hank pointed out (but not in print, of course!), watching just seven cars and no significant battles circulating around a track the size of Sebring is not a particularly good entertainment value—no matter how much you love your motor racing!

And then, right at the end, it got interesting again. The starter was standing ready at the start/finish line, checkered flag in hand, as those few remaining cars raced around on their final lap. But the two Coopers that came wailing nose-to-tail out of

Sunset Bend were McLaren's factory-green #9 and Trintignant's Walker-blue #6. Brabham's #8 was nowhere to be seen! Worried faces looked back and forth at each other in the Cooper pits even as Bruce McLaren flashed under the checker to take his first-ever Grand Prix victory. A long silence followed, and then a sweating, panting, bent-double-from-the-effort Jack Brabham came into sight, pushing his silent Cooper around the inside of Sunset Bend and onto the pit straight! His fuel pump had packed up on the very last lap, and the car coasted to a halt damn near a half-mile from the finish line! Everyone heard the sound of Brooks' lonely Ferrari V6 tearing down the back straight, downshifting for Sunset Bend, balancing through the corner on part throttle and then accelerating full-bore out onto the pit straightaway, passing the panting Brabham and his Cooper and crossing the finish line to take third. But tough, wily old Jack Brabham just kept pushing, kept sweating, kept straining and kept fighting until he got that car across the line. At which point he collapsed onto the pavement in a heaving, gasping heap. But he'd done it! Fourth place was all he needed to seal the championship over Moss and Brooks. Hank said the headline just about wrote itself afterwards: *"Brabham Walks His Way To A World Championship At Sebring!"*

To be honest, not too many folks were impressed by that first-ever U.S. Grand Prix, and the somewhat optimistic opinion in Hank's magazine story was that the race might have actually broken even. Or maybe not. But before the checker even came down there were discussions going on about just where the United States Grand Prix ought to be held next year, and naturally the East Coast types thought it should be at Watkins Glen and the West Coast types thought it was a natural for Riverside and Alec Ulmann, who had worked so hard to bring a Grand Prix to America in the first place, naturally thought it ought to stay right where it was at Sebring.

Plus there were more politics rumbling through the paddock at Sebring since the FIA in Paris had made it absolutely official that Formula One was going to change to little 1.5-liter tiddlers for 1961, and there were an awful lot of folks up in arms about it. Particularly the British teams, who didn't much like the idea that their expensive, well-developed and now even Championship-caliber 2.5-liter racecars were about to become thoroughly redundant. Or a lot of the race promoters—again, particularly in England—who didn't figure the sporting public was going to exactly turn out in droves to watch the best drivers in the world wheeling around in a bunch of kiddie toys. There were even whispers about saying *"Up Yours!"* to the FIA and starting an alternate, totally independent World Championship based on the established 2.5-liter cars.

If you're a fan, you worry and fret over this sort of thing, thinking that it might ruin, dilute or even kill off the sport you love. But the fact is that racing survives and even thrives on exactly this kind of controversy and bitter political in-fighting. Hey, it makes headlines and creates interest, you know? And you're never going to run out of people who want to—hell, *need* to—race automobiles....

Back in Passaic, the holiday season was rapidly approaching and Big Ed and me were busy taking a good, healthy look at all the new, 1960 "compacts" out of Detroit and sizing them up as potential opposition. The Plymouth Valiant and Ford Falcon were pretty straightforward dwarf versions of the same blessed sedans those companies had been building for years, and I think their biggest problem was that these were supposed to be cheap cars—pardon me, make that "economy-minded" cars—and so the bigwigs in Detroit made sure all the trim and such was the same as their bottom-of-the-line full-sized cars. The American manufacturers were always real careful about making sure that a Caddy looked snazzier and ritzier and plusher and more elegant than an Olds or a Buick or a Pontiac, and that those three also stayed a step ahead of any Chevrolet in the old sizzle, style and snoot appeal sweepstakes. And they further made sure that a base, bottom-feeder Chevy Biscayne was an obvious notch down—inside and out—from a Chevy Bel Air, and that a Bel Air was a further large step down from Chevy's wildly popular new Impala. Olds likewise had to make sure its 98 stood a wee bit taller in the public eye than its 88 (even though they were damn near the same cars underneath the sheetmetal!) and Pontiac was in the same exact fix with its Venturas, Catalinas and Bonnevilles. It got pretty damn confusing, if you want the truth of it. In fact, that's probably what caused Ford to finally give up on their "amazing new Edsel" after just a three-year run. For whatever reason, the American public just never got the Edsel properly plugged in to the usual money, status and style pecking order that made people pick out and buy whatever the hell kind of cars they wound up buying. I never pretended to understand how all that marketing stuff worked, but it seems like a lot of the bigwigs and decision makers in Detroit didn't either. And they were getting paid for it!

The one car out of the whole bunch that really caught my attention was the new, rear-engined, air-cooled Chevy Corvair. Oh, it was plain and dull and tinny as hell when it first came out, but I thought it represented a *huge* leap for an American car company. Although the Chevy dealers seemed to be a little bit puzzled about exactly what to do with them. It seems the engineers at Chevy thought they were supposed to be doing a sort of Americanized Volkswagen (which they got right clear down to an engine room smell through the heater ducts, a constant, whirring drone in back like you were being chased by the world's biggest vacuum cleaner and vicious snap oversteer if you got into a corner too hot) while the marketing guys thought they were getting some kind of shrunk-down American sedan like the Ford Falcon. And then, a year or so later when Chevy's new Corvair was in the process of laying a fairly gigantic egg, some bright wiseguy at Chevy put a couple bucket seats and some nicer trim in one and added a little "Monza" badge on the bottom of the front fender and all of a sudden you started seeing them everywhere. I thought they were pretty neat, too....

But the thing that was becoming more and more apparent to Big Ed and me was that not too many of our VW Beetle customers (in fact, hardly any at all!) were lining up to trade in their Beetles on a Studebaker Lark, Nash Rambler, Plymouth

Valiant, Ford Falcon or Chevy Corvair. In fact, most of the folks buying those cars—and they were selling quite a few—were your typical American Car buyers already! Often as not, they were either "moving up" from the second-hand ranks, replacing a used, full-size American sedan with one of those "economical new compacts" or maybe "adding a second car" for the wife at home or their snotnose kid going away to college. So while me and Big Ed started out all worried about how the new generation of "Detroit compacts" were going to affect our business, it turned out that all their commercials and advertising (and all of VW's clever, simple, gut-shot, counter-punch ads in the magazines) just brought more and more people in to buy Volkswagens! We couldn't believe it. And of course that Harry Metropolis guy was calling Big Ed every other week now, trying to get him to set some kind of price so they could get down to some serious haggling. And Big Ed was naturally stringing him along and waiting for *him* to name a price so he could get all insulted and indignant over it and slam the phone down on his ear. And after that, they'd get down to the same exact thing.

Personally, I was doing my best to avoid thinking about what might happen if we ever sold the dealership. And it was an easy thing to do since things were going so good and we were so incredibly busy all the time, which naturally makes the weeks fly by until all of a sudden you're staring Christmas and New Year's directly in the face and wondering where the hell another blessed year went. But, like I said, things were going good for us, and Big Ed and me (and our tax accountant) thought it wouldn't be such a bad idea to host a little Christmas party for the folks who worked for us and pass out a few little Christmas cards with a few little bonus checks stuffed inside. I've got to say it made me feel pretty special signing those checks. Down deep inside, you know?

Christmas Eve fell on a Thursday that year (and of course we were closed on Friday like everybody else) and it was Big Ed's idea to close up early on Thursday, shoo the last of the customers out of the shop and showroom and have this Italian catering guy he knew bring in a couple long folding tables, cover them over with red and green tablecloths and then lay out more different kinds of cheese bits and shrimp appetizers and those little cocktail hot dogs wrapped up in tiny buns and whole hams and turkeys and salads and sweet potatoes and three kinds of pasta and green beans with almonds and broccoli with cheese sauce and more different pies and cakes and pastries than you have ever seen in your life. Even if you've been to an Easter brunch out towards the tip of Long Island or a bar mitzvah spread in Scarsdale. Plus a cold keg of Knickerbocker beer to wash it all down and a big ceramic hot pot full of eggnog that, taken in sufficient quantity, could cause the wax in your ears to melt and run down both sides of your head.

Of course it was more than the bunch we had working for us at the dealership could possibly eat, but we figured we had a lot to be thankful for. Business was good and everybody was getting along with (or at least tolerating) everybody else—even Sylvester and Butch, can you believe it?—and so we also invited some of our best customers to drop by for a little holiday eggnog and face-stuffing. Some of the old racing guys, too. And of course we told all the mechanics and porters and parts guys and sales help and office girls—like I said, the VW and sportycar businesses had been *very* good to us—to have their spouses, intended spouses, best guy or girlfriend or whoever the hell they were sleeping with or not sleeping with at the time to come by as well.

Steve and J.R. were pretty good with sound systems and they'd rigged up the hi-fi in Big Ed's office so's it piped Christmas carols over the scratchy PA speaker out in the shop. Sure, it sounded like they were coming from a Russian submarine parked in 50 feet of water off the Jersey coastline (and being sung in Russian, at that) but at least the tunes were familiar and Big Ed's eggnog made it about 50/50 that we'd have a sing-along going before the afternoon was over.

I remember it was five or so and we'd been going strong since about noon-thirty (that's when the lid came off that first—of many—batches of eggnog) and damn if some four-piece Polish polka band that'd bought a VW microbus from Big Ed didn't stop by on their way to another party. Pretty soon they were knee-deep in the eggnog with the rest of us, and all of a sudden they were unpacking their instruments and we had live music! I think Big Ed maybe slipped them a couple bucks on the side. But the place was really jumping thanks to polka-speed, accordion-laced renditions of everything from *"Rudolph the Red-Nosed Reindeer"* to *"O Come All Ye Faithful"* belted out by four fat, happy, eggnog-fueled Polacks in gold sequined jackets. Julie was there with me and we'd both had enough eggnog that we were singing along like everybody else (not that you could hear yourself, but that's the real secret to all great sing-alongs anyway) and around 6:30 I happened to glance over at where Big Ed was kind of leaned back against the parts counter with one of his fat Cuban stogies shoved in the middle of a wide, self-satisfied grin. You weren't supposed to be able to get Cuban cigars here in the states anymore thanks that scraggly-looking commie Fidel Castro, but Big Ed had the connections to get stuff like genuine Cuban cigars anyway. No questions asked.

And then, right while I was looking at him, Big Ed turned kind of ashen and this strange, hollow, even frightened look came into his eyes. It was a totally foreign kind of expression for him, and I immediately felt the hairs stand up on the back of my neck. I nudged Julie and she saw it, too, and without a word we hustled over to him. *"HEY, ARE YOU OK?"* I hollered over the accordion, drum, bass and trumpet music echoing around in our shop.

The corners of Big Ed's mouth folded down in kind of a grimace. *"It's nothing,"* he said uncertainly.

"What's nothing?"

"I dunno..." he said softly, almost dreamily. *"I jus' feel kinda...."* and then his voice trailed off. But only for a second. Then—right out of nowhere!—his eyes shot wide open, his hands clutched his chest and his teeth clenched together so hard they bit his Cuban cigar clear in two.

Time froze.

So did Big Ed.

And then, what seemed at least a full minute later, he let out this long, slow groan like an overloaded rail car on bad tracks and pretty much crumpled to the floor.

"JESUS, ED!" I hollered down at him. And then to everybody in the room: *"CALL AN AMBULANCE!!! JESUS CHRIST, CALL A DAMN AMBULANCE!!!"*

Well, it seemed to take forever for the fire department to get there—even though they were just down the blessed street—and Julie and me and everybody else kind of hovered around in a panic, trying to figure out what to do.

"Lay him out flat with his feet up!"

"Make him sit up."

"NO!! DON'T TOUCH HIM!!"

"Loosen his collar!"

"It's already loose!"

"Then loosen it some more!!"

"Open his pants."

"YOU open his pants!"

"Jesus, is he breathing?"

"Breathing? He's fucking CHOKING!"

"IT'S THE CIGAR!"

"Get it out of his mouth. He'll choke to death!"

"Don't put your fingers in his mouth! He'll bite 'em off and choke on THEM!"

Julie was the one who finally reached her fingers in and got the chewed-in-two butt-end of Big Ed's stogie out of his mouth. No question it was the mommy training, I'm sure of it. Teaches 'em how to react and deal with stuff that makes most guys freeze solid in pool of their own piss and sweat.

Julie looked up at me. *"He's still breathing,"* she said hopefully.

"Fucking...right...I'm...still...breathing!" Big Ed gasped defiantly.

That was a good sign.

I heard the siren wailing down Pine Street and—jeez, it still sounded a long way away—and I remember I even prayed a little as I knelt down next to him. *"You're gonna be okay, Ed,"* I assured him in the calmest, most confident voice I could muster. *"Just relax and take it easy. The ambulance'll be here in half a minute. You're gonna be fine. Everything's gonna be okay...."*

He was panting now, like he couldn't catch his breath.

"Fuckers'r...takin'...their...own...sweet...time...about...it...aren't...they...."

Chapter 36: Beautiful Losers

As you can imagine, I spent all night Christmas Eve and most of Christmas Day at the hospital, waiting to see how things panned out, and you know how I feel about hospitals. Julie stayed at home to look after the kids, and of course I wasn't around to take the presents out of the loft part of the garage where they couldn't see them—well, not without a ladder, anyway—and put them under the tree after they fell asleep, so that was also the Christmas Santa Claus got stuck in the chimney in our house, never to return. I guess it was a pretty lousy Christmas all the way around. By noon they had Big Ed sitting up in bed and asking for one of his cigars, but he was pale and shaky and had this nervous little jiggle in his voice whenever he tried to force a laugh.

"I'm okay," he insisted (although none too convincingly), "Y'go on home now, Buddy. Fr'chrissakes, it's Christmas."

"I'll go in a little while," I told him. And I did. About 8PM. After they gave him a pill or something and he kind of drooled off to sleep. Maybe I should've asked for one of those pills myself, because I sure couldn't sleep when I got home. Even though I was as tired, worn out and exhausted as I'd ever been in my life.

Julie was a big help over those next few days while Big Ed was in the hospital. She'd go sit with him so's I could go look after things at the shop and the dealership and then naturally I'd stop by to see him after work, and I guess he was awfully damn lucky because Big Ed was pretty much okay after a short stay in the hospital and a stern talking-to by four or five different doctors who all told him to lose weight and watch what he ate and drank and exercise every day and stop screwing around with 25-year-old cocktail waitresses and….

"But that IS exercise!" Big Ed protested.

His doctors didn't look particularly convinced. Especially since cocktail waitresses usually came complete with cocktails—and plenty of them! And then came the final blow. They told him he had to stop smoking his beloved Cuban cigars.

"Jesus," he growled back at them, *"all that just to live a little longer?"*

But you could see where Big Ed's heart attack took some of the snap out of his step and some of the smartass out of his usual, freewheeling line of bullshit. And it really shook up the latest potential Mrs. B., who had been the hat-check/dice-game girl at some club a friend of his owned in the city and who now was seeing an ugly third possibility as an aging, losing-her-looks nursemaid to a fat, sickly old man superimposed between the wealthy-widow/wealthy-divorcee scenarios I believe she was pretty much counting on. But that's just my opinion, okay? In any case, Big Ed was lucky seeing as how his heart attack wasn't a real bad one (he told everybody afterwards that he probably deserved worse, and there was a lot of truth in that) and he followed his doctors' advice religiously by embarking on a stringent new health regimen that amounted mostly to skipping second helpings (at least off the dessert cart, anyway), walking around the block a few times every single morning (or was it one single time every few mornings?) and chewing on the butt end of his big, buck-fifty Cuban cigars without actually lighting them up. That last one tore him up most of all.

It was a kind of back-handed stroke of luck that Big Ed's heart attack happened over the holidays when things are generally slow in the car business, and he was back at work at the dealership—half days, anyway—before the end of January. And selling every blessed Volkswagen we could get our hands on (although, like Big Ed said, if you could operate an ink pen, you could sell Volkswagens in New Jersey). Still, the heart attack was a big wakeup call for both of us, and I found myself thinking more and more about that Harry Metropolis and the offer he'd never quite made yet for our dealership. I'd think about it sitting in my office with the big, plate-glass window facing out towards the shop, just staring off into space when I really should've been doing my paperwork on the work orders, new car pre-delivery inspections, used-car shit lists and warranty claims. I thought about it across the street at the lunch counter while I chewed on an oliveburger, a sausage sandwich, a corned beef and Swiss on rye or a pepper-and-egg sandwich on Fridays. I'd think about it riding home in my demo (the one with the Judson supercharger, right?) while The Fleetwoods sweetly harmonized *"Mr. Blue"* or Paul Anka crooned *"Put Your Head on my Shoulder"* through that fuzzy, apparently tinsel-filled speaker on the VW's dashboard. I could've driven any kind of car I wanted to, I guess—Big Ed sure did—but I kind of thought that you should drive what you sell, you know? And then Julie and me would talk about it some more at home—usually in bed at night when we couldn't get to sleep.

"How much do you think it would be?" she'd ask in a whisper so as not to wake the kids or have her mother listening in on the conversation from upstairs.

"I dunno," I told her. *"A lot...."*

"How much is 'a lot?'"

"Plenty, I guess...."

"But how much is 'plenty?'"

"A lot...."

We'd go around and around like that for half an hour sometimes, and I still couldn't get my brain wrapped around what it would be like to be sitting on a bank account full of hard, cold cash—more than I'd ever dreamed of having in one lump sum, in fact!—and moreover not having to wake up at 5:15 ayem every blessed morning so's I could be down there to put my keys in the locks to open up the dealership and the sportscar shop. And of course that was the part that was bothering and worrying and, if you want the truth of it, scaring the living shit out of me.

"What d'you think you'd do with yourself?" Julie whispered.

"I dunno," I told her. *"Something...."*

"What kind of 'something?'"

"I dunno...You know...Anything...."

"What kind of 'anything?'"

"Something...."

I always figured it's nice for a husband and wife to be able to talk that sort of stuff over, you know?

Big Ed was thinking more and more about it, too. I could see it in his eyes while that big, fat Cuban cigar with no smoke or smell coming off the end rolled across his lips from one side of his face to the other. That just didn't seem right, even if I knew he was better off not lighting up. To tell the truth, Big Ed had a lot of his old spunk back. But not all of it by any stretch of the imagination. That heart attack had aged Big Ed, and every now and then you'd catch a glimpse of that strange, lost, weary, beaten, betrayed and somewhat bewildered look that seems to creep onto the eyes of people who've taken a close-up, personal gander at the cold, black door that waits at the end of the road for all of us and maybe even caught a whiff of whatever the sweet smell or awful stench is coming through from the other side....

Speaking of death, my sister Mary Frances and her overeducated intellectual beatnik friends who didn't take nearly enough showers or baths over in Greenwich Village were all busy mourning the passing of this hotshot French existential writer named Albert Camus (pronounced Ka-moo, but you know how the French are), who got himself killed in a big car wreck outside of Paris on January 4th. Personally, I'd never heard of him, but my sister Mary Frances insisted he was a very important writer indeed.

"He wrote *The Plague,"* she told me.

"Sounds uplifting."

"And *The Myth of Sisyphus."*

"Sissy *what?"*

"Sisyphus. He's this guy who spends his whole life rolling this boulder up a hill. But the further he goes up the hill, the bigger and heavier the boulder gets and the steeper the hill gets until finally it's just too big and steep for him—no matter how hard he fights and strains and pushes."

"Sounds like running a car dealership."

She gave me a dirty look.

"So what happens?" I had to ask.

"Oh, eventually the boulder rolls right over him."

"Right over him?"

She nodded. "It rolls all the way back down to the bottom of the hill."

I could see it in my head. "So what does he do?"

"Why, he goes back down and starts all over again, of course."

"That's dumb," I told her.

"It's not dumb, it's *absurd,"* she corrected me. Like "absurd" was some wonderful, marvelous cure for anything that might ail you.

A lot of Mary Frances' highbrow/black-turtleneck/leather-patches-on-the-elbows-of-their-corduroy-jackets friends were all excited over the notion that this Albert Camus' death might have been a suicide. Like committing suicide was something unbelievably cool and trendy and fascinating, you know? And it kind of made sense seeing as how this Albert Camus guy apparently didn't think you got much out of life except agony, death and irony. He was pretty damn prolific about it, too. I personally didn't get it, of course, but I must admit I was kind of interested in the car he used to crash himself headlong into a tree, which was one of those big, rare and expensive French Facel Vegas with a hulking Chrysler FirePower V-8 under the hood. Big Ed really liked those cars (although I tended to shy away from anything French just because of the language barrier), but I must admit the notion that some guy who wrote about mostly agony, death and emptiness would get himself killed in anything as fast, stylish, powerful, classy, debonair, upscale and decadent as a Facel Vega HK-500 kind of appealed to me. But I guess none of Mary Frances' sensitive and artistic Greenwich Village friends saw the irony in it. Even though they were supposed to be real experts in the irony game.

But I was kind of happy for Mary Frances anyway, since she'd been going out pretty steady with that Pauly Martino guy who played big-band saxophone and a little cool jazz combo music now and then at clubs and lounges (but who was now moonlighting with an almost regular day job as a sort of traveling music teacher for a couple small Catholic high schools and junior highs that couldn't really afford their own fulltime music teacher on the payroll). I think Mary Frances helped get him that job, and I helped out a little with one hell of a deal—including some free-form financing that no bank would even dream of taking—on a decent-running, reasonably low-mileage '56 Beetle with faded paint, a few ugly scrapes and dings on the fenders and some rips and scratches that might have been made by a belt buckle, a bottle opener or a *very* sharp set of fingernails (or a combination of all three?) on the seat upholstery. Some guy gave it to his spoiled-rotten kid when he finally graduated high school and went off to flunk out of college. And an Ivy League school, at that.

Anyhow, I guess it was kind of a new thing for this Pauly Martino, getting up before breakfast instead of well after lunch and coming home right away after his weekend band dates instead of going out and doing whatever it is jazz saxophone players do that keeps them up all night and dead to the world until a few hours past noon in the morning. And "home" for Pauly was more and more coming to mean my sister Mary Frances' little one-bedroom apartment over on Harding, although they both took pains to sneak him in and out or make sure all the neighbors saw him leave at a reasonable hour through the front door (just so's he could sneak in over the back porch railing 15 minutes later, of course) on account of her job and her reputation and all. And that worked about as well as that sort of stuff always does, meaning that the only person on the block who wasn't on to them by the end of the first week was the husband of the poor old blind and deaf lady who lived across the hall. And he was in a coma over at the hospital. But, out of respect, all anybody in the neighborhood ever did was roll their eyes, shake their heads, tsk-tsk a few times and whisper behind Mary Frances' back about what a terrible scandal it was. And her teaching little ones over at Our Lady of Perpetual Sorrow, too!

Personally, I kind of hoped Pauly Martino would ask Mary Frances to marry him. I mean, he was an all right guy (although awfully quiet when he wasn't playing his saxophone) and the two of them seemed to get along and did an awful lot of things together. They went to concerts and plays and coffee house poetry readings and gallery openings and even went to the grand opening of the Guggenheim Museum over in Manhattan back in October. And they didn't even have a blessed TV set! Can you believe it? Mary Frances said they'd rather read books or listen to good music. That sounded pretty damn suspicious and even subversive to my dad (who, strangely enough, I wasn't even calling my "old man" anymore now that he was actually starting to turn into one). Anyhow, like I said, I was kind of hoping that Pauly Martino guy would ask Mary Frances to marry him. But he hadn't. Of course my dad had his ideas about it: *"'A course he ain't gonna marry her! Why the hell should he when she's givin' out free samples?"* But I was thinking maybe it was more because he was just too blessed shy. In fact, it was kind of a puzzle how a guy like Pauly could get up in front of a whole roomful of people and blow a jazz sax solo that floated and soared and hung in the air like the smell of a fresh-baked, homemade fruit pie cooling on a windowsill. He was that good. Although I noticed that he always had his eyes shut when he played, and seemed pretty much oblivious to everybody and everything around him. Then, when his solo was over, people would start to clap or even holler and whistle (especially if they'd been around sucking up the music and lots of other things for a few sets) and his eyes would blink open and he'd suddenly realize where he was and what was going on around him and he'd get kind of "aw, shucks" fidgety and maybe even blush a little. Or maybe even more than a little. But I eventually came to see that as a sign of character, you know? And I really wished he'd get up off his skinny jazz saxophonist ass, down a couple shooters and ask Mary Frances to marry him. Although, to be honest, I think she really kind of enjoyed the idea of just living with somebody on account the way it made everybody uneasy. Or all the people from the old neighborhood, anyway. Especially my dad. Hell, it was a way for her to strike out against all that stodgy, hypocritical, middle-class conventionality that she was really staring to crave in spite of herself as she got a little older.

Our Buddy Cal was still out in California, running a few amateur races and spending a lot of time out at Riverside or at the shop in Culver City with the Scarab crew while he tried to see Gina and waited for the sportscar and grand prix seasons to start up again down in Argentina at the end of January. Although he was still without a commitment from Ferrari either way regarding a Formula One drive. Racing *monoposto* open-wheelers on the Grand Prix circuit was the purest form—the top of the blessed mountain—for any professional road-racing driver, and Ferrari always made a habit of keeping plenty of them hanging around to pick from. He was real big on American drivers right then—it was hardly lost on him that an awful lot of his road-going sportscars were sold in the old U.S. of A., and particularly in California—and so he had Phil Hill and Cal on the line and he'd obviously been impressed as all getout with what tall, grinning, handsome and athletic ex-Marine Dan Gurney had done for him in a few sportscar drives and grand prix races the previous year. But Gurney was a little suspicious of the politics and intrigues in Maranello (not to mention their out-of-date, front-engined Grand Prix cars and a reluctance to pay much at all for the privilege of risking your neck in Ferrari's cars) and so he signed with BRM for the 1960 season, looking forward with great—if perhaps misguided—optimism to their new, rear-engined P48. But old man Ferrari was also taken with a fairly mad new Belgian driver named Willy Mairesse, who had great skills, huge balls, strange, scary eyes and an enormous appetite for taking risks. Ferrari understood and respected what men like that could do, even if they could be kind of edgy and uncomfortable to be around.

So, as you can imagine, Cal was antsy as hell. And not getting to see very much of Gina was hardly helping the situation. But she had shooting every day and then going home and working on her lines for the next day's shooting every night, and she told Cal over and over that there was just no way she could fit him while all that was going on.

"But I'm right here in town," he protested into a pay phone just a few miles away from her house.

"Yeah, I know. And I'd love to see you, too—I really, really would!—but I'd never get anything done if you were here."

"Sure, you would," Cal argued.

Gina knew better. *"Look, I've got a call every morning at 5:30 and I don't get home until eight or nine every night...."*

"I could see you then."

"No, you couldn't. I've got to go over my lines then. Sometimes until one or two in the morning."

"Hey, I could help you. I could feed you lines."

"You're feeding me one right now, aren't you?"

Cal had to chew that one over a little. *"Okay. How about if we do something after you're done going over your lines? Just for a little while."*

"All I want then is to sleep."

"We could do that."

She gave him a wicked little laugh. *"No, we couldn't."*

"Jesus, Gina. I'll be leaving for South America in a few weeks and then it's off to Europe for the season over there. I'd really like to see you a little before I go."

"I'd like to see you, too, Cal. You know I would." The receiver went silent for a moment. *"Maybe if we have a day off shooting we could. But you have to understand this is just as important to me as your career is to you. This is the first part in my life where I'm more than something to look at and lick your lips over. It's a real breakthrough for me, Cal, and I've got to do the best job I can on it. Can you understand that?"*

"Sure I can," Cal lied.

"I promise I'll make it up to you."

"You can't make up time," Cal told her without really thinking about it. *"Once it's gone, it's gone forever...."*

"Then we'll just have to wait for another 'forever' to come along, won't we?"

There wasn't much you could say to an answer like that.

Thanks to a little settling-in of the local political situation and the fact that the people were absolutely crazy nuts about motor racing, the World Manufacturers' Championship endurance racing season was once again kicking off down in Argentina, and the big news there was the incredibly low-slung and sexy new Maserati *Tipo 61* "Birdcage" fielded by Lucky Casner's new Camoradi USA team with Dan Gurney and Masten Gregory handling the driving chores. Maserati didn't have the money to field their own factory team anymore (and neither, really, did Lucky Casner, but nobody knew that yet), but the car itself was pretty damn amazing. Maserati had taken Colin Chapman's three-dimensional, multi-tubular space-frame idea to an almost ridiculous extreme, building it out of hundreds and hundreds of short, straight, small-diameter tubes welded together in all these little boxes and triangles and pyramids and trapezoids stacked and sandwiched one atop and one beside and even one inside the other from one end of the car to the other. *"Under the bodywork, it looks like it's made out of toothpicks. Or maybe a craft project some little Italian kid put together with model glue and a few boxes of raw spaghetti?"* was the way Hank put it. But the frame was light and stiff and the chassis worked really, really well. And then Maserati took a nice, simple, beautifully built little twincam four-banger and laid it halfway over on its side to get the center of gravity low and the hoodline damn near down to the wheel centers. That allowed Maserati to do a better job than anybody else of adapting to the FIA's thoroughly ridiculous new windshield rules. For reasons that seemed awfully dumb and fuzzy anywhere outside of FIA headquarters in Paris, the high and almighty world motorsports governing body (just ask them!) had decreed that, for the new season, all "prototype" sports/racing cars had to have windshields at least 25 centimeters high. Or about 10 inches in plain old English. And they had to run the full width of the cockpit, too, including in front of that extra seat that nobody except a mechanic riding back and forth from the garage or some bosomy trophy girl on a victory lap ever got to sit in. The idea (at least according to the FIA gents in Paris) was to make the cars look a little more like prototypes of actual future production models rather than the out-and-out racing machines they really were. And everybody thought it was a perfectly stupid idea, because it spoiled the smooth, supple, hopefully wind-cheating shapes of the cars—I mean, the D-Type Jags and Lotus Elevens with their now-illegal, Le Mans-style metal tonneau covers and wraparound cockpits and windscreens had to be about the sexiest racecars anybody had ever seen—not to mention that those new high windshields actually made visibility worse rather than better. First off, they were made of lightweight plexiglass, and so they'd get pitted and scratched and pock-marked from the sand, grit and flying stones, and then they'd get covered over with oil and grease and squashed bugs and whatnot as the race went on until it was like they were smeared with Vaseline. And then maybe it would get dark or rain—or, worse yet, get dark *and* rain—and Cal said it was like looking at everything through a lens that couldn't focus. A driver could at least peer over the old, low windscreens to get a good, solid look at the racetrack (and yet they did a damn good job of deflecting the wind and grit and stones and rain and bugs and what-have-you pretty much right over the driver's head!) and everybody said the new FIA windscreens were a dumb idea and made no sense at all. But the FIA wasn't really interested in "sense" when it came to making up new rules and regulations. Nope, it was more like just proving to everybody they had the power to do it. Simple as that.

The other bad part was that, except for Ferrari and Porsche—who both considered racing an integral, ongoing part of what their companies were all about—nobody else really wanted to play. Or not for very long, anyway. Like Jaguar and Vanwall before them, Aston Martin won their World Championship, swilled their champagne, smiled for the cameras, held up the trophy, packed up their tools, folded up their tent, sold off the cars and pretty much walked away. Mission accomplished. On to other things, don't you know? So it wasn't a particularly deep field of factory teams on hand down in Argentina. Not hardly. Although there were an a lot of local South American and down-for-a-holiday North American amateurs and privateers to fill out the grid and liven up the cocktail parties.

No question that new Maserati "Birdcage" was wowing everybody with its low-slung stance, looks and speed, and Dan Gurney took an immediate and ever-growing lead in the white-and-blue Camoradi USA car right from the get-go. He was still leading all the Ferraris and Porsches easily when he brought it in for fuel and tires and to hand it over to Gregory. But then the transaxle started grinding and graunching and popping out of gear, and Gregory had to park it at a little over half-distance. It was kind of a shame for the new car and the new American team running it, but everybody was pretty damn impressed with their potential. After that, the factory Ferraris cruised to an easy 1-2 finish over Jo Bonnier and Graham Hill in the first of the Porsches. The way Hank saw it, there wasn't much in the way of excitement once that new Maserati dropped out.

Another new car made an even bigger splash at the Argentine Grand Prix just two weeks later, where Colin Chapman knocked everybody for a loop when he unveiled his first-ever rear-engined Grand Prix car, the Lotus 18. Some of the scribes snickered behind their hands that Chapman held off on building a rear-engined car because he didn't want anybody to think he was copying Cooper, but once he put his mind to it, he came up with one hell of a clever and ingenious design. Although it looked even more like a spent shell casing than the Coopers, the new Lotus only weighed 800 pounds and had all kinds of clever, original and deceptively simple-looking construction details. Like using the rear halfshafts as the upper suspension links, for example. At first it looked like something was missing, you know? Or at least it did until you looked at it again and thought about it a little more until, all of a sudden, this little light came on and you appreciated all over again what you surely appreciated the very first time you ever saw a Lotus racing car.

Cal had stayed in South America between races working on his tan and lobbying to get a drive in the fourth Dino 246 the Ferrari team had brought down to Argentina, but negotiations with the organizers and promoters (and, no doubt, a sizeable wad of cash!) put retired but thoroughly beloved Argentine ace Froilan

Gonzales behind the wheel instead. Gonzalez was famous for scoring Ferrari's first-ever Grand Prix win at Silverstone in 1951 and ranked second to only Fangio in the hearts of the people, but he hadn't raced in Formula One for three years (and even that was just another one-off drive for Ferrari in Argentina). But, as Eric Gibbon told Hank: *"Business is business, and promoting a bloody car race depends entirely on putting bums on seats. And nothing puts bums on seats better than a bloody Local Hero."* Especially when you jimmy the first day's practice times to make it look like he's in with a shot at the pole. To be honest, Cal had to admit the front-engined Ferraris didn't figure to make much of an impression on the rear-engined Coopers over a full race distance in Argentina. Even though Ferrari had moved their engines back six inches—putting them almost right square in the driver's lap, in fact—and relocated the fuel tanks on either side of the cockpit to improve weight distribution and keep that weight distribution from changing so much as the fuel burned off. But if you looked at the cars side-by-side, Hank said it was like looking at dumb, lumbering dinosaurs next to slick, smart little weasels. Sure, a dinosaur could step on a weasel and crush it down to a glob of fur and guts (if that dinosaur could catch the weasel, anyway) but the weasel could sneak into the dinosaur's nest and eat its eggs. And that's what the future's really made of, isn't it?

Anyhow, the new Lotus 18 went like an absolute rocket from the very first session, even with the relatively unknown Scot Innes Ireland at the wheel. And he'd never even seen the blessed track before! Although the general chassis layout was the same, Hank said you could see a lot of differences between the new Lotus and the factory Coopers with the bodywork off. It seemed like there was just less to the Lotus, and while the Cooper frames were made out of large, stout tubes bent into graceful, gently curved arcs—like the skeleton of some great sea creature—the Lotus was made up of small, short, straight tubes welded up into triangulated, geometric, three-dimensional boxes, rectangles and alloy sheet-reinforced bulkheads. Hank said it looked pretty damn fragile, if you want the truth of it. But did it ever *go!*

Stirling Moss ultimately managed to beat out the new Lotus out for pole position—just barely—but Ireland took the lead at the start and looked to be pulling away easily until he found himself in neutral when he thought he was in gear (not an uncommon thing in a Lotus 18, as it turned out!) and had himself a quick spin. But he got it gathered up and rejoined the race while Moss retired with a broken suspension link and Bonnier inherited the lead in his front-engined BRM. The Walker pits brought Trintignant's Cooper in and put Moss in the car, and meanwhile it was Bonnier's turn to run into trouble with what sounded like a duff valve and he started dropping back. That put Ireland and the new Lotus back into the lead with just a handful of laps to go, but then something came adrift in the steering and he had to struggle on to the finish with the front wheels pointing in pretty much different directions. Which handed the win to the smart and steady Bruce McLaren in the second factory Cooper—his second Grand Prix victory in a row!—while Toly soldiered on to take a hard-driven but generally unremarkable and unremembered second place ahead of the Trintignant/Moss Cooper.

Needless to say, there were a lot of urgently whispered discussions going on during the next morning's plane flight back to London. No question Colin Chapman's new Lotus had a lot of people convinced—right there at the very beginning of the blessed season!—that everyone else was flogging last year's car. Jack Brabham, Bruce McLaren and John Cooper spent the flight busily designing the next generation Cooper in their row of seats, the BRM guys were figuring out details, modifications and refinements to get their own rear-engined car on the racetrack as soon as possible and Rob Walker was making a deal with Colin Chapman to get one of the new Lotus 18s immediately for Stirling Moss to drive. It was that damn good....

As if the loss of Aston Martin and Jaguar and the stupid new windshield rules weren't bad enough, the World Manufacturers' Championship took another hit at Sebring thanks to sponsorship. Not lack of it, but *because* of it. See, in case you somehow haven't noticed, racing costs money. *Lots* of money. Huge, piled-up mounds of it, in fact. Which is why, if you want to be brutally honest about it, racing is filled to overflowing with drivers sporting large bulges in their pants. And I'm talking the right-rear pockets here, just so there's no confusion. But other money (or free stuff that otherwise costs money) comes into the sport from gasoline companies and sparkplug companies and tire companies and damn-near-any-sort-of-enterprise-willing-to-write-a-blessed-check companies who want their names on a race—or the side of a racecar—where all the goofballs in the stands and the people reading the car magazines can see it. Plus maybe hang around the pits a little like some kind of Important Visiting Dignitary and feel like part of the action.

Anyhow, Sebring had made a deal with Amoco to supply fuel for all the cars in return for some huge but not exactly defined quantity of prestige, panache and publicity (they even called it "The Amoco 12 Hours of Sebring" and the huge winners' trophy was known far and wide as "The Amoco Trophy") only Ferrari was by now under contract with Shell and Porsche was likewise under contract with BP, and that created a few small conflicts that quickly escalated into not-so-small conflicts once the lawyers and marketing types got involved. The final upshot was that neither team would be allowed to run using some other company's fuel and oil. Period. Or that's what it said in the fine print, anyway. And you have to remember that the oil company guy who approved and signed that contract also held the pen that signed the checks that ultimately found their way into the old racing team's bank account....

But of course neither Ferrari or Porsche wanted to miss out on Sebring—or the World Manufacturers' Championship points up for grabs there—and that's how a couple of Porsche's very-latest-spec RS 60s wound up, umm, "leased" to "privateer" Jo Bonnier, along with a full complement of factory drivers and factory-trained race mechanics. Enzo Ferrari, on the other hand—out of respect for his fine and loyal fuel and lubricant sponsor Shell Oil—absolutely and positively refused to attend the race in Florida. It was impossible, and there was simply no way in hell he could do it! However, there was nothing he could do about somebody like, say, his North American agent Carlo Sebastian entering a few of Ferrari's very latest racecars for some excellent and experienced driver teams, just to keep the Porsches honest. And, at least according to Hank, there was no way you could miss all the Modenese-dialect Italian being spoken in Carlo Sebastian's pit and paddock spots. But, typically, old man Ferrari forbade his American drivers Phil Hill and Cal Carrington from taking part in the race. Hey, if the people at Sebring were going to screw with him, he was going to screw them right back by keeping the two most famous and promotable American sportycar aces in the world out of their damn race. So, there, Sebring! *Ba Fangu!*

Besides the fuel sponsorship agonies, most of the interest before the race centered on the two Camoradi USA "Birdcage" Maseratis, one of which now had the unbelievably formidable driving team of Dan Gurney and Stirling Moss behind the wheel. They ran away from everybody early on, but the Birdcage was a little fragile for long-distance racing—especially on a rough, demanding track like Sebring—and although the Moss/Gurney car had an incredible four-lap lead at sunset (when Hank said it got almost impossible to see through those dumb, pitted, scratched and greasy 10-inch-high windshields heading into the hairpin and Sunset Bend), the Maserati was out of it less than an hour later with a broken rear axle. All the best Ferraris and the other Birdcages had broken by that point, too, and damn if a pair of 1600cc Porsche RS 60s—one of Jo Bonnier's "leased" factory cars and another "privateer" entry from Brumos Porsche out of Jacksonville, Florida—didn't wind up finishing first and second overall. At *Sebring,* for gosh sakes. Now you might expect a thing like that at a twisty, tortuous place like the *Targa Florio,* but certainly not at a blood-and-guts horsepower track like Sebring.

But that's what happened. Honest.

Hank and all the rest of the racing scribes tried to find something clever and amusing to write about what happened at Sebring, and they called the big fuel sponsorship controversy "fuelish" and "fuelhardy" in their race reports. And no question it represented the very height of non-theological absurdity to anybody who knew a damn thing about racing or what actually goes on inside an automobile engine. But I guess all the whizbang marketing guys (who, by the way, don't know jack shit about cars or racing) figured it would send the wrong kind of message to old Fred Average and John Q. if one of their So-and-So-Oil-sponsored racecars wound up running (and—horror of horrors!—even *winning!)* using Brand-X gasoline.

And that was typical of what Hank and me and everybody else saw happening all over the whole blessed world. The big-money corporate advertising and marketing types were somehow getting a stranglehold on racing and sticking their bright, cheery, arrogant, misguided and generally misinformed noses in where they weren't really wanted. Or needed. Why, they looked at motor racing like it was some huge, blank billboard or an empty 30-second commercial slot just waiting for them to exploit and enjoy. On the other hand, you had to appreciate that, without all those wonderful sponsors pumping cubic yards of money in, there'd be no professional motor racing at all anymore. I mean, there was just no way you could finance a modern racing team out of prize money. Not even if you won every damn race. So I surely don't want to sound angry or bitter or upset or ungrateful or unreasonable or disparaging or anything, but fuck all those know-nothing assholes, you know?

Anyhow, Porsche won again at the Targa Florio ahead of Ferrari's new "Dino 246S" sportscar (which was nothing but one of their Dino 246 Formula One cars dressed up with fenders, lights, a second seat and one of those stupid FIA windshields) and which Ferrari fervently hoped would work a little better than their ageing *Testa Rossas* on the tighter "handling" circuits. Meanwhile Lucky Casner put *Targa* experts Umberto Maglioli and Nino Vaccarella in one of his Birdcage Maseratis, and those two battled the Jo Bonnier/Hans Herrmann Porsche for the lead after most of the Ferraris hit trouble, but then the low-slung Maserati ran over a rock and poked a hole in the fuel tank, and that was the end of it. Casner himself co-drove a Porsche 356B Carrera in the smallbore "Grand Touring" category (painted in the blue-and-white Camoradi USA colors, of course) with some local guy named Nino Todoro, and damn if they didn't finish 22nd overall and fourth in class. Hell, just *finishing* in your first-ever *Targa Florio* amounts to one hell of an accomplishment. Over at Ferrari, Toly and Cal finished a distant second to the Bonnier/Herrmann Porsche after running into a lot of small problems (and, okay, a small tree) with their Dino 246S, and they were both pretty disgusted that they couldn't have made a better fight of it. But not nearly so disgusted as old man Ferrari back in Maranello, who was never very happy about finishing second to anybody. Anywhere. And especially not to those amazing and thoroughly irritating little 1600cc Porsche RS 60s, which had now scored two outright World Manufacturers' Championship wins in a row and were getting quite a well-deserved reputation as "giant killers."

Like Brad Lackey's boss at the studio once said: *"Hey, nobody wants to play Goliath. It's a lousy part. No sympathy."*

The Thousand K's at the Nurburgring two weeks later was bedeviled with fog, mist and rain, but that actually turned out to be something of a blessing for Lucky Casner's Camoradi USA Maseratis. He had Moss and Gurney behind the wheel of the lead car again, and their skill in the near-impossible conditions, the Maserati's predictable handling and the simple fact that they could see over the top of those dumb FIA windscreens better than most other drivers allowed them to win in spite of a 15-minute stop to fix a busted oil line. And it surely didn't hurt that a slick racetrack gentles up the driving inputs and doesn't put near so much strain and shock on the engines, brakes and drivelines as a dry surface. The other Camoradi Maserati took fifth, and so Hank and all the other American motoring scribes (not to mention all us frothing-at-the-mouth fans back at home) were absolutely over the moon about the interest, promise—and now, finally, results!—this new American team was generating. Even if they *were* racing Maseratis....

But of course the all-American team everybody really had their eyes on was the Scarab Formula One crew, who finally crossed the Atlantic towards the end of May with their two-years-in-the-making/a-generation-behind-before-they-even-started Grand Prix cars. Although the cars looked absolutely gorgeous, there was a real *"ready or not, here we come!"* feel to the whole thing. The team had been testing and evaluating and building and re-building and fiddling and cutting and trying and engineering and re-engineering right up to the very last moment, and everybody on the crew knew there was a hell of a lot of stuff yet to do or get right. But there comes a time when you've either got to shit or get off the pot—especially when the FIA had decreed that the whole blessed 2.5-liter Formula was going out of date at the end of the season!—and so the Scarabs' coming out party was scheduled for the fairy-tale, street-circuit setting of the Grand Prix of Monaco on May 29th. A debut Hank and all the rest of the red-white-and-blue American scribes and fans were looking forward to with a sort of cheerful, upbeat and marvelously patriotic sense of impending doom.

And it was even worse in real life.

You have to understand that not only was the Scarab a wee bit large, clumsy, underpowered and heavy compared to the then-current state-of-the-art in Formula One, but also, of all the racing circuits on the whole blessed calendar, Monaco was probably the worst for both the cars and their drivers. Besides being tight, twisty, bumpy, lumpy, uphill and downhill, Monaco was thoroughly and completely blind most places and exceedingly hemmed-in and claustrophobic. Toly said it was like a multicolored bobsled run taken at breakneck speed, and you had to constantly be thinking ahead to what you couldn't yet see. And if you made even the tiniest mistake or miscalculation, you were bouncing off curbs and into the barriers. And yet going fast at Monaco meant sidling or sliding right up against those curbs and barriers at the entrance, apex and exit of every blessed corner. It's not the sort of thing any driver could expect to just go out and *do.* It took seat time and mileage to get acclimated first. And lots of it.

Because of the small size and narrow confines of the track, only 16 cars were ever allowed to start at the Grand Prix of Monaco. And no less than 24 showed up for time trials in May of 1960 to see who might earn the privilege. Including no less than three of the new, rear-engined BRM P48s, the two factory Coopers (which were now lower, slimmer and lighter following that plane ride back from Argentina and had new, five-speed gearboxes), three works Lotus 18s, the Scottish-blue Rob Walker Lotus 18 for Stirling Moss, eight privateer Coopers with three different kinds of engines and a new, experimental, rear-engined Ferrari for Richie Ginther to go along with the three usual Dino 246 team cars. Which were, in fact, the only other front-engined cars at Monaco besides the Scarabs. So, from the day they arrived, the goal for Lance Reventlow's crew was just to keep their chins up, look as respectable, professional and well-turned-out as possible, pass off grimaces as grins and to maybe—just maybe—put a car in the race.

Even the snootiest of the European motoring scribes—including our old pal Eric Gibbon—had to be impressed by the beautiful metallic-blue-and-white paintwork, exquisite finish, fine detailing and immaculate preparation and presentation of the Scarab racecars and the neat, clean-cut, well-organized look of the crew. Not to mention the slick, beautifully produced, full-color Scarab PR brochure all the European race promoters, car clubs and press flacks received in the mail many months before the team ever made its way to Europe. That was a real Hollywood touch, and none of the European teams ever did anything like that. But all the while guys like Eric were snickering behind their hands and making rude noises about the actual, on-track speed potential of both the Scarab racecars and their drivers.

The sad news was, they were right.

By the end of the first practice day on Thursday, Moss and the new Walker Lotus 18 had absolutely shattered the lap record (not to mention every other driver's confidence and self-esteem) with a stunning new lap record of 1:36.7, and he topped that with an even more staggering 1:36.3 the following morning, more than a second clear of World Champ Brabham's next-best Cooper on the time sheets. The best Chuck Daigh could wring out of his Scarab was a thoroughly dismal 1:49 and change. And believe me, a dozen seconds is a damn *lifetime* around a track the size of Monaco! Hank of course stopped by to ask how the cars were running and if they were having any problems, and about all Warren Olsen could do was roll his eyes and mutter: *"Where should I start?"*

The cars were stodgy and lumbering around the corners and skittish and jumpy under braking. The gears were all wrong. The drivers didn't know their way around. The tires had no grip. The engines had no power. The Ferraris and Coopers and BRMs were absolutely *rocketing* past them on Monaco's few straight sections and easily out-braking and diving underneath them in the corners. Why, they were even slower than some of the blessed Formula Juniors practicing for their curtain-raiser race before the Grand Prix! And, as if that weren't enough, every now and then the brake pedal on the Scarabs would suddenly and without warning go straight to the floor! It was just dumb luck they hadn't crashed both cars....

But what could you do? The team ordered new gearsets to be air-freighted in from Halibrand in California, and then Lance asked Stirling Moss to take one of the cars around in the next morning's practice session to see what the Best Driver in the World could do with it. And the news was maybe even more disappointing. After just two warmup laps, Moss got the car down to a 1:45! Still not near quick enough to make the field, but a solid *four seconds a lap* faster than Chuck had gone and almost six better than Lance. It was pretty damn discouraging to know that both the cars *and* the drivers were off the pace. But the team gritted its teeth and soldiered on, tracking the sudden brake failure problem to heat and/or vibration from the engine getting to the fluid in the master cylinders and then relocating them to cure it, putting in softer springs all around and, finally, taking off the Goodyears and swapping for a set of English Dunlops like most of the other teams were using. The results were mildly encouraging. Very mildly. Chuck got down to a 1:47 and Lance a 1:48.5. As Chuck told Hank afterwards: "We were out to lunch, that's all there was to it."

Sunday arrived with gloomy, threatening skies, and the Scarab team wound up watching the race from Lance's hotel suite balcony with Hank and some other Americans. Bonnier's BRM jumped the start a wee bit and grabbed the lead from the second row, but he had Brabham right behind him and Moss—who was very careful at the start and gave everybody plenty of room through the tight first corner—close behind in third. Moss waited for his opportunity to slip neatly past the Cooper, then stalked Bonnier for 16 laps before sneaking by on the 17th and pulling away. But then, a little before half-distance, a light, misty rain started to fall. It looked to Hank and Chuck like Brabham's Cooper was a lot more stable, comfortable and controllable than the Lotus in the wet conditions, and he reeled Moss in and passed him for the lead. Meanwhile cars were spinning and sliding off nearly everywhere on the greasy, rain-slicked pavement, and Brabham suddenly joined that group, going maybe just that hair too quick, getting into one of those infuriatingly slow-motion, wet-weather slides, bouncing over a curb and clouting a stack of haybales. Ouch!

Brabham's accident put Moss back in the lead with 14 seconds in hand over Bonnier's BRM, but then the Lotus' engine went flat and he pulled into the pits with what sounded like a dropped valve or something. But it was only a loose plug wire, and Moss went storming back out onto the glistening wet racetrack, reeled Bonnier in, passed him to re-take the lead, and a handful of laps later Bonnier's BRM was out of it with a broken rear suspension. Thanks to mechanical retirements, spins and crashes only four cars were still running by then, and the only real interest was a good battle for second—far behind Moss and the Lotus—between Toly's old, front-engined Ferrari and McLaren in the second factory Cooper. Hank said Toly was doing everything he could with his ageing dinosaur of a Ferrari on a track that was drying rapidly and changing diabolically every lap. But eventually McLaren slipped past and pulled away, and there was just nothing Toly could do about it. Still, he finished third and was the only Ferrari driver (or front-engined car, for that matter) to make the full race distance, and there was a certain grim satisfaction in that.

Back here in the states, nobody except us few loyal, rabid enthusiast types cared one way or the other about what happened in Monaco (and we really wouldn't know anything except the blessed final finishing order—if that—until the race reports came out in the nutball sportycar magazines three months later). The big news here was John F. Kennedy's campaign to win the Democratic nomination and put in a bid (most likely against Richard M. Nixon) to become the youngest U.S. president ever. And I must admit, he sure looked the part. At least if you wanted a handsome leading-man/touch-football-quarterback type for your commander-in-chief, anyway. Oh, a lot of folks worried that he'd be in The Pope's back pocket on account of he was Roman Catholic, but they didn't understand the difference between Irish Catholics and Italian Catholics like we do back in the old neighborhood. And his wife Jackie looked like a shoo-in for best-looking/classiest-by-far first lady this side of Princess Grace of Monaco if Kennedy got elected. And don't think that didn't sway just as many votes as his stand on the Cold War, the Space Race and those lunch-counter sit-ins down south.

Everybody and his brother was watching Robert Stack as Eliot Ness in *"The Untouchables"* on TV, and I guess it was kind of ironic that famous G-Man Melvin Purvis blew his brains out with an automatic pistol on Leap Year day. He'd led the police raid where "Pretty Boy" Floyd got gunned down and used an out-to-save-her-own-ass "girlfriend" to set up Public Enemy #1 John Dillinger like a blessed tin duck in a shooting gallery in an alley next to the Biograph Theater in Chicago. And now a bullet had found him, too. But by far the biggest headlines of the new year (not to mention an awful lot of type-heavy commentary on the editorial pages) were about the high-altitude U-2 spy plane the Russkies shot down over Soviet territory on March 1st and told the world about—complete with pictures—four days later. It was a hell of an international political scandal, torpedoed the Big Four Summit Talks and threatened the Nuclear Disarmament Conference that wasn't really getting anywhere anyway in Geneva. And it embarrassed the living hell out of all of us Americans—especially seeing as how the pilot, Francis Gary Powers, didn't have the grace, timing or patriotic decency to die in the crash like a true American hero. Or at least that's the way Butch and all my dad's union buddies at the chemical plant saw it, anyway....

But the day after Monaco, Monday, May 30th, the Indianapolis 500 became big news that hit the front pages of all the newspapers—even the *New York Times*—on account of some fast-buck artist's makeshift spectator scaffolding in the infield collapsed without warning and sent over a hundred race fans toppling and tumbling down on a whole bunch more. The damn thing was over 40 feet high, made out of old pipes and planks and thoroughly overloaded with folks who'd paid a sawbuck each to stand or sit on the top two tiers or five-bucks-per-spot on the bottom two. It was an awful mess when the thing suddenly creaked, cracked, buckled and fell, what with two people crushed to death underneath and a heck of a lot more badly injured. And especially sad when you consider they were just innocent, unsuspecting race fans out to enjoy themselves and have a good time. But that's what it takes to get car racing on the front page....

If you shuffled back to about the third or fourth page of the sports section (or right after three solid pages of all the latest hot baseball news!) you could also find out that Jim Rathmann won the Indy 500 in a Watson roadster called the Ken-Paul Special after an incredible, race-long, back-and-forth series of duels with Eddie Sachs, Troy Ruttman, Tony Bettenhausen, Sammy Speed, Johnny Thompson and, most especially, Rodger Ward. It came down to just those two at the end—Rathmann and Ward—sliding through the corners and rocketing down the straightaways nose-to-tail, side-by-side and wheel-to-wheel with the whole damn crowd standing on its feet, jumping up and down and screaming its blessed lungs out. But Rodger had to ease off right at the end on account of the cords were showing through on his right-rear tire, and the only easy lap Rathmann had in the whole blessed 500 miles was the last one. According to the record-keepers, there were no less than 29 lead changes—22 of them between Rathmann and Ward—and even a sportycar/Grand Prix nutcase like me had to admit that made your average road race look pretty tame indeed by comparison.

A week after Monaco and Indy, the Formula One Scarabs tried again at the Dutch Grand Prix at Zandvoort. Only their specially-ordered, three-racecar Fiat transporter with the custom tool boxes and parts cabinets, organized racks for damn near everything and a fairly complete machine/fabrication shop inside wasn't quite finished on time, so the cars arrived in a rented moving van while the whole blessed RAI crew found themselves jammed together in a VW Microbus. I guess it was pretty humiliating. But funny, too. And it kind of summed up the enormous gap that had opened up between young Lance Reventlow's hopes, plans and dreams for the Scarab Formula One team and how things were actually working out in real life. And nobody outside the team much cared, either. As Hank put it: "There's a lot of passion in Grand Prix motor racing, but not much in the way of *com*passion...."

Once again the Scarabs were well off the pace (although not quite so badly as at Monaco) and then Lance had a hell of a scare when a right-rear wheel flew off at damn near top speed because somebody hadn't bothered to tighten the hub nut properly. Although both he and the car survived without any serious damage, that incident really took a lot of the starch out of him, and Lance was fudging around in the mid-1:44s—way down at the very bottom of the time sheets—while Chuck was hustling around at a mildly impressive 1:38:4. But that still wasn't near quick enough to make the field. Seems the organizers were limiting the grid to only 15 cars—one fewer than Monaco, even though Zandvoort was a much bigger racetrack—simply because they couldn't afford (or at least weren't willing to pay) any more starting money than that! As you can imagine, that pissed a lot of people off—hell, some of those teams had come an awfully long way and spent an awful lot of money to race in Holland—and eventually a compromise was offered that anybody outside the top 15 qualifiers who wanted to would be welcome to start, but they wouldn't get any starting money. To which most of the team owners answered *"stuff it!"*—including Lance Reventlow. You have to understand that starting money was one of the main ways smaller teams were able to continue on in European racing, and many couldn't survive without it. It was also a question of precedent, professionalism and respect. Not to mention that just about every blessed team in the paddock—front-runners and backmarkers alike—thought the race organizers were acting like a bunch of cheap, money-grubbing assholes.

Things got even dicier when the "official" time sheets came out and Chuck's Scarab had somewhat incredibly sneaked into the very last "paid" qualifying spot thanks to a highly suspect 1:36.7 lap time—just a wee tick off what Toly and Phil

Hill were doing with their Ferrari Dinos—even though Chuck had never come close to anything like that on any of the RAI stopwatches. Or anywhere else, for that matter. Of course, the *real* story was that the race promoters desperately wanted one of the Scarabs in the field because of all the American servicemen and Army brats it might draw from the NATO base over at Wiesbaden. And they weren't above fudging things a bit to make it happen, either.

But, rather than being thrilled that one of his cars had finally qualified for its very first Grand Prix, Lance (to his everlasting credit) wasn't having any of it. He told the organizers that his car never turned anything like a 1:36.7, and if they didn't want to pay the Scarabs (and, by implication, anybody and everybody else) starting money based on their legitimate qualifying times, he was withdrawing his car from the race. Which is precisely what wound up happening. The sad part is that Chuck had worked awfully hard and driven his ass off, and in Hank's (and a lot of other people's) opinion, he wouldn't have embarrassed himself at all in the race. Sure, the car was down on power, iffy on handling and something like a generation-and-a-half out of date, but that car represented a tremendous amount of effort, hard work, blood, sweat and tears. And it was far from being a shitbox, which was more than you could say for a lot of other cars that had graced the back rows of Grand Prix starting grids over the years. On the one hand, it was nice that Lance stood up for his principles and did what he figured was the righteous and honorable thing. Even if he did do it by way of one of his angry, stalk-out-in-a-huff ultimatums. Still, Hank and a lot of other folks thought Chuck and the rest of the Scarab crew deserved better.

Jack Brabham's Cooper wound up winning the Dutch Grand Prix after a hell of an early battle with Moss in the Walker Lotus that was only settled when Moss had to pit for a tire change. And that thanks to a blowout he suffered when one of Brabham's rear tires kicked up a stone and fired it back at the Lotus like a bullet from a .44 magnum. Of course, Jack Brabham would never even *think* of doing such a thing on purpose. But dropping a wheel off in the gravel and flooring it to shower a little discouragement on the fellow just behind was a fairly common practice in Formula One....

Anyhow, Moss lost three minutes in the pits and nobody else was even close to the leaders when he pulled in, so that was pretty much the race. Then Dan Gurney had a hell of an accident when that crazy single rear brake on his BRM failed (again!) and launched him into the sand dunes at high speed. Upside-down, in fact. Dan was incredibly lucky to get off with just a few scrapes and bruises and a cracked wrist, and he was probably having a few second thoughts about signing with BRM. Although the front-engined Dino 246s were looking a little old and long in the tooth, that sort of thing never happened at Ferrari.

The Belgian Grand Prix two weeks later at Spa-Francorchamps turned out to be one of the darkest, blackest race weekends in Grand Prix history. And, although he may not have realized it at the time, that experience surely dampened whatever heart, fire and enthusiasm Lance Reventlow still had left for his Formula One adventure. You have to understand that none of the Scarab guys had ever seen a track like Spa before. It was damn near nine miles long, stitched together out of ordinary Belgian country roads through the Ardennes forest and the surrounding farm country, and it was deadly fast in a racing car and totally unforgiving. Long, high-speed straightaways led into incredibly fast, daunting sweepers and switchbacks that dove and slashed and carved their way through the undulating forests and countryside. Those corners had to be taken in massive, top-gear drifts, and even with one genuine, bog-slow first-gear hairpin at *La Source,* the average lap speed hovered around 135mph. And God only help you if you went off into the woods….

Spa was full of frightening, intimidating corners. The Masta kink, where you had to flick left-right between the blunt, hard corner of a stone barn and a wooden fence, flat out at 150-plus without lifting. Eau Rouge, where you had to descend down through a dip and then climb up over a steep crest that flattened out at the top, all the while making a snaking, slithering ess with your foot planted in top gear. Or Burnenville: a diving approach into a decreasing radius dip of a sweeper that you had to take in one long, hair-raising slide at over 140. Chuck Daigh called it *"the scariest corner on earth,"* and wondered out loud what some of the Indy 500 drivers would make of it.

Brabham typically set his jaw and got on with it, and he was fastest after first practice. Followed by Brooks in the apple-green-and-red Yeoman Credit team Cooper and then Moss in the Walker Lotus, but everybody more or less expected Moss to go quicker the second day. But that notion ended just three laps into Friday morning's first session, when a rear hub on Moss' Lotus 18 fractured at speed heading into Burnenville. Moss instinctively snapped it into a spin to scrub off some speed, but couldn't keep it from whamming *HARD!* into an embankment. It probably saved his life that he'd managed to swap ends and went in backwards. Even so, the impact catapulted him out violently, and he crash-landed on a grassy hillside with two broken legs, a broken nose, a couple fractured vertebrae and a hefty inventory of cuts, bangs and bruises. But he survived, and in the hospital Stirling was as aware as anyone how lucky he'd been not to be killed outright.

The idea that something like that could happen to the Best Damn Driver in the World at a track like Spa put a grim look on everyone's face in the paddock. And those dark expressions grew even darker when, after practice was halted to retrieve Moss and the remains of his car, it was suddenly realized that Formula One newcomer Mike Taylor and the privateer Lotus 18 he'd bought from Colin Chapman had likewise not made it around to the pits. Search parties went out and they finally found him, deep into the woods near Burnenville. He'd crashed on the same lap as Moss after his steering column apparently snapped it two and sent him crashing helplessly through the trees. And then he had to wait there in the woods for nearly 40 minutes—trapped in the car, badly injured and smelling gasoline and hot metal all around him—before he was finally rescued and sent off in another ambulance.

Needless to say, the other three Lotus 18s were immediately checked over, and the team's drivers weren't sure whether to be relieved or more frightened when cracks caused by incorrect machining were found on the rear hubs of two of the other cars, too. "That's the bloody thing about Chapman," Eric Gibbon said arily to no one in particular. "If something breaks, it's too light, but if it doesn't, it's too heavy…."

Meanwhile practice restarted and the weekend went on. Chuck Daigh was simply setting his jaw and gutting it out in the Scarab, and Hank was out on the circuit watching and saw it all during the final qualifying session. He said Chuck was taking Burnenville in the most hair-raising, graceful, inch-perfect monstrosity of a slide he had ever seen. "It was like watching a hawk swooping down to grab a rabbit, and it scared the shit out of you to watch." Even Eric Gibbon, who was standing next to Hank, shook his head and let out a respectful whistle of amazement. Still, Chuck's Scarab was well off the pace of front-row qualifiers Brabham, Brooks and a thoroughly incredible Phil Hill in one of the ungainly "dinosaur" Ferraris. Phil seemed to have a real knack for long, precise, high-speed corners, and no question the Ferrari was producing a lot of power on the long straights. But even so, his performance at Spa had a lot of drivers in "more modern" machinery pretty much muttering to themselves.

Reventlow didn't even look like he was trying. On top of all the team's mounting frustrations came that confidence-destroying wheel-coming-off incident at Zandvoort. And now, *this* place. Not to mention the brutally sobering accidents of Moss and Taylor. Clearly Lance was losing the thread of his dream. Although the "official watches" credited him with a better time than Chuck, it was actually Chuck out in the car, checking things over to see if there was any mechanical reason why Lance was more than a half-minute off Chuck's pace. Hank said it looked like he didn't want to be out there, which is no way to be in a Formula One racecar at a track like Spa….

In the race, Lance grumbled around at the very back of the pack for two laps and then his engine blew. And there were whispered rumors—even from some of the people on his own team—that he'd given it a "clutch job" and blown it up on purpose, just to get out of the damn race. But that's one of those things nobody will ever really know, of course. Plus it took an awfully long time for Lance to make it back to the pits, since he decided to take a long, solitary walk through the forest rather than trying to hitch a quick ride on one of the access roads. Hank said you could only imagine what was going through his mind as the sun filtered down through the leaves and he listened to the padding of his own footsteps and the chirp of birds and buzz of insects and the straining, almost painful wail of racing engines at top revs echoing in the distance….

Meanwhile Chuck soldiered on, driving the damn wheels off his Scarab and impressing everybody with his guts and skill if not exactly his racecar. But then it started pumping oil out and tightening as if it was about to seize (even though the oil pressure gauge was still reading okay) and so Chuck pulled in and parked it before that engine blew up, too.

Brabham still led with Phil Hill running a distant but impressive second in the old, upright Ferrari (although others were closing in) and Toly was having a nice if somewhat unnerving dice with new boy Chris Bristow in the Yeoman Credit Cooper a few positions further back. But then Toly's gearbox started acting up and he had to drop back, and that's when native Belgian and Ferrari newcomer "Wild Willy" Mairesse took up the fight with the green-and-red Cooper. It was Mairesse's first Grand Prix drive for Ferrari (and on his home track!) and it quickly escalated into a vicious battle—back and forth between two hungry young guns impatient to make an impression—and ended abruptly when Chris Bristow lost control and shot off the road at almost the same exact spot where Moss had crashed two days before. Bristow's Cooper flipped and rolled repeatedly at high speed and he was thrown out and killed instantly. His crumpled body wound up lying at the edge of the road in a grotesquely disheveled heap, where all the other drivers could see it when they passed. One of the marshals finally—mercifully—dragged it out of sight and covered it with a piece of tent canvas.

And then, just five laps later, a pheasant rose up out of the rough grass at trackside and buzzed across directly in front promising young Team Lotus Number Two Alan Stacey. It hit him square in the face at over 150. His car careened wildly off the road, crashed heavily and he, too, was dead….

Chapter 37: The Little Le Mans

Ferrari needed to win Le Mans in order to clinch another World Manufacturers' Championship, and so they showed up loaded for bear with no less than four of the very latest *Testa Rossas* backed up by a fresh, ex-works privateer entry from Carlo Sebastian. Plus a virtual swarm of their new 250 Short Wheelbase Berlinetta coupes running in the Grand Touring class (which, due to the barn-door aerodynamics of the open sports/racers thanks to those stupid FIA windshields, were almost as fast as the blessed prototypes). And there was a lot for Americans to cheer for at Le Mans that year, too. Briggs Cunningham's team arrived with three immaculate white Corvettes running fiberglass hardtops along with a sleek, "wouldn't-it-have-been-gorgeous-without-that-damn-windshield" new Jaguar prototype for Dan Gurney and Walt Hansgen to drive. Lucky Casner's Camoradi USA team showed up with two Maserati Birdcages (including one with a strange, enormous plexiglass windscreen that started halfway down the hood in an attempt to sneak a little streamlining into the new windshield rules) plus a Corvette of their own. And the French crowd really seemed to like those big old Corvettes and the rumbleguts V-8 bellow that came grumbling out their exhaust pipes. Hey, who wouldn't?

With Stirling Moss still in the hospital from his wreck at Spa and Gurney driving for Cunningham, Lucky Casner hired on Masten Gregory and Chuck Daigh to drive the Maserati "streamliner," and Hank thought that was a well-deserved chunk of recognition for all the fine drives Chuck had been putting in with the lost-cause Scarab on the Grand Prix circuit. And Hank also allowed as how it was a huge thrill to see Gregory and the white-and-blue "American" Maserati leading the whole blessed pack—including *all* the Ferraris!—at the end of lap one. Wow. And he said it got even more exciting watching Masten continue to stretch that lead every lap for the first hour and a half. Of course, Eric Gibbon sniffed that the Ferraris were just holding back and maintaining pace because they didn't expect the Birdcage to last, but it was obviously galling him a little that this newborn American team was doing so well. Especially since there were really no British teams to root for except over the long haul.

And then lightning struck the factory Ferraris, can you believe it? For once they were holding station in second, third, fourth and fifth and not racing the hell out of each other, and then *two* of them inexplicably ran out of gas on the very lap they were supposed to come in for their pit stops! Apparently they'd tried some trick new exhaust system that gave slightly more power—but also used slightly more fuel!—between the Le Mans test day in April and the race itself in June, and had somehow forgot to re-check their fuel mileage with the new setup. Willy Mairesse saw Phil's car and then Toly's car pulled off to the side of the road and instantly backed out of it and brought his car in. Hank said there was barely a quart of fuel left in the tank when he arrived at the pits to hand it over to Ginther.

And then, about 15 minutes later and with a light rain starting to fall, Gregory came in for a routine pit stop and to hand the leading Maserati "streamliner" over to Chuck Daigh. At that point they were over three minutes ahead of the Ferrari Olivier Gendebien was sharing with journalist/racer Paul Frere, who were running at an easier, more conservative pace than the other factory *Testa Rossas,* but had avoided sharing their fuel consumption problems because of it. Only then disaster struck in the Camoradi pits. Chuck climbed in, flipped the ignition switch on, listened to the reassuring click of the fuel pump and hit the starter button.

Nothing.

He hit it again.

Nothing.

Worried looks all around. The mechanics scrambled to get under that ridiculously enormous plexiglass windshield and the alloy hood underneath it and quickly checked all the electrical connections on the starter motor. Those looked okay so they checked the connections on the switch on the dash. Also fine. *Shit!* The inescapable conclusion was that the starter motor had fried, and you weren't allowed to replace components like starter motors (or push-start the car) without getting disqualified. So the only way to get back in the race was to somehow sneak the skinniest fingers on the crew in between that maddening latticework of frame tubes, unbolt the starter motor, sneak it out, rebuild it right there in the pits and re-install it.

It took exactly one hour.

During which time the Camoradi team's hopes faded, the heavens opened and rain started pouring down in buckets….

Well, the race turned into pretty much a survival contest after that—and a wet one—and Frere and Gendebien went on to win it by four laps over Carlo Sebastian's privateer *Testa Rossa,* cinching yet another World Manufacturers' Championship for Ferrari. For a change it was the Porsches that hit mechanical and crash trouble (rather than droning around like little tin robots and picking up the available placings, points and prize money after all the faster cars crapped out) and the few still running were well behind the leading Ferraris long before the closing hours. But even so, there was quite a drama playing out towards the end of the race. The Fitch/Grossman Corvette was running first in class and a highly respectable (and thoroughly unexpected, at least in the press tower) eighth overall, but it was overheating badly and coming into the Cunningham pits almost every lap with steam pouring out and foul smells and gurgling noises coming from underneath the hood. And they couldn't even add water, because then the car would be disqualified. So they'd bring it in and shut it down and let it sit awhile to cool it off, but then it wouldn't want to re-start because it was still too blessed hot. So it looked like they might be out of it with just a handful of laps to go. But then someone had the bright idea of packing the engine in ice from the drink coolers, sending it out for another lap, bringing it in and packing it in ice again, and so forth until the checker finally came down at a little after 4pm. And that's how Chevy's Corvette wound up 8th overall and scored a fine class win in their first-ever try at Le Mans. I'd never been exactly a huge fan of Corvettes (I mean, I always thought they were kind of huge cars, you know?) but I was proud as hell of those guys and what that all-American sportscar had done….

To be honest, the Scarab team already knew they were pretty much washed up in Europe after that tragic weekend at Spa. But plans and entries had already been made and all the hotel rooms and such already paid for at the French Grand Prix at Reims two weeks later, and so the team holed up in a rented garage, did their best to fix the bottom end of Chuck's engine and install a brand-new motor that had just been air-freighted in from California in Lance's car and sleep-walked their way towards the race. Only Lance had replaced himself as a driver with fast and experienced California hotshoe Richie Ginther. Some said he'd lost the old fire and desire for it after Spa, some said he wanted Ginther in the car because Richie was a savvy and sensitive test driver and, like Chuck, hands-on smart about mechanics, while still others said it was because he had to ask his mother for more money to finance RAI's continuing European escapades and, following the crashes and the two well-publicized driver deaths at Spa, she would only agree to it if he stopped driving the cars himself. Take your pick.

Although Reims was fast—rivaling even Spa for lap-average speeds—it wasn't nearly so daunting, terrifying or treacherous. Horsepower, acceleration and sheer, flat-out speed were king at Reims, and Toly and the rest of the Ferrari team were really looking forward to a race where their engines could battle—and perhaps even overcome?—the braking, handling and aerodynamic advantages of the Coopers and Lotus 18s. The Scarabs were once again the slowest cars in the field, but even then there were problems keeping them together. The Reventlow/Goossen engines apparently didn't like the long, flat-out straightaway stretches, and both cars blew up during practice and qualifying. The crew thought it might have something to do with the oiling system. There was plenty of oil pressure—even as the bottom ends started tightening up and that telltale foundry smell started drifting out from under the hood—but maybe not enough volume? In any case, it didn't much matter. They were outclassed, way off the necessary pace, out of running engines and headed for home with their tails pretty much tucked between their legs. As you can imagine, things were pretty grim around the Scarab transporter while they loaded up their silent, oil-streaked racecars well before noon on Saturday. Hank told me all about it the next time I saw him at Riverside: *"Nobody would look you in the eye. But I couldn't look them in the eye, either...."*

While the Scarabs and the rest of the team headed home, Lance and Chuck went to England for the British Grand Prix two weeks later. They already had their entries in, and so Lance made a deal on a drive in one of the factory Coopers with the understanding that whoever was quickest in practice would race it. To no one's surprise, it was Chuck, and he did fairly well in a strange car on an unfamiliar track until it came down with a case of overheating and he had to park it. But no question Lance and Chuck were impressed with the handling, braking and overall packaging of the Cooper, and were already discussing building an "RAI" version of the car before they even boarded the plane back to California.

As far as the Grand Prix circus went, with Moss still mending up from his Spa crash, Jack Brabham picked up three more wins in a row in France, England and Portugal, pretty much sewing up the World Championship (for the second season in a row!) in the process. Although Hank said English comingman Graham Hill gave him one hell of a run for his money at Silverstone in the rear-engined BRM. Brabham led easily while Hill made a thoroughly miserable start, but then he carved his way through from the back of the field, reeled Brabham in, passed him for the lead, and looked to have his first Grand Prix win in the bag when the BRM's brakes started acting up (so what's new?) and he spun out of a secure lead just six laps from the checker. Oh, well….

The other thing going on during the middle of what was *supposed* to be the 2.5-liter Grand Prix formula's final season was a groundswell movement to start a new, "Intercontinental Formula" for 2.5 and maybe even 3.0-liter cars outside of FIA jurisdiction. A lot of the British teams and race promoters were opposed to the enforced switch to little 1500cc tiddlers for the '61 season. Especially since they didn't have any competitive engines on hand except an updated version of the smaller, 1.5-liter Coventry Climax FPF that had been running around in Formula Two since 1957. It was a good, strong, solid and torquey little four-banger, but hardly powerful enough to stand up to the new V6 everybody knew Ferrari was working on.

And then the British teams got even more bent out of shape when the organizers of the Italian Grand Prix (with, no doubt, a little not-so-subtle encouragement from old man Enzo in Maranello) announced that the Italian Grand Prix at Monza would use the steeply banked oval sections of the track as part of the course. Everyone knew those bankings were sensationally fast (which would suit Ferrari's rugged and powerful Dinos nicely) and notoriously bumpy (ditto), so all the major British teams harrumphed a few times, took a snort or two of scotch, folded their arms across their chests and announced a boycott. After all, Brabham had already sewed up the championship and so had Cooper on the Constructors' side, so why the hell bother? And that's how the now ancient-looking (but oh, so damn handsome!) Ferrari Dinos scored a steamroller 1-2-3 finish ahead of a skimpy, patchwork, 16-car field of privateer, Italian hybrid Cooper/Ferraris and Cooper/Maseratis plus no less than seven Formula Two cars. Including a last-minute entry of three 1.5-liter single-seaters from Porsche, who decided to drop in and do a little free race testing for the upcoming 1500cc formula. Tavoni put Toly in Ferrari's own Formula Two car—really just a smaller, 1.5-liter version of the Dino 246—and Toly told Hank afterwards (on condition that he wouldn't be quoted) that it was more "formation flying" than real racing, seeing as how Willy Mairesse was given strict orders to hold back in his Formula One car and give Toly a "tow" to pull him away from the Porsches. That worked to perfection, and so *Scuderia Ferrari* managed a score yet another glorious triumph at Monza by winning *both* classes in perhaps the dumbest, most contrived and least interesting Grand Prix ever held there.

But even while he was rubbing their noses in it at Monza, old man Ferrari was carefully and cunningly stringing the British teams and promoters along regarding their hoped-for "Intercontinental Formula" idea. Lance Reventlow had showed a lot of enthusiasm for the new class, visualizing a Cooper-style, rear-engined Scarab with a development version of the so-far troublesome Reventlow/Goossen engine as a way to salvage some sort of respect, results and self-esteem out of the Scarab Formula One fiasco. And the blue-and-white cars would certainly be welcome to add a little color to the British Green and Scottish Blue already expected on the grids. But what they really needed to make a go of it—and all the Brits knew it—was the red cars. Sure, Ferrari had been off their game the past season, but they'd be back. And, more importantly—no matter how they were running—Ferraris brought the fans out. Bums on seats, don't you know? So Ferrari told them—indirectly, through intermediaries—that it sounded like a very good idea. After all, who in their right mind would pay good money to watch the best drivers in the world racing around in kiddie cars? Besides, Ferrari already had engines ready and his own rear-engined chassis well along in development for the new class. Why on earth wouldn't he be interested?

Why, indeed....

Meanwhile, back here in the states, the Republicans surprised absolutely no one by nominating Richard M. Nixon and Henry Cabot Lodge to go up against Kennedy and Johnson in the November elections, and old Fidel Castro managed to piss off any Americans who weren't already mad as hell at him by seizing all U.S.-owned property in Cuba on August 7th. Oh, and the Russkies tried U-2 pilot Francis Gary Powers for espionage in a big, showy trial and it wasn't exactly a blockbuster surprise when they found him guilty and sentenced him to 10 years. And my pal Sylvester Jones thought it was pretty damn ironic (although I believe the term he used was "fucked up") the way everybody here was cheering and applauding the American Negro athletes who were mopping up medals right and left at the Rome Olympics, while at the same time they were shaking their heads and *tsk-tsking* over the sit-ins, civil disobedience and forced school integration down south. Now I personally didn't believe in racial equality, seeing as how I'd noticed from close, personal observation that athletically gifted black people could pretty much run rings around athletically gifted white people. But I guess that wasn't the point, was it?

Anyhow, Nixon and Kennedy had their big, live, televised TV debates so the public could take a good, close-up gander at their presidential candidates and listen to their views on all the important subjects and issues of the day. And the consensus afterwards was just as divided—and along the exact same lines, can you believe it?—as it was before the shows aired. Although most people in the middle agreed that Kennedy was better-looking and that Nixon really needed to do something about his five-o'clock shadow and those sweat beads above his upper lip.

Fidel Castro made a rambling, four-hour speech that nobody could follow to the United Nations General Assembly (although the general gist of it was that the United States was screwing things up everywhere for all the people who didn't have anything and figured the best way to get it was to take it away from those who had) and then old Nikita Khrushchev came to town and beat his shoe on his desk in the General Assembly just to show everybody back home he wasn't afraid of us and likewise hadn't forgotten the U-2 incident and Francis Gary Powers, either. But then, who had?

Despite what was going on at the United Nations, the *real* news in New York was about how the Yankees fired longtime manager Casey Stengel—just like that!—right after the Yankees lost the World Series to the Pittsburgh Pirates in seven games. I won a double sawbuck off my dad on that series, but I still felt kind of sorry for tough, gnarly old Casey Stengel. After all, think of all the teams that never even make it to the World Series, right? Then again, loyalty and forgiveness have never been especially abundant commodities in and around New York City.

Meanwhile, back over on the Jersey side, I was working hard at the dealership, keeping a sideways eye on Big Ed and helping out Steve and J.R. a little with this Volvo sedan they were helping prepare for the fourth annual "Little Le Mans" eight-hour enduro they were having up at Lime Rock. The deal came together during one of those beer-and-bullshit sessions that inevitably seem to follow the usual Old Business, New Business and scratchy, gurgling, 16mm black-and-white British racing film at your typical wintertime sportscar club meetings. As we knew so well at the dealership, compact cars had become all the rage, and everybody in the club was chatting about the growing number of multi-hour enduros for them at Lime Rock, Marlboro and several other tracks. Anyhow, Steve and J.R. wound up sitting around a pitcher or two with an expatriate Brit MG driver named John Targett and this Porsche driver named Dave Burton, and they were pretty good friends and had moreover raced against each other a few times with the results generally split right down the middle. Although Dave said that John had to be cheating on account of no stock MG should be able to run with a Porsche and there was no way in hell (at least from what Dave had seen, anyway!) that John was out-driving him. And John countered right back that if you added up the cost of his car plus what he'd spent on various not-exactly-original-equipment parts and pieces, it was still a hell of a lot less than what a damn Porsche cost. Not to mention that there was no way Dave was out-driving him, either!

And out of such things are new racing projects and partnerships forever born….

The idea sounded deceptively simple over their second pitcher of beer: they'd go in halvsies on a car together, prepare it together, and share it together in the races. What could be simpler or more reasonable? Only of course John had his MG in *his* garage and Dave had his Porsche in *his* garage and besides, neither one of them exactly wanted their wives to catch a whiff of what they were planning. I mean, if you're married (or even close to it), can you visualize telling *your* wife that you've gone out and bought yourself a second racecar?

I thought not.

Which is of course where J.R. and Steve and our shop came in, seeing as how they were also well into that second (or was it third by now?) pitcher of beer and were easy prey for the irresistible intake suction of such an obviously marvelous idea. So it was set and decided with nothing more than a sly, knowing look shared around the table and an order for a fourth pitcher of beer. And naturally the next hour was devoted exclusively to picking a team name (they finally settled on *"The Squeelers")*, designing a team logo (a fast, low-slung cartoon pig wearing dark sunglasses and skittering around a corner on racing tires), deciding who would get to start the first race, choreographing pit stops in ornate detail and trying to settle in a fair and equitable manner whose name would go on top of whose name in the lettering over the driver's door. Oh, and picking what kind of car to use, too.

"How about one of those new Plymouth Valiants?"

"How the heck could we get one? They just came out."

"Perhaps we could get a dealer to back us?" John offered.

"Have you ever tried selling that kind of idea to a dealership?"

"No, but I've heard that's how it's done."

"That's how it's done by the guy who owns the dealership or the guy who's diddling his widow," Dave snorted.

"That's not always true," Steve corrected him. "Sometimes it's the son of the guy who owns the dealership. Or the guy who married his daughter...."

"Besides, where would you get speed parts for one of those things?"

"I thought these cars were supposed to be *stock?"* J.R. more or less asked.

John and Dave both gave him the hairy eyeball.

"My uncle's next-door neighbor bought his kid one of those '40 Ford-looking Volvo sedans the summer before last," Steve tossed in, "and the kid turned it over doing doughnuts in the railroad parking lot the first night after it snowed. Rolled it all the way down the embankment, too." He took another sip of beer. "I think it's still sitting in his driveway with a tarp over it and the roof kinda caved in...."

"You think we could get a deal on it?"

"I dunno," Steve shrugged. "But I'm pretty sure the insurance company paid off and they wound up using the money for college tuition after his dad got laid off."

John and Dave eyeballed each other slyly, and quickly agreed that such a Volvo would represent an absolutely *perfect* choice for endurance sedan racing.

"I heard Volvo engines are pretty stout."

"I understand the cars are *very* rugged."

"I heard they handle great for a car that's damn near two stories high."

"And you can't *kill* Volvos," J.R. said solemnly, lifting his glass. "You gotta beat 'em to death with a stick!"

Handshakes all around.

The deal was made.

Well, I probably don't have to tell you that the Volvo sedan project turned out to be just a wee bit more complicated, time-consuming and expensive than any of the participants (or should I say co-conspirators?) ever envisioned. But that goes without saying for any impromptu, four- or five-pitcher racecar notion, doesn't it? Still, I must admit it was kind of neat having another build-it-up-from-nothing racecar project around the shop. Although, as designated boss, I felt compelled to do my very best Old Man Finzio interpretation and got real disgusted and pissed off about it when I saw that thing out back under a tarp for the first time. Naturally I told Steve and J.R. that we really needed the space for paying-customer service work and that they'd wind up spending *way* too much time fooling around with the damn racecar instead of looking after things. I mean, you more or less *have* to make that kind of speech when you're the boss....

But the guys were pretty good about it, keeping the car out back with that ugly tarp over it—Big Ed said it looked like a four-wheeled mound of cow manure—and pushing it in after hours to work on it until, well, who really needs to know until when? And of course I got sucked in eventually, and wound up paying for the Greek over at the body shop to pound out the roof (they were going to just fill it up with Bondo, but I figured a Volvo PV544 was already plenty top-heavy) and put in new front and rear window glass. I even paid to have it painted in return for getting *"Alfredo's Foreign Car Service"* lettered across both doors.

Even so, the project dragged on about twice as long as any of the partners expected (which was no surprise to me, of course) and the fact is they never would have made the race at Lime Rock at all if it'd been held on its originally scheduled Saturday in August. But it rained like a sonofabitch that day—damn near flood conditions—and so the fourth annual Lime Rock Little Le Mans was re-scheduled for October. And October is a pretty damn fine time of year up in northwestern Connecticut on the off chance you get lucky with the weather. If you've ever been there around then, you know what I'm talking about.

So, as you well might imagine, I decided to tag along when they headed up to that re-scheduled eight-hour race at Lime Rock in October. Just to see how things worked out, you know? And so did Julie and the kids. To be honest, that trip up to Connecticut represented a pretty tough choice for me. Seems a lot of the international Big Guns like Moss in the Walker Lotus and Brabham in the factory Cooper and Salvadori in the Yeoman Credit Cooper and a whole bunch more were dropping in on the big money, FIA-sanctioned "Formula Libre" race at Watkins Glen on October 9th. Cal was even coming over and trying to set himself up with a ride for it, even though old Enzo wasn't much interested in crossing the Atlantic Ocean (or even the English Channel, for that matter) to run some fly-by-night race with no established stature, history or championship points involved. Or a sweating-fat wad of starting money, either. Especially seeing as how he'd likely get waxed by the damn Coopers and Lotuses again anyway.

I knew there was no way I could do both events, so it kind of boiled down to a question of hanging on the fences and watching the fastest, most advanced racing cars and the best damn professional drivers in the world parading by at Watkins Glen or actually participating and feeling like I was somehow Part of the Show at some little Podunk sedan race that nobody gave two shits about up at Lime Rock. And I went back and forth between the two quite a few times. On the one hand, it was a pretty long trek up to Watkins Glen (I couldn't *believe* I caught myself thinking a thing like that!), while Lime Rock was just a ways up the road. Plus I'd gotten maybe a little intimidated, bored, disappointed, out-of-touch, worn down and downright jaded where bigtime professional racing was concerned, while I found myself more or less looking forward to a homey, friendly little club race where we could all have fun and not feel like we were on a damn knife-edge all the time. Besides, Julie said she and the kids would come with if we just went up to Lime Rock for the day, and I've always figured it's more or less your sacred duty, if you're a sick, diehard racer, to try and infect your kids….

Not to mention that I was kind of curious what it might be like if we took the whole family up in one of our VW Microbus campers. I mean, we *were* selling the blessed things. And I really liked the idea that it had a little fridge in back to keep the hot dogs and lunch meat and provolone cheese and soda and juice cool for the kids (the beer was in the ice chest J.R. and Steve were bringing up in the van, natch) plus a little fold-down table where they could draw in their coloring books or play *Chutes and Ladders* and generally keep themselves amused whenever they got bored with the racing. Which figured to be about 15 minutes after we got there—tops—and this was, after all, scheduled to be an eight-hour race.

Although I have to admit I was a little concerned about how that heavily-loaded, full-of-my-beloved-wife-and-offspring VW Microbus Camper was going to handle the highways and real, open-road travel. But it wasn't too bad. I discovered I really liked sitting up high and getting that grand, commanding, over-the-road Truck Driver view through that huge expanse of windshield. Even if it did mean that our center-of-gravity was about nipple high on a junior high cheerleader. And you eventually got used to the bus-like steering wheel angle and the shift pattern with third gear halfway to the glove box and the engine noise thrumming and buzzing all around you all the time like a 30-pound bumblebee trapped in a kettledrum. Made it pretty much impossible to hear the radio except when we slowed down to go through the little towns and villages. But that was okay, since by then I'd heard about enough of Chubby Checker's blockbuster, chart-topping new dance hit *The Twist,* which it seemed like every damn disc jockey on the eastern seaboard was playing between every single commercial break and which I, personally, had grown slightly weary of after its three- or four-thousandth excursion up my ear canals. Although naturally the kids absolutely loved it, and would shriek with glee and demand that I turn the volume up as far as it would go every damn time it came on.

Which I pretended to do, of course. They also liked that funny *Please, Mr. Custer* by Larry Verne (although, like *The Twist,* it lost a little of its magic after about 600-odd playings). I was more partial to *Save the Last Dance for Me* by The Drifters, the Ventures' nifty instrumental *Walk, Don't Run* and *Chain Gang* by Sam Cooke, while Julie liked *Never on Sunday* from that naughty new movie everybody was talking about with Melina Mercouri along with Brenda Lee's sad, lush, plaintive teenage ballad *I Want to be Wanted.* And we both harmonized along with the Everly Brothers' *So Sad (To Watch Good Love Go Bad)* every single time it came on, even though I could see little Vincent holding his nose in the rearview mirror. Of course, with the general speaker quality in a VW Microbus, all those songs sounded like they were being sung through a large wad of steel wool in a cheap metal wastebasket hidden deep down somewhere behind the dashboard.

If radio reception and interior acoustics were not exactly the VW Microbus' strong suits, neither were brakes, power or handling. Not hardly. Why, that thing could barely crawl its way up to a mile a minute going up the Taconic Parkway. And that was with my foot buried a good quarter-inch into the floor mat! And God only help you if you had to stop it in a hurry from that speed! Although you most likely couldn't even get to a mile a minute if there was any kind of a hill or a headwind. But a headwind was surely better than a crosswind, which could damn near blow that big tin box clear off the road. You kept it pretty much floored all the time in a VW microbus—not that anyone much noticed!—and learned early on that you had to lead it a little and anticipate that sudden blast of wind across your bows whenever you actually managed to pull out and attempt to overtake some seriously overloaded or ill-running truck, school bus, camper, farm implement or travel trailer that was inexplicably traveling even slower than you. Not that such a thing was a common occurrence.

But people just loved those VW Microbuses—or certain people loved them, anyway—and we did pretty well with them on account of Big Ed was always happy to sell you anything you, he, or anybody else could talk you into. Big Ed was a natural born, all-American capitalist, and so it never much bothered him that VW Microbuses seemed to attract an inordinate number of bookish left-wingers, black turtleneck intellectuals, artists, PhDs, plaid-flannel-shirt types with an oversupply of facial hair and matched sets of big-boned or rail-thin females in blue jeans and sweatshirts who didn't believe in makeup. Why, Big Ed could pick VW Microbus buyers out for you before they even walked through the blessed front door.

Anyhow, it was a pretty nice trip up through the fall colors and everything into Connecticut, and I have to say I really *enjoyed* putting up the pop-up top and helping Julie and the kids set up our awning and folding table and picnic stuff right outside that VW camper's side door. Not to mention helping unload the *Alfredo's Foreign Car Service* Volvo racecar and the tools and ice chest and pit board and so forth out of our parts truck (a no-side-windows VW panel van, natch) down in the paddock. I was likewise enjoying all the waves and smiles and handshakes and *"Hey, how y'doin? Long time no see!"* I got from old club racing regulars I hadn't seen in ages.

Plus all the so-called "racecars" looked pretty damn safe, solid, slow and sturdy and also like an awful lot of fun. Which was quite a welcome change from a lot of the "pro" races I'd been to. Casual pre-race paddock handicapping had the V-8 Studebaker Larks figured as easily the most powerful cars at Lime Rock, but even they didn't look particularly intimidating. And of course Julie fell instantly, madly in love with all the little shoebox Austin Morris Mini-Minors skittering around on their tiny little 10-inch wheels. All women do. And so did I, come to think of it. I only saw one lone VW (which I noticed had some suspiciously Porsche-looking hardware underneath) plus one Fiat and two NSUs, four BMW 700s, a Renault 4CV, an English Ford and a Triumph Herald and a whole flock of those ring-ding Swedish Saabs with their unmistakable, canned-ham silhouettes and wispy, pinging little trails of oilsmoke coming out of their pea shooter-size exhausts.

Jeez, it was *fun!* And I remember thinking to myself, as I wandered through the paddock with Julie and the kids: *Why, even I could do something like this....*

But of course I didn't say anything.

After all, I knew better.

I can't say as John and Dave's race went exactly swimmingly. They somewhat optimistically drove up in the Volvo to "break in" the new (and, of course, righteously stock—*hah!)* engine J.R. put together for them, and had a friendly little seething difference of opinion along the way about who should get to start. Steve suggested they could maybe settle it with a 50-Yard Dash foot race down pit lane since it was going to be one of those Le Mans-style starts where you had to scamper across the road to the car. But John had some sort of old war wound (I think it was a burn of some kind, since I believe he was mostly a second cook, radish trimmer and potato peeler for the RAF) and Dave likewise begged off on account of he'd been out of training pretty much since he played finger-on-the-ball specialist for windy-day kickoffs on his high school football team. Not to mention that neither one of them wanted to risk embarrassing themselves by running out of gas and puking halfway down pit lane or losing to the other guy. And that was understandable. They eventually settled on flipping a coin for it—little Vincent got to do the flipping, just to make sure it was on the up-and-up—and Dave called "heads" while it turned up tails and so John got the start. He made a pretty good job of it, too. After practicing a few times in the paddock (and getting his sleeve caught on the inside door handle twice) he got away pretty quickly and was running an impressive and exciting third overall at the end of the first lap—right behind two other Volvos and just half-a-carlength ahead of a tiny but *very* healthy-sounding (not to mention madly driven) little Fiat 600, which had no doubt benefited from all the supposedly illegal hop-up parts and go-faster goodies they made for Fiats over in Italy.

Eventually one of the V-8 Studebaker Larks came lumbering up behind John and he wisely waved him by rather than risk becoming a hood ornament so early in the race. The he just more or less held station, keeping to a nice, steady pace and holding the leaders well in sight. I can't tell you how much I was enjoying it from the side-lines! I'd been away from an enduro pit stall for an awfully long time, and I'd for-gotten the giddy, all-consuming buzz of excitement that goes along with it. Especially when things are going well. Then it got even better when the Lark came in for gas after just 26 laps (had they started on light tanks like Fangio in the 1957 German Grand Prix at the Nurburgring, we all wondered?) and that put us right back into third overall again. Which felt pretty damn good, even though I knew we still had seven-and-a-half hours to go….

And then, on the 41st lap and with John doing an absolutely marvelous job, one of the rear axle hubs sheared. The wheel went flying and "our" Volvo half-spun, went off sideways, dug into the soft grass and performed the second complete roll-over maneuver of its lifetime. Although bystanders told me it was hardly one of your spectacular, high-in-the-air somersault flips or cartwheeling endos, but rather kind of a falling-over-sideways *"Thunk-Clunk-Ka-Clunk"* deals with maybe one more hefty *"THUD!"* right at the end. As John-the-Brit put it afterwards: *"I sup-pose you might call it an industrial-grade rollover."*

Of course we didn't know any of this until we noticed John was missing and sent J.R. up to the base of the tower to find out what happened. But before he even got there, little Vincent had come barreling down the hill and across the paddock to scream: *"HE FELL OVER ON HIS TOP! HE FELL OVER ON HIS TOP!"* at the top of his lungs. Naturally I went to see what'd happened, and by then the corner workers and tow truck driver had pretty much levered it back on its wheels (well, three of them, anyway) and John was waving at me somewhat sheepishly from behind where the windshield would have been if the car had still had one. So there was nothing much to do but walk back over towards the pits with little Vincent—picking up an ice cream for each of us on the way, since I didn't figure we were in any kind of hurry—and by the time we got there, John and our rather lumpy, buckled-up, three-wheeled Volvo had been towed into the paddock, where it dangled off the end of the hook like a question mark. The right-rear wheel was in the back seat, all the glass was busted out (and I'd just paid to replace it!) and there was oil all over the fenders plus steam coming out from under the front thanks to a split radiator seam. Not a very pretty sight, if you want the truth of it.

Well, I thought it was a pretty damn disappointing thing to have happen just an hour into an eight-hour race, and I guess we were all feeling disgusted about it. But then one of the other Volvo drivers came over—a guy named Art Riley, who I'd met once before at Sebring—and he allowed as how he had a whole spare axle shaft and hub assembly strapped onto his trailer. I guess he'd been racing Volvos for a while and thought he ought to carry one. He also mentioned that one of his crew guys had a street Volvo sedan and we were welcome to borrow the radiator out of it so long as we put it back when we were done. And I guess I don't have to tell you what hap-pened next, do I?

John, Dave, J.R. and me tore into that bent-up Volvo racecar while Steve made short work of getting the radiator drained and out of the crew guy's PV544 street car, and believe it or not we had Dave headed back out onto the track (only wearing his bubble shield now, seeing as how the windshield was still missing) in less than 45 minutes. And you should've heard the mighty cheer we got from all of our friends and competitors up and down pit lane! Followed by an even louder one echoing over from the small (but highly vocal!) crowd up on the spectator hill overlooking the esses when our rumpled-up, windowless Volvo sashayed back into view. Made us all feel like we'd accomplished something pretty damn special, you know?

Even Julie and the kids felt it, I could tell.

By that point we had no idea who was where anymore (and I don't think Timing and Scoring did, either), but according to the Official Hourly Reports that were coming out just like clockwork about every two-and-a-half hours, the big gas tanks, amazing momentum and great fuel mileage of the little canned-ham Saabs were almost exactly balancing out the horsepower and torque advantage of the bigger, heavier and far thirstier Studebaker Lark V-8s. Truth is, we were just damn happy to be out there again and, as impetuous driving and mechanical attrition took their inevitable toll, moving up now and then in the standings.

And then, about halfway into his second stint, Dave had the front coupling on the driveshaft come completely apart (I reckon the whole blessed driveline had been knocked around a bit during the two previous roll-overs) and the entire driveshaft assembly spit right out the bottom! Truth is, Dave was damn lucky it didn't jam into the pavement like a tent stake and flip the car right over—again!—but somewhat unlucky in that the flange or something burst a rear tire and then whanged *HARD* into the gas tank. Which responded by dumping fuel all over the hot exhaust pipe and the sparks shooting every-which-way off that dragging driveshaft and, well….

Dave managed to wrestle it over to the side of the road and then bailed out like a pilot ditching over the Atlantic before the car even came to rest. And then about all he could do was stand up, dust himself off, put his hands on his hips and watch helplessly while that Volvo burned. And burned. And burned some more. In fact, it burned so thoroughly and completely that Dave and John decided to sell the smoking remains to Art Riley on the spot rather than haul that charred hunk of blackened steel and melted rubber and plastic back to Passaic. And I couldn't say as I blamed them. As fate and the gods of accounting would have it, the money they made on the remains was just barely enough to cover the new radiator they had to buy for the crew guy's Volvo (they managed to jury-rig the bad one from earlier in the day by crushing off a couple tubes and laying on about a half-pound of solder so's he could make it back home) along with paying for most all the beer and sandwiches in the ice chest.

Hey, that's the way it goes sometimes in racing.

But the important thing was that both Dave and John were okay and—in some strange, off-the-wall way—we'd all had more fun, drama and excitement that day than any of us could remember. Even little Vincent. And you should've heard the two of them after the initial shock wore off and the giddiness set in:

"Good Lord, Dave, you didn't have to set the bloody thing on fire!"

"Well, you didn't have to roll it over, chum."

"I rolled it over TWICE, my good man. And I dare say it was a lot more spectacular than what YOU did."

"Why, I burned the damn thing clear to the ground! The corner workers said the flames went at least 50 feet in the air! Besides, I heard you only went over once. From people who saw it, too."

It went on like that all the way back to Passaic.

And meanwhile Julie and the kids were asleep in back and I was up front at the wheel, listening and laughing and now and then thinking quietly to myself: *You know, I could DO this. I really could....*

Chapter 38: A Party or a Wake?

Irish Catholic John F. Kennedy got himself elected to the presidency of these United States by the narrowest of margins on Tuesday, November 8th (a lot of people said it was Nixon's shifty eyes and the sweat over his upper lip during those TV debates that really swung the vote) and a little over a week later me and Big Ed were on a jet to Los Angeles for the U.S. Grand Prix at Riverside. Along with what Cal, Hank and everybody else said was going to be one hell of a blowout party at Lance Reventlow's enormous swanky-modern house in Beverly Hills. I must admit that Big Ed was doing pretty good by then. He'd lost about 30 pounds (although he had over twice that much still to go), had most of his color back, a faint shadow of the old glint in his eye and a kind of hesitant, iffy version of the boisterous old Big Ed swagger I'd always known. He'd gone out and bought himself one of those massive "French Thunderbird" Facel Vega HK-500s—like the one that French existential writer Albert Camus killed himself in by crashing into a tree—after he read in *Road & Track* that it was big, rare, expensive, stylish and powerful, came with an automatic transmission and that no less than Stirling Moss and Maurice Trintignant owned and drove them on the road between races. And I had to admit it actually was pretty neat—even if it was French and weighed in at over two tons—what with a great big 383-cubic-inch Chrysler engine under the hood and the most beautiful, buttery-soft, pastel mauve leather interior you have ever seen. Which went rather well with the creamy, yellowish-ivory exterior so long as it didn't make you want to puke as soon as you laid eyes on it.

Big Ed had even started dating again, even if it *was* one of the visiting nurses from the service his doctors had fixed him up with after his stay in the hospital. She was a big-boned, loud and busty southern-fried copper-blonde with a sweet (if eternally patronizing—you know how nurses are) smile named Ella May Rutabaga. And she was a full eight months past her 30th birthday, so Big Ed figured he was following his doctors' orders to a tee when it came to running around with young girls! Ella Mae moreover knew pretty much exactly what to do in any kind of medical emergency, and Big Ed figured that was like carrying a spare tire, jack, lug wrench, tool kit, a handful of fuses and maybe even an extra water pump, fuel pump, generator, fan belt, coil, set of sparkplugs, cap and rotor, point set and condenser and the number of a good towing service around with him wherever he went. But she could sure get on your nerves. She had this habit of talking to you like you were some little school kid who didn't know how to wipe his ass without getting shit all over his fingers, you know? And she talked like that to *everybody.*

You know how nurses can be.

Truth is, even though he put on a brave, confident, who-gives-a-good-goddam face about it, you could tell Big Ed was still pretty shaken by what happened back at our Christmas party and not exactly at ease with himself any more. That's a pretty scary thing to see happen to somebody you really care about and look up to. And it was Julie's idea that I should maybe take him out to California for the Grand Prix after she heard us talking about it once or twice at the dealership. "It might do him some good," she said.

"Going to a car race?"

"More like just getting away. A little change of scenery. I think he's been moping around and worrying too much. And it wouldn't be such a bad idea to get him away from that Ella Mae for a while, either. She just reinforces the idea that he's sick."

No question Julie had that part right. Fact is, Big Ed had never been much of a worrier. And I mean to a fault. Way *past* a fault, even. But now I'd catch him brooding in his office or notice one of those nervous, perpetually-watching-over-your-shoulder looks on his face when he was between customers and didn't have anything to do. I guess I was learning all over again what I learned for the first time when Butch had his accident and put himself in the hospital: how one single thing—one instant, one experience, one crushing disappointment, one terrible, terrifying moment—could change what you're made of and how you'll feel about things for the rest of your life. And the crux of it was that easy, off-hand confidence most of us are born with that whispers over and over in your ear: *"Hey, don't worry. Tomorrow is going to be pretty much like today.*"

And then one day it's gone….

As you can imagine, I absolutely jumped at the chance to take Big Ed to California. I honestly thought it would do him some good. Especially getting out from under the impossibly clean, muscular fingers and glistening, clear-polished fingernails of Nurse Ella Mae. Plus I couldn't wait to see Cal and Hank and Toly and maybe even Gina again, catch up on what was going on in the world of bigtime motor sports and maybe even casually mention the racing notions that had been circling though my own head ever since the Little Le Mans race at Lime Rock.

Big Ed and me flew out on the Thursday and even got an invite to stay in one of the rooms in Ernesto Julio's fancy apartment up in the Hollywood Hills while we were there. Right next door to Cal and Hank, in fact. That kind of surprised me, but it seems a lot of the big, international racing stars had come out after the Formula Libre race at Watkins Glen on October 9th to run a pair of "pro" sportscar races—one at Riverside and one at Laguna Seca—and Ernesto had bought himself one of those nifty new Maserati Bridcages and decided enough time and acrimony had passed that he could ask Cal to drive it. After all, by then he had a few new, not-yet discovered starlet and singer/dancer types on the line, and Gina's career had blossomed into such a huge deal that there was no point holding any hard feelings anymore. Besides, that Peter Stark character had never really worked out for Ernesto (as Hank put it: *"he had everything but the talent")* and Cal jumped at the chance. Especially since Ernesto had one of the "big-engined," 2.9-liter Birdcages with the Le Mans streamliner bodywork, and no question everybody figured that was about the best damn sports-racing car on the planet right about then. Or at least it had been a couple months before, anyway….

We got the whole story from Hank, Cal, Toly and Ernesto at dinner Thursday night at this little Italian restaurant not too far from Ernesto's place in the Hollywood hills (although Ernesto himself—and most likely one of his new starlets—would be staying at a smaller and far cozier place just up the road where they could have a little privacy away from all the houseguests). Unfortunately, Gina was missing. And I missed seeing her again, too. She was off on a publicity tour for that new Billy Wilder comedy and wouldn't make it back until midday on Friday. And then she'd be tied up again on Saturday and Sunday for some script reading and diction and dialect coaching for her next film. You could see that Cal was missing her, too.

Even so, it was great to see the whole bunch of them again. Handshakes all around. It perked Big Ed up a lot, too. Especially seeing Ernesto, who always seemed to share a special kind of insider language and understanding with Big Ed all the way back to the first time I ever saw them together back at Elkhart Lake in the fall of 1952. They were two of a kind in a lot of ways—two tough, crafty old lions growling and grumbling and swatting at flies—and it was a real tonic for Big Ed getting them back together again. And that's what Big Ed was drinking, by the way: tonic. With a squeeze of lime. And maybe just the tiniest little drop of gin to help the taste….

When we got there, Hank was in the middle of telling everybody about how Jack Brabham, John Cooper and the latest Cooper Formula One car dropped in on the Indianapolis Motor Speedway for a little private test session the week before that Formula Libre race at Watkins Glen. Naturally the USAC officials made Brabham go through the usual, dumb, one-step-at-a-time Indianapolis rookie test—even though he was the blessed World Champion!—but he did it with a smile and then put in two solid days of running the little Cooper around and around the big oval at speeds that would've qualified it just outside the top 10 for that year's Indy 500! And he did it with a 2.5-liter Climax engine running on ordinary Avgas while all the Indy regulars were using whopping 4.2-liter Meyer-Drake Offies on methanol (with maybe even a little pop of nitro for qualifying?) in their front-engined Indy roadsters. That set phone lines buzzing and made the front pages of all the local Indianapolis papers, and by the end of the second day guys like Tony Bettenhausen, A.J. Foyt, Sammy Speed, Duane Carter and Bob Wilke from the Leader Card team out of Milwaukee had driven some pretty impressive distances to get there in time to see the little Cooper for themselves. And maybe even put a watch on it as well.

Naturally that made everybody at the table feel pretty proud, seeing as how we were all dyed-in-the-wool sportycar types and had really felt the sting when Ferrari's efforts at The Speedway fizzled out like dud fireworks and then the American Indycars and drivers went over and pretty much rubbed the Europeans' noses in it at those Race of Two Worlds "Monzanapolis" races in Italy in '57 and '58. But Hank cautioned us not to get too excited about how well Brabham and the little Cooper had run at Indy. "The Dunlop tires they were running stick a hell of a lot better than the Firestones all Indy guys use, but they're much too soft to even think about racing there. Jack had to stop about every 20 laps for a new right front, and the ones they took off were worn damn near down to the canvas…."

Still, it was a hell of an encouraging story, and Hank said all the Indy regulars were really impressed with the Cooper. Not to mention Jack Brabham, who pretty much just hopped in the car and got on with it—and then some!—on a track that intimidates the crap out of everybody the first time they run there. "Now *there's* a real driver!" Sammy Speed told Hank, and Sammy was never the kind of guy to talk up another hotshoe. Especially one he might wind up racing against some day. And I guess Brabham and John Cooper were mightily impressed with the Indianapolis Motor Speedway as well, which also sent a nice swell of pride around the table. So we lifted our glasses and Hank led us in a toast to Jack Brabham and John Cooper and the Indianapolis Motor Speedway, ending with a hope that they'd all get together again sometime soon.

I always loved hearing Hank tell his racing stories. But he looked a little tired and drawn to me. And so did Cal, come to think of it. Especially around the eyes. "Hey, it's a long season," Hank explained over our second round of drinks.

"Too long," Cal agreed.

I looked at him kind of sideways. "Too much *racing??!!!"* I said like I couldn't believe my ears. "Did I hear that right?"

"Oh, I still love the racing," Cal was quick to answer. "In the car is still the only place where I really feel like I know what the hell I'm doing. The only place where everything seems to make sense." He closed his eyes and leaned his head back. "Sometimes," he continued softly, "it's almost like being immortal...."

"Immortal?" Hank-the-writer asked from beneath a set of arched eyebrows. "Are you've sure you've got the right word there?"

Cal's eyes opened a tiny sliver. "Well, what would *you* call it when you can't tell the difference between Right Now and Forever?" He curled his lips in, trying to put words on it. "That's what it feels like when you're out there and it's going well. That next stretch of road in front of you is the only thing that matters. It's like holding your future right there in your hands."

"Like you're in *control?"* Hank prodded.

Cal thought for a moment. "It's like you're in total control and just along for the ride, all at the same time," he explained, the tiniest hint of confusion and even urgency creeping into his voice. "You get to use everything you have—*everything!*—with nothing held back." He shook his head numbly. "I've never found anyplace where I've been able to do or feel or get away with anything like that..."

I remembered Cal told me pretty much the same exact thing the night the two of us sat out on the little wooden stoop of our cabin at the Seneca Lodge all those years ago, long before he'd driven his first professional race. Before he was anybody.

"When I've got somebody in my sights up ahead of me," Toly chimed in like the harmony part of a duet, "or even if it's some rat-bastard assassin threatening me in my mirrors, well..." his voice drifted off or a moment, and then returned "...I get to use all the guts, grace and guile God gave me." He looked at Hank and me. "You know, that's a very rare, very privileged opportunity."

I could feel that old static buzz standing the hairs up on the back of my neck, and wondered secretly all over again if I shouldn't maybe take a try at it myself. Not to be any kind of hero driver or paid professional like them, of course, but just to see what it felt like—touch the hem of it, you know?—and maybe get the tiniest little glimpse of that kind of challenge, sensation and satisfaction. But I didn't say anything. Not a word. I mean, I'd seen more than enough dirt-level amateurs trying to chat up genuine aces eyeball-to-eyeball like they were equals, and it never failed to make the amateurs look like blowholes.

Besides, I wanted to know more about what was going through Cal's and Toly's minds. "But if you love it so much and you're right up near the top, why the hell aren't you enjoying it?"

"Too many funerals," Toly said simply.

Cal nodded. And then added with a small choke of a laugh: "And I guess another reason is that damn Stirling Moss."

This time it was Hank who nodded like he understood.

Cal looked over at Big Ed and me. "Ever since way back when—you know this, Buddy, and so do you, Ed—it always seemed like I could take on anybody and have a decent chance of beating them. Even better than decent, so long as we had near-equal cars." Big Ed and I nodded. That went without question. Ever since I'd known him, it wasn't like Cal thought he was simply God-given *better* or *faster* than everybody else, but more like he couldn't see how anybody who put their pants on one leg at a time could be any better or faster than *him.* And he'd proved it—and then some—time and time again. But then he came up against Moss, and right at that moment—like Fangio before him and Ascari before him and Nuvolari even before him—Stirling Moss was the best damn road racing driver in the world and everybody knew it. That was hard to take if you'd grown up figuring you could run with anybody, anywhere, any time.

Like they all did.

"That shouldn't really come as any surprise," Hank reasoned. "There's always a compression of talent at the top of *any* sport—hell, that's how you all got there in the first place!—and whether it's running or jumping or knocking golf balls or shooting clay pigeons out of the sky or playing fucking tiddlywinks, at any given moment somebody or other is going to be at the top. Somebody is going to be that little bit faster or stronger or sharper or smoother or more consistent at it than everybody else. That's the way sports work," he shrugged, "and that's what makes them so much better than the aimless, mindless, meaningless slop of everyday life." He leaned in towards Cal and Toly. "You get *measured* in sports. And you can hold that time sheet in your hand and look down at it and *know* that you were just a tenth or two-tenths or whatever behind the best there is in the world. And then, maybe tomorrow or the next day or the day after that, maybe it's *you* who's a tenth or two ahead. And that's what keeps you going, because nobody ever stays at the top forever. They have their time and then they either fade or vanish,"—he hesitated for an instant after he said 'vanish'— "and then some other guy takes their place at the top or a bunch of lesser contenders wind up dog-fighting for it." Hank's eyes swept around the table, and everybody gave him a respectful little nod of agreement.

"Well," Toly finally laughed, "I sure hope it happens soon, because I'm getting damn impatient staring up Moss' exhaust pipes!" Everybody laughed, but underneath I think Toly was echoing what an awful lot of drivers secretly thought and felt. What made it even more maddening was the way Moss did it—always calm, cool, silky-smooth, surgically precise, completely unruffled and infuriatingly, even supernaturally *fast*. Not to mention polite, professional, calculating, detached and scientific. Moss always kept his eyes on the dollars, points, mechanical details and commercial opportunities more than the glittering trophies and glowing headlines, and Hank reckoned him as the first of an entirely new breed of racing driver. "He's a real professional," Hank said without making it sound like a compliment at all. "And you'll be seeing a lot more like him, I guarantee."

"Doesn't sound like much fun," Big Ed grumbled.

"It's not about fun," Hank told him. And that didn't sound like much of a compliment, either.

"Boy, that's for sure," Cal agreed.

"You're not *enjoying* it?" I asked.

"Oh, I still love my time in the car..." he started in, but Toly interrupted him:

"You know what the difference is between a professional and an amateur?" he almost demanded.

No answer.

"An amateur can go fast when he feels like it. A professional has to go fast whether he feels like it or not." Toly lit up another *Gauloise* and took a puff. "That's a pretty big difference," he said out of the side of his mouth.

"And it isn't just the racing," Cal added. "Like I said, I still love my time in the car—well, most of it, anyway—but the rest of it can start getting to you. The travel and the hospital visits and being on your own all the time and...."

"I thought there were always lots of girls?" Ernesto winked. "Or that's what I read in the funny papers, anyway."

Cal stared into Ernesto's eyes. "Sure there's girls," he said quietly. "Plenty of them. All you could ever want."

Ernesto stared back at him, and then a small, thin smile creased across his face. "My friend, you sound like a man in love."

"He doesn't know what that is!" Toly snickered while Cal did his best to stifle a blush. "I assure you, we have had many long, boring discussions on the subject. In fact, some of them have been so boring they have put me to sleep."

Then the waiter came and Ernesto insisted on ordering for all of us. Including several bottles of wine. And not his own stuff, either. Plus another round of drinks, of course. "So, how're things going with you?" I asked Hank after the waiter left.

"Same as Cal, I guess. I'm a little burned out and feeling a long way from home a lot of the time. But I guess that's pretty typical around this time of year." He took a sip of his drink. "All I know is it felt great to be back here in California for the pro races at Riverside and Laguna Seca last month. I've been here ever since."

"Don't you have the car shows to cover over in Europe?"

Hank shook his head. "Nope," he told me, looking down at the doodles on his cocktail napkin. "I told the magazine to get hold of that other guy—the one who used to cover that stuff before me?—and see if he could fill in."

"You *did?"*

Hank nodded. "I told them I needed some time back home for family stuff."

My ears perked up. *"You* have family problems?"

"Nah, not really," Hank shrugged, still looking at the table. "Just the usual stuff as your parents get older. Mending fences, mostly." He looked up at me. "But that's not for public consumption, okay?"

I nodded. "Mum's the word."

He stared back down at the table. "And I've been fooling around with that book idea a little, too."

"Oh? How's it going?"

The tiniest hint of a smile curled up at the ends of his mouth. "It's going," he said almost helplessly. "That's really as much as I know about it."

"But if you don't know, who the heck does?"

The smile got even broader. "I don't believe I can answer that one, either...."

Well, it was a fantastic dinner, what with minestrone soup and fresh clams cooked with butter and garlic and bread crumbs and fried calamari and then a salad course and a fish course and a pasta course and a meat course and so damn many side dishes they could barely all fit on the table. And the conversation was mostly about those two pro sportscar races at Riverside and Laguna Seca the month before. And also about Stirling Moss and Colin Chapman's new Lotus 19, of course....

No question Cal figured he had a pretty good ride lined up for those races with Ernesto Julio's brand-new Maserati Birdcage. After all, Toly was stuck with the same hulking Ferrari 412MI Phil Hill had driven at Riverside two years before, and although it was still fast as stink down the straightaways, racecar design had evolved by what seemed to be a whole generation in between. *"I felt like Goliath,"* Toly laughed. *"Just waiting for the stone to hit me between the eyes."*

Meanwhile Cal fell absolutely in love with the Birdcage. "You could do damn near *anything* with that car and get away with it," he said through an appreciative grin. "It was just so easy to drive, so predictable and so forgiving. And I felt safe in it, too. I was really having fun until Moss showed up with the new Lotus."

And there was the heart of it all over again. Stirling Moss had been in a blessed hospital with two broken legs, a broken nose and two cracked vertebrae after his practice accident at Spa in the middle of June, and yet he was somehow—incredibly!—back behind the wheel of a racing car in early August. And while he was laid up, crafty old Colin Chapman had been hard at work on a two-seater sports/racing version of his shatteringly quick Lotus 18 Formula One car. Hank explained that Cooper had done the same thing the year before and called their new car the "Monaco," so Chapman decided to name his new Lotus 19 sports/racer the "Monte Carlo" as a way of ever-so-gently giving John and Charlie Cooper the old razzberry. Oh, nobody took either car as a serious threat for any of the rough, tough, long-distance grinds like Sebring, Le Mans or the *Targa Florio.* But a thinly disguised, state-of-the-art Formula One car looked like just the ticket for the shorter American and European sprint-type races for sportscars. Especially the ones with big, fat purses like Riverside and Laguna Seca….

Moss tested the new Lotus 19 (and himself, if you wanted to be honest about it) at Silverstone in early August, then raced it at some track called Karlskoga in Sweden where he pretty much ran away and hid from a small but decent field. No question the car was brilliantly fast, and it looked like the wreck at Spa hadn't taken much of the luster or speed out of Moss as a driver, either.

"I don't know how you guys do that," Big Ed said to Cal and Toly, shaking his head. "Have a big wreck and damn near kill yourself, and then be back at it hard as ever a few months later."

"Well, not all of us can," Cal allowed, picking his words carefully.

"And some of us don't even get to worry about it," Toly added brightly, "because we get killed!"

A nervous laugh circled around the table.

"C'mon. I'm serious here," Big Ed insisted. You could tell he was making some kind of mental connection with his own heart attack, but it wasn't the kind of thing you could wrap your brain all the way around or put into words.

"Ah, shit," Ernesto finally scoffed. "Who the hell understands what makes people tick anyway? Certainly not the people themselves…."

I wasn't so sure about that, but the more I thought it over, the more it seemed like Ernesto might be right.

Anyhow, even after his horrendous wreck at Spa and two months on the mend, Stirling Moss was still the guy nobody could seem to beat in a straight-up fight. And he proved it all over again by coming over and winning that Formula Libre race at Watkins Glen on October 9th (this time in Rob Walker's Formula One Lotus 18) and then it was off to the west coast for the Riverside and Lagua Seca "pro" sportscar races in a brand-new, pea-soup-green Lotus 19 fielded by a bunch of English bankers who called their team UDT-Laystall and, at least according to Hank, did their best to pretend it was a serious business venture rather than a rich boys' lark. He said there was always a lot of that sort of thing going on in England.

Turns out another brand-new Lotus 19 showed up for the west coast pro races, too—a red one owned by the Arciero brothers and driven by Dan Gurney—and, in spite of just a 2.5-liter engine, Riverside's long, *long* back straightaway, billowing dust and bitter, gritty winds gusting up to 40mph, Dan shattered the lap record by almost three seconds with it in the very first session! That was pretty depressing news to surely the biggest and best damn field of no-holds-barred sports/racing cars ever assembled in these United States, including a whole fistful of Ferraris, a flock of Maseratis, Bob Drake in Max Balchowsky's chuffing Old Yaller, Dick Thompson in G.M. styling chief Bill Mitchell's gorgeous silver Stingray, both Canadian Sadlers and more quick Porsches than you ever saw on this side of the Atlantic running in the under-2.0-liter class. Not to mention grinning Wisconsin hotshoe Augie Pabst at the wheel of one of the ex-Reventlow "Meister Brauser" Scarabs that'd been tearing up the tracks in the Midwest all summer long. And that was a pretty interesting story all by itself.

So Hank told it:

Seems Augie Pabst grew up in a well-to-do, well-connected extension of a big, famous Milwaukee brewing family with a lot of land and a big dairy farm business a little ways west of Milwaukee, and he got bitten by the bug and started out racing a Triumph TR3, then graduated to a well-used, four-cylinder Ferrari Monza. He did real well with it because he was a fast, smooth and gutsy driver, and quickly got marked by just about everybody as a guy to watch. And among those watching was a young Chicago-area enthusiast and wannabe racer named Harry Heuer, whose daddy happened to be chairman of the board of yet another big brewery—the Peter Hand Brewery out of Chicago—who were well known in those parts for a very tasty and popular local midwestern beer called "Meister Brau." In one of those watch-my-hands/nothing-up-my-sleeve "marketing" arrangements that were becoming an increasingly fashionable way of passing your racing hobby off as a legit business expense and getting some big corporation (not to mention the old IRS!) to fall for it, Harry managed to convince the brewery's board of directors that they should underwrite a pair of the $17,500, Chevy-powered Scarab sports/racers Lance Reventlow put on the block after we saw them run and win at Nassau in December of 1958. He told the board he'd campaign them as "The Meister Brausers," pledged to keep expenses down, vowed they'd win all sorts of races plus a championship every single year and moreover generate all kinds of hoopla, headlines and positive publicity for the Meister Brau brand. Harry even had a nifty logo drawn up, which featured the same, stately old German-style "Meister Brau" lettering as seen on the bottles and cans plus this adorable little running-lickety-split brewmeister decked out in a crash hat and lederhosen. Everybody thought it was cute as the dickens.

But the board of directors was less than impressed once young Harry laid the numbers out. I mean, a pair of $17,500-each used racecars sounded pretty damn expensive considering that a brand-new Caddy Eldorado Biarritz convertible—with *everything!*—came in a hair shy of seventy-five hundred bucks! That amounted to an awful lot of cans, kegs and cases of Meister Brau, no matter how hard you squinted your eyes. So no matter how much young Harry pitched and pleaded and promoted and promised and cajoled, the brewery's board of directors just wasn't about to go for it. So Harry got pissed off and told them that if they didn't back his racing team idea, he'd sell all his company stock to the NAACP for 50 cents a share! And I guess they figured he was just brash, cocky, snot-nosed and hard-headed enough to do it, too, because that's about when they looked around the table, sighed, rolled their eyes, picked up their pens and signed on the dotted line….

Harry made sure the Meister Brauser Scarabs were really beautiful cars, done up in a deeper, darker metallic blue than the original RAI colors, and their team got quite a reputation all over the Midwest for looking good, winning races, getting into occasional fistfights and consuming truly impressive quantities of the old company product. They also generated a mother lode of sudsy wisecracks when Harry picked his pal Augie Pabst to drive the other car, seeing as how Augie's family name was on every single bottle of Pabst Blue Ribbon beer coming out of the big Pabst brewery in Milwaukee that was one of Peter Hand's—and Meister Brau's—biggest competitors! Although by that time Augie's family owned less than five percent of the brewery business. Even so, Harry's choice for a teammate surely turned the faces of all the board-of-directors types back at the Peter Hand Brewery in Chicago an even paler shade of their usual lily white….

But, like virtually every other driver at Riverside, Augie realized as soon as the time sheets came out that he was very definitely pedaling last year's model, and that those two new Lotus 19s were far and away the class of the field.

It wasn't even close.

"It was pretty damn disappointing," Cal laughed. "I went out there and drove my ass off in the Birdcage—and I knew I was going really *good,* too!—and then I come in and I'm third on the damn time sheets, over three seconds off the pace." He flashed an exaggerated frown. "It's like getting fixed up with a twin sister and finding out when you get there that you got the ugly one."

"You did all right," Ernesto said respectfully. "That was a pretty tough field."

"Best that's ever been," Hank agreed, and lifted his glass to toast it.

"So how'd the race go?" I wanted to know. I mean, there was no way that kind of thing would ever make the papers out east.

"I won," Cal said almost sheepishly. "But not until after both the Lotuses dropped out." He shook his head. "They had me covered—that's all there was to it. And the two of them flat ran away from me at Laguna Seca. There was just nothing I could do."

"You did all right," Ernesto repeated, rubbing his fingers together like he was holding cash. He looked over at Hank. "He even covered some of the damage you two did to my apartment when you lived there."

"That's okay," Cal assured him, "we're planning on doing more…."

The waiter brought another meat course. Veal, this time.

"So how did your races go?" I asked Toly.

"It was like dancing with an elephant on roller skates."

We all laughed.

"You know," he continued, "it's truly amazing. You get a new car and you drive it and it's wonderful and you think: *'Oh, this is marvelous! This is magnificent! If this could only go on forever....'"* He kissed his fingers and blew them into the air.

"And then what happens?"

"Oh, you drive the same exact car two or three years later and now you can't believe what an awful piece of shit it is! It doesn't stop. It doesn't go. It doesn't turn...." He slid his eyes over towards Cal. "Some people think marriage is a lot that way."

I looked at Cal, too. And that's when it suddenly began to register. "You're not thinking about getting *married,* are you?" I asked incredulously.

"Of course not!" Cal almost shouted, the color starting to rise on his face.

"Ahh, but he's *thinking* about thinking about it," Toly grinned, wagging a finger under Cal's nose. "Don't even give him a chance to try and deny it."

Now it was Ernesto's chance to raise his glass. "Here's to marriage, my friends. May those who venture in come out alive."

Naturally I had to drink to that, even though I wasn't exactly sure what it meant.

"Wasn't Toly telling us about his race?" Cal reminded us, trying hard to change the subject.

"What's to tell?" Toly shrugged, lighting up another *Gauloise.* "I had a fat old car with an ugly temperament and all the sexy new young ones blew me off."

"You had a pretty good race at Riverside. And in the first heat at Laguna Seca, too," Hank reminded him.

"Thank you," Toly nodded wryly. "It took an expert to notice."

"How do you like the tracks out here?" I asked him.

"I like your American tracks very much," he grinned. "I don't think it's quite so easy to kill yourself over here."

"A lot of the Europeans think we have sissy tracks," Hank groused. "No real risk. No real challenge." I could hear the echo of Eric Gibbon behind that one.

"Oh, those are the idiots," Toly snorted. "The writers and fans who somehow think it's glorious to get yourself killed in a racing car." He took a quick drag of his cigarette and just as quickly blew it out. "Let me assure you, the esses and turn six at Riverside are *very* exciting. And turn two at Laguna Seca..." he rolled his eyes, *"...that* will shrivel your balls up like a pair of tiny raisins!"

"But they're nothing like the Masta Kink or Burnenville at Spa," Hank scoffed almost automatically, and again I thought I was hearing Eric Gibbon's voice there in there somewhere.

"They're almost as difficult," Toly argued defensively, "just not so damnably, stupidly *dangerous!"* He leaned in close over the table and whispered: *"Let me let you in on a private little secret, my friends: there is no special joy, stature, honor or nobility to getting killed in a fucking racing car. It's just dead, like any other kind of dead."* He pulled back, took a long, deep drag off his cigarette and performed a slow, smoky French inhale. *"It just happens faster, that's all...."*

His words hung in the air like the smell of a passing fish platter.

"Then why do you keep doing it?" Hank asked.

"Oh, because I don't really believe I'll kill myself," Toly laughed. "None of us do. It's like we're all playing a little game of Russian roulette where none of us really thinks there's a bullet in the gun. Or at least not one for us, anyway. It's a little game of *'see if I can't be killed,'* you understand?" He leaned in close over the table again and lowered his voice to a soft, serious whisper. *"At some point you either decide to walk away or they eventually carry you away on a stretcher. It's simple as that."* Toly eased back in his chair and took another long, slow draw off his cigarette, savored it and exhaled. "And that's why I'm going to get out of it."

Hank's eyes widened up a few notches. "You're going to *retire?"*

A thin, secretive smile spread across Toly's face. "Not now," he said evenly. "Not until after next season." His eyes found Cal's. Bore right into them, in fact. *"Either you, I or Phil will become World Champion next year,"* he almost hissed. *"Make no mistake, my friend, I'm planning for it to be me."* Then the smile got broader, but not friendlier. *"And then I will retire...."*

"But what will you do with yourself?" I wondered out loud.

Toly leaned back in his chair and took another long, thoughtful drag off his cigarette. "I'm not entirely sure," he grinned, his eyebrows arching playfully, "but I'm sure I'll find plenty of things to keep me occupied," He looked over at Cal again. "There are other things in life besides motor racing, my friend. And I plan to find them and do them all...."

Friday's practice and qualifying sessions proved that single-seat, open-wheel Grand Prix cars were faster by far around Riverside than any sportscar—no matter how big the engine might be—but neither Big Ed or me thought they were nearly as exciting to watch. They were just too damn *good* and too much the same, you know? Sure, the times were amazing and all the drivers were right on the limit and using every blessed inch of the road—and then some—every time around. But you couldn't *see* or *feel* the speed the way you could when we watched Tommy Edwards wrestling that monster of an Allard around at Bridgehampton back at the first race we ever went to together in the spring of 1952. The cars and the drivers here were just too neat and perfect and surgically precise. And apparently we weren't the only people who felt that way, either. Just like at Sebring the previous year, the crowd was downright pitiful compared to what a Grand Prix weekend drew in Europe or South America. Of course, part of the problem was that the Los Angeles *Times-Mirror* newspapers had promoted their own big pro sportscar race at Riverside just a month before, and they were hardly about to give front-page coverage to any event they saw as a potential rival. Fact is, outside of the rabid, lunatic fringe of diehard enthusiasts like Big Ed and me who hung there on the fences all weekend long, the American public just didn't seem particularly interested in Formula One. Hank and me talked about it over a couple overpriced hot dogs at lunch time, and even he grudgingly agreed that the cars didn't offer the variety of shapes, sizes, colors and sounds that you got with the big sports/racers. Or the contrast of watching "handling" cars fighting it out with "horsepower" cars. Although that—along with a huge chunk of the usual Grand Prix magic and mystery—was missing mostly because Ferrari didn't bother to show up. Then again, why should they? Ferrari sold an awful lot of his racing and road-going sportscars in California, and no question his Formula One cars would most likely get their asses kicked again by the Lotuses and Coopers.

Of course that left both Cal and Toly pedaling second-rate, second-string privateer entries at Riverside thanks to deals that pretty much came together at the last moment. Toly was in a last-year's Cooper with a decent but too heavy Maserati engine stuffed in back, while Cal had a ride in one of the taller, fatter, older-spec 1960 Coopers with a regular-issue Climax engine owned by the Yeoman Credit team. The Riverside organizers helped put the deal together on account of Cal was a pretty big draw in Southern California, but he didn't have any illusions about running with Moss, Brabham or fellow "local hero" Dan Gurney in the latest BRM P48.

But the car that seemed to be drawing the most attention in the Riverside paddock was a backmarker, since there always seemed to be quite a crowd filing by the handsome and immaculate but washed-up-and-everybody-knew-it Reventlow Scarab. I guess there was no way Lance could resist running it one more time in the very last race of the FIA's 2.5-liter formula. Especially seeing as how it was right there in his own back yard on RAI's home track, where the team had more blessed hours and miles in than the whole rest of the field combined. The front-engined Scarab Grand Prix car was appearing for what everybody and his brother figured was probably the very last time, although Hank and a few insiders knew that Lance and Warren Olsen had already hired Eddie Miller to design them a new, rear-engined, Cooper-copy chassis to run in the loudly trumpeted (at least in England) non-FIA Intercontinental Formula series they all thought was going to take Europe by storm. Anyhow, there was a kind of a sad, romantic, bittersweet atmosphere lingering around the RAI bivouac in the paddock, and even Jersey guys like Big Ed and me, who'd never even seen the cars before except in pictures and drawings in the magazines, could sense it as we wandered by to pay our respects.

Speaking of Lance Reventlow, he hosted one hell of a party at his thoroughly unbelievable house in Beverly Hills on Friday night, and Cal managed to fix all of us up with invites. Not that it turned out you actually needed one to get in, seeing as how Lance had essentially invited the whole blessed Formula One circus over for "drinks and a few hot dogs," including everyone from team owners, managers and drivers to mechanics and rig haulers and even unloved European press flakes like Eric Gibbon. Hank thought it was just a way for Lance to thank the few people who'd really helped his team along and likewise thumb his nose at the great majority who said rude things and didn't help at all.

Did it in a pretty classy way, too.

As you can imagine, Lance's house was on the far side of simply impressive, but it was your typical California Modern Obscenely Rich rather than English or East Coast Old Money Stuffy, what with split levels, tons of glass and greenery and a rock-face waterfall tumbling down into the swimming pool. And he sure didn't skimp on the food, either. Or the, umm, "accessories." Seems he got some of the agents and studio people he knew (including his wife Jill St. John and even Ernesto Julio) to spread the word and make sure the place was filled to overflowing with gorgeous young models, starlets, dancers and would-be actresses. Including a few stop-you-in-your-tracks, *Jesus, I know that face!* types like Jill St. John, Jayne Mansfield, Gina LaScala and quite a few others. None of the gents from the Grand Prix crowd had ever seen so many beautiful—or easy to talk to!—young women. Not that any of them knew very much about racing, but they were all impressed as hell with Lance's house and so tried *very* hard to be fascinated. Better yet, a lot of them were lounging around the pool in delightfully skimpy bathing suits. Some of the Brits looked almost visibly shaken, and I got the feeling that was exactly what Lance had in mind. See, they'd never been to a Hollywood party before. Or what everybody in Hollywood wanted everybody everywhere else to *think* a Hollywood party was like, anyway....

I wandered around the house, garden and garages with Big Ed and Ernesto for a while, and even the two of them were plenty impressed with Lance's hause. It was a pretty amazing place to hang your hat, no lie. Then we went out by the pool with the three-story rock waterfall at one end, and Big Ed was holding one of his not-quite-all-tonic glasses of tonic in one hand and a fistful of cocktail shrimp in the other and all three of us were damn near walking into things because our eyes were so busy moving from faces to legs to butts to cleavages and back to faces again as we strolled around the deck. No question there was an enormous oversupply of prime female scenery around—a lot of it being actively chatted up by that point in the evening—and I was sure glad Julie wasn't there to observe where my eyes were going. But there was no way you could help yourself, you know?

Eventually I wound up out on the terrace with Gina, Cal and Toly. Geez, it was great to see her again, and as usual, she looked absolutely gorgeous. But kind of tired, too. "I just got in late this afternoon," she told me, waving a wisp of hair off her forehead, "and I've got script meetings starting up again tomorrow." She gave me a little peck on the cheek. "They want me to play a southern girl in this next one," she told me from under those incredible green eyes. "You think I can do a southern accent, Buddy?"

"Sure, why not?"

Gina looked at her drink. She *was* drinking tonic. "It doesn't matter," she half-yawned. "It's the movies. If they've got the time and budget, they can always dub it until they get it right."

Then she asked me how Julie and the kids were and we made a little small talk, but I had one ear kind of craned over, listening in on the conversation Cal and Toly were having right next to us.

"You really think one of us will be World Champion?" Cal was asking.

"Oh, there's no doubt of it. Consider the facts."

"What facts?"

Toly held up an index finger like it was the Washington Monument. *"Next year is the new formula, and only Ferrari will be ready."*

"But what about Cooper and Lotus and BRM?"

"They won't be ready. I'm sure of it. They spent too much time with their heads in the sand, arguing against the new formula...."

"I heard both BRM and Climax are working on new V-8s."

"Sure they are. But they won't be ready. They started too late. They'll both be running those old FPF Climaxes until at least the last races of the year."

"But what about the cars?"

"Ferrari's not dumb. He sees what goes on. The new rear-engined car is almost ready for testing already. And I guarantee you, that engine will have at least 20 or 30 more horsepower than any of the British cars. That's an enormous advantage in a little 1500cc racecar. And the cars will be Ferraris. They'll be a little heavier than the Lotuses and Coopers, but solid enough to finish races." He flashed an almost skull-like smile. *"There's no way we can lose."*

"But what makes you think I'll even be on the team?"

"What choice does he have? He doesn't trust Mairesse to follow team orders because Willy's a little crazy. That's why he made Willy give me that tow at Monza. Just to see if he'd do it."

"But he did it, didn't he?"

"Yes, but he grumbled about it. With Ferrari, it's not just what you do, but the way you do it...."

"So Mairesse is out?"

Toly nodded. *"He'll pay his way in for a few races, but he won't be a regular."*

Cal thought it over. *"But why me? There are a lot of other guys out there."*

"Sure there are. Ferrari wanted Gurney, but Gurney's gone to Porsche. And he wants another American. Another Californian, if possible."

"But I'm not from California."

"Sure you are!" Toly insisted, giving him a shove. *"That's why you've got this year's Cooper this weekend and I've got the old piece of shit with that lump of a Maserati engine in back."*

Cal rubbed his chin. *"But what about Phil Hill?"*

"Oh, he'll be with us," Toly assured him. *"But Ferrari doesn't entirely trust Phil because he thinks too much. He's too independent and not crazy enough. Ferrari knows he can't control and manipulate Phil the way he can with other drivers."*

Cal looked at him. *"Like who?"*

Toly stared right back, almost laughing. *"Well, like you, for one."*

Cal frowned. But then a hard, sly smile sneaked across his lips. *"If all that is true, what the hell makes you think you can beat ME?"* he asked, his nostrils kind of flaring.

Toly gave him a patronizing, almost fatherly smile. *"I'm not sure I can in equal cars and equal situations. That's something we'll just have to see, won't we?"* He paused and lit up another *Gauloise. "Besides,"* he continued, puffing to get it lit, *"it's my intention to prevent that from ever happening...."*

"Prevent what?"

"Equal cars and equal situations." Cal looked at him kind of sideways while Toly concentrated on the glowing tip of his cigarette. *"Look,"* he finally continued, *"there's no such thing as equal cars. Not on any team. And you'll be the new boy, so you'll either get what I'm done with or whatever's new and untried and hasn't been proven yet."*

"What makes you so sure you'll be Number One?"

"Simple process of elimination. It can't be Phil and it can't be you, so it has to be me. Besides, I've worked hard to get in with the mechanics—I even pay some of them off with bottles of wine and little gifts for their children and even money now and then—just to make sure I get whatever's best. And I'm the only one who can get around old man Ferrari. One side of my family was Italian, and I can speak it like a native. Even the Modenese dialect. And Ferrari came up from nothing, so he's always been awed and intimidated by real blood aristocracy like any other European peasant." Toly took another long drag and performed his patented French inhale. *"Of course you wouldn't understand that. You're American."*

Cal looked over and realized that Gina and me were eavesdropping on their conversation. "Getting an earful?" he asked.

"It's not boring," Gina smiled back at him. "I wish to hell they'd write dialogue like that for my movies."

About then Eric Gibbon wandered over—drunk, of course—and wondered out loud what was wrong with American fans and why they didn't have the good taste, breeding or appreciation of the finer points of motor sports to come out and watch the Formula One cars play. But none of us really wanted to get sucked into one of Eric's inevitable lecture/discussions, so Cal and Gina excused themselves to go find Lance so they could thank him for the nice party seeing as she had to get up so early the next morning, and I begged off on the pretext of finding Big Ed to see how he was doing. That left poor Toly alone with him, but Toly just kind of looked at Eric, looked down into his drink, drained the last of it, swirled the ice cubes once around in his glass, gave a faint, "excuse me" nod and walked away. All without saying a blessed word. But then, Toly had a real gift for languages. Even the unspoken ones.

I wandered around by myself for awhile, just listening to the chatter and taking in all the pretty girls and all the famous and/or familiar racing faces I hadn't really seen since Nassau in '58 or all the way back to Sebring in 1956, when Cal had his first-ever pro drive in a Ferrari and we both met Toly for the very first time. And I couldn't help thinking about that fascinating spaghetti dinner we all enjoyed underneath Carlo Sebastian's awning in the paddock before night practice, and in particular all those other famous faces at the far end of the table. The ones that weren't around anymore. Of course Fangio had retired. But Musso and Castellotti were dead. And so were Collins and Hawthorn and Behra and Ascari and Portago and Archie Scott-Brown and Stuart Lewis-Evans and Alan Stacey and Chris Bristow and…well, it just wasn't the kind of thing you wanted to keep thinking about, you know? Only it was hard not to, and it made what Toly was saying earlier out on the terrace sound very wise indeed.

I went to find a phone and called home—it was just about 7 in Jersey, and Julie and her mom and the kids were just finishing dinner. They were having red Jell-O with that squirty whipped cream on top for dessert, and right at that moment I kind of wished I was back home with them, you know? Especially when I was talking to little Vincent. I felt pretty lonely after I hung up, so I went off in search of Big Ed. But I couldn't find him. I saw Hank out on the terrace with Eric Gibbon, and even from a distance I could see that Hank had gotten himself sucked into one of those momentous, round-and-round, alcohol-fueled "discussions" that raise all sorts of questions about all sorts of topics, provide no answers whatsoever, cover an incredible expanse of territory and yet get absolutely nowhere. I decided it would be a good idea to give them both a wide berth, and quickly ducked back inside the house.

There was beautiful, familiar, rambling, style-to-style piano music floating out of Lance's living room, and of course it was Toly at the keyboard—head back, eyes nearly closed, cigarette dangling from lips—with a pretty young brunette at his side and a tall blond in a bathing suit standing right behind him, massaging his neck. It was the kind of image that made you shake your head, sigh and give him a helpless little nod of wonder. And maybe even envy. I don't pretend to know what happiness is, but right at that moment, Toly Wolfgang looked like the exact, spitting image of what every red-blooded American high school kid thinks it is from the day he reaches puberty onward. And that dumb, pretty dream stays with you as you grow up, even though it seems further and further away from reality every year. But it was a perfect kind of fit for a Hollywood party, you know?

Just perfect….

I wandered some more and saw Cal and Gina sitting together quietly on a little wrought iron bench out on the far corner of the lawn, right next to the reflecting pool with a bunch of fat, lazy, dressed-up-in-glistening-evening-gowns Japanese goldfish swimming around in it. I started to go up to them, but as I got closer, I could hear they were kind of arguing. Or at the very least discussing intensely. So I thought better of it. I mean, why be an asshole? They never got to see each other very much, and arguing and getting angry and maybe even yelling a little are such an important part of any major-league relationship. So I went looking for Big Ed again.

I finally located him down in the rec room with the big slate pool table in it, and he and Ernesto were playing pool for pocket change with a couple very pretty but also kind of hard-looking girls from Texas who were absolutely cleaning their clocks. But you couldn't miss that one of them was really stacked—especially when she leaned over to line up a shot—and the other was wearing a two-piece swimsuit and had fabulous legs and an incredible butt when she stretched out along the side rail, so no question Ernesto and Big Ed were getting their money's worth. And I had to admit Big Ed looked better than I'd seen him look for a long, long time. He was smiling and laughing and swearing and moreover he had a little bit of that old Big Ed glint back in his eye. I was really happy to see that. But I wasn't so happy seeing the glowing, smoky tip on the end of the big Cuban cigar rolling from one side of his mouth to the other. I knew Big Ed wasn't supposed to be smoking those things any more. But how the hell could you stop him?

We didn't leave that party until damn near two (which was of course five ayem Jersey time) and it was still going strong. Although Lance and Chuck and the rest of the RAI crew had long since vanished—hey, they had qualifying the next day—and I'd lost track of Toly after the piano music stopped and he and one or more of those girls disappeared together. And naturally I took one more peek out on the back lawn. Cal and Gina were still there, but they didn't really look like they were talking any more. In fact, they weren't doing much of anything except just sitting there, heads kind of leaned together, looking up at the sky and where the stars and moon would have been if it wasn't so overcast. I thought they looked pretty nice together, too.

Chapter 39: California Swansong

To tell the truth, race day at Riverside was a little bit of a disappointment. Especially considering it was Big Ed's and my very first Grand Prix and the Last Chance Ever to see the "real," 2.5-liter Formula One cars run in anger. So we'd more or less built up a lot of expectations, you know? But the first-ever United States Grand Prix at Riverside turned out to be pretty much an empty-looking snooze parade once the early-lap dramas played themselves out. But it was neat walking through the paddock beforehand and seeing all the cars and stars (several of whom still looked like they were suffering the after-effects of Lance's party Friday night) and dropping by to thank him personally for one heck of a swell time. Not to mention wishing Chuck the best of luck in the race. You had to about get in line to do that. Turns out Chuck and the RAI crew had done an incredible amount of work on the car since coming home from Europe—even though they all knew it was a lame-duck project—including an almost maniacal "ouncing" campaign to get the weight down and moving the fuel tank from the tail to a pair of smaller tanks on either side of the cockpit. That figured to improve weight distribution and make it so the car's handling balance didn't change so damn drastically as the fuel load burned off, but it was a fairly monumental sort of task. Why, you should've seen the complex, Chinese-box-puzzle shape they had to form up and weld together on the inside of the new tanks in order to clear all the frame tubes and hardware, and the smooth, gently curving outer skin actually served as the middle bodywork on both sides of the car. Which of course got me to thinking about what might happen if you ever got into an accident. But I guess sitting in pretty much a bathtub full of fuel was just part of the deal in Grand Prix racing, no matter what kind of car you were driving.

Everybody thought Chuck had done a heck of a job qualifying the Scarab 18th out of 23 starters, and while that may not sound too great, remember that they couldn't even qualify most of the time in Europe and that there was only one other front-engined car in the race—sometimes Ol' Yaller chauffeur Bob Drake in a thoroughly antiquated Maserati 250F—and he was way back on the last row. Plus no question Chuck was planning to give it everything he had in the race. But then, he always did.

They had a Formula Junior and a "compact sedan" race before the Grand Prix, and Walt Hansgen once again marked himself as a guy with a real future by winning them both. He took the Junior race in Briggs Cunningham's brand-new Cooper, then hopped into one of Briggs' pair of Jaguar Mark II sedans (the other was being wheeled by grinning new Cunningham recruit Augie Pabst) and the two of them simply ran away and hid from a fairly meager "compact sedan" field. But it was still a hell of a show, what with those two big Jag sedans sashaying down the esses nose-to-tail in these huge, magnificent, lock-to-lock broadslides, the cars heeled over so damn far they about needed roller skates under the rocker panels to keep from toppling right over. It sure was fun to watch, and I could almost hear the wheels turning in Big Ed's head about maybe getting himself one for the street. I think he was already getting a little bored with his new Facel Vega HK-500—especially the color combination, what with that pale pastel-mauve interior encapsulated in a paint shade that truly captured the disturbing, even nauseating gleam of badly yellowed teeth—not to mention that it handled like an overloaded garbage scow if you tried to make it go fast on anything but a straight, flat stretch of highway.

At lunchtime this professional crash tester named Tim Michnay took Chevrolet's pretty but strange CERV 1 "experimental vehicle" out for a few demonstration laps, and to tell the truth I didn't really know what to make of it. And I don't think anybody else did, either. It was an open wheel, rear-engined single-seater with pretty much the proportions of an oversized Cooper but the styling details and glistening white-with-blue paintwork of a GM Dream Car. And a hulking, inboard motorboat-sounding Chevy V-8 stuffed behind the driver with these magnificent tubular exhaust headers pointing back like a set of deck cannons on either side. Surely there was no formula or racing class for such a thing—and some of the scoops and such looked a wee bit cute and fashion-conscious for a real racing car—but it was nice to see G.M. teasing us with something like that in spite of the Detroit-wide ban on racing.

Big Ed and me both thought it was hotter than blazes by race time, what with the sun beating down through the usual Riverside heat haze, not even a blade of grass for shade and this fine, gritty, orange-yellow dust all around that got into everything. I could only imagine what it might be like on a windy day. But we had the best damn drivers in the whole damn world in front of us, with Moss in the blue Walker Lotus, world champ Brabham in the dark-green Cooper with the white racing stripes and hometown favorite Dan Gurney in the not-quite-so-dark-green BRM on the front row plus several other Americans peppered throughout the field to give us something to root for. Including Cal, Phil Hill, Chuck Daigh in the Scarab, Pete Lovely in his own, Ferrari-powered Cooper hybrid and Bob Drake in that old 250F Maserati. Not to mention tall, lanky and understated young Texas oilman Jim Hall, who'd quietly gone out and bought himself a "customer" Lotus 18 from Colin Chapman, painted it all-American white with blue racing stripes and brought it out to Riverside to see what he could do with it. I guess he had some kind of engineering background back home in Texas (although I think it was more about sucking oil up out of the ground than setting camber angles and spark advance curves), but no question he was one of those methodical, relentless, Serious Thinker types who doesn't say a whole lot but comprehends more every day. And damn if he couldn't drive pretty decent, too, qualifying a highly respectable 12th at Riverside against the very best in the world.

Like everybody else, Jim Hall had been pretty impressed by Colin Chapman's new 18 (although, to be honest, there didn't seem to be all that much to them compared to some of the other cars—but I guess that was the point) and besides his car in 12th and Moss on the pole in the blue Walker car, we had the three creamy-green "works" 18s qualified in fifth, sixth and seventh in the hands of Formula Junior graduate Jimmy Clark, ex-world motorcycle champion John Surtees and established team leader Innes Ireland. Who Eric Gibbon was quick to point out couldn't have been particularly happy getting pipped by the New Boys on the squad, even though just four-tenths of a second covered all three of them. Like Ferrari, Colin Chapman seemed to have a real knack for coming up with fresh driving talent. And, also like Ferrari, without paying very much for it, either….

Come the start Brabham took off like a shot with Gurney and Moss right behind, but Moss was up into second by the end of the first lap and seemed perfectly happy to just sit there on Brabham's gearbox and see how things developed. To my eyes, Moss looked maybe a little slicker and more graceful, but Brabham seemed somehow tougher and—if such a thing were even possible—more determined. No question we were seeing the two top guys in the world right then, and even Big Ed could appreciate the artistry. Meanwhile new-to-four-wheels John Surtees looped it at tricky turn six with new Lotus teammate Jim Clark right in his wheeltracks, and there was nothing the kid could do to keep from ramming him broadside. It happened right in front of us, and while Surtees was out on the spot, Clark managed to make it around to the pits for a fresh nosecone but had to pretty much limp through the rest of the race thanks to a leaky radiator. But I thought he looked pretty good anyway—especially for a new kid in his first big season.

And then it all fell apart. Brabham heard a big bang and saw flames in the rearview mirrors so he pulled into the pits for a little looksee, but by then it was out and they couldn't find anything. So they sent him back out again and a lap later he heard another bang and saw more flames behind him and this time they finally figured out that a misty spray from the fuel tank vent was finding its way back to the exhaust headers. They got it fixed, but by then Brabham was over a lap down and pretty much out of it.

But boy, could that guy ever *drive!* You could see it.

Then again, what else would you expect from a two-time World Champion?

Meanwhile Moss was easily pulling away from a fierce battle for second between the BRM P48s of Gurney and Bonnier, but then Dan's car split its radiator hose, steamed out its coolant and parboiled the engine. And so, with just 18 laps down and 57 yet to go, the much-ballyhooed United States Grand Prix at Riverside turned into a rather dull procession. Ho-hum. Moss and the Walker Lotus were so damn good and under so little pressure that they were almost boring to watch, and all the other cars were pretty well spaced out by that point as well (Ireland and Brabham had an entertaining little scrap, but anybody who kept track knew the Cooper was a full lap behind) so the only thing to cheer for was Chuck Daigh and the Scarab every time they completed another lap. The Scarab's front end had gotten all snarly and snaggle-toothed early on when Chuck used it to more or less "persuade" Pete Lovely's Cooper-Ferrari out of the way going down the esses—oval-track style, you know?—and that was actually kind of perfect for an old never-was dinosaur of a racecar fighting its way through its very last race.

But Chuck was having fuel feed problems on account of he'd ditched the little aluminum fuel cooler to save a few ounces, and now the fuel was percolating in the lines. But at least the thing kept running, and Chuck actually had a pretty neat-looking dice for several laps with our pal Toly in the older-spec Cooper-Maserati. Although Toly was struggling, too, what with a dead clutch pedal, a broken throttle return spring and the gearbox popping out of third gear every time he lifted off. But of course the great majority of the fans at trackside never have any idea what the drivers are dealing with in the cars (or how much the cars have to do with the final results, for that matter!), and so everybody around us was cheering like mad for Chuck's vapor-locking Scarab in its apparently valiant, tooth-and-nail battle against Toly's clutchless, throttle-sticking, popping-out-of-gear Cooper. But what can you do? The afternoon heat ultimately decided things, as it made the Scarab's fuel feed problems even worse while Toly gradually got more and more accustomed to shifting without a clutch, holding the lever in gear with one hand while steering with the other and hooking the toe of his driving shoe underneath the gas pedal to pull it back whenever it decided to stick open. So the Cooper slowly, inexorably eased away, and all the rubes around us were disappointed for Chuck in the Scarab but had to grudgingly take their hats and caps off to that lah-de-dah European guy whassizname in the Cooper. He was sure one heck of a driver. Even if he looked like a damn garden slug compared to that Stirling Moss character….

And then, right near the end, the engine in Bonnier's BRM started running rough and missing. What a shame. With just 10 laps to go, he popped and banged his way down the order from a sure and well-deserved second place to fifth at the checker behind Moss (40 second gap), Ireland (45 second gap), McLaren (yawn) and Brabham, who was still over a lap behind. To be honest, it was dull as watching paint dry in the desert, and the only spark of any kind was seeing Chuck Daigh bring that sneering, snarling, vapor-locking RAI Scarab home to score the team's first and only Grand Prix finish. He wound up a lonely 10th, a full five laps behind Moss, but even so it was like watching your kid's awful little league team finally win a game.

As we headed back towards L.A. in the rental car—hot and sweaty and absolutely coated with that horrible Riverside dust—Big Ed commented that the best thing about the whole damn day was that we didn't have to fight much traffic on the way out. I'm sure that little tidbit made a heck of an impression on the event's promoters, too.

We flew back to New York early the next morning, and it was quite a pleasant surprise to see Toly waiting in the gate area for the same flight. He said he had some kind of business to take care of in Manhattan, and you could see he was wearing a big, soft shoe on his right foot and walking sort of gingerly on account of he'd worn the top of his driving shoe clear through pulling that Cooper's sticking throttle back with his toes, and he allowed as how that didn't do his foot much good at all. "Does it hurt?" I asked.

“Of course not,” he grinned. “I’m only doing this to get sympathy from beautiful ladies.” He leaned in close and whispered: “I have it on very good authority that they fall right over on their backs for injured warriors.”

But it was really no laughing matter, since I guess he’d rubbed one hell of a bloody raw spot on the crook of his toes. Although he said the worst of it was the cramping he was getting in the car during the whole last half of the race. “It was really something,” he told us with a gaunt, pained expression on his face. “And of course you don’t want to come in for something like that because everyone will think you’re a silly little girl.” He flashed a grim smile at us. “You know how that is….”

Naturally Big Ed went up to the desk and got our seats switched around so the three of us could all fly back to New York together. First Class, no less! And the trip didn’t seem long at all thanks to the unlimited free drinks up in First Class (can you believe it?) and a rambling-all-over-the-place conversation about Toly’s race and the prospects for the new season and all the new American compact cars and Big Ed’s Facel Vega and a few Trashwagon stories and also the rumors we’d all heard that the United States Grand Prix might actually be moving to Watkins Glen following the highly disappointing fan turnout at Riverside. We also talked about Ferrari’s new 1.5-liter Grand Prix cars *(“Wait’ll you see it!”* Toly grinned) and Cal finally joining the Ferrari Formula One team. Not to mention that 3.0-liter, non-FIA “Intercontinental Formula” race series Lance Reventlow and all those privateer British teams were so hopped up about.

“It’s never going to make it,” Toly said flatly.

“Why not?” I argued. “It sounds like a swell idea to me.” I mean, I couldn’t really see using upgraded Formula Juniors as Grand Prix cars, you know?

“That’s not really the point,” Toly explained. “To begin with, they haven’t got the contracts with the tracks.”

Big Ed’s eyebrows went up knowingly. “You can’t put on a show without a hall to show it in.”

Toly nodded. “Oh, they’ve got some races scheduled in England already, but by the time they get the rest of it sorted out, the FIA’s new Formula One will be up and running—*with* Ferrari—and that should be about the end of it.”

“I thought Ferrari was going to field Intercontinental cars, too,” I told him. “Or that’s what Lance said he heard from some of the Brits, anyway.”

Toly just smiled and waited for the meaning to sink in.

“You mean he’s not?”

“I very much doubt it. Ferrari just wanted to roll another log under the legs of the British teams while he got his own cars ready for next year.”

“Geez, that’s pretty crummy.”

“That’s pretty *smart,”* Big Ed corrected me.

“Ferrari just knows how the game is played, that’s all. And you play it—how do you Americans say it?—*for keeps.”* He paused for a moment, thinking. “And there’s something else, too,” he finally added, looking me right square in the eyes.

“What’s that?”

"Everybody loves to hate the FIA in Paris because they're perceived as a bunch of stupid, pompous, officious, autocratic, out-of-touch idiots."

"That's the general impression I got," I agreed.

"But do you know what's *good* about them?"

I shook my head.

"Equality!" he proclaimed, holding up an index finger for punctuation.

"Equality?" I said.

"Equality?" Big Ed said.

Toly nodded solemnly. "The French haven't had a great racing car or team since the Bugattis before the war. So they hate everybody equally and envy everybody equally and are unfair with everybody equally."

"And that's *good?"*

"Of course it is! Otherwise you wind up with the manufacturers and car owners trying to run things, and all *they're* really interested in is getting some kind of advantage for themselves or screwing up the other guy." Toly shook his head. "It's like letting the inmates run the damn asylum…."

I thought it over a little, and there was a certain inescapable truth and symmetry at the core of it. You couldn't let the racers run the racing—they'd be stalking out of meetings and forming their own little sub-groups every time you turned around—and you sure as hell couldn't do it by committee.

"You need someone really pompous and imperious up at the top," Toly assured me. "Someone arrogant and vindictive and conceited enough to wield the authority and command the teams' respect." He leaned in a little closer and added in barely a whisper: "Believe me, my family knows all about power and politics." Toly leaned back in his seat and fished around in his jacket for his silver cigarette case. But it was empty. A small look of horror flashed across his eyes.

"Here," Big Ed offered, pulling out one of his fat Cuban cigars, "ever try one of these?"

Toly looked at it. Big Ed's cigars were about the same shape and size as a prize turd. Smelled about the same, too. "Is that your last one?" Toly asked.

"I got more in my luggage," Big Ed shrugged. "Besides, I'm not supposed to smoke 'em anyway. Just chew on 'em. Or that's what the damn doctors and nurses say, anyway."

"I couldn't take your last one."

"Okay," Big Ed nodded. And then he carefully unwrapped the cellophane, took the big stogie between his thumbs and forefingers and oh-so-artistically broke it clear in half. "Here," he said, handing Toly half a cigar. "Here's to that rat-bastard Castro down in Cuba."

Toly fished for his lighter, but Big Ed already had a book of matches out (which made me wonder if maybe he'd been sneaking a little smoke or two now and then) and fired Toly up. Then he looked at the half cigar in his own hand, looked at me kind of sideways, said, "Ah, what the hell," and lit his half up, too.

"Geez, Ed, don'cha think…" I started in, but he waved me off with just a glare.

As far as I could tell, the more Big Ed paid for his fancy Cuban cigars the worse they smelled. But I'm not what you could call a connoisseur. Although I wasn't exactly alone, seeing as how I heard a couple not-so-polite coughs coming through from the row behind us. But Big Ed didn't seem to much care. And why should he? After all, this was First Class.

We landed in New York in the middle of the afternoon and of course Big Ed had offered to give Toly a ride wherever he was going in Manhattan, and naturally that put me in the back seat of Big Ed's new Facel Vega for the very first time. And while the pastel mauve leather looked just as soft and inviting as the front, getting in and out was a real pain in the ass. Not to mention the legs, back, ankles, arms and elbows. Toly had to put the front seat all the way forward in order to make any space for my feet at all, and even then they were splayed out 180-degrees sideways like a blessed ballet dancer! Plus I could kind of smell gas back there because some French genius decided to put the huge, Monza-style flip-up gas filler in the damn trunk! I ask you: why on earth would you want a handsome, high volume, hair-trigger, polished-aluminum racing-style fuel filler hidden away in the blessed trunk of a two-ton luxury touring car? Especially since if you ever happened to spill a little gas while refueling, it got absorbed directly into the trunk carpeting roughly a foot behind where your nose wound up if you were sitting in the back seat! I mean, you *expected* that kind of thing from, say, a Triumph TR3. But not from a ten-thousand-dollar French luxury barge of a *Gran Turismo.* Still, it was a pretty neat car, and plenty fast enough to scare the living crap out of Toly and me. Or at least it was with somebody like Big Ed Baumstein at the wheel, anyway….

I recognized the building Toly was going to on Park Avenue before we even pulled up to the curb. Why, it was the same blessed address Big Ed sent us to when my sister Mary Francis needed her abortion! Only of course we were out front this time instead of creeping in through the alleyway behind. Naturally I was curious as hell about what Toly needed to do in that particular building, since I knew it was almost all doctors' offices. But I was far too polite to ask. Big Ed had no such compunctions, however. *"Say, who y'gonna see in there?"* he blurted out somewhat indelicately.

"I just have to see someone in there for a few minutes," Toly explained without really saying anything. "Thanks for the lift," Then he did his best to extract himself from the passenger side of Big Ed's Facel Vega. And that was no easy thing to do with the passenger seat all the way forward. Oh, the door was plenty big—huge, in fact—but the wraparound windshield doglegged back what looked like a good foot or so into the available opening, so getting out with the seat at the end of its tracks was a little like extricating yourself from a crashed airplane.

Big Ed and me looked back and forth at each other after Toly limped across the pavement and disappeared through the polished-brass revolving doors. But neither of us had any idea what to say. So Big Ed sighed and flipped on the radio as we pulled away from the curb. But it was Johnny Horton singing—hell, hollering—*"NORTH...to Ahl-as-KUH!"* which made us both kind of wince, so Big Ed turned it off again.

"Maybe he's going to see a foot doctor?" I finally said.

"Hey, maybe it's a psychiatrist or a psychologist?" Big Ed shrugged. "I know they got some doozies in there." We drove for a block or two in a kind of uneasy, finger-drumming silence—or as quiet as it ever gets on the streets of Manhattan, anyway—and Big Ed tried the radio again. This time he got Jerry Butler's rich, deep, from-the-gut voice singing that great, soulful ballad *"He Will Break Your Heart."* Big Ed looked at me and I nodded. The traveling music always has to be right for the mood, you know?

So the two of us cruised west across the city towards the George Washington Bridge, just listening to the radio and not saying much of anything while Big Ed dodged his way through the usual swarms of preoccupied, oblivious pedestrians, whistling traffic cops and swerving, jerking taxicabs that were always ready to burst out from behind buses, shoot across your bows or cut you off without mercy in Manhattan. It was one of those things you got used to and even bragged about if you lived in New York.

Anyhow, we were maybe halfway across the George Washington Bridge when I first noticed Big Ed kind of grimacing and holding his left arm in tight against the side of his chest. And then, right while I was looking at him, I saw all the color drain out of his face and his jaw kind of fall open a couple notches. *"You okay?"* I asked.

By that point his eyes were getting big and he was fighting to catch his breath.

"Maybe...I...don't...feel...so...good...."

Well, we made it down to the toll booths, but by then Big Ed's head was turned and he was all cinched up tight and gasping and grimacing into the vent window. It was all I could do to grab the wheel and steer with one hand, hang onto him with the other and frantically try to get my foot over his tree trunk of a leg and onto the brake pedal so's we wouldn't crash right into the damn tollbooth. I kind of hit it anyway—not that I gave a shit—and I was leaning on the horn for all I was worth even before the broken glass from the headlight and parking light lenses hit the pavement. And I was screaming like crazy at the top of my lungs: *"HELP! I NEED HELP OVER HERE! I NEED HELP OVER HERE!! HEY, I NEED SOME HELP OVER HERE!!!*

It seemed to take forever for the idiot tollbooth attendant to stop staring and gawking and realize that we had a genuine emergency going on, and by then some off-duty fireman from Weehawken came running over from the next lane. He opened the door and Big Ed kind of fell in his lap like a shot buffalo. I scrambled out the other side and ran around, and pretty soon we had him laid out as best we could on the pavement. He was all crunched up tight with pain, and there was nothing I could do but just crouch down next to him and tell him everything was going to be okay while I watched his face twist and contort. It was an awful, terrifying, helpless feeling, and I swear it seemed like it went on for hours. But I guess they have an emergency team stationed fairly close by at the George Washington Bridge and everyone said they actually got there pretty quickly. Not that you could prove it by me. A cop car got there first and then an ambulance and another cop car, and the two cops and two guys in white uniforms got Big Ed loaded up on a stretcher and shoved him into the back of the ambulance. I wanted to go with, of course, but the cop said I couldn't because I wasn't a blood relative. Plus Big Ed grabbed my arm and gasped: *"Take...care...a'th'...fucking...car!"* just before the doors closed. And so all I could do was just stand there and watch as the lights and siren came on and they carted him off to the hospital.

After that I had to answer a few dumb cop questions—mostly about the car, of course, seeing as how he'd never seen a Facel Vega before: *"Where does something like this come from?"* the cop wanted to know.

"France," I said impatiently. "It comes from France. But it's got a Chrysler engine."

The cop eyed me suspiciously. *"Why would a French car company use an American engine?"* he asked like something really sneaky or maybe even subversive or illegal might be going on.

And right there is where I knew I should have kept my damn mouth shut. *Never* offer up any free information to a police officer. Not ever. It just keeps you there longer. "Look," I told him, "why don't you ask the people from the Facel Vega dealership. There's one on the highway just outside of Passaic. They sell Renault and Citroen, too."

"Citroen?" the cop said slowly, working the word around in his mouth. "Is that some kind of French lemon?"

In spite of some of the things I'd heard, I told him I really didn't know.

He eyeballed the Facel Vega again. "Mind telling me how much something like this costs?"

Well, I knew for a fact that list price on a Facel Vega HK-500 ran right around ten thousand dollars—at least before Big Ed started haggling, anyway—but I was damned if I was going to tell the cop that. Hell, I'd be there all day. "I dunno," I deadpanned. "It's Bi—I mean, my friend's car." I gave him a New Jersey shrug. "Maybe six grand?"

That took a lot of the curiosity right out of his face. Hell, that was less than a damn Caddy Eldorado. "So," he asked, pulling a ticket book from his back pocket, "who was driving when the car hit the tollbooth island?"

"We kind of both were."

The cop looked at me sideways. "Who was at the wheel?"

Short answer, I told myself. Short answer. *Dragnet*-style, you know? "My friend was," I said simply.

"You happen to know his full name, place of residence, birth date, place of employment and driver's license number?"

"Look!" I said, getting kind of steamed. *"My best friend in the world just had a damn heart attack, and I'd sure as hell like to get over to wherever the hell they took him to see if he's okay, okay?"*

The cop actually looked hurt when I snapped at him like that. "Hey, I'm just doing my job," he almost whimpered. And then he pointed down to the hefty crumple Big Ed's two-ton Facel Vega had put in the metal guardrail strip in front of the tollbooth. One, I should point out, of probably no less than six or seven hundred thousand similar dents you, me and everybody else in creation has seen on tollbooth island guardrails over the years. "You see that?" he said.

I nodded.

"Well, that's state property there, my friend. And I guarantee you *somebody's* automobile insurance is going to have to pay for it! Otherwise it comes out of highway department tax dollars."

It was like being in high school civics class, you know?

But eventually he let me go so I could hightail it over to the hospital where they took Big Ed, and it was a pretty damn scary ride not knowing what they'd have to tell me when I finally got there. I mean, it had occurred to me more than once that Big Ed might already be dead, and I couldn't help thinking—selfishly—about what the hell I was gonna do and what sort of arrangements I'd have to make and most of all how the hell I was gonna run that damn VW business all by my lonesome if Big Ed was gone? And then of course I started feeling all guilty and shitty and cursing at myself about being so damn selfish, and right after that I started thinking and worrying and fretting about those same exact things all over again. I couldn't help it.

A nurse with a face like a musty attic had me sit in the Emergency Room waiting area for a good two hours before she finally directed me to Admissions to fill out some more dumb paperwork and then I got to sit there for another hour and a half before one of the fucking doctors finally came out to talk to me. I went to the pay phone and called home in the meantime, and before I could say much more than *"Hello, Honey"* Julie just about screeched into the phone: *"You won't BELIEVE it!"*

That threw me off guard. "I won't believe *what?"* I asked.

"IT!" she wailed excitedly. *"You simply won't believe it!"*

I started having ideas that she was maybe going to tell me she was pregnant again. "Won't believe what?" I repeated.

"YOUR SISTER'S GETTING MARRIED!!!" she screamed into the receiver like the whole blessed crowd at Ebbetts Field when the Dodgers hit a grand-slam homer against the Yankees. Complete with the echo and everything.

I could feel her waiting at the other end for me to say something. And I must admit that really *was* good news. I guess that saxophone player Pauly Martino finally got up the stones and the character to ask her. And of course Julie was going off inside like a damn fireworks display on the Fourth of July because that's the way women always get about engagement announcements. No matter what kind of ugly, disgusting or disappointing personal experiences they may have had with their own marriage.

"That's very nice," I said sullenly.

"Nice?" Julie almost growled. "Your sister Mary Francis is finally getting engaged—after all these years and after all she's been through—and all you can say is *'that's nice?'"*

So I told her where I was and about Big Ed and his heart attack and how I didn't really know anything yet, and then it was both of us feeling confused and concerned and all twisted around backwards inside instead of just me. Things get really strange in life when you have wonderful things and terrible things happening right on top of each other. Especially when none of it is happening to you personally, so there's nothing much you can do except just sit there on the sidelines laughing and crying and biting your fingernails down to the third knuckle while you wait to see how things turn out. But that's also the time when it's nice to have somebody who knows you to share all that joy and anguish and helpless frustration with, even if it's just at the other end of a phone line.

Julie offered to come right over, of course, but I told her to stay home with the kids. "You *sure?"* she asked for maybe the 10th or 12th time.

"Sure I'm sure," I told her. "There's nothing you can do here but just sit in this stupid room with your thumb up your ass reading yesterday's newspaper."

"I wish you wouldn't talk like that."

"Sorry."

"And be sure and call me as soon as you know anything."

"Of course I will."

"And you're absolutely *sure* you don't want me to come over?"

"Yeah, I'm sure," I almost laughed. And right at that moment—even though I was worried sick about Big Ed—I caught myself kind of smiling into the phone. "It's nice to be home," I whispered into the receiver.

"It's good to have you home," Julie whispered right back.

"And it's nice about my sister and Pauly Martino, too."

"That's what you said," she teased, and I could see her smiling all the way from the far end of the line.

It was well past 10:30 by the time this short, bald, maddeningly calm and sympathetic little Jewish heart doctor with a mole the color of dark chocolate on the bridge of his nose came out to bring me up to date on Big Ed's condition. His name was Dr. Silverman, and I couldn't help staring at that damn mole the whole time he talked to me. I figure he must've got that a lot. Especially seeing as how there was this one fat, black, hog-bristle of a hair sticking out of it, which made you wonder why his wife or mother or even somebody just standing next to him on the damn elevator hadn't whipped out a pair of tweezers and yanked the damn thing out for him. Things like that make you wonder if some people even have mirrors in their bathrooms at home, you know? As you can tell, I was pretty tired by then and also plenty nervous, and that sort of thing can make you giddy even in a dire crisis type of situation. I mean, nobody except priests, rabbis and undertakers really know how to act when the old health chips are down, and lots of times I think they're just faking it anyway.

Turns out Big Ed'd had what Dr. Silverman and his mole called "a moderate cardiac episode" rather than a full-blown heart attack (although he never quite spelled out the differences for me) and that Big Ed was "under observation," had been "given medication" and was "resting peacefully." Which, judging from the quick glimpse I got behind the curtain in his room, meant he was laid out with his eyes shut, tubes running in and out of his arm and his mouth hanging open like a dead carp. But at least he was snoring, and I took that to be a good sign. "You might as well go home," the doctor told me. "We'll all know a little more in the morning...."

So I drove back to Passaic in Big Ed's somewhat crunched Facel Vega with just one working headlight, and of course it was damp and dark and pissing down rain the whole way. I tried my best to think things over and sort them out, but you know how it is when you're so physically and emotionally exhausted and so damn much has happened that you just can't wrap your brain around it any more? So I mostly just listened to the radio and the rolling squish of the tires over wet pavement and the squeak and slap of the wipers backing up the music coming out of the dash. And when the D.J. hit me a sentimental broadside with Kathy Young and the Innocents singing *"A Thousand Stars"* followed by The Drifters doing *"Save The Last Dance for Me"* followed by Bert Kaempfert's instrumental *"Wonderland by Night"* and then Elvis' heart-wrenching, chart-topping single *"Are You Lonesome Tonight,"* I broke down and cried like a damn baby.

We went over to see Big Ed again the next day, and he sure looked pale, weak and haggard laid out in that hospital bed. But at the same time he seemed to have lost a lot of that iffy, nervous edge he'd had ever since his first heart attack. Like he was more relaxed and at peace with things than I think I'd ever seen him before. Although maybe that was just the drugs they were giving him, you know? They never tell you what they give people in the hospital. And even if they do tell you, it's not like you have any idea what it means. Pretty soon another doctor came in—a tall, skinny one in a white lab coat this time—checked Big Ed over for about 20 seconds, asked how he was feeling and then motioned Julie and me out into the hall.

"You're his family?" he asked.

We looked at each other. "More like friends," I explained.

"Does Mr. Baumstein have any family?"

'Not so's you'd notice' is what I wanted to say.

"Is he married?" the doc continued, looking at his clipboard.

"Several times."

"I mean currently."

I shook my head.

"Any close relatives?"

"You mean besides his ex-wives?" Ever notice how you crack jokes when you're really nervous? "He's got a brother," I told him, "but they don't talk much."

"Then who watches out for him?"

I almost said 'God,' but answered *"I guess we do,"* instead.

"Well, you'd better keep an eye on him. His life could be in your hands."

Like Julie and me needed any more responsibilities….

Then the doctor went on to explain as how Big Ed'd had himself another heart attack, but again it was a reasonably mild one with "no apparent, serious lasting damage" and he moreover looked like he was most likely "out of immediate danger" assuming "nothing else happened." But the long-term prognosis wasn't nearly so rosy. "Your friend's a very high risk for another cardiac episode," the doctor told us solemnly. "He absolutely *has* to lose some weight, watch his diet, start getting regular exercise and take better care of himself. And probably change some of his personal habits as well."

"And if he doesn't?"

"Well," the doctor allowed, looking down at his notes, "then very likely none of you will have to worry about it any more."

He couldn't have said it much plainer. And that worried me, because I couldn't really count on a guy like Big Ed overhauling his lifestyle on any kind of a permanent basis. Oh, he'd be fine when he got out of the hospital—as long as he was still scared, anyway—but then he'd start chiseling and cheating and hiding out behind the garage like a little kid with his first pack of cigarettes once he got a little of his old confidence back. And I didn't much look forward to trying to inflict that sort of advice on a guy like Big Ed Baumstein. But on the way home Julie reminded me—several different times, in fact—that if I didn't do it, no one else could. "He listens to you," she told me.

"Like hell he does," I kind of mumbled. "Big Ed doesn't listen to anybody."

"Well, he doesn't listen to you better than he doesn't listen to anybody else," Julie insisted. And even if that made no sense at all, I knew in my heart she was right.

I came by the next day on my way to work and again on my way home, and by then they had Big Ed kind of propped up in bed and he was cracking jokes with the nurses and even trying to pinch this pretty little Puerto Rican one who really filled out the top and bottom of her uniform. It was great to see him in what appeared to be higher spirits again. Although, like I said before, you never knew what they were giving him through those clear plastic tubes or inside those little paper pill cups.

After the nurses left Big Ed told me to sit down, and he had this dead serious and yet strangely serene look come over his face even before he started talking. "We've gotta get hold of that Harry Metropolis guy," he said softly.

"Whaddaya mean?" I asked him, even though I knew precisely what was coming.

Big Ed looked me right square in the eyes. "I mean I gotta bail out, Buddy. I gotta fold up my tent. I know for sure it's the right time."

"Aw, c'mon Ed," I said lamely. "You'll be up and around in no time. And you'll be selling the shit out of Volkswagens again and we'll be makin' money hand over fist and maybe we'll even get ourselves another racecar or something."

Big Ed just looked at me and smiled. "No, we won't."

Well, I wanted to argue with him, but I just couldn't. He was sure enough for both of us, I could see it in his eyes. He patted me on the arm. "And you just might think it's the right time for you to bail out, too."

I instinctively tried to pull back away from him, but he had a pretty good grip on my arm and held me there.

"You only get one shot at that brass ring, Buddy," he told me, "and I don't think you wanna try running that whole place by yourself."

"No, I guess I don't," I agreed. Whatever it took to be a wheeler-dealer and a hotshot salesman, I knew I didn't have it. Never did and never would. That's just the way things were, and I considered myself lucky to know it.

"And you sure as hell don't wanna go in partners with some fast-talking, second-generation white-shoes smartmouth like Harry Metropolis."

"That's for damn sure," I mumbled.

Big Ed nodded gently.

I inhaled, then let out a sigh so big and long and sorrowful that it smelled like a fart. "So you want me to call that Harry Metropolis jerk tomorrow and tell him you're ready to deal?"

Big Ed's eyes widened in mock horror. "Oh Jesus, didn't I teach you *anything?* You let that asshole know we want to sell and he'll try to Jew us down on the price. Sure as piss is yellow." Big Ed gave me the hairy eyeball. "And he absolutely *can't* know I've been in this place again—you haven't told anybody, have you?"

"Well, Julie knows and her mom and the kids know…."

"How about at the dealership and the shop?"

I thought it over. "I told Butch, but I think that's it. I didn't know how you were doing and so I didn't want a bunch of people coming over and bothering you."

"That's good. That's good," Big Ed mused, the wheels visibly turning behind his eyes. "Butch'll keep his mouth shut. We can count on him." He peered up at me from underneath his eyelids. "But you may have to shoot your mother-in-law."

"It'd be my pleasure," I assured him. "But I may have a hard time getting Julie to go for it."

"How about just cutting her tongue out."

I gave him a big grin. "Don't tempt me, Ed."

But Big Ed was already thinking two steps ahead. And of course that made him want one of his fat Cuban cigars. He always wheeled and dealed better with one of those damn things rolling around in his mouth. "See if there's any in my jacket in the closet, willya?" he asked. But I'd already made sure there weren't any around. I offered him a pack of gum that I'd picked up at the hospital gift shop instead. He looked at it like I'd handed him a poodle turd. "What the hell is this?"

"It's Beeman's," I said enthusiastically. "They say it aids digestion."

"There's nothing wrong with my digestion," he grumbled. "It's my fucking heart. Everybody knows it's my fucking heart."

Eventually he unwrapped three sticks and shoved them in his face. "Now the first thing," he said slowly, kneading in the gum, "is that we can't go calling this Harry Metropolis and asking for a meeting."

"We can't?"

Big Ed shook his head. "Nah, we gotta wait for him to come to us." Big Ed looked right into my eyeballs again. "Selling is more like fishing than hunting, see. Y'gotta wait for the nibble and then the bite instead of going out and chasing after it."

"Play hard to get," I said.

Big Ed gave me a nod of approval.

"Play it close to the vest," I continued.

Big Ed nodded again.

"The guy who names the first price loses," I repeated just like he'd taught me.

That put one hell of a big smile on his face. "And here I always thought you had concrete in your ears."

"I've picked up a little here and there."

"Yeah, I guess you have," he said proudly. And then he started in on the gum again, thinking. "The other thing is that we really gotta keep this thing…" he swept his eyes around his hospital room, "…real quiet. On the Q.T. He can't know about it or he'll try to come at you privately and split us apart."

"Divide and conquer, huh?"

Big Ed nodded. "That's it exactly." He patted my arm again. "Trust me. We're gonna make out fine on this deal."

"If you say so, Ed."

He shot me a warm, wide, fatherly sort of smile. "You bet we will."

Then we just sat there and listened to the metal carts wheeling by and the squeak of the nurses' shoes going up and down the hallway outside.

"So that's it," Big Ed said softly.

"Yeah, I guess it is."

"So what're you gonna do with yourself?" Big Ed asked.

"Me?"

"Sure, you. What're you gonna do with yourself?"

"Jesus, I don't know, Ed. I haven't really thought about it." I felt my future circle around the room like a hawk's shadow. "Jesus, what *will* I do?" I asked with a little bit of a choke in my voice.

"Hey, it's a big, wide world out there," he said encouragingly. "And you're young and you'll have money in your pocket and you've got a nice family," he leaned in close again and whispered: *"You're a damn lucky man to have that family of yours. I hope you know that."*

"I know it," I told him. And I did know it. More than I'd ever known anything in my life, in fact. Or at least that's the way it felt right at that moment, sitting next to Big Ed's hospital bed and listening to his voice while I fought back the stupid, dumb-ass tears that wanted to come pouring out of my eyes.

"You can probably keep *Alfredo's* if you want it," Big Ed continued, smacking his gum again. "Or you can sell it on time to Steve and J.R. and let them pay you a steady income off of it. That'd probably be better, tax-wise…."

But I wasn't even listening. It was all too sudden. Too overwhelming. Even though I'd seen it coming for a long time and from a long, long way off.

"How about you?" I asked him.

"Oh, I'll be around," he said confidently. "You haven't seen the last of me by a long shot. But the doc says I gotta take better care of myself…" he smacked his gum for me "…at least if I wanna live a little longer."

"So what will you do?"

"Oh, I dunno," he shrugged. "Maybe I'll sell my house up here and go down to live in Miami Beach in the wintertime like all the other rich Jews who've cashed in their chips. Take up golf or deepsea fishing, y'know? Get myself one a'those fancy apartments overlooking the ocean and go to all the early-bird dinners with the rest of the old farts." He leaned in close. "That's the Elephant Graveyard for rich Jews down there. They all go down to Miami Beach to die."

"You're not gonna die," I told him.

"We're *all* gonna die," he corrected me. "It's just the timing we never know about until the last fucking moment."

I knew he was pulling my leg, of course. But he was also playing with the idea himself—just kind of running it over his tongue to see what it tasted like, you know?

"But why the hell Miami Beach?"

Big Ed rolled his eyes like I didn't understand anything. "Look, the doc says I need to change my habits, right?"

"Right," I agreed.

"And I should really take better care of myself, right?"

I nodded.

"Well, there's *nobody* who can change your habits or make you take care of yourself like some rich Jewish widow."

I knew he was joking, of course, but I could sense something serious there, too. I guess having a life-threatening medical emergency can get you looking a little further into the past than yesterday and a little further into the future than tomorrow. Makes you wonder about where you came from and, when you get right down to it, if you've got anywhere left to go. Big Ed'd stopped smacking his gum and he was just sitting there, slack-jawed, looking at the rumpled mound of sheets and blankets in front of him. "I'm gonna see if I can't find somebody a little like my first wife." His eyes eased up to where his toes were sticking out at the foot of the bed. "She died, y'know."

I nodded. "Yeah. I know."

"She had a lotta heart," he said softly. "She had a lotta heart."

Chapter 40: Snakeskin Boots and Sad Souvenirs

Big Ed got out of the hospital less than a week after he went in, carrying a fist-ful of prescriptions and a list of Do's and Don'ts that covered, as he put it, "every damn enjoyable thing you'd ever want to do in this life" under the Don'ts heading and "damn near everything I hate" under the Do's. But hearing him grouse like that was music to my ears, and I was really glad to see some of the old Big Ed spark and sparkle back again. Even so, he still had his mind made up that we should sell out the VW dealership to that Harry Metropolis jerk, take the money and run. And I knew he was probably right by the way he looked like he was walking on eggs. But, like he said, we had to wait for Harry Metropolis to come to us.

It didn't take long.

In fact, a brand-new, two-tone, pewter-over-deep-metallic-silver Rolls Royce Silver Cloud II pulled up in front of our dealership the Wednesday between Christmas and New Year's who should step out but our old pal Harry, wearing his usual dark sunglasses along with these unbelievable snakeskin boots and a white fur coat that made him look like some kind of shrunken-down polar bear. He was all smiles and one-liners, of course, and spent a good portion of the first five minutes bragging about his new boots. "Made out of Egyptian Cobra skin," he cooed. "And just the hood part, too." He wiped a little New Jersey slush off the end of them with a monogrammed silk handkerchief. "I don't even want to tell you how much they cost me."

"How much did they cost you?" Big Ed asked immediately.

"Three hunnert bucks!" he crowed. "Can you believe it? Three hunnert bucks for a pair a'damn shit-kickers." He gave us a dazzling, off-kilter smile. "I must be crazy."

"If you'd spend three hunnert just on something just t'hold your smelly feet," Big Ed wondered out loud, "what kind of nutty offer d'ya think you might wanna make on our dealership?"

You could see that caught Harry off guard. But only for a heartbeat and only if you looked really close. It was just the briefest little flutter of his eyelashes, really. And the snappy patter didn't stop at all. "Hard to say. Hard to say," he allowed, kind of dancing around it while he gathered his thoughts. "I'd have to see the books first. See what kind of numbers you guys're doing and how much you're skimming off the top. Need to know about the property, too. You own or rent?"

"Own," Big Ed said casually while unwrapping himself another three sticks of Beeman's gum.

"Free and clear?"

"Y'gotta be crazy t'own anything but cash free and clear," Big Ed said like everybody knew it. "Mortgage money's the best deal in creation."

"What's your buyout?"

Big Ed gave him the Harry eyeball. "Look, I don't pull my pants down until the other guy does the same. You don't see shit until I have some kinda idea what you got in mind." He chewed a couple loud smacks out of his gum. "Decide whether I wanna waste my time with you or not, unnerstand?"

Harry's eyes narrowed a little. "You got someplace we can talk?"

"Sure," Big Ed grinned, nodding towards his office. Then he looked at me with eyes that said *'get lost'* and said: "You wanna join us, Buddy? This place is yours as much as it is mine."

On the one hand I wanted to be there to watch it—like seeing sharks devour a seal or maybe two dogs humping in a school yard during recess—but I knew Big Ed could handle it better on his own. Shit, I'm the type who can tip my hand and give things away without even saying anything. It's just the way I am. And talking about big money made me nervous. "Nah, I got some stuff to take care of out back," I told them. And then I added: "Besides, there's no reason for me to get involved unless we've actually got something serious to talk about...."

Big Ed sneaked me an appreciative wink as I headed out towards the shop.

Of course that was just the first of several serious meetings with old Harry Metropolis over the next few weeks as he and Big Ed hammered, ducked, weaseled, faked and feinted their way around each other. I'd watch them sometimes through the plate glass window when it was late and the showroom was dark and the only light was the big, brass-plated desk lamp with the dark green shade in Big Ed's office. It painted deep, dark, menacing-looking shadows on the walls and on their faces and on the stacks and reams of papers in front of them, and I'd be kind of casually hiding behind the corner of one of those pop-up VW campers, just watching their eyes and the expressions on their faces. Sometimes I'd catch a little of the conversation, too.

"Look, I can't help it if your fucking banker's out of his mind."

"Hey, that's what it's worth. You could do a lot of things with this property—a corner lot looking out on a main street at a stoplight! Hell, we had it appraised three different times. Once when we bought the burned-down apartment building behind us to build it out in the first place...."

"Yeah, and I understand you got yourselves a real Fire Sale price on it after you had some guy do a torch job on the building."

"Oh, and who the fuck are you? Dick Tracy? Joe Friday? Are you trying to buy this place or just piss me off?"

"I'm trying to buy it, but I don't mind pissing you off."

"I don't mind pissing you off, either. We're not a bunch of rubes here. We're not about to let you buy the dealership and steal the fucking property right out from under our noses while you're at it."

"I'm not trying to steal anything. I'm just trying to buy it without the fucking gold mine you seem to think is underneath it...."

They'd go on that way for hours.

But slowly, bit by bit and as if by magic, the nuts and bolts of the deal started coming together. Harry wanted the dealership *and* the property—all the property—on account of he was planning to add another franchise some day (maybe Borgward or Mercedes-Benz?) and you really don't want to be building your own building on somebody else's chunk of land. But he didn't want anything to do with *Alfredo's Foreign Car Service* in the old Sinclair. Meanwhile Big Ed was more interested in selling him the dealership but hanging on to the property and leasing the space to Harry on some kind of long-term deal because he figured we'd come out ahead tax-wise, equity-wise and investment-wise that way. To be honest, I didn't care much one way or the other once I'd made up my mind (with Julie's help, of course) that we should go through with the deal. Fact is, I just wanted it to be over with, because it tore at my gut every single day when I stuck my key in the door to open up in the morning or lock up at night and realized all over again that it was all going to belong to somebody else pretty soon.

Although that changed a little after Harry spent some time around the store and saw how smoothly things ran out in the shop and how much our service customers liked the way we took care of them. I hope it doesn't sound like I'm bragging or anything, but a lot of that was on account of me. Of course, I never thought I was doing anything particularly special—just doing the next thing that had to be done and taking care of the next person who needed to be taken care of, you know?—but Harry took me aside one afternoon before he and his lawyer and his accountant went into yet another meeting with Big Ed and our lawyer and our accountant. "I'd like you to stay on and run the back for me," he said simply, even pulling down his dark sunglasses so I could see the sincere, heartfelt look in his shifty, rat-like eyes.

I remember distinctly that happened on Friday, January 20th, and the reason I'm so sure is on account of that's the day John F. Kennedy got himself inaugurated and it was all over the newspapers and radio and television news reports. It was bitter cold with a half-foot of snow on the ground in Washington, but Kennedy wouldn't wear an overcoat, and all the news shows played it over and over again how he said from underneath the Washington Monument and the most perfect, razor-cut head of hair of any American president: *"Ask not what your country can do for you—ask what you can do for your country."* I thought that was a pretty moving sentiment, even if I didn't exactly understand what it meant.

"It means more taxes," Big Ed explained when we sat down with a couple sandwiches after Harry and his bunch left. "Democrats with big dreams always means more taxes."

"Then what do Republicans mean?" I asked.

"That's easy," Big Ed said through a mouthful of pastrami and Swiss. "More tax loopholes." He had a real knack for boiling all the grand plans, purposes, pledges and promises of our fine leaders in Washington down to their basic, how-it-affects-you-and-me essence.

I told him about Harry saying as how he wanted to keep me on at the dealership. "Hmm," Big Ed mused, rubbing his chin. "You gotta be real careful there, Buddy."

"I kind of thought I did."

"What he really wants is to just buy me out and get you to go in partners with him. It cuts his nut in half and gets me out of the picture..." Big Ed gave me a look out of the corner of his eye. "He probably thinks he can get around you one-on-one."

I could see that happening.

"Then he'll wait until you've trained up a replacement for him and then he'll do everything he can to make your life miserable—until you can't even stand it anymore—because then he gets to buy you out at a knockdown price and picks up the other half of the deal on the cheap."

"Do you really think he'd *do* that?"

"Maybe so, maybe not. I wouldn't bet against it. But either way, there's no reason in hell to leave yourself open for it." He gave me one of those grand, Big Ed smiles. "Never give a guy a chance to kick you in the nuts in a business deal, Buddy. Even if it's just to remove the temptation."

I must admit Big Ed was something of a genius when it came to orchestrating business deals. He had me sell my share of the dealership to Julie—at least on paper, anyway—so Harry had to buy the two of them out lock, stock and barrel to get his hands on the business and the blue sky above it, but he had the two of us form a separate "real estate investment" corporation that took over ownership of the property just so's we could lease it back to Harry on a 20-year deal with a buyout clause on the end of it. And that buyout was indexed to whatever the per-square-foot increase on improved land values might be at the end of 20 years, too. Everybody who understood those things (which, to be honest, didn't include me) said it was a really sweet sort of deal and that Big Ed definitely had what all the big wheelers and dealers call "long eyes."

"I probably won't be around in 20 years," Big Ed told me, "but you be sure and get yourself a sharp Jewish lawyer when the time comes."

The only part I didn't like was that Harry had an option to expand into the corner space where the old Sinclair stood so long as he gave us six months' notice. Big Ed also worked out a deal with Steve and J.R. that pretty much sold them the foreign car shop business at *Alfredo's* in return for so much a month to me and Julie for the business and about the same each month to Harry Metropolis on a sublease. All those deals put together pretty much assured Julie and me—and maybe even our kids—that we'd have a little something in the bank, a steady income, depreciation and tax deductions every year and not too much in the way of serious money worries for the rest of our lives. And if Harry Metropolis' VW dealership went down the old lemonade barrel, we'd have the property back to sell or lease all over again any way we wanted. "It's like being a damn hooker!" Big Ed grinned. "You got it, you sell it, and you still got it!"

Big Ed also spent a lot of time working out a contract deal for me to keep running the service department end of the VW business for another year—for continuity's sake, you understand—followed by an open-ended series of one-year options at a 10% salary increase every time it got renewed. Not to mention a yearly bonus based on how much business the shop did and a signed-on-the-dotted-line severance deal if Harry ever got pissed off and fired me. In fact, the one thing it didn't cover was me quitting….

As you can imagine, it took several months to hammer out all the details and get all the eyes crossed and tees dotted on the paperwork, and we finally got the closing and ownership transfer set up for Saturday, April 1st. Big Ed insisted on doing it that day because he thought it was absolutely perfect that the closing took place on April Fool's Day. But as the day approached, I could see he was having second thoughts same as me. "I know Buyer's Remorse because I see it every week," he said ruefully into his root beer one day at lunch, "but Seller's Remorse is something new for me."

I knew what he meant. To tell the truth, I was pretty much sleepwalking through my daily routine the last few weeks and dreading the day Big Ed would walk out that glass front door as my business partner for the very last time. And I didn't look forward one bit to working for a guy like Harry Metropolis who bragged about his Egyptian Cobra hood boots and wore sunglasses all the time to hide what he was thinking. But I could also see that Big Ed really needed to get out. He was pale and jittery and didn't look right anymore—like he'd been woken up in the middle of a damn nightmare or something—and I knew he wanted to get away for a while. Turns out his Italian cousin from the old scrap machinery business (who'd also recently spent some sheet time in the hospital getting his gall bladder taken out) had asked him about going down to Florida for a couple weeks to play golf and do a little deep-sea fishing. That kind of surprised me. "I didn't know you liked deep-sea fishing," I said as we were signing payroll checks together for the very last time.

"Don't know if I do," Big Ed shrugged. "But I sure as shit can't stand two solid weeks of chasing golf balls. Besides, I know a lot of people who say they get their gongs off hauling big fish out of the ocean."

"Doesn't sound like much fun to me," I allowed.

Big Ed shot me a wink. "Me, either."

"Then why do it?"

"Somehow I gotta figure out what the hell t'do with myself, Buddy. The docs all say I gotta relax and take it easy and take better care of myself. But you know me. I'm just one a'those guys who can't sit still."

And wasn't that the truth!

"Well, I sure hope you have a good time," I told him, even though I kind of doubted it. Personally, the only good reason I could think of for going to Florida in the spring was Sebring (which happened to be coming up that very weekend, by the way) and I told him as much.

Big Ed nodded. "Yeah, that was sure a lotta fun, wasn't it?"

"It sure was."

"Remember the first year we went down there with the Jag and Sammy Speed?"

"I'll never forget it."

"I went off at night and couldn't find my way back to the fucking racetrack," he laughed. "It was all weeds and busted-up concrete and I didn't know where the hell I was."

"We were wondering what happened to you."

"Yeah," he said, dabbing at his eyes, "we sure had a lotta fun."

"That we did."

Then, very slowly, his smile melted into one of the saddest frowns I'd ever seen on his face. "Y'know, sometimes I wonder what the hell happened to me, Buddy…."

And that's when I realized all over again that he really needed to get away. He'd get these sudden, overpowering waves of emotion flooding through his system that made it hard for him to even keep himself together. That wasn't like him at all. "The docs all said it's pretty typical," he told me in a near approximation of the old Big Ed voice. "They gave me pills for it, but I haven't started taking 'em yet."

"Maybe you should?"

"I dunno," he answered, measuring his words carefully. "I think maybe I'll like 'em too much."

That night I got a call from Hank down at Sebring. Said he was coming up to New York after the races were over and looked forward to maybe seeing me. "New York?" I said. "Why the hell would anyone want to come to New York?"

"Beats me," he agreed. "But that's where all the damn book publishers are."

"You actually *finished* that story you were working on?"

"Well, not exactly," he said kind of sheepishly. "But I've ruined a lot of paper and I'm far enough along that I want to see if anybody's interested."

"I'm sure it's great," I told him. And I meant it. "I always enjoy reading the stuff you write."

"Thanks," he told me. "But I'm not sure your opinion is worth much of anything in the publishing world."

"I read, don't I?"

"You *do?"* he said with an edge in his voice. "Then tell me: what was the last novel you read?"

I thought it over, and the best I could come up with was *Moby Dick* back in senior year of high school. And that was mostly the *Classics Illustrated* comic book version, come to think of it. Not to mention that movie with Gregory Peck.

"You see?" Hank laughed into the phone.

"Yeah, I guess," I laughed right back. Then I asked him how things were going at Sebring.

"Well, today was probably a hell of a lot more entertaining than the 12 Hour is going to be." For the second year in a row, the Sebring organizers held a four-hour enduro for little 1.0-liter-and-under production car tiddlers on Friday, and Hank said it was fun to watch seeing as how some of the manufacturers and importer/distributors took it pretty seriously and got some of the top-rank aces like Stirling Moss and Dan Gurney and Walt Hansgen and Bruce McLaren recruited out of the paddock to handle some of the driving chores. I guess Stirling Moss' sister Pat was in the race, too.

"Is she any good?" I wanted to know.

"You bet your sweet ass she is! She's made quite a name for herself driving rallye cars—big Healeys, mostly—and she was mixing it up pretty good with Walt Hansgen in a pair of those Sebring Sprites."

"Walt Hansgen? Wow!"

Then Hank told me all about the Sebring Sprites Donald Healey sent over, which were a wee bit breathed upon compared to the little buzz-boxes and Bugeyes we were used to seeing on the street. "Jesus, you should've seen them!" Hank laughed into the phone. "Moss and McLaren were swapping positions every lap for the first hour or so. It was hysterical."

"Did they win?"

"Nah, they weren't quite fast enough to stay with those slick little Fiat-Abarth 1000s." I'd only seen magazine photos, but knew they were about the sexiest (and most expensive!) little 1.0-liter GTs ever built. "They put Dan Gurney in one—had to about fold him double to get him inside!—and he was pretty much running away with it until the car ran out of brakes with something like an hour to go."

"Another Dan Gurney hard-luck story," I tossed in.

"There sure are a lot to choose from, aren't there?" Hank agreed.

At the end of the four hours and the usual pit stop disasters, it was two of Gurney's teammates in a pair of those Fiat-Abarth 1000s coming home first and second followed by Walt Hansgen, Bruce McLaren, Stirling Moss, Ed Leavens, Pat Moss and Briggs Cunningham himself in a spread-out swarm of Sebring Sprites. "That race was worth the price of admission all by itself," he told me.

"But you're a blessed scribe," I ribbed him. "You don't pay to get in."

"Well, it was worth it even if you paid," he insisted. "And so will the party in the infield be tonight."

"You be careful," I teased. "It gets crazy there at night in Green Park. I understand there were a couple human sacrifices last year."

"I'll be all right," he said bravely. "I speak the native tongue."

Then I asked him how things looked for the 12 Hour.

"I think it's pretty much pick your favorite Ferrari as far as the overall goes. There really isn't anybody to challenge them except the Cunningham and Camoradi Maseratis. They've each got a couple regular, front-engined Birdcages plus one each of the new, rear-engined Type 63s…"

"How do they look?" I had to ask. I mean, new Maserati racecars had always done a lot for my pulse rate and blood pressure.

"They look like turds with wheels," Hank said sadly. "Maybe the ugliest damn cars I've ever seen. Their pictures don't do them justice."

"I haven't seen any," I told him.

"Well, trust me on this: they look even worse in person."

"Jeez, that's too bad."

"Oh, they've got some great driver lineups—Moss, Graham Hill, Masten Gregory, Bruce McLaren, Walt Hansgen—but nobody expects the cars to last. And once they're gone, it'll just be a question of which Ferrari you prefer."

"How're Cal and Toly doing?"

"Mixed bag, really. They're sharing a brand-new, rear-engined Ferrari sports model called the 246SP. I think it's basically that rear-engined Grand Prix car they tried at the end of last season wrapped up in two-seater bodywork. And all the Ferraris have split-nostril noses this year and these bulky, raised-up rear ends with little spoiler lips across the top to help with the aerodynamics. I guess Carlo Chiti—he's Ferrari's head racing engineer—talked the Old Man into buying himself a wind tunnel and that's what they came up with. But boy, are those cars ever *ugly!"*

"An ugly Ferrari?" It didn't sound possible.

"Well, maybe just homely. Useta be a guy with a little taste and talent would sculpt out a car's shape based on his thumb and his eyeball and what he thought the wind might like. And most of the cars looked pretty damn swell."

"Yeah, they sure did," I agreed.

"But then you had guys like Frank Costin coming in from aircraft streamlining and aerodynamics, so now it's turning into some kind of damn science," he paused for a moment, fishing for words. "I guess I just don't like it as well...."

Naturally I asked him about Cal and Toly's chances, and the way he saw it—even though the new 246SP was lighter and quicker and handled a hell of a lot better than the old warhorse, front-engined V-12s—it was too new and untested and probably wouldn't go the distance. "Even Cal and Toly think they'd be better off with one of the old 250 *Testa Rossas,"* Hank told me. "At least for this race, anyway."

"To finish first, you first must finish," I repeated for maybe the five hundred thousandth time in my life.

"Isn't that the truth!" Hank agreed. "And even then it comes down to who has the luck and who gets the breaks."

"Yeah," I added. "Or the breakages."

And that's exactly the way it happened, as Hank explained in detail after I picked him up at LaGuardia on Tuesday afternoon. "At the start Cal got stuck way down deep in the pack when the engine wouldn't catch right away, but he waited for all the banzai crazies to sort themselves out and then just worked his way forward. He took the lead pretty easily about 50 minutes in and after that he and Toly were pulling away from everybody right through the first and second round of pit stops. Nobody could touch them. But then Cal banged a curb when he swerved to dodge some backmarker pulling out to pass some other backmarker, and that wrecked the steering gear and they were out of it."

"Sounds a little impatient of him. Especially with a big lead."

"I thought so, too," Hank allowed. "And so did he, judging by the look on his face afterward."

"Why the hell was he pushing so hard?"

"Oh, I guess he and Toly had a couple little side bets going. Not for money, of course. Just for a little slice of honor."

"What kind of side bets?"

"Oh, best lap average and best number of laps between fuel stops, tightest window between slowest lap and fastest lap, that sort of thing."

"Hmm. I always figured Cal had a little in hand over Toly."

"So did I," Hank admitted. "But Toly's got kind of a new look in his eye this year."

"What do you mean?"

"It's hard to explain. You've really got to see it for yourself."

"C'mon, Hank. You're supposed to be the big, hot-shit writer."

Hank curled his lip under. "I dunno. He just looks *hungrier* this year. A little more focused and urgent, maybe. It's hard to miss."

"He said he wants to win the World Championship this year."

"He just might at that. Especially based on the way he was running at Sebring."

"Was he actually *faster* than Cal?"

"Let's just call it a tossup, okay? But no question he was pushing Cal. Pushing him pretty hard, in fact."

I rolled that around in my mind. Like so many things in racing, it didn't sound right, but there it was. "So what happened to everybody else?" I finally asked.

"Oh, all the Maseratis broke down except for the 2.0-liter Type 60 Birdcage Briggs Cunningham was sharing with our old buddy Creighton Pendleton the Third. They took it easy the whole time, suffered through the usual mechanical disasters and limped home in 19th at the flag. Behind two MGAs, a Sebring Sprite and a Sunbeam Alpine…."

"That's pretty damn embarrassing."

"Hey, at least they made the distance. That's more than you could say for any of the other Maseratis. And just think how good it made the guys in the MGs, the Sprite and the Alpine feel."

He had a point there.

"At the end it was Ferrari, Ferrari, Ferrari, Ferrari with *Testa Rossas* sweeping the first four places. Hill and Gendebien won it again, and I thought the Rodriguez brothers did a hell of a nice, steady job to come home third in one of Carlo Sebastian's cars. Another one of Carlo's cars—one of the older, front-engined 246S Dinos—took sixth overall and won the 2.5-liter sports/prototype class with Jim Hall and George Constantine doing the driving, and you would have been proud as hell of Denise McCluggage."

"Oh? What'd she do to the boys this time?"

"She entered her own Ferrari GT—one of those nifty 250 Short Wheelbase Berlinettas…"

"I *love* those cars!" I blurted out.

"Hey, who doesn't?" Hank agreed. "Anyhow, Denise and her co-driver Allen Eager came home in 10th overall and won the Grand Touring class. Came in two laps ahead of the first Corvette."

"Good for her!"

"And it wasn't any expensive, well-manned pro effort, either. They took care of almost everything by themselves, with just a couple volunteer helpers. They made a pretty damn swell job of it."

"Good for them," I repeated. "Good for them."

Hank nodded.

"Anything else worth mentioning?"

"Oh, I thought the Elva Couriers looked like a lot of fun. That Carl Haas guy out of Chicago entered a couple of them, but they ran into problems. And one of those gorgeous little Climax-powered Lola sports/racers finished up 13th overall with just an 1100cc engine. Have you seen one of those things yet?"

I shook my head.

"Well, they're a real work of art as far as I'm concerned. Make a Lotus Eleven look bulky and fat by comparison."

That was hard to believe, but I knew better than to doubt Hank's word.

"Oh, and you'll be happy to know that your beloved Arnolt-Bristols finished 21st, 23rd and 24th overall, first, second and third in class and won the team prize. They weren't the fastest cars out there by a long shot, but their teamwork and discipline are really first-class and they're built like tanks."

"So did you have a lot of fun?" I asked him.

"It was okay," Hank allowed. "I survived the Friday night mess in the infield without any visible permanent damage and at least it didn't rain this year…" his voice trailed off, but then he added, very quietly: "I'm thinking of not going back to Europe this summer."

"Y-you *are?"* I stammered. I couldn't believe what I was hearing.

"Yeah," he said slowly, "I've been thinking about it a lot lately. I've been doing this for—what is it, going on five years now?—and I think I may finally be getting burned out."

"But I thought this was what you always wanted?"

"It was."

"But what happened? Didn't it turn out to be what you thought it'd be?"

"No, it turned out to be exactly what I thought it'd be. Maybe even better."

"But it wasn't what you really wanted?" I was trying hard to understand.

Hank scratched his head. "It was exactly what I wanted then," he said softly but deliberately. "But maybe it's not what I want any more. Hell, you cover enough races and it all starts running together. Like you're writing the same damn story over and over again."

"You get stale?"

"Not so much 'stale' as used up. I gotta face it: I'm out of gas and I'm homesick as hell, Buddy. If nothing else, I need to at least take some kind of break."

"So you're not going back to Europe."

"Nope," he shook his head. "I told the magazine to give the job back to the other guy. The one who had it before. I guess he's been bugging them about it for quite awhile."

"He's not as good as you," I warned.

"Hey," Hank laughed, "who the heck is?"

I gave him a tight sort of smile. "I'll miss your stories."

"Oh, don't worry. I'll still be writing stuff for the magazine. And I'll still be covering races here in the states. I've never done the Indy 500 and I'd like to do that. Maybe even write something about it for one of the English magazines. I hear rumors that Brabham may be coming over with one of the Coopers this year."

"That'd be interesting."

"It sure would," Hank agreed, "even if he doesn't really have a shot at winning anything. And I'd like to try some other kinds of writing, too. Nobody thinks I can write about anything except cars and racing."

"That's what I always thought," I said, giving him the old needle.

"Hey, that's what everybody thinks! That's why I'd like to maybe try something different for a change."

"Like what?"

"I dunno. Maybe do a few articles for some of those travel magazines. Maybe even something for *Playboy."*

"Playboy? Who the hell reads *Playboy?"*

"Nobody. They just look at the titty pictures, same as you and me. But I hear it pays pretty good."

"It pays good because so many guys buy it to look at the titty pictures."

"I don't mind. Having a piece in *Playboy* gives a writer a perfectly legitimate excuse to thumb through the magazine himself. Even right out in public if he wants to."

We got a pretty good laugh off that.

"And there's something else, too," Hank added, patting the battered leather briefcase underneath his legs, "I want to see if I can do anything with this thing."

"Is that your book?"

Hank gave me a solid half a nod.

"What is it?"

"Well, I *hope* it's about three-quarters of a blockbuster best-seller," he grinned.

"Boy, wouldn't that be swell," I grinned right back.

"Wouldn't it ever," Hank agreed. "Wouldn't it ever."

I dropped him off in front of the famous old Flat Iron building on the wedge-shaped corner of 5th Avenue and Broadway where 23rd Street cuts across. "You know," he told me, "this is supposed to be the oldest skyscraper in New York."

It looked like a tall slice of old wedding cake with dried-out masonry frosting. "Doesn't look like much compared to the Chrysler Building and the Empire State," I observed.

"Yeah," Hank grinned. "And it's Chicago school architecture on top of it!"

Naturally I offered to wait outside and also told Hank he was more than welcome to come home to dinner and stay with us over on the Jersey side. But he said he had another book publisher appointment later that afternoon plus two more and meetings with a couple so-called "literary agents" the next day, so he was going to stay in the city. "Besides," he laughed as he climbed out of the car, "I'm so used to being on my own in small, strange rooms that I'm probably not fit to be around family life any more. You develop some pretty disgusting habits when you're alone all the time."

"I don't care if you pick your nose with your toes," I told him, "you're always welcome at our house. Always."

I meant it, too.

Hank called me from the airport to thank me again on his way out of town late Thursday afternoon, and I got the feeling that his big literary meetings hadn't exactly gone the way he'd hoped. "Nah," he told me disgustedly, "nobody was very interested in a novel about cars and racing. One agent said he'd read it—for a fee, of course—and give me a critique, but everybody else basically blew me off."

"Just like that?"

"Just like that."

"Without even reading any of it?"

"Yeah," he sighed into the receiver. "They all pretty much agreed there's no market for it, even if it's a great read."

"No market for it? That stinks."

"I thought so, too. But that's the way it is. They're a pretty snotty, stuck-up bunch here in Manhattan. Like it's some kind of a closed, secret society, and you have to know somebody who knows somebody to even get your foot in the door."

"That stinks," I repeated.

"And they're so damn arrogant and holier-than-thou about it. Like they're the only ones who know what people like or what they might want to read." I could feel Hank's anger and frustration all the way from the other end of the line. "They think they know more about everything than anybody. Hell, they think they know more about everything than God."

"Hey," I told him, "most New Yorkers think civilization ends at the Hudson River…."

"You know what this one publishing lady told me?" he snarled into the phone.

"No, what?"

"She told me there was no market for my book because *'THOSE people don't read!'"* He said it mimicking her tight-ass, snotty, down-your-nose New York twang. And then he didn't say anything. He just steamed.

"So what're you going to do?" I finally asked.

"Fly back to California and finish it anyway. Just to prove I can do it if nothing else. And besides," I could hear a little of the helpless old 'what-can-you-do' Hank humor creeping into his voice, "I *gotta* keep writing."

"Why's that?"

"Hey, I gotta find out what happens…."

We closed the deal on the VW dealership as planned on Saturday, April 1st, Big Ed took off for Florida with his cousin on Sunday and come Monday morning Harry called me into Big Ed's old office to tell me how happy he was that I was working for him and what great plans he had for the dealership and that, oh, by the way, he wanted to exercise his option on the old Sinclair and could I please have *Alfredo's Foreign Car Service* moved the hell out of there by Monday, October 2nd. Although sooner would really be better.

So I went over at lunchtime and told Steve and J.R., and also promised that I'd help them find a new and even better shop and help them get things moved and set up. I mean, *Alfredo's* was basically just a dirty old gas station with a leaky roof and two mismatched additions tacked on, and it was always hotter than hell in the summer and frigid cold in the winter and one of the lifts leaked pressure so's you had to keep bumping the lever every 10 minutes or it'd creep right down on you and there was a big crack in the ceiling beam where we used to hang the chain hoist before the first time we tried hauling a Big Healey engine and transmission out and....

And I swear it was as much a part of me as any of my internal organs and the thought of it not being there any more was just tearing me right in half.

But you soldier on, right?

So me and Steve and J.R. went scouting around for new space on evenings and weekends and meanwhile old Harry Metropolis was showing me how he figured things *should* be done in the service department end of a successful new car dealership. Like fr'instance how every single VeeDub that came in for *anything* should also get new wiper blades, a new fan belt and an eight-ounce can of Marvin's Magical Mystery Oil additive in its crankcase.

"But what if it doesn't *need* new wiper blades or a new fan belt?" I asked.

"Every car needs new wiper blades and a new fan belt," Harry insisted. "Some need them more than others, but those things always wear out, don't they?"

"Yeah, eventually," I grudgingly agreed. "But I usually don't replace them unless the cars really need it and the customer wants it."

"Absolutely!" Harry nodded through a big, slimy smile. "And that's why it's *our* job to make them want it. For their own peace of mind, see?"

"And the Marvin's Magical Mystery Oil?"

"Same thing. For their own peace of mind. It's a great product, and it doesn't hurt a thing. It's just too bad these VWs don't have radiators."

"Radiators?"

"Sure, radiators. Because then you can help everybody out with a radiator flush and new radiator hoses once a year, too. It's all part of *merchandising* your service department, see?"

I saw, all right. "You ever know a guy named Colin St. John?" I asked him.

"I don't think so. Why?"

"I think you guys maybe went to the same school together, that's all."

But if I didn't much like fixing my customers up with fan belts and wiper blades and eight-ounce cans of Marvin's Magical Mystery Oil additive that they didn't actually need, I drew the line at putting new plug wires on with every blessed tuneup and selling full clutch jobs—and I mean disc, pressure plate, throwout bearing and flywheel resurfacing—to people who really only needed a damn cable adjustment.

"They're going to need that new clutch sooner or later," Harry argued.

And that's when I told him where he could stick it and reminded him in very plain English about my severance package just in case he felt like firing me. To tell the truth, we were less than three weeks into our new deal together, and already I was thinking about just how the hell I was going to get out of it. I talked to Julie about it, of course, and she thought I should try my best to gut it out because there was a nice payout at the end and also because I don't think she really wanted me hanging around the damn house all day. Come to think of it, I wasn't real wild about that notion, either.

Especially with her mother hanging around.

I talked to Big Ed about it when he came over for lunch the day after he got back from Florida. He looked pretty good, too. Although Big Ed didn't exactly tan, he got this nice, rosy sort of glow that generally lasted until his skin started to peel.

"So how was your trip?" I asked him after we ordered our sandwiches.

"Oh, it's hard to say which was worse," he smiled grimly, "the golfing or the deep-sea fishing."

"You didn't like it?"

"Aw, it was okay," he groused, "but it's nothing like the fun we used to have."

"You don't like golf?"

"It's more like I didn't like the golfers. Maybe there's something wrong with me, but I think it's dumb and boring. And yet you should hear some of these assholes around the bar after they've finished up 18 holes. Why, you'd think they'd climbed a fucking mountain or fought each other with swords and dueling pistols instead of just whacking little white balls around somebody's lawn."

"Maybe you just don't get it?"

"Yeah. Maybe I don't. My cousin likes it, and I told him I'd try again."

"How about the deep-sea fishing?"

"I guess that was kinda fun. It was hot and the sea was up and my cousin got seasick and spent most of the day with his head over the side."

"Sounds delightful."

"It was. But at least I got to eat his sandwich at lunchtime."

"You catch anything?"

"Hell, *yes!"* Big Ed sneered. "I got two barracudas—they're nasty-looking things!—but I guess they're no damn good to eat. And I got wahoo, too…"

"A *'wha' who two?'"*

"That's what I said: *'a wahoo, too.'* And then my cousin hooked into this big-ass blue marlin. But he got sick again and so I had to reel the damn thing in." Big Ed eyeballed me. "You know what the difference is between deep-sea fishermen and weight lifters?"

I shook my head. "No idea."

"Weight lifters don't clutter up their dens and rec rooms with stuffed barbells."

After the deep-sea fishing story, Big Ed filled me in about all the highly pissed-off Cuban refugees from the old Batista regime who were hanging around the southern tip of Florida and talking and plotting about launching an invasion to take their country back from that scraggly-beard rat-bastard Fidel Castro and his fatigue-wearing communist buddies. Big Ed heard from the captain of his charter boat that they even had some help promised from the good old U.S. government, although that was supposed to be very hush-hush so only a few hundred thousand people knew about it.

That of course got us around to East-West relations and the Cold War and how the damn Russkies had beaten us into the headlines once again by launching this human astronaut—pardon me, *"cosmonaut"*—named Yuri Gagarin into space, sending him once around the planet and then bringing him safely back home afterwards. Hell, the best our ex-Nazi German rocket scientists had managed was to shoot this chimpanzee named Ham 150 miles or so straight up and bring him right back down again. And while neither Big Ed or me could see any actual practical value in orbiting around the earth in some kind of scientifically enhanced sardine tin, no question it had great propaganda value and was yet another serious International Prestige black eye for the old U.S. of A.

We talked about Kennedy and the Freedom Riders and rednecks down south and how a bunch of the new native leaders in those new black republics in Africa that used to be European colonies were finding politics a pretty damn chancy line of work. Like Patrice Lumumba, for example, who went from being a rabble-rousing nobody when the Belgians were in charge to becoming Premier once the Congo was granted its independence in June of 1960. But he wound up locked in a pretty vicious power struggle with President Kasavubu (Big Ed allowed as how it's probably trouble anyway when you've got both a President *and* a Premier) and there was rioting and mutinies and some really vicious attacks on the remaining Europeans. Kasavubu came to New York with a bunch of his buddies to try and get himself seated as the new Congolese government at the U.N. general assembly, and meanwhile Lumumba more or less disappeared. Or at least he did until he turned up arrested by Moise Tshombe, who was president of the Katanga province where all the copper mines were that fueled the whole blessed economy. But he didn't stay arrested for very long, seeing as how he got killed "trying to escape from prison." That smelled like week-old fish to everybody, and so the U.N. ordered an investigation. But Tshombe told them basically to take a hike, and that it was, and I'm quoting from the newspaper here: "solely an internal matter." Only then the old pendulum swung back the other way and it was Tshombe getting himself arrested by his old political buddies just two months later.

"It's hard to follow unless you got a damn scorecard," Big Ed observed.

I had to agree. Although we both figured the other real loser was this guy named Mark Dinning, who had a novelty hit record climbing the charts called *Top 40, News, Weather and Sports* that was all about some high school kid doing his homework while he was listening to the radio and then getting all the facts and the songs mixed up on his test the next day. Pretty cute idea, right? Only he had this one cute, bouncy line: *"I had-a Lu-mum-buh a-doing the rhumba to the tune of the Blue Tango,"* that obviously didn't seem quite so cute and bouncy once the news got out that he'd been murdered.

"You take your chances when you hang your star on current events," was the way Big Ed saw it.

I finally got around to mentioning what was going on at the dealership, and Big Ed didn't look particularly happy when I laid it out for him. "You know, it takes a whole lifetime to make a good reputation," he almost snarled, "but it only takes some smartmouth angle-shooter five minutes to screw it up."

He obviously understood how I felt.

"Maybe you should try to get him to fire you," Big Ed offered.

"How would I do it?" I wondered out loud.

"Do you know what pisses him off?"

"Honesty."

"I mean besides that."

I couldn't really think of a thing. It's hard to get the upper hand on a guy with no character because they just flat don't give a shit.

"Well, the only advice I can give you is to find something he really hates and then do it as often as you can."

But of course that wasn't the sort of thing I could do, even if I knew how to do it.

Just like Big Ed said, those Cuban exiles launched a counter-revolutionary revolutionary invasion on Tuesday, April 25th, and the place they picked to strike at the heart of Castro's Cuba was called, appropriately enough, the Bay of Pigs. And general consensus in the old neighborhood was that it would go down as one of the most thoroughly botched, bungled, under-thought and over-reached military operations since Pickett's Charge at Gettysburg and Custer's Last Stand put together. Not only did it fail, fall apart and fizzle out miserably, but the supposedly promised "American assistance" (meaning mostly fighter planes and bombers, of course) never bothered to show up. Which left the so-called "invaders" pretty much scrambling back to the Florida and Louisiana swamps and beaches with their ears down and their collective tails between their legs. And you can bet by that time they were more pissed off at our government in Washington than Castro down in Cuba.

Speaking of pissed off, I was getting more and more that way every day about old Harry Metropolis. He'd brought in a sales manager named Salvatore *"Call me Sal"* Carpino to run the front end of the store, and he was your typical slick, smooth-talking, shined-shoes/perfectly-creased-pants/razor-cut-hairdo car sales pro like you've seen a kazillion times at American car dealerships. *"Call me Sal"* was thoughtful, caring, earnest and sincere on the outside but bitter, mean, devious and insincere where it counted, and I took an immediate dislike to him that ripened with age like fine cheese.

Worse yet was the sad-eyed con artist of an Assistant Service Manager Harry hired to work with me out back. His name was Eugene Phlemn, and he had these droopy, look-right-down-into-my-soul Basset Hound eyes that he could level at you like a pair of high-caliber sympathy cannons even while he was lying right through his blessed teeth at you. It got to where I'd go hide in the john whenever he was telling some customer with barely 20,000 miles on the clock that they needed a clutch job, wiper blades and a new fan belt.

Meanwhile, over at *Alfredo's,* Steve had located a nice, clean, solid-looking block building with decent lighting, high ceilings, radiant heat and plenty of space inside plus a fenced parking area outside that was just on the other side of the main highway and that he thought we could get a good deal on seeing as how the previous tenant went bust and took off for parts unknown owing about six months' back rent. But Big Ed was never a fan of renting anything from anybody, and after he got done with the actual negotiating, he and I were buying the place outright all fixed up with a brand-new compressor and tank, a re-tarred roof and three hydraulic lifts included in the sale price. He set it up so that our so-called "real estate investment company" leased it back to *Alfredo's,* and the plan was to start moving in as soon as all the paperwork was signed and the improvements were completed and approved.

By then that sad-looking, insincere rat-bastard Eugene Phlemn had fired Sylvester for showing up late now and then, but of course I immediately arranged to have Steve and J.R. hire him on again over at *Alfredo's* (although I did have to guarantee his salary against the cars he fixed just in case there wasn't enough work to go around). It wasn't two weeks later that Harry himself fired my friend Butch—right out of his blessed wheelchair, can you believe it—for taking a thoroughly deserved and not-even-close-to-making-contact swing at old Eugene.

And that was enough for me.

"You can shove this job right up your ass," I told Harry.

"I'm sorry you feel that way," Harry lied.

"We're both sorry you feel that way," Eugene lied some more.

"Ah, go fuck yourselves. Both of you."

So in the end I guess everybody got what they wanted. Harry got me to hold the leash on the service department while he transitioned over and put his new people in place, J.R. and Steve got a nice new shop where it was warm in the wintertime and not quite so damn unbearably hot in the summertime and I got the hell out. Sure, Julie was a little pissed about the extra income and that year-end bonus but, to tell the truth, we didn't really need it. "I'm thinking of maybe using part of J.R. and Steve's new shop for myself," I told her. "It's really a lot bigger than they need right now, and I'm thinking I could take in maybe two or three project cars at a time and just work on them myself. Do 'em the way they *should* be done."

"Is that what you really want?" Julie asked me. "To work on fricking *cars* again?"

"More than you'll ever know," I told her. And I meant it, too.

A couple weeks later I cruised by the VW dealership and saw that they'd put chainlink fences up all around the old Sinclair and a big, dusty yellow bulldozer fired up to start knocking it down. It really tore my heart open when I saw that thing churn and grind and groan its way into the side wall, and I finally couldn't take it any more and headed over to the new shop to help Steve and J.R. set up the parts shelving and run the metal compressor-line piping along the side walls. Sylvester was finishing up a Jag valve job that we had to move over from the old shop in pieces on account of the head needed a couple new valve seats installed and wasn't back from the machine shop in time and Butch was up front in the office figuring out what sort of parts inventory we ought to carry on hand and how he wanted it organized. It felt a lot like old times, you know? At the end of the day we all split a six-pack of Knickerbocker together and toasted our new shop, but it seemed awfully damn clean and organized and well-lit and warm and quiet and not one little bit like home.

I left the new shop around 9 and drove past the corner where the old Sinclair had been standing as recently as that morning. It was nothing but a big, empty foundation hole, a couple recognizable scraps of the old peaked tarpaper roof and several low mounds of old, yellowed bricks. I stopped and got out—I don't really know why—and I had this sudden impulse to go in and save just one brick to use as a paperweight or a door stop or something. Or even to not use it for anything, but just to have around as a souvenir. You know how that sentimental shit is. But the demolition fencing went all the way around and the gate was padlocked so I couldn't get in. And that's where I was, just kind of standing there with my fingers curled through the fence wire, when I heard somebody coming up behind me.

"Oh, it's you," Eugene Phlemn's so-sad-and-earnest-it-made-you-want-to-puke voice said from behind me. "I was just locking up and thought you might have been a vandal or a burglar or something."

"Have you got the key to this gate?" I asked him.

"I think I do."

"D'ya think you could open it up so I could grab one of those bricks?"

"Oh, I don't think I could do that," he said. "Those bricks belong to Mr. Metropolis. They're his property."

"We're only talking about one fucking brick here," I argued.

"I'm pretty sure he's sold them all to the demolition company. Every one of them. It wouldn't be right."

Well, of course all he wanted was for me to slip him some cash. But I wasn't about to do that. It'd spoil the meaning of the whole thing, you know? Besides, what the old Sinclair meant to me wasn't in the damn bricks, and I knew it. And that's when I noticed the cheesy little cardboard sign Old Man Finzio used to have tacked up behind the cash register sticking out of a pile of rubble. The one that said: *"CREDIT MAKES ENEMIES—LET'S BE FRIENDS."* It made me smile just a little.

After that I said goodbye to that asshole Eugene Phlemn, got in my Karmann-Ghia and drove all the way to the Turnpike and back just to give him time to leave. Then I got out, climbed right over the top of that fence and grabbed that sign out of the rubbish. Took one of the bricks, too. I cut my hand so it damn near needed stitches and tore the shit out of my left knee doing it, but I didn't really care....

Chapter 41: Spiders and Sharks

It always feels weird when you move anyplace new. You leave someplace where you know where everything is because that's where you've always left it and arrive at someplace where you have to figure out where the heck you're going to put it, and it just doesn't feel right even if you know it's much bigger and better and everybody and his brother is patting you on the back and congratulating you and maybe even looking a little envious about it. And that's the way it was with the new shop. First off, it was absolutely huge (or at least that's the way it looked when it was empty, anyway) at something just over 10,000 square feet, and our deal was that I got three generous, well-lit stalls in the back corner across from our brand-new air compressor, where I had my own metal workbench and plenty of elbow room for me and space for all my tools plus a set of metal shelves for the parts and pieces of whatever projects I might have in progress. Me and Big Ed made absolutely sure we had everything you might want or need in that shop: gas welder, arc welder, grinder, hydraulic press, distributor machine, brand-new floor jacks, three lifts, big iron bench vises, one of those fancy Sun electrical testers I really didn't know how to use, a perfectly flat concrete pad for alignments in the other back corner—you name it. Fact is, it was the first really well-organized, well-set-up personal work area I'd ever had in my life. And when it was done, I remember just sitting there in the middle of it on top of Butch's beat-up old toolbox, looking at those three nice, clean, empty, well-organized work stalls and wondering just where the hell I was going to find the kind of cars I really wanted to work on to fill them up? I knew only too well how easy it is to clog up shop space with dust-collecting, non-income generating long-term projects that just never seem to get finished. Or sad orphan racecars that just need a place to rest and recuperate between ugly race weekend blowups and breakdowns. Or wonderful but totally hopeless vehicles belonging to what turn out to be pretty much absentee owners:

"Say, I've got this old Rolls-Royce [or Bentley or Bugatti or Cadillac or Packard or Ferrari 212 or Mercedes 540 or pre-war Maserati Grand Prix car] *here, and if I have it towed over, d'ya think you could work me out an estimate on it?"*

"What do you want done to it?"

"I dunno. Whatever it needs."

I warn you: do not be deceived by what appears to be an open wound of financial opportunity. Do not say:

"Sure. Why the heck not? When are you bringing it over?"

Because the answer is more than likely going to be:

"The towtruck's here right now. I gotta get it out of here today because they're tearing the building down tomorrow to build a shopping mall…."

That's when the alarm bells should start going off like a blessed crash dive on a submarine. Even though the mere mention of those kind of cars gets your ears perked up and your blood rate hiked. Which is why a seasoned, certified and experienced master car mechanic needs to learn how to pull back on the reins a bit and calmly reply: *"Say, why don't I come look at it over by you? I'll charge you the regular hourly rate for however long it takes to talk over what you want done and how much it's liable to cost, and if I wind up working on it for you, the consultation's on the house. Fair enough?"*

But of course no wrench twister who really loves cars is ever quite that smart. And that's precisely how I wound up with this stately, sad, arthritic and badly listing old mummy of a Duesenberg Model J Murphy-bodied roadster sitting right square in the middle of my brand-new floor space less than a week later. It belonged to some business associate/junk trader buddy of Big Ed's from his old scrap machinery business—one of those guys who called himself a "collector" but really just bought old dead cars, stuck them in a barn or commercial garage or the dark, damp basement of an industrial building someplace and never quite got around to fixing them up—and I guess Big Ed had seen this thing once or twice and decided to recommend me as an "honest, experienced expert" who could restore it for him. Totally. And at a really good price, too….

"Thanks a lot, Ed," I told him as we stood there staring at it. Sure, you could see as how it'd been a really noble and magnificent car in its day. Only now there were rats' nests and blocks of D-Con where the upholstery used to be, the instruments and a lot of the interior hardware were scattered all over the trunk in bits and pieces, one fender was badly dinged and the door on that side was hanging off its hinges, the convertible top was in tatters and caved in on one side where something obviously fell on it, the steering wheel was gone so you had to steer it with a pair of vise-grips, the carburetor and one headlight were missing, the engine didn't hardly turn and the entire mess was covered with a layer of dust the same color, texture and thickness as mouse fur. We watched it drool the first-ever little pool of greasy-black oil onto the nice, shiny gray cement paint on my floor. "Thanks a lot," I repeated.

"Hey," he said, putting an arm around my shoulder. "Just look at this car. It *needs* you, Buddy."

"What it needs is a decent burial," I muttered, sounding an awful lot like the ghost of Old Man Finzio.

"Listen, Buddy," Big Ed argued, "it'll take a mechanical genius like you to resurrect a disaster like this. Who else could do it?" He stared at that tall, proud, dust-covered and badly discolored front grille with a couple of its slats missing. "A car like this really *deserves* it, Buddy," he added gently. "And I got you front money, too…."

I looked at it again, but it was like I couldn't get my eyes to focus.

"Jesus, Ed, I don't know where to begin!"

Big Ed patted me on the shoulder. "You'll figure it out," he told me. "You'll see. You'll figure it out."

I wasn't convinced at all. But that hadn't stopped Big Ed from doing one hell of a sales job on the guy who owned that Duesenberg, and he was more than willing to give me a thousand-dollar deposit to get started on it—you heard me right, *a thousand bucks!*—and that marked the beginning of what turned out to be the longest, most drawn-out, most agonizing, most fascinating, most frustrating, most occasionally (*very* occasionally!) rewarding but generally up-blind-alleys and down-the-garden-path discouraging car adventures I'd ever been on in my life. Believe me, raising children is only slightly more difficult than restoring great old automobiles. And at least you have a wife to help with the kids. But you meet some really neat, quirky, sometimes wonderful and sometimes downright unnerving characters lurking in the backwaters of the car restoration business along the way. And the research and parts-finding is kind of interesting, too. In fact, sometimes it's a little *too* interesting, seeing as how you can easily get side-tracked into more fascinating shit that you really don't have the time to fool around with than you can imagine....

Like did you know that back in their heyday during the 1920s and early 1930s, Duesenbergs were considered the best damn automobiles in the world? About the most expensive, too. But that's because they had stuff like twin-overhead-cam, four-valve-per-cylinder engines when most car manufacturers were still fooling around with flatheads. And did you know that Clark Gable, Gary Cooper and Marlene Dietrich all owned Duesenbergs? Or that Duesenbergs were the first cars ever with hydraulic brakes? Which, by the way, gave them one heck of an advantage when a team of Duesenbergs went overseas in 1921 and beat the hell out of all the Europeans in the French Grand Prix at Le Mans. That was the biggest damn race in all of Europe at the time, and a lot of the snooty French locals felt it was way beneath their dignity to get waxed by a bunch of American yahoos. Especially considering that American oval-track ace Jimmy Murphy rolled his car over during practice and had to crawl out of a damn hospital bed to take the start and then went on—internal injuries, taped-up ribs and all—to win the blessed race! Why, it got the organizers so upset that they made their first champagne toast at the victory banquet to the French car and driver that came home third instead of to Murphy and the winning Duesenberg! And that's when most of the American team just stood up and walked out. Now I don't know what you're exactly supposed to *do* with information like that, but it sure seems important as hell when you stumble over it while flipping through a bunch of pages looking for something else.

I also learned that taking fat deposits on restorations can turn out to be the worst deal you ever made in your life once you get a handle on how much time and effort is actually involved in bringing old, dead cars back to life. Oh, and never do a job like that for a friend (or even a friend of a friend) because it makes you feel guilty as hell about asking for more money when the damn thing is still in a million pieces and a million miles from done and maybe even looks a lot less like a car than when it originally came in on the end of a tow hook. But that's exactly what you've got to do once you add everything up and discover that—not even counting parts and sublet work—your actual return on time invested has dropped below the Federal minimum wage.

Much to my surprise, Sylvester turned out to be an enormous help with that car. But that's because he worked almost exclusively on worn-out, hopeless-case projects at the late-night, back-alley garage he had going up in Harlem. "Shit, man, you lucky," he told me. "Your customers kin at least *pay* to have shit done."

By that time Sylvester was only coming in two or three days a week—afternoons and early evenings mostly, plus occasional Saturday afternoons—and he'd go right over to whatever project he was on at the time and work relentlessly and disgustedly and angrily and methodically like he always did until he decided it was time for him to go. And then he'd just up and vanish until the next time you saw him. But his work was good and thorough and he knew what the hell he was doing, and Steve and J.R. and me all figured we really could have used him a lot more. But, like I said, Sylvester had beat-up old cars lined up to be fixed outside his ramshackle garage back in Harlem, and I guess he figured that was something he really needed to do. Even if it took him an awful long time to get paid now and then. And not always in cash, if you know what I mean. But of course he never talked about it that way. Instead he'd say: *"Why th'fuck Ah wants t'wuk for you pale, tired white boys anyway when I gots all the car work Ah kin handle at m'own fuckin' shop?"* Then he'd give me that cold, crooked, sneering smile of his with a bent-up Lucky sticking out of one side and add: *"—Ah only does it outta pity."*

Memorial Day was a really big deal for American sportycar types seeing as how Kleenex heir/diehard enthusiast "Gentleman Jim" Kimberly paid to have reigning World Champion Jack Brabham and a modified "Indianapolis" Cooper come over and run the Indy 500. It was still way shy on horsepower (some said by as much as 150!) compared to the 80-cubic-inch-bigger, alcohol-burning Meyer-Drake Offys in the traditional Indianapolis roadsters, but it was light and handy and no question Black Jack Brabham was there to collect some finishing money and do the best he could rather than dazzling everybody. But he dazzled them anyway in a quiet, methodical kind of way. He qualified 13th and ran smoothly, steadily and intelligently to a ninth-place finish while Eddie Sachs pitted three laps from the end and handed the overall win to some new oval-track phenom out of Texas named A.J. Foyt. Sammy Speed said we'd be hearing a lot about that guy before too long, and Sammy wasn't the kind of guy to toot his horn about other drivers unless he figured they were really something special. "He looks like he's got a little bit of a temper, though," Sammy allowed, "so I don't think you want to get on his bad side." Needless to say, all of us sportycar types were pretty damn thrilled about the way Brabham and that little underdog Cooper-Climax had run at Indy, and no doubt a lot of heads were being scratched and chins were being rubbed in oval-track shops and garages all over the country because of it.

I was also pretty damn thrilled two weekends later when my sister Mary Frances and that Pauly Martino saxophone player finally got married, and I was really happy for both of them. I figured it was kind of a nice fit, and Julie even agreed, which made it even better. We had a swell time at the wedding, too, even though most of the rest of the family spent the whole time rolling their eyeballs and talking behind their hands about what a horror it was that they were already living together and what a crime and a shame and a sin it was that they didn't try to hide it a little better from the neighbors. But Pauly got some of his musician friends to drop by and they made up—by far—the best damn wedding band you ever heard in your life. At least if you like cool jazz and hot trumpet solos, anyway. Although you had to be a little careful about waltzing into the men's room when the band was on break on account of it smelled like somebody was burning a dead horse's tail and you could come out feeling very light-headed and agreeable indeed. Not to mention hungry. Which is, I believe, how I wound up devouring an entire layer of the wedding cake all by my lonesome and then went looking around for any leftover relish trays from before dinner. Especially those little candied gherkins.

Anyhow, by that time our once-empty and supposedly enormous new shop was filled wall-to-wall with customer work, long-term projects and slumbering racecars, and I didn't have to worry one bit about what the hell I was going to do with myself every day. Not hardly. Although it was a little tough getting back into the swing of actually working on stuff with my own two hands again. My wrists and fingers and forearms ached for two weeks straight, I found cricks in my shoulders and back I never knew I had before, and I also came to realize all over again—in bright blood-red and iridescent, purplish-black Technicolor—how blessed easy it is to bang your head or burn the back of your hand or hit your thumb with a hammer or run your knuckles full tilt into a jagged radiator core when you're working on cars for a living. I also discovered that those quiet little pinnacle moments of appreciation I enjoyed so much don't come around very often at all on a long-term restoration project.

But I made up for that a little by working here and there on other jobs around the shop, and our original idea that I'd just have my own, separate stalls and work pretty much solo while leaving the day-to-day *Alfredo's* business to Steve and J.R. didn't even last two weeks. It's not like we had any formal meeting of the minds about it or anything, but it's just the way things worked out, and I found myself pitching in whenever and wherever stuff needed to get done—especially during the run-up to a race weekend—and Steve and J.R. would help me out, too, whenever I happened to need it. Plus everybody, including a lot of our customers and Butch in the parts department and Sylvester when he came in and even Steve and J.R. themselves, seemed to look to me when it came to figuring out what had to be done or how it needed to be done or what needed to be done next. Force of habit, I guess. And it felt pretty good, if you want the truth of it. No question every shop needs some kind of skipper to guide it along, and we needed one more than most seeing as how we were up to our eyeballs with work. We had Buster Jones' brand-new E-Type getting a roll bar and some competition seat belts and brake pads put in, a top-end job and new gearbox synchros on an AC-Bristol, an old four-cylinder Ferrari Monza waiting on a few rear end pieces from Italy and a check from its owner, my torn-down-into-a-kazillion-pieces Duesenberg Model J restoration, a Morgan with a banged-up front end and an Elva that needed a clutch, a Fiat-Abarth with the back deck lid propped up and no compression on the two middle cylinders, a Lotus Eleven with a couple cracks in its frame plus a Lotus 7 kit we were trying to turn into a whole car (well, most of a whole car, anyway) for some guy who took one look and decided there was no way he could do it himself, a once-raced Stanguellini Formula Junior that was essentially just resting seeing as how the new, rear-engined Cooper and Lotus Juniors had rendered it pretty much obsolete barely two months and two races after our customer took delivery (at least he was good about paying storage!) plus more damn MGs, Jags, Sprites, Alpines, Big Healeys and TR3s than you could shake a torque wrench at.

Business was *good.*

Plus I had a few dreams circling around in my head that we could maybe get a Lotus and an Elva and maybe even an Alfa Romeo franchise for ourselves one day. Oh, I didn't delude myself that we'd ever make a lot of money on new car sales, but I loved those cars and figured they sure couldn't hurt the work coming in on the service end. Not hardly! But I wasn't in any great hurry to have all the complications and responsibilities of a full-blown car dealership fall in my lap again on account of I was getting a pretty bad case of the old racing itch. We had John Targett's MG and Dave Burton's Porsche and my brother-in-law Carson Flegley's new triple-carb Healey 3000 in pretty regularly, and naturally I went up to the races with those guys now and then and so I was really starting to feel the tug. Carson wasn't racing all that much any more—my sister Sarah Jean didn't much like it because she thought it made him feel a little too dashing and independent, even if he was just trundling around at the back, waving people by—but I was catching a little bit of the heat and the glow off all three of them. And I was pretty much enjoying the race weekends again, too. That's what happens when you're no longer trying to take care of a four-man job with just one pair of hands and one pair of feet. But all of a sudden just hanging around and enjoying it from the sidelines wasn't enough. Hell, I'd worked hard and had a little money in the bank, and I had this feeling like I *deserved* it. Like I owed it to myself, you know? Although, if I'm really honest, most of it boiled down to this hunger and curiosity and longtime, slumbering yearning I'd always had about what racing actually felt like from the *inside.* Not that I was ever going to be a hero-driver type like Cal or Toly or Tommy Edwards or Sammy Speed or even Creighton Pendleton the Third. But I'd watched the guys at those little local club races at Lime Rock and Thompson and Marlboro and the way I had it figured, at least half of them were maybe even worse than me. Maybe even a little bit more than half. But of course that's just a bunch of daydreaming and cocktail-hour bullshit until you go out and prove it. To yourself as much as anybody else….

Naturally I mentioned it to Julie a couple times and, as you can imagine, she chose to not take me very seriously. That wasn't near as taxing or messy as snapping her back up straight as a ramrod, folding her arms across her chest, glaring at me with those death-ray eyes and asking me just what the hell I thought I was thinking. Or telling me flat-out there was no way in hell she would allow it. Or that the only way I could ever do it would be over her dead body. Or my dead body, more likely. And that would of course be followed by the Lyrical Chorus Response part where Julie handled all the low, teeth-grinding bass growls while her mom added in all the high, hard, owl-screechy notes and the kids screamed at each other in the background as backup. Or at least that's what I thought would happen, anyway. But there was no reason to push anything with Julie (or even talk seriously about it) until I figured out what kind of car I wanted to drive. Not to mention how the hell I was going to get my hands on one.

But of course that was logic talking and, as anyone with any background in motorsports whatsoever can tell you, logic has little if anything to do with the purchase of a first racecar. Not that you know it at the time. Nope, no matter how much you know (or think you know) or how many times you've been around the block or even how many *"Jeez, all it needs is..."* racing horror stories you've personally been involved in, I'm thoroughly convinced that the selection of a first racecar is primarily controlled by fate, happenstance and heartstrings. In other words, it's an emotional rather than a logical decision. Or maybe it's not really a decision at all...unless it's the *car* that's doing the deciding, that is.

Oh, you start out rational enough. Fact is, I've seen racers poring over magazine road test data panels and scribbling out comparative spec sheets on engine displacement and quoted *(hah!)* horsepower and torque figures, tire sizes and curb weights, frontal area and aerodynamic profiles, wheelbases and track widths, carefully thinking and considering and evaluating until they come to the inescapable conclusion that the new *Fuggi-Manouli Bastardo Berlinetta GT 1000 Allemano* will absolutely blow the doors off any damn Brighton-Crudley Elf in creation. And it should. At least according to the spec sheets, anyway. Only those spec sheets don't take into account that the horsepower figures quoted for the *Bastardo Berlinetta GT* were actually copied off the right-hand column of the carry-out menu at some deli in Bologna seeing as how Fuggi-Manouli's brand-new dynomometer hadn't quite been paid for or delivered yet. Not to mention that the *Bastardo Berlinetta* was priced at something like twice what a Brighton-Crudley Elf would cost, you couldn't get any speed parts (or even regular parts sometimes, come to that) for them and both the North American distributor and the parent company back in Italy worked out of dingy four-stall garages and were teetering on the brink of bankruptcy. Besides, nobody in their right mind buys a brand-new car and turns it into a damn racecar. That's only for rich idiots and genuine sponsored racers with genuine factory connections.

Truth is, I was really just at the jawing-around stage. And according to pretty much everybody, the most obvious and ideal First Racecar on the planet was the cute, cheap and cheeky little Austin-Healey Sprite. But I'd noticed that there were already an awful lot of them around and it was becoming crystal-clear that there were Sprites and then there were *SPRITES,* if you know what I mean. Plus it was competitive as hell at the front with an awful lot of questionably legal speed parts and top-secret tuning tricks hidden behind those grinning Healey Sprite grilles (and more coming every race weekend!) and I could see as how you could easily wind up spending Jaguar or Corvette or even Ferrari money trying to build yourself the best damn racing Sprite in the world. Or even in the greater metropolitan New York area.

Then there was Formula Junior. That was supposed to be the "nursery class" for wannabe race drivers, and no question I could get myself one hell of a hell of a deal on that handsome, hardly-used and by now thoroughly obsolete Stanguellini we had sitting right there on our shop floor. And you can bet I climbed in and out of it a few times late at night after everybody else had gone home when I was supposed to be fooling around with that blessed Duesenberg. I could squint my eyes and grab the wheel in both hands and make motor sounds with my mouth and pretend I was up on the bankings at Monza or, better yet, whipping through the streets of Monaco with Juan Manuel Fangio in one mirror and Stirling Moss in the other. Only I must admit I was a little iffy about racing an open-wheeled car. It sure looked naked and unprotected out there by the tires, and I couldn't help thinking about how many professional drivers had graduated themselves directly from open-wheel single-seaters into ambulances or hearses. No question I'd have a much tougher time trying to talk Julie into something like that. Not to mention that a front-engined Stanguellini was already a mid-pack backmarker at best and sinking fast. But there was an awful lot of magic in the view through its wraparound plexiglass windscreen from behind its riveted wood-rim wheel, and I did love that it was Italian…

And that's when the Alfa came out of nowhere. You have to understand that you don't really pick your first racecar—it picks *you.* And this Alfa must've seen me coming from a long way off. It was a pretty little powder-blue '57 *Giulietta Spider* convertible that some retired old widower stockbroker up near Tuckahoe bought, drove for a while and most likely fell in love with like people usually do with Alfa Romeos. Only then he got cancer and it sat in his garage for a few years while he went from sick to sicker to dead, and by then the car had kind of gotten sick right along with him out of sympathy like sportycars—and most especially Italian sportycars—often do. Particularly when there's nobody around to drive them or pay attention to them or pat them on the dashboard after a really good late-afternoon run through the countryside.

Anyhow, it turns out the guy had two sons, and one was a shyster criminal lawyer with a lot of shady friends in Manhattan while the other was a head doctor in Boston who'd made himself a few unwanted headlines by supposedly messing around with other parts of some of his better-endowed female patients besides their heads. Although he never got tried or convicted or anything seeing as how none of the women really wanted to come forward and testify. But the point is that neither of them gave two shits about that car. Or the old family house up in Tuckahoe, which by the way was sitting on a particularly prime piece of corner real estate and was pretty much a shambles thanks to an older guy living there all by his lonesome for several years with just his memories and old furniture and crap memorabilia for company. Both kids agreed there was some really wonderful, valuable, heartwarming family stuff up there that neither one of them really cared about or knew what to do with, and as you can imagine they were both busy as hell with their own lives and families and practices and poker nights and near-divorces. So it just seemed ever so much simpler for the shady Manhattan shyster lawyer to put in a call to a friend of his who was supposedly handy with a matchbook and a five-gallon can of gasoline and settle things that way.

Well, the poor car was sitting in the attached garage when the house went up one early Thursday morning like a boy scout campfire, but the wind was blowing the other way and about all the Alfa got was a few singes and a bunch of smoke damage that turned it the general color of a dirty street pigeon. Plus a squashed top, a crushed windshield, some flattened-out spots on the front fenders where the roof caved in on it and a bunch of fire-hose water in the interior. Naturally the police were more than a little curious as to why this particular unlived-in house with the gas and power shut off decided to erupt in the middle of the night like a damn homecoming bonfire, and meanwhile the poor Alfa wound up pretty much belonging to the insurance company and sitting behind a nearby gas station without even a tarp over it while they tried to figure out what the hell to do with the damn thing. And that's where Steve saw it one day when he was out chasing a few Duesenberg parts for me up near White Plains.

"It'd make a hell of a nice first racecar," he told me between bites of his turkey-and-Swiss sandwich the next day at lunchtime.

"You think?"

"Well, it's not a *Veloce,"* he allowed as he eyeballed his pickle spear, "which means it's just got the single carburetor, the regular compression ratio and the wimpy cams. But you can put all that *Veloce* stuff on afterwards if you want to. No sweat."

You have to understand here that Alfa had been making two distinct versions of its 1300cc *Giulietta Sprint* coupes and *Giulietta Spider* convertibles since almost the very beginning: the ordinary, everyday, rank-and-file single-carb version and the much rarer, quicker and more expensive *Giulietta Sprint Veloce* and *Giulietta Spider Veloce* with a higher compression ratio, twin side-draft/two-barrel Weber carburetors and intake- and exhaust-cam profiles that reminded you of what you might find on either side of Sophia Loren's cleavage. But, like Steve said, you could upgrade any *Giulietta* to *Veloce* specs if you had the cash to buy the parts. That is if you could find them.

"But you think it would make a good racecar?" I asked him again.

"Hey," Steve shrugged, "what I think doesn't mean shit. But I think you might want to take a look at it."

"That might be hard to do. We got a lot of work in right now and I'm pretty busy…."

"No problem," he told me. "I don't think it's going anywhere."

And that's how I wound up standing behind that gas station up near Tuckahoe on a dreary, drizzly, rainy Saturday afternoon, looking at that poor little beat-up, betrayed and abandoned Alfa Spider and wondering why on earth I wanted it so much. But of course the answer was obvious. It *needed* me!

Naturally it was tough keeping up with what was going on with Cal and Toly and the European racing scene without Hank over there covering it and sending me letters or giving me a phone call now and then to keep me up to date. You couldn't count on the stateside papers at all—not even the *Times*—so I sent in five bucks for a subscription to Denise McCluggage's new *Competition Press* and even re-subscribed to *Autosport* to keep up on things. But it just wasn't the same. I was on the outside now with all the other rubes and fence-hangers, and it felt almost like some really close friend had died. Not to mention that Eric Gibbon's columns and race reports were always ever-so-slightly skewed in favor of the British cars, teams and drivers (can you imagine?) and more than a little sour-grapes bitter about the way Ferrari had caught them all with their pants down when the new-for-1961, 1500cc FIA Formula One cars finally hit the racetracks.

The season opened at Monaco in the middle of May that year (although we didn't see the full race reports in this country until the September issues of the magazines, which for some reason came out about the middle of August) and Ferrari showed up with a trio of tough, tested, torpedo-shaped cars with sinister-looking split-nostril front ends and an almost obscenely powerful—for 1500cc, anyway—V-6 that had maybe 20 or more horsepower in hand over the Coventry Climax four-bangers being used by the British teams. The scribes immediately dubbed them the "shark-nose" Ferraris, and as you can imagine, the name stuck instantly. Everybody figured they had the other teams covered, and Eric Gibbon's commentary made it sound an awful lot like the blessed Battle of Britain, what with the small, brave, resourceful and patriotic English teams up against a cruel, unfair and far more powerful foreign enemy. And I guess there was some truth in that. Mind you, I'd always had a lot of respect and admiration for all the British teams and drivers—in spite of Eric's whimpering—and they really *did* have a lot of that *carry on,* "Battle of Britain" spirit. You could always count on their sense of duty, dignity, purpose, patriotism, honor, order, loyalty, resourcefulness and fair play to produce some truly heroic efforts against even the most overwhelming odds. And no question they were still ahead of everybody when it came to the art and science of making cars handle. But still you couldn't help thinking that if they'd gotten off their damn English duffs and started working on new engines when the 1500cc formula was first announced (like Ferrari did) instead of just moaning and arguing and grousing about it, they wouldn't have been in that kind of fix to begin with.

Porsche was taking a somewhat different approach. They were fielding their first-ever, full-blown Grand Prix team for the new formula, but the cars were really just open-wheel, single-seater developments of their existing RSK, RS60 and RS61 sports/racers. Everybody thought they looked kind of tall, blunt and stubby compared to the British cars and the Ferraris, but they figured to be rugged, proven and reliable (if a bit out of date) and Porsche thought that might count for a lot in a year when everybody else was fooling around with something new. Not to mention that they had BRM refugees Dan Gurney and Jo Bonnier signed on as drivers, and no question those guys were both genuine aces.

Still, Ferrari was the team to beat, and I'm sure the other teams felt like definite underdogs when those dangerous-looking, shark-nosed Ferraris rolled out of the transporter and lined up in the pit lane at Monaco for the very first time. They'd already run one of them in a non-championship race at Syracuse in April with emerging young Italian hotshoe Giancarlo Baghetti at the controls, and he simply blew the rest of the field away. Sure it wasn't a Grand Prix, but it wasn't much of a contest, either. And Ferrari wasn't about to stop there. They'd set Cal up with a new, experimental, wide-angle/120-degree V6 engine, which was supposedly lighter and more powerful than the old, narrow-angle V6s in the other two cars, plus it got the weight down a little lower and further forward in the chassis to make the car handle better. It was just one more sign of how far ahead Ferrari was, testing a new, second-generation engine at the first damn race of the season! And Cal was making the most of it, too. Or at least he did once he started getting a handle on the place after Toly took him for a long walk around the circuit on Thursday afternoon. Cal allowed as how Monaco was really tough to learn on account of it was so blind and busy and hemmed in and claustrophobic and overflowing with all sorts of distractions. Both on and off the track, seeing as how there were parties and receptions and unbelievable yachts parked out in the harbor with unbelievable beauties sunbathing on the decks. And then Gina arrived, too. She'd been shooting a Hitchcock espionage picture in London and kind of casually dropped in for the weekend as a surprise. Not that she had to sneak away or anything, seeing as how her agent and the producer and all of Brad Lackey's studio publicity hacks knew the value of getting her face plastered all over the tabloids in the company of famous, handsome and dashing professional racing drivers. And two was even better than one, you know? Eric Gibbon somehow got his hands on this really great shot of all three of them—Cal, Gina and Toly—having coffee under an umbrella at this lovely little oceanfront café, and naturally it made a lot of the supermarket tabloids and almost all of the movie gossip magazines. Only some of them showed it cropped so it was just Cal and Gina while others showed just Gina and Toly and still others ran both versions side-by-side with the not-so-subtle implication that there was an awful lot of swap-around, Hollywood-style hanky panky going on. All thanks to our old friend Eric Gibbon, of course.

As you can imagine, I was pulling like hell for Cal (and, okay, Toly too) and I just about jumped out of my skin when I read that he'd qualified that Ferrari with the new, experimental engine in the middle of the front row! In his first-ever Grand Prix and his first-ever race at Monaco—can you believe it? It was a hell of a run! But on the tight, twisty streets of Monaco with no long straightaways where the Ferraris could flex their horsepower, Stirling Moss had once again done the incredible and put his old, four-banger Rob Walker Lotus on pole. And on Cal's other side was comingman Jim Clark in Colin Chapman's latest Grand Prix design: the unbelievably sleek, graceful and delicate-looking little Lotus 21. Graham Hill had done a heck of a job to qualify his temporarily Climax-powered BRM in fourth spot on the grid—he seemed to do particularly well at Monaco—while Phil Hill and Toly were stuck back in fifth and sixth. That made things just a wee bit awkward around the Ferrari pits, and Gina allowed as how Cal had a tough time being gracious about it with his teammates. But then, you had to wonder how hard he really tried….

According to Eric Gibbon's race report, Cal used the Ferrari's power to out-drag Moss and Clark at the start, but no question the Lotus chassis still had the edge under braking and going around corners. Plus the Ferrari's power was all up at the top end, so although it would absolutely shriek through the gears heading up the hill towards Casino Square or along the harbor front straightaway, it would fluff up, stutter and stumble coming out of the tight hairpins, while the torquey Climax four-banger in Moss' car pulled cleanly. So although Cal managed to edge away a little over the first two laps, it wasn't long before Stirling gobbled it back up through the twisty stuff and was sitting right on his gearbox. And you have to realize this was all a new experience for Cal, leading his very first Grand Prix—at Monaco, no less!—with a guy like Stirling Moss sitting right in his mirrors. Had to be a wee bit more unnerving than racing his ratty old MG TC at Bridgehampton, don't you think? Plus it was early and the cars were heavy with fuel, and after 14 pretty amazing laps with nothing but empty track ahead of him, Cal finally went just that little bit too hard and too deep into one of the corners. The front end started to push wide and he had no choice but to lift off for a heartbeat to keep from clipping the damn curbing on the outside….

That's all Moss needed. He was through in a flash and instantly began pulling away. But not by yards and car-lengths. More like inches and feet. Cal said it was frustrating as hell seeing Moss ease slowly away from him—especially when he was trying as hard as he could and saw the distance shrinking a little down the few, short straightaways thanks to the Ferrari's superior power. No question it was driving him nuts, and so he started trying even harder. But that was a mistake. It just made him lose his flow and rhythm and pretty soon the other two Ferraris were right behind him. Phil Hill sneaked by under braking and then Toly got him, too, and no question Cal was feeling pretty damn demoralized about then. But it's always easier to chase than to lead, and once he was at the back end of that three-car Ferrari freight train, things started falling into place again. Cal found he could stay with the other two cars pretty easily—not pushing at all—and he began to relax and regroup and get back into the rhythm of the race. There was still a long, long way to go.

A few laps later it was Toly's turn to have problems. The little welded-on, curved metal toe pad on the throttle pedal snapped off—the one that allowed a driver to angle his foot for heel-and-toe downshifts while braking—and all of a sudden he had a choice of brake or gas but never both together. That left Toly fishing uncoordinatedly for gears in the middle of corners and squirreling around up on tiptoes braking into them, and Cal passed him easily. Toly faded quickly in Cal's mirrors and now Phil was just ahead, driving neatly and expertly but still losing ground in maddening tenths, quarter- and half-seconds to Moss in the Lotus. It stayed that way for many laps, and Phil finally and sportingly pulled aside on the run along the harbor front and waved Cal past to see if he could do anything about Moss and the Lotus. It was a hell of a noble gesture and the mark of a driver who truly believed in his duty to the team, and Cal resolved he'd do his very best with the opportunity. And this time it was all coming to him the right way—all smooth, all flowing, all happening in some kind of dreamy, unhurried slow motion. With the cars now down to fighting weight and just 22 laps to go, the Ferrari pits hung out the *"GO!"* sign. Cal responded with a new lap record and cut into Moss' lead. But then Moss fought back, going two-tenths faster yet. I guess the crowd was going absolutely bananas as the two of them flew around the racetrack, the gap stretching out and shrinking from lap to lap and even corner to corner like the cars were connected with an elastic band. And now the Lotus was starting to puff out little clouds of smoke with every shift!

But there was to be no miracle finish. Moss was still in front by a scant 3.6 seconds when the checker fluttered down at the end of 100 laps and two-and-three-quarters hours. And from the photographs, you could see both of them looked damn near used up afterwards. Sure, it was disappointing for Cal. But he'd still done one hell of a job. And finished ahead of both of his Ferrari teammates, too. Better yet, the shark-nose red cars had come home second, third and fourth in their race debut on the only track on the entire Grand Prix calendar that didn't figure to suit them. Although it had to be somewhat discouraging getting beat by some English guy who put his pants on one leg at a time like anybody else driving what was basically last year's chassis and with a far less powerful engine nestled behind his backside.

Things were different a week later at the Dutch Grand Prix, where the shark-nose Ferraris finally had a little room to show off their muscle. All three of the cars now had the wide-angle "experimental" engines Cal had tried at Monaco, and Phil, Toly and Cal filled the front row with Phil and Toly tied exactly at 1:35.7 and Cal just a faint tick behind at 1:35.9. Moss was the best of the rest at 1:36.2 with all the other top Coventry Climax runners right behind him, and I guess there was some kind of problem getting the race off when Phil's Ferrari had trouble with its clutch hydraulics. The organizers more or less held up the start until the mechanics could get it fixed, and needless to say, that didn't go down especially well with some of the other team managers. There was apparently a lot of arguing and grousing and protesting and screaming in Modenese Italian going on before the cars finally got away.

Poor Cal's engine went all soft and spluttery on the very first lap with some kind of phantom ignition problem and he started dropping back, which gave third place to Graham Hill's BRM. Jim Clark in the slippery new Lotus came absolutely rocketing through the pack from his 10th qualifying spot, passed Cal and then Graham Hill and locked onto the back of the two Ferraris. He was the only car or driver with any hope of keeping the Ferraris in sight, and Eric Gibbon's race report was over the moon about the way Clark drove and the incredible handling of the new Lotus. But it still wasn't enough to match the horsepower advantage of the Ferraris. Toly got the jump at the start, Phil fell in step behind him—Tavoni had brokered a kind of gentlemen's agreement that they wouldn't race the shit out of each other when they already had the rest of the field covered—and that was pretty much the race.

It wasn't even close.

Spa in the middle of June was more of the same. Only this time the positions got swapped around with Phil winning, Toly less than a second behind and Cal 19 seconds further back in his first-ever race at Spa. Ferrari even added a fourth car for experienced Belgian favorite Olivier Gendebien, and he brought it home fourth in a crushing show of supremacy for the red cars. And the point got driven home even more emphatically at the French Grand Prix at Reims. The team again brought a fourth car for 26-year-old Italian hopeful Giancarlo Baghetti, who came from a wealthy, well-connected Milanese industrial family and had already won two minor, non-championship Formula One races in Naples and Syracuse—against fairly meager opposition—in a "borrowed" factory shark-nose. For a change Phil and Cal and Toly all ran into engine problems, and Baghetti came through to win by a few inches (and about twenty horsepower!) over Gurney's Porsche after the other three Ferraris all dropped out while leading. It was a pretty bitter pill for Cal, since he'd led fair-and-square from the start and thought he was on his way to his first Grand Prix victory when his engine lost power and the oil pressure faded away. The same thing happened to Phil and Toly a few laps later, and imagine how Baghetti felt! Why, he'd entered and won his very first Grand Prix! Nobody else had ever done that! Although a closer look showed that he'd qualified no better than 12th while his teammates took the top three spots on the grid and he was battling with a bunch of lesser cars for fourth—far behind the other Ferraris—when they ran into trouble. Even so, the Italian press and fans went thoroughly insane over their new hero. And why not? After all, he'd driven just three races in a Formula One car and won all three of them! Needless to say, the pressure in Italy to add this oh-so-promising young Italian star to the regular factory team—even at the expense of one of the established "foreign" drivers—began building immediately.

Cal finally had everything go right for him in Spain, where a brand-new track provided an unusually level playing field and Cal qualified on pole and led every lap. But Toly and Phil were only a few precious ticks behind at the end of qualifying and they both ran into problems in the race. Phil's car developed a bad oil leak while running a close secoind and the spray was going all over Toly, who was right behind. Toly tried to pull out and pass so he could signal Phil about the problem, but Phil didn't know about the leak and thought he was trying to get by. All Toly got for his trouble was a face full of oil and oil all over his left front tire, and he spun while trying to switch to his spare set of goggles. It was at the slowest part of the track and he lightly tagged a guardrail—barely more than a touch—but it tweaked the front end and he was out of it. And Phil was out from his oil leak barely a lap later. That left Cal to simply cruise on home to an easy—if lonely—victory.

It was Cal's first Grand Prix win in just his fifth race, but even so it felt kind of hollow. He didn't say it in so many words, but I could see it in his eyes when we talked about it later. And I guess he was worried about Toly by then, too. Sure, they laughed and joked about Cal's too-easy win and Toly's stupid spin while changing goggles, but Cal didn't like the gaunt look of his face or the grim look in his eye or the way his complexion had lost its tan, healthy coloring. He'd even heard rumors about drugs, and one day he thought he saw a little zippered leather case with what looked like the plunger end of a syringe poking out of it in Toly's helmet bag. But it wasn't the kind of thing he could or would confront him about. In fact, it was none of his damn business. They were friends as well as teammates, but in that light, circumspect, arm's-length way you have to be whenever risk and competition are involved. Even so, Cal could see that Toly was struggling with something inside even as he was going faster and faster and driving better and better on the racetrack.

"You know, you get to where it's not so easy anymore," Toly laughed that night as they celebrated Cal's win with a serious oversupply of the local sherry.

"What do you mean?" Cal asked.

"Maybe I'm getting old, but now it seems like I have to think about doing what I used to do without thinking."

"No question about it," Cal agreed, lifting his glass and putting the needle in at the same time, *"you're getting old, all right...."*

"It's not the age," Toly corrected him as their glasses clinked together, *"it's the damn mileage...."*

It was more of the same at a wet British Grand Prix at Aintree in the middle of July, where Toly, Phil and Cal once again finished 1-2-3, well clear of the opposition. By that point, the only real question was which one of the Ferrari drivers would win the World Championship. It was almost like they could've drawn lots for it among themselves. And the team seemed to be favoring Toly, if only to keep them from fighting among themselves. Not to mention that he was the only one of the three with some genuine Italian blood in his veins—all the way down from the Borgias, in fact—spoke the language like a native and had done plenty of lobbying, paying off and politicking in Maranello before the season even began. He'd told us all that he was going to win the world championship that year and then retire, and it looked like fate and destiny were both on his side. Not to mention several of the hard working race mechanics on the *Scuderia Ferrari* team.

But that all changed at the German Grand Prix at The Nurburgring the first weekend in August, when the long-rumored new engines from England finally made their debut. BRM ran their new V-8 briefly in practice but were planning to race the old 4-cylinder cars, while Cooper showed up with the prototype of the new and exquisite little Coventry Climax V-8 engine that all the rest of the British teams had been waiting so desperately for stuck in the back of Brabham's car. Although it was all very slap-dash and last-minute and riddled with teething problems, the new

Climax V-8 made a fine, crisp yowl and was immediately 7 or 8mph faster than the older four-cylinder cars on the straightaways. But first the distributor drive seized because they'd turned it around to clear something and blocked an oil hole and then it was overheating and worse yet the oil pan was too low and bottoming out over some of the track's rougher humps and jumps. The team wound up literally jacking the engine up and adding spacers underneath and switching to larger rear tires to gain enough clearance to keep it from banging on the pavement. And they couldn't seem to get the overheating to go away. But it was still fast enough to have Tavoni staring at his stopwatch every time it went by. And Stirling Moss in Rob Walker's upgraded, four-cylinder Lotus 18/21 was once again showing what a real genius of a driver and a great-handling car could do around a track as long, complex, daunting and difficult to master as the *Nordschleife.* Phil had used his experience to put his Ferrari on pole with the first sub-9 minute lap ever recorded around The 'Ring's 14 miles, but Brabham, Moss and Bonnier in the stubby-looking Porsche had all taken their cars by the scruff of the neck and forced them into second, third and fourth on the grid ahead of Toly and Cal.

And then, on race day, a sunny morning turned overcast and a soft, gentle rain began to sprinkle down less than an hour before the start….

As you can imagine there was a scurry to put on rain tires, but then it looked like it might clear and Ferrari took them off again on Phil and Toly's cars but left Cal on rains to cover all bets. Brabham was in worse shape since Dunlop didn't have any rain tires in the larger size he had to run on the rear, and so he started the race with the softer "wet" comound tires on the front and the harder "drys" in back. He led away from the start with the new Climax V-8 making a wonderfully lean, hard noise, but the tire combination caught him out and he spun on the slick pavement—fortunately without hurting himself or causing any serious damage—and after that it was all Stirling Moss. Cal fought with him briefly thanks to his wet-weather tires, but then the track started to dry out and Moss once again just pulled off into the distance, smooth and unruffled, while Cal eased off to cool his tires and then let Phil past to see if he could make any impression on Moss. But he couldn't. So it was the dark blue Lotus all by itself in the lead with Phil, Cal and Toly running pretty much together about 20 seconds behind. Then Toly surprised the heck out of Cal by making a sudden, desperate and unexpected dive down the inside, and Cal had to fight the urge to chop him right off. *"He wasn't supposed to do that,"* Cal said bitterly afterwards. *"If Tavoni showed me a MOVE OVER sign, that's one thing. But to just make a fucking dive-bomb move on your own teammate, well…."*

Cal was pretty damn upset about it. But he wisely didn't make an issue of it on the racetrack. *"I could have crowded him and tried to take the corner away, but he was already over-committed and it probably would've taken us both out. I don't think that would've gone down too well with Mr. Ferrari."* As soon as he was past, Toly started putting the pressure on Phil. *"The thing about the Nurburgring is that you can only see a little bit of it from the pits, and so Toly would go by there all nice in a line behind Phil and then race the shit out of him as soon as they were out of sight!"* He finally barged past to take second place behind Moss with another let-me-by-or-I'll-wreck-us-both move a few laps later. *"I saw the whole thing,"* Cal said. *"It was pretty damn disgusting."* At any rate, that's how it finished—Moss, Toly, Phil and Cal—with Clark and Surtees filling out the top six but not anywhere near within striking distance.

I was just finishing up the race reports in *Autosport* and *Competition Press* a week or so later when I got an unexpected phone call from Hank. "You got room at the inn?" he asked.

"Why? You coming to town?"

"Through it more than to it. And just for a day, really. I'm on my way back to Europe."

"You *are?"*

"Yep. On my way to do a little reporting at the Italian Grand Prix at Monza."

"I thought you were all through with all that?"

"I thought I was, too."

"So what happened?"

"Lots of things. Money. Need. Opportunity. I'll tell you when I see you."

I thought about it for a moment. "How about your book?" I had to ask.

"Well, that's the other reason I'm coming to town." A happy, excited edge came into his voice. "I think I might be done with it…."

"You *think* you might be done with it?" I shook my head and laughed. "Jesus, Hank, if you don't know, who the heck would?"

"I guess nobody," he said sheepishly.

So Hank flew into Idlewild on Thursday, August 31st, and naturally the first thing we talked about was the thing *everybody* was talking about that particular day: how the communists had put up a wall overnight through the middle of town to seal the border between East Berlin and West Berlin. It was the first time the Cold War had a real monument to itself you could look at and try to understand.

"Aren't you worried going back to Europe with all that going on?" I asked him.

"I don't think it'll really affect me," Hank allowed. "It's just local politics. The communists are sick and tired of all the brains and money oozing across the border into West Berlin. They're just trying to put a stop to it."

"You think that's *right?"* I said incredulously.

"Hell, no. It stinks, in fact. But that's the way things are and there isn't much of anything you can do about it. Besides," Hank gave me a knowing smile, "this war won't be won with machine guns and concrete blocks."

"It won't?"

Hank shook his head and rubbed his fingers together like he was holding cash.

I could see his point.

Turns out Hank was on his way to a meeting with some feature editor at *Sports Illustrated* who'd happened to hear that some American he'd never heard of might very well win that year's World Grand Prix Driving Championship. And also as how that championship was a very big deal over in Europe and that a whole bunch of sniffy, old-world Europeans would likely be very unhappy to see an American win it. Not to mention the snoot factor what with this renegade, black-market nobleman Wolfgang in the running plus the glamour-and-floodlights angle with Gina LaScala. Sounded like a hell of a story, even if Fred Average and old John Q. had no idea who any of these people were and moreover didn't really give a good God damn about what went on over in Europe. Even if the last race in the championship *was* going to be held at Watkins Glen in upper New York State. And, since Hank knew the cast of characters and moreover had a little credibility with the nutcases who actually followed this stupid sport, he sounded like the right man for the job. Especially since he'd work reasonably cheap, understood how to write simple, declarative sentences and respected deadlines.

"You're gonna write for *Sports Illustrated?"*

"Don't get too excited," Hank said, kind of blushing. "It's just a one-off, freelance job. But I'm hoping it'll help get my name around."

"It sure as hell should!"

"Hard to say," he said. "Hard to say. It's like you have to beat people over the head to get any recognition in this business."

I knew he was talking about his book. He had the manuscript in the briefcase under his legs. "How's that coming?" I asked.

"I'm gonna see another publisher this afternoon and some agent I got out of the phone book after that. Maybe I can get one of them to actually sit down and read it."

"I'll read it," I told him.

"That's a very nice offer, Buddy, but I don't think your opinion is worth very much in the publishing world."

"Why not?" I said, trying to sound a little bit insulted.

Hank gave me the old eyeball. "Look, you're my friend, right?"

"Right."

"And you love racing?"

"Does a chicken have lips?"

"So what are you going to tell me, huh? That you hate it? That you think the plot is thin and the characters are two-dimensional?"

"I'm sure they're not."

"Exactly! And that's why your opinion isn't worth two shits in a snowstorm."

"You're making me feel bad," I told him, doing my best to sound a little hurt.

"Well, the publishers are making *me* feel bad," Hank groused, "I'm just spreading it around a little, that's all…."

Chapter 42: Head Gaskets and Headlines

Everybody and his brother figured the Italian Grand Prix at Monza was going to be some kind of motorized Italian coronation ceremony where Ferrari sewed up the Formula One Constructor's Championship in glorious, resurgent style in front of an ecstatically cheering hometown crowd while one of its drivers—either Phil or Toly, but most likely Toly—clinched the World Driving Championship as icing on the cake. Oh, Moss and Cal were still in there with feeble, mathematical shots at the title, but no way were the Ferraris going to get beat by a better-handling racecar on a power track like Monza. And it wasn't real likely that Phil and Toly would both break down while Cal went on to win. Which, the way the points shook out, was pretty much what had to happen for Cal to have a shot at the title at the very last race of the season at Watkins Glen. Where he'd also have to beat out Phil and Toly and possibly also Stirling Moss.

But it was shaping up as a great story as far as Hank was concerned, what with *Scuderia Ferrari* about to win its first Grand Prix championship since 1958—and right in front of its greatest fans!—after getting kicked all over Europe, Argentina and America by the top British teams for the past two years. Plus you had two Americans in the hunt for the title—the quiet, serious, fast, nervous and oh-so-deserving Phil Hill on one side and this entirely-too-likable punk rich kid from New Jersey with the easy smile and good looks on the other—along with this incredibly suave, fascinating and mysterious continental aristocrat with all the style, flair, playboy reputation and dark family pedigree you could ask for. Hank said you couldn't script it up any better as fiction, you know?

Of course, Toly didn't seem all that dark and mysterious to any of us any more—except maybe when he was flipping back and forth between languages or playing some of that incredible piano music of his—and even though Phil Hill was a heck of a driver who had earned every bit of where he was (and who was, after all, an American), I caught myself kind of pulling for Toly down in my heart of hearts. And I kind of think Hank was, too, even though he would never say such a thing out loud or—horrors!—ever write anything like that for *Sports Illustrated.*

As you can imagine, I was pretty surprised when Hank called me on an overseas phone hookup about 6:30 ayem Passaic time Friday morning to tell me what was going on at Monza. Julie was over at the stove whipping up a mess of Friday-morning peppers-and-eggs with toast and I was in the middle of trying to get the kids up and ready for school, but I was always all ears when it came to the latest racing news from Europe. It was a lousy connection—all crackles and static—and I kind of wondered what was so damn important that Hank had to make an overseas call. "You won't *believe* what I heard this afternoon!" he said kind of breathlessly. And then he gave it a little dramatic pause like all good storytellers do.

"Hey, it's your nickel," I prodded.

He continued in a fast, urgent whisper, as if somebody might be listening. *"Stirling Moss is going to drive a Ferrari next year!"* he hissed into my ear.

"You're shitting me!" I about yelped. *"Stirling Moss?!! Driving for Ferrari?!!"* I had notions in my head already of what that would mean for everybody else. Especially considering the way those shark-nosed Ferraris had been steamrollering

everybody all year long plus what Stirling Moss had been doing pretty decisively to just about every other driver on the planet ever since he set foot in a racecar. It almost didn't seem fair. Although I remembered the story Eric Gibbon told us at Nassau about the other time Moss was supposedly going to drive for Ferrari. Back in 1951. That's when he was just a promising young pup of 21 and right at the beginning of his stunning career. Old Enzo always had a shrewd eye for talent—and especially talent with a little money behind it—and so Stirling and his dad were cordially invited down to Maranello for a little face-to-face sit down with *Signore* Ferrari about a deal for the upcoming season. Formula One was scheduled to drop down to essentially 2.0-liter, un-supercharged Formula Two cars in 1952 to make the machinery a little simpler, cheaper, more plentiful and easier to come by and hopefully improve the show. And everybody pretty much figured Ferrari was going to have the best and most reliable cars—or at the very least the best and most reliable engines—and when they left Maranello, Stirling and his old man thought they had a deal set. But when they showed up as agreed at some minor race in Bari to try out one of the cars and show the team what he could do, Moss and his father were in for a rude awakening. Stirling arrived in the pits and immediately sat down in what he thought was "his" car to try it on for size, and one of the Italian mechanics promptly shooed him out and told him the car was for old "Silver Fox" Piero Taruffi and that there was no Ferrari racing car on hand for any short, eager and impetuous young Englishman. As you can imagine, that left a mark. *"Stirling Moss driving for Ferrari?"* I repeated slowly, tasting the meaning of the words. *"WOW!"* And then something else occurred to me. "If Moss is headed for Ferrari, who the heck's going to leave?" Sure, Ferrari would occasionally run an extra car here and there for a local hero or a promising young Italian (assuming an appropriate wad of cash changed hands, anyway), but he already had a three-car team with Toly, Cal and Phil and it didn't make sense that he would want to run four. Hell, most of the other factory teams only ran two.

"That's the $64,000 question, isn't it?" Hank agreed. *"There's no official word—in fact, nobody's even supposed to know about it yet—but there's rumors flying around all over the place."*

"What about Cal?" I asked instinctively.

"Well, he'd be the guy on the bubble, wouldn't he?"

I let out a low whistle.

"But there's another possibility, too," Hank whispered with his mouth even closer to the phone. *"A really intriguing possibility...."* And then he let it dangle for a moment, like all good storytellers know how to do.

"So are you going to tell me or do I have to reach my fingers right through this damn phone line and strangle you with it?'

He let me wait a little more. *"What would you say if I told you Moss might not be driving FOR Ferrari?"* Hank asked mysteriously.

"But you just said..."

"I said he might be driving A Ferrari, not necessarily FOR Ferrari."

It took a minute for the difference to sink in. I already knew from the magazines that Moss had been driving a Scottish-blue, Rob Walker-entered Ferrari Short Wheelbase *Berlinetta* in various English GT races and was pretty much cleaning up with it. “But I thought Ferrari never sold their Grand Prix cars?”

“Normally they don’t. But after Moss beat their whole damn team even-up with that four-cylinder Lotus at Monaco and The ’Ring, I guess the old man had a few second thoughts.” He pulled in close to the receiver and started whispering again. *“Nobody’s supposed to know anything about it yet, but I know for a fact that Alf Francis—he’s Stirling’s own mechanic—spent most of last week down at Maranello going over the cars. Of course, it’s all VERY hush-hush.”*

“Wow,” I whispered back. *“How’s it going to work?”*

“The way I understand it, Ferrari is going to sell or rent or lease a car to Rob Walker’s team, and they’re going to paint it Scottish blue with a white band around its nose and run it out of Rob’s shop in England—just like they did with the Cooper and the Lotus.”

“Wow,” I said again, the vision of a dark-blue, shark-nostril Ferrari with a white band around its nose shimmering in my head. *“That’s one hell of a story!”*

“It sure is,” Hank agreed.

“Why are you whispering?” Julie asked as she set a heaping plate of peppers-and-eggs in front of me. She made great peppers-and-eggs.

I looked at her kind of sheepishly with my hand over the receiver. “It’s nothing. Just car talk.”

She gave me the snake eyes. Not like she was really suspicious or anything, but just to keep me on my toes.

“I-it’s Hank,” I stammered, sounding guilty as hell (like husbands always do, even when they haven’t got one blessed thing to feel guilty about). “He’s calling all the way from Italy.”

“My God, what time is it over there?”

“What time is it over there?” I whispered into the phone. Hank told me. “It’s the middle of the afternoon,” I reported to Julie through the straightest face you have ever seen. “Right after second practice.”

Julie gave me an impatient grimace. “You’d better be getting the kids up. And I sure hope that’s not a collect call.”

I yelled upstairs again for little Vincent to get his sister out of bed and into the bathroom. Then I went back to Hank. In a whisper, of course: *“So what happens at Ferrari if Walker gets a privateer car?”*

“Hard to say. Cal may still not be out of the woods. There’s a lot of pressure in Italy to hire Baghetti on.”

“Is he any good?”

“Yeah, he’s pretty good. I mean, he’s won three out of three races for Ferrari. But two of them were against nobodies and he was awfully lucky in France. They’ve got a fourth car again for him this weekend to keep the Italian fans happy, but I

don't think he's really in Cal's class. Or Phil's or Toly's, either. And I'm sure old man Ferrari's sharp enough to see that, too. But, like I said, he's done a good job and there's a LOT of local pressure...."

I took a forkful of peppers-and-eggs and thought it over while I chewed and swallowed. "So what else is going on?" I asked him.

He allowed as how the British teams were plenty miffed that the race was being run on the layout that included the steep, rough bankings again, and on top of that the Italian organizers had brought in a whole bunch of uniformed "security police" from Sardinia to maintain order and keep souvenir-hunting locals out of the pits, but who were spending most of their time making life miserable for the visiting race teams and pushing foreign journalists around. *"I think they must be leftovers from Mussolini's black shirts,"* Hank whispered. *"The track apparently has some sort of deal with a big Italian press service, and I guess they told these goons they don't want anybody else out there shooting pictures and selling them. I can't shoot anywhere except around the paddock and from the normal spectator areas."*

"That kind of stinks."

"It sure does. And you know what's even worse?"

"What?"

"Would you believe that rat-bastard Eric Gibbon got himself an all-access photo pass?"

"How'd he swing that?"

"Beats me. Probably knew who to pay off. Or maybe he bought it off some local Italian newspaper flake who'd rather sit in the press room and drink Campari."

"Figures. He's cheap as hell except when it comes to greasing palms."

"And you can bet he's not doing it with his own money, either."

I looked at the clock and yelled upstairs again for little Vincent and littler Roberta to get their sweet little butts downstairs. "Ahh, domestic bliss," Hank chuckled at the other end.

"You're just jealous," I said as I stared at the whopping plate of peppers-and-eggs growing cold in front of me. "I'm like a damn king in his castle," I told him. "Maybe even an emperor."

"I understand you get to sweep out the stables, too."

"All part of the job," I assured him while shoveling up another forkful of eggs. "All part of the job." Julie made some pretty fantastic peppers-and-eggs on Friday mornings. "So what else is going on? How's the race shaping up?"

"Well, it's a *huge* field—I think they've got every blessed Italian privateer and piece-of-crap hybrid in creation here—but it looks like a Ferrari benefit so far. They've been at the top of the top of the time sheets in both sessions so far. They even brought two extra cars—the one I told you about for Baghetti plus one of the old, narrow-angle hacks for Ricardo Rodriguez. You can bet that cost Rodriguez's father plenty. And I'm sure the race promoters kicked in a little something for Baghetti, too."

"You think?"

"Hey, the red cars are a huge draw in Italy—especially here at Monza—and an Italian driver in a red car is even better. Believe me, money changed hands."

"How're Cal and Toly doing?"

"About the same. Second and fourth right now, but you could put a handkerchief over the whole bunch of them. And slipstreaming is so damn important. A lucky tow can work wonders for your lap times here at Monza."

"Really?"

"Oh, hell yes! Rodriguez in the old V-6 got a really good suck off the back of Toly's car and actually closed up a good 20 yards on him going down the pit straight! And that's with an engine anybody on the team will tell you is down 10 to 15 horsepower on the newer ones…."

"Wow. And how about all those new British engines?" I asked.

"Pretty much crap so far. They put fuel injection on the BRM V-8s, but they can't seem to make them run right. Especially up on the bankings. They can get them to run—how did Graham Hill say it?—*'flat as a kipper or fluffy as a kitten,'* but they can't seem to make them run clean."

"How about the new Climax?"

"Well, there's two of them here—one in Brabham's Cooper and another one stuffed in the back of Stirling's Lotus—but they're both overheating. They'll run a few laps and then start steaming and pumping water out, and nobody seems to be able to figure out why. Or at least not yet, anyway."

"Then it's just a question of which Ferrari is going to win, right?"

"Well, that's what everybody's expecting and that's how it looks to me. But the slipstreaming could always throw a wrench in the works. If you can stay with somebody, you've always got a chance to jink out and dive-bomb by under braking. It'll be hard for even the Ferraris to break away from the rest here at Monza. Or the best of the rest, anyway. The cars seem to always wind up running in packs at this place. Hell, they're all practicing for it already."

"Practicing?"

"Sure. Practicing trying to stay with the Ferraris by tucking into their slipstream." Hank allowed himself a little laugh. "Shit, when the Ferraris pull out to practice, all the British cars and Porsches pull out right behind them like hounds after a bitch in heat."

"What a colorful image," I laughed right back. "You must be a writer."

"And you must be a grease monkey. I can smell the 90-weight under your fingernails from here."

Julie looked at the uneaten mound of eggs on the plate in front of me and gave me a scowl. "Look, I gotta run," I told Hank.

"I gotta run, too. The next session's gonna start in about 10 minutes."

"Hey, good luck with your story," I told him. "And give me a call now and then to let me know what's happening, okay?"

"Sure, if I can get through. It took me damn near an hour this time. And I figure it'll be even worse on the weekend."

"Do your best."

"Sure I will. But you can bet I'll be calling collect next time. This is gonna cost me a fortune!"

"You've got to learn to keep things short and sweet," I teased.

"When I've got a story to tell?" he laughed. "Not too likely."

"And listen," I whispered before I hung up, kind of swiveling my back around towards Julie, *"after I'm off, go ahead and reverse the charges...."*

Naturally I thought about what was going on at Monza all day long at the shop. It was better than listening to the radio, where the DJs seemed to be playing Chubby Checker's hot new dance craze *The Twist* between every single soft drink and acne cream commercial. Sure, I liked pop music, but I could only stand so much of it before the sheer repetition got the better of me. It was almost like they were being paid to play certain songs, you know? So sometimes I'd switch stations and try a little oldster music like my mom liked to listen to in her kitchen—you know, all the old crooners and torch singers and big bands and that kind of stuff—or maybe the weak little station from Greenwich Village Pauly Martino showed me that had all the latest hot and cool jazz and by far the mellowest-sounding disc jockeys on the planet. Or the black blues and gospel station Sylvester always listened to or the country station Butch liked or sometimes even a little classical. I guess I picked that last one up from Toly. And also that it was okay to switch around from one style of music to another and enjoy them all. It was a lot like cars, as far as I could see. If you loved an MG or a Ferrari or a Porsche, that didn't mean you couldn't appreciate something like a nicely-done hot rod or a Bonneville streamliner or a Chrysler 300 convertible or an Indianapolis roadster or something like that fabulous old hulk of a Duesenberg I had torn down into a kazillion pieces behind me. They were all good, you know? Just in different ways. And that's why, on that particular day with the Duesenberg on one side and my Alfa racecar project on the other and the blessed Italian Grand Prix weekend just kicking off all the way on the other side of the world with three of my best friends not only just there, but acting as key players, I decided to listen to a little opera for a change. Puccini, in fact. It just seemed like the right thing to do....

We'd made some genuine progress on the Duesenberg and had the body stripped off and the block, crank and head over at Roman Szymanski's shop for a little machine work while I messed around rebuilding the brakes, suspension and running gear. But the thing about a restoration project is that it moves at a snail's pace on account of you're always running into situations where you suddenly realize you need a this or a that or a whatsis or a whatchamacallit or some seal, gasket set, packing piece or brake cylinder repair kit that hasn't been available over-the-counter since the blessed Roosevelt administration. Or maybe some special shouldered bolt or one-of-a-kind tapered steel pin with a flat edge on one side that you have to get machined up from scratch. And then that particular little sub-assembly is pretty much frozen solid until you get what you need, and so you move to some other part of the car and do that until you find you need a this or a that or a whatsis or a whatchamacallit or some seal or gasket set or…you get the idea.

But whenever that happened, I could always sneak over into the next stall and do a little fiddling with the Alfa to cheer myself up. I'd cleaned the car up as best I could (although it was still going to need paint), changed all the fluids and gone through all the electrics and brake hydraulics, took off the broken windshield and windshield frame, got rid of the top, pulled out the seats and had Butch weld me in a nice, stout roll bar.

I'd also pulled the head off—as much for a little look-see as anything else—and reground the valves, and of course I had notions about milling the head a little and putting on the hotter cams and dual Weber carburetors from the *Veloce* version. But I was having a little trouble locating the parts I needed, and it went against the grain of my natural, inbred cheapness to pay a small king's ransom (and small kings were running damn near as much as big kings when it came to Alfa speed parts!) to order them brand-new from Italy. Better to wait until a wreck, fire, theft, divorce or some other horrific natural disaster made a used set available at a reasonable price. Besides, it might actually be better to start out with the car in ordinary, two-barrel trim. Why, it was a foolproof, built-in natural excuse in case I got waxed by all the other Alfas. Or the MGAs and Sprites, for that matter.

I must admit I was really enjoying working on that Alfa, and appreciating more and more the way it was designed and put together. Especially the engine. Or at least I was until I got to where I was re-installing the cylinder head and dropped the damn timing chain down inside the front cover of the motor. After I already had all the head nuts torqued down, too. I remember it made this dull, clattery, jangling noise that sent chills up my spine as I watched the last few links slip out of sight like a snake's tail disappearing down a rat hole. And then I just stood there—staring at it!—like you always do whenever you've done something incredibly, unbelievably stupid.

"SHIT!" I said to nobody in particular.

"You drop the cam chain?" J.R. chuckled from behind me.

"What's it to you if I did?" I snapped at him.

"Sorry," he said. But I could still hear a trace of a snicker behind his voice.

Well, I wasn't about to ask for any help—I mean, I was *supposed* to be pretty much the damn boss, you know?—even though I knew as well as anyone that every make and model ever built has its own little tricks and gimmicks. I peered down the front of the engine with a flashlight, but I couldn't see much of anything. So I got myself a fresh cup of coffee, wiped off all my tools and spent the rest of the damn day taking the head and front cover back off, re-threading the timing chain and re-assembling everything again. With a brand-new head gasket, of course. And you don't really want to know what those things cost, either. Naturally that's right about when J.R. poked his head over my shoulder again and whispered: *"Y'know, you COULD have gone fishing for it down the front cover with a piece of coat-hanger wire."*

I stared at him. "Does that *work?"*

"Well," he allowed, his face a monument to feigned sincerity, "it takes a little practice and finesse, but it's worked for me a time or two...."

"Why didn't you tell me that before??!!" I snarled at him.

He looked me right, square in the eyes. "Why didn't you *ask?"*

He had me there. And then he smilingly showed me how a really *smart* Alfa wrench-twister ties the ends of the cam chain up with little strands of mechanic's wire so's they can't go falling down inside the front engine cover. Again.

"Thanks for telling me now," I snorted.

"Hey, no problem," he smiled. "I'm here to help."

So now I had the head back on and the head nuts re-torqued and the camshafts bolted in and properly lined up with their marks on either side, and that's when I *very* carefully draped the ends of the timing chain over the cam sprockets and fastened them together in the middle with the master link. Bingo! Piece of cake! Then all I had to do was re-install the little blue-black spring clip that prevents the master link from coming apart so the timing chain goes flailing merrily off its sprockets while the valves go crashing into the pistons and each other like bumper cars at Coney Island. And you'd really rather not have that happen, you know? But putting that little spring clip on is one of those difficult jobs where it takes a lot of force and yet you're working small and cramped for finger space and can't get any blessed leverage and nothing wants to stay still for you. And I just about had it—squeezing for all I was worth with my left hand while pressing down *hard* on a screwdriver blade with my right—when suddenly the damn screwdriver slipped and dug itself a gouge the approximate size and shape of the Panama Canal across the top of my thumb knuckle. But I didn't hardly feel it, because I was too busy listening to the faint, horrifying little *"ping!"* followed by an even fainter, even more unsettling little *"ting!"* followed by the tiniest, most heart-rending little echo of a tinkling noise you ever heard as that spring clip tinked, clinked and tumbled its way down into the bottom of the engine. *"OHMYGOD!"* I hissed through clenched teeth.

"You drop the Jesus clip?" J.R. asked from two stalls over.

"The *what?"* I had to ask.

"The Jesus clip."

"Why do you call it a Jesus clip?"

"Because that's what you always say—*JEE-ZUS!!!*—when you drop one of those damn things down into the engine and realize that you've got to take the oil pan off to get it out. And that's if you're lucky...."

If we'd had a pet dog around that shop, I would've kicked it.

"You better go home for the night," J.R. laughed. And I had to agree. This just wasn't turning out to be my day at all....

A nice, Friday-night pasta-with-calamari-sauce dinner plus a glass or two of wine, a little playing with the kids and a good night's sleep put a little better complexion on things come Saturday morning, and it only took me three-quarters of an hour to get the Alfa up on stands and drop the oilpan once J.R. showed me how you could come at it from the bottom to get it off. Although even then several of the pan bolts were of the maddeningly-tiny/impossible-to-get-at/I-need-eyeballs-on-the-end-of-my-damn-fingers variety where you spend more time groping and grasping and grunting than anything else. But eventually I got the pan down far enough to sneak a magnet in sideways and fish around for that damn Jesus clip, and it didn't take more than a few minutes and my entire supply of available cuss words to retrieve it. And there it was, sitting just as innocent as you please in the palm of my hand. Naturally my first instinct was to hurl the damn thing as far as my anger and arm strength would carry it. But then I knew I'd just have to go all the way into the city to the franchised Alfa dealership for another one. Or maybe more than one, seeing as how I just might have learned a little something from the experience.

I was almost finished buttoning everything up—for the second time!—when the phone rang. It was Hank again on yet another crackly, static-y trans-Atlantic hookup. And collect this time, of course. "This is a *terrible* connection," I told him.

"Don't hang up!" he hollered into the other end. *"It took me damn near two hours to get this one!"*

It was the middle of the night over at Monza, and he said qualifying had gone pretty much as expected. The five Ferraris had qualified 1-2-3-4-6 with just Graham Hill's BRM sneaking into fifth spot ahead of Baghetti and mostly thanks to a real monster of a tow behind two of the red cars. After that came a big gap down to Jim Clark's sleek but underpowered Lotus 21, which hadn't gotten near so lucky catching a slipstream.

"What about Moss and Brabham and the Climax V-8s?" I asked.

"Not so good. They're both still boiling over after a few laps. Brabham's got no choice but to run his, but Team Lotus offered Moss Ireland's car because of the points situation. Pretty sporting gesture, actually. Although I wouldn't be surprised if some money changed hands, too."

"Hey, everybody's got to make a living."

"He still hasn't got a prayer against the Ferraris—not here at Monza, anyway—but at least the four-cylinder Lotus might actually go the distance and score some points. But it looks pretty hopeless as far as the championship is concerned."

"So it'll probably come down to Phil or Toly, right?"

"Probably? I'd say 'definitely' is more like it. Although Cal's still in with an outside shot."

"That should work right into your story."

"Like they say in the pressroom, *'it almost writes itself.'*"

"Anything else going on?"

It was silent for a moment at the other end. "Well," Hank said finally, "I got to do my interviews today at lunchtime...." And then his voice kind of trailed off.

I waited a few heartbeats, but nothing came out of the receiver. "Anything wrong?" I asked.

"I dunno," Hank said slowly, kind of drawing out the words. "Toly didn't look real good to me today."

"Whaddaya mean?"

"I dunno," Hank repeated. "It's his coloring. And his cheeks and eyes. They looked kind of sunken, you know? Like a skull."

"You think he's *sick?"*

Another pause. Then, softly: "Yeah. Maybe. Or that's what it looked like to me, anyway…."

"Has he got a flu or something?"

"No, I don't think it's that kind of sick. I think it's maybe the other kind of sick."

It took a moment for the meaning to sink in.

"Oh, he says he's feeling fine and itching to go racing and get things settled in the championship once and for all. And he's really driving well. Better than I've ever seen him, I think. He's on the pole with a little in hand over Phil and Cal. But he sure doesn't look right. Or at least not to me, anyway…."

Hank didn't have to say anything more.

I was surprised when I didn't get a call from Hank Sunday afternoon or evening or even early the next morning to fill me in on what had happened at Monza, but I understood as soon as I picked the early edition of the *Times* up off my breakfast table and saw that the sport I loved had once again made it to the front page. I'd learned through bitter experience that was never, ever a good thing. And there it was, down at the bottom of the front page, a large, grainy picture of the short, fast straightaway between the Ascari Curve and the South Curve at Monza with the remains of two wrecked Ferraris and a Lotus scattered all over like a damn plane crash, people running everywhere, a wicked, horrifying gash of splintered spectator fencing and awkwardly twisted bodies up on the hillside in the background and another body—this one in a driving suit—crumpled up on the pavement below. The headline was short, brutal and to the point: *"DRIVER AND 11 SPECTATORS KILLED AT ITALIAN GRAND PRIX!"*

The impact was like getting hit with a damn wrecking ball, and I had to stifle the immediate urge to wad that front page up and throw it away before I could read any more. As if I could somehow change things back to how they were if I could only get rid of that damn newspaper….

But I just had to keep reading it. I had no choice.

It was only a short, few-column story that started at the bottom of page one and continued on page 33. Toly had apparently gotten off to a bad start while Phil and Cal jumped out ahead of the field, and he was working his way back to the front when, on just the second lap, he blew past Clark and somehow got tangled up with Cal's wheels at over 150mph. Both Ferraris spun, and Toly's bounced off of Clark's

Lotus, launched up an embankment, tore through a fence and carved a wicked, merciless arc through the crowd before crashing back down to the pavement again. I had instant, nightmare visions of what that must have looked like from inside that car—hearing the horrified screams and the thud of flesh and the *crack!* of breaking bones over the flat-out howl of the engine and seeing all the blood and the body parts flying and all those terrified, disbelieving, flashbulb-pop faces whipping past just before everything went black….

Toly was dead on the spot and so were 11 spectators.

Over 30 more were injured—many of them critically.

Cal and Clark were apparently all right with just minor injuries.

And the race went on….

The story said ambulances ran pretty much a shuttle service back and forth from the crash site for the better part of an hour, and not a word about the wreck was broadcast over the track PA system. The Italian Grand Prix finally ended about an hour later with Phil Hill scoring a hollow, shell-shocked Ferrari victory roughly 20 seconds ahead of Dan Gurney's Porsche. Oh, and he clinched the World Driving Championship, too.

But it was hardly a time for celebrations....

You don't get over something like that. Not quickly, not slowly, not all at once, and certainly not ever. And for some stupid, morbid reason, you want to—you *need* to—know all the grisly little details, as if that will somehow explain things and make it easier to accept. But of course it doesn't. I got to talk to Hank again when he arrived in New York a few days later to turn in his story and pictures to *Sports Illustrated.* He called me from the airport and of course I offered to pick him up, but he said he was in kind of a hurry and taking a cab into the city, but maybe we could meet later on for dinner. He sounded tired and rushed and like he really didn't feel much like talking. Although no question the headlines and notoriety had turned his story into quite a hot property. In fact, it even prodded that Manhattan literary agent to finally take a look at his manuscript—or at least pay some N.Y.U. grad student a few bucks to skim through it, anyway—and he also wanted to talk to Hank while he was in town. So they met for coffee after Hank was done at *Sports Illustrated,* and the agent told Hank he thought the manuscript just might have a future somewhere. Although Hank allowed as how 'might' was really the key word in that sentence when I picked him up later that afternoon on Fifth Avenue, just a few blocks down from the Flat Iron Building. "Those literary agents are all working on the come," he grumbled. "They don't pay you anything and they don't cover any expenses, but they sure as hell take their cut if anything sells." He shook his head. "The only thing they have to trade in is hope."

"Hope's a nice thing to have."

"Money's better," he answered sullenly. It smelled like he'd been drinking. And he sure didn't look like he wanted to talk much about what happened at Monza. But then, he'd just finished writing about it on the plane over from Italy, and that couldn't have been very pleasant. "I had a hard time writing about it," he said like he was really talking to himself. "Or a hard time getting started, anyway. But then it just came out like diarrhea. I couldn't stop it. Filled up two fucking notebooks."

"Is it any good?"

"I told you, it's like diarrhea. Shit." He looked down at his hands. There were ink smudges on the ends of his fingers and they were shaking just a little. "But that's what editors are for, aren't they?" he added so softly I could hardly hear.

"You want to go get some dinner or something?"

"Nah," he sighed. "My insides are all screwed up from traveling and the time changes and all. Besides, it's—what?—four in the afternoon here? That's way too early for dinner."

"Everywhere but Miami Beach," I said, trying to make a joke. Hank didn't so much as flick an eyelash. So I tried again: "You maybe want to go out for a drink?"

"I already had a drink," Hank grumbled. "In fact I had three. Or maybe it was four. They didn't do much for me." He was staring out the side window with blank, vacant eyes, watching the Manhattan street traffic wheel by.

"You wanna come over by our house and maybe shower and take a nap?"

He started to say something mean, but stopped himself. "Y'know," he allowed dreamily, "maybe that wouldn't be so bad. Being in a real home again for a change." He looked at me. "Cal says you put him up a couple times and he liked it."

"How's Cal doing?" I had to ask.

"Like a guy who got shot with a cannon and lived through it. You can still see the hole." Hank's eyes looked like something out of a horror movie. "They've been pretty rough on him over there. A lot of the press reports said he caused the wreck."

"You think he did?"

Hank gave me half a shrug. "Does it make any difference?"

I turned and headed crosstown towards the George Washington Bridge, and it seemed to me like Hank really wanted to talk about it. *Needed* to talk about it. If only to try and get it out of his system, you know? "So the press was pretty hard on Cal?" I prodded to get him going again.

"Some of the columns damn near called him a murderer."

"Eric Gibbon?"

Hank nodded grimly. "Give that rat-bastard an opening and he'll disembowel you just for the sheer, fucking fun of it!"

"Maybe that's what his audience likes."

"They can all go to hell. The whole fucking bunch of them." Hank stared out at the sidewalk again, watching the reflections of buses, cars, taxicabs, newspaper stands and all those faceless heads and headless torsos moving across the plate glass windows.

"Can you tell me what happened?" I asked him gently.

At first he didn't answer. Just kept staring out the window. But then he told me everything in this weary, worn-down voice that sounded like it was coming from very far away. *"It was just another racing accident,"* he began softly. *"That's all.*

A really fast one. A really bad one. A really unlucky one. But just another racing accident when you get right down to it." He let out a long, heavy sigh. "Toly had the pole, and he'd really had a little something extra on Phil and Cal all through practice and qualifying. He told Cal and Phil that he'd bribed two of the mechanics to give him the best engine, but I'm sure he was just winding them up. He was really driving well—maybe better than I'd ever seen him—and he looked so damn determined it was almost scary. Especially with his eyes kind of sunken the way they were. It was almost like it wouldn't be enough to just win the damn championship. No, he was going to win the race as well. And all the flakes and flacks in the pressroom thought he'd do it, too. There was something in the air that made it seem almost pre-ordained…."

His voice trailed off and I had to nudge him again to get him started: "But what happened in the race?"

"Oh, Toly's car started to creep a little on the line because the clutch was dragging and he lifted off so he wouldn't jump the start and maybe get black-flagged. And of course that's when they waved the green. Hell, *everybody* went streaming by him. He was down around ninth or tenth by the time they got to the first corner. From fucking pole position!" He shook his head disgustedly.

"Then how did he catch up to Cal again?"

"You have to understand that Monza is almost all long straights and fast, sweeping corners. And that Toly's Ferrari had one hell of a horsepower advantage. Plus you always go faster when you're running in the suction of a bunch of cars lined up ahead of you…"

In my mind's eye, I could almost see and feel what it must have been like inside that car—saw the shimmering curtain of heat waves rising up off the pavement and the eerie, wavering line of green and red cars stacked almost one on top of the other in front of me, the gearbox and tailpipes of the last one drawing slowly, inexorably closer like it was on a damn conveyor belt.

"It's like Toly had the power of God or the devil or both of them mixed together that day, the way he came leapfrogging through the field. He passed Moss and Brabham and Baghetti's Ferrari and Graham Hill's BRM and now—in just a little over a lap—he's drawing in on the slipstreaming battle between Clark and Rodriguez just a few car lengths behind Phil and Cal's Ferraris at the front of the pack. The suck from those four cars is tremendous, and he's already got himself up one heck of a head of steam. He jinks out and sweeps past Rodriguez's Ferrari and Clark's Lotus both on the run down to the Ascari Curve, and now he's still got a huge amount of momentum and already feeling the pull off the back of Phil and Cal's cars…"

Again I could see it and feel it—just the way Hank was telling it—as I pulled out of the slipstream and slipped past the red Ferrari and the green Lotus like they were sliding gently backwards. Effortless, you know? And meanwhile the two Ferraris ahead were falling easily into my grasp….

"...Toly kept his foot down all the way through Ascari, taking a really smooth, delicate line so he wouldn't scrub off any speed. It was brilliant, really. And he was just easing out to slide underneath Cal when Cal pulled out to try and go under Phil..."

"My God, didn't he see him coming?"

Hank shook his head. "Maybe the mirror on the right side got knocked around or wasn't aimed properly—you can't see a whole lot out of them anyway—and the last time he'd checked was down the long straight to Ascari, and all he saw then was the nose of Clark's Lotus with Rodriguez right behind. He knew the Lotus didn't have the power to draw in on him, and neither did Rodriguez's Ferrari with the old V-6 in it. He couldn't even see Toly at that point because it was a fraction of a second before he pulled out of the slipstream to pass them both." Hank curled his lip under, and it almost looked like he was going to cry. "There was just no way a car could make up that much distance," he continued, his voice cracking just a little. "It just wasn't possible...."

"But Toly did it?" I finally asked.

"Yeah," Hank nodded heavily. "Toly did it." He took in a deep breath and slowly exhaled. "Oh, Cal saw him coming at the last second. Saw the red tip of that shark nose flashing into his peripheral vision just before he felt the bump when the wheels touched..." Hank rolled up his palms.

"It must have been awful for him."

"Cal went for quite a ride. Spun down the middle of the road at well over 150, but that's what probably saved him. It scrubbed off a lot of speed before the car finally skated off onto the grass and hit one of the barriers. But it wasn't much of a crash. And at least he was facing the other way so he couldn't see what was happening behind him."

"It must've been terrible for Toly, going into the crowd like that."

"He may have been spared that," Hank said softly. "He got thrown out of the car, and nobody seems sure if that happened when it was going up the embankment or coming down the other side. There was an awful lot of dirt and dust and flying parts and fence posts..." I watched a shiver go through Hank. "There was no way you could really tell. It looked like a damn explosion."

I licked my lips and thought about it for a minute or two. Then finally asked: "What actually killed him?"

"Crushed skull. Broken neck. Take your pick," Hank looked at me again with those tired, beaten eyes. "It doesn't much matter, does it?"

"No," I had to agree, "I guess it really doesn't....

Chapter 43: Hollywood Endings

The 1961 United States Grand Prix was scheduled to take place right in our own back yard at Watkins Glen exactly four weeks after that tragic race at Monza, Italy, and naturally Big Ed and Carson and me already had plans and reservations made. We of course wanted to be right there on the sidelines, cheering like mad, as our old pal Cal (or our old pal Toly or our old pal Phil) swept to yet another magnificent Ferrari victory and clinched the World Grand Prix Driving Championship right in front of our eyes at the very last race of the season. After which we would all go downtown (or up to The Seneca Lodge or out to the Glen Motor Inn on Route 14 overlooking the lake), have a nice dinner and guzzle champagne until we were drunk as hooty-owls.

But of course all that changed at Monza, and in spite of Phil Hill clinching the first World Championship ever for an American driver, there was a sad, hollow gloom hanging over everything because of what happened to Toly. In fact, Ferrari wasn't even sending his cars to that first-ever United States Grand Prix at Watkins Glen. The public excuse was that the team was still deep in mourning over Toly's death and that both championships were already won, so what was the point? But Hank said Ferrari also couldn't come close to terms with the Glen organizers over starting money—his cars hadn't showed at either of the other U.S. Grand Prix rounds at Sebring or Riverside for much the same reason—and he was damned if he was going to take anything less than both ears and the tail to bring the biggest damn draw in racing to Watkins Glen. Especially with the new Climax and BRM V-8s starting to show so much promise and at a new track with a lot of fast, sinewy, sweeping corners where high-speed handling really counted for a lot. Rumor had it Ferrari used his American drivers—popular local boy Cal Carrington and brand-new World Champion Phil Hill—for leverage during the negotiations, threatening to keep them from racing anything else at The Glen if his ransom for bringing *Scuderia Ferrari* wasn't met. And that's pretty much what happened. Naturally we all thought it stunk, but old man Ferrari had never been in the business of pleasing other people. Only himself.

"The guy sure knows how to play hard ball," Big Ed allowed around his unlit cigar as we tooled up towards Watkins Glen in his brand new, 3.8-liter Jaguar Mk. II Sedan. I personally thought we would've been better off in one of his old Caddy Eldorados or Chrysler 300s considering the size of the back seat and the trunk space. Or maybe even seeing if we could rent one of those sale-proof VW campers that none of Harry Metropolis' hotshot new salesmen could seem to move at our old VW dealership. But then, Harry didn't like paying salesmen very much—word had it his hand shook any time he had to sign a check with more than three digits to the left of the decimal point—and none of his bright, young, cheery and magnificently insincere rookie salespeople had Big Ed's knack for picking out likely camper buyers before they even walked through the front door.

Although things seemed to be going along just fine at *Alfredo's Sports Car Service,* the front page of the *New York Times* proclaimed that the Cold War was getting even colder and that international tensions were at an all-time high thanks to the Berlin wall, Castro's communists barely spitting distance away from our Florida coastline, turmoil (emphasis on the "oil") in the Mideast, another possible Korea brewing in some Southeast Asian country nobody ever heard of called Viet Nam plus all sorts of bloody civil unrest in those unstable, violent and self-important little emerging nations in black Africa. Even so, the big news all over the greater New York metropolitan area was the battle between Roger Maris and Mickey Mantle to see which one of them would break Babe Ruth's home run record while the Yankees continued yet another steamroller run towards the World Series. That naturally squeezed racing pretty much right off the sports pages, and there wasn't much pre-race hoopla at all prior to that first-ever World Championship Grand Prix at Watkins Glen.

But we didn't care.

We were going anyway.

I'd even asked Pauly Martino if he wanted to come along with us. You know, for one of those Weekend With The Guys/Welcome To The Family deals where everybody feels clumsy, awkward and uncomfortable around everybody else from about 3 o'clock Friday afternoon clear through Sunday evening. But Mary Frances thought it was a real nice gesture anyway, and you could see he was surprised and highly thankful that I'd made the offer. In fact, my sister Mary Frances gave me a smile as warm as a fireplace on Christmas Eve as a kind of reward, and that felt pretty damn nice. Although Pauly had to beg off on account he had a saxophone gig at some little jazz club in Manhattan on Friday plus a wedding on Sunday afternoon, and he'd promised Mary Frances that they'd go down to this place called Gerde's Folk City in The Village on Saturday night to hear this new, long-haired shrimp of a folk singer from Minnesota named Bob Dylan (although I understood he was actually Jewish rather than Welsh and his real last name was Zimmerman) who played guitar, carried his harmonica on a little wire stand strapped in front of his narrow, scrawny shoulders and had a voice like something you might find running around a barnyard. But he was all the rage anyway because his songs were all about social injustice, loneliness, alienation and the general pain of living, and so all the in-the-know/down-your-nose New York tastemaker types in Manhattan were convinced he was The Next New Thing. And of course once those folks have made up their oversized minds about something, who the hell are the rest of us to disagree?

Big Ed was looking a lot better by then—he'd lost more weight and had about two-thirds of his color back—but he still had a little of that walking-on-eggs uncertainty in his voice and the way he moved made me nervous now and then when I was around him. Not that I didn't enjoy his company—far from it!—but I'd catch myself looking for any kind of little tics or twitches or any other telltale signs that he was starting to seize up again like a motor running out of oil and start worrying about where the hell the nearest fire department rescue squad or hospital emergency room might be. And that sort of thing can keep you very much on edge.

But even with the gloom and the worry and the fact that we didn't figure we'd be seeing either Cal or Phil—or Toly, of course—in the race, there was still a little of that old, on-the-road-again feeling of escape and adventure. We'd left before daybreak, and I must admit it felt pretty damn good as we tooled across upper New York State toward Watkins Glen in Big Ed's new Jaguar sedan, watching the early morning countryside wheel by and listening to the pleasant, familiar, six-cylinder growl purring out the tailpipe behind us. It was the same exact sound I remembered from that very first race Big Ed and me ever went to together, back when we took his brand-new, creamy-ivory XK120 across an empty, early-Sunday-morning Manhattan and Long Island towards Bridgehampton in the spring of 1952. Top down, of course. Why, I could close my eyes and feel it all over again: the powerful growl of the Jag's engine and the rolling vibration of the road and the chilly, early-morning air whipping over and around that split-screen, fighter-style windshield while we shielded our eyes from a brilliant and perfect sunrise. I could even smell the fresh spring grass around us and the vapor scent of the *Castrollo* upper cylinder lube I'd insisted on putting in Big Ed's gas tank and the steaming hot coffee in carry-out paper cups we held between our knees. It seemed like just yesterday and a million years ago all at the same time, you know?

We talked about a lot of stuff along the way. About the prospects for Hank's book and Roger Maris breaking The Bambino's record by hitting his 61st home run and of course about that terrible and unforgettable accident at Monza. But what was there really to say? And of course about Cal and where his career was going and the thing he apparently had going with Gina LaScala whenever the two of them could sneak in a little time together. And also how proud we all were of him. And how sad we felt about Toly, too. Then we'd just kind of sit there, listening to the engine and the wind and the tires, watching the scenery roll by and hoping that at least one of us could come up with something else to say.

"How's the Duesenberg project coming?" Big Ed finally asked.

"I may live to see the end of it," I told him.

"Slow going, huh?"

"You really need long eyes and an awful lot of patience to be in the restoration business. And God only knows how you make any money at it."

"But you're enjoying it?"

I thought it over. "I don't think 'enjoying' is exactly the right word," I tried to explain: "It's more like I'm doing something—I don't know—*worthwhile* for a change. Something that'll last awhile and maybe even be important to other people."

"That's nice," Big Ed nodded.

"Yeah, I guess. And it's nice working on something where I can take my time and get it right instead of rushing like crazy to get a million things rushed together at the last minute for a damn race weekend."

Big Ed looked over at me and smiled. I always hated when he did that while he was driving. "You miss it though, don'cha?" He said with a deliberate wink.

"Yeah, I guess I do," I admitted. "That's why I'm having so much fun with that Alfa. I guess you could say it's become kind of a pet project for me."

"When're y'planning to take her out?"

I pretended like I hadn't much thought about it. "Well, it's pretty much almost done—just paint and cosmetics, really—and I've been kind of looking at that SCMA school and regional race up at Lime Rock the third weekend in October…."

Big Ed's eyebrows eased up. "That soon?"

"Sure. Why not?"

"Have you told Julie about it yet?" Carson asked from the back seat.

I didn't say anything.

"I SAID HAVE YOU TOLD JULIE ABOUT IT YET?" Carson yelled from behind my ear.

"I heard you."

"Oh. I thought maybe you didn't because of the wind noise or something."

"I heard you just fine."

"Well," Big Ed asked like a prosecuting attorney, *"have you told her yet or not?"*

I stared at the gleaming little chrome-plated glove box lock in front of me on the Jag's polished walnut dash. "Uh…not quite yet," I more or less mumbled.

Big Ed eased back into his seat and sighed. "Well, you'd better start getting around to it, pal." He gave me a solid nudge with his elbow. "Trust me, it ain't gonna get any easier…."

That was for sure.

We got to Watkins Glen a little after 10 and met up with Hank at the foot of the stands just before Friday morning's second practice, and we were all surprised when he pointed out Cal's helmet in one of the privateer Coopers. "Hey, I thought Ferrari wasn't letting any of his drivers race here?" I wondered out loud.

"Cal doesn't have a contract for next year yet," Hank explained.

But iddn't he still under contract for this year?" Big Ed asked.

"You'd think he still would be," Hank allowed. "But the promoters here wanted Cal pretty bad. They even helped arrange the ride for him. Briggs Cunningham actually owns the car."

I watched the white Cooper with the two narrow blue stripes tool past. "Is the car any good?"

Hank made an uneven, wavering motion with his hand. "It's decent enough—and you know it's well prepared if it came out of Alf Momo's shop!—but it's an older T-53 chassis with a regular customer Climax in it, and it's just not fast enough to run at the front. Not even with Jesus Christ himself behind the wheel."

"How about Captain Marvel?" Big Ed joked.

"You think old man Ferrari will be pissed off?" I asked Hank.

"I don't think there's any question about it. But maybe that's the point. Cal's pissed off that he hasn't been offered a contract yet for next year. Maybe this is just his way of putting a little pressure on."

"Maybe this is just his way of telling old man Ferrari to fuck off," Big Ed mused around the soggy end of his unlit cigar.

"You think that's *smart?"* Carson asked, and Hank just shrugged.

But I figured I knew Cal better than anyone—except maybe Gina—and I doubted that he'd really thought things through. He'd always been a bit of a gunslinger type, and I could see him jumping at the opportunity to race again in his own back yard without thinking all that much about the consequences.

We watched for a while from down at the last corner, and I think the thing that impressed me most was how good even the damn backmarkers were in Formula One, taking smooth, fluid arcs through the turn—all on the same exact line—and using every bit of pavement right down to the final inch. But it wasn't terribly exciting to watch. As Hank pointed out, that's what always made grassroots-level amateur racing so stupidly entertaining—everybody was ragged and all over the road and making all sorts of dumb mistakes—but this was more like watching a damn ballet. Or maybe a bunch of heart surgeons hard at work in an operating room. Sure, it was life and death. But it also seemed a little bit dull, boring and sterile. And it was damn near impossible to get torqued up over the FIA's new so-called "Grand Prix" cars with their screaming little 1500cc engines and pea-shooter exhaust pipes. Oh, the noise they made was crisp and lean all right, but it was high and thin and didn't do much more than fuzz your eardrums instead of making your spine jangle and the ground tremble under your feet.

After the session we went back into the paddock and found Cal over by the Cunningham Cooper, talking over a gear ratio change with one of the mechanics. It surprised me a little how serious, matter-of-fact and mechanically savvy he'd become. *"I want to go up a tooth on second and third,"* he was telling the guy in the coveralls, *"but maybe down a tooth on top. It may have me at the redline before I get to the banked horseshoe at the end of that long chute—especially if I get a good tow—but I'll need the acceleration coming up out of the top of the esses. The car's just flat out of breath up there...."*

"Well, listen to the mechanical genius," I teased from behind Cal's shoulder. He spun around and flashed an instant and enormous smile at us.

"HEY!" he shouted, giving me a shake, an elbow to the ribs and half a hug in quick succession. "Jesus, you're a sight for sore eyes! It's great to see you!"

"It's great to be seen."

"How're things going?"

"I have a feeling I should be asking *you* that question."

Half the smile faded off Cal's face. "You know how it is," he said, looking down into the Cooper's cockpit. "You read the funny papers."

"To tell the truth, they haven't been real funny lately."

"No, they haven't," he agreed without looking up.

Then we just kind of stood there, shuffling our feet and looking at the ground or off towards the clouds and the treetops. "So how're things going with Gina?" I finally asked.

"I'll be seeing her again in a couple of days!" he answered eagerly. "I've got a pretty decent ride lined up for the West-Coast money races at Riverside and Laguna Seca, and she's out in Hollywood again."

"What kind of car is it?"

"It's a Cooper Monaco. But with a Buick V-8 in the back."

"A *Buick?"* Big Ed asked, his eyebrows inching up.

"Isn't that kinda *heavy?"* I wondered.

"No, not one of the big iron V-8s like Max Balchowsky uses. This is one of those new, all-aluminum GM jobs out of that new Buick Special. Momo thinks it ought to have a lot of potential."

It sounded good, but I had my doubts. After all, it was a brand-new engine with no previous racing history, and there are always a bagful of tricks and weaknesses to muddle through with any new race motor. Plus there wasn't any transaxle I knew of capable of handling the torque and power of a Detroit V-8. Or not over a full race distance, anyway. But those are the kind of things you always wind up learning on the fly. "Well, good luck with it," I told him. "And good luck with Gina, too."

"Thanks. It looks like we'll get to spend a few days together after the Riverside race. We're planning to drive up to Carmel and stay a few days at this place she knows. Maybe even the whole week. Then I go racing and she's off to New York for some stupid press deal for her new movie."

"You guys live busy lives."

"Yeah," he agreed sullenly. "Maybe too busy." But then his face brightened. "So how're things going with the Palumbos these days?"

"Fine."

"Wife and kids?"

"Fine. Just fine."

"And Ed's taking care of himself?" Cal gave Big Ed a little bank shot with his shoulder. "Is he staying away from old whiskey and young girls?"

"I'm being s'God damn good, life's not worth living," Big Ed assured him.

"Glad to hear it," Cal grinned.

I ran my eyes over the Cooper. "How's the car?"

"Oh, it handles great," Cal said with measured enthusiasm, "I wish to hell our Ferraris handled that well. But the gearbox is clunky as hell and the motor doesn't have enough power to peel the icing off a cake…"

"Wait a minute!" Hank laughed. "Let me get my notebook! A line like that deserves to be immortalized."

"Go ahead if you want to," Cal shrugged. "But don't give me the credit, OK? I'm not that clever. I'm sure I heard it someplace." And then a slow, dark cloud passed across Cal's face. "I remember now," he almost whispered. "Toly's the one who said it…."

There wasn't much to say after that.

On our way out of the paddock, Big Ed treated Hank, Carson and me to some particularly mediocre but nicely-overpriced sausage sandwiches, a bag of greasy French fries each and a round of watery Cokes from the concession stand, and then we watched the afternoon practice from near the top of the hill overlooking the esses. It was almost eerie how those cars skated up through there like so many brightly colored waterbugs darting across the skin of a pond. “It ain’t much for spectacle, is it?” Big Ed observed.

“No, but it’s beautiful anyway,” Hank argued lamely. “It’s just you have to look a little harder to appreciate it.”

Big Ed gave him the hairy eyeball. “Hey, spectating’s not supposed to be about working harder to appreciate stuff. Just look at boxing or roller derby or pro football. Y’gotta serve it up like raw meat if y’wanna draw fans….”

As always, there was a lot of truth in what Big Ed had to say.

We went over by the press room after the session to check on the times, and it was Brabham and Moss with the Climax V-8s at the head of the pack—although both of them were running hot by the time they pulled in—followed by Graham Hill in the BRM, Clark in the Lotus, McLaren in the other Cooper and so forth. Cal’s time put him right about mid-pack, which was better than most of the privateers and independents but a few solid ticks adrift of the genuine factory teams. Which is I guess the best you could expect. I didn’t want to say anything, but Cal hadn’t looked all that special to me during the session. Good, but not *special.* And I’d always been convinced that Cal was one of those special drivers. The rare ones, you know? The ones that only come along once or twice in a generation. But I guess that’s what people think about every up-and-coming new hotshot racer. Or at least that’s what their friends think, anyway….

That night we all went out to dinner together at the Seneca Lodge, and at first it seemed kind of taut and strained while we waited in the bar for a table to open up for us. The place was full of racing people and a jumble of foreign accents—but mostly British and Australian—and everybody was jabbering away about how the various teams were running and what their prospects were for the race. Naturally we talked a lot about Cal’s ride in the Cunningham Cooper and how it might affect his future.

“Well, the old man won’t be very happy about it, that’s for sure,” Cal allowed over the glass of local red he’d been nursing through two rounds. “But, hell, he hasn’t come across with a contract offer for next year, so I figure we’re about even. I know Phil’s already got his.”

“Hey, he’s the new World Champion. What do you expect?”

“You think Ferrari wants you back?”

“Hard to say. There’s an awful lot of stuff in play. It’s an open secret that Walker’s getting a Ferrari for Moss to drive. And every damn race fan in Italy wants Baghetti and maybe even Bandini to get a seat on the factory team. They want to see their hometown Italian boys in, and you can’t really blame them. And Rodriguez’s father wants him to get a shot, too, and he’s got the money to make it happen.” Cal rolled his palms up. “I may be the odd man out, simple as that.”

“That’s kind of a shitty deal.”

"Hey, what can you do? Plus there's a lot of other strange stuff going on at Ferrari these days, too…"

Hank's ears perked up. "Like what?"

Cal's eyes swept around to see if there were any extra ears listening in. Then he leaned in close and whispered: "Dissatisfaction. Dissension in the ranks. Maybe even mutiny…" he shot Hank a wink. "The natives are definitely restless." And then, in a voice so low we had to crane our necks to hear, Cal told us how team manager Tavoni, chief racing engineer Chiti, designer/engineer Giotto Bizzarrini and a few other key players were at serious loggerheads with *Signore* Ferrari. Part of it was apparently about Ferrari's wife, Laura, who went to most of the races in place of her husband and always had her nose stuck deep into the team's business. Everyone knew she was old man Ferrari's agent, spy, eyes and ears when he wasn't around, and so naturally everyone was afraid of her. Not to mention that she rubbed a lot of people the wrong way. Plus there was a lot of ego-driven shit about who got credit for what and serious differences of opinion about how the cars should be built and how the team ought to be run.

Hank pounded down the rest of his third Black Label and water and allowed as how it was the same old story all over again: struggle and adversity generally spawns cooperation, camaraderie and spirit on a racing team, while success—and especially great success—always seems to breed more in the way of pride, pettiness, jealousy and dissatisfaction. "It's just the way things are," Hank observed. "That's why nobody stays on top forever."

"Hey, when you're winning, it always seems easy," Cal agreed. "In fact, you start wondering what the hell's wrong with everybody else."

"What about when you're losing?" I had to ask.

Cal thought about it for a minute while Big Ed bought another round. "When you're losing, you just try harder, that's all," Cal answered evenly. "But it seems like the harder you try, the harder everything gets."

"It's almost like there's a rhythm and melody to it when you're doing well," Hank added in a dreamy, faraway voice. You could see he was getting a little plastered. "And when you lose that magic, there's just no way to force your way back again…."

"I'll drink to that," Cal agreed, lifting his glass. But he only took a sip.

Then the guy at the bar called for *"BAUMSTEIN!"* and we all filed into the noisy, bustling, caramel-colored Seneca Lodge dining hall with its high ceilings and varnished log cabin walls and roof beams. It was a friendly, familiar and nostalgic place for all of us, and naturally it didn't hurt at all that we'd been through four rounds of pre-dinner cocktails (all except Cal, that is) plus another round with our appetizers and salads followed by a few bottles of beer with our steaks, green beans, grilled mushrooms, onion rings and baked potatoes. The food tasted great as always and there was a lot of fun and laughter in that room, and it could really get under your skin if you let it. And we did.

Big Ed and Cal and even Carson jerked me around about my Alfa project and I ribbed Cal right back about being stuck in mid-pack and off his usual best on the racetrack that day. *"Or that's what it looked like to me, anyway,"* I told him. At first he looked surprised and maybe even a little hurt. That caught me off guard, since you could usually shoot an arrow point-blank into a guy like Cal Carrington and not even leave a mark. No question Cal had changed a lot over the past few years. Gotten a little smoother and tougher and smarter on the outside but maybe a little softer and more vulnerable on the inside. Maybe even matured, as unlikely as that seemed. Like Hank once said: *"With experience comes wisdom, but you usually get its three ugly stepsisters—Doubt, Hesitation and Uncertainty—right along with it."* That thought sent a quick chill up my spine, since you don't really want to see that sort of thing happening to your friends. And even more especially to your heroes. But then that sly, familiar cobra smile creased its way across Cal's face and the old, smartass gleam I hadn't seen for so long flickered up again in his eyes.

"You just pay attention tomorrow, when it counts," he said through a self-assured grin. "I'm planning on surprising a few people." And with that he excused himself and headed off to get some sleep.

"He never used to do that," Big Ed grumbled as we wandered back into the bar after dessert. "Hell, he used to close the fucking place down with us. And then we'd go down the road to the next place and close that one down, too. And then he'd go out and beat the pants off everybody the next morning." Big Ed'd had himself a few gin-and-tonics, even though he wasn't supposed to. But it didn't look like they were doing him any harm. In fact, much the opposite. And for some reason, I wasn't worried about him or that something bad was going to happen. But then, I'd had a few myself, you know?

Big Ed bought us all another round and raised his glass as soon as it arrived. He smiled as his eyes swept slowly around the Seneca bar, and you could almost see tears welling up in them. "We used to have us a hell of a good time up here, didn't we?"

"We sure did," we all agreed.

"Here's to it."

"Here's to it."

"May you get what you want."

"May you want what you get."

The smile on Big Ed's face slowly faded. "Jesus, when the hell did it all get s'damn *serious?"*

"When it got *serious,"* Hank answered importantly, his head bobbing up-and-down like drunks do. He'd been pouring 'em down pretty good ever since we got to the Seneca, which wasn't his usual style. But I guess he still hadn't heard anything about his book from his agent or the publishers—not a word—and on top of that it'd been a long, depressing month for just about everybody. So there was a lot to forget. And it'd also been a long, long time since we'd all been around a table at the Seneca Lodge together, so there was a lot to remember, too. To tell the truth, I'd rarely seen Hank get himself shit-faced. Hardly ever, in fact. But now he was getting into that deep, meandering, grandly philosophical state drunks have a habit of falling into as the evening wears on. He was rotating his empty beer bottle around in front of him like some kind of alcoholic lighthouse, staring at the front and back labels as they went by. *"This all came out wrong,"* he announced somberly.

"What came out wrong?"

"This!" He waved his hand around the table so it included just about everything. "This season. This weekend. Our friends' lives and futures. It all came out wrong."

"Whaddaya mean?" Big Ed asked as he passed around some more beers.

Hank drained about a third of his in one long swallow. "Things just never come out like you picture them. Never how you want them to be. I mean, if *I* was writing this, it would've all come out right."

"You thinking about writing about it?"

"Another novel?"

Hank stared at me around both sides of his beer bottle. "Not a *novel,"* he corrected me. "This one'd have to be a screenplay."

"A what?" Big Ed asked.

"A screenplay! A screenplay!" Hank insisted. "Every waiter and cab driver in Los Angeles has a fucking screenplay." He glared at Big Ed. "Hell, I was *born* in Los Angeles. Why can't I have one, too?" He was getting belligerent, as drunks often do.

"Hey, who's stopping you?" Big Ed snapped, a little flush of color rising around his neck. Believe me, you don't want to see two friends who've had a little too much to drink start getting into an argument. That can get ugly in no time at all.

"What's the difference between a book and a screenplay anyway?" I interrupted, as much to change the conversation's direction as anything else.

Hank stared at me like I had a brain the size of a pea. "In a screenplay," he explained disdainfully, "everybody gets what they deserve and everything turns out all right in the end."

"But life's not like that," I reminded him.

"Sssurrrre life's not like that," Hank slurred as he rotated his beer bottle lighthouse in front of him. "That's why people go to the fucking movies!" He stopped turning the bottle and started picking at the edges of the label with his fingernails. "There's already enough shit you can't make heads or tails of in real life. Who the hell wants to pay admission to see more of it at the fucking movies?"

Big Ed shot me a pair of raised eyebrows. "Then tell me," he asked Hank, "if you was to write it, how would it come out in the end?"

"Would Toly live?" I wanted to know.

Hank shook his head slowly as he peeled the label off his bottle. "Nah, can't do that," he said, still shaking his head. "Like to, but I can't. Toly's gotta die."

"Why?" we both echoed.

"Y'gotta have a little heartbreak and tragedy," Hank explained without looking up. "That's one of the prime requirements for any Hollywood screenplay. Only it can't happen to the hero, of course…" He wadded up the label between his fingers and flicked it into the ashtray. "Besides, he was sick."

"Sick?" Big Ed asked.

"You sure?"

"Pretty sure," Hank nodded. "Just like his father, I think. The kind of sick you don't get better from." He turned the bottle around and started working on the label on the other side. "And even if he wasn't, what can you do with a character like Toly Wolfgang? Have him ride off by himself into the fucking sunset? That's no way to end a love story."

"So this is a love story?"

Hank thought it over while he worked on the label. "Yeah," he finally sighed, "I guess it is. They're all love stories when you get right down to it…."

Big Ed, Carson and me looked at each other.

"So how does it end?" I asked again.

Hank looked up from the bottle. "I guess I'd have Toly die just like it really happened. Only maybe I wouldn't kill off so many spectators. Or maybe I'd kill off even more. People love all that blood and guts shit. Especially if it's really spectacular and you don't actually see all the gore and broken bodies on camera. You've got to leave the worst of that to the imagination. It's better that way." The back label was gone now, too, and Hank's eyes scanned around the table, looking for another bottle.

"Here, take mine," I said, and pushed it over. He drank what was left in one swallow and started in on the label with his fingernail again. "So what happens after the crash at Monza?" I finally asked.

"Oh, you'd probably have to have the big Hollywood death scene. You know, the one where Cal gets out of his car and runs over and cradles Toly in his arms while Toly asks him to beat Moss in the next race so he can still win the championship…."

"Even though he's dying?"

"Sssurre, even though he's dying!" Hank insisted. "Don't you ever go to the fucking movies? This is a real key moment here. You can always tell by the soft lighting and the music. The actor'll have a black smudge on his cheek and a little blood trickling out of the corner of his mouth—not too much, just a little—and of course he's breathing like his chest got crushed under a road grader..."

"I've *seen* that scene!" I had to laugh.

"At least a hunnert times!" Big Ed agreed.

"…and there's got to be music," Hank continued. "Strings mostly. But piano, too. And right at the end it builds up into this big, swelling crescendo while the camera raises up to show the cars still sliding around the corner and the fans screaming and cheering for more up in the grandstands…."

"I think I've seen that one, too."

Big Ed looked at Hank appreciatively. "Y'know, you're pretty damn good at this shit."

"S'nothing," Hank blushed. "Just a serious oversupply of imagination." He tried taking another swig out of my beer, but it was empty.

Big Ed ordered us another round. Only cocktails again this time. A gin-and-tonic for Big Ed, a rum and coke with a squeeze of lime for me—that was really Julie's drink—and another Black Label and water for Hank. Like he needed it, you know?

"So that's how you end it?" I asked. "With the death scene?"

"Oh, hell no," Hank insisted, waving his hand through the air. "Y'can't have somebody die right at the end. You'll give the audience indigestion. Maybe even nightmares. And besides, the hero's gotta *prove* himself."

"Prove himself?"

"To who?"

Hank looked at the three of us like we'd never gotten out of fourth grade. "Why to himself, of course," he said like it was obvious. "And the girl, too."

"What girl?"

"The girl. There's always a girl. Can't have a movie without one. He's gotta win that last race of the season—beat the best fucking driver in the world!—in order to prove himself to the girl and clinch the World Championship and some small, everlasting sliver of immortality for his friend."

"But his friend is dead," Big Ed reminded him.

"Of course he's dead!" Hank growled impatiently. "That's what makes it such a fucking noble gesture, see."

Well, no question it was all a bunch of high-alcohol-content bullshit. And really pretty damn grim considering what had actually happened. Even so, none of us could wait to hear the rest of it.

Hank took a gulp of his new Johnnie Walker Black and stared off in the distance. "Maybe we'd even have the ghost visit him in the run-up to that final race."

"Toly's ghost?" Big Ed mused. "That sounds like a good title."

"So now it's a ghost story?" Carson wondered.

"Sssurre it's a ghost story!" Hank nodded enthusiastically. "Why the fuck not?" He took another gulp of his whiskey. "Hell, Shakespeare used ghosts all the time! It's a time-honored tradition." By that point, Hank's eyes were wandering off regularly in two different directions.

"How would'ja do it?" Big Ed wanted to know.

"Oh, that's easy. Y'just make it a little creepy, that's all." He thought for a minute. "Let's say fr'instance Toly's car goes under a guardrail in the wreck and it cleaves his head clear off. Like what happened to de Portago on the *Mille Miglia."*

"That's pretty damn gruesome, Hank."

"Suurreee it is! Hell, maybe we even open with that shot—before the credits or anything!" He closed his eyes, and you could see him imagining it all back there somewhere behind his eyelids. "We show the start like some newsreel footage of

the race, see? The cars slipstreaming and battling back-and-forth for the lead. And then we show the crash. And then we follow this fat, roly-poly little photographer scurrying out onto the track to take some horrible pictures of the wreck and the bodies so he can sell 'em to…"

"Eric Gibbon?"

"That's who I see in the part," Hank nodded. "Anyhow, we follow this fat asshole as he runs up to the head—it's just sitting there on the edge of the pavement, upright and all covered in blood with the helmet and goggles still on—only the eyes are still open and alive behind the shattered lenses and the lips are twitching and moving like it's trying to say something. Only no words are coming out because its fucking larynx is still 20 yards up the road with the rest of the body…"

"Jesus Christ, Hank!" I almost screamed. *"That's horrible!"*

"It's okay! It's okay!" he insisted drunkenly. "We'll shoot it like we're looking through the camera's viewfinder, see. Have it go all artsy black-and-white again, so the blood won't really show."

"It's still pretty damn grisly," I told him.

"Sure it is!" he nodded enthusiastically. "That's what it's supposed to be! We're trying to make a hit movie here."

"Who's gonna star in this fucking picture?" Big Ed asked. "Vincent Price?"

"He'd be good," Hank answered seriously. "But he's way too tall."

"And ain't cuttin' his head off gonna make that death scene where his pal cradles him in his arms a little messy?" Big Ed argued.

"No! No! That's the other movie!" Hank snapped back at him. *"This one is the ghost story."* He looked at us like we were stupid again.

"So then what happens?" I had to ask.

"Well, let's say the ghost comes to him in his hotel room. The night before the final race, right? Only you don't know if it's a real ghost or just some sort of terrible nightmare. That's real important because a lot of people don't believe in ghosts."

"Do you believe in ghosts?"

"I'm a Hollywood screenwriter here," Hank explained. "The only thing I believe in is selling screenplays…."

At that point Hank laid his head down on the table and looked like he was about to fall asleep.

"Hey, you can't nod off yet!" I yelled at him, and gave his shoulder a rough shake. *"Y'gotta finish. Y'gotta tell us the rest!"*

Hank's head came up slowly and unsteadily and he looked around like he didn't know exactly where he was. But then took a deep breath, another sip of scotch and continued like he'd never missed a beat: "Well, first off there's gotta be music in the background—piano music, just like the ghost used to play—and of course he's just the way he was when he got killed. He's wearing the driving suit with blood all over the neck and chest and carrying his head tucked underneath his arm like a damn basketball. And it's still got the shattered goggles and the its racing helmet on, of course." It was spooky and just a little sickening how clearly I could see it: the body standing there in light blue, blood-stained Dunlop coveralls carrying Toly's head under its arm—the face as sly, wry and alive as ever, of course—still wearing the broken goggles and that familiar, scraped and stone-chipped black helmet with the faded family crest on the front.

"Jesus, Hank, that's pretty damn horrible," I told him.

"It's supposed to be."

"So what happens then?" Carson asked breathlessly.

Hank allowed himself a satisfied smile. "Oh, the ghost lights itself up a *Gauloises* and smokes it right there under its arm—French inhale and everything—while that haunting, dissonant piano music keeps playing in the background..."

I could see it and hear it, and it was eerie as hell.

"...and then they have a conversation, the hero and the ghost. And the ghost explains about how it had this tragic, incurable disease and about the slow, agonizing death that it would have had to suffer through. So the hero really did him a favor by causing the accident."

"That lets him off the hook, right?"

"Of course it does," Hank nodded. "In the movies, they always make it seem better to go out the express..."

"It's like that in real life, too," Big Ed observed.

"Yeah," Carson agreed solemnly, "only who's ever ready to go?"

Hank silenced them both with a glance. "...Anyhow, then the ghost asks the hero to go out and win that last race—to beat out Moss and Hill and whoever the hell else—so the ghost can win the championship and get him and his family a little gold-plated slice of immortality."

"And of course he does," I added disgustedly, "and everything gets wrapped up in a nice, neat little package."

"Not so fast!" Hank growled at me. "Not so fast...You forget, there's still the love angle to work out...."

"So now it's a love story again?"

"It's always been a love story!" Hank snarled. "Only the hero and the heroine have never been able to find the time and space to make it happen, see? They're too busy with their lives and careers...."

"This isn't *like* real life," I told Hank, "it *is* real life!"

"With ghosts?" Big Ed asked.

He had me there.

"So what happens then?" we all needed to know.

"Well, it comes down to the last race of the season, of course—right here at Watkins Glen!—and the hero out-qualifies his teammates..."

"So Ferrari's here?"

Hank stared at us. "Of course Ferrari's here! What the hell kind of Grand Prix would you have without Ferrari?"

Big Ed, Carson and me looked at each other.

"So the hero out-qualifies his teammates?" I prodded to get him going again.

Hank nodded. "But he's behind Moss in the V-8 Climax…"

"He'll never make the bloody finish!" one of the eavesdropping BRM mechanics from the next table over tossed in, and the rest of them laughed. Hank had gathered up quite a little audience for himself.

Big Ed glared at them. But we didn't have to prod Hank at all to get him started again. He was rolling: "…So the race starts and at first our hero drops back a few spots because he's too anxious with the clutch and throttle off the line. But the Ferrari's got the power and he's got the bit between his teeth, and he picks off Clark and Brabham and then his teammates one right after the other. But he's still got Moss running out in front of him. The best fucking driver in the world! And he tries and he tries, but he can't seem to close the gap. In fact, it even looks like Moss may be inching away from him!"

"All the blokes know what *that* one feels like!" one of the BRM guys from the next table observed.

"Does he catch him?" Big Ed wanted to know.

"Well, he's driving for all he's worth, but he's not making much of an impression on Moss. And then he looks in his mirror, and here comes this red #4 Ferrari with Toly's helmet in it, closing in on him from the rear. And so he starts driving harder and harder to get away from it, but even so it's getting closer and closer until he can see the determined sneer on the face and the fierce look in the eyes right through the shattered goggles—why, they're glowing like hot coals!—and it's almost right on top of him when suddenly…." Hank stopped and let it dangle there for a moment while his eyes made a lap around the table. I swear, you could've heard a damn pin drop!

"Jesus, Hank!" Big Ed demanded.

"C'mon, Hank!" I almost begged.

"What in bloody hell happens?" the BRM mechanic and his pals at the next table wanted to know.

A wicked storyteller's smile blossomed across Hank's face. "Why, the same thing that would happen in real life, of course!" he said simply.

"But what's that?" we all said in unison.

"Moss' Climax V-8 overheats, of course."

There was an audible groan from the next table.

"So Cal wins the race?"

"And Toly wins the championship?"

Hank rubbed his jaw, looking vaguely unsatisfied. "I think it needs just one more twist," he said thoughtfully. "Why don't we make it so that if our hero wins the race and also scores the point for fastest lap, then *he* beats out the ghost for the championship!"

"They don't give out points for fastest lap anymore," I pointed out.

"Does a movie audience know that?"

"But that means you gotta go all the way back to the beginning t'change everything!" Big Ed groused.

Hank smiled at him. "In real life, yes. In a novel, yes. But this is a Hollywood screenplay. We wouldn't even need a fucking eraser…."

"So what finally happens?" I wanted to know.

"Oh, this part almost writes itself. Let's say our hero cuts the fastest lap while he's chasing after Moss and being chased by the ghost in the phantom Ferrari. And he knows it because the team manager showed it to him on the pit board. So now he's got the lead and he knows he's got the point for fastest lap and it's just a few laps from the end and he's gotta figure out what the hell he's going to do. If he just stays out there, he's going to win the race and become World Champion—at his dead friend's expense, of course—and that's when…." Hank paused one more time to let us all twist in the wind.

"When *what??!!"* I just about screamed.

"What the hell happens?!" Big Ed bellowed.

"How's it end?!" the gents at the next table demanded.

Hank gave us another slow, self-satisfied smile. "That's when he pulls into the pits and retires, doing the first selfless thing he's ever done in his life and handing his dead friend the World Championship on a silver platter."

Big Ed, Carson and me looked at each other, blinking. It was perfect.

"And that's it?"

"Not quite."

"Who wins the bloody race?" the English mechanics wanted to know.

Hank picked up his Johnny Walker Black, looked into it fondly and drained the last quarter-inch. "When our hero pulls in, of course the mechanics and the team manager are all over him, screaming at him in English and Italian and wanting to know what went wrong. But he just calmly switches off and climbs up out of the car. By that point the team manager is right in his face—nose to nose as soon as he's got his fucking helmet off!—demanding to know what broke and why the hell he pulled in. But the hero just looks at him and says: *'Sorry, I just don't feel up to winning today.'* Then he drops his helmet and goggles into the seat and walks away…."

"And that's *it?"* I asked.

"No, there's one more little bit. You always need something small and light right at the end to keep the audience happy." Hank looked at me with those dreamy, far-away eyes. "And that's where *you* come in."

"Me?"

Hank nodded. "Right after he walks away from the car, the hero comes looking for you—his old, trusted friend, confidant and sidekick."

"For what?" Big Ed wanted to know.

"Why, to borrow a little loose change so he can call his girlfriend out in California, of course…."

It took a moment for the image to sink in. "That's almost *too* realistic," I laughed, and tilted my glass in Hank's direction.

"We still want to know who won the bloody Grand Prix!" the guys at the next table insisted.

"Oh, I don't know," Hank sighed, looking very sleepy indeed. "Take your pick."

"But it's your bloody story, mate!"

"All right. All right." Hank closed his eyes and thought for a moment. "Why not make it Innes Ireland for Team Lotus? Neither of them has ever won a Grand Prix. And everyone says Chapman's yanking his ride for next year anyway. It'd be just desserts for all the effort he's put in and all the wheels coming off and retirements he's suffered through at Lotus. I've always thought of Ireland as a kind of monument to all the gutsy Hard Tryers of this world."

"Ireland?" one of the guys at the next table said incredulously.

"Team Lotus?" another one chimed in.

The first BRM mechanic turned to his friends: *"Y'see, I told you it was all a bloody fiction!"*

As you can imagine, we had to damn near set off a bomb to get Hank out of bed and over to the track the next morning. He looked just terrible, and spent most of the day sitting in the front passenger seat of Big Ed's Jaguar with the door wide open for a little fresh air and to give him an easy shot at the ground whenever he felt sick. Which was often. I borrowed his press pass and made the runs to the tower to pick up the latest timing sheets for him, and the only real news was that Moss elected to use the proven four-cylinder engine in his Lotus instead of trusting that prone-to-overheating new Climax V-8 like the one Brabham was stuck with over in the Cooper team. That turn of events left Brabham on the pole, an up-and-coming Graham Hill in the quickly improving V-8 BRM, Moss in the four-cylinder Walker Lotus, McLaren, Clark, Brooks in the second BRM and then Gurney and Bonnier in the Porsches split by Ireland in the second Team Lotus entry. And then came Cal, who did indeed come through with a hell of an effort in a second-tier car, putting it at the head of the privateer list and just a heartbeat behind the second drivers on the full factory teams. Sure, we wanted him to do better, but it was really all you could hope for in real life.

We made an easy and early night of it on Saturday—that's one of the inevitable penalties for going way over the edge on Friday—and the race on Sunday started out exciting but then degenerated into another one of those dull, droning, stretched-out processions where the great majority of position changes come from retirements rather than racing. At the start Moss rocketed away to grab the lead, but Brabham battled back in the V-8 Cooper and those two put on a hell of a great show until a little past half-distance, swapping the lead back and forth several times to the great delight of the somewhat disappointing but highly enthusiastic Glen crowd. And

Ireland, who had certainly heard the rumors and was surely feeling pressure on his job, fought his way through from eighth qualifying spot to take a strong third position behind that riveting Moss/Brabham duel.

And then it all fell apart. Brabham's Climax V-8 started overheating again and he had to pull in and retire, and 12 laps later Moss was also out with mechanical problems. That left Innes Ireland firmly in the lead, but he was having fuel pressure problems and you could hear that his engine wasn't running right. But he was doing better than the guys chasing him, as Graham Hill had the BRM's magneto fall off just when it looked like he was closing in on the Lotus, and then damn if it wasn't our boy Cal in second place, well behind but cutting three- four- and even five-second chunks out of Ireland's lead every lap. Cal was driving the snot out of that Cooper—and you could see it, too!—right on the smooth, brilliant, perfectly judged edge of control and physics at every braking point, turn-in, apex and corner exit. He was running it right to the redline (and maybe even a little past?) in every gear and turning qualifying times every single lap, and we were frantically clicking our stopwatches and doing the calculations in our heads and on the tips of our fingers, figuring what it would take and how many laps were left and moreover what a huge, enormous deal it would be if Cal Carrington won the damn race in Briggs Cunningham's blue-and-white, American-entered privateer Cooper! An American—and a local guy at that!—winning the first-ever United States Grand Prix at Watkins Glen? Why, it was too much to even hope for….

And of course it was. With just a few laps to go, Cal's car failed to come around on schedule. There was just this empty hole where the white Cooper should have been and a silence as loud as a damn freight train passing by. Hank and me looked at each other. And with every passing heartbeat our expressions got deeper, darker and more concerned. But then we heard it: the flat, backfiring, party-razzberry exhaust note of a four-cylinder engine running on just three. Or maybe even two. The Cooper appeared at the far end of the straightaway—just a tiny white speck in the distance, really—trundling slowly around the bottom of the banked horseshoe bend with a trail of bluish-white smoke streaming out the exhaust pipe. And then the sound cut completely as Cal switched off and pulled onto the grass, done for the day.

Naturally we tried to make out way up to him, but by the time we got close the race was over, Ireland had won his and Team Lotus' first-ever Grand Prix victory (and probably figured that his job was now secure) and the towtruck had arrived to haul Cal and his dead Cooper back to the paddock. So we headed back to the paddock ourselves, and found Cal sitting in a lawn chair with an unopened beer in his hand, looking neither happy, sad, angry, disappointed or disgusted. In fact, there was no expression on his face at all. "That was a heck of a nice drive," I told him.

"It was okay," he said, his eyes a million miles away.

"You damn near pulled it off."

"Yep," he agreed without emotion. "It was a pretty good run there for awhile." He opened his beer and took a tiny sip, made a face like it tasted terribly bitter and set it down. He looked absolutely drained.

"Everybody thought you did a great job," Carson said encouragingly.

"Hey," Cal answered with just the tiniest hint of his old, cobra smile curling up at the corners of his mouth. "That's what I'm here for."

I rummaged in my pocket for a handful of change and held it out to him. "You wanna call Gina?" I asked.

He cocked his head towards me. "How'd you know?"

I pulled my shoulders up in a minor-league version of a New Jersey shrug. "Just a lucky guess…."

Chapter 44: A Race Dance at Lime Rock Park

Back at *Alfredo's,* my Alfa racecar project was progressing along nicely. In fact, I had just about everything finished, figured out and buttoned up except for what color I ought to paint it. I didn't particularly like the smoke-damaged robin's-egg blue, and I was kind of split right down the middle between brilliant Italian red and a sinister, glistening black. With white, offset number circles in either case, of course. And naturally I asked Steve and J.R. and Butch and Big Ed and Carson and even Sylvester when he came in for their opinion, and even more naturally it was likewise split right down the middle between the red and the black. Except for Big Ed, who thought it ought to be bright school-bus yellow. I guess the lesson here is that you really shouldn't ask anybody what color you ought to paint your new race-car, because it never accomplishes anything except getting you more confused.

The big fly in the ointment was that I still hadn't quite gotten around to mentioning my plans to run the Alfa in the SCMA Drivers' School and Regional Race up at Lime Rock to Julie, and it was starting to worry me quite a bit what she might have to say. I mean, the last thing in the world I wanted was to get into a big argument with her over it. Or, worse yet, her *and* her mother. I never seemed to come out ahead on those deals, even when I felt absolutely, positively certain that I was right. Or at least not wrong, you know? Sure, I'd had thoughts about simply sneaking off for the weekend under some lame cover story like I was just going to help out some of the other guys, but no question she'd find out what really happened sooner or later, and that would be the end of my so-called racing career right then and there. She'd make sure of it, just out of spite. And I'd really kind of deserve it for sneaking around on her in the first place, if you know what I mean.

But the notion of just casually mentioning it to her some morning over coffee or evening after dessert made my palms sweat and chills go up and down my spine. In fact, confronting Julie with my racing plans was far more unnerving than the thought of actually strapping myself into the Alfa and venturing out on the racetrack for the very first time. Why, it wasn't even close….

With barely 10 days to go, I finally concocted a scheme. It started with buying us a couple tickets to see Julie Newmar in a dinner theater production of *Damn Yankees* over in Cedar Grove on Saturday night. I could see by Julie's eyes she knew something was up. *"So what's this all about?"* she asked like I was plotting the assassination of President Lincoln.

"Why, nothing," I lied unconvincingly. "I just thought, you know, what with you letting me go up to Watkins Glen with the guys and all, that maybe you deserved a little night out on the town, too…."

She gave me the look all wives seem to have that says: *'Okay, Buster, but don't think for one minute I'm buying it!'*

So we got all dressed up and Big Ed lent me his new Jag sedan for old time's sake and we left the kids with her mother and my folks came over, too, and they all had take-out pizza from Pete and Pasquale's Palermo Room while we went out to the show. And it was pretty good, too. Even though I had mistakenly assumed it was a musical comedy about the Civil War, not baseball. But I guess it would be kind of tough to script a musical comedy around the battles of Gettysburg and Bull Run or General Sherman's march to the sea. Anyhow, it was really about how the underdog Washington Senators beat the New York Yankees in the World Series thanks to a deal this long-suffering Senators fan makes with the devil. And that was quite a timely tonic for me seeing as how the Yankees had just wrapped up their 17th World Series championship only a week or so before, and my insanely rabid Yankee-fan father would not let you, me or anyone else on the planet forget it. You know how he always was about the damn Yankees. So it was really a pretty good show and I actually enjoyed it very much. Especially the hot, steamy *"Whatever Lola Wants"* number Julie Newmar did in a rather skin-tight, undersized and revealing costume that had my own Julie elbowing me in the ribs on account of my eyes were about stuck out on stalks.

But all through the dinner and dessert and coffee and even later during the show's intermission, I just couldn't find the right moment, words, or get up the stones to tell Julie about my racing plans. So now we were on our way home and it was damn near boiling up inside me like steam in a pressure cooker. I was desperate, and yet I still couldn't seem to find the right words or approach to get the subject rolling. Hell, this was harder than asking her to marry me, you know? And no question she could tell I was stewing in my own damn juices, too. Wives have a real sixth sense about that sort of thing.

"You have something you want to tell me?" she finally asked about three blocks from our house. She had this mysterious smile on her face that reminded me of the bright, gleaming edge on a good butcher knife.

"Uhh…yeah…kinda…" I more or less mumbled.

"Something like that you've been building that Alfa Romeo into a racecar over at the shop, and that you want to go through Drivers' School and race it up at Lime Rock next weekend?"

My jaw fell open until it landed on the knot in my tie. "H-how the heck did *you* know?" I stammered.

Her smile opened up even wider. Only now I could see it was a friendly one, and a huge wave of relief rolled over me. "Big Ed and Carson told me," she laughed. "I know all about it."

"And you're n-not *mad??!!"*

"Why should I be?" she asked, patting me on the arm. "I think I can trust you not to do anything stupid."

"Y-you CAN?" This was not what I'd expected.

Julie nodded. "Big Ed and Carson talked it over with me. Oh, I was a little upset about it at first. But they brought me around. They convinced me you'd be careful and use your head. And also that you maybe deserve this…"

"I D-DO?" I couldn't believe what I was hearing, you know?

"Yeah," Julie said, giving me a light jab in the ribs with her elbow, "I really think you do."

I didn't know what to say.

"I-I don't know what to say," I told her.

She shrugged like it was nothing and gave my arm a nice squeeze. "There's just one thing...."

'Uh-oh,' I thought, *'here it comes!'* I had this premonition like I'd accidentally wandered under the shadow of the world's biggest sledgehammer, only I couldn't for the life of me figure out what Julie was thinking. "What've you got in mind?" I finally asked.

"No big thing. You've just gotta let *me* take the Alfa Romeo through drivers' school next spring."

The hammer slammed down, but the blow wasn't anything like I expected. *"Wh-WHAT??!!"* I gasped.

"You heard me. You've got to let *me* take it through drivers' school next spring. And maybe even try racing it if I want to...."

I couldn't believe my ears. *"Y-you really WANT to?"*

"Sure. Why not?" She shot me a pirate wink. "It's not fair that you should have all the fun."

Well, needless to say I agreed enthusiastically, wholeheartedly and immediately. And then I couldn't wait to pull into our driveway and stop the car so's I could kiss her and kiss her again and kiss her a few times more after that and then wrap her up in my arms with our mouths and lips and hands all over each other until we were grabbing and groping and kissing and hugging and petting and pawing and getting ourselves all stretched out and twisted up together on that Jaguar sedan's front seat like a couple high school kids at the drive-in. Or at least until Julie got her damn high heel caught in the horn ring, anyway. And I mean jammed right in—*stuck!*—so's it wouldn't turn off. As you can imagine, that jerked us upright in a pretty big hurry. Just in time to see Julie's mom and my folks and all three of the kids looking out at us through the living room and bedroom windows, in fact. Not to mention the neighbors all up and down the street.

If you must know, it was just a little bit embarrassing.

I got to the shop Monday morning to find that Steve, J.R., Sylvester and the Greek from the body shop had quietly come in over the weekend and sanded, masked and painted the Alfa for me. But they'd split it right down the middle and painted it gleaming lipstick red on the driver's side and glistening midnight black on the other. Just so's I could see what both colors looked like and make up my mind, you know? It was quite a surprise, and an even bigger surprise to find out that Julie'd put them up to it behind my back. So all I had to do was pick which side I liked better and then they'd re-paint the other one to match and we'd be ready to have this sign painter Big Ed knew come in and do the number circles and detailing. Only the longer I stared at it, the better I liked it just the way it was. "All we need is maybe a narrow little racing stripe right down the middle to separate the red from the black," I told them. So they had the sign-painter guy come in and put a perfect little Italian tricolor racing stripe down the center with a thin gold pinstripe on either side, and then he added offset white number circles on the hood and deck with perfect little gold pinstripes around them plus small, gold *"Alfredo's Sports Car Service"* lettering on the front fenders and *"Buddy and Julie"* with a tiny heart dotting the *"i"* along the top edge of the driver's-side door. It looked pretty damn swell, if you want the truth of it.

As you can imagine, I was pretty damn excited about going up to that first-ever race and driving school at Lime Rock. Even though I'd been around the sport from just about as far back as I could remember and considered myself something of an old hand. But believe me, it sure feels different when you're the one who's going to be climbing behind the wheel! We'd decided that I'd tow up on Friday afternoon in a sort-of Rig Caravan with Carson (who had taken to pulling the trailer with his Healey 3000 on it with one of the family funeral home's semi-retired Cadillac hearses) and that he'd help get me through the drivers' school on Saturday and then we'd more or less crew for each other on Sunday. Big Ed and Julie and the kids and Sarah Jean and Carson's kids and maybe even Butch and my Aunt Rosamarina and Mary Frances and Pauly Martino were all planning to come up and join us on Sunday (along with a huge, sort-of potluck picnic lunch, of course) and we'd all make a day of it together. And the weather cooperated, too, what with cool but sunny fall skies and all the leaves turned those gorgeous golds and reds and russets and yellows and oranges like you see on all the fall picture postcards and seasonal Chamber of Commerce brochures up in that part of Connecticut.

We got in late Friday night and bunked in at a quaint, charming and thoroughly overpriced little broken-down country inn not far from the racetrack that was justly famous for its coffee and breakfast pastries, thin walls, bad plumbing, creaky wooden floors and naked 100-watt light bulbs over the sinks in the bathrooms. There wasn't even a radio in our room, but we got a nice hour-and-a-half show from the room down at the end of the hall where some fortunate gent was getting incredibly lucky.

Imagine my surprise the next morning when I stepped out in the hall just in time to see a terrifically relaxed-looking Creighton Pendleton the Third and one of the barely college-age waitresses from the White Hart Inn coming out of that room down the hall. She was a tall, pretty, athletic-looking girl in that kind of preppy, jeans-and-Weejuns/little-silver-hoop-earrings/No-Obvious-Makeup style that's so popular up in Connecticut. Creighton gave me about a one-quarter-inch nod of recognition as he passed by in the hall, and I watched her long, dark blond ponytail bounce and bob up and down (along with those two fascinating things inside her black turtleneck) as she followed him silently down the stairs.

"I wonder what the hell he's doing up here?" I said to nobody in particular.

"You heard what he was doing for more than an hour last night!" Carson snickered. I guess that was about the funniest and raciest thing I'd ever heard him say.

We arrived at the track a little before 8 and got the cars unloaded and the Alfa through tech inspection, and that's when I had to decide what car number I wanted. I hadn't really thought much about it, but Carson was quick to remind me that you could make anything with a "1," a "4" or a "7" in it out of straight-cut pieces of tape or contact paper, while all the other numbers took a steady hand and a little artistic talent or they looked like what you generally see on some six-year-old's lemonade stand. Plus if you're up for a Drivers' School/First Race weekend, you pretty much have to take whatever's left over after all the regulars have entered for Sunday's race. Turns out "1" was open, but I always thought it was kind of brash and cheeky to put a "1" on your racecar unless you'd already won a championship or something. And naturally "7," "11" and "77" were already spoken for. But nobody had "74," so that's what I picked. And I did a pretty damn good job of laying those numbers out with some black tape and a razor blade, if I do say so myself. And I do.

Then there was barely time to check the fluids and the tire pressures before they called us to this meeting under the starter's stand at the start/finish line where the head instructor—some flinty-eyed little Scotsman in a green Tam o'Shanter cap named Gordon MacKenzie—went over the school schedule and the rules of the road and the location of the corner stations and what the flags all meant. Of course I already knew most of that stuff, but it all tends to take on a different sort of meaning when you're going out on the track yourself for the very first time. And imagine my surprise when I discovered I none other than our old moans, squeals, grunts and bed-banging-against-the-wall-at-the-end-of-the-hall buddy Creighton Pendleton the Third as my blessed driving instructor! Can you believe it? But he gave me a full half-inch nod of recognition when we got paired off and he was actually pretty nice about it. Even if he did still sound like an arrogant, spoiled, stuck-up, down-your-nose, cake-eating son-of-a-bitch now and then. But I guess guys like him just can't help it, you know? It's the way they were brought up. Along with a dash or two of prep school plus way too much money and privilege and nobody around to call "bullshit" on them when they're growing up and sorely need it. I believe that kind of upbringing tends to do something to the posture of a person's nose.

Next up were "Station Wagon Runs" to show all of us rookies the proper line around Lime Rock Park, and Creighton the Third was naturally there with his new white Ferrari Pininfarina 250GT coupe (which most likely played a key supporting role in landing that tall, pretty young girl with the ponytail the night before), so he borrowed Carson's Cadillac hearse to take me and a couple other students around the track. I of course grabbed the shotgun seat while the other guys climbed and clambered in back (where, to be honest, there really isn't a lot of stuff to hang onto or brace yourself against in a Cadillac hearse) and off we went.

I couldn't believe how different Lime Rock looked from inside a car out on the racetrack. Even a blessed Cadillac hearse! I could see right away that the safe, open, plenty-of-room-to-screw-up feeling you got through Big Bend and the left-hander that followed quickly evaporated as soon as you went through the tricky little humpbacked right onto No Name Straight. From that point on, the track got a whole lot faster, what felt like a whole lot narrower and incredibly less forgiving with every heartbeat and bend in the road.

"Momentum is the key here at Lime Rock," Creighton told us as he lurched the big Caddy hearse almost sideways and hurled it into The Uphill. I could feel my breakfast doing about the same and all the other students' legs bracing and hands hanging on for dear life on the seatback behind me, and I was sure their stomachs were feeling every bit as queasy and uneasy as my own. "You have to be a little careful here," Creighton said casually as that big, long Cadillac wheezed and careened its way towards West Bend. "If you're going to lift here, do it before the corner and then get back on the power to stabilize things through the turn. If you wait until you get *into* the corner to decide to back off, you're most likely going to wind up in the barriers over there," he pointed to a little dirt embankment dead ahead with a piece of scarred guardrail and some stacks of old tires in front of it, "or you'll go off and try to catch it and wind up shooting back across the track and into the barriers over there," he pointed to some more heavily dimpled guardrail on the other side of the road, "and very possibly upside down…."

Now there was a comforting thought!

Then he grabbed himself a smooth, sudden handful of steering lock and heaved that big Caddy into West Bend without hardly touching the brakes! My fingernails dug into the armrest upholstery and I swear that car damn near went up on two wheels as Creighton wallowed and squealed and sashayed it across the apex on the inside and then half-slid/half-squirmed it back across the pavement to the opposite side on four howling, overloaded whitewalls. *Wow!* But there wasn't even time to shake my head in wonder, since we were now approaching an absolutely blind crest with nothing but fall-color treetops ahead of it at what felt like an astonishingly high rate of speed.

"Now *this,"* Creighton continued calmly as we rocketed over the top and plunged downhill at an impossibly steep angle, "is the most important corner on the entire track here at Lime Rock. You really want to get this one right. Get the car gathered up and get on the power early in order to get maximum drive out onto the pit straight. It's the only way you'll ever pass anyone here." And with that he rolled on about seven-eighths of a full turn of steering and heeled that big Caddy halfway over onto its rocker panels while I held the armrest in a death grip and braced for the impact that never came….

That guy could really drive, no lie!

I felt the automatic kick down into passing gear for a second as we wheezed and groaned our way onto the front straight with Creighton's right foot buried into the floor carpeting, but then it kind of slipped its way back into Drive and we were suddenly surrounded by the kind of high-speed silence and serenity you might expect inside a fine Cadillac hearse. "Driving is more like dancing than anything else," Creighton explained like he'd said it a million times before. "And I mean graceful, elegant, ballroom dancing like we always had at the cotillions, not that twisting, awkward, hopping-around jive stuff like the high school kids do." He looked over at me for a moment, and for a change only halfway down his nose. "The car is your partner, and you've got to lead it along gently and treat it properly like you would any other dance partner. At least if you want to get the very best out of it."

By then we were hurtling into Big Bend again, and I went from listening to mostly just trying to hang on. And then, halfway through the left-hander, one of the guys in back got sick all over the other guy in back. As you can imagine, Creighton the Third pulled in at the end of the lap and promptly returned the car to Carson. "Thanks so very much," he told Carson airily. "And I'd suggest you'll want to leave the windows down for a little while...."

After the station wagon runs we had a break while the guys in the Formula Cars and the guys with the big V-8s and the modified cars went out for their sessions, and then it was our turn again. First we took the Alfa out with Creighton driving and me riding shotgun—he scared the living shit out of me, and I think on purpose!—and then we came in and switched around so I got a turn at the wheel with him in the passenger seat. On the one hand I wanted to impress him and maybe even get back at him a little for damn near making me crap my pants in the Cadillac. But on the other I was pretty damn nervous, worried, uncertain and intimidated by the whole thing. Not to mention that I really wanted to pass the school, you know?

I tried to do what Creighton had showed me and just follow the proper line, but it embarrassed me more than a little that I was backing out of it, braking and even downshifting for corners he was taking damn near flat-out in third. Or even top. But I must've been doing okay, because at the end of the session he climbed out, gave me the closest thing to a genuine smile I'd ever seen out of him and said: *"You're on your own now. And you're doing just fine."*

He might as well have pinned a damn medal of honor on my chest, you know?

Well, I passed the school and so I was automatically eligible for the race the next day, and that night Carson and me went over to The White Hart in Salisbury for a pair of fat, juicy cheeseburgers and a few celebratory beers. We got that tall, pretty girl with the small hoop earrings who'd spent the previous night making jungle music with Creighton Pendleton down at the end of the hall as our waitress, only now she was wearing this kind of scoop-necked black leotard top and matching black stockings with a red plaid skirt. She immediately had us pegged for nobodies and acted like she'd never seen either one of us before, and that was fine with Carson and me so long as she kept bending over to drop off rounds of drinks or pick up dirty dishes and ashtrays. It was a hell of a nice view when she did.

The White Hart was filling up more and more with racing people as the evening wore on, and I had to remind myself over and over again to go easy on the booze and beer on account of it was race day tomorrow and I really wanted to be at my best and sharpest. Although that can get hard to do when rounds are being bought and there's racing chatter going on all around you and there's this waitress coming around who makes you squirm in your chair every time she bends over. But we did our best, and I'm proud to say Carson and me left the White Hart a good solid half-hour before closing time and managed to walk all the way from our parking spot outside to our upstairs room at the inn without hardly stumbling or falling down much at all. Although I guess we did leave the car with one of its back wheels kind of parked in the goldfish pond….

Sunday morning kicked off with a little pre-sunrise matinee encore performance going on in Creighton Pendleton's room at the end of the hall. At right around five ayem, you know? Only this time the voice doing all the little bite-your-lip squeals, gasps, squawks and shrieks was different. And I recognized it immediately. *"Jesus Christ, that's Sally Enderle's voice!"* I whispered through clenched teeth.

"I don't know why you're bothering to whisper," he observed candidly, "they sure as hell aren't…."

He had a point there.

Well, naturally neither of us could get back to sleep, so we took a couple Anacin apiece with a glass of bicarb for a chaser, showered, dressed, went down by the kitchen to see about a couple cups of coffee to go and headed for the racetrack. The sun was just coming up over the green and red and russet and orange and gold of fall in the Berkshires, and no question it was going to be another brilliant, bright and scrumptiously beautiful fall day. Inside the track we tidied up our area in the paddock and got all the folding chairs and tables set up, and I'm glad we did because not long after first practice our friends and families started showing up. And I mean *everybody.* Including Julie and the kids and her mother and Sarah Jean and her kids and my mom and dad and Big Ed and Steve and J.R. and Butch and my Aunt Rosamarina and my sister Mary Frances and her Pauly Martino and even Sam and Irma Green from over in Eastchester, N.Y., who once bought a VW bus from Big Ed back when we owned the dealership. Not to mention—and much to my surprise!—none other than Cal Carrington and Gina LaScala! Which, as you can surely imagine, created quite a bit of foot traffic congestion plus an awful lot of head-swiveling and walking into things around our paddock space. *"Jesus, what the hell are you two doing here?"* I yelped as I gave them both a big hug. *"I thought you were supposed to be racing at Laguna Seca this weekend."*

"The gearbox broke at Riverside," Cal said kind of sheepishly. "There weren't any parts to fix it and Gina had to come to New York for this thing on Monday anyway, so I figured, you know, what the hell?"

"Jeez, it's *great* to see you two!" I looked at Cal and then over at Gina. God, was she ever beautiful! Why, it almost boiled the glop in your eyeballs just to look at her. And they made a hell of a handsome-looking couple, too. "You know everybody here?" I asked Gina. And of course everybody who didn't was already lined up in front of her with their jaws dangling open and their eyes bugged out. Including my folks and Julie's mother. So I introduced her all around and Gina was as sweet and patient and pleasant as could be with everybody. Which made me feel pretty damn special, you know? And then I took Cal aside and asked him privately how things were going and how his prospects were looking for next season. "Any word yet from Ferrari?" I asked.

"Nothing to speak of. I know they want me for the sportscar races, so that's something. But no word yet on Formula One."

"So what will you do?"

"Oh, I've had some feelers from other teams. But you really have to be careful about where you wind up when it comes to Formula One. Ferrari hasn't always had the best cars, but at least they don't fall apart underneath you like some others we could both mention."

I knew what he was talking about. "Then what happens if the Ferrari deal falls through and you can't get a good ride someplace else?"

"If I can't get a decent ride, then maybe the smart thing might be to just get out."

"Quit??!!" I couldn't believe my ears! "Wouldn't you miss it?"

"Oh, Jesus *YES* I'd miss it!" he said emphatically. "I'm like an addict, Buddy. I've got to have my speed fix. And—let's face it—this is the only life I really know." He looked me right in the eye. "But you know what Toly always used to say: *'In this game, you either decide to walk away at some point or they wind up carrying you away on a stretcher.'"* He gave his shoulders a little shrug. "That's just the way things are in professional racing."

"But you still love doing it?"

That sly, cobra smile creased its way across his face. "It's the second-best thing I know, Buddy," he said with a wink. "And I'm not even sure I've got the rankings right."

That gave me an idea. *"Lissen,"* I told him, *"if you'd like to step in and drive my car today, that'd be just fine with me."*

"Oh, no," Cal laughed. "You're not getting out of it *that* easy! This is *your* turn to be the big hero driver today. I'm only here for the beer and sandwiches."

"Y'know, I don't feel much like a hero," I admitted to him quietly. And I didn't. In fact, my guts were churning like the inside of a cement truck at that very moment.

"No problem, Buddy," Cal grinned. "Just do what the rest of us do."

"What's that?"

A terribly heavy, serious look drew down over his face like a window shade. He drew in close by my ear and whispered: *"Hey, when you don't feel it—fake it!"* and punctuated with a soft little nudge in the ribs. "Believe me, Buddy, it's good advice."

"Thanks," I told him. And I meant it. Cal sure had a way of taking the edge and awe off of things. But I guess a lifetime of not giving much of a good God damn about anybody or anything probably helped.

A half-hour later I went out for qualifying, and it was really pretty intimidating. But it was also about the most damn fun I'd ever had, trying to go as fast as I dared without worrying about cops or speed limits or oncoming traffic or little old ladies in bifocals creeping unexpectedly out of hidden driveways. I did my best to remember everything everybody had been telling me about staying on the line and watching out for faster cars coming up behind me, and by the end I'd somehow managed to qualify solidly and respectably about three-quarters of the way down on the grid. Which I thought was pretty damn decent for my first-ever race. And particularly with an ordinary, two-barrel-carb Alfa engine under the hood, too.

Around noon the girls put out a big lunch spread with all kinds of Italian-style submarine sandwiches and more different kinds of side dishes, salads, condiments and such than you've ever seen. And meanwhile I stationed myself at the barbecue grill and doled out fat, kosher-style all-beef hot dogs and sirloin hamburgers that Big Ed brought from some deli he knew in Teaneck. Cal wandered over to get a couple for him and Gina, and I asked him again what he planned to do if things didn't exactly work out for him in Europe. And his answer kind of surprised me.

"Oh, maybe I'll find some things to do and cars to race out in California."

"It wouldn't have anything to do with the fact that Gina's out there, would it?"

He shot me a wink. "I suppose the thought has crossed my mind." But then he actually looked a little serious. Or as serious as you could ever expect a guy like Cal to get. "I heard you can get stunt work driving in chases pretty easy, and Gina says I really ought to get a screen test for myself."

"YOU??" I nearly choked. "In the *movies?"*

"Oh, I know I haven't got any acting talent. But maybe I could be just another pretty face, you know?"

I thought it over, and suddenly it didn't seem so far-fetched. I mean, anything was possible in Hollywood so long as you had the right connections. And Lord knows Cal didn't really need the money. "Come to think of it," I told him, "you've been living your life like it's a damn movie for as long as I've known you."

"You see? It makes perfect sense."

"If you say so."

"I heard Bruce Kessler's been doing a bunch of assistant directing in the movie business out there. He says it's almost as interesting and involving as racing."

"And you believe him?"

"Not for a minute," Cal grinned. "But it couldn't hurt to check it out."

"That reminds me: how's Hank doing? You seen him lately?"

"Day before we left. We had dinner with him in Carmel. He came up to cover the races at Laguna for the magazine."

"Any word yet on his book?"

"I guess the agent had some New York publisher a little interested. He said they really liked it. But then they had some big meeting and it turned into the same old shit. *'There's no market for it'* and *'THOSE people don't read!'"*

"That's a damn shame. I sure hope it works out for him."

"Hey, all anyone can do is keep on plugging."

"You throw enough shit at a wall and some of it's bound to stick."

"Well, we all hope it does, anyway."

"Hey, hope's a good thing, too."

"I find I'm counting on it more and more every day...."

Later on I spent a little time with Mary Frances and was pleased to hear that things were going really well so far with her and Pauly. And also that they were thinking about maybe adopting a kid since she couldn't really have any of her own any more. "That's a pretty big step," I advised her cautiously.

"Nah, it's just a whole bunch of little steps all strung together. I think we'll be all right if we do it."

"How about money?"

"How about money!" she shot right back at me. "It's a bitch now and it'll be a bitch if we have a kid. That's just the way things are."

"But you really want to do it?"

She put her hand on my arm. "I really think I do, Buddy. I love working with those kids at school, and I'm sure I could make a really good job of it."

"Well, if that's what you want...."

"That's what I want."

I leaned over and gave her a little peck on the cheek and whispered: *"Well, you know who you can call if the shit hits the fan."*

"Sure," she whispered back, *"Dial-A-Prayer."*

"Hey, that's our number."

I also got a chance to talk with Gina a little. Privately, you know, when Cal went off to the john. "So I understand Cal may be coming out to L.A. if things don't work out for him in Europe for next year."

"That's what he says."

"How do you feel about that?"

"I'm not really sure yet. It sounds great sometimes and sometimes it sounds scary as hell. You have to understand how it is with movie actresses. We don't know shit about how we actually feel unless we have writers and directors figuring it out for us and telling us what to do. Without them, we're pretty much flying blind."

"But are you excited?"

"Yeah. I guess."

"Worried?"

"Yeah, that, too."

I wanted to come up with something clever and positive and uplifting to say, but I couldn't think of a thing. "Well, I sure hope it works out for you two."

"So do I," she said with what sounded like genuine feeling. "But you know how it always is with performers."

"What kind of performers?"

"Any kind of performers...."

I waited for her to go on.

She looked up at the hillside over the esses, took a sip of her iced tea and continued. "We're only at our best when you see us doing whatever it is that we do. Everything you find out about us beyond that usually turns into a huge disappointment."

"That's a pretty bleak outlook."

She folded her lips into a dry little smile. "It's just the truth, that's all. People get fooled too easily. They have a habit of confusing talent with character…."

"Well," I told her as I stood up to get little Vincent another hot dog, "all you can do is your best. Just remember to clean up after yourselves in the bathroom and leave a little room for each other everyplace else."

"That sounds like some pretty good advice."

We were standing around the grill a little later when Carson came over carrying the time sheets, and wouldn't you know it we were side-by-side on the ninth row with Carson's 3.0-liter Healey on the inside and me and the Alfa on the outside, barely a quarter-second behind. Not that my friend and brother-in-law Carson Flegley was ever what you would consider any kind of Major Threat as a racing talent. Even so, I could tell that Julie and the kids were pretty proud of me. Although little Vincent did ask what those other Alfas that looked exactly the same as mine were doing way up at the front end of the grid?

"They've got better engines and more experienced drivers," I explained.

"Bigger engines?" he asked the way kids do.

"Not bigger…*better!*" I told him.

He looked up at me with those big, round, questioning seven-year-old eyes. "But you're supposed to be a car mechanic, aren't you, Daddy?"

"Yes, I am," I smiled down at him.

"Then why can't you make a better engine, too?"

"I will," I assured him, roughing up his hair. "When wintertime comes, you just bet I will."

"So you'll get a better engine for Christmas?"

"I've already sent my letter off to Santa Claus."

Well, I can't really describe the feeling of putting on your driving suit, helmet and racing gloves and strapping yourself in for your very first race. You feel so blessed light-headed that you're afraid you'll rise right up into the air, and there's this hollow, empty buzz in your gut that's half fear, half excitement and at least an additional one-third wondering what the hell you're doing there and wishing you were someplace else. But, like some condemned nobleman mindlessly sleepwalking his way towards the guillotine at the end of a famous novel, you just keep going through the motions and doing the next thing that needs to be done until you find yourself all snuggled into your silent metal cocoon on the false grid, waiting for the signal to fire up the engines….

Way up at the front of the line you see the familiar Porsche coupe and MGA roadster of Dave Burton and John Targett along with another Porsche and the two fastest Alfa *Veloces*, and the marshal standing right in front of them suddenly raises his hand, blows a piercing blast through his whistle and waves his arm around over his head in a wide, circular motion. Engines fire up all around you, and you fight that last, urgent impulse to undo the lap belts and leap out like a pilot jumping out of a burning fighter plane. But instead you reach out with a shaking, unsteady hand and twist the key on your own dash as well. You know the starter is turning your engine over, but you can't really hear it what with the noise of all those other un-muffled engines running and revving and blipping up-and-down all around you. But you can feel when it catches through the wheel and the seat of your pants and see the tach needle rise and flicker happily and steadily at just under 1000 rpm. You give the gas pedal a good prod and watch with satisfaction as the needle sweeps up through its arc, but you still can't hear your own engine against the chorus of all the other noise.

Then the pace car swings out and Dave and John and the other Porsche and the two Alfas and the rest of the cars at the front of the line begin to move—one after the other—while you wait there, adjusting and re-adjusting yourself in the seat and flexing and un-flexing your fingers around the steering wheel as you watch the cars ahead of you peel off one after the other and head out onto the racetrack, where a marshal is pointing them alternately, deliberately and decisively to the outside or the inside to make up the two even rows forming up behind the pace car. You don't even think about it when your turn comes. All by themselves the revs come up and the clutch pedal eases out and you're rolling—parallel to the fence at first and then angling out onto the racetrack and into your place in line behind a blue MG in the outside row with another Alfa just to his right on the inside and your friend and brother-in-law Carson Flegly right beside you in his big, grumbling Healey 3000.

You're *rolling!*

You twist the wheel back and forth a little on the pace lap to heat up the tires just like you've seen some of your heroes do, and everybody ahead of and beside and behind you is doing the same. You check your mirrors for the umpty-umpth time heading up the green, russet, red and gold valley of No Name Straight and maybe you and Carson exchange nervous thumbs-up signals back and forth to each other. You give the belts one final tug on the run towards West Bend, then feel your hands tense up on the wheel as the cars seem to pack together even tighter at the top of that daunting, downhill plunge into the last corner….

Way up towards the front—out of the corner of your eye—you see the pace car and the front rows disappearing out of sight around to the right. And you wonder in a sudden panic if you should be in second or in third and when exactly you should be hammering the gas pedal clear to the floorboards. You're far enough back that you don't even see the pace car pulling into the pit lane, and the sudden crescendo of sound is the first thing that tips you off the race is *on!* It comes from ahead at first, but instantly it's beside and all around you like an artillery barrage, and damn if you haven't already got your right foot planted like everybody else before you even have time to think about it….

Down the straight you go, past the pits and under the waving green flag while the cars jostle and feint for position ahead of you while you look around for some kind of opening of your own. And keeping your eye on the tach, too, because no way can you hear when to shift on account of all the noise. But there's no place to go because you're in a box behind the MG with the big six in Carson's Healey more than enough to keep you hemmed in there down the straightaway and into Big Bend. In fact. that's were you sit for most of the lap, with cars all around you and no place to go even though you think somewhere, deep in your heart, that if you could just find your way through all those bozos you could maybe get away from them.

It takes a few laps to figure out that the only place you're ever going to get around anybody cleanly at Lime Rock is under braking into Big Bend. But to do it—and especially in an ordinary, plain-Jane Alfa Spider sucking through a dinky little two-pot carburetor—you need to have a lot more momentum coming out of that last, daunting, sweeping corner called The Downhill. And there's just no way to do that with Carson's big, fat Healey clogging up the racetrack ahead of you. You *know* that you're faster than him through there, but it's hard to make yourself drop back and take a run when there's some other guy in an overstimulated MG TD filling up your mirrors to overflowing and hunting for a way by. But it finally dawns on you that he can't get by, either—same as you—and there isn't much of anything he can about it when you back way off at the crest of the hill, wait for what seems like at least 10 seconds and then floor it for the charge into The Downhill. But you're up on Carson's bumper again before you're halfway through the turn and there's no choice but to back out of it again before you're even on the straightaway….

Fact is, it took me about four tries to finally get it timed just right (and you can bet it was driving the guy in the TD behind me absolutely nuts!) but finally I did, and came drifting out of that last turn like Tazio Nuvolari himself, foot to the floor, using every inch of pavement and closing rapidly on the back end of Carson's Healey. Hell, I could read the slanted red *"3000"* lettering across the decklid like it was right in front of my eyes. I still had some momentum on him as I jinked out to the right to set up the pass, and I think he was a little surprised to see me there, if you want the truth of it. But the Healey still had more torque and horsepower than my Alfa, and by less than halfway down the pit straight things had equalized. And then they started going the other way as the Healey began creeping forward and easing away from me again. But I was on the inside, and he didn't figure to get clear enough for a driver of Carson's caliber to try to yank across to the inside and block the pass. So all I had to do was wait it out and keep it floored and not even flinch for the brakes until I saw Carson give up and back out of it. He did it with plenty of room to spare, and the Healey disappeared from my peripheral vision like someone had yanked it back with a tow chain. And then I went in maybe even a little deeper than I needed to just to make a point, getting the ass end a little up-on-tiptoes squirrelly in the process. Then I just drove my line and concentrated ahead of me and tried to be as damn smooth and deft and careful and smart and judiciously brave as I dared. And when I checked my mirrors again next time down the pit straight, Carson was way, *way* behind—just a blob in my mirror—and had that TD for company, trying to find a way past. Boy, you would've thought I'd passed Fangio himself for the lead at the blessed Nurburgring!

But the glory and self-appreciation didn't last long, as suddenly I saw Dave Burton's Porsche and John Targett's MG and those two fast Alfas plus that other 356 coming up in my mirrors like a salvo of rockets. I stayed over to the left on No Name Straight and eased off a bit to let them all by, and I couldn't believe the harsh, hollow rasp off that Porsche or the howl of the MG or the snapping, feline snarl of those two Alfas as they backed off and dropped down a gear for The Uphill. Jesus, those engines sounded like all lean meat, you know?

In fact, by the time I got to the bottom of The Downhill, the four of them were halfway down the pit straightaway and pulling away, flying underneath a waving, sunlit checkered flag in a formation so blessed tight I didn't have any idea which one of them had actually won. But even before I got to the flagstand myself, I was already thinking and wondering and planning and plotting and rolling it over in my mind what might happen if I milled a little off the cylinder head and got my hands on a pair of sidedraft Webers and a set of those hot *Veloce* cams….